THE PENGUIN BOOK OF

GREEK VERSE

INTRODUCED AND EDITED BY

CONSTANTINE A. TRYPANIS

WITH
PLAIN PROSE TRANSLATIONS
OF EACH POEM

PENGUIN BOOKS

PENGUIN BOOKS

Published by the Penguin Group
Penguin Books Ltd, 27 Wrights Lane, London W8 5TZ, England
Penguin Books USA Inc., 375 Hudson Street, New York, New York 10014, USA
Penguin Books Australia Ltd, Ringwood, Victoria, Australia
Penguin Books Canada Ltd, 10 Alcorn Avenue, Toronto, Ontario, Canada M4V 3B2
Penguin Books (NZ) Ltd, 182 190 Wairau Road, Auckland 10, New Zealand

Penguin Books Ltd, Registered Offices: Harmondsworth, Middlesex, England

First published 1971
7 9 10 8 6

Printed in England by Clays Ltd, St Ives plc
Set in Monotype Fournier and
New Hellenic Greek

TO
ALIKI TRYPANIS

ἣ μεγάλα χάρις δώρῳ σὺν ὀλίγῳ

CONTENTS

vii

CONTENTS

PHOCYLIDES (*fl.* 544 B.C.)

ANACREON (*c.* 563–478 B.C.)

ANACREONTEA (date unknown)

THEOGNIS (*fl.* 520 B.C.)

SIMONIDES (556–467 B.C.)

ANONYMOUS (late 6th century B.C.)

AESCHYLUS (525–456 B.C.)

PINDAR (522–? 448 B.C.)

BACCHYLIDES (505–450 B.C.)

SOPHOCLES (495–406 B.C.)

EURIPIDES (480–406 B.C.)

CONTENTS

ARISTOPHANES (450–385 B.C.)

TIMOTHEUS (c. 447–357 B.C.)

PLATO (429–347 B.C.)

ARISTOTLE (384–322 B.C.)

II. THE HELLENISTIC WORLD

MENANDER (? 343–293 B.C.)

CLEANTHES (331–232 B.C.)

ANYTE (*fl.* 300 B.C.)

THEOCRITUS (*c.* 316–*c.* 260 B.C.)

ARATUS (*c.* 315–240 B.C.)

CALLIMACHUS (310–*c.* 240 B.C.)

ASCLEPIADES (*fl.* 290 B.C.)

POSEIDIPPUS (*fl.* 280 B.C.)

? POSEIDIPPUS

HEDYLUS (*fl.* 280 B.C.)

APOLLONIUS RHODIUS (295–215 B.C.)

LEONIDAS OF TARENTUM (*fl.* 274 B.C.)

HERODAS (*fl.* 240 B.C.)

ALCAEUS OF MESSENE (*fl.* 197 B.C.)

PHILIP V, KING OF MACEDON (238–179 B.C.)

DIOSCORIDES (*fl.* 180 B.C.)

MOSCHUS (*fl.* 150 B.C.)

BION (*fl.* 120 B.C.)

CONTENTS

GREGORY OF NAZIANZUS (*c.* 329–89)

ANONYMOUS (? 4th century)

SYNESIUS (*c.* 370–413)

CYRUS OF PANOPOLIS (*fl. c.* 440)

NONNUS (*fl. c.* 450)

ANONYMOUS (5th century)

ANONYMOUS (? 5th century)

PAMPREPIUS OF PANOPOLIS (*fl. c.* 500)

ANONYMOUS (? 5th century)

AGATHIAS SCHOLASTICUS (*c.* 536–82)

IV. THE BYZANTINE EMPIRE

CONTENTS

xviii

ANONYMOUS (15th century)

ANONYMOUS (? early 15th century)

ANONYMOUS (? early 15th century)

V. UNDER FRANKISH AND TURKISH RULE

ANONYMOUS FOLK-SONGS
(18th- and 19th-century versions. The origins of
some go deep into the Byzantine period.)

? VIZENTZOS CORNAROS (16th–17th century)

GEORGE CHORTATZIS (*fl. c.* 1590)

CONTENTS

VIZENTZOS CORNAROS (16th–17th century)

RHIGAS PHERRHAIOS (1759–98)

VI. MODERN GREECE

DIONYSIOS SOLOMOS (1798–1857)

ANDREAS KALVOS (1792–1869)

ALEXANDER SOUTSOS (1803–63)

GEORGE ZALOKOSTAS (1805–58)

ALEXANDER RIZOS RANGAVIS (1809–92)

JULIUS TYPALDOS (1814–83)

CONTENTS

CONTENTS

Contents

PREFACE

In this anthology I have tried to show the uninterrupted development of Greek poetry from the Homeric epics to the present day. In dealing with the vast and varied material that ancient, medieval and modern Greek poetry has to offer, I have been guided not only by literary historical considerations, but also by the poetic excellence of the poems, or extracts, selected. At the same time, when dealing with longer poetic forms, I have tried to include at least one complete specimen, if that were possible* – one complete Pindaric Ode for example, one complete Theocritean Idyll, more than one complete *kontakion*, etc. – so that the reader can have the opportunity of becoming acquainted with the various types of poetry in which the Greek genius expressed itself.

In regard to the translations which accompany the text, I should like to stress that they make no literary claims. Their aim is to help the reader of the original to understand the text at the points at which he finds it difficult. Moreover, I should like to emphasize that they owe a great deal to a number of printed books, as well as to many of my friends and pupils, who have most kindly helped me in the rendering of various passages into English. Their number is too great to mention them here by name, but this by no means makes my debt of gratitude to them any less. One exception, however, must be made. I must single out Mr Christopher Walker, who so ably and so carefully 'edited' the present book, and who with extreme care and ability went once again through all the translations, correcting, adapting and often recasting them into a more suitable and homogeneous style.

As in a book of this nature a set orthography for the poems in demotic Greek – a quality not apparent in the writings of the poets – is necessary, I have followed the rules given in the *Neohellenike Grammatike tes Demotikes*, of the Greek government's Department of Educational Books, which

---

* This was, naturally, impossible for epic and drama.

was published in 1941 by a committee under the presidency of Manolis Triantaphyllides.* A further difficulty is presented by the transliteration into English of the names of the poets. In this consistency is not possible. Famous ancient names have been given as traditionally rendered – e.g. Callinus, Alcman, Alcaeus etc. – whereas the names of modern Greek poets like Valaoritis, Kavafis, Seferis, etc. have been phonetically transliterated, because that is the form in which the English-speaking world knows them.

An anthology is indeed a vulnerable book to compile. Every reader conversant with the material is bound to find that some of his favourite poems have been left out, and that the English translations do not convey the 'poetry' of the original. But in spite of this and of many other shortcomings, of which the author is fully aware, this book can safely claim to include a great deal of the finest poetry ever written in any language in the world.

Chicago
May 1970   CONSTANTINE A. TRYPANIS

* A shorter and more accessible version of this is: M. Triantaphyllides, *Neohellenike Grammatike*, Athens, 1948.

INTRODUCTION

I. ANCIENT GREECE

Epic Poetry

NOTHING is known of the works of Orpheus, Linus or Musaeus, to whom the Greeks attributed the 'origins' of Greek song and poetry. The history of Greek poetry, indeed the history of Western literature, begins for us, therefore, with Homer and the two heroic epics of the *Iliad* and the *Odyssey*. Recent research has confirmed that the great Homeric poems are the outcome of a long poetic tradition covering roughly five hundred years, which developed in the hands of gifted professional or semi-professional singers, who originally accompanied their recitations with music. It is probable that in the course of the ninth or the eighth century B.C. the long monumental epic, such as we know it from the *Iliad* and the *Odyssey*, was composed by the Ionian Greeks, and that the two Homeric poems were later committed to writing, sometime between the seventh and the sixth centuries B.C., when their texts became more or less static. The Homeric picture is, therefore, an amalgam derived from different periods, and it is not surprising that a number of Mycenaean elements are to be found side by side with others from the three centuries following the collapse of the Mycenaean world (*c.* 1100 B.C.), as well as a few taken from the late ninth and the eighth centuries. Thus some weapons are Mycenaean, others are post-Mycenaean; inhumations and cremation are sometimes conflated; the relation of the supreme king with the other Achaean leaders, and their relations with the subordinate members of their households, are compendious, reflecting Mycenaean customs as well as certain developments of the subsequent Dark Age; and clothes, cults, marriage customs, and so on show a similar blend of the older and the newer.

It is not only an amalgam of cultures we find in the *Iliad* and the *Odyssey*, but also a linguistic mixture, in which early Peloponnesian, Aeolic, Ionic and even some Attic elements can be traced, which in a sense show the course the epic tradition followed, the lands to which it spread, before the final monumental compositions were committed to writing. So every single line of the great Homeric epics must be assessed in the terms of a traditional and formalized language and a traditional subject-matter. But the problems of who Homer was, and at what point of this long and fluctuating epic tradition he should be placed, remain unsolved. Most contemporary scholars are inclined to consider him an outstanding oral Ionian singer, and to attribute to him the monumental composition of the *Iliad*. But there is little proof that can be offered for this, and we are today as ignorant as the classical Greeks, who had no certain or accepted facts about the poet's life.

The broad structure of the Homeric epics is not difficult to master. It possesses a certain simplicity, which facilitated oral composition as well as oral recitation. In the *Iliad* the whole poem hangs on the wrath of Achilles, and, though many other episodes are introduced, this gives a unity to the whole. The *Odyssey*, which is remarkable for the economy of its structure – 'the despair of all its imitators' – tells of Odysseus, who after many years of wandering comes home to find his wife encircled by contemptible suitors and kills them.

There is a great difference of temper between the *Iliad* and the *Odyssey*, and the change is not in language, nor in metre, nor, superficially at least, in handling. It is a change in the meaning of poetry, and this in its turn is due to a change in the way of regarding and interpreting life. An ancient critic compared Homer in the *Odyssey* to the setting sun, whose greatness remains without violence, and he was right. A softer, a more romantic approach to life has taken the place of primitive directness and the all-significant valour in battle of the *Iliad*. The two monumental epics could hardly have been composed at the same time, or by the same man. Their overwhelming effect lies in their unmatched power to express the sense of human greatness; they are the incarnation of the whole strength and splendour of life. And this is achieved – if such achievement can be summarized in a few words – by the nobility and the depth of the emotions portrayed, by the effective contrast of the characters introduced, by the clarity and variety of the scenes described; by the musical flow of the hexameter and the wealth and brilliance of the epic diction; and not least by the recurrent descriptive epithets and the magnificent similes, always drawn from the poet's own world, as well as the moral sentences, which convey a light on the whole of life. Nor should the plainness of thought, the rapidity of the narrative and the blending of divine with human action be overlooked.

The admiration of the whole Greek world for the Homeric epics was unique, and their influence upon the subsequent development of Greek literature, art and culture in general cannot be overrated. Homer was the Poet *par excellence* for the whole of antiquity; ἅλις πάντεσσιν Ὅμηρος, 'Homer is enough for everybody', as Theocritus so succinctly and despairingly put it in one of his Idylls. Few works, and probably none which are not scriptural, have ever had such a hold on a nation for so many centuries.

The second great name in Greek poetry is that of Hesiod (? seventh century), the founder of the didactic epic, and the first tangible personality in the history of Greek literature. The *Theogony* – or such of it as belongs to him – is a poem of grand scope attempting to work into a system the floating legends of the gods and goddesses and their offspring. Far more interesting, however, is his *Works and Days* with their fervent exhortation to work and justice, their farmer's calendar and their appendix on seafaring and housekeeping. They contain a number of myths, such as that of Pandora, in which woman is first shown as the source of evil, and the first fable in Greek, that of the hawk and the nightingale. Hesiod teaches in the real sense of the word. He gives practical advice on agriculture, navigation, housekeeping, astronomy and divination. He makes clear that heroism exists not only in the old Homeric aristocratic ideal of valour in battle, but also in the long silent struggle of the farmer with the 'black' earth and with the elements. The sober and practical character of Hesiod's poetry remained one of the basic factors in Greek civilization, and his literary progeny was prolific.

Elegiac Poetry

The origins of the word 'elegy' are obscure. Originally it may have been a dirge metre, but we first find it in war-songs, and in the course of time it became the special verse for love-poetry. The elegiac war-songs of Callinus of Ephesus (*fl. c.* 660 B.C.) – probably the oldest known – and of Tyrtaeus of Aphidna (*fl. c.* 670 B.C.) are direct and powerful poems, appealing to a sense of honour and describing the horrors and the glory of war. The greatest among the early elegists was Mimnermus of Colophon (*fl. c.* 630 B.C.), who developed the amatory side of the elegy. He is the first hedonist in Western literature, who in a nostalgic and romantic style proclaimed that all that matters in life is pleasure and love. By far the best-preserved elegiac writer is Theognis of Megara (*fl. c.* 520 B.C.), who expressed the views of the old aristocratic world at a time when its privileges were being challenged. There is a tinge of pessimism and a masked didactic tone in his writing, but brighter flights of personal feeling are also found.

Iambic Poetry

The word 'iambus' is also of unknown origin, and may well be Asiatic. As a metre iambics are closer to common speech than either the epic hexameter or the elegiac couplet. Their first appearance in literature has a pronounced satirical colour, no doubt deriving from the improvised iambic repartee which was a general practice at the early Greek festivals of Dionysus. Of the three iambic poets considered as 'classical' by the Alexandrians, Archilochus of Paros (*fl. c.*

648 B.C.) is the greatest. He has a light-hearted cynicism and a sharp dislike for anything heroic. The realistic humour of his verses shows that the old morality which feared and honoured public opinion was changing in the framework of the city-state. But no matter how much he gave vent to his personal feelings there is a clear exhortatory aspect in his poetry, without which he would not have been placed next to Homer, recited at public festivals, or worshipped at Paros after his death. The debt of Catullus and Horace to Archilochus has been rightly stressed. Lesser in every respect are the other two 'classical' iambic poets, Semonides of Amorgos (*fl. c.* 630 B.C.) and Hipponax of Ephesus (*fl. c.* 540 B.C.). Tradition makes the latter a lame and deformed beggar, whose invective drove those he attacked to commit suicide. He is also credited with the invention of the 'halting iambus', a trimeter with a spondee or a trochee in the last foot. Hipponax influenced Attic comedy, and was much admired and imitated in the Hellenistic world.

Melic Poetry

Melic poetry, which includes both personal and choral lyric, differs in both content and form from elegiac and iambic. In content it is on the whole personal and emotional, with no didactic or satirical elements. In form it consists of strophic compositions, in which the many complicated rhythms employed are closely integrated with the music that accompanied them. Moreover, by contrast with most elegiac and iambic poetry, the personal lyrics were not sung in public, but before a private gathering of friends. The most famous examples of Personal Lyric come from Lesbos, so it is natural that Aeolic dialect and Aeolic rhythms prevail in it.

Alcaeus (*fl.* ? 600 B.C.) was a native of Mytilene, and the political convulsions of his time are reflected in his poetry. There are passion and venom in his political songs, and a dionysiac debauchery in his drinking-songs; but there are also gentle and serene lines, and a precise vision of the natural world. His style is direct and clear.

If Alcaeus gave voice to a number of intimate subjective emotions, it was Sappho of Eressus (*fl.* ? 600 B.C.), who probed into the last recesses of the personal world of passion. Her name cast such a spell on Greece and Rome that it is hard to distinguish fact from fiction in the stories surrounding her. It is certain that she was married and had a daughter; but that she went into exile or committed suicide at Leucas cannot be confirmed. The world of her poetry is the girl's life between childhood and marriage. Love is the source of her inspiration, Eros, as it releases the forces of the spirit and joins souls in the sensuous grace of dance and play. Her feeling for nature is unique, and it is true to say that no other Greek love-poetry ever approached the passion, tenderness and tragic exaltation of Sappho's verse. It is for this that Plato called her the Tenth Muse.

Very different are the light-hearted, hedonistic verses of Anacreon of Teos (*c.* 563–478 B.C.). He wrote in an Ionic vernacular with a few Aeolic traces and in simple metres. Though he loved pleasure and had no prejudices about drink or sex, he is usually decorous and dignified. In the extant fragments he appears very different from the inebriated debauched old man late antiquity represented him to be.

The Dorians, the last comers to Greece, had so far – with the exception of Tyrtaeus – contributed nothing to Greek literature. But with the dawn of the sixth century a new school of poetry arose in Sparta under the guidance of a Sardian whom the Dorians called Alcman, and it spread among Doric-speaking peoples. Its contribution was the Choral Lyric, voicing not individual sentiments but those of a community, or part of a community. The chief fragment of Alcman (*fl. c.* 630 B.C.) which survives comes from a *Partheneion*, a song for a chorus of girls. It is extremely beautiful, and is still individual in tone, the members of the choir addressing all manner of remarks to each other. In

Sicily a greater writer arose in the person of Stesichorus (*fl. c.* 600 B.C.), who wrote choral pieces on a grand scale, dealing with epic themes. Little of his work has survived. Ibycus of Rhegium (*fl.* 560 B.C.) should also be mentioned; his songs for boy-choirs were especially praised.

But the great figures of the age were Simonides and Pindar, who showed what a master could make of the choral ode. Simonides of Ceos (556–467 B.C.) was a many-sided poet who excelled in an extraordinary range of types and occasions of poetry. He introduced the *Epinikion*, the serious choral ode in honour of victories at the games. His severe style is free of sentimentality, but flares into a sudden brilliance when a simile or a metaphor is introduced. The restrained beauty of his art reached its peak in the epigrams which he wrote for the tombs of the heroic dead of the Persian wars. Most celebrated of these is his epitaph on the Spartans who fell at Thermopylae.

Pindar (522–?448 B.C.), 'by far the most famous of all the lyricists' as Quintilian calls him, was born at Cynoscephalae near Thebes. Although he travelled widely, and his life reached well into the Periclean Age, his whole outlook belongs to the period before the Persian wars. His were the old-fashioned aristocratic ideals, according to which human excellence was connected with blood, and its heroic or divine origin. The bulk of Pindar's work consists of choral songs written for victors at the four great athletic festivals of Greece. These have been supplemented in recent years by fragments of Paeans, Dithyrambs and Maiden-songs. His language is the literary Doric with a few Aeolic elements; the influence of the epic diction is also evident. His style is lofty and even elaborate, and not always easy to enjoy. This is due to the complicated word-order and his allusive treatment of mythology. On the whole he composed in triads – strophe, antistrophe and epode – but there are also a few monostrophic compositions. Pindar's renown during and after his lifetime was immense. The city of Athens gave him honorary rights, and a gift of 10,000 drachmae; at Delphi he was invited for years by a special herald's cry to partake of the meal at the god's festival; when Alexander captured and destroyed Thebes, he spared only the house of Pindar as a sign of honour to his genius, and the Alexandrians and the Romans considered him by far the greatest of all lyric poets.

Bacchylides (505–450 B.C.), the nephew of Simonides, also wrote choral lyrics for festal occasions, but their tone differs from that of the two great masters of the period. There is an effortless simplicity and hardly anything didactic in his writings. They point to a new age, when the choral lyric ceased to be a popular form. Its features were partly absorbed in the lyrical section of drama, and partly in the forms of Dithyramb, in which words were increasingly subjugated to music. The bombastic remains of Timotheus' (c. 447–357 B.C.) *Persians* show how far the change was to go.

Drama

TRAGEDY. If lyric poetry had close ties with tyranny and the traditional aristocracy from which it drew its patrons, the patron of drama – both tragedy and comedy – was the city of Athens, the democratic city *par excellence*. The origins of Greek tragedy are obscure. It probably developed from the Dorian 'goat-choirs' of the northern Peloponnese, but the first steps of the transformation seem to have taken place in Attica. It is not surprising that in sixth-century Greece there were experiments seeking to bring lyric poetry into an organic relationship with ancient ritual, and that Dionysus was the god who was the particular focal point. We are told that Thespis of Icaria – an Attic deme – was the first who 'to rest the chorus and vary the entertainment' recited to the public a speech in trochaic hexameters. His first 'victory' was later in 534 B.C. at the great festival of Dionysus. In tragedy the Attic genius found its characteristic poetry, for throughout the fifth century that was the chief literary art of Athens, indeed of the whole Greek world, for every artistic, intellectual and political activity was then centred there.

Most tragedians made their appearance at the Greater or City Dionysia, held in the early spring. On the second day of the festival five comedies were presented, and then came the competition in tragedy, which extended over three full days, one assigned to each competing playwright. Each tragedian composed three tragedies for the occasion, which might or might not be connected in subject, to form a trilogy, and a fourth play of an entirely different genre, a grotesque satyr-play, in which satyrs formed the chorus. Of early Attic tragedy nothing survives. All the extant plays – with the possible exception of the *Rhesus* – were composed by the three tragedians the Greeks considered the greatest: Aeschylus, Sophocles and Euripides. Athenian tragedy, in full maturity, is a majestic achievement. It belongs to the Theatre of Convention, and clung to the end to the marks of its religious origins – the chorus, the mask and the pre-eminently serious character. The plots, with few exceptions, were taken from mythology. Without being invariably tragic in the modern sense, Greek tragedy was always concerned with the great issues of life and death, and with the relation of man to the gods.

Aeschylus (525–456 B.C.) belongs to the great generation that defeated the Persians in 490 and 480 B.C. He, more than anyone else, gave to tragedy the form we know. By introducing a second actor, he rendered the dialogue independent of the chorus, whose number he reduced. To him are further ascribed the system of trilogy and tetralogy, as well as various improvements of detail in costume and the like. The titanic inspiration of Aeschylus, the gravity of his thoughts, the rugged grandeur of his language and the majestic simplicity of the structure of his plays have secured for him a unique place in the history of Greek poetry. He believed in the overwhelming power of the gods and the weakness and dependence of all human beings, but he dealt with his lofty themes primarily as an artist, not as a preacher. His characters are no puppets in the hands of destiny, nor are they mere symbols. The appalling conflicts which they sustain come from their own will. There is no trace of fatalism in the whole of Aeschylus. The *Oresteia* – a trilogy consisting of *Agamemnon*, the *Libation-bearers* and the *Eumenides* – produced in 458 B.C., is his masterpiece, and has been acclaimed as the highest achievement of all Greek drama. Of equal inspiration is *Prometheus Bound*, the first and only surviving play of a trilogy, where the poet moves in a world of gods and Titans. With the *Persians*, which deals with the battle of Salamis and the defeat of the Persian invaders, Aeschylus showed that he could equally well handle a historical subject, and proclaim the old moral message that the gods overthrow the arrogant. His other surviving plays – the *Suppliant Women* and the *Seven against Thebes* – are less impressive and far more archaic and stiff. The general recognition accorded to Aeschylus in his lifetime – he is said to have won twenty-eight victories at the festival of Dionysus – continued long after his death, and the posthumous production of his plays was ensured by public enactment in Athens.

The splendour and balance of the generation that built the Periclean state was somehow imaged in the life and person of Sophocles (495–406 B.C.). Affable, witty, sensitive, brilliant, handsome and wealthy: that is the picture of the poet antiquity has handed down to us. Sophocles is reputed to have written 123 tragedies, of which only seven survive. He also made technical improvements, such as the introduction of a third actor and of painted scenery, and won a prodigious number of first prizes – twenty as opposed to the fifteen of Aeschylus or the five of Euripides. The triumph of Sophoclean tragedy is its character-drawing. Sophocles' tragic men and women with their violent passions and their tender emotions are alive behind their idealizing masks, even if in nobility and dignity they belong to a different world from ours. The tragic element centres round the inevitability of suffering as seen through the eyes of the individual. By a series of sharply contrasting scenes the poet uncovers the true nature of a suffering human being, his fulfilment of destiny, and his self-fulfilment. He thus draws from the agony of his heroes a deep tragic lyricism, which is stressed by every device of the dramatist's imagination. He does not purport to explain or to justify life with its great reversals of fortune. He simply observes and portrays it. Perhaps nowhere is that strange fusion of character and fate more movingly presented than in the two Oedipus plays. In *King Oedipus* – produced in 430 B.C. – the play Aristotle considered the most perfect tragedy, Sophocles showed with unsurpassed power the hideous misfortunes which had fallen upon the Theban king and which brought about his downfall. In *Oedipus at Colonus*, his last play, published after the poet's death, Oedipus the accused man, the apogee of infamy and pollution, is lifted to become a symbol of peace and a blessing to the land that receives him – an end as incomprehensible and as unbelievable as the act of the gods that had shattered him at the peak of his glory. Sophocles was a traditionalist. He challenged the modernism of the Sophists and their arrogant trust in the powers of human reason. In *Antigone*, the most celebrated Sophoclean drama, he wonderfully demonstrated the superiority of the 'higher laws' of the gods to any man-made law that crossed them. At the same time Sophocles was the first to present women, not only men, as worthy representatives of humanity. His great tragic heroines – Antigone, Deianeira, Tecmessa, Jocasta, even Electra – are unparalleled on the Greek stage. But whereas Sophocles mistrusted the powers of human intellect and stressed man's dependence on the gods, he believed deeply in the dignity of man, the dignity always present in his great heroic figures at the moment of their downfall, that of an Ajax or an Oedipus. The Attic grace of Sophocles' diction, the superb lyricism he is capable of, and his effortless calm and sense of proportion placed him above the uncouth archaism of Aeschylus – however grand – and the sophisticated subjectivism of Euripides. When 'Atticism' triumphed (from the first century B.C. onwards), it was he who was acclaimed as the great master of the Greek theatre, a view which remained unchallenged till the twentieth century.

The crisis through which the age was passing can be clearly seen in the tragedies of Euripides (480–406 B.C.). He became the mouthpiece of the new Sophistic rationalism which had gradually permeated all the great cultural forces, religion, morality, political theory and poetry. Tradition raved against him. We are told he was a morose cynic, privately vicious; that his slaves or private acquaintances wrote his plays; that his father was a fraudulent bankrupt and his mother a greengrocer. Most of these stories can be proved untrue. In reality he belonged to a middle-class, landowning family, and his mother was probably of noble descent. The new elements which came to form Euripides' style were bourgeois realism, rhetoric and philosophy. They transformed not only the myths, but also the poetic language of tragedy, as well as its traditional form and tone. It was Euripides who invented domestic drama. *Medea*, for example, portrays Athenian bourgeois reality, for the poet infused into Jason's desertion of Medea passions and problems unknown to the original myth, but which were hotly discussed in the society of his day. Euripides was constantly experimenting and innovating. Thus it is a far cry from *Medea*, which in tone is perhaps nearest to the works of his predecessors, to *Orestes*, where tragedy is changed into something quite unconventional and different from anything Aeschylus or Sophocles had done with that myth. Moreover, Euripides imported from the elaborate art of forensic oratory the new devices of polished argument into the speeches and the dialogue of his tragedy. They helped him in presenting the various views of older and contemporary philosophers that excited him. His works have been called the debating platform of every movement of his age. And indeed there is hardly anything from the sublimely religious to the frankly frivolous which is alien to his theatre. His treatment of women and slaves, and his presentation on the stage of love and madness in all their manifestations, should be singled out. With these Euripides opened an entirely new field to tragedy, and he did so with relentless realism. This we can see for example in the way he revealed the pathology of unfulfilled desire in *Hippolytus*; or, in *Hecuba*, how extreme suffering can distort and debase a noble character. Superb is the manner in which he depicts the human infirmities which originate in the world of the instincts and affect the destiny of man. Perhaps nobody has plumbed the depths of the irrational as deeply as this poet of rationalism in his last play, the *Bacchae*, where he deliberately escapes from rational self-knowledge into irrational ecstasy. At other levels too Euripides was an innovator. He made extensive use of the Prologue – so necessary in an age where there were no playbills – and of the *deus ex machina*, which served as a kind of epilogue to his plays. He developed the lyrical element in drama, extending it from the chorus to the characters; he detached the chorus songs from the organic structure of the plays, and developed 'recognition' as a dramatic climax to a point hitherto unknown. He also presented his characters in realistic costumes, which caused a huge outcry on the grounds that he was debasing tragedy!

Euripides has been rightly seen as the last great classical poet, and as the first of the new, the Alexandrian era. His diction became the basis of the diction of nearly all poetry for centuries to come; his portrayal of love and his broad, humane approach to the problems of women and slaves, as well as the soft romantic mood of much of his poetry, were widely imitated and further developed in the era which followed. It was long before the Athenians gave Euripides any support, but he triumphed in the end, and dominated not only the Attic stage, but the whole Hellenistic world.

OLD COMEDY. Greek comedy grew from the mysteries of fertility and procreation, ceremonies in which ithyphallic processions, rustic ribaldry and miming were combined. But when comedy first appears as an artistic form it belongs entirely to Athens, and like tragedy is associated with the god Dionysus. Its climax was reached in the work of Aristophanes (450–385 B.C.). His eleven extant plays – the only complete plays surviving from Old Comedy – are amazing creations and a unique phenomenon in the history of literature. Athenian society and the Athenian state are transformed there into a world of pure fancy, in which satire, wit, buffoonery, obscenity and magnificent lyricism abound. They reflect perhaps more than anything else the spirit of fifth-century Athens in its freedom, vitality, exuberance, and self-confidence, and that superb 'civilized' capacity of laughing at oneself.

The *Birds*, produced in 414 B.C., is unquestionably Aristophanes' masterpiece. Apart from the clever skits, the bright jokes and the fantastic flights of imagination, the lyricism which pervades the whole is breathtaking. Other plays of his, like the *Acharnians* (425 B.C.) or *Lysistrata*, are satires on the war-party, or a plea for peace, in which topical allusions or daring indecency prevail. In the *Knights* (424 B.C.) the demagogue Cleon is violently attacked; in the *Clouds* (423 B.C.) Socrates is held up to ridicule, and the intellectual movement of the Sophists is debunked; and the *Frogs* (406 B.C.) criticizes the new poetry as symbolized by Euripides. Imperceptibly Aristophanes slides into fantastic exaggerations, so that Euripides is finally revealed as the incarnation of all the evils of the day.

With the *Frogs* the great days of Aristophanes and of Old Comedy come to an end. The defeat of Athens in 404 B.C. brought an end to the conditions under which Old Comedy was possible. It was too expensive and too outspoken to suit a defeated people. The *Parliament of Women* and *Wealth*, both written after that, have less of the real Aristophanes in them. Aristophanes was not a unique figure in Old Comedy. Though he had the greatest success in winning prizes – he won four first prizes, three second and one third during his career – writers such as Eupolis and Cratinus were not far behind.

II. THE HELLENISTIC WORLD

New Comedy

In Greek literature, the Hellenistic Age starts with New Comedy. But whereas all other forms of Hellenistic poetry flourished chiefly in Egypt and Asia, New Comedy remained an exclusively Attic product. Menander (?343–293 B.C.) was for Rome, as he is for us, the classic of New Comedy. He abandoned all broad political and social issues, and turned to a safe 'middle-class' theatre with fictitious characters and conventionalized plots. He created the comedy of manners. His plays are full of love-affairs, violations of girls, exposure of infants, intriguing slaves, improbable recognitions, flatterers and angry fathers; together with these we find moralizing about the uncertainty of human affairs, and a recurrence of the virtue-triumphant motif. Menander's debt to Euripides can hardly be overrated. He took over from Euripidean tragedy the love-motif – which to this day we associate with the comedy of manners – the realistic interest in character, the use of the Prologue and the chorus-songs which were mere 'interludes', and not organically connected with the plot. Menander's world is undoubtedly narrow: no reflection can be seen in it of the world-stirring events that were taking place in his day. But it is also a wide-hearted world, with a broad understanding of suffering and a humane attitude proclaiming that all men are equal, the rich and the poor, the free and the enslaved. It points to the new and broader Hellenistic culture which was to follow. With the exception of Homer, no other Greek poet influenced world literature as strongly as Menander. In the forms that

Plautus and Terence gave his poetry, it captivated the world. Yet only fragments of Menander's works have survived, and only one complete (and rather disappointing) play, *Dyskolos*, which was recently retrieved. Menander was not the only distinguished poet of New Comedy; there were many others, but their works have disappeared.

Alexandrian Poetry (323–146 B.C.)

The victory of the Macedonians at Chaeronea (338 B.C.) meant the end of 'classical' Greece. Greek civilization was carried by Alexander to the East, and his successors honoured and cultivated it in the Hellenized kingdoms of Egypt, Syria and Pergamum; but the character of Greek literature changed when it was transplanted to the newly conquered lands, and the political and cultural significance of the city-state disappeared. The spiritual world of Hellenistic Greece severed itself from the multitude. Scholars and poets withdrew from the world and worked as individuals. Secluded in their libraries, supported by the kings, studying the great works of the past, they took little interest in the present and the 'many'. The famous Callimachean words σικχαίνω πάντα τὰ δημόσια, 'I hate everything public', summarize admirably their attitude. Thus poetry lost its centre, and ceased to deal with life as a whole, with what really here and now interested people, what they cared for, thought and felt. The splendid achievements of classical poetry that were being collected, classified and annotated in great scientific institutions like the Museum of Alexandria or the libraries of the Hellenistic world became more of an obsession than an inspiration. Great art overshadowed and checked new growth, as it is wont to do. The beginnings of the new Alexandrian poetry (323–146 B.C.) can be traced to the works of the Colophonian Antimachus and the Coan Philetas. They tried to rescue verse from the decrepitude into which it had fallen among debased dithyrambists and academic dramatists by setting an example of learned poetry appealing only to the learned

few. Antimachus of Colophon (*c.* 380 B.C.) was the founder
of narrative elegy, but the central figure of the Alexandrian
revival was undoubtedly Philetas of Cos (*fl. c.* 320 B.C.). He
became tutor to Ptolemy II, and a circle of distinguished
scholars and poets clustered round him. It was as an elegist
that he won lasting fame, and he was the first real 'scholar-
poet', the ideal the Alexandrians admired and imitated. Two
decades of fairly intensive activity form a prelude to Alex-
andria's Golden Age (*c.* 280–*c.* 240 B.C.), which Aratus of
Soli (*c.* 315–240 B.C.) can be fairly said to have initiated with
his polished astronomical poem entitled *Phaenomena*.

The three great names in Alexandrian poetry are Theo-
critus, Callimachus and Apollonius of Rhodes. Of these,
Theocritus (*c.* 316–*c.* 260 B.C.) is by far the most attractive
to the modern world. A native of Syracuse, he was drawn to
the eastern Aegean and to the court of the Ptolemies, the
greatest literary centre of his day. He wrote many kinds of
poetry – bucolic idylls (the term 'idyll' simply means short
poem), town mimes, short epics, hymns, lyrics and epi-
grams – but he owes his fame chiefly to his bucolic idylls,
whose theme was pastoral life, and whose unique charm lies
in a strange combination of realism and romanticism. He is
the founder of pastoral poetry, whose 'unclassical' yearning
for the tranquillity and the simplicity of country life could be
felt only by those living in over-populated cities like the vast
new cosmopolitan cities of the Hellenistic world. Theocritus
was an accomplished craftsman, and modern scholarship has
emphasized the element of parody, pastiche and topical
allusion in his bucolics; though disguised references to indi-
viduals – the *mascarade bucolique* – are unproved except for
Idyll VII, the masterpiece of the *merae rusticae*. But Theo-
critus' highest achievement in pure art is *Idyll II*, the town
mime in which Simaetha, deserted by Delphis, tells the story
of her love to the moon. It is the greatest Alexandrian love-
poem which has survived. Theocritus uses the literary Doric
for most of his poems, but there are some in the Epic Ionic

and Aeolic dialects. In the manipulation of the hexameter he varies the metrical form according to his material.

Though Theocritus may seem more attractive today, the chief figure of the Alexandrian movement was Callimachus (310–c. 240 B.C.). He came from Cyrene to Alexandria, where he joined the court of Ptolemy II, and was commissioned to prepare the famous *Pinakes*, the catalogue of the books of the Alexandrian library. He combined the qualities of scholar, poet and critic, and rose to be the chief representative of the school of poetry which cultivated the short and highly finished poem. His most famous works were the *Causes*, an elegiac poem in four books containing a series of aetiological legends connected with Greek history, customs and rites, and *Hecale*, a short epic (roughly 1000 lines), describing the victory of Theseus over the bull of Marathon and the rustic hospitality extended to him by Hecale. But his *Iambi* – thirteen poems of miscellaneous content and character – and his other poems were much admired, and display the same mastery of form. On the whole his poetry – which with the exception of six hymns and some sixty epigrams we know only from fragments – though admirably polished, is dry, appealing more to the intellect than to the heart. An exception should be made of his epigrams. Some of these, especially the epitaphs, are among the most moving poems written in Greek. In the bitter controversy between the writers of long, traditional epics and those who preferred the short and highly polished poem, Callimachus took a leading part. The details of the dispute escape us, but the quarrel between Callimachus and his pupil Apollonius, which culminated in the latter's withdrawal to Rhodes, seems to have been one of the important episodes in it. Though Callimachus' critics were numerous and persistent, his fame and popularity after his death exceeded that of every other Alexandrian poet. To no other writer, except Homer, do the later grammarians pay such honour.

Apollonius (295–215 B.C.), called 'of Rhodes' because of

his retirement to that island, was born in Alexandria, or less probably in Naucratis. He is the only Alexandrian poet of distinction who was a native of Egypt. He headed the literary revolution against his teacher Callimachus, and sustained it practically single-handed; his effective result, however, is to be found two hundred years later in Virgil, whose own genius absorbed and transfigured Apollonius. The *Argonautica*, Apollonius' *magnum opus*, narrates in four books Jason's journey to Colchis, the winning with Medea's aid of the Golden Fleece, and his return. It is the first Romantic Epic, for the fame and the lasting charm of this work rest on Book III, where the love of Medea for Jason is masterfully portrayed. Apollonius is capable of beautiful episodes, excellent similes, and *genre*-scenes of great charm, but he does not have the constructive power to give his work an organic unity; moreover his character-drawing is extremely weak. No epic has a less inspiring or more colourless hero than Jason! Apollonius' vocabulary is mainly taken from Homer, but in the Alexandrian manner he is continually varying and interpreting the Homeric words and phrases. Metrically his hexameter follows Homer rather than Callimachus.

Though Apollonius did not found a school, he did not lack admirers and imitators and even translators into Latin. His true successors, however, are the late Hellenistic prose Romances, which took over and further developed the elements of romantic love and adventure. Much of the finest work of the period is to be found within the narrow limits of the Epigram, to which the Hellenistic age made several fundamental changes. It cultivated purely artificial, epideictic epitaphs and votive inscriptions, never intended to be carved on a tomb or on a votive offering; and it infused into that concise poetic form the subjective emotions of the elegy and of the drinking-songs. The epigrammatists of this age can be grouped into two schools, the Ionian and the Peloponnesian.

The Ionian School was centred in Samos and Alexandria. It is social and sophisticated and treats of love and wine and literature and art in a complex style and vocabulary. Its leader is Asclepiades of Samos (*fl. c.* 290 B.C.), the most brilliant of all Alexandrian epigrammatists. Some forty of his tender, economical and imaginative poems have survived. He introduced a number of erotic themes and symbols which became part of world poetry, and influenced more than anyone else the development of the epigram. Closely associated with him are the poets Poseidippus of Pella (*fl. c.* 280 B.C.) and Hedylus (*fl. c.* 280 B.C.), whose work, though not as brilliant, is of a similar nature. These were followed by Callimachus – a brilliant epigrammatist as we saw – and by the skilful, realistic conceits of Dioscorides (*fl. c.* 180 B.C.), often called the last of the Alexandrian poets.

The Peloponnesian School wrote chiefly in Doric about country life and scenery in a realistic, straightforward manner. To it belong Anyte of Tegea (*fl. c.* 300 B.C.), whose mock-epitaphs on pet animals (a conceit she invented) and short nature lyrics are full of pure emotion and charm, Nossis (*c.* 299 B.C.) from the South Italian Locri, and Perses of Thebes (*c.* 315 B.C.). But the most important representative of that school was Leonidas of Tarentum (*fl. c.* 274 B.C.), one of the greatest Greek epigrammatists, whose influence was widely felt. About a hundred of his epigrams have survived, nearly all dealing with the life of the poor in a highly mannered and rhetorical style. This contrast of style and content is strangely effective. Finally Alcaeus of Messene (*fl. c.* 197 B.C.) should be mentioned as the inaugurator of the invective epigram, taken over by Catullus and many lampoonists after him. Nearly all the epigrammatists of that period wrote other kinds of poetry too, but it has all disappeared.

Though elegiac verse was the chosen medium for the new Alexandrian poetry, almost nothing has survived of Alexandrian elegy. The works of Euphorion of Chalcis (*c.* 300 B.C.) and Phanocles (date of birth unknown) are inferior poetry and insufficient to give a picture of Alexandrian elegy.

There is nothing, however, that suggests that the personal love-elegy, such as we know it from the great Roman elegists, was cultivated by the Alexandrians.

Even less can be recaptured of Alexandrian drama. Alexandria boasted of a Pleiad of tragic poets, and the names of some sixty-odd dramatists are recorded, but we know nothing about their works. The one complete play which has survived, *Alexandra*, in which recondite material and dark myths are treated in an extravagant style, has been attributed to Lycophron (*c.* 300 B.C.), but internal evidence shows it probably belongs to the second century B.C. Nor were the Mimes of Herodas (*fl.* 240 B.C.) intended for production in the theatre. Those realistic pictures of contemporary life, with a particular emphasis on the seamy side, were written for recitation, just like the town mimes of Theocritus.

Post-Alexandrian Hellenistic Poetry (146 B.C.–A.D. 330)

The political upheavals in Egypt in the middle of the second century B.C. caused the learned men, including Aristarchus, to flee from Alexandria. This brought about the end of Alexandrian poetry. The city lost her undisputed literary supremacy, and was henceforth rivalled by Pergamum, Athens, Rhodes, Antioch and Beirut. The most important poems composed in Greek in post-Alexandrian antiquity are by Moschus (*fl. c.* 150 B.C.) and Bion (*fl. c.* 120 B.C.), the last examples of the Hellenistic pastoral. The vast output of didactic poetry, ranging from controversial grammatical problems to the migration of birds, are of negligible poetic value, as can be seen from even the most significant of these, the *Theriaca* and the *Alexipharmaca* of Nicander of Colophon (second century B.C.). By far the most popular poetry of the time was the epigram, where little originality is displayed. Two Syrian epigrammatists should perhaps be singled out: Antipater of Sidon (*fl. c.* 120 B.C.) and Meleager of Gadara (*fl. c.* 90 B.C.), the compiler of the *Garland*, the oldest anthology of epigrams we know. In the Greek East both the spirit and the material for great poetic creations were absent.

After the Roman conquest of Greece and of the Hellenistic East, the centre of Greek culture swung to the West, to Rome. It was in Rome that the literary and artistic disputes which began in the Greek world were fought out. Above all, it was the dispute about style in prose which caused the greatest excitement. But we also meet some excitement in connexion with poetry, when in the days of Sulla (137–78 B.C.) the refined and scholarly style of the Alexandrians was introduced to the Roman world by Valerius Cato and the Greek poet Parthenius. Parthenius of Nicaea (first century B.C.) is the most important figure in Greek poetry of the period. He was enslaved during the Third Mithridatic War and taken to Italy, where he was freed. His writings, mostly elegiac – all lost to us now – were greatly admired, and the Alexandrian style he advocated was immediately adopted by Catullus and the other great Roman elegists. At the same time, the classicists were also acclaimed by Horace and by Augustus himself. Thus, Roman literature, refreshed by the Greek spirit, blossomed out into a splendour that far outshone contemporary Greek writing. The years A.D. 100–330 are marked by the active interest the Roman emperors took in the Greek East. From the days of Hadrian Athens became once more the 'capital' of Greece. The movement which sought to revive Greek literature started under the banner of 'classicism' raised by Quintilian and Pliny the Younger; but it was the Second Sophistic which took the lead in this with the main emphasis on oratory and prose style. This mummified Atticism flourished by the middle of the second century, and its influence continued for centuries to come, until the end of the Byzantine Empire. Its aftermath is still felt in the *Katharevousa*, the purist style of modern Greek. This romantic Atticism dominated all forms of literature, art and thought of the Graeco-Roman world, and its artificial rhetoric had disastrous effects upon the further development of Greek poetry. A dead rhetoric, a heavy didactic flavour colours the

inferior verse of those days, when Sophists with their elabo-
rate and artificial style were the masters of poetry. Various
rhetorical *genres*, like the Encomium, the Address (προσ-
φώνησις), the Funeral Oration, as well as various exercises
(προγυμνάσματα), were now composed in verse, a detri-
mental practice which was handed over to the Byzantine
Greeks. An interesting point which should be noted is the
complete absence of any influence of the great Roman poets
upon poetry written in Greek. Such was the undisputed
supremacy of Greek literature in the Graeco-Roman world.

III. THE PERIOD OF TRANSITION

The rise of Christianity among educated Greeks was by far
the most important event in the life of the Greek nation in
the first Christian centuries, and the reign of Constantine the
Great (A.D. 324–37) may well be regarded as the beginning of
a new era for the Greeks, both politically and spiritually.
Whatever the intention of Constantine may have been, the
founding of Constantinople in 330 proved tantamount
to the creation of a new Greek state. The preponderance of
the Greek element in the Eastern provinces, as well as the
fact that from Hadrian's day Greek language and literature
had been recognized as the universal language and literature,
gradually led to the full Hellenization of the Eastern Roman
state. From the beginning of the seventh century Byzantium
is Greek both in its leadership and in its members. The far-
reaching consequences of this in the development of Greek
letters need hardly be stressed.

The newly founded capital, which was to combine Roman
valour and Hellenic learning, was enriched from the start
with all that Greek art and letters could give it. A vast number
of precious manuscripts were collected in its schools and
libraries, and numerous works of art were brought from the
centres of the ancient world to embellish it. Moreover,

Constantinople, *the* City, gradually drew to herself nearly all important men of letters from the East and the West of the Empire. The Byzantine genius found admirable expression in many fields, but in literature, it must be admitted, creative spontaneity is on the whole lacking. And this is largely due to the fact that the majority of Byzantine literary works laboured under the Classical and Hellenistic linguistic and literary tradition, which smothered all originality. Only in religious poetry did the Byzantine Greeks ever approach greatness, because there they ventured to break away from the great Classical inheritance.

The transitional character of Greek literature in the first three centuries of the Byzantine Empire has rightly been stressed. In it, beside the last spasms of ancient culture, the first important expressions of the Christian world appear. Of the many writers of elegiacs of this period perhaps only one epigrammatist, Palladas (*c.* 360–430), should be singled out, who with the same ferocity preached against the flesh and attacked the Christian monks who sought to mortify it. At the same time we come across an ambitious 'revival' of the grand epic. Quintus of Smyrna (*fl. c.* 400) composed the *Posthomerica*, where with little passion or heroism he attempted in fourteen books to fill the gap between the *Iliad* and the *Odyssey*. He was followed by Nonnus of Panopolis (*fl. c.* 450), who in the forty-eight books of his ingenious and baroque *Dionysiaca* tells of the exploits – usually amorous – of Dionysus during his triumphal progress to India; an utterly unenjoyable work. Finally, we find what has been called the 'last flower in the garden of Antiquity', the romantic epic of Musaeus (fourth century), *Hero and Leander*. There is something fierce and tender in the mannered style of this much shorter work, as it describes the story of the separated lovers and, especially, Leander's last swim and death. But the triumph of Christianity had turned attention to a new mythology and to a new scale of values. Such inspiration as existed was now put to the service of the

1

Church, with the exception of the epigram, which in the works of Rufinus (*fl. c.* 550), Paul the Silentiary (*fl. c.* 563), Agathias (*c.* 536–582) and Macedonius (*fl. c.* 550) still clung to the old Hellenistic models – a last autumnal glow of the dying ancient world. The Hellenistic *ecphrasis* also reached considerable heights in the long elaborate description of St Sophia by Paul the Silentiary, who in stilted, archaic hexameters stressed the twin grandeurs of church and state around which Byzantine life was to revolve.

IV. THE BYZANTINE EMPIRE

The end of the period of transition is marked by the writings of George Pisidis (seventh century), one of the few distinguished Byzantine poets. He was deacon and keeper of the archives of St Sophia, and wrote verse on a variety of subjects, philosophical, theological and political. He also celebrated in an epic Encomium in iambic trimeters, the victory of the emperor Heraclius over the Persians. The epic Encomium continued to be cultivated till much later, as can be seen from the works of Theodosius the Deacon (tenth century) and Constantine Manasses (twelfth century), but its poetic value became negligible. George Pisidis was much admired and imitated by the Byzantine Greeks. He was even compared with Euripides! In his hands the new Byzantine metres begin to take shape, in particular the Byzantine iambic twelve-syllable verse, which became the principal metre in subsequent 'highbrow' Greek poetry. Pisidis had to tackle the great problem of the 'new' pronunciation of Greek, which from roughly A.D. 200 had lost the distinction between long and short vowels on which the ancient world had based its metrical rules. A rhythmic effect could now be achieved only by a set number of syllables and set accents in every line. This new metrical system was superimposed on the ancient iambic trimeter (to whose rules of prosody Pisidis faithfully adhered), though it was no longer discernible by ear, when read aloud. Pisidis was followed by nearly all subsequent Byzantine poets who used the 'iambic trimeter'. It was a *tour de force*, and the quality of the poetry, as would be expected, greatly suffered.

Religious Poetry

In the period of transition we also meet the first flowering of the new Christian religious poetry, the only original Byzantine literary achievement. Inspired by a deep devotion to the new faith, it broke away from the literary tradition, so closely connected with the pagan past. Its subjects were popular and significant for the men and women of that period, and its language was closer to the spoken idiom of the day, although the influence of traditional 'Attic Greek' and of 'Translation Greek' (that of Scripture) is also evident. It replaced quantitative with accentual metre in which there were a definite number of syllables in each colon; lines of different lengths were joined into balanced units, and these again were joined into strophes, whose structure was closely connected with the melody which accompanied them, when chanted in church. Originally, Christian religious poetry had also employed Classical metres – hexameters, elegiacs, iambics, anacreontics and anapaests – as can be seen from the works of Methodius (fourth century), Synesius (*c.* 370–413) and Gregory of Nazianzus (*c.* 329–89). But it soon abandoned that sterile effort and turned to the new 'rhythmic system, though followers of the classical heritage occasionally appeared up to the eighth century. At first (fourth and fifth centuries) short hymns, the *troparia*, and certain Isostichic Prayers were composed. But they soon gave way to the long elaborate metrical sermons, the *kontakia* of the sixth and seventh centuries. The view has been put forward, and appears to be well founded, that the impulse to this new type of poetry was given by Syrian models. But the complete control of metre and thought we find in the great Byzantine *kontakia* is purely Greek. The chief representative of the metrical homily is Romanos (*fl. c.* 540), the greatest poet of the Greek middle ages. He was a Hellenized Jew from Emesa (Homs), who came to live in Constantinople, and whose poetic and musical genius commanded universal admiration. Some eighty-five *kontakia* attributed to him have survived, some of which – like those on the Person of Christ – are of extraordinary skill and beauty. Clarity of style, striking imagery, arresting similes and metaphors, and a dexterous use of dialogue characterize his writing. Occasionally, however, he becomes grandiloquent and prone to an oriental love of size. The music of the hymns of Romanos is unfortunately lost, but the dramatic character of their content suggests that they were chanted in a kind of recitative, resembling oratorio. Romanos was not the only important composer of *kontakia* in the sixth century. There are others, mainly anonymous, like the author of the famous *Akathistos Hymn*, whose poems show impressive workmanship and a deep religious feeling.

In the second half of the seventh century Byzantine religious poetry entered its final stage with a new type of hymn, the *kanon*. The great length of this – each *kanon* consists of eight or nine long odes – led to an expansion of motives and an agonizing search after variety. Moreover, the music was more important than the words, which is always to the detriment of poetry. Andrew of Crete (*c.* 660–740), whose most important work, the *Major Kanon*, comprises no fewer than 250 strophes, is the initiator of this literary *genre*. He was followed by a vast number of religious poets of varying ability. The two most admired representatives of the *kanon* are St John Damascene (*fl.* 730) and his half-brother Cosmas of Maiouma. St John Damascene even returned to the use of quantitative metres and arranged some of his acrostics as elegiac epigrams on the subjects of his hymns, but rhetoric and erudition smother the works of both these authors, as well as the striving after effect. The storm

of the iconoclastic controversy which broke out in the life-
time of St John Damascene resulted in a second spring of
hymn-writing. It is works of this period, mostly anonymous,
which finally found their way into the liturgy of the Eastern
Church, replacing the hymns of the older school. On the
whole these are the creations of minor poets, whose pompous
style is full of platitudes and unsuccessfully coined epithets.
There is, however, one exception, Cassia (*fl. c.* 840),
the only poetess Byzantium can boast. Her poetry has been
on the whole overrated – she has even been called the Sappho
of Byzantium – but at least one short hymn, *Mary Magdalene*,
is a real masterpiece, and is chanted to this day during Holy
Week in the Eastern Orthodox Church.

Of all the post-iconoclast religious poets Symeon the
Mystic (949–1022) ranks highest. After Romanos he is the
figure second in importance in Byzantine poetry, because of
his striking originality. His long mystic hymns are inspired
and sincere pieces of writing, in spite of a cumbersome form-
lessness and many tedious repetitions. Symeon is also a
milestone in the history of Greek metre, for he is the first
to use in personal poetry the 'political' fifteen-syllable line,
the verse which was to become supreme, almost exclusive, in
later Greek demotic poetry. The origins of this verse are
obscure, but it appears to go back to the early days of the
Eastern Empire, or even further.

By the eleventh century hymnography had lost its signifi-
cance. Religious feeling had waned, and the attention of
church, court and society had turned to the dogmatic
quarrels between the Roman Catholic and the Greek·Ortho-
dox churches. Moreover the Greek Orthodox liturgy had
been completed; all the feast-days had their hymns, and there
was no room for more. The parodies of religious poetry
which appear in the eleventh century testify to this decline,
even if in the West, at Grotta Ferrata near Rome, new hymns
continued to be written in Greek. Byzantine religious poetry
was to accomplish a great historical mission. In the Greek

world it helped to keep Christian feeling and national consciousness alive in the face of the barbarian invasions, and during the long years of servitude under the Turks; to the East, West and North it scattered the seeds that later blossomed into the literature and culture of other peoples, the Russians, the Southern Slavs, the Rumanians, the Syrians, the Copts and the Armenians.

Lay Poetry

With the decline of hymnography, Byzantine poetry indeed presents a melancholy picture. There is no dramatic poetry – the only surviving drama, *The Sufferings of Christ*, is a miserable eleventh-century cento made up of verses of the ancient tragedians – and hardly any lyric poetry worthy of the name was written. The bigoted monk and the pedantic scholar excluded sensuous love and the body from their verse, and the dead weight of the ancient forms smothered any original expression. Poetry once again came to rival rhetoric, and was rarely the expression of an inner necessity. The metres used are the iambic twelve-syllable trimeter, the epic hexameter and inferior anacreontics. Moral Admonitions, Prayers of Sinners, and Laments full of the ascetic spirit of the time came to take the place of true lyrical verse. Some of these, though inferior works, should be singled out, like the *Lament on Human Life* by George Pisidis, or the lament *On the Death of his Sister Anastasia* by Christopher of Mytilene (c. 1000–1050), or the lament *Athens in the Middle Ages* by Michael Acominatos (c. 1140–1220), in which the poet mourns over the lost splendour of the city; but they are drops in an ocean of dead verse.

Didactic poetry flourished. The Byzantine Greeks assiduously cultivated it for centuries both in the purist idiom and later in the demotic. None of these prose-in-verse creations is poetry in any sense of the word, nor can the voluminous and artificial learned verse-romances of the twelfth century by Theodore Prodromos or Nicetas Evgenianos be regarded as poetry. Only in the epigram, the poetic *genre* the Byzantine Greeks cultivated right through the long centuries of the Eastern Empire, can a real exception be made. There we find some noteworthy names. First Theodore the Studite (759–826), abbot of the famous monastery of the Studion in Constantinople, and one of the great champions of the icons in the iconoclast controversy. His epigrams express vividly and with originality the religious spirit of his time, and the subjects he chooses – churches, monastic life, religious feasts, holy icons and holy relics – had a real meaning for his contemporaries. Then in the tenth and eleventh centuries, when with the Macedonian dynasty (867–1057) Byzantium reached its military and scholastic peak, we find John Geometres (Kyriotes), Christopher of Mytilene and John Mavropous, in whose epigrams taste, restraint, feeling and even a refined humour are clearly at work among a mass of Classical and Hellenistic influences. Finally, perhaps, one should also mention the beggar poet Manuel Philes (*c.* 1275–1345), whose epigrams display a spark of ingenuity and stand above much of the work of the last centuries of the Empire. All the profane poetry worth mentioning written in the highbrow style by the Byzantine Greeks makes, in fact, a poor and scanty crop.

V. UNDER FRANKISH AND TURKISH RULE

It is a mistake to regard the fall of Constantinople to the Turks in 1453 as a sharp dividing line between Byzantine and Modern Greek literature. It is true that 1453 marks the end of what is usually known as 'Byzantinism', or literature written in a 'purist' form of Greek, except in so far as this was artificially revived at a later date. But the germs of Modern Greek popular poetry can be traced as far back as the tenth century in the epic cycle of Digenis Akritas, and still more in the verse-romances of the thirteenth and the fourteenth centuries. Away from Constantinople in the provinces of the East, environment and conditions in the tenth century were conducive to the birth of an epic cycle, and it was then and there that the *Epic of Digenis Akritas* came into being. Unfortunately, we possess only a few remnants of that epic cycle woven around a hero unknown to history, the son of a Saracen father and a Greek mother. He symbolizes the heroism of those involved in the perennial struggle of the Byzantine Greeks against the Saracens on the Eastern borders of the Empire. This epic cycle apparently originated in Comagene, or Euphratesia, and later spread from the frozen steppes of Russia to the burning deserts of Syria, and reached even the remote western colonies of southern Italy. From it there survives only a small number of isolated folk-songs – committed to writing in the nineteenth and twentieth centuries – and half a dozen versions of a long poem, the so-called *Epic of Basil Digenis Akritas* ranging from the fourteenth to the seventeenth centuries. They all differ in language and style and even in the sequence of the episodes, which points to the existence of an oral poetry and tradition in the Greek world of that period. The Epic itself, which appears to have been fashioned on the pattern of the late Hellenistic romances, is of little poetic value, but some of the folk-songs belonging to that cycle are of great vigour and beauty.

Elements of Modern Greek can also be found in the satirical *Prodromic* poems, attributed to the beggar-poet Theodore Prodromos, which are of the twelfth century. They display a peculiar, mordant humour, but have limited poetic merits. Of much greater interest are the Byzantine Verse Romances which appeared after 1204, when Constantinople fell to the Franks of the Fourth Crusade. They use a language close to the spoken idiom of the time, and were also transmitted through the 'oral' tradition. Some of these, such as *Belthandros and Chrysantza*, while retaining marked Oriental features, have been enlivened by the influence of Western romance; conversely, others, such as *Imperios and Margarona*, though essentially French, have in their Greek adaptations received many Greek popular features. Their poetic value is unfortunately very limited. However, the literary debt of Modern Greece to the Crusades should not be overlooked, for among other things they were responsible for the introduction of rhyming verse to Greek poetry.

Greek Literature Under Frankish Rule

The beginnings of Modern Greek lyric poetry can be detected in writings which appeared in the seventeenth century in Rhodes and Cyprus, then under the rule of the Knights Templar and the Lusignans. But it was in Crete that the most vigorous literature flourished in the sixteenth and seventeenth centuries, when the island was under Venetian occupation. This was brought to an abrupt end by the Turkish capture of Crete in 1669. We can trace there the development of the fifteen-syllable 'political' lines from the rude-rhymed paraphrase of Genesis and Exodus by Georgios Choumis to the finished handling of the same metre by Vizentzos Cornaros in his great romantic poem *Erotocritos*, which probably dates from the beginning of the seventeenth century. It describes the trials and sorrows of two lovers, Erotocritos and Aretousa, whose love is finally crowned with a happy issue. Though based on a French work, *Paris et Vienne*, which Cornaros probably knew through an Italian version, the *Erotocritos* has a large number of purely Greek local elements, and was for centuries the national poem of Crete. It has passages of real poetic merit and became very popular among the Greeks beyond the boundaries of Crete. In connexion with this an interesting series of Cretan dramas should be mentioned. The best known of the tragedies is *Erophile* by George Chortatzis, inspired by Giraldi's *Orbecche*, a sanguinary melodrama, written about 1600. Of the comedies, *Katsourbos* and *Fortunatos*, though in the main borrowed from Italian and ultimately going back to Plautine and

Terentine comedy, are interesting for the introduction of local character and colouring; mention should also be made of the *Gyparis*, a pastoral comedy by the author of *Erophile*. But the real gem of Cretan drama is the mystery-play *The Sacrifice of Abraham*, also fashioned on an Italian model, the *Isaach* of L. Groto. It is anonymous, though Cornaros has been considered by some modern scholars to be the author. Crete possesses an interesting series of popular songs, and a charming pastoral poem, *The Fair Shepherdess*, attributed to Nicholas Drymitinos. The language of this attractive Cretan literature has incorporated some Venetian words, but its character is that of a vigorous native tongue with a number of Cretan forms and idioms. Had Crete not fallen to the Turks in 1669, when all literary activity ceased, it would have probably become the Modern Greek literary language, and the course of Modern Greek poetry might have been entirely different.

Greek Lands Under Turkish Rule

In the Greek lands under Turkish domination, the only note-worthy poetry is to be found in the folk-songs and the klephtic ballads. The subjects, indeed the roots, of many of these go back to the Byzantine era, and one, the *Swallow Song*, has even been traced as far back as Greek antiquity. Greek folk-songs fall into three main divisions: historical folk-songs, treating of historical events as seen through the people's eyes; songs of everyday life, that is love-songs, lullabies, marriage-songs, dirges, carols, etc. and the *Para-loges*, short narratives, often the summaries of folk-traditions or folk-tales. Some of the most beautiful and vivid poetry composed in Greek can be found in the folk-songs. They mainly use the fifteen-syllable verse, rhymed and unrhymed, and are full of the breath of the forests and the mountains, personifying trees, rocks and rivers, and even death. The family feelings they express are deep and noble, as well as the love for their native land. Their heyday was the eighteenth century, but they have been a source of constant inspiration and rejuvenation for Modern Greek poetry.

In the eighteenth century we also meet the first important influence of French literature upon the Phanariot Greeks – the educated Greeks who had clustered round the Oecumenical Patriarch in Constantinople – which largely determined the writings of the precursors of Modern Greek poetry as it appeared after the liberation of Greece: Athanasios Chrestopoulos (1772–1849), John Velaras (1771–1823) and Rhigas Pherrhaios (1759–98).

VI. MODERN GREECE

The Greek Romantics

The liberation of Greece in 1828, finally achieved after a long and bitter war of independence (1821–8), made the capital of the new kingdom – first Nauplia and then Athens – the centre of all Greek political and intellectual life. It was in the mixed and unsettled society of the capital of those days that the Romantic School of Athens flourished. Alexander Soutsos (1803–63), its founder and leading spirit, having studied in Paris, came under the influence of the French Romantics, but his exuberant and patriotic writings hardly captured the spirit of their models. As a satirist, however, he is often terse and vigorous, and the influence he exercised upon Greek poetry was felt for many years. The other main early representatives of the Romantic School of Athens, Panagiotis Soutsos (1805–68), Alexander Rizos Rangavis (1809–92), George Zalokostas (1805–58), Theodore Orphanides (1818–86), Elias Tantalidis (1818–76) and John Karasoutsas (1824–73), though varying in character and quality, are all slaves of a boundless romanticism; they mainly use a stilted purist diction, and are painstakingly patriotic. Achilles Paraschos (1838–95) is the leading figure in the last period of the school. Alfred de Musset, Victor Hugo and Lord Byron were his models, but the mock-heroic patriotism and the rhetorical profuseness of his verse prevented him from rising anywhere near their level, though a spark of true poetry is occasionally evident. His contemporaries George Paraschos (1822–86), Angelos Vlachos (1838–1919), Alexander Vizantios (1841–98), Demetrios Paparrhegopoulos (1843–73), and George Vizyenos (1848–94) were all overshadowed by his reputation, in spite of their greater directness and often more delicate technique.

The School of the Ionian Islands

Contemporary with the Romantic School of Athens another school of poetry flourished in the Ionian Islands, which had been under Venetian, and then under French and British, rule till 1864. Its founder and greatest representative is Dionysios Solomos (1798–1857), a native of Zante. Like others of the Ionian aristocracy of his day, he received his education in Italy, and wrote his first poems in Italian. He soon, however, aspired to become the Dante of Greece and started writing in Greek. His early works are short lyrics, but the War of Independence stirred him to more ambitious projects. With the years his approach to art and life deepened, and expressed itself in verses of great delicacy and balance, unsurpassed to this day in Modern Greek. From the *Ode to Liberty* (the first stanzas of which became the Greek national anthem) to *The Free Besieged*, which sings of the heroic resistance of Missolonghi, the development of a highly spiritual nature can be traced. Unfortunately, most of his mature work is known only from fragments, as the instability of his disposition and an overdeveloped self-criticism prevented him from completing any of his major works. In the struggle that continued from Byzantine days between the purist form of Greek (the *Katharevousa*) and the demotic as the language for literature, Solomos marks a turning point. By choosing the latter he pointed the way Greek poetry was to follow after the Demotic Movement of the 1880s. Moreover, he introduced a number of Western

metrical forms, which freed Modern Greek poetry from the
monotony of the fifteen-syllable line mainly in use previously.

Of the other poets of the Ionian School, George Tertsetis
(1800–74), Julius Typaldos (1814–83), Gerasimos Markoras
(1826–1911) and Lorentzos Mavilis (1860–1912) – one of the
most distinguished Greek sonnet-writers – must be men-
tioned, but Andreas Kalvos (1792–1869) and Aristotle
Valaoritis (1824–79) are by far the most distinguished. The
poetry of Andreas Kalvos is austere, patriotic and moral-
izing; it used a classicizing form of the language, and had
little influence upon subsequent literature. Aristotle Valao-
ritis, on the other hand, was deeply romantic and exuberant,
often grandiloquent; and by adopting spoken Greek as the
language of poetry he had a considerable influence on later
poets. He is the link that connects the Ionian School with
the New School of Athens, just as in his own way Solomos had
been the link that connected seventeenth-century Cretan
literature with the Ionian School.

The New School of Athens

In the progress of the two literary and linguistic streams, the
consciously classicizing and the living popular language,
which Modern Greece had inherited from the Byzantine
world, the Demotic Movement of the 1880s marks a turning-
point. This was a violent reaction not only against the dead
and conventional classicizing language and the flabby exu-
berance of the Greek Romantics, but also against the weight
of the whole classical tradition. It advocated a return of
Greek art and literature to contemporary life. John Psycharis
with the publication in 1888 of his book *My Journey* (osten-
sibly a series of traveller's impressions, but really intended
to awaken the linguistic conscience of the Greeks) became
the leader of the movement. The battle flared up and a
number of distinguished critics, scholars and writers joined
the struggle, which was greatly helped by the study of
modern Greek folk-lore, then promoted by Nicolas Polites,

and the researches into medieval and modern Greek history of Constantine Paparrhegopoulos. The battle ended with the decisive victory of the demotic language for all writings of an imaginative character, and the founding of the so-called New School of Athens in poetry, whose central figure was Kostis Palamas. The New School aspired to become the Greek Parnassians, masters of a restrained and objective art but at the same time drawing inspiration from contemporary Greece and using the living idiom. Kostis Palamas (1859–1943), a native of Missolonghi, was a man of versatile talent and wide reading. His many important poetical works portray modern Greek life, the continuity of Greek history, and a number of social and spiritual convulsions of the late nineteenth and early twentieth centuries. His long lyrical philosophic poem, *The Twelve Lays of the Gypsy* is perhaps his greatest achievement. The Gypsy-musician, the central figure of the poem, symbol of freedom and art, gradually deepens into the patriot, the Greek, and finally into the 'Hellene', citizen and teacher of the world. A variety of philosophic and historical elements are interwoven, and a vigorous lyricism permeates the work. Together with the *Twelve Lays, The King's Flute,* a long historical epic intended to awaken the heroic spirit in modern Greece, and to stress the Christian and pagan elements which are 'the fabric of the Greek soul', as well as *Motionless Life,* Palamas' most important collection of lyrics, have established his reputation not only in Greek letters, but throughout the Western world. His influence upon all subsequent Greek literature has been paramount.

In poetry his contemporaries George Drosinis (1859–1951), John Polemis (1862–1925) and Kostas Krystallis (1868–94), as well has his immediate successors John Gryparis (1871–1942), Constantine Hatzopoulos (1871–1920), Miltiades Malakasis (1870–1943) and Lambros Porphyras (1879–1932) have all felt and acknowledged their debt to the leader of the school, wide as is the variety of their styles and personalities. It is the poets of this school who explored the great phrastic and metrical possibilities of the spoken idiom, and who introduced free verse and symbolism into Greek poetry, which has much enriched and enlivened it in the course of the twentieth century. Of the women writers of the New School of Athens, Myrtiotissa (Madame Theone Dracopoulos, 1883–1967), Emily S. Daphne (1887–1941) and Maria Polydoure (1905–30) are noteworthy for the elegance and passion of their verses. After Palamas the most important figure in Greek poetry is Angelos Sikelianos (1884–1951). The roots of his vigorous verse are in the New School of Athens, but he follows a different and often obscurer course. Greek nature and history are seen in the light of a Dionysiac mysticism. His striking lyrical gift and his rich, incisive diction have produced some of the most arresting lyrical poetry written in the twentieth century.

Constantine Kavafis (1863–1933) is the one significant Greek poet who remained untouched by the influence of Palamas and the New School of Athens. An Alexandrian by birth, Kavafis discerned behind present-day Alexandria the lineaments of the decadent Hellenistic past, out of which he built his 'myth' of a personal and at the same time perennial human condition. Perhaps no other Greek poet has expressed the tragedy of life more sensually, or felt sensuality more tragically; but elements of relief abound, exquisitely lyrical and often ironical. His writings have been widely translated, and universally acknowledged.

Of the many other remarkable poets who have written since the end of the First World War only four will be mentioned here. Firstly, Kostas Karyotakis (1896–1928), whose strange, pessimistic and often sarcastic poems are indeed arresting. Secondly, Nikos Kazantzakis (1885–1957), better known as a novelist, who is the author of a long philosophic epic called *The Odyssey*. The size (it is 33,333 lines long) and style of this are overwhelming, and the nihilism that permeates the whole work depressing, but there are long passages of vigour and beauty, and a remarkable wealth in the use of language. Thirdly, George Seferis (1909–1971): the leading poet of the thirties, he was a genuine symbolist, whose intense poetic response to the history of his race is indeed impressive. But he also moves beyond the limits of Greece and records with great sensitivity and purity of diction the fate of modern man. His poetry has a remarkable Greek quality in which pessimism and resilience in the face of adversity are strangely fused. In 1963 he was awarded the Nobel Prize for Literature. And finally Odysseus Elytis (b. 1911), whose surrealist technique owes much to the French writers of the period between the two world wars, but whose verses are full of the light and colour of the Aegean world.

Modern Greek poetry is mainly lyrical, and little satirical and hardly any dramatic verse of merit has been written. The satire of Andrew Laskaratos (1811–1901) and George Souris (1853–1919) – who created a peculiar form of political satire in his weekly paper *Romios* – must be recorded, but it has lost much of its flavour today.

Poetry written in Greek constitutes the longest uninterrupted tradition in the Western world. From Homer to the present day not a single generation of Greeks has lived without expressing its joys and sorrows in verse, and frequently in verse of outstanding originality and beauty. It is Greek poetry which has given the world the various poetic *genres* in which Western man has expressed his emotions and so many of his thoughts to the present day; and in many of these *genres* – the epic, the lyric and the dramatic – the achievements of the Greeks have yet to be superseded. It is a happy augury that in the last hundred years better poetry has been written in Greek than in all the fourteen preceding centuries; and that in the last fifty years, by the surrender of its political or purely national aspirations, Greek poetry has again achieved universal validity and significance.

I
ANCIENT GREECE

HOMER
date unknown

1. The Wrath of Achilles

Μῆνιν ἄειδε, θεά, Πηληϊάδεω Ἀχιλῆος
οὐλομένην, ἣ μυρί᾽ Ἀχαιοῖς ἄλγε᾽ ἔθηκε,
πολλὰς δ᾽ ἰφθίμους ψυχὰς Ἄϊδι προΐαψεν
ἡρώων, αὐτοὺς δὲ ἑλώρια τεῦχε κύνεσσιν
οἰωνοῖσί τε πᾶσι, Διὸς δ᾽ ἐτελείετο βουλή,
ἐξ οὗ δὴ τὰ πρῶτα διαστήτην ἐρίσαντε
Ἀτρεΐδης τε ἄναξ ἀνδρῶν καὶ δῖος Ἀχιλλεύς.

Τίς τ᾽ ἄρ σφωε θεῶν ἔριδι ξυνέηκε μάχεσθαι;
Λητοῦς καὶ Διὸς υἱός· ὁ γὰρ βασιλῆϊ χολωθεὶς
νοῦσον ἀνὰ στρατὸν ὦρσε κακήν, ὀλέκοντο δὲ λαοί,
οὕνεκα τὸν Χρύσην ἠτίμασεν ἀρητῆρα
Ἀτρεΐδης· ὁ γὰρ ἦλθε θοὰς ἐπὶ νῆας Ἀχαιῶν
λυσόμενός τε θύγατρα φέρων τ᾽ ἀπερείσι᾽ ἄποινα,
στέμματ᾽ ἔχων ἐν χερσὶν ἑκηβόλου Ἀπόλλωνος
χρυσέῳ ἀνὰ σκήπτρῳ, καὶ λίσσετο πάντας Ἀχαιούς,
Ἀτρεΐδα δὲ μάλιστα δύω, κοσμήτορε λαῶν·
‹Ἀτρεΐδαι τε καὶ ἄλλοι ἐϋκνήμιδες Ἀχαιοί,
ὑμῖν μὲν θεοὶ δοῖεν Ὀλύμπια δώματ᾽ ἔχοντες
ἐκπέρσαι Πριάμοιο πόλιν, εὖ δ᾽ οἴκαδ᾽ ἱκέσθαι·

SING, goddess, of the cursed wrath of Achilles, Peleus' son, that brought to the Achaeans immeasurable suffering, and hurled away to Hades many mighty souls of heroes, making their bodies carrion for the dogs and every bird of prey: so the will of Zeus was accomplished. [Sing] from the day when first the son of Atreus [Agamemnon], king of men, and godly Achilles quarrelled and parted.

Which of the gods set them to fight against one another? [It was Apollo] the son of Leto and Zeus; in his anger with the king he sent an evil plague to the army, and the soldiers died; for the son of Atreus had slighted Chryses the priest. For he [Chryses] had come to the swift ships of the Achaeans to free his daughter, bringing a vast ransom and holding in his hands the fillet of far-shafting Apollo on a golden staff; he made this plea to all the Achaeans, and especially to the two sons of Atreus, marshals of men: 'Sons of Atreus, and the other finely greaved Achaeans, may the gods that live in halls of Olympus grant you the sack of the city of Priam, and a safe homecoming; but set my dear child

3

παῖδα δ' ἐμοὶ λύσαιτε φίλην, τὰ δ' ἄποινα δέχεσθαι,
ἁζόμενοι Διὸς υἱὸν ἐκηβόλον Ἀπόλλωνα.⟩
Ἔνθ' ἄλλοι μὲν πάντες ἐπευφήμησαν Ἀχαιοὶ
αἰδεῖσθαί θ' ἱερῆα καὶ ἀγλαὰ δέχθαι ἄποινα·
ἀλλ' οὐκ Ἀτρείδη Ἀγαμέμνονι ἥνδανε θυμῷ,
ἀλλὰ κακῶς ἀφίει, κρατερὸν δ' ἐπὶ μῦθον ἔτελλε·
⟨μή σε, γέρον, κοίλησιν ἐγὼ παρὰ νηυσὶ κιχείω
ἢ νῦν δηθύνοντ' ἢ ὕστερον αὖτις ἰόντα,
μή νύ τοι οὐ χραίσμη σκῆπτρον καὶ στέμμα θεοῖο·
τὴν δ' ἐγὼ οὐ λύσω· πρίν μιν καὶ γῆρας ἔπεισιν
ἡμετέρῳ ἐνὶ οἴκῳ, ἐν Ἄργεϊ, τηλόθι πάτρης,
ἱστὸν ἐποιχομένην καὶ ἐμὸν λέχος ἀντιόωσαν·
ἀλλ' ἴθι, μή μ' ἐρέθιζε, σαώτερος ὥς κε νέηαι.⟩
Ὣς ἔφατ', ἔδεισεν δ' ὁ γέρων καὶ ἐπείθετο μύθῳ·
βῆ δ' ἀκέων παρὰ θῖνα πολυφλοίσβοιο θαλάσσης·
πολλὰ δ' ἔπειτ' ἀπάνευθε κιὼν ἠρᾶθ' ὁ γεραιὸς
Ἀπόλλωνι ἄνακτι, τὸν ἠύκομος τέκε Λητώ·
⟨κλῦθί μευ, ἀργυρότοξ', ὃς Χρύσην ἀμφιβέβηκας
Κίλλαν τε ζαθέην Τενέδοιό τε ἶφι ἀνάσσεις,
Σμινθεῦ, εἴ ποτέ τοι χαρίεντ' ἐπὶ νηὸν ἔρεψα,
ἢ εἰ δή ποτέ τοι κατὰ πίονα μηρί' ἔκηα

free, and accept the ransom, in reverence for the son of Zeus, far-shafting Apollo.'

Then all the other Achaeans cried out that he should respect the priest and accept the splendid ransom; but this did not please the heart of Agamemnon, son of Atreus. He sent him away roughly, with harsh words: 'Do not let me catch you, old man, lingering any longer near the hollow ships now, or coming back again later; or the staff and fillet of the god may be of no use to you. I will not set her free before old age comes upon her in my house, in Argos, far from her native land. There shall she weave at her loom and be in my bed my companion. Go; do not provoke me if you wish to leave unhurt.'

So he spoke, and the old man was afraid and obeyed his words; and he walked silently along the shore of the loud-roaring sea. But when he was well away, the old man prayed fervently to king Apollo, whom Leto with the lovely tresses bore: 'Hear me, god of the silver bow, you who stand over Chrysa and holy Killa and rule Tenedos with might; Smintheus, if ever I put roof to a temple that delighted you, or if ever I burnt in your honour the fat thighs of bulls or goats, fulfil this

ταύρων ἠδ' αἰγῶν, τόδε μοι κρήηνον ἐέλδωρ·
τείσειαν Δαναοὶ ἐμὰ δάκρυα σοῖσι βέλεσσιν.〉

'Ὣς ἔφατ' εὐχόμενος, τοῦ δ' ἔκλυε Φοῖβος 'Απόλλων,
βῆ δὲ κατ' Οὐλύμποιο καρήνων χωόμενος κῆρ,
τόξ' ὤμοισιν ἔχων ἀμφηρεφέα τε φαρέτρην·
ἔκλαγξαν δ' ἄρ' ὀϊστοὶ ἐπ' ὤμων χωομένοιο,
αὐτοῦ κινηθέντος· ὁ δ' ἤϊε νυκτὶ ἐοικώς.
ἕζετ' ἔπειτ' ἀπάνευθε νεῶν, μετὰ δ' ἰὸν ἔηκε·
δεινὴ δὲ κλαγγὴ γένετ' ἀργυρέοιο βιοῖο·
οὐρῆας μὲν πρῶτον ἐπῴχετο καὶ κύνας ἀργούς,
αὐτὰρ ἔπειτ' αὐτοῖσι βέλος ἐχεπευκὲς ἐφιεὶς
βάλλ'· αἰεὶ δὲ πυραὶ νεκύων καίοντο θαμειαί.

'Εννῆμαρ μὲν ἀνὰ στρατὸν ᾤχετο κῆλα θεοῖο,
τῇ δεκάτῃ δ' ἀγορήνδε καλέσσατο λαὸν 'Αχιλλεύς·
τῷ γὰρ ἐπὶ φρεσὶ θῆκε θεὰ λευκώλενος "Ηρη·
κήδετο γὰρ Δαναῶν, ὅτι ῥα θνῄσκοντας ὁρᾶτο.
οἱ δ' ἐπεὶ οὖν ἤγερθεν ὁμηγερέες τ' ἐγένοντο,
τοῖσι δ' ἀνιστάμενος μετέφη πόδας ὠκὺς 'Αχιλλεύς·
〈'Ατρεΐδη, νῦν ἄμμε παλιμπλαγχθέντας ὀΐω
ἂψ ἀπονοστήσειν, εἴ κεν θάνατόν γε φύγοιμεν,
εἰ δὴ ὁμοῦ πόλεμός τε δαμᾷ καὶ λοιμὸς 'Αχαιούς·

wish of mine, let the Danaans pay with your arrows for my tears.'

So he prayed, and Phoebus Apollo heard him, and came down from the peaks of Olympus angry at heart, with his bow and his covered quiver on his shoulders. And the arrows clanged on his shoulders as the angry god moved; he came like nightfall. Then he sat at a distance from the ships, and shot an arrow; and there came a terrible clang from the silver bow. First he assailed the mules and the swift dogs, but later he aimed and fired his piercing shaft at the men; and many pyres for the dead burnt constantly.

For nine days the god's arrows fell on the army; but on the tenth Achilles summoned the men to assemble. The goddess Hera of the white arms put the thought in his mind, because she pitied the Danaans, when she saw them dying. And when they had gathered, and the assembly was complete, swift-footed Achilles stood up and spoke to them; 'Son of Atreus, I suppose that we shall make a wandering return home again – always assuming we escape death – if war and pestilence together ravage the Achaeans. Would it not be better to ask some prophet

ἀλλ' ἄγε δή τινα μάντιν ἐρείομεν ἢ ἱερῆα,
ἢ καὶ ὀνειροπόλον, καὶ γάρ τ' ὄναρ ἐκ Διός ἐστιν,
ὅς κ' εἴποι ὅ τι τόσσον ἐχώσατο Φοῖβος Ἀπόλλων,
εἴτ' ἄρ' ὅ γ' εὐχωλῆς ἐπιμέμφεται εἴθ' ἑκατόμβης,
αἴ κέν πως ἀρνῶν κνίσης αἰγῶν τε τελείων
βούλεται ἀντιάσας ἡμῖν ἀπὸ λοιγὸν ἀμῦναι.›
   Ἤτοι ὅ γ' ὣς εἰπὼν κατ' ἄρ' ἕζετο· τοῖσι δ' ἀνέστη
Κάλχας Θεστορίδης, οἰωνοπόλων ὄχ' ἄριστος,
ὃς ᾔδη τά τ' ἐόντα τά τ' ἐσσόμενα πρό τ' ἐόντα,
καὶ νήεσσ' ἡγήσατ' Ἀχαιῶν Ἴλιον εἴσω
ἣν διὰ μαντοσύνην, τήν οἱ πόρε Φοῖβος Ἀπόλλων·
ὅ σφιν ἐϋφρονέων ἀγορήσατο καὶ μετέειπεν·
‹ὦ Ἀχιλεῦ, κέλεαί με, Διῒ φίλε, μυθήσασθαι
μῆνιν Ἀπόλλωνος ἑκατηβελέταο ἄνακτος·
τοιγὰρ ἐγὼν ἐρέω· σὺ δὲ σύνθεο καί μοι ὄμοσσον
ἦ μέν μοι πρόφρων ἔπεσιν καὶ χερσὶν ἀρήξειν·
ἦ γὰρ ὀΐομαι ἄνδρα χολωσέμεν, ὃς μέγα πάντων
Ἀργείων κρατέει καί οἱ πείθονται Ἀχαιοί·
κρείσσων γὰρ βασιλεὺς ὅτε χώσεται ἀνδρὶ χέρηϊ·
εἴ περ γάρ τε χόλον γε καὶ αὐτῆμαρ καταπέψῃ,
ἀλλά τε καὶ μετόπισθεν ἔχει κότον, ὄφρα τελέσσῃ,
ἐν στήθεσσιν ἑοῖσι· σὺ δὲ φράσαι εἴ με σαώσεις.›

or priest, or even an interpreter of dreams – for a dream too comes from Zeus – to tell us why Phoebus Apollo is so angry? Does he blame us for some promise [we broke], or some hecatomb [we did not offer]? Perhaps he will accept the burning fat of lambs and of faultless goats, to hold off the pestilence from us.'

So he spoke, and sat down; and Calchas, son of Thestor, stood up among them, most excellent of seers, who knew the present, the future and the past, and who had guided the ships of the Achaeans to Troy by the art of prophecy which Phoebus Apollo had given him. Being well disposed to them, he spoke in the assembly and said: 'Achilles, loved by Zeus, you propose I explain the anger of far-shafting lord Apollo. I will therefore speak; but you must covenant with me on your oath you are willing to help me by word and deed. I believe I shall anger a man who is the great ruler of all the Argives, and whom the Achaeans obey. For a king who is angry with a lesser man is more powerful than he; even though for that day he swallows his anger, his wrath lingers on in his breast till he settles his account; consider then, whether you will protect me.'

Τὸν δ' ἀπαμειβόμενος προσέφη πόδας ὠκὺς Ἀχιλλεύς·
‹θαρσήσας μάλα εἰπὲ θεοπρόπιον ὅ τι οἶσθα·
οὐ μὰ γὰρ Ἀπόλλωνα Διὶ φίλον, ᾧ τε σύ, Κάλχαν,
εὐχόμενος Δαναοῖσι θεοπροπίας ἀναφαίνεις,
οὔ τις ἐμεῦ ζῶντος καὶ ἐπὶ χθονὶ δερκομένοιο
σοὶ κοίλης παρὰ νηυσὶ βαρείας χεῖρας ἐποίσει
συμπάντων Δαναῶν, οὐδ' ἢν Ἀγαμέμνονα εἴπῃς,
ὃς νῦν πολλὸν ἄριστος Ἀχαιῶν εὔχεται εἶναι.›
   Καὶ τότε δὴ θάρσησε καὶ ηὔδα μάντις ἀμύμων·
‹οὔτ' ἄρ ὅ γ' εὐχωλῆς ἐπιμέμφεται οὔθ' ἑκατόμβης,
ἀλλ' ἕνεκ' ἀρητῆρος, ὃν ἠτίμησ' Ἀγαμέμνων
οὐδ' ἀπέλυσε θύγατρα καὶ οὐκ ἀπεδέξατ' ἄποινα,
τοὔνεκ' ἄρ ἄλγε' ἔδωκεν ἑκηβόλος ἠδ' ἔτι δώσει·
οὐδ' ὅ γε πρὶν Δαναοῖσιν ἀεικέα λοιγὸν ἀπώσει,
πρίν γ' ἀπὸ πατρὶ φίλῳ δόμεναι ἑλικώπιδα κούρην
ἀπριάτην ἀνάποινον, ἄγειν θ' ἱερὴν ἑκατόμβην
ἐς Χρύσην· τότε κέν μιν ἱλασσάμενοι πεπίθοιμεν.›
   Ἤτοι ὅ γ' ὣς εἰπὼν κατ' ἄρ ἕζετο· τοῖσι δ' ἀνέστη
ἥρως Ἀτρεΐδης εὐρὺ κρείων Ἀγαμέμνων
ἀχνύμενος· μένεος δὲ μέγα φρένες ἀμφὶ μέλαιναι

And swift-footed Achilles answered and said to him: 'Take full courage, and speak any prophecy you know; for, by Apollo, dear to Zeus, to whom you, Calchas, pray, when you reveal your oracles to the Danaans, no man shall lay his heavy hands upon you near the hollow ships, as long as I live and see the light, not one of the Greeks, not even if you mean Agamemnon, who now claims to be, by far the greatest of the Achaeans.'

And then the blameless seer took courage and spoke: 'He [Apollo] is not displeased because of a [broken] vow, nor because of a hecatomb. He is displeased because of his priest whom Agamemnon dishonoured when he did not set his daughter free, and did not accept the ransom; for this the far-shafting god has brought suffering upon us, and will bring still more. Nor will he take the hated pestilence away from the Danaans, till we have given the girl with the flashing eyes to her father, unbought, unransomed, and brought a holy hecatomb to Chrysa; then we might soothe his anger and persuade him to relent.'

So he spoke and sat down, and the hero son of Atreus, wide-ruling Agamemnon, stood up full of anger; his dark heart was brimming with

7

πίμπλαντ', ὄσσε δέ οἱ πυρὶ λαμπετόωντι ἔΐκτην·
Κάλχαντα πρώτιστα κάκ' ὀσσόμενος προσέειπε·
‹μάντι κακῶν, οὐ πώ ποτέ μοι τὸ κρήγυον εἶπας·
αἰεί τοι τὰ κάκ' ἐστὶ φίλα φρεσὶ μαντεύεσθαι,
ἐσθλὸν δ' οὔτε τί πω εἶπας ἔπος οὔτ' ἐτέλεσσας·
καὶ νῦν ἐν Δαναοῖσι θεοπροπέων ἀγορεύεις
ὡς δὴ τοῦδ' ἕνεκά σφιν ἑκηβόλος ἄλγεα τεύχει,
οὕνεκ' ἐγὼ κούρης Χρυσηίδος ἀγλά' ἄποινα
οὐκ ἔθελον δέξασθαι, ἐπεὶ πολὺ βούλομαι αὐτὴν
οἴκοι ἔχειν· καὶ γάρ ῥα Κλυταιμνήστρης προβέβουλα
κουριδίης ἀλόχου, ἐπεὶ οὔ ἕθέν ἐστι χερείων,
οὐ δέμας οὐδὲ φυήν, οὔτ' ἂρ φρένας οὔτε τι ἔργα.
ἀλλὰ καὶ ὣς ἐθέλω δόμεναι πάλιν, εἰ τό γ' ἄμεινον·
βούλομ' ἐγὼ λαὸν σῶν ἔμμεναι ἢ ἀπολέσθαι·
αὐτὰρ ἐμοὶ γέρας αὐτίχ' ἑτοιμάσατ', ὄφρα μὴ οἶος
Ἀργείων ἀγέραστος ἔω, ἐπεὶ οὐδὲ ἔοικε·
λεύσσετε γὰρ τό γε πάντες, ὅ μοι γέρας ἔρχεται ἄλλῃ.›
      Τὸν δ' ἠμείβετ' ἔπειτα ποδάρκης δῖος Ἀχιλλεύς·
‹Ἀτρεΐδη κύδιστε, φιλοκτεανώτατε πάντων,
πῶς γάρ τοι δώσουσι γέρας μεγάθυμοι Ἀχαιοί;
οὐδέ τί που ἴδμεν ξυνήϊα κείμενα πολλά·

wrath, and his eyes were like flashing fire. He first spoke to Calchas, eyeing him balefully: 'Seer of evil, you have never yet told me one pleasant thing. To tell of evil is always the joy of your heart, but you have never yet said, or done, anything good. And now you tell the Danaans in your oracle that the far-shafting god brings suffering upon them, because I would not accept the rich ransom for the girl Chryseis, as I would much rather keep her in my house; for yes, I prefer her to Clytaemnestra my wedded wife, for in no way is she worse, neither in body, nor in nature, nor in intelligence, nor in skills. Yet, even so, I will give her back, if that is better; I want my men to be safe, not to be ruined. But you must find for me a gift at once, lest I alone of all the Argives be without a prize, for that would not be proper; for you all see that my prize is going elsewhere.'

Swift-footed, godly Achilles then answered him: 'Most glorious son of Atreus, most covetous of men, how shall the great-hearted Achaeans give you a prize? We do not know where many gifts lie stored; the

ἀλλὰ τὰ μὲν πολίων ἐξεπράθομεν, τὰ δέδασται,
λαοὺς δ' οὐκ ἐπέοικε παλίλλογα ταῦτ' ἐπαγείρειν.
ἀλλὰ σὺ μὲν νῦν τήνδε θεῷ πρόες· αὐτὰρ Ἀχαιοὶ
τριπλῇ τετραπλῇ τ' ἀποτείσομεν, αἴ κέ ποθι Ζεὺς
δῷσι πόλιν Τροίην εὐτείχεον ἐξαλαπάξαι.⟩
    Τὸν δ' ἀπαμειβόμενος προσέφη κρείων Ἀγαμέμνων·
⟨μὴ δὴ οὕτως, ἀγαθός περ ἐών, θεοείκελ' Ἀχιλλεῦ,
κλέπτε νόῳ, ἐπεὶ οὐ παρελεύσεαι οὐδέ με πείσεις.
ἦ ἐθέλεις, ὄφρ' αὐτὸς ἔχῃς γέρας, αὐτὰρ ἔμ' αὔτως
ἧσθαι δευόμενον, κέλεαι δέ με τήνδ' ἀποδοῦναι;
ἀλλ' εἰ μὲν δώσουσι γέρας μεγάθυμοι Ἀχαιοί,
ἄρσαντες κατὰ θυμόν, ὅπως ἀντάξιον ἔσται·
εἰ δέ κε μὴ δώωσιν, ἐγὼ δέ κεν αὐτὸς ἕλωμαι
ἢ τεὸν ἢ Αἴαντος ἰὼν γέρας, ἢ Ὀδυσῆος
ἄξω ἑλών· ὁ δέ κεν κεχολώσεται, ὃν κεν ἵκωμαι.
ἀλλ' ἤτοι μὲν ταῦτα μεταφρασόμεσθα καὶ αὖτις,
νῦν δ' ἄγε νῆα μέλαιναν ἐρύσσομεν εἰς ἅλα δῖαν,
ἐν δ' ἐρέτας ἐπιτηδὲς ἀγείρομεν, ἐς δ' ἑκατόμβην
θείομεν, ἂν δ' αὐτὴν Χρυσηίδα καλλιπάρῃον
βήσομεν· εἰς δέ τις ἀρχὸς ἀνὴρ βουληφόρος ἔστω,
ἢ Αἴας ἢ Ἰδομενεὺς ἢ δῖος Ὀδυσσεὺς

plunder we took from captured towns has been distributed, and it is not proper to collect it back from the people. But give up this girl to the god now, and we Achaeans will pay you back threefold and four-fold, if Zeus grant us to sack the well-walled city of Troy.'

King Agamemnon answered him and said: 'Godlike Achilles, though you are brave, do not try to trick me in this way. You will not outwit me, nor persuade me. Do you want to keep your gift of honour, and me of all people to sit idle with nothing? Are you telling me to give her back? Either the great-hearted Achaeans will give me a gift as I wish, an equal recompense – or, if they do not give it, then I will go myself and carry away a prize of honour, either yours, or that of Ajax or of Odysseus. The man to whom I go will be angry. But this we shall consider again later. Now let us launch a black ship on the godly sea, select oarsmen for it, put a hecatomb on board, and send Chryseis of the beautiful cheeks herself; and let one of our counsellors be captain, Ajax, or Idomeneus, or godly Odysseus, or you, son of Peleus, most

ἠὲ σύ, Πηλεΐδη, πάντων ἐκπαγλότατ' ἀνδρῶν,
ὄφρ' ἡμῖν ἑκάεργον ἱλάσσεαι ἱερὰ ῥέξας.)
    Τὸν δ' ἄρ' ὑπόδρα ἰδὼν προσέφη πόδας ὠκὺς Ἀχιλλεύς·
(ὤ μοι, ἀναιδείην ἐπιειμένε, κερδαλεόφρον,
πῶς τίς τοι πρόφρων ἔπεσιν πείθηται Ἀχαιῶν
ἢ ὁδὸν ἐλθέμεναι ἢ ἀνδράσιν Ἶφι μάχεσθαι;
οὐ γὰρ ἐγὼ Τρώων ἕνεκ' ἤλυθον αἰχμητάων
δεῦρο μαχησόμενος, ἐπεὶ οὔ τί μοι αἴτιοί εἰσιν·
οὐ γὰρ πώ ποτ' ἐμὰς βοῦς ἤλασαν οὐδὲ μὲν ἵππους,
οὐδέ ποτ' ἐν Φθίῃ ἐριβώλακι βωτιανείρῃ
καρπὸν ἐδηλήσαντ', ἐπεὶ ἦ μάλα πολλὰ μεταξὺ
οὔρεά τε σκιόεντα θάλασσά τε ἠχήεσσα·
ἀλλὰ σοί, ὦ μέγ' ἀναιδές, ἅμ' ἑσπόμεθ', ὄφρα σὺ χαίρῃς,
τιμὴν ἀρνύμενοι Μενελάῳ σοί τε, κυνῶπα,
πρὸς Τρώων· τῶν οὔ τι μετατρέπῃ οὐδ' ἀλεγίζεις·
καὶ δή μοι γέρας αὐτὸς ἀφαιρήσεσθαι ἀπειλεῖς,
ᾧ ἔπι πολλὰ μόγησα, δόσαν δέ μοι υἷες Ἀχαιῶν.
οὐ μὲν σοί ποτε ἶσον ἔχω γέρας, ὁππότ' Ἀχαιοὶ
Τρώων ἐκπέρσωσ' εὖ ναιόμενον πτολίεθρον·
ἀλλὰ τὸ μὲν πλεῖον πολυάϊκος πολέμοιο
χεῖρες ἐμαὶ διέπουσ'· ἀτὰρ ἤν ποτε δασμὸς ἵκηται,
σοὶ τὸ γέρας πολὺ μεῖζον, ἐγὼ δ' ὀλίγον τε φίλον τε

fierce of men, to offer sacrifices for us and appease the far-shafting god.'

Then swift-footed Achilles looked at him scowling, and said: 'Ah! shameless, greedy man, how can any Achaean willingly go on a journey or fight valiantly against men in answer to words from you? I did not come here to fight because of the Trojan spearsmen; they did not provoke me. They never yet drove away my oxen or my horses, nor did they ravage my harvest in Phthia, nurse of men, where soil does not crumble to dust under the plough; for many shadowy mountains and the loud-roaring sea lie between us; but we followed you here, most shameless man, to please you by earning glory for Menelaus and for you, you dog-face, at the expense of the Trojans. All this you do not consider, nor do you care about it; and now you yourself threaten to take my prize, for which I laboured much, and which the sons of the Achaeans gave me. I never get a prize equal to yours, when the Achaeans sack some richly populated city of the Trojans; my hands fight most of the furious war, but, when the division of the booty comes, your prize is far bigger; I, having fought to exhaustion, go to

ἔρχομ' ἔχων ἐπὶ νῆας, ἐπεί κε κάμω πολεμίζων.
νῦν δ' εἶμι Φθίηνδ', ἐπεὶ ἦ πολὺ φέρτερόν ἐστιν
οἴκαδ' ἴμεν σὺν νηυσὶ κορωνίσιν, οὐδέ σ' ὀΐω
ἐνθάδ' ἄτιμος ἐὼν ἄφενος καὶ πλοῦτον ἀφύξειν.›
    Τὸν δ' ἠμείβετ' ἔπειτα ἄναξ ἀνδρῶν 'Αγαμέμνων·
‹φεῦγε μάλ', εἴ τοι θυμὸς ἐπέσσυται, οὐδέ σ' ἔγωγε
λίσσομαι εἴνεκ' ἐμεῖο μένειν· πάρ' ἐμοιγε καὶ ἄλλοι
οἵ κέ με τιμήσουσι, μάλιστα δὲ μητίετα Ζεύς.
ἔχθιστος δέ μοί ἐσσι διοτρεφέων βασιλήων·
αἰεὶ γάρ τοι ἔρις τε φίλη πόλεμοί τε μάχαι τε·
εἰ μάλα καρτερός ἐσσι, θεός που σοὶ τό γ' ἔδωκεν·
οἴκαδ' ἰὼν σὺν νηυσί τε σῆς καὶ σοῖς ἑτάροισι
Μυρμιδόνεσσιν ἄνασσε, σέθεν δ' ἐγὼ οὐκ ἀλεγίζω,
οὐδ' ὄθομαι κοτέοντος· ἀπειλήσω δέ τοι ὧδε·
ὡς ἔμ' ἀφαιρεῖται Χρυσηΐδα Φοῖβος 'Απόλλων,
τὴν μὲν ἐγὼ σὺν νηΐ τ' ἐμῇ καὶ ἐμοῖς ἑτάροισι
πέμψω, ἐγὼ δέ κ' ἄγω Βρισηΐδα καλλιπάρηον
αὐτὸς ἰὼν κλισίηνδε, τὸ σὸν γέρας, ὄφρ' ἐῢ εἰδῇς
ὅσσον φέρτερός εἰμι σέθεν, στυγέῃ δὲ καὶ ἄλλος
ἶσον ἐμοὶ φάσθαι καὶ ὁμοιωθήμεναι ἄντην.›

the ships with some small thing, for my own. Now I will leave for
Phthia, because it is far better to return home on my beaked ships; nor
do I intend to stay here dishonoured to pile up wealth and riches for
you.'
    Then Agamemnon, king of men, answered him: 'Leave quickly, if
your heart is set on it. I do not beg you to stay on for my sake; I have
others with me who will honour me, above all Zeus, the counsellor;
most hateful to me are you of all the god-reared kings; you always love
quarrels, wars and fighting. If you are very strong, it is only a gift of a
god. Go home with your ships and your companions, and rule among
Myrmidons; I have no regard for you, nor do I care if you are angry
And this is my threat to you: since Phoebus Apollo takes Chryseis
away from me, her I shall send back, with my ship and my companions;
and I myself shall go to your hut, and take Briseis of the beautiful
cheeks, your own prize, so that you will clearly know how far greater
I am than you, and so that others later shall fear to match their words
with mine, and to compare themselves with me to my face.'

Ὣς φάτο· Πηλεΐωνι δ' ἄχος γένετ', ἐν δέ οἱ ἦτορ
στήθεσσιν λασίοισι διάνδιχα μερμήριξεν,
ἢ ὅ γε φάσγανον ὀξὺ ἐρυσσάμενος παρὰ μηροῦ
τοὺς μὲν ἀναστήσειεν, ὁ δ' Ἀτρεΐδην ἐναρίζοι,
ἦε χόλον παύσειεν ἐρητύσειέ τε θυμόν.
ἧος ὁ ταῦθ' ὥρμαινε κατὰ φρένα καὶ κατὰ θυμόν,
ἕλκετο δ' ἐκ κολεοῖο μέγα ξίφος, ἦλθε δ' Ἀθήνη
οὐρανόθεν· πρὸ γὰρ ἧκε θεὰ λευκώλενος Ἥρη,
ἄμφω ὁμῶς θυμῷ φιλέουσά τε κηδομένη τε·
στῆ δ' ὄπιθεν, ξανθῆς δὲ κόμης ἕλε Πηλεΐωνα
οἴῳ φαινομένη· τῶν δ' ἄλλων οὔ τις ὁρᾶτο·
θάμβησεν δ' Ἀχιλεύς, μετὰ δ' ἐτράπετ', αὐτίκα δ' ἔγνω
Παλλάδ' Ἀθηναίην· δεινὼ δέ οἱ ὄσσε φάανθεν·
καί μιν φωνήσας ἔπεα πτερόεντα προσηύδα·
‹τίπτ' αὖτ', αἰγιόχοιο Διὸς τέκος, εἰλήλουθας;
ἦ ἵνα ὕβριν ἴδῃ Ἀγαμέμνονος Ἀτρεΐδαο;
ἀλλ' ἔκ τοι ἐρέω, τὸ δὲ καὶ τελέεσθαι ὀίω·
ἧς ὑπεροπλίῃσι τάχ' ἄν ποτε θυμὸν ὀλέσσῃ.›
    Τὸν δ' αὖτε προσέειπε θεὰ γλαυκῶπις Ἀθήνη·
‹ἦλθον ἐγὼ παύσουσα τὸ σὸν μένος, αἴ κε πίθηαι,
οὐρανόθεν· πρὸ δέ μ' ἧκε θεὰ λευκώλενος Ἥρη

So he said, and pain seized the son of Peleus, and his heart within his shaggy breast was divided, considering whether to draw his sharp sword from his thigh, break up the assembly, and kill the son of Atreus, or to hold back his anger and curb his heart. While he was considering this in his heart and in his mind, and as he was drawing his great sword from its sheath, Athene came down from heaven. For the white-armed goddess Hera sent her, whose heart loved both equally, and cared for them. She stood behind Peleus' son and caught him by his golden hair, visible only to him; none of the others saw her. And Achilles marvelled and turned round, and recognized Pallas Athene at once; her eyes shone frighteningly. He spoke to her with winged words, and said: 'Why have you come back again, daughter of aegis-carrying Zeus? To see the insolence of Agamemnon, son of Atreus? But I will tell you this, and I believe it will come true: for his insolence he shall soon lose his own life.'
    Then the bright-eyed goddess Athene spoke to him again: 'I came from heaven to still your anger, if you would listen to me; I was sent by the white-armed goddess Hera, who loves you both equally in her

ἄμφω ὁμῶς θυμῷ φιλέουσά τε κηδομένη τε·
ἀλλ' ἄγε λῆγ' ἔριδος, μηδὲ ξίφος ἕλκεο χειρί·
ἀλλ' ἤτοι ἔπεσιν μὲν ὀνείδισον ὡς ἔσεταί περ·
ὧδε γὰρ ἐξερέω, τὸ δὲ καὶ τετελεσμένον ἔσται·
καί ποτέ τοι τρὶς τόσσα παρέσσεται ἀγλαὰ δῶρα
ὕβριος εἵνεκα τῆσδε· σὺ δ' ἴσχεο, πείθεο δ' ἡμῖν.〉

    Τὴν δ' ἀπαμειβόμενος προσέφη πόδας ὠκὺς Ἀχιλλεύς·
〈χρὴ μὲν σφωΐτερόν γε, θεά, ἔπος εἰρύσσασθαι
καὶ μάλα περ θυμῷ κεχολωμένον· ὣς γὰρ ἄμεινον·
ὅς κε θεοῖς ἐπιπείθηται, μάλα τ' ἔκλυον αὐτοῦ.〉

    Ἦ καὶ ἐπ' ἀργυρέῃ κώπῃ σχέθε χεῖρα βαρεῖαν,
ἂψ δ' ἐς κουλεὸν ὦσε μέγα ξίφος, οὐδ' ἀπίθησε
μύθῳ Ἀθηναίης· ἡ δ' Οὔλυμπόνδε βεβήκει
δώματ' ἐς αἰγιόχοιο Διὸς μετὰ δαίμονας ἄλλους.

    Πηλεΐδης δ' ἐξαῦτις ἀταρτηροῖς ἐπέεσσιν
Ἀτρεΐδην προσέειπε, καὶ οὔ πω λῆγε χόλοιο·
〈οἰνοβαρές, κυνὸς ὄμματ' ἔχων, κραδίην δ' ἐλάφοιο,
οὔτε ποτ' ἐς πόλεμον ἅμα λαῷ θωρηχθῆναι
οὔτε λόχονδ' ἰέναι σὺν ἀριστήεσσιν Ἀχαιῶν
τέτληκας θυμῷ· τὸ δέ τοι κὴρ εἴδεται εἶναι.
ἦ πολὺ λώϊόν ἐστι κατὰ στρατὸν εὐρὺν Ἀχαιῶν

heart, and cares for you. Come now, stop the quarrel, and do not with your hand draw the sword; but with words rebuke him and tell him that this will happen. For so I will tell you, and so it shall be fulfilled: some day three times as many splendid gifts as these will come to you, because of this insult; hold your hand and be advised by us.'

And swift-footed Achilles answered and said to her: 'Goddess, a man must observe what you two [goddesses] say, even though he is very angry at heart; for it is better so. The gods listen gladly to him who obeys them.'

He spoke, and kept his heavy hand on the silver hilt, and thrust the great sword back into the sheath, and did not disobey the words of Athene; and she left for Olympus, to join the other gods, in the halls of aegis-carrying Zeus.

Then the son of Peleus again spoke savage words to Atreus' son, and did not stifle his anger at all: 'Sodden with drink, with the face of a dog and the heart of a deer, you never had the courage to arm for battle with your soldiers, or to lie in ambush with the best of the Achaeans; for you, that would equal death. Indeed, it is far more pleasant to go through the great encampment of the Achaeans and take

δῶρ' ἀποαιρεῖσθαι ὅς τις σέθεν ἀντίον εἴπῃ·
δημοβόρος βασιλεύς, ἐπεὶ οὐτιδανοῖσιν ἀνάσσεις·
ἦ γὰρ ἄν, Ἀτρεΐδη, νῦν ὕστατα λωβήσαιο.
ἀλλ' ἔκ τοι ἐρέω καὶ ἐπὶ μέγαν ὅρκον ὀμοῦμαι·
ναὶ μὰ τόδε σκῆπτρον, τὸ μὲν οὔ ποτε φύλλα καὶ ὄζους
φύσει, ἐπεὶ δὴ πρῶτα τομὴν ἐν ὄρεσσι λέλοιπεν,
οὐδ' ἀναθηλήσει· περὶ γάρ ῥά ἑ χαλκὸς ἔλεψε
φύλλα τε καὶ φλοιόν· νῦν αὖτέ μιν υἷες Ἀχαιῶν
ἐν παλάμῃς φορέουσι δικασπόλοι, οἵ τε θέμιστας
πρὸς Διὸς εἰρύαται· ὁ δέ τοι μέγας ἔσσεται ὅρκος·
ἦ ποτ' Ἀχιλλῆος ποθὴ ἵξεται υἷας Ἀχαιῶν
σύμπαντας· τότε δ' οὔ τι δυνήσεαι ἀχνύμενός περ
χραισμεῖν, εὖτ' ἂν πολλοὶ ὑφ' Ἕκτορος ἀνδροφόνοιο
θνήσκοντες πίπτωσι· σὺ δ' ἔνδοθι θυμὸν ἀμύξεις
χωόμενος ὅ τ' ἄριστον Ἀχαιῶν οὐδὲν ἔτεισας.›
   Ὣς φάτο Πηλεΐδης, ποτὶ δὲ σκῆπτρον βάλε γαίῃ
χρυσείοις ἥλοισι πεπαρμένον, ἕζετο δ' αὐτός·
Ἀτρεΐδης δ' ἑτέρωθεν ἐμήνιε· τοῖσι δὲ Νέστωρ
ἡδυεπὴς ἀνόρουσε, λιγὺς Πυλίων ἀγορητής,
τοῦ καὶ ἀπὸ γλώσσης μέλιτος γλυκίων ῥέεν αὐδή·
τῷ δ' ἤδη δύο μὲν γενεαὶ μερόπων ἀνθρώπων

your prize from the man who speaks against you. You are a king who can feast on his people because you rule men who are worth nothing – otherwise this insult, son of Atreus, would have been your last. But I will speak out to you, and swear a mighty oath: yes, by this staff that shall no more sprout leaf or twig, as it has for ever left its stump in the hills, and will not bud again, because the bronze has stripped it of leaves and bark, and which now the sons of the Achaeans that pronounce judgement carry in their hands, they that by Zeus' command watch over the laws – so this shall be a mighty oath for you: Some day all the sons of the Achaeans will long for Achilles; and then you will not be able to help them, for all your grief, when many fall dying at the hands of man-killing Hector. Then you will tear your heart within you with anger that you failed to honour the best of the Achaeans.'

So spoke the son of Peleus, and he threw on the earth the staff studded with golden nails, and he himself sat down; and on the other side the son of Atreus was wild with fury. Then sweet-speaking Nestor rose up from among them, the clear-voiced orator of the Pylians, from whose tongue flowed a voice sweeter than honey. Two generations of

ἐφθίαθ', οἳ οἱ πρόσθεν ἅμα τράφεν ἠδ' ἐγένοντο
ἐν Πύλῳ ἠγαθέῃ, μετὰ δὲ τριτάτοισιν ἄνασσεν·
ὅ σφιν ἐϋφρονέων ἀγορήσατο καὶ μετέειπεν·
‹ὦ πόποι, ἦ μέγα πένθος Ἀχαιΐδα γαῖαν ἱκάνει·
ἦ κεν γηθήσαι Πρίαμος Πριάμοιό τε παῖδες
ἄλλοι τε Τρῶες μέγα κεν κεχαροίατο θυμῷ,
εἰ σφῶϊν τάδε πάντα πυθοίατο μαρναμένοιϊν,
οἳ περὶ μὲν βουλὴν Δαναῶν, περὶ δ' ἐστὲ μάχεσθαι.
ἀλλὰ πίθεσθ'· ἄμφω δὲ νεωτέρω ἐστὸν ἐμεῖο·
ἤδη γάρ ποτ' ἐγὼ καὶ ἀρείοσιν ἠέ περ ὑμῖν
ἀνδράσιν ὡμίλησα, καὶ οὔ ποτέ μ' οἵ γ' ἀθέριζον.
οὐ γάρ πω τοίους ἴδον ἀνέρας οὐδὲ ἴδωμαι,
οἷον Πειρίθοόν τε Δρύαντά τε, ποιμένα λαῶν,
Καινέα τ' Ἐξάδιόν τε καὶ ἀντίθεον Πολύφημον,
Θησέα τ' Αἰγεΐδην, ἐπιείκελον ἀθανάτοισιν·
κάρτιστοι δὴ κεῖνοι ἐπιχθονίων τράφεν ἀνδρῶν·
κάρτιστοι μὲν ἔσαν καὶ καρτίστοις ἐμάχοντο,
φηρσὶν ὀρεσκῴοισι, καὶ ἐκπάγλως ἀπόλεσσαν.
καὶ μὲν τοῖσιν ἐγὼ μεθομίλεον ἐκ Πύλου ἐλθών,
τηλόθεν ἐξ ἀπίης γαίης· καλέσαντο γὰρ αὐτοί·
καὶ μαχόμην κατ' ἔμ' αὐτὸν ἐγώ· κείνοισι δ' ἂν οὔ τις

mortal men that had in the past been born and reared with him in holy Pylos he had already seen perish, and he was king among the third. Being well-disposed to them, he made this speech to the assembly: 'Alas, a great cause for mourning comes to the land of Achaea; Priam and Priam's sons would be truly glad, and all the other Trojans would greatly rejoice in their hearts, if they heard of this quarrel between you two who are the leaders of the Danaans in counsel and in battle. But listen to me; you are both younger than I. Already, in the past, I have had dealings with better men than you, and they never disregarded me. I never saw such warriors, nor shall see, as were Peirithous and Dryas, the shepherd of men, and Caineus and Exadios and godlike Polyphemus and Theseus, son of Aigeus, that looked like a god. They were brought up to be the mightiest of all men on the earth, they were the mightiest and they fought with the mightiest, with the wild beasts of the mountain caves, and marvellously destroyed them. And with these I dealt, when I came from far away, from Pylos, a distant land; for they themselves invited me. And I fought in single-combat; but none of the men

τῶν οἳ νῦν βροτοί εἰσιν ἐπιχθόνιοι μαχέοιτο·
καὶ μέν μευ βουλέων ξύνιεν πείθοντό τε μύθῳ·
ἀλλὰ πίθεσθε καὶ ὕμμες, ἐπεὶ πείθεσθαι ἄμεινον·
μήτε σὺ τόνδ' ἀγαθός περ ἐὼν ἀποαίρεο κούρην,
ἀλλ' ἔα, ὥς οἱ πρῶτα δόσαν γέρας υἷες Ἀχαιῶν·
μήτε σύ, Πηλεΐδη, ἔθελ' ἐριζέμεναι βασιλῆϊ
ἀντιβίην, ἐπεὶ οὔ ποθ' ὁμοίης ἔμμορε τιμῆς
σκηπτοῦχος βασιλεύς, ᾧ τε Ζεὺς κῦδος ἔδωκεν.
εἰ δὲ σὺ καρτερός ἐσσι, θεὰ δέ σε γείνατο μήτηρ,
ἀλλ' ὅ γε φέρτερός ἐστιν, ἐπεὶ πλεόνεσσιν ἀνάσσει.
Ἀτρεΐδη, σὺ δὲ παῦε τεὸν μένος· αὐτὰρ ἔγωγε
λίσσομ' Ἀχιλλῆϊ μεθέμεν χόλον, ὃς μέγα πᾶσιν
ἕρκος Ἀχαιοῖσιν πέλεται πολέμοιο κακοῖο.⟩
   Τὸν δ' ἀπαμειβόμενος προσέφη κρείων Ἀγαμέμνων·
⟨ναὶ δὴ ταῦτά γε πάντα, γέρον, κατὰ μοῖραν ἔειπες·
ἀλλ' ὅδ' ἀνὴρ ἐθέλει περὶ πάντων ἔμμεναι ἄλλων,
πάντων μὲν κρατέειν ἐθέλει, πάντεσσι δ' ἀνάσσειν,
πᾶσι δὲ σημαίνειν, ἅ τιν' οὐ πείσεσθαι ὀΐω·
εἰ δέ μιν αἰχμητὴν ἔθεσαν θεοὶ αἰὲν ἐόντες,
τοὔνεκά οἱ προθέουσιν ὀνείδεα μυθήσασθαι;⟩
   Τὸν δ' ἄρ' ὑποβλήδην ἠμείβετο δῖος Ἀχιλλεύς·

who are now on earth could fight against them. And they heard my
advice, and listened to my words. You too listen to me, for it is better
so. You [Agamemnon], though you are a great man, do not seize the
girl from him, but leave her to be a prize of honour as she was given
from the beginning by the sons of the Achaeans; nor, son of Peleus,
should you harbour any wish to stir up strife with a king, might against
might; for a sceptred king merits no ordinary share of honour, since
Zeus gave him glory. Though you are strong and the son of a goddess,
yet he is superior, for he rules over more men. And you, son of Atreus,
stifle your rage; I beg you to put aside your anger with Achilles. He is
for all the Achaeans a great bulwark against evil war.'

   Then King Agamemnon answered him and said: 'Time-honoured
lord, all this that you say is certainly right. But this man wants to be
above all the others, he wants to be master of all, be king of all, be com-
mander of all; I believe no one will listen to him. Even if the immortal
gods did make him a warrior, does that mean that they also want him
to speak abuse?'

   Then godlike Achilles broke in on him and answered: 'Yes, for I

‹ἦ γάρ κεν δειλός τε καὶ οὐτιδανὸς καλεοίμην,
εἰ δὴ σοὶ πᾶν ἔργον ὑπείξομαι ὅττι κεν εἴπῃς·
ἄλλοισιν δὴ ταῦτ' ἐπιτέλλεο, μὴ γὰρ ἔμοιγε
σήμαιν'· οὐ γὰρ ἔγωγ' ἔτι σοὶ πείσεσθαι ὀΐω·
ἄλλο δέ τοι ἐρέω, σὺ δ' ἐνὶ φρεσὶ βάλλεο σῇσι·
χερσὶ μὲν οὔ τοι ἔγωγε μαχήσομαι εἵνεκα κούρης
οὔτε σοὶ οὔτε τῳ ἄλλῳ, ἐπεί μ' ἀφέλεσθέ γε δόντες·
τῶν δ' ἄλλων ἅ μοί ἐστι θοῇ παρὰ νηΐ μελαίνῃ,
τῶν οὐκ ἄν τι φέροις ἀνελὼν ἀέκοντος ἐμεῖο·
εἰ δ' ἄγε μὴν πείρησαι, ἵνα γνώωσι καὶ οἵδε·
αἶψά τοι αἷμα κελαινὸν ἐρωήσει περὶ δουρί.›

    Ὣς τώ γ' ἀντιβίοισι μαχεσσαμένω ἐπέεσσιν
ἀνστήτην, λῦσαν δ' ἀγορὴν παρὰ νηυσὶν Ἀχαιῶν·
Πηλεΐδης μὲν ἐπὶ κλισίας καὶ νῆας ἐΐσας
ἤϊε σύν τε Μενοιτιάδῃ καὶ οἷς ἑτάροισιν·
Ἀτρεΐδης δ' ἄρα νῆα θοὴν ἅλαδε προέρυσσεν,
ἐν δ' ἐρέτας ἔκρινεν ἐείκοσιν, ἐς δ' ἑκατόμβην
βῆσε θεῷ, ἀνὰ δὲ Χρυσηΐδα καλλιπάρηον
εἷσεν ἄγων· ἐν δ' ἀρχὸς ἔβη πολύμητις Ὀδυσσεύς.

(Iliad)

would be called a coward, a good-for-nothing, if I always gave in to you, no matter what you said. Order others in this way, not me; for I do not think that I shall obey you any more. This, too, I will tell you; keep it in mind: I will not fight with my hands for the girl's sake, not with you, nor with anyone else; as you gave her to me, you have taken her away. But you shall not seize and carry away against my will anything else that is my own, near my fast black ship. Go now, and try, so that these others may see; your dark blood will soon flow round my spear.'

When the two had finished the battle of violent words, they stood up and dissolved the assembly near the Achaean ships. The son of Peleus went to his huts and well-balanced ships with Menoetius' son and his companions; and the son of Atreus launched a swift ship on the sea, and chose twenty oarsmen for it, and embarked a hecatomb for the god, and brought Chryseis of the beautiful cheeks and put her in; and Odysseus of many counsels stepped in as their leader.

2. Hector and Andromache

Τὴν δ' αὖτε προσέειπε μέγας κορυθαίολος Ἕκτωρ·
‹ἦ καὶ ἐμοὶ τάδε πάντα μέλει, γύναι· ἀλλὰ μάλ' αἰνῶς
αἰδέομαι Τρῶας καὶ Τρῳάδας ἑλκεσιπέπλους,
αἴ κε κακὸς ὣς νόσφιν ἀλυσκάζω πολέμοιο·
οὐδέ με θυμὸς ἄνωγεν, ἐπεὶ μάθον ἔμμεναι ἐσθλὸς
αἰεὶ καὶ πρώτοισι μετὰ Τρώεσσι μάχεσθαι,
ἀρνύμενος πατρός τε μέγα κλέος ἠδ' ἐμὸν αὐτοῦ.
εὖ γὰρ ἐγὼ τόδε οἶδα κατὰ φρένα καὶ κατὰ θυμόν·
ἔσσεται ἦμαρ ὅτ' ἄν ποτ' ὀλώλῃ Ἴλιος ἱρὴ
καὶ Πρίαμος καὶ λαὸς ἐϋμμελίω Πριάμοιο.
ἀλλ' οὔ μοι Τρώων τόσσον μέλει ἄλγος ὀπίσσω,
οὔτ' αὐτῆς Ἑκάβης οὔτε Πριάμοιο ἄνακτος
οὔτε κασιγνήτων, οἵ κεν πολέες τε καὶ ἐσθλοὶ
ἐν κονίῃσι πέσοιεν ὑπ' ἀνδράσι δυσμενέεσσιν,
ὅσσον σεῦ, ὅτε κέν τις Ἀχαιῶν χαλκοχιτώνων
δακρυόεσσαν ἄγηται, ἐλεύθερον ἦμαρ ἀπούρας·
καί κεν ἐν Ἄργει ἐοῦσα πρὸς ἄλλης ἱστὸν ὑφαίνοις,
καί κεν ὕδωρ φορέοις Μεσσηΐδος ἢ Ὑπερείης
πόλλ' ἀεκαζομένη, κρατερὴ δ' ἐπικείσετ' ἀνάγκη·
καί ποτέ τις εἴπῃσιν ἰδὼν κατὰ δάκρυ χέουσαν·

THEN great Hector of the flashing helmet answered her [Andromache]: 'I too am considering all these things, my wife, but I shall be deeply ashamed of the scorn of the Trojans and the Trojan women with their long robes, if like a coward I shrink away from the battle; nor does my heart urge me to do so, for I have learned to be brave always and to fight among the first of the Trojans, striving to maintain my father's great glory and my own. For I know this well in my mind and in my heart: a day will come when sacred Ilium will perish, and Priam and the people of Priam of the fine ashen spear. But I do not feel such pain when I think of the Trojans, or even of Hecuba herself, or King Priam, or of my many brave brothers who may fall in the dust at enemy hands, as when I think of you, when an Achaean in a bronze tunic shall lead you away weeping, robbing you of the light of freedom. And you may find yourself in Argos, weaving the loom at another woman's orders, or carrying water from the fountain Messeis, or Hyperia, much against your will; but hard necessity will press upon you, and someone, seeing

«Ἕκτορος ἥδε γυνή, ὃς ἀριστεύεσκε μάχεσθαι
Τρώων ἱπποδάμων, ὅτε Ἴλιον ἀμφιμάχοντο.»
ὥς ποτέ τις ἐρέει· σοὶ δ' αὖ νέον ἔσσεται ἄλγος
χήτεϊ τοιοῦδ' ἀνδρὸς ἀμύνειν δούλιον ἦμαρ.
ἀλλά με τεθνηῶτα χυτὴ κατὰ γαῖα καλύπτοι,
πρίν γέ τι σῆς τε βοῆς σοῦ θ' ἑλκηθμοῖο πυθέσθαι.»
   Ὣς εἰπὼν οὗ παιδὸς ὀρέξατο φαίδιμος Ἕκτωρ·
ἂψ δ' ὁ πάϊς πρὸς κόλπον ἐϋζώνοιο τιθήνης
ἐκλίνθη ἰάχων, πατρὸς φίλου ὄψιν ἀτυχθείς,
ταρβήσας χαλκόν τε ἰδὲ λόφον ἱππιοχαίτην,
δεινὸν ἀπ' ἀκροτάτης κόρυθος νεύοντα νοήσας.
ἐκ δὲ γέλασσε πατήρ τε φίλος καὶ πότνια μήτηρ·
αὐτίκ' ἀπὸ κρατὸς κόρυθ' εἵλετο φαίδιμος Ἕκτωρ,
καὶ τὴν μὲν κατέθηκεν ἐπὶ χθονὶ παμφανόωσαν·
αὐτὰρ ὅ γ' ὃν φίλον υἱὸν ἐπεὶ κύσε πῆλέ τε χερσίν,
εἶπε δ' ἐπευξάμενος Διί τ' ἄλλοισίν τε θεοῖσι·
‹Ζεῦ ἄλλοι τε θεοί, δότε δὴ καὶ τόνδε γενέσθαι
παῖδ' ἐμόν, ὡς καὶ ἐγώ περ, ἀριπρεπέα Τρώεσσιν,
ὧδε βίην τ' ἀγαθόν, καὶ Ἰλίου ἶφι ἀνάσσειν·
καί ποτέ τις εἴποι «πατρός γ' ὅδε πολλὸν ἀμείνων»

your tears streaming, will say: "This is the wife of Hector, who was the bravest in battle of the horse-breaking Trojans when they fought round Ilium." So they will say; and fresh suffering will come to you, lacking such a husband to keep away the day of slavery. I pray the heaped earth may enshroud me, a dead man, before I hear of your lamentation and of your being dragged into captivity.'

When he said this, glorious Hector stretched out his arms for his son; but the child screamed and shrank back to the bosom of the well-girdled nurse, frightened at the sight of his father, terrified of the bronze and the horse-haired crest, when he saw it nod menacingly from the top of the helmet; at this his loving father and his honoured mother laughed, and at once glorious Hector took the helmet off his head, and put it, flashing brightly, on the ground; and then he kissed his dear child, and swung him in his arms, and prayed to Zeus and to the other gods, and said: 'Zeus and all the other gods, grant that this son of mine may become distinguished amongst the Trojans like myself, as great in strength, and that he may rule Ilium powerfully. And may someone say on seeing him return from war: "This man is much braver than

ἐκ πολέμου ἀνιόντα· φέροι δ' ἔναρα βροτόεντα
κτείνας δήϊον ἄνδρα, χαρείη δὲ φρένα μήτηρ.〉
  ῞Ως εἰπὼν ἀλόχοιο φίλης ἐν χερσὶν ἔθηκε
παῖδ' ἑόν· ἡ δ' ἄρα μιν κηώδεϊ δέξατο κόλπῳ
δακρυόεν γελάσασα· πόσις δ' ἐλέησε νοήσας,
χειρί τέ μιν κατέρεξεν ἔπος τ' ἔφατ' ἔκ τ' ὀνόμαζε·
〈δαιμονίη, μή μοί τι λίην ἀκαχίζεο θυμῷ·
οὐ γάρ τίς μ' ὑπὲρ αἶσαν ἀνὴρ ῞Αϊδι προϊάψει·
μοῖραν δ' οὔ τινά φημι πεφυγμένον ἔμμεναι ἀνδρῶν,
οὐ κακόν, οὐδὲ μὲν ἐσθλόν, ἐπὴν τὰ πρῶτα γένηται.
ἀλλ' εἰς οἶκον ἰοῦσα τὰ σ' αὐτῆς ἔργα κόμιζε,
ἱστόν τ' ἠλακάτην τε, καὶ ἀμφιπόλοισι κέλευε
ἔργον ἐποίχεσθαι· πόλεμος δ' ἄνδρεσσι μελήσει
πᾶσι, μάλιστα δ' ἐμοί, τοὶ Ἰλίῳ ἐγγεγάασιν.〉
  ῞Ως ἄρα φωνήσας κόρυθ' εἵλετο φαίδιμος ῞Εκτωρ
ἵππουριν· ἄλοχος δὲ φίλη οἶκόνδε βεβήκει
ἐντροπαλιζομένη, θαλερὸν κατὰ δάκρυ χέουσα.

                                          (*Iliad*)

his father." May he kill his enemy and bring back the blood-covered spoils, and may his mother rejoice in her heart.'

Having said this, he put the boy in the hands of his dear wife, and she, smiling through her tears, took him to her sweet breast. Her husband saw and pitied her, and stroked her with his hand, and spoke to her, calling her by name: 'Dear one, do not grieve too much in your heart because of me. For no man shall send me to Hades before my time. But no one, I say, has escaped death, neither the coward nor the brave man, once he has been born; go home and carry on with your work, your loom and your distaff, and order your servants to do their work; the men will see to the war I most of all of those who are in Ilium.'

When he said that, glorious Hector took up the horse-haired helmet, and his dear wife went to her home, looking back from time to time, her tears falling fast.

HOMER

3. Mighty Poseidon

Οὐδ' ἀλαοσκοπίην εἶχε κρείων ἐνοσίχθων·
καὶ γὰρ ὁ θαυμάζων ἧστο πτόλεμόν τε μάχην τε
ὑψοῦ ἐπ' ἀκροτάτης κορυφῆς Σάμου ὑληέσσης
Θρηϊκίης· ἔνθεν γὰρ ἐφαίνετο πᾶσα μὲν Ἴδη,
φαίνετο δὲ Πριάμοιο πόλις καὶ νῆες Ἀχαιῶν.
ἔνθ' ἄρ' ὅ γ' ἐξ ἁλὸς ἕζετ' ἰών, ἐλέαιρε δ' Ἀχαιούς
Τρωσὶν δαμναμένους, Διὶ δὲ κρατερῶς ἐνεμέσσα.

Αὐτίκα δ' ἐξ ὄρεος κατεβήσετο παιπαλόεντος
κραιπνὰ ποσὶ προβιβάς· τρέμε δ' οὔρεα μακρὰ καὶ ὕλη
ποσσὶν ὑπ' ἀθανάτοισι Ποσειδάωνος ἰόντος.
τρὶς μὲν ὀρέξατ' ἰών, τὸ δὲ τέτρατον ἵκετο τέκμωρ,
Αἰγάς, ἔνθα δέ οἱ κλυτὰ δώματα βένθεσι λίμνης
χρύσεα μαρμαίροντα τετεύχαται, ἄφθιτα αἰεί.
ἔνθ' ἐλθὼν ὑπ' ὄχεσφι τιτύσκετο χαλκόποδ' ἵππω,
ὠκυπέτα, χρυσέῃσιν ἐθείρῃσιν κομόωντε,
χρυσὸν δ' αὐτὸς ἔδυνε περὶ χροΐ, γέντο δ' ἱμάσθλην
χρυσείην εὔτυκτον, ἑοῦ δ' ἐπιβήσετο δίφρου,
βῆ δ' ἐλάαν ἐπὶ κύματ'· ἄταλλε δὲ κήτε' ὑπ' αὐτοῦ
πάντοθεν ἐκ κευθμῶν, οὐδ' ἠγνοίησεν ἄνακτα·

AND it was no blind look-out place that the mighty Earthshaker had, for he sat upon the highest peak of wooded Samothrace and looked in wonder at the war and the battle; all Ida could be seen from there, and the city of Priam, and the ships of the Achaeans. He went from the sea, and sat down there and felt pity for the Achaeans, who were defeated by the Trojans, and was very angry with Zeus.

He went straight down from the rocky mountain, stepping out swiftly. And the high hills and the forest lands trembled under the deathless feet of Poseidon as he moved. Three strides he made, and with the fourth he reached his goal, Aigae, where his famous palace was built in the depths of the water, glistening and golden, for ever imperishable. When he came there, he harnessed to his chariot his two bronze-hooved, swift horses with their golden manes. He girt his own golden armour round his body, picked up his well-made golden whip, mounted his chariot and drove across the waves. And the sea beasts from the deeps gambolled on all sides under him, for they recognized

γηθοσύνη δὲ θάλασσα διίστατο· τοὶ δὲ πέτοντο
ῥίμφα μάλ', οὐδ' ὑπένερθε διαίνετο χάλκεος ἄξων·
τὸν δ' ἐς 'Αχαιῶν νῆας ἐϋσκάρθμοι φέρον ἵπποι.

(Iliad)

4. Achilles' Immortal Horses

'Ως οἱ μὲν μάρναντο, σιδήρειος δ' ὀρυμαγδὸς
χάλκεον οὐρανὸν ἷκε δι' αἰθέρος ἀτρυγέτοιο·
ἵπποι δ' Αἰακίδαο μάχης ἀπάνευθεν ἐόντες
κλαῖον, ἐπεὶ δὴ πρῶτα πυθέσθην ἡνιόχοιο
ἐν κονίῃσι πεσόντος ὑφ' 'Εκτορος ἀνδροφόνοιο.
ἦ μὰν Αὐτομέδων, Διώρεος ἄλκιμος υἱός,
πολλὰ μὲν ἄρ μάστιγι θοῇ ἐπεμαίετο θείνων,
πολλὰ δὲ μειλιχίοισι προσηύδα, πολλὰ δ' ἀρειῇ·
τὼ δ' οὔτ' ἄψ ἐπὶ νῆας ἐπὶ πλατὺν 'Ελλήσποντον
ἠθελέτην ἰέναι οὔτ' ἐς πόλεμον μετ' 'Αχαιούς,
ἀλλ' ὡς τε στήλη μένει ἔμπεδον, ἥ τ' ἐπὶ τύμβῳ
ἀνέρος ἐστήκῃ τεθνηότος ἠὲ γυναικός,
ὣς μένον ἀσφαλέως περικαλλέα δίφρον ἔχοντες,
οὔδει ἐνισκίμψαντε καρήατα· δάκρυά δέ σφι
θερμὰ κατὰ βλεφάρων χαμάδις ῥέε μυρομένοισιν

their king; and in pleasure the sea opened a path for him. They flew very swiftly, and below the bronze axle was not moistened; and the bounding horses brought him to the ships of the Achaeans.

So they fought, and the clash of iron reached to the bronze heaven through the barren air. But the horses of the grandson of Aeacus [Achilles], away from the battle, wept when they first realized that their charioteer [Patroclus] had been thrown in the dust by man-killing Hector. It is true Automedon, the brave son of Diores, urged them on, beating them many times with the sharp whip, and spoke to them mildly many times, and threatened them many times; but they would not return to the ships near the wide Hellespont, nor go into battle among the Achaeans; but like the stone that stands unmoved on the tomb of a dead man or woman, so they remained motionless, holding back the splendid chariot, with their heads dropping to the earth. And warm tears flowed from their eyes to the earth as they wept because

ἡνιόχοιο πόθῳ· θαλερὴ δ' ἐμιαίνετο χαίτη
ζεύγλης ἐξεριποῦσα παρὰ ζυγὸν ἀμφοτέρωθεν.

Μυρομένω δ' ἄρα τώ γε ἰδὼν ἐλέησε Κρονίων,
κινήσας δὲ κάρη προτὶ ὃν μυθήσατο θυμόν·
‹ἆ δειλώ, τί σφῶϊ δόμεν Πηλῆϊ ἄνακτι
θνητῷ, ὑμεῖς δ' ἐστὸν ἀγήρω τ' ἀθανάτω τε;
ἦ ἵνα δυστήνοισι μετ' ἀνδράσιν ἄλγε' ἔχητον;
οὐ μὲν γάρ τί πού ἐστιν ὀϊζυρώτερον ἀνδρὸς
πάντων ὅσσα τε γαῖαν ἔπι πνείει τε καὶ ἕρπει.
ἀλλ' οὐ μὰν ὑμῖν γε καὶ ἅρμασι δαιδαλέοισιν
Ἕκτωρ Πριαμίδης ἐποχήσεται· οὐ γὰρ ἐάσω.
ἦ οὐχ ἅλις ὡς καὶ τεύχε' ἔχει καὶ ἐπεύχεται αὔτως;
σφῶϊν δ' ἐν γούνεσσι βαλῶ μένος ἠδ' ἐνὶ θυμῷ,
ὄφρα καὶ Αὐτομέδοντα σαώσετον ἐκ πολέμοιο
νῆας ἔπι γλαφυράς· ἔτι γάρ σφισι κῦδος ὀρέξω,
κτείνειν, εἰς ὅ κε νῆας ἐϋσσέλμους ἀφίκωνται
δύη τ' ἠέλιος καὶ ἐπὶ κνέφας ἱερὸν ἔλθῃ.›

Ὣς εἰπὼν ἵπποισιν ἐνέπνευσεν μένος ἠΰ.
τὼ δ' ἀπὸ χαιτάων κονίην οὔδάσδε βαλόντε
ῥίμφα φέρον θοὸν ἅρμα μετὰ Τρῶας καὶ Ἀχαιούς.

(*Iliad*)

they longed for their charioteer; and their thick manes were soiled as
they fell down from under the collarstraps and flowed over the yoke
from both sides.

But the son of Cronos saw them weeping, and felt compassion; he
shook his head and said to his own heart: 'Ah, unlucky pair, why did
we give you to King Peleus, a mortal, when you are free from old age
and immortal? Was it for you to suffer with the unhappy mortals?
For of all that breathes and moves upon the earth there is nothing more
wretched than man. But Hector, the son of Priam, shall not ride a
richly decorated chariot pulled by you, for I will not permit it. Is it
not enough that he holds that armour, and that he boasts about it? I
will give strength to your knees and your heart, so that you can carry
Automedon safely from the battle to the hollow ships; for I will give
success in killing to them [the Trojans], until they reach the well-
benched ships, and the sun sets, and holy darkness comes.'

So he spoke, and he breathed great vigour into the horses. And they,
shaking the dust from their manes to the ground, quickly brought the
swift chariot among the Trojans and the Greeks.

5. The Shield of Achilles

Ποίει δὲ πρώτιστα σάκος μέγα τε στιβαρόν τε
πάντοσε δαιδάλλων, περὶ δ' ἄντυγα βάλλε φαεινὴν
τρίπλακα μαρμαρέην, ἐκ δ' ἀργύρεον τελαμῶνα.
πέντε δ' ἄρ' αὐτοῦ ἔσαν σάκεος πτύχες· αὐτὰρ ἐν αὐτῷ
ποίει δαίδαλα πολλὰ ἰδυίῃσι πραπίδεσσιν.

  Ἐν μὲν γαῖαν ἔτευξ', ἐν δ' οὐρανόν, ἐν δὲ θάλασσαν,
ἠέλιόν τ' ἀκάμαντα σελήνην τε πλήθουσαν,
ἐν δὲ τὰ τείρεα πάντα, τά τ' οὐρανὸς ἐστεφάνωται,
Πληϊάδας θ' Ὑάδας τε τό τε σθένος Ὡρίωνος
Ἄρκτον θ', ἣν καὶ Ἄμαξαν ἐπίκλησιν καλέουσιν,
ἥ τ' αὐτοῦ στρέφεται καί τ' Ὠρίωνα δοκεύει,
οἴη δ' ἄμμορός ἐστι λοετρῶν Ὠκεανοῖο.

  Ἐν δὲ δύω ποίησε πόλεις μερόπων ἀνθρώπων
καλάς. ἐν τῇ μέν ῥα γάμοι τ' ἔσαν εἰλαπίναι τε,
νύμφας δ' ἐκ θαλάμων δαΐδων ὕπο λαμπομενάων
ἠγίνεον ἀνὰ ἄστυ, πολὺς δ' ὑμέναιος ὀρώρει·
κοῦροι δ' ὀρχηστῆρες ἐδίνεον, ἐν δ' ἄρα τοῖσιν
αὐλοὶ φόρμιγγές τε βοὴν ἔχον· αἱ δὲ γυναῖκες
ἱστάμεναι θαύμαζον ἐπὶ προθύροισιν ἑκάστη.
λαοὶ δ' εἰν ἀγορῇ ἔσαν ἀθρόοι· ἔνθα δὲ νεῖκος

First of all he [Hephaestus] made a great strong shield, decorating it all over, and fitted round it a triple rim, flashing brightly, and to it a silver baldrick. There were five layers to the shield itself, and on it his skilled mind fashioned much cunning work.

He wrought thereon the earth and the sky, and the sea and the unwearying sun and the full moon and all the stars with which the sky is crowned; the Pleiades and the Hyades and mighty Orion and the Bear, which men also call the Wain, which turns in her place and watches Orion and is the only one of the stars which does not dip in the Ocean.

And on it he depicted two beautiful cities of mortal men. In the one were weddings and festivities; under the blaze of torches they were leading the brides from their rooms through the city, and the bridal song rose loud. And dancing young men were whirling round, and among them flutes and lyres were sounding, and the women stood each at her door and marvelled. And people were crowded in the assembly place; for a quarrel had arisen there; two men were quarrelling

HOMER

ὠρώρει, δύο δ' ἄνδρες ἐνείκεον εἵνεκα ποινῆς
ἀνδρὸς ἀποφθιμένου· ὁ μὲν εὔχετο πάντ' ἀποδοῦναι
δήμῳ πιφαύσκων, ὁ δ' ἀναίνετο μηδὲν ἑλέσθαι·
ἄμφω δ' ἱέσθην ἐπὶ ἴστορι πεῖραρ ἑλέσθαι.
λαοὶ δ' ἀμφοτέροισιν ἐπήπυον, ἀμφὶς ἀρωγοί·
κήρυκες δ' ἄρα λαὸν ἐρήτυον· οἱ δὲ γέροντες
ἥατ' ἐπὶ ξεστοῖσι λίθοις ἱερῷ ἐνὶ κύκλῳ,
σκῆπτρα δὲ κηρύκων ἐν χέρσ' ἔχον ἠεροφώνων·
τοῖσιν ἔπειτ' ἤϊσσον, ἀμοιβηδὶς δὲ δίκαζον.
κεῖτο δ' ἄρ' ἐν μέσσοισι δύω χρυσοῖο τάλαντα,
τῷ δόμεν ὃς μετὰ τοῖσι δίκην ἰθύντατα εἴποι.

  Τὴν δ' ἑτέρην πόλιν ἀμφὶ δύω στρατοὶ ἥατο λαῶν
τεύχεσι λαμπόμενοι· δίχα δέ σφισιν ἥνδανε βουλή,
ἠὲ διαπραθέειν ἢ ἄνδιχα πάντα δάσασθαι,
κτῆσιν ὅσην πτολίεθρον ἐπήρατον ἐντὸς ἔεργεν·
οἱ δ' οὔ πω πείθοντο, λόχῳ δ' ὑπεθωρήσσοντο.
τεῖχος μέν ῥ' ἄλοχοί τε φίλαι καὶ νήπια τέκνα
ῥύατ' ἐφεσταότες, μετὰ δ' ἀνέρες οὓς ἔχε γῆρας·
οἱ δ' ἴσαν· ἦρχε δ' ἄρα σφιν Ἄρης καὶ Παλλὰς Ἀθήνη,
ἄμφω χρυσείω, χρύσεια δὲ εἵματα ἔσθην,
καλὼ καὶ μεγάλω σὺν τεύχεσιν, ὥς τε θεὼ περ

about the blood-price for a man who had been killed; the one insisted on paying in full and was explaining this to the people, but the other refused and would take nothing; both were willing to accept the decision of an adjudicator. And the people were shouting in applause, supporting both sides. And heralds kept order among the people, while the elders sat on polished stones in the sacred circle, holding in their hands the staffs of clear-voiced heralds. They then stood up before them and gave judgement each in turn. And in the middle lay two talents of gold, to be given to the one who should plead most justly among them.

  Round the other city were two besieging armies with glittering armour. They could not decide whether they should sack the town, or share with the townspeople all the wealth the coveted city held. But the besieged were not yet compliant and were arming for an ambush. Their dear wives and small children stood on the wall to guard it, and with them the old men; but the rest went out, and their leaders were Ares and Pallas Athene, both made of gold, and golden were the garments they wore. They were big and beautiful in this armour and like

ἀμφὶς ἀριζήλω· λαοὶ δ' ὑπολίζονες ἦσαν.
οἱ δ' ὅτε δή ῥ' ἵκανον ὅθι σφίσιν εἶκε λοχῆσαι,
ἐν ποταμῷ, ὅθι τ' ἀρδμὸς ἔην πάντεσσι βοτοῖσιν,
ἔνθ' ἄρα τοί γ' ἵζοντ' εἰλυμένοι αἴθοπι χαλκῷ.
τοῖσι δ' ἔπειτ' ἀπάνευθε δύω σκοποὶ ἥατο λαῶν,
δέγμενοι ὁππότε μῆλα ἰδοίατο καὶ ἕλικας βοῦς.
οἱ δὲ τάχα προγένοντο, δύω δ' ἅμ' ἔποντο νομῆες
τερπόμενοι σύριγξι· δόλον δ' οὔ τι προνόησαν.
οἱ μὲν τὰ προϊδόντες ἐπέδραμον, ὦκα δ' ἔπειτα
τάμνοντ' ἀμφὶ βοῶν ἀγέλας καὶ πώεα καλὰ
ἀργεννέων οἰῶν, κτεῖνον δ' ἐπὶ μηλοβοτῆρας.
οἱ δ' ὡς οὖν ἐπύθοντο πολὺν κέλαδον παρὰ βουσὶν
εἰράων προπάροιθε καθήμενοι, αὐτίκ' ἐφ' ἵππων
βάντες ἀερσιπόδων μετεκίαθον, αἶψα δ' ἵκοντο.
στησάμενοι δ' ἐμάχοντο μάχην ποταμοῖο παρ' ὄχθας,
βάλλον δ' ἀλλήλους χαλκήρεσιν ἐγχείῃσιν.
ἐν δ' Ἔρις ἐν δὲ Κυδοιμὸς ὁμίλεον, ἐν δ' ὀλοὴ Κήρ,
ἄλλον ζωὸν ἔχουσα νεούτατον, ἄλλον ἄουτον,
ἄλλον τεθνηῶτα κατὰ μόθον ἕλκε ποδοῖιν·
εἷμα δ' ἔχ' ἀμφ' ὤμοισι δαφοινεὸν αἵματι φωτῶν.
ὡμίλευν δ' ὥς τε ζωοὶ βροτοὶ ἠδ' ἐμάχοντο,

gods, easily picked out, and the people at their feet were smaller. And when they came to where they thought it good to set the ambush, in a river bed, where there was a watering-place used by all the herds, they sat down there covered in glittering bronze. And they posted two guards at a distance from them, to watch for flocks and oxen with crooked horns approaching. And they came soon, and with them followed two herdsmen delighting in their pipes; they did not notice the ambush. The others, when they saw them, attacked them and swiftly cut down the herds of oxen and the fine flocks of white sheep. They also killed the shepherds. And when [the besiegers], sitting at the place of assembly, heard the great din among the oxen, they immediately mounted [their chariots] behind their high-striding horses and came up quickly. A battle followed on the banks of the river, as they struck one another with bronzed-tipped spears. And with them mingled Strife and Panic, and dreadful Death, snatching one man alive but just wounded, and another with no wound, and dragging another away by the feet, dead, through the crowd; and the cloak on his shoulders was red with men's blood. Like living mortals they joined battle and fought, and hauled away the corpses of their enemies' dead.

νεκρούς τ' ἀλλήλων ἔρυον κατατεθνηῶτας.
  Ἐν δ' ἐτίθει νειὸν μαλακήν, πίειραν ἄρουραν,
εὐρεῖαν τρίπολον· πολλοὶ δ' ἀροτῆρες ἐν αὐτῇ
ζεύγεα δινεύοντες ἐλάστρεον ἔνθα καὶ ἔνθα.
οἱ δ' ὁπότε στρέψαντες ἱκοίατο τέλσον ἀρούρης,
τοῖσι δ' ἔπειτ' ἐν χερσὶ δέπας μελιηδέος οἴνου
δόσκεν ἀνὴρ ἐπιών· τοὶ δὲ στρέψασκον ἀν' ὄγμους,
ἱέμενοι νειοῖο βαθείης τέλσον ἱκέσθαι.
ἡ δὲ μελαίνετ' ὄπισθεν, ἀρηρομένη δὲ ἐῴκει,
χρυσείη περ ἐοῦσα· τὸ δὴ περὶ θαῦμα τέτυκτο.
  Ἐν δ' ἐτίθει τέμενος βασιλήϊον· ἔνθα δ' ἔριθοι
ἤμων ὀξείας δρεπάνας ἐν χερσὶν ἔχοντες.
δράγματα δ' ἄλλα μετ' ὄγμον ἐπήτριμα πῖπτον ἔραζε,
ἄλλα δ' ἀμαλλοδετῆρες ἐν ἐλλεδανοῖσι δέοντο.
τρεῖς δ' ἄρ' ἀμαλλοδετῆρες ἐφέστασαν· αὐτὰρ ὄπισθε
παῖδες δραγμεύοντες, ἐν ἀγκαλίδεσσι φέροντες,
ἀσπερχὲς πάρεχον· βασιλεὺς δ' ἐν τοῖσι σιωπῇ
σκῆπτρον ἔχων ἑστήκει ἐπ' ὄγμου γηθόσυνος κῆρ.
κήρυκες δ' ἀπάνευθεν ὑπὸ δρυῒ δαῖτα πένοντο,
βοῦν δ' ἱερεύσαντες μέγαν ἄμφεπον· αἱ δὲ γυναῖκες
δεῖπνον ἐρίθοισιν λεύκ' ἄλφιτα πολλὰ πάλυνον.

And then he set in the shield a wide field of soft, rich fallow, being ploughed for the third time; and many ploughmen drove their teams in it to and fro as they circled. Whenever they came to the end of the field and turned, a man would come and put a cup of sweet wine in their hands; then they turned back along the furrows, making for the other end of the deep fallow soil. And the field behind them grew black and looked like a new ploughland, although made of gold: such was the wondrous quality of the craftsmanship.

And then he set in a king's estate where hired reapers were reaping with sharp sickles in their hands. Cuts of corn were falling to the earth in rows along the furrows, while the sheaf-binders were tying others in bands of straw. Three sheaf-binders stood there, while behind them boys were gathering the corn and carrying it in their arms to the binders, giving them a constant supply; and the king was standing silently among them by the cut row of corn, holding his staff, happy at heart. And at a distance, under an oak, attendants were preparing a feast. They were preparing a great ox they had killed, while the women were sprinkling much white barley, a supper for the labourers.

'Εν δὲ τίθει σταφυλῇσι μέγα βρίθουσαν ἀλωὴν
καλὴν χρυσείην· μέλανες δ' ἀνὰ βότρυες ἦσαν,
ἑστήκει δὲ κάμαξι διαμπερὲς ἀργυρέῃσιν.
ἀμφὶ δὲ κυανέην κάπετον, περὶ δ' ἕρκος ἔλασσε
κασσιτέρου· μία δ' οἴη ἀταρπιτὸς ἦεν ἐπ' αὐτήν,
τῇ νίσσοντο φορῆες, ὅτε τρυγόῳεν ἀλωήν.
παρθενικαὶ δὲ καὶ ἠίθεοι ἀταλὰ φρονέοντες
πλεκτοῖς ἐν ταλάροισι φέρον μελιηδέα καρπόν.
τοῖσιν ἐν μέσσοισι πάϊς φόρμιγγι λιγείῃ
ἱμερόεν κιθάριζε, λίνον δ' ὑπὸ καλὸν ἄειδε
λεπταλέῃ φωνῇ· τοὶ δὲ ῥήσσοντες ἁμαρτῇ
μολπῇ τ' ἰυγμῷ τε ποσὶ σκαίροντες ἕποντο.
'Εν δ' ἀγέλην ποίησε βοῶν ὀρθοκραιράων·
αἱ δὲ βόες χρυσοῖο τετεύχατο κασσιτέρου τε,
μυκηθμῷ δ' ἀπὸ κόπρου ἐπεσσεύοντο νομόνδε
πὰρ ποταμὸν κελάδοντα, παρὰ ῥοδανὸν δονακῆα.
χρύσειοι δὲ νομῆες ἅμ' ἐστιχόωντο βόεσσι
τέσσαρες, ἐννέα δέ σφι κύνες πόδας ἀργοὶ ἕποντο.
σμερδαλέω δὲ λέοντε δύ' ἐν πρώτῃσι βόεσσι
ταῦρον ἐρύγμηλον ἐχέτην· ὁ δὲ μακρὰ μεμυκὼς
ἕλκετο· τὸν δὲ κύνες μετεκίαθον ἠδ' αἰζηοί.

He also fashioned in gold a beautiful vineyard richly laden with grapes; the grapes were black, but the supporting poles showed up throughout in silver. And round it he ran a ditch of blue enamel, and round that a fence of tin; and only one path led to it, which the pickers might use whenever they gathered the grapes. And young girls and youths merrily carried the sweet fruit in plaited baskets. And among them a boy played sweetly on a clear-toned lyre and with soft voice sang the Linos-song beautifully, while the rest kept time with him and followed the music and the words with dancing feet.

And he wrought on it a herd of straight-horned cattle and the cows were made of gold and tin, and they hurried lowing from the byre to feed beside a river murmuring by the swaying rushes. And herdsmen of gold were following with the cattle, four of them, and nine swift-footed dogs came after them. But at the head of the herd two savage lions had seized a loud-roaring bull that bellowed mightily as they hauled him away, and the dogs and the young men ran after him. The

τὼ μὲν ἀναρρήξαντε βοὸς μεγάλοιο βοείην
ἔγκατα καὶ μέλαν αἷμα λαφύσσετον· οἱ δὲ νομῆες
αὔτως ἐνδίεσαν ταχέας κύνας ὀτρύνοντες.
οἱ δ' ἤτοι δακέειν μὲν ἀπετρωπῶντο λεόντων,
ἱστάμενοι δὲ μάλ' ἐγγὺς ὑλάκτεον ἔκ τ' ἀλέοντο.
    Ἐν δὲ νομὸν ποίησε περικλυτὸς ἀμφιγυήεις
ἐν καλῇ βήσσῃ μέγαν οἰῶν ἀργεννάων,
σταθμούς τε κλισίας τε κατηρεφέας ἰδὲ σηκούς.
    Ἐν δὲ χορὸν ποίκιλλε περικλυτὸς ἀμφιγυήεις,
τῷ ἴκελον οἷόν ποτ' ἐνὶ Κνωσῷ εὐρείῃ
Δαίδαλος ἤσκησεν καλλιπλοκάμῳ Ἀριάδνῃ.
ἔνθα μὲν ἠίθεοι καὶ παρθένοι ἀλφεσίβοιαι
ὠρχεῦντ', ἀλλήλων ἐπὶ καρπῷ χεῖρας ἔχοντες.
τῶν δ' αἱ μὲν λεπτὰς ὀθόνας ἔχον, οἱ δὲ χιτῶνας
εἴατ' ἐϋννήτους, ἦκα στίλβοντας ἐλαίῳ·
καί ῥ' αἱ μὲν καλὰς στεφάνας ἔχον, οἱ δὲ μαχαίρας
εἶχον χρυσείας ἐξ ἀργυρέων τελαμώνων.
οἱ δ' ὁτὲ μὲν θρέξασκον ἐπισταμένοισι πόδεσσι
ῥεῖα μάλ', ὡς ὅτε τις τροχὸν ἄρμενον ἐν παλάμῃσιν
ἑζόμενος κεραμεὺς πειρήσεται, αἴ κε θέῃσιν·
ἄλλοτε δ' αὖ θρέξασκον ἐπὶ στίχας ἀλλήλοισι.

two lions had torn the great bull's hide and were devouring his en-
trails and his black blood. In vain the herdsmen urged their fast dogs
to attack, for they shrank from biting the lions; they stood very close
and barked, but avoided them.

And the glorious lame god fashioned in the shield a pasture in a
beautiful valley, a great grazing ground with white sheep and its farm-
buildings and roofed huts and pens.

And [on the shield] the glorious lame god also devised a dancing
place, like that which Daidalus once designed in spacious Knossos for
Ariadne of the lovely locks. There danced youths and young girls,
whose suitors bring oxen in dowry; their hands were on one another's
wrists; the girls wore fine linen clothes, and the youths closely woven
tunics, faintly gleaming with oil; the girls had beautiful wreaths [on
their heads], and the youths daggers of gold hanging from silver bald-
ricks. And sometimes they ran round very lightly with accomplished
movements of their feet, like a potter sitting by the wheel that fits
between his hands trying it out, [to see] if it will twirl; and then again
they ran in lines to meet each other. And a great delighted company

πολλὸς δ' ἱμερόεντα χορὸν περίσταθ' ὅμιλος
τερπόμενοι· δοιὼ δὲ κυβιστητῆρε κατ' αὐτοὺς
μολπῆς ἐξάρχοντες ἐδίνευον κατὰ μέσσους.

Ἐν δὲ τίθει ποταμοῖο μέγα σθένος Ὠκεανοῖο
ἄντυγα πὰρ πυμάτην σάκεος πύκα ποιητοῖο.

(Iliad)

6. The Death of Hector

Ὣς εἰπὼν προτὶ ἄστυ μέγα φρονέων ἐβεβήκει,
σευάμενος ὥς θ' ἵππος ἀεθλοφόρος σὺν ὄχεσφιν,
ὅς ῥά τε ῥεῖα θέησι τιταινόμενος πεδίοιο·
ὣς Ἀχιλεὺς λαιψηρὰ πόδας καὶ γούνατ' ἐνώμα.

Τὸν δ' ὁ γέρων Πρίαμος πρῶτος ἴδεν ὀφθαλμοῖσι,
παμφαίνονθ' ὥς τ' ἀστέρ' ἐπεσσύμενον πεδίοιο,
ὅς ῥά τ' ὀπώρης εἶσιν, ἀρίζηλοι δέ οἱ αὐγαὶ
φαίνονται πολλοῖσι μετ' ἀστράσι νυκτὸς ἀμολγῷ·
ὅν τε κύν' Ὠρίωνος ἐπίκλησιν καλέουσι.
λαμπρότατος μὲν ὅ γ' ἐστί, κακὸν δέ τε σῆμα τέτυκται,
καί τε φέρει πολλὸν πυρετὸν δειλοῖσι βροτοῖσιν·
ὣς τοῦ χαλκὸς ἔλαμπε περὶ στήθεσσι θέοντος.
ᾤμωξεν δ' ὁ γέρων, κεφαλὴν δ' ὅ γε κόψατο χερσὶν

stood round the lovely dance, while a couple of acrobats keeping time
with the music turned cartwheels in and out among the people.

And he set round the outermost rim of the solidly fashioned shield
the mighty stream of Ocean.

So he [Achilles] spoke, and headed for the city greatly elated, plying
feet and knees in his charge just like a prize-winning horse in the
chariot-race that strains as he gallops fast across the plain.

Old Priam was the first to see him (with his eyes), rushing over the
plain, blazing like the star which rises at harvest time and whose clear
rays shine among the many stars in the darkness of the night, the star
they call the Dog of Orion. Very bright indeed it is, but an evil sign,
bringing much fever to poor mortals. So shone the bronze round his
breast as he ran. But the old man groaned and beat his head with his
hands, lifting them high as he groaned, and cried out loudly in prayer

ὑψόσ᾽ ἀνασχόμενος, μέγα δ᾽ οἰμώξας ἐγεγώνει
λισσόμενος φίλον υἱόν· ὁ δὲ προπάροιθε πυλάων
ἑστήκει, ἄμοτον μεμαὼς Ἀχιλῆϊ μάχεσθαι·
τὸν δ᾽ ὁ γέρων ἐλεεινὰ προσηύδα χεῖρας ὀρεγνύς·
«Ἕκτορ, μή μοι μίμνε, φίλον τέκος, ἀνέρα τοῦτον
οἶος ἄνευθ᾽ ἄλλων, ἵνα μὴ τάχα πότμον ἐπίσπῃς
Πηλεΐωνι δαμείς, ἐπεὶ ἦ πολὺ φέρτερός ἐστι,
σχέτλιος· αἴθε θεοῖσι φίλος τοσσόνδε γένοιτο
ὅσσον ἐμοί· τάχα κέν ἑ κύνες καὶ γῦπες ἔδοιεν
κείμενον· ἦ κέ μοι αἰνὸν ἀπὸ πραπίδων ἄχος ἔλθοι·
ὅς μ᾽ υἱῶν πολλῶν τε καὶ ἐσθλῶν εὖνιν ἔθηκε,
κτείνων καὶ περνὰς νήσων ἔπι τηλεδαπάων.
καὶ γὰρ νῦν δύο παῖδε, Λυκάονα καὶ Πολύδωρον,
οὐ δύναμαι ἰδέειν Τρώων εἰς ἄστυ ἀλέντων,
τούς μοι Λαοθόη τέκετο, κρείουσα γυναικῶν.
ἀλλ᾽ εἰ μὲν ζώουσι μετὰ στρατῷ, ἦ τ᾽ ἂν ἔπειτα
χαλκοῦ τε χρυσοῦ τ᾽ ἀπολυσόμεθ᾽· ἔστι γὰρ ἔνδον·
πολλὰ γὰρ ὤπασε παιδὶ γέρων ὀνομάκλυτος Ἄλτης.
εἰ δ᾽ ἤδη τεθνᾶσι καὶ εἰν Ἀΐδαο δόμοισιν,
ἄλγος ἐμῷ θυμῷ καὶ μητέρι, τοὶ τεκόμεσθα·
λαοῖσιν δ᾽ ἄλλοισι μινυνθαδιώτερον ἄλγος

to his dear son. But he [Hector] stood before the gates, thirsting to fight with Achilles; the old man stretching out his hands addressed him piteously: 'Hector, my dear son, do not wait for this man alone, far from the others, lest you quickly find death at the hands of the son of Peleus, since he is much more powerful than you. The cruel man! Would he were as dear to the gods as he is to me; soon dogs and the vultures would devour him as he lay on the ground dead; great sorrow would then be lifted from my heart. For he has deprived me of many brave sons, killing and selling them to the islands far away. Even now among the Trojans who took refuge in the city I cannot see two of my sons, Lycaon and Polydorus, whom Laothoë, a queen among women, bore to me. But if they are still alive in the camp we shall ransom them later with bronze and gold; for there is [plenty] in the palace, since Altes, the distinguished old man, gave much wealth to his daughter. But if they are already dead and in the halls of Hades, sorrow is in store for me and their mother, we who bore them. For other men there will be a shorter time of mourning, unless you die as well, killed by

ἔσσεται, ἢν μὴ καὶ σὺ θάνῃς Ἀχιλῆϊ δαμασθείς.
ἀλλ' εἰσέρχεο τεῖχος, ἐμὸν τέκος, ὄφρα σαώσῃς
Τρῶας καὶ Τρωάς, μηδὲ μέγα κῦδος ὀρέξῃς
Πηλείδῃ, αὐτὸς δὲ φίλης αἰῶνος ἀμερθῇς.
πρὸς δ' ἐμὲ τὸν δύστηνον ἔτι φρονέοντ' ἐλέησον,
δύσμορον, ὅν ῥα πατὴρ Κρονίδης ἐπὶ γήραος οὐδῷ
αἴσῃ ἐν ἀργαλέῃ φθίσει, κακὰ πόλλ' ἐπιδόντα,
υἷάς τ' ὀλλυμένους ἑλκηθείσας τε θύγατρας,
καὶ θαλάμους κεραϊζομένους, καὶ νήπια τέκνα
βαλλόμενα προτὶ γαίῃ ἐν αἰνῇ δηϊοτῆτι,
ἑλκομένας τε νυοὺς ὀλοῇς ὑπὸ χερσὶν Ἀχαιῶν.
αὐτὸν δ' ἂν πύματόν με κύνες πρώτῃσι θύρῃσιν
ὠμησταὶ ἐρύουσιν, ἐπεί κέ τις ὀξέϊ χαλκῷ
τύψας ἠὲ βαλὼν ῥεθέων ἐκ θυμὸν ἕληται,
οὓς τρέφον ἐν μεγάροισι τραπεζῆας θυραωρούς,
οἵ κ' ἐμὸν αἷμα πιόντες ἀλύσσοντες περὶ θυμῷ
κείσοντ' ἐν προθύροισι. νέῳ δέ τε πάντ' ἐπέοικεν
ἀρηϊκταμένῳ, δεδαϊγμένῳ ὀξέϊ χαλκῷ,
κεῖσθαι· πάντα δὲ καλὰ θανόντι περ, ὅττι φανήῃ·
ἀλλ' ὅτε δὴ πολιόν τε κάρη πολιόν τε γένειον
αἰδῶ τ' αἰσχύνωσι κύνες κταμένοιο γέροντος,
τοῦτο δὴ οἴκτιστον πέλεται δειλοῖσι βροτοῖσιν.›

Achilles. But come inside the wall, my son, to save the Trojan men and women, and do not give great glory to the son of Peleus, nor you yourself lose your dear life. And also pity me, an unhappy man who can still feel and think, whom father Zeus, the son of Cronos, will destroy with a painful death at the threshold of old age when I have seen many evils: my sons killed, my daughters dragged to slavery, their rooms plundered, their babies dashed to the ground in the dreadful fighting, my daughters-in-law hauled away by the cruel hands of the Achaeans. And myself perhaps, last of all, the flesh-devouring dogs will tear to pieces at the outer gates when someone has struck or wounded me with sharp bronze and taken away the life from my limbs; the dogs that I have fed at the table in my palace, the guards of my doors will drink my blood and lie, appetites maddened, in the porch. It is quite seemly for a young man to lie dead in battle, torn by sharp bronze. Everything is proper, when he is dead, whatever may be seen; but when dogs defile the grey head, the grey beard and privy parts of a dead old man, that is the saddest thing for miserable mortals.'

Ἦ ῥ' ὁ γέρων, πολιὰς δ' ἄρ' ἀνὰ τρίχας ἕλκετο χερσὶ
τίλλων ἐκ κεφαλῆς· οὐδ' Ἕκτορι θυμὸν ἔπειθε.
μήτηρ δ' αὖθ' ἑτέρωθεν ὀδύρετο δάκρυ χέουσα,
κόλπον ἀνιεμένη, ἑτέρηφι δὲ μαζὸν ἀνέσχε·
καί μιν δάκρυ χέουσ' ἔπεα πτερόεντα προσηύδα·
‹Ἕκτορ, τέκνον ἐμόν, τάδε τ' αἴδεο καί μ' ἐλέησον
αὐτήν, εἴ ποτέ τοι λαθικηδέα μαζὸν ἐπέσχον·
τῶν μνῆσαι, φίλε τέκνον, ἄμυνε δὲ δήϊον ἄνδρα
τείχεος ἐντὸς ἐών, μηδὲ πρόμος ἵστασο τούτῳ,
σχέτλιος· εἴ περ γάρ σε κατακτάνῃ, οὔ σ' ἔτ' ἔγωγε
κλαύσομαι ἐν λεχέεσσι, φίλον θάλος, ὃν τέκον αὐτή,
οὐδ' ἄλοχος πολύδωρος· ἄνευθε δέ σε μέγα νῶϊν
Ἀργείων παρὰ νηυσὶ κύνες ταχέες κατέδονται.›
  Ὣς τώ γε κλαίοντε προσαυδήτην φίλον υἱόν,
πολλὰ λισσομένω· οὐδ' Ἕκτορι θυμὸν ἔπειθον,
ἀλλ' ὅ γε μίμν' Ἀχιλῆα πελώριον ἆσσον ἰόντα.
ὡς δὲ δράκων ἐπὶ χειῇ ὀρέστερος ἄνδρα μένῃσι,
βεβρωκὼς κακὰ φάρμακ', ἔδυ δέ τέ μιν χόλος αἰνός,
σμερδαλέον δὲ δέδορκεν ἑλισσόμενος περὶ χειῇ·
ὣς Ἕκτωρ ἄσβεστον ἔχων μένος οὐχ ὑπεχώρει,
πύργῳ ἔπι προὔχοντι φαεινὴν ἀσπίδ' ἐρείσας·

The old man spoke, and pulled at his grey hair with his hands, tearing it from his head; but he did not weaken the resolve of Hector. And his mother on the other side wailed and shed tears; she let fall the fold of her robe and with the other hand held up her breast; in tears she spoke winged words to him: 'Hector, my son, if ever I gave you my breast to soothe your sorrows, respect it and pity me; remember that, dear son; come inside the walls to keep off [that] ruinous man; do not stand foremost and alone against him; he is savage! For, if he kills you, I shall not mourn you lying on a funeral-couch, dear child I brought to life, nor will your richly dowered wife, but far away from both of us the swift dogs will devour you by the ships of the Argives.'

So the two addressed their dear son, weeping and entreating him many times, but they did not weaken Hector's resolve; he waited there to face the terrible Achilles, who was approaching. And, as a mountain snake fed on poisonous herbs, brimming with evil anger, waits for a man, lying coiled about its den, and glares horribly, so Hector, with unflinching courage, stood firm and rested his gli.tering shield against a

ὀχθήσας δ' ἄρα εἶπε πρὸς ὃν μεγαλήτορα θυμόν·
‹ὤ μοι ἐγών, εἰ μέν κε πύλας καὶ τείχεα δύω,
Πουλυδάμας μοι πρῶτος ἐλεγχείην ἀναθήσει,
ὅς μ' ἐκέλευε Τρωσὶ ποτὶ πτόλιν ἡγήσασθαι
νύχθ' ὕπο τήνδ' ὀλοήν, ὅτε τ' ὤρετο δῖος Ἀχιλλεύς.
ἀλλ' ἐγὼ οὐ πιθόμην· ἦ τ' ἂν πολὺ κέρδιον ἦεν.
νῦν δ' ἐπεὶ ὤλεσα λαὸν ἀτασθαλίῃσιν ἐμῇσιν,
αἰδέομαι Τρῶας καὶ Τρῳάδας ἑλκεσιπέπλους,
μή ποτέ τις εἴπῃσι κακώτερος ἄλλος ἐμεῖο·
‹Ἕκτωρ ἦφι βίηφι πιθήσας ὤλεσε λαόν.›
ὣς ἐρέουσιν· ἐμοὶ δὲ τότ' ἂν πολὺ κέρδιον εἴη
ἄντην ἢ Ἀχιλῆα κατακτείναντα νέεσθαι,
ἠέ κεν αὐτῷ ὀλέσθαι ἐϋκλειῶς πρὸ πόληος.
εἰ δέ κεν ἀσπίδα μὲν καταθείομαι ὀμφαλόεσσαν
καὶ κόρυθα βριαρήν, δόρυ δὲ πρὸς τεῖχος ἐρείσας
αὐτὸς ἰὼν Ἀχιλῆος ἀμύμονος ἀντίος ἔλθω
καί οἱ ὑπόσχωμαι Ἑλένην καὶ κτήμαθ' ἅμ' αὐτῇ,
πάντα μάλ' ὅσσα τ' Ἀλέξανδρος κοίλῃς ἐνὶ νηυσὶν
ἠγάγετο Τροίηνδ', ἥ τ' ἔπλετο νείκεος ἀρχή,
δωσέμεν Ἀτρεΐδῃσιν ἄγειν, ἅμα δ' ἀμφὶς Ἀχαιοῖς
ἄλλ' ἀποδάσσεσθαι, ὅσα τε πτόλις ἥδε κέκευθε·
Τρωσὶν δ' αὖ μετόπισθε γερούσιον ὅρκον ἕλωμαι

projecting tower; heavy at heart, he addressed his indomitable soul:
'How miserable I am! If I enter the gates and the wall the first to re-
proach me will be Polydamas, who urged me to lead the Trojans back
to the city in this disastrous night, when godlike Achilles rose to battle.
But I did not listen to him; it would certainly have been much better.
And now, since by my own recklessness I have destroyed the army, I
fear the scorn of Trojan men and long-robed Trojan women and fear
that someone lesser than I will say: "Hector, relying on his own
strength, destroyed the army." So they will say; then it would have
been much better for me either to kill Achilles in single combat and
return, or to die honourably at his hands for the sake of the city. On
the other hand, suppose I put down my bossed shield and tough hel-
met, rest my spear against the wall and go to meet noble Achilles face
to face. I would promise that we would give Helen, the cause of the war,
to the sons of Atreus, and with her all the possessions that Paris
brought to Troy in his hollow ships, and also that we would share with
the Achaeans all that this city contains, then I should exact an oath

μή τι κατακρύψειν, ἀλλ' ἄνδιχα πάντα δάσασθαι
κτῆσιν ὅσην πτολίεθρον ἐπήρατον ἐντὸς ἐέργει·
ἀλλὰ τίη μοι ταῦτα φίλος διελέξατο θυμός;
μή μιν ἐγὼ μὲν ἵκωμαι ἰών, ὁ δέ μ' οὐκ ἐλεήσει
οὐδέ τί μ' αἰδέσεται, κτενέει δέ με γυμνὸν ἐόντα
αὔτως ὥς τε γυναῖκα, ἐπεί κ' ἀπὸ τεύχεα δύω.
οὐ μέν πως νῦν ἔστιν ἀπὸ δρυὸς οὐδ' ἀπὸ πέτρης
τῷ ὀαριζέμεναι, ἅ τε παρθένος ἠΐθεός τε,
παρθένος ἠΐθεός τ' ὀαρίζετον ἀλλήλοιιν.
βέλτερον αὖτ' ἔριδι ξυνελαυνέμεν ὅττι τάχιστα·
εἴδομεν ὁπποτέρῳ κεν 'Ολύμπιος εὖχος ὀρέξῃ.›
῝Ως ὅρμαινε μένων, ὁ δέ οἱ σχεδὸν ἦλθεν 'Αχιλλεὺς
Ἶσος 'Ενυαλίῳ, κορυθάϊκι πτολεμιστῇ,
σείων Πηλιάδα μελίην κατὰ δεξιὸν ὦμον
δεινήν· ἀμφὶ δὲ χαλκὸς ἐλάμπετο εἴκελος αὐγῇ
ἢ πυρὸς αἰθομένου ἢ ἠελίου ἀνιόντος.
῝Εκτορα δ', ὡς ἐνόησεν, ἕλε τρόμος· οὐδ' ἄρ' ἔτ' ἔτλη
αὖθι μένειν, ὀπίσω δὲ πύλας λίπε, βῆ δὲ φοβηθείς·
Πηλείδης δ' ἐπόρουσε ποσὶ κραιπνοῖσι πεποιθώς.
ἠΰτε κίρκος ὄρεσφιν, ἐλαφρότατος πετεηνῶν,
ῥηϊδίως οἴμησε μετὰ τρήρωνα πέλειαν,

from the elders of the Trojans that they would hide nothing, but divide everything into two parts, all the treasure this delightful city holds. But why does my heart consider this? Perhaps, if I approach him, he will show no pity or regard for me, but will kill me unarmed just as if I were a woman, once I take off my weapons. Now is no time to chatter with him from an oak or from a rock like a girl talking to a young man: it is only girls and young men who have such conversations. It is nobler to engage in battle with him as soon as possible, so that we may know to whom the Olympian [Zeus] will give glory.'

These were his thoughts as he waited; and Achilles came at him like the warrior Ares who wears the waving plume, brandishing in his right arm the dreadful Pelian ash; and the bronze shone round like the light of a blazing fire, or of the rising sun. Hector, as he saw him, was seized by terror; and did not have the courage to remain there any longer but left the gates behind him, and fled in a panic; and the son of Peleus rushed on after him, trusting his swift feet. As in the mountains a falcon, the swiftest of birds, swoops easily on a timid dove; she flies

ἡ δέ θ' ὕπαιθα φοβεῖται, ὁ δ' ἐγγύθεν ὀξὺ λεληκὼς
ταρφέ' ἐπαΐσσει, ἑλέειν τέ ἑ θυμὸς ἀνώγει·
ὣς ἄρ' ὁ γ' ἐμμεμαὼς ἰθὺς πέτετο, τρέσε δ' Ἕκτωρ
τεῖχος ὕπο Τρώων, λαιψηρὰ δὲ γούνατ' ἐνώμα.
οἱ δὲ παρὰ σκοπιὴν καὶ ἐρινεὸν ἠνεμόεντα
τείχεος αἰὲν ὑπὲκ κατ' ἀμαξιτὸν ἐσσεύοντο,
κρουνὼ δ' ἵκανον καλλιρρόω· ἔνθα δὲ πηγαὶ
δοιαὶ ἀναΐσσουσι Σκαμάνδρου διηέντος.
ἡ μὲν γάρ θ' ὕδατι λιαρῷ ῥέει, ἀμφὶ δὲ καπνὸς
γίγνεται ἐξ αὐτῆς ὡς εἰ πυρὸς αἰθομένοιο·
ἡ δ' ἑτέρη θέρεϊ προρέει ἐϊκυῖα χαλάζῃ,
ἢ χιόνι ψυχρῇ, ἢ ἐξ ὕδατος κρυστάλλῳ.
ἔνθα δ' ἐπ' αὐτάων πλυνοὶ εὐρέες ἐγγὺς ἔασι
καλοὶ λαΐνεοι, ὅθι εἵματα σιγαλόεντα
πλύνεσκον Τρώων ἄλοχοι καλαί τε θύγατρες
τὸ πρὶν ἐπ' εἰρήνης, πρὶν ἐλθεῖν υἷας Ἀχαιῶν.
τῇ ῥα παραδραμέτην, φεύγων, ὁ δ' ὄπισθε διώκων·
πρόσθε μὲν ἐσθλὸς ἔφευγε, δίωκε δέ μιν μέγ' ἀμείνων
καρπαλίμως, ἐπεὶ οὐχ ἱερήϊον οὐδὲ βοείην
ἀρνύσθην, ἅ τε ποσσὶν ἀέθλια γίγνεται ἀνδρῶν,
ἀλλὰ περὶ ψυχῆς θέον Ἕκτορος ἱπποδάμοιο.
ὡς δ' ὅτ' ἀεθλοφόροι περὶ τέρματα μώνυχες ἵπποι

before him; but he, screaming harshly, urged by his instinct to seize her from close behind keeps darting at her: so he flew straight on eagerly; but Hector fled in terror beneath the wall of the Trojans, and swiftly plied his limbs. Then they rushed past the look-out place and the wind-swept fig-tree, keeping under the wall, along the cart-track, and reached the two richly flowing springs, where the double sources of the eddying Scamander gush forth. The one flows with hot water, and steam rises from it as if from a burning fire; while the other flows, in the summer, cold, like hail, or freezing snow, or water turned to ice. Close to them are the beautiful wide stone basins where the wives and lovely daughters of the Trojans used in the past to wash their shimmering clothes, in the peaceful days before the sons of the Achaeans came. The chase went on beyond them, [the one] running away, the other following after him. In front a brave man was escaping, but a much braver followed swiftly after him, as they were not competing for a sacrificial victim or a bull's hide, which are the men's prizes for running, but for the life of horse-breaking Hector. And, as prize-winning, solid-hooved

HOMER

ῥίμφα μάλα τρωχῶσι· τὸ δὲ μέγα κεῖται ἄεθλον,
ἢ τρίπος ἠὲ γυνή, ἀνδρὸς κατατεθνηῶτος·
ὣς τὼ τρὶς Πριάμοιο πόλιν πέρι δινηθήτην
καρπαλίμοισι πόδεσσι· θεοὶ δ' ἐς πάντες ὁρῶντο·
τοῖσι δὲ μύθων ἦρχε πατὴρ ἀνδρῶν τε θεῶν τε·
‹ὢ πόποι, ἦ φίλον ἄνδρα διωκόμενον περὶ τεῖχος
ὀφθαλμοῖσιν ὁρῶμαι· ἐμὸν δ' ὀλοφύρεται ἦτορ
Ἕκτορος, ὅς μοι πολλὰ βοῶν ἐπὶ μηρί' ἔκηεν
Ἴδης ἐν κορυφῇσι πολυπτύχου, ἄλλοτε δ' αὖτε
ἐν πόλει ἀκροτάτῃ· νῦν αὖτέ ἑ δῖος Ἀχιλλεὺς
ἄστυ πέρι Πριάμοιο ποσὶν ταχέεσσι διώκει.
ἀλλ' ἄγετε φράζεσθε, θεοί, καὶ μητιάασθε
ἠέ μιν ἐκ θανάτοιο σαώσομεν, ἦέ μιν ἤδη
Πηλεΐδῃ Ἀχιλῆϊ δαμάσσομεν ἐσθλὸν ἐόντα.›
    Τὸν δ' αὖτε προσέειπε θεὰ γλαυκῶπις Ἀθήνη·
‹ὢ πάτερ ἀργικέραυνε, κελαινεφές, οἷον ἔειπες·
ἄνδρα θνητὸν ἐόντα, πάλαι πεπρωμένον αἴσῃ,
ἂψ ἐθέλεις θανάτοιο δυσηχέος ἐξαναλῦσαι;
ἔρδ'· ἀτὰρ οὔ τοι πάντες ἐπαινέομεν θεοὶ ἄλλοι.›
    Τὴν δ' ἀπαμειβόμενος προσέφη νεφεληγερέτα Ζεύς·
‹θάρσει, Τριτογένεια, φίλον τέκος· οὔ νύ τι θυμῷ

horses run very fast round the turning-post when a great prize is at
stake, such as a tripod or a woman, [at games] after a man's death; so
they circled the city of Priam three times on their swift feet; and all
the gods were watching. Then the Father of Men and Gods spoke first
to them: 'Alas! I see with my eyes a man dear to me chased round the
wall; my heart is weeping for Hector, who has sacrificed the thighs of
many oxen to me on the peaks of many-valed Ida, and at other times
again at the highest point of the city; but now on swift feet noble
Achilles is pursuing him round the city of Priam. But come, gods,
think and consider whether we should save him from death, or let him
fall, brave though he is, to Achilles, the son of Peleus.'

    To him the bright-eyed goddess Athene spoke and said: 'Father,
hurler of the white thunderbolt, gatherer of black clouds, what did you
say? Do you want to reprieve from death, of which news is always
hateful, a man who is mortal, and whose fate has been settled long ago?
Do so: but we, all the other gods, will not praise you for it.'

    Zeus, the cloud-gatherer, answered her and said: 'Take courage,
Tritonia my dear child; I did not really say this seriously, and I want

37

πρόφρονι μυθέομαι, ἐθέλω δέ τοι ἤπιος εἶναι·
ἔρξον ὅπη δή τοι νόος ἔπλετο, μηδ' ἔτ' ἐρώει.›
   Ὣς εἰπὼν ὄτρυνε πάρος μεμαυῖαν Ἀθήνην·
βῆ δὲ κατ' Οὐλύμποιο καρήνων ἀΐξασα.
   Ἕκτορα δ' ἀσπερχὲς κλονέων ἔφεπ' ὠκὺς Ἀχιλλεύς.
ὡς δ' ὅτε νεβρὸν ὄρεσφι κύων ἐλάφοιο δίηται,
ὄρσας ἐξ εὐνῆς, διά τ' ἄγκεα καὶ διὰ βήσσας·
τὸν δ' εἴ πέρ τε λάθῃσι καταπτήξας ὑπὸ θάμνῳ,
ἀλλά τ' ἀνιχνεύων θέει ἔμπεδον, ὄφρα κεν εὕρῃ·
ὣς Ἕκτωρ οὐ λῆθε ποδώκεα Πηλεΐωνα.
ὁσσάκι δ' ὁρμήσειε πυλάων Δαρδανιάων
ἀντίον ἀΐξασθαι ἐϋδμήτους ὑπὸ πύργους,
εἴ πώς οἱ καθύπερθεν ἀλάλκοιεν βελέεσσι,
τοσσάκι μιν προπάροιθεν ἀποστρέψασκε παραφθὰς
πρὸς πεδίον· αὐτὸς δὲ ποτὶ πτόλιος πέτετ' αἰεί.
ὡς δ' ἐν ὀνείρῳ οὐ δύναται φεύγοντα διώκειν·
οὔτ' ἄρ' ὁ τὸν δύναται ὑποφεύγειν οὔθ' ὁ διώκειν·
ὣς ὁ τὸν οὐ δύνατο μάρψαι ποσίν, οὐδ' ὃς ἀλύξαι.
πῶς δέ κεν Ἕκτωρ κῆρας ὑπεξέφυγεν θανάτοιο,
εἰ μή οἱ πύματόν τε καὶ ὕστατον ἤντετ' Ἀπόλλων
ἐγγύθεν, ὅς οἱ ἐπῶρσε μένος λαιψηρά τε γοῦνα;

to be kind to you. Do as your heart is inclined, delay no longer.'
   Saying this he spurred Athene on, who was already eager [for action],
and she now came darting down from the peaks of Olympus.
   Meanwhile swift Achilles chased Hector relentlessly. Just as a hound
rouses the fawn of a deer from its lair, pursues it through glens and
thickets in the mountains, and, although it crouches down panic-
stricken under a bush, he picks up its trail and runs on till he finds it:
so Hector did not escape the swift-footed son of Peleus. Whenever he
rushed for the Dardanian gates, under the well-built towers, in the
hope that they might hold him [Achilles] back with arrows from
above, he [Achilles] was always in time to turn him away towards the
plain; while he himself always flew along nearest to the city. And as in
a dream you cannot catch someone running away – the one cannot
escape, nor the other catch up – so Achilles could not overtake Hector
in the race, nor Hector escape him. How could Hector have escaped
the fate of death, if Apollo had not for the last time met him and roused
in him strength and swiftness of limb? And noble Achilles made a sign

λαοῖσιν δ' ἀνένευε καρήατι δῖος Ἀχιλλεύς,
οὐδ' ἔα ἱέμεναι ἐπὶ Ἕκτορι πικρὰ βέλεμνα,
μή τις κῦδος ἄροιτο βαλών, ὁ δὲ δεύτερος ἔλθοι.
ἀλλ' ὅτε δὴ τὸ τέταρτον ἐπὶ κρουνοὺς ἀφίκοντο,
καὶ τότε δὴ χρύσεια πατὴρ ἐτίταινε τάλαντα,
ἐν δὲ τίθει δύο κῆρε τανηλεγέος θανάτοιο,
τὴν μὲν Ἀχιλλῆος, τὴν δ' Ἕκτορος ἱπποδάμοιο,
ἕλκε δὲ μέσσα λαβών· ῥέπε δ' Ἕκτορος αἴσιμον ἦμαρ,
ᾤχετο δ' εἰς Ἀΐδαο, λίπεν δέ ἑ Φοῖβος Ἀπόλλων.
Πηλείωνα δ' ἵκανε θεὰ γλαυκῶπις Ἀθήνη,
ἀγχοῦ δ' ἱσταμένη ἔπεα πτερόεντα προσηύδα·
‹νῦν δὴ νῶϊ ἔολπα, Διῒ φίλε φαίδιμ' Ἀχιλλεῦ,
οἴσεσθαι μέγα κῦδος Ἀχαιοῖσι προτὶ νῆας,
Ἕκτορα δῃώσαντε μάχης ἄατόν περ ἐόντα.
οὔ οἱ νῦν ἔτι γ' ἔστι πεφυγμένον ἄμμε γενέσθαι,
οὐδ' εἴ κεν μάλα πολλὰ πάθοι ἑκάεργος Ἀπόλλων
προπροκυλινδόμενος πατρὸς Διὸς αἰγιόχοιο.
ἀλλὰ σὺ μὲν νῦν στῆθι καὶ ἄμπνυε, τόνδε δ' ἐγώ τοι
οἰχομένη πεπιθήσω ἐναντίβιον μαχέσασθαι.›
Ὣς φάτ' Ἀθηναίη, ὁ δ' ἐπείθετο, χαῖρε δὲ θυμῷ,
στῆ δ' ἄρ' ἐπὶ μελίης χαλκογλώχινος ἐρεισθείς.

with his head to the soldiers, and would not allow them to cast their sharp shafts at Hector, lest someone else should get the glory of wounding him and he come second. But, when for the fourth time they reached the fountains, the Father [of the gods] lifted up his golden scales, and placed in them two lots of death, the bringer of deep sorrow: the one of Achilles and the other of horse-breaking Hector. He held them up by the middle of the beam; and Hector's day of death fell sinking down to Hades, and Phoebus Apollo deserted him. Then the bright-eyed goddess Athene came up to the son of Peleus, and, standing near, spoke winged words to him: 'Now, illustrious Achilles, dear to Zeus, I hope we two shall bring great glory to the Achaeans at their ships; we shall kill Hector, though he will battle to the end. Now he can no longer escape us, even if far-shafting Apollo were to struggle hard and roll at the feet of his aegis-carrying father Zeus. But you stand still now, and take your breath, while I go to him [Hector], and persuade him to fight and face you man to man.'

So spoke Athene, and he obeyed, rejoicing in his mind; and stood leaning on his ashen, bronze-pointed spear. And then she left him, and

ἡ δ' ἄρα τὸν μὲν ἔλειπε, κιχήσατο δ' Ἕκτορα δῖον
Δηϊφόβῳ ἐΐκυῖα δέμας καὶ ἀτειρέα φωνήν·
ἀγχοῦ δ' ἱσταμένη ἔπεα πτερόεντα προσηύδα·
‹ἠθεῖ', ἦ μάλα δή σε βιάζεται ὠκὺς Ἀχιλλεύς,
ἄστυ πέρι Πριάμοιο ποσὶν ταχέεσσι διώκων·
ἀλλ' ἄγε δὴ στέωμεν καὶ ἀλεξώμεσθα μένοντες.›

Τὴν δ' αὖτε προσέειπε μέγας κορυθαίολος Ἕκτωρ·
‹Δηΐφοβ', ἦ μέν μοι τὸ πάρος πολὺ φίλτατος ἦσθα
γνωτῶν, οὓς Ἑκάβη ἠδὲ Πρίαμος τέκε παῖδας·
νῦν δ' ἔτι καὶ μᾶλλον νοέω φρεσὶ τιμήσασθαι,
ὃς ἔτλης ἐμοῦ εἵνεκ', ἐπεὶ ἴδες ὀφθαλμοῖσι,
τείχεος ἐξελθεῖν, ἄλλοι δ' ἔντοσθε μένουσι.›

Τὸν δ' αὖτε προσέειπε θεὰ γλαυκῶπις Ἀθήνη·
‹ἠθεῖ', ἦ μὲν πολλὰ πατὴρ καὶ πότνια μήτηρ
λίσσονθ' ἑξείης γουνούμενοι, ἀμφὶ δ' ἑταῖροι,
αὖθι μένειν· τοῖον γὰρ ὑποτρομέουσιν ἅπαντες·
ἀλλ' ἐμὸς ἔνδοθι θυμὸς ἐτείρετο πένθεϊ λυγρῷ.
νῦν δ' ἰθὺς μεμαῶτε μαχώμεθα, μηδέ τι δούρων
ἔστω φειδωλή, ἵνα εἴδομεν εἴ κεν Ἀχιλλεὺς
νῶϊ κατακτείνας ἔναρα βροτόεντα φέρηται
νῆας ἔπι γλαφυράς, ἦ κεν σῷ δουρὶ δαμήῃ.›

came to noble Hector, looking like Deiphobus in body and with his strong voice; standing close, she spoke winged words to him: 'My dear brother, swift Achilles now presses on you hard, chasing you round the city of Priam on his quick feet. But come, let us make a stand, let us wait for him and beat him back.'

Powerful Hector of the flashing helmet spoke to her in turn: 'Deiphobus, you were always the dearest of my brothers, the sons of Hecuba and Priam. But now I think I shall honour you still more, since, when you saw me with your own eyes, you dared for my sake to come out of the walls [of the city], while the others remain inside.'

The bright-eyed goddess Athene said to him: 'My dear brother, my father and my respected mother begged me many times to stay there, touching my knees in turn, and my companions were all around, so full of fear are they all; but my heart within was torn with fearful grief. And now let us go and fight eagerly, let us no longer spare our spears, that we may find out whether Achilles will kill us both, and carry our blood-covered spoils to the hollow ships, or if he will be killed by your spear.'

Ὣς φαμένη καὶ κερδοσύνη ἡγήσατ' Ἀθήνη·
οἱ δ' ὅτε δὴ σχεδὸν ἦσαν ἐπ' ἀλλήλοισιν ἰόντες,
τὸν πρότερος προσέειπε μέγας κορυθαίολος Ἕκτωρ·
⟨οὔ σ' ἔτι, Πηλέος υἱέ, φοβήσομαι, ὡς τὸ πάρος περ
τρὶς περὶ ἄστυ μέγα Πριάμου δίον, οὐδέ ποτ' ἔτλην
μεῖναι ἐπερχόμενον· νῦν αὖτέ με θυμὸς ἀνῆκε
στήμεναι ἀντία σεῖο· ἕλοιμί κεν, ἤ κεν ἁλοίην.
ἀλλ' ἄγε δεῦρο θεοὺς ἐπιδώμεθα· τοὶ γὰρ ἄριστοι
μάρτυροι ἔσσονται καὶ ἐπίσκοποι ἁρμονιάων·
οὐ γὰρ ἐγώ σ' ἔκπαγλον ἀεικιῶ, αἴ κεν ἐμοὶ Ζεὺς
δώῃ καμμονίην, σὴν δὲ ψυχὴν ἀφέλωμαι·
ἀλλ' ἐπεὶ ἄρ κέ σε συλήσω κλυτὰ τεύχε', Ἀχιλλεῦ,
νεκρὸν Ἀχαιοῖσιν δώσω πάλιν· ὣς δὲ σὺ ῥέζειν.⟩
    Τὸν δ' ἄρ' ὑπόδρα ἰδὼν προσέφη πόδας ὠκὺς Ἀχιλλεύς·
⟨Ἕκτορ, μή μοι, ἄλαστε, συνημοσύνας ἀγόρευε·
ὡς οὐκ ἔστι λέουσι καὶ ἀνδράσιν ὅρκια πιστά,
οὐδὲ λύκοι τε καὶ ἄρνες ὁμόφρονα θυμὸν ἔχουσιν,
ἀλλὰ κακὰ φρονέουσι διαμπερὲς ἀλλήλοισιν,
ὣς οὐκ ἔστ' ἐμὲ καὶ σὲ φιλήμεναι, οὐδέ τι νῶϊν
ὅρκια ἔσσονται, πρίν γ' ἢ ἕτερόν γε πεσόντα
αἵματος ἆσαι Ἄρηα, ταλαύρινον πολεμιστήν.

Saying this, Athene led him on deceitfully. But when, as they advanced, they came close to one another, great Hector of the flashing helmet addressed Achilles first: 'Son of Peleus, no longer will I fly before you, as I did before. Three times have I run round the great and noble city of Priam, and never dared to wait for you to catch up; but now my heart has urged me to stand against you. I shall kill you, or be killed. But come, let us swear by the gods, for they will be the best witnesses and observers of agreement. I will not outrage you brutally, if Zeus should give me victory and I take your life away; but after I have stripped you of your famous armour, Achilles, I will give your body back to the Achaeans; and you do the same.'

And swift-footed Achilles looked at him grimly and said: 'Hector, do not talk to me about pacts, accursed one. As there are no faithful promises between lions and men, nor do wolves and lambs think in the same way, but always plan evil against one another, so it is not possible for you and me to be friends, nor will there be any pacts between us, until one of us falls and satisfies with his blood the hunger of the warrior Ares who carries the ox-hide shield. Call to your mind all your

παντοίης ἀρετῆς μιμνήσκεο· νῦν σε μάλα χρή
αἰχμητήν τ' ἔμεναι καὶ θαρσαλέον πολεμιστήν.
οὔ τοι ἔτ' ἔσθ' ὑπάλυξις, ἄφαρ δέ σε Παλλὰς Ἀθήνη
ἔγχει ἐμῷ δαμάᾳ· νῦν δ' ἀθρόα πάντ' ἀποτίσεις
κήδε' ἐμῶν ἑτάρων, οὓς ἔκτανες ἔγχεϊ θύων.)
    Ἦ ῥα, καὶ ἀμπεπαλὼν προΐει δολιχόσκιον ἔγχος·
καὶ τὸ μὲν ἄντα ἰδὼν ἠλεύατο φαίδιμος Ἕκτωρ·
ἕζετο γὰρ προϊδών, τὸ δ' ὑπέρπτατο χάλκεον ἔγχος,
ἐν γαίῃ δ' ἐπάγη· ἀνὰ δ' ἥρπασε Παλλὰς Ἀθήνη,
ἂψ δ' Ἀχιλῆϊ δίδου, λάθε δ' Ἕκτορα, ποιμένα λαῶν.
Ἕκτωρ δὲ προσέειπεν ἀμύμονα Πηλεΐωνα·
‹ἤμβροτες, οὐδ' ἄρα πώ τι, θεοῖς ἐπιείκελ' Ἀχιλλεῦ,
ἐκ Διὸς ἠείδης τὸν ἐμὸν μόρον· ἦ τοι ἔφης γε·
ἀλλά τις ἀρτιεπὴς καὶ ἐπίκλοπος ἔπλεο μύθων,
ὄφρα σ' ὑποδείσας μένεος ἀλκῆς τε λάθωμαι.
οὐ μέν μοι φεύγοντι μεταφρένῳ ἐν δόρυ πήξεις,
ἀλλ' ἰθὺς μεμαῶτι διὰ στήθεσφιν ἔλασσον,
εἴ τοι ἔδωκε θεός· νῦν αὖτ' ἐμὸν ἔγχος ἄλευαι
χάλκεον· ὡς δή μιν σῷ ἐν χροῒ πᾶν κομίσαιο.
καί κεν ἐλαφρότερος πόλεμος Τρώεσσι γένοιτο
σεῖο καταφθιμένοιο· σὺ γάρ σφισι πῆμα μέγιστον.)

courage; now more than ever it is necessary for you to be a spearman
and a fearless fighter. There is no escape for you any longer, for Pallas
Athene will fell you at once with my spear; now you shall pay for all
the sorrows of my companions, whom in your fury you killed with
your spear.'

With these words, he swung back his long-shafted spear and hurled
it; but illustrious Hector watched its coming and avoided it; seeing it
in time, he crouched down, and the bronze spear flew over him and
stuck in the ground. But Pallas Athene snatched it up and gave it back
to Achilles; she concealed her action from Hector, shepherd of men.
Then Hector spoke to the noble son of Peleus: 'You missed, godlike
Achilles, and Zeus has not yet shown you when I will die, as, indeed,
you said. You are a subtle man and glib in your speech; [you wished]
to frighten me and make me lose my courage and strength. But you
will not thrust your spear into my back as I flee; pierce me, if the god
allows you, through my breast as I charge. But now in your turn dodge
my bronze-tipped spear! May all [the head] be buried in your flesh.
For with you dead, the war will be easier for the Trojans, for you are
their greatest scourge.'

Ἦ ῥα, καὶ ἀμπεπαλὼν προΐει δολιχόσκιον ἔγχος,
καὶ βάλε Πηλεΐδαο μέσον σάκος οὐδ' ἀφάμαρτε·
τῆλε δ' ἀπεπλάγχθη σάκεος δόρυ· χώσατο δ' Ἕκτωρ
ὅττι ῥά οἱ βέλος ὠκὺ ἐτώσιον ἔκφυγε χειρός,
στῆ δὲ κατηφήσας, οὐδ' ἄλλ' ἔχε μείλινον ἔγχος.
Δηΐφοβον δὲ κάλει λευκάσπιδα μακρὸν ἀΰσας·
ᾔτεέ μιν δόρυ μακρόν· ὁ δ' οὔ τί οἱ ἐγγύθεν ἦεν·
Ἕκτωρ δ' ἔγνω ᾗσιν ἐνὶ φρεσὶ φώνησέν τε·
‹ὢ πόποι, ἦ μάλα δή με θεοὶ θάνατόνδε κάλεσσαν·
Δηΐφοβον γὰρ ἔγωγ' ἐφάμην ἥρωα παρεῖναι·
ἀλλ' ὁ μὲν ἐν τείχει, ἐμὲ δ' ἐξαπάτησεν Ἀθήνη.
νῦν δὲ δὴ ἐγγύθι μοι θάνατος κακός, οὐδ' ἔτ' ἄνευθεν,
οὐδ' ἀλέη· ἦ γάρ ῥα πάλαι τό γε φίλτερον ἦεν
Ζηνί τε καὶ Διὸς υἷι ἑκηβόλῳ, οἵ με πάρος γε
πρόφρονες εἰρύατο· νῦν αὖτέ με μοῖρα κιχάνει.
μὴ μὰν ἀσπουδί γε καὶ ἀκλειῶς ἀπολοίμην,
ἀλλὰ μέγα ῥέξας τι καὶ ἐσσομένοισι πυθέσθαι.›
  Ὣς ἄρα φωνήσας εἰρύσσατο φάσγανον ὀξύ,
τό οἱ ὑπὸ λαπάρην τέτατο μέγα τε στιβαρόν τε,
οἴμησεν δὲ ἀλεὶς ὥς τ' αἰετὸς ὑψιπετήεις,
ὅς τ' εἶσιν πεδίονδε διὰ νεφέων ἐρεβεννῶν

With these words he swung back and hurled his long-shafted spear;
he did not miss, the spear struck the centre of Achilles' shield, but
it bounced off. And Hector was angry, because the swift weapon had
left his hand for nothing; and he stood dejected, for he had no other
ashen spear. And he called Deiphobus of the white shield, shouting out
for a long spear; but he was nowhere near; and Hector realized what
had happened and cried out: 'Alas! It is certain that the gods have sum-
moned me to death. For I thought the hero Deiphobus was at my side,
but he is behind the city wall, and Athene has deceived me. And now
evil death is near me, no longer far away, and there is no escape. This
must long have been the wish of Zeus and of his far-shafting son, who
had willingly helped me before; but now doom overtakes me. At least
let me not die without a struggle, with no glory, but after accomplishing
some great deed for posterity to hear of.'
  So he spoke, and drew his sharp sword, which hung big and power-
ful below his loins, and he braced himself and swooped like a high-
soaring eagle, which drops to the plain through the black clouds to

ἁρπάξων ἢ ἄρν' ἀμαλὴν ἢ πτῶκα λαγωόν·
ὣς Ἕκτωρ οἴμησε τινάσσων φάσγανον ὀξύ.
ὁρμήθη δ' Ἀχιλεύς, μένεος δ' ἐμπλήσατο θυμὸν
ἀγρίου, πρόσθεν δὲ σάκος στέρνοιο κάλυψε
καλὸν δαιδάλεον, κόρυθι δ' ἐπένευε φαεινῇ
τετραφάλῳ· καλαὶ δὲ περισσείοντο ἔθειραι
χρύσεαι, ἃς Ἥφαιστος ἵει λόφον ἀμφὶ θαμειάς.
οἷος δ' ἀστὴρ εἶσι μετ' ἀστράσι νυκτὸς ἀμολγῷ
ἕσπερος, ὃς κάλλιστος ἐν οὐρανῷ ἵσταται ἀστήρ,
ὣς αἰχμῆς ἀπέλαμπ' εὐήκεος, ἣν ἄρ' Ἀχιλεύς
πάλλεν δεξιτερῇ φρονέων κακὸν Ἕκτορι δίῳ,
εἰσορόων χρόα καλόν, ὅπη εἴξειε μάλιστα.
τοῦ δὲ καὶ ἄλλο τόσον μὲν ἔχε χρόα χάλκεα τεύχεα,
καλά, τὰ Πατρόκλοιο βίην ἐνάριξε κατακτάς·
φαίνετο δ' ᾗ κληῗδες ἀπ' ὤμων αὐχέν' ἔχουσι,
λαυκανίην, ἵνα τε ψυχῆς ὤκιστος ὄλεθρος·
τῇ ῥ' ἐπὶ οἷ μεμαῶτ' ἔλασ' ἔγχεϊ δῖος Ἀχιλλεύς,
ἀντικρὺ δ' ἁπαλοῖο δι' αὐχένος ἤλυθ' ἀκωκή·
οὐδ' ἄρ' ἀπ' ἀσφάραγον μελίη τάμε χαλκοβάρεια,
ὄφρα τί μιν προτιείποι ἀμειβόμενος ἐπέεσσιν.
ἤριπε δ' ἐν κονίῃς· ὁ δ' ἐπεύξατο δῖος Ἀχιλλεύς·

snatch a tender lamb or a timid hare; so Hector rushed forward,
brandishing his sharp sword. Achilles also charged, his soul full of
fierce rage. He held before his chest the beautiful, decorated shield his
flashing helmet with its four projections bobbing on his head; and the
lovely golden plumes which Hephaestus had set thickly on the crest
waved around it. And as the evening star, which is the most beautiful
in the sky, rises among the other stars in the twilight, so the sharp point
flashed on the spear which Achilles, intent on killing godly Hector,
brandished in his right hand, searching his [enemy's] fine flesh for
the place likeliest to yield. The beautiful bronze armour, which he
had seized when he killed powerful Patroclus, fully covered all of
[Hector's] body; except [that there was a gap] at the throat, the point
where the collar-bones separate the neck from the shoulders and where
death comes quickest. As he charged, noble Achilles thrust with his
spear at this spot and the point came out on the other side through the
tender neck. But the ash, heavy with bronze, did not cut the windpipe,
so that he could speak and answer him (with words). He fell in the dust,
and noble Achilles triumphed over him. 'Hector, you had once thought,

‹"Εκτορ, ἀτάρ που ἔφης Πατροκλῆ' ἐξεναρίζων
σῶς ἔσσεσθ', ἐμὲ δ' οὐδὲν ὀπίζεο νόσφιν ἐόντα,
νήπιε· τοῖο δ' ἄνευθεν ἀοσσητὴρ μέγ' ἀμείνων
νηυσὶν ἔπι γλαφυρῇσιν ἐγὼ μετόπισθε λελείμμην,
ὅς τοι γούνατ' ἔλυσα· σὲ μὲν κύνες ἠδ' οἰωνοὶ
ἑλκήσουσ' ἀϊκῶς, τὸν δὲ κτεριοῦσιν Ἀχαιοί.›

Τὸν δ' ὀλιγοδρανέων προσέφη κορυθαίολος Ἕκτωρ·
‹λίσσομ' ὑπὲρ ψυχῆς καὶ γούνων σῶν τε τοκήων,
μή με ἔα παρὰ νηυσὶ κύνας καταδάψαι Ἀχαιῶν,
ἀλλὰ σὺ μὲν χαλκόν τε ἅλις χρυσόν τε δέδεξο,
δῶρα τά τοι δώσουσι πατὴρ καὶ πότνια μήτηρ,
σῶμα δὲ οἴκαδ' ἐμὸν δόμεναι πάλιν, ὄφρα πυρός με
Τρῶες καὶ Τρώων ἄλοχοι λελάχωσι θανόντα.›

Τὸν δ' ἄρ' ὑπόδρα ἰδὼν προσέφη πόδας ὠκὺς Ἀχιλλεύς·
‹μή με, κύον, γούνων γουνάζεο μηδὲ τοκήων·
αἲ γάρ πως αὐτόν με μένος καὶ θυμὸς ἀνείη
ὤμ' ἀποταμνόμενον κρέα ἔδμεναι, οἷα μ' ἔοργας,
ὡς οὐκ ἔσθ' ὃς σῆς γε κύνας κεφαλῆς ἀπαλάλκοι,
οὐδ' εἴ κεν δεκάκις τε καὶ εἰκοσινήριτ' ἄποινα
στήσωσ' ἐνθάδ' ἄγοντες, ὑπόσχωνται δὲ καὶ ἄλλα,

when stripping the armour off Patroclus, that you would be safe, and did not fear me at all, because I was far away. Fool; for the avenger of his death, much greater than you, was not there but left behind at the hollow ships – I, who have unstrung your limbs. The dogs and the birds shall tear you shamefully, but the Achaeans will bury him [Patroclus] with all honour.'

And Hector of the flashing helmet, losing his strength, said to him: 'I beg you by your life, your knees, and your parents, do not leave me to be torn by the dogs near the ships of the Achaeans; accept the bronze and much gold, which my father and my honoured mother will give you, and send my body back home, so that the Trojans and their wives may put me on a funeral pyre.'

But swift-footed Achilles looked at him grimly and said: 'Dog, do not entreat me by my knees or by my parents, for I wish my angry heart could urge me to cut up your flesh and devour it raw myself, such things have you done to me; so there is nobody who can drive away the dogs from your head, not even if they bring gifts ten and twenty times as great and set them here before me and even promise

οὐδ' εἴ κέν σ' αὐτὸν χρυσῷ ἐρύσασθαι ἀνώγοι
Δαρδανίδης Πρίαμος· οὐδ' ὥς σέ γε πότνια μήτηρ
ἐνθεμένη λεχέεσσι γοήσεται, ὃν τέκεν αὐτή,
ἀλλὰ κύνες τε καὶ οἰωνοὶ κατὰ πάντα δάσονται.›
   Τὸν δὲ καταθνῄσκων προσέφη κορυθαίολος Ἕκτωρ·
‹ἦ σ' εὖ γιγνώσκων προτιόσσομαι, οὐδ' ἄρ' ἔμελλον
πείσειν· ἦ γὰρ σοί γε σιδήρεος ἐν φρεσὶ θυμός.
φράζεο νῦν, μή τοί τι θεῶν μήνιμα γένωμαι
ἤματι τῷ ὅτε κέν σε Πάρις καὶ Φοῖβος Ἀπόλλων
ἐσθλὸν ἐόντ' ὀλέσωσιν ἐνὶ Σκαιῇσι πύλῃσιν.›
   Ὣς ἄρα μιν εἰπόντα τέλος θανάτοιο κάλυψε,
ψυχὴ δ' ἐκ ῥεθέων πταμένη Ἄϊδόσδε βεβήκει,
ὃν πότμον γοόωσα, λιποῦσ' ἀνδροτῆτα καὶ ἥβην.
τὸν καὶ τεθνηῶτα προσηύδα δῖος Ἀχιλλεύς·
‹τέθναθι· κῆρα δ' ἐγὼ τότε δέξομαι, ὁππότε κεν δὴ
Ζεὺς ἐθέλῃ τελέσαι ἠδ' ἀθάνατοι θεοὶ ἄλλοι.›
   Ἦ ῥα, καὶ ἐκ νεκροῖο ἐρύσσατο χάλκεον ἔγχος,
καὶ τό γ' ἄνευθεν ἔθηχ', ὁ δ' ἀπ' ὤμων τεύχε' ἐσύλα
αἱματόεντ'· ἄλλοι δὲ περίδραμον υἷες Ἀχαιῶν,
οἳ καὶ θηήσαντο φυὴν καὶ εἶδος ἀγητὸν

more; not even if Pri·am, the son of Dardanus, would wish to pay your
weight in gold, not even then shall your honoured mother lay you on
a bed and weep for you, but the dogs and the birds shall tear you up
completely.'
   And, as he was dying, Hector of the glancing helmet said this to him:
'I know you well, and I foresaw this; I did not expect to persuade you,
for within you, you truly have an iron heart. But take care now, lest I
be the cause of the wrath of the gods against you on the day when
Paris and Phoebus Apollo shall kill you, at the Scaean gates, brave
though you are.'
   As he said this, death covered him; and his soul flew from his limbs,
and went down to Hades wailing for its fate, at leaving its manly vigour
and its youth. But although he was dead, noble Achilles spoke to him:
'Die; and I will accept my death, whenever Zeus and the other im-
mortal gods want to bring it about.'
   With these words he pulled out his bronze-tipped spear from the
corpse; then put it aside and took the blood-streaked armour off his
shoulders. The other sons of the Achaeans ran up and gathered round,
gazing in wonder at the build and marvellous good looks of Hector;

Ἕκτορος· οὐδ' ἄρα οἵ τις ἀνουτητί γε παρέστη.
ὧδε δέ τις εἴπεσκεν ἰδὼν ἐς πλησίον ἄλλον·
‹ὢ πόποι, ἦ μάλα δὴ μαλακώτερος ἀμφαφάασθαι
Ἕκτωρ ἢ ὅτε νῆας ἐνέπρησεν πυρὶ κηλέῳ.›
   Ὣς ἄρα τις εἴπεσκε καὶ οὐτήσασκε παραστάς.

(*Iliad*)

7. The Burial of Patroclus

Ὣς οἱ μὲν στενάχοντο κατὰ πτόλιν· αὐτὰρ Ἀχαιοὶ
ἐπεὶ δὴ νῆάς τε καὶ Ἑλλήσποντον ἵκοντο,
οἱ μὲν ἄρ' ἐσκίδναντο ἑὴν ἐπὶ νῆα ἕκαστος,
Μυρμιδόνας δ' οὐκ εἴα ἀποσκίδνασθαι Ἀχιλλεύς,
ἀλλ' ὅ γε οἷς ἑτάροισι φιλοπτολέμοισι μετηύδα·
‹Μυρμιδόνες ταχύπωλοι, ἐμοὶ ἐρίηρες ἑταῖροι,
μὴ δή πω ὑπ' ὄχεσφι λυώμεθα μώνυχας ἵππους,
ἀλλ' αὐτοῖς ἵπποισι καὶ ἅρμασιν ἄσσον ἰόντες
Πάτροκλον κλαίωμεν· ὃ γὰρ γέρας ἐστὶ θανόντων.
αὐτὰρ ἐπεί κ' ὀλοοῖο τεταρπώμεσθα γόοιο,
ἵππους λυσάμενοι δορπήσομεν ἐνθάδε πάντες.›
   Ὣς ἔφαθ', οἱ δ' ὤμωξαν ἀολλέες, ἦρχε δ' Ἀχιλλεύς.

and not one stood by without inflicting a wound. And looking at his neighbour one would say: 'How strange! Hector is certainly much easier to manage now than when he burned the ships with blazing fire.'

This would they say as they stood by him and wounded him.

So they [the Trojans] mourned through the city; but the Achaeans, when they reached the ships and the Hellespont, split up and each went to his own ship. Achilles, however, did not allow the Myrmidons to disperse, but spoke to his war-loving companions: 'Swift-horsed Myrmidons, my loyal comrades, let us not unyoke the solid-hooved horses from their chariots yet, but let us go up with horses and chariots and mourn Patroclus; for this is the privilege of the dead. And when we have had our fill of sad lamentation, we shall unyoke our horses and have our meal here.'

So he spoke, and they all mourned together as Achilles led the way.

οἱ δὲ τρὶς περὶ νεκρὸν ἐΰτριχας ἤλασαν ἵππους
μυρόμενοι· μετὰ δέ σφι Θέτις γόου ἵμερον ὦρσε.
δεύοντο ψάμαθοι, δεύοντο δὲ τεύχεα φωτῶν
δάκρυσι· τοῖον γὰρ πόθεον μήστωρα φόβοιο.
τοῖσι δὲ Πηλεΐδης ἁδινοῦ ἐξῆρχε γόοιο,
χεῖρας ἐπ' ἀνδροφόνους θέμενος στήθεσσιν ἑταίρου·
‹χαῖρέ μοι, ὦ Πάτροκλε, καὶ εἰν Ἀΐδαο δόμοισι·
πάντα γὰρ ἤδη τοι τελέω τὰ πάροιθεν ὑπέστην,
Ἕκτορα δεῦρ' ἐρύσας δώσειν κυσὶν ὠμὰ δάσασθαι,
δώδεκα δὲ προπάροιθε πυρῆς ἀποδειροτομήσειν
Τρώων ἀγλαὰ τέκνα, σέθεν κταμένοιο χολωθείς.›
Ἦ ῥα, καὶ Ἕκτορα δῖον ἀεικέα μήδετο ἔργα,
πρηνέα πὰρ λεχέεσσι Μενοιτιάδαο τανύσσας
ἐν κονίῃς· οἱ δ' ἔντε' ἀφοπλίζοντο ἕκαστος
χάλκεα μαρμαίροντα, λύον δ' ὑψηχέας ἵππους,
κὰδ δ' ἷζον παρὰ νηΐ ποδώκεος Αἰακίδαο
μυρίοι· αὐτὰρ ὁ τοῖσι τάφον μενοεικέα δαίνυ.
πολλοὶ μὲν βόες ἀργοὶ ὀρέχθεον ἀμφὶ σιδήρῳ
σφαζόμενοι, πολλοὶ δ' ὄϊες καὶ μηκάδες αἶγες·
πολλοὶ δ' ἀργιόδοντες ὕες, θαλέθοντες ἀλοιφῇ,
εὐόμενοι τανύοντο διὰ φλογὸς Ἡφαίστοιο·

Three times they drove their fine-maned horses round the body,
grieving; and Thetis kindled their desire for lamentation. The sands
grew wet and the armour of the men grew wet with tears; for they
longed for the man who could so well inspire fear. The son of Peleus
led their rich lamentation, putting his man-slaying hands on the breast
of his companion: 'I greet you, Patroclus, even in the Halls of Hades.
Now I will do all that I promised before: that I would drag Hector
here and give him to the dogs to be torn up raw; and that in front of
your pyre I would cut the throats of twelve highborn sons of the
Trojans to vent my anger at your death.'

He spoke, and thought of outrages for noble Hector's [body], as he
flung him face down in the dust near the bier of the son of Menoetius.
And they all stripped off their glittering bronze armour and unyoked
their loud-neighing horses; they sat in crowds round the ship of the
swift-footed grandson of Aeacus, and he offered them a funeral feast
after their own hearts. Many white oxen lay stretched out, their
throats cut with steel, and many sheep and bleating goats, and many
white-tusked boars rich in fat were stretched to roast in the flame of

πάντη δ' ἀμφὶ νέκυν κοτυλήρυτον ἔρρεεν αἷμα.
    Αὐτὰρ τόν γε ἄνακτα ποδώκεα Πηλεΐωνα
εἰς Ἀγαμέμνονα δῖον ἄγον βασιλῆες Ἀχαιῶν,
σπουδῇ παρπεπιθόντες ἑταίρου χωόμενον κῆρ.
οἱ δ' ὅτε δὴ κλισίην Ἀγαμέμνονος ἷξον ἰόντες,
αὐτίκα κηρύκεσσι λιγυφθόγγοισι κέλευσαν
ἀμφὶ πυρὶ στῆσαι τρίποδα μέγαν, εἰ πεπίθοιεν
Πηλεΐδην λούσασθαι ἄπο βρότον αἱματόεντα.
αὐτὰρ ὅ γ' ἠρνεῖτο στερεῶς, ἐπὶ δ' ὅρκον ὄμοσσεν·
‹οὐ μὰ Ζῆν', ὅς τίς τε θεῶν ὕπατος καὶ ἄριστος,
οὐ θέμις ἐστὶ λοετρὰ καρήατος ἆσσον ἱκέσθαι,
πρίν γ' ἐνὶ Πάτροκλον θέμεναι πυρὶ σῆμά τε χεῦαι
κείρασθαί τε κόμην, ἐπεὶ οὔ μ' ἔτι δεύτερον ὧδε
ἵξετ' ἄχος κραδίην, ὄφρα ζωοῖσι μετείω.
ἀλλ' ἤτοι νῦν μὲν στυγερῇ πειθώμεθα δαιτί·
ἠῶθεν δ' ὄτρυνε, ἄναξ ἀνδρῶν Ἀγάμεμνον,
ὕλην τ' ἀξέμεναι παρά τε σχεῖν ὅσσ' ἐπιεικὲς
νεκρὸν ἔχοντα νέεσθαι ὑπὸ ζόφον ἠερόεντα,
ὄφρ' ἤτοι τοῦτον μὲν ἐπιφλέγῃ ἀκάματον πῦρ
θᾶσσον ἀπ' ὀφθαλμῶν, λαοὶ δ' ἐπὶ ἔργα τράπωνται.›
    Ὣς ἔφαθ', οἱ δ' ἄρα τοῦ μάλα μὲν κλύον ἠδὲ πίθοντο.

Hephaestus, and on every side of the dead body blood flowed in streams.
    But the chiefs of the Achaeans led their king, the swift-footed son of
Peleus, to noble Agamemnon, though it was hard to persuade him [to
come], enraged as he was at heart on account of his comrade. But when
they reached the tent of Agamemnon, they immediately ordered the
clear-voiced heralds to place a large tripod on the fire, hoping they could
persuade the son of Peleus to wash away the bloody gore [from his
body]. But he refused firmly and also took an oath: 'No, by Zeus, who
is the greatest and the best of gods, it is not proper to bring water to
my head, before I put Patroclus on a pyre and pile up a barrow [for
him], and cut off my hair, since such sorrow will never touch my heart
again as long as I live. But now, let us yield to the hateful feast. And
at dawn, Agamemnon, king of men, send men to bring wood and to
prepare all that is proper for a dead body to have when it descends into
misty darkness, so that the untiring fire may most swiftly consume him
from our eyes and the men return to their duties.'
    So he spoke, and they listened to him carefully and obeyed. Then

ἐσσυμένως δ' ἄρα δόρπον ἐφοπλίσσαντες ἕκαστοι
δαίνυντ', οὐδέ τι θυμὸς ἐδεύετο δαιτὸς ἐΐσης.
αὐτὰρ ἐπεὶ πόσιος καὶ ἐδητύος ἐξ ἔρον ἕντο,
οἱ μὲν κακκείοντες ἔβαν κλισίηνδε ἕκαστος,
Πηλεΐδης δ' ἐπὶ θινὶ πολυφλοίσβοιο θαλάσσης
κεῖτο βαρὺ στενάχων, πολέσιν μετὰ Μυρμιδόνεσσιν,
ἐν καθαρῷ, ὅθι κύματ' ἐπ' ἠϊόνος κλύζεσκον·
εὖτε τὸν ὕπνος ἔμαρπτε, λύων μελεδήματα θυμοῦ,
νήδυμος ἀμφιχυθείς — μάλα γὰρ κάμε φαίδιμα γυῖα
Ἕκτορ' ἐπαΐσσων προτὶ Ἴλιον ἠνεμόεσσαν —
ἦλθε δ' ἐπὶ ψυχὴ Πατροκλῆος δειλοῖο,
πάντ' αὐτῷ μέγεθός τε καὶ ὄμματα κάλ' ἐϊκυῖα,
καὶ φωνήν, καὶ τοῖα περὶ χροΐ εἵματα ἕστο·
στῆ δ' ἄρ' ὑπὲρ κεφαλῆς καί μιν πρὸς μῦθον ἔειπεν·
‹εὕδεις, αὐτὰρ ἐμεῖο λελασμένος ἔπλευ, Ἀχιλλεῦ.
οὐ μέν μευ ζώοντος ἀκήδεις, ἀλλὰ θανόντος·
θάπτε με ὅττι τάχιστα, πύλας Ἀΐδαο περήσω.
τῆλέ με εἴργουσι ψυχαί, εἴδωλα καμόντων,
οὐδέ μέ πω μίσγεσθαι ὑπὲρ ποταμοῖο ἐῶσιν,
ἀλλ' αὕτως ἀλάλημαι ἀν' εὐρυπυλὲς Ἄϊδος δῶ.
καί μοι δὸς τὴν χεῖρ', ὀλοφύρομαι· οὐ γὰρ ἔτ' αὖτις

they prepared their meal swiftly, nor was their appetite lacking for
their communal meal, and they shared it out separately. When they
had satisfied the urge for food and drink, the rest left to lie down, each
in his tent. But the son of Peleus lay among his many Myrmidons,
lamenting bitterly on the shore of the loud-roaring sea, in a clear spot
where the waves were breaking on the shore; and when sleep took hold
of him, easing the cares of his heart — sleep that fell heavily on him, for
his splendid limbs were very tired after chasing Hector at windswept
Ilium — the spirit of unhappy Patroclus came to him in every way like
his living self, in stature, and beautiful eyes and voice; and the clothes
on his body were the same; and he stood over Achilles' head and spoke
to him: 'You sleep, Achilles, and you have forgotten me. You never
neglected me when I was living, but [you do so now I am] dead. Bury
me as soon as possible that I may pass through the gates of Hades. The
spirits, the phantoms of the dead, drive me away and do not allow me to
mingle with them beyond the river; I wander vainly by the wide-
gated palace of Hades. Give me your hand, I beg you, for I shall not

νίσομαι ἐξ Ἀΐδαο, ἐπήν με πυρὸς λελάχητε.
οὐ μὲν γὰρ ζωοί γε φίλων ἀπάνευθεν ἑταίρων
βουλὰς ἑζόμενοι βουλεύσομεν, ἀλλ' ἐμὲ μὲν κήρ
ἀμφέχανε στυγερή, ἥ περ λάχε γιγνόμενόν περ·
καὶ δὲ σοὶ αὐτῷ μοῖρα, θεοῖς ἐπιείκελ' Ἀχιλλεῦ,
τείχει ὑπο Τρώων εὐηφενέων ἀπολέσθαι.
ἄλλο δέ τοι ἐρέω καὶ ἐφήσομαι, αἴ κε πίθηαι·
μὴ ἐμὰ σῶν ἀπάνευθε τιθήμεναι ὀστέ', Ἀχιλλεῦ,
ἀλλ' ὁμοῦ, ὡς τράφομέν περ ἐν ὑμετέροισι δόμοισιν,
εὖτέ με τυτθὸν ἐόντα Μενοίτιος ἐξ Ὀπόεντος
ἤγαγεν ὑμέτερόνδ' ἀνδροκτασίης ὑπο λυγρῆς,
ἤματι τῷ, ὅτε παῖδα κατέκτανον Ἀμφιδάμαντος,
νήπιος, οὐκ ἐθέλων, ἀμφ' ἀστραγάλοισι χολωθείς·
ἔνθα με δεξάμενος ἐν δώμασιν ἱππότα Πηλεὺς
ἔτραφέ τ' ἐνδυκέως καὶ σὸν θεράποντ' ὀνόμηνεν·
ὡς δὲ καὶ ὀστέα νῶϊν ὁμὴ σορὸς ἀμφικαλύπτοι
χρύσεος ἀμφιφορεύς, τόν τοι πόρε πότνια μήτηρ.›
   Τὸν δ' ἀπαμειβόμενος προσέφη πόδας ὠκὺς Ἀχιλλεύς·
‹τίπτε μοι, ἠθείη κεφαλή, δεῦρ' εἰλήλουθας,
καί μοι ταῦτα ἕκαστ' ἐπιτέλλεαι; αὐτὰρ ἐγώ τοι
πάντα μάλ' ἐκτελέω καὶ πείσομαι ὡς σὺ κελεύεις.

return again from Hades once you hand me to the flames. Never [again] alive shall we sit apart from our dear companions to discuss things together; the harsh fate which was allotted to me when I was born has fallen on me. And you too, godlike Achilles, are fated to perish at the foot of the city wall of the wealthy Trojans. But I will tell you another thing, and ask you, Achilles, if you will obey me, not to lay my bones apart from yours; but as we were reared together in your house, when Menoetius brought me there from Opus just a small boy after the grim murder on the day when I killed the son of Amphidamas, foolishly, without meaning to do so, because of my anger over the dice; Peleus the horseman received me in his house then and brought me up lovingly and named me your attendant: so may the same urn hold our bones, the golden two-handled vase which your honourable mother gave you.'
   And swift-footed Achilles answered him and said: 'Why, dear friend, have you come here and why do you ask me all these things? Of course I will do all this. I will obey your orders. But come, stand

ἀλλά μοι ἆσσον στῆθι· μίνυνθά περ ἀμφιβαλόντε
ἀλλήλους ὀλοοῖο τεταρπώμεσθα γόοιο.›

"Ως ἄρα φωνήσας ὠρέξατο χερσὶ φίλῃσιν,
οὐδ᾽ ἔλαβε· ψυχὴ δὲ κατὰ χθονὸς ἠΰτε καπνὸς
ᾤχετο τετριγυῖα· ταφὼν δ᾽ ἀνόρουσεν ᾿Αχιλλεὺς
χερσί τε συμπλατάγησεν, ἔπος δ᾽ ὀλοφυδνὸν ἔειπεν·
‹ὢ πόποι, ἦ ῥά τίς ἐστι καὶ εἰν ᾿Αΐδαο δόμοισι
ψυχὴ καὶ εἴδωλον, ἀτὰρ φρένες οὐκ ἔνι πάμπαν·
παννυχίη γάρ μοι Πατροκλῆος δειλοῖο
ψυχὴ ἐφεστήκει γοόωσά τε μυρομένη τε,
καί μοι ἕκαστ᾽ ἐπέτελλεν, ἔϊκτο δὲ θέσκελον αὐτῷ.›

"Ως φάτο, τοῖσι δὲ πᾶσιν ὑφ᾽ ἵμερον ὦρσε γόοιο·
μυρομένοισι δὲ τοῖσι φάνη ῥοδοδάκτυλος ᾿Ηὼς
ἀμφὶ νέκυν ἐλεεινόν...

. . . .

Αὐτὰρ ἐπεὶ τό γ᾽ ἄκουσεν ἄναξ ἀνδρῶν ᾿Αγαμέμνων,
αὐτίκα λαὸν μὲν σκέδασεν κατὰ νῆας ἐΐσας,
κηδεμόνες δὲ παρ᾽ αὖθι μένον καὶ νήεον ὕλην,
ποίησαν δὲ πυρὴν ἑκατόμπεδον ἔνθα καὶ ἔνθα,
ἐν δὲ πυρῇ ὑπάτῃ νεκρὸν θέσαν ἀχνύμενοι κῆρ.

---

closer to me, that we may embrace each other even for a little and in-
dulge in sad lamentation.'

When he said this, he stretched out his arms, but did not touch him;
for like smoke his soul vanished gibbering under the earth. Achilles
sprang up astonished, and clapped his hands together and said these
sad words: 'Alas! Then there really is in the Halls of Hades a soul and
an image [of the dead], but with no life in it. For all night the spirit of
miserable Patroclus stood by me grieving and lamenting, and told me
all that I should do, and was wonderfully like his living self.'

So he spoke; and there arose in them all a longing for lamentation,
and rosy-fingered Dawn appeared as they were weeping round the
pathetic corpse...

And when the king of men, Agamemnon, heard this, at once he dis-
persed the men to their evenly proportioned ships; but the mourners
remained there and heaped up the wood. They made a pile a hundred
feet in length and breadth, and with grief in their heart laid the body on
the top of the pile. They skinned many fat sheep and shambling,

πολλὰ δὲ ἴφια μῆλα καὶ εἰλίποδας ἕλικας βοῦς
πρόσθε πυρῆς ἔδερόν τε καὶ ἄμφεπον· ἐκ δ' ἄρα πάντων
δημὸν ἑλὼν ἐκάλυψε νέκυν μεγάθυμος Ἀχιλλεύς
ἐς πόδας ἐκ κεφαλῆς, περὶ δὲ δρατὰ σώματα νήει.
ἐν δ' ἐτίθει μέλιτος καὶ ἀλείφατος ἀμφιφορῆας,
πρὸς λέχεα κλίνων· πίσυρας δ' ἐριαύχενας ἵππους
ἐσσυμένως ἐνέβαλλε πυρῆ μεγάλα στεναχίζων.
ἐννέα τῷ γε ἄνακτι τραπεζῆες κύνες ἦσαν,
καὶ μὲν τῶν ἐνέβαλλε πυρῆ δύο δειροτομήσας,
δώδεκα δὲ Τρώων μεγαθύμων υἱέας ἐσθλούς
χαλκῷ δηϊόων· κακὰ δὲ φρεσὶ μήδετο ἔργα·
ἐν δὲ πυρὸς μένος ἧκε σιδήρεον, ὄφρα νέμοιτο.
ᾤμωξέν τ' ἄρ' ἔπειτα, φίλον δ' ὀνόμηνεν ἑταῖρον·
‹χαῖρέ μοι, ὦ Πάτροκλε, καὶ εἰν Ἀΐδαο δόμοισι·
πάντα γὰρ ἤδη τοι τελέω τὰ πάροιθεν ὑπέστην.
δώδεκα μὲν Τρώων μεγαθύμων υἱέας ἐσθλούς
τοὺς ἅμα σοὶ πάντας πῦρ ἐσθίει· Ἕκτορα δ' οὔ τι
δώσω Πριαμίδην πυρὶ δαπτέμεν, ἀλλὰ κύνεσσιν.›
    Ὣς φάτ' ἀπειλήσας· τὸν δ' οὐ κύνες ἀμφεπένοντο,
ἀλλὰ κύνας μὲν ἄλαλκε Διὸς θυγάτηρ Ἀφροδίτη
ἤματα καὶ νύκτας, ῥοδόεντι δὲ χρῖεν ἐλαίῳ

crooked-horned oxen and prepared them before the pyre; great-hearted Achilles took the fat from all of them and covered the dead body of Patroclus from head to feet, and heaped round it the skinned carcasses. He also set down three two-handled jars of honey and oil, and leaned them against the bier; groaning deeply, he threw with great violence four high-necked horses upon the pyre. Nine dogs the king had fed at his table; two of them he killed and threw them on the pyre. He also killed with his bronze sword twelve noble sons of the brave Trojans, for his mind was full of malice; and then he set the iron strength of fire to the pyre to feed upon it. With a loud groan he called his dear comrade by name: 'I greet you, Patroclus, even in the Halls of Hades; I now fulfil all that I promised to you formerly: twelve brave sons of the noble Trojans, all these the fire devours together with you; but Hector, the son of Priam, I will not give to the flames to be devoured, but to the dogs.'

So he spoke, threatening; but dogs did not worry him [Hector]. For Aphrodite, the daughter of Zeus, drove them off by day and night, and anointed him with ambrosial oil of roses, so that he would not be

ἀμβροσίῳ, ἵνα μή μιν ἀποδρύφοι ἑλκυστάζων.
τῷ δ' ἐπὶ κυάνεον νέφος ἤγαγε Φοῖβος Ἀπόλλων
οὐρανόθεν πεδίονδε, κάλυψε δὲ χῶρον ἅπαντα
ὅσσον ἐπεῖχε νέκυς, μὴ πρὶν μένος ἠελίοιο
σκήλει' ἀμφὶ περὶ χρόα ἵνεσιν ἠδὲ μέλεσσιν.

Οὐδὲ πυρὴ Πατρόκλου ἐκαίετο τεθνηῶτος·
ἔνθ' αὖτ' ἄλλ' ἐνόησε ποδάρκης δῖος Ἀχιλλεύς·
στὰς ἀπάνευθε πυρῆς δοιοῖς ἠρᾶτ' ἀνέμοισι,
Βορέῃ καὶ Ζεφύρῳ, καὶ ὑπίσχετο ἱερὰ καλά·
πολλὰ δὲ καὶ σπένδων χρυσέῳ δέπαϊ λιτάνευεν
ἐλθέμεν, ὄφρα τάχιστα πυρὶ φλεγεθοίατο νεκροί,
ὕλη τε σεύαιτο καήμεναι. ὦκα δὲ Ἶρις
ἀράων ἀΐουσα μετάγγελος ἦλθ' ἀνέμοισιν.
οἱ μὲν ἄρα Ζεφύροιο δυσαέος ἀθρόοι ἔνδον
εἰλαπίνην δαίνυντο· θέουσα δὲ Ἶρις ἐπέστη
βηλῷ ἔπι λιθέῳ· τοὶ δ' ὡς ἴδον ὀφθαλμοῖσι,
πάντες ἀνήϊξαν, κάλεόν τέ μιν εἰς ἓ ἕκαστος·
ἡ δ' αὖθ' ἕζεσθαι μὲν ἀνήνατο, εἶπε δὲ μῦθον·
‹οὐχ ἕδος· εἶμι γὰρ αὖτις ἐπ' Ὠκεανοῖο ῥέεθρα,
Αἰθιόπων ἐς γαῖαν, ὅθι ῥέζουσ' ἑκατόμβας
ἀθανάτοις, ἵνα δὴ καὶ ἐγὼ μεταδαίσομαι ἱρῶν·

lacerated when dragged along [by Achilles]; Phoebus Apollo, too, pulled a dark cloud from the sky to the plain and overshadowed the whole space covered by the dead body, lest the power of the sun shrivel the flesh on his sinews and his limbs.

But the pyre of dead Patroclus did not burn. Then swift-footed Achilles had a further thought. Standing away from the pyre, he prayed to two winds, Boreas and Zephyrus, and promised them beautiful sacrifices; pouring out many libations from a golden cup, he begged them to come, so that the corpses might be burned as soon as possible (with fire), and the wood might blaze up quickly. And Iris, hearing his prayers, went swiftly as a messenger to the winds. They were at home with fierce-breathing Zephyrus, celebrating a feast, when Iris came running up and stood on the stone threshold. But when they saw her (with their eyes) they all rose up and invited her, each one of them, to sit by him. But she refused to sit down, and said: 'No seat [for me]; I must go back to the streams of the Ocean, to the lands of the Aethiopians, where they sacrifice hecatombs to the immortal gods, so that I too can have a share in their offerings. But Achilles is praying to

ἀλλ' Ἀχιλεὺς Βορέην ἠδὲ Ζέφυρον κελαδεινὸν
ἐλθεῖν ἀρᾶται, καὶ ὑπίσχεται ἱερὰ καλά,
ὄφρα πυρὴν ὄρσητε καήμεναι, ᾗ ἔνι κεῖται
Πάτροκλος, τὸν πάντες ἀναστενάχουσιν Ἀχαιοί.›
   Ἡ μὲν ἄρ' ὣς εἰποῦσ' ἀπεβήσετο, τοὶ δ' ὀρέοντο
ἠχῇ θεσπεσίη, νέφεα κλονέοντε πάροιθεν.
αἶψα δὲ πόντον ἵκανον ἀήμεναι, ὦρτο δὲ κῦμα
πνοιῇ ὕπο λιγυρῇ· Τροίην δ' ἐρίβωλον ἵκέσθην,
ἐν δὲ πυρῇ πεσέτην, μέγα δ' ἴαχε θεσπιδαὲς πῦρ.
παννύχιοι δ' ἄρα τοί γε πυρῆς ἄμυδις φλόγ' ἔβαλλον,
φυσῶντες λιγέως· ὁ δὲ πάννυχος ὠκὺς Ἀχιλλεὺς
χρυσέου ἐκ κρητῆρος, ἑλὼν δέπας ἀμφικύπελλον,
οἶνον ἀφυσσόμενος χαμάδις χέε, δεῦε δὲ γαῖαν,
ψυχὴν κικλήσκων Πατροκλῆος δειλοῖο.
ὡς δὲ πατὴρ οὗ παιδὸς ὀδύρεται ὀστέα καίων,
νυμφίου, ὅς τε θανὼν δειλοὺς ἀκάχησε τοκῆας,
ὣς Ἀχιλεὺς ἑτάροιο ὀδύρετο ὀστέα καίων,
ἑρπύζων παρὰ πυρκαϊήν, ἀδινὰ στεναχίζων.
   Ἦμος δ' ἑωσφόρος εἶσι φόως ἐρέων ἐπὶ γαῖαν,
ὅν τε μέτα κροκόπεπλος ὑπεὶρ ἅλα κίδναται ἠώς,
τῆμος πυρκαϊὴ ἐμαραίνετο, παύσατο δὲ φλόξ.

Boreas and to loud Zephyrus and promises beautiful sacrifices for them
to come and kindle the pile on which Patroclus lies, for whom all the
Achaeans are lamenting.'

She said this, and left; and they rose with a tumultuous noise, rolling
the clouds before them. Swiftly they came, blowing over the sea, and
the waves rose at their sharp blast; and they reached rich-soiled Troy
and fell upon the pyre, and the mighty fire roared loudly. All night,
together, blowing shrilly, they fanned the blaze of the pyre; and all
night swift Achilles, holding a two-handled cup, poured wine on the
ground from a golden bowl and soaked the earth as he called the spirit
of unhappy Patroclus. And as a father mourns as he burns the bones of
his son, a bridegroom who has saddened his luckless parents by his
death, so mourned Achilles as he burned the bones of his comrade,
pacing slowly round the blazing pyre, groaning continually.

But when the morning star came, heralding light to the earth – the
star that is followed by saffron-mantled dawn that spreads over the
sea – then the pyre shrivelled away and the flames died down; and the

οἱ δ' ἄνεμοι πάλιν αὖτις ἔβαν οἰκόνδε νέεσθαι
Θρηίκιον κατὰ πόντον· ὁ δ' ἔστενεν οἴδματι θύων.
Πηλεΐδης δ' ἀπὸ πυρκαϊῆς ἑτέρωσε λιασθεὶς
κλίνθη κεκμηώς, ἐπὶ δὲ γλυκὺς ὕπνος ὄρουσεν·
οἱ δ' ἀμφ' Ἀτρεΐωνα ἀολλέες ἠγερέθοντο·
τῶν μιν ἐπερχομένων ὅμαδος καὶ δοῦπος ἔγειρεν,
ἕζετο δ' ὀρθωθεὶς καί σφεας πρὸς μῦθον ἔειπεν·
‹Ἀτρεΐδη τε καὶ ἄλλοι ἀριστῆες Παναχαιῶν,
πρῶτον μὲν κατὰ πυρκαϊὴν σβέσατ' αἴθοπι οἴνῳ
πᾶσαν, ὁπόσσον ἐπέσχε πυρὸς μένος· αὐτὰρ ἔπειτα
ὀστέα Πατρόκλοιο Μενοιτιάδαο λέγωμεν
εὖ διαγιγνώσκοντες· ἀριφραδέα δὲ τέτυκται·
ἐν μέσσῃ γὰρ ἔκειτο πυρῇ, τοὶ δ' ἄλλοι ἄνευθεν
ἐσχατιῇ καίοντ' ἐπιμὶξ ἵπποι τε καὶ ἄνδρες.
καὶ τὰ μὲν ἐν χρυσέῃ φιάλῃ καὶ δίπλακι δημῷ
θείομεν, εἰς ὅ κεν αὐτὸς ἐγὼν Ἄϊδι κεύθωμαι.
τύμβον δ' οὐ μάλα πολλὸν ἐγὼ πονέεσθαι ἄνωγα,
ἀλλ' ἐπιεικέα τοῖον· ἔπειτα δὲ καὶ τὸν Ἀχαιοὶ
εὐρύν θ' ὑψηλόν τε τιθήμεναι, οἵ κεν ἐμεῖο
δεύτεροι ἐν νήεσσι πολυκλήϊσι λίπησθε.›
Ὣς ἔφαθ', οἱ δ' ἐπίθοντο ποδώκεϊ Πηλεΐωνι.
πρῶτον μὲν κατὰ πυρκαϊὴν σβέσαν αἴθοπι οἴνῳ,

winds went back again to their home over the Thracian sea; and it roared with a violent swell. Then the son of Peleus turned away from the funeral pyre and, wearied, lay down and sweet sleep leapt upon him. But the others crowded round the son of Atreus, the noise and the din they made as they approached woke him, and he sat upright and spoke to them: 'Sons of Atreus, and you other chiefs of the Achaeans, first put out the whole pyre – all that the might of the fire has gripped – with bright wine, and then let us collect the bones of Patroclus, the son of Menoetius, singling them out carefully – for they are easy to distinguish, as he lay in the centre of the pyre, while the others, horses and men, were burned together at the edge – and let us put them in a golden urn with a double layer of fat, till I myself be hidden in Hades. And I want a barrow built, not very large, but of a fitting size. Then, later, Achaeans, you must make it broad and high, those of you who are left at the many-oared ships after my death.'

So he spoke; and they obeyed the swift-footed son of Peleus. First they put out the pyre with bright wine, all that the flame had touched,

ὅσσον ἐπὶ φλὸξ ἦλθε, βαθεῖα δὲ κάππεσε τέφρη·
κλαίοντες δ' ἑτάροιο ἐνηέος ὀστέα λευκὰ
ἄλλεγον ἐς χρυσέην φιάλην καὶ δίπλακα δημόν,
ἐν κλισίῃσι δὲ θέντες ἑανῷ λιτὶ κάλυψαν·
τορνώσαντο δὲ σῆμα θεμείλιά τε προβάλοντο
ἀμφὶ πυρήν· εἶθαρ δὲ χυτὴν ἐπὶ γαῖαν ἔχευαν,
χεύαντες δὲ τὸ σῆμα πάλιν κίον. αὐτὰρ 'Αχιλλεὺς
νηῶν δ' ἔκφερ' ἄεθλα, λέβητάς τε τρίποδάς τε
αὐτοῦ λαὸν ἔρυκε καὶ ἵζανεν εὐρὺν ἀγῶνα,
ἵππους θ' ἡμιόνους τε βοῶν τ' ἴφθιμα κάρηνα,
ἠδὲ γυναῖκας ἐϋζώνους πολιόν τε σίδηρον.

(Iliad)

8. Priam and Achilles

"Ως ἄρα φωνήσας ἀπέβη πρὸς μακρὸν "Ολυμπον
'Ερμείας· Πρίαμος δ' ἐξ ἵππων ἄλτο χαμᾶζε,
'Ιδαῖον δὲ κατ' αὖθι λίπεν· ὁ δὲ μίμνεν ἐρύκων
ἵππους ἡμιόνους τε· γέρων δ' ἰθὺς κίεν οἴκου,
τῇ ρ' 'Αχιλεὺς ἵζεσκε Διἲ φίλος· ἐν δέ μιν αὐτὸν
εὖρ', ἕταροι δ' ἀπάνευθε καθήατο· τὼ δὲ δύ' οἴω,

and the deep ash fell in; and, weeping, they collected the white bones
of their dear comrade and put them in a golden urn with a double
layer of fat, and then set them in the tent, and covered them with soft
linen. And they marked out the circle of the barrow and set its founda-
tions round the pyre, and straightaway piled a heap of earth upon it;
when they had heaped up the tomb, they left. But Achilles kept the men
there, and made them sit down in a wide assembly for the funeral
games, and from the ships he brought out prizes, cauldrons and tripods
and horses and mules and strong (heads of) oxen, and women wearing
fine girdles, and grey iron.

So spoke Hermes, and he left for high Olympus; and Priam leapt from
his carriage to the ground, and left Idaeus there. He [Idaeus] stayed to
guard the horses and the mules, while the old man went straight to the
hut where Achilles, dear to Zeus, was sitting. He found him within,
and his companions were sitting apart from him; two only, the hero

ἥρως Αὐτομέδων τε καὶ Ἄλκιμος, ὄζος Ἄρηος,
ποίπνυον παρεόντε· νέον δ' ἀπέληγεν ἐδωδῆς
ἔσθων καὶ πίνων· ἔτι καὶ παρέκειτο τράπεζα.
τοὺς δ' ἔλαθ' εἰσελθὼν Πρίαμος μέγας, ἄγχι δ' ἄρα στὰς
χερσὶν Ἀχιλλῆος λάβε γούνατα καὶ κύσε χεῖρας
δεινὰς ἀνδροφόνους, αἵ οἱ πολέας κτάνον υἷας.
ὡς δ' ὅτ' ἂν ἄνδρ' ἄτη πυκινὴ λάβῃ, ὅς τ' ἐνὶ πάτρῃ
φῶτα κατακτείνας ἄλλων ἐξίκετο δῆμον,
ἀνδρὸς ἐς ἀφνειοῦ, θάμβος δ' ἔχει εἰσορόωντας,
ὣς Ἀχιλεὺς θάμβησεν ἰδὼν Πρίαμον θεοειδέα·
θάμβησαν δὲ καὶ ἄλλοι, ἐς ἀλλήλους δὲ ἴδοντο.
τὸν καὶ λισσόμενος Πρίαμος πρὸς μῦθον ἔειπε·
‹μνῆσαι πατρὸς σοῖο, θεοῖς ἐπιείκελ' Ἀχιλλεῦ,
τηλίκου ὥς περ ἐγών, ὀλοῷ ἐπὶ γήραος οὐδῷ·
καὶ μέν που κεῖνον περιναιέται ἀμφὶς ἐόντες
τείρουσ', οὐδέ τίς ἐστιν ἀρὴν καὶ λοιγὸν ἀμῦναι.
ἀλλ' ἤτοι κεῖνός γε σέθεν ζώοντος ἀκούων
χαίρει τ' ἐν θυμῷ, ἐπί τ' ἔλπεται ἤματα πάντα
ὄψεσθαι φίλον υἱὸν ἀπὸ Τροίηθεν ἰόντα·
αὐτὰρ ἐγὼ πανάποτμος, ἐπεὶ τέκον υἷας ἀρίστους
Τροίῃ ἐν εὐρείῃ, τῶν δ' οὔ τινά φημι λελεῖφθαι.

Automedon and Alcimus of the stock of Ares, were busy in attendance.
He had just finished eating and drinking, and the table still stood beside
him. But great Priam was not noticed, as he entered, and, standing near,
clasped Achilles' knees with his hands, and kissed the dreadful man-
slaughtering hands that had killed many of his sons. And, as when a
heavy curse comes on a man who has murdered someone in his own
country, and gone to a foreign land, to some wealthy person's house,
and those who see him are amazed, so Achilles was amazed when he
saw godlike Priam; and the others were amazed as well, and looked at
one another. And Priam said to him in supplication: 'Remember your
own father, godlike Achilles, who is the same age as I am [and stands]
upon the dreadful threshold of old age. And perhaps his neighbours all
round are oppressing him, and there is nobody to defend him from
havoc and destruction. But even so, when he hears that you are alive,
he rejoices in his heart, and every day hopes to see his dear son coming
back from Troy. But I am altogether wretched, for I gave life to the
bravest sons in wide Troy, not one of whom, I say, is left. Fifty I had,

πεντήκοντά μοι ἦσαν, ὅτ' ἤλυθον υἷες 'Αχαιῶν·
ἐννεακαίδεκα μέν μοι ἰῆς ἐκ νηδύος ἦσαν,
τοὺς δ' ἄλλους μοι ἔτικτον ἐνὶ μεγάροισι γυναῖκες.
τῶν μὲν πολλῶν θοῦρος ''Αρης ὑπὸ γούνατ' ἔλυσεν·
ὃς δέ μοι οἶος ἔην, εἴρυτο δὲ ἄστυ καὶ αὐτούς,
τὸν σὺ πρῴην κτείνας ἀμυνόμενον περὶ πάτρης,
'Έκτορα· τοῦ νῦν εἵνεχ' ἱκάνω νῆας 'Αχαιῶν
λυσόμενος παρὰ σεῖο, φέρω δ' ἀπερείσι' ἄποινα.
ἀλλ' αἰδεῖο θεούς, 'Αχιλεῦ, αὐτόν τ' ἐλέησον,
μνησάμενος σοῦ πατρός· ἐγὼ δ' ἐλεεινότερός περ,
ἔτλην δ' οἶ' οὔ πώ τις ἐπιχθόνιος βροτὸς ἄλλος,
ἀνδρὸς παιδοφόνοιο ποτὶ στόμα χεῖρ' ὀρέγεσθαι.⟩
   'Ὣς φάτο, τῷ δ' ἄρα πατρὸς ὑφ' ἵμερον ὦρσε γόοιο·
ἁψάμενος δ' ἄρα χειρὸς ἀπώσατο ἦκα γέροντα.
τὼ δὲ μνησαμένω, ὁ μὲν 'Έκτορος ἀνδροφόνοιο
κλαῖ' ἀδινὰ προπάροιθε ποδῶν 'Αχιλῆος ἐλυσθείς,
αὐτὰρ 'Αχιλλεὺς κλαῖεν ἑὸν πατέρ', ἄλλοτε δ' αὖτε
Πάτροκλον· τῶν δὲ στοναχὴ κατὰ δώματ' ὀρώρει.
αὐτὰρ ἐπεί ῥα γόοιο τετάρπετο δῖος 'Αχιλλεύς,
καί οἱ ἀπὸ πραπίδων ἦλθ' ἵμερος ἠδ' ἀπὸ γυίων,
αὐτίκ' ἀπὸ θρόνου ὦρτο, γέροντα δὲ χειρὸς ἀνίστη,

when the sons of the Achaeans arrived; nineteen were from one mother, and the others other women bore to me in my palace. Fierce Ares has unstrung the knees of most of them, but Hector, who was my favourite, and who defended us and the city, you have just killed fighting for his country; for his sake I come now to the ships of the Achaeans, and bring countless riches to ransom him from you. Fear the gods, Achilles, and have pity on me, remembering your own father; I am even more miserable, for I have brought myself to do what no other man on earth has done, to lift to my mouth the hand of the man who killed my sons.'

   So he spoke, and he stirred in him the wish to lament for his father; and he took the old man's hand, and gently pushed him away. And they both remembered, and the one, rolling before Achilles' feet, wept profusely for man-slaying Hector, and Achilles wept for his own father, and then again for Patroclus; and their lamentation went up throughout the house. But when noble Achilles had his fill of tears and the wish to weep had left his heart and his limbs, he immediately sprang from his seat; he raised up the old man with his hands, pitying his white head

οἰκτείρων πολιόν τε κάρη πολιόν τε γένειον,
καί μιν φωνήσας ἔπεα πτερόεντα προσηύδα·
‹ἆ δείλ', ἦ δὴ πολλὰ κάκ' ἄνσχεο σὸν κατὰ θυμόν.
πῶς ἔτλης ἐπὶ νῆας 'Αχαιῶν ἐλθέμεν οἶος,
ἀνδρὸς ἐς ὀφθαλμοὺς ὅς τοι πολέας τε καὶ ἐσθλοὺς
υἱέας ἐξενάριξα; σιδήρειόν νύ τοι ἦτορ.
ἀλλ' ἄγε δὴ κατ' ἄρ' ἕζευ ἐπὶ θρόνου, ἄλγεα δ' ἔμπης
ἐν θυμῷ κατακεῖσθαι ἐάσομεν ἀχνύμενοί περ·
οὐ γάρ τις πρῆξις πέλεται κρυεροῖο γόοιο·
ὡς γὰρ ἐπεκλώσαντο θεοὶ δειλοῖσι βροτοῖσι,
ζώειν ἀχνυμένοις· αὐτοὶ δέ τ' ἀκηδέες εἰσί.
δοιοὶ γάρ τε πίθοι κατακείαται ἐν Διὸς οὔδει
δώρων οἷα δίδωσι κακῶν, ἕτερος δὲ ἑάων·
ᾧ μέν κ' ἀμμείξας δώῃ Ζεὺς τερπικέραυνος,
ἄλλοτε μέν τε κακῷ ὅ γε κύρεται, ἄλλοτε δ' ἐσθλῷ·
ᾧ δέ κε τῶν λυγρῶν δώῃ, λωβητὸν ἔθηκε,
καί ἑ κακὴ βούβρωστις ἐπὶ χθόνα δῖαν ἐλαύνει,
φοιτᾷ δ' οὔτε θεοῖσι τετιμένος οὔτε βροτοῖσιν.
ὡς μὲν καὶ Πηλῆϊ θεοὶ δόσαν ἀγλαὰ δῶρα
ἐκ γενετῆς· πάντας γὰρ ἐπ' ἀνθρώπους ἐκέκαστο
ὄλβῳ τε πλούτῳ τε, ἄνασσε δὲ Μυρμιδόνεσσι,
καί οἱ θνητῷ ἐόντι θεὰν ποίησαν ἄκοιτιν.

and his white beard, and spoke winged words to him and said: 'Alas, wretched man, you have certainly suffered much evil in your heart; how did you dare to come alone to the ships of the Achaeans to meet the eyes of the man who killed many of your brave sons? Your heart is of iron. But come now, sit on a seat; and let us leave our sorrows to rest in our heart, for all our pain; for there is no use in cold lamentation. For the gods have so woven the life of unhappy mortals that they should live in sorrow, while they themselves are free from care. Two jars of gifts lie at the threshold of Zeus' halls to be distributed, one of evil, and the other of good gifts. Those who receive from thunder-loving Zeus a mixture of the two sometimes have evil and sometimes good luck, but the man to whom he gives evil he makes an outcast, and dreadful hunger drives him across the sacred earth, as he wanders honoured by neither gods nor men. So the gods gave shining gifts to Peleus from his birth; for he surpassed all other men both in riches and in happiness, and he ruled over the Myrmidons, and, though a mortal, they gave him a goddess for a wife. But some god gave him misfortune too, no child

ἀλλ' ἐπὶ καὶ τῷ θῆκε θεὸς κακόν, ὅττι οἱ οὔ τι
παίδων ἐν μεγάροισι γονὴ γένετο κρειόντων,
ἀλλ' ἕνα παῖδα τέκεν παναώριον· οὐδέ νυ τόν γε
γηράσκοντα κομίζω, ἐπεὶ μάλα τηλόθι πάτρης
ἧμαι ἐνὶ Τροίῃ, σέ τε κήδων ἠδὲ σὰ τέκνα.
καὶ σέ, γέρον, τὸ πρὶν μὲν ἀκούομεν ὄλβιον εἶναι·
ὅσσον Λέσβος ἄνω, Μάκαρος ἕδος, ἐντὸς ἐέργει
καὶ Φρυγίη καθύπερθε καὶ Ἑλλήσποντος ἀπείρων,
τῶν σε, γέρον, πλούτῳ τε καὶ υἱάσι φασὶ κεκάσθαι.
αὐτὰρ ἐπεί τοι πῆμα τόδ' ἤγαγον Οὐρανίωνες,
αἰεί τοι περὶ ἄστυ μάχαι τ' ἀνδροκτασίαι τε.
ἄνσχεο, μηδ' ἀλίαστον ὀδύρεο σὸν κατὰ θυμόν·
οὐ γάρ τι πρήξεις ἀκαχήμενος υἷος ἑῆος,
οὐδέ μιν ἀνστήσεις, πρὶν καὶ κακὸν ἄλλο πάθῃσθα.›
    Τὸν δ' ἠμείβετ' ἔπειτα γέρων Πρίαμος θεοειδής·
‹μή πώ μ' ἐς θρόνον ἷζε, διοτρεφές, ὄφρα κεν Ἕκτωρ
κεῖται ἐνὶ κλισίῃσιν ἀκηδής, ἀλλὰ τάχιστα
λῦσον, ἵν' ὀφθαλμοῖσιν ἴδω· σὺ δὲ δέξαι ἄποινα
πολλά, τά τοι φέρομεν· σὺ δὲ τῶνδ' ἀπόναιο, καὶ ἔλθοις
σὴν ἐς πατρίδα γαῖαν, ἐπεί με πρῶτον ἔασας
αὐτόν τε ζώειν καὶ ὁρᾶν φάος ἠελίοιο.›

in his palaces, no offspring of the ruling kings, but only one son,
doomed to an early death; and I do not look after him now he is getting
old, for I am in Troy very far away from my homeland, bringing sor-
row to you and to your sons. And you too, old man, we have heard,
were happy in the past – for in all the lands that Lesbos in the north,
where Macar reigned, and upper Phrygia and the boundless Hellespont
contain they say that you, old man, were the most famous for your
wealth and for your sons. But since the gods of the sky have brought
this calamity on you, battles and the killing [of men] are always round
your city; have courage and do not grieve for ever in your heart; you
will achieve nothing by weeping for your son, you will not bring him
back to life, before you suffer some other misfortune.'

    The old man, godlike Priam, then answered him: 'Do not offer me
a seat, god-reared Achilles, as long as Hector lies unburied in your huts;
give him back as soon as possible for me to see him with my eyes, and
accept the great ransoms which we bring you. May you enjoy them
and reach your homeland safely, since you have first let me live and see
the light of the sun.'

Τὸν δ' ἄρ' ὑπόδρα ἰδὼν προσέφη πόδας ὠκὺς Ἀχιλλεύς·
⟨μηκέτι νῦν μ' ἐρέθιζε, γέρον· νοέω δὲ καὶ αὐτὸς
Ἕκτορά τοι λῦσαι, Διόθεν δέ μοι ἄγγελος ἦλθε
μήτηρ, ἥ μ' ἔτεκεν, θυγάτηρ ἁλίοιο γέροντος.
καὶ δέ σε γιγνώσκω, Πρίαμε, φρεσίν, οὐδέ με λήθεις,
ὅττι θεῶν τίς σ' ἦγε θοὰς ἐπὶ νῆας Ἀχαιῶν.
οὐ γάρ κε τλαίη βροτὸς ἐλθέμεν, οὐδὲ μάλ' ἡβῶν,
ἐς στρατόν· οὐδὲ γὰρ ἂν φυλάκους λάθοι, οὐδέ κ' ὀχῆα
ῥεῖα μετοχλίσσειε θυράων ἡμετεράων.
τῶ νῦν μή μοι μᾶλλον ἐν ἄλγεσι θυμὸν ὀρίνῃς,
μή σε, γέρον, οὐδ' αὐτὸν ἐνὶ κλισίῃσιν ἐάσω
καὶ ἱκέτην περ ἐόντα, Διὸς δ' ἀλίτωμαι ἐφετμάς.⟩
Ὣς ἔφατ', ἔδεισεν δ' ὁ γέρων καὶ ἐπείθετο μύθῳ.
Πηλεΐδης δ' οἴκοιο λέων ὣς ἆλτο θύραζε,
οὐκ οἶος, ἅμα τῷ γε δύω θεράποντες ἕποντο,
ἥρως Αὐτομέδων ἠδ' Ἄλκιμος, οὕς ῥα μάλιστα
τῖ' Ἀχιλεὺς ἑτάρων μετὰ Πάτροκλόν γε θανόντα,
οἳ τόθ' ὑπὸ ζυγόφιν λύον ἵππους ἡμιόνους τε,
ἐς δ' ἄγαγον κήρυκα καλήτορα τοῖο γέροντος,
κὰδ δ' ἐπὶ δίφρου εἷσαν· ἐϋξέστου δ' ἀπ' ἀπήνης
ᾕρεον Ἑκτορέης κεφαλῆς ἀπερείσι' ἄποινα.

Then swift-footed Achilles sternly looked at him and said: 'Do not provoke me any more, old man; I myself am thinking of giving Hector back to you, for the mother who gave me birth, the daughter of the old man of the sea, came with a message from Zeus [to me]. And I realize in my mind that some god has led you too, Priam, to the swift ships of the Achaeans; you do not deceive me; for a mortal man would not have dared to come into the camp, not even if he were in the flower of his youth; he could not have escaped the guards, nor easily have pushed back the bolts of our doors. Therefore in my sorrow do not try my heart any more, lest I do not spare even you, old man, although you are a suppliant in my huts, and so disobey the commands of Zeus.'

So he spoke; and the old man was afraid and obeyed. But the son of Peleus leaped like a lion from the door of the hut; not alone, for two attendants accompanied him, the hero Automedon, and Alcimus, whom Achilles honoured most of his companions after the death of Patroclus. These then unharnessed the horses and mules from the yoke, and led in the old man's clear-voiced herald and showed him to a seat. They also took down from the well-polished carriage the great ransom for Hector's head. And they left two cloaks and a well-woven tunic

κὰδ δ' ἔλιπον δύο φάρε' ἐϋννητόν τε χιτῶνα,
ὄφρα νέκυν πυκάσας δοίη οἰκόνδε φέρεσθαι.
δμωὰς δ' ἐκκαλέσας λοῦσαι κέλετ' ἀμφί τ' ἀλεῖψαι,
νόσφιν ἀειράσας, ὡς μὴ Πρίαμος ἴδοι υἱόν,
μὴ ὁ μὲν ἀχνυμένῃ κραδίῃ χόλον οὐκ ἐρύσαιτο
παῖδα ἰδών, Ἀχιλῆϊ δ' ὀρινθείη φίλον ἦτορ,
καί ἑ κατακτείνειε, Διὸς δ' ἀλίτηται ἐφετμάς.
τὸν δ' ἐπεὶ οὖν δμωαὶ λοῦσαν καὶ χρῖσαν ἐλαίῳ,
ἀμφὶ δέ μιν φᾶρος καλὸν βάλον ἠδὲ χιτῶνα,
αὐτὸς τόν γ' Ἀχιλεὺς λεχέων ἐπέθηκεν ἀείρας,
σὺν δ' ἕταροι ἤειραν ἐϋξέστην ἐπ' ἀπήνην.
ᾤμωξέν τ' ἄρ' ἔπειτα, φίλον δ' ὀνόμηνεν ἑταῖρον·
‹μή μοι, Πάτροκλε, σκυδμαινέμεν, αἴ κε πύθηαι
εἰν Ἀϊδός περ ἐὼν ὅτι Ἕκτορα δῖον ἔλυσα
πατρὶ φίλῳ, ἐπεὶ οὔ μοι ἀεικέα δῶκεν ἄποινα.
σοὶ δ' αὖ ἐγὼ καὶ τῶνδ' ἀποδάσσομαι ὅσσ' ἐπέοικεν.›
    Ἦ ῥα, καὶ ἐς κλισίην πάλιν ἤϊε δῖος Ἀχιλλεύς,
ἕζετο δ' ἐν κλισμῷ πολυδαιδάλῳ, ἔνθεν ἀνέστη,
τοίχου τοῦ ἑτέρου, ποτὶ δὲ Πρίαμον φάτο μῦθον·
‹υἱὸς μὲν δή τοι λέλυται, γέρον, ὡς ἐκέλευες,
κεῖται δ' ἐν λεχέεσσ'· ἅμα δ' ἠοῖ φαινομένηφιν

[for Achilles] to cover the body when he gave it [to Priam] to carry home. Then he called his women-servants and ordered them to wash and anoint the body all over, moving it away, so that Priam would not see his son, in case, if he saw (his son), he could not hold back the anger in his grieving heart, and so arouse the spirit of Achilles to kill him and so violate the command of Zeus. But when the servants had washed and anointed the body of Hector with oil, they threw over it a beautiful cloak and a tunic; Achilles himself raised it up and placed it on a bier and together with his companions lifted it on to the well-polished carriage. But then he lamented and called his dear comrade by name: 'Patroclus, do not be angry with me, if you hear, though in Hades, that I have ransomed noble Hector to his dear father, since he gave ransoms that were not unworthy. And I will give you a proper share, even of these.'

Noble Achilles spoke, and returned to the tent and sat down on the richly decorated couch which he had left on the opposite side of the room, and addressed Priam: 'Your son, old man, is given back to you as you asked, and lies on a bier; and when dawn appears you shall see

ὄψεαι αὐτὸς ἄγων· νῦν δὲ μνησώμεθα δόρπου.
καὶ γάρ τ' ἠΰκομος Νιόβη ἐμνήσατο σίτου,
τῇ περ δώδεκα παῖδες ἐνὶ μεγάροισιν ὄλοντο,
ἓξ μὲν θυγατέρες, ἓξ δ' υἱέες ἡβώοντες,
τοὺς μὲν Ἀπόλλων πέφνεν ἀπ' ἀργυρέοιο βιοῖο
χωόμενος Νιόβῃ, τὰς δ' Ἄρτεμις ἰοχέαιρα,
οὕνεκ' ἄρα Λητοῖ ἰσάσκετο καλλιπαρήῳ·
φῆ δοιὼ τεκέειν, ἡ δ' αὐτὴ γείνατο πολλούς·
τὼ δ' ἄρα καὶ δοιώ περ ἐόντ' ἀπὸ πάντας ὄλεσσαν.
οἱ μὲν ἄρ' ἐννῆμαρ κέατ' ἐν φόνῳ, οὐδέ τις ἦεν
κατθάψαι, λαοὺς δὲ λίθους ποίησε Κρονίων·
τοὺς δ' ἄρα τῇ δεκάτῃ θάψαν θεοὶ Οὐρανίωνες.
ἡ δ' ἄρα σίτου μνήσατ', ἐπεὶ κάμε δάκρυ χέουσα.
νῦν δέ που ἐν πέτρῃσιν, ἐν οὔρεσιν οἰοπόλοισιν,
ἐν Σιπύλῳ, ὅθι φασὶ θεάων ἔμμεναι εὐνὰς
νυμφάων, αἵ τ' ἀμφ' Ἀχελώϊον ἐρρώσαντο,
ἔνθα λίθος περ ἐοῦσα θεῶν ἐκ κήδεα πέσσει.
ἀλλ' ἄγε δὴ καὶ νῶϊ μεδώμεθα, δῖε γεραιέ,
σίτου· ἔπειτά κεν αὖτε φίλον παῖδα κλαίοισθα,
Ἴλιον εἰσαγαγών· πολυδάκρυτος δέ τοι ἔσται.›

him yourself and carry him away. But now let us turn our thoughts to food; even Niobe of the beautiful hair remembered to eat, whose twelve children died in her palace, six daughters and six youthful sons; the sons Apollo killed with his silver bow, because he was angry with Niobe; and the daughters arrow-loving Artemis killed, because Niobe had compared herself with lovely-faced Leto. She had said that she [Leto] had given birth to only two, whereas she had borne many; they [Apollo and Artemis], though only two, destroyed all [her children]. Nine days they lay in blood, and there was nobody to bury them, for the son of Cronos had turned the people to stones; but on the tenth day the gods of the sky buried them. And Niobe turned her thoughts to food, when she was exhausted with weeping. Now somewhere in the rocks of the lonely mountains in Sipylus, where they say are the haunts of the godly Nymphs, who dance round Acheloüs, there, although a stone, she broods over the sorrows sent from the gods. But come now, noble old man, let us too think of eating, and later you can lament your dear son, when you have taken him to Troy; and many tears will you shed over him.'

῏Η, καὶ ἀναΐξας ὄϊν ἄργυφον ὠκὺς Ἀχιλλεύς
σφάξ᾽· ἕταροι δὲ δερόν τε καὶ ἄμφεπον εὖ κατὰ κόσμον,
μίστυλλόν τ᾽ ἄρ᾽ ἐπισταμένως πεῖράν τ᾽ ὀβελοῖσιν,
ὤπτησάν τε περιφραδέως, ἐρύσαντό τε πάντα.
Αὐτομέδων δ᾽ ἄρα σῖτον ἑλὼν ἐπένειμε τραπέζῃ
καλοῖς ἐν κανέοισιν· ἀτὰρ κρέα νεῖμεν Ἀχιλλεύς.
οἱ δ᾽ ἐπ᾽ ὀνείαθ᾽ ἑτοῖμα προκείμενα χεῖρας ἴαλλον.
αὐτὰρ ἐπεὶ πόσιος καὶ ἐδητύος ἐξ ἔρον ἔντο,
ἤτοι Δαρδανίδης Πρίαμος θαύμαζ᾽ Ἀχιλῆα,
ὅσσος ἔην οἷός τε· θεοῖσι γὰρ ἄντα ἐῴκει·
αὐτὰρ ὁ Δαρδανίδην Πρίαμον θαύμαζεν Ἀχιλλεύς,
εἰσορόων ὄψίν τ᾽ ἀγαθὴν καὶ μῦθον ἀκούων.
αὐτὰρ ἐπεὶ τάρπησαν ἐς ἀλλήλους ὁρόωντες,
τὸν πρότερος προσέειπε γέρων Πρίαμος θεοειδής·
⟨λέξον νῦν με τάχιστα, διοτρεφές, ὄφρα καὶ ἤδη
ὕπνῳ ὕπο γλυκερῷ ταρπώμεθα κοιμηθέντες·
οὐ γάρ πω μύσαν ὄσσε ὑπὸ βλεφάροισιν ἐμοῖσιν
ἐξ οὗ σῆς ὑπὸ χερσὶν ἐμὸς πάϊς ὤλεσε θυμόν,
ἀλλ᾽ αἰεὶ στενάχω καὶ κήδεα μυρία πέσσω,
αὐλῆς ἐν χόρτοισι κυλινδόμενος κατὰ κόπρον.
νῦν δὴ καὶ σίτου πασάμην καὶ αἴθοπα οἶνον
λαυκανίης καθέηκα· πάρος γε μὲν οὔ τι πεπάσμην.⟩

Swift Achilles spoke, and, leaping up, killed a silver-white sheep, and his companions flayed it and dressed it properly; then they cut it skilfully into small pieces, pierced them with spits, roasted them carefully, and pulled them all off the fire. And Automedon took bread and distributed it round the table in beautiful baskets, as Achilles gave out the meat and they all stretched out their hands to the food, which was lying ready before them. But when they had satisfied the desire for food and drink, Dardanian Priam, as he watched Achilles, marvelled at how big and splendid he was, for he looked exactly like a god; and Achilles admired Dardanian Priam, looking at his noble face and hearing his words. When they were satisfied with looking at each other, the old man, godlike Priam, addressed him first: 'Let me now lie down as soon as possible, offspring of Zeus, that, reclining, I may rest and enjoy sweet sleep; for my eyes have not closed under my eyelids since my son lost his life at your hands; but I have been weeping all the time and brooding over my many griefs, rolling amid the dung of the livestock's feeding-place in my courtyard. Now at last I have tasted food and poured bright wine down my throat, for before I had eaten nothing.'

Ἦ ῥ', Ἀχιλεὺς δ' ἑτάροισιν ἰδὲ δμωῇσι κέλευσε
δέμνι' ὑπ' αἰθούσῃ θέμεναι καὶ ῥήγεα καλὰ
πορφύρε' ἐμβαλέειν, στορέσαι τ' ἐφύπερθε τάπητας,
χλαίνας τ' ἐνθέμεναι οὔλας καθύπερθεν ἕσασθαι.
αἱ δ' ἴσαν ἐκ μεγάροιο δάος μετὰ χερσὶν ἔχουσαι,
αἶψα δ' ἄρα στόρεσαν δοιὼ λέχε' ἐγκονέουσαι.
τὸν δ' ἐπικερτομέων προσέφη πόδας ὠκὺς Ἀχιλλεύς·
‹ἐκτὸς μὲν δὴ λέξο, γέρον φίλε, μή τις Ἀχαιῶν
ἐνθάδ' ἐπέλθῃσιν βουληφόρος, οἵ τέ μοι αἰεὶ
βουλὰς βουλεύουσι παρήμενοι, ἣ θέμις ἐστί·
τῶν εἴ τίς σε ἴδοιτο θοὴν διὰ νύκτα μέλαιναν,
αὐτίκ' ἂν ἐξείποι Ἀγαμέμνονι ποιμένι λαῶν,
καί κεν ἀνάβλησις λύσιος νεκροῖο γένηται.
ἀλλ' ἄγε μοι τόδε εἰπὲ καὶ ἀτρεκέως κατάλεξον,
ποσσῆμαρ μέμονας κτερεϊζέμεν Ἕκτορα δῖον,
ὄφρα τέως αὐτός τε μένω καὶ λαὸν ἐρύκω.›
    Τὸν δ' ἠμείβετ' ἔπειτα γέρων Πρίαμος θεοειδής·
‹εἰ μὲν δή μ' ἐθέλεις τελέσαι τάφον Ἕκτορι δίῳ,
ὧδέ κέ μοι ῥέζων, Ἀχιλεῦ, κεχαρισμένα θείης.
οἶσθα γὰρ ὡς κατὰ ἄστυ ἐέλμεθα, τηλόθι δ' ὕλη
ἀξέμεν ἐξ ὄρεος, μάλα δὲ Τρῶες δεδίασιν.

He spoke; and Achilles ordered his companions and his women-
servants to put couches in the porch and to lay beautiful purple rugs
on them, spread blankets over them, and to lay thick cloaks on top for
them [Priam and the herald] to cover themselves with. And they went
out of the hut, holding torches in their hands and quickly spread two
couches. And swift-footed Achilles, addressing him, said sharply:
'Lie outside, my old friend, lest some Counsellor of the Achaeans
comes here, one of those who are always sitting with me discussing
things as they should. If any of these sees you in the short dark night,
he would tell Agamemnon, the shepherd of men, at once, and there
might be a delay in giving back the body. But come, tell me this, and
tell me exactly: how many days do you want for the funeral rites of
noble Hector, so that I may hold myself back for so long and restrain
the army?'
    And then the old man, godlike Priam, answered him: 'If you are
really willing to let me give a funeral to noble Hector, you will win my
gratitude, Achilles, for it. For you know how we are hemmed in the
city, and it is a long way for us to carry wood from the mountain; and
the Trojans are greatly afraid [to do so]. For nine days we would lament

ἐννῆμαρ μέν κ' αὐτὸν ἐνὶ μεγάροις γοάοιμεν,
τῇ δεκάτῃ δέ κε θάπτοιμεν δαινῦτό τε λαός,
ἐνδεκάτῃ δέ κε τύμβον ἐπ' αὐτῷ ποιήσαιμεν,
τῇ δὲ δυωδεκάτῃ πολεμίξομεν, εἴ περ ἀνάγκη.›
    Τὸν δ' αὖτε προσέειπε ποδάρκης δῖος Ἀχιλλεύς·
‹ἔσται τοι καὶ ταῦτα, γέρον Πρίαμ', ὡς σὺ κελεύεις·
σχήσω γὰρ πόλεμον τόσσον χρόνον ὅσσον ἄνωγας.›
    Ὣς ἄρα φωνήσας ἐπὶ καρπῷ χεῖρα γέροντος
ἕλλαβε δεξιτερήν, μή πως δείσει' ἐνὶ θυμῷ.
οἱ μὲν ἄρ' ἐν προδόμῳ δόμου αὐτόθι κοιμήσαντο,
κῆρυξ καὶ Πρίαμος, πυκινὰ φρεσὶ μήδε' ἔχοντες,
αὐτὰρ Ἀχιλλεὺς εὗδε μυχῷ κλισίης ἐϋπήκτου·
τῷ δὲ Βρισηῒς παρελέξατο καλλιπάρηος.

(Iliad)

9. Invocation to the Muse

Ἄνδρα μοι ἔννεπε, Μοῦσα, πολύτροπον, ὃς μάλα πολλὰ
πλάγχθη, ἐπεὶ Τροίης ἱερὸν πτολίεθρον ἔπερσε·
πολλῶν δ' ἀνθρώπων ἴδεν ἄστεα καὶ νόον ἔγνω,
πολλὰ δ' ὅ γ' ἐν πόντῳ πάθεν ἄλγεα ὃν κατὰ θυμόν,

him in our palace, and on the tenth we would bury him, and the people would hold the funeral feast; and on the eleventh we would make a tomb for him, and on the twelfth shall fight, if we must.'

And swift-footed Achilles spoke to him again: 'These things too, old Priam, will be done as you wish, for I shall hold back the fight for the time you tell me.'

Saying this, he clasped the old man's right hand at the wrist, lest he should feel fear in his heart. And the herald and Priam slept there in the porch of the hut with many thoughts in their minds; but Achilles slept in a corner of the well-built tent; and Briseis of the beautiful cheeks lay beside him.

TELL me, Muse, of the resourceful man who wandered very far after he had sacked the holy city of Troy. He saw the cities of many men, and learned their thoughts. He suffered many hardships in his heart as

ἀρνύμενος ἥν τε ψυχὴν καὶ νόστον ἑταίρων.
ἀλλ᾽ οὐδ᾽ ὧς ἑτάρους ἐρρύσατο, ἱέμενός περ·
αὐτῶν γὰρ σφετέρησιν ἀτασθαλίησιν ὄλοντο,
νήπιοι, οἳ κατὰ βοῦς Ὑπερίονος Ἠελίοιο
ἤσθιον· αὐτὰρ ὁ τοῖσιν ἀφείλετο νόστιμον ἦμαρ.
τῶν ἀμόθεν γε, θεά, θύγατερ Διός, εἰπὲ καὶ ἡμῖν.

    Ἔνθ᾽ ἄλλοι μὲν πάντες, ὅσοι φύγον αἰπὺν ὄλεθρον,
οἴκοι ἔσαν, πόλεμόν τε πεφευγότες ἠδὲ θάλασσαν·
τὸν δ᾽ οἶον, νόστου κεχρημένον ἠδὲ γυναικός,
νύμφη πότνι᾽ ἔρυκε Καλυψώ, δῖα θεάων,
ἐν σπέσσι γλαφυροῖσι, λιλαιομένη πόσιν εἶναι.
ἀλλ᾽ ὅτε δὴ ἔτος ἦλθε περιπλομένων ἐνιαυτῶν,
τῷ οἱ ἐπεκλώσαντο θεοὶ οἶκόνδε νέεσθαι
εἰς Ἰθάκην, οὐδ᾽ ἔνθα πεφυγμένος ἦεν ἀέθλων,
καὶ μετὰ οἷσι φίλοισι. θεοὶ δ᾽ ἐλέαιρον ἅπαντες
νόσφι Ποσειδάωνος· ὁ δ᾽ ἀσπερχὲς μενέαινεν
ἀντιθέῳ Ὀδυσῆι πάρος ἣν γαῖαν ἱκέσθαι.

(Odyssey)

on the sea, he struggled to save his life and bring his comrades home.
But even so, in spite of his efforts, he failed to save his comrades. It was
their own folly that destroyed them; for the fools devoured the oxen
of Hyperion the Sun, and so the god robbed them of the day of their
return home. Goddess, daughter of Zeus, tell us too of these things,
starting at the point you wish.

At this time all the other survivors of utter destruction had reached
their homes, having escaped the war and the sea. Him alone, longing
for his return and for his wife, Calypso the Nymph, the beautiful
goddess, detained in her hollow cave; for she longed for him to be her
husband. Even when, as the years rolled on, the time came which the
gods had allotted for his homecoming to Ithaca he was not free from
troubles, even among his friends. Yet all the gods were sorry for him,
except Poseidon; he raged continually against godlike Odysseus until
the day he reached his own land.

10. Calypso's Island

Σεύατ' ἔπειτ' ἐπὶ κῦμα λάρῳ ὄρνιθι ἐοικώς,
ὅς τε κατὰ δεινοὺς κόλπους ἁλὸς ἀτρυγέτοιο
ἰχθῦς ἀγρώσσων πυκινὰ πτερὰ δεύεται ἅλμῃ·
τῷ ἴκελος πολέεσσιν ὀχήσατο κύμασιν Ἑρμῆς.
ἀλλ' ὅτε δὴ τὴν νῆσον ἀφίκετο τηλόθ' ἐοῦσαν,
ἔνθ' ἐκ πόντου βὰς ἰοειδέος ἠπειρόνδε
ἤιεν, ὄφρα μέγα σπέος ἵκετο, τῷ ἔνι νύμφη
ναῖεν ἐϋπλόκαμος· τὴν δ' ἔνδοθι τέτμεν ἐοῦσαν.
πῦρ μὲν ἐπ' ἐσχαρόφιν μέγα καίετο, τηλόθι δ' ὀδμὴ
κέδρου τ' εὐκεάτοιο θύου τ' ἀνὰ νῆσον ὀδώδει
δαιομένων· ἡ δ' ἔνδον ἀοιδιάουσ' ὀπὶ καλῇ
ἱστὸν ἐποιχομένη χρυσείῃ κερκίδ' ὕφαινεν.
ὕλη δὲ σπέος ἀμφὶ πεφύκει τηλεθόωσα,
κλήθρη τ' αἴγειρός τε καὶ εὐώδης κυπάρισσος.
ἔνθα δέ τ' ὄρνιθες τανυσίπτεροι εὐνάζοντο,
σκῶπές τ' ἴρηκές τε τανύγλωσσοί τε κορῶναι
εἰνάλιαι, τῇσίν τε θαλάσσια ἔργα μέμηλεν.
ἡ δ' αὐτοῦ τετάνυστο περὶ σπείους γλαφυροῖο
ἡμερὶς ἡβώωσα, τεθήλει δὲ σταφυλῇσι·

HE then swooped down on the waves like a seagull drenching its thickly feathered wings with spray as it hunts the fish down the fearful gulfs of the waste sea. So Hermes rode the many waves; but when he reached the remote island [of Ogygia] he stepped on to the land from the blue sea and walked along till he reached the great cavern where [Calypso] the Nymph with the beautiful locks was living. He found her at home; a big fire was blazing on the hearth, and the scent from the burning, easily split cedar and juniper was wafted across the island. Inside she was singing in a beautiful voice as she wove at the loom and moved her golden shuttle. About the cave grew a thick wood: alders, aspens and fragrant cypresses. In it roosted wide-winged birds, horned owls and falcons and garrulous choughs, birds of the coast whose business takes them down to the sea. Round the hollow cavern itself a garden vine bloomed vigorously, heavy with bunches of grapes; from

κρῆναι δ' ἑξείης πίσυρες ῥέον ὕδατι λευκῷ,
πλησίαι ἀλλήλων τετραμμέναι ἄλλυδις ἄλλη.
ἀμφὶ δὲ λειμῶνες μαλακοὶ ἴου ἠδὲ σελίνου
θήλεον· ἔνθα κ' ἔπειτα καὶ ἀθάνατός περ ἐπελθὼν
θηήσαιτο ἰδὼν καὶ τερφθείη φρεσὶν ᾗσιν.
ἔνθα στὰς θηεῖτο διάκτορος ἀργειφόντης.
αὐτὰρ ἐπεὶ δὴ πάντα ἑῷ θηήσατο θυμῷ,
αὐτίκ' ἄρ' εἰς εὐρὺ σπέος ἤλυθεν· οὐδέ μιν ἄντην
ἠγνοίησεν ἰδοῦσα Καλυψώ, δῖα θεάων,
οὐ γάρ τ' ἀγνῶτες θεοὶ ἀλλήλοισι πέλονται
ἀθάνατοι, οὐδ' εἴ τις ἀπόπροθι δώματα ναίει.
οὐδ' ἄρ' Ὀδυσσῆα μεγαλήτορα ἔνδον ἔτετμεν,
ἀλλ' ὅ γ' ἐπ' ἀκτῆς κλαῖε καθήμενος, ἔνθα πάρος περ,
δάκρυσι καὶ στοναχῇσι καὶ ἄλγεσι θυμὸν ἐρέχθων.

(*Odyssey*)

four near-by springs clear water poured out; [they were] close to one another, but faced in different directions, and in lush meadows on either side the iris and the parsley flourished. It was a spot which even an immortal god, if he came there, would admire when he saw it, and would be delighted in his heart. There the Messenger, the killer of Argos, stood still, and looked on in admiration. When he had enjoyed everything to his heart's content he moved swiftly into the great cavern; Calypso, the honoured goddess, knew him when she looked at him, for none of the immortal gods is a stranger to his fellows even though his home may be remote from theirs. But he [Hermes] did not find great-hearted Odysseus in the cave; for, as in the past, he sat weeping on the shore, tormenting his heart with tears, sighs and suffering.

11. Wrecked at Sea

Ἔνθα δύω νύκτας δύο τ᾽ ἤματα κύματι πηγῷ
πλάζετο, πολλὰ δέ οἱ κραδίη προτιόσσετ᾽ ὄλεθρον.
ἀλλ᾽ ὅτε δὴ τρίτον ἦμαρ ἐϋπλόκαμος τέλεσ᾽ Ἠώς,
καὶ τότ᾽ ἔπειτ᾽ ἄνεμος μὲν ἐπαύσατο ἠδὲ γαλήνη
ἔπλετο νηνεμίη, ὁ δ᾽ ἄρα σχεδὸν εἴσιδε γαῖαν
ὀξὺ μάλα προϊδών, μεγάλου ὑπὸ κύματος ἀρθείς.
ὡς δ᾽ ὅτ᾽ ἂν ἀσπάσιος βίοτος παίδεσσι φανήῃ
πατρός, ὃς ἐν νούσῳ κεῖται κρατέρ᾽ ἄλγεα πάσχων,
δηρὸν τηκόμενος, στυγερὸς δέ οἱ ἔχραε δαίμων,
ἀσπάσιον δ᾽ ἄρα τόν γε θεοὶ κακότητος ἔλυσαν,
ὣς Ὀδυσῆ᾽ ἀσπαστὸν ἐείσατο γαῖα καὶ ὕλη,
νῆχε δ᾽ ἐπειγόμενος ποσὶν ἠπείρου ἐπιβῆναι.
ἀλλ᾽ ὅτε τόσσον ἀπῆν ὅσσον τε γέγωνε βοήσας,
καὶ δὴ δοῦπον ἄκουσε ποτὶ σπιλάδεσσι θαλάσσης·
ῥόχθει γὰρ μέγα κῦμα ποτὶ ξερὸν ἠπείροιο
δεινὸν ἐρευγόμενον, εἴλυτο δὲ πάνθ᾽ ἁλὸς ἄχνη·
οὐ γὰρ ἔσαν λιμένες νηῶν ὄχοι, οὐδ᾽ ἐπιωγαί,
ἀλλ᾽ ἀκταὶ προβλῆτες ἔσαν σπιλάδες τε πάγοι τε·
καὶ τότ᾽ Ὀδυσσῆος λύτο γούνατα καὶ φίλον ἦτορ,
ὀχθήσας δ᾽ ἄρα εἶπε πρὸς ὃν μεγαλήτορα θυμόν·

AND then for two nights and two days he was wandering in the swelling sea, and often his heart foresaw destruction. But when at last lovely-tressed Dawn brought the third day, the wind fell and a breathless calm spread across, and with a quick glance ahead as he was lifted on a great wave, he saw land near by. And as the sight of a father's life is most welcome to his children when he lies sick in great pain and has been wasting away for a long time, since some angry god had attacked him, but to their delight the gods release him from his trouble, so welcome appeared earth and forest to Odysseus; and he swam on eager to set foot on land. But when he was within earshot of the shore, and heard the thunder of the sea against the reefs – for the great wave crashed against the dry land, roaring terribly, and the foam of the sea covered everything, for there were no harbours for ships nor shelters, but jutting headlands and reefs and cliffs – then the knees of Odysseus were loosened, and his heart melted, and in despair he spoke to his own

‹ὤ μοι, ἐπεὶ δὴ γαῖαν ἀελπέα δῶκεν ἰδέσθαι
Ζεύς, καὶ δὴ τόδε λαῖτμα διατμήξας ἐτέλεσσα,
ἔκβασις οὔ πη φαίνεθ᾽ ἁλὸς πολιοῖο θύραζε·
ἔκτοσθεν μὲν γὰρ πάγοι ὀξέες, ἀμφὶ δὲ κῦμα
βέβρυχεν ῥόθιον, λισσὴ δ᾽ ἀναδέδρομε πέτρη,
ἀγχιβαθὴς δὲ θάλασσα, καὶ οὔ πως ἔστι πόδεσσι
στήμεναι ἀμφοτέροισι καὶ ἐκφυγέειν κακότητα·
μή πώς μ᾽ ἐκβαίνοντα βάλῃ λίθακι ποτὶ πέτρῃ
κῦμα μέγ᾽ ἁρπάξαν· μελέη δέ μοι ἔσσεται ὁρμή.
εἰ δέ κ᾽ ἔτι προτέρω παρανήξομαι, ἤν που ἐφεύρω
ἠιόνας τε παραπλῆγας λιμένας τε θαλάσσης,
δείδω μή μ᾽ ἐξαῦτις ἀναρπάξασα θύελλα
πόντον ἐπ᾽ ἰχθυόεντα φέρῃ βαρέα στενάχοντα,
ἠέ τί μοι καὶ κῆτος ἐπισσεύῃ μέγα δαίμων
ἐξ ἁλός, οἷά τε πολλὰ τρέφει κλυτὸς Ἀμφιτρίτη·
οἶδα γὰρ ὥς μοι ὀδώδυσται κλυτὸς ἐννοσίγαιος.›
Ἧος ὁ ταῦθ᾽ ὥρμαινε κατὰ φρένα καὶ κατὰ θυμόν,
τόφρα δέ μιν μέγα κῦμα φέρε τρηχεῖαν ἐπ᾽ ἀκτήν.
ἔνθα κ᾽ ἀπὸ ῥινοὺς δρύφθη, σὺν δ᾽ ὀστέ᾽ ἀράχθη,
εἰ μὴ ἐπὶ φρεσὶ θῆκε θεὰ γλαυκῶπις Ἀθήνη·

brave heart: 'Alas! now that, beyond all hope, Zeus has given me sight of land and I have indeed opened my way across this gulf of the sea, yet there seems no way out of the grey water. Outside there are sharp cliffs, and the waves roar surging round them, and the smooth rock rises sheer and the sea is deep near there, so that I cannot find a foothold for both my feet anywhere and escape destruction; for, if I were to go ashore, a great wave might catch me and dash me on the jagged rock, and a wretched struggle that would be. But if I swim further along the coast and try to find shores that take the waves aslant, and to find refuge from the sea, I fear the storm-winds will catch me again and carry me over the fish-rich sea groaning deeply; or else some god may even send a monster from the sea against me, one of the many that renowned Amphitrite feeds; for I know how angry the great Earth-shaker is with me.'

As he pondered these things in his heart and in his mind, a great wave carried him to the rugged shore. There he would have been stripped of his skin and his bones would have been broken, had not the goddess, grey-eyed Athene, put a thought into his head. He rushed in

ἀμφοτέρῃσι δὲ χερσὶν ἐπεσσύμενος λάβε πέτρης,
τῆς ἔχετο στενάχων, εἵως μέγα κῦμα παρῆλθε.
καὶ τὸ μὲν ὣς ὑπάλυξε, παλιρρόθιον δέ μιν αὖτις
πλῆξεν ἐπεσσύμενον, τηλοῦ δέ μιν ἔμβαλε πόντῳ.
ὡς δ' ὅτε πουλύποδος θαλάμης ἐξελκομένοιο
πρὸς κοτυληδονόφιν πυκιναὶ λάϊγγες ἔχονται,
ὣς τοῦ πρὸς πέτρῃσι θρασειάων ἀπὸ χειρῶν
ῥινοὶ ἀπέδρυφθεν· τὸν δὲ μέγα κῦμα κάλυψεν.
ἔνθα κε δὴ δύστηνος ὑπὲρ μόρον ὤλετ' Ὀδυσσεύς,
εἰ μὴ ἐπιφροσύνην δῶκε γλαυκῶπις Ἀθήνη.
κύματος ἐξαναδύς, τά τ' ἐρεύγεται ἠπειρόνδε,
νῆχε παρέξ, ἐς γαῖαν ὁρώμενος, εἴ που ἐφεύροι
ἠιόνας τε παραπλῆγας λιμένας τε θαλάσσης.
ἀλλ' ὅτε δὴ ποταμοῖο κατὰ στόμα καλλιρόοιο
ἷξε νέων, τῇ δή οἱ ἐείσατο χῶρος ἄριστος,
λεῖος πετράων, καὶ ἐπὶ σκέπας ἦν ἀνέμοιο.
ἔγνω δὲ προρέοντα καὶ εὔξατο ὃν κατὰ θυμόν·
«κλῦθι, ἄναξ, ὅτις ἐσσί· πολυλλίστον δέ σ' ἱκάνω,
φεύγων ἐκ πόντοιο Ποσειδάωνος ἐνιπάς.
αἰδοῖος μέν τ' ἐστὶ καὶ ἀθανάτοισι θεοῖσιν
ἀνδρῶν ὅς τις ἵκηται ἀλώμενος, ὡς καὶ ἐγὼ νῦν

and with both his hands clutched a rock, to which he clung, groaning,
till the great wave went by. So he escaped that danger; but the rush of
the backwash caught him a second time and threw him far out to sea.
And as when an octopus is dragged from its haunt many pebbles cling
to its suckers, so the skin was stripped from his strong hands by the
rocks, and the great wave closed over him. There unlucky Odysseus
would certainly have perished, beyond what was ordained by the
Fates, had not grey-eyed Athene given him sure counsel. He left the
breakers that roar on the shore, and swam along away from the shore
but looking towards the land, to see if he could find shores that took
the waves aslant, and find refuge from the sea. But when, as he swam,
he came to the mouth of a beautifully flowing river, where the ground
seemed most suitable, free from rocks, and also with shelter from the
wind, Odysseus felt the river running, and prayed to him in his heart:
'Hear me, King, whoever you are. To you I come, to whom many
prayers are made, as I flee from the sea and Poseidon's threats. Even
the deathless gods respect the man who comes as a wanderer, as I,

σόν τε ῥόον σά τε γούναθ' ἱκάνω πολλὰ μογήσας.
ἀλλ' ἐλέαιρε, ἄναξ· ἱκέτης δέ τοι εὔχομαι εἶναι.〉

"Ὥς φάθ', ὁ δ' αὐτίκα παῦσεν ἑὸν ῥόον, ἔσχε δὲ κῦμα,
πρόσθε δέ οἱ ποίησε γαλήνην, τὸν δ' ἐσάωσεν
ἐς ποταμοῦ προχοάς· ὁ δ' ἄρ' ἄμφω γούνατ' ἔκαμψε
χεῖράς τε στιβαράς· ἁλὶ γὰρ δέδμητο φίλον κῆρ.
ᾤδεε δὲ χρόα πάντα, θάλασσα δὲ κήκιε πολλὴ
ἂν στόμα τε ῥῖνάς θ'· ὁ δ' ἄρ' ἄπνευστος καὶ ἄναυδος
κεῖτ' ὀλιγηπελέων, κάματος δέ μιν αἰνὸς ἵκανεν.
ἀλλ' ὅτε δή ῥ' ἄμπνυτο καὶ ἐς φρένα θυμὸς ἀγέρθη,
καὶ τότε δὴ κρήδεμνον ἀπὸ ἕο λῦσε θεοῖο.
καὶ τὸ μὲν ἐς ποταμὸν ἁλιμυρήεντα μεθῆκεν,
ἂψ δ' ἔφερεν μέγα κῦμα κατὰ ῥόον, αἶψα δ' ἄρ' Ἰνὼ
δέξατο χερσὶ φίλῃσιν· ὁ δ' ἐκ ποταμοῖο λιασθεὶς
σχοίνῳ ὑπεκλίνθη, κύσε δὲ ζείδωρον ἄρουραν·
ὀχθήσας δ' ἄρα εἶπε πρὸς ὃν μεγαλήτορα θυμόν·
〈ὤ μοι ἐγώ, τί πάθω; τί νύ μοι μήκιστα γένηται;
εἰ μέν κ' ἐν ποταμῷ δυσκηδέα νύκτα φυλάσσω,
μή μ' ἄμυδις στίβη τε κακὴ καὶ θῆλυς ἐέρση
ἐξ ὀλιγηπελίης δαμάσῃ κεκαφηότα θυμόν·

after many hardships, now have come to your stream, and to your knees. Pity me, King, for I call myself your suppliant.'

So he spoke, and he [the river-god] at once stopped his stream, held back his waves, and made the water calm before him; and brought him safely to the river-mouth. And he bent both his knees and his strong arms, for his heart was broken by the salt water. And his flesh was all swollen, and a great stream of sea-water gushed up through his mouth and his nostrils. So he lay, without breath or speech, quite helpless; and a terrible weariness came over him. But when his breath returned and his spirit came to him again, he unfastened the veil of the goddess and let it fall into the sea-flowing river. And a great wave carried it back down the stream and soon Ino caught it in her hands. Then he [Odysseus] turned from the river and bent down to the reeds and kissed the life-giving earth; in despair he spoke to his own brave heart: 'Alas! What will happen to me? What will become of me in the end? If I keep watch in the river-bed all through the care-ridden night, I fear that the bitter frost and the fresh dew will be too much for me and I will breathe out my life, because I am so weak and the river breeze

αὔρη δ' ἐκ ποταμοῦ ψυχρὴ πνέει ἠῶθι πρό.
εἰ δέ κεν ἐς κλιτὺν ἀναβὰς καὶ δάσκιον ὕλην
θάμνοις ἐν πυκινοῖσι καταδράθω, εἴ με μεθήῃ
ῥῖγος καὶ κάματος, γλυκερὸς δέ μοι ὕπνος ἐπέλθῃ,
δείδω μὴ θήρεσσιν ἕλωρ καὶ κύρμα γένωμαι.›
  Ὣς ἄρα οἱ φρονέοντι δοάσσατο κέρδιον εἶναι·
βῆ ῥ' ἴμεν εἰς ὕλην· τὴν δὲ σχεδὸν ὕδατος εὗρεν
ἐν περιφαινομένῳ· δοιοὺς δ' ἄρ' ὑπήλυθε θάμνους,
ἐξ ὁμόθεν πεφυῶτας· ὁ μὲν φυλίης, ὁ δ' ἐλαίης.
τοὺς μὲν ἄρ' οὔτ' ἀνέμων διάη μένος ὑγρὸν ἀέντων,
οὔτε ποτ' ἠέλιος φαέθων ἀκτῖσιν ἔβαλλεν,
οὔτ' ὄμβρος περάασκε διαμπερές· ὣς ἄρα πυκνοὶ
ἀλλήλοισιν ἔφυν ἐπαμοιβαδίς· οὓς ὑπ' Ὀδυσσεὺς
δύσετ'. ἄφαρ δ' εὐνὴν ἐπαμήσατο χερσὶ φίλῃσιν
εὐρεῖαν· φύλλων γὰρ ἔην χύσις ἤλιθα πολλή,
ὅσσον τ' ἠὲ δύω ἠὲ τρεῖς ἄνδρας ἔρυσθαι
ὥρῃ χειμερίῃ, εἰ καὶ μάλα περ χαλεπαίνοι.
τὴν μὲν ἰδὼν γήθησε πολύτλας δῖος Ὀδυσσεύς,
ἐν δ' ἄρα μέσσῃ λέκτο, χύσιν δ' ἐπεχεύατο φύλλων.
ὡς δ' ὅτε τις δαλὸν σποδιῇ ἐνέκρυψε μελαίνῃ
ἀγροῦ ἐπ' ἐσχατιῆς, ᾧ μὴ πάρα γείτονες ἄλλοι,

blows cold in the early morning. But, if I climb up the hillside to the shady wood and fall asleep in the thickets, even if the cold and fatigue leave me, and sweet sleep does come over me, I fear that I will become the spoil and the prey of wild beasts.'

As he thought about it, this seemed the better way. He went up to the wood; he found it near the water in a place clearly visible. So he crept under two bushes that grew from one stem, both olive trees, one of them wild olive. Through these the force of the wet winds never blew, nor did the bright sun ever strike through them with his rays, nor could the rain pierce through, so close were they twined to one another; and under tnem crept Odysseus, and at once he heaped up a wide bed with his hands, for there was a large pile of fallen leaves — enough to cover two or three men in wintertime, however hard the weather. And long-suffering noble Odysseus saw it and rejoiced, and he lay in the middle of it and poured the fallen leaves over him. And, as when a man has hidden a brand in the black embers at the far end of his farm, where there are no neighbours near, and so saves a seed of the

σπέρμα πυρὸς σώζων, ἵνα μή ποθεν ἄλλοθεν αὔῃ,
ὡς 'Οδυσεὺς φύλλοισι καλύψατο· τῷ δ' ἄρ' 'Αθήνη
ὕπνον ἐπ' ὄμμασι χεῦ', ἵνα μιν παύσειε τάχιστα
δυσπονέος καμάτοιο, φίλα βλέφαρ' ἀμφικαλύψας.

(Odyssey)

12. Nausicaa

Αἱ δ' ὅτε δὴ ποταμοῖο ῥόον περικαλλέ' ἵκοντο,
ἔνθ' ἦ τοι πλυνοὶ ἦσαν ἐπηετανοί, πολὺ δ' ὕδωρ
καλὸν ὑπεκπρορέει μάλα περ ῥυπόωντα καθῆραι,
ἔνθ' αἵ γ' ἡμιόνους μὲν ὑπεκπροέλυσαν ἀπήνης.
καὶ τὰς μὲν σεῦαν ποταμὸν πάρα δινήεντα
τρώγειν ἄγρωστιν μελιηδέα· ταὶ δ' ἀπ' ἀπήνης
εἵματα χερσὶν ἕλοντο καὶ ἐσφόρεον μέλαν ὕδωρ,
στεῖβον δ' ἐν βόθροισι θοῶς ἔριδα προφέρουσαι.
αὐτὰρ ἐπεὶ πλῦνάν τε κάθηράν τε ῥύπα πάντα,
ἑξείης πέτασαν παρὰ θῖν' ἁλός, ἧχι μάλιστα
λάϊγγας ποτὶ χέρσον ἀποπλύνεσκε θάλασσα.
αἱ δὲ λοεσσάμεναι καὶ χρισάμεναι λίπ' ἐλαίῳ
δεῖπνον ἔπειθ' εἵλοντο παρ' ὄχθῃσιν ποταμοῖο,

fire so that he does not have to look for a light elsewhere, so did
Odysseus cover himself with the leaves. And Athene shed sleep on his
eyes, to close his eyelids and release him quickly from his painful
fatigue.

Now when they came to the beautiful stream of the river, where the
pools were always full, and much bright water gushed up from under
and flowed past, enough to clean the dirtiest clothes, there the girls un-
harnessed the mules from under the chariot, and turned them loose
along the banks of the swirling river to graze on the honey-sweet
clover. Then they took the clothes from the carriage in their hands and
carried them to the dark water and swiftly trod them in the trenches,
in busy rivalry. Now when they had washed and cleaned all the stains,
they spread them all out in a line along the seashore, where the sea
washed the shingle clean on the coast. And having bathed and anointed
themselves with rich oil, they took their midday meal on the river-
bank, waiting for the clothes to dry in the sunshine. And when they had

εἵματα δ' ἠελίοιο μένον τερσήμεναι αὐγῇ.
αὐτὰρ ἐπεὶ σίτου τάρφθεν δμῳαί τε καὶ αὐτή,
σφαίρῃ ταί γ' ἄρα παῖζον, ἀπὸ κρήδεμνα βαλοῦσαι·
τῇσι δὲ Ναυσικάα λευκώλενος ἄρχετο μολπῆς.
οἵη δ' Ἄρτεμις εἶσι κατ' οὔρεα ἰοχέαιρα,
ἢ κατὰ Τηΰγετον περιμήκετον ἢ Ἐρύμανθον,
τερπομένη κάπροισι καὶ ὠκείῃς ἐλάφοισι·
τῇ δέ θ' ἅμα νύμφαι, κοῦραι Διὸς αἰγιόχοιο,
ἀγρονόμοι παίζουσι· γέγηθε δέ τε φρένα Λητώ·
πασάων δ' ὑπὲρ ἥ γε κάρη ἔχει ἠδὲ μέτωπα,
ῥεῖά τ' ἀριγνώτη πέλεται, καλαὶ δέ τε πᾶσαι·
ὣς ἥ γ' ἀμφιπόλοισι μετέπρεπε παρθένος ἀδμής.
  Ἀλλ' ὅτε δὴ ἄρ' ἔμελλε πάλιν οἰκόνδε νέεσθαι
ζεύξασ' ἡμιόνους πτύξασά τε εἵματα καλά,
ἔνθ' αὖτ' ἄλλ' ἐνόησε θεὰ γλαυκῶπις Ἀθήνη,
ὡς Ὀδυσεὺς ἔγροιτο, ἴδοι τ' εὐώπιδα κούρην,
ἥ οἱ Φαιήκων ἀνδρῶν πόλιν ἡγήσαιτο.
σφαῖραν ἔπειτ' ἔρριψε μετ' ἀμφίπολον βασίλεια·
ἀμφιπόλου μὲν ἅμαρτε, βαθείῃ δ' ἔμβαλε δίνῃ,
αἱ δ' ἐπὶ μακρὸν ἄϋσαν. ὁ δ' ἔγρετο δῖος Ὀδυσσεύς,
ἑζόμενος δ' ὅρμαινε κατὰ φρένα καὶ κατὰ θυμόν·
‹ὤ μοι ἐγώ, τέων αὖτε βροτῶν ἐς γαῖαν ἱκάνω;

had enough food, the servants and herself [Nausicaa], they started playing at ball, throwing away their veils; and among them Nausicaa of the white arms began a song. And as Artemis, the archer, moves along the mountain ridges of very high Taygetus or of Erymanthus, enjoying the chase of boars and swift deer, and with her play the wild wood-nymphs, the daughters of Zeus, lord of the aegis; and Leto is happy in her heart as high over all she [Artemis] holds her head and brows, and she is easily distinguishable, though all are beautiful – so the unwedded girl outshone her servants.

But when she was about to return home, after yoking the mules and folding up the beautiful clothes, grey-eyed Athene turned to other thoughts, so that Odysseus might wake up and see the lovely girl who was to be his guide to the city of the Phaeacian men. Then the princess threw the ball to one of her attendants; her throw fell wide of the girl, and the ball landed in the deep-eddying current, and they all cried out loudly. And godlike Odysseus woke up, and sat up thinking in his heart and his spirit: 'Alas, to what men's land have I come now? Are

ἦ ῥ' οἵ γ' ὑβρισταί τε καὶ ἄγριοι οὐδὲ δίκαιοι,
ἦε φιλόξεινοι, καί σφιν νόος ἐστὶ θεουδής;
ὥς τέ με κουράων ἀμφήλυθε θῆλυς ἀϋτή,
νυμφάων, αἳ ἔχουσ' ὀρέων αἰπεινὰ κάρηνα
καὶ πηγὰς ποταμῶν καὶ πίσεα ποιήεντα.
ἦ νύ που ἀνθρώπων εἰμὶ σχεδὸν αὐδηέντων;
ἀλλ' ἄγ', ἐγὼν αὐτὸς πειρήσομαι ἠδὲ ἴδωμαι.›
  Ὣς εἰπὼν θάμνων ὑπεδύσετο δῖος Ὀδυσσεύς,
ἐκ πυκινῆς δ' ὕλης πτόρθον κλάσε χειρὶ παχείῃ
φύλλων, ὡς ῥύσαιτο περὶ χροῒ μήδεα φωτός.
βῆ δ' ἴμεν ὥς τε λέων ὀρεσίτροφος, ἀλκὶ πεποιθώς,
ὅς τ' εἶσ' ὑόμενος καὶ ἀήμενος, ἐν δέ οἱ ὄσσε
δαίεται· αὐτὰρ ὁ βουσὶ μετέρχεται ἢ ὀίεσσιν
ἠὲ μετ' ἀγροτέρας ἐλάφους· κέλεται δέ ἑ γαστὴρ
μήλων πειρήσοντα καὶ ἐς πυκινὸν δόμον ἐλθεῖν·
ὣς Ὀδυσεὺς κούρῃσιν ἐϋπλοκάμοισιν ἔμελλε
μίξεσθαι, γυμνός περ ἐών· χρειὼ γὰρ ἵκανε.
σμερδαλέος δ' αὐτῇσι φάνη κεκακωμένος ἅλμῃ,
τρέσσαν δ' ἄλλυδις ἄλλη ἐπ' ἠιόνας προὐχούσας·
οἴη δ' Ἀλκινόου θυγάτηρ μένε· τῇ γὰρ Ἀθήνη
θάρσος ἐνὶ φρεσὶ θῆκε καὶ ἐκ δέος εἵλετο γυίων.

they proud and wild and unjust, or are they hospitable and of a god-
fearing mind? What shrill girls' cry rings round me from the nymphs
that live on the steep hilltops and the river-springs, and the grassy
water-meadows! Am I now near people of human speech? Come, I will
discover for myself and see.'

So he thought, and the godly Odysseus crept from under the bushes,
and with his strong hand broke a leafy bough from the thick wood to
hold against his body, that it might hide his manhood. And he rushed
out like a mountain-bred lion who goes, trusting in his strength, wind-
beaten and rained upon with flaming eyes; among the oxen or sheep he
goes, or on the track of wild deer; his belly makes him go even to the
well-built homestead to try and attack sheep. So was Odysseus about
to approach the beautiful-tressed girls, though he was naked; for it was
necessary. But he looked frightening to them, bleached with the salt
sea-foam, and they fled in all directions over the jutting beaches of the
shore. Only the daughter of Alcinous stood firm, for Athene gave her
heart courage, and stopped the trembling in her limbs. And she stood

στῆ δ' ἄντα σχομένη· ὁ δὲ μερμήριξεν Ὀδυσσεύς,
ἢ γούνων λίσσοιτο λαβὼν εὐώπιδα κούρην,
ἢ αὔτως ἐπέεσσιν ἀποσταδὰ μειλιχίοισι
λίσσοιτ', εἰ δείξειε πόλιν καὶ εἵματα δοίη.
ὣς ἄρα οἱ φρονέοντι δοάσσατο κέρδιον εἶναι,
λίσσεσθαι ἐπέεσσιν ἀποσταδὰ μειλιχίοισι,
μή οἱ γοῦνα λαβόντι χολώσαιτο φρένα κούρη.
αὐτίκα μειλίχιον καὶ κερδαλέον φάτο μῦθον·
‹γουνοῦμαί σε, ἄνασσα· θεός νύ τις ἢ βροτός ἐσσι;
εἰ μέν τις θεός ἐσσι, τοὶ οὐρανὸν εὐρὺν ἔχουσιν,
Ἀρτέμιδί σε ἐγώ γε, Διὸς κούρη μεγάλοιο,
εἶδός τε μέγεθός τε φυήν τ' ἄγχιστα ἐΐσκω·
εἰ δέ τίς ἐσσι βροτῶν, τοὶ ἐπὶ χθονὶ ναιετάουσι,
τρισμάκαρες μὲν σοί γε πατὴρ καὶ πότνια μήτηρ,
τρισμάκαρες δὲ κασίγνητοι· μάλα πού σφισι θυμὸς
αἰὲν ἐϋφροσύνῃσιν ἰαίνεται εἵνεκα σεῖο,
λευσσόντων τοιόνδε θάλος χορὸν εἰσοιχνεῦσαν.
κεῖνος δ' αὖ περὶ κῆρι μακάρτατος ἔξοχον ἄλλων,
ὅς κέ σ' ἐέδνοισι βρίσας οἰκόνδ' ἀγάγηται.
οὐ γάρ πω τοιοῦτον ἐγὼ ἴδον ὀφθαλμοῖσιν,
οὔτ' ἄνδρ' οὔτε γυναῖκα· σέβας μ' ἔχει εἰσορόωντα.

still, facing him; and Odysseus considered whether he should clasp the knees of the lovely maiden, and so make his prayer, or should stand as he was, away from her, and ask her with gentle words whether she would show him the town and give him clothes. And, as he was thinking, it seemed better to him to keep away, and to ask her with gentle words, lest the girl be angry with him if he touched her knees; so he spoke at once gentle and cunning words: 'I come to you as a suppliant, Queen; are you a goddess or a human being? If you are a goddess, one of those that hold the wide heaven, to Artemis then, the daughter of great Zeus, I liken you most in beauty and stature and form; but if you are a daughter of the men who live on the earth, most blessed are your father and honourable mother, and most blessed your brothers and sisters. Surely their hearts always glow with delight for your sake each time they see such a flower of a girl entering the dance. But happiest beyond all others is the man who shall win you with gifts and take you to his home. Never have my eyes seen such a man or woman among mortals. I am seized by wonder as I look at you. Yet

Δήλῳ δή ποτε τοῖον ᾿Απόλλωνος παρὰ βωμῷ
φοίνικος νέον ἔρνος ἀνερχόμενον ἐνόησα·
ἦλθον γὰρ καὶ κεῖσε, πολὺς δέ μοι ἕσπετο λαὸς
τὴν ὁδὸν ᾗ δὴ μέλλεν ἐμοὶ κακὰ κήδε᾿ ἔσεσθαι.
ὡς δ᾿ αὔτως καὶ κεῖνο ἰδὼν ἐτεθήπεα θυμῷ
δήν, ἐπεὶ οὔ πω τοῖον ἀνήλυθεν ἐκ δόρυ γαίης,
ὡς σέ, γύναι, ἄγαμαί τε τέθηπά τε δείδιά τ᾿ αἰνῶς
γούνων ἅψασθαι· χαλεπὸν δέ με πένθος ἱκάνει.
χθιζὸς ἐεικοστῷ φύγον ἤματι οἴνοπα πόντον·
τόφρα δέ μ᾿ αἰεὶ κῦμ᾿ ἐφόρει κραιπναί τε θύελλαι
νήσου ἀπ᾿ ᾿Ωγυγίης· νῦν δ᾿ ἐνθάδε κάββαλε δαίμων,
ὄφρα τί που καὶ τῇδε πάθω κακόν· οὐ γὰρ ὀΐω
παύσεσθ᾿, ἀλλ᾿ ἔτι πολλὰ θεοὶ τελέουσι πάροιθεν.
ἀλλά, ἄνασσ᾿, ἐλέαιρε· σὲ γὰρ κακὰ πολλὰ μογήσας
ἐς πρώτην ἱκόμην, τῶν δ᾿ ἄλλων οὔ τινα οἶδα
ἀνθρώπων, οἳ τήνδε πόλιν καὶ γαῖαν ἔχουσιν.
ἄστυ δέ μοι δεῖξον, δὸς δὲ ῥάκος ἀμφιβαλέσθαι,
εἴ τί που εἴλυμα σπείρων ἔχες ἐνθάδ᾿ ἰοῦσα.
σοὶ δὲ θεοὶ τόσα δοῖεν ὅσα φρεσὶ σῇσι μενοινᾷς,
ἄνδρα τε καὶ οἶκον καὶ ὁμοφροσύνην ὀπάσειαν
ἐσθλήν· οὐ μὲν γὰρ τοῦ γε κρεῖσσον καὶ ἄρειον,

in Delos once I saw as beautiful a thing: a young sapling of a palm-tree springing by the altar of Apollo. For there too I went, and many men came with me, on that journey, where dreadful troubles were in store for me. And as I looked on it for a long time, I marvelled in my heart – for never yet had so beautiful a tree grown from the ground. In such a manner I marvel at you, lady, and I am astonished and fear greatly to touch your knees, though heavy sorrows are upon me. Yesterday, on the twentieth day, I escaped from the wine-dark sea, but all that time the wave and the rushing storms carried me on from the island of Ogygia. And now some god has put me on this shore, that here too, perhaps, I may suffer some evil; for I do not believe that the trouble will cease; the gods will yet do much to me before that. But, Queen, pity me, for, after suffering much, I have come first to you, and I know none of the others who live in this city and this land. Show me the town, give me a rag to put round me, if you brought any wrap for the linen, when you came here. And may the gods grant you all your heart's desires, a husband and a home, and a mind at one with his – a good gift, for there is nothing greater and nobler than when

ἦ δθ' ὁμοφρονέοντε νοήμασιν οἶκον ἔχητον
ἀνὴρ ἠδὲ γυνή· πόλλ' ἄλγεα δυσμενέεσσι,
χάρματα δ' εὐμενέτησι· μάλιστα δέ τ' ἔκλυον αὐτοί.⟩

(Odyssey)

13. The Cyclops

Ὣς ἐφάμην, ὁ δὲ δέκτο καὶ ἔκπιεν· ἥσατο δ' αἰνῶς
ἡδὺ ποτὸν πίνων, καί μ' ἤτεε δεύτερον αὖτις·
⟨ Δός μοι ἔτι πρόφρων, καί μοι τεὸν οὔνομα εἰπὲ
αὐτίκα νῦν, ἵνα τοι δῶ ξείνιον, ᾧ κε σὺ χαίρης.
καὶ γὰρ Κυκλώπεσσι φέρει ζείδωρος ἄρουρα
οἶνον ἐρισταφυλον, καί σφιν Διὸς ὄμβρος ἀέξει·
ἀλλὰ τόδ' ἀμβροσίης καὶ νέκταρός ἐστιν ἀπορρώξ.⟩
Ὣς ἔφατ'· αὐτάρ οἱ αὖτις πόρον αἴθοπα οἶνον·
τρὶς μὲν ἔδωκα φέρων, τρὶς δ' ἔκπιεν ἀφραδίησιν.
αὐτάρ ἐπεὶ Κύκλωπα περὶ φρένας ἤλυθεν οἶνος,
καὶ τότε δή μιν ἔπεσσι προσηύδων μειλιχίοισι·
⟨Κύκλωψ, εἰρωτᾷς μ' ὄνομα κλυτόν; αὐτὰρ ἐγώ τοι
ἐξερέω· σὺ δέ μοι δὸς ξείνιον, ὥς περ ὑπέστης.

man and wife are of one heart and mind in a house, a great grief to
their enemies and much joy to their friends; but they themselves know
it best.'

So I spoke, and he [the Cyclops] took the cup and drank it up, and
had great delight in drinking the sweet drink, and asked me for a
second cup.

'Of your kindness give me some more, and tell me your name now,
so that I can give you a stranger's gift, in which you will delight. For
the earth, the grain-giver, bears for the Cyclopes wine from mighty
clusters of grapes, and the rain of Zeus makes them grow; but this is a
portion of nectar and ambrosia.'

So he spoke, and I handed him the bright wine again. Three times I
brought it and gave it to him, and three times in his folly he drank it
to the dregs. Now when the wine had gone to the head of the Cyclops,
(then) I spoke to him with soft words: 'Cyclops, you ask me my
glorious name, and I will tell it to you, and you give me a stranger's

Οὖτις ἐμοί γ' ὄνομα· Οὖτιν δέ με κικλήσκουσι
μήτηρ ἠδὲ πατὴρ ἠδ' ἄλλοι πάντες ἑταῖροι.›
  Ὣς ἐφάμην, ὁ δέ μ' αὐτίκ' ἀμείβετο νηλέϊ θυμῷ·
‹Οὖτιν ἐγὼ πύματον ἔδομαι μετὰ οἷς ἑτάροισι,
τοὺς δ' ἄλλους πρόσθεν· τὸ δέ τοι ξεινήϊον ἔσται.›
  Ἦ καὶ ἀνακλινθεὶς πέσεν ὕπτιος, αὐτὰρ ἔπειτα
κεῖτ' ἀποδοχμώσας παχὺν αὐχένα, κὰδ δέ μιν ὕπνος
ἥρει πανδαμάτωρ· φάρυγος δ' ἐξέσσυτο οἶνος
ψωμοί τ' ἀνδρόμεοι· ὁ δ' ἐρεύγετο οἰνοβαρείων.
καὶ τότ' ἐγὼ τὸν μοχλὸν ὑπὸ σποδοῦ ἤλασα πολλῆς,
ἧος θερμαίνοιτο· ἔπεσσί τε πάντας ἑταίρους
θάρσυνον, μή τίς μοι ὑποδείσας ἀναδύη.
ἀλλ' ὅτε δὴ τάχ' ὁ μοχλὸς ἐλάϊνος ἐν πυρὶ μέλλεν
ἅψεσθαι, χλωρός περ ἐών, διεφαίνετο δ' αἰνῶς,
καὶ τότ' ἐγὼν ἆσσον φέρον ἐκ πυρός, ἀμφὶ δ' ἑταῖροι
ἵσταντ'· αὐτὰρ θάρσος ἐνέπνευσεν μέγα δαίμων.
οἱ μὲν μοχλὸν ἑλόντες ἐλάϊνον, ὀξὺν ἐπ' ἄκρῳ,
ὀφθαλμῷ ἐνέρεισαν· ἐγὼ δ' ἐφύπερθεν ἐρεισθεὶς
δίνεον, ὡς ὅτε τις τρυπῷ δόρυ νήϊον ἀνὴρ
τρυπάνῳ, οἱ δέ τ' ἔνερθεν ὑποσσείουσιν ἱμάντι
ἁψάμενοι ἑκάτερθε, τὸ δὲ τρέχει ἐμμενὲς αἰεί·

gift, as you promised. No One is my name, and No One they call me,
my father and my mother and all my companions.'

So I spoke, and at once he answered me from his pitiless heart: 'I
will eat No One last, after his fellows; all the others before him. That
shall be your gift.'

He spoke, and sank backwards, and fell with his face turned up-
wards, and there he lay with his great neck bent round, and all-con-
quering sleep overcame him. And the wine and the pieces of men's
flesh poured out of his mouth, as he vomited, heavy with drink. Then
I thrust that stake under the deep ashes, until it was hot, and I spoke
to my companions, encouraging them, lest anyone should hang back
from me in fear. But when that bar of olive wood was just about to
catch fire in the flame, green though it was, and began to glow terribly,
then I went close and drew it from the fire, and my companions
gathered round me, and a god breathed great courage into us. They
seized the bar of olive wood that was sharpened at the point, and
thrust it into his eye; while I leaned on it above and turned it round,
as when a man bores a ship's beam with a drill, while his fellows below

ὣς τοῦ ἐν ὀφθαλμῷ πυριήκεα μοχλὸν ἑλόντες
δινέομεν, τὸν δ' αἷμα περίρρεε θερμὸν ἐόντα.
πάντα δέ οἱ βλέφαρ' ἀμφὶ καὶ ὀφρύας εὗσεν ἀϋτμὴ
γλήνης καιομένης· σφαραγεῦντο δέ οἱ πυρὶ ῥίζαι.
ὡς δ' ὅτ' ἀνὴρ χαλκεὺς πέλεκυν μέγαν ἠὲ σκέπαρνον
εἰν ὕδατι ψυχρῷ βάπτῃ μεγάλα ἰάχοντα
φαρμάσσων· τὸ γὰρ αὖτε σιδήρου γε κράτος ἐστίν·
ὣς τοῦ σίζ' ὀφθαλμὸς ἐλαϊνέῳ περὶ μοχλῷ.
σμερδαλέον δὲ μέγ' ᾤμωξεν, περὶ δ' ἴαχε πέτρη,
ἡμεῖς δὲ δείσαντες ἀπεσσύμεθ'. αὐτὰρ ὁ μοχλὸν
ἐξέρυσ' ὀφθαλμοῖο πεφυρμένον αἵματι πολλῷ.
τὸν μὲν ἔπειτ' ἔρριψεν ἀπὸ ἕο χερσὶν ἀλύων,
αὐτὰρ ὁ Κύκλωπας μεγάλ' ἤπυεν, οἵ ῥά μιν ἀμφὶς
ᾤκεον ἐν σπήεσσι δι' ἄκριας ἠνεμοέσσας.
οἱ δὲ βοῆς ἀΐοντες ἐφοίτων ἄλλοθεν ἄλλος,
ἱστάμενοι δ' εἴροντο περὶ σπέος ὅττι ἑ κήδοι·
‹τίπτε τόσον, Πολύφημ', ἀρημένος ὧδ' ἐβόησας
νύκτα δι' ἀμβροσίην, καὶ ἀΰπνους ἄμμε τίθησθα;
ἦ μή τίς σευ μῆλα βροτῶν ἀέκοντος ἐλαύνει;
ἦ μή τίς σ' αὐτὸν κτείνει δόλῳ ἠὲ βίηφιν;›
    Τοὺς δ' αὖτ' ἐξ ἄντρου προσέφη κρατερὸς Πολύφημος·

spin it with a strap, which they hold at either end, and it runs round
continually. So we gripped the fiery pointed wood, and whirled it
round in his eye, and the blood flowed round the heated bar. And the
breath of the flame singed all his eyelids and his brows, as the ball of
the eye burnt away, and its roots crackled in the flame. And as when a
smith dips a great axe or adze in cold water, hissing fiercely as he tem-
pers it – for through this the iron is strengthened – so his eye hissed
round the olive bar. And he raised so great and terrible a cry that the
rock rang round, and we fled away in terror, as he pulled the brand out
of his eye, covered with blood. Then, maddened with pain, he threw
it away with his hands, and called with a loud voice to the Cyclopes
who lived round about in the caves on the windy peaks. And they
heard the cry and came together from all sides, and standing round the
cave, asked him what troubled him: 'What has hurt you, Polyphemus,
so much that you cry aloud through the immortal night, and make us
sleepless? Is some mortal man driving away your flocks against your
will? Is someone trying to kill you by cunning or by force?'

‹ὦ φίλοι, Οὖτίς με κτείνει δόλῳ οὐδὲ βίηφιν.›

Οἱ δ' ἀπαμειβόμενοι ἔπεα πτερόεντ' ἀγόρευον·
‹εἰ μὲν δὴ μή τίς σε βιάζεται οἶον ἐόντα,
νοῦσόν γ' οὔ πως ἔστι Διὸς μεγάλου ἀλέασθαι,
ἀλλὰ σύ γ' εὔχεο πατρὶ Ποσειδάωνι ἄνακτι.›

Ὣς ἄρ' ἔφαν ἀπιόντες· ἐμὸν δ' ἐγέλασσε φίλον κῆρ,
ὡς ὄνομ' ἐξαπάτησεν ἐμὸν καὶ μῆτις ἀμύμων.

(*Odyssey*)

14. Circe

Εὗρον δ' ἐν βήσσησι τετυγμένα δώματα Κίρκης
ξεστοῖσιν λάεσσι, περισκέπτῳ ἐνὶ χώρῳ.
ἀμφὶ δέ μιν λύκοι ἦσαν ὀρέστεροι ἠδὲ λέοντες,
τοὺς αὐτὴ κατέθελξεν, ἐπεὶ κακὰ φάρμακ' ἔδωκεν.
οὐδ' οἵ γ' ὡρμήθησαν ἐπ' ἀνδράσιν, ἀλλ' ἄρα τοί γε
οὐρῇσιν μακρῇσι περισσαίνοντες ἀνέσταν.
ὡς δ' ὅτ' ἂν ἀμφὶ ἄνακτα κύνες δαίτηθεν ἰόντα
σαίνωσ'· αἰεὶ γάρ τε φέρει μειλίγματα θυμοῦ·
ὣς τοὺς ἀμφὶ λύκοι κρατερώνυχες ἠδὲ λέοντες
σαῖνον· τοὶ δ' ἔδεισαν, ἐπεὶ ἴδον αἰνὰ πέλωρα.

And strong Polyphemus replied to them from the cave: 'My friends, No One is killing me by cunning or by force.'

And they answered, speaking winged words: 'If then no one is handling you violently, and you are alone, you can in no way escape a sickness sent by great Zeus. But pray to your father, the lord Poseidon.'

So they spoke and left; and I laughed in my heart to see how my name and my excellent cunning had deceived them.

THEY found in the forest glades the palace of Circe, built of polished stone, in a place visible from all sides. And all around it were mountain-bred wolves and lions, which she herself had bewitched, by giving them harmful drugs. They did not set on the men, but jumped up at them and fawned about them, wagging their long tails. And, as dogs fawn about their master when he comes from the feast, for he always brings them bits that ease their hunger, so the strong-clawed wolves and the lions fawned round them. But the men were frightened, when they saw the strange and terrible creatures. So they stood at the outer gate

ἔσταν δ' ἐν προθύροισι θεᾶς καλλιπλοκάμοιο,
Κίρκης δ' ἔνδον ἄκουον ἀειδούσης ὀπὶ καλῇ,
ἱστὸν ἐποιχομένης μέγαν ἄμβροτον, οἷα θεάων
λεπτά τε καὶ χαρίεντα καὶ ἀγλαὰ ἔργα πέλονται.
τοῖσι δὲ μύθων ἦρχε Πολίτης, ὄρχαμος ἀνδρῶν,
ὅς μοι κήδιστος ἑτάρων ἦν κεδνότατός τε·
‹ὦ φίλοι, ἔνδον γάρ τις ἐποιχομένη μέγαν ἱστὸν
καλὸν ἀοιδιάει, δάπεδον δ' ἅπαν ἀμφιμέμυκεν,
ἢ θεὸς ἠὲ γυνή· ἀλλὰ φθεγγώμεθα θᾶσσον.›
    Ὣς ἄρ' ἐφώνησεν, τοὶ δ' ἐφθέγγοντο καλεῦντες.
ἡ δ' αἶψ' ἐξελθοῦσα θύρας ὤϊξε φαεινὰς
καὶ κάλει· οἱ δ' ἅμα πάντες ἀϊδρείῃσιν ἕποντο·
Εὐρύλοχος δ' ὑπέμεινεν, ὀϊσάμενος δόλον εἶναι.
εἷσεν δ' εἰσαγαγοῦσα κατὰ κλισμούς τε θρόνους τε,
ἐν δέ σφιν τυρόν τε καὶ ἄλφιτα καὶ μέλι χλωρὸν
οἴνῳ Πραμνείῳ ἐκύκα· ἀνέμισγε δὲ σίτῳ
φάρμακα λύγρ', ἵνα πάγχυ λαθοίατο πατρίδος αἴης.
αὐτὰρ ἐπεὶ δῶκέν τε καὶ ἔκπιον, αὐτίκ' ἔπειτα
ῥάβδῳ πεπληγυῖα κατὰ συφεοῖσιν ἐέργνυ.
οἱ δὲ συῶν μὲν ἔχον κεφαλὰς φωνήν τε τρίχας τε
καὶ δέμας, αὐτὰρ νοῦς ἦν ἔμπεδος ὡς τὸ πάρος περ.

of the fair-tressed goddess's house, and they heard Circe inside singing
in a beautiful voice, as she worked at her great, godly web – such as is
the handiwork of goddesses, delicate, graceful and splendid. Then
Polites, a leader of men, dearest to me and most glorious of all my
companions, spoke first: 'Friends, in the palace is someone working
at a large and beautiful web and singing – the whole floor [of the
palace] is resounding; [someone who is] either a woman or a goddess.
Let us quickly call to her.'

So he spoke, and they cried out, calling her. And she came forward,
opened the bright doors and invited them in; they, in their ignorance,
all went in together with her. But Eurylochus stayed behind, for he
guessed that there was some deceit. And she led them in, and sat them
on chairs and high seats, and she mixed for them in Pramnian wine
cheese and barley-meal and fresh honey, and mixed harmful drugs with
the food to make them forget their homeland completely. Now when
she had given them [the cup], and they had drunk it to the dregs, she
swiftly struck them with a wand and penned them in the pigsties of
the swine. Thus they had the head and voice, the bristles and the shape
of swine, but their mind was as sound as it had been in the past. Thus

ὣς οἱ μὲν κλαίοντες ἐέρχατο· τοῖσι δὲ Κίρκη
πάρ ῥ' ἄκυλον βάλανόν τ' ἔβαλεν καρπόν τε κρανείης
ἔδμεναι, οἷα σύες χαμαιευνάδες αἰὲν ἔδουσιν.

(*Odyssey*)

15. The Shade of Ajax

Αἱ δ' ἄλλαι ψυχαὶ νεκύων κατατεθνηώτων
ἕστασαν ἀχνύμεναι, εἴροντο δὲ κήδε' ἑκάστη.
οἴη δ' Αἴαντος ψυχὴ Τελαμωνιάδαο
νόσφιν ἀφεστήκει, κεχολωμένη εἵνεκα νίκης,
τήν μιν ἐγὼ νίκησα δικαζόμενος παρὰ νηυσὶ
τεύχεσιν ἀμφ' Ἀχιλῆος· ἔθηκε δὲ πότνια μήτηρ.
παῖδες δὲ Τρώων δίκασαν καὶ Παλλὰς Ἀθήνη.
ὡς δὴ μὴ ὄφελον νικᾶν τοιῷδ' ἐπ' ἀέθλῳ·
τοίην γὰρ κεφαλὴν ἕνεκ' αὐτῶν γαῖα κατέσχεν,
Αἴανθ', ὃς περὶ μὲν εἶδος, περὶ δ' ἔργα τέτυκτο
τῶν ἄλλων Δαναῶν μετ' ἀμύμονα Πηλείωνα.
τὸν μὲν ἐγὼν ἐπέεσσι προσηύδων μειλιχίοισιν·
‹Αἶαν, παῖ Τελαμῶνος ἀμύμονος, οὐκ ἄρ' ἔμελλες
οὐδὲ θανὼν λήσεσθαι ἐμοὶ χόλου εἵνεκα τευχέων
οὐλομένων; τὰ δὲ πῆμα θεοὶ θέσαν Ἀργείοισι,

they were penned in, weeping; and Circe threw acorns to them and mast and fruit of the cornel tree to eat, which the swine that sleep on the ground always feed on.

THE other souls of the dead stood sorrowing, and each one asked about those that were dear to him. Only the soul of Ajax, the son of Telamon, stood apart, angry at my victory over him, when we had competed by the ships for the arms of Achilles which his [Achilles'] honoured mother had set for a prize, and which the sons of the Trojans and Pallas Athene had awarded. I wish I had never won such a prize! So splendid a man did the earth close over for the sake of those arms: Ajax, who in appearance and in feats of war excelled all the other Danaans, after the noble son of Peleus. To him then I spoke gently and said: 'Ajax, son of noble Telamon, even in death were you not to forget your anger against me, because of those cursed arms which the gods determined to be a cause of destruction to the Argives? For what

τοῖος γάρ σφιν πύργος ἀπώλεο· σεῖο δ' Ἀχαιοὶ
ἶσον Ἀχιλλῆος κεφαλῇ Πηληϊάδαο
ἀχνύμεθα φθιμένοιο διαμπερές· οὐδέ τις ἄλλος
αἴτιος, ἀλλὰ Ζεὺς Δαναῶν στρατὸν αἰχμητάων
ἐκπάγλως ἔχθαιρε, τεῒν δ' ἐπὶ μοῖραν ἔθηκεν.
ἀλλ' ἄγε δεῦρο, ἄναξ, ἵν' ἔπος καὶ μῦθον ἀκούσῃς
ἡμέτερον· δάμασον δὲ μένος καὶ ἀγήνορα θυμόν.›
    Ὣς ἐφάμην, ὁ δέ μ' οὐδὲν ἀμείβετο, βῆ δὲ μετ' ἄλλας
ψυχὰς εἰς Ἔρεβος νεκύων κατατεθνηώτων.

(*Odyssey*)

16. The Sirens

Ἦ τοι ἐγὼ τὰ ἕκαστα λέγων ἑτάροισι πίφαυσκον·
τόφρα δὲ καρπαλίμως ἐξίκετο νηῦς εὐεργὴς
νῆσον Σειρήνοιϊν· ἔπειγε γὰρ οὖρος ἀπήμων.
αὐτίκ' ἔπειτ' ἄνεμος μὲν ἐπαύσατο ἠδὲ γαλήνη
ἔπλετο νηνεμίη, κοίμησε δὲ κύματα δαίμων.
ἀνστάντες δ' ἕταροι νεὸς ἱστία μηρύσαντο,
καὶ τὰ μὲν ἐν νηῒ γλαφυρῇ θέσαν, οἱ δ' ἐπ' ἐρετμὰ
ἑζόμενοι λεύκαινον ὕδωρ ξεστῇς ἐλάτῃσιν.

a tower of strength fell when you fell! And we Achaeans always mourn for you as much as for the death of Achilles, the son of Peleus! There is no one to blame but Zeus, who hated the army of the Danaan spearmen so violently and brought your fate upon you. But come near, my lord, to hear my words and my speech; master your anger and your proud spirit.'

So I spoke, but he did not answer a word, and moved away to Erebus to join the other souls of the dead.

So I repeated all these things, one after the other, and made them clear to my companions. Meanwhile the well-made ship came swiftly to the island of the two Sirens, for a gentle breeze sped her along. Then suddenly the wind ceased, and there was a breathless calm; and some god lulled the waves to sleep. My companions rose up, drew in the ship's sails and stowed them in the hollow ship, and then they sat at the oars and whitened the water with their polished pine-blades. But I

αὐτὰρ ἐγὼ κηροῖο μέγαν τροχὸν ὀξέϊ χαλκῷ
τυτθὰ διατμήξας χερσὶ στιβαρῇσι πίεζον.
αἶψα δ' ἰαίνετο κηρός, ἐπεὶ κέλετο μεγάλη ἲς
Ἠελίου τ' αὐγὴ Ὑπεριονίδαο ἄνακτος·
ἑξείης δ' ἑτάροισιν ἐπ' οὔατα πᾶσιν ἄλειψα.
οἱ δ' ἐν νηΐ μ' ἔδησαν ὁμοῦ χεῖράς τε πόδας τε
ὀρθὸν ἐν ἱστοπέδῃ, ἐκ δ' αὐτοῦ πείρατ' ἀνῆπτον·
αὐτοὶ δ' ἑζόμενοι πολιὴν ἅλα τύπτον ἐρετμοῖς.
ἀλλ' ὅτε τόσσον ἀπῆν ὅσσον τε γέγωνε βοήσας,
ῥίμφα διώκοντες, τὰς δ' οὐ λάθεν ὠκύαλος νηῦς
ἐγγύθεν ὀρνυμένη, λιγυρὴν δ' ἔντυνον ἀοιδήν·
‹δεῦρ' ἄγ' ἰών, πολύαιν' Ὀδυσεῦ, μέγα κῦδος Ἀχαιῶν,
νῆα κατάστησον, ἵνα νωϊτέρην ὄπ' ἀκούσῃς.
οὐ γάρ πώ τις τῇδε παρήλασε νηΐ μελαίνῃ,
πρίν γ' ἡμέων μελίγηρυν ἀπὸ στομάτων ὄπ' ἀκοῦσαι,
ἀλλ' ὅ γε τερψάμενος νεῖται καὶ πλείονα εἰδώς.
ἴδμεν γάρ τοι πάνθ' ὅσ' ἐνὶ Τροίῃ εὐρείῃ
Ἀργεῖοι Τρῶές τε θεῶν ἰότητι μόγησαν·
ἴδμεν δ' ὅσσα γένηται ἐπὶ χθονὶ πουλυβοτείρῃ.›
Ὣς φάσαν ἱεῖσαι ὄπα κάλλιμον· αὐτὰρ ἐμὸν κῆρ

with my sharp bronze [sword] cut a large disc of wax in pieces, and kneaded it with my strong hands. And soon the wax grew warm, when my great might and the rays of the lord Helios, son of Hyperion, asserted their power over it. And I filled the ears of all my men with it, one after the other, and they tied me up in the ship hand and foot, standing in the mast-socket, and fastened the rope-ends to the mast itself; and they themselves sat down and beat the grey sea-water with their oars. But when the ship was at the distance at which a man's shout from the land could be heard, and we were moving swiftly on our way, they [the Sirens] noticed the quick ship moving along close by, and they lifted up their clear song: 'Come here, much-praised Odysseus, great glory of the Achaeans; stop your ship to listen to our voice. For no one has ever passed by this way in his black ship without listening to the voice from our lips, sweet as the honeycomb, and without enjoying it, and so gone wiser on his way. For we know all the hardships the Argives and the Trojans suffered in the wide land of Troy at the gods' designs, and we know all that is to be on the all-nourishing earth.'

So they spoke, lifting up their sweet voices; and my heart longed to

ἤθελ' ἀκουέμεναι, λῦσαί τ' ἐκέλευον ἑταίρους,
ὀφρύσι νευστάζων· οἱ δὲ προπεσόντες ἔρεσσον.
αὐτίκα δ' ἀνστάντες Περιμήδης Εὐρύλοχός τε
πλείοσί μ' ἐν δεσμοῖσι δέον μᾶλλόν τε πίεζον.
αὐτὰρ ἐπεὶ δὴ τάς γε παρήλασαν, οὐδ' ἔτ' ἔπειτα
φθογγῆς Σειρήνων ἠκούσαμεν οὐδέ τ' ἀοιδῆς,
αἶψ' ἀπὸ κηρὸν ἕλοντο ἐμοὶ ἐρίηρες ἑταῖροι,
ὅν σφιν ἐπ' ὠσὶν ἄλειψ', ἐμέ τ' ἐκ δεσμῶν ἀνέλυσαν.

(*Odyssey*)

27. Scylla and Charybdis

Ἡμεῖς δὲ στεινωπὸν ἀνεπλέομεν γοόωντες·
ἔνθεν γὰρ Σκύλλη, ἑτέρωθι δὲ δῖα Χάρυβδις
δεινὸν ἀνερροίβδησε θαλάσσης ἁλμυρὸν ὕδωρ.
ἤ τοι ὅτ' ἐξεμέσειε, λέβης ὡς ἐν πυρὶ πολλῷ
πᾶσ' ἀναμορμύρεσκε κυκωμένη· ὑψόσε δ' ἄχνη
ἄκροισι σκοπέλοισιν ἐπ' ἀμφοτέροισιν ἔπιπτεν.
ἀλλ' ὅτ' ἀναβρόξειε θαλάσσης ἁλμυρὸν ὕδωρ,
πᾶσ' ἔντοσθε φάνεσκε κυκωμένη, ἀμφὶ δὲ πέτρη
δεινὸν βεβρύχει, ὑπένερθε δὲ γαῖα φάνεσκε

listen, and I ordered my companions to unbind me, nodding at them with my brow; but they bent over their oars and rowed on. Then Perimedes and Eurylochus rose up quickly and bound me still tighter [against the mast] with more ropes. But when they had moved past them, and we no longer heard the sound of the Sirens or their song, my dear companions at once removed the wax, with which I had filled their ears, and set me free from my bonds.

AND we sailed up the narrow strait, lamenting. For on the one side was Scylla, and on the other mighty Charybdis sucked down the salt sea-water in a terrifying manner. Whenever she belched it forth, she seethed and boiled up like a cauldron on a great fire; and overhead the spray fell on the tops of the cliffs on both sides. But when she gulped the salt sea-water down, she appeared turbulent to her depths, and the rock around roared terribly, and the earth could be seen beneath, dark

ψάμμῳ κυανέη· τοὺς δὲ χλωρὸν δέος ᾕρει.
ἡμεῖς μὲν πρὸς τὴν ἴδομεν δείσαντες ὄλεθρον·
τόφρα δέ μοι Σκύλλη κοίλης ἐκ νηὸς ἑταίρους
ἓξ ἕλεθ', οἳ χερσίν τε βίηφί τε φέρτατοι ἦσαν·
σκεψάμενος δ' ἐς νῆα θοὴν ἅμα καὶ μεθ' ἑταίρους
ἤδη τῶν ἐνόησα πόδας καὶ χεῖρας ὕπερθεν
ὑψόσ' ἀειρομένων· ἐμὲ δὲ φθέγγοντο καλεῦντες
ἐξονομακλήδην, τότε γ' ὕστατον, ἀχνύμενοι κῆρ.
ὡς δ' ὅτ' ἐπὶ προβόλῳ ἁλιεὺς περιμήκεϊ ῥάβδῳ
ἰχθύσι τοῖς ὀλίγοισι δόλον κατὰ εἴδατα βάλλων
ἐς πόντον προΐησι βοὸς κέρας ἀγραύλοιο,
ἀσπαίροντα δ' ἔπειτα λαβὼν ἔρριψε θύραζε,
ὣς οἵ γ' ἀσπαίροντες ἀείροντο προτὶ πέτρας·
αὐτοῦ δ' εἰνὶ θύρῃσι κατήσθιε κεκλήγοντας,
χεῖρας ἐμοὶ ὀρέγοντας ἐν αἰνῇ δηϊοτῆτι.
οἴκτιστον δὴ κεῖνο ἐμοῖς ἴδον ὀφθαλμοῖσι
πάντων ὅσσ' ἐμόγησα πόρους ἁλὸς ἐξερεείνων.

(*Odyssey*)

with sand; and pale fear took hold of the men. We looked towards
her, fearing destruction; but Scylla picked up from my hollow ship six
of my companions, the most powerful and hardiest of hand. And look-
ing into the swift ship to find my men, I saw their feet and hands as
they were lifted high up; and they cried out aloud to me in their agony,
and called me by my name – then for the last time. And, as when a
fisherman on some headland lets his baits down with a long rod to
snare the little fishes below, and casts into the water the horn of an ox
that lives on the fields, and, catching each, flings them writhing on the
shore, so were they lifted up writhing on to the cliff. And there, in her
home, she devoured them, as they shrieked and stretched out their
hands to me in the terrible death-struggle. And that was the most pitiful
thing my eyes have seen in all my labours as I have searched out paths
across the sea.

18. Homecoming

Εὖτ' ἀστὴρ ὑπερέσχε φαάντατος, ὅς τε μάλιστα
ἔρχεται ἀγγέλλων φάος Ἠοῦς ἠριγενείης,
τῆμος δὴ νήσῳ προσεπίλνατο ποντοπόρος νηῦς.

Φόρκυνος δέ τίς ἐστι λιμήν, ἁλίοιο γέροντος,
ἐν δήμῳ Ἰθάκης· δύο δὲ προβλῆτες ἐν αὐτῷ
ἀκταὶ ἀπορρῶγες, λιμένος ποτιπεπτηυῖαι,
αἵ τ' ἀνέμων σκεπόωσι δυσαήων μέγα κῦμα
ἔκτοθεν· ἔντοσθεν δέ τ' ἄνευ δεσμοῖο μένουσι
νῆες ἐΰσσελμοι, ὅτ' ἂν ὅρμου μέτρον ἵκωνται.
αὐτὰρ ἐπὶ κρατὸς λιμένος τανύφυλλος ἐλαίη,
ἀγχόθι δ' αὐτῆς ἄντρον ἐπήρατον ἠεροειδές,
ἱρὸν νυμφάων αἳ νηϊάδες καλέονται.
ἐν δὲ κρητῆρές τε καὶ ἀμφιφορῆες ἔασι
λάϊνοι· ἔνθα δ' ἔπειτα τιθαιβώσσουσι μέλισσαι.
ἐν δ' ἱστοὶ λίθεοι περιμήκεες, ἔνθα τε νύμφαι
φάρε' ὑφαίνουσιν ἁλιπόρφυρα, θαῦμα ἰδέσθαι·
ἐν δ' ὕδατ' ἀενάοντα. δύω δέ τέ οἱ θύραι εἰσίν,
αἱ μὲν πρὸς Βορέαο καταιβαταὶ ἀνθρώποισιν,
αἱ δ' αὖ πρὸς Νότου εἰσὶ θεώτεραι· οὐδέ τι κείνη
ἄνδρες ἐσέρχονται, ἀλλ' ἀθανάτων ὁδός ἐστιν.

WHEN the brightest of all stars rose, that which comes heralding the light of early dawn, then the seafaring ship drew near the island.

There is in the land of Ithaca a certain harbour of Phorcys, the old man of the sea, with two headlands, sheer cliffs which close in together round the harbour and break the mighty waves that the stormy winds roll outside; inside, well-decked ships ride without moorings, when once they have reached the place of anchorage. Now at the head of the harbour there is a long-leaved olive tree, and close by is a lovely shadowy cave, sacred to the nymphs called the Naiads. And in it are mixing bowls and stone jars, and bees also hive there. There, too, are long looms of stone, on which the nymphs weave cloth dyed in purple, a marvel to see, and there are springs of water always flowing. There are two entrances to the cave, one facing Boreas [the north wind] through which men may go down, but that facing Notos [the south] is rather for the gods; through it no men enter, for it is the path of the immortals.

"Ενθ' οἵ γ' εἰσέλασαν πρὶν εἰδότες. ἡ μὲν ἔπειτα
ἠπείρῳ ἐπέκελσεν, ὅσον τ' ἐπὶ ἥμισυ πάσης,
σπερχομένη· τοίων γὰρ ἐπείγετο χέρσ' ἐρετάων·
οἱ δ' ἐκ νηὸς βάντες ἐϋζύγου ἠπειρόνδε
πρῶτον Ὀδυσσῆα γλαφυρῆς ἐκ νηὸς ἄειραν
αὐτῷ σύν τε λίνῳ καὶ ῥήγεϊ σιγαλόεντι,
κὰδ δ' ἄρ' ἐπὶ ψαμάθῳ ἔθεσαν δεδμημένον ὕπνῳ.

(*Odyssey*)

19. The Dog Argos

"Ὣς οἱ μὲν τοιαῦτα πρὸς ἀλλήλους ἀγόρευον·
ἂν δὲ κύων κεφαλήν τε καὶ οὔατα κείμενος ἔσχεν,
Ἄργος, Ὀδυσσῆος ταλασίφρονος, ὅν ῥά ποτ' αὐτὸς
θρέψε μέν, οὐδ' ἀπόνητο, πάρος δ' εἰς Ἴλιον ἱρὴν
ᾤχετο. τὸν δὲ πάροιθεν ἀγίνεσκον νέοι ἄνδρες
αἶγας ἐπ' ἀγροτέρας ἠδὲ πρόκας ἠδὲ λαγωούς·
δὴ τότε κεῖτ' ἀπόθεστος ἀποιχομένοιο ἄνακτος,
ἐν πολλῇ κόπρῳ, ἥ οἱ προπάροιθε θυράων
ἡμιόνων τε βοῶν τε ἅλις κέχυτ', ὄφρ' ἂν ἄγοιεν
δμῶες Ὀδυσσῆος τέμενος μέγα κοπρήσοντες·

Having knowledge of the place, they brought [their ship] in there; and in full course the vessel ran half her length up the shore; for she was driven by the hands of such strong oarsmen. They alighted on to the land from the well-benched ship, and first lifted Odysseus out of the hollow ship, just as he was, in the sheet of linen and the bright rug, and put him on the sand still heavy with sleep.

So they spoke to one another. And a dog raised his head and pricked up his ears there where he lay – Argos, [the dog] of stout-hearted Odysseus, which he himself had once bred, but had not been able to enjoy; for he had left for sacred Ilium too soon. In the past the young men used to take the dog to chase wild goats and deer and hares; but then, his master far away, he lay despised in the deep dung of mules and bulls which lay in heaps in front of the doors until the servants of Odysseus carried it away to fertilize his large estate. There the dog

ἔνθα κύων κεῖτ' Ἄργος, ἐνίπλειος κυνοραιστέων.
δὴ τότε γ', ὡς ἐνόησεν Ὀδυσσέα ἐγγὺς ἐόντα,
οὐρῇ μέν ῥ' ὅ γ' ἔσηνε καὶ οὔατα κάββαλεν ἄμφω,
ἄσσον δ' οὐκέτ' ἔπειτα δυνήσατο οἷο ἄνακτος
ἐλθέμεν· αὐτὰρ ὁ νόσφιν ἰδὼν ἀπομόρξατο δάκρυ,
ῥεῖα λαθὼν Εὔμαιον, ἄφαρ δ' ἐρεείνετο μύθῳ·
‹Εὔμαι', ἦ μάλα θαῦμα κύων ὅδε κεῖτ' ἐνὶ κόπρῳ.
καλὸς μὲν δέμας ἐστίν, ἀτὰρ τόδε γ' οὐ σάφα οἶδα,
εἰ δὴ καὶ ταχὺς ἔσκε θέειν ἐπὶ εἴδεϊ τῷδε,
ἦ αὔτως οἷοί τε τραπεζῆες κύνες ἀνδρῶν
γίγνοντ', ἀγλαΐης δ' ἕνεκεν κομέουσιν ἄνακτες.›
    Τὸν δ' ἀπαμειβόμενος προσέφης, Εὔμαιε συβῶτα·
‹καὶ λίην ἀνδρός γε κύων ὅδε τῆλε θανόντος.
εἰ τοιόσδ' εἴη ἠμὲν δέμας ἠδὲ καὶ ἔργα,
οἷόν μιν Τροίηνδε κιὼν κατέλειπεν Ὀδυσσεύς,
αἶψά κε θηήσαιο ἰδὼν ταχυτῆτα καὶ ἀλκήν.
οὐ μὲν γάρ τι φύγεσκε βαθείης βένθεσιν ὕλης
κνώδαλον, ὅττι δίοιτο· καὶ ἴχνεσι γὰρ περιῄδη·
νῦν δ' ἔχεται κακότητι, ἄναξ δέ οἱ ἄλλοθι πάτρης
ὤλετο, τὸν δὲ γυναῖκες ἀκηδέες οὐ κομέουσι.

Argos lay, full of vermin. Yet, even now, when he was aware of
Odysseus standing close by, he wagged his tail and dropped his ears;
but he no longer had the strength to come nearer to his master. And he
[Odysseus] looked away, and wiped a tear away, without difficulty
avoiding Eumaeus' notice; and at once asked him, saying: 'Eumaeus,
it is really most strange [to find] this hound lying here in the dung. He
is well built, but I do not know for certain whether he has speed with
this beauty, or whether he is only good-looking like the dogs men
feed at their table, looking after them simply to show them off.'
    Then, swineherd Eumaeus, you answered: 'This is in fact the dog of
a man that has died in a land far away; if he was now what he once was
in limb and in achievements, when Odysseus left him to go to Troy,
you would soon marvel at the sight of his swiftness and his strength.
There was no beast that could escape him in the depths of the thick
wood when he was hunting; for on the scent, too, he was the keenest
hound. But now he is ugly, and his master has perished far away from
his own country, and the heartless women take no care of him. Ser-

93

δμῶες δ', εὖτ' ἄν μηκέτ' ἐπικρατέωσιν ἄνακτες,
οὐκέτ' ἔπειτ' ἐθέλουσιν ἐναίσιμα ἐργάζεσθαι·
ἥμισυ γάρ τ' ἀρετῆς ἀποαίνυται εὐρύοπα Ζεὺς
ἀνέρος, εὖτ' ἄν μιν κατὰ δούλιον ἦμαρ ἕλησιν.)
  Ὣς εἰπὼν εἰσῆλθε δόμους εὐναιετάοντας,
βῆ δ' ἰθὺς μεγάροιο μετὰ μνηστῆρας ἀγαυούς.
Ἄργον δ' αὖ κατὰ μοῖρ' ἔλαβεν μέλανος θανάτοιο,
αὐτίκ' ἰδόντ' Ὀδυσῆα ἐεικοστῷ ἐνιαυτῷ.

(*Odyssey*)

20. The Slaying of the Suitors

Σιγῇ δ' ἐξ οἴκοιο Φιλοίτιος ἆλτο θύραζε,
κλήϊσεν δ' ἄρ' ἔπειτα θύρας εὐερκέος αὐλῆς.
κεῖτο δ' ὑπ' αἰθούσῃ ὅπλον νεὸς ἀμφιελίσσης
βύβλινον, ᾧ ῥ' ἐπέδησε θύρας, ἐς δ' ἥϊεν αὐτός·
ἕζετ' ἔπειτ' ἐπὶ δίφρον ἰών, ἔνθεν περ ἀνέστη,
εἰσορόων Ὀδυσῆα. ὁ δ' ἤδη τόξον ἐνώμα
πάντῃ ἀναστρωφῶν, πειρώμενος ἔνθα καὶ ἔνθα,
μὴ κέρα' ἶπες ἔδοιεν ἀποιχομένοιο ἄνακτος.
ὧδε δέ τις εἴπεσκεν ἰδὼν ἐς πλησίον ἄλλον·

vants are not inclined to honest service when their masters are not ruling over them; for far-sounding Zeus takes away the half of a man's virtue when the day of slavery comes upon him.'

So he spoke, and entered the well-placed house, and went straight to the hall to join the proud suitors. But the fate of black death came upon Argos, the moment he saw Odysseus in the twentieth year.

THEN Philoetius jumped silently out of the house, and barred the gates of the well-fenced court. Beneath the gallery lay the cable of a curved ship made of the byblus plant; with this he fastened the gates, and then he came in himself. After that he went and sat on the seat from which he had risen, and watched Odysseus. He [Odysseus] was already handling the bow, turning it about every way, and trying it out on this side and on that, lest the worms had eaten the horns when the master of the bow was away. Looking at his neighbour, a man would say:

‹ἤ τις θηητὴρ καὶ ἐπίκλοπος ἔπλετο τόξων.
ἦ ῥά νύ που τοιαῦτα καὶ αὐτῷ οἴκοθι κεῖται,
ἦ ὅ γ' ἐφορμᾶται ποιησέμεν, ὡς ἐνὶ χερσὶ
νωμᾷ ἔνθα καὶ ἔνθα κακῶν ἔμπαιος ἀλήτης.›
   Ἄλλος δ' αὖ εἴπεσκε νέων ὑπερηνορεόντων·
‹αἲ γὰρ δὴ τοσσοῦτον ὀνήσιος ἀντιάσειεν
ὡς οὗτός ποτε τοῦτο δυνήσεται ἐντανύσασθαι.›
   Ὣς ἄρ' ἔφαν μνηστῆρες· ἀτὰρ πολύμητις Ὀδυσσεύς,
αὐτίκ' ἐπεὶ μέγα τόξον ἐβάστασε καὶ ἴδε πάντη,
ὡς ὅτ' ἀνὴρ φόρμιγγος ἐπιστάμενος καὶ ἀοιδῆς
ῥηϊδίως ἐτάνυσσε νέῳ περὶ κόλλοπι χορδήν,
ἅψας ἀμφοτέρωθεν ἐϋστρεφὲς ἔντερον οἰός,
ὣς ἄρ' ἄτερ σπουδῆς τάνυσεν μέγα τόξον Ὀδυσσεύς.
δεξιτερῇ δ' ἄρα χειρὶ λαβὼν πειρήσατο νευρῆς·
ἡ δ' ὑπὸ καλὸν ἄεισε, χελιδόνι εἰκέλη αὐδήν.
μνηστῆρσιν δ' ἄρ' ἄχος γένετο μέγα, πᾶσι δ' ἄρα χρὼς
ἐτράπετο. Ζεὺς δὲ μεγάλ' ἔκτυπε σήματα φαίνων·
γήθησέν τ' ἄρ' ἔπειτα πολύτλας δῖος Ὀδυσσεύς,
ὅττι ῥά οἱ τέρας ἧκε Κρόνου πάϊς ἀγκυλομήτεω·
εἵλετο δ' ὠκὺν ὀϊστόν, ὅ οἱ παρέκειτο τραπέζῃ
γυμνός· τοὶ δ' ἄλλοι κοίλης ἔντοσθε φαρέτρης

'He has indeed a good eye, and a shrewd turn for a bow! It looks as if he himself has such a bow lying at home, or else he is set on making one; so does this evil-witted beggar turn it this side and that in his hands.'

And again another of the haughty young men would say: 'May that fellow have as much profit from that bow as ever he has chance of managing to bend it!'

So spoke the suitors, but Odysseus of many counsels had swiftly lifted the great bow and examined it on every side, as a man skilled in the lyre and in minstrelsy easily stretches a string round a new peg after tying the twisted sheep-gut at both ends; so without effort Odysseus bent the great bow. And he took it in his right hand and tried out the bow-string, which rang sweetly at the touch like a swallow singing. Then great terror seized the suitors, and the colour of their skin was changed; and Zeus thundered loudly, making his omen clear. And long-suffering, godly Odysseus was glad because the son of sharp-witted Cronos had sent him a sign. Then he took up a swift arrow which lay bare on his table; the other arrows were in the hollow quiver, those

κείατο, τῶν τάχ' ἔμελλον 'Αχαιοὶ πειρήσεσθαι.
τόν ῥ' ἐπὶ πήχει ἑλὼν ἕλκεν νευρὴν γλυφίδας τε,
αὐτόθεν ἐκ δίφροιο καθήμενος, ἧκε δ' ὀϊστὸν
ἄντα τιτυσκόμενος, πελέκεων δ' οὐκ ἤμβροτε πάντων
πρώτης στειλειῆς, διὰ δ' ἀμπερὲς ἦλθε θύραζε
ἰὸς χαλκοβαρής· ὁ δὲ Τηλέμαχον προσέειπε·
‹Τηλέμαχ', οὔ σ' ὁ ξεῖνος ἐνὶ μεγάροισιν ἐλέγχει
ἥμενος, οὐδέ τι τοῦ σκοποῦ ἤμβροτον οὐδέ τι τόξον
δὴν ἔκαμον τανύων· ἔτι μοι μένος ἔμπεδόν ἐστιν,
οὐχ ὥς με μνηστῆρες ἀτιμάζοντες ὄνονται.
νῦν δ' ὥρη καὶ δόρπον 'Αχαιοῖσιν τετυκέσθαι
ἐν φάει, αὐτὰρ ἔπειτα καὶ ἄλλως ἑψιάασθαι
μολπῇ καὶ φόρμιγγι· τὰ γάρ τ' ἀναθήματα δαιτός.›
῏Η καὶ ἐπ' ὀφρύσι νεῦσεν· ὁ δ' ἀμφέθετο ξίφος ὀξὺ
Τηλέμαχος, φίλος υἱὸς 'Οδυσσῆος θείοιο,
ἀμφὶ δὲ χεῖρα φίλην βάλεν ἔγχεϊ, ἄγχι δ' ἄρ' αὐτοῦ
πὰρ θρόνον ἑστήκει κεκορυθμένος αἴθοπι χαλκῷ.

Αὐτὰρ ὁ γυμνώθη ῥακέων πολύμητις 'Οδυσσεύς,
ἆλτο δ' ἐπὶ μέγαν οὐδόν, ἔχων βιὸν ἠδὲ φαρέτρην
ἰῶν ἐμπλείην, ταχέας δ' ἐκχεύατ' ὀϊστοὺς

which the Achaeans were soon to feel. He put this one on the bridge of the bow, and held the notch and drew back the string from the seat on which he sat, and with straight aim shot the arrow, and did not miss one of the axes, beginning from the first axe-handle; and the bronze-weighted arrow passed clean through, and out. And he said to Telemachus: 'Telemachus, your guest who sits in the palace does not shame you. I did not miss my mark, nor did I weary myself much in bending the bow. My strength is still steady, despite the suitors' insults and contempt. But now, while it is still light, it is time for dinner to be prepared for the Achaeans, and then especially we must amuse ourselves with dancing and the lyre, for these are the crown of the feast.'

He said this and nodded with his brows; and Telemachus, the dear son of divine Odysseus, buckled on his sharp sword about him, and took the spear in his hand, and stood by his seat at his father's side, armed with the flashing bronze.

Then cunning Odysseus stripped off his rags and leaped on to the great threshold with his bow and quiver full of arrows, and poured out all the swift shafts, there before his feet, and spoke among the suitors:

αὐτοῦ πρόσθε ποδῶν, μετὰ δὲ μνηστῆρσιν ἔειπεν·
⟨οὗτος μὲν δὴ ἄεθλος ἀάατος ἐκτετέλεσται·
νῦν αὖτε σκοπὸν ἄλλον, ὃν οὔ πώ τις βάλεν ἀνήρ,
εἴσομαι, αἴ κε τύχωμι, πόρῃ δέ μοι εὖχος Ἀπόλλων.⟩
ἦ καὶ ἐπ᾽ Ἀντινόῳ ἰθύνετο πικρὸν ὀϊστόν.

. . . .

Πάπτηνεν δ᾽ Ὀδυσεὺς καθ᾽ ἑὸν δόμον, εἴ τις ἔτ᾽ ἀνδρῶν
ζωὸς ὑποκλοπέοιτο, ἀλύσκων κῆρα μέλαιναν.
τοὺς δὲ ἴδεν μάλα πάντας ἐν αἵματι καὶ κονίῃσι
πεπτεῶτας πολλούς, ὥς τ᾽ ἰχθύας, οὕς θ᾽ ἁλιῆες
κοῖλον ἐς αἰγιαλὸν πολιῆς ἔκτοσθε θαλάσσης
δικτύῳ ἐξέρυσαν πολυωπῷ· οἱ δέ τε πάντες
κύμαθ᾽ ἁλὸς ποθέοντες ἐπὶ ψαμάθοισι κέχυνται·
τῶν μέν τ᾽ Ἠέλιος φαέθων ἐξείλετο θυμόν·
ὣς τότ᾽ ἄρα μνηστῆρες ἐπ᾽ ἀλλήλοισι κέχυντο.

(Odyssey)

'Now at last this terrible trial is over, and now I will see if Apollo will
grant me fame and I may hit another target, one which no man has yet
hit.'

He spoke, and aimed the bitter arrow at Antinous...

And Odysseus peered through his house to see if any man was still alive
and hiding to escape black death. But he found them all fallen in their
blood in the dust, like the fish that the fishermen with their fine-meshed
net draw from the grey sea to the hollow of a beach; all the fish longing
for the salt sea waves are heaped upon the sand, and the shining sun
takes their life away. So now the suitors lay heaped upon each other.

21. The Recognition

Ὣς φάτο, τῆς δ' αὐτοῦ λύτο γούνατα καὶ φίλον ἦτορ,
σήματ' ἀναγνούσῃ τά οἱ ἔμπεδα πέφραδ' Ὀδυσσεύς·
δακρύσασα δ' ἔπειτ' ἰθὺς δράμεν, ἀμφὶ δὲ χεῖρας
δειρῇ βάλλ' Ὀδυσῆϊ, κάρη δ' ἔκυσ' ἠδὲ προσηύδα·
‹μή μοι, Ὀδυσσεῦ, σκύζευ, ἐπεὶ τά περ ἄλλα μάλιστα
ἀνθρώπων πέπνυσο· θεοὶ δ' ὤπαζον ὀϊζύν,
οἳ νῶϊν ἀγάσαντο παρ' ἀλλήλοισι μένοντε
ἥβης ταρπῆναι καὶ γήραος οὐδὸν ἱκέσθαι.
αὐτὰρ μὴ νῦν μα τόδε χώεο μηδὲ νεμέσσα,
οὕνεκά σ' οὐ τὸ πρῶτον, ἐπεὶ ἴδον, ὧδ' ἀγάπησα.
αἰεὶ γάρ μοι θυμὸς ἐνὶ στήθεσσι φίλοισιν
ἐρρίγει μή τίς με βροτῶν ἀπάφοιτο ἔπεσσιν
ἐλθών· πολλοὶ γὰρ κακὰ κέρδεα βουλεύουσιν.
οὐδέ κεν Ἀργείη Ἑλένη, Διὸς ἐκγεγαυῖα,
ἀνδρὶ παρ' ἀλλοδαπῷ ἐμίγη φιλότητι καὶ εὐνῇ,
εἰ ᾔδη ὅ μιν αὖτις ἀρήϊοι υἷες Ἀχαιῶν
ἀξέμεναι οἴκόνδε φίλην ἐς πατρίδ' ἔμελλον.
τὴν δ' ἦ τοι ῥέξαι θεὸς ὦρσεν ἔργον ἀεικές·
τὴν δ' ἄτην οὐ πρόσθεν ἑῷ ἐγκάτθετο θυμῷ

So he spoke, and at once her knees were loosened and her heart melted
in her as she recognized the clear indications that Odysseus gave her.
Then she wept and ran straight towards him and threw her arms round
Odysseus' neck, and kissed his head and said: 'Do not be angry with
me, Odysseus; for you were always the wisest of men. It is the gods
that gave us sorrow, who begrudged us that we should stay together
and enjoy our youth, and so come to the threshold of old age. So now
do not be angry with me, nor hold it against me that I did not welcome
you thus as soon as I saw you. For the heart in my breast always
shuddered in fear that some man should come and deceive me with his
words; for there are many who devise evil schemes for gain. No, even
Argive Helen, the daughter of Zeus, would not have lain with a
stranger and taken him for lover, had she known that the warlike sons
of the Achaeans would bring her home again to her own dear country.
However, it was a god that urged her to that shameful deed; never be-
fore that did she have in her heart the thought of this bitter folly, from

λυγρήν, ἐξ ἧς πρῶτα καὶ ἡμέας ἵκετο πένθος.
νῦν δ᾽, ἐπεὶ ἤδη σήματ᾽ ἀριφραδέα κατέλεξας
εὐνῆς ἡμετέρης, τὴν οὐ βροτὸς ἄλλος ὀπώπει,
ἀλλ᾽ οἶοι σύ τ᾽ ἐγώ τε καὶ ἀμφίπολος μία μούνη,
᾽Ακτορίς, ἥν μοι δῶκε πατὴρ ἔτι δεῦρο κιούσῃ,
ἣ νῶϊν εἴρυτο θύρας πυκινοῦ θαλάμοιο,
πείθεις δή μευ θυμόν, ἀπηνέα περ μάλ᾽ ἐόντα.)
    ῝Ως φάτο, τῷ δ᾽ ἔτι μᾶλλον ὑφ᾽ ἵμερον ὦρσε γόοιο·
κλαῖε δ᾽ ἔχων ἄλοχον θυμαρέα, κεδνὰ ἰδυῖαν.
ὡς δ᾽ ὅτ᾽ ἄν ἀσπάσιος γῆ νηχομένοισι φανήῃ,
ὦν τε Ποσειδάων εὐεργέα νῆ᾽ ἐνὶ πόντῳ
ῥαίσῃ, ἐπειγομένην ἀνέμῳ καὶ κύματι πηγῷ·
παῦροι δ᾽ ἐξέφυγον πολιῆς ἁλὸς ἠπειρόνδε
νηχόμενοι, πολλὴ δὲ περὶ χροΐ τέτροφεν ἅλμη,
ἀσπάσιοι δ᾽ ἐπέβαν γαίης, κακότητα φυγόντες·
ὣς ἄρα τῇ ἀσπαστὸς ἔην πόσις εἰσοροώσῃ,
δειρῆς δ᾽ οὔ πω πάμπαν ἀφίετο πήχεε λευκώ.

(Odyssey)

which sorrow first came to us too. But now that you have given me a clear description of our bed, which no other mortal man has seen, except you and I and one single servant, the daughter of Actor, whom my father gave me before I came here – the one who guarded the doors of our strong bridal chamber – now you convince my mind, although it is a mind hard to persuade.'

So she spoke, and stirred in him a still greater longing to weep. And he wept as he embraced his beloved and faithful wife. And, as the sight of land is welcome to swimmers, when Poseidon has broken their well-made ship on the sea, driven by the wind and the swelling waves, and only a few have escaped the grey sea-water and swum to the shore, their bodies crusted all over with brine, and with joy have set foot on land and escaped an evil death; so welcome to her was the sight of her husband, and she would not let her white arms go from his neck.

99

HOMER

22. The Suitors' Last Journey

Ἑρμῆς δὲ ψυχὰς Κυλλήνιος ἐξεκαλεῖτο
ἀνδρῶν μνηστήρων· ἔχε δὲ ῥάβδον μετὰ χερσὶ
καλὴν χρυσείην, τῇ τ' ἀνδρῶν ὄμματα θέλγει
ὧν ἐθέλει, τοὺς δ' αὖτε καὶ ὑπνώοντας ἐγείρει·
τῇ ῥ' ἄγε κινήσας, ταὶ δὲ τρίζουσαι ἕποντο.
ὡς δ' ὅτε νυκτερίδες μυχῷ ἄντρου θεσπεσίοιο
τρίζουσαι ποτέονται, ἐπεί κέ τις ἀποπέσῃσιν
ὁρμαθοῦ ἐκ πέτρης, ἀνά τ' ἀλλήλῃσιν ἔχονται,
ὣς αἱ τετριγυῖαι ἅμ' ἤισαν· ἦρχε δ' ἄρα σφιν
Ἑρμείας ἀκάκητα κατ' εὐρώεντα κέλευθα.
πὰρ δ' ἴσαν Ὠκεανοῦ τε ῥοὰς καὶ Λευκάδα πέτρην,
ἠδὲ παρ' Ἡελίοιο πύλας καὶ δῆμον ὀνείρων
ἤισαν· αἶψα δ' ἵκοντο κατ' ἀσφοδελὸν λειμῶνα,
ἔνθα τε ναίουσι ψυχαί, εἴδωλα καμόντων.

(Odyssey)

Now Cyllenian Hermes called the souls of the suitors out [of the palace], and he held in his hand his beautiful golden wand with which he lulls to sleep the eyes of those he chooses, and [with which he] wakes up others though they are sleeping. With this he roused [the souls] and led them, and they followed him gibbering. And as bats flit gibbering in the depths of a wonderful cave, when one has fallen down from the cluster on the rock where they cling to one another high up, so the souls gibbered as they set out together; and Hermes the gracious one led them down the dank paths. They passed the streams of Ocean and the White Rock, and they passed beyond the gates of the Sun, and the land of dreams; and soon they came to the meadow of asphodel, where souls live, the phantoms of the dead.

HESIOD

date unknown

23. Pandora

Κρύψαντες γὰρ ἔχουσι θεοὶ βίον ἀνθρώποισιν·
ῥηιδίως γάρ κεν καὶ ἐπ' ἤματι ἐργάσσαιο,
ὥστε σε κεἰς ἐνιαυτὸν ἔχειν καὶ ἀεργὸν ἐόντα·
αἶψά κε πηδάλιον μὲν ὑπὲρ καπνοῦ καταθεῖο,
ἔργα βοῶν δ' ἀπόλοιτο καὶ ἡμιόνων ταλαεργῶν.
ἀλλὰ Ζεὺς ἔκρυψε χολωσάμενος φρεσὶν ᾗσιν,
ὅττι μιν ἐξαπάτησε Προμηθεὺς ἀγκυλομήτης·
τούνεκ' ἄρ' ἀνθρώποισιν ἐμήσατο κήδεα λυγρά.
κρύψε δὲ πῦρ· τὸ μὲν αὖτις ἐὺς πάϊς Ἰαπετοῖο
ἔκλεψ' ἀνθρώποισι Διὸς πάρα μητιόεντος
ἐν κοΐλῳ νάρθηκι λαθὼν Δία τερπικέραυνον.
τὸν δὲ χολωσάμενος προσέφη νεφεληγερέτα Ζεύς·
‹Ἰαπετιονίδη, πάντων πέρι μήδεα εἰδώς,
χαίρεις πῦρ κλέψας καὶ ἐμὰς φρένας ἠπεροπεύσας,
σοί τ' αὐτῷ μέγα πῆμα καὶ ἀνδράσιν ἐσσομένοισιν.
τοῖς δ' ἐγὼ ἀντὶ πυρὸς δώσω κακόν, ᾧ κεν ἅπαντες
τέρπωνται κατὰ θυμὸν ἑὸν κακὸν ἀμφαγαπῶντες.›
Ὣς ἔφατ'· ἐκ δ' ἐγέλασσε πατὴρ ἀνδρῶν τε θεῶν τε.

FOR the gods keep hidden from men the means of livelihood. Otherwise, working even for one day only you would easily make enough to provide you for a whole year without working; soon you would put aside the rudder [of your ship] over the smoke [of your hearth], and the work of the oxen and the sturdy mules would disappear. But Zeus grew angry at heart and hid it, because crafty Prometheus had deceived him. For this he devised sorrow and suffering for men. He hid fire; but for the sake of mankind the noble son of Iapetus stole this away again from Zeus wise in counsel, in a hollow fennel-stalk, escaping the notice of Zeus who delights in thunder. And Zeus the cloud-gatherer said to him in anger:

'Son of Iapetus, most cunning of all men, you are pleased that you have stolen fire and outwitted me; but it will be a great evil for you and for the men that are to come. In exchange for fire I will give them an evil in which in their hearts they will all rejoice as they embrace their own destruction.'

So said the father of men and gods, and he laughed aloud. And he

Ἥφαιστον δ' ἐκέλευσε περικλυτὸν ὅττι τάχιστα
γαῖαν ὕδει φύρειν, ἐν δ' ἀνθρώπου θέμεν αὐδὴν
καὶ σθένος, ἀθανάτῃς δὲ θεῇς εἰς ὦπα ἐίσκειν
παρθενικῆς καλὸν εἶδος ἐπήρατον· αὐτὰρ Ἀθήνην
ἔργα διδασκῆσαι, πολυδαίδαλον ἱστὸν ὑφαίνειν·
καὶ χάριν ἀμφιχέαι κεφαλῇ χρυσέην Ἀφροδίτην
καὶ πόθον ἀργαλέον καὶ γυιοκόρους μελεδώνας·
ἐν δὲ θέμεν κύνεόν τε νόον καὶ ἐπίκλοπον ἦθος
Ἑρμείην ἤνωγε, διάκτορον Ἀργεϊφόντην.

Ὣς ἔφαθ'· οἱ δ' ἐπίθοντο Διὶ Κρονίωνι ἄνακτι.
αὐτίκα δ' ἐκ γαίης πλάσσεν κλυτὸς Ἀμφιγυήεις
παρθένῳ αἰδοίῃ ἴκελον Κρονίδεω διὰ βουλάς·
ζῶσε δὲ καὶ κόσμησε θεὰ γλαυκῶπις Ἀθήνη·
ἀμφὶ δέ οἱ Χάριτές τε θεαὶ καὶ πότνια Πειθὼ
ὅρμους χρυσείους ἔθεσαν χροΐ· ἀμφὶ δὲ τήν γε
Ὧραι καλλίκομοι στέφον ἄνθεσιν εἰαρινοῖσιν·
ἐν δ' ἄρα οἱ στήθεσσι διάκτορος Ἀργεϊφόντης
ψεύδεά θ' αἱμυλίους τε λόγους καὶ ἐπίκλοπον ἦθος
θῆκε θεῶν κῆρυξ, ὀνόμηνε δὲ τήνδε γυναῖκα
Πανδώρην, ὅτι πάντες Ὀλύμπια δώματ' ἔχοντες
δῶρον ἐδώρησαν, πῆμ' ἀνδράσιν ἀλφηστῇσιν.

ordered famous Hephaestus speedily to mix earth with water and put in
it human speech and strength, and give to the beautiful, lovable form
of a maiden a face like that of the immortal goddesses; and he ordered
Athene to teach her the crafts, how to weave a richly-wrought web;
and [he ordered] golden Aphrodite to shed grace round her head, and
painful desire and cares that weary the limbs; and he told Hermes the
guide, the slayer of Argus, to put in her a shameless mind and a nature
full of deceit.

So he spoke, and they obeyed king Zeus, the son of Cronos. At
once the famous lame god shaped out of earth the likeness of a modest
maiden according to the wishes of the son of Cronos. And the goddess
grey-eyed Athene girdled her and dressed her, and the divine Graces
and venerable Persuasion put necklaces of gold round her neck, and
the fair-tressed Hours put round her head a garland of spring flowers.
Moreover, the Guide, the Slayer of Argus, the herald of the gods, put
in her breast lies and cunning words and a deceitful nature, and he
called this woman Pandora, because all who dwell in the halls of
Olympus gave her a gift, to be an evil to men who eat bread.

Αὐτὰρ ἐπεὶ δόλον αἰπὺν ἀμήχανον ἐξετέλεσσεν,
εἰς Ἐπιμηθέα πέμπε πατὴρ κλυτὸν Ἀργεϊφόντην
δῶρον ἄγοντα, θεῶν ταχὺν ἄγγελον· οὐδ᾽ Ἐπιμηθεὺς
ἐφράσαθ᾽, ὥς οἱ ἔειπε Προμηθεὺς μή ποτε δῶρον
δέξασθαι πὰρ Ζηνὸς Ὀλυμπίου, ἀλλ᾽ ἀποπέμπειν
ἐξοπίσω, μή πού τι κακὸν θνητοῖσι γένηται.
αὐτὰρ ὁ δεξάμενος, ὅτε δὴ κακὸν εἶχ᾽, ἐνόησεν.

Πρὶν μὲν γὰρ ζώεσκον ἐπὶ χθονὶ φῦλ᾽ ἀνθρώπων
νόσφιν ἄτερ τε κακῶν καὶ ἄτερ χαλεποῖο πόνοιο
νούσων τ᾽ ἀργαλέων, αἵ τ᾽ ἀνδράσι Κῆρας ἔδωκαν.
ἀλλὰ γυνὴ χείρεσσι πίθου μέγα πῶμ᾽ ἀφελοῦσα
ἐσκέδασ᾽. ἀνθρώποισι δ᾽ ἐμήσατο κήδεα λυγρά.
μούνη δ᾽ αὐτόθι Ἐλπὶς ἐν ἀρρήκτοισι δόμοισιν
ἔνδον ἔμιμνε πίθου ὑπὸ χείλεσιν, οὐδὲ θύραζε
ἐξέπτη· πρόσθεν γὰρ ἐπέλλαβε πῶμα πίθοιο.
ἄλλα δὲ μυρία λυγρὰ κατ᾽ ἀνθρώπους ἀλάληται·
πλείη μὲν γὰρ γαῖα κακῶν, πλείη δὲ θάλασσα·
νοῦσοι δ᾽ ἀνθρώποισιν ἐφ᾽ ἡμέρῃ, αἱ δ᾽ ἐπὶ νυκτὶ
αὐτόματοι φοιτῶσι κακὰ θνητοῖσι φέρουσαι
σιγῇ, ἐπεὶ φωνὴν ἐξείλετο μητίετα Ζεύς.

(*Works and Days*)

But when he had finished the perilous, irresistible snare, the Father sent glorious Argus-Slayer, the swift messenger of the gods, to take it as a gift to Epimetheus. And Epimetheus did not think of what Prometheus had told him, never to accept a gift from Olympian Zeus, but to send it back lest it turn out to be something harmful to men. Instead he accepted the gift, and when he possessed the evil thing, he learnt its meaning.

For, before this time, the tribes of men lived on the earth free from evil, from hard work and from painful diseases, which the Fates give to men. But the woman took the great lid off the jar with her hands and scattered them about. Her plans brought painful suffering to men. Only Hope remained there in the unbreakable home under the lip of the jar, and did not fly away; for before that the lid of the jar stopped her. But other countless evils wander among men: full is the earth of evils, and full the sea. Day and night diseases come upon men of their own accord, silently bringing suffering to mortals, for wise Zeus took speech away from them.

HESIOD

24. The Fifth Generation

Μηκέτ᾽ ἔπειτ᾽ ὤφελλον ἐγὼ πέμπτοισι μετεῖναι
ἀνδράσιν, ἀλλ᾽ ἢ πρόσθε θανεῖν ἢ ἔπειτα γενέσθαι.
νῦν γὰρ δὴ γένος ἐστὶ σιδήρεον· οὐδέ ποτ᾽ ἦμαρ
παύονται καμάτου καὶ ὀϊζύος, οὐδέ τι νύκτωρ
φθειρόμενοι. χαλεπὰς δὲ θεοὶ δώσουσι μερίμνας.
ἀλλ᾽ ἔμπης καὶ τοῖσι μεμείξεται ἐσθλὰ κακοῖσιν.
Ζεὺς δ᾽ ὀλέσει καὶ τοῦτο γένος μερόπων ἀνθρώπων,
εὖτ᾽ ἂν γεινόμενοι πολιοκρόταφοι τελέθωσιν.
οὐδὲ πατὴρ παίδεσσιν ὁμοίιος οὐδέ τι παῖδες,
οὐδὲ ξεῖνος ξεινοδόκῳ καὶ ἑταῖρος ἑταίρῳ,
οὐδὲ κασίγνητος φίλος ἔσσεται, ὡς τὸ πάρος περ.
αἶψα δὲ γηράσκοντας ἀτιμήσουσι τοκῆας·
μέμψονται δ᾽ ἄρα τοὺς χαλεποῖς βάζοντες ἔπεσσι
σχέτλιοι οὐδὲ θεῶν ὄπιν εἰδότες· οὐδέ κεν οἵ γε
γηράντεσσι τοκεῦσιν ἀπὸ θρεπτήρια δοῖεν
χειροδίκαι· ἕτερος δ᾽ ἑτέρου πόλιν ἐξαλαπάξει.
οὐδέ τις εὐόρκου χάρις ἔσσεται οὔτε δικαίου
οὔτ᾽ ἀγαθοῦ, μᾶλλον δὲ κακῶν ῥεκτῆρα καὶ ὕβριν
ἀνέρες αἰνήσουσι· δίκη δ᾽ ἐν χερσί, καὶ αἰδὼς
οὐκ ἔσται· βλάψει δ᾽ ὁ κακὸς τὸν ἀρείονα φῶτα

I WISH, then, I were not among the men of the fifth generation, but either had died before, or been born afterwards. For without doubt today's is a race of iron. They never rest from labour and suffering by day, nor from destruction by night; and the gods shall give them painful cares. But even so, even these shall have some good mingled with their evils. And Zeus will destroy this race of mortal men too, when they shall be born with grey hair on their temples at birth. And the father will not agree with his children, nor the guest with his host, nor friend with friend, nor will brother love brother as in the past. To their parents, as they begin to grow old, children will pay no respect, but will reproach them, addressing them with harsh words – the reckless fools, ignorant of the vengeance of the gods. They will not pay back [anything] to their elderly parents for rearing them; for them might shall be right. One man will sack another's city. There will be no respect for a man who keeps his oath, or for the just or the good; men will rather praise the evil-doer and the man of insolence. Justice will be decided by force, and there will be no honour. The evil will harm the better

μύθοισιν σκολιοῖς ἐνέπων, ἐπὶ δ' ὅρκον ὀμεῖται.
ζῆλος δ' ἀνθρώποισιν ὀιζυροῖσιν ἅπασι
δυσκέλαδος κακόχαρτος ὁμαρτήσει, στυγερώπης.
καὶ τότε δὴ πρὸς Ὄλυμπον ἀπὸ χθονὸς εὐρυοδείης
λευκοῖσιν φάρεσσι καλυψαμένα χρόα καλὸν
ἀθανάτων μετὰ φῦλον ἴτον προλιπόντ' ἀνθρώπους
Αἰδὼς καὶ Νέμεσις· τὰ δὲ λείψεται ἄλγεα λυγρὰ
θνητοῖς ἀνθρώποισι· κακοῦ δ' οὐκ ἔσσεται ἀλκή.

(Works and Days)

25. Power and Right

I

Νῦν δ' αἶνον βασιλεῦσιν ἐρέω φρονέουσι καὶ αὐτοῖς·
ὧδ' ἴρηξ προσέειπεν ἀηδόνα ποικιλόδειρον
ὕψι μάλ' ἐν νεφέεσσι φέρων ὀνύχεσσι μεμαρπώς·
ἣ δ' ἐλεόν, γναμπτοῖσι πεπαρμένη ἀμφ' ὀνύχεσσι,
μύρετο· τὴν ὅ γ' ἐπικρατέως πρὸς μῦθον ἔειπεν·
«Δαιμονίη, τί λέληκας; ἔχει νύ σε πολλὸν ἀρείων·
τῇ δ' εἶς, ᾗ σ' ἂν ἐγώ περ ἄγω καὶ ἀοιδὸν ἐοῦσαν·

man, speaking crooked words against him, and will swear an oath upon it. Envy, ugly-voiced, delighting in evil, sour-faced, will accompany all wretched men. And then Respect and just Retribution, wrapping their beautiful shapes in white robes, will leave the wide-pathed earth, and forsake mankind to go to Olympus and join the race of the deathless gods; and bitter sorrows will be left for mortal men; and there will be no defence against evil.

I

AND now I shall tell a fable to the kings, who are themselves wise. Thus said the hawk to the spotted-necked nightingale as he carried her high up in the clouds, gripping her with his talons; and she, pierced by his crooked talons, was lamenting pitifully. He spoke to her harshly: 'My good lady, why do you scream? One much stronger than you holds you now, and you will go wherever I take you, even though you

δεῖπνον δ', αἴ κ' ἐθέλω, ποιήσομαι ἠὲ μεθήσω.
ἄφρων δ', ὅς κ' ἐθέλῃ πρὸς κρείσσονας ἀντιφερίζειν·
νίκης τε στέρεται πρός τ' αἴσχεσιν ἄλγεα πάσχει.)
ὣς ἔφατ' ὠκυπέτης ἴρηξ, τανυσίπτερος ὄρνις.

II

Ὦ βασιλῆς, ὑμεῖς δὲ καταφράζεσθε καὶ αὐτοὶ
τήνδε δίκην· ἐγγὺς γὰρ ἐν ἀνθρώποισιν ἐόντες
ἀθάνατοι φράζονται, ὅσοι σκολιῇσι δίκησιν
ἀλλήλους τρίβουσι θεῶν ὄπιν οὐκ ἀλέγοντες.
τρὶς γὰρ μύριοί εἰσιν ἐπὶ χθονὶ πουλυβοτείρῃ
ἀθάνατοι Ζηνὸς φύλακες θνητῶν ἀνθρώπων·
οἵ ῥα φυλάσσουσίν τε δίκας καὶ σχέτλια ἔργα
ἠέρα ἑσσάμενοι, πάντη φοιτῶντες ἐπ' αἶαν.

III

Οἳ γ' αὐτῷ κακὰ τεύχει ἀνὴρ ἄλλῳ κακὰ τεύχων,
ἡ δὲ κακὴ βουλὴ τῷ βουλεύσαντι κακίστη.

(*Works and Days*)

---

are a singer. And I shall make a meal of you if I wish, or set you free.
A man who wants to fight against one stronger is a fool; he is deprived
of victory and suffers pain on top of his shame.' So said the swiftly
flying hawk, the long-winged bird.

II

You, kings, mark this punishment well, even you: for the deathless
gods are close among men, and mark those who destroy one another
with crooked judgements, disregarding the vengeance of the gods. For
on the many-feeding earth there are thrice ten thousand immortal
observers set there by Zeus to watch over mortal men; they keep
watch on judgements and evil deeds as they move, clothed in mist, all
over the earth.

III

The man who damages another damages himself, and evil schemes are
most harmful to the schemer.

26. The Cry of the Crane

Φράζεσθαι δ', εὖτ' ἂν γεράνου φωνὴν ἐπακούσῃς
ὑψόθεν ἐκ νεφέων ἐνιαύσια κεκληγυίης·
ἥτ' ἀρότοιό τε σῆμα φέρει καὶ χείματος ὥρην
δεικνύει ὀμβρηροῦ· κραδίην δ' ἔδακ' ἀνδρὸς ἀβούτεω·
δὴ τότε χορτάζειν ἕλικας βόας ἔνδον ἐόντας·
ῥηίδιον γὰρ ἔπος εἰπεῖν· βόε δὸς καὶ ἄμαξαν·
ῥηίδιον δ' ἀπανήνασθαι· πάρα ἔργα βόεσσιν.
φησὶ δ' ἀνὴρ φρένας ἀφενειὸς πήξασθαι ἄμαξαν,
νήπιος, οὐδὲ τὸ οἶδ'· ἑκατὸν δέ τε δούρατ' ἀμάξης,
τῶν πρόσθεν μελέτην ἐχέμεν οἰκήια θέσθαι.
    Εὖτ' ἂν δὲ πρώτιστ' ἄροτος θνητοῖσι φανείη,
δὴ τότ' ἐφορμηθῆναι ὁμῶς δμῶές τε καὶ αὐτὸς
αὔην καὶ διερὴν ἀρόων ἀρότοιο καθ' ὥρην,
πρωὶ μάλα σπεύδων, ἵνα τοι πλήθωσιν ἄρουραι.
ἦρι πολεῖν· θέρεος δὲ νεωμένη οὔ σ' ἀπατήσει.
νειὸν δὲ σπείρειν ἔτι κουφίζουσαν ἄρουραν·
νειὸς ἀλεξιάρη παίδων εὐκηλήτειρα.
    Εὔχεσθαι δὲ Διὶ χθονίῳ Δημήτερί θ' ἁγνῇ,
ἐκτελέα βρίθειν Δημήτερος ἱερὸν ἀκτήν,

Take note, when you hear the voice of the crane, who cries every year
from high in the clouds; she gives the signal for ploughing, and points
to the season of rainy winter; she pains the heart of the man with no
oxen. Then you must feed up your twisted-horned oxen in the cow-
house; for it is easy to say: 'Give me a pair of oxen and a waggon',
and it is easy to refuse: 'There is work for the oxen to do.' The man
who is rich only in imagination thinks his waggon is [already] built –
the fool, he does not even know this: 'There are a hundred timbers to
a waggon.' Take care that you store these up beforehand at home.

As soon as the time for ploughing is announced to men, then set out
quickly, you and your slaves, in dry and in wet, to plough in the season
for ploughing, hurrying out very early in the morning, so that your
fields will be full. Plough in the spring; but fallow land just broken up
in the summer will not disappoint your hopes. Sow the fallow land
when the soil is still light; fallow land will protect you from harm, will
comfort your children.

When you first begin ploughing, pray to Zeus of the Earth and to
pure Demeter, to make Demeter's holy grain ripe and thick, as you

ἀρχόμενος τὰ πρῶτ' ἀρότου, ὅτ' ἂν ἄκρον ἐχέτλης
χειρὶ λαβὼν ὁρπηκα βοῶν ἐπὶ νῶτον ἵκηαι
ἔνδρυον ἑλκόντων μεσάβων. ὁ δὲ τυτθὸς ὄπισθε
δμῷος ἔχων μακέλην πόνον ὀρνίθεσσι τιθείη
σπέρμα κατακρύπτων· εὐθημοσύνη γὰρ ἀρίστη
θνητοῖς ἀνθρώποις, κακοθημοσύνη δὲ κακίστη.
ὧδέ κεν ἀδροσύνῃ στάχυες νεύοιεν ἔραζε,
εἰ τέλος αὐτὸς ὄπισθεν Ὀλύμπιος ἐσθλὸν ὀπάζοι,
ἐκ δ' ἀγγέων ἐλάσειας ἀράχνια· καί σε ἔολπα
γηθήσειν βιότου αἱρεύμενον ἔνδον ἐόντος.
εὐοχθέων δ' ἵξεαι πολιὸν ἔαρ, οὐδὲ πρὸς ἄλλους
αὐγάσεαι· σέο δ' ἄλλος ἀνὴρ κεχρημένος ἔσται.

Εἰ δέ κεν ἠελίοιο τροπῇς ἀρόῳς χθόνα δῖαν,
ἥμενος ἀμήσεις ὀλίγον περὶ χειρὸς ἐέργων,
ἀντία δεσμεύων κεκονιμένος, οὐ μάλα χαίρων,
οἴσεις δ' ἐν φορμῷ· παῦροι δέ σε θηήσονται.
ἄλλοτε δ' ἀλλοῖος Ζηνὸς νόος αἰγιόχοιο,
ἀργαλέος δ' ἄνδρεσσι καταθνητοῖσι νοῆσαι.
εἰ δέ κεν ὄψ' ἀρόσῃς, τόδε κέν τοι φάρμακον εἴη·
ἦμος κόκκυξ κοκκύζει δρυὸς ἐν πετάλοισι

hold the end of the plough-handle in your hand and bring your stick down on the back of the oxen while they pull the pole-bar by the yoke-straps. And let a young slave follow behind with a mattock and make it difficult for the birds by covering the seed well; for the habit of good management is the best there is for mortal men, and that of bad management the worst. If you do this, your corn-ears will bow to the ground in abundance, if the Olympian later grants a good outcome, and you will drive the cobwebs from your storage-vessels. And I expect you will be glad when you live off the things that are stored in your house. In plenty will you reach grey springtime, and you will not turn to others for help, but another will have need of you.

But if you plough the holy earth at the solstice, you will grasp a thin [crop] with your hand as you reap, stooping down and, far from rejoicing, binding the sheaves cross-wise, covered with dust; you will bring it all back in a basket, and few will admire you. But the thoughts of aegis-bearing Zeus are different at different times, and it is hard for mortal men to understand them. Should you plough late, this may be the remedy: when the cuckoo first cuckoos in the leaves of the oak

τὸ πρῶτον, τέρπει δὲ βροτοὺς ἐπ' ἀπείρονα γαῖαν,
τῆμος Ζεὺς ὕοι τρίτῳ ἤματι μηδ' ἀπολήγοι,
μήτ' ἄρ' ὑπερβάλλων βοὸς ὁπλὴν μήτ' ἀπολείπων·
οὕτω κ' ὀψαρότης πρωηρότῃ ἰσοφαρίζοι.
ἐν θυμῷ δ' εὖ πάντα φυλάσσεο· μηδέ σε λήθοι
μήτ' ἔαρ γιγνόμενον πολιὸν μήθ' ὥριος ὄμβρος.

(Works and Days)

27. Winter

Μῆνα δὲ Ληναιῶνα, κάκ' ἤματα, βουδόρα πάντα,
τοῦτον ἀλεύασθαι, καὶ πηγάδας, αἵ τ' ἐπὶ γαῖαν
πνεύσαντος Βορέαο δυσηλεγέες τελέθουσιν,
ὅς τε διὰ Θρήκης ἱπποτόφου εὐρέϊ πόντῳ
ἐμπνεύσας ὤρινε· μέμυκε δὲ γαῖα καὶ ὕλη·
πολλὰς δὲ δρῦς ὑψικόμους ἐλάτας τε παχείας
οὔρεος ἐν βήσσῃς πίλνα χθονὶ πουλυβοτείρῃ
ἐμπίπτων, καὶ πᾶσα βοᾷ τότε νήριτος ὕλη.
θῆρες δὲ φρίσσουσ', οὐρὰς δ' ὑπὸ μέζε' ἔθεντο,
τῶν καὶ λάχνῃ δέρμα κατάσκιον· ἀλλά νυ καὶ τῶν
ψυχρὸς ἐὼν διάησι δασυστέρνων περ ἐόντων.

and delights men over the boundless earth, if Zeus then sends rain on the third day and does not cease – not rising above the ox's hoof nor falling short of it – in this way the late plougher would catch up with the early. Keep all this well in your mind, and do not let the approach of grey spring and the rainy season escape you.

AVOID the month of Lenaeon – ugly days, all suitable for ox-skinning – and [avoid] the frosts which are cruel, when Boreas [the north wind] blows over the earth. He blows across horse-breeding Thrace, and stirs up the wide sea; the earth and the forests roar. He falls on many lofty-branched oaks and thick pines and brings them down to the bounteous earth in the mountain glens; and all the vast woods roar, and the beasts shudder and put their tails beneath their genitals, even those whose hide is shaded with fur; for his cold blast blows even through them, though they are shaggy-breasted. He [Boreas] goes

καί τε διὰ ῥινοῦ βοὸς ἔρχεται, οὐδέ μιν ἴσχει·
καί τε δι' αἶγα ἄησι τανύτριχα· πώεα δ' οὔ τι,
οὕνεκ' ἐπηετανοὶ τρίχες αὐτῶν, οὐ διάησιν
ἲς ἀνέμου Βορέου· τροχαλὸν δὲ γέροντα τίθησιν.
καὶ διὰ παρθενικῆς ἁπαλόχροος οὐ διάησιν,
ἥ τε δόμων ἔντοσθε φίλη παρὰ μητέρι μίμνει
οὔ πω ἔργα ἰδυῖα πολυχρύσου Ἀφροδίτης·
εὖ τε λοεσσαμένη τέρενα χρόα καὶ λίπ' ἐλαίῳ
χρισαμένη μυχίη καταλέξεται ἔνδοθι οἴκου
ἤματι χειμερίῳ, ὅτ' ἀνόστεος ὃν πόδα τένδει
ἔν τ' ἀπύρῳ οἴκῳ καὶ ἤθεσι λευγαλέοισιν.
οὐδέ οἱ ἠέλιος δείκνυ νομὸν ὁρμηθῆναι·
ἀλλ' ἐπὶ κυανέων ἀνδρῶν δῆμόν τε πόλιν τε
στρωφᾶται, βράδιον δὲ Πανελλήνεσσι φαείνει.
καὶ τότε δὴ κεραοὶ καὶ νήκεροι ὑληκοῖται
λυγρὸν μυλιόωντες ἀνὰ δρία βησσήεντα
φεύγουσιν· καὶ πᾶσιν ἐνὶ φρεσὶ τοῦτο μέμηλεν,
ὡς σκέπα μαιόμενοι πυκινοὺς κευθμῶνας ἔχωσι
καὶ γλάφυ πετρῆεν· τότε δὴ τρίποδι βροτῷ ἶσοι,
οὔ τ' ἐπὶ νῶτα ἔαγε, κάρη δ' εἰς οὔδας ὁρᾶται,
τῷ ἴκελοι φοιτῶσιν, ἀλευόμενοι νίφα λευκήν.

through even the ox's hide; it does not hold him back. He also blows through the long-haired goat's skin. But through the sheep's fleeces, because their wool is thick, Boreas' strength does not pierce at all; but he makes the old man run quickly. Yet he does not blow through the soft-skinned girl, who stays at home with her mother, ignorant as yet of the ways of Aphrodite rich in gold; she washes her soft skin carefully and she anoints herself richly with oil, and will lie down in an inner part of the house on a winter's day when the boneless one [the octopus] gnaws his own foot in his fireless house, his miserable abode; for the sun shows him no ground to move to, but circles round the land and the homes of swarthy men, and [only] later shines upon all the Hellenes. Then the creatures of the wood, horned and unhorned, dismally grinding their teeth, flee through the brushwood of the glens, and all have one desire: in their search for shelter to reach some well-protected hiding-place, some rocky cave. Then, like the three-legged man [the old man] whose back is broken and whose head looks down to the ground, they wander to escape the white snow.

Καὶ τότε ἕσσασθαι ἔρυμα χροός, ὥς σε κελεύω,
χλαῖνάν τε μαλακὴν καὶ τερμιόεντα χιτῶνα·
στήμονι δ' ἐν παύρῳ πολλὴν κρόκα μηρύσασθαι·
τὴν περιέσσασθαι, ἵνα τοι τρίχες ἀτρεμέωσι,
μηδ' ὀρθαὶ φρίσσωσιν ἀειρόμεναι κατὰ σῶμα.
ἀμφὶ δὲ ποσσὶ πέδιλα βοὸς Ἶφι κταμένοιο
ἄρμενα δήσασθαι, πίλοις ἔντοσθε πυκάσσας.
πρωτογόνων δ' ἐρίφων, ὁπότ' ἂν κρύος ὥριον ἔλθῃ,
δέρματα συρράπτειν νεύρῳ βοός, ὄφρ' ἐπὶ νώτῳ
ὑετοῦ ἀμφιβάλῃ ἀλέην· κεφαλῆφι δ' ὕπερθεν
πῖλον ἔχειν ἀσκητόν, ἵν' οὔατα μὴ καταδεύῃ·
ψυχρὴ γάρ τ' ἠὼς πέλεται Βορέαο πεσόντος,
ἠῷος δ' ἐπὶ γαῖαν ἀπ' οὐρανοῦ ἀστερόεντος
ἀὴρ πυροφόρος τέταται μακάρων ἐπὶ ἔργοις·
ὅς τε ἀρυσσάμενος ποταμῶν ἄπο αἰεναόντων,
ὑψοῦ ὑπὲρ γαίης ἀρθεὶς ἀνέμοιο θυέλλῃ
ἄλλοτε μέν θ' ὕει ποτὶ ἕσπερον, ἄλλοτ' ἄησι
πυκνὰ Θρηϊκίου Βορέου νέφεα κλονέοντος.

(*Works and Days*)

And in that season put on, as I tell you, a soft cloak and a fringed tunic to protect your body; and weave a lot of wool on thin warp. Wind this well round you, so that your hair keeps still and does not bristle and stand up all over your body. Lace round your feet well-fitting boots made of the hide of a slaughtered ox, covered thickly inside with felt. And when the season of the frost comes, stitch together skins of firstling kids with ox-sinew to put over your back to keep off the rain. On top, on your head, wear a close-fitting cap of felt to keep your ears dry; for the dawn is cold at the onset of Boreas, and far from the starry sky a mist that will produce good wheat-crops is stretched out across the earth, over the farmlands of blessed men; this is drawn from the ever-flowing rivers, and is lifted high above the earth by wind-storms; and sometimes it turns to rain towards evening, and sometimes to wind, when Thracian Boreas shakes the thick clouds.

HESIOD

28. Time for Sailing

Ἤματα πεντήκοντα μετὰ τροπὰς ἠελίοιο,
ἐς τέλος ἐλθόντος θέρεος καματώδεος ὥρης,
ὡραῖος πέλεται θνητοῖς πλόος· οὔτε κε νῆα
καυάξαις οὔτ' ἄνδρας ἀποφθείσειε θάλασσα,
εἰ δὴ μὴ πρόφρων γε Ποσειδάων ἐνοσίχθων
ἢ Ζεὺς ἀθανάτων βασιλεὺς ἐθέλησιν ὀλέσσαι·
ἐν τοῖς γὰρ τέλος ἐστὶν ὁμῶς ἀγαθῶν τε κακῶν τε.
τῆμος δ' εὐκρινέες τ' αὖραι καὶ πόντος ἀπήμων·
εὔκηλος τότε νῆα θοὴν ἀνέμοισι πιθήσας
ἑλκέμεν ἐς πόντον φόρτον τ' ἐς πάντα τίθεσθαι,
σπεύδειν δ' ὅττι τάχιστα πάλιν οἰκόνδε νέεσθαι·
μηδὲ μένειν οἶνόν τε νέον καὶ ὀπωρινὸν ὄμβρον
καὶ χειμῶν' ἐπιόντα Νότοιό τε δεινὰς ἀήτας,
ὅστ' ὤρινε θάλασσαν ὁμαρτήσας Διὸς ὄμβρῳ
πολλῷ ὀπωρινῷ, χαλεπὸν δέ τε πόντον ἔθηκεν.
    Ἄλλος δ' εἰαρινὸς πέλεται πλόος ἀνθρώποισιν·
ἦμος δὴ τὸ πρῶτον, ὅσον τ' ἐπιβᾶσα κορώνη
ἴχνος ἐποίησεν, τόσσον πέταλ' ἀνδρὶ φανείη
ἐν κράδῃ ἀκροτάτῃ, τότε δ' ἄμβατός ἐστι θάλασσα·
εἰαρινὸς δ' οὗτος πέλεται πλόος. οὔ μιν ἔγωγε

FIFTY days after the solstice, when the season of exhausting summer has finished, is the right time for men to sail. You will not wreck your ship, nor will the sea bring death to the sailors, unless Poseidon the Earthshaker is not propitious, or Zeus, the king of the deathless gods, wishes to destroy them; for the accomplishment of good and evil alike is in their hands. At that time winds are steady and the sea is harmless. Then, free from care, trust the winds, and haul your swift ship to the sea, and put all the cargo aboard; but hurry, that you may return home again as quickly as possible; do not wait for the time of the new wine and the autumn rain of the oncoming storms and the terrible blasts of Notos [the south wind] which comes with the heavy autumn rains of Zeus and stirs up the sea and makes it dangerous.

Another time for men to sail is spring, when a man first sees leaves on the end of a branch as large as the footprint of a crow as it alights; then the sea can be crossed, and this is the spring sailing time. I, for

αἴνημ'· οὐ γὰρ ἐμῷ θυμῷ κεχαρισμένος ἐστίν·
ἁρπακτός· χαλεπῶς κε φύγοις κακόν· ἀλλά νυ καὶ τὰ
ἄνθρωποι ῥέζουσιν ἀϊδρείῃσι νόοιο·
χρήματα γὰρ ψυχὴ πέλεται δειλοῖσι βροτοῖσιν.
δεινὸν δ' ἐστὶ θανεῖν μετὰ κύμασιν. ἀλλά σ' ἄνωγα
φράζεσθαι τάδε πάντα μετὰ φρεσίν, ὡς ἀγορεύω.
μηδ' ἐν νηυσὶν ἅπαντα βίον κοίλῃσι τίθεσθαι·
ἀλλὰ πλέω λείπειν, τὰ δὲ μείονα φορτίζεσθαι.
δεινὸν γὰρ πόντου μετὰ κύμασι πήματι κύρσαι.
δεινὸν δ', εἴ κ' ἐπ' ἄμαξαν ὑπέρβιον ἄχθος ἀείρας
ἄξονα καυάξαις καὶ φορτία μαυρωθείη.
μέτρα φυλάσσεσθαι· καιρὸς δ' ἐπὶ πᾶσιν ἄριστος.

(*Works and Days*)

29. The Gift of the Muses

I

Μουσάων Ἑλικωνιάδων ἀρχώμεθ' ἀείδειν,
αἵ θ' Ἑλικῶνος ἔχουσιν ὄρος μέγα τε ζάθεόν τε
καί τε περὶ κρήνην ἰοειδέα πόσσ' ἁπαλοῖσιν
ὀρχεῦνται καὶ βωμὸν ἐρισθενέος Κρονίωνος.

. . . .

one, do not approve of it, for it does not please my heart. Such sailing
is rushed; only with difficulty will you avoid harm. Yet in their ignor-
ance men do this too, for wealth means life to miserable mortals; but
it is terrible to die in the waves. But I advise you to consider all these
things as I say. And do not put your entire livelihood in hollow ships;
leave most things behind, and load the smaller part on board. For it is
terrible to meet with disaster in the waves of the sea, as it is terrible if,
having piled too heavy a load on your waggon you break an axle, and
your load is ruined. Observe moderation. The right time is in all
things the best.

I

LET us begin our song with the Heliconian Muses who dwell in
great and most holy Mount Helicon, and dance with delicate feet
round the dark spring and the altar of the most powerful son of Cronos.

αἵ νύ ποθ' Ἡσίοδον καλὴν ἐδίδαξαν ἀοιδήν,
ἄρνας ποιμαίνονθ' Ἑλικῶνος ὕπο ζαθέοιο.
τόνδε δέ με πρώτιστα θεαὶ πρὸς μῦθον ἔειπον,
Μοῦσαι Ὀλυμπιάδες, κοῦραι Διὸς αἰγιόχοιο·
  ‹Ποιμένες ἄγραυλοι, κάκ' ἐλέγχεα, γαστέρες οἶον,
ἴδμεν ψεύδεα πολλὰ λέγειν ἐτύμοισιν ὁμοῖα,
ἴδμεν δ', εὖτ' ἐθέλωμεν, ἀληθέα γηρύσασθαι.›
  Ὣς ἔφασαν κοῦραι μεγάλου Διὸς ἀρτιέπειαι·
καί μοι σκῆπτρον ἔδον δάφνης ἐριθηλέος ὄζον
δρέψασαι, θηητόν· ἐνέπνευσαν δέ μοι αὐδὴν
θέσπιν, ἵνα κλείοιμι τά τ' ἐσσόμενα πρό τ' ἐόντα.
καί μ' ἐκέλονθ' ὑμνεῖν μακάρων γένος αἰὲν ἐόντων,
σφᾶς δ' αὐτὰς πρῶτόν τε καὶ ὕστατον αἰὲν ἀείδειν.
ἀλλὰ τί ἦ μοι ταῦτα ‹περὶ δρῦν ἢ περὶ πέτρην›;

II

Ὅν τινα τιμήσωσι Διὸς κοῦραι μεγάλοιο
γεινόμενόν τε ἴδωσι διοτρεφέων βασιλήων,
τῷ μὲν ἐπὶ γλώσσῃ γλυκερὴν χείουσιν ἐέρσην,
τοῦ δ' ἔπε' ἐκ στόματος ῥεῖ μείλιχα· οἱ δέ τε λαοὶ

It was they who once taught Hesiod how to sing beautifully, as he was shepherding his lambs under most holy Helicon. These words the goddesses first told me, the Muses of Olympus, daughters of aegis-bearing Zeus:

'You shepherds, who live in the fields, evil, disgraceful creatures, mere bellies, we know how to tell many lies, as though they were true; but we know, when we wish, how to speak the truth.'

So spoke the ready-voiced daughters of great Zeus, and they cut a staff and gave it to me, a branch of blooming laurel, a thing to marvel at. And they breathed into me a godly voice that I should celebrate the things to come and the things of the past, and ordered me to sing of the race of the blessed gods that live for ever, always to celebrate them at the beginning and at the end. But why all this 'concerning oak, or rock'?

II

Whenever the daughters of great Zeus honour one of the kings cherished by Zeus and watch over him at his birth, they pour sweet dew upon his tongue and out of his mouth flow gentle words. All the

πάντες ἐς αὐτὸν ὁρῶσι διακρίνοντα θέμιστας
ἰθείῃσι δίκῃσιν· ὁ δ' ἀσφαλέως ἀγορεύων
αἶψά κε καὶ μέγα νεῖκος ἐπισταμένως κατέπαυσεν·
τοὔνεκα γὰρ βασιλῆες ἐχέφρονες, οὕνεκα λαοῖς
βλαπτομένοις ἀγορῆφι μετάτροπα ἔργα τελεῦσι
ῥηιδίως, μαλακοῖσι παραιφάμενοι ἐπέεσσιν.
ἐρχόμενον δ' ἀν' ἀγῶνα θεὸν ὣς ἱλάσκονται
αἰδοῖ μειλιχίῃ, μετὰ δὲ πρέπει ἀγρομένοισιν·
τοίη Μουσάων ἱερὴ δόσις ἀνθρώποισιν.
ἐκ γάρ τοι Μουσέων καὶ ἑκηβόλου Ἀπόλλωνος
ἄνδρες ἀοιδοὶ ἔασιν ἐπὶ χθόνα καὶ κιθαρισταί,
ἐκ δὲ Διὸς βασιλῆες· ὁ δ' ὄλβιος, ὅν τινα Μοῦσαι
φίλωνται· γλυκερή οἱ ἀπὸ στόματος ῥέει αὐδή.
εἰ γάρ τις καὶ πένθος ἔχων νεοκηδέϊ θυμῷ
ἄζηται κραδίην ἀκαχήμενος, αὐτὰρ ἀοιδὸς
Μουσάων θεράπων κλέεα προτέρων ἀνθρώπων
ὑμνήσῃ μάκαράς τε θεούς, οἳ Ὄλυμπον ἔχουσιν,
αἶψ' ὁ γε δυσφροσυνέων ἐπιλήθεται οὐδέ τι κηδέων
μέμνηται· ταχέως δὲ παρέτραπε δῶρα θεάων.

(*Theogony*)

people look to him as he gives judgements with true justice, and with his authority he would swiftly stop even a great quarrel in a short time. For kings are prudent in that when the people is injured by its assembly they easily set the matter right again by appeasing it with soft words. And when he passes through a gathering they respect him like a god with sweet reverence, and he stands out among the crowd; such is the Muses' sacred gift to men. For the singers and the lyre-players on earth come from the Muses and far-shafting Apollo, but the kings are of Zeus. Happy is the man whom the Muses love; a sweet voice flows out from his mouth. For even if a man has sorrow and grief in his newly saddened mind, and lives in fear because his heart is distressed, yet when a singer, a servant of the Muses, sings of the deeds of former men and of the blessed gods who dwell in Olympus, he swiftly forgets his worries, and does not remember his sorrows; the gifts of the goddesses soon take him [from those thoughts].

30. The End of the Titans

Οὐδ' ἄρ' ἔτι Ζεὺς ἴσχεν ἑὸν μένος, ἀλλά νυ τοῦ γε
εἶθαρ μὲν μένεος πλῆντο φρένες, ἐκ δέ τε πᾶσαν
φαῖνε βίην· ἄμυδις δ' ἄρ' ἀπ' οὐρανοῦ ἠδ' ἀπ' 'Ολύμπου
ἀστράπτων ἔστειχε συνωχαδόν· οἱ δὲ κεραυνοὶ
ἵκταρ ἅμα βροντῇ τε καὶ ἀστεροπῇ ποτέοντο
χειρὸς ἄπο στιβαρῆς, ἱερὴν φλόγα εἰλυφόωντες
ταρφέες· ἀμφὶ δὲ γαῖα φερέσβιος ἐσμαράγιζε
καιομένη, λάκε δ' ἀμφὶ πυρὶ μεγάλ' ἄσπετος ὕλη.
ἔζεε δὲ χθὼν πᾶσα καὶ 'Ωκεανοῖο ῥέεθρα
πόντος τ' ἀτρύγετος· τοὺς δ' ἄμφεπε θερμὸς ἀϋτμὴ
Τιτῆνας χθονίους, φλὸξ δ' αἰθέρα δῖαν ἵκανεν
ἄσπετος, ὄσσε δ' ἄμερδε καὶ ἰφθίμων περ ἐόντων
αὐγὴ μαρμαίρουσα κεραυνοῦ τε στεροπῆς τε.
καῦμα δὲ θεσπέσιον κάτεχεν Χάος· εἴσατο δ' ἄντα
ὀφθαλμοῖσιν ἰδεῖν ἠδ' οὔασι ὄσσαν ἀκοῦσαι
αὔτως, ὡς εἰ Γαῖα καὶ Οὐρανὸς εὐρὺς ὕπερθε
πίλνατο· τοῖος γάρ κε μέγας ὑπὸ δοῦπος ὀρώρει
τῆς μὲν ἐρειπομένης, τοῦ δ' ὑψόθεν ἐξεριπόντος·

ZEUS restrained his might no longer, but immediately his mind was filled with fury, and he revealed all his power. He went straight down from the sky and from Olympus, flashing lightning all the way. With thunder and lightning the thunderbolts flew thick and fast from his sturdy hand, one after the other rolling along the holy flames. The life-giving earth crashed around as it burned, and the great woods crackled loudly in the fire. The whole earth seethed, and Ocean's streams and the barren sea. The hot steam covered the earth-born Titans, and giant flames reached to the holy aether; the blazing light of the thunderbolt and the lightning blinded their eyes, mighty though they were. Chaos was possessed of a dreadful heat; and looking straight at it with your eyes and hearing the noise in your ears, it seemed as if the earth and the wide sky above had been driven together, for such a great roar would have arisen if the earth had fallen

τόσσος δοῦπος ἔγεντο θεῶν ἔριδι ξυνιόντων.
σὺν δ' ἄνεμοι ἔνοσίν τε κονίην τ' ἐσφαράγιζον
βροντήν τε στεροπήν τε καὶ αἰθαλόεντα κεραυνόν,
κῆλα Διὸς μεγάλοιο, φέρον δ' ἰαχήν τ' ἐνοπήν τε
ἐς μέσον ἀμφοτέρων· ὄτοβος δ' ἄπλητος ὀρώρει
σμερδαλέης ἔριδος, κάρτος δ' ἀνεφαίνετο ἔργων.
ἐκλίνθη δὲ μάχη· πρὶν δ' ἀλλήλοις ἐπέχοντες
ἐμμενέως ἐμάχοντο διὰ κρατερὰς ὑσμίνας.

Οἳ δ' ἄρ' ἐνὶ πρώτοισι μάχην δριμεῖαν ἔγειραν
Κόττος τε Βριάρεώς τε Γύης τ' ἄατος πολέμοιο,
οἵ ῥα τριηκοσίας πέτρας στιβαρῶν ἀπὸ χειρῶν
πέμπον ἐπασσυτέρας, κατὰ δ' ἐσκίασαν βελέεσσι
Τιτῆνας, καὶ τούς μὲν ὑπὸ χθονὸς εὐρυοδείης
πέμψαν καὶ δεσμοῖσιν ἐν ἀργαλέοισιν ἔδησαν
χερσὶν νικήσαντες ὑπερθύμους περ ἐόντας.

(*Theogony*)

in ruins and the sky fallen down from above. So great was the roar
which arose as the gods attacked one another in their anger. And the
winds rose howling and stirred up earthquake and dust-storm, thunder
and lightning and the smoke-black thunderbolt, the weapons of great
Zeus; and they carried the shouts and the cries between the two
[armies]. A tremendous din arose from the terrible battle, and their
might was revealed in their fighting. The tide of the battle turned;
until then they had kept at one another and battled steadily on through
the heavy fighting.

Cottus and Briareos and Gyes, ever hungry for war, fought fiercely
in the front line. Three hundred rocks, one after the other, they hurled
from their sturdy hands, and covered the Titans with their missiles,
and threw them under the wide-pathed earth and bound them in pain-
ful fetters, conquering them despite their high courage.

HOMERIC HYMNS

date unknown

31. Persephone Snatched Away

Δήμητρ' ἠΰκομον σεμνὴν θεὸν ἄρχομ' ἀείδειν,
αὐτὴν ἠδὲ θύγατρα τανύσφυρον ἣν Ἀϊδωνεὺς
ἥρπαξεν, δῶκεν δὲ βαρύκτυπος εὐρύοπα Ζεύς,
νόσφιν Δήμητρος χρυσαόρου ἀγλαοκάρπου
παίζουσαν κούρῃσι σὺν Ὠκεανοῦ βαθυκόλποις,
ἄνθεά τ' αἰνυμένην ῥόδα καὶ κρόκον ἠδ' ἴα καλὰ
λειμῶν' ἀμ μαλακὸν καὶ ἀγαλλίδας ἠδ' ὑάκινθον
νάρκισσόν θ', ὃν φῦσε δόλον καλυκώπιδι κούρῃ
Γαῖα Διὸς βουλῇσι χαριζομένη Πολυδέκτῃ,
θαυμαστὸν γανόωντα, σέβας τότε πᾶσιν ἰδέσθαι
ἀθανάτοις τε θεοῖς ἠδὲ θνητοῖς ἀνθρώποις·
τοῦ καὶ ἀπὸ ῥίζης ἑκατὸν κάρα ἐξεπεφύκει,
κῶζ' ἥδιστ' ὀδμή, πᾶς δ' οὐρανὸς εὐρὺς ὕπερθε
γαῖά τε πᾶσ' ἐγέλασσε καὶ ἁλμυρὸν οἶδμα θαλάσσης.
ἡ δ' ἄρα θαμβήσασ' ὠρέξατο χερσὶν ἅμ' ἄμφω
καλὸν ἄθυρμα λαβεῖν· χάνε δὲ χθὼν εὐρυάγυια
Νύσιον ἀμ πεδίον τῇ ὄρουσεν ἄναξ πολυδέγμων
ἵπποις ἀθανάτοισι Κρόνου πολυώνυμος υἱός.

I SHALL begin by singing of fair-haired Demeter, the venerable goddess, and her slender-ankled daughter, whom the king of Hades snatched away, and who was given to him by loud-thundering, all-watching Zeus, as she was playing with the daughters of Ocean, whose dresses fall in deep folds, far from gold-sworded Demeter, the giver of splendid fruit; she was gathering flowers in a lush meadow – the rose, the crocus, beautiful violets and irises and the hyacinth, and a narcissus which the Earth had grown to deceive the blushing girl, and so please the king of Hades, according to the wishes of Zeus; it sparkled marvellously, a wonder to all who saw it, whether immortal gods or mortal men. From its root had grown a hundred blossoms, and it had the sweetest perfume, and the whole wide sky above, the whole earth and the salty swell of the sea smiled [in reflection of it]. And she [Persephone] was amazed and stretched out both her hands to take hold of the beautiful toy; but the wide-pathed earth yawned in the plain of Nysa, and the many-titled son of Cronos, the king who receives all, leapt up

ἁρπάξας δ' ἀέκουσαν ἐπὶ χρυσέοισιν ὄχοισιν
ἦγ' ὀλοφυρομένην· ἴαχησε δ' ἄρ' ὄρθια φωνῇ
κεκλομένη πατέρα Κρονίδην ὕπατον καὶ ἄριστον.
οὐδέ τις ἀθανάτων οὐδὲ θνητῶν ἀνθρώπων
ἤκουσεν φωνῆς, οὐδ' ἀγλαόκαρποι ἐλαῖαι.

(Hymn II)

32. Demeter at the House of Celeus

Ὣς ἔφαθ'· ἡ δ' ἐπένευσε καρήατι, ταὶ δὲ φαεινὰ
πλησάμεναι ὕδατος φέρον ἄγγεα κυδιάουσαι.
ῥίμφα δὲ πατρὸς ἵκοντο μέγαν δόμον, ὦκα δὲ μητρὶ
ἔννεπον ὡς εἶδόν τε καὶ ἔκλυον. ἡ δὲ μάλ' ὦκα
ἐλθούσας ἐκέλευε καλεῖν ἐπ' ἀπείρονι μισθῷ.
αἱ δ' ὡς τ' ἢ ἔλαφοι ἢ πόρτιες ἤαρος ὥρη
ἄλλοντ' ἂν λειμῶνα κορεσσάμεναι φρένα φορβῇ
ὣς αἱ ἐπισχόμεναι ἑανῶν πτύχας ἱμεροέντων
ἤϊξαν κοίλην κατ' ἀμαξιτόν, ἀμφὶ δὲ χαῖται
ὤμοις ἀΐσσοντο κροκηΐῳ ἄνθει ὁμοῖαι.
τέτμον δ' ἐγγὺς ὁδοῦ κυδρὴν θεὸν ἔνθα πάρος περ

with his immortal horses. Against her will he seized her, and took her away weeping on his golden chariot. She cried out, calling shrilly to her father, the son of Cronos, the first and the best of the gods. But no god, nor mortal man, heard her voice, nor did the bright-berried olives.

So she [Callidice, daughter of Celeus] spoke; and the goddess bowed her head in agreement. And they filled their bright pitchers with water and carried them off proudly. They soon came to their father's great house, and at once told their mother what they had seen and heard. She then ordered them to run to the stranger and ask her to come for a rich reward. And like deer or young calves in spring, which skit about the meadow when they have grazed their fill, so they held up the folds of their lovely dresses, and darted down the rutted cart track, and their hair streamed over their shoulders like a crocus flower. They found the noble goddess by the wayside, where they had left her before; and then

κάλλιπον· αὐτὰρ ἔπειτα φίλα πρὸς δώματα πατρὸς
ἠγεῦνθ', ἡ δ' ἄρ' ὄπισθε φίλον τετιημένη ἦτορ
στεῖχε κατὰ κρῆθεν κεκαλυμμένη, ἀμφὶ δὲ πέπλος
κυάνεος ῥαδινοῖσι θεᾶς ἐλελίζετο ποσσίν.
αἶψα δὲ δώμαθ' ἵκοντο διοτρεφέος Κελεοῖο,
βὰν δὲ δι' αἰθούσης ἔνθα σφίσι πότνια μήτηρ
ἧστο παρὰ σταθμὸν τέγεος πύκα ποιητοῖο,
παῖδ' ὑπὸ κόλπῳ ἔχουσα νέον θάλος· αἱ δὲ παρ' αὐτὴν
ἔδραμον, ἡ δ' ἄρ' ἐπ' οὐδὸν ἔβη ποσὶ καί ῥα μελάθρου
κῦρε κάρη, πλῆσεν δὲ θύρας σέλαος θείοιο.
τὴν δ' αἰδώς τε σέβας τε ἰδὲ χλωρὸν δέος εἷλεν·
εἶξε δέ οἱ κλισμοῖο καὶ ἐδριάασθαι ἄνωγεν.

(Hymn II)

33. The Delian Festival

Ἀλλὰ σὺ Δήλῳ Φοῖβε μάλιστ' ἐπιτέρπεαι ἦτορ,
ἔνθα τοι ἑλκεχίτωνες Ἰάονες ἠγερέθονται
αὐτοῖς σὺν παίδεσσι καὶ αἰδοίῃς ἀλόχοισιν.
οἱ δέ σε πυγμαχίῃ τε καὶ ὀρχηθμῷ καὶ ἀοιδῇ
μνησάμενοι τέρπουσιν ὅταν στήσωνται ἀγῶνα.

they led her to the house of their dear father. And she walked behind
them sad at heart, with her head covered, and a dark dress swung about
the goddess's slender feet. Soon they came to the house of god-reared
Celeus, and crossed the portico, where their honoured mother sat by
a pillar of the well-fitted roof, holding in her bosom her son, a young
scion. And the girls ran to her, but the goddess stepped on the
threshold; and her head reached the roof of the palace, and she filled
the doorway with a godly light. Then awe and reverence and pale
fear seized her [Metaneira, wife of Celeus], and she rose from her couch
and asked her [Demeter] to be seated.

BUT your heart, Phoebus, takes most delight in Delos, where the long-
robed Ionians gather with their children and their honoured wives;
and they commemorate and delight you with boxing and dancing and
song whenever they hold their competitions. A man who came across

φαίη κ' ἀθανάτους καὶ ἀγήρως ἔμμεναι αἰεὶ
ὅς τότ' ἐπαντιάσει' ὅτ' Ἰάονες ἀθρόοι εἶεν·
πάντων γάρ κεν ἴδοιτο χάριν, τέρψαιτο δὲ θυμὸν
ἄνδρας τ' εἰσορόων καλλιζώνους τε γυναῖκας
νῆάς τ' ὠκείας ἠδ' αὐτῶν κτήματα πολλά.
πρὸς δὲ τόδε μέγα θαῦμα, ὅου κλέος οὔποτ' ὀλεῖται,
κοῦραι Δηλιάδες Ἑκατηβελέταο θεράπναι·
αἴ τ' ἐπεὶ ἄρ πρῶτον μὲν Ἀπόλλων' ὑμνήσωσιν,
αὖτις δ' αὖ Λητώ τε καὶ Ἄρτεμιν ἰοχέαιραν,
μνησάμεναι ἀνδρῶν τε παλαιῶν ἠδὲ γυναικῶν
ὕμνον ἀείδουσιν, θέλγουσι δὲ φῦλ' ἀνθρώπων.
πάντων δ' ἀνθρώπων φωνὰς καὶ κρεμβαλιαστὺν
μιμεῖσθ' ἴσασιν· φαίη δέ κεν αὐτὸς ἕκαστος
φθέγγεσθ'· οὕτω σφιν καλὴ συνάρηρεν ἀοιδή.

Ἀλλ' ἄγεθ' ἱλήκοι μὲν Ἀπόλλων Ἀρτέμιδι ξύν,
χαίρετε δ' ὑμεῖς πᾶσαι· ἐμεῖο δὲ καὶ μετόπισθε
μνήσασθ', ὁππότε κέν τις ἐπιχθονίων ἀνθρώπων
ἐνθάδ' ἀνείρηται ξεῖνος ταλαπείριος ἐλθών·
‹ὦ κοῦραι, τίς δ' ὕμμιν ἀνὴρ ἥδιστος ἀοιδῶν
ἐνθάδε πωλεῖται, καὶ τέῳ τέρπεσθε μάλιστα;›
ὑμεῖς δ' εὖ μάλα πᾶσαι ὑποκρίνασθ' ἀμφ' ἡμέων·
‹τυφλὸς ἀνήρ, οἰκεῖ δὲ Χίῳ ἔνι παιπαλοέσσῃ,

the Ionians gathered together would say they were a deathless and un-
ageing people; for he would see how graceful they all are, and he
would delight his heart in watching the men and the well-girdled
women and the fast ships and their many possessions. Moreover there
is this great marvel whose glory will never die: the Delian maidens,
the servants of the Far-shooter. For, after praising Apollo, and then
Leto and Artemis the archer, they sing a song about the men and
women of old, and enchant the tribes of men; and they know how to
imitate the tongues of all men, and their rattling music. One would say
those men themselves were speaking, so realistic is their beautiful song.

But come, Apollo and Artemis, be propitious; and [maidens] fare-
well to you all. Remember me in times to come, when a foreigner who
has seen and suffered much comes and asks [a local person]: 'Whom do
you think, girls, is the sweetest of the singers who often visit you here?
Who gives you the greatest pleasure?' With one voice, all together
answer him: 'The blind man who lives in rocky Chios; all his songs

τοῦ πᾶσαι μετόπισθεν ἀριστεύουσιν ἀοιδαί.
ἡμεῖς δ' ὑμέτερον κλέος οἴσομεν ὅσσον ἐπ' αἶαν
ἀνθρώπων στρεφόμεσθα πόλεις εὖ ναιεταώσας·)
οἱ δ' ἐπὶ δὴ πείσονται, ἐπεὶ καὶ ἐτήτυμόν ἐστιν.
αὐτὰρ ἐγὼν οὐ λήξω ἑκηβόλον 'Απόλλωνα
ὑμνέων ἀργυρότοξον ὃν ἠύκομος τέκε Λητώ.

(Hymn III)

34. The Baby Cattle-thief

Φῆ ῥ' ὁ γέρων· ὁ δὲ θᾶσσον ὁδὸν κίε μῦθον ἀκούσας.
οἰωνὸν δ' ἐνόει τανυσίπτερον, αὐτίκα δ' ἔγνω
φηλητὴν γεγαῶτα Διὸς παῖδα Κρονίωνος.
ἐσσυμένως δ' ἤιξεν ἄναξ Διὸς υἱὸς 'Απόλλων
ἐς Πύλον ἠγαθέην διζήμενος εἰλίποδας βοῦς,
πορφυρέῃ νεφέλῃ κεκαλυμμένος εὐρέας ὤμους·
ἴχνιά τ' εἰσενόησεν 'Εκηβόλος εἶπέ τε μῦθον·
‹᾽Ω πόποι ἦ μέγα θαῦμα τόδ' ὀφθαλμοῖσιν ὁρῶμαι·
ἴχνια μὲν τάδε γ' ἐστὶ βοῶν ὀρθοκραιράων,
ἀλλὰ πάλιν τέτραπται ἐς ἀσφοδελὸν λειμῶνα·
βήματα δ' οὔτ' ἀνδρὸς τάδε γίγνεται οὔτε γυναικὸς

[are, and] in time to come will be, the best.' And I shall spread your glory, as long as I wander over the earth to visit the well-situated cities of men. And then they will believe me, because it is true. Moreover, I shall never cease praising far-shooting Apollo, master of the silver bow, the son of fair-tressed Leto.

The old man spoke; and when he [Apollo] heard these words, he went faster on his way; and he saw a broad-winged bird, and he knew at once that the thief was the child of Zeus, the son of Cronos. So the lord Apollo, son of Zeus, hurried on to most holy Pylos, searching for his shambling oxen, his broad shoulders covered in a dark cloud. And the Far-shooter noticed some tracks and said:

'Oh ho! This is indeed a great marvel that I see before my eyes. These are for certain tracks of straight-horned oxen, but they are turned backwards towards the flowery meadow. And these are not the footprints of a man or of a woman, or of grey wolves, or bears or

οὔτε λύκων πολιῶν οὔτ' ἄρκτων οὔτε λεόντων·
οὔτε τι κενταύρου λασιαύχενος ἔλπομαι εἶναι
ὅς τις τοῖα πέλωρα βιβᾷ ποσὶ καρπαλίμοισιν·
αἰνὰ μὲν ἔνθεν ὁδοῖο, τὰ δ' αἰνότερ' ἔνθεν ὁδοῖο.⟩
Ὣς εἰπὼν ἤϊξεν ἄναξ Διὸς υἱὸς Ἀπόλλων,.
Κυλλήνης δ' ἀφίκανεν ὄρος καταείμενον ὕλῃ
πέτρης εἰς κευθμῶνα βαθύσκιον, ἔνθα τε νύμφη
ἀμβροσίη ἐλόχευσε Διὸς παῖδα Κρονίωνος.
ὀδμὴ δ' ἱμερόεσσα δι' οὔρεος ἠγαθέοιο
κίδνατο, πολλὰ δὲ μῆλα ταναύποδα βόσκετο ποίην.
ἔνθα τότε σπεύδων κατεβήσατο λάϊνον οὐδὸν
ἄντρον ἐς ἠερόεν ἑκατηβόλος αὐτὸς Ἀπόλλων.

Τὸν δ' ὡς οὖν ἐνόησε Διὸς καὶ Μαιάδος υἱὸς
χωόμενον περὶ βουσὶν ἑκηβόλον Ἀπόλλωνα,
σπάργαν' ἔσω κατέδυνε θυήεντ'· ἠΰτε πολλὴν
πρέμνων ἀνθρακιὴν ὕλης σποδὸς ἀμφικαλύπτει,
ὣς Ἑρμῆς Ἑκάεργον ἰδὼν ἀνεείλε᾿ ἓ αὐτόν.
ἐν δ' ὀλίγῳ συνέλασσε κάρη χεῖράς τε πόδας τε
φῆ ῥα νεόλλουτος προκαλεύμενος ἥδυμον ὕπνον
ἐγρήσσων ἐτεόν γε· χέλυν δ' ὑπὸ μασχάλῃ εἶχε.
γνῶ δ' οὐδ' ἠγνοίησε Διὸς καὶ Λητοῦς υἱὸς

lions; nor I think are they of a rough-maned Centaur, who makes such monstrous foot-marks with his swift feet; the tracks on this side of the road are strange, but those on the other are even stranger.'

When he said this, the lord Apollo, the son of Zeus, glided on and came to the thickly wooded mountain of Cyllene and the deep-shadowed cave in the rock, where the divine nymph bore the child of Zeus, the son of Cronos. A lovely scent spread over the sacred hill, and many long-shanked sheep were grazing on the grass. Then far-shafting Apollo himself stepped swiftly down over the stone threshold into the misty cave.

When [Hermes] the son of Zeus and Maia realized long-shafting Apollo was angry about his cattle, he buried himself in his fragrant swaddling-clothes; and just as wood-ash covers over the deep embers of logs, so Hermes curled himself up, when he saw the Far-shooter. He squeezed head and hands and feet together in a little space, like a child that has just been bathed and longs for sleep, but in truth he was wide awake and he kept his lyre under his arm. But the son of Zeus and Leto realized this, and did not fail to see the beautiful mountain-nymph

νύμφην τ' οὐρείην περικαλλέα καὶ φίλον υἱόν,
παῖδ' ὀλίγον δολίης εἰλυμένον ἐντροπίῃσι.
παπτήνας δ' ἀνὰ πάντα μυχὸν μεγάλοιο δόμοιο
τρεῖς ἀδύτους ἀνέῳγε λαβὼν κληῖδα φαεινὴν
νέκταρος ἐμπλείους ἠδ' ἀμβροσίης ἐρατεινῆς·
πολλὸς δὲ χρυσός τε καὶ ἄργυρος ἔνδον ἔκειτο,
πολλὰ δὲ φοινικόεντα καὶ ἄργυφα εἵματα νύμφης,
οἷα θεῶν μακάρων ἱεροὶ δόμοι ἐντὸς ἔχουσιν.
ἔνθ' ἐπεὶ ἐξερέεινε μυχοὺς μεγάλοιο δόμοιο
Λητοΐδης μύθοισι προσηύδα κύδιμον Ἑρμῆν·
‹Ὦ παῖ ὃς ἐν λίκνῳ κατάκειαι, μήνυέ μοι βοῦς
θᾶττον· ἐπεὶ τάχα νῶϊ διοισόμεθ' οὐ κατὰ κόσμον.
ῥίψω γάρ σε λαβὼν ἐς Τάρταρον ἠερόεντα,
εἰς ζόφον αἰνόμορον καὶ ἀμήχανον· οὐδέ σε μήτηρ
ἐς φάος οὐδὲ πατὴρ ἀναλύσεται, ἀλλ' ὑπὸ γαίῃ
ἐρρήσεις ὀλίγοισι μετ' ἀνδράσιν ἡγεμονεύων.›
Τὸν δ' Ἑρμῆς μύθοισιν ἀμείβετο κερδαλέοισι·
‹Λητοΐδη τίνα τοῦτον ἀπηνέα μῦθον ἔειπας
καὶ βοῦς ἀγραύλους διζήμενος ἐνθάδ' ἱκάνεις;
οὐκ ἴδον, οὐ πυθόμην, οὐκ ἄλλου μῦθον ἄκουσα·

and her dear son, a little child so cunningly concealed. He looked into every corner of the great house, then took a bright key, and he opened three boxes full of nectar and lovely ambrosia. And there was much gold and silver lying in them, and many of the nymph's garments in purple and silver like those kept in the sacred houses of the blessed gods. Then, after the son of Leto had fully searched the deep recesses of the great house, he spoke to glorious Hermes:

'Child, lying there in the cradle, tell me quickly about my cattle, or we two will very soon have an ugly quarrel. For I will take hold of you and throw you into misty Tartarus, into a dreadful and hopeless darkness, and neither your mother nor your father shall bring you back to the light, but you will wander under the earth, the leader only of children.'

And Hermes answered him with cunning words: 'Son of Leto, what harsh words are these you have spoken? And have you come here to look for cattle that live in the fields? I have not seen them; I have not heard of them; no one has told me of them. I could not give news of

οὐκ ἂν μηνύσαιμ', οὐκ ἂν μήνυτρον ἀροίμην·
οὐδὲ βοῶν ἐλατῆρι κραταιῷ φωτὶ ἔοικα,
οὐδ' ἐμὸν ἔργον τοῦτο, πάρος δέ μοι ἄλλα μέμηλεν·
ὕπνος ἐμοί γε μέμηλε καὶ ἡμετέρης γάλα μητρός,
σπάργανά τ' ἀμφ' ὤμοισιν ἔχειν καὶ θερμὰ λοετρά.
μή τις τοῦτο πύθοιτο πόθεν τόδε νεῖκος ἐτύχθη·
καί κεν δὴ μέγα θαῦμα μετ' ἀθανάτοισι γένοιτο
παῖδα νέον γεγαῶτα διὰ προθύροιο περῆσαι
βουσὶ μετ' ἀγραύλοισι· τὸ δ' ἀπρεπέως ἀγορεύεις.
χθὲς γενόμην, ἁπαλοὶ δὲ πόδες, τρηχεῖα δ' ὑπὸ χθών.
εἰ δὲ θέλεις πατρὸς κεφαλὴν μέγαν ὅρκον ὀμοῦμαι·
μὴ μὲν ἐγὼ μήτ' αὐτὸς ὑπίσχομαι αἴτιος εἶναι,
μήτε τιν' ἄλλον ὄπωπα βοῶν κλοπὸν ὑμετεράων,
αἵ τινες αἱ βόες εἰσί· τὸ δὲ κλέος οἷον ἀκούω.)
    Ὣς ἄρ' ἔφη καὶ πυκνὸν ἀπὸ βλεφάρων ἀμαρύσσων
ὀφρύσι ῥιπτάζεσκεν ὀρώμενος ἔνθα καὶ ἔνθα,
μάκρ' ἀποσυρίζων, ἄλιον τὸν μῦθον ἀκούων.

(*Hymn IV*)

them, nor take the reward for such information; I don't look like a
cattle-thief, a strong man; that is no work for me. I care for other
things instead; I care for sleep, and my mother's milk, to have swad-
dling-clothes round my shoulders, and to take warm baths. Don't let
anyone hear how this quarrel started; for it would be a very strange
thing indeed among the deathless gods for a newly born child to come
in through the doorway of the house with cattle from the field; what
you say is impossible. I was born yesterday, and my feet are tender,
and the ground under is rough; but, if you wish, I will swear a great
oath by my father's head, and promise you that I am not guilty myself,
nor have I seen anyone else steal your cattle, whatever these cattle may
be; for I hear only rumours about them.'
    So he spoke; and he looked from side to side with quick darts of his
eyes and kept moving his brows up and down, whistling loudly as he
listened to wasted words.

HOMERIC EPIGRAM

date unknown

35. Midas' Tomb

Χαλκῆ παρθένος εἰμί, Μίδεω δ' ἐπὶ σήματι κεῖμαι·
ἔστ' ἂν ὕδωρ τε νάῃ καὶ δένδρεα μακρὰ τεθήλῃ
ἠέλιός τ' ἀνιὼν λάμπῃ, λαμπρά τε σελήνη,
καὶ ποταμοί γε ῥέωσιν ἀνακλύζῃ δὲ θάλασσα
αὐτοῦ τῇδε μένουσα πολυκλαύτου ἐπὶ τύμβου
ἀγγελέω παριοῦσι Μίδης ὅτι τῇδε τέθαπται.

TYRTAEUS
fl. 685–668 B.C.

36. The Proper Way to Die

Τεθνάμεναι γὰρ καλὸν ἐπὶ προμάχοισι πεσόντα
    ἄνδρ' ἀγαθὸν περὶ ᾗ πατρίδι μαρνάμενον.
τὴν δ' αὐτοῦ προλιπόντα πόλιν καὶ πίονας ἀγροὺς
    πτωχεύειν πάντων ἔστ' ἀνιηρότατον,
πλαζόμενον σὺν μητρὶ φίλῃ καὶ πατρὶ γέροντι
    παισί τε σὺν μικροῖς κουριδίῃ τ' ἀλόχῳ.
ἐχθρὸς μὲν γὰρ τοῖσι μετέσσεται, οὕς κεν ἵκηται
    χρησμοσύνῃ τ' εἴκων καὶ στυγερῇ πενίῃ,

I AM a bronze maiden and I stand on the tomb of Midas. As long as water flows, and the tall trees bloom, and the rising sun shines, and the bright moon, and the rivers run, and the sea swells, standing here on the tomb of many tears I shall announce to those that pass that this is where Midas is buried.

IT is noble for a brave man to fall in the front line of battle, fighting for his country; and most wretched is the man who leaves his city and his rich fields and goes begging, wandering with his mother and his old father, with his young children and his wedded wife. He will be an enemy to those he will mix with, of those he will come to, driven by necessity and hateful poverty. He shames his family and insults his

αἰσχύνει τε γένος, κατὰ δ' ἀγλαὸν εἶδος ἐλέγχει,
  πᾶσα δ' ἀτιμία καὶ κακότης ἕπεται.
εἰ δ' οὕτως ἀνδρός τοι ἀλωμένου οὐδεμί' ὥρη
  γίγνεται, οὔτ' αἰδὼς οὔτ' ὀπίσω γένεος,
θυμῷ γῆς περὶ τῆσδε μαχώμεθα καὶ περὶ παίδων
  θνῄσκωμεν ψυχέων μηκέτι φειδόμενοι.
ὦ νέοι, ἀλλὰ μάχεσθε παρ' ἀλλήλοισι μένοντες,
  μηδὲ φυγῆς αἰσχρᾶς ἄρχετε μηδὲ φόβου,
ἀλλὰ μέγαν ποιεῖσθε καὶ ἄλκιμον ἐν φρεσὶ θυμόν,
  μηδὲ φιλοψυχεῖτ' ἀνδράσι μαρνάμενοι·
τοὺς δὲ παλαιοτέρους, ὧν οὐκέτι γούνατ' ἐλαφρά,
  μὴ καταλείποντες φεύγετε, τοὺς γεραιούς·
αἰσχρὸν γὰρ δὴ τοῦτο μετὰ προμάχοισι πεσόντα
  κεῖσθαι πρόσθε νέων ἄνδρα παλαιότερον,
ἤδη λευκὸν ἔχοντα κάρη πολιόν τε γένειον,
  θυμὸν ἀποπνείοντ' ἄλκιμον ἐν κονίῃ,
αἱματόεντ' αἰδοῖα φίλαις ἐν χερσὶν ἔχοντα —
  αἰσχρὰ τά γ' ὀφθαλμοῖς καὶ νεμεσητὸν ἰδεῖν —
καὶ χρόα γυμνωθέντα· νέοισι δὲ πάντ' ἐπέοικεν,
  ὄφρ' ἐρατῆς ἥβης ἀγλαὸν ἄνθος ἔχῃ·
ἀνδράσι μὲν θηητὸς ἰδεῖν, ἐρατὸς δὲ γυναιξίν,
  ζωὸς ἐών, καλὸς δ' ἐν προμάχοισι πεσών.

handsome looks; every infamy and every misery follow. If then there
is no regard for the homeless man, no honour and no children, let us
fight bravely for this land, let us die for our children, and spare our
lives no more. Young men, fight close to one another, and never be the
first to fly disgracefully, or to be seized by panic, but fill your heart and
your thoughts with ample courage; never consider your own life,
when you are fighting with men. Do not run and abandon the older
men, who no longer have agile knees; do not abandon the old. For it
is shameful when an older man falls in the front line and lies before the
young, one whose hair is white and whose beard is grey, breathing out
his brave spirit in the dust, holding his private parts blood-covered in
his hands — it is an ugly and reproachful sight for the eyes — and his
body naked. Nothing is improper for the young, nothing as long as a
man has the bright flower of lovely youth. While he is alive the men
who see him admire him and the women desire him; and he is beautiful

ἀλλά τις εὖ διαβὰς μενέτω ποσὶν ἀμφοτέροισιν
στηριχθεὶς ἐπὶ γῆς, χεῖλος ὀδοῦσι δακών.

CALLINUS
fl. 660 B.C.

37. *War Is Upon Us*

Μέχρις τεῦ κατάκεισθε; κότ' ἄλκιμον ἕξετε θυμόν,
  ὦ νέοι; οὐδ' αἰδεῖσθ' ἀμφιπερικτίονας,
ὧδε λίην μεθιέντες, ἐν εἰρήνη δὲ δοκεῖτε
  ἧσθαι, ἀτὰρ πόλεμος γαῖαν ἅπασαν ἔχει.

. . . .

καί τις ἀποθνήσκων ὕστατ' ἀκοντισάτω.
τιμῆέν τε γάρ ἐστι καὶ ἀγλαὸν ἀνδρὶ μάχεσθαι
  γῆς πέρι καὶ παίδων κουριδίης τ' ἀλόχου
δυσμενέσιν· θάνατος δὲ τότ' ἔσσεται, ὁππότε κεν δὴ
  Μοῖραι ἐπικλώσωσ'· ἀλλά τις ἰθὺς ἴτω
ἔγχος ἀνασχόμενος καὶ ὑπ' ἀσπίδος ἄλκιμον ἦτορ
  ἔλσας, τὸ πρῶτον μιγνυμένου πολέμου.
οὐ γάρ κως θάνατόν γε φυγεῖν εἱμαρμένον ἐστὶν
  ἄνδρ', οὐδ' εἰ προγόνων ἦ γένος ἀθανάτων.

when killed in the first line of battle. Stand steadfast, with both feet set firm on the ground, biting your lip with your teeth.

How much longer will you be idle? When will you have a stout heart, young men? Are you, so slovenly, not ashamed of your neighbours? You think you are resting in peace, but war grips all the land . . .

And let each cast his javelin for the last time as he dies. For it is an honourable and splendid thing for a man to fight against the enemy for his country, his children and his wedded wife. Death shall come whenever the Fates spin it in their thread; so, as soon as battle is joined, let each man go forward with his spear poised and a stout heart behind his shield. For it is decreed that no man at all shall escape death, even if he is the offspring of immortal forefathers. Often he

πολλάκι δηϊοτῆτα φυγὼν καὶ δοῦπον ἀκόντων·
ἔρχεται, ἐν δ’ οἴκῳ μοῖρα κίχεν θανάτου·
ἀλλ’ ὁ μὲν οὐκ ἔμπης δήμῳ φίλος οὐδὲ ποθεινός,
τὸν δ’ ὀλίγος στενάχει καὶ μέγας, ἤν τι πάθῃ·
λαῷ γὰρ σύμπαντι πόθος κρατερόφρονος ἀνδρὸς
θνήσκοντος· ζώων δ’ ἄξιος ἡμιθέων·
ὥσπερ γάρ μιν πύργον ἐν ὀφθαλμοῖσιν ὁρῶσιν·
ἔρδει γὰρ πολλῶν ἄξια μοῦνος ἐών.

ARCHILOCHUS
fl. 648 B.C.

38. A Poet's Spear

Ἐν δορὶ μέν μοι μᾶζα μεμαγμένη, ἐν δορὶ δ’ οἶνος
Ἰσμαρικός, πίνω δ’ ἐν δορὶ κεκλιμένος.

39. A Poet's Shield

Ἀσπίδι μὲν Σαΐων τις ἀγάλλεται, ἣν παρὰ θάμνῳ
ἔντος ἀμώμητον κάλλιπον οὐκ ἐθέλων·

escapes alive from battle and from the din of the spears, but the fate of death comes on him in his home. This latter man is not dear to the people, nor is he missed; whereas, should something befall the former, men of small and of great means alike lament him. When a brave man dies, it is a loss to the whole people; and while he lives, he is treated as a demigod. For in their eyes he is like a fortress; for single-handed he does the work of many.

My bread is kneaded with my spear, my Ismarian wine is [mixed] by my spear, and I drink reclining on my spear.

Some Thracian [now] is pleased with my shield, which unwillingly I left on a bush in perfect condition on our side [of the battlefield];

αὐτὸς δ' ἐξέφυγον θανάτου τέλος· ἀσπὶς ἐκείνη
ἐρρέτω· ἐξαῦτις κτήσομαι οὐ κακίω.

40. The Real General

Οὐ φιλέω μέγαν στρατηγὸν οὐδὲ διαπεπλιγμένον,
οὐδὲ βοστρύχοισι γαῦρον οὐδ' ὑπεξυρημένον,
ἀλλά μοι σμικρός τις εἴη καὶ περὶ κνήμας ἰδεῖν
ῥοικός, ἀσφαλέως βεβηκὼς ποσσί, καρδίης πλέως.

41. Anything May Happen

Χρημάτων ἄελπτον οὐδέν ἐστιν οὐδ' ἀπώμοτον,
οὐδὲ θαυμάσιον, ἐπειδὴ Ζεὺς πατὴρ Ὀλυμπίων
ἐκ μεσημβρίης ἔθηκε νύκτ' ἀποκρύψας φάος
ἡλίου λάμποντος· λυγρὸν δ' ἦλθ' ἐπ' ἀνθρώπους δέος.
ἐκ δὲ τοῦ καὶ πιστὰ πάντα κἀπίελπτα γίγνεται
ἀνδράσιν· μηδεὶς ἔθ' ὑμῶν εἰσορῶν θαυμαζέτω,
μηδ' ὅταν δελφῖσι θῆρες ἀνταμείψωνται νομὸν
ἐνάλιον καί σφιν θαλάσσης ἠχέεντα κύματα
φίλτερ' ἠπείρου γένηται, τοῖσι δ' ἡδὺ ᾖ ὄρος.

but I escaped death. To hell with that shield! I shall get another, no worse.

I DO not like a tall general, nor a long-shanked one, nor one who is proud of his hair, nor one who is partly shaved. Give me one who is short and bandy-legged to look at, but who walks firmly and is full of courage.

NOTHING is unexpected or can be declared impossible on oath, or strange, since Zeus the father of the Olympians made night out of midday, hiding the light of the shining sun, and dreadful terror came upon the human race. Because of this men can believe and expect anything. Let no one be surprised if he sees the wild beasts take in exchange the salty pastures from the dolphins, and prefer the loud-sounding waves of the ocean to the land, and if they [the dolphins] find the mountains delightful.

ALCMAN

fl. 630 B.C.

42. Hagesichora

Ἔστι τις σιῶν τίσις·
ὁ δ' ὄλβιος, ὅστις εὔφρων
ἀμέραν διαπλέκει
ἄκλαυτος· ἐγὼν δ' ἀείδω
Ἀγιδῶς τὸ φῶς· ὁρῶ
ϝ' ὧτ' ἄλιον, ὅνπερ ἄμιν
Ἀγιδὼ μαρτύρεται
φαίνην· ἐμὲ δ' οὔτ' ἐπαινῆν
οὔτε μωμήσθαι νιν ἁ κλεννὰ χοραγὸς
οὐδ' ἁμῶς ἐῆ· δοκεῖ γὰρ ἤμεν αὔτα
ἐκπρεπὴς τώς, ὥσπερ αἴ τις
ἐν βοτοῖς στάσειεν ἵππον
παγὸν ἀεθλοφόρον καναχάποδα
  τῶν ὑποπετριδίων ὀνείρων.

ἦ οὐχ ὁρῆς; ὁ μὲν κέλης
Ἐνετικός· ἁ δὲ χαίτα
τᾶς ἐμᾶς ἀνεψιᾶς
Ἀγησιχόρας ἐπανθεῖ
χρυσὸς ὡς ἀκήρατος·
τὸ τ' ἀργύριον πρόσωπον,
διαφάδαν τί τοι λέγω;
Ἁγησιχόρα μὲν αὔτα·

THERE is such a thing as the gods' vengeance. But blessed is the man who in wisdom weaves together his days without tears. And so I sing the radiance of Agido. I see her as the sun, to which Agido appeals to shine on us. But the glorious leader of the choir [Hagesichora] does not allow me to praise or to blame her at all. For she herself appears pre-eminent; as if one were to set among the grazing beasts a strong prize-winning horse with ringing hooves, like those in our fleeting dreams.

Do you not see? The race-horse is Venetian: but the hair of my cousin Hagesichora blossoms like pure gold; and her silver face — what can I tell you to make it manifest? This is Hagesichora. She is

ἁ δὲ δευτέρα πεδ' Ἀγιδὼ τὸ ϝεῖδος
ἵππος Ἰβηνῷ Κολαξαῖος δραμήται·
ταὶ Πεληάδες γὰρ ἇμιν
ὀρθρίαι φᾶρος φεροίσαις
νύκτα δι' ἀμβροσίαν ἅτε Σήριον
    ἄστρον αὐηρομέναι μάχονται.

οὔτε γάρ τι πορφύρας
τόσσος κόρος, ὥστ' ἀμύναι,
οὔτε ποικίλος δράκων
παγχρύσιος, οὐδὲ μίτρα
Λυδία, νεανίδων
ἰανογλεφάρων ἄγαλμα,
οὐδὲ ταὶ Ναννῶς κόμαι,
ἀλλ' οὐδ' Ἀρέτα σιειδής,
οὐδὲ Σύλακίς τε καὶ Κλεησισήρα,
οὐδ' ἐς Αἰνησιμβρότας ἐνθοῖσα φασεῖς·
⟨Ἀσταφίς τέ μοι γένοιτο
καὶ ποτιγλέποι Φίλυλλα
Δαμαρέτα τ' ἐρατά τε ϝιανθεμίς⟩ —
    ἀλλ' Ἀγησιχόρα με τείρει.

second to Agido in beauty, but a Scythian horse will run against a
Lydian. For the Pleiades of the dawn, rising through the holy night
like the star of Sirius, compete with us who hold the plough.*

For we do not have enough purple to protect ourselves from them,
or a dappled snake, all of gold, or a Lydian headband, the delight of
soft-eyed maidens, or even the hair of Nanno, or Areta who looks like
a goddess, or Sylacis and Cleësisera. Nor shall you go to Aenisimbrota's
house and say: 'May Astaphis be mine, and may Philylla look at me,
and Damareta and lovely Ianthemis.' But Hagesichora makes me
suffer.

* It is thought the Pleiades were a rival choir and that the plough
was a sacred plough connected with the worship of a god. The whole
passage is doubtful.

οὐ γὰρ ἀ καλλίσφυρος
Ἀγησιχόρα πάρ' αὐτεῖ·
Ἀγιδοῖ δ' ἴκταρ μένει
θωστήριά τ' ἀμ' ἐπαινεῖ.
ἀλλὰ τᾶν εὐχάς, σιοί,
δέξασθε· σιῶν γὰρ ἄνα
καὶ τέλος· χοροστάτις,
ϝείποιμί κ', ἐγὼν μὲν αὐτὰ
παρσένος μάταν ἀπὸ θράνω λέλακα
γλαύξ· ἐγὼν δὲ τᾷ μὲν Ἀώτι μάλιστα
ϝανδάνην ἐρῶ· πόνων γὰρ
ἄμιν ἰάτωρ ἔγεντο·
ἐξ Ἀγησιχόρας δὲ νεάνιδες
    ἰρήνας ἐρατᾶς ἐπέβαν.

τῷ τε γὰρ σηραφόρῳ
αὐτῶς ἕπεται μέγ' ἄρμα,
τῷ κυβερνάτα δὲ χρὴ
κἠν νᾷ μάλιστ' ἀκούην·
ἀ δὲ τᾶν Σηρηνίδων
ἀοιδοτέρα μὲν οὐχί,
σιαὶ γάρ, ἀντὶ δ' ἕνδεκα
παίδων δεκὰς ἄδ' ἀείδει·
φθέγγεται δ' ἄρ' ὥτ' ἐπὶ Ξάνθω ῥοαῖσι
κύκνος· ἀ δ' ἐπιμέρῳ ξανθᾷ κομίσκᾳ. . .

For fair-ankled Hagesichora is not here by my side; she is waiting
close by Agido, and is praising our festival. But, gods, accept their
prayers; for to the gods belong the accomplishment and the fulfilment.
Teacher of the choir, I should say, I, a maiden myself, have screeched
in vain like an owl from the roof-beam. But I wish most of all to please
the Lady of the Dawn. For she has been the healer of our pains; and,
because of Hagesichora, the maidens have found the peace that they
desire.

A great chariot simply follows its trace-horse, and the captain in a
ship must be obeyed swiftly. They may not be more melodious than
the Sirens, for they are goddesses, but these ten young girls sing
against eleven. Their voice is like the swan's on the streams of Xanthus.
And she with her lovely fair hair . . .

ALCMAN

43. Sleep

Εὕδουσι δ' ὀρέων κορυφαί τε καὶ φάραγγες
πρώονές τε καὶ χαράδραι
φῦλά τ' ἑρπέτ' ὅσα τρέφει μέλαινα γαῖα
θῆρές τ' ὀρεσκῷοι καὶ γένος μελισσᾶν
καὶ κνώδαλ' ἐν βένθεσσι πορφυρέας ἁλός·
εὕδουσι δ' οἰωνῶν φῦλα τανυπτερύγων.

MIMNERMUS
fl. 630 B.C.

44. There Is No Joy without Aphrodite

Τίς δὲ βίος, τί δὲ τερπνὸν ἄτερ χρυσῆς Ἀφροδίτης;
τεθναίην, ὅτε μοι μηκέτι ταῦτα μέλοι,
κρυπταδίη φιλότης καὶ μείλιχα δῶρα καὶ εὐνή·
οἷ' ἥβης ἄνθεα γίγνεται ἁρπαλέα
ἀνδράσιν ἠδὲ γυναιξίν· ἐπεὶ δ' ὀδυνηρὸν ἐπέλθῃ
γῆρας, ὅ τ' αἰσχρὸν ὁμῶς καὶ κακὸν ἄνδρα τιθεῖ,
αἰεί μιν φρένας ἀμφὶ κακαὶ τείρουσι μέριμναι,
οὐδ' αὐγὰς προσορῶν τέρπεται ἠελίου,
ἀλλ' ἐχθρὸς μὲν παισίν, ἀτίμαστος δὲ γυναιξίν·
οὕτως ἀργαλέον γῆρας ἔθηκε θεός.

ASLEEP are the peaks and watercourses of the mountains, the head-lands and ravines, all creeping things which the black earth feeds, wild beasts and the race of the bees, and monsters in the depths of the dark sea; asleep are the tribes of the broad-winged birds.

WHAT would life be, what pleasure, without golden Aphrodite? May I die when secret love and sweet gifts and the bed mean nothing to me any more, the things that are the flowers of youth, delightful to men and women. And when painful old age comes, which makes man both ugly and evil, ugly cares always press on his mind, and he finds no pleasure in looking at the light of the sun, but is hated by the boys and scorned by the women. Thus full of suffering has the god made old age.

45. Like the Generations of the Leaves . . .

'Ημεῖς δ' οἷά τε φύλλα φύει πολυάνθεμος ὥρη
ἔαρος, ὅτ' αἶψ' αὐγῆς αὔξεται ἠελίου,
τοῖς ἴκελοι πήχυιον ἐπὶ χρόνον ἄνθεσιν ἥβης
τερπόμεθα, πρὸς θεῶν εἰδότες οὔτε κακὸν
οὔτ' ἀγαθόν· Κῆρες δὲ παρεστήκασι μέλαιναι,
ἡ μὲν ἔχουσα τέλος γήραος ἀργαλέου,
ἡ δ' ἑτέρη θανάτοιο· μίνυνθα δὲ γίγνεται ἥβης
καρπός, ὅσον τ' ἐπὶ γῆν κίδναται ἠέλιος·
αὐτὰρ ἐπὴν δὴ τοῦτο τέλος παραμείψεται ὥρης,
αὐτίκα τεθνάμεναι βέλτιον ἢ βίοτος·
πολλὰ γὰρ ἐν θυμῷ κακὰ γίγνεται· ἄλλοτε οἶκος
τρυχοῦται, πενίης δ' ἔργ' ὀδυνηρὰ πέλει·
ἄλλος δ' αὖ παίδων ἐπιδεύεται, ὧν τε μάλιστα
ἱμείρων κατὰ γῆς ἔρχεται εἰς 'Αΐδην·
ἄλλος νοῦσον ἔχει θυμοφθόρον· οὐδέ τις ἔστιν
ἀνθρώπων, ᾧ Ζεὺς μὴ κακὰ πολλὰ διδοῖ.

But like the leaves that the many-blossomed season of spring brings forth when they grow swiftly in the light of the sun; like them we enjoy the flowers of our youth for a short span of time, not knowing if the gods have good or bad in store for us. But the black Fates stand beside us, one holding out as our fate an old age full of suffering, the other death. The fruit of youth is short-lived, as short as the time the sun is spread out across the earth. But when the time of maturity is over, then at once death is better than living. For much suffering comes to the heart. Sometimes the home is wasted, and poverty's painful work is there; one man has no children, and goes under the earth to Hades longing for them more than anything else; another is in the grip of heart-wasting sickness. There is no mortal to whom Zeus does not give many evils.

SEMONIDES OF AMORGOS

fl. 630 B.C.

46. Hope is Misleading

Ἐν δὲ τὸ κάλλιστον Χῖος ἔειπεν ἀνήρ·
⟨ οἵη περ φύλλων γενεή, τοίη δὲ καὶ ἀνδρῶν.⟩
παῦροι μὴν θνητῶν οὔασι δεξάμενοι
στέρνοισ' ἐγκατέθεντο· πάρεστι γὰρ ἐλπὶς ἑκάστῳ
ἀνδρῶν, ἥ τε νέων στήθεσιν ἐμφύεται.
θνητῶν δ' ὄφρα τις ἄνθος ἔχῃ πολυήρατον ἥβης,
κοῦφον ἔχων θυμὸν πόλλ' ἀτέλεστα νοεῖ·
οὔτε γὰρ ἐλπίδ' ἔχει γηρασέμεν οὔτε θανεῖσθαι
οὐδ', ὑγιὴς ὅταν ᾖ, φροντίδ' ἔχει καμάτου.
νήπιοι, οἷς ταύτῃ κεῖται νόος, οὐ δὲ ἴσασιν,
ὡς χρόνος ἔσθ' ἥβης καὶ βιότου ὀλίγος
θνητοῖσ'. ἀλλὰ σὺ ταῦτα μαθὼν βιότου ποτὶ τέρμα
ψυχῇ τῶν ἀγαθῶν τλῆθι χαριζόμενος.

The man from Chios said one thing, the most beautiful thing: 'Like the generation of the leaves is that of men.' Few mortals who have heard this have taken it truly to heart, for hope is ever present in every man, hope which takes root in the breast of men in their youth. For when a mortal has the lovely blossom of youth, light-heartedly he hopes for many impossible things. He does not believe he will grow old or die; nor when he is well does he bother about sickness. Fools, who think in this way; they do not know that for mortals the time of youth and of life is short. But now that you have learnt this towards the end of your life, treat yourself to the good things [in life].

ANONYMOUS

?7th century B.C.

47. Swallow Song

Ἦλθ', ἦλθε χελιδών,
καλὰς ὥρας ἄγουσα,
καλοὺς ἐνιαυτούς,
ἐπὶ γαστέρα λευκά,
ἐπὶ νῶτα μέλαινα.
παλάθαν σὺ προκύκλει
ἐκ πίονος οἴκου
οἴνου τε δέπαστρον
τυροῦ τε κάνυστρον·
καὶ πύρνα χελιδὼν
καὶ λεκιθίταν
οὐκ ἀπωθεῖται. πότερ' ἀπίωμες, ἢ λαβώμεθα;
εἰ μέν τι δώσεις· εἰ δὲ μή, οὐκ ἐάσομες
ἢ τὰν θύραν φέρωμες ἢ τοὐπέρθυρον,
ἢ τὰν γυναῖκα τὰν ἔσω καθημέναν·
μικρὰ μέν ἐστι, ῥᾳδίως μιν οἴσομες.
ἀλλ' εἰ φέρῃς τι,
μέγα δή τι φέροις.
ἄνοιγ', ἄνοιγε τὰν θύραν χελιδόνι·
οὐ γὰρ γέροντές ἐσμεν, ἀλλὰ παιδία.

SHE has come, the swallow has come, bringing hours of beauty, years of beauty, on her white belly, on her black back. Bring fruit and cake from your rich house and offer it to us, and a cup of wine and a basket of cheese. The swallow does not disdain even wheaten bread or pulse bread. Shall we go, or are we to get something [to eat]? If you give us something, [good], but if you don't we shall not let you be; we shall carry away the door or the lintel, or your wife sitting inside. She is small; we shall carry her easily. But if you give us something, let it be something big. Open, open the door to the swallow; for we are not old men, but children.

ALCAEUS

fl. ?600 B.C.

48. The Great House Flashes

Μαρμαίρει δὲ μέγας δόμος   χάλκῳ· παῖσα δ' "Αρη κεκό-
σμηται στέγα

λάμπραισιν κυνίαισι, κὰτ   τᾶν λεῦκοι κατύπερθεν ἴππιοι
λόφοι

νεύοισιν, κεφάλαισιν ἀν-   δρων ἀγάλματα· χάλκιαι δὲ
πασσάλοις

κρύπτοισιν περικείμεναι   λάμπραι κνάμιδες, ἄρκος ἰσχύρω
βέλεος,

θόρρακές τε νέω λίνω   κόϊλαί τε κὰτ ἀσπίδες βεβλήμεναι·

πὰρ δὲ Χαλκίδικαι σπάθαι,   πὰρ δὲ ζώματα πόλλα καὶ
κυπάσσιδες·

τῶν οὐκ ἔστι λάθεσθ' ἐπει-   δὴ πρώτιστ' ὐπὰ τῶργον
ἔσταμεν τόδε.

49. The Ship of State

I

'Ασυννέτημμι τὼν ἀνέμων στάσιν·
τὸ μὲν γὰρ ἔνθεν κῦμα κυλίνδεται,
τὸ δ' ἔνθεν· ἄμμες δ' ὂν τὸ μέσσον
ναῖ φορήμμεθα συν μελαίνᾳ,

THE great house flashes with bronze; the whole roof is thickly arrayed with shining helmets, from the top of which swing white horsehair plumes that adorn men's heads, ready for battle. And shining bronze greaves, defences against powerful missiles, hang hiding the pegs; and fresh linen breastplates and hollow shields lie on the floor. Near them are swords of Chalcis and next to them many belts and short tunics. We cannot forget these things since first we stood ready for this deed.

I

I AM baffled by the quarrelling winds. One wave rolls up on this side, another on that, and we with our black ship are carried in the middle,

χείμωνι μόχθεντες μεγάλῳ μάλα·
πὲρ μὲν γὰρ ἄντλος ἰστοπέδαν ἔχει,
λαῖφος δὲ πὰν ζάδηλον ἤδη,
καὶ λάκιδες μέγαλαι κὰτ αὖτο,

χόλαισι δ' ἄγκονναι, τὰ δ' ὀήϊα...

II

Τόδ' αὖτε κῦμα τῶν προτέρων ὄνω
στείχει, παρέξει δ' ἄμμι πόνον πόλυν
ἄντλην, ἐπεί κε νᾶος ἔμβαι

. . . .

φαρξώμεθ' ὡς ὤκιστα τοίχοις,
ἒς δ' ἔχυρον λίμενα δρόμωμεν.

καὶ μή τιν' ὄκνος μόλθακος ἀμμέων
λάχῃ· πρόδηλον γὰρ μέγ' ἀέθλιον·
μνάσθητε τὼ πάροιθα μόχθω·
νῦν τις ἄνηρ δόκιμος γενέσθω.

struggling hard against the storm. The bilge-water has reached the mast-socket, and the sail is already worn through, and there are great rents along it and the sheets are slackening, the rudders...

II

This wave is coming again on top of the ones before, and it will give us much hard work to bale out, when it enters the ship.... Let us patch the walls [of the ship] as quickly as we can, and run to a safe harbour. Let none of us be seized by cowardly hesitation, for there is clearly a great struggle ahead. Remember how we suffered in the past. Let each man now prove himself steadfast.

50. Drinking Songs

I

Ὕει μὲν ὁ Ζεῦς, ἐκ δ' ὀράνω μέγας
χείμων, πεπάγαισιν δ' ὑδάτων ῥόαι

. . . .

κάββαλλε τὸν χείμων', ἐπὶ μὲν τίθεις
πῦρ, ἐν δὲ κέρναις οἶνον ἀφειδέως
μέλιχρον, αὔτὰρ ἀμφὶ κόρσαι
μόλθακον ἀμφι . . . γνόφαλλον . . .

II

Τέγγε πλεύμονας οἴνῳ· τὸ γὰρ ἄστρον περιτέλλεται,
ἀ δ' ὤρα χαλέπα, πάντα δὲ δίψαισ' ὑπὰ καύματος,

ἄχει δ' ἐκ πετάλων ἄδεα τέττιξ, πτερύγων δ' ὕπα
κακχέει λιγύραν πύκνον ἀοίδαν, θέρος ὅππατα

φλόγιον κατὰ γᾶν πεπτάμενον πάντα καταυλέῃ.

. . . .

I

Zeus is raining and a great storm comes from the sky, and the streams of water are frozen. . . . Defy the storm, lay on the fire, and mix sweet wine unsparingly and put a soft cushion round . . .

II

Soak your lungs with wine, for the Dog Star is circling, and the season is cruel, and the heat makes all things thirsty. The cicada shrills sweetly from the leaves, and pours an endless clear song from under his wings, now that blazing summer charms all the winged things of the earth. . . .

ἄνθει δὲ σκόλυμος· νῦν δε γύναικες μιαρώταται,
·λέπτοι δ' ἄνδρες, ἐπεὶ δὴ κεφάλαν καὶ γόνα Σείριος

ἄσδει . . .

III

Πώνωμεν· τί τὰ λύχν' ὀμμένομεν; δάκτυλος ἀμέρα·
κὰδ δ' ἄερρε κυλίχναις μεγάλαις αἶταποίκιλλις·

οἶνον γὰρ Σεμέλας καὶ Δίος υἶος λαθικάδεον
ἀνθρώποισιν ἔδωκ'. ἔγχεε κέρναις ἔνα καὶ δύο

πλήαις κὰκ κεφάλας, ἀ δ' ἀτέρα τὰν ἀτέραν κύλιξ
ὠθήτω . . .

51. Drink and Get Drunk With Me

Πῶνε καὶ μέθυ', ὦ Μελάνιππ', ἄμ' ἔμοι· τί φαῖς,
ὄταμε . . . διννάεντ' 'Αχέροντα μέγαν πόρον

ζάβαις, ἀελίω κόθαρον φάος ἄψερον
ὄψεσθ'; ἀλλ' ἄγι μὴ μεγάλων ἐπιβάλλεο·

The artichoke is in bloom; now are women most lustful, but men are weak, because the Dog Star dries up their head and knees . . .

III

Let us drink. Why are we waiting for the lamps? Daylight [has only] a finger [left]. Get hold of the big embellished cups. The son of Semele and Zeus gave men wine to drown their sorrows; mix one of water to two of wine, fill them to the top, let one cup follow hard upon the other . . .

DRINK, and get drunk with me, Melanippus. Why do you think that, when you have crossed the wide stream of swirling Acheron, you will see the pure sunlight again? Come, do not set your heart on great

καὶ γὰρ Σίσυφος Αἰολίδαις βασίλευς ἔφα
ἄνδρων πλεῖστα νοησάμενος θάνατον φύγην

ἀλλὰ καὶ πολύιδρις ἔων ὐπὰ κᾶρι δὶς
διννάεντ' 'Αχέροντ' ἐπέραισε· μέγαν δ' ὦν

αὔτῳ μόχθον ἔχην Κρονίδαις βασίλευς κάτω
μελαίνας χθόνος. ἀλλ' ἄγι μὴ τάδ' ἐπέλπεο ...

52. Helen and Thetis

'Ως λόγος, κάκων ἄχος ἔννεκ' ἔργων
Περράμῳ καὶ παῖσί ποτ', "Ωλεν', ἦλθεν
ἐκ σέθεν πίκρον, πύρι δ' ὤλεσε Ζεῦς
"Ιλιον ἴραν.

οὐ τεαύταν Αἰακίδαις ποθέννην
πάντας ἐς γάμον μάκαρας καλέσσαις
ἄγετ' ἐκ Νήρηος ἔλων μελάθρων
πάρθενον ἄβραν

ἐς δόμον Χέρρωνος· ἔλυσε δ' ἄγνας
ζῶμα παρθένω· φιλότας δ' ἔγεντο
Πήλεος καὶ Νηρείδων ἀρίστας.
ἐς δ' ἐνίαυτον

things. For even King Sisyphus, the son of Aeolus, the most cunning of men, claimed he could escape death; but for all his cunning, he crossed the swirling Acheron twice at the command of Fate; and the king below, the son of Cronos, decreed a heavy labour for him to perform under the black earth. Come, do not hope for these things ...

THE tale runs that, because of their evil deeds, bitter suffering once came from you, Helen, to Priam and his sons, and Zeus destroyed holy Ilium by fire. It was not such a woman the son of Aeacus [Peleus] desired, the gentle girl [Thetis] he led from the palace of Nereus to the house of Cheiron, when he invited all the gods to the wedding. He unfastened the pure maiden's belt, and Peleus and the fairest of the

παῖδα γέννατ' αἰμιθέων φέριστον,
ὄλβιον ξάνθαν ἐλάτηρα πώλων·
οἰ δ' ἀπώλοντ' ἀμφ' Ἐλένᾳ Φρύγες τε
καὶ πόλις αὔτων.

53. *The Dioscuri*

Δεῦτέ μοι νᾶσον Πέλοπος λίποντες
παῖδες ἴφθιμοι Δίος ἠδὲ Λήδας,
ἰλλάῳ θύμῳ προφάνητε, Κάστορ
καὶ Πολύδευκες,

οἰ κὰτ εὔρηαν χθόνα καὶ θάλασσαν
παῖσαν ἔρχεσθ' ὠκυπόδων ἐπ' ἴππων,
ῥῆα δ' ἀνθρώποις θανάτω ῥύεσθε
ζακρυόεντος

εὐσδύγων θρώσκοντες ὂν ἄκρα νάων
πήλοθεν λάμπροι πρότον' ὀντρέχοντες
ἀργαλέᾳ δ' ἐν νύκτι φάος φέροντες
νᾶϊ μελαίνᾳ.

Nereids made love, and in a year's time she bore a son, the greatest of
the demigods, a blessed driver of gold-maned horses. But the Phrygians
and their city perished, because of Helen.

COME to me, strong sons of Zeus and Leda, and leave the island of
Pelops; appear with kindly heart, Castor and Polydeuces, you who go
across the wide earth and over the whole sea upon swift horses, and
who with ease save men from freezing death, brilliant from afar as you
run up the forestays of the well-benched ships, bringing light to the
black ship in the cruel night.

SAPPHO
fl. ?600 B.C.

54. A Prayer to Aphrodite

Ποικιλόθρον' ἀθανάτ' 'Αφρόδιτα,
παῖ Δίος δολόπλοκε, λίσσομαί σε,
μή μ' ἄσαισι μήδ' ὀνίαισι δάμνα,
πότνια, θῦμον·

ἀλλὰ τυίδ' ἔλθ', αἴ ποτα κἀτέρωτα
τὰς ἔμας αὔδας ἀίοισα πήλοι
ἔκλυες, πάτρος δὲ δόμον λίποισα
χρύσιον ἦλθες

ἄρμ' ὑπασδεύξαισα· κάλοι δέ σ' ἆγον
ὤκεες στροῦθοι περὶ γᾶς μελαίνας
πύκνα δίννεντες πτέρ' ἀπ' ὠράνω αἴθ-
ρος διὰ μέσσω,

αἶψα δ' ἐξίκοντο· σὺ δ', ὦ μάκαιρα,
μειδιάσαισ' ἀθανάτῳ προσώπῳ
ἦρε' ὄττι δηῦτε πέπονθα κὤττι
δηῦτε κάλημμι

IMMORTAL Aphrodite on your richly decorated throne, beguiling daughter of Zeus, I beg you, honoured goddess, do not crush my heart with pain and anguish;

But come [now to me] here, if ever in the past, hearing my cries of love from afar, you left your father's golden house and came,

Your chariot yoked. With the flutter of their many wings, beautiful, swift sparrows brought you from the sky through the mid-air to the black earth,

And swiftly did they reach me. And you, Blessed One, smiling with your immortal face, asked what again had happened to me, why again I was begging you [to come here],

κὤττι μοι μάλιστα θέλω γένεσθαι
μαινόλᾳ θύμῳ· ‹τίνα δηῦτε Πείθω
ἄψ σ᾿ ἄγην ἐς σὰν φιλότατα; τίς σ᾿, ὦ
Ψάπφ᾿, ἀδικήει;

‹καὶ γὰρ αἰ φεύγει, ταχέως διώξει·
αἰ δὲ δῶρα μὴ δέκετ᾿, ἀλλὰ δώσει·
αἰ δὲ μὴ φίλει, τάχεως φιλήσει
κωὐκ ἐθέλοισα.›

Ἔλθε μοι καὶ νῦν, χαλέπαν δὲ λῦσον
ἐκ μερίμναν, ὄσσα δέ μοι τέλεσσαι
θῦμος ἰμέρρει, τέλεσον· σὺ δ᾿ αὔτα
σύμμαχος ἔσσο.

55. *To a Young Girl*

Φαίνεταί μοι κῆνος ἴσος θέοισιν
ἔμμεν᾿ ὤνηρ, ὄττις ἐνάντιός τοι
ἰσδάνει καὶ πλάσιον ἆδυ φωνεί-
σας ὐπακούει

And what was the greatest wish of my mad heart: 'Who is it that
now you wish Persuasion to lead back to your friendship? Who wrongs
you, Sappho?

'For if she avoids you [now], soon will she pursue you; and if she
does not accept gifts, [soon] will she offer them; and if she does not
love you, soon will she love you, even against her will.'

Come to me, even now, and free me from my crushing cares; fulfil
all that my heart desires; you yourself be my ally.

EQUAL of the gods seems to me that man who sits opposite you and,
close to you, listens to your sweet words

καὶ γελαίσας ἰμέροεν, τό μ' ἦ μὰν
καρδίαν ἐν στήθεσιν ἐπτόαισεν,
ὡς γὰρ ἔς σ' ἴδω βρόχε', ὥς με φώναις
οὐδ' ἓν ἔτ' εἴκει,

ἀλλ' ἄκαν μὲν γλῶσσα πέπαγε, λέπτον δ'
αὔτικα χρῷ πῦρ ὑπαδεδρόμηκεν,
ὀππάτεσσι δ' οὐδ' ἓν ὄρημμ', ἐπιρρόμ-
βεισι δ' ἄκουαι,

κὰδ δέ μ' ἴδρως κακχέεται, τρόμος δὲ
παῖσαν ἄγρει, χλωροτέρα δὲ ποίας
ἔμμι, τεθνάκην δ' ὀλίγω 'πιδεύης
φαίνομ' ἔμ' αὔτᾳ.

56. The Stars and the Moon

Ἄστερες μὲν ἀμφὶ κάλαν σελάνναν
ἂψ ἀπυκρύπτοισι φάεννον εἶδος,
ὅπποτα πλήθοισα μάλιστα λάμπη
γᾶν ἐπὶ παῖσαν.

And lovely laugh, which has passionately excited the heart in my breast. For whenever I look at you, even for a moment, no voice comes to me,

But my tongue is frozen, and at once a delicate fire flickers under my skin. I no longer see anything with my eyes, and my ears are full of strange sounds.

Sweat pours down me, and trembling seizes me all over. I am paler than grass, and I seem to be little short of death . . .

THE stars about the beautiful moon again hide their radiant shapes, when she is full and shines at her brightest on all the earth.

146

57. Absent from Atthis

. . . .

Σε θέᾳ σ' ἰκέλαν ἀρι-
γνώτᾳ, σᾷ δὲ μάλιστ' ἔχαιρε μόλπᾳ.

νῦν δὲ Λύδαισιν ἐμπρέπεται γυναί-
κεσσιν, ὡς ποτ' ἀελίω
δύντος ἁ βροδοδάκτυλος σελάννα

πάντα περρέχοισ' ἄστρα· φάος δ' ἐπί-
σχει θάλασσαν ἐπ' ἀλμύραν
ἴσως καὶ πολυανθέμοις ἀρούραις·

ἁ δ' ἐέρσα κάλα κέχυται τεθά-
λαισι δὲ βρόδα κἄπαλ' ἄν-
θρυσκα καὶ μελίλωτος ἀνθεμώδης·

πόλλα δὲ ζαφοίταισ' ἀγάνας ἐπι-
μνάσθεισ' Ἄτθιδος ἰμέρῳ
λέπταν ποι φρένα, κῆρ δ' ἄσᾳ βόρηται.

. . . .

[? When we lived together with constancy] she saw you [Atthis] as a
well-known goddess, and took the greatest pleasure in your song.

But now she is pre-eminent among Lydian women, as, when the sun
has set, the rosy-fingered moon

Surpasses all the stars. It throws its light over the salt sea, and
equally over the richly flowered fields.

The lovely dew falls, the roses bloom, the tender chervil and the
flowering honey clover.

And often she walks up and down remembering gentle Atthis with
desire in her tender heart, and her soul is devoured by longing.

58. The Evening Star

Ἔσπερε πάντα φέρων ὄσα φαίνολις ἐσκέδασ' αὔως,
φέρεις ὄιν, φέρεις αἶγα, φέρεις ἄπυ μάτερι παῖδα.

59. Parting

Τεθνάκην δ' ἀδόλως θέλω·
ἄ με ψισδομένα κατελίμπανε,

πόλλα καὶ τόδ' ἔειπέ μοι·
‹ὤιμ' ὡς δεῖνα πεπόνθαμεν,
Ψάπφ', ἦ μάν σ' ἀέκοισ' ἀπυλιμπάνω.›

τὰν δ' ἔγω τάδ' ἀμειβόμαν·
‹χαίροισ' ἔρχεο κἄμεθεν
μέμναισ', οἶσθα γὰρ ὥς σε πεδήπομεν·

‹αἰ δὲ μή, ἀλλά σ' ἔγω θέλω
ὄμμναισαι, σὺ δὲ λάθεαι
ὄσσα μόλθακα καὶ κάλ' ἐπάσχομεν.

HESPERUS, bringing [back] all things which bright dawn scattered;
you bring the sheep, you bring the goat, you bring the child back to
its mother.

TRULY I wish I were dead. She was leaving me in tears,
　And this she told me many times: 'Oh, what unhappiness has struck
us, Sappho; against my deepest wish do I leave you.'
　And this answer I gave to her: 'Go and be happy, and remember me,
for you know how we cared for you.
　'If not, I would remind you, should you forget, of the soft delights
we shared.

‹πόλλοις γὰρ στεφάνοις ἴων
καὶ βρόδων κροκίων τ' ὔμοι
κἀνήτω πὰρ ἔμοι περεθήκαο

‹καὶ πόλλαις ὐπαθύμιδας
πλέκταις ἀμφ' ἀπάλα δέρα
ἀνθέων ἐράτων πεποημμέναις

‹καὶ πόλλῳ θάμακις μύρῳ
βρενθείῳ κεφάλαν ἔμαν
ἐξαλείψαο καὶ βασιληίῳ.›

60. A Young Bride

I

Οἶον τὸ γλυκύμαλον ἐρεύθεται ἄκρῳ ἐπ' ὔσδῳ,
ἄκρον ἐπ' ἀκροτάτῳ, λελάθοντο δὲ μαλοδρόπηες,
οὐ μὰν ἐκλελάθοντ', ἀλλ' οὐκ ἐδύναντ' ἐπίκεσθαι.

'For many wreaths of violet and rose, crocus and dill did you put on your head beside me,

'And round your soft neck many garlands woven of lovely flowers;

'And often you spread much costly myrrh, fit even for a queen, upon my head.'

I

LIKE the sweet apple that reddens at the top of a branch, at the top of the topmost bough; the apple-pickers forgot it – no, they did not forget it, they could not reach so far.

II

οἶαν τὰν ὑάκινθον ἐν ὥρεσι ποίμενες ἄνδρες
πόσσι καταστείβοισι, χάμαι δέ τε πόρφυρον ἄνθος . . .

61. *Bitter-sweet Love*

῎Ερος δηὖτέ μ᾽ ὁ λυσιμέλης δόνει,
γλυκύπικρον ἀμάχανον ὄρπετον.

62. *I Sleep Alone*

Δέδυκε μὲν ἀ σελάννα
καὶ Πληιάδες, μέσαι δὲ
νύκτες, παρὰ δ᾽ ἔρχετ᾽ ὤρα,
ἔγω δὲ μόνα κατεύδω.

63. *Love's Attack*

῎Ερος δ᾽ ἐτίναξέ μοι
φρένας, ὡς ἄνεμος κὰτ ὄρος δρύσιν ἐμπέτων.

II

Like the hyacinth trodden under the shepherds' feet on the hills, when on the ground the purple flower . . .

LOVE the loosener of limbs shakes me again, an inescapable bitter-sweet creature.

THE moon has set, and the Pleiades; it is midnight, the night-watch goes by, and I sleep alone.

LOVE shook my heart, like a mountain-wind that falls upon the oak trees.

64. The Most Lovely Thing

Οἱ μὲν ἰππήων στρότον, οἱ δὲ πέσδων,
οἱ δὲ νάων φαῖσ' ἐπὶ γᾶν μέλαιναν
ἔμμεναι κάλλιστον, ἔγω δὲ κῆν' ὅτ-
τω τις ἔραται·

πάγχυ δ' εὔμαρες σύνετον πόησαι
πάντι τοῦτ', ἀ γὰρ πόλυ περσκέθοισα
κάλλος ἀνθρώπων Ἐλένα τὸν ἄνδρα
τὸν πανάριστον

καλλίποισ' ἔβα 'ς Τροΐαν πλέοισα
κωὐδὲ παῖδος οὐδὲ φίλων τοκήων
πάμπαν ἐμνάσθη, ἀλλὰ παράγαγ' αὔταν
Κύπρις ἔραισαν.

. . . .
. . . .
. . . με νῦν Ἀνακτορίας ὀνέμναι-
σ' οὐ παρεοίσας·

τᾶς κε βολλοίμαν ἔρατόν τε βᾶμα
κἀμάρυχμα λάμπρον ἴδην προσώπω
ἦ τὰ Λύδων ἄρματα καὶ πανόπλοις
πεσδομάχεντας.

SOME say that the most beautiful thing on the black earth is an army of
horsemen, others an army of foot-soldiers, others a fleet of ships; but
I say it is the person you love.

Very easy it is to make this clear to all; for she who far surpassed all
human beings in beauty, Helen,

Deserted her most noble husband and sailed to Troy, and did not
think at all of her child or her dear parents; the Cyprian goddess led
her astray in love.

. . . [Which] now puts me in mind of Anactoria, far away;

Her lovely way of walking, and the bright radiance of her face, I
would rather see than the Lydian chariots and fully armed infantry.

PSEUDO-SAPPHO

65. Andromache's Wedding

‹"Εκτωρ καὶ συνέταιροι ἄγοισ' ἐλικώπιδα
Θήβας ἐξ ἰέρας Πλακίας τ' ἀπ' ἀιννάω
ἄβραν 'Ανδρομάχαν ἐνὶ ναῦσιν ἐπ' ἄλμυρον
πόντον· πόλλα δ' ἐλίγματα χρύσια κἄμματα
πορφύρα κὰτ ἀύτμενα, ποίκιλ' ἀθύρματα,
ἀργύρα τ' ἀνάριθμα ποτήρια κἀλέφαις.›
ὡς εἶπ'· ὀτραλέως δ' ἀνόρουσε πάτηρ φίλος.
φάμα δ' ἦλθε κατὰ πτόλιν εὐρύχορον φίλοις.
αὔτικ' 'Ιλίαδαι σατίναις ὑπ' ἐϋτρόχοις
ἄγον αἰμιόνοις, ἐπέβαινε δὲ παῖς ὄχλος
γυναίκων τ' ἄμα παρθενίκαν τε τανυσφύρων·
χῶρις δ' αὖ Περάμοιο θύγατρες ἐπήισαν.
ἴπποις δ' ἄνδρες ὕπαγον ὑπ' ἄρματα κάμπυλα
πάντες ἠίθεοι . . .
αὖλος δ' ἀδυμέλης κιθάρα τ' ὀνεμίγνυτο
καὶ ψόφος κροτάλων, λιγέως δ' ἄρα πάρθενοι
ἄειδον μέλος ἄγνον, ἴκανε δ' ἐς αἴθερα
ἄχω θεσπεσία . .

'ACROSS the salty sea in their ships, from holy Thebes and from the ever-flowing streams of Placia, Hector and his comrades are bringing the girl with the swift-glancing eyes, delicate Andromache. And they bring many jewels of twisted gold and richly perfumed purple robes, many embroidered things, countless silver cups and [carved] ivory.' So he spoke. And [Hector's] loving father rose quickly. And the news went round the wide city to his friends. At once the men of Troy harnessed mules to the well-wheeled carriages, and the whole crowd of women and slender-ankled girls ascended; but the daughters of Priam went separately; and the men were harnessing their horses under the curved chariot, all young men in their prime . . .

And the sweet-singing pipe was mixed with the lyre and the sound of cymbals, and the maidens sang clearly a pure song, and a wondrous echo reached to the sky . . .

μύρρα καὶ κασία λίβανος τ' ὀνεμείχνυτο·
γύναικες δ' ἐλέλυσδον ὅσαι προγενέστεραι
πάντες δ' ἄνδρες ἐπήρατον ἴαχον ὄρθιον
Πάον' ὀνκαλέοντες ἑκάβολον εὐλύραν,
ὕμνην δ' "Εκτορα κ' 'Ανδρομάχαν θεοεικέλοις.

SOLON
fl. 594 B.C.

66. They Hurry Here and There

Σπεύδει δ' ἄλλοθεν ἄλλος· ὁ μὲν κατὰ πόντον ἀλᾶται
  ἐν νηυσὶν χρήζων οἴκαδε κέρδος ἄγειν
ἰχθυόεντ', ἀνέμοισι φορεύμενος ἀργαλέοισιν,
  φειδωλὴν ψυχῆς οὐδεμίαν θέμενος·
ἄλλος γῆν τέμνων πολυδένδρεον εἰς ἐνιαυτὸν
  λατρεύει, τοῖσιν καμπύλ' ἄροτρα μέλει·
ἄλλος 'Αθηναίης τε καὶ 'Ηφαίστου πολυτέχνεω
  ἔργα δαεὶς χειροῖν ξυλλέγεται βίοτον·
ἄλλος 'Ολυμπιάδων Μουσέων πάρα δῶρα διδαχθείς,
  ἱμερτῆς σοφίης μέτρον ἐπιστάμενος·

Myrrh and cassia and frankincense were mingled together, and all the older women raised a joyous shout; and all the men sang forth their lovely loud song, invoking Paean, the far-shafting god, the splendid harper. And they sang of Hector and Andromache, who looked like gods.

THEY hurry here and there; one man roams over the fish-breeding sea in the hope of shipping home some profit, driven by terrible winds, quite careless of his life; another cultivates the land, ploughing [it] every tree-rich year with curved ploughshares; another, trained in the skills of Athene and Hephaestus of many trades, makes a living by the labour of his hands; another has learned the gifts of the Olympian Muses and mastered the measures of the wisdom men long for; far-

ἄλλον μάντιν ἔθηκεν ἄναξ ἑκάεργος Ἀπόλλων,
   ἔγνω δ' ἀνδρὶ κακὸν τηλόθεν ἐρχόμενον,
ᾧ συνομαρτήσωσι θεοί· τὰ δὲ μόρσιμα πάντως
   οὔτε τις οἰωνὸς ῥύσεται οὔθ' ἱερά·
ἄλλοι Παιῶνος πολυφαρμάκου ἔργον ἔχοντες
   ἰητροί, καὶ τοῖς οὐδὲν ἔπεστι τέλος·
πολλάκι δ' ἐξ ὀλίγης ὀδύνης μέγα γίγνεται ἄλγος,
   κοὐκ ἄν τις λύσαιτ' ἤπια φάρμακα δούς·
τὸν δὲ κακαῖς νούσοισι κυκώμενον ἀργαλέαις τε
   ἁψάμενος χειροῖν αἶψα τίθησ' ὑγιῆ.

STESICHORUS
c. 630–c. 553 B.C.

67. The Setting Sun

Ἀέλιος δ' Ὑπεριονίδας δέπας ἐσκατέβαινε
χρύσεον, ὄφρα δι' Ὠκεανοῖο περάσας
ἀφίκοιθ' ἱερᾶς ποτὶ βένθεα νυκτὸς ἐρεμνᾶς
ποτὶ ματέρα κουριδίαν τ' ἄλοχον παῖδάς τε φίλους·
ὁ δ' ἐς ἄλσος ἔβα δάφναισι κατάσκιον
ποσσὶ πάϊς Διός.

shafting king Apollo makes another a seer, and he sees from a distance the evil coming to the men on whom the gods attend; but what is fated neither bird[-omen] nor sacrifice can avert. Others are doctors with the skill of Paeon of the many drugs, and there is no end to them. But often great suffering springs from a small pain, and no one can cure it by administering soothing medicines, whereas a touch of the hand can swiftly cure one who is in the throes of painful sickness.

THE sun, the child of Hyperion, was descending into the golden bowl to cross the Ocean and reach the depths of holy dark night, [to come] to his mother, his lawful wife and his dear children. And the son of Zeus went on foot to the grove, which was deeply shaded by laurels.

IBYCUS
fl. 560 B.C.

68. No Rest from Love

Ἦρι μὲν αἵ τε Κυδώνιαι
μηλίδες ἀρδόμεναι ῥοᾶν
ἐκ ποταμῶν, ἵνα Παρθένων
κῆπος ἀκήρατος, αἵ τ᾽ οἰνανθίδες
αὐξόμεναι σκιεροῖσιν ὑφ᾽ ἔρνεσιν
οἰαρέοις θαλέθοισιν· ἐμοὶ δ᾽ ἔρος
οὐδεμίαν κατάκοιτος ὥραν,
ἄθ᾽ ὑπὸ στεροπᾶς φλέγων
Θρηΐκιος βορέας,
ἀΐσσων παρὰ Κύπριδος ἀζαλέ-
αις μανίαισιν ἐρεμνὸς ἀθαμβὴς
ἐγκρατέως πεδόθεν φυλάσσει
ἡμετέρας φρένας.

69. The Wide Nets of Cypris

Ἔρος αὖτέ με κυανέοισιν ὑπὸ
βλεφάροις τακέρ᾽ ὄμμασι δερκόμενος
κηλήμασι παντοδαποῖς ἐς ἄπει-
ρα δίκτυα Κύπριδος ἐσβάλλει·

In spring the Cydonian quinces, watered by the river streams
where the Maidens' inviolate garden lies, and the vine-blossoms, grow
thickly under the shady vine-sprays. But for me love sleeps in no
season; like Thracian Boreas [the north wind] aflame with lightning it
rushes from Cypris, dark and shameless, with withering madness, and
clings powerfully to the roots of my heart.

Again tender Love, looking (with his eyes) from under his dark
eyelids, throws me with his various spells into Cypris' inescapable nets.

ἦ μὰν τρομέω νιν ἐπερχόμενον,
ὥστε φερέζυγος ἵππος ἀεθλοφόρος ποτὶ γήραϊ
ἀέκων σὺν ὄχεσφι θοοῖς ἐς ἅμιλλαν ἔβα.

PHOCYLIDES
fl. 544 B.C.

70. The Evil Lerians

Καὶ τόδε Φωκυλίδου· Λέριοι κακοί· οὐχ ὁ μέν, ὃς δ᾽ οὔ·
πάντες, πλὴν Προκλέους· καὶ Προκλέης Λέριος.

ANACREON
c. 563–478 B.C.

71. To Artemis

Γουνοῦμαι σ᾽, ἐλαφηβόλε,
ξανθὴ παῖ Διός, ἀγρίων
δέσποιν᾽ Ἄρτεμι θηρῶν·
ἦ κου νῦν ἐπὶ Ληθαίου
δίνῃσι θρασυκαρδίων
ἀνδρῶν ἐσκατορᾷς πόλιν
χαίρουσ᾽· οὐ γὰρ ἀνημέρους
ποιμαίνεις πολιήτας.

I am truly afraid of his onslaught, like an ageing champion team-horse
that unwillingly enters the competition with his swift chariot.

AND this is by Phocylides: The Lerians are evil. Not one man [evil],
another not; but all, except Procles; and Procles too is a Lerian.

I BESEECH you, Artemis, fair-haired child of Zeus, huntress of the deer,
mistress of wild beasts; now from the whirling waters of Lethaeus be
happy to watch this city of brave-hearted men; for you do not shepherd
savage citizens.

72. *To Dionysus*

Ὦναξ, ᾧ δαμάλης Ἔρως
καὶ Νύμφαι κυανώπιδες
πορφυρῆ τ' Ἀφροδίτη
συμπαίζουσιν, ἐπιστρέφεαι
δ' ὑψηλὰς ὀρέων κορυφάς·
γουνοῦμαί σε, σὺ δ' εὐμενὴς
ἔλθ' ἡμίν, κεχαρισμένης
δ' εὐχωλῆς ἐπακούειν·
Κλεοβούλῳ δ' ἀγαθὸς γένεο
σύμβουλος, τὸν ἐμὸν γ' ἔρω-
τ', ὦ Δεόνυσε, δέχεσθαι.

73. *The Motley-sandalled Girl*

Σφαίρη δηῦτέ με πορφυρῆ
βάλλων χρυσοκόμης Ἔρως
νήνι ποικιλοσαμβάλῳ
συμπαίζειν προκαλεῖται·
ἡ δ', ἐστὶν γὰρ ἀπ' εὐκτίτου
Λέσβου, τὴν μὲν ἐμὴν κόμην,
λευκὴ γάρ, καταμέμφεται,
πρὸς δ' ἄλλην τινὰ χάσκει.

LORD, with whom Love the conqueror and the dark-eyed Nymphs and rosy Aphrodite play; you who haunt the high peaks of the mountains, I pray to you: come benevolently to me, let my prayer please you, and hearken to it. Be a good counsellor to Cleobulus, and may he, O Dionysus, accept my love.

GOLDEN-HAIRED Love strikes me again with a purple ball, and calls me out to play with a motley-sandalled girl. But she — for she comes from well-built Lesbos — finds fault with my hair, for it is white, and gapes after another girl.

74. My Hair is Already Grey

Πολιοὶ μὲν ἡμὶν ἤδη
κρόταφοι κάρη τε λευκόν,
χαρίεσσα δ' οὐκέθ' ἥβη
πάρα, γηραλέοι δ' ὀδόντες.
γλυκεροῦ δ' οὐκέτι πολλὸς
βιότου χρόνος λέλειπται·

διὰ ταῦτ' ἀνασταλύζω
θαμὰ Τάρταρον δεδοικώς.
'Αΐδεω γάρ ἐστι δεινὸς
μυχός, ἀργαλέη δ' ἐς αὐτὸν
κάτοδος· καὶ γὰρ ἐτοῖμον
καταβάντι μὴ ἀναβῆναι.

75. Bring Wine

I

Φέρ' ὕδωρ, φέρ' οἶνον, ὦ παῖ, φέρε δ' ἀνθεμόεντας ἡμὶν
στεφάνους ἔνεικον, ὡς δὴ πρὸς Ἔρωτα πυκταλίζω.

My temples are already grey and my head is white; graceful youth is
no longer with me, and my teeth are old. No longer is there a long span
of sweet life left to me.

For this I often lament, in fear of Tartarus; for the depth of Hades
is terrible, and the way down to it painful. And also it is certain that for
him who has descended there is no ascent.

I

Boy, bring water, bring wine, bring us garlands of flowers that I may
box with Love.

II

"Αγε δή, φέρ' ἡμίν, ὦ παῖ,
κελέβην, ὅκως ἄμυστιν
προπίω, τὰ μὲν δέκ' ἐγχέας
ὕδατος, τὰ πέντε δ' οἴνου
κυάθους, ὡς ἀνυβριστὶ
ἀνὰ δηῦτε βασσαρήσω.

III

"Αγε δηῦτε μηκέθ' οὕτω
πατάγῳ τε κἀλαλητῷ
Σκυθικὴν πόσιν παρ' οἴνῳ
μελετῶμεν, ἀλλὰ καλοῖς
ὑποπίνοντες ἐν ὕμνοις.

76. The Thracian Filly

Πῶλε Θρηκίη, τί δή με λοξὸν ὄμμασιν βλέπουσα
νηλέως φεύγεις, δοκέεις δέ μ' οὐδὲν εἰδέναι σοφόν;

ἴσθι τοι, καλῶς μὲν ἄν τοι τὸν χαλινὸν ἐμβάλοιμι,
ἡνίας δ' ἔχων στρέφοιμί σ' ἀμφὶ τέρματα δρόμου.

νῦν δὲ λειμῶνάς τε βόσκεαι κοῦφά τε σκιρτῶσα παίζεις,
δεξιὸν γὰρ ἱπποπείρην οὐκ ἔχεις ἐπεμβάτην.

II

Come, boy, bring us a cup to drink deep, mixing ten ladles of water with five of wine, so that I may again break out in Bacchic frenzy without disrespect.

III

Come, let us not think of another Scythian drinking-bout with noise and shouts, but let us drink gently with beautiful songs.

THRACIAN filly, why do you cruelly avoid me, looking askance and thinking that I have no skill at all? Know that I could put a bridle on you correctly, and hold the reins, and turn you round the end of the racecourse. But now you graze on the meadows, and play about, skipping lightly; for you have no able horseman to mount you.

ANACREONTEA
date unknown

77. *Love Stood at My Door*

Μεσονυκτίοις ποτ' ὥραις,
στρέφετην ὅτ' Ἄρκτος ἤδη
κατὰ χεῖρα τὴν Βοώτου,
μερόπων δὲ φῦλα πάντα
κέαται κόπῳ δαμέντα·
τότ' Ἔρως ἐπισταθείς μευ
θυρέων ἔκοπτ' ὀχῆας.
‹τίς, ἔφην, θύρας ἀράσσει;
κατά μευ σχίζεις ὀνείρους.›
ὁ δ' Ἔρως, ‹ἄνοιγε, φησίν·
βρέφος εἰμί, μὴ φόβησαι·
βρέχομαι δὲ κἀσέληνον
κατὰ νύκτα πεπλάνημαι.›
ἐλέησα ταῦτ' ἀκούσας,
ἀνὰ δ' εὐθὺ λύχνον ἅψας
ἀνέῳξα, καὶ βρέφος μὲν
ἐσορῶ φέροντα τόξον
πτέρυγάς τε καὶ φαρέτρην.
παρὰ δ' ἱστίην καθίσας
παλάμαις τε χεῖρας αὐτοῦ
ἀνέθαλπον, ἐκ δὲ χαίτης
ἀπέθλιβον ὑγρὸν ὕδωρ.
ὁ δ', ἐπεὶ κρύος μεθῆκεν,
‹φέρε, φησί, πειράσωμεν
τόδε τόξον, εἴ τι μοι νῦν

At the midnight hour, when the Bear is already turning to the arm of the Waggoner, and all the tribes of mortal men, overcome by fatigue, are lying [asleep], then Love stood at my door and knocked on the bolt. 'Who', I said, 'is knocking at the door? You are breaking up my dreams.' And Love said: 'Open. I am a little boy, do not be afraid. I am standing in the rain and I have lost my way in the moonless night.' I felt sorry when I heard this and at once lit the lamp and opened the door, and I saw a little boy with wings carrying a bow and a quiver. I sat him by the hearth; I warmed his hands between my palms, and squeezed the (damp) water out of his hair. And he, when he no longer felt cold, said, 'Come, let us try this bow, to see if the string is at all

βλάβεται βραχεῖσα νευρή.›
τανύει δὲ καί με τύπτει
μέσον ἧπαρ, ὥσπερ οἶστρος·
ἀνὰ δ' ἄλλεται καχάζων,
‹ξένε δ', εἶπε, συγχάρηθι·
κέρας ἀβλαβὲς μὲν ἦν μοι,
σὺ δὲ καρδίαν πονήσεις.›

78. A Cicada

Μακαρίζομέν σε, τέττιξ,
ὅτε δενδρέων ἐπ' ἄκρων
ὀλίγην δρόσον πεπωκὼς
βασιλεὺς ὅπως ἀείδεις·
σὰ γάρ ἐστι κεῖνα πάντα,
ὁπόσα βλέπεις ἐν ἀγροῖς,
ὁπόσα τρέφουσιν ὗλαι.
σὺ δὲ φιλία γεωργῶν
ἀπὸ μηδενός τι βλάπτων·
σὺ δὲ τίμιος βροτοῖσιν,
θέρεος γλυκὺς προφήτης.
φιλέουσι μέν σε Μοῦσαι,
φιλέει δὲ Φοῖβος αὐτός,
λιγυρὴν δ' ἔδωκεν οἴμην.
τὸ δὲ γῆρας οὔ σε τείρει,
σοφέ, γηγενής, φίλυμνε·
ἀπαθής, ἀναιμόσαρκε,
σχεδὸν εἶ θεοῖς ὅμοιος.

damaged by the damp.' He draws [the bow], and strikes me in the middle of my heart, like a maddening sting. He jumps up, laughing loudly. 'My host,' he said, 'rejoice with me. My bow has suffered no damage, but your heart will ache.'

WE bless you, cicada, when, having sipped a little dew, from the tops of trees you sing like a king; for yours are all the things that you see in the fields; all that the woods grow is yours; you are a friend of the farmers, for you damage nothing. And you are honoured by mankind, the sweet prophet of spring. The Muses love you, and Phoebus himself – for he gave you your shrill song. Old age does not weigh upon you, wise one, earth-born, lover of song. Undisturbed, of bloodless flesh, you are almost like the gods.

THEOGNIS

fl. 520 B.C.

79. Cyrnus

Σοὶ μὲν ἐγὼ πτέρ' ἔδωκα, σὺν οἷς ἐπ' ἀπείρονα πόντον
  πωτήσῃ καὶ γῆν πᾶσαν ἀειράμενος
ῥηϊδίως· θοίνῃς δὲ καὶ εἰλαπίνῃσι παρέσσῃ
  ἐν πάσαις, πολλῶν κείμενος ἐν στόμασιν·
καί σε σὺν αὐλίσκοισι λιγυφθόγγοις νέοι ἄνδρες
  ἐν κώμοις ἐρατοῖς καλά τε καὶ λιγέα
ᾄσονται· καὶ ὅταν δνοφερῆς ὑπὸ κεύθεσι γαίης
  βῇς πολυκωκύτους εἰς Ἀΐδαο δόμους,
οὐδὲ τότ' οὐδὲ θανὼν ἀπολεῖς κλέος, ἀλλὰ μελήσεις
  ἄφθιτον ἀνθρώποις αἰὲν ἔχων ὄνομα,
Κύρνε, καθ' Ἑλλάδα γῆν στρωφώμενος ἠδ' ἀνὰ νήσους,
  ἰχθυόεντα περῶν πόντον ἐπ' ἀτρύγετον,
οὐχ ἵπποις θνητοῖσιν ἐφήμενος· ἀλλά σε πέμψει
  ἀγλαὰ Μουσάων δῶρα ἰοστεφάνων·
πᾶσι γάρ, οἷσι μέμηλε, καὶ ἐσσομένοισιν ἀοιδὴ
  ἔσσῃ ὁμῶς, ὄφρ' ἂν ᾖ γῆ τε καὶ ἠέλιος·
αὐτὰρ ἐγὼν ὀλίγης παρὰ σεῦ οὐ τυγχάνω αἰδοῦς,
  ἀλλ' ὥσπερ μικρὸν παῖδα λόγοις μ' ἀπατᾷς.

I HAVE given you wings on which you may rise and fly with ease over
the endless sea and over the whole earth. You will be present at all
feasts and banquets, on the tongues of many men; and young men will
sing loud and clear of you during [their] lovely revels accompanied by
their little clear-toned flutes. And, when you pass into the hiding-
places of the dark earth, into the house of Hades filled with lamentation,
not even then, not even when dead, will you lose your glory, but, since
your name will be undying among men, you will be famous, Cyrnus,
as you circle round the land of Greece and the islands, crossing the
unharvested fish-rich sea, not riding on mortal horses. The glorious
gifts of the violet-crowned Muses will send you on your way, for you
will be with all who care and who will care for songs, as long as there
is earth and sun. Yet I do not have even a little respect from you, but
you deceive me with your talk, as if I were a little child.

SIMONIDES
556–467 B.C.

80. *The Greek Dead at Thermopylae*

Τῶν ἐν Θερμοπύλαις θανόντων
εὐκλεὴς μὲν ἁ τύχα, καλὸς δ' ὁ πότμος,
βωμὸς δ' ὁ τάφος, πρὸ γόων δὲ μνᾶστις, ὁ δ' οἶκτος ἔπαινος·
ἐντάφιον δὲ τοιοῦτον οὔτ' εὐρὼς
οὔθ' ὁ πανδαμάτωρ ἀμαυρώσει χρόνος.
ἀνδρῶν ἀγαθῶν ὅδε σηκὸς οἰκέταν εὐδοξίαν
Ἑλλάδος εἵλετο· μαρτυρεῖ δὲ καὶ Λεωνίδας,
Σπάρτας βασιλεύς, ἀρετᾶς μέγαν λελοιπὼς
κόσμον ἀέναόν τε κλέος.

81. *Danae*

Ὅτε λάρνακι
ἐν δαιδαλέᾳ
ἄνεμός τε μιν πνέων
κινηθεῖσά τε λίμνα δείματι
ἔρειπεν, οὐκ ἀδιάντοισι παρειαῖς
ἀμφί τε Περσέϊ βάλλε φίλαν χέρα

GLORIOUS is the fate of those who died at Thermopylae, and beautiful their death; their tomb is an altar; for lamentation they have remembrance, for sorrow praise. Mould will never darken such a winding-sheet, nor all-conquering time. This shrine of brave men has taken the glory of Greece to itself; Leonidas, King of Sparta, too, is witness, who has left behind him the great glory of his valour, and undying fame.

WHEN the wind blew on her in the carved chest, and the water was rough, she fell back with fear, her cheeks wet with tears, and put her hand round Perseus and said: 'Child, how much I suffer, but you sleep,

εἶπέν τ'· ‹ὦ τέκος, οἶον ἔχω πόνον·
σὺ δ' ἀωτεῖς, γαλαθηνῷ
δ' ἤθεϊ κνοώσσεις
ἐν ἀτερπέϊ δούρατι χαλκεογόμφῳ
τῷδε νυκτιλαμπεῖ,
κυανέῳ δνόφῳ ταθείς·
ἄχναν δ' ὕπερθε τεᾶν κομᾶν
βαθεῖαν παριόντος
κύματος οὐκ ἀλέγεις, οὐδ' ἀνέμου
φθόγγον, πορφυρέᾳ
κείμενος ἐν χλανίδι, πρόσωπον καλόν.
εἰ δέ τοι δεινὸν τό γε δεινὸν ἦν,
καί κεν ἐμῶν ῥημάτων
λεπτὸν ὑπεῖχες οὖας.
κέλομαι δ', εὗδε βρέφος,
εὑδέτω δὲ πόντος, εὑδέτω δ' ἄμετρον κακόν·
μεταβουλία δέ τις φανείη,
Ζεῦ πάτερ, ἐκ σέο·
ὅττι δὲ θαρσαλέον ἔπος εὔχομαι
ἢ νόσφι δίκας,
σύγγνωθί μοι.›

and like a tender baby slumber in this joyless, bronze-studded chest
that shines in the night, lying stretched out in black gloom. You do
not notice the deep foam of the wave passing over your hair, nor the
cry of the wind as you lie in a purple blanket, with your face so beauti-
ful. If what is terrible were terrible for you, you would open your soft
ear to my words. Sleep, child, I bid you, and sleep the sea, and sleep
the measureless suffering. May some change appear from you, father
Zeus. Forgive me, if I speak too bold a word, or what is beyond my
rights.'

82. On the Spartan Dead at Thermopylae

'Ω ξεῖν', ἀγγέλλειν Λακεδαιμονίοις ὅτι τῇδε
κείμεθα τοῖς κείνων ῥήμασι πειθόμενοι.

83. On the Seer Megistias

Μνῆμα τόδε κλεινοῖο Μεγιστίου, ὅν ποτε Μῆδοι
Σπερχειὸν ποταμὸν κτεῖναν ἀμειψάμενοι,
μάντιος, ὅς τότε κῆρας ἐπερχομένας σάφα εἰδὼς
οὐκ ἔτλη Σπάρτης ἡγεμόνας προλιπεῖν.

84. Pausanias' Offering at Delphi

Ἑλλήνων ἀρχηγὸς ἐπεὶ στρατὸν ὤλεσα Μήδων
Παυσανίας, Φοίβῳ μνῆμ' ἀνέθηκα τόδε.

STRANGER, take this message to the Spartans: that here we lie, obedient to their orders.

THIS is the tomb of renowned Megistias, whom the Persians killed when they crossed the river Spercheius; a seer, though he knew well then that death was coming, he did not allow himself to abandon the leaders of Sparta.

I, PAUSANIAS, the leader of the Greeks, dedicated this monument to Phoebus, when I destroyed the army of the Medes.

85. On the Spartan Dead

Ἄσβεστον κλέος οἵδε φίλῃ περὶ πατρίδι θέντες
κυάνεον θανάτου ἀμφεβάλοντο νέφος·
οὐδὲ τεθνᾶσι θανόντες, ἐπεί σφ' ἀρετὴ καθύπερθεν
κυδαίνουσ' ἀνάγει δώματος ἐξ Ἀίδεω.

86. On the Defenders of Tegea

Τῶνδε δι' ἀνθρώπων ἀρετὰν οὐχ ἵκετο καπνὸς
αἰθέρα δαιομένης εὐρυχόρου Τεγέας,
οἳ βούλοντο πόλιν μὲν ἐλευθερίᾳ τεθαλυῖαν
παισὶ λιπεῖν, αὐτοὶ δ' ἐν προμάχοισι θανεῖν.

87. Timocreon

Πολλὰ φαγὼν καὶ πολλὰ πιὼν καὶ πολλὰ κάκ' εἰπὼν
ἀνθρώπους κεῖμαι Τιμοκρέων Ῥόδιος.

THESE men bestowed ever-blazing glory upon their fatherland, and folded around themselves the dark cloud of death. But, though they have died, they are not dead, since their valour which sheds glory on them from above lifts them from the house of Hades.

BECAUSE of the valour of these men, smoke from the burning of spacious Tegea did not reach the sky; they wished to leave to their children a city blossoming with freedom, and to die themselves in the forefront of the battle.

AFTER eating much and drinking much and speaking much abuse against mankind, I lie here, Timocreon of Rhodes.

ANONYMOUS

late 6th century B.C.

88. Harmodius and Aristogeiton

'Εν μύρτου κλαδὶ τὸ ξίφος φορήσω
ὥσπερ Ἁρμόδιος καὶ Ἀριστογείτων,
ὅτε τὸν τύραννον κανέτην
ἰσονόμους τ' Ἀθήνας ἐποιησάτην.

Φίλταθ' Ἁρμόδι', οὔ τί πω τέθνηκας,
νήσοις δ' ἐν μακάρων σέ φασιν εἶναι,
ἵνα περ ποδώκης Ἀχιλεύς,
Τυδείδην τέ φασιν ἐσθλὸν Διομήδεα.

'Εν μύρτου κλαδὶ τὸ ξίφος φορήσω,
ὥσπερ Ἁρμόδιος καὶ Ἀριστογείτων,
ὅτ' Ἀθηναίης ἐν θυσίαις
ἄνδρα τύραννον Ἵππαρχον ἐκαινέτην.

Αἰεὶ σφῶν κλέος ἔσσεται κατ' αἶαν,
φίλταθ' Ἁρμόδιε καὶ Ἀριστόγειτον,
ὅτι τὸν τύραννον κανέτην,
ἰσονόμους τ' Ἀθήνας ἐποιησάτην.

I SHALL carry my sword within a myrtle branch, as did Harmodius and Aristogeiton when they slew the tyrant and made Athens a city of just laws.

Dearest Harmodius, you are not yet dead, but they say that you are in the Islands of the Blessed, where swift-footed Achilles is and, they say, the son of Tydeus, brave Diomedes.

I shall carry my sword within a myrtle branch, as did Harmodius and Aristogeiton when at the sacrifice to Athene they slew Hipparchos, the tyrant.

Their fame shall live on the earth for ever, dearest Harmodius and Aristogeiton, because they slew the tyrant and made Athens a city of just laws.

AESCHYLUS
525–456 B.C.

89. Salamis

ΑΓΓΕΛΟΣ

Ἦρξεν μέν, ὦ δέσποινα, τοῦ παντὸς κακοῦ
φανεὶς ἀλάστωρ ἢ κακὸς δαίμων ποθέν.
ἀνὴρ γὰρ Ἕλλην ἐξ Ἀθηναίων στρατοῦ
ἐλθὼν ἔλεξε παιδὶ σῷ Ξέρξῃ τάδε,
ὡς εἰ μελαίνης νυκτὸς ἵξεται κνέφας,
Ἕλληνες οὐ μενοῖεν, ἀλλὰ σέλμασιν
ναῶν ἐπενθορόντες ἄλλος ἄλλοσε
δρασμῷ κρυφαίῳ βίοτον ἐκσωσοίατο.
ὁ δ᾽ εὐθὺς ὡς ἤκουσεν, οὐ ξυνεὶς δόλον
Ἕλληνος ἀνδρὸς οὐδὲ τὸν θεῶν φθόνον,
πᾶσιν προφωνεῖ τόνδε ναυάρχοις λόγον,
εὖτ᾽ ἂν φλέγων ἀκτῖσιν ἥλιος χθόνα
λήξῃ, κνέφας δὲ τέμενος αἰθέρος λάβῃ,
τάξαι νεῶν μὲν στῖφος ἐν στοίχοις τρισὶν
ἔκπλους φυλάσσειν καὶ πόρους ἁλιρρόθους,
ἄλλας δὲ κύκλῳ νῆσον Αἴαντος πέριξ·
ὡς εἰ μόρον φευξοίαθ᾽ Ἕλληνες κακόν,
ναυσὶν κρυφαίως δρασμὸν εὑρόντες τινά,
πᾶσιν στέρεσθαι κρατὸς ἦν προκείμενον.

MESSENGER: Madam, an avenging spirit or evil power appeared and began all these calamities. For a Grecian man came from the Athenian army and told your son Xerxes this: that once the darkness of black night came the Greeks would wait no more, but jump on to the benches of their ships and save their lives in secret flight, scattering right and left. And as soon as he heard this, not seeing the Grecian's trick or the jealousy of the gods, he gave these orders to all his captains: when the sun ceased burning the earth with its rays and darkness seized the domain of the air, they should draw up the pack of our ships in three lines to guard the exits, the pathways of the roaring sea, and the others in a circle round the island of Ajax; and that if the Greeks escaped an evil death, finding some secret way of flight in their ships, it had been decided to behead all [the Persian captains]. All this he said in the

τοσαῦτ' ἔλεξε κάρθ' ὑπ' εὐθύμου φρενός·
οὐ γὰρ τὸ μέλλον ἐκ θεῶν ἠπίστατο.
οἱ δ' οὐκ ἀκόσμως, ἀλλὰ πειθάρχῳ φρενὶ
δεῖπνόν τ' ἐπορσύνοντο, ναυβάτης τ' ἀνὴρ
τροποῦτο κώπην σκαλμὸν ἀμφ' εὐήρετμον.
ἐπεὶ δὲ φέγγος ἡλίου κατέφθιτο
καὶ νὺξ ἐπήει, πᾶς ἀνὴρ κώπης ἄναξ
ἐς ναῦν ἐχώρει πᾶς θ' ὅπλων ἐπιστάτης·
τάξις δὲ τάξιν παρεκάλει νεὼς μακρᾶς·
πλέουσι δ' ὡς ἕκαστος ἦν τεταγμένος,
καὶ πάννυχοι δὴ διάπλοον καθίστασαν
ναῶν ἄνακτες πάντα ναυτικὸν λεών.
καὶ νὺξ ἐχώρει, κοὐ μάλ' Ἑλλήνων στρατὸς
κρυφαῖον ἔκπλουν οὐδαμῇ καθίστατο·
ἐπεί γε μέντοι λευκόπωλος ἡμέρα
πᾶσαν κατέσχε γαῖαν εὐφεγγὴς ἰδεῖν,
πρῶτον μὲν ἠχῇ κέλαδος Ἑλλήνων πάρα
μολπηδὸν ηὐφήμησεν, ὄρθιον δ' ἅμα
ἀντηλάλαξε νησιώτιδος πέτρας
ἠχώ· φόβος δὲ πᾶσι βαρβάροις παρῆν
γνώμης ἀποσφαλεῖσιν· οὐ γὰρ ὡς φυγῇ
παιᾶν' ἐφύμνουν σεμνὸν Ἕλληνες τότε,
ἀλλ' ἐς μάχην ὁρμῶντες εὐψύχῳ θράσει·
σάλπιγξ δ' ἀϋτῇ πάντ' ἐκεῖν' ἐπέφλεγεν.

best of spirits, for he did not know what the gods had in store. And
they [the Persians], not in disorder, but with obedient hearts, prepared
the meal, and each sailor looped his oar on the well-shaped thole-pin.
And when the light of the sun was extinguished and night came, each
[sailor], master of his oar, went to his ship, and each [soldier] as well,
the master of his arms. And the word was passed from rank to rank of
battleships, and they set sail in the order in which they were set, and
the captains of the ships kept all the sailors at the oar the whole night.
The night moved on, but there was no sign of any secret flight by the
Greek fleet. But when day of the white horses gripped all the land,
brilliant to see, the first sound was a shout of triumph from the Greeks,
like a song, and the echo rang back clearly from the island rocks;
terror seized all the barbarians [the Persians] [fearing] that their plan
had failed. For the Greeks were singing a solemn battle-song, not as
men in flight, but as though rushing to battle with fine courage; and
the bugle set all aflame there, with its call. At once at the helmsman's

εὐθὺς δὲ κώπης ῥοθιάδος ξυνεμβολῇ
ἔπαισαν ἅλμην βρύχιον ἐκ κελεύματος,
θοῶς δὲ πάντες ἦσαν ἐκφανεῖς ἰδεῖν.
τὸ δεξιὸν μὲν πρῶτον εὐτάκτως κέρας
ἡγεῖτο κόσμῳ, δεύτερον δ' ὁ πᾶς στόλος
ἐπεξεχώρει, καὶ παρῆν ὁμοῦ κλύειν
πολλὴν βοήν, ⟨ὦ παῖδες Ἑλλήνων ἴτε,
ἐλευθεροῦτε πατρίδ', ἐλευθεροῦτε δὲ
παῖδας, γυναῖκας, θεῶν τε πατρῴων ἕδη,
θήκας τε προγόνων· νῦν ὑπὲρ πάντων ἀγών.⟩
καὶ μὴν παρ' ἡμῶν Περσίδος γλώσσης ῥόθος
ὑπηντίαζε, κοὐκέτ' ἦν μέλλειν ἀκμή.
εὐθὺς δὲ ναῦς ἐν νηὶ χαλκήρη στόλον
ἔπαισεν· ἦρξε δ' ἐμβολῆς Ἑλληνικὴ
ναῦς, κἀποθραύει πάντα Φοινίσσης νεὼς
κόρυμβ', ἐπ' ἄλλην δ' ἄλλος ηὔθυνεν δόρυ.
τὰ πρῶτα μέν νυν ῥεῦμα Περσικοῦ στρατοῦ
ἀντεῖχεν· ὡς δὲ πλῆθος ἐν στενῷ νεῶν
ἤθροιστ', ἀρωγὴ δ' οὔτις ἀλλήλοις παρῆν,
αὐτοὶ θ' ὑφ' αὑτῶν ἐμβόλοις χαλκοστόμοις
παίοντ', ἔθραυον πάντα κωπήρη στόλον,
Ἑλληνικαί τε νῆες οὐκ ἀφρασμόνως
κύκλῳ πέριξ ἔθεινον, ὑπτιοῦτο δὲ

word, with regular dip of the foaming oars, they beat the deep sea; and soon they could all be seen. The right wing (first) led the van in due order, and (secondly) the whole fleet sailed out; and you could hear one great shout: 'Forward sons of the Greeks! Liberate your homeland, liberate your children, your wives, the shrines of your ancestral gods, your fathers' tombs. Now is the struggle for everything!' And from our side the sound of Persian voices answered; but there was no time to wait. At once ship struck ship with its bronze-capped prow; the first to ram was a Greek ship, which sheered away the entire high-pointed stern of a Phoenician ship; then all directed their ships against each other. At first the flood of the Persian fleet held out, but as great numbers of ships gathered in the narrows, and no assistance was possible from one to another, they themselves hit one another with their own bronze beaks; they shattered all the oared fleet, and, not without skill, the Greek ships [had come] round in a circle [and] were charging.

σκάφη νεῶν, θάλασσα δ' οὐκέτ' ἦν ἰδεῖν,
ναυαγίων πλήθουσα καὶ φόνου βροτῶν,
ἀκταὶ δὲ νεκρῶν χοιράδες τ' ἐπλήθυον.
φυγῇ δ' ἀκόσμῳ πᾶσα ναῦς ἡρέσσετο,
ὅσαιπερ ἦσαν βαρβάρου στρατεύματος.
τοὶ δ' ὥστε θύννους ἤ τιν' ἰχθύων βόλον
ἀγαῖσι κωπῶν θραύμασίν τ' ἐρειπίων
ἔπαιον, ἐρράχιζον· οἰμωγὴ δ' ὁμοῦ
κωκύμασιν κατεῖχε πελαγίαν ἅλα,
ἕως κελαινῆς νυκτὸς ὄμμ' ἀφείλετο.
κακῶν δὲ πλῆθος, οὐδ' ἂν εἰ δέκ' ἤματα
στοιχηγοροίην, οὐκ ἂν ἐκπλήσαιμί σοι.
εὖ γὰρ τόδ' ἴσθι, μηδάμ' ἡμέρᾳ μιᾷ
πλῆθος τοσουτάριθμον ἀνθρώπων θανεῖν.

(Persians)

90. *Prometheus Bound*

ΠΡΟΜΗΘΕΥΣ

ˉΩ δῖος αἰθὴρ καὶ ταχύπτεροι πνοαί,
ποταμῶν τε πηγαί, ποντίων τε κυμάτων
ἀνήριθμον γέλασμα, παμμῆτόρ τε γῆ,
καὶ τὸν πανόπτην κύκλον ἡλίου καλῶ·
ἴδεσθέ μ' οἷα πρὸς θεῶν πάσχω θεός.

The hulls of the ships were overturned; and the sea, covered with wreckage and slaughter of men, could no longer be seen. The rocky shores were full of corpses, and all the ships rowed away in a disorderly flight – all those which belonged to the barbarian army. And they [the Greeks], like [men killing] tunny or some other catch of fish, were beating, hacking at them with broken oars and fragments from the wrecks. Cries and lamentation filled the wide sea, until the dark night's eye bore them away. Even if I spoke in order for ten whole days I could not finish telling you all the suffering. Know this for certain, that never in one day have so many men lost their lives.

PROMETHEUS: O divine air, and swift-winged winds, springs of the rivers and numberless laughing flashes of the sea's waves, earth, mother of all, and the all-seeing circle of the sun, I call upon you: see what I, a god, suffer from the gods.

δέρχθηθ' οἵαις αἰκίαισιν
διακναιόμενος τὸν μυριετῆ
χρόνον ἀθλεύσω.
τοιόνδ' ὁ νέος ταγὸς μακάρων
ἐξηῦρ' ἐπ' ἐμοὶ δεσμὸν ἀεικῆ.
φεῦ φεῦ, τὸ παρὸν τό τ' ἐπερχόμενον
πῆμα στενάχω· πῇ ποτε μόχθων
χρὴ τέρματα τῶνδ' ἐπιτεῖλαι;

καίτοι τί φημι; πάντα προυξεπίσταμαι
σκεθρῶς τὰ μέλλοντ', οὐδέ μοι ποταίνιον
πῆμ' οὐδὲν ἥξει. τὴν πεπρωμένην δὲ χρὴ
αἶσαν φέρειν ὡς ῥᾷστα, γιγνώσκονθ' ὅτι
τὸ τῆς ἀνάγκης ἔστ' ἀδήριτον σθένος.
ἀλλ' οὔτε σιγᾶν οὔτε μὴ σιγᾶν τύχας
οἷόν τέ μοι τάσδ' ἐστί. θνητοῖς γὰρ γέρα
πορὼν ἀνάγκαις ταῖσδ' ἐνέζευγμαι τάλας·
ναρθηκοπλήρωτον δὲ θηρῶμαι πυρὸς
πηγὴν κλοπαίαν, ἣ διδάσκαλος τέχνης
πάσης βροτοῖς πέφηνε καὶ μέγας πόρος.
τοιῶνδε ποινὰς ἀμπλακημάτων τίνω
ὑπαιθρίοις δεσμοῖς πεπασσαλευμένος.

(*Prometheus Bound*)

Look upon me, as I am racked with torments, and shall wrestle with them through numberless years. Such shameful bonds has the new king of the gods contrived for me. Alas, alas, I grieve for my present suffering and for the suffering to come; how is there to be an end to these hardships?

Yet, what do I say? Even now I know fully in advance all that is to be, and no misfortune will come unexpected to me. But I must carry my fated destiny as lightly as I can, knowing that the power of necessity is unconquerable. But I can neither be silent, nor can I speak, about this fate of mine; for since I brought a gift to mortals, I have been yoked in this torture, a wretched man. I discovered within a fennel-stalk the stolen fountain of fire, which has proved the teacher of all arts to men, and a great pathway [to achievement]. For such wrongs I pay the penalty, pinned down in shackles beneath the sky.

91. The Sacrifice of Iphigenia

ΧΟΡΟΣ

Ζεύς, ὅστις ποτ' ἐστίν, εἰ τόδ' αὐ-
τῷ φίλον κεκλημένῳ,
τοῦτό νιν προσεννέπω.
οὐκ ἔχω προσεικάσαι
πάντ' ἐπισταθμώμενος
πλὴν Διός, εἰ τὸ μάταν
ἀπὸ φροντίδος ἄχθος
χρὴ βαλεῖν ἐτητύμως.

οὐδ' ὅστις πάροιθεν ἦν μέγας,
παμμάχῳ θράσει βρύων,
οὐδὲ λέξεται πρὶν ὤν·
ὃς δ' ἔπειτ' ἔφυ, τρια-
κτῆρος οἴχεται τυχών.
Ζῆνα δέ τις προφρόνως
ἐπινίκια κλάζων
τεύξεται φρενῶν τὸ πᾶν,

τὸν φρονεῖν βροτοὺς ὁδώ-
σαντα, τὸν πάθει μάθος
θέντα κυρίως ἔχειν.
στάζει δ' ἀνθ' ὕπνου πρὸ καρδίας

CHORUS: Zeus – whosoever he be – if it pleases him to be called this, then I address him so: I have weighed all in the balance, and have nothing to compare him with, (except Zeus,) if truly I am to cast away the futile burden of care-laden thoughts.

He [Uranus] who in the past was great, swelling with the courage that conquers every opponent, shall not even be mentioned as being of the past; and he [Cronos] who was born later, met his victor and is gone. But if with all your heart you cry out 'Zeus is the victor,' you will in all ways attain wisdom,

He [Zeus], who set men on the road to wisdom, who firmly established the law to hold good: 'We learn by suffering.' Instead of sleep, the anguish of painful memory drips before the heart; wisdom comes

μνησιπήμων πόνος· καὶ παρ' ἄ-
κοντας ἦλθε σωφρονεῖν.
δαιμόνων δέ που χάρις βίαιος
σέλμα σεμνὸν ἡμένων.

καὶ τόθ' ἡγεμὼν ὁ πρέ-
σβυς νεῶν 'Αχαιϊκῶν,
μάντιν οὔτινα ψέγων,
ἐμπαίοις τύχαισι συμπνέων,
εὖτ' ἀπλοίᾳ κεναγγεῖ βαρύ-
νοντ' 'Αχαιϊκὸς λεώς,
Χαλκίδος πέραν ἔχων παλιρρό-
χθοις ἐν Αὐλίδος τόποις·

πνοαὶ δ' ἀπὸ Στρυμόνος μολοῦσαι
κακόσχολοι, νήστιδες, δύσορμοι,
βροτῶν ἄλαι,
ναῶν τε καὶ πεισμάτων ἀφειδεῖς,
παλιμμήκη χρόνον τιθεῖσαι
τρίβῳ κατέξαινον ἄνθος 'Αργεί-
ων· ἐπεὶ δὲ καὶ πικροῦ
χείματος ἄλλο μῆχαρ
βριθύτερον πρόμοισιν
μάντις ἔκλαγξεν προφέρων "Αρτεμιν, ὥστε χθόνα βά-
κτροις ἐπικρούσαντας 'Ατρείδας δάκρυ μὴ κατασχεῖν·

even to those who do not want it. It is a gift from the gods, who sit on
the majestic high bench of the helmsman, that cannot be refused.

So it was then, with the elder leader of the Achaean ships; speaking
no word of blame against any prophet, following the sudden wind of
destiny, when the army of the Achaeans was pressed by delay in port
and by starvation on the coast facing Chalcis, in the tide-roaring land
of Aulis;

And the winds from the Strymon, which brought harmful idleness,
hunger, which made anchorage unsafe, which drove men to madness,
and which never spared ships and cables, but prolonged the delay, wore
away, wasted the flower of the Argives. And when the prophet pro-
claimed to the leaders another, harsher remedy for the cruel storm,
bringing forward Artemis [as authority], so that the Atreidae struck
the ground with their staves and could not hold back their tears,

ἄναξ δ' ὁ πρέσβυς τότ' εἶπε φωνῶν·
‹βαρεῖα μὲν κὴρ τὸ μὴ πιθέσθαι,
βαρεῖα δ', εἰ
τέκνον δαΐξω, δόμων ἄγαλμα,
μιαίνων παρθενοσφάγοισι
ῥείθροις πατρῴους χέρας πέλας βω-
μοῦ. τί τῶνδ' ἄνευ κακῶν,
πῶς λιπόναυς γένωμαι
ξυμμαχίας ἁμαρτών;
παυσανέμου γὰρ θυσίας παρθενίου θ' αἵματος ὀρ-
γᾷ περιόργῳ σφ' ἐπιθυμεῖν θέμις. εὖ γὰρ εἴη.›

ἐπεὶ δ' ἀνάγκας ἔδυ λέπαδνον
φρενὸς πνέων δυσσεβῆ τροπαίαν
ἄναγνον, ἀνίερον, τόθεν
τὸ παντότολμον φρονεῖν μετέγνω.
βροτοὺς θρασύνει γὰρ αἰσχρόμητις
τάλαινα παρακοπὰ πρωτοπήμων.
ἔτλα δ' οὖν θυτὴρ γενέ-
σθαι θυγατρός, γυναικοποί-
νων πολέμων ἀρωγὰν
καὶ προτέλεια ναῶν.

Then the elder king spoke thus and said: 'Terrible is the punishment of the disobedient, but terrible is it too if I murder my child, my home's delight, defiling by the altar a father's hands with the streams of blood of a young girl. Which of the two is without suffering? How can I betray my allies, and desert the fleet? It is right that they should long passionately for the sacrifice and the blood of the virgin to make the winds cease. [I shall do it.] May all be well.'

And when he slipped his neck under the yoke of necessity, and the wind of his thoughts veered and blew impious, defiled, unholy, from that moment he turned his thoughts to reckless insolence. For accursed derangement, that makes men do degrading things and that is the beginning of suffering, too much emboldens men. And so he had the heart to sacrifice his daughter, aiding a war to avenge the abduction of a wife – an offering on behalf of the fleet.

λιτὰς δὲ καὶ κληδόνας πατρῴους
παρ' οὐδὲν αἰῶ τε παρθένειον
ἔθεντο φιλόμαχοι βραβῆς.
φράσεν δ' ἀόζοις πατὴρ μετ' εὐχὰν
δίκαν χιμαίρας ὕπερθε βωμοῦ
πέπλοισι περιπετῆ παντὶ θυμῷ
προνωπῆ λαβεῖν ἀέρ-
δην, στόματός τε καλλιπρῴ-
ρου φυλακᾷ κατασχεῖν
φθόγγον ἀραῖον οἴκοις,

βίᾳ χαλινῶν τ' ἀναύδῳ μένει.
κρόκου βαφὰς δ' ἐς πέδον χέουσα
ἔβαλλ' ἕκαστον θυτή-
ρων ἀπ' ὄμματος βέλει φιλοίκτῳ,
πρέπουσά θ' ὡς ἐν γραφαῖς, προσεννέπειν
θέλουσ', ἐπεὶ πολλάκις
πατρὸς κατ' ἀνδρῶνας εὐτραπέζους
ἔμελψεν, ἁγνᾷ δ' ἀταύρωτος αὐδᾷ πατρὸς
φίλου τριτόσπονδον εὔποτμον
παιᾶνα φίλως ἐτίμα.

τὰ δ' ἔνθεν οὔτ' εἶδον οὔτ' ἐννέπω·
τέχναι δὲ Κάλχαντος οὐκ ἄκραντοι.

Her entreaties and her cries of 'Father' and her virgin years the war-
loving leaders thought nothing of. After the prayer, her father told the
attendants resolutely to lift her up above the altar like a kid, wrapped
in her robes and facing downwards, and by covering her beautiful
mouth to retrain the voice that would bring a curse upon his house

By force and by the voiceless strength of the bridle. And she, pour-
ing her saffron-dyed robe towards the ground, from her eyes cast to
each of her killers a shaft which yearned for pity, lovely as in a picture,
trying to call them by name; for many times she had sung in her
father's halls when the men were feasting well, and, [as a heifer] un-
bulled, had lovingly honoured [in song] with pure voice her dear
father's paean of good fortune, as it accompanied the third libation.
What followed I did not see, nor do I relate; but the art of Calchas

Δίκα δὲ τοῖς μὲν παθοῦ-
σιν μαθεῖν ἐπιρρέπει· τὸ μέλλον δ᾽
ἐπεὶ γένοιτ᾽ ἂν κλύοις· πρὸ χαιρέτω·
ἴσον δὲ τῷ προστένειν.
τορὸν γὰρ ἥξει σύνορθρον αὐγαῖς.

(Agamemnon)

92. The Beacons

ΚΛΥΤΑΙΜΗΣΤΡΑ

Ἥφαιστος Ἴδης λαμπρὸν ἐκπέμπων σέλας.
φρυκτὸς δὲ φρυκτὸν δεῦρ᾽ ἀπ᾽ ἀγγάρου πυρὸς
ἔπεμπεν· Ἴδη μὲν πρὸς Ἑρμαῖον λέπας
Λήμνου· μέγαν δὲ πανὸν ἐκ νήσου τρίτον
Ἀθῷον αἶπος Ζηνὸς ἐξεδέξατο,
ὑπερτελής τε, πόντον ὥστε νωτίσαι,
ἰσχὺς πορευτοῦ λαμπάδος πρὸς ἡδονὴν

· · · · · · · ·

πεύκη τὸ χρυσοφεγγές, ὥς τις ἥλιος,
σέλας παραγγείλασα Μακίστου σκοπαῖς·
ὁ δ᾽ οὔτι μέλλων οὐδ᾽ ἀφρασμόνως ὕπνῳ
νικώμενος παρῆκεν ἀγγέλου μέρος·
ἑκὰς δὲ φρυκτοῦ φῶς ἐπ᾽ Εὐρίπου ῥοὰς

is always fulfilled. Justice measures out understanding to those who have suffered. And the future – you may hear about that, when it comes. Let it be greeted in advance; but that is the same as weeping for it [in advance], for it will become clear with the light of dawn.

CLYTAEMNESTRA: Hephaestus, sending out bright light from Ida; beacon sent beacon hither from the [first] courier-fire. Ida to the rock of Hermes in Lemnos; and Athos, third, the peak of Zeus, took the great torch from the island; and leaping over, so as to skim the back of the sea, joyfully, the strength of the courier-fire . . . the pine-tree blaze, passing on its gold-lit radiance like a sun to the watch-towers of Makistos. And these, not delaying, or overcome by sleep through heedlessness, did not neglect their role as messenger; and, from afar, the light of the beacon passed the signal to the guards of Messapion of

Μεσσαπίου φύλαξι σημαίνει μολόν.
οἱ δ' ἀντέλαμψαν καὶ παρήγγειλαν πρόσω
γραίας ἐρείκης θωμὸν ἅψαντες πυρί.
σθένουσα λαμπὰς δ' οὐδέπω μαυρουμένη,
ὑπερθοροῦσα πεδίον Ἀσωποῦ, δίκην
φαιδρᾶς σελήνης, πρὸς Κιθαιρῶνος λέπας,
ἤγειρεν ἄλλην ἐκδοχὴν πομποῦ πυρός,
φάος δὲ τηλέπομπον οὐκ ἠναίνετο
φρουρὰ πλέον καίουσα τῶν εἰρημένων·
λίμνην δ' ὑπὲρ Γοργῶπιν ἔσκηψεν φάος.
ὄρος τ' ἔπ' Αἰγίπλαγκτον ἐξικνούμενον
ὤτρυνε θεσμὸν μὴ χατίζεσθαι πυρός·
πέμπουσι δ' ἀνδαίοντες ἀφθόνῳ μένει
φλογὸς μέγαν πώγωνα, καὶ Σαρωνικοῦ
πορθμοῦ κάτοπτον πρῶν' ὑπερβάλλειν πρόσω
φλέγουσαν· εἶτ' ἔσκηψεν, εὖτ' ἀφίκετο
Ἀραχναῖον αἶπος, ἀστυγείτονας σκοπάς·
κἄπειτ' Ἀτρειδῶν ἐς τόδε σκήπτει στέγος
φάος τόδ' οὐκ ἄπαππον Ἰδαίου πυρός.
τοιοίδε τοί μοι λαμπαδηφόρων νόμοι,
ἄλλος παρ' ἄλλου διαδοχαῖς πληρούμενοι·
νικᾷ δ' ὁ πρῶτος καὶ τελευταῖος δραμών.

(*Agamemnon*)

its coming across the streams of Euripus. They lit [there] a flame in answer, and sent the message on by setting fire to a pile of old heather. And the torch, full of vigour, not yet losing its light, leaped like the bright moon over the plain of Asopus to the rock of Cithaeron, and there roused a new relay of signal-fire. And the watch-post, making a larger fire than had been commanded, did not refuse the light sent from afar; and the light swooped down over the Gorgon-eyed lake, reached the Mountain where Goats roam, and spurred [the watch-post] not to neglect the law of the beacon fire. And with all their might they lit a great beard of flame and sent it onwards, and it went blazing on beyond the headland that looks on the Saronic straits, and hurled itself downwards when it reached the Arachnean peak, that watch-post neighbouring the city. Then it hurled itself down here to the house of the Atreidae, this light, whose ancestor was the fire from Mount Ida. Such are the rules I set my torch-bearers, supplied in succession one after another. He who ran first and last gets the prize.

93. Orestes Sees the Furies

ΟΡΕΣΤΗΣ, ΧΟΡΟΣ

Ορ. Ἴδεσθε χώρας τὴν διπλῆν τυραννίδα
πατροκτόνους τε δωμάτων πορθήτορας.
σεμνοὶ μὲν ἦσαν ἐν θρόνοις τόθ᾽ ἥμενοι,
φίλοι δὲ καὶ νῦν, ὡς ἐπεικάσαι πάθη
πάρεστιν, ὅρκος τ᾽ ἐμμένει πιστώμασι.
ξυνώμοσαν μὲν θάνατον ἀθλίῳ πατρὶ
καὶ ξυνθανεῖσθαι· καὶ τάδ᾽ εὐόρκως ἔχει.
ἴδεσθε δ᾽ αὖτε, τῶνδ᾽ ἐπήκοοι κακῶν,
τὸ μηχάνημα, δεσμὸν ἀθλίῳ πατρί,
πέδας τε χειροῖν καὶ ποδοῖν ξυνωρίδα.
ἐκτείνατ᾽ αὐτὸ καὶ κύκλῳ παρασταδὸν
στέγαστρον ἀνδρὸς δείξαθ᾽, ὡς ἴδῃ πατήρ,
οὐχ οὑμός, ἀλλ᾽ ὁ πάντ᾽ ἐποπτεύων τάδε
Ἥλιος, ἄναγνα μητρὸς ἔργα τῆς ἐμῆς,
ὡς ἂν παρῇ μοι μάρτυς ἐν δίκῃ ποτέ,
ὡς τόνδ᾽ ἐγὼ μετῆλθον ἐνδίκως μόρον
τὸν μητρός· Αἰγίσθου γὰρ οὐ λέγω μόρον·
ἔχει γὰρ αἰσχυντῆρος, ὡς νόμος, δίκην·

ORESTES: Look at the two tyrants of this land [Clytaemnestra and Aegisthus], murderers of my father and plunderers of my house. They were stately when seated on their thrones, and even now they are lovers, as one can see by comparing their fates, and their oath remains true to their pledge. Together they swore death to my unhappy father, and to die together; and they have kept these vows. Look, too, you who have [only] heard about these crimes, at the subtle snare, a shackle for my poor father, with manacles for his hands and fetters for his feet. Spread it [the net] out, stand about it in a circle, and show the man's shroud, so that the father – not mine, but the Sun who looks upon all things here – may see the unholy deeds of my mother, so that he can be a witness for me in some future trial, [testifying] that I justly brought this death on my mother. I am not speaking of Aegisthus' death; for he found, as the law has it, the punishment of an adulterer. But a woman who contrived this horror

ἥτις δ' ἐπ' ἀνδρὶ τοῦτ' ἐμήσατο στύγος,
ἐξ οὗ τέκνων ἤνεγχ' ὑπὸ ζώνην βάρος,
φίλον τέως, νῦν δ' ἐχθρόν, ὡς φαίνει, κακόν,
τί σοι δοκεῖ; μύραινά γ' εἴτ' ἔχιδν' ἔφυ
σήπειν θιγοῦσ' ἂν ἄλλον οὐ δεδηγμένον
τόλμης ἕκατι κἀδίκου φρονήματος.
τοιάδ' ἐμοὶ ξύνοικος ἐν δόμοισι μὴ
γένοιτ'· ὀλοίμην πρόσθεν ἐκ θεῶν ἄπαις.

Χο. αἰαῖ αἰαῖ μελέων ἔργων·
στυγερῷ θανάτῳ διεπράχθης.
αἰαῖ, αἰαῖ,
μίμνοντι δὲ καὶ πάθος ἀνθεῖ.

Ορ. ἔδρασεν ἢ οὐκ ἔδρασε; μαρτυρεῖ δέ μοι
φᾶρος τόδ', ὡς ἔβαψεν Αἰγίσθου ξίφος.
φόνου δὲ κηκὶς ξὺν χρόνῳ ξυμβάλλεται,
πολλὰς βαφὰς φθείρουσα τοῦ ποικίλματος.
νῦν αὐτὸν αἰνῶ, νῦν ἀποιμώζω παρών,
πατροκτόνον θ' ὕφασμα προσφωνῶν τόδε
ἀλγῶ μὲν ἔργα καὶ πάθος γένος τε πᾶν,
ἄζηλα νίκης τῆσδ' ἔχων μιάσματα.

against her husband, the burden of whose children she carried be-
neath her girdle, [a burden] once fond towards her, now, as is
apparent, bitterly hating; how does she look to you? If she had been
a sea-serpent or a viper, her touch alone, without a bite from her
fangs, would breed corruption; such was her cruel and lawless spirit.
May such a woman never live in my house. May the gods grant that
I die childless before that should happen.

CHORUS: Alas, alas, for these unhappy deeds! You [Agamemnon] died
a hateful death. Ah, ah, for the one who survives, too, suffering is
flowering.

ORESTES: Did she do it, or did she not? This cloak is my witness,
since Aegisthus' sword has dyed it red. The gushing blood of mur-
der works with time to destroy the many colours of the woven cloth.
Now I praise him, now, here, I grieve for him, and, speaking of this
web that killed my father, I grieve for deeds and sufferings and for
my whole race, since I have the unenviable taint of guilt as trophy
for this victory.

Χο. οὔτις μερόπων ἀσινῆ βίοτον
  διὰ παντὸς ἄνατος ἀμείψει.
  αἰαῖ, αἰαῖ,
  μόχθος δ' ὁ μὲν αὐτίχ', ὁ δ' ἥξει.

Ορ. ἀλλ' ὡς ἂν εἰδῆτ', οὐ γὰρ οἶδ' ὅπη τελεῖ,
  ὥσπερ ξὺν ἵπποις ἡνιοστροφῶ δρόμου
  ἐξωτέρω· φέρουσι γὰρ νικώμενον
  φρένες δύσαρκτοι· πρὸς δὲ καρδίᾳ φόβος
  ᾄδειν ἕτοιμος ἠδ' ὑπορχεῖσθαι κότῳ.
  ἕως δ' ἔτ' ἔμφρων εἰμί, κηρύσσω φίλοις,
  κτανεῖν τέ φημι μητέρ' οὐκ ἄνευ δίκης,
  πατροκτόνον μίασμα καὶ θεῶν στύγος.
  καὶ φίλτρα τόλμης τῆσδε πλειστηρίζομαι
  τὸν πυθόμαντιν Λοξίαν, χρήσαντ' ἐμοὶ
  πράξαντι μὲν ταῦτ' ἐκτὸς αἰτίας κακῆς
  εἶναι, παρέντα δ' — οὐκ ἐρῶ τὴν ζημίαν·
  τόξῳ γὰρ οὔτις πημάτων προσίξεται.
  καὶ νῦν ὁρᾶτέ μ', ὡς παρεσκευασμένος
  ξὺν τῷδε θαλλῷ καὶ στέφει προσίξομαι
  μεσόμφαλόν θ' ἵδρυμα, Λοξίου πέδον,

CHORUS: No mortal man shall ever pass his life unscathed, intact through everything. Ah, ah, there is suffering now, there is suffering to come.

ORESTES: But you should know — for I do not know where this shall end — that [I stand] like a charioteer with his horses far outside the course; for my mind, hard to govern, is carrying me away in defeat; in my heart terror is ready to sing out and to dance in wrath. But, while I am still in my senses, I cry out to my friends, I say that I have not unjustly killed my mother — that defilement who killed my father and who is hated by the gods. And above all I name Loxias, the prophet of Pytho, as the one who drew me to this rash deed; for he gave me the oracular answer that if I did this I would be free from evil blame, but if I failed — I dare not name the price. That appalling suffering no man's arrow can reach. And now you see me, ready with this branch and crown, as I am going as a suppliant to the temple at the navel of the earth, the land of Loxias, to that famous

πυρός τε φέγγος ἄφθιτον κεκλημένον,
φεύγων τόδ' αἷμα κοινόν· οὐδ' ἐφ' ἑστίαν
ἄλλην τραπέσθαι Λοξίας ἐφίετο.
καὶ μαρτυρεῖν μὲν ὡς ἐπορσύνθη κακὰ
τάδ' ἐν χρόνῳ μοι πάντας 'Αργείους λέγω·
φεύγω δ' ἀλήτης τῆσδε γῆς ἀπόξενος,
ζῶν καὶ τεθνηκὼς τάσδε κληδόνας λιπών.

Χο. ἀλλ' εὖ γ' ἔπραξας, μηδ' ἐπιζευχθῇς στόμα
φήμῃ πονηρᾷ μηδ' ἐπιγλωσσῶ κακά,
ἐλευθερώσας πᾶσαν 'Αργείων πόλιν,
δυοῖν δρακόντοιν εὐπετῶς τεμὼν κάρα.

Ορ. ἆ, ἆ.
δμωαὶ γυναῖκες αἴδε, Γοργόνων δίκην,
φαιοχίτωνες καὶ πεπλεκτανημέναι
πυκνοῖς δράκουσιν· οὐκέτ' ἂν μείναιμ' ἐγώ.

Χο. τίνες σε δόξαι, φίλτατ' ἀνθρώπων πατρί,
στροβοῦσιν; ἴσχε, μὴ φοβοῦ νικῶν πολύ.

Ορ. οὐκ εἰσὶ δόξαι τῶνδε πημάτων ἐμοί·
σαφῶς γὰρ αἵδε μητρὸς ἔγκοτοι κύνες.

undying glow of fire, to escape from the blood of my kin; Loxias
did not wish me to turn to any other hearth. And I call on all the
Argives to testify for me in the future how this evil came about. But
I go into exile, a wanderer, a stranger to this land, alive or dead,
leaving behind this tale.

CHORUS: But you triumphed. Do not let your mouth be fastened to
words of ill fortune, or speak of suffering, when you have liberated
the whole city of the Argives by successfully severing the heads of
two snakes.

ORESTES: Ah, ah! These are captive women, like Gorgons, robed in
grey and coiled with swarming snakes; I can stay no longer!

CHORUS: What shapes of fantasy derange you, son most beloved to his
father? Stay; do not fear, you who have known such victories.

ORESTES: These are not fantasies that torment me. Unmistakably
these are the avenging hounds of my mother.

Χο. ποταίνιον γὰρ αἶμά σοι χεροῖν ἔτι·
  ἐκ τῶνδέ τοι ταραγμὸς ἐς φρένας πίτνει.
Ορ. ἄναξ Ἄπολλον, αἵδε πληθύουσι δή,
  κἀξ ὀμμάτων στάζουσιν αἶμα δυσφιλές.
Χο. εἷς σοὶ καθαρμός· Λοξίας δὲ προσθιγὼν
  ἐλεύθερόν σε τῶνδε πημάτων κτίσει.
Ορ. ὑμεῖς μὲν οὐχ ὁρᾶτε τάσδ᾽, ἐγὼ δ᾽ ὁρῶ·
  ἐλαύνομαι δὲ κοὐκέτ᾽ ἂν μείναιμ᾽ ἐγώ.

(*The Libation-bearers*)

94. His Own Epitaph

Αἰσχύλον Εὐφορίωνος Ἀθηναῖον τόδε κεύθει
μνῆμα καταφθίμενον πυροφόροιο Γέλας·
ἀλκὴν δ᾽ εὐδόκιμον Μαραθώνιον ἄλσος ἂν εἴποι
καὶ βαθυχαιτήεις Μῆδος ἐπιστάμενος.

CHORUS: Still fresh is the blood on your hands; from this, turmoil falls upon your mind.
ORESTES: King Apollo, more and more they come, and loathsome blood drips from their eyes.
CHORUS: Only one can cleanse you. When Loxias touches you, he will set you free from this suffering.
ORESTES: You cannot see them, but I see them. I am driven away, and I can stay no longer.

THIS tomb at Gela, rich in corn, covers [the body of] Aeschylus, son of Euphorion the Athenian. However, the glorious grove of Marathon could speak of his valour, and the long-haired Medes who experienced it.

PINDAR
522–?448 B.C.

95. Pelops

Πρὸς εὐάνθεμον δ' ὅτε φυὰν
λάχναι νιν μέλαν γένειον ἔρεφον,
ἑτοῖμον ἀνεφρόντισεν γάμον

Πισάτα παρὰ πατρὸς εὔ-
    δοξον Ἱπποδάμειαν
σχεθέμεν. ἐγγὺς ἐλ-
    θὼν πολιᾶς ἁλὸς οἶος ἐν ὄρφνᾳ
ἄπυεν βαρύκτυπον
Εὐτρίαιναν· ὁ δ' αὐτῷ
πὰρ ποδὶ σχεδὸν φάνη.
τῷ μὲν εἶπε· ‹Φίλια δῶρα
    Κυπρίας ἄγ' εἴ τι, Ποσεί-
        δαον, ἐς χάριν
τέλλεται, πέδασον ἔγχος
    Οἰνομάου χάλκεον,
ἐμὲ δ' ἐπὶ ταχυτάτων πόρευσον ἁρμάτων
ἐς Ἆλιν, κράτει δὲ πέλασον.
ἐπεὶ τρεῖς τε καὶ δέκ' ἄνδρας ὀλέσαις
μναστῆρας ἀναβάλλεται γάμον

WHEN he grew to the sweet-flowering time, and down was covering
his darkening cheek, he turned his thoughts keenly to marriage;
    To winning glorious Hippodameia from her Pisatan father. He went
down alone beside the grey sea, and cried in the darkness to the loud-
thundering god of the Good Trident. And he appeared close by his feet;
and Pelops said to him: 'If the passionate gifts of Cypris, Poseidon, can, I
pray, be turned to kindness, shackle the bronze spear of Oenomaus,
lead me on the swiftest chariot to Elis, and give me victory. For he has
killed thirteen men, suitors of his daughter, and puts off her wedding.

θυγατρός. ὁ μέγας δὲ κίν-
  δυνος ἄναλκιν οὐ φῶτα λαμβάνει.
θανεῖν δ' οἷσιν ἀνάγ-
  κα, τά κέ τις ἀνώνυμον
γῆρας ἐν σκότῳ καθ-
  ήμενος ἕψοι μάταν,
ἁπάντων καλῶν ἄμμορος; ἀλλ' ἐμοὶ
  μὲν οὗτος ἄεθλος
ὑποκείσεται· τὺ δὲ πρᾶ-
  ξιν φίλαν δίδοι.)
ὣς ἔννεπεν· οὐδ' ἀκράν-
  τοις ἐφάψατο
ἔπεσι. τὸν μὲν ἀγάλλων θεὸς
ἔδωκεν δίφρον τε χρύσεον πτεροῖ-
  σίν τ' ἀκάμαντας ἵππους.

ἕλεν δ' Οἰνομάου βίαν
  παρθένον τε σύνευνον·
ἃ τέκε λαγέτας
  ἐξ ἀρεταῖσι μεμαότας υἱούς.
νῦν δ' ἐν αἱμακουρίαις
  ἀγλααῖσι μέμεικται,
'Αλφεοῦ πόρῳ κλιθείς,
τύμβον ἀμφίπολον ἔχων πο-
  λυξενωτάτῳ παρὰ βωμῷ.

(*Olympian I*)

'Great danger does not wrestle with a cowardly man. But why should those who are doomed to die seek an old age that has no glory, pointlessly sitting in darkness, with no share in anything great? I shall take this contest on; and, you, grant me the issue dear [to my heart].' So he spoke and he used words which were not idle. The god honoured him, and gave him a golden chariot and wing-swift untiring horses.

He conquered powerful Oenomaus and took the maiden as his bride, who bore him six sons – leaders of men, eager for noble deeds. Now buried by the ford of Alphaeus in a well-attended tomb, he shares in the splendid blood-offerings at an altar, where numberless strangers come.

96. Evadne

Ἅ τοι Ποσειδάωνι μει-
    χθεῖσα Κρονίῳ λέγεται
παῖδα ἰόπλοκον Εὐάδναν τεκέμεν.
κρύψε δὲ παρθενίαν ὠδῖνα κόλποις·
κυρίῳ δ' ἐν μηνὶ πέμποισ'
    ἀμφιπόλους ἐκέλευσεν
ἥρωι πορσαίνειν δόμεν
    Εἰλατίδᾳ βρέφος,
ὃς ἀνδρῶν Ἀρκάδων ἄνασσε Φαισά-
    νᾳ, λάχε τ' Ἀλφεὸν οἰκεῖν·
ἔνθα τραφεῖσ' ὑπ' Ἀπόλλω-
    νι γλυκείας πρῶτον ἔψαυσ' Ἀφροδίτας.

οὐδ' ἔλαθ' Αἴπυτον ἐν παν-
    τὶ χρόνῳ κλέπτοισα θεοῖο γόνον·
ἀλλ' ὁ μὲν Πυθῶνάδ', ἐν θυμῷ πιέσαις
    χόλον οὐ φατὸν ὀξείᾳ μελέτᾳ,
ᾤχετ' ἰὼν μαντευσόμενος ταύ-
    τας περ' ἀτλάτου πάθας.
ἁ δὲ φοινικόκροκον ζώ-
    ναν καταθηκαμένα
κάλπιδά τ' ἀργυρέαν λό-
    χμας ὑπὸ κυανέας

SHE [Pitane], who had slept with Poseidon, the son of Cronos, is said to have borne a dark-haired child, Evadne; and she hid her maiden offspring under the folds of her robe. But in the appointed month she ordered her servants to bring the baby and give her to [Aepytus] the heroic son of Eilatus to rear – to him who ruled over the Arcadians at Phaesane, and was living by the river Alpheus. There she grew up, and first touched [the gifts of] sweet Aphrodite beneath Apollo's embrace;

But she did not manage to conceal her pregnancy by the god from Aepytus all the time. With the utmost care he suppressed the unspeakable anger in his heart and went to Delphi to ask the oracle about this unbearable disaster. And she, lowering her purple and saffron belt, and putting down her silver pitcher, bore a godly son in a dark thicket; the

τίκτε θεόφρονα κοῦρον.
τᾷ μὲν ὁ χρυσοκόμας
πραΰμητίν τ' Ἐλείθυι-
αν παρέστασέν τε Μοίρας·

ἦλθεν δ' ὑπὸ σπλάγχνων ὑπ' ὠ-
δῖνός τ' ἐρατᾶς Ἴαμος
ἐς φάος αὐτίκα. τὸν μὲν κνιζομένα
λεῖπε χαμαί· δύο δὲ γλαυκῶπες αὐτὸν
δαιμόνων βουλαῖσιν ἐθρέ-
ψαντο δράκοντες ἀμεμφεῖ
ἰῷ μελισσᾶν καδόμε-
νοι. βασιλεὺς δ' ἐπεὶ
πετραέσσας ἐλαύνων ἵκετ' ἐκ Πυ-
θῶνος, ἅπαντας ἐν οἴκῳ
εἴρετο παῖδα, τὸν Εὐά-
δνα τέκοι· Φοίβου γὰρ αὐτὸν φᾶ γεγάκειν

πατρός, περὶ θνατῶν δ' ἔσε-
σθαι μάντιν ἐπιχθονίοις
ἔξοχον, οὐδέ ποτ' ἐκλείψειν γενεάν.
ὣς ἄρα μάνυε. τοὶ δ' οὔτ' ὦν ἀκοῦσαι
οὔτ' ἰδεῖν εὔχοντο πεμπταῖ-
ον γεγενημένον. ἀλλ' ἐν
κέκρυπτο γὰρ σχοίνῳ βατι-
ᾷ τ' ἐν ἀπειρίτῳ,

golden-haired god sent to her side gentle Eileithyia and the Fates.
And from her womb came Iamos swiftly to the light with the loving
pain of childbirth. In her anxiety she left him on the ground; and by the
will of the gods, two grey-eyed serpents fed him with the bees' harmless
poison [honey]. When the king came riding back from rocky Pytho,
he asked all in the house about the boy whom Evadne had borne; for
he said he was a son of Phoebus,

And would be above all mortals the best prophet for the men on
earth and that his race would never die; thus he revealed the god's
answer. But they declared they had not seen or heard about the five-day-
old child; for it was hidden in the rushes and the pathless briars, its tender
body bathed in the yellow and dark purple light of violets. For that

Ἴων ξανθαῖσι καὶ παμπορφύροις ἀ-
    κτῖσι βεβρεγμένος ἁβρὸν
σῶμα· τὸ καὶ κατεφάμι-
    ξεν καλεῖσθαί νιν χρόνῳ σύμπαντι μάτηρ

τοῦτ' ὄνυμ' ἀθάνατον. τερ-
    πνᾶς δ' ἐπεὶ χρυσοστεφάνοιο λάβεν
καρπὸν Ἥβας, Ἀλφεῷ μέσσῳ καταβὰς
    ἐκάλεσσε Ποσειδᾶν' εὐρυβίαν,
ὃν πρόγονον, καὶ τοξοφόρον Δά-
    λου θεοδμάτας σκοπόν,
αἰτέων λαοτρόφον τι-
    μάν τιν' ἑᾷ κεφαλᾷ,
νυκτὸς ὑπαίθριος. ἀντε-
    φθέγξατο δ' ἀρτιεπὴς
πατρία ὄσσα, μετάλλα-
    σέν τέ νιν· ‹Ὄρσο, τέκος,
δεῦρο πάγκοινον ἐς χώ-
    ραν ἴμεν φάμας ὄπισθεν.›

ἵκοντο δ' ὑψηλοῖο πέ-
    τραν ἀλίβατον Κρονίου·
ἔνθα οἱ ὤπασε θησαυρὸν δίδυμον
μαντοσύνας, τόκα μὲν φωνὰν ἀκούειν

reason his mother vowed that he should always be called

By that immortal name [Iamos]. And when he [Iamos] received
the blossom of lovely, golden-garlanded Youth, he went under the
bare sky at night to the middle of the river Alpheus, and called
mighty Poseidon, his forefather, and the Bow-carrying Guardian of
god-built Delos [Apollo], and asked for himself the honour of caring
for his people. And his father's faultless voice rang out in response
'Rise, child; come, follow my voice, let us go to the land which all men
share.'

And they reached the steep rock of the mighty son of Cronos,
where he gave him a double gift of prophecy: to hear the voice that

ψευδέων ἄγνωτον, εὖτ' ἄν
  δὲ θρασυμάχανος ἐλθὼν
Ἡρακλέης, σεμνὸν θάλος
  Ἀλκαϊδᾶν, πατρὶ
ἑορτάν τε κτίσῃ πλειστόμβροτον τε-
  θμόν τε μέγιστον ἀέθλων,
Ζηνὸς ἐπ' ἀκροτάτῳ βω-
  μῷ τότ' αὖ χρηστήριον θέσθαι κέλευσεν.

(*Olympian VI*)

97. Hieron's Pythian Victory

Χρυσέα φόρμιγξ, Ἀπόλλωνος καὶ ἰοπλοκάμων
σύνδικον Μοισᾶν κτέανον· τᾶς ἀκούει
  μὲν βάσις ἀγλαΐας ἀρχά,
πείθονται δ' ἀοιδοὶ σάμασιν
ἀγησιχόρων ὁπόταν προοιμίων
  ἀμβολὰς τεύχῃς ἐλελιζομένα.
καὶ τὸν αἰχματὰν κεραυνὸν σβεννύεις
αἰενάου πυρός. εὕδει δ' ἀνὰ σκά-
  πτῳ Διὸς αἰετός, ὠκεῖ-
  αν πτέρυγ' ἀμφοτέρωθεν χαλάξαις,

cannot lie; and when Heracles, the holy scion from Alcaeus' sons, had
come, bold in his designs, and had established for his father a festival
crowded with people and the greatest of the games, then, [he told him],
he would place an oracle at the highest point of the Altar, in honour
of Zeus.

LYRE of gold, the shared possession of Apollo and the violet-haired
Muses, you, whom footsteps follow as they begin the festive dance,
and whose calls the singers obey whenever with trembling strings you
strike the prelude to lead the chorus: you quench even the pointed
thunderbolt made of everlasting fire; and the eagle sleeps on the
sceptre of Zeus, letting his swift wings droop on either side,
  He, the king of birds. On his beaked head you poured a dark cloud,

ἀρχὸς οἰωνῶν, κελαινῶπιν δ' ἐπί οἱ νεφέλαν
ἀγκύλῳ κρατί, γλεφάρων ἀδὺ κλάϊ-
        θρον, κατέχευας· ὁ δὲ κνώσσων
ὑγρὸν νῶτον αἰωρεῖ, τεαῖς
        ῥιπαῖσι κατασχόμενος. καὶ γὰρ βια-
            τὰς Ἄρης, τραχεῖαν ἄνευθε λιπὼν
ἐγχέων ἀκμάν, ἰαίνει καρδίαν
κώματι, κῆλα δὲ καὶ δαιμόνων θέλ-
        γει φρένας ἀμφί τε Λατοί-
        δα σοφίᾳ βαθυκόλπων τε Μοισᾶν.

ὅσσα δὲ μὴ πεφίληκε Ζεύς, ἀτύζονται βοὰν
Πιερίδων ἀΐοντα, γᾶν τε καὶ πόν-
        τον κατ' ἀμαιμάκετον,
ὅς τ' ἐν αἰνᾷ Ταρτάρῳ κεῖται, θεῶν πολέμιος,
Τυφὼς ἑκατοντακάρανος· τόν ποτε
Κιλίκιον θρέψεν πολυώνυμον ἄντρον· νῦν γε μάν
ταί θ' ὑπὲρ Κύμας ἁλιερκέες ὄχθαι
Σικελία τ' αὐτοῦ πιέζει
        στέρνα λαχνάεντα· κίων δ' οὐρανία συνέχει,
νιφόεσσ' Αἴτνα, πάνετες χιόνος ὀξείας τιθήνα·

τᾶς ἐρεύγονται μὲν ἀπλάτου πυρὸς ἁγνόταται
ἐκ μυχῶν παγαί· ποταμοὶ δ' ἀμέραισιν
        μὲν προχέοντι ῥόον καπνοῦ

a sweet sealing of his eyelids; as he sleeps he heaves his soft back,
possessed by your quivering strings. Even powerful Ares puts the
sharp point of his spears far aside, and nurses his heart in drowsiness;
your arrows charm even the thoughts of the gods through the skill of
Leto's son and of the high-girded Muses.

But all things that Zeus has not loved are struck with terror when
they hear the voice of the Pierian Muses, whether on earth or in the
unfathomable sea; [among these is] he who lies in terrible Tartarus,
an enemy of the gods, Typhon with the hundred heads, whom the
famous Cilician cave once reared, though now too the water-
stemming shores of Cyme and Sicily lie heavy on his shaggy chest,
and a sky-reaching column holds him fast: Aetna, deep in snow, the
eternal nurse of sharp frost.

From her depth are spumed out purest fountains of unapproachable
fire; in daytime her rivers pour out a fiery stream of smoke; but in the

αἴθων᾽· ἀλλ᾽ ἐν ὄρφναισιν πέτρας
φοίνισσα κυλινδομένα φλὸξ ἐς βαθεῖ-
αν φέρει πόντου πλάκα σὺν πατάγῳ.
κεῖνο δ᾽ Ἀφαίστοιο κρουνοὺς ἑρπετόν
δεινοτάτους ἀναπέμπει· τέρας μὲν
θαυμάσιον προσιδέσθαι,
θαῦμα δὲ καὶ παρεόντων ἀκοῦσαι,

οἷον Αἴτνας ἐν μελαμφύλλοις δέδεται κορυφαῖς
καὶ πέδῳ, στρωμνὰ δὲ χαράσσοισ᾽ ἅπαν νῶ-
τον ποτικεκλιμένον κεντεῖ.
εἴη, Ζεῦ, τὶν εἴη ἀνδάνειν,
ὃς τοῦτ᾽ ἐφέπεις ὄρος, εὐκάρποιο γαί-
ας μέτωπον, τοῦ μὲν ἐπωνυμίαν
κλεινὸς οἰκιστὴρ ἐκύδανεν πόλιν
γείτονα, Πυθιάδος δ᾽ ἐν δρόμῳ κά-
ρυξ ἀνέειπέ νιν ἀγγέλ-
λων Ἱέρωνος ὑπὲρ καλλινίκου

ἅρμασι. ναυσιφορήτοις δ᾽ ἀνδράσι πρῶτα χάρις
ἐς πλόον ἀρχομένοις πομπαῖον ἐλθεῖν
οὖρον· ἐοικότα γάρ
κἄν τελευτᾷ φερτέρου νόστου τυχεῖν. ὁ δὲ λόγος

darkness of the night the red rolling flame brings the rocks to the deep stretch of the sea with a huge crash. That monster flings out most fearful spouts of fire, a wonder marvellous to watch, a marvel even to hear from those who have seen it.

Such is the one who is bound under the dark-leaved summits of Aetna and the plain below, while his bed, making furrows along his entire back as it is stretched along it, goads him on. May that, Zeus, may that please you, who frequent this mountain, the forehead of a fertile land – [the mountain] whose namesake city near by was made glorious by its famous founder, when the herald proclaimed her name on the Pythian track when announcing the splendid victory of Hieron's chariot.

For seafaring men the greatest blessing is to have a favourable wind as they start their voyage, for then it looks probable that at the accomplishment [of their voyage] they will have a better return home; in the

ταύταις ἐπὶ συντυχίαις δόξαν φέρει
λοιπὸν ἔσσεσθαι στεφάνοισί νιν ἵπποις τε κλυτὰν
καὶ σὺν εὐφώνοις θαλίαις ὀνυμαστάν.
Λύκιε καὶ Δάλοι᾽ ἀνάσσων

    Φοῖβε Παρνασσοῦ τε κράναν Κασταλίαν φιλέων,
ἐθελήσαις ταῦτα νόῳ τιθέμεν εὔανδρόν τε χώραν.

ἐκ θεῶν γὰρ μαχαναὶ πᾶσαι βροτέαις ἀρεταῖς,
καὶ σοφοὶ καὶ χερσὶ βιαταὶ περίγλωσ-
    σοί τ᾽ ἔφυν. ἄνδρα δ᾽ ἐγὼ κεῖνον
αἰνῆσαι μενοινῶν ἔλπομαι
μὴ χαλκοπάραον ἄκονθ᾽ ὡσείτ᾽ ἀγῶ-
    νος βαλεῖν ἔξω παλάμᾳ δονέων,
μακρὰ δὲ ῥίψαις ἀμεύσασθ᾽ ἀντίους.
εἰ γὰρ ὁ πᾶς χρόνος ὄλβον μὲν οὕτω
    καὶ κτεάνων δόσιν εὐθύ-
    νοι, καμάτων δ᾽ ἐπίλασιν παράσχοι·

ἦ κεν ἀμνάσειεν, οἵαις ἐν πολέμοισι μάχαις
τλάμονι ψυχᾷ παρέμειν᾽, ἁνίχ᾽ εὑρί-
    σκοντο θεῶν παλάμαις τιμὰν
οἵαν οὔτις Ἑλλάνων δρέπει
πλούτου στεφάνωμ᾽ ἀγέρωχον. νῦν γε μὰν

same way, so does the thought inspired by his [Hieron's] good fortune bring confidence that this city will for the rest of time be glorious with wreaths [of victory] for its chariots, and that [its name] will be famous in the tuneful festivities. Phoebus, lord of Lycia and of Delos, you who love the Castalian fountain of Parnassus, may you desire to make this prayer of mine good, and this land a home of noble men.

For from the gods come all the means of mortal triumph. [Through them] men are wise, strong in hand and eloquent in speech; and, keen to praise that man [Hieron], I trust I shall not, as in a contest, cast outside the course the bronze-cheeked spear which I brandish in my hand, but with my long throw far surpass my rivals. May all future time keep him thus in the straight course of prosperity and of wealth, and may it grant oblivion of his pains.

Then would he be reminded of the battles of war in which he stood his ground with a brave heart, when at the hands of the gods he and his brothers were winning honour such as none of the Greeks reaps

τὰν Φιλοκτήταο δίκαν ἐφέπων
ἐστρατεύθη· σὺν δ' ἀνάγκᾳ μιν φίλον
καί τις ἐὼν μεγαλάνωρ ἔσανεν.
    φαντὶ δὲ Λαμνόθεν ἕλκει
    τειρόμενον μεταβάσοντας ἐλθεῖν

ἥροας ἀντιθέους Ποίαντος υἱὸν τοξόταν·
ὃς Πριάμοιο πόλιν πέρσεν, τελεύτα-
    σέν τε πόνους Δαναοῖς,
ἀσθενεῖ μὲν χρωτὶ βαίνων, ἀλλὰ μοιρίδιον ἦν.
οὕτω δ' Ἱέρωνι θεὸς ὀρθωτὴρ πέλοι
τὸν προσέρποντα χρόνον, ὧν ἔραται και-
    ρὸν διδούς.
Μοῖσα, καὶ πὰρ Δεινομένει κελαδῆσαι
πίθεό μοι ποινὰν τεθρίππων·
    χάρμα δ' οὐκ ἀλλότριον νικαφορίᾳ πατέρος.
ἄγ' ἔπειτ' Αἴτνας βασιλεῖ φίλιον ἐξεύρωμεν ὕμνον·

τῷ πόλιν κείναν θεοδμάτῳ σὺν ἐλευθερίᾳ
Ὑλλίδος στάθμας Ἱέρων ἐν νόμοις ἔ-
    κτισσε· θέλοντι δὲ Παμφύλου
καὶ μὰν Ἡρακλειδᾶν ἔκγονοι
ὄχθαις ὕπο Ταϋγέτου ναίοντες αἰ-
εὶ μένειν τεθμοῖσιν ἐν Αἰγιμιοῦ

[today], a noble crown of riches. But on this occasion he took to the
field in the manner of Philoctetes; for through necessity even a proud
man fawned for his friendship. They say that the godlike heroes went
to fetch from Lemnos

The bowman, son of Poeas, who was afflicted by his wound; he
sacked the city of Priam, and ended the labours of the Danaans,
although he walked with weak limbs; but that is what the Fates had
ordained. May the god in the time drawing near be a preserver to
Hieron in the same way, giving him all that he wishes at the right
season. Muse, yield to my wishes to sing in Deinomenes' house his
reward [victory] with the four-horsed [chariot]; the father's victory is
no alien joy [to the son]. Come, let us compose a friendly song to
honour the king of Aetna;

For him for whom Hieron built that divinely established city with
the laws of the Dorian people. And the sons of Pamphylus, true des-
cendants of Heracles, dwelling under the hills of Taygetus, are willing

Δωριεῖς. ἔσχον δ' Ἀμύκλας ὄλβιοι
Πινδόθεν ὀρνύμενοι, λευκοπώλων
    Τυνδαριδᾶν βαθύδοξοι
    γείτονες, ὧν κλέος ἄνθησεν αἰχμᾶς.

Ζεῦ τέλει', αἰεὶ δὲ τοιαύταν Ἀμένα παρ' ὕδωρ
αἶσαν ἀστοῖς καὶ βασιλεῦσιν διακρί-
    νειν ἔτυμον λόγον ἀνθρώπων.
σύν τοι τίν κεν ἀγητὴρ ἀνήρ,
υἱῷ τ' ἐπιτελλόμενος, δᾶμον γεραί-
    ρων τράποι σύμφωνον ἐς ἡσυχίαν.
λίσσομαι νεῦσον, Κρονίων, ἥμερον
ὄφρα κατ' οἶκον ὁ Φοίνιξ ὁ Τυρσα-
    νῶν τ' ἀλαλατὸς ἔχῃ, ναυ-
    σίστονον ὕβριν ἰδὼν τὰν πρὸ Κύμας,

οἷα Συρακοσίων ἀρχῷ δαμασθέντες πάθον,
ὠκυπόρων ἀπὸ ναῶν ὅ σφιν ἐν πόν-
    τῳ βάλεθ' ἁλικίαν,
Ἑλλάδ' ἐξέλκων βαρείας δουλίας. ἀρέομαι
πὰρ μὲν Σαλαμῖνος Ἀθαναίων χάριν

to live for ever as Dorians under the laws of Aegimius; they conquered Amyclae having set out from Pindus, rich men; now neighbours of the Tyndaridae, the masters of white horses, [they live] deep in glory; and the fame of their spears burst into flower.

Zeus, the accomplisher, [grant that] beside the waters of Amenas the truthful words of men may assign good fortune to citizens and princes alike. With your help, may the leader who instructs his son honour the people and turn them to harmonious peace. Grant, I beg, son of Cronos, that the battle-shout of the Carthaginians and the Etruscans may die out in peace at home, now they have seen that pride has brought disaster to their ships off Cumae:

Such were their losses at the hands of the master of Syracuse – a defeat which flung their young warriors from their swift ships into the sea, delivering Greece from her weight of slavery. From Salamis I win the thanks of the Athenians, but in Sparta I will speak of the battles before Cithaeron – those in which the Medes with their

μισθόν, ἐν Σπάρτᾳ δ' ἀπὸ τᾶν πρὸ Κιθαιρῶ-
    νος μαχᾶν,
ταῖσι Μήδειοι κάμον ἀγκυλότοξοι,
παρὰ δὲ τὰν εὔυδρον ἀκτὰν
   'Ιμέρα παίδεσσιν ὕμνον Δεινομένεος τελέσαις,
τὸν ἐδέξαντ' ἀμφ' ἀρετᾷ πολεμίων ἀνδρῶν καμόντων.

καιρὸν εἰ φθέγξαιο, πολλῶν πείρατα συντανύσαις
ἐν βραχεῖ, μείων ἕπεται μῶμος ἀνθρώ-
   πων· ἀπὸ γὰρ κόρος ἀμβλύνει
αἰανὴς ταχείας ἐλπίδας,
ἀστῶν δ' ἀκοὰ κρύφιον θυμὸν βαρύ-
   νει μάλιστ' ἐσλοῖσιν ἐπ' ἀλλοτρίοις.
ἀλλ' ὅμως, κρέσσον γὰρ οἰκτιρμοῦ φθόνος,
μὴ παρίει καλά. νώμα δικαίῳ
   πηδαλίῳ στρατόν· ἀψευ-
   δεῖ δὲ πρὸς ἄκμονι χάλκευε γλῶσσαν.

εἴ τι καὶ φλαῦρον παραιθύσσει, μέγα τοι φέρεται
πὰρ σέθεν. πολλῶν ταμίας ἐσσί· πολλοὶ
   μάρτυρες ἀμφοτέροις πιστοί.
εὐανθεῖ δ' ἐν ὀργᾷ παρμένων,
εἴπερ τι φιλεῖς ἀκοὰν ἀδεῖαν αἰ-
   εἰ κλύειν, μὴ κάμνε λίαν δαπάναις·

curved bows were beaten; but on the well-watered bank of Himera I
shall win it by paying a tribute in song to the sons of Deinomenes –
praise which they won by their valour when their foes were defeated.

If you speak at the right time, joining the strands of many enter-
prises in a few words, men will be less critical of you. For boring per-
petual satisfaction blunts the thrill of expectation. Most of all, when
citizens hear of the great achievements of others, secretly their spirits
are depressed. But even so – for it is better to be envied than to be
pitied – do not by-pass nobility. Rule your people with the rudder of
justice, and forge your tongue on the anvil of truth.

If even a trivial word falls from your mouth, it is considered weighty
[because it comes] from you. You are the steward of a rich store;
many are the reliable witnesses to both [your good and your evil]
deeds. But abide in a temper that blossoms in beauty, and, if you delight
in ever hearing something sweet, do not grow tired of spending

ἐξίει δ' ὥσπερ κυβερνάτας ἀνὴρ
ἱστίον ἀνεμόεν. μὴ δολωθῇς,
ὦ φίλε, κέρδεσιν εὐτραπέ-
λοις· ὀπιθόμβροτον αὔχημα δόξας

οἶον ἀποιχομένων ἀνδρῶν δίαιταν μανύει
καὶ λογίοις καὶ ἀοιδοῖς. οὐ φθίνει Κροί-
σου φιλόφρων ἀρετά.
τὸν δὲ ταύρῳ χαλκέῳ καυτῆρα νηλέα νόον
ἐχθρὰ Φάλαριν κατέχει παντᾷ φάτις,
οὐδέ μιν φόρμιγγες ὑπωρόφιαι κοινανίαν
μαλθακὰν παίδων ὀάροισι δέκονται.
τὸ δὲ παθεῖν εὖ πρῶτον ἀέθλων·
εὖ δ' ἀκούειν δευτέρα μοῖρ'· ἀμφοτέροισι δ' ἀνὴρ
ὃς ἂν ἐγκύρσῃ καὶ ἕλῃ, στέφανον ὕψιστον δέδεκται.

(Pythian I)

98. Athens

Ὦ ταὶ λιπαραὶ καὶ ἰοστέφανοι καὶ ἀοίδιμοι,
Ἑλλάδος ἔρεισμα, κλειναὶ Ἀθᾶναι, δαιμόνιον πτολίεθρον.

lavishly. Like a helmsman, set full sail to the wind. Do not be lured, my friend, by deceitful gains.

When men are dead and gone, the posthumous report of their glory alone proclaims their way of life to chroniclers and poets. The generous excellence of Croesus does not fade away; while Phalaris, ruthless in spirit, who burnt men in a bronze bull, is forever possessed by a report of loathing, and no lyres in the roofed halls welcome him as a gentle companion to the songs of boys. To have good fortune is first among prizes; the second is to be well spoken of; but the man who finds and wins both has received the supreme crown.

O GLORIOUS Athens — shining, violet-crowned, worthy of song, bulwark of Greece, city of the gods.

99. *Theoxenus*

Χρῆν μὲν κατὰ καιρὸν ἐρώ-
    των δρέπεσθαι, θυμέ, σὺν ἁλικίᾳ·
τὰς δὲ Θεοξένου ἀκτῖ-
    νας πρὸς ὄσσων μαρμαρυζοίσας δρακεὶς
ὃς μὴ πόθῳ κυμαίνεται, ἐξ ἀδάμαντος
ἢ σιδάρου κεχάλκευ-
    ται μέλαιναν καρδίαν

ψυχρᾷ φλογί, πρὸς δ᾽ Ἀφροδί-
    τας ἀτιμασθεὶς ἑλικογλεφάρου
ἢ περὶ χρήμασι μοχθί-
    ζει βιαίως, ἢ γυναικείῳ θράσει
ψυχρὰν φορεῖται πᾶσαν ὁδὸν θεραπεύων.
ἀλλ᾽ ἐγὼ θεᾶς ἕκατι
    κηρὸς ὣς δαχθεὶς ἕλᾳ

ἱρᾶν μελισσᾶν τάκομαι, εὖτ᾽ ἂν ἴδω
παιδὸς νεόγυιον ἐς ἥ-
    βαν· ἐν δ᾽ ἄρα καὶ Τενέδῳ
Πειθώ τ᾽ ἔναιεν καὶ Χάρις
    υἱὸν ἀνᾶγ᾽ Ἀγησίλα.

You should gather the blossoms of love at the right time, my heart –
in the prime of life; but the man who sees the rays of light shimmering
from the eyes of Theoxenus and is not seized by a storm of desire has
a black heart of steel or iron beaten on the anvil

In a cold flame; dishonoured by quick-glancing Aphrodite, he is
either slaving hard after riches, or, with a woman's rash confidence,
concerning himself with every icy pathway, he is being driven onwards.
But I, by the grace of the goddess, when stung by the flame

Melt like the wax of holy bees, whenever I look at the youthful
vigour of the boy's fresh limbs. So too in Tenedos lived Persuasion,
and Charm raised Agesilas' son.

BACCHYLIDES

505–450 B.C.

100. Croesus

Βρύει μὲν ἱερὰ βουθύτοις ἑορταῖς,
βρύουσι φιλοξενίας ἀγυιαί·
λάμπει δ' ὑπὸ μαρμαρυγαῖς ὁ χρυσὸς
ὑψιδαιδάλτων τριπόδων σταθέντων

πάροιθε ναοῦ, τόθι μέγιστον ἄλσος
Φοίβου παρὰ Κασταλίας ῥεέθροις
Δελφοὶ διέπουσι. θεόν, θεόν τις
ἀγλαϊζέτω, ὁ γὰρ ἄριστος ὄλβῳ.

ἐπεί ποτε καὶ δαμασίππου
Λυδίας ἀρχαγέταν,
εὖτε τὰν πεπρωμέναν
Ζηνὸς τελειοῦσαι κρίσιν
Σάρδιες Περσᾶν ἐπορθεῦντο στρατῷ,
Κροῖσον ὁ χρυσάορος

THE shrines are full for sacrificial feasts, the streets are full of welcome foreigners, and flashes shine from the gold of the tall, carved tripods that are set

Before the temple where Delphi rules the great grove of Phoebus near the Castalian spring. The god, celebrate the god, for he is the first in blessedness.

For once when Sardis, in fulfilment of Zeus' fated decision, was being sacked by the Persian army, Apollo of the golden sword protected Croesus, the lord of horse-taming Lydia.

φύλαξ' 'Απόλλων. ὁ δ' ἐς ἀέλπτον ἆμαρ
μολὼν πολυδάκρυον οὐκ ἔμελλε
μίμνειν ἔτι δουλοσύναν· πυρὰν δὲ
χαλκοτείχεος προπάροιθεν αὐλᾶς

ναῆσατ', ἔνθα σὺν ἀλόχῳ τε κεδνᾷ
σὺν εὐπλοκάμοις τ' ἐπέβαιν' ἄλαστον
θυγατράσι δυρομέναις· χέρας δ' ἐς
αἰπὺν αἰθέρα σφετέρας ἀείρας

γέγωνεν· ‹ὑπέρβιε δαῖμον,
    ποῦ θεῶν ἐστὶν χάρις;
ποῦ δὲ Λατοίδας ἄναξ;
    πίτνουσιν 'Αλυάττα δόμοι,
τίς δὲ νῦν δώρων ἀμοιβὰ μυρίων
    φαίνεται Πυθωνόθεν;

‹πέρθουσι Μῆδοι δοριάλωτον ἄστυ,
φοινίσσεται αἵματι χρυσοδίνας
Πακτωλός· ἀεικελίως γυναῖκες
    ἐξ ἐϋκτίτων μεγάρων ἄγονται·

But when he [Croesus] came to that unlooked-for day, he was not
going to wait further for slavery of many tears. Before his courtyard,
walled in bronze, a pyre

He built which he mounted with his honoured wife and fair-tressed
daughters who were weeping bitterly. He raised his hands to the sheer
vault of the sky

And cried: 'All-powerful god, where is the gratitude of the gods?
Where is the lordly son of Leto? Alyattes' house is falling in ruins, and
what recompense is there now from Delphi for the countless gifts I
offered?

'The Medes are ravaging the conquered city, and Pactolus, whose
waters swirl with gold, is reddened by blood; women are shamefully
driven away from the well-built palaces.

⟨τὰ πρόσθε δ' ἐχθρὰ φίλα· θανεῖν γλύκιστον.⟩
τόσ' εἶπε, καὶ ἁβροβάταν κέλευσεν
ἅπτειν ξύλινον δόμον. ἔκλαγον δὲ
    παρθένοι, φίλας τ' ἀνὰ ματρὶ χεῖρας

ἔβαλλον· ὁ γὰρ προφανὴς θνα-
    τοῖσιν ἔχθιστος φόνων·
ἀλλ' ἐπεὶ δεινοῦ πυρὸς
    λαμπρὸν διάϊσσεν μένος,
Ζεὺς ἐπιστάσας μελαγκευθὲς νέφος
    σβέννυεν ξανθὰν φλόγα.

ἄπιστον οὐδέν, ὅ τι θεῶν μέριμνα
τεύχει· τότε Δαλογενὴς Ἀπόλλων
φέρων ἐς Ὑπερβορέους γέροντα
    σὺν τανισφύροις κατένασσε κούραις

δι' εὐσέβειαν, ὅτι μέγιστα θνατῶν
ἐς ἀγαθέαν ἀνέπεμψε Πυθώ.

'What was once] oathed is now loved: sweetest of all is to die.' So he
spoke; and he ordered a softly-stepping boy to set fire to the pile of
wood. The girls were crying and threw their arms round their mother;
    For a death before men's eyes is the most hateful. But when the
brilliant strength of the dreadful fire leapt up, Zeus set a heavy black
cloud above it, and quenched the yellow flame.
    Nothing the gods do in their concern for us is unbelievable. Then
Delos-born Apollo brought the old man and his slender-ankled daugh-
ters to the Hyperboreans, and put them there to live
    In return for [Croesus'] piety, for of all mortal men he had sent the
greatest gifts to blessed Delphi.

SOPHOCLES
495–406 B.C.

101. *Long and Immeasurable Time*

ΑΙΑΣ

Ἄπανθ' ὁ μακρὸς κἀναρίθμητος χρόνος
φύει τ' ἄδηλα καὶ φανέντα κρύπτεται·
κοὐκ ἔστ' ἄελπτον οὐδέν, ἀλλ' ἁλίσκεται
χὠ δεινὸς ὅρκος χαἰ περισκελεῖς φρένες.
κἀγὼ γάρ, ὃς τὰ δείν' ἐκαρτέρουν τότε,
βαφῇ σίδηρος ὥς, ἐθηλύνθην στόμα
πρὸς τῆσδε τῆς γυναικός· οἰκτίρω δέ νιν
χήραν παρ' ἐχθροῖς παῖδά τ' ὀρφανὸν λιπεῖν.
ἀλλ' εἶμι πρός τε λουτρὰ καὶ παρακτίους
λειμῶνας, ὡς ἂν λύμαθ' ἁγνίσας ἐμὰ
μῆνιν βαρεῖαν ἐξαλύξωμαι θεᾶς·
μολών τε χῶρον ἔνθ' ἂν ἀστιβῆ κίχω
κρύψω τόδ' ἔγχος τοὐμόν, ἔχθιστον βελῶν,
γαίας ὀρύξας ἔνθα μή τις ὄψεται·
ἀλλ' αὐτὸ νὺξ Ἅιδης τε σῳζόντων κάτω.
ἐγὼ γὰρ ἐξ οὗ χειρὶ τοῦτ' ἐδεξάμην
παρ' Ἕκτορος δώρημα δυσμενεστάτου,

AJAX: Long and immeasurable Time reveals all hidden things, and covers what has been seen, and there is nothing unexpected; the sternest oath is overruled, and the firmest will. Even I, who, like tempered iron, then [in the past] endured terrible things, have grown soft at the words of this woman. I pity her and cannot leave her a widow among enemies, or leave an orphaned child. But I shall go to the bathing-places and the meadows by the sea-shore, where I can cleanse these stains and so appease the goddess's oppressive anger. There will I find some untrodden place, where I will hide this sword of mine, most loathed of weapons. I will dig the earth [and bury it] where no man will see it. Let Night and Hades keep it below. For from the time my hand accepted it as a gift from Hector, deadliest of my enemies, I have had

οὔπω τι κεδνὸν ἔσχον Ἀργείων πάρα.
ἀλλ᾽ ἔστ᾽ ἀληθὴς ἡ βροτῶν παροιμία,
ἐχθρῶν ἄδωρα δῶρα κοὐκ ὀνήσιμα.
τοιγὰρ τὸ λοιπὸν εἰσόμεσθα μὲν θεοῖς
εἴκειν, μαθησόμεσθα δ᾽ Ἀτρείδας σέβειν.
ἄρχοντές εἰσιν, ὥσθ᾽ ὑπεικτέον. τί μήν;
καὶ γὰρ τὰ δεινὰ καὶ τὰ καρτερώτατα
τιμαῖς ὑπείκει· τοῦτο μὲν νιφοστιβεῖς
χειμῶνες ἐκχωροῦσιν εὐκάρπῳ θέρει·
ἐξίσταται δὲ νυκτὸς αἰανὴς κύκλος
τῇ λευκοπώλῳ φέγγος ἡμέρα φλέγειν·
δεινῶν τ᾽ ἄημα πνευμάτων ἐκοίμισε
στένοντα πόντον· ἐν δ᾽ ὁ παγκρατὴς ὕπνος
λύει πεδήσας, οὐδ᾽ ἀεὶ λαβὼν ἔχει.
ἡμεῖς δε πῶς οὐ γνωσόμεθα σωφρονεῖν;
ἐγὼ δ᾽ ἐπίσταμαι γὰρ ἀρτίως ὅτι
ὅ τ᾽ ἐχθρὸς ἡμῖν ἐς τοσόνδ᾽ ἐχθαρτέος,
ὡς καὶ φιλήσων αὖθις, ἔς τε τὸν φίλον
τοσαῦθ᾽ ὑπουργῶν ὠφελεῖν βουλήσομαι,
ὡς αἰὲν οὐ μενοῦντα. τοῖς πολλοῖσι γὰρ
βροτῶν ἄπιστός ἐσθ᾽ ἑταιρείας λιμήν.

(*Ajax*)

nothing good from the Greeks. So the proverb men have is true: 'The gifts of an enemy are no gifts; they bring no profit.' From now on, we shall know that we must obey the gods, and we shall learn to respect the sons of Atreus. They are our leaders, so we must obey. What else? For the terrible and most powerful things yield to authority. Just as winter, heavy with snow, gives way to summer with its many crops, and the immortal circle of Night moves away for Day of the white horses to kindle her light; and the blast of fierce winds lulls the moaning sea to sleep, and sleep the all-powerful, which has bound us, sets us free; he does not hold us for ever. Why should I not learn [this] wisdom? I, who have just been taught that we should hate our enemies only to the point where [until] they can become friends again, shall wish to help a friend as though he will not always be a friend; for friendship is not a safe harbour for most men.

102. *None is More Wonderful Than Man*

ΧΟΡΟΣ

Πολλὰ τὰ δεινὰ κοὐδὲν ἀν-
θρώπου δεινότερον πέλει·
τοῦτο καὶ πολιοῦ πέραν
πόντου χειμερίῳ νότῳ
χωρεῖ, περιβρυχίοισιν
περῶν ὑπ' οἴδμασιν, θεῶν
τε τὰν ὑπερτάταν, Γᾶν
ἄφθιτον, ἀκαμάταν ἀποτρύεται,
Ἰλλομένων ἀρότρων ἔτος εἰς ἔτος,
Ἱππείῳ γένει πολεύων.

κουφονόων τε φῦλον ὀρ-
νίθων ἀμφιβαλὼν ἄγρει
καὶ θηρῶν· ἀγρίων ἔθνη
πόντου τ' εἰναλίαν φύσιν
σπείραισι δικτυοκλώστοις,
περιφραδὴς ἀνήρ· κρατεῖ
δὲ μηχαναῖς ἀγραύλου
θηρὸς ὀρεσσιβάτα, λασιαύχενά θ'
Ἱππον ὑπαξέμεν ἀμφίλοφον ζυγὸν
οὔρειόν τ' ἀκμῆτα ταῦρον.

CHORUS: Many wonders there are, and yet none is more wonderful than man. He journeys over the grey ocean with stormy Notos [the south wind] crossing through waves that surge about him; Earth, the immortal, the greatest of the gods, the tireless one, he wears away, turning the soil with his horses as his ploughs pass up and down, year after year.

With woven nets he snares the race of thoughtless birds, the tribes of savage beasts, the sea-brood of the deep, man of subtle wit. By his cunning he masters the animals that nest in the wilderness, that roam across the hills; he tames the rich-maned horse, putting a yoke upon its neck, and the unwearied mountain bull.

καὶ φθέγμα καὶ ἀνεμόεν
φρόνημα καὶ ἀστυνόμους
ὀργὰς ἐδιδάξατο καὶ δυσαύλων
πάγων ὑπαίθρεια καὶ
δύσομβρα φεύγειν βέλη
παντοπόρος· ἄπορος ἐπ᾽ οὐδὲν ἔρχεται
τὸ μέλλον· Ἅιδα μόνον
φεῦξιν οὐκ ἐπάξεται·
νόσων δ᾽ ἀμαχάνων φυγὰς
ξυμπέφρασται.

σοφόν τι τὸ μαχανόεν
τέχνας ὑπὲρ ἐλπίδ᾽ ἔχων
τοτὲ μὲν κακόν, ἄλλοτ᾽ ἐπ᾽ ἐσθλὸν ἕρπει,
νόμους περαίνων χθονὸς
θεῶν τ᾽ ἔνορκον δίκαν·
ὑψίπολις· ἄπολις ὅτῳ τὸ μὴ καλὸν
ξύνεστι τόλμας χάριν.
μήτ᾽ ἐμοὶ παρέστιος
γένοιτο μήτ᾽ ἴσον φρονῶν
ὃς τάδ᾽ ἔρδοι.

(*Antigone*)

And he has taught himself speech and wind-swift thought, and the
ways of building an ordered state, and he has taught himself to escape
the arrows of the frost and of the rain, when it is hard to sleep under
the open sky – the all-resourceful; he is never at a loss whatever comes
his way. Only from death will he not devise an escape; although he
has found ways of curing hopeless sicknesses.

How skilful, passing belief, are the arts that lead him sometimes to
evil and sometimes to good! When he honours the laws of the land
and justice sanctioned by the gods, his cities stand proud and tall; but
he who rashly embraces evil is homeless. May the man who acts thus
never share my hearth, or my thoughts.

SOPHOCLES

103. Love

ΧΟΡΟΣ

Ἔρως ἀνίκατε μάχαν,
Ἔρως, ὃς ἐν κτήμασι πίπτεις,
ὃς ἐν μαλακαῖς παρειαῖς
νεάνιδος ἐννυχεύεις,
φοιτᾷς δ' ὑπερπόντιος ἔν τ'
ἀγρονόμοις αὐλαῖς·
καί σ' οὔτ' ἀθανάτων φύξιμος οὐδεὶς
οὔθ' ἁμερίων σέ γ' ἀνθρώ-
πων, ὁ δ' ἔχων μέμηνεν.

σὺ καὶ δικαίων ἀδίκους
φρένας παρασπᾷς ἐπὶ λώβᾳ·
σὺ καὶ τόδε νεῖκος ἀνδρῶν
ξύναιμον ἔχεις ταράξας·
νικᾷ δ' ἐναργὴς βλεφάρων
ἵμερος εὐλέκτρου
νύμφας, τῶν μεγάλων πάρεδρος ἐν ἀρχαῖς
θεσμῶν· ἄμαχος γὰρ ἐμπαί-
ζει θεὸς Ἀφροδίτα.

(*Antigone*)

CHORUS: Love, unconquered in battle, Love, you who fall upon men's
wealth, who keep your night-watch on the soft cheeks of a girl, who
travel across the sea or to men's country dwellings; not one of the im-
mortals can escape you, nor any mortal man. He who touches you is
seized by madness.

Even the mind of the just you drag from its course to injustice and
to dishonour. It is you who stirred these men of common blood to
fight. Sharp desire, kindled by the eyes of the lovely bride, is the
conqueror: desire sits enthroned and rules together with the great
Laws; and Aphrodite playfully mocks, the goddess none can defeat.

SOPHOCLES

104. Orestes' Chariot-race

ΠΑΙΔΑΓΩΓΟΣ

Κεῖνος γὰρ ἐλθὼν ἐς τὸ κλεινὸν Ἑλλάδος
πρόσχημ' ἀγῶνος Δελφικῶν ἄθλων χάριν,
ὅτ' ᾔσθετ', ἀνδρὸς ὀρθίων κηρυγμάτων
δρόμον προκηρύξαντος, οὗ πρώτη κρίσις,
εἰσῆλθε λαμπρός, πᾶσι τοῖς ἐκεῖ σέβας·
δρόμον δ' ἰσώσας τῇ φύσει τά τ' ἔργματα
νίκης ἔχων ἐξῆλθε πάντιμον γέρας.
χὤπως μὲν ἐν πολλοῖσι παῦρά σοι λέγω,
οὐκ οἶδα τοιοῦδ' ἀνδρὸς ἔργα καὶ κράτη·
ἐν δ' ἴσθ'· ὅσων γὰρ εἰσεκήρυξαν βραβῆς
τούτων ἐνεγκὼν πάντα κἀπινίκια
ὠλβίζετ', Ἀργεῖος μὲν ἀνακαλούμενος,
⟨ὄνομα δ' Ὀρέστης, τοῦ τὸ κλεινὸν Ἑλλάδος
Ἀγαμέμνονος στράτευμ' ἀγείραντός ποτε.⟩
καὶ ταῦτα μὲν τοιαῦθ'· ὅταν δέ τις θεῶν
βλάπτῃ, δύναιτ' ἂν οὐδ' ἂν ἰσχύων φυγεῖν.
κεῖνος γὰρ ἄλλης ἡμέρας, ὅθ' ἱππικῶν
ἦν ἡλίου τέλλοντος ὠκύπους ἀγών,
εἰσῆλθε πολλῶν ἁρματηλατῶν μέτα.

TUTOR: He [Orestes] went to the famous festival, the pride of Greece,
for the games of Delphi; and when he heard the man proclaim in a loud
voice the foot-race, which was the first event to be decided, he entered
the contest – a brilliant sight, a wonder to all who were there. And
having finished the course, an achievement as brilliant as his appear-
ance, he left carrying the all-honoured prize of victory. And, to tell a
long story in a few words, I never saw such a man competing and win-
ning. One thing you should know: in all the contests announced by
the judges, he carried away the prize; men called him a happy man
[when the herald cried out]: 'He is an Argive, his name is Orestes, son
of Agamemnon who once gathered together the famous army of the
Greeks.' And that was so. But when a god sets out to do harm, not
even the strong can escape. For, on another day, when the chariots
were to show their speed (of foot) at sunrise, he entered the race with
many other charioteers. One was an Achaean, one from Sparta, two

εἷς ἦν Ἀχαιός, εἷς ἀπὸ Σπάρτης, δύο
Λίβυες ζυγωτῶν ἁρμάτων ἐπιστάται·
κἀκεῖνος ἐν τούτοισι Θεσσαλὰς ἔχων
ἵππους, ὁ πέμπτος· ἕκτος ἐξ Αἰτωλίας
ξανθαῖσι πώλοις· ἕβδομος Μάγνης ἀνήρ·
ὁ δ᾽ ὄγδοος λεύκιππος, Αἰνιὰν γένος·
ἔνατος Ἀθηνῶν τῶν θεοδμήτων ἄπο·
Βοιωτὸς ἄλλος, δέκατον ἐκπληρῶν ὄχον.
στάντες δ᾽ ὅθ᾽ αὐτοὺς οἱ τεταγμένοι βραβῆς
κλήροις ἔπηλαν καὶ κατέστησαν δίφρους,
χαλκῆς ὑπαὶ σάλπιγγος ᾖξαν. οἱ δ᾽ ἅμα
ἵπποις ὁμοκλήσαντες ἡνίας χεροῖν
ἔσεισαν· ἐν δὲ πᾶς ἐμεστώθη δρόμος
κτύπου κροτητῶν ἁρμάτων· κόνις δ᾽ ἄνω
φορεῖθ᾽· ὁμοῦ δὲ πάντες ἀναμεμειγμένοι
φείδοντο κέντρων οὐδέν, ὡς ὑπερβάλοι
χνόας τις αὐτῶν καὶ φρυάγμαθ᾽ ἱππικά.
ὁμοῦ γὰρ ἀμφὶ νῶτα καὶ τροχῶν βάσεις
ἤφριζον, εἰσέβαλλον ἱππικαὶ πνοαί.
καὶ πρὶν μὲν ὀρθοὶ πάντες ἕστασαν δίφροι·
ἔπειτα δ᾽ Αἰνιᾶνος ἀνδρὸς ἄστομοι
πῶλοι βίᾳ φέρουσιν, ἐκ δ᾽ ὑποστροφῆς

masters of the yoked chariots were Libyans and he [Orestes] was the
fifth, driving Thessalian mares; the sixth an Aetolian with chestnut
colts, the seventh a Magnesian man, the eighth with white horses was
of Aenean stock; the ninth from Athens, the god-built city, another a
Boeotian, making the tenth chariot. They took their stations where the
appointed judges placed them by lot, and ranged their chariots; the
bronze trumpet cried out, and they leapt forward. All shouted at their
horses and shook the reins in their hands. The whole course was filled
with the din of rattling chariots, and the dust blew up; all, in a confused
bunch, used their whips unsparingly trying to pass the wheels and the
snorting horses. For the breath of the steeds spumed and struck the
rolling wheels and the backs of the drivers. Until that time no chariot
had been overturned; but then the hard-mouthed colts of the Aenean
broke away violently and, swerving as they passed from the sixth to

τελοῦντες ἕκτον ἕβδομόν τ' ἤδη δρόμον
μέτωπα συμπαίουσι Βαρκαίοις ὄχοις·
κἀντεῦθεν ἄλλος ἄλλον ἐξ ἑνὸς κακοῦ
ἔθραυε κἀνέπιπτε, πᾶν δ' ἐπίμπλατο
ναυαγίων Κρισαῖον ἱππικῶν πέδον.
γνοὺς δ' οὐξ Ἀθηνῶν δεινὸς ἡνιοστρόφος
ἔξω παρασπᾷ κἀνοκωχεύει παρεὶς
κλύδων' ἔφιππον ἐν μέσῳ κυκώμενον.
ἤλαυνε δ' ἔσχατος μὲν ὑστέρας δ' ἔχων
πώλους Ὀρέστης, τῷ τέλει πίστιν φέρων·
ὁ δ' ὡς ὁρᾷ μόνον νιν ἐλλελειμμένον,
ὀξὺν δι' ὤτων κέλαδον ἐνσείσας θοαῖς
πώλοις διώκει, κἀξισώσαντε ζυγὰ
ἠλαυνέτην, τότ' ἄλλος, ἄλλοθ' ἄτερος
κάρα προβάλλων ἱππικῶν ὀχημάτων.
καὶ τοὺς μὲν ἄλλους πάντας ἀσφαλεῖς δρόμους
ὠρθοῦθ' ὁ τλήμων ὀρθὸς ἐξ ὀρθῶν δίφρων·
ἔπειτα λύων ἡνίαν ἀριστερὰν
κάμπτοντος ἵππου λανθάνει στήλην ἄκραν
παίσας· ἔθραυσε δ' ἄξονος μέσας χνόας,
κἀξ ἀντύγων ὤλισθεν· ἐν δ' ἐλίσσεται
τμητοῖς ἱμᾶσι· τοῦ δὲ πίπτοντος πέδῳ

the seventh lap, crashed headlong into the chariot of the Barcean. After this accident one crashed onto the other until the whole plain of Crissa was filled with the wrecks of chariots. The cunning Athenian charioteer, seeing this, drew aside and paused, leaving the surge of horses and wheels seething in mid course. Orestes was driving last, holding his horses back, his trust in the finish. But when he saw him [the Athenian] alone left in, he raised a shrill cry that pierced the ears of his swift colts, and gave chase. They raced; team was level with team, first the one then the other showing his head in front of the [two] chariots. Until then unlucky [Orestes] had passed safely through all the laps standing fast on his upright chariot. But then he slackened his left rein as the horses turned, and, unawares, struck the edge of the post. He smashed the axle in two, and was thrown over the chariot-rail. He was caught in the trimmed reins; as he fell to the ground, his

πῶλοι διεσπάρησαν ἐς μέσον δρόμον.
στρατὸς δ' ὅπως ὁρᾷ νιν ἐκπεπτωκότα
δίφρων, ἀνωλόλυξε τὸν νεανίαν,
οἷ' ἔργα δράσας οἷα λαγχάνει κακά,
φορούμενος πρὸς οὖδας, ἄλλοτ' οὐρανῷ
σκέλη προφαίνων, ἔστε νιν διφρηλάται,
μόλις κατασχεθόντες ἱππικὸν δρόμον,
ἔλυσαν αἱματηρόν, ὥστε μηδένα
γνῶναι φίλων ἰδόντ' ἂν ἄθλιον δέμας.
καί νιν πυρᾷ κέαντες εὐθὺς ἐν βραχεῖ
χαλκῷ μέγιστον σῶμα δειλαίας σποδοῦ
φέρουσιν ἄνδρες Φωκέων τεταγμένοι,
ὅπως πατρῴας τύμβον ἐκλάχῃ χθονός.
τοιαῦτά σοι ταῦτ' ἐστίν, ὡς μὲν ἐν λόγοις
ἀλγεινά, τοῖς δ' ἰδοῦσιν, οἵπερ εἴδομεν,
μέγιστα πάντων ὧν ὅπωπ' ἐγὼ κακῶν.

(*Electra*)

colts were scattered into the middle of the course. The spectators, seeing him fallen from the chariot, screamed out in pity for the young man who had achieved so much and had met with such misfortune; now he was dragged on the earth, and now his legs rose skywards, until the charioteers, with difficulty checking his horses' impetuosity, released him, streaked with blood; no friend who saw that miserable body would have recognized him. They burnt it at once on a pyre; and chosen men of Phocis are bringing the sad dust of that broad body in a small bronze urn, so that he may have a grave in his native land. Such is my story, painful to tell; but for those of us who saw it, the greatest sorrow that I have ever seen.

SOPHOCLES

105. Thebes in Time of Pestilence

ΧΟΡΟΣ

Ὦ Διὸς ἀδυεπὲς φάτι, τίς ποτε
τᾶς πολυχρύσου
Πυθῶνος ἀγλαὰς ἔβας
Θήβας; ἐκτέταμαι φοβερὰν φρένα
δείματι πάλλων
ἰήιε Δάλιε Παιάν,
ἀμφὶ σοὶ ἁζόμενος τί μοι ἢ νέον
ἢ περιτελλομέναις ὥραις πάλιν
ἐξανύσεις χρέος.
εἰπέ μοι, ὦ χρυσέας τέκνον Ἐλπίδος,
ἄμβροτε Φάμα.

πρῶτά σε κεκλόμενος, θύγατερ Διός,
ἄμβροτ᾽ Ἀθάνα,
γαιάοχόν τ᾽ ἀδελφεὰν
Ἄρτεμιν, ἃ κυκλόεντ᾽ ἀγορᾶς θρόνον
Εὔκλεα θάσσει,
καὶ Φοῖβον ἑκαβόλον, ἰὼ
τρισσοὶ ἀλεξίμοροι προφάνητέ μοι,
εἴ ποτε καὶ προτέρας ἄτας ὕπερ
ὀρνυμένας πόλει
ἠνύσατ᾽ ἐκτοπίαν φλόγα πήματος,
ἔλθετε καὶ νῦν.

CHORUS: O sweet-speaking voice of Zeus, what message do you bring
to glorious Thebes from Pytho rich in gold? I am racked with suspense,
my fearful heart shakes in terror; Healer of Delos, to whom wild cries
of 'Ie, ie' rise, I stand in holy fear before you; will you demand some
new submission, or one that will return with the circling years? Tell
me, voice immortal, child of golden Hope.

First I call on you, goddess Athene, daughter of Zeus, and on
Artemis your sister, guardian of our land, who sits on her throne of
fame over the Agora's circle, and [I call] on far-shafting Phoebus;
come, appear in threefold help; if ever in time past, as ruin spread over
the city, you drove the flames of havoc past our land, come now again.

ὦ πόποι, ἀνάριθμα γὰρ φέρω
πήματα· νοσεῖ δέ μοι πρόπας
στόλος, οὐδ᾽ ἔνι φροντίδος ἔγχος
ᾧ τις ἀλέξεται. οὔτε γὰρ ἔκγονα
κλυτᾶς χθονὸς αὔξεται οὔτε τόκοισιν
        ἰηίων
καμάτων ἀνέχουσι γυναῖκες·
        ἄλλον δ᾽ ἂν ἄλ-
λῳ προσίδοις ἅπερ εὔπτερον ὄρνιν
κρεῖσσον ἀμαιμακέτου πυρὸς ὄρμενον
        ἀκτὰν πρὸς ἑσπέρου θεοῦ·

        ὧν πόλις ἀνάριθμος ὄλλυται·
        νηλέα δὲ γένεθλα πρὸς πέδῳ
θαναταφόρα κεῖται ἀνοίκτως·
ἐν δ᾽ ἄλοχοι πολιαί τ᾽ ἔπι ματέρες
ἀκτὰν παρὰ βώμιον ἄλλοθεν ἄλλαι
        λυγρῶν πόνων
ἱκτῆρες ἐπιστενάχουσιν.
        παιὰν δὲ λάμ-
·πει στονόεσσά τε γῆρυς ὁμαυλος·
ὧν ὕπερ, ὦ χρυσέα θύγατερ Διός,
        εὐῶπα πέμψον ἀλκάν·

Alas, I bear countless sorrows. A plague is on all our people, and thought can find no weapon for defence. The fruits of this famous earth do not grow, nor do women rise from the crying agony of child-birth with their children [alive]. One after another, like swift-winged birds, and faster than irresistible fire, you see them hurrying to the shore of the western god.

By such countless deaths the city is ruined; her children lie un-pitied on the ground, with none to mourn them, spreading death. And the wives and the grey-haired mothers wail at the altar steps on every side, begging for an end to their bitter pain. Clear rises the prayer to the Healer, and with it are blended the sighs and the voices of men. For these things, golden daughter of Zeus, send us the bright face of help.

Αρεά τε τὸν μαλερόν, ὃς
νῦν ἄχαλκος ἀσπίδων
φλέγει με περιβόατος ἀντιάζων,
παλίσσυτον δράμημα νωτίσαι πάτρας
ἄπουρον, εἴτ' ἐς μέγαν
θάλαμον 'Αμφιτρίτας
εἴτ' ἐς τὸν ἀπόξενον ὅρμων
Θρήκιον κλύδωνα·
τέλει γάρ, εἴ τι νὺξ ἀφῇ,
τοῦτ' ἐπ' ἆμαρ ἔρχεται·
τόν, ὦ τᾶν πυρφόρων
ἀστραπᾶν κράτη νέμων,
ὦ Ζεῦ πάτερ, ὑπὸ σῷ φθίσον κεραυνῷ.

Λύκει' ἄναξ, τά τε σὰ χρυ-
σοστρόφων ἀπ' ἀγκυλᾶν
βέλεα θέλοιμ' ἂν ἀδάματ' ἐνδατεῖσθαι
ἀρωγὰ προσταθέντα, τάς τε πυρφόρους
'Αρτέμιδος αἴγλας, ξὺν αἷς
Λύκι' ὄρεα διάσσει·
τὸν χρυσομίτραν τε κικλήσκω,
τᾶσδ' ἐπώνυμον γᾶς,
οἰνῶπα Βάκχον, εὔιον
Μαινάδων ὁμόστολον,

And let Ares, the fierce god of Death, who, though with no bronze shield, attacks me with war-cries and flame, let him turn in rapid flight away from our land to the great water-palace of Amphitrite, or to the angry, harbourless Thracian sea that is friend to none. For, if the night leaves anything undone, the day that follows shall accomplish it. Father Zeus, master of the flame-bearing lightning, destroy him beneath your thunderbolt.

Lycean King, I wish the irresistible arrows that fly from your bent bow, strung with twisted gold, would come to my help, and that Artemis' flash of flame, with which she leaps across the Lycian hills, would come, too. And I call on him, the gold-crowned god, named by the name of this land, wine-faced Bacchus, companion of the Maenads,

πελασθῆναι φλέγοντ'
ἀγλαῶπι σύμμαχον
πεύκᾳ 'πὶ τὸν ἀπότιμον ἐν θεοῖς θεόν.

(King Oedipus)

106. Oedipus Finds Out

ΟΙΔΙΠΟΥΣ, ΙΟΚΑΣΤΗ, ΑΓΓΕΛΟΣ, ΧΟΡΟΣ, ΘΕΡΑΠΩΝ

Οι. ὦ φίλτατον γυναικὸς Ἰοκάστης κάρα,
τί μ' ἐξεπέμψω δεῦρο τῶνδε δωμάτων;

Ιο. ἄκουε τἀνδρὸς τοῦδε, καὶ σκόπει κλύων
τὰ σέμν' ἵν' ἥκει τοῦ θεοῦ μαντεύματα.

Οι. οὗτος δὲ τίς ποτ' ἐστὶ καὶ τί μοι λέγει;

Ιο. ἐκ τῆς Κορίνθου, πατέρα τὸν σὸν ἀγγελῶν
ὡς οὐκέτ' ὄντα Πόλυβον, ἀλλ' ὀλωλότα.

Οι. τί φής, ξεν'; αὐτός μοι σὺ σημήνας γενοῦ.

Αγ. εἰ τοῦτο πρῶτον δεῖ μ' ἀπαγγεῖλαι σαφῶς,
εὖ ἴσθ' ἐκεῖνον θανάσιμον βεβηκότα.

to whom the Bacchants raise their cry, to come near with the blaze of his brilliant torch, an ally against the one god who is dishonoured among the gods [Ares].

OEDIPUS: Jocasta, my dearest wife, why did you call me here out of the house?

JOCASTA: Listen to this man, and as you listen see what the dreaded oracles of the god have come to.

OEDIPUS: Who can he be, and what has he got to tell me?

JOCASTA: He comes from Corinth to bring a message that your father Polybus is alive no longer, but dead.

OEDIPUS: What did you say, stranger? Make it clear yourself.

MESSENGER: If I must make this clear to you first, know for certain that he is dead and gone.

Οι. πότερα δόλοισιν, ἢ νόσου ξυναλλαγῇ;
Αγ. σμικρὰ παλαιὰ σώματ᾽ εὐνάζει ῥοπή.
Οι. νόσοις ὁ τλήμων, ὡς ἔοικεν, ἔφθιτο.
Αγ. καὶ τῷ μακρῷ γε συμμετρούμενος χρόνῳ.
Οι. φεῦ φεῦ, τί δῆτ᾽ ἄν, ὦ γύναι, σκοποῖτό τις
τὴν Πυθόμαντιν ἑστίαν, ἢ τοὺς ἄνω
κλάζοντας ὄρνις, ὧν ὑφηγητῶν ἐγὼ
κτενεῖν ἔμελλον πατέρα τὸν ἐμόν; ὁ δὲ θανὼν
κεύθει κάτω δὴ γῆς. ἐγὼ δ᾽ ὅδ᾽ ἐνθάδε
ἄψαυστος ἔγχους, εἴ τι μὴ τὠμῷ πόθῳ
κατέφθιθ᾽· οὕτω δ᾽ ἂν θανὼν εἴη 'ξ ἐμοῦ.
τὰ δ᾽ οὖν παρόντα συλλαβὼν θεσπίσματα
κεῖται παρ᾽ Ἅιδη Πόλυβος ἀξι᾽ οὐδενός.
Ιο. οὔκουν ἐγώ σοι ταῦτα προύλεγον πάλαι;
Οι. ηὔδας· ἐγὼ δὲ τῷ φόβῳ παρηγόμην.
Ιο. μὴ νῦν ἔτ᾽ αὐτῶν μηδὲν ἐς θυμὸν βάλῃς.
Οι. καὶ πῶς τὸ μητρὸς οὐκ ὀκνεῖν λέχος με δεῖ;
Ιο. τί δ᾽ ἂν φοβοῖτ᾽ ἄνθρωπος, ᾧ τὰ τῆς τύχης
κρατεῖ, πρόνοια δ᾽ ἐστὶν οὐδενὸς σαφής;
εἰκῆ κράτιστον ζῆν, ὅπως δύναιτό τις.

OEDIPUS: But how? By treachery or by sickness?
MESSENGER: A small touch on the balance sends the old to their rest.
OEDIPUS: It seems that the poor man died of sickness.
MESSENGER: And by the great age to which he had lived.
OEDIPUS: Alas, alas; then why indeed, my wife, should one look to
the hearth of the Pythian seer or to the birds that scream over our
heads, that led me to believe that I would kill my father? He is dead
and hidden under the earth, and I am here, and have not touched a
spear, unless perhaps he died of longing for me; then I could be
guilty of his death. But Polybus has swept into his tomb the present
prophecies; they are worth nothing.
JOCASTA: Did I not foretell you this long ago?
OEDIPUS: You said so; but I was led astray by fear.
JOCASTA: Now think no more about these things.
OEDIPUS: But how can I not fear my mother's bed?
JOCASTA: Why should men be afraid when they are at the hands of
Fortune, and can foresee no single thing with certainty? One should
live as life comes, as best one can. But do not fear a marriage with

  σὺ δ' ἐς τὰ μητρὸς μὴ φοβοῦ νυμφεύματα·
  πολλοὶ γὰρ ἤδη κἀν ὀνείρασιν βροτῶν
  μητρὶ ξυνηυνάσθησαν. ἀλλὰ ταῦθ' ὅτῳ
  παρ' οὐδέν ἐστι, ῥᾷστα τὸν βίον φέρει.
Οι. καλῶς ἅπαντα ταῦτ' ἂν ἐξείρητό σοι,
  εἰ μὴ 'κύρει ζῶσ' ἡ τεκοῦσα· νῦν δ' ἐπεὶ
  ζῇ, πᾶσ' ἀνάγκη, κεἰ καλῶς λέγεις, ὀκνεῖν.
Ιο. καὶ μὴν μέγας γ' ὀφθαλμὸς οἱ πατρὸς τάφοι.
Οι. μέγας, ξυνίημ'· ἀλλὰ τῆς ζώσης φόβος.
Αγ. ποίας δὲ καὶ γυναικὸς ἐκφοβεῖσθ' ὕπερ;
Οι. Μερόπης, γεραιέ, Πόλυβος ἧς ᾤκει μέτα.
Αγ. τί δ' ἔστ' ἐκείνης ὑμὶν ἐς φόβον φέρον;
Οι. θεήλατον μάντευμα δεινόν, ὦ ξένε.
Αγ. ἦ ῥητόν; ἢ οὐχὶ θεμιτὸν ἄλλον εἰδέναι;
Οι. μάλιστά γ'· εἶπε γάρ με Λοξίας ποτὲ
  χρῆναι μιγῆναι μητρὶ τἠμαυτοῦ, τό τε
  πατρῷον αἷμα χερσὶ ταῖς ἐμαῖς ἑλεῖν.
  ὧν οὕνεχ' ἡ Κόρινθος ἐξ ἐμοῦ πάλαι
  μακρὰν ἀπῳκεῖτ'· εὐτυχῶς μέν, ἀλλ' ὅμως
  τὰ τῶν τεκόντων ὄμμαθ' ἥδιστον βλέπειν.
Αγ. ἦ γὰρ τάδ' ὀκνῶν κεῖθεν ἦσθ' ἀπόπτολις;

your mother. For many men before now have slept with their mothers in their dreams. The man who gives no thought to such things bears life most easily.

OEDIPUS: All this would have been well said by you, if my mother were not still alive. But now, as she is alive, I must still fear — even though you speak well.

JOCASTA: But your father's death is a great relief.

OEDIPUS: Great, I know; but I fear the woman who lives.

MESSENGER: And who is the woman you fear?

OEDIPUS: Merope, old man; the woman Polybus lived with.

MESSENGER: And what is it about her that can frighten you?

OEDIPUS: An oracle sent by the god, full of horror, stranger.

MESSENGER: Can you tell it to us? Or should no one else know?

OEDIPUS: Yes, you can hear. Loxias once said that I must marry my own mother and shed the blood of my father with my own hands. That is why I have been living for so long away from Corinth. I was lucky; yet it is sweetest to see your parents' face.

MESSENGER: For fear of that you kept away from your city?

Οι. πατρός τε χρήζων μὴ φονεὺς εἶναι, γέρον.

Αγ. τί δῆτ' ἐγὼ οὐχὶ τοῦδε τοῦ φόβου σ', ἄναξ,
ἐπείπερ εὔνους ἦλθον, ἐξελυσάμην;

Οι. καὶ μὴν χάριν γ' ἂν ἀξίαν λάβοις ἐμοῦ.

Αγ. καὶ μὴν μάλιστα τοῦτ' ἀφικόμην, ὅπως
σοῦ πρὸς δόμους ἐλθόντος εὖ πράξαιμί τι.

Οι. ἀλλ' οὔποτ' εἶμι τοῖς φυτεύσασίν γ' ὁμοῦ.

Αγ. ὦ παῖ, καλῶς εἶ δῆλος οὐκ εἰδὼς τί δρᾷς.

Οι. πῶς, ὦ γεραιέ; πρὸς θεῶν δίδασκέ με.

Αγ. εἰ τῶνδε φεύγεις οὕνεκ' εἰς οἴκους μολεῖν.

Οι. ταρβῶ γε μή μοι Φοῖβος ἐξέλθῃ σαφής.

Αγ. ἦ μὴ μίασμα τῶν φυτευσάντων λάβῃς;

Οι. τοῦτ' αὐτό, πρέσβυ, τοῦτό μ' εἰσαεὶ φοβεῖ.

Αγ. ἆρ' οἶσθα δῆτα πρὸς δίκης οὐδὲν τρέμων;

Οι. πῶς δ' οὐχί, παῖς γ' εἰ τῶνδε γεννητῶν ἔφυν;

Αγ. ὁθούνεκ' ἦν σοι Πόλυβος οὐδὲν ἐν γένει.

Οι. πῶς εἶπας; οὐ γὰρ Πόλυβος ἐξέφυσέ με;

Αγ. οὐ μᾶλλον οὐδὲν τοῦδε τἀνδρός, ἀλλ' ἴσον.

OEDIPUS: And because I would not be the killer of my father, old man.

MESSENGER: I should have freed you from this fear, my king, since I came with good intentions.

OEDIPUS: You would certainly have had a proper reward from me.

MESSENGER: And that is exactly why I came — to get a good reward when you return to your home.

OEDIPUS: But I will never go where I will be with my parents.

MESSENGER: My son, it is very clear that you do not know what you are doing.

OEDIPUS: How, old man? For the gods' sake tell me.

MESSENGER: If that is why you keep away from your house.

OEDIPUS: I fear Apollo may come true for me.

MESSENGER: Afraid lest you incur guilt over your parents?

OEDIPUS: Exactly, old man; I am always afraid of that.

MESSENGER: Well, do you know that you have no reason to fear?

OEDIPUS: Why not, if I am the child of those parents?

MESSENGER: Because Polybus was no relation of yours.

OEDIPUS: What did you say? Was not Polybus my father?

MESSENGER: No more than this man here [*pointing to himself*], but just as much.

216

Οι. καὶ πῶς ὁ φύσας ἐξ ἴσου τῷ μηδενί;

Αγ. ἀλλ' οὔ σ' ἐγείνατ' οὔτ' ἐκεῖνος οὔτ' ἐγώ.

Οι. ἀλλ' ἀντὶ τοῦ δὴ παῖδά μ' ὠνομάζετο;

Αγ. δῶρόν ποτ', ἴσθι, τῶν ἐμῶν χειρῶν λαβών.

Οι. κᾆθ' ὧδ' ἀπ' ἄλλης χειρὸς ἔστερξεν μέγα;

Αγ. ἡ γὰρ πρὶν αὐτὸν ἐξέπεισ' ἀπαιδία.

Οι. σὺ δ' ἐμπολήσας ἢ τυχών μ' αὐτῷ δίδως;

Αγ. εὑρὼν ναπαίαις ἐν Κιθαιρῶνος πτυχαῖς.

Οι. ὡδοιπόρεις δὲ πρὸς τί τούσδε τοὺς τόπους;

Αγ. ἐνταῦθ' ὀρείοις ποιμνίοις ἐπεστάτουν.

Οι. ποιμὴν γὰρ ἦσθα κἀπὶ θητείᾳ πλάνης;

Αγ. σοῦ δ', ὦ τέκνον, σωτήρ γε τῷ τότ' ἐν χρόνῳ.

Οι. τί δ' ἄλγος ἴσχοντ' ἐν χεροῖν με λαμβάνεις;

Αγ. ποδῶν ἂν ἄρθρα μαρτυρήσειεν τὰ σά.

Οι. οἴμοι, τί τοῦτ' ἀρχαῖον ἐννέπεις κακόν;

Αγ. λύω σ' ἔχοντα διατόρους ποδοῖν ἀκμάς.

Οι. δεινόν γ' ὄνειδος σπαργάνων ἀνειλόμην.

OEDIPUS: How can my father be the same to me as someone who is nothing to me?

MESSENGER: Neither is he, nor am I your father.

OEDIPUS: Then why did he call me his son?

MESSENGER: Because, you should know, he received you as a gift from my own hands.

OEDIPUS: And then, though coming thus from the hand of another, he loved me so much?

MESSENGER: He was childless before; that persuaded him.

OEDIPUS: And you – had you bought me or did you find me and give me to him?

MESSENGER: I found you in a winding glen of Cithaeron.

OEDIPUS: Why were you journeying in those lands?

MESSENGER: I was the shepherd there of a mountain flock.

OEDIPUS: You were a travelling shepherd, working for hire?

MESSENGER: And your rescuer, my son, at that time.

OEDIPUS: And what was my suffering when you picked me up?

MESSENGER: The ankles of your feet could tell us that.

OEDIPUS: Ah! Why do you mention that old evil?

MESSENGER: I set you free when your ankles were pierced.

OEDIPUS: A dreadful scar of shame I picked up from my cradle.

Αγ. ὥστ' ὠνομάσθης ἐκ τύχης ταύτης ὃς εἶ.

Οι. ὦ πρὸς θεῶν, πρὸς μητρός, ἢ πατρός; φράσον.

Αγ. οὐκ οἶδ'· ὁ δοὺς δὲ ταῦτ' ἐμοῦ λῷον φρονεῖ.

Οι. ἦ γὰρ παρ' ἄλλου μ' ἔλαβες οὐδ' αὐτὸς τυχών;

Αγ. οὔκ, ἀλλὰ ποιμὴν ἄλλος ἐκδίδωσί μοι.

Οι. τίς οὗτος; ἦ κάτοισθα δηλῶσαι λόγῳ;

Αγ. τῶν Λαΐου δήπου τις ὠνομάζετο.

Οι. ἦ τοῦ τυράννου τῆσδε γῆς πάλαι ποτέ;

Αγ. μάλιστα· τούτου τἀνδρὸς οὗτος ἦν βοτήρ.

Οι. ἦ κἄστ' ἔτι ζῶν οὗτος, ὥστ' ἰδεῖν ἐμέ;

Αγ. ὑμεῖς γ' ἄριστ' εἰδεῖτ' ἂν οὑπιχώριοι.

Οι. ἔστιν τις ὑμῶν τῶν παρεστώτων πέλας,
    ὅστις κάτοιδε τὸν βοτῆρ', ὃν ἐννέπει,
    εἴτ' οὖν ἐπ' ἀγρῶν εἴτε κἀνθάδ' εἰσιδών;
    σημήναθ', ὡς ὁ καιρὸς εὑρῆσθαι τάδε.

Χο. οἶμαι μὲν οὐδέν' ἄλλον ἢ τὸν ἐξ ἀγρῶν,
    ὃν κἀμάτευες πρόσθεν εἰσιδεῖν· ἀτὰρ
    ἥδ' ἂν τάδ' οὐχ ἥκιστ' ἂν Ἰοκάστη λέγοι.

MESSENGER: So that you were given the name you have, because of that misfortune.

OEDIPUS: O for the gods' sake, tell me. Was it my mother's or my father's doing?

MESSENGER: I do not know. The man who gave you to me knows better.

OEDIPUS: Did you take me from someone else? Didn't you find me yourself?

MESSENGER: No, another shepherd gave you to me.

OEDIPUS: Who was he? Do you know, can you tell who he was?

MESSENGER: He was, I think, called one of Laius' men.

OEDIPUS: The king who ruled this country long before?

MESSENGER: Yes, he was one of that man's shepherds.

OEDIPUS: Is he still alive, so that I can see him?

MESSENGER: You, who live here, should know best.

OEDIPUS: Is there any of you standing near who knows the shepherd he speaks of? Have you seen him in the fields or near here? Tell me. The time has come when we must find this out.

CHORUS: I think that this is no other than the man from the fields whom you wanted to see earlier. But Jocasta here could best tell you that.

Οι. γύναι, νοεῖς ἐκεῖνον, ὅντιν' ἀρτίως
μολεῖν ἐφιέμεσθα; τόνδ' οὗτος λέγει;

Ιο. τί δ' ὅντιν' εἶπε; μηδὲν ἐντραπῇς. τὰ δὲ
ῥηθέντα βούλου μηδὲ μεμνῆσθαι μάτην.

Οι. οὐκ ἂν γένοιτο τοῦθ', ὅπως ἐγὼ λαβὼν
σημεῖα τοιαῦτ' οὐ φανῶ τοὐμὸν γένος.

Ιο. μὴ πρὸς θεῶν, εἴπερ τι τοῦ σαυτοῦ βίου
κήδει, ματεύσῃς τοῦθ'· ἅλις νοσοῦσ' ἐγώ.

Οι. θάρσει· σὺ μὲν γὰρ οὐδ' ἐὰν τρίτης ἐγὼ
μητρὸς φανῶ τρίδουλος, ἐκφανῇ κακή.

Ιο. ὅμως πιθοῦ μοι, λίσσομαι· μὴ δρᾶ τάδε.

Οι. οὐκ ἂν πιθοίμην μὴ οὐ τάδ' ἐκμαθεῖν σαφῶς.

Ιο. καὶ μὴν φρονοῦσά γ' εὖ τὰ λῷστά σοι λέγω.

Οι. τὰ λῷστα τοίνυν ταῦτά μ' ἀλγύνει πάλαι.

Ιο. ὦ δύσποτμ', εἴθε μήποτε γνοίης ὃς εἶ.

Οι. ἄξει τις ἐλθὼν δεῦρο τὸν βοτῆρά μοι;
ταύτην δ' ἐᾶτε πλουσίῳ χαίρειν γένει.

Ιο. ἰοὺ ἰού, δύστηνε· τοῦτο γάρ σ' ἔχω
μόνον προσειπεῖν, ἄλλο δ' οὔποθ' ὕστερον.

OEDIPUS: My wife, you know the man whom we wanted to summon
here a little while ago. Is it he that this man is speaking of?

JOCASTA: Why [ask] about the man he spoke of? Take no notice. Don't
try to remember what was idly spoken.

OEDIPUS: With such clues in my hands I cannot fail to solve the prob-
lem of my birth.

JOCASTA: No, by the gods! If you care about your life at all, stop this
search. My suffering is enough.

OEDIPUS: Courage. Even if I were found to be slave-born three times
over, son of three slave mothers, your honour would be untouched.

JOCASTA: But listen to me, I beg you. Do not do this.

OEDIPUS: I could not be persuaded by anyone not to discover the
whole truth clearly.

JOCASTA: And yet for your own good I tell you what is best.

OEDIPUS: The best! That has always made me suffer in the past.

JOCASTA: Doomed man. May you never learn who you are.

OEDIPUS: Will someone go and fetch the shepherd here? Let her gloat
over her noble birth.

JOCASTA: Alas, alas! Wretched man. That is all I can call you; nothing
after that.

Χο. τί ποτε βέβηκεν, Οἰδίπους, ὑπ' ἀγρίας
    ᾄξασα λύπης ἡ γυνή; δέδοιχ' ὅπως
    μὴ 'κ τῆς σιωπῆς τῆσδ' ἀναρρήξει κακά.

Οι. ὁποῖα χρῄζει ῥηγνύτω· τοὐμὸν δ' ἐγώ,
    κεἰ σμικρόν ἐστι, σπέρμ' ἰδεῖν βουλήσομαι.
    αὕτη δ' ἴσως, φρονεῖ γὰρ ὡς γυνὴ μέγα,
    τὴν δυσγένειαν τὴν ἐμὴν αἰσχύνεται.
    ἐγὼ δ' ἐμαυτὸν παῖδα τῆς Τύχης νέμων
    τῆς εὖ διδούσης οὐκ ἀτιμασθήσομαι.
    τῆς γὰρ πέφυκα μητρός· οἱ δὲ συγγενεῖς
    μῆνές με μικρὸν καὶ μέγαν διώρισαν.
    τοιόσδε δ' ἐκφὺς οὐκ ἂν ἐξέλθοιμ' ἔτι
    ποτ' ἄλλος, ὥστε μὴ 'κμαθεῖν τοὐμὸν γένος.

Χο. εἴπερ ἐγὼ μάντις εἰμὶ καὶ κατὰ γνώμαν ἴδρις,
    οὐ τὸν Ὄλυμπον ἀπείρων,
    ὦ Κιθαιρών, οὐκ ἔσει τὰν αὔριον
    πανσέληνον, μὴ οὐ σέ γε καὶ πατριώταν Οἰδίπου
    καὶ τροφὸν καὶ ματέρ' αὔξειν,
    καὶ χορεύεσθαι πρὸς ἡμῶν, ὡς ἐπίηρα φέροντα' τοῖς
        ἐμοῖς τυράννοις.
    ἰήϊε Φοῖβε, σοὶ δὲ ταῦτ' ἀρέστ' εἴη.

CHORUS: Oedipus, why has the woman left us shaken by wild grief? I fear a storm of sorrow may break out of this silence.

OEDIPUS: Let all that must burst out. I shall want to know my birth, even if it is low. Perhaps she, with a woman's pride, feels shame for my low birth. I consider myself the child of Good Fortune, and I shall not be shamed. She is my mother; the Months are my nearest of kin; they made me both small and great. This being my lineage, I will never be other than the man I am, therefore why avoid finding out my birth?

CHORUS: If I can tell the future, and if I can judge with wisdom, O Cithaeron, you will not fail – no, by Olympus, you will not fail – to know at tomorrow's full moon that Oedipus honours you as his native land, as his nurse and his mother; and that we dance and sing in your honour, because you are pleasing to our king. Phoebus, to whom we cry, may this be pleasing to you.

τίς σε, τέκνον, τίς σ' ἔτικτε τᾶν μακραιώνων ἄρα
Πανὸς ὀρεσσιβάτα πα-
τρὸς πελασθεῖσ'; ἦ σέ γ' εὐνάτειρά τις
Λοξίου, τῷ γὰρ πλάκες ἀγρόνομοι πᾶσαι φίλαι;
εἴθ' ὁ Κυλλάνας ἀνάσσων,
εἴθ' ὁ Βακχεῖος θεὸς ναίων ἐπ' ἄκρων ὀρέων σ' εὕρημα
    δέξατ' ἔκ του
Νυμφᾶν Ἑλικωνίδων, αἷς πλεῖστα συμπαίζει.

Οι. εἰ χρή τι κἀμὲ μὴ συναλλάξαντά πω,
πρέσβεις, σταθμᾶσθαι, τὸν βοτῆρ' ὁρᾶν δοκῶ,
ὅνπερ πάλαι ζητοῦμεν. ἔν τε γὰρ μακρῷ
γήρᾳ ξυνᾴδει τῷδε τἀνδρὶ σύμμετρος,
ἄλλως τε τοὺς ἄγοντας ὥσπερ οἰκέτας
ἔγνωκ' ἐμαυτοῦ· τῇ δ' ἐπιστήμῃ σύ μου
προὔχοις τάχ' ἄν που, τὸν βοτῆρ' ἰδὼν πάρος.
Χο. ἔγνωκα γάρ, σάφ' ἴσθι· Λαΐου γὰρ ἦν
εἴπερ τις ἄλλος πιστὸς ὡς νομεὺς ἀνήρ.
Οι. σὲ πρῶτ' ἐρωτῶ, τὸν Κορίνθιον ξένον,
ἦ τόνδε φράζεις;   Αγ. τοῦτον, ὅνπερ εἰσορᾷς.
Οι. οὗτος, σύ, πρέσβυ, δεῦρό μοι φώνει βλέπων
ὅσ' ἄν σ' ἐρωτῶ. Λαΐου ποτ' ἦσθα σύ;

Who was it, my son, which of the long-living Nymphs bore you,
embraced by mountain-roving Pan? Or was it a bride of Loxias,
who loves all upland pasturage? Or was it the master of Cyllene
[Hermes], or the Bacchic god, who dwells on the mountain-tops,
that received you, a new-born joy, from one of the Nymphs of
Helicon, his special playmates?

OEDIPUS: Elders, if I can judge, I think – though I have had no deal-
ings with him – that I too see the shepherd we have so long been
looking for. His long years equal those of this man here; moreover,
I recognize those who bring him as my own servants. But you would
know better than I, as you have seen the shepherd before.

CHORUS: I recognize him; you can be sure of that. For he was one of
Laius' men, as faithful as any of his herdsmen.

OEDIPUS: I ask you first, Corinthian stranger: do you recognize him?

MESSENGER: It is he. The man you see.

OEDIPUS: You there, old man, look at me and answer all I ask you.
Were you one of Laius' men?

Θε. ἦ δοῦλος, οὐκ ὠνητός, ἀλλ' οἴκοι τραφείς.
Οι. ἔργον μεριμνῶν ποῖον ἢ βίον τίνα;
Θε. ποίμναις τὰ πλεῖστα τοῦ βίου συνειπόμην.
Οι. χώροις μάλιστα πρὸς τίσι ξύναυλος ὤν;
Θε. ἦν μὲν Κιθαιρών, ἦν δὲ πρόσχωρος τόπος.
Οι. τὸν ἄνδρα τόνδ' οὖν οἶσθα τῇδέ που μαθών;
Θε. τί χρῆμα δρῶντα; ποῖον ἄνδρα καὶ λέγεις;
Οι. τόνδ' ὃς πάρεστιν· ἢ ξυνήλλαξάς τί πω;
Θε. οὐχ ὥστε γ' εἰπεῖν ἐν τάχει μνήμης ἄπο.
Αγ. κοὐδέν γε θαῦμα, δέσποτ'. ἀλλ' ἐγὼ σαφῶς
    ἀγνῶτ' ἀναμνήσω νιν. εὖ γὰρ οἶδ' ὅτι
    κάτοιδεν ἦμος τὸν Κιθαιρῶνος τόπον
    ὁ μὲν διπλοῖσι ποιμνίοις, ἐγὼ δ' ἑνὶ
    ἐπλησίαζον τῷδε τἀνδρὶ τρεῖς ὅλους
    ἐξ ἦρος εἰς ἀρκτοῦρον ἐκμήνους χρόνους·
    χειμῶνι δ' ἤδη τἀμά τ' εἰς ἔπαυλ' ἐγὼ
    ἤλαυνον οὗτός τ' εἰς τὰ Λαΐου σταθμά.
    λέγω τι τούτων, ἢ οὐ λέγω πεπραγμένον;
Θε. λέγεις ἀληθῆ, καίπερ ἐκ μακροῦ χρόνου.

SERVANT: Yes, one of his slaves, not one he bought, but born and bred in his house.

OEDIPUS: What did you look after? How did you earn your living?

SERVANT: Most of my life I tended flocks of sheep.

OEDIPUS: In what part of the land did you spend most of your time?

SERVANT: It was Cithaeron, and the country round there.

OEDIPUS: Well, do you know this man? Did you meet him anywhere there?

SERVANT: Doing what? Which man are you talking about?

OEDIPUS: This man here. Did you have any dealings with him before?

MESSENGER: And it is no wonder, master. But I will make him remember clearly, though now he has forgotten. I am sure that he remembers when he tended two flocks of sheep in a part of Cithaeron and I was near him with one flock for three whole seasons of six months each, from spring to autumn. In winter I used to lead mine to my fold, and he led his to the folds of Laius. Am I speaking of something that happened, or not?

SERVANT: You speak the truth, though it is of a long time ago.

Αγ. φέρ' εἰπὲ νῦν, τότ' οἶσθα παῖδά μοί τινα
  δούς, ὡς ἐμαυτῷ θρέμμα θρεψαίμην ἐγώ;
Θε. τί δ' ἔστι; πρὸς τί τοῦτο τοὔπος ἱστορεῖς;
Αγ. ὅδ' ἐστίν, ὦ τᾶν, κεῖνος ὃς τότ' ἦν νέος.
Θε. οὐκ εἰς ὄλεθρον; οὐ σιωπήσας ἔσῃ;
Οι. ἄ, μὴ κόλαζε, πρέσβυ, τόνδ', ἐπεὶ τὰ σὰ
  δεῖται κολαστοῦ μᾶλλον ἢ τὰ τοῦδ' ἔπη.
Θε. τί δ', ὦ φέριστε δεσποτῶν, ἁμαρτάνω;
Οι. οὐκ ἐννέπων τὸν παῖδ' ὃν οὗτος ἱστορεῖ.
Θε. λέγει γὰρ εἰδὼς οὐδέν, ἀλλ' ἄλλως πονεῖ.
Οι. σὺ πρὸς χάριν μὲν οὐκ ἐρεῖς, κλαίων δ' ἐρεῖς.
Θε. μὴ δῆτα, πρὸς θεῶν, τὸν γέροντά μ' αἰκίσῃ.
Οι. οὐχ ὡς τάχος τις τοῦδ' ἀποστρέψει χέρας;
Θε. δύστηνος, ἀντὶ τοῦ; τί προσχρῄζων μαθεῖν;
Οι. τὸν παῖδ' ἔδωκας τῷδ' ὃν οὗτος ἱστορεῖ;
Θε. ἔδωκ'· ὀλέσθαι δ' ὤφελον τῇδ' ἡμέρᾳ.
Οι. ἀλλ' ἐς τόδ' ἥξεις μὴ λέγων γε τοὐνδικον.
Θε. πολλῷ γε μᾶλλον, ἢν φράσω, διόλλυμαι.
Οι. ἀνὴρ ὅδ', ὡς ἔοικεν, ἐς τριβὰς ἐλᾷ.

MESSENGER: Come now, tell me, do you remember giving me a child to bring up as my own?

SERVANT: What's this? Why do you tell that story?

MESSENGER: This is he, my friend; the man who was then a baby.

SERVANT: Damn you – won't you hold your tongue?

OEDIPUS: Don't scold him, old man; your words should be punished more than his.

SERVANT: What wrong have I done, O best of masters?

OEDIPUS: You are not telling us about the child he speaks of.

SERVANT: He speaks in ignorance – he is wasting his efforts.

OEDIPUS: You will not talk to please me; but you will talk if you suffer.

SERVANT: For the sake of the gods, do not torture me, an old man.

OEDIPUS: Will nobody quickly twist his arms behind his back?

SERVANT: Poor me! What for? What do you want to know?

OEDIPUS: Did you give him the child he speaks about?

SERVANT: I gave it. I wish I had died that day.

OEDIPUS: That is where you'll end, if you do not tell the truth.

SERVANT: I am far more lost if I speak.

OEDIPUS: It seems that this man is trying to delay us.

SOPHOCLES

Θε. οὐ δῆτ' ἔγωγ', ἀλλ' εἶπον ὡς δοίην πάλαι.
Οι. πόθεν λαβών; οἰκεῖον, ἢ 'ξ ἄλλου τινός·
Θε. ἐμὸν μὲν οὐκ ἔγωγ', ἐδεξάμην δέ του.
Οι. τίνος πολιτῶν τῶνδε κἀκ ποίας στέγης;
Θε. μὴ πρὸς θεῶν, μή, δέσποθ', ἱστόρει πλέον.
Οι. ὄλωλας, εἴ σε ταῦτ' ἐρήσομαι πάλιν.
Θε. τῶν Λαΐου τοίνυν τις ἦν γεννημάτων.
Οι. ἦ δοῦλος, ἢ κείνου τις ἐγγενὴς γεγώς;
Θε. οἴμοι, πρὸς αὐτῷ γ' εἰμὶ τῷ δεινῷ λέγειν.
Οι. κἄγωγ' ἀκούειν. ἀλλ' ὅμως ἀκουστέον.
Θε. κείνου γέ τοι δὴ παῖς ἐκλήζεθ'· ἡ δ' ἔσω
κάλλιστ' ἂν εἴποι σὴ γυνὴ τάδ' ὡς ἔχει.
Οι. ἦ γὰρ δίδωσιν ἥδε σοι;   Θε. μάλιστ', ἄναξ.
Οι. ὡς πρὸς τί χρείας;   Θε. ὡς ἀναλώσαιμί νιν.
Οι. τεκοῦσα τλήμων;   Θε. θεσφάτων γ' ὄκνῳ κακῶν.
Οι. ποίων;   Θε. κτενεῖν νιν τοὺς τεκόντας ἦν λόγος.
Οι. πῶς δῆτ' ἀφῆκας τῷ γέροντι τῷδε σύ;

SERVANT: No, no, not I; I have already said long ago that I gave it.
OEDIPUS: Where did you get it from? Your own home, or from someone else?
SERVANT: It was certainly not mine. Somebody gave it to me.
OEDIPUS: Which of these citizens, from what home?
SERVANT: For the love of the gods, master, ask no more.
OEDIPUS: You are lost, if I ask you this again.
SERVANT: Well; it was a child from the household of Laius.
OEDIPUS: A slave, or one born of his blood?
SERVANT: Alas! I am about to say the terrible thing.
OEDIPUS: And I to hear it; but it must be heard.
SERVANT: It was said to be a child of his. But your wife in the palace could best tell you of these things.
OEDIPUS: Did she give it to you?
SERVANT: Yes, my king.
OEDIPUS: To do what with it?
SERVANT: To kill it.
OEDIPUS: Her own child, the wretched woman?
SERVANT: In fear of an evil prophecy.
OEDIPUS: What prophecy?
SERVANT: It was said it would kill its own parents.
OEDIPUS: Why then did you give it to this old man?

224

Θε. κατοικτίσας, ὦ δέσποθ', ὡς ἄλλην χθόνα
δοκῶν ἀποίσειν, αὐτὸς ἔνθεν ἦν· ὁ δὲ
κάκ' ἐς μέγιστ' ἔσωσεν. εἰ γὰρ οὗτος εἶ
ὅν φησιν οὗτος, ἴσθι δύσποτμος γεγώς.

Οι. ἰοὺ ἰού· τὰ πάντ' ἂν ἐξήκοι σαφῆ.
ὦ φῶς, τελευταῖόν σε προσβλέψαιμι νῦν,
ὅστις πέφασμαι φύς τ' ἀφ' ὧν οὐ χρῆν, ξὺν οἷς τ'
οὐ χρῆν ὁμιλῶν, οὕς τέ μ' οὐκ ἔδει κτανών.

(*King Oedipus*)

107. *The Grove of Colonus*

ΧΟΡΟΣ

Εὐίππου, ξένε, τᾶσδε χώ-
ρας ἵκου τὰ κράτιστα γᾶς ἔπαυλα,
τὸν ἀργῆτα Κολωνόν, ἔνθ'
ἁ λίγεια μινύρεται
θαμίζουσα μάλιστ' ἀη-
δὼν χλωραῖς ὑπὸ βάσσαις,
τὸν οἰνωπὸν ἔχουσα κισ-
σὸν καὶ τὰν ἄβατον θεοῦ

SERVANT: I felt sorry for it, master. I thought that he would take it to another land, the one he came from. But he saved it for the greatest evil. If you are the man he says you are, know that you were born to misfortune.

OEDIPUS: Alas, alas! Everything must have come true! Light, may I see you now for the last time, I who have been found born of those of whom I should not have been born, living with those with whom I should not live, and the killer of those I should not have killed.

CHORUS: Stranger, you have come to white Colonus, the best dwelling in this land of fine horses, where the clear-singing nightingale warbles her song in the green glens, clinging to the wine-dark ivy, and to the untrodden grove of the god, thick with leaves and berry-clusters,

φυλλάδα μυριόκαρπον ἀνάλιον
ἀνήνεμόν τε πάντων
χειμώνων· ἵν' ὁ βακχιώ-
τας ἀεὶ Διόνυσος ἐμβατεύει
θείαις ἀμφιπολῶν τιθήναις.

θάλλει δ' οὐρανίας ὑπ' ἄ-
χνας ὁ καλλίβοτρυς κατ' ἦμαρ αἰεὶ
νάρκισσος, μεγάλοιν θεοῖν
ἀρχαῖον στεφάνωμ', ὅ τε
χρυσαυγὴς κρόκος· οὐδ' ἄϋ-
πνοι κρῆναι μινύθουσιν
Κηφισοῦ νομάδες ῥεέ-
θρων, ἀλλ' αἰὲν ἐπ' ἤματι
ὠκυτόκος πεδίων ἐπινίσεται
ἀκηράτῳ σὺν ὄμβρῳ
στερνούχου χθονός· οὐδὲ Μου-
σᾶν χοροί νιν ἀπεστύγησαν, οὐδ' αὖ
ἁ χρυσάνιος Ἀφροδίτα.

ἔστιν δ' οἷον ἐγὼ γᾶς
Ἀσίας οὐκ ἐπακούω,
οὐδ' ἐν τᾷ μεγάλᾳ Δωρίδι νάσῳ
Πέλοπος πώποτε βλαστὸν

without sun and without the blast of storms, which Dionysus in ecstasy always haunts with his godlike nurses [the nymphs of Nysa].

Day by day the narcissus blooms in lovely clusters, fed by the dew of the sky, from long ago a crown for the great goddesses, and with it the gold-lit crocus; the sleepless wandering springs of the streams of the river Cephisus do not fail; but each day it [Cephisus] moves across the plains giving rapid birth with its pure water to [the plants of] the swelling earth. The chorus of the Muses does not despise this place, nor does Aphrodite of the golden reins.

And here is found the foliage of the grey olive that feeds children, a plant such, I hear, as cannot be found in the land of Asia, nor ever grows in the great Doric island of Pelops; a deathless, self-sown plant

φύτευμ' ἀχείρωτον αὐτοποιόν,
  ἐγχέων φόβημα δαΐων,
ὃ τᾷδε θάλλει μέγιστα χώρᾳ,
γλαυκᾶς παιδοτρόφου φύλλον ἐλαίας·
τὸ μέν τις οὐ νεαρὸς οὐδὲ γήρᾳ
συνναίων ἁλιώσει χερὶ πέρσας· ὁ
  γὰρ εἰσαιὲν ὁρῶν κύκλος
  λεύσσει νιν Μορίου Διὸς
  χἀ γλαυκῶπις Ἀθάνα.

ἄλλον δ' αἶνον ἔχω μα-
  τροπόλει τᾷδε κράτιστον,
δῶρον τοῦ μεγάλου δαίμονος, εἰπεῖν,
  χθονὸς αὔχημα μέγιστον,
  εὔιππον, εὔπωλον, εὐθάλασσον.
  ὦ παῖ Κρόνου, σὺ γάρ νιν ἐς
τόδ' εἶσας αὔχημ', ἄναξ Ποσειδάν,
ἵπποισιν τὸν ἀκεστῆρα χαλινὸν
πρώταισι ταῖσδε κτίσας ἀγυιαῖς.
ἁ δ' εὐήρετμος ἔκπαγλ' ἁλία χερσὶ
  παραπτυσσομένα πλάτα
  θρῴσκει, τῶν ἑκατομπόδων
  Νηρήδων ἀκόλουθος.

(Oedipus at Colonus)

— a terror to the spears of the enemy — which grows in greatest abundance in this land. No young person, nor anyone who dwells with old age, will damage or destroy it with his hand; for the sleepless eye of Morian Zeus watches over it, and grey-eyed Athene.

Yet more great praise have I for this our mother-city — a gift of the great god, the greatest glory of our land with its splendid horses, its splendid colts, its great sea-power. Son of Cronos, king Poseidon, you established her in this glory, by showing first in this city the use of the bit that curbs the horses' rage; and the well-rowed oars leap splendidly from the waves, sped by men's hands in the track of the hundred-footed Nereids.

108. Old Age

ΧΟΡΟΣ

Ὅστις τοῦ πλέονος μέρους
χρῄζει τοῦ μετρίου παρεὶς
ζώειν, σκαιοσύναν φυλάσ-
σων ἐν ἐμοὶ κατάδηλος ἔσται.
ἐπεὶ πολλὰ μὲν αἱ μακραὶ
ἀμέραι κατέθεντο δὴ
λύπας ἐγγυτέρω, τὰ τέρ-
ποντα δ᾽ οὐκ ἂν ἴδοις ὅπου,
ὅταν τις ἐς πλέον πέσῃ
τοῦ δέοντος· ὁ δ᾽ ἐπίκουρος ἰσοτέλεστος,
Ἄϊδος ὅτε μοῖρ᾽ ἀνυμέναιος
ἄλυρος ἄχορος ἀναπέφηνε,
θάνατος ἐς τελευτάν.

μὴ φῦναι τὸν ἅπαντα νι-
κᾷ λόγον· τὸ δ᾽, ἐπεὶ φανῇ,
βῆναι κεῖσ᾽ ὁπόθεν περ ἥ-
κει πολὺ δεύτερον ὡς τάχιστα.
ὡς εὖτ᾽ ἂν τὸ νέον παρῇ
κούφας ἀφροσύνας φέρον,
τίς πλάγχθη πολὺ μόχθος ἔ-
ξω; τίς οὐ καμάτων ἔνι;
φθόνος, στάσεις, ἔρις, μάχαι

CHORUS: He who is not content with a modest length of life, but de-
sires a larger portion, will, in my opinion, clearly be the man who
clings to foolishness. For the long days store up many things that are
closer to sorrow [than to joy]; when a man falls beyond the proper
length of life, there is nowhere where he may see things that give de-
light; and the deliverer comes at last to all alike – when the doom of
Hades suddenly appears, without a marriage-song or lyre or dance –
death at the last.

Not to be born is [best] beyond all estimate. But when a man has
been born, by far the second best is to go as soon as possible to the
place from which he has come. For when youth recedes, taking with it
its light follies, what trouble will he escape? What suffering that will
not be his? Envy, disputes, strife, battles and bloodshed; and, last of

SOPHOCLES

καὶ φόνοι· τό τε κατάμεμπτον ἐπιλέλογχε
πύματον ἀκρατὲς ἀπροσόμιλον
γῆρας ἄφιλον, ἵνα πρόπαντα
κακὰ κακῶν ξυνοικεῖ.

ἐν ᾧ τλάμων ὅδ', οὐκ ἐγὼ μόνος,
πάντοθεν βόρειος ὥς τις ἀκτὰ
κυματοπλὴξ χειμερία κλονεῖται,
ὡς καὶ τόνδε κατ' ἄκρας
δειναὶ κυματοαγεῖς
ἆται κλονέουσιν ἀεὶ ξυνοῦσαι,
αἱ μὲν ἀπ' ἀελίου δυσμᾶν,
αἱ δ' ἀνατέλλοντος,
αἱ δ' ἀνὰ μέσσαν ἀκτῖν',
αἱ δ' ἐννυχιᾶν ἀπὸ Ῥιπᾶν.

(*Oedipus at Colonus*)

109. The End of Oedipus

ΑΓΓΕΛΟΣ

'Ὡς μὲν γὰρ ἐνθένδ' εἷρπε, καὶ σύ που παρὼν
ἔξοισθ', ὑφηγητῆρος οὐδενὸς φίλων,
ἀλλ' αὐτὸς ἡμῖν πᾶσιν ἐξηγούμενος·
ἐπεὶ δ' ἀφῖκτο τὸν καταρράκτην ὁδὸν
χαλκοῖς βάθροισι γῆθεν ἐρριζωμένον,
ἔστη κελεύθων ἐν πολυσχίστων μιᾷ,

all, old age falls to his lot, hated by all, infirm, friendless, lonely old age, the home of the worst of ills.

Thus is the unhappy man here, not I alone; and like a wave-beaten coast, facing north, battered by storms on all sides, he is battered through and through by violent, ever-present troubles that break over him like waves – some from the setting sun, some from the rising sun, some from the region of the midday light, and some from the dark Ripaean hills.

MESSENGER: You saw how he left here – you were present too, so you know – with no friend to guide him, but leading the way himself for us all to follow. Now when he reached the Steep Threshold, rooted to the earth by its bronze steps, he paused in one of the branching paths

229

κοίλου πέλας κρατῆρος, οὗ τὰ Θησέως
Περίθου τε κεῖται πίστ' ἀεὶ ξυνθήματα·
ἀφ' οὗ μέσος στὰς τοῦ τε Θορικίου πέτρου
κοίλης τ' ἀχέρδου κἀπὸ λαΐνου τάφου
καθέζετ'· εἶτ' ἔλυσε δυσπινεῖς στολάς.
κἄπειτ' ἀύσας παῖδας ἠνώγει ῥυτῶν
ὑδάτων ἐνεγκεῖν λουτρὰ καὶ χοάς ποθεν·
τὼ δ' εὐχλόου Δήμητρος εἰς ἐπόψιον
πάγον μολοῦσαι τάσδ' ἐπιστολὰς πατρὶ
ταχεῖ 'πόρευσαν σὺν χρόνῳ, λουτροῖς τέ νιν
ἐσθῆτί τ' ἐξήσκησαν ᾗ νομίζεται.
ἐπεὶ δὲ παντὸς εἶχε δρῶντος ἡδονήν,
κοὐκ ἦν ἔτ' οὐδὲν ἀργὸν ὧν ἐφίετο,
κτύπησε μὲν Ζεὺς χθόνιος, αἱ δὲ παρθένοι
ῥίγησαν ὡς ἤκουσαν· ἐς δὲ γούνατα
πατρὸς πεσοῦσαι κλαῖον, οὐδ' ἀνίεσαν
στέρνων ἀραγμοὺς οὐδὲ παμμήκεις γόους.
ὁ δ' ὡς ἀκούει φθόγγον ἐξαίφνης πικρόν,
πτύξας ἐπ' αὐταῖς χεῖρας εἶπεν· ‹ὦ τέκνα,
οὐκ ἔστ' ἔθ' ὑμῖν τῇδ' ἐν ἡμέρᾳ πατήρ.
ὄλωλε γὰρ δὴ πάντα τἀμά, κοὐκέτι
τὴν δυσπόνητον ἕξετ' ἀμφ' ἐμοὶ τροφήν·
σκληρὰν μέν, οἶδα, παῖδες· ἀλλ' ἓν γὰρ μόνον
τὰ πάντα λύει ταῦτ' ἔπος μοχθήματα.

near the hollow basin, the place where the binding agreement made
between Theseus and Peirithous has its eternal memorial. He stood
half-way between that and the Thorician Stone – the hollow pear-tree
and the marble tomb; then he sat down and took off his soiled
clothes. And he called his daughters, and asked them to bring fresh
water from some fountain, so that he could wash and pour a libation.
And the two of them went to the Hill of Demeter, guardian of young
plants, which was visible from there, and in a little time brought what
their father had told them; and they washed and dressed him as is
customary [for the dead]. And when he was content that he had done
everything, that no wish of his was unfulfilled, thunder beat from Zeus
of the Dead. The girls shuddered when they heard it, and fell on their
father's knees and wept for long, beating their breasts and crying out
endlessly. And as soon as he heard their bitter lamentation, he put his
arms round them and said: 'Children, this day ends your father's life,
for all that was mine is gone; no longer will you bear the heavy burden
of looking after me – I know it was hard, my children. Yet one word

τὸ γὰρ φιλεῖν οὐκ ἔστιν ἐξ ὅτου πλέον
ἢ τοῦδε τἀνδρὸς ἔσχεθ᾽, οὗ τητώμεναι
τὸ λοιπὸν ἤδη τὸν βίον διάξετον.⟩
   τοιαῦτ᾽ ἐπ᾽ ἀλλήλοισιν ἀμφικείμενοι
λύγδην ἔκλαιον πάντες. ὡς δὲ πρὸς τέλος
γόων ἀφίκοντ᾽ οὐδ᾽ ἔτ᾽ ὠρώρει βοή,
ἦν μὲν σιωπή, φθέγμα δ᾽ ἐξαίφνης τινὸς
θώϋξεν αὐτόν, ὥστε πάντας ὀρθίας
στῆσαι φόβῳ δείσαντας ἐξαίφνης τρίχας.
καλεῖ γὰρ αὐτὸν πολλὰ πολλαχῇ θεός·
⟨ὦ οὗτος οὗτος, Οἰδίπους, τί μέλλομεν
χωρεῖν; πάλαι δὴ τἀπὸ σοῦ βραδύνεται.⟩
ὁ δ᾽ ὡς ἐπῄσθετ᾽ ἐκ θεοῦ καλούμενος,
αὐδᾷ μολεῖν οἱ γῆς ἄνακτα Θησέα.
κἀπεὶ προσῆλθεν, εἶπεν· ⟨ὦ φίλον κάρα,
δός μοι χερὸς σῆς πίστιν ὁρκίαν τέκνοις,
ὑμεῖς τε, παῖδες, τῷδε· καὶ καταίνεσον
μήποτε προδώσειν τάσδ᾽ ἑκών, τελεῖν δ᾽ ὅσ᾽ ἂν
μέλλῃς φρονῶν εὖ ξυμφέροντ᾽ αὐταῖς ἀεί.⟩
ὁ δ᾽, ὡς ἀνὴρ γενναῖος, οὐκ οἴκτου μέτα
κατῄνεσεν τάδ᾽ ὅρκιος δράσειν ξένῳ.
ὅπως δὲ ταῦτ᾽ ἔδρασεν, εὐθὺς Οἰδίπους
ψαύσας ἀμαυραῖς χερσὶν ὧν παίδων λέγει·

alone makes all these sufferings as nothing: *love* you had from this man here as from no other. Bereaved of him you must now pass the rest of your life.'

   With such words, all three clinging closely to one another wept with sobs. But as they came to the end of their lamentation, and no sound came from them any more, there was silence; and suddenly a voice called out aloud to him, so that the hair of those who heard it at once stood up in terror; for the god was calling him many times and in many ways: 'Oedipus, Oedipus, why are we delaying our departure? You delay too long.' No sooner had he recognized that the god was calling him than he asked for Theseus, the king of this land, to come near. And when he came close, he said: 'My dear friend, give me the pledge of your hand for my children, and you, my daughters, for him. And promise that you will never willingly forsake them, that you will always do what is good for them as their friend.' And he, a noble man, controlling his feelings, agreed under oath to do so for his friend. When Theseus had done that, Oedipus at once touched his children with his

⟨ὦ παῖδε, τλάσας χρὴ τὸ γενναῖον φρενὶ
χωρεῖν τόπων ἐκ τῶνδε, μηδ' ἃ μὴ θέμις
λεύσσειν δικαιοῦν, μηδὲ φωνούντων κλύειν.
ἀλλ' ἕρπεθ' ὡς τάχιστα· πλὴν ὁ κύριος
Θησεὺς παρέστω μανθάνων τὰ δρώμενα.⟩
    τοσαῦτα φωνήσαντος εἰσηκούσαμεν
ξύμπαντες· ἀστακτὶ δὲ σὺν ταῖς παρθένοις
στένοντες ὡμαρτοῦμεν. ὡς δ' ἀπήλθομεν,
χρόνῳ βραχεῖ στραφέντες, ἐξαπείδομεν
τὸν ἄνδρα τὸν μὲν οὐδαμοῦ παρόντ' ἔτι,
ἄνακτα δ' αὐτὸν ὀμμάτων ἐπίσκιον
χεῖρ' ἀντέχοντα κρατός, ὡς δεινοῦ τινος
φόβου φανέντος οὐδ' ἀνασχετοῦ βλέπειν.
ἔπειτα μέντοι βαιὸν οὐδὲ σὺν χρόνῳ
ὁρῶμεν αὐτὸν γῆν τε προσκυνοῦνθ' ἅμα
καὶ τὸν θεῶν Ὄλυμπον ἐν ταὐτῷ λόγῳ.
μόρῳ δ' ὁποίῳ κεῖνος ὤλετ' οὐδ' ἂν εἷς
θνητῶν φράσειε πλὴν τὸ Θησέως κάρα.
οὐ γάρ τις αὐτὸν οὔτε πυρφόρος θεοῦ
κεραυνὸς ἐξέπραξεν οὔτε ποντία
θύελλα κινηθεῖσα τῷ τότ' ἐν χρόνῳ,
ἀλλ' ἤ τις ἐκ θεῶν πομπός, ἢ τὸ νερτέρων
εὔνουν διαστὰν γῆς ἀλάμπετον βάθρον.

blind hands and said: 'You must be brave at heart and go now, children, from this place, and do not ask to see what should not be seen, nor hear what is forbidden. Leave, as quickly as you can. Let only Theseus, master of this land, stay to witness what will happen.'

So much he said, and we all heard him; and with streaming tears and with lamentation we followed the girls away. But when we had gone, after a little we turned our heads and saw that Oedipus was there no more; only the king, holding his hand across his face to shade his eyes as from some dreadful sight which had appeared – the kind no man can bear to see. And then, in a short time, we saw him salute the earth and Olympus, [the home] of the gods, both together in one prayer. But by what death Oedipus died no man can tell except Theseus. For no fire-bringing thunderbolt of the god took away his life then, nor a storm that sprang from the sea. But either a messenger came from the gods, or the dark lower world of the dead, being well-disposed, opened a painless passage for him; for the man passed away with no

ἀνὴρ γὰρ οὐ στενακτὸς οὐδὲ σὺν νόσοις
ἀλγεινὸς ἐξεπέμπετ', ἀλλ' εἴ τις βροτῶν
θαυμαστός. εἰ δὲ μὴ δοκῶ φρονῶν λέγειν,
οὐκ ἂν παρείμην οἷσι μὴ δοκῶ φρονεῖν.

(*Oedipus at Colonus*)

EURIPIDES
480–406 B.C.

110. The Cyclops

ΚΥΚΛΩΨ

Ὁ πλοῦτος, ἀνθρωπίσκε, τοῖς σοφοῖς θεός,
τὰ δ' ἄλλα κόμποι καὶ λόγων εὐμορφίαι.
ἄκρας δ' ἐναλίας ἃς καθίδρυται πατὴρ
χαίρειν κελεύω· τί τάδε προύστήσω λόγῳ;
Ζηνὸς δ' ἐγὼ κεραυνὸν οὐ φρίσσω, ξένε,
οὐδ' οἶδ' ὅ τι Ζεύς ἐστ' ἐμοῦ κρείσσων θεός.
οὔ μοι μέλει τὸ λοιπόν· ὡς δ' οὔ μοι μέλει,
ἄκουσον. ὅταν ἄνωθεν ὄμβρον ἐκχέῃ,
ἐν τῇδε πέτρα στέγν' ἔχων σκηνώματα,
ἢ μόσχον ὀπτὸν ἤ τι θήρειον δάκος
δαινύμενος, εὖ τέγγων τε γαστέρ' ὑπτίαν,

lamentation, not in sickness or suffering; something wonderful, beyond the world of men. If what I tell you does not seem to make sense, I would not try to win over those who consider me foolish.

CYCLOPS: Little man, wealth is the god of the wise, the rest is show and fancy talk. The shores of the sea, which are dedicated to my father, mean nothing to me. Why did you speak to me about them? I do not dread the thunderbolt of Zeus, stranger, nor do I acknowledge that Zeus is a greater god than myself. I do not care about the future; hear why I do not care. When he [Zeus] pours rain from above, I, with dry quarters in this rock, and feasting on roast calf or on some wild beast, lie upon my back and thoroughly soak my belly, draining a

ἐπεκπιὼν γάλακτος ἀμφορέα, πέπλον
κρούω, Διὸς βρονταῖσιν εἰς ἔριν κτυπῶν.
ὅταν δὲ βορέας χιόνα Θρήκιος χέῃ,
δοραῖσι θηρῶν σῶμα περιβαλὼν ἐμὸν
καὶ πῦρ ἀναίθων — χιόνος οὐδέν μοι μέλει.
ἡ γῆ δ᾽ ἀνάγκῃ, κἂν θέλῃ κἂν μὴ θέλῃ,
τίκτουσα ποίαν τἀμὰ πιαίνει βοτά.
ἐγὼ οὔτινι θύω πλὴν ἐμοί, θεοῖσι δ᾽ οὔ,
καὶ τῇ μεγίστῃ, γαστρὶ τῇδε, δαιμόνων.
ὡς τοὐμπιεῖν γε κἀμφαγεῖν τοὐφ᾽ ἡμέραν
Ζεὺς οὗτος ἀνθρώποισι τοῖσι σώφροσιν,
λυπεῖν δὲ μηδὲν αὐτόν. οἳ δὲ τοὺς νόμους
ἔθεντο ποικίλλοντες ἀνθρώπων βίον,
κλαίειν ἄνωγα· τὴν δ᾽ ἐμὴν ψυχὴν ἐγὼ
οὐ παύσομαι δρῶν εὖ — κατεσθίων τε σέ.
ξένιά τε λήψῃ τοιάδ᾽, ὡς ἄμεμπτος ὦ,
πῦρ καὶ πατρῷον τόνδε λέβητά γ᾽, ὃς ζέσας
σὴν σάρκα διαφόρητον ἀμφέξει καλῶς.
ἀλλ᾽ ἕρπετ᾽ εἴσω, τῷ κατ᾽ αὔλιον θεῷ
ἵν᾽ ἀμφὶ βωμὸν στάντες εὐωχῆτέ με.

(*Cyclops*)

jar of milk, and I fart against my cloak, vying in noise with the thunder-
claps of Zeus. And, when Thracian Boreas [the north wind] pours down
snow, I cover my body with the hides of beasts, and I light a fire —
snow is nothing to me. The earth must, whether she wants it or not,
grow grass and fatten my sheep. And these I sacrifice to nobody but
myself — not to the gods — and to the greatest of deities, this belly. To
drink and to eat each day, that is the Zeus of the wise men, and to be
worried by nothing. I wish them misery who make laws to dress up
men's lives, I shall never cease from doing good to myself — devouring
you, too. You will get gifts of hospitality, so that I may be beyond re-
proach — these gifts: fire and this ancestral cauldron which will hold
the pieces of your flesh quite admirably once it boils. Now step inside,
that, standing at the altar, you may honour the god of this fold and give
me a fine feast.

111. *Alcestis*

ΧΟΡΟΣ

Ὦ Πελίου θύγατερ,
χαίρουσά μοι εἰν Ἀίδαο δόμοις
τὸν ἀνάλιον οἶκον οἰκετεύοις.
ἴστω δ' Ἀίδας ὁ μελαγχαίτας θεὸς ὅς τ' ἐπὶ κώπᾳ
πηδαλίῳ τε γέρων
νεκροπομπὸς ἵζει,
πολὺ δὴ πολὺ δὴ γυναῖκ' ἀρίσταν
λίμναν Ἀχεροντίαν πορεύ-
σας ἐλάτᾳ δικώπῳ.

πολλά σε μουσοπόλοι
μέλψουσι καθ' ἑπτάτονόν τ' ὀρείαν
χέλυν ἔν τ' ἀλύροις κλέοντες ὕμνοις,
Σπάρτᾳ κύκλος ἁνίκα Καρνείου περινίσσεται ὥρας
μηνός, ἀειρομένας
παννύχου σελάνας,
λιπαραῖσί τ' ἐν ὀλβίαις Ἀθάναις.
τοίαν ἔλιπες θανοῦσα μολ-
πὰν μελέων ἀοιδοῖς.

CHORUS: O daughter of Pelias, may you be happy in your sunless home, the house of Hades. Let Hades, the black-haired god, the old man who sits at his oar and rudder conducting the dead, know that he ferried the very best of women across the lake of Acheron in his two-oared boat.

The servants of the Muses will sing many songs in your honour to the seven-toned lyre-shell of the mountain tortoise, and in wild dirges, when in Sparta the circling season brings back the month of Carneius, and the moon is up all night, and in rich, happy Athens. Such a song by your death have you left for the poets to sing.

I wish it were in my power, I wish I could bring you back to the

εἴθ' ἐπ' ἐμοὶ μὲν εἴη,
δυναίμαν δέ σε πέμψαι
φάος ἐξ 'Αίδα τεράμνων
καὶ Κωκυτοῖο ῥεέθρων
    ποταμίᾳ νερτέρᾳ τε κώπᾳ.
σὺ γὰρ ὦ, μόνα, ὦ φίλα γυναικῶν,
σὺ τὸν αὑτᾶς
ἔτλας πόσιν ἀντὶ σᾶς ἀμεῖψαι
ψυχᾶς ἐξ "Αιδα. κούφα σοι
χθὼν ἐπάνωθε πέσοι, γύναι. εἰ δέ τι
καινὸν ἕλοιτο πόσις λέχος, ἦ μάλ' ἂν ἔμοιγ' ἂν εἴη
    στυγηθεὶς τέκνοις τε τοῖς σοῖς.

                                        (*Alcestis*)

112. Medea's Revenge

ΜΗΔΕΙΑ

Ὦ Ζεῦ Δίκη τε Ζηνὸς Ἡλίου τε φῶς,
νῦν καλλίνικοι τῶν ἐμῶν ἐχθρῶν, φίλαι,
γενησόμεσθα κεἰς ὁδὸν βεβήκαμεν·
νῦν ἐλπὶς ἐχθροὺς τοὺς ἐμοὺς τείσειν δίκην.
οὗτος γὰρ ἀνὴρ ᾗ μάλιστ' ἐκάμνομεν
λιμὴν πέφανται τῶν ἐμῶν βουλευμάτων·

light from the halls of Hades and the streams of Cocytus, with the oars
of the river of the dead. For you alone, beloved woman, had the
courage to give up your life to bring back your husband from Hades.
May the earth lie lightly upon you, woman. If your husband should
choose a new bridal-bed, he would certainly incur my hatred and your
children's.

MEDEA: O Zeus, and Justice, daughter of Zeus, and light of the Sun,
we shall now, my friends, have a splendid triumph over my enemies,
and we are well on the way to it. Now there is hope my enemies will
pay the penalty. This man, who was our greatest weakness, has proved
a harbour for my plans; on him we shall tie the hawsers of our ship's

ἐκ τοῦδ' ἀναψόμεσθα πρυμνήτην κάλων,
μολόντες ἄστυ καὶ πόλισμα Παλλάδος.
ἤδη δὲ πάντα τἀμά σοι βουλεύματα
λέξω· δέχου δὲ μὴ πρὸς ἡδονὴν λόγους.
πέμψασ' ἐμῶν τιν' οἰκετῶν Ἰάσονα
ἐς ὄψιν ἐλθεῖν τὴν ἐμὴν αἰτήσομαι·
μολόντι δ' αὐτῷ μαλθακοὺς λέξω λόγους,
ὡς καὶ δοκεῖ μοι ταῦτά, καὶ καλῶς ἔχειν
γάμους τυράννων οὓς προδοὺς ἡμᾶς ἔχει·
καὶ ξύμφορ' εἶναι καὶ καλῶς ἐγνωσμένα.
παῖδας δὲ μεῖναι τοὺς ἐμοὺς αἰτήσομαι,
οὐχ ὡς λιποῦσ' ἂν πολεμίας ἐπὶ χθονὸς
ἐχθροῖσι παῖδας τοὺς ἐμοὺς καθυβρίσαι,
ἀλλ' ὡς δόλοισι παῖδα βασιλέως κτάνω.
πέμψω γὰρ αὐτοὺς δῶρ' ἔχοντας ἐν χεροῖν,
νύμφῃ φέροντας, τήνδε μὴ φυγεῖν χθόνα,
λεπτόν τε πέπλον καὶ πλόκον χρυσήλατον·
κἄνπερ λαβοῦσα κόσμον ἀμφιθῇ χροΐ,
κακῶς ὀλεῖται πᾶς θ' ὃς ἂν θίγῃ κόρης·
τοιοῖσδε χρίσω φαρμάκοις δωρήματα.
ἐνταῦθα μέντοι τόνδ' ἀπαλλάσσω λόγον·

prow when we reach the city and the citadel of Pallas. And now I will
tell you all my schemes; listen to my unlovely words. I shall send one
of my servants to Jason, and ask him to come here to meet me face to
face. And, when he comes, I shall speak soft words to him, as though I
agree with him that it is well he entered in that royal marriage by which
he betrayed me; that it is for my advantage, and a good decision. I
shall ask him if my sons can stay – not that I would leave my sons to
be insulted by my enemies in a hostile land – but that I may kill the
daughter of the king by treachery! For I shall send them with presents
in their hands for the bride, so that she never leaves the land: a delicate
robe and gold-wrought wreath. If she accepts this finery and puts it
about her, she, and all who touch her, will die a horrible death. With
such poison shall I anoint the presents. Now I shall end this story, and

ᾤμωξα δ' οἷον ἔργον ἔστ' ἐργαστέον
τοὐντεῦθεν ἡμῖν· τέκνα γὰρ κατακτενῶ
τἄμ'· οὔτις ἔστιν ὅστις ἐξαιρήσεται·
δόμον τε πάντα συγχέασ' Ἰάσονος
ἔξειμι γαίας, φιλτάτων παίδων φόνον
φεύγουσα καὶ τλᾶσ' ἔργον ἀνοσιώτατον.
οὐ γὰρ γελᾶσθαι τλητὸν ἐξ ἐχθρῶν, φίλαι.
ἴτω· τί μοι ζῆν κέρδος; οὔτε μοι πατρὶς
οὔτ' οἶκος ἔστιν οὔτ' ἀποστροφὴ κακῶν.
ἡμάρτανον τόθ' ἡνίκ' ἐξελίμπανον
δόμους πατρῴους, ἀνδρὸς Ἕλληνος λόγοις
πεισθεῖσ', ὃς ἡμῖν σὺν θεῷ τείσει δίκην.
οὔτ' ἐξ ἐμοῦ γὰρ παῖδας ὄψεταί ποτε
ζῶντας τὸ λοιπὸν οὔτε τῆς νεοζύγου
νύμφης τεκνώσει παῖδ', ἐπεὶ κακῶς κακὴν
θανεῖν σφ' ἀνάγκη τοῖς ἐμοῖσι φαρμάκοις.
μηδείς με φαύλην κἀσθενῆ νομιζέτω
μηδ' ἡσυχαίαν, ἀλλὰ θατέρου τρόπου,
βαρεῖαν ἐχθροῖς καὶ φίλοισιν εὐμενῆ·
τῶν γὰρ τοιούτων εὐκλεέστατος βίος.

(*Medea*)

lament the dreadful thing that remains for me to do thereafter. For I shall kill my own children; no man shall take them from me. And when I cave ruined the house of Jason, I shall leave this land, setting my dearest children's death behind me, having brought myself to commit a most unholy crime. For to be laughed at by one's enemies is not to be borne, my friends. But there. For what profit is life to me? I have no country, no home, no escape from misery. I made my mistake the day I left my father's house, trusting the words of a Greek man, who with a god's help will pay me for it. After this day, he will never see alive the sons I bore him, nor will he get a son by his newly wedded bride, for the evil girl must die an evil death from my poisons. Let no one think me a coward, or weak, or gentle, but quite the contrary: inexorable to my enemies and kindly to my friends. For such are they whose life men most esteem.

113. I Wish I Could Take Shelter

ΧΟΡΟΣ

'Ηλιβάτοις ὑπὸ κευθμῶσι γενοίμαν,
ἵνα με πτεροῦσσαν ὄρνιν ἀγέλῃσι
    ποταναῖς θεὸς ἐνθείη·
ἀρθείην δ' ἐπὶ πόντιον
    κῦμα τᾶς 'Αδριηνᾶς
ἀκτᾶς 'Ηριδανοῦ θ' ὕδωρ·
ἔνθα πορφύρεον σταλάσ-
σουσιν ἐς οἶδμα πατρὸς τάλαι-
ναι κόραι Φαέθοντος οἴ-
    κτῳ δακρύων
τὰς ἠλεκτροφαεῖς αὐγάς.

'Εσπερίδων δ' ἐπὶ μηλόσπορον ἀκτὰν
ἀνύσαιμι τᾶν ἀοιδῶν, ἵν' ὁ ποντο-
μέδων πορφυρέας λίμνας
ναύταις οὐκέθ' ὁδὸν νέμει,
    σεμνὸν τέρμονα κυρῶν
οὐρανοῦ, τὸν "Ατλας ἔχει·
κρῆναί τ' ἀμβρόσιαι χέον-
ται Ζηνὸς μελάθρων παρὰ κοί-
ταις, ἵν' ἀ βιόδωρος αὔ-
    ξει ζαθέα
χθὼν εὐδαιμονίαν θεοῖς.

(*Hippolytus*)

CHORUS: I wish I could take shelter in some steep cavern, where the god would set me, a winged bird, among the flocks of flying creatures; and I would rise above the sea-waves of the Adriatic shore and the stream of Eridanus, where, weeping for Phaethon, his father's unhappy daughters let drop the amber-bright beams of their tears into the dark wave.

I wish I could reach the apple-sown shore of the singing Hesperides, where the master of the dark sea no longer gives a path to sailors; and come to the sacred boundary of the sky, which Atlas holds; the ambrosial fountains flow past the palace and the couch of Zeus, where the life-giving, most holy earth brings happiness to the gods.

114. Song of the Slaves

ΧΟΡΟΣ

Αὔρα, ποντιὰς αὔρα,
ἅτε ποντοπόρους κομί-
ζεις θοὰς ἀκάτους ἐπ' οἶδμα λίμνας,
ποῖ με τὰν μελέαν πορεύ-
σεις; τῷ δουλόσυνος πρὸς οἶ-
κον κτηθεῖσ' ἀφίξομαι; ἢ
Δωρίδος ὅρμον αἴας;
ἢ Φθιάδος, ἔνθα τὸν
καλλίστων ὑδάτων πατέρα
φασὶν 'Απιδανὸν πεδία λιπαίνειν;

ἢ νάσων, ἁλιήρει
κώπᾳ πεμπομέναν τάλαι-
ναν, οἰκτρὰν βιοτὰν ἔχουσαν οἴκοις,
ἔνθα πρωτόγονός τε φοῖ-
νιξ δάφνα θ' ἱερούς ἀνέ-
σχε πτόρθους Λατοῖ φίλα ὠ-
δῖνος ἄγαλμα δίας;
σὺν Δηλιάσιν τε κού-
ραισιν 'Αρτέμιδος θεᾶς
χρυσέαν ἄμπυκα τόξα τ' εὐλογήσω;

(Hecuba)

CHORUS: Breeze, sea-breeze, you who carry the swift sea-crossing boats on the swell of the water, where will you take me in my misery? Who will take me as his slave? Whose house will I reach? Will it be a haven in the Dorian land? Or one in Phthia where, it is said, Apidanus, father of the best waters, fattens the plains?

Or to one of the islands — a miserable woman, sent by the oars that sweep the sea to have a wretched domestic existence, where the first palm and the first laurel-tree lifted their sacred branches for dear Leto to honour her holy travail? Shall I praise with the maidens of Delos the golden diadem and the bow of the goddess Artemis?

EURIPIDES

115. Youth

ΧΟΡΟΣ

Ἁ νεότας μοι φίλον αἰ-
εί· τὸ δὲ γῆρας ἄχθος
βαρύτερον Αἴτνας σκοπέλων
ἐπὶ κρατὶ κεῖται, βλεφάρων
σκοτεινὸν φάος ἐπικαλύψαν.
μή μοι μήτ' Ἀσιήτιδος
τυραννίδος ὄλβος εἴη,
μὴ χρυσοῦ δώματα πλήρη
τᾶς ἥβας ἀντιλαβεῖν,
ἃ καλλίστα μὲν ἐν ὄλβῳ,
καλλίστα δ' ἐν πενίᾳ.
τὸ δὲ λυγρὸν φόνιόν τε γῆ-
ρας μισῶ· κατὰ κυμάτων δ'
ἔρροι, μηδέ ποτ' ὤφελεν
θνατῶν δώματα καὶ πόλεις
ἐλθεῖν, ἀλλὰ κατ' αἰθέρ' αἰ-
εὶ πτεροῖσι φορείσθω.

εἰ δὲ θεοῖς ἦν ξύνεσις
καὶ σοφία κατ' ἄνδρας,
δίδυμον ἂν ἥβαν ἔφερον
φανερὸν χαρακτῆρ' ἀρετᾶς

CHORUS: I always love youth; old age weighs on the head, a burden heavier than the rocks of Aetna, and covers the light of the eyes with darkness. I would not have the wealth of the kings of Asia, nor a house full of gold, in place of youth, most beautiful in riches and most beautiful in poverty. I hate murderous, sad old age. I wish it were cast in the waves of the sea; it should never have come to the homes and the cities of men; let it be carried away on wings to the sky for ever.

If the gods had the sense and wisdom of men, they would have given a double youth, a clear mark of virtue for those who had it, and after

ὅσοισιν μέτα, κατθανόντες τ᾽
εἰς αὐγὰς πάλιν ἁλίου
διssοὺς ἂν ἔβαν διαύλους,
ἁ δυσγένεια δ᾽ ἁπλοῦν ἂν
εἶχεν ζόας βίοτον,
καὶ τῷδ᾽ ἦν τούς τε κακοὺς ἂν
γνῶναι καὶ τοὺς ἀγαθούς,
ἴσον ἅτ᾽ ἐν νεφέλαισιν ἄ-
στρων ναύταις ἀριθμὸς πέλει.
νῦν δ᾽ οὐδεὶς ὅρος ἐκ θεῶν
χρηστοῖς οὐδὲ κακοῖς σαφής,
ἀλλ᾽ εἱλισσόμενός τις αἰ-
ὼν πλοῦτον μόνον αὔξει.

οὐ παύσομαι τὰς Χάριτας
Μούσαις συγκαταμειγνύς,
ἁδίσταν συζυγίαν.
μὴ ζῴην μετ᾽ ἀμουσίας,
αἰεὶ δ᾽ ἐν στεφάνοισιν εἴ-
ην· ἔτι τοι γέρων ἀοι-
δὸς κελαδεῖ Μναμοσύναν·
ἔτι τὰν Ἡρακλέους
καλλίνικον ἀείδω
παρά τε Βρόμιον οἰνοδόταν
παρά τε χέλυος ἑπτατόνου
μολπὰν καὶ Λίβυν αὐλόν·

death they would retrace their course back into the light of the sun;
but mean natures would have had only one term of life, and this would
be the distinction between the good and the bad, just as the number of
stars in a cloudy sky guides sailors. As it is, the gods have set no clear
mark to distinguish the good from the bad; but some circling year
brings only more wealth.

I shall not cease from joining the Graces with the Muses, the
sweetest of all partnerships. May I never live without poetry, and
always have garlands around me. The old singer still sings of Mnemo-
syne; I still sing the song of victory for Hercules, with Bromius, the
giver of wine, and the sound of the seven-toned lyre-shell and the

οὔπω καταπαύσομεν
    Μούσας, αἵ μ᾽ ἐχόρευσαν.

παιᾶνα μὲν Δηλιάδες
    ὑμνοῦσ᾽ ἀμφὶ πύλας τὸν
Λατοῦς εὔπαιδα γόνον
    εἰλίσσουσαι καλλίχορον·
παιᾶνας δ᾽ ἐπὶ σοῖς μελά-
θροις κύκνος ὡς γέρων ἀοι-
δὸς πολιᾶν ἐκ γενύων
    κελαδήσω· τὸ γὰρ εὖ
    τοῖς ὑμνοισιν ὑπάρχει·
Διὸς ὁ παῖς· τᾶς δ᾽ εὐγενίας
    πλέον ὑπερβάλλων ἀρετᾷ
    μοχθήσας τὸν ἄκυμον
θῆκεν βίοτον βροτοῖς
    πέρσας δείματα θηρῶν.

(*Mad Hercules*)

Libyan pipe. I shall never turn aside from the Muses, who rouse me to the dance.

The Delian maidens sing a paean by the gates of the Temple, and circle in beautiful dance in honour of Leto's noble son. So I too will shout out paeans at your palace doors from my mouth, though my beard is grey, like an old singing swan, for this is a good occasion for songs. He is the son of Zeus, and with courage yet greater than his noble descent he laboured, and gave men an untroubled life by destroying the dreaded monsters.

116. Delphic Dawn

ΙΩΝ

Ἄρματα μὲν τάδε λαμπρὰ τεθρίππων
Ἥλιος ἤδη λάμπει κατὰ γῆν,
ἄστρα δὲ φεύγει πυρὶ τῷδ᾽ αἰθέρος
ἐς νύχθ᾽ ἱεράν·
Παρνησιάδες δ᾽ ἄβατοι κορυφαὶ
καταλαμπόμεναι τὴν ἡμερίαν
    ἀψῖδα βροτοῖσι δέχονται.
σμύρνης δ᾽ ἀνύδρου καπνὸς εἰς ὀρόφους
Φοίβου πέταται.
θάσσει δὲ γυνὴ τρίποδα ζάθεον
Δελφίς, ἀείδουσ᾽ Ἕλλησι βοάς,
    ἃς ἂν Ἀπόλλων κελαδήσῃ.
ἀλλ᾽, ὦ Φοίβου Δελφοὶ θέραπες,
τὰς Κασταλίας ἀργυροειδεῖς
βαίνετε δίνας, καθαραῖς δὲ δρόσοις
ἀφυδρανάμενοι στείχετε ναούς·
στόμα τ᾽ εὔφημον φρουρεῖν ἀγαθόν,
φήμας τ᾽ ἀγαθὰς
τοῖς ἐθέλουσιν μαντεύεσθαι
    γλώσσης ἰδίας ἀποφαίνειν.

ION: Already the sun lights over the earth its flashing four-horsed chariot, and, driven by this fire, the stars fly from the sky into the holy night; the untrodden peaks of Parnassus are covered with light, and welcome for men the daylight's arc. The smoke of dry myrrh rises to Phoebus' roof, and the Delphic woman sits on the most holy tripod, chanting for the Greeks the things Apollo sings. Delphic servants of Apollo, come to the silver-faced streams of Castalia, and wash your-selves with the clear water, and walk to the temple. It is good to keep your mouth in religious silence, and let your tongue speak pure words only to those who wish to ask for an oracle. And I will make pure the

ἡμεῖς δέ, πόνους οὓς ἐκ παιδὸς
μοχθοῦμεν ἀεί, πτόρθοισι δάφνης
στέφεσίν θ' ἱεροῖς ἐσόδους Φοίβου
καθαρὰς θήσομεν, ὑγραῖς τε πέδον
ῥανίσιν νοτερόν· πτηνῶν τ' ἀγέλας,
αἳ βλάπτουσιν σέμν' ἀναθήματα,
τόξοισιν ἐμοῖς φυγάδας θήσομεν·
ὡς γὰρ ἀμήτωρ ἀπάτωρ τε γεγὼς
τοὺς θρέψαντας
   Φοίβου ναοὺς θεραπεύω.

(Ion)

117. O, the Many Drops of Tears

ΧΟΡΟΣ

Ὄρνις, ἃ παρὰ πετρίνας
πόντου δειράδας, ἀλκυών,
ἔλεγον οἶτον ἀείδεις,
εὐξύνετον ξυνετοῖς βοάν,
ὅτι πόσιν κελαδεῖς ἀεὶ μολπαῖς,
ἐγώ σοι παραβάλλομαι
θρήνους, ἄπτερος ὄρνις,
ποθοῦσ' Ἑλλάνων ἀγόρους,
ποθοῦσ' Ἄρτεμιν λοχίαν,

entrance to Phoebus' temple with laurel branches and sacred garlands, and the floor moist with water-drops, tasks I have always performed since my childhood; and with my arrows I will drive away the flocks of birds which damage the sacred offerings. For, since I have no father and no mother, I serve the temple of Phoebus, which raised me.

CHORUS: Bird, you who sing a sad song round the rocky headlands of the sea, a cry easily understood by those who know you are always calling your mate, kingfisher; I, a wingless bird, compete with you in lamentation, as I long for the market-places of the Greeks; for Artemis,

ἃ παρὰ Κύνθιον ὄχθον οἰ-
κεῖ φοίνικά θ' ἁβροκόμαν
    δάφναν τ' εὐερνέα καὶ
γλαυκᾶς θαλλὸν ἱερὸν ἐλαί-
ας, Λατοῦς ὠδῖνα φίλαν,
λίμναν θ' εἱλίσσουσαν ὕδωρ
κύκλιον, ἔνθα κύκνος μελῳ-
    δὸς Μούσας θεραπεύει.

ὦ πολλαὶ δακρύων λιβάδες,
αἳ παρηίδας εἰς ἐμὰς
    ἔπεσον, ἁνίκα πύργων
ὀλομένων ἐν ναυσὶν ἔβαν
πολεμίων ἐρετμοῖσι καὶ λόγχαις.
ζαχρύσου δὲ δι' ἐμπολᾶς
    νόστον βάρβαρον ἦλθον,
ἔνθα τᾶς ἐλαφοκτόνου
θεᾶς ἀμφίπολον κόραν
παῖδ' Ἀγαμεμνονίαν λατρεύ-
ω βωμούς τ' οὐ μηλοθύτας,
    ζηλοῦσ' ἄταν διὰ παν-
τὸς δυσδαίμον'· ἐν γὰρ ἀνάγ-
καις οὐ κάμνεις σύντροφος ὤν.
μεταβάλλει δυσδαιμονία·
τὸ δὲ μετ' εὐτυχίας κακοῦ-
    σθαι θνατοῖς βαρὺς αἰών.

the helper at childbirth, who lives by Mount Cynthus, and the rich-leaved palm and the thick-branched laurel and the sacred branch of the grey olive-tree, which soothed Leto as she gave birth, and the round lake's circling water, where the singing swan pays homage to the Muses.

O, the many drops of tears that fell on my cheeks, when the towers [of Troy] were destroyed, and I entered the enemy's ships with their oars and their spears! Sold for much gold, I came to this barbaric home, where I serve the stag-killing goddess's maiden priestess, the child of Agamemnon, and altars where it is not sheep that are sacrificed – a fate forever unhappy. For if you have always been in misery you do not suffer. It is change that causes pain. But to suffer when you are happy makes mortals' life heavy to bear.

καὶ σὲ μέν, πότνι᾽, Ἀργεία
πεντηκόντορος οἶκον ἄξει·
συρίζων θ᾽ ὁ κηροδέτας
κάλαμος οὐρείου Πανὸς
  κώπαις ἐπιθωΰξει,
ὁ Φοῖβός θ᾽ ὁ μάντις ἔχων
κέλαδον ἑπτατόνου λύρας
ἀείδων ἄξει λιπαρὰν
εὖ σ᾽ Ἀθηναίων ἐπὶ γᾶν.
  ἐμὲ δ᾽ αὐτοῦ λιποῦσα
βήσῃ ῥοθίοισι πλάταις·
ἀέρι δὲ πρότονοι κατὰ πρῷραν ὑ-
πὲρ στόλον ἐκπετάσουσι πόδα
  ναὸς ὠκυπόμπου.

λαμπροὺς ἱπποδρόμους βαίην,
ἔνθ᾽ εὐάλιον ἔρχεται πῦρ·
οἰκείων δ᾽ ὑπὲρ θαλάμων
πτέρυγας ἐν νώτοις ἀμοῖς
  λήξαιμι θοάζουσα·
χοροῖς δ᾽ ἐσταίην, ὅθι καὶ
παρθένος, εὐδοκίμων γάμων,
παρὰ πόδ᾽ εἱλίσσουσα φίλας
ματρὸς ἡλίκων θιάσους,
  χαρίτων εἰς ἀμίλλας,
  χαίτας ἁβρόπλουτον ἔριν,

You, mistress, a fifty-oared Argive ship will carry home; and the wax-bound reed of mountain Pan will pipe, and speed the oars; and the seer, Phoebus, singing to the sound of the seven-toned lyre, will bring you safely to the rich land of the Athenians. But me you will abandon here, as you leave with the splashing of oars; and the fore-stays at the prow of the fast ship will stretch out the sail to catch the wind for the journey.

I wish I could step on the splendid racecourse, where the bright fire of the sun rises; stay the wings on my back to alight in my father's house, and stand, as when a young girl at a happy wedding, dancing near my dear mother with groups of my own age, competing in grace,

ὀρνυμένα, πολυποίκιλα φάρεα
καὶ πλοκάμους περιβαλλομένα
γένυσιν ἐσκίαζον.

(*Iphigenia in Tauris*)

118. The Furies

ΧΟΡΟΣ

Αἰαῖ,
δρομάδες ὦ πτεροφόροι
ποτνιάδες θεαί,
ἀβάκχευτον αἳ θίασον ἐλάχετ᾽ ἐν
δάκρυσι καὶ γόοις,
μελάγχρωτες εὐμενίδες, αἵτε τὸν
τανὰον αἰθέρ᾽ ἀμπάλλεσθ᾽, αἵματος
τινύμεναι δίκαν, τινύμεναι φόνον,
καθικετεύομαι καθικετεύομαι,
τὸν Ἀγαμέμνονος
γόνον ἐάσατ᾽ ἐκλαθέσθαι λύσσας
μανιάδος φοιταλέου. φεῦ μόχθων,
οἵων, ὦ τάλας, ὀρεχθεὶς ἔρρεις,
τρίποδος ἄπο φάτιν, ἃν ὁ Φοῖβος ἔλακε, δε-
ξάμενος ἀνὰ δάπεδον,
ἵνα μεσόμφαλοι λέγονται μυχοί.

competing in richness of hair, moving in richly-embroidered clothes,
and shading my cheeks with the locks of my hair.

CHORUS: Alas, raging wing-swift goddesses, whose worshippers do
not revel in wine, but in tears and sighs, dark-skinned Eumenides: you,
who disturb the outspread air as you fly avenging bloodshed, avenging
murder, I beg, I beg you fervently, let the son of Agamemnon escape
the rabid madness that visits him. Alas, miserable man, what labours
you took upon yourself, to ruin you, when you received the oracle
Phoebus uttered from the [Delphic] tripod, in the building where they
say is the innermost navel of the earth.

Ἰὼ Ζεῦ,
τίς ἔλεος, τίς δδ᾽ ἀγὼν
φόνιος ἔρχεται,
θοάζων σε τὸν μέλεον, ᾧ δάκρυα
δάκρυσι συμβάλλει
πορεύων τις ἐς δόμον ἀλαστόρων
ματέρος αἷμα σᾶς, ὅ σ᾽ ἀναβακχεύει;
ὁ μέγας ὄλβος οὐ μόνιμος ἐν βροτοῖς·
κατολοφύρομαι κατολοφύρομαι.
ἀνὰ δὲ λαῖφος ὡς
τις ἀκάτου θοᾶς τινάξας δαίμων
κατέκλυσεν δεινῶν πόνων ὡς πόντου
λάβροις ὀλεθρίοισιν ἐν κύμασιν.
τίνα γὰρ ἔτι πάρος οἶκον ἕτερον ἢ τὸν ἀπὸ
θεογόνων γάμων,
τὸν ἀπὸ Ταντάλου, σέβεσθαί με χρή;

(*Orestes*)

119. Receive This God, Whoever He May Be

ΑΓΓΕΛΟΣ

᾽Αγελαῖα μὲν βοσκήματ᾽ ἄρτι πρὸς λέπας
μόσχων ὑπεξήκριζον, ἡνίχ᾽ ἥλιος
ἀκτῖνας ἐξίησι θερμαίνων χθόνα.
ὁρῶ δὲ θιάσους τρεῖς γυναικείων χορῶν,

Alas, Zeus! What pity is there, what is this struggle for blood now coming, which descends upon you, wretched man, piling tears upon tears; what avenging spirit, that maddens you, drives to the house the blood of your mother? Great happiness is not lasting among mortals. I lament for you, I lament for you. For like a fast ship, whose sail was shaken by a god, you are thrown into a sea of terrible suffering, in wild destructive waves. What other house than this, born of the seed of the gods, [born] of Tantalus, should I revere?

MESSENGER: The herds of young bulls and heifers were just moving up to the rocks when the sun was lifting his first rays, warming the earth. And I saw three groups of women; Autonoe led one, your

ὧν ἦρχ' ἑνὸς μὲν Αὐτονόη, τοῦ δευτέρου
μήτηρ Ἀγαύη σή, τρίτου δ' Ἰνὼ χοροῦ.
ηὗδον δὲ πᾶσαι σώμασιν παρειμέναι,
αἳ μὲν πρὸς ἐλάτης νῶτ' ἐρείσασαι φόβην,
αἳ δ' ἐν δρυὸς φύλλοισι πρὸς πέδῳ κάρα
εἰκῇ βαλοῦσαι σωφρόνως, οὐχ ὡς σὺ φῂς
ᾠνωμένας κρατῆρι καὶ λωτοῦ ψόφῳ
θηρᾶν καθ' ὕλην Κύπριν ἠρημωμένας.
ἡ σὴ δὲ μήτηρ ὠλόλυξεν ἐν μέσαις
σταθεῖσα βάκχαις, ἐξ ὕπνου κινεῖν δέμας,
μυκήμαθ' ὡς ἤκουσε κεροφόρων βοῶν.
αἳ δ' ἀποβαλοῦσαι θαλερὸν ὀμμάτων ὕπνον
ἀνῇξαν ὀρθαί, θαῦμ' ἰδεῖν εὐκοσμίας,
νέαι παλαιαὶ παρθένοι τ' ἔτ' ἄζυγες.
καὶ πρῶτα μὲν καθεῖσαν εἰς ὤμους κόμας
νεβρίδας τ' ἀνεστείλανθ' ὅσαισιν ἀμμάτων
σύνδεσμ' ἐλέλυτο, καὶ καταστίκτους δορὰς
ὄφεσι κατεζώσαντο λιχμῶσιν γένυν.
αἳ δ' ἀγκάλαισι δορκάδ' ἢ σκύμνους λύκων
ἀγρίους ἔχουσαι λευκὸν ἐδίδοσαν γάλα,
ὅσαις νεοτόκοις μαστὸς ἦν σπαργῶν ἔτι
βρέφη λιπούσαις· ἐπὶ δ' ἔθεντο κισσίνους

mother Agave the second, and the third was led by Ino. And they all
slept, sprawled out, some leaning back against the branches of fir-
trees, others just letting their heads fall on the oak-leaves on the
ground; but they were sober, not, as you say, intoxicated by the
wine-bowl, and excited by the sound of the flute to search for Cypris
[Love], through the forest's loneliness. And your mother, when she
heard the lowing of the horned bulls, stood up in the middle of the
Bacchants, and called out to them to shake their bodies from sleep.
And they, casting refreshing sleep from their eyes, jumped up —
young, old, and girls not yet married; a marvel of discipline to see.
And first they let their hair loose on their shoulders, and fastened the
fawn-skins — those whose clasps had been loosened — and tied the
dappled skins tightly around them with snakes that licked their jaws;
those who were young mothers, whose breasts were still swollen and
who had left their infants, held in their arms a fawn or the wild cub of a
wolf, and gave them their white milk to suck. Then they put on gar-

στεφάνους δρυός τε μίλακός τ᾽ ἀνθεσφόρου.
θύρσον δέ τις λαβοῦσ᾽ ἔπαισεν ἐς πέτραν,
ὅθεν δροσώδης ὕδατος ἐκπηδᾷ νοτίς·
ἄλλη δὲ νάρθηκ᾽ ἐς πέδον καθῆκε γῆς,
καὶ τῇδε κρήνην ἐξανῆκ᾽ οἴνου θεός·
ὅσαις δὲ λευκοῦ πώματος πόθος παρῆν,
ἄκροισι δακτύλοισι διαμῶσαι χθόνα
γάλακτος ἐσμοὺς εἶχον· ἐκ δὲ κισσίνων
θύρσων γλυκεῖαι μέλιτος ἔσταζον ῥοαί.
ὥστ᾽, εἰ παρῆσθα, τὸν θεὸν τὸν νῦν ψέγεις
εὐχαῖσιν ἂν μετῆλθες εἰσιδὼν τάδε.

ξυνήλθομεν δὲ βουκόλοι καὶ ποιμένες,
κοινῶν λόγων δώσοντες ἀλλήλοις ἔριν
ὡς δεινὰ δρῶσι θαυμάτων τ᾽ ἐπάξια·
καί τις πλάνης κατ᾽ ἄστυ καὶ τρίβων λόγων
ἔλεξεν εἰς ἅπαντας· ʿὮ σεμνὰς πλάκας
ναίοντες ὀρέων, θέλετε θηρασώμεθα
Πενθέως Ἀγαύην μητέρ᾽ ἐκ βακχευμάτων
χάριν τ᾽ ἄνακτι θώμεθα;ʾ εὖ δ᾽ ἡμῖν λέγειν
ἔδοξε, θάμνων δ᾽ ἐλλοχίζομεν φόβαις
κρύψαντες αὐτούς· αἱ δὲ τὴν τεταγμένην
ὥραν ἐκίνουν θύρσον ἐς βακχεύματα,

lands of ivy and of oak-leaves and of flowering briony; and one took hold of the thyrsus, and struck the rock, from which a cool jet of water sprang up; another struck the earth with her staff and the god sent a fountain of wine from there. And those who wanted a drink of white milk scratched the earth with their finger-tips, and had streams of milk; and from the ivy-covered wands dripped sweet rivers of honey. So that if you had been there and seen these things, you would have followed with prayers the god whom you now accuse.

We got together, cowherds and shepherds, to match reports on their strange and wondrous doings. And one who had visited the city and had a way with words said to us all: 'You, who live on the solemn mountain flats, do you think we should catch Agave, Pentheus' mother, and keep her away from these Bacchic revelries, and so oblige the king?' We thought he was right in what he said, so we hid ourselves in the thick bushes and lay in wait. And they shook the thyrsus at the set hour to start the Bacchic rites, calling with united voice

Ἴακχον ἀθρόῳ στόματι τὸν Διὸς γόνον
Βρόμιον καλοῦσαι· πᾶν δὲ συνεβάκχευ' ὄρος
καὶ θῆρες, οὐδὲν δ' ἦν ἀκίνητον δρόμῳ.

κυρεῖ δ' Ἀγαύη πλησίον θρῴσκουσά μου·
κἀγὼ 'ξεπήδησ' ὡς συναρπάσαι θέλων,
λόχμην κενώσας ἔνθ' ἐκρυπτόμην δέμας.
ἡ δ' ἀνεβόησεν· ⟨Ὦ δρομάδες ἐμαὶ κύνες,
θηρώμεθ' ἀνδρῶν τῶνδ' ὕπ'· ἀλλ' ἕπεσθέ μοι,
ἕπεσθε θύρσοις διὰ χερῶν ὡπλισμέναι.⟩

ἡμεῖς μὲν οὖν φεύγοντες ἐξηλύξαμεν
βακχῶν σπαραγμόν, αἱ δὲ νεμομέναις χλόην
μόσχοις ἐπῆλθον χειρὸς ἀσιδήρου μέτα.
καὶ τὴν μὲν ἂν προσεῖδες εὔθηλον πόριν
μυκωμένην ἔχουσαν ἐν χεροῖν δίχα,
ἄλλαι δὲ δαμάλας διεφόρουν σπαράγμασιν.
εἶδες δ' ἂν ἢ πλεύρ' ἢ δίχηλον ἔμβασιν
ῥιπτόμεν' ἄνω τε καὶ κάτω· κρεμαστὰ δὲ
ἔσταζ' ὑπ' ἐλάταις ἀναπεφυρμέν' αἵματι.
ταῦροι δ' ὑβρισταὶ κἀς κέρας θυμούμενοι
τὸ πρόσθεν ἐσφάλλοντο πρὸς γαῖαν δέμας,
μυριάσι χειρῶν ἀγόμενοι νεανίδων.
θᾶσσον δὲ διεφοροῦντο σαρκὸς ἐνδυτὰ

Iacchos, the son of Zeus, Bromius; and the whole mountain was seized with Bacchic frenzy, and the wild animals – there was nothing that was not running with them.

And Agave jumped near me, and I leapt out to seize her, leaving the thicket where I was hiding; and she cried out: 'My hounds that run with me, we are hunted by these men. But follow me, follow me armed with your thyrsus in your hand.'

So we fled and escaped being torn to pieces by the Bacchants; but they attacked, with their hands unarmed, the herds that were grazing on the grass. And you could see one holding in her hands a great-uddered cow, torn in the middle and bellowing, while others were tearing the heifers in pieces and tossing them about. And you could see ribs and cloven hoofs thrown up and down. Bits were hanging on the fir-trees, smeared with blood. And the bulls, once insolent, their anger rising to their horns, were thrown to the ground, dragged by the hands of thousands of young girls. The skins were scattered in less time than you would close the eyelids over your royal eyes. And they

ἤ σὲ ξυνάψαι βλέφαρα βασιλείοις κόραις.
χωροῦσι δ' ὥστ' ὄρνιθες ἀρθεῖσαι δρόμῳ
πεδίων ὑποτάσεις, αἱ παρ' Ἀσωποῦ ῥοαῖς
εὔκαρπον ἐκβάλλουσι Θηβαίων στάχυν·
Ὑσιάς τ' Ἐρυθράς θ', αἱ Κιθαιρῶνος λέπας
νέρθεν κατῳκήκασιν, ὥστε πολέμιοι,
ἐπεσπεσοῦσαι πάντ' ἄνω τε καὶ κάτω
διέφερον· ἥρπαζον μὲν ἐκ δόμων τέκνα·
ὁπόσα δ' ἐπ' ὤμοις ἔθεσαν, οὐ δεσμῶν ὕπο
προσείχετ' οὐδ' ἔπιπτεν ἐς μέλαν πέδον,
οὐ χαλκός, οὐ σίδηρος· ἐπὶ δὲ βοστρύχοις
πῦρ ἔφερον, οὐδ' ἔκαιεν. οἱ δ' ὀργῆς ὕπο
ἐς ὅπλ' ἐχώρουν φερόμενοι βακχῶν ὕπο·
οὗπερ τὸ δεινὸν ἦν θέαμ' ἰδεῖν, ἄναξ.
τοῖς μὲν γὰρ οὐχ ἥμασσε λογχωτὸν βέλος,
κεῖναι δὲ θύρσους ἐξανιεῖσαι χερῶν
ἐτραυμάτιζον κἀπενώτιζον φυγῇ
γυναῖκες ἄνδρας, οὐκ ἄνευ θεῶν τινος.
πάλιν δ' ἐχώρουν ὅθεν ἐκίνησαν πόδα,
κρήνας ἐπ' αὐτὰς ἃς ἀνῆκ' αὐταῖς θεός.
νίψαντο δ' αἷμα, σταγόνα δ' ἐκ παρηίδων
γλώσσῃ δράκοντες ἐξεφαίδρυνον χροός.

moved like birds which fly swiftly over the plains stretching below them that put forth the rich Theban crops by the streams of Aesopus. They fell like an enemy on Hysiae and Erythrae, that nestle under rocks of Cithaeron, and turned everything upside down. They snatched children from their homes; and the things they put on their shoulders were not strapped on them but yet did not fall to the dark ground; and they had neither bronze, nor iron [weapons]; and they carried blazing fire on their hair, but it did not burn. And they [the villagers], angered by the Bacchants, took up arms. And that, my king, was a strange sight to see. The barbed spears did not draw blood from them; but by throwing their staves (with their hands) the women wounded the men and turned them to flight, which could not have been without the help of some god. And they returned to the place whence they had set out, to the fountains that the god had sent them. And they washed off the blood and snakes licked the drops of blood off the skin of their cheeks with their tongues.

τὸν δαίμον' οὖν τόνδ' ὅστις ἔστ', ὦ δέσποτα,
δέχου πόλει τῇδ'· ὡς τά τ' ἄλλ' ἐστὶν μέγας,
κἀκεῖνό φασιν αὐτόν, ὡς ἐγὼ κλύω,
τὴν παυσίλυπον ἄμπελον δοῦναι βροτοῖς.
οἴνου δὲ μηκέτ' ὄντος οὐκ ἔστιν Κύπρις
οὐδ' ἄλλο τερπνὸν οὐδὲν ἀνθρώποις ἔτι.

(Bacchae)

120. What is Wisdom?

ΧΟΡΟΣ

Ἆρ' ἐν παννυχίοις χοροῖς
θήσω ποτὲ λευκὸν
πόδ' ἀναβακχεύουσα, δέραν
εἰς αἰθέρα δροσερὸν ῥίπτουσ',
ὡς νεβρὸς χλοεραῖς ἐμπαί-
ζουσα λείμακος ἡδοναῖς,
ἡνίκ' ἂν φοβερὰν φύγῃ
θήραν ἔξω φυλακᾶς
εὐπλέκτων ὑπὲρ ἀρκύων,
θωΰσσων δὲ κυναγέτας
συντείνῃ δράμημα κυνῶν·
μόχθοις τ' ὠκυδρόμοις τ' ἀέλ-
λαις θρῴσκει πεδίον

So, master, receive this god, whoever he may be, in the city; for he is powerful in other things too; but they also say, so I am told, that he gave the pain-quenching vine to men. And if there is no more wine, there can be no more love, nor anything else that delights mankind.

CHORUS: Shall I ever set my white foot in night-long dances, breaking into Bacchic frenzy, throwing back my head in the dewy air — like a fawn at play in the grassy delights of a meadow, when it escapes the dreadful hunt, out of the ambush, leaping the well-woven nets, although the hurrying hunter urges on the running hounds; with an effort, with

παραποτάμιον, ἡδομένα
βροτῶν ἐρημίαις σκιαρο-
κόμοιό τ' ἔρνεσιν ὕλας.

τί τὸ σοφόν; ἢ τί τὸ κάλλιον
παρὰ θεῶν γέρας ἐν βροτοῖς
ἢ χεῖρ' ὑπὲρ κορυφᾶς
τῶν ἐχθρῶν κρείσσω κατέχειν;
ὅ τι καλὸν φίλον ἀεί.

. . . .

εὐδαίμων μὲν ὃς ἐκ θαλάσσας
ἔφυγε χεῖμα, λιμένα δ' ἔκιχεν·
εὐδαίμων δ' ὃς ὕπερθε μόχθων
ἐγένεθ'· ἑτέρᾳ δ' ἕτερος ἕτερον
ὄλβῳ καὶ δυνάμει παρῆλθεν.
μυρίαι δ' ἔτι μυρίοις
εἰσὶν ἐλπίδες· αἱ μὲν
τελευτῶσιν ἐν ὄλβῳ
βροτοῖς, αἱ δ' ἀπέβησαν·
τὸ δὲ κατ' ἦμαρ ὅτῳ βίοτος
εὐδαίμων, μακαρίζω.

(*Bacchae*)

swift bounds, it springs across the plain by the river, rejoicing in the young trees of the shady forest, away from all men?

What is wisdom? What greater prize has been given to men by the gods than to hold one's hand in mastery over the head of an enemy? What is good is always loved. . . . Happy is the man who escapes the storm at sea, and finds a harbour; happy the man who overcomes hardships. In different ways one man surpasses the next in wealth or power; moreover, countless are the hopes of countless people – some are fulfilled, bringing happiness to mortals, others come to nought. But him whose life from day to day is happy I consider blessed.

121. Old Age

Κείσθω δόρυ μοι μίτον ἀμφιπλέκειν ἀράχναις.
μετὰ δ’ ἡσυχίας πολιῷ γήρᾳ συνοικοίην·
ἀείδοιμι δὲ στεφάνοις κάρα πολιὸν στεφανώσας
Θρήικιον πέλταν πρὸς Ἀθάνας
περικίοσιν ἀγκρεμάσας θαλάμοις
δέλτων τ’ ἀναπτύσσοιμι γῆρυν
ἃν σοφοὶ κλέονται.

(*Erechtheus*)

122. Daybreak

Μέλπει δ’ ἐν δένδρεσι λεπτὰν
ἀηδὼν ἁρμονίαν
ὀρθρευομένα γόοις
Ἴτυν Ἴτυν πολύθρηνον.
σύριγγας δ’ οὐριβάται
κινοῦσιν ποίμνας ἐλάται·
ἔγρονται δ’ εἰς βοτάναν
ξανθᾶν πώλων συζυγίαι.
ἤδη δ’ εἰς ἔργα κυναγοὶ
στείχουσιν θηροφόνοι,
παγαῖς τ’ ἐπ’ Ὠκεανοῦ
μελιβόας κύκνος ἀχεῖ.

LET my spear lie idle for spiders to weave their web around it. May I
live in peace in white old age. May I sing with garlands around my
white head, having hung up my Thracian shield on the pillared house
of Athene; may I unfold the voice of books, which the wise honour.

THE nightingale sings her delicate song in the trees, greeting the dawn
with laments for Itys, Itys much-lamented; and shepherds of the flocks
who wander on the mountains start playing their pipes; the pairs of
gold-maned colts awaken to their pasture; already the beast-killing
hunters are striding to their work, and at the Ocean's sources the
honey-voiced swan is singing. The boats are setting out, moved by the

ἄκατοι δ' ἀνάγονται ὑπ' εἰρεσίας
ἀνέμων τ' εὐαέσσιν ῥοθίοις
ἀνὰ δ' ἱστία λευκὰ πετάννυται,
σινδὼν δὲ πρότονον ἐπὶ μέσον πελάζει.

(*Phaethon*)

ARISTOPHANES
450–385 B.C.

123. *Have No Grudge Against Me*

ΔΙΚΑΙΟΠΟΛΙΣ

Μή μοι φθονήσητ' ἄνδρες οἱ θεώμενοι,
εἰ πτωχὸς ὢν ἔπειτ' ἐν Ἀθηναίοις λέγειν
μέλλω περὶ τῆς πόλεως, τρυγῳδίαν ποιῶν.
τὸ γὰρ δίκαιον οἶδε καὶ τρυγῳδία.
ἐγὼ δὲ λέξω δεινὰ μὲν δίκαια δέ.
οὐ γάρ με νῦν γε διαβαλεῖ Κλέων ὅτι
ξένων παρόντων τὴν πόλιν κακῶς λέγω.
αὐτοὶ γάρ ἐσμεν οὑπὶ Ληναίῳ τ' ἀγών,
κοὔπω ξένοι πάρεισιν· οὔτε γὰρ φόροι
ἥκουσιν οὔτ' ἐκ τῶν πόλεων οἱ ξύμμαχοι·
ἀλλ' ἐσμὲν αὐτοὶ νῦν γε περιεπτισμένοι·

oars and by fair gusts of wind; white sails are hoisted, and the cloth comes close to the middle of the forestay.

DIKAIOPOLIS: Have no grudge against me, spectators, if, although poor, I speak before the Athenian people about the city, and make a comedy of it. For even comedy knows what is right, and I shall tell things terrible but just. Cleon will not accuse me now of defaming the city in the presence of strangers. We are alone, and it is the competition at the Lenaea – no strangers are here yet; for the tributes have not come, nor the allied troops from their cities. We are now on our own, clean-winnowed, for I call the alien residents [of Athens] the chaff of

τοὺς γὰρ μετοίκους ἄχυρα τῶν ἀστῶν λέγω
ἐγὼ δὲ μισῶ μὲν Λακεδαιμονίους σφόδρα,
καὐτοῖς ὁ Ποσειδῶν οὑπὶ Ταινάρῳ θεὸς
σείσας ἅπασιν ἐμβάλοι τὰς οἰκίας·
κἀμοὶ γάρ ἐστ' ἀμπέλια διακεκομμένα.
ἀτὰρ φίλοι γὰρ οἱ παρόντες ἐν λόγῳ,
τί ταῦτα τοὺς Λάκωνας αἰτιώμεθα;
ἡμῶν γὰρ ἄνδρες, κοὐχὶ τὴν πόλιν λέγω,
μέμνησθε τοῦθ' ὅτι οὐχὶ τὴν πόλιν λέγω,
ἀλλ' ἀνδράρια μοχθηρά, παρακεκομμένα,
ἄτιμα καὶ παράσημα καὶ παράξενα,
ἐσυκοφάντει Μεγαρέων τὰ χλανίσκια·
κεἴ που σίκυον ἴδοιεν ἢ λαγῴδιον
ἢ χοιρίδιον ἢ σκόροδον ἢ χόνδρους ἅλας,
ταῦτ' ἦν Μεγαρικὰ κἀπέπρατ' αὐθημερόν.
καὶ ταῦτα μὲν δὴ σμικρὰ κἀπιχώρια,
πόρνην δὲ Σιμαίθαν ἰόντες Μεγαράδε
νεανίαι κλέπτουσι μεθυσοκότταβοι·
κᾆθ' οἱ Μεγαρῆς ὀδύναις πεφυσιγγωμένοι
ἀντεξέκλεψαν Ἀσπασίας πόρνα δύο·
κἀντεῦθεν ἀρχὴ τοῦ πολέμου κατερράγη
Ἕλλησι πᾶσιν ἐκ τριῶν λαικαστριῶν.
ἐντεῦθεν ὀργῇ Περικλέης οὑλύμπιος

the citizens. I hate the Lacedaemonians violently, and may Poseidon, the god of Taenaron, throw all their houses down with an earthquake; for my little vines too have been cut through. But after all — and only friends are present at this speech — why do we blame the Laconians for this? Men from among us, not the city — remember this, I do not say the city — but villainous little men, base-minted coins, worthless, counterfeit, false half-foreign friends kept pointing the finger at the little cloaks of Megara. And if they saw a cucumber lying about, or a young hare, or a piglet, or a garlic, or lumps of salt, all these were Megarian and were sold on the same day. These were small things that happened at home; but some young drunkards, cottabus-players, went to Megara and seized the prostitute Simaetha. The Megarians, goaded to rage by garlic and their suffering, stole two of Aspasia's whores in return; and from this, war broke out among all the Greeks — from three whores! Olympian Pericles flashed lightning, thundered, shook

ἤστραπτ' ἐβρόντα ξυνεκύκα τὴν Ἑλλάδα,
ἐτίθει νόμους ὥσπερ σκόλια γεγραμμένους,
ὡς χρὴ Μεγαρέας μήτε γῇ μήτ' ἐν ἀγορᾷ
μήτ' ἐν θαλάττῃ μήτ' ἐν οὐρανῷ μένειν.
ἐντεῦθεν οἱ Μεγαρῆς, ὅτε δὴ 'πείνων βάδην,
Λακεδαιμονίων ἐδέοντο τὸ ψήφισμ' ὅπως
μεταστραφείη τὸ διὰ τὰς λαικαστρίας·
κοὐκ ἠθέλομεν ἡμεῖς δεομένων πολλάκις.
κἀντεῦθεν ἤδη πάταγος ἦν τῶν ἀσπίδων.
ἐρεῖ τις, οὐ χρῆν· ἀλλὰ τί ἐχρῆν, εἴπατε.
φέρ' εἰ Λακεδαιμονίων τις ἐκπλεύσας σκάφει
ἀπέδοτο φήνας κυνίδιον Σεριφίων,
καθῆσθ' ἂν ἐν δόμοισιν; ἦ πολλοῦ γε δεῖ·
καὶ κάρτα μέντἂν εὐθέως καθείλκετε
τριακοσίας ναῦς, ἦν δ' ἂν ἡ πόλις πλέα
θορύβου στρατιωτῶν, περὶ τριηράρχου βοῆς,
μισθοῦ διδομένου, παλλαδίων χρυσουμένων,
στοᾶς στεναχούσης, σιτίων μετρουμένων,
ἀσκῶν, τροπωτήρων, κάδους ὠνουμένων,
σκορόδων, ἐλαῶν, κρομμύων ἐν δικτύοις,
στεφάνων, τριχίδων, αὐλητρίδων, ὑπωπίων·
τὸ νεώριον δ' αὖ κωπέων πλατουμένων,
τύλων ψοφούντων, θαλαμιῶν τροπουμένων,

the whole of Greece, passed decrees composed like drinking-songs that the Megarians should be wiped off the earth, out of the market-places, off the sea and the sky. So the Megarians, as they starved by slow stages, begged the Lacedaemonians to get the law about the whores altered; but, though they asked us many times, we did not agree. Then instantly there was a clash of shields. One could say: 'They shouldn't have done it'; but tell me, what should they have done? Come now, if a Lacedaemonian, sailing in a boat, denounced a small Seriphian dog as contraband and sold it, would you have stayed at home? Far from it indeed. You would have launched three hundred ships immediately, and the city would be alive with the din of soldiers, shouts about a trierarch, the paying of wages, gilding of statues of Pallas, colonnades resounding, rations measured out, wine-skins, oar-loops, casks bought, garlics, olives, onions in nets, garlands, pilchards, flute-girls and black eyes. And the dockyard would be full of the planing of oars, hammering of pegs, shaping of oar-holes, flute-playing, boatswains, trills and

αὐλῶν, κελευστῶν, νιγλάρων, συριγμάτων.
ταῦτ' οἶδ' ὅτι ἂν ἐδρᾶτε· τὸν δὲ Τήλεφον
οὐκ οἰόμεσθα; νοῦς ἄρ' ἡμῖν οὐκ ἔνι.

(Acharnians)

124. A Rude, Bilious Master

ΔΗΜΟΣΘΕΝΗΣ

Λέγοιμ' ἂν ἤδη. νῦν γάρ ἐστι δεσπότης
ἄγροικος ὀργὴν κυαμοτρὼξ ἀκράχολος,
Δῆμος πυκνίτης, δύσκολον γερόντιον
ὑπόκωφον. οὗτος τῇ προτέρᾳ νουμηνίᾳ
ἐπρίατο δοῦλον, βυρσοδέψην Παφλαγόνα,
πανουργότατον καὶ διαβολώτατόν τινα.
οὗτος καταγνοὺς τοῦ γέροντος τοὺς τρόπους,
ὁ βυρσοπαφλαγών, ὑποπεσὼν τὸν δεσπότην
ἤκαλλ' ἐθώπευ' ἐκολάκευ' ἐξηπάτα
κοσκυλματίοις ἄκροισι τοιαυτὶ λέγων·
‹ὦ Δῆμε λοῦσαι πρῶτον ἐκδικάσας μίαν,
ἔνθου ῥόφησον ἔντραγ' ἔχε τριώβολον.
βούλει παραθῶ σοι δόρπον;› εἶτ' ἀναρπάσας

whistles. I know you would have done so. Why should we not expect Telephus to do this? We have no sense.

DEMOSTHENES: I wish to speak. For we have a boorish, bilious, testy, bean- [vote-]eating master, Demos from the deme of Pnyx, a difficult little old man, slightly deaf. At the beginning of last month he bought a slave, a Paphlagonian tanner, a most villainous and slanderous creature. When he learnt the old man's ways, the Paphlagonian leatherman cringed to his master, flattered him, pampered him, fawned before him, and deceived him with a tanner's scraps of adulation, saying things like this: 'Demos, you have judged one lawsuit, it is time to take your bath; put this in your mouth, gulp this down, gobble this sweetmeat, take your three obols of juryman's pay. Do you want me to set out

ὅ τι ἂν τις ἡμῶν σκευάσῃ, τῷ δεσπότῃ
Παφλαγὼν κεχάρισται τοῦτο. καὶ πρώην γ᾽ ἐμοῦ
μᾶζαν μεμαχότος ἐν Πύλῳ Λακωνικήν,
πανουργότατά πως περιδραμὼν ὑφαρπάσας
αὐτὸς παρέθηκε τὴν ὑπ᾽ ἐμοῦ μεμαγμένην.
ἡμᾶς δ᾽ ἀπελαύνει κοὐκ ἐᾷ τὸν δεσπότην
ἄλλον θεραπεύειν, ἀλλὰ βυρσίνην ἔχων
δειπνοῦντος ἑστὼς ἀποσοβεῖ τοὺς ῥήτορας.
ᾄδει δὲ χρησμούς· ὁ δὲ γέρων σιβυλλιᾷ.
ὁ δ᾽ αὐτὸν ὡς ὁρᾷ μεμακκοακότα,
τέχνην πεποίηται. τοὺς γὰρ ἔνδον ἄντικρυς
ψευδῆ διαβάλλει· κᾆτα μαστιγούμεθα
ἡμεῖς· Παφλαγὼν δὲ περιθέων τοὺς οἰκέτας
αἰτεῖ ταράττει δωροδοκεῖ λέγων τάδε·
‹ὁρᾶτε τὸν Ὕλαν δι᾽ ἐμὲ μαστιγούμενον;
εἰ μή μ᾽ ἀναπείσετ᾽, ἀποθανεῖσθε τήμερον.›
ἡμεῖς δὲ δίδομεν· εἰ δὲ μή, πατούμενοι
ὑπὸ τοῦ γέροντος ὀκταπλάσιον χέζομεν.

(*Knights*)

dinner for you?' Then, snatching whatever one of us is preparing, the
Paphlagonian offers it to his master as a favour coming from him. And
a short time ago, when I had mixed a Spartan dough in Pylos, in his
villainous way the tanner crept up and stole it, and set at his master's
table what I had kneaded. And he drives us all away, and will allow no
one else to wait upon his master, but stands with a leather whisk and
flaps away the orators from his table. He chants out oracles, and the
old man plays the Sibyl; and he, seeing the old man mooning, starts his
tricks. Those of the household he slanders outright and afterwards we
are whipped; and the Paphlagonian goes round questioning the ser-
vants, worries them, bribes them and tells them: 'You see how Hylas
is whipped because of me? If you do not convince me to the contrary,
you will die today.' And we hand things over. Otherwise the old man
treads on us and we shit out eight times as much.

ARISTOPHANES

125. The Clouds

ΧΟΡΟΣ

Ἀέναοι Νεφέλαι
ἀρθῶμεν φανεραὶ δροσερὰν φύσιν εὐάγητον,
πατρὸς ἀπ' Ὠκεανοῦ βαρυαχέος
ὑψηλῶν ὀρέων κορυφὰς ἐπὶ
  δενδροκόμους, ἵνα
τηλεφανεῖς σκοπιὰς ἀφορώμεθα,
καρπούς τ' ἀρδομέναν ἱερὰν χθόνα,
καὶ ποταμῶν ζαθέων κελαδήματα,
καὶ πόντον κελάδοντα βαρύβρομον·
δμμα γὰρ αἰθέρος ἀκάματον σελαγεῖται
  μαρμαρέαις ἐν αὐγαῖς.
ἀλλ' ἀποσεισάμεναι νέφος ὄμβριον
ἀθανάτας ἰδέας ἐπιδώμεθα
  τηλεσκόπῳ ὄμματι γαῖαν.

. . . .

παρθένοι ὀμβροφόροι
Ἔλθωμεν λιπαρὰν χθόνα Παλλάδος, εὔανδρον γᾶν
  Κέκροπος ὀψόμεναι πολυήρατον·
οὗ σέβας ἀρρήτων ἱερῶν, ἵνα
  μυστοδόκος δόμος
ἐν τελεταῖς ἁγίαις ἀναδείκνυται,

CHORUS: Eternal clouds, let us rise up and show our dewy, radiant natures; let us rise up from our loud-roaring father, the Ocean, to the peaks of high mountains, shaggy with trees; so that we may gaze upon hilltops that are clear from afar, and upon the holy earth watering her fruits, and upon the rushing of sacred rivers, and the loud sound of the thundering sea: for now the unwearying eye of the sky shines out with flashing ray. Let us shake off the rain-cloud from our immortal shapes, and look upon the earth with far-seeing eye. . .

Rain-bringing maidens, let us go to the fruitful land of Pallas, to see the much-loved country of Cecrops, nurse of good men, where the religious ceremonies of which no one may speak are honoured, where

οὐρανίοις τε θεοῖς δωρήματα,
ναοί θ' ὑψερεφεῖς καὶ ἀγάλματα,
καὶ πρόσοδοι μακάρων ἱερώταται,
εὐστέφανοί τε θεῶν θυσίαι θαλίαι τε
    παντοδαπαῖς ἐν ὥραις,
ἦρί τ' ἐπερχομένῳ Βρομία χάρις,
εὐκελάδων τε χορῶν ἐρεθίσματα,
καὶ μοῦσα βαρύβρομος αὐλῶν.

(*Clouds*)

126. *The Hoopoe*

ΕΠΟΨ

I

Ἄγε σύννομέ μοι παῦσαι μὲν ὕπνου,
λῦσον δὲ νόμους ἱερῶν ὕμνων,
οὓς διὰ θείου στόματος θρηνεῖς
τὸν ἐμὸν καὶ σὸν πολύδακρυν Ἴτυν·

the house for the Mysteries is opened in the holy rites; and where there
are gifts to the gods of the sky, and high-roofed temples and statues,
and most holy processions for the blessed ones, and sacrifices to the
gods with lovely wreaths, and feasts in all seasons; and, when spring
is coming, the graceful celebrations to honour Bromius, the rousing of
sweet-singing choruses, and the loud-sounding music of flutes.

I

THE HOOPOE: Come, my comrade, wake from your sleep, set loose
the music of your holy songs with which your godly mouth laments
Itys, for whom you and I have shed many tears. And, as your bright-

ἑλελιζομένης δ' ἱεροῖς μέλεσιν
  γένυος ξουθῆς
καθαρὰ χωρεῖ διὰ φυλλοκόμου
μίλακος ἠχὼ πρὸς Διὸς ἕδρας,
ἵν' ὁ χρυσοκόμας Φοῖβος ἀκούων
τοῖς σοῖς ἐλέγοις ἀντιψάλλων
ἐλεφαντόδετον φόρμιγγα θεῶν
ἵστησι χορούς· διὰ δ' ἀθανάτων
στομάτων χωρεῖ ξύμφωνος ὁμοῦ
  θεία μακάρων ὀλολυγή.

II

ἐποποῖ ποποποποποποποῖ,
ἰὼ ἰὼ ἰτὼ ἰτὼ ἰτὼ ἰτώ,
ἴτω τις ὧδε τῶν ἐμῶν ὁμοπτέρων·
ὅσοι τ' εὐσπόρους ἀγροίκων γύας
νέμεσθε, φῦλα μυρία κριθοτράγων
  σπερμολόγων τε γένη
ταχὺ πετόμενα, μαλθακὴν ἱέντα γῆρυν·
  ὅσα τ' ἐν ἄλοκι θαμὰ
βῶλον ἀμφιτιττυβίζεθ' ὧδε λεπτὸν
  ἡδομένα φωνᾷ·
τιὸ τιὸ τιὸ τιὸ τιὸ τιὸ τιὸ τιό.

brown throat trills that holy song, the sound rings clear through the rich leaves of briony to the seat of Zeus, where golden-haired Phoebus listens, and answers your elegies with his lyre, inlaid with ivory, and establishes a chorus of the gods. So from immortal mouths pours out a holy lamentation of the blessed ones that blends with your voice.

II

Epopoi, popopopopopopoi, io, io, ito, ito, ito, ito, ito; let one, let all my winged fellows come here, you who live on the well-sown farm-land of the peasants, the countless tribes of barley-eaters, and the swift-winged families of seed-pickers, [come] calling softly. All who twitter so often around the clods in the furrow [come singing] with joyful voice – tio, tio, tio, tio, tio, tio, tio, tio; all who dwell in gardens

δσα θ' ὑμῶν κατὰ κήπους ἐπὶ κισσοῦ
   κλάδεσι νομὸν ἔχει,
τά τε κατ' ὄρεα τά τε κοτινοτράγα τά τε κομαροφάγα,
ἀνύσατε πετόμενα πρὸς ἐμὰν αὐδάν·
   τριοτὸ τριοτὸ τοτοβρίξ·
οἵ θ' ἑλείας παρ' αὐλῶνας ὀξυστόμους
ἐμπίδας κάπτεθ', ὅσα τ' εὐδρόσους γῆς τόπους
ἔχετε λειμῶνά τ' ἐρόεντα Μαραθῶνος, ὄρ-
νις πτερυγοποίκιλός τ' ἀτταγᾶς ἀτταγᾶς.
   ὧν τ' ἐπὶ πόντιον οἶδμα θαλάσσης
φῦλα μετ' ἀλκυόνεσσι ποτῆται,
δεῦρ' ἴτε πευσόμενοι τὰ νεώτερα,
πάντα γὰρ ἐνθάδε φῦλ' ἀθροίζομεν
   οἰωνῶν ταναοδείρων.

(Birds)

127. The Birds

ΧΟΡΟΣ

Ἤδη 'μοὶ τῷ παντόπτᾳ
καὶ παντάρχᾳ θνητοὶ πάντες
θύσουσ' εὐκταίαις εὐχαῖς.
πᾶσαν μὲν γὰρ γᾶν ὀπτεύω,

among ivy branches, all who live on the mountains, all who strip wild
olives, all who nibble arbutus, hurry, fly to my voice – trioto, trioto,
totobrix – and with them you, who by marshy dykes snap down the
sharp-stinging gnats; and all who keep to the dew-covered meadows
and the lovely plain of Marathon, and the bird with the many-coloured
wings, francolin, francolin; and flocks of birds that fly with the king-
fishers over the swelling waves of the sea, come here to learn the news,
for here we are gathering all the tribes of long-necked birds.

CHORUS: Now all mortals shall sacrifice to me, the all-seeing, the ruler
of all, with votive offerings and prayers; for I look on the whole world,

σῴζω δ᾽ εὐθαλεῖς καρπούς
κτείνων παμφύλων γένναν
θηρῶν, ἃ πάντ᾽ ἐν γαίᾳ
ἐκ κάλυκος αὐξανόμενον γένυσι παμφάγοις
δένδρεσί τ᾽ ἐφημένα καρπὸν ἀποβόσκεται·
κτείνω δ᾽ οἳ κήπους εὐώδεις
φθείρουσιν λύμαις ἐχθίσταις,
ἑρπετά τε καὶ δάκετα πάνθ᾽ ὅσαπερ
ἔστιν ὑπ᾽ ἐμᾶς πτέρυγος ἐν φοναῖς ὄλλυται.

. . . .

εὔδαιμον φῦλον πτηνῶν
οἰωνῶν, οἳ χειμῶνος μὲν
χλαίνας οὐκ ἀμπισχνοῦνται·
οὐδ᾽ αὖ θερμὴ πνίγους ἡμᾶς
ἀκτὶς τηλαυγὴς θάλπει·
ἀλλ᾽ ἀνθηρῶν λειμώνων
φύλλων τ᾽ ἐν κόλποις ναίω,
ἡνίκ᾽ ἂν ὁ θεσπέσιος ὀξὺ μέλος ἀχέτας
θάλπεσι μεσημβρινοῖς ἡλιομανὴς βοᾷ.
χειμάζω δ᾽ ἐν κοίλοις ἄντροις
νύμφαις οὐρείαις ξυμπαίζων·
ἠρινά τε βοσκόμεθα παρθένια
λευκότροφα μύρτα Χαρίτων τε κηπεύματα.

(*Birds*)

and preserve the ripe fruits by killing all the many tribes of animals that eat with greedy jaws everything on earth that grows from bud, or that sit on trees and feed off the fruit. I kill those that ruin the fragrant garden with hateful destruction; snakes and all creatures with a bite, above which I fly, meet a bloody end. . .

O happy race of flying birds, who do not wear cloaks in winter, we whom the far-flashing ray of choking heat does not make hot! When the divine-voiced cicada is chirping his sharp song, sun-mad at the midday heat, I live in flowering meadows and in the folds of leaves; I spend my winter in hollow caves, playing with the nymphs of the mountains; and in spring we feed off the virgin white-berried myrtle, and off the gardens of the Muses.

128. The Women Will Stop War

ΠΡΟΒΟΥΛΟΣ, ΛΥΣΙΣΤΡΑΤΗ

Πρ. Πῶς οὖν ὑμεῖς δυναταὶ παῦσαι τεταραγμένα πράγματα
  πολλὰ
  ἐν ταῖς χώραις καὶ διαλῦσαι;   Λυ. φαύλως πάνυ.
  Πρ. πῶς; ἀπόδειξον.

Λυ. ὥσπερ κλωστῆρ', ὅταν ἡμῖν ᾖ τεταραγμένος, ὧδε λαβοῦ-
  σαι,
  ὑπενεγκοῦσαι τοῖσιν ἀτράκτοις τὸ μὲν ἐνταυθοῖ τὸ δ'
  ἐκεῖσε,
  οὕτως καὶ τὸν πόλεμον τοῦτον διαλύσομεν, ἤν τις ἐάσῃ,
  διενεγκοῦσαι διὰ πρεσβειῶν τὸ μὲν ἐνταυθοῖ τὸ δ' ἐκεῖσε.

Πρ. ἐξ ἐρίων δὴ καὶ κλωστήρων καὶ ἀτράκτων πράγματα
  δεινὰ
  παύσειν οἴεσθ', ὦ ἀνόητοι;   Λυ. κἂν ὑμῖν γ' εἴ τις ἐνῆν
  νοῦς,
  ἐκ τῶν ἐρίων τῶν ἡμετέρων ἐπολιτεύεσθ' ἂν ἅπαντα.

Πρ. πῶς δή; φέρ' ἴδω.   Λυ. πρῶτον μὲν ἐχρῆν, ὥσπερ
  πόκου ἐν βαλανείῳ
  ἐκπλύναντας τὴν οἰσπώτην, ἐκ τῆς πόλεως ἐπὶ κλίνης
  ἐκραβδίζειν τοὺς μοχθηροὺς καὶ τοὺς τριβόλους ἀπολέξαι,

MEMBER OF THE STANDING COMMITTEE OF TEN: How could you find
  a cure for so much confusion in our countries? How could you un-
  ravel it?

LYSISTRATA: Very easily.

MEMBER: How? Tell me.

LYSISTRATA: Like a skein. When it is tangled, we get hold of it like
  this, we put it on the spindles, one bit this side, the other that side.
  That is how we shall disentangle this war too, if they let us – un-
  ravelling it with embassies, a bit this side, a bit that side.

MEMBER: Silly women. You think that with wool and skeins and
  spindles you can stop these terrible things!

LYSISTRATA: If you had any sense in your heads, you would deal with
  everything the way we deal with wool.

MEMBER: But how? Come, show me.

LYSISTRATA: First of all, just as you wash the sheep-dung off the wool
  in the bath, you should beat the evil men out of the city, pick out
  the prickly thorns, card out those who bring these people together

καὶ τούς γε συνισταμένους τούτους καὶ τοὺς πιλοῦντας
    ἑαυτούς
ἐπὶ ταῖς ἀρχαῖσι διαξῆναι καὶ τὰς κεφαλὰς ἀποτῖλαι·
εἶτα ξαίνειν ἐς καλαθίσκον κοινὴν εὔνοιαν, ἅπαντας
καταμιγνύντας τούς τε μετοίκους κεἴ τις ξένος ἢ φίλος
    ὑμῖν,
κεἴ τις ὀφείλει τῷ δημοσίῳ, καὶ τούτους ἐγκαταμεῖξαι·
καὶ νὴ Δία τάς γε πόλεις, ὁπόσαι τῆς γῆς τῆσδ᾽ εἰσὶν
    ἄποικοι,
διαγιγνώσκειν ὅτι ταῦθ᾽ ἡμῖν ὥσπερ τὰ κατάγματα
    κεῖται
χωρὶς ἕκαστον· κᾆτ᾽ ἀπὸ τούτων πάντων τὸ κάταγμα
    λαβόντας
δεῦρο ξυνάγειν καὶ συναθροίζειν εἰς ἕν, κᾆπειτα ποιῆσαι
τολύπην μεγάλην κᾆτ᾽ ἐκ ταύτης τῷ δήμῳ χλαῖναν ὑφῆ-
    ναι.
Πρ. οὔκουν δεινὸν ταυτὶ ταύτας ῥαβδίζειν καὶ τολυπεύειν,
    αἷς οὐδὲ μετῆν πάνυ τοῦ πολέμου;   Λυ. καὶ μήν, ὦ
        παγκατάρατε,
    πλεῖν ἢ γε διπλοῦν αὐτὸν φέρομεν, πρώτιστον μέν γε
        τεκοῦσαι
    κἀκπέμψασαι παῖδας ὁπλίτας.   Πρ. σίγα, μὴ μνησικα-
        κήσῃς.

and those who compact themselves into a felt to win office, and
pluck off their heads; then you should dress the wool which is well-
disposed to the city in a small basket, and mix up with it all the alien
residents, and if there is any visitor or friend of yours, even if they
are in debt to the public treasury, mix them in too. And, by Zeus,
the cities that are colonies of this land, you should realize that they
are like shreds of wool scattered about. And then collect the shreds
from all these, bring them here, put them together, and wind them
all into a big ball and weave a cloak from it for the people.

MEMBER: But is it not shocking to beat in those who have had nothing
    whatsoever to do with the war, and wind them into our ball?
LYSISTRATA: But we, you cursed man, feel it more than twice over.
    First of all we give birth to our sons, and then we send them out to
    war as heavy-armed soldiers.
MEMBER: Stop. You mustn't bear grudges.

Λυ. εἶθ' ἡνίκα χρῆν εὐφρανθῆναι καὶ τῆς ἥβης ἀπολαῦσαι,
μονοκοιτοῦμεν διὰ τὰς στρατιάς. καὶ θἠμέτερον μὲν ἐᾶτε,
περὶ τῶν δὲ κορῶν ἐν τοῖς θαλάμοις γηρασκουσῶν ἀνιῶ-
μαι.

Πρ. οὔκουν χἄνδρες γηράσκουσιν;   Λυ. μὰ Δί' ἀλλ' οὐκ
εἶπας ὅμοιον.

ὁ μὲν ἥκων γάρ, κἄν ᾖ πολιός, ταχὺ παῖδα κόρην γεγά-
μηκεν·

τῆς δὲ γυναικὸς σμικρὸς ὁ καιρός, κἄν τούτου μὴ 'πιλάβη-
ται,

οὐδεὶς ἐθέλει γῆμαι ταύτην, ὀττευομένη δὲ κάθηται.

(Lysistrata)

129. Peace

ΧΟΡΟΣ ΑΘΗΝΑΙΩΝ

Πρόσαγε χορόν, ἔπαγε δὲ Χάριτας,
ἐπὶ δὲ κάλεσον Ἄρτεμιν,
ἐπὶ δὲ δίδυμον ἀγέχορον
Ἰήιον
εὔφρον', ἐπὶ δὲ Νύσιον,
ὃς μετὰ μαινάσι Βάκχιος ὄμμασι δαίεται,

LYSISTRATA: Then, when we should be happy, and be enjoying our
youth, we sleep alone, because of the campaigns; and to put aside
our own troubles – I worry about our daughters, who grow old at
home [unmarried].

MEMBER: But don't men grow old as well?

LYSISTRATA: By Zeus, you can't say it is the same. When a man comes
back from the war, even if he is grey-haired, he quickly gets mar-
ried to a young girl. But for a woman the time of her prime is short,
and, if she does not take advantage of it, no one wants to marry her,
and she sits there, looking out for omens.

CHORUS OF ATHENIANS: Bring here a chorus, bring forward the
Graces, and call upon Artemis and her twin brother Apollo, the
kindly leader of the dance, to whom we cry 'Ie'; call upon the god
of Nyssa, Bacchus, whose eyes blaze among his Maenads; call upon

Δία τε πυρὶ φλεγόμενον, ἐπί τε
πότνιαν ἄλοχον ὀλβίαν·
εἶτα δὲ δαίμονας, οἷς ἐπιμάρτυσι
χρησόμεθ᾽ οὐκ ἐπιλήσμοσιν
Ἡσυχίας πέρι τῆς ἀγανόφρονος,
ἣν ἐποίησε θεὰ Κύπρις.
ἀλαλαὶ ἰὴ παιήων·
αἴρεσθ᾽ ἄνω ἰαί,
ὡς ἐπὶ νίκῃ ἰαί.
εὐοῖ εὐοῖ, εὐαί εὐαί.

ΧΟΡΟΣ ΛΑΚΕΔΑΙΜΟΝΙΩΝ

Ταΰγετον αὖτ᾽ ἐραννὸν ἐκλιπῶα
Μῶα μόλε Λάκαινα πρεπτὸν ἀμὶν
κλέωα τὸν Ἀμύκλαις σιὸν
καὶ χαλκίοικον Ἀσάναν,
Τυνδαρίδας τ᾽ ἀγασώς,
τοὶ δὴ πὰρ Εὐρώταν ψιάδδοντι.
εἶα μάλ᾽ ἔμβη
ὢ εἶα κοῦφα πάλλων,
ὡς Σπάρταν ὑμνίωμες,
τᾷ σιῶν χοροὶ μέλοντι
καὶ ποδῶν κτύπος,
ᾇ τε πῶλοι ταὶ κόραι
πὰρ τὸν Εὐρώταν

Zeus, ablaze with fire; call upon his happy honoured consort. And
then call upon the gods, whom we shall use as witnesses who will
not forget about gentle Peace, whom the goddess Cypris created.
Alalae, ie, the healer! Rise high, ie! As for a victory, rise high,
ie! Evoi, evoi, evae, evae!

CHORUS OF SPARTANS: Laconian Muse, once more abandon lovely
Taygetus and come; you are the one who praises for us the noble
god of Amyclae and Athene of the Bronze House and the virtuous
Tyndarids, who play by the Eurotas. Come, step in, come, leap
lightly so that we may sing of Sparta that loves the chorus honour-
ing her gods and the beat of dancing feet, whose daughters leap like
foals near the Eurotas, raising thick dust with their feet, their hair

ἀμπάλλοντι πυκνὰ ποδοῖν
ἀγκονίωαι,
ταὶ δὲ κόμαι σείονθ᾿ ἅπερ Βακχᾶν
θυρσαδδωᾶν καὶ παιδδωᾶν.
ἀγεῖται δ᾿ ἁ Λήδας παῖς
ἁγνὰ χοραγὸς εὐπρεπής.
ἀλλ᾿ ἄγε κόμαν παραμπύκιδδε χερί, ποδοῖν τε πάδη
ᾇ τις ἔλαφος· κρότον δ᾿ ἁμᾷ ποίει χορωφελήταν.
καὶ τὰν σιὰν δ᾿ αὖ τὰν κρατίσταν Χαλκίοικον ὕμνει
τὰν πάμμαχον.

(Lysistrata)

130. A Battle of Poets

ΧΟΡΟΣ

Ἦ που δεινὸν ἐριβρεμέτας χόλον ἔνδοθεν ἕξει,
ἡνίκ᾿ ἂν ὀξύλαλον παρίδῃ θήγοντος ὀδόντα
ἀντιτέχνου· τότε δὴ μανίας ὑπὸ δεινῆς
ὄμματα στροβήσεται.

ἔσται δ᾿ ἱππολόφων τε λόγων κορυθαίολα νείκη
σχινδαλάμων τε παραξόνια σμιλεύματά τ᾿ ἔργων,
φωτὸς ἀμυνομένου φρενοτέκτονος ἀνδρὸς
ῥήμαθ᾿ ἱπποβάμονα.

shaking like that of Bacchants brandishing their thyrsi and playing;
the daughter of Leda leads the dance beautiful and pure. But come,
hold back your hair with your hand, and jump on your feet like a
roe; make a beat to help the dance; and praise once again the most
powerful goddess of the Bronze House, the ever-victorious.

CHORUS: The loud-bellowing man will feel terrible anger in his heart
when he glances at the sharp-tongued fellow, his rival in art, whetting
his tusks. Then, seized by a terrible frenzy, he will roll his eyes.
And there will be flashing-helmeted struggles of horsehair-crested
words, and linchpins in splinters, and words being chipped, man ward-
ing off ingenious man, words charging on horseback.

φρίξας δ' αὐτοκόμου λοφιᾶς λασιαύχενα χαίταν,
δεινὸν ἐπισκύνιον ξυνάγων βρυχώμενος ἥσει
ῥήματα γομφοπαγῆ πινακηδὸν ἀποσπῶν
γηγενεῖ φυσήματι·

ἔνθεν δὴ στοματουργὸς ἐπῶν βασανίστρια λίσφη
γλῶσσ' ἀνελισσομένη φθονεροὺς κινοῦσα χαλινοὺς
ῥήματα δαιομένη καταλεπτολογήσει
πλευμόνων πολὺν πόνον.

(Frogs)

131. Poverty

ΧΡΕΜΥΛΟΣ

Σὺ γὰρ ἂν πορίσαι τί δύναι' ἀγαθὸν πλὴν φῴδων ἐκ βαλα-
νείου
καὶ παιδαρίων ὑποπεινώντων καὶ γραϊδίων κολοσυρτόν;
φθειρῶν τ' ἀριθμὸν καὶ κωνώπων καὶ ψυλλῶν οὐδὲ λέγω σοι
ὑπὸ τοῦ πλήθους, αἳ βομβοῦσαι περὶ τὴν κεφαλὴν ἀνιῶσιν,
ἐπεγείρουσαι καὶ φράζουσαι, ‹πεινήσεις, ἀλλ' ἐπανίστω.›
πρὸς δέ γε τούτοις ἀνθ' ἱματίου μὲν ἔχειν ῥάκος· ἀντὶ δὲ κλίνης
στιβάδα σχοίνων κορέων μεστήν, ἣ τοὺς εὕδοντας ἐγείρει·

When he has shaken the mane of hair that lies thick on his neck, drawing his brows down in a terrible frown, he will roar and hurl words, riveted like planks, wrenching them out with a titanic blast.

Then no doubt the polished tongue, the mouth-worker, word-tester, unfolding, giving rein to its envy, will feast on the details of words; hard work for the lungs.

CHREMYLUS: What good could you [Poverty] offer except sores from the public baths, and the noisy rabble of little half-starved children and bent old women? I will not tell you of the number of lice and mosquitoes and fleas – there are so many – buzzing round the head, and worrying us; they wake us up calling: 'You will starve, get up.' Moreover, instead of a cloak you have rags, instead of a bed a mattress of rushes full of bugs, that wakes up those sleeping on it. And you have a

καὶ φορμὸν ἔχειν ἀντὶ τάπητος σαπρόν· ἀντὶ δὲ προσκεφα-
   λαίου
λίθον εὐμεγέθη πρὸς τῇ κεφαλῇ· σιτεῖσθαι δ' ἀντὶ μὲν ἄρτων
μαλάχης πτόρθους, ἀντὶ δὲ μάζης φυλλεῖ' ἰσχνῶν ῥαφανίδων,
ἀντὶ δὲ θράνους στάμνου κεφαλὴν κατεαγότος, ἀντὶ δὲ μάκτρας
φιδάκνης πλευρὰν ἐρρωγυῖαν καὶ ταύτην. ἆρά γε πολλῶν
ἀγαθῶν πᾶσιν τοῖς ἀνθρώποις ἀποφαίνω σ' αἴτιον οὖσαν;

(Wealth)

TIMOTHEUS
c. 447–357 B.C.

132. A Defeat at Sea

'Επεὶ δὲ ἀμβόλιμος ἅλ-
  μα στόματος ὑπερέθνιεν,
ὀξυπαραυδήτῳ
  φωνᾷ παρακόπῳ
  τε δόξᾳ φρενῶν
  κατακορὴς ἀπείλει
γόμφοισ' ἐμπρίων
μιμούμενος λυμεῶ-
  νι σώματος θαλάσσᾳ·
⟨ᾖδη θρασεῖα καὶ πάρος
λάβρον αὐχέν' ἔσχες ἔμ θ
  πέδα καταζευχθεῖσα λινοδέτῳ τεόν.

rotten reed mat in the place of a carpet, and instead of a pillow a big
stone under your head. You feed on mallow-shoots instead of bread,
and thin radish-tops instead of barley-cakes, [and you have] the top of
a broken wine-jar for a chair, and the side of a cask – and that broken –
for a kneading-trough. Well, [Poverty,] do I prove you the giver of
blessings to all mankind?

WHEN the upsurging brine foamed over his mouth, with harshly
yelling voice and insane flights of thought, he angrily threatened it,
gnashing his teeth in imitation of the sea, the destroyer of his body:
'You are arrogant now, but formerly you had your violent neck yoked

νῦν δέ σ' ἀναταράξει
ἐμὸς ἄναξ, ἐμὸς
πεύκαισιν ὀριγόνοισιν, ἐγ-
κλήσει δὲ πεδία πλόϊμα νομάσιν αὐγαῖς,
οἰστρομανὲς παλεομί-
σημ' ἄπιστον τ' ἀγκάλι-
σμα κλυσιδρομάδος αὔρας.⟩
φάτ' ἄσθματι στρευγόμενος,
βλοσυρὰν δ' ἐξέβαλλεν
ἄχναν ἐπανερευγόμενος
στόματι βρύχιον ἅλμαν.
φυγᾷ δὲ πάλιν ἵετο Πέρ-
σης στρατὸς βάρβαρος ἐπισπέρχων.
ἄλλα δ' ἄλλαν θραῦεν σύρτις,
μακραυχενόπλους
χειρῶν δ' ἔγβαλλον ὀρείους
πόδας ναός. στόματος
δ' ἐξήλλοντο μαρμαροφεγ-
γεῖς παῖδες συγκρουόμενοι·
κατάστερος δὲ πόντος
ἐγ λιποπνόης λιπαστέρεσσιν
ἐγάργαιρε σώμασιν,
ἐβρίθοντο δ' ἀϊόνες.

(*Persians*)

in shackles of hemp. But now, my master – yes, my master – will rouse you to frenzy with pines from the hills, and he will imprison your meadows fit for sailing in wandering lights, you ancient frenzied abomination, faithless in the embrace of the rushing foaming wind.' So he spoke, worn out with panting, and threw up a fearful foam as he vomited forth (from his mouth) brine, from the depths. Again, the barbarian Persian army was rushing back in flight. Here and there the shallows smashed them, and knocked out of the men's hands the long-necked mountain-born legs of the ship [the oars]; from their mouths there leapt out the bright-flashing children [their teeth] crashing together. The sea was bestarred, and swarmed with breathless, lightless bodies; and the shores were laden [with corpses].

PLATO
429–347 B.C.

133. Agathon

Τὴν ψυχήν, Ἀγάθωνα φιλῶν, ἐπὶ χείλεσιν ἔσχον·
ἦλθε γὰρ ἡ τλήμων ὡς διαβησομένη.

134. Aster

Ἀστὴρ πρὶν μὲν ἔλαμπες ἐνὶ ζωοῖσιν Ἑῷος·
νῦν δὲ θανὼν λάμπεις Ἕσπερος ἐν φθιμένοις.

135. Dion

Δάκρυα μὲν Ἑκάβῃ τε καὶ Ἰλιάδεσσι γυναιξὶ
Μοῖραι ἐπέκλωσαν δή ποτε γεινομέναις·
σοὶ δέ, Δίων, ῥέξαντι καλῶν ἐπινίκιον ἔργων
δαίμονες εὐρείας ἐλπίδας ἐξέχεαν.
κεῖσαι δ᾽ εὐρυχόρῳ ἐν πατρίδι τίμιος ἀστοῖς,
ὦ ἐμὸν ἐκμήνας θυμὸν ἔρωτι Δίων.

KISSING Agathon, my soul was on my lips; for it came forward,
poor thing, as though it would cross over to him.

As the Morning Star you shone in the past among the living; but now,
dead, you shine like the Evening Star among those that have perished.

THE Fates wove tears for Hecuba and the Trojan women at the hour
of their birth; and the gods poured away your far-reaching hopes,
Dion, after you had celebrated the triumph for your noble deeds. You
lie in your spacious homeland, honoured by your citizens, Dion — you,
who maddened my soul with love.

136. *On the Dead of Eretria*

Οἴδε ποτ' Αἰγαίοιο βαρύβρομον οἶδμα λιπόντες
 Ἐκβατάνων πεδίῳ κείμεθ' ἐνὶ μεσάτῳ.
χαῖρε, κλυτὴ ποτε πατρὶς Ἐρέτρια· χαίρετ', Ἀθῆναι
 γείτονες Εὐβοίης· χαῖρε, θάλασσα φίλη.

ARISTOTLE
384–322 B.C.

137. *Virtue*

Ἀρετὰ πολύμοχθε γένει βροτείῳ,
 θήραμα κάλλιστον βίῳ,
σᾶς πέρι, παρθένε, μορφᾶς
 καὶ θανεῖν ζηλωτὸς ἐν Ἑλλάδι πότμος
καὶ πόνους τλῆναι μαλεροὺς ἀκάμαντας·
τοῖον ἐπὶ φρένα βάλλεις
 καρπὸν ἰσαθάνατον χρυσοῦ τε κρείσσω
καὶ γονέων μαλακαυγήτοιό θ' ὕπνου.
σεῦ δ' ἕνεκεν καὶ ὁ δῖος
 Ἡρακλῆς Λήδας τε κοῦροι
πόλλ' ἀνέτλασαν ἐν ἔργοις
 σὰν . . ἕποντες δύναμιν·

WE, here, once left the loud-sounding waves of the Aegean, and now lie in the middle of the plain of Ecbatana. Farewell, Eretria, once our glorious home; farewell, Athens, the neighbour of Euboea; farewell, beloved sea.

VIRTUE, cause of much labour to the human race, the best prize to seize in life; even to die for your countenance, virgin goddess, and to suffer ravaging, unending hardships, is in Greece an enviable fate. You give the soul such an immortal reward, more precious than gold, more precious than our parents or the soft light of sleep. For your sake, godly Heracles and the sons of Leda suffered much in their labours, [? proclaiming] your power. For love of you, Achilles and Ajax came to

σοῖς τε πόθοις Ἀχιλεὺς Αἴ-
    ας τ' Ἀΐδαο δόμους ἦλθον·
σᾶς δ' ἕνεκεν φιλίου μορφᾶς Ἀταρνέος
    ἔντροφος ἀελίου χήρωσεν αὐγάς.
τοιγὰρ ἀοίδιμος ἔργοις,
    ἀθάνατόν τέ μιν αὐξήσουσι Μοῦσαι,
Μναμοσύνας θύγατρες, Δι-
    ὸς ξενίου σέβας αὔξου-
    σαι φιλίας τε γέρας βεβαίου.

the house of Hades, and for the sake of your beautiful countenance, the nursling of Atarneus was bereft of the light of the sun. Therefore songs will praise his deeds, and the Muses, daughters of Mnemosyne, will raise him to immortality, increasing respect for Zeus of Hospitality, and for the gift of true friendship.

II
THE HELLENISTIC WORLD

MENANDER
?343–293 B.C.

138. *Whom the Gods Love*

Ὅν οἱ θεοὶ φιλοῦσιν ἀποθνῄσκει νέος.

139. *Watch Ungrieving*

Τοῦτον εὐτυχέστατον λέγω,
ὅστις θεωρήσας ἀλύπως, Παρμένων,
τὰ σεμνὰ ταῦτ᾽ ἀπῆλθεν, ὅθεν ἦλθεν, ταχύ,
τὸν ἥλιον τὸν κοινόν, ἄστρ᾽, ὕδωρ, νέφη,
πῦρ· ταῦτά, κἂν ἑκατὸν ἔτη βιῷς, ἀεὶ
ὄψει παρόντα, κἂν ἐνιαυτοὺς σφόδρ᾽ ὀλίγους,
σεμνότερα τούτων ἕτερα δ᾽ οὐκ ὄψει ποτέ.
πανήγυριν νόμισόν τιν᾽ εἶναι τὸν χρόνον,
ὃν φημι, τοῦτον ἢ 'πιδημίαν ἐν ᾧ
ὄχλος, ἀγορά, κλεπταί, κυβεῖαι, διατριβαί.
ἂν πρῷος ἀπίῃς καταλύσεις, βελτίονα
ἐφόδι᾽ ἔχων ἀπῆλθες, ἐχθρὸς οὐδενί·
ὁ προσδιατρίβων δ᾽ ἐκοπίασεν ἀπολέσας

He whom the gods love dies young.

I call him happiest, Parmeno, who watched ungrieving these magnificent things — the sun, common [to all], the stars, water, clouds, fire — and then departed to the land whence he came. You will always see the same things before you, whether you live for one hundred years or for a very few years; more magnificent things than these you will never see. Look on the span of time of which I speak as a festival or a visit to a foreign land in which there are crowds, and buying and selling, thieving, dice-playing and amusements. If you leave your place of lodging early you will have left better provided, nobody's enemy. But the man who prolongs his stay gets weary, loses his fare, and, coming

κακῶς τε γηρῶν ἐνδεής του γίνεται,
ρεμβόμενος ἐχθροὺς ηὗρ', ἐπεβουλεύθη ποθέν,
οὐκ εὐθανάτως ἀπῆλθεν ἐλθὼν εἰς χρόνον.

(*The Supposititious Baby*)

140. Vanitas Vanitatum

Ὅταν εἰδέναι θέλῃς σεαυτὸν ὅστις εἶ,
ἔμβλεψον εἰς τὰ μνήμαθ' ὡς ὁδοιπορεῖς.
ἐνταῦθ' ἔνεστ' ὀστᾶ τε καὶ κούφη κόνις
ἀνδρῶν βασιλέων καὶ τυράννων καὶ σοφῶν
καὶ μέγα φρονούντων ἐπὶ γένει καὶ χρήμασιν
αὐτῶν τε δόξῃ κἀπὶ κάλλει σωμάτων.
κᾆτ' οὐδὲν αὐτοῖς τῶνδ' ἐπήρκεσεν χρόνον.
κοινὸν τὸν Ἅιδην ἔσχον οἱ πάντες βροτοί.
πρὸς ταῦθ' ὁρῶν γίνωσκε σαυτὸν ὅστις εἶ.

141. All that Injures Lies Within

Μειράκιον, οὔ μοι κατανοεῖν δοκεῖς ὅτι
ὑπὸ τῆς ἰδίας ἕκαστα κακίας σήπεται,
καὶ πᾶν τὸ λυμαινόμενόν ἐστιν ἔνδοθεν.
οἷον ὁ μὲν ἰός, ἂν σκοπῇς, τὸ σιδήριον,

to an ugly old age, is always lacking something; roaming about, he
finds enemies who plot against him; and, when the time comes, he
leaves with no easy death.

WHEN you want to find out who you are, look at the tombs as you
walk along. Inside them are the bones and fine dust of men, who were
kings and tyrants, wise men, and men proud of their [noble] descent,
of their wealth, of their glory, and of the beauty of their bodies. And
then, afterwards, not one of these things protected them against time.
All mortals come to the same death. Look at these and learn what you
are yourself.

MY boy, you do not seem to understand that all things that decay do so
because of their own corruption, and all that destroys lies within. Thus
rust, if you look, destroys the iron, moths the [woollen] cloak, and

τὸ δ' ἱμάτιον οἱ σῆτες, ὁ δὲ θρὶψ τὸ ξύλον.
ὃ δὲ τὸ κάκιστον τῶν κακῶν πάντων, φθόνος
φθισικὸν πεπόηκε καὶ ποήσει καὶ ποεῖ,
ψυχῆς πονηρᾶς δυσσεβῆς παράστασις.

142. Poverty

Τὸ κουφότατον σε τῶν κακῶν πάντων δάκνει,
πενία. τί γὰρ τοῦτ' ἔστιν; ἧς γένοιτ' ἂν εἷς
φίλος βοηθήσας ἰατρὸς ῥαδίως.

CLEANTHES
331–232 B.C.

143. Hymn to Zeus

Κύδιστ' ἀθανάτων, πολυώνυμε παγκρατὲς αἰεί,
Ζεῦ φύσεως ἀρχηγέ, νόμου μετὰ πάντα κυβερνῶν,
χαῖρε· σὲ γὰρ καὶ πᾶσι θέμις θνητοῖσι προσαυδᾶν.
ἐκ σοῦ γὰρ γενόμεσθα, θεοῦ μίμημα λαχόντες

worm the wood. But the worst of all evils is envy, the godless companion of the evil soul, and this has consumed you, it consumes you now, and will continue to do so.

THE lightest of all evils gnaws at you — poverty. For what is it? It is an ill for which a single friend's help would be the easy cure.

HAIL, O Zeus, most glorious of the immortals, named by many names, forever all-powerful, leader of nature, you who govern the universe with laws; for it is proper that all mortals should call upon you. For from you we are born; of all the mortal things that live and move upon

μοῦνοι, ὅσα ζώει τε καὶ ἕρπει θνήτ' ἐπὶ γαῖαν·
τῷ σε καθυμνήσω, καὶ σὸν κράτος αἰὲν ἀείσω.
σοὶ δὴ πᾶς ὅδε κόσμος ἑλισσόμενος περὶ γαῖαν
πείθεται ᾗ κεν ἄγῃς, καὶ ἑκὼν ὑπὸ σεῖο κρατεῖται·
τοῖον ἔχεις ὑποεργὸν ἀνικήτοις ἐνὶ χερσὶν
ἀμφήκη πυρόεντ' αἰεζώοντα κεραυνόν·
τοῦ γὰρ ὑπὸ πληγῆς φύσεως πάντ' ἔργα βέβηκεν,
ᾧ σὺ κατευθύνεις κοινὸν λόγον, ὃς διὰ πάντων
φοιτᾷ μιγνύμενος μεγάλῳ μικροῖς τε φάεσσιν.
οὐδέ τι γίγνεται ἔργον ἐπὶ χθονὶ σοῦ δίχα, δαῖμον,
οὔτε κατ' αἰθέριον θεῖον πόλον, οὔτ' ἐνὶ πόντῳ,
πλὴν ὁπόσα ῥέζουσι κακοὶ σφετέραισιν ἀνοίαις.
ἀλλὰ σὺ καὶ τὰ περισσὰ ἐπίστασαι ἄρτια θεῖναι,
καὶ κοσμεῖν τἄκοσμα, καὶ οὐ φίλα σοὶ φίλα ἐστίν.
ὧδε γὰρ εἰς ἓν πάντα συνήρμοκας ἐσθλὰ κακοῖσιν,
ὥσθ' ἕνα γίγνεσθαι πάντων λόγον αἰὲν ἐόντα,
ὃν φεύγοντες ἐῶσιν ὅσοι θνητῶν κακοί εἰσιν,
δύσμοροι, οἵ τ' ἀγαθῶν μὲν ἀεὶ κτῆσιν ποθέοντες
οὔτ' ἐσορῶσι θεοῦ κοινὸν νόμον οὔτε κλύουσιν,
ᾧ κεν πειθόμενοι σὺν νῷ βίον ἐσθλὸν ἔχοιεν·
αὐτοὶ δ' αὖθ' ὁρμῶσιν ἄνοι κακὸν ἄλλος ἐπ' ἄλλο,

the earth the only ones created in god's image. So I will praise you, and always sing of your power. The entire universe which moves round the earth follows where you lead it, and is willingly mastered by you. So powerful is the servant you hold in your unconquerable hands; the two-edged, flaming, eternal thunderbolt. For all the works of creation pass under its strokes [of lightning]; through it you direct the common Word, which moves through all things and mingles with the great star [the sun] and the small stars. Nothing is done in the world without you, god, neither in the holy air of the sky, nor in the sea, except for what the evil do in their folly. But you know how to make extraordinary things normal, and to make order out of chaos; you love even unlovely things. In this way you have joined everything into one, the evil and the good, so that the eternal Word becomes one, which those who are evil among mortals avoid and abandon. Poor wretches, who always desire to acquire riches, but do not see, nor hear, the common law of the god; yet if they were sensible and obeyed it, they would have a noble life. But they senselessly hurry after all kinds of evil – some

οἳ μὲν ὑπὲρ δόξης σπουδὴν δυσέριστον ἔχοντες,
οἳ δ' ἐπὶ κερδοσύνας τετραμμένοι οὐδενὶ κόσμῳ
ἄλλοι δ' εἰς ἄνεσιν καὶ σώματος ἡδέα ἔργα
ὧδ' ἀνόητ' ἔρδουσιν ἐπ' ἄλλοτε δ' ἄλλα φέρονται,
σπεύδοντες μάλα πάμπαν ἐναντία τῶνδε γενέσθαι.
ἀλλὰ Ζεῦ πάνδωρε κελαινεφὲς ἀργικέραυνε,
ἀνθρώπους ῥύου μὲν ἀπειροσύνης ἀπὸ λυγρῆς,
ἣν σύ, πάτερ, σκέδασον ψυχῆς ἄπο, δὸς δὲ κυρῆσαι
γνώμης, ᾗ πίσυνος σὺ δίκης μέτα πάντα κυβερνᾷς,
ὄφρ' ἂν τιμηθέντες ἀμειβώμεσθά σε τιμῇ,
ὑμνοῦντες τὰ σὰ ἔργα διηνεκές, ὡς ἐπέοικε
θνητὸν ἐόντ', ἐπεὶ οὔτε βροτοῖς γέρας ἄλλο τι μεῖζον
οὔτε θεοῖς, ἢ κοινὸν ἀεὶ νόμον ἐν δίκῃ ὑμνεῖν.

rushing in the hard race for fame, others chaotically set on making money, and others on the ease and the pleasures of the body; they do these foolish things, and rush to and fro, altogether hastening the defeat of these ends. But, O Zeus, giver of all, shrouded in dark clouds, master of the bright thunderbolt, save men from painful ignorance. Scatter it, Father, from their hearts, and grant that they may find wisdom, that wisdom in which you trust and so rule everything with justice; so that, honoured thus, we may pay you back with honour, always celebrating your works, as is proper for mortals; for there is no greater prize for men and gods than justly to praise the common law.

ANYTE

fl. 300 B.C.

144. The Goat

Ἡνία δή τοι παῖδες ἐνί, τράγε, φοινικόεντα
θέντες καὶ λασίῳ φιμὰ περὶ στόματι,
ἵππια παιδεύουσι θεοῦ περὶ ναὸν ἄεθλα,
ὄφρ' αὐτοὺς ἐφορῇ νήπια τερπομένους.

145. Myro's Pets

Ἀκρίδι τᾷ κατ' ἄρουραν ἀηδόνι, καὶ δρυοκοίτᾳ
τέττιγι ξυνὸν τύμβον ἔτευξε Μυρώ,
παρθένιον στάξασα κόρα δάκρυ· δισσὰ γὰρ αὐτᾶς
παίγνι' ὁ δυσπειθὴς ᾤχετ' ἔχων Ἀΐδας.

146. The Tomb of Damis' Horse

Μνᾶμα τόδε φθιμένου μενεδαΐου εἴσατο Δᾶμις
ἵππου, ἐπεὶ στέρνον τοῦδε δαφοινὸς Ἄρης
τύψε· μέλαν δέ οἱ αἷμα ταλαυρίνου διὰ χρωτὸς
ζέσσ', ἐπὶ δ' ἀργαλέᾳ βῶλον ἔδευσε φονᾷ.

THE children put purple reins on you, billy-goat, and a muzzle on
your bearded face, and train you to run like a racehorse round the
temple of the god that he may see them happy in their childish games.

FOR her cricket, the nightingale of the fields, and for her cicada
that lived in the trees, Myro made one grave, shedding the tears of a
young girl; for inexorable Hades had borne away both her pets.

DAMIS built this tomb for his brave war-horse, when bloody Ares
pierced it through the breast. The black blood bubbled through its
thick hide, and drenched the earth at its painful death.

THEOCRITUS

c. 316–c. 260 B.C.

147. The Cup

ΑΙΠΟΛΟΣ

Τῶ ποτὶ μὲν χείλη μαρύεται ὑψόθι κισσός,
κισσὸς ἑλιχρύσῳ κεκονιμένος· ἁ δὲ κατ' αὐτὸν
καρπῷ ἕλιξ εἱλεῖται ἀγαλλομένα κροκόεντι.
ἔντοσθεν δὲ γυνά τι θεῶν δαίδαλμα τέτυκται,
ἀσκητὰ πέπλῳ τε καὶ ἄμπυκι· πὰρ δέ οἱ ἄνδρες
καλὸν ἐθειράζοντες ἀμοιβαδὶς ἄλλοθεν ἄλλος
νεικείουσ' ἐπέεσσι. τὰ δ' οὐ φρενὸς ἅπτεται αὐτᾶς·
ἀλλ' ὅκα μὲν τῆνον ποτιδέρκεται ἄνδρα γέλαισα,
ἄλλοκα δ' αὖ ποτὶ τὸν ῥιπτεῖ νόον. οἱ δ' ὑπ' ἔρωτος
δηθὰ κυλοιδιόωντες ἐτώσια μοχθίζοντι.
τοῖς δὲ μέτα γριπεύς τε γέρων πέτρα τε τέτυκται
λεπράς, ἐφ' ᾇ σπεύδων μέγα δίκτυον ἐς βόλον ἕλκει
ὁ πρέσβυς, κάμνοντι τὸ καρτερὸν ἀνδρὶ ἐοικώς.
φαίης κα γυίων νιν ὅσον σθένος ἐλλοπιεύειν·
ὧδέ οἱ ᾠδήκαντι κατ' αὐχένα πάντοθεν ἶνες
καὶ πολιῷ περ ἐόντι, τὸ δὲ σθένος ἄξιον ἅβας.
τυτθὸν δ' ὅσσον ἄπωθεν ἁλιτρύτοιο γέροντος
πυρραίαις σταφυλαῖσι καλὸν βέβριθεν ἁλωά,

GOATHERD: Above, around the lips [of the cup], winds ivy, ivy dotted with golden berries, and along it winds the tendril delighting in its saffron fruit. And within is fashioned a woman, such as the gods might fashion, adorned with cloak and circlet. And, from either side of her, two men with beautiful long hair are quarrelling, speaking in turn. Yet these things do not touch her heart, but she glances for a time at the one and smiles, and then she shifts her thoughts to the other; while they, hollow-eyed from passionate longing, struggle in vain. Beside these, there is carved an old fisherman, and a rugged rock, on which the old man is eagerly gathering up a great net for a cast, like a man straining hard. You would say that he was fishing with all the strength of his limbs, the sinews down his neck stand out so much, grey-haired though he is; he has a young man's strength. And a little way from the sea-worn old man, there is a vineyard with a beautiful crop of blushing

τὰν ὀλίγος τις κῶρός ἐφ' αἱμασιαῖσι φυλάσσει
ἥμενος· ἀμφὶ δέ νιν δύ' ἀλώπεκες ἃ μὲν ἀν' ὄρχως
φοιτῇ σινομένα τὰν τρώξιμον, ἃ δ' ἐπὶ πήρᾳ
πάντα δόλον τεύχοισα τὸ παιδίον οὐ πρὶν ἀνησεῖν
φατὶ πρὶν ἢ ἀκράτιστον ἐπὶ ξηροῖσι καθίξῃ.
αὐτὰρ ὅγ' ἀνθερίκοισι καλὰν πλέκει ἀκριδοθήραν
σχοίνῳ ἐφαρμόσδων· μέλεται δέ οἱ οὔτε τι πήρας
οὔτε φυτῶν τοσσῆνον, ὅσον περὶ πλέγματι γαθεῖ.
παντᾷ δ' ἀμφὶ δέπας περιπέπταται ὑγρὸς ἄκανθος.
αἰπολικὸν θάημα· τέρας κέ τυ θυμὸν ἀτύξαι.

(*Idyll I*)

148. The Death of Daphnis

ΘΥΡΣΙΣ

‹Ὦ Πάν Πάν, εἴτ' ἐσσὶ κατ' ὤρεα μακρὰ Λυκαίω,
εἴτε τύγ' ἀμφιπολεῖς μέγα Μαίναλον, ἔνθ' ἐπὶ νᾶσον
τὰν Σικελάν, Ἑλίκας δὲ λίπε ῥίον αἰπύ τε σᾶμα
τῆνο Λυκαονίδαο, τὸ καὶ μακάρεσσιν ἀγητόν.›

grapes, which a little boy, who sits on a dry-stone wall, guards. About him are two foxes, and one goes in and out among the vine-rows, plundering the eating-grapes, while the other uses all her cunning to get hold of [the boy's] wallet, and vows she will not let the boy alone until she has wrecked [deprived him of] his breakfast. But the lad is plaiting a pretty cricket-cage by joining rushes and asphodel, and is more delighted with his plaiting than worried about the vines or the wallet. And all about the cup the flowing acanthus spreads. It is a wonderful thing to a goatherd's eyes, a marvel that would amaze your heart.

THYRSIS: 'Pan, Pan, whether you are on the high hills of Lycaeus, or keeping watch on great Maenalus, come to the island of Sicily, and leave the mountain-peak of Helice, and that sheer tomb of Lycaon's son, in which even the Blessed Ones delight.'

λήγετε βουκολικᾶς Μοῖσαι, ἴτε λήγετ' ἀοιδᾶς.
‹ἔνθ', ὦναξ, καὶ τάνδε φέρευ πακτοῖο μελίπνουν
ἐκ κηρῶ σύριγγα καλὸν περὶ χεῖλος ἑλικτάν·
ἦ γὰρ ἐγὼν ὑπ' ἔρωτος ἐς Ἄιδαν ἕλκομαι ἤδη.›
λήγετε βουκολικᾶς Μοῖσαι, ἴτε λήγετ' ἀοιδᾶς.
‹νῦν ἴα μὲν φορέοιτε βάτοι, φορέοιτε δ' ἄκανθαι,
ἀ δὲ καλὰ νάρκισσος ἐπ' ἀρκεύθοισι κομάσαι·
πάντα δ' ἄναλλα γένοιτο, καὶ ἀ πίτυς ὄχνας ἐνείκαι,
Δάφνις ἐπεὶ θνάσκει, καὶ τὰς κύνας ὤλαφος ἕλκοι,
κἠξ ὀρέων τοὶ σκῶπες ἀηδόσι γαρύσαιντο.›
λήγετε βουκολικᾶς Μοῖσαι, ἴτε λήγετ' ἀοιδᾶς.
χὠ μὲν τόσσ' εἰπὼν ἀπεπαύσατο· τὸν δ' Ἀφροδίτα
ἤθελ' ἀνορθῶσαι· τά γε μὰν λίνα πάντα λελοίπει
ἐκ Μοιρᾶν, χὠ Δάφνις ἔβα ῥόον. ἔκλυσε δίνα
τὸν Μοίσαις φίλον ἄνδρα, τὸν οὐ Νύμφαισιν ἀπεχθῆ.
λήγετε βουκολικᾶς Μοῖσαι, ἴτε λήγετ' ἀοιδᾶς.

(Idyll I)

Cease, Muses, come, cease the pastoral song.
'Come, my Lord [Pan], and take this pipe, honey-scented from its thick wax, with binding about its beautiful lip, for now I am truly dragged to Hades by Love.'
Cease, Muses, come, cease the pastoral song.
'Now, brambles, may you bear violets, and you, thorns, may you bear violets, and may the beautiful narcissus blossom on the juniper. May all be changed, and may the pine bear pears, since Daphnis is dying. May the stag tear at the hounds, and may the owls from the mountains compete with the nightingales.'
Cease, Muses, come, cease the pastoral song.
So much he [Daphnis] said, and ended; and Aphrodite wished to raise him again, but all the thread of the Fates was run, and Daphnis departed into the stream [of Acheron]. The waters closed over the man whom the Muses loved, whom the Nymphs did not despise.
Cease, Muses, come, cease the pastoral song.

149. Simaetha

ΣΙΜΑΙΘΑ

Νῦν δὴ μῶνα ἐοῖσα πόθεν τὸν ἔρωτα δακρύσω;
ἐκ τίνος ἄρξωμαι; τίς μοι κακὸν ἄγαγε τοῦτο;
ἦνθ' ἁ τωὐβούλοιο καναφόρος ἄμμιν Ἀναξὼ
ἄλσος ἐς Ἀρτέμιδος, τᾷ δὴ τόκα πολλὰ μὲν ἄλλα
θηρία πομπεύεσκε περισταδόν, ἐν δὲ λέαινα.

    φράζεό μευ τὸν ἔρωθ' ὅθεν ἵκετο, πότνα Σελάνα.

καί μ' ἁ Θευμαρίδα Θρᾷσσα τροφός, ἁ μακαρῖτις,
ἀγχίθυρος ναίοισα κατεύξατο καὶ λιτάνευσε
τὰν πομπὰν θάσασθαι· ἐγὼ δέ οἱ ἁ μεγάλοιτος
ὡμάρτευν βύσσοιο καλὸν σύροισα χιτῶνα
κἀμφιστειλαμένα τὰν ξυστίδα τὰν Κλεαρίστας.

    φράζεό μευ τὸν ἔρωθ' ὅθεν ἵκετο, πότνα Σελάνα.

ἤδη δ' εὖσα μέσαν κατ' ἀμαξιτόν, ᾇ τὰ Λύκωνος,
εἶδον Δέλφιν ὁμοῦ τε καὶ Εὐδάμιππον ἰόντας·
τοῖς δ' ἦς ξανθοτέρα μὲν ἑλιχρύσοιο γενειάς,
στήθεα δὲ στίλβοντα πολὺ πλέον ἢ τύ, Σελάνα,
ὡς ἀπὸ γυμνασίοιο καλὸν πόνον ἄρτι λιπόντων.

    φράζεό μευ τὸν ἔρωθ' ὅθεν ἵκετο, πότνα Σελάνα.

SIMAETHA: Now that I am alone, where shall I start to lament my love?
Where shall I begin? Who brought this evil upon me? Eubulus'
daughter, our Anaxo, went as basket-bearer to the grove of Artemis,
and that day many (other) wild beasts paraded round in honour of the
goddess, and among them a lioness.
    Consider, Lady Moon, whence came my love.
    And Theumaridas' Thracian nurse, now dead, who lived next
door, had begged and entreated me to come and see the pageant. And
I, unhappy wretch, went with her, wearing a lovely long linen dress,
and Clearista's fine cloak over it.
    Consider, Lady Moon, whence came my love.
    And when I was already halfway along the road to where Lycon's
is, I saw Delphis and Eudamippus walking together. Fairer than heli-
chryse were their beards, and their chests shone far brighter than you,
Moon, for they had just left the manly toil of the wrestling-school.
    Consider, Lady Moon, whence came my love.

χὼς ἴδον ὡς ἐμάνην, ὥς μοι πυρὶ θυμὸς ἰάφθη
δειλαίας, τὸ δὲ κάλλος ἐτάκετο. οὐκέτι πομπᾶς
τήνας ἐφρασάμαν, οὐδ' ὡς πάλιν οἴκαδ' ἀπῆνθον
ἔγνων, ἀλλά μέ τις καπυρὰ νόσος ἐξεσάλαξεν
κείμαν δ' ἐν κλιντῆρι δέκ' ἄματα καὶ δέκα νύκτας.

    φράζεό μευ τὸν ἔρωθ' ὅθεν ἵκετο, πότνα Σελάνα.

καί μευ χρὼς μὲν ὁμοῖος ἐγίνετο πολλάκι θάψῳ,
ἔρρευν δ' ἐκ κεφαλᾶς πᾶσαι τρίχες, αὐτὰ δὲ λοιπὰ
ὀστί' ἔτ' ἦς καὶ δέρμα. καὶ ἐς τίνος οὐκ ἐπέρασα
ἢ ποίας ἔλιπον γραίας δόμον ἅτις ἐπᾷδεν;
ἀλλ' ἦς οὐδὲν ἐλαφρόν, ὁ δὲ χρόνος ἄνυτο φεύγων.

    φράζεό μευ τὸν ἔρωθ' ὅθεν ἵκετο, πότνα Σελάνα.

χοὖτω τᾷ δώλᾳ τὸν ἀλαθέα μῦθον ἔλεξα·
‹εἰ δ' ἄγε, Θεστυλί, μοι χαλεπᾶς νόσω εὑρέ τι μᾶχος.
πᾶσαν ἔχει με τάλαιναν ὁ Μύνδιος· ἀλλὰ μολοῖσα
τήρησον ποτὶ τὰν Τιμαγήτοιο παλαίστραν·
τηνεὶ γὰρ φοιτῇ, τηνεὶ δέ οἱ ἀδὺ καθῆσθαι.›

    φράζεό μευ τὸν ἔρωθ' ὅθεν ἵκετο, πότνα Σελάνα.

‹κἠπεί κά νιν ἐόντα μάθῃς μόνον, ἄσυχα νεῦσον,
κεῖφ' ὅτι «Σιμαίθα τυ καλεῖ,» καὶ ὑφαγέο τεῖδε.›

As I saw, madness seized me, and my poor heart was on fire. My looks faded away, and I thought no more of that pageant, nor do I know how I came home again; but a parching sickness shook me, and I lay on my bed for ten days and ten nights.

Consider, Lady Moon, whence came my love.

And often my skin would turn as pale as fustic; all my hair was falling from my head, and all that was left of me was bones and skin. And to whose house did I not go – what hag's home did I pass by – of those that had skill in charms? But it was no light matter, and time was flying on.

Consider, Lady Moon, whence came my love.

And so I told my maid the real story. 'Come, Thestylis, find me some cure for this harsh sickness. The Myndian [Delphis] possesses me completely, unhappy that I am. But go, and keep watch by Timagetus' wrestling-school, for he goes there often, and likes to sit there.'

Consider, Lady Moon, whence came my love.

'And when you are sure that he is alone, signal to him secretly, and say: "Simaetha asks you to come," and lead him here.' So I spoke.

ὡς ἔφαμαν· ἃ δ' ἦνθε καὶ ἄγαγε τὸν λιπαρόχρων
εἰς ἐμὰ δώματα Δέλφιν· ἐγὼ δέ νιν ὡς ἐνόησα
ἄρτι θύρας ὑπὲρ οὐδὸν ἀμειβόμενον ποδὶ κούφῳ—

    φράζεό μευ τὸν ἔρωθ' ὅθεν ἵκετο, πότνα Σελάνα—
πᾶσα μὲν ἐψύχθην χιόνος πλέον, ἐκ δὲ μετώπω
ἱδρώς μευ κοχύδεσκεν ἴσον νοτίαισιν ἐέρσαις,
οὐδέ τι φωνῆσαι δυνάμαν, οὐδ' ὅσσον ἐν ὕπνῳ
κνυζεῦνται φωνεῦντα φίλαν ποτὶ ματέρα τέκνα·
ἀλλ' ἐπάγην δαγῦδι καλὸν χρόα πάντοθεν ἴσα.

    φράζεό μευ τὸν ἔρωθ' ὅθεν ἵκετο, πότνα Σελάνα.
καί μ' ἐσιδὼν ὥστοργος ἐπὶ χθονὸς ὄμματα πάξας
ἕζετ' ἐπὶ κλιντῆρι καὶ ἑζόμενος φάτο μῦθον·
‹ἦ ῥά με, Σιμαίθα, τόσον ἔφθασας, ὅσσον ἐγώ θην
πρᾶν ποκα τὸν χαρίεντα τράχων ἔφθασσα Φιλῖνον,
ἐς τὸ τεὸν καλέσασα τόδε στέγος ἢ 'μὲ παρῆμεν.›

    φράζεό μευ τὸν ἔρωθ' ὅθεν ἵκετο, πότνα Σελάνα.
‹ἦνθον γάρ κεν ἐγώ, ναὶ τὸν γλυκὺν ἦνθον Ἔρωτα,
ἢ τρίτος ἠὲ τέταρτος ἐὼν φίλος αὐτίκα νυκτός,
μᾶλα μὲν ἐν κόλποισι Διωνύσοιο φυλάσσων,
κρατὶ δ' ἔχων λεύκαν, Ἡρακλέος ἱερὸν ἔρνος,

And she went, and brought the sleek-skinned Delphis to my house,
and I, as soon as I knew he was stepping light-footed over the
threshold of my door –

Consider, Lady Moon, whence came my love.

I turned colder than snow from head to foot, the sweat rolled from
my brow like damp dew and I could not speak a word – not as much
as children whimper in their sleep as they call to their dear mother; but
all my beautiful body grew stiff like a wax doll's.

Consider, Lady Moon, whence came my love.

And when he glanced at me, the cruel one fixed his eyes on the
ground, and sat down upon the couch and, sitting there, said: 'Truly,
Simaetha, by inviting me to your house, you have out-distanced my
coming by no more than I recently out-distanced graceful Philinus in
the race.'

Consider, Lady Moon, whence came my love.

'For I would have come, by sweet Love I would, as soon as it got
dark, with two friends, or with three, carrying in my bosom apples of

πάντοθι πορφυρέαισι περὶ ζώστραισιν ἑλικτάν.›
φράζεό μευ τὸν ἔρωθ' ὅθεν ἵκετο, πότνα Σελάνα.
‹καί κ', εἰ μέν μ' ἐδέχεσθε, τάδ' ἦς φίλα (καὶ γὰρ ἐλαφρὸς
καὶ καλὸς πάντεσσι μετ' ἀιθέοισι καλεῦμαι)
εὗδόν τ', εἰ μῶνον τὸ καλὸν στόμα τεῦς ἐφίλησα·
εἰ δ' ἄλλα μ' ὠθεῖτε καὶ ἁ θύρα εἴχετο μοχλῷ,
πάντως κα πελέκεις καὶ λαμπάδες ἦνθον ἐφ' ὑμέας.›
φράζεό μευ τὸν ἔρωθ' ὅθεν ἵκετο, πότνα Σελάνα.
‹νῦν δὲ χάριν μὲν ἔφαν τᾷ Κύπριδι πρᾶτον ὀφείλειν,
καὶ μετὰ τὰν Κύπριν τύ με δευτέρα ἐκ πυρὸς εἵλευ,
ὦ γύναι, ἐσκαλέσασα τεὸν ποτὶ τοῦτο μέλαθρον
αὔτως ἡμίφλεκτον· Ἔρως δ' ἄρα καὶ Λιπαραίω
πολλάκις Ἀφαίστοιο σέλας φλογερώτερον αἴθει.›
φράζεό μευ τὸν ἔρωθ' ὅθεν ἵκετο, πότνα Σελάνα,
‹σὺν δὲ κακαῖς μανίαις καὶ παρθένον ἐκ θαλάμοιο
καὶ νύμφαν ἐφόβησ' ἔτι δέμνια θερμὰ λιποῖσαν
ἀνέρος.› ὣς ὁ μὲν εἶπεν· ἐγὼ δέ οἱ ἁ ταχυπειθὴς
χειρὸς ἐφαψαμένα μαλακῶν ἔκλιν' ἐπὶ λέκτρων·
καὶ ταχὺ χρὼς ἐπὶ χρωτὶ πεπαίνετο, καὶ τὰ πρόσωπα
θερμότερ' ἦς ἢ πρόσθε, καὶ ἐψιθυρίσδομες ἁδύ.

Dionysus, and on my head white poplar, the holy plant of Heracles, twined all around with crimson bands.'

Consider, Lady Moon, whence came my love.

'And if you had received me that would have been pleasant, for I am called nimble and fair among all the young men. And, if I had only kissed your beautiful mouth, I should have slept. But, had you tried to push me out of this house and had the door been barred, assuredly axes and torches would have come against you.'

Consider, Lady Moon, whence came my love.

'But as it is, my thanks are due first to Cypris, I say, and after her to you, lady, who saved me from the flame half-burnt, by summoning me to this house of yours; for truly Love often kindles a blaze hotter than Hephaestus on Lipara.'

Consider, Lady Moon, whence came my love.

'And with terrible madness he scares a girl from her room, and makes a bride leave her husband's bed while it is still warm.' So he spoke; and I, always too easily won over, took him by the hand, and drew him down upon the soft couch. And quickly skin warmed to skin, and our faces burned hotter than before, and we whispered sweetly. And, to

χὤς ἄρα τοι μὴ μακρὰ φίλα θρυλέοιμι Σελάνα,
ἐπράχθη τὰ μέγιστα, καὶ ἐς πόθον ἤνθομες ἄμφω.
κοὔτε τι τῆνος ἐμὶν ἀπεμέμψατο μέσφα τό γ' ἐχθές,
οὔτ' ἐγὼ αὖ τήνῳ. ἀλλ' ἦνθέ μοι ἅ τε Φιλίστας
μάτηρ τᾶς ἁμᾶς αὐλητρίδος ἅ τε Μελιξοῦς
σάμερον, ἁνίκα πέρ τε ποτ' ὠρανὸν ἔτραχον ἵπποι
'Αῶ τὰν ῥοδόεσσαν ἀπ' ὠκεανοῖο φέροισαι,
κεῖπέ μοι ἄλλα τε πολλὰ καὶ ὡς ἄρα Δέλφις ἔραται.
κεῖτε νιν αὖτε γυναικὸς ἔχει πόθος εἴτε καὶ ἀνδρός,
οὐκ ἔφατ' ἀτρεκὲς ἴδμεν, ἀτὰρ τόσον· αἰὲν Ἔρωτος
ἀκράτω ἐπεχεῖτο καὶ ἐς τέλος ᾤχετο φεύγων,
καὶ φάτο οἱ στεφάνοισι τὰ δώματα τῆνα πυκαξεῖν.
ταῦτά μοι ἁ ξείνα μυθήσατο, ἔστι δ' ἀλαθής.
ἦ γάρ μοι καὶ τρὶς καὶ τετράκις ἄλλοκ' ἐφοίτη,
καὶ παρ' ἐμὶν ἐτίθει τὰν Δωρίδα πολλάκις ὄλπαν·
νῦν δὲ τί; δωδεκαταῖος ἀφ' ὧτέ νιν οὐδὲ ποτεῖδον.
ἦ ῥ' οὐκ ἄλλο τι τερπνὸν ἔχει, ἁμῶν δὲ λέλασται;
νῦν μὰν τοῖς φίλτροις καταδήσομαι· αἱ δ' ἔτι κά με
λυπῇ, τὰν 'Αΐδαο πύλαν, ναὶ Μοίρας, ἀραξεῖ.
τοῖά οἱ ἐν κίστᾳ κακὰ φάρμακα φαμὶ φυλάσσειν,
'Ασσυρίω, δέσποινα, παρὰ ξείνοιο μαθοῖσα.

cut short my prattling, dear Moon, the ultimate was accomplished, and
we both attained our desire. And he did not find any fault with me till
yesterday, nor I with him. But today, when the horses of rosy
Dawn were bringing her swiftly from the Ocean to the sky, the mother
of Philista our flute-player, and of Melixo, came to me; and she told me
many other things, and also that Delphis was in love. She did not say
for certain if it was a woman he desired or a man; but only this, that
he was constantly toasting Love with unmixed wine, and that in the
end he went off in a hurry and said he would wreathe that house with
garlands. Such was the story my guest told me, and she is no liar. For,
truly, before, he would come to me three and four times a day, and
often he would leave his Dorian oil-flask with me. But now what?
Eleven days have passed since I have even seen him. Must he not have
some other delight, and have forgotten me? Now with my love-magic
I will bind him fast; but if he still vexes me, by the Fates, he shall beat
upon the gate of Hades; such evil drugs, I vow, I keep for him in my
box — practices I learned, Lady, from an Assyrian stranger. But

ἀλλὰ τὺ μὲν χαίροισα ποτ' ὠκεανὸν τρέπε πώλως,
πότνι'· ἐγὼ δ' οἰσῶ τὸν ἐμὸν πόθον ὥσπερ ὑπέσταν.
χαῖρε Σελαναία λιπαρόθρονε, χαίρετε δ' ἄλλοι
ἀστέρες, εὐκάλοιο κατ' ἄντυγα Νυκτὸς ὀπαδοί.

(*Idyll II*)

150. Harvest-time in Cos

Ἧς χρόνος ἁνίκ' ἐγώ τε καὶ Εὔκριτος εἰς τὸν Ἄλεντα
εἵρπομες ἐκ πόλιος, σὺν καὶ τρίτος ἄμμιν Ἀμύντας.
τᾷ Δηοῖ γὰρ ἔτευχε θαλύσια καὶ Φρασίδαμος
κ'Ἀντιγένης, δύο τέκνα Λυκωπέος, εἴ τί περ ἐσθλὸν
χαῶν τῶν ἐπάνωθεν· ἀπὸ Κλυτίας τε καὶ αὐτῶ
Χάλκωνος, Βούριναν ὃς ἐκ ποδὸς ἄνυε κράναν
εὖ ἐνερεισάμενος πέτρᾳ γόνυ· ταὶ δὲ παρ' αὐτὰν
αἴγειροι πτελέαι τε εὔσκιον ἄλσος ὕφαινον
χλωροῖσιν πετάλοισι κατηρεφέες κομόωσαι.
κοὔπω τὰν μεσάταν ὁδὸν ἄνυμες, οὐδὲ τὸ σᾶμα
ἁμῖν τὸ Βρασίλα κατεφαίνετο, καί τιν' ὁδίταν
ἐσθλὸν σὺν Μοίσαισι Κυδωνικὸν εὕρομες ἄνδρα,

farewell Lady, and turn your horses to the Ocean. And I will bear my
longing as I have endured it till now. Farewell, Moon, on your
gleaming throne, and farewell you other stars that follow the chariot
of quiet Night.

THERE was a time when Eucritus and I [Simichidas] were going from
the town to the Haleis, and Amyntas made a third with us. For
Phrasidamus and Antigenes were making harvest-offerings to Deo —
the two sons of Lycopeus, noble, if any, among men of noble blood,
being descended from Clytia and Chalcon himself, the man who
pressed his knee firmly against the rock and made the spring Burina
flow under his foot; and beside it [the spring] poplars and elms wove a
shady sacred grove with green foliage arched thickly above. And we
had not yet gone half the way, and could not see the tomb of Brasilas,
when by the Muses' grace we met a traveller, a good man of Cydonia.

οὔνομα μὲν Λυκίδαν, ἦς δ᾽ αἰπόλος, οὐδέ κέ τίς νιν
ἠγνοίησεν ἰδών ἐπεὶ αἰπόλῳ ἔξοχ᾽ ἐῴκει.
ἐκ μὲν γὰρ λασίοιο δασύτριχος εἶχε τράγοιο
κνακὸν δέρμ᾽ ὤμοισι νέας ταμίσοιο ποτόσδον,
ἀμφὶ δέ οἱ στήθεσσι γέρων ἐσφίγγετο πέπλος
ζωστῆρι πλακερῷ, ῥοικὰν δ᾽ εἶχεν ἀγριελαίω
δεξιτερᾷ κορύναν. καί μ᾽ ἀτρέμας εἶπε σεσαρὼς
ὄμματι μειδιόωντι, γέλως δέ οἱ εἴχετο χείλευς·
‹Σιμιχίδα, πᾷ δὴ τὺ μεσαμέριον πόδας ἕλκεις,
ἁνίκα δὴ καὶ σαῦρος ἐν αἱμασιαῖσι καθεύδει,
οὐδ᾽ ἐπιτυμβίδιοι κορυδαλλίδες ἠλαίνοντι;
ἦ μετὰ δαῖτ᾽ ἄκλητος ἐπείγεαι, ἤ τινος ἀστῶν
λανὸν ἔπι θρῴσκεις; ὡς τοι ποσὶ νισσομένοιο
πᾶσα λίθος πταίοισα ποτ᾽ ἀρβυλίδεσσιν ἀείδει.›
τὸν δ᾽ ἐγὼ ἀμείφθην· ‹Λυκίδα φίλε, φαντί τυ πάντες
ἦμεν συρικτὰν μέγ᾽ ὑπείροχον ἔν τε νομεῦσιν
ἔν τ᾽ ἀματήρεσσι. τὸ δὴ μάλα θυμὸν ἰαίνει
ἀμέτερον· καίτοι κατ᾽ ἐμὸν νόον ἰσοφαρίζειν
ἔλπομαι. ἁ δ᾽ ὁδὸς ἅδε θαλυσιάς· ἦ γὰρ ἑταῖροι
ἀνέρες εὐπέπλῳ Δαμάτερι δαῖτα τελεῦντι
ὄλβω ἀπαρχόμενοι· μάλα γάρ σφισι πίονι μέτρῳ
ἁ δαίμων εὔκριθον ἀνεπλήρωσεν ἀλωάν.

His name was Lycidas and he was a goatherd; no one that saw him
could have mistaken him, for he looked exactly like a goatherd. On his
shoulders he had the tawny skin of a thick-haired, shaggy goat, reeking
of fresh rennet, and an old tunic was buckled round his chest with a
broad belt, and in his right hand he held a crooked club of wild olive.
With a quiet smile and a twinkle in his eye he spoke to me, and laughter
rested on his lips: 'Simichidas, where are you going on foot in the
middle of the day, when even the lizard sleeps in the walls, and the
tomb-haunting larks do not flit about? Are you hurrying to a banquet
to which you have not been invited, or rushing to some townsman's
winepress? For, as you go, all the pebbles spin singing off your shoes.'
And I answered: 'Friend Lycidas, all men say you are by far the best
piper among the herdsmen and the reapers, and this cheers my heart
greatly; and yet in my mind, I fancy myself your equal. This journey
is to a harvest festival, for friends of mine are celebrating a feast for
beautifully robed Demeter, giving the first fruits of their wealth; for in
fullest measure has the goddess piled their threshing-floor with barley.

ἀλλ' ἄγε δή, ξυνὰ γὰρ ὁδὸς ξυνὰ δὲ καὶ ἀώς,
βουκολιασδώμεσθα· τάχ' ὥτερος ἄλλον ὀνασεῖ.
καὶ γὰρ ἐγὼ Μοισᾶν καπυρὸν στόμα, κἠμὲ λέγοντι
πάντες ἀοιδὸν ἄριστον· ἐγὼ δέ τις οὐ ταχυπειθής,
οὐ Δᾶν· οὐ γάρ πω κατ' ἐμὸν νόον οὔτε τὸν ἐσθλὸν
Σικελίδαν νίκημι τὸν ἐκ Σάμω οὔτε Φιλίταν
ἀείδων, βάτραχος δὲ ποτ' ἀκρίδας ὥς τις ἐρίσδω.›
ὣς ἐφάμαν ἐπίταδες· ὁ δ' αἰπόλος ἁδὺ γελάσσας,
‹τάν τοι›, ἔφα, ‹κορύναν δωρύττομαι, οὕνεκεν ἐσσὶ
πᾶν ἐπ' ἀλαθείᾳ πεπλασμένον ἐκ Διὸς ἔρνος.
ὥς μοι καὶ τέκτων μέγ' ἀπέχθεται ὅστις ἐρευνῇ
ἶσον ὄρευς κορυφᾷ τελέσαι δόμον Ὠρομέδοντος,
καὶ Μοισᾶν ὄρνιχες ὅσοι ποτὶ Χῖον ἀοιδὸν
ἀντία κοκκύζοντες ἐτώσια μοχθίζοντι.
ἀλλ' ἄγε βουκολικᾶς ταχέως ἀρξώμεθ' ἀοιδᾶς,
Σιμιχίδα· κἠγὼ μέν — ὅρη, φίλος, εἴ τοι ἀρέσκει
τοῦθ' ὅτι πρᾶν ἐν ὄρει τὸ μελύδριον ἐξεπόνασα.

‹Ἔσσεται Ἀγεάνακτι καλὸς πλόος ἐς Μιτυλήναν,
χὥταν ἐφ' ἑσπερίοις Ἐρίφοις νότος ὑγρὰ διώκῃ
κύματα, χὠρίων ὅτ' ἐπ' ὠκεανῷ πόδας ἴσχει,
αἴ κα τὸν Λυκίδαν ὀπτεύμενον ἐξ Ἀφροδίτας

But come, the day and the journey are yours and mine to share; let us sing pastoral songs, and we shall perhaps give each other pleasure. For I too am a clear-sounding mouth for the Muses, and all call me too the best of singers; but I am not easily convinced – by Zeus no. For I do not believe that I can beat in song either the famous Sicelidas from Samos, or Philetas, but I compete with them like a frog against crickets.' So I spoke, cunningly; and with a sweet laugh the goatherd answered: 'I will give you my stick, for you are a sapling whom Zeus has shaped all for truth. I particularly hate a builder who tries to raise his house as high as the peak of mount Oromedon, and those cocks of the Muses, who waste their labour crowing against the singer of Chios. But come, let us begin our pastoral song quickly, Simichidas; as I shall – see, friend, if it pleases you, this little song I recently finished on the hill:

'Ageanax shall have a fair voyage to Mitylene, when the Haedi stand in the evening sky, and Notos [the south wind] chases the wet waves, and when Orion sets his feet upon the Ocean, if he saves Lycidas

ῥύσηται· θερμὸς γὰρ ἔρως αὐτῶ με καταίθει.
χάλκυόνες στορεσεῦντι τὰ κύματα τάν τε θάλασσαν
τόν τε νότον τόν τ' εὖρον, ὃς ἔσχατα φυκία κινεῖ,
ἀλκυόνες, γλαυκαῖς Νηρηίσι ταί τε μάλιστα
ὀρνίχων ἐφίληθεν, ὅσοις τέ περ ἐξ ἀλὸς ἄγρα.
Ἀγεάνακτι πλόον διζημένῳ ἐς Μιτυλήναν
ὥρια πάντα γένοιτο, καὶ εὔπλοος ὅρμον ἵκοιτο.
κἠγὼ τῆνο κατ' ἆμαρ ἀνήτινον ἢ ῥοδόεντα
ἢ καὶ λευκοΐων στέφανον περὶ κρατὶ φυλάσσων
τὸν Πτελεατικὸν οἶνον ἀπὸ κρατῆρος ἀφυξῶ
πὰρ πυρὶ κεκλιμένος, κύαμον δέ τις ἐν πυρὶ φρυξεῖ.
χἀ στιβὰς ἐσσεῖται πεπυκασμένα ἔστ' ἐπὶ πᾶχυν
κνύζᾳ τ' ἀσφοδέλῳ τε πολυγνάμπτῳ τε σελίνῳ.
καὶ πίομαι μαλακῶς μεμναμένος Ἀγεάνακτος
αὐταῖς ἐν κυλίκεσσι καὶ ἐς τρύγα χεῖλος ἐρείδων.
αὐλησεῦντι δέ μοι δύο ποιμένες, εἷς μὲν Ἀχαρνεύς,
εἷς δὲ Λυκωπίτας· ὁ δὲ Τίτυρος ἐγγύθεν ᾀσεῖ
ὡς ποκα τᾶς Ξενέας ἠράσσατο Δάφνις ὁ βούτας,
χὡς ὄρος ἀμφεπονεῖτό καὶ ὡς δρύες αὐτὸν ἐθρήνευν
Ἱμέρα αἵτε φύοντι παρ' ὄχθαισιν ποταμοῖο,
εὖτε χιὼν ὥς τις κατετάκετο μακρὸν ὑφ' Αἷμον

from the fire of Aphrodite; for hot love for him consumes me. And the kingfishers shall lay the waves and the sea to rest, and Notos [the south wind] and Euros [the east] that stirs the deepest seaweeds – the kingfishers, dearest to the grey-blue Nereids of those birds whose prey comes from the sea. May all things favour Ageanax, who wishes to sail to Mitylene, and may he reach a safe anchorage. And I, on that day, shall wreathe my head with dill, roses, or white stocks, and reclining by the fire shall draw the wine of Ptelea from the bowl, and someone shall roast beans on the fire for me. And my couch shall be strewn elbow-deep with fleabane and asphodel and richly curling celery, and I shall drink happily, remembering Ageanax in my very cups, as I press my lip to the dregs. And two shepherds shall pipe to me, one from Acharnae, and one from Lycope. Close by me Tityrus shall sing, how once Daphnis, the herdsman, loved Xenia; and how the mountain suffered for him, and the oak trees, which grow on the banks of the river Himera, lamented for him as he wasted away like snow under high Haemus or Athos or Rhodope or

ἢ Ἄθω ἢ Ῥοδόπαν ἢ Καύκασον ἐσχατόωντα.
ἀσεῖ δ᾽ ὥς ποκ᾽ ἔδεκτο τὸν αἰπόλον εὐρέα λάρναξ
ζωὸν ἐόντα κακαῖσιν ἀτασθαλίαισιν ἄνακτος,
ὥς τέ νιν αἱ σιμαὶ λειμωνόθε φέρβον ἰοῖσαι
κέδρον ἐς ἀδεῖαν μαλακοῖς ἄνθεσσι μέλισσαι
οὕνεκά οἱ γλυκὺ Μοῖσα κατὰ στόματος χέε νέκταρ.
ὦ μακαριστὲ Κομᾶτα, τύ θην τάδε τερπνὰ πεπόνθεις·
καὶ τὺ κατεκλάσθης ἐς λάρνακα, καὶ τὺ μελισσᾶν
κηρία φερβόμενος ἔτος ὥριον ἐξεπόνασας.
αἴθ᾽ ἐπ᾽ ἐμεῦ ζωοῖς ἐναρίθμιος ὠφελὲς ἦμεν
ὥς τοι ἐγὼν ἐνόμευον ἀν᾽ ὤρεα τὰς καλὰς αἶγας
φωνᾶς εἰσαΐων, τὺ δ᾽ ὑπὸ δρυσὶν ἢ ὑπὸ πεύκαις
ἁδὺ μελισδόμενος κατεκέκλισο, θεῖε Κομᾶτα.⟩

Χὠ μὲν τόσσ᾽ εἰπὼν ἀπεπαύσατο· τὸν δὲ μέτ᾽ αὖθις
κἠγὼν τοῖ᾽ ἐφάμαν· ⟨Λυκίδα φίλε, πολλὰ μὲν ἄλλα
Νύμφαι κἠμὲ δίδαξαν ἀν᾽ ὤρεα βουκολέοντα
ἐσθλά, τά που καὶ Ζηνὸς ἐπὶ θρόνον ἄγαγε φάμα·
ἀλλὰ τόγ᾽ ἐκ πάντων μέγ᾽ ὑπείροχον, ᾧ τυ γεραίρειν
ἀρξεῦμ᾽· ἀλλ᾽ ὑπάκουσον, ἐπεὶ φίλος ἔπλεο Μοίσαις·

remotest Caucasus. And he shall sing how once, through a king's evil wickedness, the goatherd was put alive into a broad chest; and how the blunt-nosed bees came from the meadows to the sweet-smelling chest of cedar and fed him on tender flowers, because the Muse poured sweet nectar on his mouth. Ah, blessed Comatas, you experienced these delights, you too were enclosed in a chest; you too were fed on honeycomb and suffered through the springtime of the year. I wish you had been numbered with the living in my day, that I might have herded your beautiful goats on the hills, and listened to your voice; while you, godly Comatas, lay under the oaks or the pines, singing sweetly.'

So much he said, and ended; and after him I too followed with these words: 'Friend Lycidas, the Nymphs have also taught me many other fine songs, as I shepherded my herd on the hills, whose fame perhaps has been reported even to the throne of Zeus; but this with which I will begin to honour you is by far the best of all. Listen then, for you are a friend of the Muses:

⟨Σιμιχίδᾳ μὲν Ἔρωτες ἐπέπταρον· ἦ γὰρ ὁ δειλός
τόσσον ἐρᾷ Μυρτοῦς ὅσον εἴαρος αἶγες ἔρανται.
Ἄρατος δ' ὁ τὰ πάντα φιλαίτατος ἀνέρι τήνῳ
παιδὸς ὑπὸ σπλάγχνοισιν ἔχει πόθον. οἶδεν Ἄριστις,
ἐσθλὸς ἀνήρ, μέγ' ἄριστος, ὃν οὐδέ κεν αὐτὸς ἀείδειν
Φοῖβος σὺν φόρμιγγι παρὰ τριπόδεσσι μεγαίροι,
ὡς ἐκ παιδὸς Ἄρατος ὑπ' ὀστίον αἴθετ' ἔρωτι.
τόν μοι, Πάν, Ὁμόλας ἐρατὸν πέδον ὅστε λέλογχας,
ἄκλητον τήνοιο φίλας ἐς χεῖρας ἐρείσαις,
εἴτ' ἔστ' ἄρα Φιλῖνος ὁ μαλθακὸς εἴτε τις ἄλλος.
κεἰ μὲν ταῦτ' ἔρδοις, ὦ Πὰν φίλε, μήτι τυ παῖδες
Ἀρκαδικοὶ σκίλλαισιν ὑπὸ πλευράς τε καὶ ὤμως
τανίκα μαστίζοιεν ὅτε κρέα τυτθὰ παρείη·
εἰ δ' ἄλλως νεύσαις, κατὰ μὲν χρόα πάντ' ὀνύχεσσι
δακνόμενος κνάσαιο καὶ ἐν κνίδαισι καθεύδοις·
εἴης δ' Ἠδωνῶν μὲν ἐν ὤρεσι χείματι μέσσῳ
Ἕβρον πὰρ ποταμὸν τετραμμένος ἐγγύθεν Ἄρκτω,
ἐν δὲ θέρει πιμάτοισι παρ' Αἰθιόπεσσι νομεύοις
πέτρᾳ ὕπο Βλεμύων, ὅθεν οὐκέτι Νεῖλος ὁρατός.

'The gods of Love sneezed for [favoured] Simichidas; for he, poor
man, loves Myrto as dearly as goats love the spring. But Aratus,
dearest in everything to that man, holds deep in his heart the desire
for a boy. Aristis knows this, an excellent man, the best of the best –
Phoebus himself by his own tripods would not object to his singing
with the lyre – he knows how under his bones Aratus is burning with
love for a boy. Ah, Pan, to whom the lovely plain of Homole has
been given, put him unsummoned in my friend's arms, be it the gentle
Philinus or another. And if you do that, dear Pan, then may the
Arcadian lads never flog you with squills on the flanks and the
shoulders, when they find only a little meat. But if you order other-
wise, then may you be bitten, and scratch yourself all over with your
nails, and may you sleep in nettles; and in midwinter may you find
yourself on the mountains of the Edonians, turned towards the river
Hebrus, close to the Pole; and in summer may you herd your flock
among the furthest of the Ethiopians under the rock of the Blemyes,
from where the Nile can no longer be seen. But you, gods of Love,

ὔμμες δ' Ὑετίδος καὶ Βυβλίδος ἁδὺ λιπόντες
νᾶμα καὶ Οἰκοῦντα, ξανθᾶς ἕδος αἰπὺ Διώνας,
ὦ μάλοισιν Ἔρωτες ἐρευθομένοισιν ὁμοῖοι,
βάλλετέ μοι τόξοισι τὸν ἱμερόεντα Φιλῖνον,
βάλλετ', ἐπεὶ τὸν ξεῖνον ὁ δύσμορος οὐκ ἐλεεῖ μευ.
καὶ δὴ μὰν ἀπίοιο πεπαίτερος, αἱ δὲ γυναῖκες,
«αἰαῖ, φαντί, Φιλῖνε, τό τοι καλὸν ἄνθος ἀπορρεῖ.»
μηκέτι τοι φρουρέωμες ἐπὶ προθύροισιν, Ἄρατε,
μηδὲ πόδας τρίβωμες· ὁ δ' ὄρθριος ἄλλον ἀλέκτωρ
κοκκύσδων ναρκαῖσιν ἀνιαραῖσι διδοίη·
εἷς δ' ἀπὸ τᾶσδε, φέριστε, Μόλων ἄγχοιτο παλαίστρας.
ἄμμιν δ' ἁσυχία τε μέλοι, γραῖά τε παρείη
ἄτις ἐπιφθύζοισα τὰ μὴ καλὰ νόσφιν ἐρύκοι.»

   Τόσσ' ἐφάμαν· ὁ δέ μοι τὸ λαγωβόλον, ἁδὺ γελάσσας
ὡς πάρος, ἐκ Μοισᾶν ξεινήιον ὤπασεν ἦμεν.
χὠ μὲν ἀποκλίνας ἐπ' ἀριστερὰ τὰν ἐπὶ Πύξας
εἷρφ' ὁδόν· αὐτὰρ ἐγών τε καὶ Εὔκριτος ἐς Φρασιδάμω
στραφθέντες χὠ καλὸς Ἀμύντιχος ἔν τε βαθείαις
ἁδείας σχοίνοιο χαμευνίσιν ἐκλίνθημες

rosy as apples, leave the sweet stream of Hyetis and Byblis, and
Oecus, that steep seat of fair-haired Dione, and wound for me with
your bows the lovely Philinus, wound him; for the wretch has no
pity on my friend. And truly he is riper than a pear, and the women
cry: "Ah, Philinus, your beautiful blossoms are falling away." Let
us no longer keep guard by his doorway, Aratus, nor wear our feet
away; but let the morning cock, with his crowing, hand over some-
one else to the numbing cold [of dawn]. My friend, let Molon alone
from that wrestling-school be strangled, and our minds be set at
peace, and may an old crone come to spit, to drive unlovely things
away.'

So much I said; and Lycidas, laughing sweetly as before, gave me his
shepherd's staff as a token of friendship in the Muses. And he turned
away to the left, and took the road to Pyxa; but I and Eucritus and the
handsome Amyntichus turned towards Phrasidamus' farm, and laid
ourselves happily on deep couches of sweet rushes and on the fresh-

ἔν τε νεοτμάτοισι γεγαθότες οἰναρέοισι.
πολλαὶ δ' ἄμμιν ὕπερθε κατὰ κρατὸς δονέοντο
αἴγειροι πτελέαι τε· τὸ δ' ἐγγύθεν ἱερὸν ὕδωρ
Νυμφᾶν ἐξ ἄντροιο κατειβόμενον κελάρυζε.
τοὶ δὲ ποτὶ σκιαραῖς ὀροδαμνίσιν αἰθαλίωνες
τέττιγες λαλαγεῦντες ἔχον πόνον· ἁ δ' ὀλολυγὼν
τηλόθεν ἐν πυκιναῖσι βάτων τρύζεσκεν ἀκάνθαις·
ἄειδον κόρυδοι καὶ ἀκανθίδες, ἔστενε τρυγών,
πωτῶντο ξουθαὶ περὶ πίδακας ἀμφὶ μέλισσαι.
πάντ' ὦσδεν θέρεος μάλα πίονος, ὦσδε δ' ὀπώρας.
ὄχναι μὲν πὰρ ποσσί, παρὰ πλευραῖσι δὲ μᾶλα
δαψιλέως ἁμῖν ἐκυλίνδετο, τοὶ δ' ἐκέχυντο
ὄρπακες βραβίλοισι καταβρίθοντες ἔραζε·
τετράενες δὲ πίθων ἀπελύετο κρατὸς ἄλειφαρ.
Νύμφαι Κασταλίδες Παρνάσιον αἶπος ἔχοισαι,
ἆρά γέ πᾳ τοιόνδε Φόλω κατὰ λάϊνον ἄντρον
κρατῆρ' Ἡρακλῆϊ γέρων ἐστάσατο Χίρων;
ἆρά γέ πᾳ τῆνον τὸν ποιμένα τὸν ποτ' Ἀνάπῳ,
τὸν κρατερὸν Πολύφαμον, ὃς ὤρεσι νᾶας ἔβαλλε,
τοῖον νέκταρ ἔπεισε κατ' αὔλια ποσσὶ χορεῦσαι,
οἷον δὴ τόκα πῶμα διεκρανάσατε, Νύμφαι,

stripped vine-leaves. Many poplars and elms were swaying over our heads; and near by, the sacred water from the cave of the Nymphs sang as it flowed down. On the shady boughs the dark cicadas were chattering busily, and the tree-frog cried far off in the thick thornbrake. Larks and finches sang, the dove sighed, and the yellow bees flitted about the springs. All things smelt of a very rich harvest and of fruit-time. Pears were rolling in abundance at our feet and apples at our side, and the branches, heavy with sloes, drooped down to the ground. And the four-year seal was loosened from the head of the wine jar. Nymphs of Castalia, you that haunt steep Parnassus, was it a bowl like this that old Chiron set before Heracles in Pholus' rocky cave? Was it such nectar that drove that shepherd by the Anapus to dance in his sheep-folds, the mighty Polyphemus, who pelted ships with mountain-crags — such nectar as you, Nymphs, mixed for us to drink that day by the altar of Demeter of the Threshing Floor? May I again plant the great

βωμῷ πὰρ Δάματρος ἀλωίδος; ἇς ἐπὶ σωρῷ
αὖτις ἐγὼ πάξαιμι μέγα πτύον, ἁ δὲ γελάσσαι
δράγματα καὶ μάκωνας ἐν ἀμφοτέραισιν ἔχοισα.

(*Idyll VII*)

151. Bombyca

ΒΑΤΤΟΣ

Μῶσαι Πιερίδες, συναείσατε τὰν ῥαδινάν μοι
παῖδ᾿· ὧν γὰρ χ᾿ ἅψησθε, θεαί, καλὰ πάντα ποεῖτε.
Βομβύκα χαρίεσσα, Σύραν καλέοντί τυ πάντες,
ἰσχνὰν ἁλιόκαυστον, ἐγὼ δὲ μόνος μελίχλωρον.
καὶ τὸ ἴον μέλαν ἐστὶ καὶ ἁ γραπτὰ ὑάκινθος,
ἀλλ᾿ ἔμπας ἐν τοῖς στεφάνοις τὰ πρᾶτα λέγονται.
ἁ αἲξ τὰν κύτισον, ὁ λύκος τὰν αἶγα διώκει,
ἁ γέρανος τὤροτρον, ἐγὼ δ᾿ ἐπὶ τὶν μεμάνημαι.
αἴθε μοι ἦς ὅσσα Κροῖσόν ποκα φαντὶ πεπᾶσθαι.
χρύσεοι ἀμφότεροί κ᾿ ἀνεκείμεθα τᾷ ᾿Αφροδίτᾳ,
τὼς αὐλὼς μὲν ἔχοισα καὶ ἢ ῥόδον ἢ τύγε μᾶλον,
σχῆμα δ᾿ ἐγὼ καὶ καινὰς ἐπ᾿ ἀμφοτέροισιν ἀμύκλας.
Βομβύκα χαρίεσσ᾿, οἱ μὲν πόδες ἀστράγαλοί τευς,
ἁ φωνὰ δὲ τρύχνος· τὸν μὰν τρόπον οὐκ ἔχω εἰπεῖν.

(*Idyll X*)

winnowing-shovel on her heap of corn, while she smiles on us with sheaves and poppies in both hands.

BATTUS: Pierian Muses, sing with me of the slender girl; for, goddesses, you make whatever you touch beautiful. Graceful Bombyca, all call you the Syrian, lean and sun-scorched, but I alone, honey-gold. The violet and the painted hyacinth are dark, but none the less they are the first choice for garlands. The goat follows the moon-clover, the wolf the goat, the crane the plough, and I am mad for you. I wish I had the wealth they say Croesus once possessed. Then we should stand in gold as offerings to Aphrodite, you holding your pipes and a rose or an apple, and I with new clothes, and new shoes from Amyclae on both my feet. Graceful Bombyca, your feet are like knuckle-bones, and your voice nightshade; your ways, I cannot describe.

303

THEOCRITUS

152. Gorgo and Praxinoa

ΓΟΡΓΩ, ΠΡΑΞΙΝΟΑ

‹Ἔνδοι Πραξινόα;› ‹Γοργοῖ φίλα, ὡς χρόνῳ, ἔνδοι.
θαῦμ' ὅτι καὶ νῦν ἦνθες. ὅρη δίφρον Εὐνόα αὐτᾷ·
ἔμβαλε καὶ ποτίκρανον.› ‹ἔχει κάλλιστα.› ‹καθίζευ.›
‹ὢ τᾶς ἀλεμάτω ψυχᾶς· μόλις ὔμμιν ἐσώθην,
Πραξινόα, πολλῶ μὲν ὄχλω, πολλῶν δὲ τεθρίππων·
παντᾷ κρηπῖδες, παντᾷ χλαμυδηφόροι ἄνδρες·
ἁ δ' ὁδὸς ἄτρυτος· τὺ δ' ἑκαστέρω αἰὲν ἀποικεῖς.›
‹ταῦθ' ὁ πάραρος τῆνος· ἐπ' ἔσχατα γᾶς ἔλαβ' ἐνθὼν
ἰλεόν, οὐκ οἴκησιν, ὅπως μὴ γείτονες ὦμες
ἀλλάλαις, ποτ' ἔριν, φθονερὸν κακόν, αἰὲν ὅμοιος.›
‹μὴ λέγε τὸν τεὸν ἄνδρα, φίλα, Δίνωνα τοιαῦτα
τῶ μικκῶ παρεόντος· ὅρη γύναι, ὡς ποθορῇ τυ.
θάρσει Ζωπύριον, γλυκερὸν τέκος· οὐ λέγει ἀπφῦν.›
‹αἰσθάνεται τὸ βρέφος, ναὶ τὰν πότνιαν.› ‹καλὸς ἀπφῦς.›
‹ἀπφῦς μὰν τῆνός γα πρόαν — λέγομες δὲ πρόαν θην

GORGO: Is Praxinoa at home?

PRAXINOA: Gorgo dear! Such a long time! She is at home – I'm sur
prised you got here even now. Eunoa, see to a chair for her, and
put a cushion on it.

GORGO: It's fine as it is.

PRAXINOA: Do sit down.

GORGO: Poor soul that I am! I hardly got here alive, Praxinoa, in all
that crowd and so many carriages – everywhere hob-nailed boots
and men in cloaks; and the road is never-ending – you live farther
and farther away.

PRAXINOA: That's that lunatic! He comes to the end of the earth and
buys a cave, not a house, so that we can't be neighbours – out of
spite, the mean brute; he's always the same!

GORGO: Don't talk like that about your husband Dinon, my dear,
when the little one is here. See how he's looking at you, woman.
Never mind, Zopyrion, sweet child, she doesn't mean daddy.

PRAXINOA: By the goddess! The child understands.

GORGO: Nice daddy!

PRAXINOA: Still, that daddy, the other day, really just the other day,

‹πάππα, νίτρον καὶ φῦκος ἀπὸ σκανᾶς ἀγοράσδειν› —
ἦνθε φέρων ἅλας ἅμμιν, ἀνὴρ τρισκαιδεκάπαχυς.›
‹χὡμὸς ταυτᾷ ἔχει· φθόρος ἀργυρίω Διοκλείδας·
ἑπταδράχμως κυνάδας, γραιᾶν ἀποτίλματα πηρᾶν,
πέντε πόκως ἔλαβ' ἐχθές, ἅπαν ῥύπον, ἔργον ἐπ' ἔργῳ.
ἀλλ' ἴθι τὡμπέχονον καὶ τὰν περονατρίδα λάζευ.
βᾶμες τῶ βασιλῆος ἐς ἀφνειῶ Πτολεμαίω
θασόμεναι τὸν Ἄδωνιν· ἀκούω χρῆμα καλόν τι
κοσμεῖν τὰν βασίλισσαν.› ‹ἐν ὀλβίῳ ὄλβια πάντα.›
‹ὧν ἴδες, ὧν εἶπες καὶ ἰδοῖσά τυ τῷ μὴ ἰδόντι.
ἕρπειν ὥρα κ' εἴη.› ‹ἀεργοῖς αἰὲν ἑορτά.
Εὐνόα, αἶρε τὸ νῆμα καὶ ἐς μέσον αἰνόδρυπτε
θὲς πάλιν· αἱ γαλέαι μαλακῶς χρῄζοντι καθεύδειν.
κινεῦ δή, φέρε θᾶσσον ὕδωρ. ὕδατος πρότερον δεῖ,
ἁ δὲ σμᾶμα φέρει. δὸς ὅμως. μὴ δὴ πολύ, λᾳστρί·
ἔγχει ὕδωρ. δύστανε, τί μευ τὸ χιτώνιον ἄρδεις;
παῦε. ὁποῖα θεοῖς ἐδόκει, τοιαῦτα νένιμμαι.
ἁ κλᾲξ τᾶς μεγάλας πεῖ λάρνακος; ὧδε φέρ' αὐτάν.›

I said to him: 'Papa, go and get some soda and rouge at the stall,'
and he brought me back salt, great lumbering giant!

GORGO: Mine's like that too, a waster of money, Diocleidas. Yesterday
for seven drachmas he bought five fleeces of dog's hair, shavings off
old saddlebags, nothing but dirt, just work upon work. But come,
put on your shawl and your wrap. Let's go and see *Adonis* in rich
King Ptolemy's palace. I'm told the Queen is preparing something
fine.

PRAXINOA: Everything's grand in grand houses.

GORGO: When you have seen a thing, you can talk about it to others
who haven't. It's time to be going.

PRAXINOA: It's always holiday for the idle. Eunoa, pick up that thread
and bring it back here, or I'll beat you. Cats like soft beds to sleep
on. Move, and bring me some water at once. I need water first, and
she brings soap! Still, let me have it. Not so much, you thief. Now
the water. You wretch, what are you wetting my dress for? That'll
do. I've washed as well as the gods allow. Where's the key of the
big chest? Bring it here.

‹Πραξινόα μάλα τοι τὸ καταπτυχὲς ἐμπερόναμα
τοῦτο πρέπει· λέγε μοι, πόσσω κατέβα τοι ἀφ᾽ ἱστῶ;›
‹μὴ μνάσῃς Γοργοῖ· πλέον ἀργυρίω καθαρῶ μνᾶν
ἢ δύο· τοῖς δ᾽ ἔργοις καὶ τὰν ψυχὰν ποτέθηκα.›
‹ἀλλὰ κατὰ γνώμαν ἀπέβα τοι.› ‹τοῦτο κάλ᾽ εἶπες.
τὠμπέχονον φέρε μοι καὶ τὰν θολίαν κατὰ κόσμον
ἀμφίθες. οὐκ ἀξῶ τε τέκνον. μορμώ, δάκνει ἵππος.
δάκρυ᾽ ὅσσα θέλεις, χωλὸν δ᾽ οὐ δεῖ τυ γενέσθαι.
ἕρπωμες. Φρυγία τὸν μικκὸν παῖσδε λαβοῖσα,
τὰν κύν᾽ ἔσω κάλεσον, τὰν αὐλείαν ἀπόκλαξον.›

(Idyll XV)

153. The Distaff

Γλαύκας, ὦ φιλέριθ᾽ ἀλακάτα, δῶρον ᾽Αθανάας
γύναιξιν, νόος οἰκωφελίας αἷσιν ἐπάβολος,
θέρσεισ᾽ ἅμμιν ὑμάρτῃ πόλιν ἐς Νείλεος ἀγλάαν,
ὅππα Κύπριδος ἱρον καλάμῳ χλῶρον ὑπ᾽ ἀπάλῳ.
τυῖδε γὰρ πλόον εὐάνεμον αἰτήμεθα πὰρ Δίος,

GORGO: That dress with its deep pleats suits you very well, Praxinoa. Tell me, what did the material cost you?

PRAXINOA: Don't remind me of that, Gorgo; more than two minas of good money, and as for the work! I put my very life into it.

GORGO: But it's just what you wanted.

PRAXINOA: That's true. Bring me my wrap and my sun-hat; put them on properly. I shan't take you, baby. Boo, Bogey! Horsey bite! Cry as much as you like, but we mustn't have you getting lame. Let's be going. Phrygia, take the little one, and call the dog in, and lock the front door.

DISTAFF, friend of those who spin, grey-eyed Athene's gift to women who know the art of being a housewife, take courage, come with me to the rich town of Neileus where the sanctuary of Cypris lies, green with its soft rushes. For there we sail; and we ask Zeus for fair winds for our sea-journey, that I may enjoy the sight of my friend Nicias, that

ὅππως ξέννον ἔμον τέρψομ' ἰδὼν κἀντιφιληθέω,
Νικίαν, Χαρίτων ἱμεροφώνων ἱερὸν φύτον,
καὶ σὲ τὰν ἐλέφαντος πολυμόχθω γεγενημέναν
δῶρον Νικιάας εἰς ἀλόχω χέρρας ὀπάσσομεν,
σὺν τῷ πόλλα μὲν ἔργ' ἐκτελέσῃς ἀνδρείοις πέπλοις,
πόλλα δ' οἶα γύναικες φορέοισ' ὑδάτινα βράκη.
δὶς γὰρ μάτερες ἄρνων μαλάκοις ἐν βοτάνᾳ πόκοις
πέξαιντ' αὐτοέτει, Θευγενίδος γ' ἔννεκ' ἐυσφύρω·
οὕτως ἀνυσίεργος, φιλέει δ' ὅσσα σαόφρονες.
οὐ γὰρ εἰς ἀκίρας οὐδ' ἐς ἀέργω κεν ἐβολλόμαν
ὀπασσαί σε δόμοις ἀμμετέρας ἔσσαν ἀπὺ χθόνος.
καὶ γάρ τοι πάτρις, ἂν ὡς Ἐφύρας κτίσσε ποτ' Ἀρχίας,
νάσω Τρινακρίας μύελον, ἀνδρῶν δοκίμων πόλιν.
νῦν μὰν οἶκον ἔχοισ' ἄνερος, ὃς πόλλ' ἐδάη σόφα
ἀνθρώποισι νόσοις φάρμακα λύγραις ἀπαλαλκέμεν,
οἰκήσῃς κατὰ Μίλλατον ἐράνναν πεδ' Ἰαόνων,
ὡς εὐαλάκατος Θεύγενις ἐν δαμότισιν πέλῃ,
καί οἱ μνᾶστιν ἀεὶ τῶ φιλαοίδω παρέχῃς ξένω.
κῆνο γάρ τις ἔρει τὤπος ἰδὼν σ'· ⟨ἦ μεγάλα χάρις
δώρῳ σὺν ὀλίγῳ· πάντα δὲ τίματα τὰ πὰρ φίλων.⟩

(Idyll XXVIII)

sacred offspring of the sweet-voiced Graces, and be welcomed in return, and put you, my gift of well-carved ivory, in the hands of his wife. With her you will accomplish much work on men's clothes, and much on the flowing robes that women wear; for, to please fair-ankled Theugenis, the mothers of the lambs are shorn of their soft fleeces in the pastures twice in the same year; so industrious is she, so prudent in her ways. I would not wish to place you in the home of a weak or idle wife, for you come from my own country; your native town is that which Archias of Ephyra once founded, the very marrow of the island of Trinacria, a city of famous men. Now, in the home of a man skilled in the use of many drugs that protect men from grim sicknesses, you shall dwell with the Ionians in lovely Miletus, so that Theugenis may be famous among the women of her town for her distaff, and so that you may always remind her of her song-loving friend. For, seeing you, this is what men will say: 'Truly great goodwill goes with a small gift; yet all that comes from friends is precious.'

ARATUS
c. 315–240 B.C.

154. Proem

'Εκ Διὸς ἀρχώμεσθα, τὸν οὐδέποτ' ἄνδρες ἐῶμεν
ἄρρητον· μεσταὶ δὲ Διὸς πᾶσαι μὲν ἀγυιαί,
πᾶσαι δ' ἀνθρώπων ἀγοραί, μεστὴ δὲ θάλασσα
καὶ λιμένες· πάντη δὲ Διὸς κεχρήμεθα πάντες.
τοῦ γὰρ καὶ γένος εἰμέν· ὁ δ' ἤπιος ἀνθρώποισιν
δεξιὰ σημαίνει, λαοὺς δ' ἐπὶ ἔργον ἐγείρει,
μιμνήσκων βιότοιο, λέγει δ' ὅτε βῶλος ἀρίστη
βουσί τε καὶ μακέλῃσι, λέγει δ' ὅτε δεξιαὶ ὧραι
καὶ φυτὰ γυρῶσαι καὶ σπέρματα πάντα βαλέσθαι.
αὐτὸς γὰρ τά γε σήματ' ἐν οὐρανῷ ἐστήριξεν,
ἄστρα διακρίνας, ἐσκέψατο δ' εἰς ἐνιαυτὸν
ἀστέρας οἵ κε μάλιστα τετυγμένα σημαίνοιεν
ἀνδράσιν ὡράων, ὄφρ' ἔμπεδα πάντα φύωνται.
τῷ μιν ἀεὶ πρῶτόν τε καὶ ὕστατον ἱλάσκονται.
χαῖρε, πάτερ, μέγα θαῦμα, μέγ' ἀνθρώποισιν ὄνειαρ,
αὐτὸς καὶ προτέρη γενεή. χαίροιτε δὲ Μοῦσαι
μειλίχιαι μάλα πᾶσαι· ἐμοί γε μὲν ἀστέρας εἰπεῖν
ᾗ θέμις εὐχομένῳ τεκμήρατε πᾶσαν ἀοιδήν.

(Astronomy)

LET us begin with Zeus, whom we mortals never leave unnamed. Full
of Zeus are all the streets, and all the market-places of men, the sea is
full of him and so are the harbours; we have all had need of Zeus in all
places. For we are also his progeny; and he, well-disposed towards
mankind, gives them good omens, and wakes people to their work,
reminding them of their livelihood. He tells when the land is best for
the oxen and the mattocks, and he tells when the season is right for
planting plants and for sowing all kinds of seeds. For he made the signs
in heaven into stars; and when he had distinguished between the stars,
he decided which of them during the year would best indicate the sea-
sons to men, so that all things might grow without failing. For this,
men always pray to him first and last. Hail, Father, great wonder,
great blessing to men, you and the Earlier Race. And hail, Muses, all
of you most kind; guide my entire song and help me tell the stars, as is
proper, since I pray to you.

155. Against his Critics

Οἶδ' ὅτι μοι Τελχῖνες ἐπιτρύζουσιν ἀοιδῇ,
νήιδες οἳ Μούσης οὐκ ἐγένοντο φίλοι . . .

• • • • • • • •

⟨Ἔλλετε Βασκανίης ὀλοὸν γένος· αὖθι δὲ τέχνῃ
κρίνετε, μὴ σχοίνῳ Περσίδι τὴν σοφίην.
μηδ' ἀπ' ἐμεῦ διφᾶτε μέγα ψοφέουσαν ἀοιδήν
τίκτεσθαι· βροντᾶν οὐκ ἐμόν, ἀλλὰ Διός.⟩
καὶ γὰρ ὅτε πρώτιστον ἐμοῖς ἐπὶ δέλτον ἔθηκα
γούνασιν, Ἀπόλλων εἶπεν ὅ μοι Λύκιος·
⟨. . . ἀοιδέ, τὸ μὲν θύος ὅττι πάχιστον
θρέψαι, τὴν Μοῦσαν δ' ὠγαθὲ λεπταλέην·
πρὸς δέ σε καὶ τόδ' ἄνωγα, τὰ μὴ πατέουσιν ἅμαξαι
τὰ στείβειν, ἑτέρων δ' ἴχνια μὴ καθ' ὁμά
δίφρον ἐλᾶν μηδ' οἶμον ἀνὰ πλατύν, ἀλλὰ κελεύθους
ἀτρίπτους, εἰ καὶ στεινοτέρην ἐλάσεις.
τεττίγων ἐνὶ τοῖς γὰρ ἀείδομεν οἳ λιγὺν ἦχον
. . . θόρυβον δ' οὐκ ἐφίλησαν ὄνων.⟩

I know that the Telchines, who are ignorant and no friends of the Muse, grumble at my poetry. . . . 'Begone you murderous race of Jealousy! Hereafter judge poetry by [the canons of] art, and not by the Persian measuring-chain, nor seek from me a loudly resounding song. It is not for me to thunder; that is the business of Zeus.' And indeed when I first placed a writing tablet on my knees Lycian Apollo said to me: '. . . poet, feed the victim to be as fat as possible; but, my friend, keep the Muse slender. This too I bid you: tread a path which carriages do not tread down; do not drive your chariot upon the common track of others, nor along a wide road, but on unworn paths, though your course be narrower. For we sing among those who love the shrill ringing of the cicada, and not the clamour of . . . asses.' Let others bray

θηρὶ μὲν οὐατόεντι πανείκελον ὀγκήσαιτο
    ἄλλος, ἐγὼ δ' εἴην οὐλαχύς, ὁ πτερόεις,
ἂ πάντως, ἵνα γῆρας ἵνα δρόσον ἢν μὲν ἀείδω
    προίκιον ἐκ δίης ἠέρος εἶδαρ ἔδων,
αὖθι τὸ δ' ἐκδύοιμι, τό μοι βάρος ὅσσον ἔπεστι
    τριγλώχιν ὀλοῷ νῆσος ἐπ' Ἐγκελάδῳ.
οὐ νέμεσις· Μοῦσαι γὰρ ὅσους ἴδον ὄθματι παῖδας
    μὴ λοξῷ, πολιοὺς οὐκ ἀπέθεντο φίλους.

(Causes)

156. The Things I Keep

Καὶ γὰρ ἐγὼ τὰ μὲν ὅσσα καρήατι τῆμος ἔδωκα
    ξανθὰ σὺν εὐόδμοις ἁβρὰ λίπη στεφάνοις,
ἄπνοα πάντ' ἐγένοντο παρὰ χρέος, ὅσσα τ' ὀδόντων
    ἔνδοθι νείαιράν τ' εἰς ἀχάριστον ἔδυ,
καὶ τῶν οὐδὲν ἔμεινεν ἐς αὔριον· ὅσσα δ' ἀκουαῖς
    εἰσεθέμην, ἔτι μοι μοῦνα πάρεστι τάδε.

(Causes)

just like the long-eared brute, but let me be the delicate one, the winged one. Oh yes indeed! That I may sing, living on dew-drops, free sustenance from the divine air; that I may then shed old age, which weighs upon me like the Three-cornered Island upon deadly Enceladus. But never mind! For if the Muses have not looked askance at you in your childhood, they do not cast you from their friendship when you are grey.

For all the soft, gold-gleaming ointments which I then put on my head, together with fragrant garlands, certainly lost their scent in no time; and of all that passed between my teeth and plunged into my ungrateful belly nothing remained next morning; but the only things which I still keep are those that I took in through my ears.

157. Acontius and Cydippe

Αὐτὸς Ἔρως ἐδίδαξεν Ἀκόντιον, ὁππότε καλῇ
   ἤθετο Κυδίππῃ παῖς ἐπὶ παρθενικῇ,
τέχνην — οὐ γὰρ ὅγ᾽ ἔσκε πολύκροτος — ὄφρα λέγοιτο
   τοῦτο διὰ ζωῆς οὔνομα κουρίδιον.
ἦ γάρ, ἄναξ, ὁ μὲν ἦλθεν Ἰουλίδος ἡ δ᾽ ἀπὸ Νάξου,
   Κύνθιε, τὴν Δήλῳ σὴν ἐπὶ βουφονίην,
αἷμα τὸ μὲν γενεῆς Εὐξαντίδος, ἡ δὲ Προμηθίς,
   καλοὶ νησάων ἀστέρες ἀμφότεροι.
πολλαὶ Κυδίππην ὀλίγην ἔτι μητέρες υἱοῖς
   ἐδνῆστιν κεραῶν ᾔτεον ἀντὶ βοῶν·
κείνης οὐχ ἑτέρη γὰρ ἐπὶ λασίοιο γέροντος
   Σιληνοῦ νοτίην ἵκετο πιδυλίδα
ἠοῖ εἰδομένη μάλιον ῥέθος οὐδ᾽ Ἀριήδης
   ἐς χορὸν εὐδούσης ἁβρὸν ἔθηκε πόδα·

    • • • • • • • •

ἤδη καὶ κούρῳ παρθένος εὐνάσατο,
τέθμιον ὡς ἐκέλευε προνύμφιον ὕπνον ἰαῦσαι
   ἄρσενι τὴν τᾶλιν παιδὶ σὺν ἀμφιθαλεῖ.
Ἥρην γάρ κοτέ φασι — κύον, κύον, ἴσχεο, λαιδρὲ
   θυμέ, σύ γ᾽ ἀείσῃ καὶ τά περ οὐχ ὁσίη·

EROS himself taught Acontius, when the youth was ablaze with love
for the beautiful maiden Cydippe — for he was not cunning — the art of
gaining for his whole life the name of a lawful husband. For, Lord of
Cynthus [Apollo], he came from Iulis and she from Naxos to your ox
sacrifice in Delos; his blood was of the family of Euxantius, and she
was a descendant of Promethus, both beautiful stars of the islands.
Many mothers asked for Cydippe as a bride for their sons while she
was still a child, offering horned oxen as gifts. For no one with a gentle
face more like the dawn's came to the moist spring of hairy old Silenus,
nor set her delicate foot in dance when Ariadne was asleep . . . and the
maiden was already in bed with the boy, as ritual ordered that the
bride should sleep her pre-nuptial sleep with a boy whose parents were
both alive. For they say that, once upon a time, Hera — dog, dog, re-
frain, my shameless soul! You would sing even of that which it is
blasphemous to tell. It is a great blessing for you that you have not

ὤναο κάρτ' ἕνεκ' οὔ τι θεῆς ἴδες ἱερὰ φρικτῆς,
ἐξ ἂν ἐπεὶ καὶ τῶν ἤρυγες ἱστορίην.
ἦ πολυιδρείη χαλεπὸν κακόν, ὅστις ἀκαρτεῖ
γλώσσης· ὡς ἐτεὸν παῖς ὅδε μαῦλιν ἔχει.
ἠῷοι μὲν ἔμελλον ἐν ὕδατι θυμὸν ἀμύξειν
οἱ βόες ὀξεῖαν δερκόμενοι δορίδα,
δειελινὴν τὴν δ' εἷλε κακὸς χλόος, ἦλθε δὲ νοῦσος,
αἶγας ἐς ἀγριάδας τὴν ἀποπεμπόμεθα,
ψευδόμενοι δ' ἱερὴν φημίζομεν· ἣ τότ' ἀνιγρὴ
τὴν κούρην 'Αίδεω μέχρις ἔτηξε δόμων.
δεύτερον ἐστόρνυντο τὰ κλισμία, δεύτερον ἡ παῖς
ἑπτὰ τεταρταίῳ μῆνας ἔκαμνε πυρί.
τὸ τρίτον ἐμνήσαντο γάμου κάτα, τὸ τρίτον αὖτε
Κυδίππην ὀλοὸς κρυμὸς ἐσῳκίσατο.
τέτρατον οὐκέτ' ἔμεινε πατὴρ . . . .
Φοῖβον· ὁ δ' ἐννύχιον τοῦτ' ἔπος ηὐδάσατο·
‹'Αρτέμιδος τῇ παιδὶ γάμον βαρὺς ὅρκος ἐνικλᾷ·
Λύγδαμιν οὐ γὰρ ἐμὴ τῆμος ἔκηδε κάσις
οὐδ' ἐν 'Αμυκλαίῳ θρύον ἔπλεκεν οὐδ' ἀπὸ θήρης
ἔκλυζεν ποταμῷ λύματα Παρθενίῳ,

seen the rites of the goddess at which men shudder [Demeter], or else you would have blurted out their story too. Truly much knowledge is a grievous thing for a man who does not control his tongue; this man is really a child with a knife. In the morning the oxen were about to tear their hearts seeing the sharp blade reflected before them in the water. But in the afternoon an evil pallor came upon her [Cydippe]; she was taken by the disease which we exorcize into the wild goats – the one we falsely call the holy disease. That grievous sickness then wasted the girl even to the Halls of Hades. A second time the couches were spread; a second time the maiden was sick for seven months with a quartan fever. A third time they thought of marriage; a third time again a deadly chill settled on Cydippe. The fourth time her father could endure it no more, but [set off to Delphic] Phoebus, who in the night spoke and said: 'A solemn oath by Artemis frustrates your child's marriage. For my sister was not at that time distressing Lygdamis, nor weaving rushes in Amyclae's shrine, nor washing off the stains from the hunt in the river Parthenios; she was at home in Delos when your

Δήλῳ δ' ἦν ἐπίδημος, Ἀκόντιον ὁππότε σὴ παῖς
  ὤμοσεν, οὐκ ἄλλον, νυμφίον ἐξέμεναι.
ὦ Κήϋξ, ἀλλ' ἤν με θέλῃς συμφράδμονα θέσθαι,
  .... τελευτήσεις ὅρκια θυγατέρος·
ἀργύρῳ οὐ μόλιβον γὰρ Ἀκόντιον, ἀλλὰ φαεινῷ
  ἤλεκτρον χρυσῷ φημί σε μειξέμεναι.
Κοδρείδης σύ γ' ἄνωθεν ὁ πενθερός, αὐτὰρ ὁ Κεῖος
  γαμβρὸς Ἀρισταίου Ζηνὸς ἀφ' ἱερέων
Ἰκμίου οἷσι μέμηλεν ἐπ' οὔρεος ἀμβώνεσσιν
  πρηΰνειν χαλεπὴν Μαῖραν ἀνερχομένην,
αἰτεῖθαι τὸ δ' ἄημα παραὶ Διὸς ᾧ τε θαμεινοὶ
  πλήσσονται λινέαις ὄρτυγες ἐν νεφέλαις.›
ἢ θεός· αὐτὰρ ὁ Νάξον ἔβη πάλιν, εἴρετο δ' αὐτὴν
  κούρην, ἡ δ' ἀν' ἐτῶς πᾶν ἐκάλυψεν ἔπος
κὴν αὖ σῶς· ... λοιπόν, Ἀκόντιε, σεῖο μετελθεῖν
  .... ἐς Διονυσιάδα.
χἠ θεὸς εὐορκεῖτο καὶ ἥλικες αὐτίχ' ἑταίρης
  εἶπον ὑμηναίους οὐκ ἀναβαλλομένους.
οὔ σε δοκέω τημοῦτος, Ἀκόντιε, νυκτὸς ἐκείνης
  ἀντί κε, τῇ μίτρης ἥψαο παρθενίης,
οὐ σφυρὸν Ἰφίκλειον ἐπιτρέχον ἀσταχύεσσιν
  οὐδ' ἃ Κελαινίτης ἐκτεάτιστο Μίδης

child swore that she would have Acontius, none other, for bridegroom.
But, Ceyx, if you will take me for your counsellor, you will fulfil your
daughter's oath.... For I say that, with Acontius, you will not be
mingling lead with silver, but electrum with shining gold. You, the
father of the bride, are sprung from Codrus; the Cean bridegroom
springs from the priests of Zeus Aristaeus the Icmian, priests whose
business on the mountain tops is to placate the awkward Maera, when
she rises, and to entreat from Zeus the wind whereby many a quail is
entangled in the linen nets.' So spoke the god. And her father went
back to Naxos, and questioned the maiden herself; and she disclosed
everything truthfully. And she became well again. For the rest,
Acontius, it will be your business to go ... to Dionysias [Naxos]. So
faith was kept with the goddess, and straightway the girls of her age
sang their friend's marriage-hymn, deferring no longer. Then, I think,
Acontius, that for that night, when you touched her maiden girdle, you
would have accepted neither the ankle of Iphicles [the swift runner]
who ran upon the ears of corn [without bending them], nor the

313

δέξασθαι, ψήφου δ' ἂν ἐμῆς ἐπιμάρτυρες εἶεν
  οἵτινες οὐ χαλεποῦ νήιδές εἰσι θεοῦ.
ἐκ δὲ γάμου κείνοιο μέγ' οὔνομα μέλλε νέεσθαι·
  δὴ γὰρ ἔθ' ὑμέτερον φῦλον Ἀκοντιάδαι
πουλύ τι καὶ περίτιμον Ἰουλίδι ναιετάουσιν,
  Κεῖε, τεὸν δ' ἡμεῖς ἵμερον ἐκλύομεν
τόνδε παρ' ἀρχαίου Ξενομήδεος, ὅς ποτε πᾶσαν
  νῆσον ἐνὶ μνήμῃ κάτθετο μυθολόγῳ,
ἀρχμενος ὡς νύμφῃσιν ἐναίετο Κωρυκίῃσιν,
  τὰς ἀπὸ Παρνησσοῦ λῖς ἐδίωξε μέγας,
Ὑδροῦσσαν τῷ καί μιν ἐφήμισαν, ὥς τε Κιρώδης
  . . . . . . ᾤκεεν ἐν Καρύαις·
ὥς τέ μιν ἐννάσσαντο τέων Ἀλαλάξιος αἰεὶ
  Ζεὺς ἐπὶ σαλπίγγων ἱρὰ βοῇ δέχεται
Κᾶρες ὁμοῦ Λελέγεσσι, μετ' οὔνομα δ' ἄλλο βαλέσθαι
  Φοίβου καὶ Μελίης ἶνις ἔθηκε Κέως·
ἐν δ' ὕβριν θάνατόν τε κεραύνιον, ἐν δὲ γόητας
  Τελχῖνας μακάρων τ' οὐκ ἀλέγοντα θεῶν
ἠλεὰ Δημώνακτα γέρων ἐνεθήκατο δέλτοις
  καὶ γρηῦν Μακελώ, μητέρα Δεξιθέης,
ἃς μούνας, ὅτε νῆσον ἀνέτρεπον εἵνεκ' ἀλιτρῆς
  ὕβριος, ἀσκηθεῖς Ἔλλιπον ἀθάνατοι·

possessions of Midas of Celaenae. And my verdict would be attested
by all who are not ignorant of the stern god [Eros]. And from that
marriage a great name was destined to arise. For, man of Cea, your
clan, the Acontiadae, still dwell at Iulis, numerous and honoured. And
this love of yours we heard from old Xenomedes, who once set down
[the history of] the whole island in a mythological record, beginning
with the tale of how it was inhabited by the Corycian nymphs, whom
a great lion drove away from Parnassus; for that reason also they called
it Hydrussa, and how Cirodes ... dwelt in Caryae. And how they
settled in the country whose offerings Zeus Alalaxius always receives to
the sound of trumpets – Carians and Leleges together; and how Ceos,
son of Phoebus and Melia, made it take another name. The insolence
and the lightning death and the Telchinian wizards and Demonax who
foolishly disregarded the blessed gods, these the old man put on his
writing tablets; aged Macelo too, Dexithea's mother, the two whom
alone the deathless gods left unscathed, when they overthrew the
island for its sinful insolence. And how, of its four cities, Megacles

τέσσαρας ὥς τε πόληας ὁ μὲν τείχισσε Μεγακλῆς
Κάρθαιαν, Χρυσοῦς δ' Εὔπυλος ἡμιθέης
εὔκρηνον πτολίεθρον Ἰουλίδος, αὐτὰρ Ἀκαῖος
Ποιήσσαν Χαρίτων ἵδρυμ' ἐϋπλοκάμων,
ἄστυρον Ἄφραστος δὲ Κορήσιον, εἶπε δέ, Κεῖε,
ξυγκραθέντ' αὐταῖς ὀξὺν ἔρωτα σέθεν
πρέσβυς ἐτητυμίῃ μεμελημένος, ἔνθεν ὁ παιδὸς
μῦθος ἐς ἡμετέρην ἔδραμε Καλλιόπην.

(*Causes*)

158. *The Olive and the Laurel*

Εἶς — οὐ γάρ; — ἡμέων, παῖ Χαριτάδεω, καὶ σὺ

. . . .

ἄκουε δὴ τὸν αἶνον· ἔν κοτε Τμώλῳ
δάφνην ἐλαίη νεῖκος οἱ πάλαι Λυδοὶ
λέγουσι θέσθαι· καὶ γὰρ
καλόν τε δένδρεον

. . . .

‹ὡριστερὸς μὲν λευκὸς ὡς ὕδρου γαστήρ,
ὁ δ' ἡλιοπλὴξ ὃς τὰ πολλὰ γυμνοῦται.

built Carthaea, and Eupylus, son of the demi-goddess Chryso, the fair-fountained city of Iulis, and Acaeus Poeessa, seat of the fair-tressed Graces, and how Aphrastus built the city of Coresus. And, O Cean, along with this, that old man, a lover of truth, told of your passionate love; from there the maiden's story came to my Muse.

You also [claim] — is it not so? — son of Charitades, to be one of us. . . . Well, listen to this tale. Once upon a time the ancient Lydians say the laurel had a quarrel with the olive on Tmolus . . . a beautiful tree . . .: '. . . the left side is white like the belly of a water-snake, the other, which is mostly exposed, is scorched by the sun. What house is there

τίς δ' οἶκος οὗπερ οὐκ ἐγὼ παρὰ φλιῇ;
τίς δ' οὔ με μάντις ἢ τίς οὐ θύτης ἕλκει;
καὶ Πυθίη γὰρ ἐν δάφνῃ μὲν ἵδρυται,
δάφνην δ' ἀείδει καὶ δάφνην ὑπέστρωται.
ὤφρων ἐλαίη, τοὺς δὲ παῖδας οὐ Βράγχος
τοὺς τῶν Ἰώνων, οἷς ὁ Φοῖβος ὠργίσθη,
δάφνῃ τε κρούων κἦπος οὐ . . .
δὶς ἢ τρὶς εἰπὼν ἀρτεμέας ἐποίησε;
κἠγὼ μὲν ἢ 'πὶ δαῖτας ἢ 'ς χορὸν φοιτέω
τὸν Πυθαϊστήν· γίνομαι δὲ κἄεθλον·
οἱ Δωριῆς δὲ Τεμπόθεν με τέμνουσιν
ὀρέων ἀπ' ἄκρων καὶ φέρουσιν ἐς Δελφούς,
ἐπὴν τὰ τὠπόλλωνος ἱρ' ἀγινῆται.
ὤφρων ἐλαίη, πῆμα δ' οὐχὶ γινώσκω
οὐδ' οἶδ' ὁκοίην οὐλαφηφόρος κάμπτει,
ἁγνὴ γάρ εἰμι, κοὔ πατεῦσί μ' ἄνθρωποι,
ἱρὴ γάρ εἰμι· σοὶ δὲ χὠπότ' ἂν νεκρόν
μέλλωσι καίειν ἢ τάφῳ περιστέλλειν,
αὐτοί τ' ἀνεστέψαντο χὐπὸ τὰ πλευρά
τοῦ μὴ πνέοντος . . . παξ ὑπέστρωσαν.⟩
ἢ μὲν τάδ', οὐκέτ' ἄλλα· τὴν δ' ἀπήλλαξε
μάλ' ἀτρεμαίως ἡ τεκοῦσα τὸ χρῖμα·

where I am not beside the doorpost? What seer or priest of sacrifice
does not carry me? In fact the Pythian Priestess has her seat on laurel,
laurel she sings, and she has laurel for a couch. Stupid olive, did not
Branchus restore to health the sons of the Ionians, with whom Phoebus
was angry, by striking them with laurel, and uttering his mystic spell
two or three times? And I also go to feasts and Pytho's dance, and I am
the prize of victory. The Dorians cut me on the hilltops of Tempe and
carry me to Delphi whenever Apollo's festival is celebrated. Stupid
olive, I know no sorrow, nor the path trod by the carriers of the dead,
for I am pure and men do not tread on me; for I am holy. But you,
whenever men are to burn a corpse or lay it in a grave, they use you
for their wreaths and [alas] they spread you under the sides of the man
who breathes no more.' So much the one said; no more. But the oil-
bearing tree dealt with her very quietly: 'Friend, fair in all respects,

‹ὦ πάντα καλή, τῶν ἐμῶν τὸ κάλλιστον
ἐν τῇ τελευτῇ κύκνος ὡς . . . . . .
ἤεισας· οὕτω μὴ κάμοιμ . . . . . .
ἐγὼ μὲν ἄνδρας, οὓς Ἄρης ἀνήλωσε
συνέκ τε πέμπω χὐπὸ . . . . . .
. . . ων ἀριστέων, οἳ κα . . . . . .
ἐγὼ δὲ λευκὴν ἡνίκ' ἐς τάφον Τηθὺν
φέρουσι παῖδες ἢ γέροντα Τιθωνόν,
αὐτή θ' ὁμαρτέω κἠπὶ τὴν ὁδὸν κεῖμαι·
γηθέω δὲ πλεῖον ἢ σὺ τοῖς ἀγινεῦσιν
ἐκ τῶν σε Τεμπέων. ἀλλ' ἐπεὶ γὰρ ἐμνήσθης
καὶ τοῦτο· κῶς ἄεθλον οὐκ ἐγὼ κρέσσων
σεῦ; καὶ γὰρ ὡγὼν οὖν Ὀλυμπίη μέζων
ἢ 'ν τοῖσι Δελφοῖς· ἀλλ' ἄριστον ἡ σωπή.
ἐγὼ μὲν οὔτε χρηστὸν οὔτε σε γρύζω
ἀπηνὲς οὐδέν· ἀλλά μοι δύ' ὄρνιθες
ἐν τοῖσι φύλλοις ταῦτα τινθυρίζουσαι
πάλαι κάθηνται· κωτίλον δὲ τὸ ζεῦγος.
‹τίς δ' εὗρε δάφνην;› ‹γῆ τε καὶ . . .
ὡς πρῖνον, ὡς δρῦν, ὡς κύπειρον, ὡς πεύκην.›
‹τίς δ' εὗρ' ἐλαίην;› ‹Παλλάς, ἧμος ἤριζε
τῷ φυκιόκῳ κἠδίκαζεν ἀρχαίοις
ἀνὴρ ὄφις τὰ νέρθεν ἀμφὶ τῆς Ἀκτῆς.›

like the swan . . . you sang my greatest beauty at the end of your song.
May I never tire of doing this. I escort the men whom Ares has slain,
and beneath . . . of princes, who . . . and when the children carry to the
grave a white-haired Tethys [old woman], or some old Tithonus, it is
I who go with them and lie strewn on the path; and I find more joy in
this than you in those who bring you from Tempe. But since you spoke
of this too, am I not better than you as a prize? For certainly the
Olympic games are greater than those held at Delphi. But silence is
best. For my part I mutter no word of praise or blame for you. But
two birds which have long been perched in my leaves are muttering
this – they are a chattering couple: "Who discovered the laurel?"
"Earth and . . . just like the ilex, the oak, the galingale and the pine."
"Who discovered the olive?" "Pallas, when she contended for
Attica with the Seaweed Dweller in days of old, with a snake-tailed

‹ἐν ᾗ δάφνη πέπτωκε. τῶν δ᾽ ἀειζώων
τίς τὴν ἐλαίην, τίς δὲ τὴν δάφνην τιμᾷ;›
‹δάφνην ᾽Απόλλων, ἡ δὲ Παλλὰς ἣν εὗρε.›
‹ξυνὸν τόδ᾽ αὐταῖς, θεοὺς γὰρ οὐ διακρίνω.
τί τῆς δάφνης ὁ καρπός; ἐς τί χρήσωμαι;›
‹μήτ᾽ ἔσθε μήτε πῖνε μήτ᾽ ἐπιχρίσῃ.
ὁ τῆς δ᾽ ἐλαίης ἓν μὲν ... μάσταξ
ὁ στέμφυλον καλεῦσιν, ἓν δὲ τὸ χρῖμα,
ἓν δ᾽ ἡ κολυμβὰς ἣν ἔπωνε χὠ Θησεύς·›
‹τὸ δεύτερον τίθημι τῇ δάφνῃ πτῶμα.
τεῦ γὰρ τὸ φύλλον οἱ ἱκέται προτείνουσι;›
‹τὸ τῆς ἐλαίης·› ‹τὰ τρί᾽ ἡ δάφνη κεῖται.›
(φεῦ τῶν ἀτρύτων, οἷα κωτιλίζουσι·
λαιδρὴ κορώνη, κῶς τὸ χεῖλος οὐκ ἀλγεῖς;)
‹τεῦ γὰρ τὸ πρέμνον Δήλιοι φυλάσσουσι;›
‹τὸ τῆς ἐλαίης ἣ ἀνέπαυσε τὴν Λητώ.›

. . . . ›

ὣς εἶπε· τῇ δ᾽ ὁ θυμὸς ἀμφὶ τῇ ῥήσει
ἤλγησε, μέζων δ᾽ ἢ τὸ πρόσθεν ἠγέρθη
τὰ δεύτερ᾽ ἐς τὸ νεῖκος, ἔστε ...

man [Cecrops] as judge." "One fall against the laurel. Which god honours the laurel, which the olive-tree?" "Apollo honours the laurel, Pallas the olive, which she herself discovered." "This is a tie, for I do not distinguish between gods. What is the laurel's fruit? What use can I make of it?" "Don't eat it, don't drink it, don't use it for ointment. But the olive's fruit is first that which [the poor] chew, the olive-cake as they call it, second [it produces] oil, and third the pickled olive which even Theseus swallowed." "I count this a second fall for the laurel. Whose is the leaf the suppliants offer in appeal?" "The olive's." "The laurel has had three falls now." Alas! those creatures, how they chatter on! Shameless crow, doesn't your lip grow sore? "Whose trunk do the Delians preserve?" "The olive's, which gave rest to Leto . . ." . . .' So she spoke; and the other's heart was pained by her speech, and she was even more anxious than before to compete a second time, until ... a bramble-bush spoke, the thorny ... of the

βάτος τὸ τρηχὺ τειχέων . . . .
ἔλεξεν (ἦν γὰρ οὐκ ἄπωθε τῶν δενδρέων)·
⟨οὐκ ὦ τάλαιναι παυσόμεσθα, μὴ χαρταὶ
γενώμεθ᾽ ἐχθροῖς, μηδ᾽ ἐροῦμεν ἀλλήλας
ἄνολβ᾽ ἀναιδέως, ἀλλὰ ταῦτά γ᾽ . . . .;⟩
τὴν δ᾽ ἄρ᾽ ὑποδρὰξ οἷα ταῦρος ἡ δάφνη
ἔβλεψε καὶ τάδ᾽ εἶπεν ⟨ὦ κακὴ λώβη,
ὡς δὴ μί᾽ ἡμέων καὶ σύ; μή με ποιῆσαι
Ζεὺς τοῦτο· καὶ γὰρ γειτονεῦσ᾽ ἀποπνίγεις
. . . οὐ μὰ Φοῖβον, οὐ μὰ δέσποιναν,
τῇ κύμβαλοι ψοθεῦσιν, οὐ μὰ Πακτωλόν . . .⟩

(Iambus IV)

159. The City Waking Up

Τὴν μὲν ἄρ᾽ ὡς φαμένην ὕπνος λάβε, τὴν δ᾽ ἀίουσαν.
καδδραθέτην δ᾽ οὐ πολλὸν ἐπὶ χρόνον, αἶψα γὰρ ἦλθεν
στιβῆεις ἄγχαυρος, ὅτ᾽ οὐκέτι χεῖρες ἔπαγροι
φιλητέων· ἤδη γὰρ ἐωθινὰ λύχνα φαείνει·
ἀείδει καί πού τις ἀνὴρ ὑδατηγὸς ἱμαῖον·
ἔγρει καί τιν᾽ ἔχοντα παρὰ πλόον οἰκίον ἄξων
τετριγὼς ὑπ᾽ ἄμαξαν, ἀνιάζουσι δὲ πυκνοῖς
δμῶοι χαλκῆες κωφώμενοι ἔνδον ἀκουήν . . .

(Hecale)

walls – for it was not far off from the trees: 'Wretches, let us stop, lest we give pleasure to our foes; let us not rashly say evil [things] of one another; but . . . '. The laurel-tree looked grimly at it like a wild bull and said: 'You disgraceful wretch, you pass yourself off as one of us? Preserve me, Zeus, from that! For even having you near me stifles me. . . . No, by Phoebus, by the Lady for whom the Cymbals clash [Cybele], no, by Pactolus . . .'

WHILE she said this, sleep overcame her and her hearer. They slept soundly, but not for long; for soon the frosty early dawn came, when thieves' hands are no longer seeking their prey, for already the lamps of dawn are shining; many a water-carrier is singing his song of the well, and the axle, creaking under the wagons, wakes the man whose house is beside the highway, while the blacksmith slaves, their own hearing deafened, torment the ear with repeated . . .

160. The Epiphany of Apollo

Οἶον ὁ τὠπόλλωνος ἐσείσατο δάφνινος ὅρπηξ,
οἷα δ᾽ ὅλον τὸ μέλαθρον· ἑκὰς ἑκὰς ὅστις ἀλιτρός.
καὶ δή που τὰ θύρετρα καλῷ ποδὶ Φοῖβος ἀράσσει.
οὐχ ὁράᾳς; ἐπένευσεν ὁ Δήλιος ἡδύ τι φοῖνιξ
ἐξαπίνης, ὁ δὲ κύκνος ἐν ἠέρι καλὸν ἀείδει.
αὐτοὶ νῦν κατοχῆες ἀνακλίνασθε πυλάων,
αὐταὶ δὲ κληῖδες· ὁ γὰρ θεὸς οὐκέτι μακρήν.
οἱ δὲ νέοι μολπήν τε καὶ ἐς χορὸν ἐντύνεσθε.
ὡπόλλων οὐ παντὶ φαείνεται, ἀλλ᾽ ὅτις ἐσθλός·
ὅς μιν ἴδῃ, μέγας οὗτος, ὃς οὐκ ἴδε, λιτὸς ἐκεῖνος.
ὀψόμεθ᾽, ὦ Ἑκάεργε, καὶ ἐσσόμεθ᾽ οὔποτε λιτοί.
μήτε σιωπηλὴν κίθαριν μήτ᾽ ἄψοφον ἴχνος
τοῦ Φοίβου τοὺς παῖδας ἔχειν ἐπιδημήσαντος,
εἰ τελέειν μέλλουσι γάμον πολιήν τε κερεῖσθαι,
ἑστήξειν δὲ τὸ τεῖχος ἐπ᾽ ἀρχαίοισι θεμέθλοις.
ἡγασάμην τοὺς παῖδας, ἐπεὶ χέλυς οὐκέτ᾽ ἀεργός.
εὐφημεῖτ᾽ ἀίοντες ἐπ᾽ Ἀπόλλωνος ἀοιδῇ.
εὐφημεῖ καὶ πόντος, ὅτε κλείουσιν ἀοιδοὶ
ἢ κίθαριν ἢ τόξα, Λυκωρέος ἔντεα Φοίβου.

How the laurel sapling of Apollo shook, how the whole temple shook!
Away, away, whoever is sinful! Surely now Phoebus is knocking at
the door with his shapely foot. Can you not see? Suddenly the Delian
palm nodded sweetly, and the swan sings beautifully in the air. You
door-bolts, open of your own accord, of your own accord, bars [open];
for the god is no longer far away. And you, young men, prepare your-
selves for the song and for the dance.

Apollo does not appear to everyone, but only to those who are
good. The man who sees him is great; the man who has not seen him
is worthless. We shall see you, far-shafting god, and we shall never be
worthless. Let the boys not keep the lyre silent, nor their feet quiet,
when Apollo makes his visit, if they are to reach marriage and to cut
the grey hair [of old age] and if the wall is to stand upon its old founda-
tions. I applaud the boys because the lyre is no longer idle.

Be silent, you that hear, at the song to Apollo. Even the sea is silent
when the singers praise the lyre, or the bow, the weapons of Lycoreian

οὐδὲ Θέτις Ἀχιλῆα κινύρεται αἴλινα μήτηρ,
ὁππόθ' ἰὴ παιῆον ἰὴ παιῆον ἀκούσῃ.

καὶ μὲν ὁ δακρυόεις ἀναβάλλεται ἄλγεα πέτρος,
ὅστις ἐνὶ Φρυγίῃ διερὸς λίθος ἐστήρικται,
μάρμαρον ἀντὶ γυναικὸς ὀιζυρόν τι χανούσης.

(Hymn II)

161. Artemis and the Cyclopes

Αὖθι δὲ Κύκλωπας μετεκίαθε· τοὺς μὲν ἔτετμε
νήσῳ ἐνὶ Λιπάρῃ (Λιπάρη νέον, ἀλλὰ τότ' ἔσκεν
οὔνομά οἱ Μελιγουνίς) ἐπ' ἄκμοσιν Ἡφαίστοιο
ἑσταότας περὶ μύδρον· ἐπείγετο γὰρ μέγα ἔργον·
ἱππείην τετύκοντο Ποσειδάωνι ποτίστρην.
αἱ νύμφαι δ' ἔδδεισαν, ὅπως ἴδον αἰνὰ πέλωρα
πρηόσιν Ὀσσαίοισιν ἐοικότα (πᾶσι δ' ὑπ' ὀφρὺν
φάεα μουνόγληνα σάκει ἴσα τετραβοείῳ
δεινὸν ὑπογλαύσσοντα) καὶ ὁππότε δοῦπον ἄκουσαν
ἄκμονος ἠχήσαντος ἐπὶ μέγα πουλύ τ' ἄημα
φυσάων αὐτῶν τε βαρὺν στόνον· αὖε γὰρ Αἴτνη,

Phoebus. Nor does Thetis, his mother, wail her dirges for Achilles
when she hears 'Hie Paeeon, Hie Paeeon' – the holy cry.

Yes, even the weeping rock forgets its pain, the wet rock that is set
in Phrygia, a marble block like a woman with her mouth gaping in
suffering.

AND at once she went to visit the Cyclopes. She found them in the
island of Lipara – Lipara in later times, but then it was named Meli-
gunis – at the anvils of Hephaestus, standing round a red-hot lump of
iron. For an important work was being hurried through; they were
making a horse-trough for Poseidon. And the Nymphs were frightened,
when they saw the terrible monsters looking like the crags of Ossa –
all had one eye as big as a shield of fourfold hide, which gleamed ter-
ribly out from under their brows – and when they heard the din of the
anvil echoing loudly, and the great blast of the bellows, and the heavy
groaning of the Cyclopes themselves. For Aetna cried out, and

αὖε δὲ Τρινακίη Σικανῶν ἕδος, αὖε δὲ γείτων
Ἰταλίη, μεγάλην δὲ βοὴν ἐπὶ Κύρνος ἀύτει.
εὖθ' οἵ γε ῥαιστῆρας ἀειράμενοι ὑπὲρ ὤμων
ἢ χαλκὸν ζείοντα καμινόθεν ἠὲ σίδηρον
ἀμβολαδὶς τετυπόντες ἐπὶ μέγα μυχθίσσειαν.
τῷ σφέας οὐκ ἐτάλασσαν ἀκηδέες Ὠκεανῖναι
οὔτ' ἄντην ἰδέειν οὔτε κτύπον οὔασι δέχθαι.
οὐ νέμεσις· κείνους γε καὶ αἱ μάλα μηκέτι τυτθαὶ
οὐδέποτ' ἀφρικτὶ μακάρων ὁρόωσι θύγατρες.
ἀλλ' ὅτε κουράων τις ἀπειθέα μητέρι τεύχοι,
μήτηρ μὲν Κύκλωπας ἑῇ ἐπὶ παιδὶ καλιστρεῖ,
Ἄργην ἢ Στερόπην· ὁ δὲ δώματος ἐκ μυχάτοιο
ἔρχεται Ἑρμείης σποδιῇ κεχριμένος αἰθῇ.
αὐτίκα τὴν κούρην μορμύσσεται, ἡ δὲ τεκούσης
δύνει ἔσω κόλπους θεμένη ἐπὶ φάεσι χεῖρας.

(*Hymn III*)

162. Nicoteles

Δωδεκέτη τὸν παῖδα πατὴρ ἀπέθηκε Φίλιππος
ἐνθάδε τὴν πολλὴν ἐλπίδα Νικοτέλην.

Trinacia, the seat of the Sicanians, cried out, and neighbouring Italy
cried out, and Cyrnus screamed with a loud cry. And when they lifted
their hammers above their shoulders, taking turns to smite the bronze
boiling from the furnaces, or the iron, they snorted loudly. Because of
this the daughters of Oceanus could not look at them face to face with-
out terror, nor could they endure the din in their ears. No fault of
theirs! Not even the daughters of the Blessed Ones, even when they
are no longer children, look on those Cyclopes without shuddering.
But, when one of the young girls disobeys her mother, the mother
calls on the Cyclopes to punish her child – Arges or Steropes; and
Hermes comes from the farthest end of the house covered with burnt
ash. At once he plays bogeyman to the child, and she sinks into her
mother's lap, with her hands over her eyes.

PHILIP, the father, laid here his twelve-year-old son, his one great
hope, Nicoteles.

163. Heraclitus

Εἶπέ τις, Ἡράκλειτε, τεὸν μόρον, ἐς δέ με δάκρυ
ἤγαγεν, ἐμνήσθην δ᾽ ὁσσάκις ἀμφότεροι
ἥλιον ἐν λέσχῃ κατεδύσαμεν· ἀλλὰ σὺ μέν που
ξεῖν᾽ Ἁλικαρνησεῦ τετράπαλαι σποδιή·
αἱ δὲ τεαὶ ζώουσιν ἀηδόνες, ᾗσιν ὁ πάντων
ἁρπακτὴς Ἀίδης οὐκ ἐπὶ χεῖρα βαλεῖ.

164. All Public Things Disgust Me

Ἐχθαίρω τὸ ποίημα τὸ κυκλικόν, οὐδὲ κελεύθῳ
χαίρω, τίς πολλοὺς ὧδε καὶ ὧδε φέρει·
μισέω καὶ περίφοιτον ἐρώμενον, οὐδ᾽ ἀπὸ κρήνης
πίνω· σικχαίνω πάντα τὰ δημόσια.
Λυσανίη, σὺ δὲ ναίχι καλός, καλός — ἀλλὰ πρὶν εἰπεῖν
τοῦτο σαφῶς, ἠχώ φησί τις· ⟨ἄλλος ἔχει.⟩

SOMEONE spoke of your death, Heraclitus, and it moved me to tears, and I remembered how often we put the sun to sleep as we were talking. You, my friend from Halicarnassus, lie somewhere, long long ago gone to dust; but your nightingales [poems] are living, and Hades who snatches everything will never lay his hand upon them.

I HATE the poems of the epic cycle, and take no pleasure in a road that carries many men to and fro. I also hate a beloved whom many go after; and I do not drink water from a [public] fountain. All public things disgust me. Lysanias, yes indeed you are handsome, handsome. But, before I have had the chance to say this clearly, an echo says, 'Another man has him.'*

* Echo would have answered ⟨ἔχει ἄλλος⟩ to ⟨ναίχι καλός⟩.

ASCLEPIADES
fl. 290 B.C.

165. *Zeus, Too, is a Victim*

Νῖφε, χαλαζοβόλει, ποίει σκότος, αἴθε, κεραύνου,
   πάντα τὰ πορφύροντ' ἐν χθονὶ σεῖε νέφη.
ἢν γάρ με κτείνῃς, τότε παύσομαι· ἢν δὲ μ' ἀφῇς ζῆν,
   καὶ διαδὺς τούτων χεῖρον, κωμάσομαι·
ἕλκει γάρ μ' ὁ κρατῶν καὶ σοῦ θεός, ᾧ ποτε πεισθείς,
   Ζεῦ, διὰ χαλκείων χρυσὸς ἔδυς θαλάμων.

166. *Nicarete*

Νικαρέτης τὸ πόθοισι βεβλημένον ἡδὺ πρόσωπον,
   πυκνὰ δι' ὑψορόφων φαινόμενον θυρίδων,
αἱ χαροπαὶ Κλεοφῶντος ἐπὶ προθύροις ἐμάραναν,
   Κύπρι φίλη, γλυκεροῦ βλέμματος ἀστεροπαί.

SEND snow, hurl hail, make darkness, lightning, thunder; shake all the dark clouds on the earth. If you kill me, then I shall stop; but if you allow me to live, even though I go through worse than this, I will serenade my love. For the god is dragging me on, he who is even stronger than you, Zeus; he who once persuaded you to turn yourself into gold and make your way into the bronze chamber.

NICARETE's sweet face – often seen through her high windows – struck by the arrows of desire, was blasted, dear Cypris, by the joyful lightning that shot from Cleophon's sweet eyes as he stood at her doorway.

167. Tryphera

Εἰς ἀγορὰν βαδίσας, Δημήτριε, τρεῖς παρ' Ἀμύντου
γλαυκίσκους αἴτει, καὶ δέκα φυκίδια·
καὶ κυφὰς καρῖδας — ἀριθμήσει δέ σοι αὐτός —
εἴκοσι καὶ τέτορας δεῦρο λαβών ἄπιθι.
καὶ παρὰ Θαυβορίου ῥοδίνους ἓξ πρόσλαβε · · ·
καὶ Τρυφέραν ταχέως ἐν παρόδῳ κάλεσον.

168. Drink, Asclepiades

Πίν', Ἀσκληπιάδη· τί τὰ δάκρυα ταῦτα; τί πάσχεις;
οὐ σὲ μόνον χαλεπὴ Κύπρις ἐληίσατο,
οὐδ' ἐπὶ σοὶ μούνῳ κατεθήξατο τόξα καὶ ἰοὺς
πικρὸς Ἔρως. τί ζῶν ἐν σποδιῇ τίθεσαι;
πίνωμεν Βάκχου ζωρὸν πόμα· δάκτυλος ἀώς·
ἦ πάλιν κοιμιστὰν λύχνον μένομεν;
πίνωμεν, δύσερως· μετά τοι χρόνον οὐκέτι πουλύν,
σχέτλιε, τὴν μακρὰν νύκτ' ἀναπαυσόμεθα.

Go along to the market, Demetrius, and get three small grey-fish and ten little wrasses [cheap fish] from Amyntas' shop; and get two dozen humped prawns – he will count them for you – and come straight back. And also get six rose-garlands from Thauborius; and, as you go by, nip in and invite Tryphera.

DRINK, Asclepiades. Why these tears? What is the trouble? Cruel Cypris did not devastate only you; sharp-stinging Eros did not sharpen his bow and arrows against you alone. Why put yourself among the ashes of the dead, when still alive? Let us drink the draught of Bacchus unmixed. Daylight is but a finger. Shall we wait to see again the lamp that calls us to sleep? Let us drink, unhappy lover. Before long, poor wretch, we shall rest through the long night.

169. *Wine is the Test of Love*

Οἶνος ἔρωτος ἔλεγχος· ἐρᾶν ἀρνεύμενον ἡμῖν
ἤτασαν αἱ πολλαὶ Νικαγόρην προπόσεις.
καὶ γὰρ ἐδάκρυσεν καὶ ἐνύστασε, καί τι κατηφὲς
ἔβλεπε, χὠ σφιχθεὶς οὐκ ἔμενε στέφανος.

POSEIDIPPUS
fl. 280 B.C.

170. *Archianax*

Τὸν τριετῆ παίζοντα περὶ φρέαρ ᾽Αρχιάνακτα
εἴδωλον μορφᾶς κωφὸν ἐπεσπάσατο·
ἐκ δ᾽ ὕδατος τὸν παῖδα διάβροχον ἥρπασε μάτηρ
σκεπτομένα ζωᾶς εἴ τινα μοῖραν ἔχει·
Νύμφας δ᾽ οὐκ ἐμίηνεν ὁ νήπιος, ἀλλ᾽ ἐπὶ γούνων
ματρὸς κοιμαθεὶς τὸν βαθὺν ὕπνον ἔχει.

WINE is the test of love. The many toasts distressed Nicagoras, who was telling us he was not in love. For he dropped a tear, his head drooped, he cast his glances somewhat downwards, and the tightly bound garland did not keep its place.

THE dumb image of his own form drew down Archianax, the three-year-old boy, as he was playing by the well. His mother snatched the boy out of the water, soaked through, wondering if any measure of life was left to him. The poor innocent did not defile the Nymphs with his death, but fell asleep on his mother's knees, and is sleeping the deep slumber.

? POSEIDIPPUS

171. You Are Not Being Fair

Στρογγύλη, εὐτόρνευτε, μονούατε, μακροτράχηλε,
ὑψαύχην, στεινῷ φθεγγομένη στόματι,
Βάκχου καὶ Μουσέων ἱλαρὴ λάτρι καὶ Κυθερείης,
ἡδύγελως, τερπνὴ συμβολικῶν ταμίη,
τίφθ' ὁπόταν νήφω, μεθύεις σύ μοι, ἢν δὲ μεθυσθῶ,
ἐκνήφεις; ἀδικεῖς συμποτικὴν φιλίην.

HEDYLUS
fl. 280 B.C.

172. Let Us Drink

Πίνωμεν· καὶ γάρ τι νέον, καὶ γάρ τι παρ' οἶνον
εὕροιμεν λεπτὸν καί τι μελιχρὸν ἔπος.
'Αλλὰ κάδοις Χίου με κατάβρεχε, καὶ λέγε· ‹Παῖζε,
Ἡδύλε.› μισῶ ζῆν εἰς κενὸν οὐ μεθύων.

ROUND, well-wrought, one-eared, long-throated, with your neck held high, speaking with your narrow mouth, merry worshipper of Bacchus, the Muses and Cythereia, sweetly laughing, delightful treasurer of our dining-club contributions, why when I am sober are you full of wine, and why when I get tipsy do you become sober? You break the laws of drinkers' friendship.

LET us drink. For, indeed, over wine we may find some new, some elegant, some honey-sweet turn of speech. Soak me with jars of Chian wine and say: 'Enjoy yourself, Hedylus.' I hate living emptily, not drunk with wine.

APOLLONIUS RHODIUS
295–215 B.C.

173. The Sailing of the Argo

Οἱ δ', ὥστ' ἠίθεοι Φοίβῳ χορὸν ἢ ἐνὶ Πυθοῖ
ἢ που ἐν Ὀρτυγίῃ, ἢ ἐφ' ὕδασιν Ἰσμηνοῖο
στησάμενοι, φόρμιγγος ὑπαὶ περὶ βωμὸν ὁμαρτῇ
ἐμμελέως κραιπνοῖσι πέδον ῥήσσωσι πόδεσσιν·
ὣς οἱ ὑπ' Ὀρφῆος κιθάρῃ πέπληγον ἐρετμοῖς
πόντου λάβρον ὕδωρ, ἐπὶ δὲ ῥόθια κλύζοντο·
ἀφρῷ δ' ἔνθα καὶ ἔνθα κελαινὴ κήκιεν ἅλμη
δεινὸν μορμύρουσα περισθενέων μένει ἀνδρῶν.
στράπτε δ' ὑπ' ἠελίῳ φλογὶ εἴκελα νηὸς ἰούσης
τεύχεα· μακραὶ δ' αἰὲν ἐλευκαίνοντο κέλευθοι,
ἀτραπὸς ὣς χλοεροῖο διειδομένη πεδίοιο.
πάντες δ' οὐρανόθεν λεῦσσον θεοὶ ἤματι κείνῳ
νῆα καὶ ἡμιθέων ἀνδρῶν γένος, οἳ τότ' ἄριστοι
πόντον ἐπιπλώεσκον· ἐπ' ἀκροτάτῃσι δὲ νύμφαι
Πηλιάδες σκοπιῇσιν ἐθάμβεον, εἰσορόωσαι
ἔργον Ἀθηναίης Ἰτωνίδος ἠδὲ καὶ αὐτοὺς
ἥρωας χείρεσσιν ἐπικραδάοντας ἐρετμά.
αὐτὰρ ὅγ' ἐξ ὑπάτου ὄρεος κίεν ἄγχι θαλάσσης
Χείρων Φιλλυρίδης, πολιῇ δ' ἐπὶ κύματος ἀγῇ

AND, just like young men who create a dance to honour Phoebus, in Delphi or Delos or by the waters of Ismenus, and all bring their quick feet down on the ground together round the altar in time to the sound of the lyre, so they struck the turbulent sea with their oars to Orpheus' lyre, and the rushing waves surged up. And on either side the dark salt water broke into foam, seething angrily at the might of such sturdy men. As the ship moved on their armour glittered in the sunshine like fire; and all the time a long white wake followed behind, which could be seen like a path across a grassy plain. On that day all the gods looked down from heaven on the ship and the might of her heroic men, the finest of their time to sail the sea. And from the highest peaks the nymphs of Pelion marvelled as they watched the work of Itonian Athene, and the heroes themselves wielding the oars in their hands. And Cheiron, the son of Philyra, came down from the highest mountain to the sea-shore, and wet his feet where the white surf broke, and,

τέγγε πόδας, καὶ πολλὰ βαρείῃ χειρὶ κελεύων
νόστον ἐπευφήμησεν ἀπηρέα νισσομένοισιν.
σὺν καὶ οἱ παράκοιτις, ἐπωλένιον φορέουσα
Πηλείδην Ἀχιλῆα, φίλῳ δειδίσκετο πατρί.

(*Voyage of the* Argo)

174. Eros and Aphrodite

Ἦ ῥα, καὶ ἔλλιπε θῶκον, ἐφωμάρτησε δ' Ἀθήνη·
ἐκ δ' ἴσαν ἄμφω ταίγε παλίσσυτοι· ἡ δὲ καὶ αὐτὴ
βῆ ῥ' ἴμεν Οὐλύμποιο κατὰ πτύχας, εἴ μιν ἐφεύροι·
εὖρε δὲ τόνγ' ἀπάνευθε, Διὸς θαλερῇ ἐν ἀλωῇ,
οὐκ οἶον, μετὰ καὶ Γανυμήδεα, τόν ῥά ποτε Ζεὺς
οὐρανῷ ἐγκατένασσεν ἐφέστιον ἀθανάτοισιν,
κάλλεος ἱμερθείς. ἀμφ' ἀστραγάλοισι δὲ τώγε
χρυσείοις, ἅ τε κοῦροι ὁμήθεες, ἐψιόωντο.
καί ῥ' ὁ μὲν ἤδη πάμπαν ἐνίπλεον ᾧ ὑπὸ μαζῷ
μάργος Ἔρως λαιῆς ὑποΐσχανε χειρὸς ἀγοστόν,
ὀρθὸς ἐφεστηώς, γλυκερὸν δέ οἱ ἀμφὶ παρειὰς
χροιῆς θάλλεν ἔρευθος· ὁ δ' ἐγγύθεν ὀκλαδὸν ἧστο
σῖγα κατηφιόων, δοιὼ δ' ἔχεν, ἄλλον ἔτ' αὔτως

waving many times with his great hand, wished the travellers a painless
return. With him was his wife, carrying in her arms Achilles the son of
Peleus, whom she held up for his beloved father to see.

SHE [Hera] spoke and left her seat; and Athene followed her, and they
both set out so as to return soon. And she [Aphrodite] also went on her
way through the glens of Olympus to find him [Eros]. And she found
him far away in the fruit-laden orchard of Zeus, not alone, but with him
Ganymede, whom once Zeus had brought home to live with the im-
mortal gods in heaven, desiring his beauty. And these two, similar
boys, were playing with golden knuckle-bones [dice]. And greedy
Eros was already standing up with the palm of his left hand full of
them clutched under his breast; on his cheeks blossomed a sweet red

329

ἄλλῳ ἐπιπροϊείς, κεχόλωτο δὲ καγχαλόωντι.
καί μὴν τούσγε παρᾶσσον ἐπί προτέροισιν ὀλέσσας
βῆ κενεαῖς σὺν χερσίν ἀμήχανος, οὐδ᾽ ἐνόησεν
Κύπριν ἐπιπλομένην· ἡ δ᾽ ἀντίη ἵστατο παιδός,
καί μιν ἄφαρ γναθμοῖο κατασχομένη προσέειπεν·
‹ Τίπτ᾽ ἐπιμειδιάᾳς, ἄφατον κακόν; ἦέ μιν αὔτως
ἤπαφες οὐδὲ δίκῃ περιέπλεο, νῆιν ἐόντα;
εἰ δ᾽ ἄγε μοι πρόφρων τέλεσον χρέος ὅττι κεν εἴπω,
καί κέν τοι ὀπάσαιμι Διὸς περικαλλὲς ἄθυρμα
κεῖνο, τό οἱ ποίησε φίλη τροφὸς Ἀδρήστεια
ἄντρῳ ἐν Ἰδαίῳ ἔτι νήπια κουρίζοντι,
σφαῖραν ἐυτρόχαλον, τῆς οὐ σύγε μείλιον ἄλλο
χειρῶν Ἡφαίστοιο κατακτεατίσσῃ ἄρειον.›

(*Voyage of the* Argo)

175. Medea

Νύξ μὲν ἔπειτ᾽ ἐπί γαῖαν ἄγεν κνέφας, οἱ δ᾽ ἐνί πόντῳ
ναυτίλοι εἰς Ἑλίκην τε καί ἀστέρας Ὠρίωνος
ἔδρακον ἐκ νηῶν, ὕπνοιο δὲ καί τις ὁδίτης
ἤδη καί πυλαωρὸς ἐέλδετο, καί τινα παίδων

glow; near him the other was sitting on his haunches silent and down-cast; he had two [dice] left, which he threw one after the other endlessly, and was angry at Eros' loud laughter. And, of course, losing them as quickly as the others, he went off empty-handed, helpless; he did not notice Cypris approaching. And she stood, facing her son, and, taking his chin in her hand, said:

'Why do you smile in triumph, you unspeakable rascal? You cheated him, didn't you? Didn't you beat him unfairly, because he doesn't know the game? Come, do me the favour readily that I'm going to ask of you, and I will give you that beautiful toy of Zeus – the one which his dear nurse Adrasteia made for him in the Idaean cave when he was still a child and liked children's things – a well-rounded ball; you could get no better toy from the hands of Hephaestus.'

THEN night brought darkness over the earth; and the sailors on the sea looked from their ships to the Bear and the stars of Orion; and now the traveller and the watchmen long for sleep, and a sad sleep covers

μητέρα τεθνεώτων ἀδινὸν περὶ κῶμ' ἐκάλυπτεν,
οὐδὲ κυνῶν ὑλακὴ ἔτ' ἀνὰ πτόλιν, οὐ θρόος ἦεν
ἠχήεις, σιγὴ δὲ μελαινομένην ἔχεν ὀρφνην·
ἀλλὰ μάλ' οὐ Μήδειαν ἐπὶ γλυκερὸς λάβεν ὕπνος.
πολλὰ γὰρ Αἰσονίδαο πόθῳ μελεδήματ' ἔγειρεν
δειδυῖαν ταύρων κρατερὸν μένος, οἷσιν ἔμελλεν
φθεῖσθαι ἀεικελίῃ μοίρῃ κατὰ νειὸν Ἄρηος.
δάκρυ δ' ἀπ' ὀφθαλμῶν ἐλέῳ ῥέεν· ἔνδοθι δ' αἰεὶ
τεῖρ' ὀδύνη, σμύχουσα διὰ χροὸς ἀμφί τ' ἀραιὰς
ἶνας καὶ κεφαλῆς ὑπὸ νείατον ἰνίον ἄχρις,
ἔνθ' ἀλεγεινότατον δύνει ἄχος, ὁππότ' ἀνίας
ἀκάματοι πραπίδεσσιν ἐνισκίμψωσιν ἔρωτες.
πυκνὰ δέ οἱ κραδίη στηθέων ἔντοσθεν ἔθυιεν,
ἠελίου ὥς τίς τε δόμοις ἔνι πάλλεται αἴγλη,
ὕδατος ἐξανιοῦσα τὸ δὴ νέον ἠὲ λέβητι
ἠέ που ἐν γαυλῷ κέχυται, ἡ δ' ἔνθα καὶ ἔνθα
ὠκείῃ στροφάλιγγι τινάσσεται ἀίσσουσα —
ὣς δὲ καὶ ἐν στήθεσσι κέαρ ἐλελίζετο κούρης,
φῆ δέ οἱ ἄλλοτε μὲν θελκτήρια φάρμακα ταύρων
δωσέμεν· ἄλλοτε δ' οὔτι, καταφθίσθαι δὲ καὶ αὐτή·
αὐτίκα δ' οὔτ' αὐτὴ θανέειν, οὐ φάρμακα δώσειν,
ἀλλ' αὔτως εὔκηλος ἐὴν ὀτλησέμεν ἄτην.

the mother whose children have died; there was no longer any barking from the dogs in the city, nor loud voices of men; silence held the blackening gloom. But sweet sleep did not come to Medea; for, in love with Aeson's son, many cares kept her awake, and she feared the violent strength of the bulls, which would give him an ugly death in the field of Ares. And the tears flowed from her eyes, for she pitied him. And always in her heart pain tortured her, and burnt through her skin, and across the soft sinews, and deep down under the nape of the neck where pain dives sharpest, when the untiring gods of Love attack the heart with suffering. And in her breast her heart beat fast, as a sunbeam quivers on the walls of a house when it is reflected from water which has just been poured into a cauldron, or perhaps a pail; and the reflection jumps and shakes here and there as the water whirls swiftly. Even so in the girl's breast her heart whirled. And one moment she thought she would give him the charms to put a spell on the bulls, and at another that she would not, and that she herself would die; and then suddenly that she would not die and not give the charms, but bear her

ἐζομένη δῆπειτα δοάσσατο, φώνησέν τε·
‹Δειλὴ ἐγώ, νῦν ἔνθα κακῶν ἢ ἔνθα γένωμαι;
πάντη μοι φρένες εἰσὶν ἀμήχανοι, οὐδέ τις ἀλκὴ
πήματος, ἀλλ' αὕτως φλέγει ἔμπεδον. ὡς ὄφελόν γε
Ἀρτέμιδος κραιπνοῖσι πάρος βελέεσσι δαμῆναι,
πρὶν τόνγ' εἰσιδέειν, πρὶν Ἀχαιίδα νῆα κομίσσαι
Χαλκιόπης υἷας· τοὺς μὲν θεὸς ἤ τις Ἐρινὺς
ἄμμι πολυκλαύτους δεῦρ' ἤγαγε κεῖθεν ἀνίας. —
φθίσθω ἀεθλεύων, εἴ οἱ κατὰ νειὸν ὀλέσθαι
μοῖρα πέλει· πῶς γάρ κεν ἐμοὺς λελάθοιμι τοκῆας
φάρμακα μησαμένη, ποῖον δ' ἐπὶ μῦθον ἐνίψω;
τίς δὲ δόλος, τίς μῆτις ἐπίκλοπος ἔσσετ' ἀρωγῆς; —
ἢ μιν ἄνευθ' ἑτάρων προσπτύξομαι οἶον ἰδοῦσα;
δύσμορος· οὐ μὲν ἔολπα καταφθιμένοιό περ ἔμπης
λωφήσειν ἀχέων, τότε δ' ἂν κακὸν ἄμμι πέλοιτο
κεῖνος ὅτε ζωῆς ἀπαμείρεται. ἐρρέτω αἰδώς,
ἐρρέτω ἀγλαΐη, ὁ δ' ἐμῇ ἰότητι σαωθεὶς
ἀσκηθής, ἵνα οἱ θυμῷ φίλον, ἔνθα νέοιτο·
αὐτὰρ ἐγὼν αὐτῆμαρ, ὅτ' ἐξανύσειεν ἄεθλον,
τεθναίην, ἢ λαιμὸν ἀναρτήσασα μελάθρῳ
ἢ καὶ πασσαμένη ῥαιστήρια φάρμακα θυμοῦ. —

fate, just as she was, patiently. Then, sitting down, she hesitated in doubt, and said:

'Poor me, which of the evils must I choose now? I am utterly bewildered; there is no cure for my pain, but it burns on unceasingly despite all. I wish I had been killed by Artemis' swift shafts before I had set eyes on him, before Chalciope's sons brought the Achaean ship here. Some god, or some fury, brought them here to cause us suffering and many tears. Let him die in the battle, if his fate is to die on the field. For how could I prepare the charms behind my parent's back? What story can I tell them? What trick, what clever plan can I find to help me? If I see him alone, away from his companions, shall I greet him? I am unlucky! I can never hope to find rest from my sorrows, even if he is killed; then misery would come to me when he loses his life. Away with modesty, away with my good name! May he go unharmed, wherever his heart wishes, saved by my efforts. But as for me, on the very day he successfully finishes the contest, may I die – either within the palace hanging my neck in a noose, or swallowing fatal drugs. Yet

ἀλλὰ καὶ ὣς φθιμένῃ μοι ἐπιλλίξουσιν ὀπίσσω
κερτομίας, τηλοῦ δὲ πόλις περὶ πᾶσα βοήσει
πότμον ἐμόν· καί κέν με διὰ στόματος φορέουσαι
Κολχίδες ἄλλυδις ἄλλαι ἀεικέα μωμήσονται·
«ἥτις κηδομένη τόσον ἀνέρος ἀλλοδαποῖο
κάτθανεν, ἥτις δῶμα καὶ οὓς ᾔσχυνε τοκῆας,
μαργοσύνῃ εἴξασα.» — τί δ᾽ οὐκ ἐμὸν ἔσσεται αἶσχος;
ὤ μοι ἐμῆς ἄτης. ἦ τ᾽ ἂν πολὺ κέρδιον εἴη
τῇδ᾽ αὐτῇ ἐν νυκτὶ λιπεῖν βίον ἐν θαλάμοισιν,
πότμῳ ἀνωίστῳ κάκ᾽ ἐλέγχεα πάντα φυγοῦσαν,
πρὶν τάδε λωβήεντα καὶ οὐκ ὀνομαστὰ τελέσσαι.»
Ἦ, καὶ φωριαμὸν μετεκίαθεν, ᾗ ἔνι πολλὰ
φάρμακά οἱ, τὰ μὲν ἐσθλά, τὰ δὲ ῥαιστήρι᾽, ἔκειτο.
ἐνθεμένη δ᾽ ἐπὶ γούνατ᾽ ὀδύρετο, δεῦε δὲ κόλπους
ἄλληκτον δακρύοισι, τὰ δ᾽ ἔρρεεν ἀσταγὲς αὔτως,
αἴν᾽ ὀλοφυρομένης τὸν ἑὸν μόρον. ἵετο δ᾽ ἥγε
φάρμακα λέξασθαι θυμοφθόρα τόφρα πάσαιτο,
ἤδη καὶ δεσμοὺς ἀνελύετο φωριαμοῖο,
ἐξελέειν μεμαυῖα, δυσάμμορος· ἀλλά οἱ ἄφνω
δεῖμ᾽ ὀλοὸν στυγεροῖο κατὰ φρένας ἦλθ᾽ Ἀίδαο,
ἔσχετο δ᾽ ἀμφασίῃ δηρὸν χρόνον. ἀμφὶ δὲ πᾶσαι
θυμηδεῖς βιότοιο μεληδόνες ἰνδάλλοντο·

even so, when I am dead, they will fling taunts at me; and every distant
city will ring with my fate, and the Colchian women, tossing my name
on their lips, will revile me everywhere, and mock me – "The girl who
cared so much for a stranger that she killed herself; the girl who dis-
graced her home and her parents, overcome by a mad passion." And
what disgrace will not be mine? Alas, the madness of my passion. It
would be far better for me to take leave of life by some mysterious
death in my room this very night, escaping all slander and reproach,
before I do such dreadful, unspeakable things.'

She spoke, and fetched a box in which were many drugs, some good
ones, others for killing; and, putting this upon her knees, she wept.
And she wet her bosom with endless tears, which, as before, flowed in
torrents, as she wept bitterly for her own fate. And she longed to
choose a murderous drug to take, and she was already loosening the
clasp of the box eager to pull it out, the unhappy girl. But suddenly a
terrible fear of hateful Hades seized her. And she held back for long in
silence, and all the pleasant things for which she cared in life flashed

μνήσατο μὲν τερπνῶν, ὅσ' ἐνὶ ζωοῖσι πέλονται
μνήσαθ' ὁμηλικίης περιγηθέος, οἷά τε κούρη·
καί τέ οἱ ἠέλιος γλυκίων γένετ' εἰσοράασθαι,
ἢ πάρος, εἰ ἐτεόν γε νόῳ ἐπεμαίεθ' ἔκαστα.
καὶ τὴν μέν ῥα πάλιν σφετέρων ἀποκάτθετο γούνων
Ἥρης ἐννεσίῃσι μετάτροπος· οὐδ' ἔτι βουλὰς
ἄλλῃ δοιάζεσκεν, ἐέλδετο δ' αἶψα φανῆναι
ἠῶ τελλομένην, ἵνα οἱ θελκτήρια δοίη
φάρμακα συνθεσίῃσι καὶ ἀντήσειεν ἐς ὠπήν.
πυκνὰ δ' ἀνὰ κληῖδας ἑῶν λύεσκε θυράων,
αἴγλην σκεπτομένη· τῇ δ' ἀσπάσιον βάλε φέγγος
Ἠριγενής, κίνυντο δ' ἀνὰ πτολίεθρον ἕκαστοι.

(*Voyage of the* Argo)

176. The Light of Love

Ὣς φάτο, κυδαίνων· ἡ δ' ἐγκλιδὸν ὄσσε βαλοῦσα
νεκτάρεον μείδησε, χύθη δέ οἱ ἔνδοθι θυμὸς
αἴνῳ ἀειρομένης· καὶ ἀνέδρακεν ὄμμασιν ἄντην,
οὐδ' ἔχεν ὅττι πάροιθεν ἔπος προτιμυθήσαιτο,
ἀλλ' ἄμυδις μενέαινεν ἀολλέα πάντ' ἀγορεῦσαι.

before her. She thought of the delights that there are for the living; she thought of her happy friends, as a young girl does; and the sun grew sweeter than ever to see, as her heart truly longed for all these things. And she put the box aside, [taking it] off her knees; her mind changed at Hera's prompting and she wavered no longer in her purpose, but longed for the dawn to rise quickly so that she could give him, as she had promised, the charms to work the spell, and meet him face to face. And she often loosened the bolts of her door to watch for the first glimmer of day; and she rejoiced when Dawn shed her light, and people in the town began to stir.

So he [Jason] spoke, paying court to her [Medea]; and she cast her eyes down with a nectar-sweet smile; and her heart melted within her, elated by his praise, and she gazed straight into his eyes. She did not know what to say first, but longed to tell him everything at once. She

προπρὸ δ' ἀφειδήσασα θυώδεος ἔξελε μίτρης
φάρμακον· αὐτὰρ ὅγ' αἶψα χεροῖν ὑπέδεκτο γεγηθώς.
καί νύ κέ οἱ καὶ πᾶσαν ἀπὸ στηθέων ἀρύσασα
ψυχὴν ἐγγυάλιξεν ἀγαιομένη χατέοντι·
τοῖος ἀπὸ ξανθοῖο καρήατος Αἰσονίδαο
στράπτεν Ἔρως ἡδεῖαν ἀπὸ φλόγα, τῆς δ' ἀμαρυγὰς
ὀφθαλμῶν ἥρπαζεν, ἰαίνετο δὲ φρένας εἴσω
τηκομένη, οἷόν τε περὶ ῥοδέησιν ἐέρση
τήκεται ἠῴοισιν ἰαινομένη φαέεσσιν.
ἄμφω δ' ἄλλοτε μέν τε κατ' οὔδεος ὄμματ' ἔρειδον
αἰδόμενοι, ὁτὲ δ' αὖτις ἐπὶ σφίσι βάλλον ὀπωπὰς
ἱμερόεν φαιδρῇσιν ὑπ' ὀφρύσι μειδιόωντες.

(Voyage of the Argo)

177. Argo *Sails through the Wandering Rocks*

Ἔνθα σφιν κοῦραι Νηρηΐδες ἄλλοθεν ἄλλαι
ἤντεον, ἡ δ' ὄπιθε πτέρυγος θίγε πηδαλίοιο
δῖα Θέτις, Πλαγκτῇσιν ἐνὶ σπιλάδεσσιν ἔρυσθαι.
ὡς δ' ὁπόταν δελφῖνες ὑπὲξ ἁλὸς εὐδιόωντες
σπερχομένην ἀγεληδὸν ἑλίσσωνται περὶ νῆα,

did not hesitate, and from her fragrant girdle brought out the charm, and at once he took it in his hands with joy. She would have even drawn out her whole soul from her breast, and given it to him, exulting in his desire [for her]; such was the sweet flame which Love flashed from the golden head of Aeson's son; and he [Love] held her gleaming eyes. And her heart grew warm within, melting away as the dew melts round roses when warmed by the morning light. And at one moment both were fixing their eyes on the ground in embarrassment, and then again they were casting glances at each other, smiling with the light of love under their radiant brows.

THE Nereids met them here, swimming in from all sides; and Lady Thetis, coming up astern, laid her hand on the rudder-blade to guide them through the Wandering Rocks. And, as when in fair weather schools of dolphins come up from the depths of the sea and circle round a fast-sailing ship — seen now ahead, now astern, now abeam of

ἄλλοτε μὲν προπάροιθεν ὁρώμενοι ἄλλοτ' ὄπισθεν
ἄλλοτε παρβολάδην, ναύτῃσι δὲ χάρμα τέτυκται —
ὣς αἱ ὑπεκπροθέουσαι ἐπήτριμοι εἱλίσσοντο
'Αργώῃ περὶ νηί· Θέτις δ' ἴθυνε κέλευθον.
καὶ ῥ' ὅτε δὴ Πλαγκτῇσιν ἐνιχρίμψεσθαι ἔμελλον,
αὐτίκ' ἀνασχόμεναι λευκοῖς ἐπὶ γούνασι πέζας,
ὑψοῦ ἐπ' αὐτάων σπιλάδων καὶ κύματος ἀγῆς
ῥώοντ' ἔνθα καὶ ἔνθα διασταδὸν ἀλλήλῃσιν.
τὴν δὲ παρηορίην κόπτεν ῥόος· ἀμφὶ δὲ κῦμα
λάβρον ἀειρόμενον πέτραις ἐπικαχλάζεσκεν,
αἵ θ' ὁτὲ μὲν κρημνοῖς ἐναλίγκιαι ἠέρι κῦρον,
ἄλλοτε δὲ βρύχιαι νεάτῳ ὑπὸ κεύθεϊ πόντου
ἠρήρεινθ', ὅθι πολλὸν ὑπείρεχεν ἄγριον οἶδμα.
αἱ δ', ὥστ' ἠμαθόεντος ἐπισχεδὸν αἰγιαλοῖο
παρθενικαί, δίχα κόλπον ἐπ' ἰξύας εἱλίξασαι,
σφαίρῃ ἀθύρουσιν περιηγέϊ· αἱ μὲν ἔπειτα
ἄλλη ὑπ' ἐξ ἄλλης δέχεται καὶ ἐς ἠέρα πέμπει
ὕψι μεταχρονίην, ἡ δ' οὔ ποτε πίλναται οὔδει —
ὣς αἱ νῆα θέουσαν ἀμοιβαδὶς ἄλλοθεν ἄλλη
πέμπε διηερίην ἐπὶ κύμασιν, αἰὲν ἄπωθεν
πετράων· περὶ δέ σφιν ἐρευγόμενον ζέεν ὕδωρ.

her, to the delight of the sailors – so the Nereids darted up, one after the other, and circled round the ship Argo as Thetis guided its course. And when she was about to touch the Wandering Rocks, they quickly lifted their dresses above their white knees, and hurried up, at a distance from one another, on to the rocks themselves, where the waves broke, on both sides of the ship. The current struck the side of the ship and all around the furious waves rose and crashed over the rocks, which one moment touched the sky like beetling crags, and then, down in the lowest depths, were fixed fast at the bottom of the sea, where the wild waves stood far above them. And they [the Nereids] – just as young girls by a sandy beach roll their skirts up to their waists on either side, and play with a round ball; they catch it, one from the other, and throw it high into the air, and it never touches the ground – so they in turn, one after the other, sent the ship through the air over the waves, always keeping her away from the rocks; and the water spouted and seethed around them. And lord Hephaestus himself,

τὰς δὲ καὶ αὐτὸς ἄναξ κορυφῆς ἔπι λισσάδος ἄκρης
ὀρθός, ἐπὶ στελεῇ τυπίδος βαρὺν ὦμον ἐρείσας,
Ἥφαιστος θηεῖτο, καὶ αἰγλήεντος ὕπερθεν
οὐρανοῦ ἑστηυῖα Διὸς δάμαρ, ἀμφὶ δ' Ἀθήνη
βάλλε χέρας, τοῖόν μιν ἔχεν δέος εἰσορόωσαν.
ὅσση δ' εἰαρινοῦ μηκύνεται ἤματος αἶσα,
τοσσάτιον μογέεσκον ἐπὶ χρόνον ὀχλίζουσαι
νῆα διὲκ πέτρας πολυηχέας. οἱ δ' ἄνεμοιο
αὖτις ἐπαυρόμενοι προτέρω θέον· ὦκα δ' ἄμειβον
Θρινακίης λειμῶνα, βοῶν τροφὸν Ἠελίοιο.
ἔνθ' αἱ μὲν κατὰ βένθος ἁλίγκιαι αἰθυίῃσιν
δῦνον, ἐπεί ῥ' ἀλόχοιο Διὸς πόρσυνον ἐφετμάς·

(*Voyage of the* Argo)

LEONIDAS OF TARENTUM
fl. 274 B.C.

178. The Season for Sailing

Ὁ πλόος ὡραῖος· καὶ γὰρ λαλαγεῦσα χελιδὼν
ἤδη μέμβλωκεν, χὠ χαρίεις Ζέφυρος·
λειμῶνες δ' ἀνθεῦσι, σεσίγηκεν δὲ θάλασσα
κύματι καὶ τρηχεῖ πνεύματι βρασσομένη.

standing on the top of a smooth rock and resting his heavy shoulder
on the handle of his hammer, watched them, and the wife of Zeus
watched them, as she stood above the flashing heaven; and she threw
her arms round Athene, so great was the fear that seized her as she
watched. And for as long as daylight in spring draws on into the
evening, they [the Nereids] toiled, heaving the ship between the loud-
echoing rocks; then they [the Argonauts] caught the wind again and
sped on, and soon passed the meadow of Thrinacia, which fed the oxen
of Helios. There, the nymphs plunged to the depths of the sea like sea-
mews, since they had fulfilled the request of the wife of Zeus.

IT is the season for sailing; already the chattering swallow has come,
and gentle Zephyrus [the west wind]; the meadows are in flower; and
the sea, seething with waves and rough winds, has sunk to silence.

ἀγκύρας ἀνέλοιο, καὶ ἐκλύσαιο γύαια,
    ναυτίλε, καὶ πλώοις πᾶσαν ἐφεὶς ὀθόνην.
ταῦτ' ὁ Πρίηπος ἐγών ἐπιτέλλομαι ὁ λιμενίτας,
    ὤνθρωφ', ὡς πλώοις πᾶσαν ἐπ' ἐμπορίην.

179. The Vine and the Billy-goat

Ἴξαλος εὐπώγων αἰγὸς πόσις ἔν ποθ' ἀλωῆ
    οἴνης τοὺς ἁπαλοὺς πάντας ἔδαψε κλάδους.
τῷ δ' ἔπος ἐκ γαίης τόσον ἄπυε· ‹κεῖρε, κάκιστε,
    γναθμοῖς ἡμέτερον κλῆμα τὸ καρποφόρον·
ῥίζα γὰρ ἔμπεδος εὖσα πάλιν γλυκὺ νέκταρ ἀνήσει,
    ὅσσον ἐπισπεῖσαί σοι, τράγε, θυομένῳ.›

180. The Relics of his Ancient Craft

Εὐκαπὲς ἄγκιστρον, καὶ δούρατα δουλιχόεντα,
    χώρμιήν, καὶ τὰς ἰχθυδόκους σπυρίδας,
καὶ τοῦτον νηκτοῖσιν ἐπ' ἰχθύσι τεχνασθέντα
    κύρτον, ἁλιπλάγκτων εὕρεμα δικτυβόλων,
τρηχύν τε τριόδοντα, Ποσειδαώνιον ἔγχος,
    καὶ τοὺς ἐξ ἀκάτων διχθαδίους ἐρέτας,

Lift the anchors and untie the hawsers, sailor, and sail with all the canvas set; I, Priapus, [the god] of the harbour, tell you to do this, my man, so that you may sail for all kinds of cargo.

THE bounding, well-bearded husband of the nanny-goat once nibbled all the tender shoots of a vine in a vineyard. From the ground the vine said to him these words only: 'Tear off with your jaws, most evil creature, my branches that bear the fruit; for my root holds fast and will again send up sweet nectar, enough for a libation over you, billy-goat, when you are being sacrificed.'

As is customary and right, the fisherman Diophantus dedicates to the patron of his art these relics of his ancient craft: the easily swallowed hook, the slender poles, the line, the creels to hold the fish, this wicker-pot devised to trap the swimming fish, an invention of sea-roaming

ὁ γριπεὺς Διόφαντος ἀνάκτορι θήκατο τέχνας,
ὡς θέμις, ἀρχαίας λείψανα τεχνοσύνας.

181. His Own Epitaph

Πολλὸν ἀπ' Ἰταλίης κεῖμαι χθονός, ἔκ τε Τάραντος
πάτρης· τοῦτο δέ μοι πικρότερον θανάτου.
τοιοῦτος πλανίων ἄβιος βίος· ἀλλά με Μοῦσαι
ἔστερξαν, λυγρῶν δ' ἀντὶ μελιχρὸν ἔχω.
οὔνομα δ' οὐκ ἤμυσε Λεωνίδου· αὐτά με δῶρα
κηρύσσει Μουσέων πάντας ἐπ' ἠελίους.

HERODAS
fl. 240 B.C.

182. Law and Order

ΒΑΤΤΑΡΟΣ

Ἐρεῖ τάχ' ὑμῖν· ‹ἐξ Ἄκης ἐλήλουθα
πυροὺς ἄγων κἤστησα τὴν κακὴν λιμόν,›
ἐγὼ δὲ πόρνας ἐκ Τύρου· τί τῷ δήμῳ
τοῦτ' ἐστί; δωρεὴν γὰρ οὔθ' οὗτος πυροὺς
δίδωσ' ἀλήθειν οὔτ' ἐγὼ πάλιν κείνην.

fishermen, his rough trident, a weapon of Poseidon, and the two oars
of his boat.

I LIE far from the soil of Italy and from Tarentum, my mother-town.
This for me is more bitter than death. Such is the wanderer's life – no
life at all. But the Muses loved me, and so, in return for sadness, I
possess something sweet. The name of Leonidas is not lost; the Muses'
gifts themselves make me known under all the suns.

BATTAROS: Perhaps he [Thales the pimp] will tell you: 'I once came
from Acre bringing wheat, and ended the evil famine'; whereas *I* bring
whores from Tyre. What is that to the people? His gift, of wheat to

εἰ δ' οὕνεκεν πλεῖ τὴν θάλασσαν ἢ χλαῖναν
ἔχει τριῶν μνέων 'Αττικῶν, ἐγὼ δ' οἰκέω
ἐν γῇ τρίβωνα καὶ ἀσκέρας σαπρὰς ἕλκων,
βίη τιν' ἄξει τῶν ἐμῶν ἔμ' οὐ πείσας,
καὶ ταῦτα νυκτός, οἴχετ' ἥμιν ἡ ἀλεωρὴ
τῆς πόλιος, ἄνδρες, κἀφ' ὅτῳ σεμνύνεσθε,
τὴν αὐτονομίην ὑμέων Θαλῆς λύσει.
ὃν χρῆν ἑαυτὸν ὅστις ἐστὶ κἀκ ποίου
πηλοῦ πεφύρητ' εἰδότ' ὡς ἐγὼ ζώειν
τῶν δημοτέων φρίσσοντα καὶ τὸν ἥκιστον.
νῦν δ' οἱ μὲν ἐόντες τῆς πόλιος καλυπτῆρες
καὶ τῇ γενῇ φυσῶντες οὐκ ἴσον τούτῳ
πρὸς τοὺς νόμους βλέπουσι κἠμὲ τὸν ξεῖνον
οὐδεὶς πολίτης ἠλόησεν οὐδ' ἦλθεν
πρὸς τὰς θύρας μευ νυκτὸς οὐδ' ἔχων δᾷδας
τὴν οἰκίην ὑφῆψεν οὐδὲ τῶν πορνέων
βίη λαβὼν οἴχωκεν· ἀλλ' ὁ Φρὺξ οὗτος
ὁ νῦν Θαλῆς ἐών, πρόσθε δ', ἄνδρες, 'Αρτίμμης,
ἅπαντα ταῦτ' ἔπρηξε κοὐκ ἐπῃδέσθη
οὔτε νόμον οὔτε προστάτην οὔτ' ἄρχοντα.

(*The Pander*)

grind, is not free, nor is mine. If, because he sails the sea or has a cloak
worth three Attic minae, while I live ashore and trail a threadbare coat
and rotten slippers, he can drag one of my girls away by force, against
my will, and that after dark – goodbye to the safety of the city and all
that you, gentlemen, pride yourselves on; Thales will bring an end to
your independence. He should remember who he is, and the clay from
which he is made, and live as I do, cringing before even the least of the
citizens. But now, those who are the defenders of the city, and who
pride themselves on their birth, have more regard for the law than he
has; and no citizen has laid his hands upon me, the foreigner, nor has
come to my doors at night, nor set fire to my house with his torches,
nor seized any of my whores and dragged them away by force. But
this Phrygian – now called Thales, but before, gentlemen, Artimmes –
did all that, and had no respect for law, or patron, or magistrate.

ALCAEUS OF MESSENE
fl. 197 B.C.

183. Philip, King of Macedon

Ἄκλαυστοι καὶ ἄθαπτοι, ὁδοιπόρε, τῷδ' ἐπὶ τύμβῳ
Θεσσαλίας τρισσαὶ κείμεθα μυριάδες,
Ἠμαθίῃ μέγα πῆμα· τὸ δὲ θρασὺ κεῖνο Φιλίππου
πνεῦμα θοῶν ἐλάφων ᾤχετ' ἐλαφρότερον.

PHILIP V, KING OF MACEDON
238–179 B.C.

184. Alcaeus of Messene

Ἄφλοιος καὶ ἄφυλλος, ὁδοίπορε, τῷδ' ἐπὶ νώτῳ
Ἀλκαίῳ σταυρὸς πήγνυται ἠλίβατος.

DIOSCORIDES
fl. 180 B.C.

185. A Faithful Servant

Λυδὸς ἐγώ, ναὶ Λυδός, ἐλευθερίῳ δέ με τύμβῳ,
δέσποτα, Τιμάνθη τὸν σὸν ἔθευ τροφέα.
εὐαίων ἀσινῆ τείνοις βίον· ἢν δ' ὑπὸ γήρως
πρός με μόλῃς, σὸς ἐγώ, δέσποτα, κἠν Ἀΐδῃ.

UNWEPT and unburied we lie, traveller, in this Thessalian tomb, the thirty thousand, a great scourge to Macedonia; and that insolent spirit of Philip vanished more lightly than swift deer.

BARKLESS and leafless, traveller, a towering cross is being set up on this hill for Alcaeus.

I AM Lydian, yes, a Lydian; but, master, you put Timanthes, your slave [tutor], in a tomb fit for a freeman. May you spend a happy life untroubled. And if you come to me in old age, I am yours, master, even in Hades.

341

MOSCHUS

fl. 150 B.C.

186. Europa and the Bull

Ὡς φαμένη νώτοισιν ἐφίζανε μειδιόωσα,
αἱ δ' ἄλλαι μέλλεσκον, ἄφαρ δ' ἀνεπήλατο ταῦρος,
ἣν θέλεν ἁρπάξας· ὠκὺς δ' ἐπὶ πόντον ἵκανεν.
ἡ δὲ μεταστρεφθεῖσα φίλας καλέεσκεν ἑταίρας
χεῖρας ὀρεγνυμένη, ταὶ δ' οὐκ ἐδύναντο κιχάνειν.
ἀκτάων δ' ἐπιβὰς πρόσσω θέεν, ἠῢτε δελφὶς
χηλαῖς ἀβρέκτοισιν ἐπ' εὐρέα κύματα βαίνων.
ἡ δὲ τότ' ἐρχομένοιο γαληνιάασκε θάλασσα,
κήτεα δ' ἀμφὶς ἄταλλε Διὸς προπάροιθε ποδοῖιν,
γηθόσυνος δ' ὑπὲρ οἶδμα κυβίστεε βυσσόθε δελφίς.
Νηρεΐδες δ' ἀνέδυσαν ὑπὲξ ἁλός, αἱ δ' ἄρα πᾶσαι
κητείοις νώτοισιν ἐφήμεναι ἐστιχόωντο.
καὶ δ' αὐτὸς βαρύδουπος ὑπεὶρ ἅλα Ἐννοσίγαιος
κῦμα κατιθύνων ἁλίης ἡγεῖτο κελεύθου
αὐτοκασιγνήτῳ· τοὶ δ' ἀμφί μιν ἠγερέθοντο
Τρίτωνες, πόντοιο βαρύθροοι αὐλητῆρες,
κόχλοισιν ταναοῖς γάμιον μέλος ἠπύοντες.
ἡ δ' ἄρ' ἐφεζομένη Ζηνὸς βοέοις ἐπὶ νώτοις

So she [Europa] spoke, and sat on his back smiling; the others hesitated, but suddenly the bull leapt up, carrying off the one he wanted. He quickly reached the sea; and she turned round and called to her friends, with outstretched arms, but they could not reach her. Stepping on to the beach he ran forward, and like a dolphin strode the broad waves with his hooves dry. And then the sea grew calm as he entered it, and the sea-monsters gambolled before the feet of Zeus, and the dolphin from the deep tumbled joyfully over the waves. And the Nereids came up from the sea, all riding on the backs of sea-monsters, and ranged themselves in rows. And the loud-crashing Shaker of the Earth himself went across the surface of the sea calming the waves, and led his brother along the ocean path. And around him the Tritons gathered, the gruff flute-players of the sea, playing a wedding song on their slender shells. And she, sitting on the bovine back of Zeus, held the

τῇ μὲν ἔχεν ταύρου δολιχὸν κέρας, ἐν χερὶ δ' ἄλλῃ
εἴρυε πορφυρέην κόλπου πτύχα, ὄφρα κε μή μιν
δεύοι ἐφελκόμενον πολιῆς ἁλὸς ἄσπετον ὕδωρ.
κολπώθη δ' ὤμοισι πέπλος βαθὺς Εὐρωπείης,
ἱστίον οἷά τε νηός, ἐλαφρίζεσκε δὲ κούρην.

BION

fl. 120 B.C.

187. Lament for Adonis

Αἰάζω τὸν Ἄδωνιν ‹ἀπώλετο καλὸς Ἄδωνις.›
‹ὤλετο καλὸς Ἄδωνις› ἐπαιάζουσιν Ἔρωτες.

μηκέτι πορφυρέοις ἐνὶ φάρεσι Κύπρι κάθευδε·
ἔγρεο δειλαία, κυανόστολα καὶ πλατάγησον
στήθεα καὶ λέγε πᾶσιν ‹ἀπώλετο καλὸς Ἄδωνις.›
αἰάζω τὸν Ἄδωνιν· ἐπαιάζουσιν Ἔρωτες.

κεῖται καλὸς Ἄδωνις ἐν ὤρεσι μηρὸν ὀδόντι,
λευκῷ λευκὸν ὀδόντι τυπείς, καὶ Κύπριν ἀνιῆ
λεπτὸν ἀποψύχων, τὸ δέ οἱ μέλαν εἴβεται αἷμα
χιονέας κατὰ σαρκός, ὑπ' ὀφρύσι δ' ὄμματα ναρκῆ,
καὶ τὸ ῥόδον φεύγει τῶ χείλεος, ἀμφὶ δὲ τήνῳ
θνᾴσκει καὶ τὸ φίλημα, τὸ μήποτε Κύπρις ἀποισεῖ.

bull's long horn with one hand and pulled up the purple pleats of her
robe with the other, so that the endless water of the grey sea would not
wet it as it trailed along. The deep folds of Europa's mantle swelled
out round her shoulders, like the sail of a ship, and lifted the maiden up.

I WEEP for Adonis: 'Beautiful Adonis is dead.' 'Beautiful Adonis is
dead,' the gods of Love weep in answer.

Cypris, sleep no longer on bedspreads of purple; rise, unhappy
[goddess], wear black and beat your breast, crying out to all: 'Beautiful
Adonis is dead.' I weep for Adonis; the gods of Love weep in answer.

Beautiful Adonis lies on the hills, his white thigh gashed by a white
tusk, and Cypris mourns as his breath ebbs faintly and his black blood
drops down his snow-white flesh; under his brow his eyes are clouded,
and the rose flies from his lips and with it dies the kiss which Cypris

343

Κύπριδι μὲν τὸ φίλημα καὶ οὐ ζώοντος ἀρέσκει,
ἀλλ' οὐκ οἶδεν Ἄδωνις ὅ νιν θνάσκοντα φίλησεν.
αἰάζω τὸν Ἄδωνιν· ἐπαιάζουσιν Ἔρωτες.

ἄγριον ἄγριον ἕλκος ἔχει κατὰ μηρὸν Ἄδωνις,
μεῖζον δ' ἁ Κυθέρεια φέρει ποτικάρδιον ἕλκος.
τῆνον μὲν περὶ παῖδα φίλοι κύνες ὠδύραντο,
καὶ Νύμφαι κλαίουσιν ὀρειάδες, ἁ δ' Ἀφροδίτα
λυσαμένα πλοκαμῖδας ἀνὰ δρυμὼς ἀλάληται
πενθαλέα, νήπλεκτος, ἀσάνδαλος, αἱ δὲ βάτοι νιν
ἐρχομέναν κείροντι καὶ ἱερὸν αἷμα δρέπονται,
ὀξὺ δὲ κωκύουσα δι' ἄγκεα μακρὰ φορεῖται
Ἀσσύριον βοόωσα πόσιν καὶ παῖδα καλεῦσα.
ἀμφὶ δέ νιν μέλαν εἷμα παρ' ὀμφαλὸν αἰωρεῖτο,
στήθεα δ' ἐκ μηρῶ φοινίσσετο, τοὶ δ' ὑπὸ μαζοὶ
χιόνεοι τὸ πάροιθεν Ἀδώνιδι πορφύροντο.
⟨αἰαῖ τὰν Κυθέρειαν⟩ ἐπαιάζουσιν Ἔρωτες.
ὤλεσε τὸν καλὸν ἄνδρα, σὺν ὤλεσεν ἱερὸν εἶδος.

Κύπριδι μὲν καλὸν εἶδος, ὅτε ζώεσκεν Ἄδωνις,
κάτθανε δ' ἁ μορφὰ σὺν Ἀδώνιδι, τὸν Κύπριν αἰαῖ
ὤρεα πάντα λέγοντι καὶ αἱ δρύες ⟨αἱ τὸν Ἄδωνιν⟩,
καὶ ποταμοὶ κλαίοντι τὰ πένθεα τᾶς Ἀφροδίτας,

will never receive. To kiss him, though dead, is pleasure for Cypris; but Adonis does not know that she kissed him as he died. I weep for Adonis, the gods of Love weep in answer.

Adonis has a cruel, cruel wound in his thigh, but greater is the wound that Cytherea carries in her heart. Around the youth the friendly hounds lament, and the mountain Nymphs weep; and Aphrodite with her hair loose wanders in the thicket, distraught, her hair dishevelled, without her sandals, and the thorns tear her feet as she walks, and draw her sacred blood; crying harshly she wanders through the long glens, crying out for her Assyrian husband and calling the boy. And the black dress gathers round her navel, and her breast is reddened from the wound in his thigh, and below, her breasts that once were snow-white are red because of Adonis. 'Alas for Cytherea,' weep the gods of Love in answer; she lost her beautiful man, and with him her godly beauty.

Cypris was beautiful, when Adonis was alive, but her beauty died with Adonis. Alas for Cypris; all the mountains and the oaks cry, 'Alas for Adonis.' And the rivers weep for Aphrodite's mourning, and

καὶ παγαὶ τὸν Ἄδωνιν ἐν ὤρεσι δακρύοντι,
ἄνθεα δ' ἐξ ὀδύνας ἐρυθαίνεται, ἀ δὲ Κυθήρα
πάντας ἀνὰ κναμώς, ἀνὰ πᾶν νάπος οἰκτρὸν ἀείδει
⟨αἰαῖ τὰν Κυθέρειαν, ἀπώλετο καλὸς Ἄδωνις.⟩
ἀχὼ δ' ἀντεβόασεν ⟨ἀπώλετο καλὸς Ἄδωνις.⟩
Κύπριδος αἰνὸν ἔρωτα τίς οὐκ ἔκλαυσεν ἂν αἰαῖ;
   ὡς ἴδεν, ὡς ἐνόησεν Ἀδώνιδος ἄσχετον ἕλκος,
ὡς ἴδε φοίνιον αἷμα μαραινομένῳ περὶ μηρῷ,
πάχεας ἀμπετάσασα κινύρετο ⟨μεῖνον Ἄδωνι,
δύσποτμε μεῖνον Ἄδωνι, πανύστατον ὥς σε κιχείω,
ὥς σε περιπτύξω καὶ χείλεα χείλεσι μείξω.
ἔγρεο τυτθὸν Ἄδωνι, τὸ δ' αὖ πύματόν με φίλησον,
τοσσοῦτόν με φίλησον, ὅσον ζώει τὸ φίλημα,
ἄχρις ἀπὸ ψυχᾶς ἐς ἐμὸν στόμα κεἰς ἐμὸν ἧπαρ
πνεῦμα τεὸν ῥεύσῃ, τὸ δέ σευ γλυκὺ φίλτρον ἀμέλξω,
ἐκ δὲ πίω τὸν ἔρωτα, φίλημα δὲ τοῦτο φυλάξω
ὡς αὐτὸν τὸν Ἄδωνιν, ἐπεὶ σύ με δύσμορε φεύγεις,
φεύγεις μακρὸν Ἄδωνι καὶ ἔρχεαι εἰς Ἀχέροντα
καὶ στυγνὸν βασιλῆα καὶ ἄγριον, ἀ δέ τάλαινα
ζώω καὶ θεός ἐμμι καὶ οὐ δύναμαί σε διώκειν.
λάμβανε Περσεφόνα τὸν ἐμὸν πόσιν, ἐσσὶ γὰρ αὐτὰ

the fountains on the hills weep for Adonis, and the flowers turn red with pain, and Cytherea sings sadly, wandering across all the ridges and the glens: 'Weep for Cytherea, beautiful Adonis is dead.' And Echo cried back: 'Beautiful Adonis is dead.' Alas! Who would not weep for Cypris' sad love?

When she saw, when she perceived Adonis' incurable wound, when she saw the deadly blood round the withering thigh, she flung up her arms and wailed: 'Stay, Adonis, stay with me, unlucky Adonis, for me to hold you for the last time, to embrace you and join my lips to your lips. Rise for one moment; Adonis, kiss me for the last time, kiss me no longer than the lifetime of a kiss, as long as it takes your breath to flow from your soul to my mouth and my heart; and I will suck your sweet love-charm and drink up your love; and I will keep this kiss as if it were Adonis himself, because, ill-fated one, you are leaving me. You leave, Adonis, for a long journey; you go to Acheron and the cruel, wild king, and I in my misery go on living, and, though a goddess, cannot follow you. Persephone, take my husband, for you are

πολλὸν ἐμεῦ κρέσσων, τὸ δὲ πᾶν καλὸν ἐς σὲ καταρρεῖ.
ἐμμὶ δ᾽ ἐγὼ πανάποτμος, ἔχω δ᾽ ἀκόρεστον ἀνίαν
καὶ κλαίω τὸν Ἄδωνιν, ὅ μοι θάνε, καί σε φοβεῦμαι.
θνάσκεις, ὦ τριπόθητε, πόθος δέ μοι ὡς ὄναρ ἔπτα,
χήρα δ᾽ ἁ Κυθέρεια, κενοὶ δ᾽ ἀνὰ δώματ᾽ Ἔρωτες.
σοὶ δ᾽ ἅμα κεστὸς ὄλωλε. τί γὰρ τολμηρὲ κυνάγεις;
καλὸς ἐὼν τοσσοῦτον ἐμήναο θηρὶ παλαίειν;›
ὥδ᾽ ὀλοφύρατο Κύπρις, ἐπαιάζουσιν Ἔρωτες,
‹αἰαῖ τὰν Κυθέρειαν· ἀπώλετο καλὸς Ἄδωνις.›

ANONYMOUS

c. 100 B.C.

188. Lament for Bion

Ἄρχετε Σικελικαί, τῶ πένθεος ἄρχετε Μοῖσαι.
αἰαῖ, ταὶ μαλάχαι μέν, ἐπὰν κατὰ κᾶπον ὄλωνται,
ἠδὲ τὰ χλωρὰ σέλινα τό τ᾽ εὐθαλὲς οὖλον ἄνηθον
ὕστερον αὖ ζώοντι καὶ εἰς ἔτος ἄλλο φύοντι·
ἄμμες δ᾽ οἱ μεγάλοι καὶ καρτεροί, οἱ σοφοὶ ἄνδρες,
ὁππότε πρᾶτα θάνωμες, ἀνάκοοι ἐν χθονὶ κοίλᾳ
εὕδομες εὖ μάλα μακρὸν ἀτέρμονα νήγρετον ὕπνον.

much better than I; everything beautiful comes down to you. I am
totally wretched; I have a grief that cannot be quenched, I weep for
Adonis, who is dead to me, and I fear you [Persephone]. You die,
thrice-longed-for man, and my desire has taken wings like a dream;
Cytherea is a widow, the gods of Love are left lonely in the house;
with you, my magic girdle is gone. Reckless man, why did you go
hunting? How could a man so beautiful lose his senses completely and
fight with a wild beast?' Thus Cypris lamented, and the gods of Love
wept in answer: 'Alas for Cytherea, beautiful Adonis is dead.'

BEGIN, Muses of Sicily, begin your mourning. Alas! When the mallow
dies in the garden, or the green parsley, or the thriving, curly dill, [yet]
they come to life again and spring forth into another year. But we men,
the great and powerful, the wise, when once we die, hear nothing in
the hollow earth, and sleep a very long, endless sleep, from which there
is no waking.

ANTIPATER OF SIDON

fl. 120 B.C.

189. No Longer, Orpheus

Οὐκέτι θελγομένας, Ὀρφεῦ, δρύας, οὐκέτι πέτρας
ἄξεις, οὐ θηρῶν αὐτονόμους ἀγέλας·
οὐκέτι κοιμάσεις ἀνέμων βρόμον, οὐχὶ χάλαζαν,
οὐ νιφετῶν συρμούς, οὐ παταγεῦσαν ἅλα.
ὤλεο γάρ· σὲ δὲ πολλὰ κατωδύραντο θύγατρες
Μναμοσύνας, μάτηρ δ᾽ ἔξοχα Καλλιόπα.
τί φθιμένοις στοναχεῦμεν ἐφ᾽ υἱάσιν, ἁνίκ᾽ ἀλαλκεῖν
τῶν παίδων Ἀΐδην οὐδὲ θεοῖς δύναμις;

MELEAGER

fl. 90 B.C.

190. Heliodora

Ὁ στέφανος περὶ κρατὶ μαραίνεται Ἡλιοδώρας·
αὐτὴ δ᾽ ἐκλάμπει τοῦ στεφάνου στέφανος.

No longer, Orpheus, will you lead the enchanted oak-trees, no longer
the rocks, nor the shepherdless herds of wild beasts. No more will you
lull to sleep the howl of the winds, nor the hail, nor the drifts of snow,
nor the roaring sea. For you are dead; the daughters of Mnemosyne
wailed long over you, and, above all, your mother Calliope. Why
do we mourn for our dead sons, when not even gods have the power to
ward off Death from their children?

THE garland is fading round the head of Heliodora; but she glows
brightly, a garland for the garland.

347

191. The Cup-bearer

Ἔγχει, καὶ πάλιν εἰπέ, πάλιν, πάλιν ‹Ἡλιοδώρας›
εἰπέ, σὺν ἀκρήτῳ τὸ γλυκὺ μίσγ᾽ ὄνομα·
καί μοι τὸν βρεχθέντα μύροις καὶ χθιζὸν ἐόντα,
μναμόσυνον κείνας, ἀμφιτίθει στέφανον.
δακρύει φιλέραστον ἰδοὺ ῥόδον, οὕνεκα κείναν
ἄλλοθι, κοὐ κόλποις ἀμετέροις ἐσορᾷ.

192. Heliodora's Wreath

Πλέξω λευκόϊον, πλέξω δ᾽ ἁπαλὴν ἅμα μύρτοις
νάρκισσον, πλέξω καὶ τὰ γελῶντα κρίνα,
πλέξω καὶ κρόκον ἡδύν· ἐπιπλέξω δ᾽ ὑάκινθον
πορφυρέην, πλέξω καὶ φιλέραστα ῥόδα,
ὡς ἂν ἐπὶ κροτάφοις μυροβοστρύχου Ἡλιοδώρας
εὐπλόκαμον χαίτην ἀνθοβολῇ στέφανος.

193. Noisy Cicada

Ἀχήεις τέττιξ, δροσεραῖς σταγόνεσσι μεθυσθείς,
ἀγρονόμαν μέλπεις μοῦσαν ἐρημολάλον·
ἄκρα δ᾽ ἐφεζόμενος πετάλοις, πριονώδεσι κώλοις
αἰθίοπι κλάζεις χρωτὶ μέλισμα λύρας.

FILL the cup and say again, again, again: 'To Heliodora.' Speak the sweet name, mix with it the unmixed wine. And place round my forehead the garland dripping with scent, though it be yesterday's, to remind myself of her. Look how the rose, dear to lovers, is weeping, because it sees her elsewhere and not in my arms.

I SHALL plait white violets, I shall plait the soft narcissus, together with myrtle-berries, and I shall plait the laughing lilies, and plait sweet crocus; I shall weave red hyacinths and roses, dear to lovers, so that the garland on the temples of Heliodora with the perfumed curls shall wreathe with flowers her beautiful cascade of hair.

NOISY cicada, drunk with dew-drops, you sing your country song that fills the desolate places with chattering; and, sitting on the edge of the leaves, with saw-like legs and sunburnt skin you shriek out music like

ἀλλά, φίλος, φθέγγου τι νέον δενδρώδεσι Νύμφαις
παίγνιον, ἀντῳδὸν Πανὶ κρέκων κέλαδον,
ὄφρα φυγὼν τὸν Ἔρωτα, μεσημβρινὸν ὕπνον ἀγρεύσω
ἐνθάδ᾽ ὑπὸ σκιερᾷ κεκλιμένος πλατάνῳ.

POMPEIUS
1st century B.C.

194. Mycenae

Εἰ καὶ ἐρημαίη κέχυμαι κόνις ἔνθα Μυκήνη,
  εἰ καὶ ἀμαυροτέρη παντὸς ἰδεῖν σκοπέλου,
Ἰλίου τις καθορῶν κλεινὴν πόλιν, ἧς ἐπάτησα
  τείχεα, καὶ Πριάμου πάντ᾽ ἐκένωσα δόμον,
γνώσεται ἔνθεν ὅσον πάρος ἔσθενον. εἰ δέ με γῆρας
  ὕβρισεν, ἀρκοῦμαι μάρτυρι Μαιονίδῃ.

ANTIPHILUS
fl. A.D. 53

195. On the Ship's Poop

Κἢν πρύμνῃ λαχέτω μέ ποτε στιβάς, αἵ θ᾽ ὑπὲρ αὐτῆς
  ἠχεῦσαι ψακάδων τύμματι διφθερίδες,
καὶ πῦρ ἐκ μυλάκων βεβιημένον, ἥ τ᾽ ἐπὶ τούτων
  χύτρη, καὶ κενεὸς πομφολύγων θόρυβος,

the lyre's. But, my friend, speak some new playful tune for the Nymphs of the woods and strike up a song in answer to Pan's music, so that I may escape from Love and snatch a midday sleep as I lie here under a shady plane-tree.

ALTHOUGH I, Mycenae, lie abandoned, a heap of dust, and although I am less conspicuous than any rock, the man who looks at the glorious city of Ilium, whose walls I trampled over, and emptied Priam's whole house, will know from that how powerful I was in the past. If old age has abused me, Homer's testimony is enough for me.

SOME time let my straw mattress [again] be on the [ship's] poop, with the weatherskins above it, sounding with the beating spray, and the fire breaking out from the stone fireplace, and the pot on it and the

καί κε ῥυπῶντ' ἐσίδοιμι διήκονον· ἡ δὲ τράπεζα
ἔστω μοι στρωτὴ νηὸς ὕπερθε σανίς·
δὸς λάβε, καὶ ψιθύρισμα τὸ ναυτικόν· εἶχε τύχη τις
πρῴην τοιαύτη τὸν φιλόκοινον ἐμέ.

ANONYMOUS
? 1st century A.D.

196. Flute Song

Εἶδες ἔαρ, χειμῶνα, θέρος· ταῦτ' ἐστὶ διόλου·
ἥλιος αὐτὸς ἔδυ, καὶ νὺξ τὰ τεταγμέν' ἀπέχει·
μὴ κοπία ζητεῖν πόθεν ἥλιος ἢ πόθεν ὕδωρ,
ἀλλὰ πόθεν τὸ μύρον καὶ τοὺς στεφάνους ἀγοράσῃς.
                              Αὔλει μοι.

Κρήνας αὐτορύτους μέλιτος τρεῖς ἤθελον ἔχειν,
πέντε γαλακτορύτους, οἴνου δέκα, δώδεκα μύρου,
καὶ δύο πηγαίων ὑδάτων, καὶ τρεῖς χιονέων·
παῖδα κατὰ κρήνην καὶ παρθένον ἤθελον ἔχειν.
                              Αὔλει μοι.

empty noise of bubbling. Let me look at the unwashed cabin-boy, and let my table be laid on deck, a plank; and let there be a game of pitch-and-toss, and sailors' talk. Just lately I had such luck, I, who love to share the common lot.

You saw spring, winter, summer; these always exist. When the sun goes down, the night comes into her own. Do not strive to find out whence the sun comes, or whence water, but where you can buy the scent and the garlands. Pipe for me, piper.

I would like to have three self-flowing fountains of honey, five flowing with milk, ten with wine, twelve with scents, two with fresh water, and three with snowy [water]; I would like to have a boy and a girl for every fountain. Pipe for me, piper.

ANONYMOUS

Λύδιος αὐλὸς ἐμοὶ τὰ δὲ Λύδια παίγματα λύρας,
καὶ Φρύγιος κάλαμος τὰ δὲ ταύρεα τύμπανα πονεῖ·
ταῦτα ζῶν ᾆσαί τ' ἔραμαι, καί, ὅταν ἀποθάνω,
αὐλὸν ὑπὲρ κεφαλῆς θέτε μοι, παρὰ ποσσὶ δὲ λύραν.
Αὔλει μοι.

SATYRUS
2nd century A.D.

197. Pastoral Solitude

Ποιμενίαν ἄγλωσσος ἀν' ὀργάδα μέλπεται Ἀχὼ
ἀντίθρουν πτανοῖς ὑστερόφωνον ὄπα.

For me the Lydian pipe, and the Lydian songs of the lyre, and a Phrygian reed; and the drums of ox-hide beating. I long to sing these things while I live; and when I die, put over my head a pipe, and at my feet a lyre. Pipe for me, piper.

ALONG this fertile pasture-land tongueless Echo sings in answer to the birds, with late-crying voice.

III

THE PERIOD OF TRANSITION

QUINTUS SMYRNAEUS

4th century A.D.

198. The Return from Troy

Οὐδέ τις ἐλπωρὴ βιότου πέλεν, οὕνεκ' ἐρεμνὴ
νὺξ ἅμα καὶ μέγα χεῖμα καὶ ἀθανάτων χόλος αἰνὸς
ὦρτο· Ποσειδάων γὰρ ἀνηλέα πόντον ὄρινεν
ἦρα κασιγνήτοιο φέρων ἐρικυδέι κούρῃ,
ἥ ῥα καὶ αὐτὴ ὕπερθεν ἀμείλιχα μαιμώωσα
θῦνε μετ' ἀστεροπῆσιν· ἐπέκτυπε δ' οὐρανόθεν Ζεὺς
κυδαίνων ἀνὰ θυμὸν ἑὸν τέκος, ἀμφὶ δὲ πᾶσαι
νῆσοί τ' ἤπειροί τε κατεκλύζοντο θαλάσσῃ
Εὐβοίης οὐ πολλὸν ἀπόπροθεν, ἧχι μάλιστα
τεῦχεν ἀμειλίκτοισιν ἐπ' ἄλγεσιν ἄλγεα δαίμων
Ἀργείοις· στοναχὴ δὲ καὶ οἰμωγὴ κατὰ νῆας
ἔπλετ' ἀπολλυμένων· κανάχιζε δὲ δούρατα νηῶν
ἀγνυμένων· αἱ γάρ ῥα συνωχαδὸν ἀλλήλῃσιν
αἰὲν ἐνερρήγνυντο. πόνος δ' ἄπρηκτος ὀρώρει·
καί ῥ' οἱ μὲν κώπῃσιν ἀπωσέμεναι μεμαῶτες
νῆας ἐπεσσυμένας αὐτοῖς ἅμα δούρασι λυγροὶ
κάππεσον ἐς μέγα βένθος, ἀμειλίκτῳ δ' ὑπὸ πότμῳ
κάτθανον, οὕνεκ' ἄρα σφιν ἐπέχραον ἄλλοθεν ἄλλα
νηῶν δούρατα μακρά· συνηλοίηντο δὲ πάντων
σώματα λευγαλέως· οἱ δ' ἐν νήεσσι πεσόντες

THERE was no hope of life as the night came on dark, and, with it, a great storm and the terrible anger of the gods. For Poseidon stirred the merciless sea to please his brother's noble daughter, who, from up above, quivered relentlessly with rage, and darted with lightning flashes. And Zeus thundered from the sky above, wishing to pay honour to his child; and all the islands and the land about Euboea were covered by the sea, where, above all, the goddess piled cruelty upon relentless cruelty against the Argives. Cries and the groans of drowning men filled the ships, the crashing of timbers rang out as the vessels broke up, for they were being smashed against each other all the time. Any efforts they made were useless; some, straining with the oars to push apart the ships as they were colliding, fell wretchedly along with the oars into the great depths of the sea, and died a merciless death because the long ship-beams, tossing this way and that, caught them, and crushed all their bodies hideously. Those who had fallen in the

κεῖντο καταφθιμένοισιν ἐοικότες· οἱ δ᾽ ὑπ᾽ ἀνάγκης
νήχοντ᾽ ἀμφιπεσόντες ἐϋξέστοισιν ἐρετμοῖς·
ἄλλοι δ᾽ αὖ σανίδεσσιν ἐπέπλεον· ἔβραχε δ᾽ ἅλμη
βυσσόθεν, ὥς τε θάλασσαν ἰδ᾽ οὐρανὸν ἠδὲ καὶ αἶαν
φαίνεσθ᾽ ἀλλήλοισιν ὁμῶς συναρηρότα πάντα.

ANONYMOUS
4th century A.D.

199. The Ancient Gods are Dead

Εἴπατε τῷ βασιλῆϊ· χαμαὶ πέσε δαίδαλος αὐλά·
οὐκέτι Φοῖβος ἔχει καλύβαν, οὐ μάντιδα δάφνην,
οὐ παγὰν λαλέουσαν· ἀπέσβετο καὶ λάλον ὕδωρ.

MUSAEUS
4th century A.D.

200. Leander's Death

Νὺξ ἦν, εὖτε μάλιστα βαρυπνείοντες ἀῆται,
χειμερίαις πνοιῇσιν ἀκοντίζοντες ἰωάς,
ἀθρόον ἐμπίπτουσιν ἐπὶ ῥηγμῖνι θαλάσσης.
καὶ τότε δὴ Λείανδρος ἐθήμονος ἐλπίδι νύμφης
δυσκελάδων πεφόρητο θαλασσαίων ἐπὶ νώτων.
ἤδη κύματι κῦμα κυλίνδετο, σύγχυτο δ᾽ ὕδωρ,
αἰθέρι μίσγετο πόντος, ἀνέγρετο πάντοθεν ἠχὴ

ships lay like dead men; others, forced into the sea, swam astride the smooth-planed oars, while others floated on wooden planks. And the ocean roared from its depth, so that water, sky and earth all seemed to be joined together.

TELL this to the king: the decorated court has fallen to the ground, Phoebus no longer has a cell, nor laurel of prophecy, nor babbling fountain; even the chattering water has dried up.

IT was night, when the heavy-blowing winds cast most strongly the spears of their cries in stormy blasts and fell in force upon the shore of the sea. Then it was that Leander, in the hope of meeting the girl as usual, was carried upon the cruelly roaring ridges of the sea. Already, wave was rolling on wave, the waters were stirred up, the sea was merged with the sky and from all sides arose the shriek of battling

356

μαρναμένων ἀνέμων· Ζεφύρῳ δ' ἀντέπνεεν Εὖρος
καὶ Νότος εἰς Βορέην μεγάλας ἐφέηκεν ἀπειλάς·
καὶ κτύπος ἦν ἀλίαστος ἐρισμαράγοιο θαλάσσης.
αἰνοπαθὴς δὲ Λέανδρος ἀκηλήτοις ἐνὶ δίναις
πολλάκι μὲν λιτάνευε θαλασσαίην Ἀφροδίτην,
πολλάκι δ' αὐτὸν ἄνακτα Ποσειδάωνα θαλάσσης.
ἀλλά οἱ οὔ τις ἄρηγεν, Ἔρως δ' οὐκ ἤρκεσε Μοίρας.
πάντοθι δ' ἀγρομένοιο δυσάντεϊ κύματος ὁλκῷ
τυπτόμενος πεφόρητο, ποδῶν δέ οἱ ὤκλασεν ὁρμὴ
καὶ σθένος ἦν ἀνόνητον ἀκοιμήτων παλαμάων.
πολλὴ δ' αὐτομάτη χύσις ὕδατος ἔρρεε λαιμῷ,
καὶ ποτὸν ἀχρήιστον ἀμαιμακέτου πίεν ἄλμης.
καὶ δὴ λύχνον ἄπιστον ἀπέσβεσε πικρὸς ἀήτης
καὶ ψυχὴν καὶ ἔρωτα πολυτλήτοιο Λεάνδρου...
νείκεσε δ' ἀγριόθυμον ἐπεσβολίῃσιν ἀήτην·
ἤδη γὰρ φθιμένοιο μόρον θέσπισσε Λεάνδρου
εἰσέτι δηθύνοντος· ἐπαγρύπνοισι δ' ὀπωπαῖς
ἵστατο, κυμαίνουσα πολυκλαύτοισι μερίμναις·
ἤλυθε δ' ἠριγένεια, καὶ οὐκ ἴδε νυμφίον Ἡρώ.
πάντοθι δ' ὄμμα τίταινεν ἐς εὐρέα νῶτα θαλάσσης,
εἴ που ἐσαθρήσειεν ἀλωόμενον παρακοίτην
λύχνου σβεννυμένοιο· παρὰ κρηπῖδα δὲ πύργου

winds. Eurus, the east wind, blew against Zephyrus, the west, Notus the south, wildly threatened Boreas, the north; and endless was the crashing of the loud-thundering sea. Leander, suffering dreadfully in the inexorable swirl, prayed many times to Aphrodite of the sea, many times to Poseidon himself, master of the Ocean. But no one came to his aid: Love could not hold back the Fates. He was buffeted, carried here and there by the powerful sucking of the gathering waves; the vigour of his legs faded; the power of his unresting hands was of no avail. Of its own force much water poured down his throat, and he swallowed the useless drink of the irresistible sea. And the bitter wind put out the faithless lamp, and the life and the love of long-suffering Leander. With violent words Hero reviled the savage-hearted wind, for now she foresaw the fate of Leander as he lost his strength while still held back. With sleepless eyes she stood, heavy with tears at her troubles. Dawn came, but Hero did not see her lover. She strained her eyes in every direction over the wide ridges of the sea, in case she should catch a sight of her lover who had lost his way when the light

δρυπτόμενον σπιλάδεσσιν ὅτ' ἔδρακε νεκρὸν ἀκοίτην,
δαιδαλέον ῥήξασα περὶ στήθεσσι χιτῶνα
ῥοιζηδὸν προκάρηνος ἀπ' ἠλιβάτου πέσε πύργου
καὶ διερὴ τέθνηκε σὺν ὀλλυμένῳ παρακοίτῃ·
ἀλλήλων δ' ἀπόναντο καὶ ἐν πυμάτῳ περ ὀλέθρῳ.

(*Hero and Leander*)

GREGORY OF NAZIANZUS
c. 329–389

201. The Storm Which Converted Him

Ἤδη μοι πολιόν τε κάρη, καὶ ἅψεα ῥικνὰ
ἐκλίνθη βιότοιο πρὸς ἕσπερον ἀλγινόεντος.
Ἀλλ' οὔπω τοιόνδε τοσόνδε τε ἄλγος ἀνέτλην·
οὐδ' ὅτε μαινομένοισι κορυσσόμενον ἀνέμοισι
γαίης ἐκ Φαρίης ἐπ' Ἀχαιΐδα πόντον ἔτετμον
ἀντολίη Ταύροιο, τὸν ἐρρίγασι μάλιστα
ναῦται, χειμερίου, παῦροι δέ τε πείσματ' ἔλυσαν.
Ἔνθα δ' ἐγὼ νύκτας τε καὶ ἤματα εἴκοσι πάντα
νηὸς ἔνι πρύμνῃ κείμην, θεὸν ὑψιμέδοντα
κικλήσκων λιτῇσι. Τὸ δ' ἄφρεε κῦμ' ἐπὶ νῆα,
οὔρεσιν ἢ σκοπέλοισιν ὁμοίϊον ἔνθα καὶ ἔνθα,
πολλὸν δ' ἐντὸς ἔπιπτε· τινάσσετο δ' ἄρμενα πάντα,

had gone out. And when she saw her lover dead by the base of the tower, his body torn by the rocks, she ripped the finely wrought mantle from around her breasts and rushed to plunge headlong from the steep tower to die in the waves with her dead lover. So even in the final disaster they had joy of one another.

Now my head is white, and my emaciated limbs incline to the eventide of life that is full of pain; yet never have I suffered such a pain, nor one so great [as now]: no, not even when, from the land of the Pharos to Greece, at the time of the rising of wintry Taurus, I crossed the ocean when it was whipped by the raging winds, which sailors dread most of all and [in which] few of them unfasten their hawsers. Then I lay there in the stern of the ship twenty days and nights together, and with prayers made entreaty to the God who rules high above. The waves foamed on both sides of the ship, like mountains or rocks, and much [water] fell on board. All the rigging was shaken by the shrill whistling blasts of

ὀξέα συρίζοντος ἐπὶ προτόνοισιν ἀήτου·
αἰθὴρ δ' ἐν νεφέεσι μελαίνετο, καὶ στεροπῇσι
λάμπετο, καὶ κρατεραῖς περιάγνυτο πάντοσε φωναῖς.
Τῆμος ἐμαυτὸν ἔδωκα θεῷ, καὶ πόντον ἄλυξα
ἄγριον εὐαγέεσσιν ὑποσχεσίῃσι πεσόντα.

(On Himself)

202. On Himself

Ἑλλὰς ἐμή, νεότης τε φίλη, καὶ ὅσσα πεπάσμην,
καὶ δέμας, ὡς Χριστῷ εἴξατε προφρονέως.
Εἰ δ' ἱερῆα φίλον με θεῷ θέτο μητέρος εὐχὴ
καὶ πατρὸς παλάμη, τίς φθόνος; Ἀλλά, μάκαρ,
σοῖς με, Χριστέ, χοροῖσι δέχου, καὶ κῦδος ὀπάζοις
υἱέϊ Γρηγορίου σῷ λάτρι Γρηγορίῳ.

ANONYMOUS
?4th century

203. Joyful Light*

Φῶς ἱλαρὸν ἁγίας δόξης,
ἀθανάτου πατρὸς οὐρανίου,
ἁγίου, μάκαρος,
Ἰησοῦ Χριστέ,

wind upon the forestays, and the heavens were black with clouds, lit up with lightning flashes and rent by loud cries from every side. Then I gave myself to God, and escaped the raging sea which fell still at my holy promises.

O MY Greece, my youth, my body, all that I possess, how gladly you gave way to Christ! Who would bear a grudge if my mother's wish and my father's hand made me a priest, beloved of God? And may you, blessed Christ, receive me in your choirs, and grant glory to your servant Gregory, the son of Gregory.

JOYFUL light of holy glory, Christ Jesus, son of a deathless heavenly

*An Evensong hymn.

ἐλθόντες ἐπὶ τὴν ἡλίου δύσιν,
ἰδόντες φῶς ἑσπερινὸν
ὑμνοῦμεν πατέρα, υἱὸν
καὶ ἅγιον πνεῦμα θεόν.
Ἄξιος εἶ ἐν πᾶσι καιροῖς
ὑμνεῖσθαι φωναῖς αἰσίαις,
υἱὲ θεοῦ, ζωὴν ὁ διδούς·
διὸ κόσμος σε δοξάζει.

ANONYMOUS
?4th century

204. Evensong

Σὲ καὶ νῦν εὐλογοῦμεν,   Χριστέ μου Λόγε θεοῦ,
φῶς ἐκ φωτὸς ἀνάρχου   καὶ πνεῦμα ἐξ ἀνάρχου
τριττοῦ φωτὸς εἰς μίαν   δόξαν ἀθροιζομένου·

ὃς ἔλυσας τὸ σκότος,   ὃς ὑπέστησας τὸ φῶς,
ἵν᾽ ἐν φωτὶ κτίσῃς τὰ πάντα   καὶ τὴν ἄστατον ὕλην
στήσῃς μορφῶν εἰς κόσμον   καὶ τὴν νῦν εὐκοσμίαν·

Father, holy and blessed; we have come to the setting of the sun, and seeing the light of evening we celebrate the Father, Son and Holy Ghost as God. You are worthy to be praised at all times with voices of propitiation, son of God, giver of life; for this the world glorifies you.

Now again do we bless your name, my Christ, Word of God, light of light without beginning, spirit of triple light without beginning, all gathered into one glory.

You scattered the darkness and set up the light, so that in light you might build all that there is, and make fast the shifting matter, shaping it into a universe and into the fair order that it now has.

ὃς νοῦν ἐφώτισας ἀνθρώπου   λόγῳ τε καὶ σοφίᾳ
λαμπρότητος τῆς ἄνω   καὶ κάτω θεὶς εἰκόνα,
ἵνα φωτὶ βλέπῃ τὸ φῶς   καὶ γένηται φῶς ὅλον.

Σὺ φωστῆρσιν οὐρανὸν   κατηύγασας ποικίλοις,
σὺ νύκτα καὶ ἡμέραν   ἀλλήλαις εἴκειν ἠπίως
ἔταξας νόμον τιμῶν   ἀδελφότητος καὶ φιλίας.

Καὶ τῇ μὲν ἔπαυσας κόπους   τῆς πολυμόχθου σαρκός,
τῇ δ' ἤγειρας εἰς ἔργον   καὶ πράξεις τάς σοι φίλας,
ἵνα τὸ σκότος φυγόντες   φθάσωμεν εἰς ἡμέραν.

Σὺ μέν βάλοις ἐλαφρὸν   ὕπνον ἐμοῖς βλεφάροις
ὡς μὴ γλῶσσαν ὑμνῳδὸν   ἐπὶ πολὺ νεκροῦσθαι,
μήτ' ἀντίφωνον ἀγγέλων   πλάσμα σὸν ἡσυχάζειν.

Σὺν σοὶ δὲ κοίτη εὐσεβεῖς   ἐννοίας ἐταζέτω,
μήδ' ἔτι τῶν ῥυπαρῶν   ἡμέρας νὺξ ἐλέγξῃ,
μηδὲ παίγνια νυκτὸς   ἐνύπνια θροείτω.

Νοῦς δὲ καὶ σώματος δίχα   σοί, θεέ, προσλαλείτω,
τῷ πατρὶ καὶ τῷ υἱῷ   καὶ τῷ ἁγίῳ πνεύματι,
ᾧ τιμὴ δόξα κράτος   εἰς τοὺς αἰῶνας. Ἀμήν.

And you illuminated the mind of man with word and wisdom, placing below an image of the brilliance that is above, that in light he might see the light and become light entirely.

With diversity of lanterns you illumined the sky, and commanded the night and day gently to yield one to the other, honouring the laws of brotherhood and friendship;

By the one you brought an end to the labours of the much-wearied flesh, and with the other you roused men to work and to action dear to you, so that we might escape the darkness and come unto the day.

May you lay light sleep upon my eyes, so that my hymning tongue may not for long lie still; and may your creation [man] not be silent, he who sings in chorus with the angels.

With your help may my bed reveal pious thoughts; may the night not reproach the vileness of the day, and may frivolities not disturb the dreams of night.

May the mind alone, without the body, hold converse with you, O God, Father and Son, and Holy Ghost, to whom be honour, glory, and power for ever and ever. Amen.

SYNESIUS

c. 370–413

205. Christ's Journey to Heaven

Ἀνιόντα σε, κοίρανε,
τὰ κατ' ἠέρος ἄσπετα
τρέσεν ἔθνεα δαιμόνων·
θάμβησε δ' ἀκηράτων
χορὸς ἄμβροτος ἀστέρων·
αἰθὴρ δὲ γελάσσας,
σοφὸς ἁρμονίας πατήρ,
ἐξ ἑπτατόνου λύρας
ἐκεράσσατο μουσικὰν
ἐπινίκιον ἐς μέλος.
Μείδησεν Ἑωσφόρος,
ὁ διάκτορος ἀμέρας,
καὶ χρύσεος Ἕσπερος,
Κυθερήϊος ἀστήρ·
ἁ μὲν κερόεν σέλας
πλήσασα ῥόου πυρὸς
ἀγεῖτο σελάνα,
ποιμὴν νυχίων θεῶν·
τὰν δ' εὐρυφαῆ κόμαν
Τιτὰν ἐπετάσσατο
ἄρρητον ὑπ' ἴχνιον·
ἔγνω δὲ γόνον θεοῦ,
τὸν ἀριστοτέχναν νόον,
ἰδίου πυρὸς ἀρχάν.
Σὺ δὲ ταρσὸν ἐλάσσας,

THE countless tribes of heavenly spirits trembled when they saw you
ascending, Lord; and the immortal chorus of pure stars was astounded.
Aether, the wise father of Harmony, laughed and composed some
music, a song of victory, on the seven-toned lyre. The Morning Star,
the messenger of day, smiled and so did golden Hesperus, the star of
Aphrodite. The Moon, shepherd of the gods of night, filled her horn-
shaped light with a flood of fire and led the way, and the Sun shook out
his far-flashing hair along his indescribable path; he recognized the son
of God, the great creating mind, origin of his own fire. And you lifted
your feet and jumped over the back of the blue-rimmed sky and stood

362

κυανάντυγος οὐρανοῦ
ὑπερήλαο νώτων,
σφαίρῃσι δ' ἐπεστάθης
νοεραῖσιν ἀκηράτοις,
ἀγαθῶν ὅθι παγά,
στγώμενος οὐρανός.
Ἔνθ' οὔτε βαθύρροος
ἀκαμαντοπόδας χρόνος
χθονὸς ἔκγονα σύρων,
οὐ κῆρες ἀναιδέες
βαθυκύμονος ὕλας,
ἀλλ' αὐτὸς ἀγήρως
αἰὼν ὁ παλαιγενής,
νέος ὢν ἅμα καὶ γέρων,
τᾶς ἀενάω μονᾶς
ταμίας πέλεται θεοῖς.

CYRUS OF PANOPOLIS
fl. c. 440

206. On the Stylite Daniel

Μεσσηγὺς γαίης τε καὶ οὐρανοῦ ἵσταται ἀνὴρ
πάντοθεν ὀρνυμένους οὐ τρομέων ἀνέμους·
τοὔνομα μὲν Δανήλ, μεγάλῳ Συμεῶνι δ' ἐρίζει,
ἴχνια ῥιζώσας κίονι διχθαδίῳ·
λιμῷ δ' ἀμβροσίᾳ τρέφεται καὶ ἀναίμονι δίψῃ,
υἱέα κηρύσσων μητρὸς ἀπειρογάμου.

on the pure spheres of the spirit, the fountain of all that is good, the silent sky. There deep-flowing and unwearied time does not trawl in the children of earth, nor is there any death to insult deep-surging matter; but Eternity himself, founded of old and yet unageing, at once young and old, is in existence, the steward of unending permanence for the gods.

BETWEEN the earth and the sky he stands, a man who does not fear the winds that rise from all around him. His name is Daniel, and he rivals great Symeon; for he has planted his feet upon a double column. Divine hunger sustains him, and bloodless thirst; and he proclaims the son of an unwedded mother.

NONNUS

fl. c. 450

207. Chalcomede and Her Lover

Εἶπε μόθους γελόωσα φιλομμειδὴς Ἀφροδίτη,
Ἄρεα κερτομέουσα γαμοστόλον· ἄγχι δὲ πόντου
καλλείψας ἀκόμιστον ἐπ' αἰγιαλοῖο χιτῶνα
θαλπόμενος γλυκερῇσι μεληδόσι λούσατο Μορρεύς,
γυμνὸς ἐών· ψυχρῇ δὲ δέμας φαίδρυνε θαλάσσῃ,
θερμὸν ἔχων Παφίης ὀλίγον βέλος· ἐν δὲ ῥεέθροις
Ἰνδῴην ἱκέτευεν Ἐρυθραίην Ἀφροδίτην,
εἰσαΐων, ὅτι Κύπρις ἀπόσπορός ἐστι θαλάσσης·
λουσάμενος δ' ἀνέβαινε μέλας πάλιν· εἶχε δὲ μορφὴν
ὡς φύσις ἐβλάστησε, καὶ ἀνέρος οὐ δέμας ἅλμη,
οὐ χροιὴν μετάμειψεν, ἐρευθαλέη περ ἐοῦσα.
καὶ κενεῇ χρόα λοῦσεν ἐπ' ἐλπίδι· χιόνεος γὰρ
ἱμερόεις μενέαινε φανήμεναι ἄζυγι κούρῃ·
καὶ λινέῳ κόσμησε δέμας χιονώδεϊ πέπλῳ,
οἷον ἔσω θώρηκος ἀεὶ φορέουσι μαχηταί.
    Ἱσταμένη δ' ἄφθογγος ἐπ' ἠόνος εἶχε σιωπὴν
Χαλκομέδη δολόεσσα. μεταστρεφθεῖσα δὲ κούρη
Μορρέος ἀχλαίνοιο σαόφρονας εἷλκεν ὀπωπάς,
ἀσκεπὲς αἰδομένη δέμας ἀνέρος· εἰσιδέειν γὰρ

SMILING Aphrodite said this and laughed, mocking Ares the marriage-maker and his battles. And Morrheus left his tunic untended on the beach near the sea and bathed naked, warmed as he was by the sweet sorrows of love. His body took pleasure in the water's coolness, but the tiny shaft of Paphian Aphrodite was hot within him. And among the billows he prayed to Indian Aphrodite of the Red Sea; for he had heard that Cyprian Aphrodite was born from the sea. Even so, when he had bathed he was still black; his form was just as nature had made it, and the salt water had not changed his body nor his colour, for all that the sea was the Red Sea. But he washed his skin in the vain hope of becoming white and so being desired by the unmarried maiden. So he adorned his body in a snowy linen robe such as warriors always wear under their breastplates.

Full of guile stood Chalcomede silent upon the shore and said nothing, but, like a maiden, turned aside and averted her chaste eyes from the naked Morrheus, ashamed to see the unclad body of a man;

ἅζετο θῆλυς ἐοῦσα λελουμένον ἄρσενα κούρη.

ἀλλ᾽ ὅτε χῶρον ἔρημον ἐσέδρακεν ἄρμενον εὐναῖς,
τολμηρὴν παλάμην ὀρέγων αἰδήμονι νύμφῃ
εἵματος ἀψαύστοιο σαόφρονος ἥψατο κούρης·
καί νύ κεν ἀμφίζωστον ἑλὼν εὐήνορι δεσμῷ
νυμφιδίῳ σπινθῆρι βιήσατο θυιάδα κούρην·
ἀλλά τις ἀχράντοιο δράκων ἀνεπήλατο κόλπου,
παρθενικῆς ἀγάμοιο βοηθόος, ἀμφὶ δὲ μίτρην
ἀμφιλαφὴς κυκλοῦτο φυλάκτορι γαστέρος ὁλκῷ·
ὀξὺ δὲ συρίζοντος ἀσιγήτων ἀπὸ λαιμῶν
πέτραι ἐμυκήσαντο· φόβῳ δ᾽ ἐλελίζετο Μορρεὺς
αὐχένιον μύκημα νόθης σάλπιγγος ἀκούων,
παπταίνων ἀγάμοιο προασπιστῆρα κορείης.

(Dionysiaca)

ANONYMOUS
5th century

208. On Sabinus

Τοῦτό τοι ἡμετέρης μνημήϊον, ἐσθλὲ Σαβῖνε,
ἡ λίθος ἡ μικρή, τῆς μεγάλης φιλίης.
αἰεὶ ζητήσω σε· σὺ δ᾽, εἰ θέμις, ἐν φθιμένοισι
τοῦ Λήθης ἐπ᾽ ἐμοὶ μή τι πίῃς ὕδατος.

being a woman, the maiden was abashed to see a man bathing.
But, when he had seen a lonely spot suitable for lying down, he boldly stretched forth his hand to the shy virgin and touched the chaste girl's garment which had never before been touched by man. And now he would have held her in both hands in a manly grip, and would have forced the frantic maiden with the flaming desire of a bridegroom; but from her immaculate bosom there sprang a serpent to save the unwedded virgin, and it thickly encircled her girdle with the protecting coils of its body. Unceasing shrill cries from its throat made the rocks resound. Morrheus trembled with fear, when he heard the trumpet-like bellow from the throat of the animal, and saw the champion of unwedded maidenhood.

GOOD Sabinus, this is the memorial of our friendship, our great friendship: a little stone. I shall always miss you. And, if it is permissible among those who have died, for my sake do not drink any of the water of Lethe.

ANONYMOUS

?5th century

209. On Vibius

Ἄνθεα πολλὰ γένοιτο νεοδμήτῳ ἐπὶ τύμβῳ,
μὴ βάτος αὐχμηρή, μὴ κακὸν αἰγίπυρον,
ἀλλ' ἴα καὶ σάμψουχα καὶ ὑδατίνη νάρκισσος,
Οὐείβιε, καὶ περὶ σοῦ πάντα γένοιτο ῥόδα.

ANONYMOUS

?5th century

210. Evening Prayer

Ἡ ἀσώματος φύσις τῶν Χερουβὶμ
ἀσιγήτοις σε ὕμνοις δοξολογεῖ·
ἑξαπτέρυγα ζῷα, τὰ Σεραφίμ,
ταῖς ἀπαύστοις φωναῖς σε ὑπερυψοῖ·
τῶν ἀγγέλων δὲ πᾶσαι αἱ στρατιαὶ
τρισαγίοις σε ᾄσμασιν εὐφημεῖ·
πρὸ γὰρ πάντων ὑπάρχεις ὁ ὢν πατὴρ
καὶ συνάναρχον ἔχεις τὸν υἱόν,
καὶ ἰσότιμον φέρων πνεῦμα ζωῆς
τῆς τριάδος δεικνύεις τὸ ἀμερές.
Παναγία παρθένε, μήτηρ Χριστοῦ,
οἱ τοῦ λόγου αὐτόπται καὶ ὑπουργοί,
προφητῶν καὶ μαρτύρων πάντες χοροὶ
ὡς ἀθάνατον ἔχοντες τὴν ζωήν,

MAY many flowers blossom on your new-built tomb; not the dry bramble, not the ugly rest-harrow, but violets and marjoram and water-loving narcissus, Vibius; and may every rose surround you.

THE incorporeal form of the cherubim celebrates you in hymns never silent; the six-winged beasts, the seraphim, extol you in voices without ceasing; and all the hosts of angels acclaim you in songs thrice-sacred. For you, the Father, who exist before all things, and have your son of like eternity, and hold the spirit of life as a partner of equal honour, reveal the indivisibility of the Holy Trinity. Our Lady, virgin, mother of Christ, and you, eye witnesses and ministers of the Word, and all the choruses of prophets and martyrs who have eternal life, intercede for

ὑπὲρ πάντων πρεσβεύσατε ἱλασμόν,
ὅτι πάντες ὑπάρχομεν ἐν δεινοῖς·
τῆς δὲ πλάνης ῥυσθέντες τοῦ πονηροῦ
τῶν ἀγγέλων βοήσωμεν τὴν ᾠδήν·

ANONYMOUS

?5th century

211. On Adam

Τῆς σοφίας ὁδηγέ,   φρονήσεως χορηγέ,
τῶν ἀφρόνων παιδευτὰ   καὶ πτωχῶν ὑπερασπιστά,
στήριξον, συνέτισον   τὴν καρδίαν μου, δέσποτα·

σὺ δίδου μοι λόγον   ὁ τοῦ πατρὸς Λόγος·
ἰδοὺ γὰρ τὰ χείλη μου   οὐ κωλύσω ἐν τῷ κράζειν σοι·
⟨ἐλεῆμον,   ἐλέησον   τὸν παραπεσόντα.⟩

Ἐκάθισεν Ἀδὰμ τότε   καὶ ἔκλαυσεν   ἀπέναντι
τῆς τρυφῆς τοῦ παραδείσου   χερσὶ τύπτων τὰς ὄψεις,
καὶ ἔλεγεν   ⟨ἐλεῆμον,   ἐλέησον   τὸν παραπεσόντα.⟩

Ἰδὼν Ἀδὰμ   τὸν ἄγγελον   ὠθήσαντα   καὶ κλείσαντα
τὴν τοῦ θείου κήπου θύραν   ἀνεστέναξε μέγα
καὶ ἔλεγεν·   ⟨ἐλεῆμον,   ἐλέησον   τὸν παραπεσόντα.⟩

propitiation for all men, for we are all in sore straits; that we, preserved from the guile of the evil one, may sing aloud the song of the angels.

LEADER of wisdom, provider of prudence, teacher of the foolish, defender of the poor, uphold and make wise my heart, O master.

Give to me reason, Word of the Father; see, I shall never allow my lips to cease crying to you: 'Have mercy, O merciful one, upon him who fell.'

Then Adam sat and wept before the delights of Paradise, beating his face with his hands, and said: 'Have mercy, O merciful one, upon him who fell.'

As Adam saw the angel push and close the door of the heavenly garden, he lamented loudly and said: 'Have mercy, O merciful one, upon him who fell.

‹Συνάλγησον, παράδεισε, τῷ κτήτορι πτωχεύσαντι
καὶ τῷ ἤχῳ σου τῶν φύλλων ἱκέτευσον τὸν πλάστην,
μὴ κλείσῃ σε· ἐλεῆμον, ἐλέησον τὸν παραπεσόντα.

‹Τὰ δένδρα σου κατάκαμψον ὡς ἔμψυχα καὶ πρόσ-
πεσον
τῷ κλειδούχῳ, ἵνα οὕτως μείνῃς ἀνεῳγμένος
τῷ κράζοντι· «ἐλεῆμον, ἐλέησον τὸν παραπεσόν-
τα.»

‹Ὀσφραίνομαι τοῦ κάλλους σου καὶ τήκομαι μνη-
σκόμενος,
πῶς ἐν τούτῳ ηὐφραινόμην ἀπὸ τῆς εὐοσμίας
τῶν ἄνθεων. ἐλεῆμον, ἐλέησον τὸν παραπεσόν-
τα.

‹Νῦν ἔμαθον, ἃ ἔπαθον, νῦν ἔγνωκα, ἃ εἶπέ μοι
ὁ θεὸς ἐν παραδείσῳ, ὅτι «Εὔαν λαμβάνων
λανθάνεις με·» ἐλεῆμον, ἐλέησον τὸν παραπεσόντα.

‹Παράδεισε, πανάρετε, πανάγιε, πανόλβιε,
δι᾽ Ἀδὰμ πεφυτευμένε, δι᾽ Εὔαν κεκλεισμένε,
πῶς κλαύσω σε; ἐλεῆμον, ἐλέησον τὸν παρα-
πεσόντα.

'Share, O Paradise, your impoverished master's pain, and with the rustling of your leaves beseech the Creator not to close your gates. Have mercy, O merciful one, upon him who fell.

'Make your trees to bow down like living beings, to fall down before him who holds the key, that thus you may remain open for him who cries: "Have mercy, O merciful one, upon him who fell."

'I breathe the perfume of your beauty and I melt as I remember the delights that I had there from the sweet scent of the flowers; have mercy, O merciful one, upon him who fell.

'Now have I learnt what has befallen me, now have I grasped what God told me in Paradise: "By taking Eve you slip away from me." Have mercy, O merciful one, upon him who fell.

'Paradise, full of virtue, holiness and happiness, planted for Adam, closed because of Eve, how shall I bewail you? Have mercy, O merciful one, upon him who fell.

‹ Ῥερύπωμαι,   ἠφάνισμαι,   δεδούλωμαι   τοῖς δούλοις
   μου·
ἑρπετὰ γὰρ καὶ θηρία,   ἃ ὑπέταξα φόβῳ,
πτοοῦσί με·   ἐλεῆμον,   ἐλέησον   τὸν παραπεσόντα.

‹ Οὐκέτι μοι   τὰ ἄνθεα   προσάγουσιν   ἀπόλαυσιν,
ἀλλ᾽ ἀκάνθας καὶ τριβόλους   ἡ γῆ μοι ἀνατέλλει,
οὐ πρόσοδον·   ἐλεῆμον,   ἐλέησον   τὸν παραπεσόν-
τα.

‹ Τὴν τράπεζαν   τὴν ἄμοχθον   κατέστρεψα   θελήματι·
καὶ λοιπὸν ἐν τῷ ἱδρῶτι   τοῦ προσώπου μου ἐσθίω
τὸν ἄρτον μου·   ἐλεῆμον,   ἐλέησον   τὸν παραπε-
σόντα.

‹ Ὁ λάρυγξ μου,   ὃν ἥδυναν   τὰ νάματα   τὰ ἅγια,
ἐπικράνθη ἀπὸ πλήθους   τῶν ἀναστεναγμῶν μου,
βοῶντός μου·   ‹ Ἐλεῆμον,   ἐλέησον   τὸν παραπεσόν-
τα. ›

‹ Πῶς ἔπεσα;   ποῦ ἔφθασα;   Ἐκ βήματος   εἰς ἔδαφος·
ἀπὸ θείας νουθεσίας   εἰς ἀθλίαν οὐσίαν
κατήντησα.   ἐλεῆμον,   ἐλέησον   τὸν παραπεσόντα.

'I am polluted, I am ruined, of my slaves I am a slave; for the wild
beasts and reptiles that I mastered by fear fill me with terror; have
mercy, O merciful one, upon him who fell.
'No longer do the flowers give me joy; thorns and brambles the
earth raises for me, not harvest; have mercy, O merciful one, upon him
who fell.
'Of my own will I overthrew the table spread without toil, and in
the days to come I shall eat my bread in the sweat of my brow; have
mercy, O merciful one, upon him who fell.
'My throat that was made sweet from the holy waters has become
bitter from the multitude of my sighs, as I cry out: "Have mercy, O
merciful one, upon him who fell."
'How have I fallen? Where have I come? From a pedestal to the
ground; from divine wisdom [communion] to wretched physical exist-
ence. Have mercy, O merciful one, upon him who fell.

ANONYMOUS

‹Λοιπὸν Σατὰν ἀγάλλεται γυμνώσας με τῆς δόξης
μου·
ἀλλ’ οὐ χαίρεται ἐν τούτῳ· ἰδοὺ γὰρ ὁ θεός μου
ἐνδύει με· ἐλεῆμον, ἐλέησον τὸν παραπεσόντα.

‹Αὐτὸς θεὸς οἰκτείρας μου τὴν γύμνωσιν ἐνδύει με·
διὰ τοῦτο μοι δεικνύει, ὅτι καὶ παραβάντος
φροντίζει μου· ἐλεῆμον, ἐλέησον τὸν παραπεσόν-
τα.

‹Σημαίνει μοι τὸ ἔνδυμα τὴν μέλλουσαν κατάστασιν·
ὁ γὰρ ἄρτι με ἐνδύσας μετ’ ὀλίγον φορεῖ με
καὶ σῴζει με· ἐλεῆμον ἐλέησον τὸν παραπεσόν-
τα.›

‹Ταχύ, Ἀδάμ, ἐγνώρισας τὸ θέλημα τῶν σπλάγ-
χνων μου·
διὰ τοῦτο οὐ στερῶ σε τῆς ἐλπίδος σου ταύτης
κραυγάζοντα· «ἐλεῆμον, ἐλέησον τὸν παραπεσόν-
τα.»

‹Οὐ θέλω, οὐδὲ βούλομαι, τὸν θάνατον, οὗ ἔπλασα·
σωφρονίσας δὲ μετρίως, αἰωνίως δοξάσω
τὸν κράζοντα· «ἐλεῆμον, ἐλέησον τὸν παραπεσόν-
τα.»»

'And now Satan rejoices that he has stripped me of my glory; but he
shall have no joy in this, for see, my God will clothe me. Have mercy,
O merciful one, upon him who fell.
'God himself has taken pity on my nakedness, and gives me clothes.
By this he shows me that, although I have sinned, he still takes care of
me. Have mercy, O merciful one, upon him who fell.
'The raiment is a sign of the state that is to come; for he who has
just clothed me shall in a little time carry me and save me. Have mercy,
O merciful one, upon him who fell.'
'Swiftly, Adam, have you understood the will of my heart, and so I
shall not bereave you of this hope of yours as you cry: "Have mercy,
O merciful one, upon him who fell."
'I do not wish nor desire the death of him whom I created; and, if he
is sensible and moderate, I shall give eternal glory to him who cries:
"Have mercy, O merciful one, upon him who fell."'

370

Νῦν οὖν, σωτήρ,   κἀμὲ σῶσον   τὸν πόθῳ με ζητοῦντα σε·
ἐγὼ κλέψαι σε οὐ θέλω;   κλαπῆναι δέ σοι θέλω
καὶ κράζειν σοι·   ⟨ἐλεῆμον,   ἐλέησον   τὸν παραπεσον-
τα.⟩

PAMPREPIUS OF PANOPOLIS
fl. c. 500

212. The Storm

Σήμερον ἀμφ' ἐμὲ κῶμος ἀείδεται, οὐχ ὅσον αὐλῶν,
οὐχ ὅσον ἑπτατόνοιο λύρης ἀναβάλλεται ἠχὼ
ἡδὺν ἀμειβομένη μελέων θρόον, οὔθ' ὃν ἀείδει
οὔρεος ὀμφήεντος ὑπὸ κλίτος ἠχέτα κύκνος
γηραλέης σειρῆνος ἀκήρατον ἄχθος ἀμείβων,
ἀκροτάτοις πτερύγεσσιν ὅτε πνείουσιν ἀῆται·
ἀλλ' ὅσον ἐκ Θρήικης νιφετώδεος ἔμπνοος αὔρη
χειμερίοις πελάγεσσιν ἐπισκαίρουσα θαλάσσης
ὄρθριον ἀείδει ῥοθίῳ μέλος· ἡδὺ δὲ μέλπει
χιονέην Φαέθοντος ἐριφλεγέος πυρὸς αἴγλην
χεύμασιν ὀμβροτόκων σβεῖσαν διεροῖς νεφελάων
καὶ κυνὸς ἀστραίοιο πυραιθέα . . .
ὑγροπόροις νιφάδεσσι κατασβεσθέντα . . .
χεύματι γὰρ χλοάουσι καὶ ἀστέρες, οὐκέτι μήνην
σύνδρομον ἠελίῳ κυανώπιδα πότναν ὁρῶμεν

    Now, O Saviour, save me too as with passion I seek after you. It is
not my desire to deceive you, but to be taken in by you, and to call out
to you: 'Have mercy, O merciful one, upon him who fell.'

TODAY a festival is resounding about me. Not that of flutes, not that
which the voice of the seven-stringed lyre sends up in response to the
sweet sound of songs, nor that which under the slope of the prophetic
mountain is sung by the shrill swan, when he casts off his pure burden
of melodious old age as the breezes blow through his feather-tips; but
a song the wind-rich blast from snowy Thrace sings to the breakers at
dawn as it dances on the winter waters. And sweetly it sings, of how the
snow-white gleam of Phaethon's golden fire is quenched by the wet
streams of the rainclouds, and the burning . . . of the dog-star is ex-
tinguished by melting snow. For even stars go pale before the waters;
no longer do we see the moon, that dark-eyed Lady who follows the

ψυχομένῳ νεφέεσσι καλυπτομενο . . .
οὐκέτι νυκτὸς ἔρευθος ἴτυν περίβαλλεν ἑῷον.

. . . .

ἤδη γὰρ νεφέων ἀνεφαίνετο μέσσοθι κύκλος
ἄκρον ἐρευθιόων, λεπτὴ δ' ἀνεθήλεεν αἴγλη
βοσκομένη τινὰ χῶρον, ὅσον νέφος ἐκτὸς ἐρύκει,
ἠερίην δ' ὤιξεν ἀνήλυσιν· ἠελίου δὲ
αὐγὴ πρῶτον ἔλαμψε βοώπιδος οἷα σελήνης,
ὑψίπορος δ' ἤστραψεν ὀϊστεύουσα κολώνας
ἀκτάς τε κλονέουσα· μόγις δ' ἐκέδασσεν ὀμίχλην
ὑψόθεν ἀμφιέλικτον, ἀλαμπέα μητέρα πάχνης.
πᾶσα δὲ γαῖα γέλασσε, πάλιν μείδησε γαλήνη.
ἤέρα δ' ἠέλιος πυριλαμπέος ἔμπλεον αἴγλης
θέρμε τε καὶ πέλαγος· νηυσὶν δ' ἀνεπάλλετο δελφὶς
ἡμιφανὴς ῥοθίοισιν ἐν ἠέρι πόντον ἐρέσσων.
στέρνα δὲ νυμφάων ἐζώσατο παντρόφον αἴγλην
μαρναμένην χιόνεσσι, φύσις δ' ἤμειπτο χαλάζης
εἰς ῥόον ὀμβρήεντα, χιὼν δ' ἐτινάσσετο γαίῃ,
φέγγει νικηθεῖσα· βιαζομένη δὲ γαλήνη
ἔρρεε ποικιλόδακρυς ἀνηναμένη μόθον αἴγλης.

course of the sun, covered and frozen by the clouds . . . no longer does
the redness of the dawn embrace the circle of the night . . .

For now a circle appeared in the clouds, red about its rim; and a thin
glow reached up and coloured a place the clouds did not guard, and it
opened a misty way for the return [of the sun]. At first the rays of the
sun shone like the glow of the ox-eyed moon; then they soared high
and flashed, striking the hills and shaking the shores. Barely did they
disperse the mist, the dark mother of frost, which swirled around from
above. There was laughter in all the land; calm smiled again. The sun
filled the air with fiery brilliance and warmed the sea; the dolphin leapt
up, half seen by the tossing ships as, in the air, it skimmed the water.
The breasts of the Nymphs were clothed with the life-giving brightness
[of the sun] that fought against the snow; hail was changed into a
showery stream. Snow, conquered by the light, was shaken to the
ground; forced by the calm weather it flowed away in tears of many
shapes, declining to battle with brightness. The sinews of springs
roared aloud in their channels, straitened by the snow-floods of the
heavens' outpouring; their breasts were swollen with the streams. The

πηγάων δὲ τένοντες ἐμυκήσαντο ῥεέθροις
στεινόμενοι νιφάδεσσι διιπετέων προχοάων,
μαζοὶ δ' ἐσφριγόωντο ῥοώδεες· ἐκ δὲ χαράδρης
ὦρτο ῥόος παλίνορσος, ὅπη πιτυώδεος ὕλης
νειόθεν ἐρρίζωντο συνήλικες ἔρνεσι νύμφαι.

• • • • • • • • • •

ἤδη μὲν Φαέθοντος ἐφ' ἑσπερίης πόμα λίμνης
αἰθερίην κροτέοντες ὑπ' ἴχνεσιν ἀτραπὸν ἵπποι
ἄντυγα μυδαλέην λιποφεγγέος ἕλκον ἀπήνης.
ἠέρι δ' ἠγερέθοντο πάλιν νεφελώδεες ἀτμοὶ
ἐκ χθονὸς ἀντέλλοντες, ἀποκρύπτοντο δὲ πάντα
τείρεα πουλυθέμεθλα καὶ οὐκέτι φαίνετο μήνη.
ὑψιπέτης δ' ὄρμαινε μέγας βρονταῖος ἀήτης
λάβρος ἐπαιγίζων, νεφέων δ' ἐξέσσυτο δαλὸς
ῥηγνυμένων ἑκάτερθε καὶ ἀλλήλοισι χυθέντων.
παῖδα δὲ νηπιάχοντα πατὴρ ἐπὶ κόλπον ἀείρας
οὔασι χεῖρας ἔβαλλεν, ὅπως μὴ δοῦπον ἀκούσῃ
ὑψόθεν ἀλλήλῃσιν ἀρασσομένων νεφελάων.
αἰθὴρ δ' ἐσμαράγησεν, ὀρινομένη δὲ καὶ αὐτὴ
παρθένος ἑλκεσίπεπλος ἑὴν ἐκάλεσσε τιθήνην.
γαῖα δὲ καρποτόκων λαγόνων ὠδῖνας ἀνέσχεν
αἰθέρι καὶ νεφέεσσιν ἐπιτρέψασα γενέθλην.

torrents rose out from their ravines and flowed back to where the Nymphs, as old as the trees, were rooted deep in the pine-wood . . .

And now the horses of Phaethon, beating the path of heaven with their hooves, were drawing the damp rail of their darkened chariot to their drinking pool in the western sea. And the clouds of mist were again gathering in the sky, rising from the earth; all the deep-rooted stars were hidden, and the moon was no longer seen. And on high a great thundering gale started up, furiously rushing; and a fire-brand leapt from the clouds as they burst open on either side, and poured into one another. The father lifted his infant child on to his lap, and put his hands over its ears so that it would not hear the crash above of clouds striking clouds. The heavens roared loudly, and a little girl in a trailing robe was woken up and called her nurse. The earth ended the pains of her fruit-bearing belly, and committed her child-bearing to the sky and the clouds.

ANONYMOUS
?5th century

213. The Akathistos Hymn

(later Procemium by Sergius, 7th century)

Τῇ ὑπερμάχῳ στρατηγῷ τὰ νικητήρια,
ὡς λυτρωθεῖσα τῶν δεινῶν, εὐχαριστήρια
ἀναγράφω σοι ἡ πόλις σου, θεοτόκε·
ἀλλ᾿ ὡς ἔχουσα τὸ κράτος ἀπροσμάχητον
ἐκ παντοίων με κινδύνων ἐλευθέρωσον,
ἵνα κράζω σοι· ‹χαῖρε, νύμφη ἀνύμφευτε.›

Ἄγγελος πρωτοστάτης   οὐρανόθεν ἐπέμφθη
  εἰπεῖν τῇ θεοτόκῳ τὸ ‹χαῖρε›·
καὶ σὺν τῇ ἀσωμάτῳ φωνῇ
  σωματούμενόν σε θεωρῶν, κύριε,
ἐξίστατο καὶ ἵστατο,   κραυγάζων πρὸς αὐτὴν τοιαῦτα·
‹χαῖρε, δι᾿ ἧς ἡ χαρὰ ἐκλάμψει·
  χαῖρε, δι᾿ ἧς ἡ ἀρὰ ἐκλείψει·
χαῖρε, τοῦ πεσόντος Ἀδὰμ ἡ ἀνάκλησις·
  χαῖρε, τῶν δακρύων τῆς Εὔας ἡ λύτρωσις·
χαῖρε, ὕψος δυσανάβατον   ἀνθρωπίνοις λογισμοῖς·

To you, Mother of God, champion and leader, I, your city [Constantinople], delivered from sufferings, ascribe the prize of victory and my thanks. And may you, in your invincible power, free me from all kinds of dangers, that I may cry to you: 'Hail, wedded maiden and virgin.'

A leading angel was sent from heaven to say to the Virgin: 'Hail.' And when he saw you, O Lord, becoming flesh, he was amazed and arose and cried to her with voice incorporeal:
  'Hail to you through whom joy will shine out;
  hail to you through whom the curse shall pass away;
  hail, redemption of fallen Adam;
  hail, deliverance of the tears of Eve;
  hail, height unattainable by human thought;

374

χαῖρε, βάθος δυσθεώρητον   καὶ ἀγγέλων ὀφθαλμοῖς·
χαῖρε, ὅτι ὑπάρχεις   βασιλέως καθέδρα·
    χαῖρε, ὅτι βαστάζεις   τὸν βαστάζοντα πάντα·
χαῖρε, ἀστὴρ ἐμφαίνων τὸν ἥλιον·
    χαῖρε, γαστὴρ ἐνθέου σαρκώσεως·
χαῖρε, δι᾽ ἧς νεουργεῖται ἡ κτίσις·
    χαῖρε, δι᾽ ἧς βρεφουργεῖται ὁ κτίστης·
        χαῖρε, νύμφη ἀνύμφευτε.>

Βλέπουσα ἡ ἁγία   ἑαυτὴν ἐν ἁγνείᾳ
    φησὶ τῷ Γαβριὴλ θαρσαλέως·
<Τὸ παράδοξόν σου τῆς φωνῆς
    δυσπαράδεκτόν μου τῇ ψυχῇ φαίνεται·
ἀσπόρου γὰρ συλλήψεως   τὴν κύησιν πῶς λέγεις κράζων·
    «Ἀλληλούϊα.»>

Γνῶσιν ἄγνωστον γνῶναι   ἡ παρθένος ζητοῦσα
    ἐβόησε πρὸς τὸν λειτουργοῦντα·
<ἐκ λαγόνων ἁγνῶν υἱὸν
    πῶς ἐστὶ τεχθῆναι δυνατόν; λέξον μοι·>

hail, depth invisible even to the eyes of angels;
hail to you, the throne of the king;
hail to you who bear him, the bearer of all;
hail, star that heralds the sun;
hail, womb of divine incarnation;
hail to you through whom creation is reborn;
hail to you through whom the Creator becomes a child:
hail, wedded maiden and virgin.'
The holy lady, seeing herself to be chaste, spoke boldly to Gabriel:
'The paradox of your words I find hard for my soul to accept; what
do you mean when you speak of childbirth from a conception without
seed, crying "Alleluia"?'
The Virgin, yearning to grasp a knowledge unknowable, cried to
the ministering angel: 'How can a son be born of chaste loins, tell me?'

πρὸς ἣν ἐκεῖνος ἔφησεν ἐν φόβῳ,   πλὴν κραυγάζων οὕτω·
‹χαῖρε, βουλῆς ἀπορρήτου μύστις
  χαῖρε, σιγῆς δεομένων πίστις·
χαῖρε, τῶν θαυμάτων Χριστοῦ τὸ προοίμιον·
  χαῖρε, τῶν δογμάτων αὐτοῦ τὸ κεφάλαιον·
χαῖρε, κλῖμαξ ἐπουράνιε,   ᾗ κατέβη ὁ θεός·
  χαῖρε, γέφυρα μετάγουσα   τοὺς ἐκ γῆς πρὸς οὐρανόν·
χαῖρε, τὸ τῶν ἀγγέλων   πολυθρύλητον θαῦμα·
  χαῖρε, τὸ τῶν δαιμόνων   πολυθρήνητον τραῦμα·
χαῖρε, τὸ φῶς ἀρρήτως γεννήσασα·
  χαῖρε, τὸ «πῶς» μηδένα διδάξασα·
χαῖρε, σοφῶν ὑπερβαίνουσα γνῶσιν·
  χαῖρε, πιστῶν καταυγάζουσα φρένας·
   χαῖρε, νύμφη ἀνύμφευτε.›

Δύναμις τοῦ ὑψίστου   ἐπεσκίασε τότε
  πρὸς σύλληψιν τῇ ἀπειρογάμῳ·
καὶ τὴν εὔκαρπον ταύτης νηδὺν
  ὡς ἀγρὸν ὑπέδειξεν ἡδὺν ἅπασι

He himself spoke to her in fear; yet this he cried:
 'Hail, initiate of secret counsel;
 hail to you, the proof of knowledge that demands silence;
 hail, prelude to the miracles of Christ;
 hail, the sum of his teachings;
 hail, celestial ladder by which God has descended;
 hail, bridge that bears men from earth to heaven;
 hail, far-famed miracle of the angels;
 hail, much-mourned affliction of the spirits of evil;
 hail to you, mysterious mother of light;
 hail to you, who taught nobody "how";
 hail to you, surpassing the knowledge of the wise;
 hail to you, illuminating the minds of the faithful;
 hail, wedded maiden and virgin.'
Then the power of the All-highest overshadowed her, planning the
conception of one without experience of marriage; and she showed

τοῖς θέλουσι θερίζειν σωτηρίαν   ἐν τῷ ψάλλειν οὕτως·
    ‹Ἀλληλούϊα.›

Ἔχουσα θεοδόχον   ἡ παρθένος τὴν μήτραν
    ἀνέδραμε πρὸς τὴν Ἐλισάβετ·
τὸ δὲ βρέφος ἐκείνης εὐθὺς
    ἐπιγνοῦν τὸν ταύτης ἀσπασμὸν ἔχαιρε
καὶ ἅλμασιν ὡς ᾄσμασιν   ἐβόα πρὸς τὴν θεοτόκον·
‹χαῖρε, βλαστοῦ ἀμαράντου κλῆμα·
    χαῖρε, καρποῦ ἀκηράτου κτῆμα·
χαῖρε, γεωργὸν γεωργοῦσα φιλάνθρωπον·
    χαῖρε, φυτουργὸν τῆς ζωῆς ἡμῶν φύουσα·
χαῖρε, ἄρουρα βλαστάνουσα   εὐφορίαν οἰκτιρμῶν·
    χαῖρε, τράπεζα βαστάζουσα   εὐθηνίαν ἱλασμῶν·
χαῖρε, ὅτι λειμῶνα   τῆς τρυφῆς ἀναθάλλεις·
    χαῖρε, ὅτι λιμένα   τῶν ψυχῶν ἑτοιμάζεις·
χαῖρε, δεκτὸν πρεσβείας θυμίαμα·
    χαῖρε, παντὸς τοῦ κόσμου ἐξίλασμα·
χαῖρε, θεοῦ πρὸς θνητοὺς εὐδοκία·

forth her fruitful womb as a sweet field for all who would harvest salvation by singing thus: 'Alleluia.'

The Virgin, holding God in her womb, hastened to Elisabeth. And Elisabeth's little child knew at once her embrace, and rejoiced, and with leaps like songs cried to the mother of God:
    'Hail, vine of the unwithered shoot;
hail, field of the immortal crop;
hail to you who harvest the harvester, friend of man;
hail to you who plant the planter of our life;
hail, field that flourishes with a fertility of compassion;
hail, table that bears a wealth of mercy;
hail to you who make a meadow of delight to blossom;
hail to you who make ready a haven for souls;
hail, incense of mediation, gladly received;
hail, propitiation of all the world;
hail, goodwill of God to mortal men;

χαῖρε, θνητῶν πρὸς θεὸν παρρησία·
χαῖρε, νύμφη ἀνύμφευτε.)

Ζάλην ἔνδοθεν ἔχων   λογισμῶν ἀμφιβόλων
ὁ σώφρων Ἰωσὴφ ἐταράχθη,
πρὸς τὴν ἄγαμόν σε θεωρῶν
καὶ κλεψίγαμον ὑπονοῶν, ἄμεμπτε·
μαθὼν δέ σου τὴν σύλληψιν   ἐκ πνεύματος ἁγίου ἔφη·
(Ἀλληλούϊα.)

Ἤκουσαν οἱ ποιμένες   τῶν ἀγγέλων ὑμνούντων
τὴν ἔνσαρκον Χριστοῦ παρουσίαν·
καὶ δραμόντες ὡς πρὸς ποιμένα
θεωροῦσι τοῦτον ὡς ἀμνὸν ἄμωμον
ἐν τῇ γαστρὶ Μαρίας βοσκηθέντα,   ἣν ὑμνοῦντες εἶπον·
(χαῖρε, ἀμνοῦ καὶ ποιμένος μήτηρ·
χαῖρε, αὐλὴ λογικῶν προβάτων·
χαῖρε, ἀοράτων ἐχθρῶν ἀμυντήριον·
χαῖρε, παραδείσου θυρῶν ἀνοικτήριον·
χαῖρε, ὅτι τὰ οὐράνια   συναγάλλεται τῇ γῇ·
χαῖρε, ὅτι τὰ ἐπίγεια   συγχορεύει οὐρανοῖς·

hail, boldness of mortal speech to God;
hail, wedded maiden and virgin.'

Joseph, a prudent man, was troubled within himself by a tumult of cares and doubts. He saw you unwedded and suspected illicit love, lady of no blame. But when he learnt of your conception by the Holy Ghost, he said 'Alleluia.'

The shepherds heard the angels singing of the incarnate presence of Christ; and, running as if to their shepherd, they saw him, a blameless lamb, pastured in Mary's womb; and in praise of her they cried:

'Hail, mother of lamb and shepherd;
hail, fold of the flock endowed with reason;
hail, protection against unseen foes;
hail, key of the gates of paradise;
hail, for the skies rejoice with the earth;
hail, for the earth chants in chorus with the heavens;

χαῖρε, τῶν ἀποστόλων   τὸ ἀσίγητον στόμα·
    χαῖρε, τῶν ἀθλοφόρων   τὸ ἀνίκητον θάρσος·
χαῖρε, στερρὸν τῆς πίστεως ἔρεισμα·
    χαῖρε, λαμπρὸν ·τῆς χάριτος γνώρισμα·
χαῖρε, δι' ἧς ἐγυμνώθη ὁ Ἅιδης·
    χαῖρε, δι' ἧς ἐνεδύθημεν δόξαν·
      χαῖρε, νύμφη ἀνύμφευτε.›

Θεοδρόμον ἀστέρα   θεωρήσαντες μάγοι
    τῇ τούτου ἠκολούθησαν αἴγλῃ·
καὶ ὡς λύχνον κρατοῦντες αὐτόν,
    δι' αὐτοῦ ἠρεύνων κραταιὸν ἄνακτα·
καὶ φθάσαντες τὸν ἄφθαστον   ἐχάρησαν, αὐτῷ βοῶντες·
      ‹Ἀλληλούϊα.›

Ἴδον παῖδες Χαλδαίων   ἐν χερσὶ τῆς παρθένου
    τὸν πλάσαντα χειρὶ τοὺς ἀνθρώπους·
καὶ δεσπότην νοοῦντες αὐτόν,
    εἰ καὶ δούλου ἔλαβε μορφήν, ἔσπευσαν
τοῖς δώροις θεραπεῦσαι καὶ   βοῆσαι τῇ εὐλογημένῃ·
‹χαῖρε, ἀστέρος ἀδύτου μήτηρ·
    χαῖρε, αὐγὴ μυστικῆς ἡμέρας·

    hail, unsilenced mouth of the apostles;
    hail, invincible courage of the martyrs;
    hail, unshaken bastion of the faith;
    hail, brilliant token of grace;
    hail to you, through whom Hades was laid bare;
    hail to you, through whom we were clothed in glory;
    hail, wedded maiden and virgin.'
The Wise Men saw a star moving towards God, and followed its
lustre, held it as a lantern, and by it searched for the mighty king. And,
when they reached him whom no man can reach, they were joyful, and
cried to him 'Alleluia.'
    The sons of the Chaldaeans saw in the virgin's hands him who with
his hand created men; they recognized him as master, although he had
taken the shape of a slave, and hastened to do him grace with gifts, and
cry to the blessed virgin:
    'Hail, mother of a star that does not set;
    hail, dawn of a mystic day;

χαῖρε, τῆς ἀπάτης τὴν κάμινον σβέσασα·
  χαῖρε, τῆς τριάδος τοὺς μύστας φωτίζουσα·
χαῖρε, τύραννον ἀπάνθρωπον ἐκβαλοῦσα τῆς ἀρχῆς·
  χαῖρε, κύριον φιλάνθρωπον ἐπιδείξασα Χριστόν·
χαῖρε, ἡ τῆς βαρβάρου λυτρουμένη θρησκείας·
  χαῖρε, ἡ τοῦ βορβόρου ῥυομένη τῶν ἔργων·
χαῖρε, πυρὸς προσκύνησιν παύσασα·
  χαῖρε, φλογὸς παθῶν ἀπαλλάττουσα·
χαῖρε, πιστῶν ὁδηγὲ σωφροσύνης·
  χαῖρε, πασῶν γενεῶν εὐφροσύνη·
    χαῖρε, νύμφη ἀνύμφευτε.)

Κήρυκες θεοφόροι γεγονότες οἱ μάγοι
  ὑπέστρεψαν εἰς τὴν Βαβυλῶνα,
ἐκτελέσαντές σου τὸν χρησμὸν
  καὶ κηρύξαντές σε τὸν Χριστὸν ἅπασιν,
ἀφέντες τὸν Ἡρώδην ὡς ληρώδη, μὴ εἰδότα ψάλλειν·
    (ʾΑλληλούϊα.)

Λάμψας ἐν τῇ Αἰγύπτῳ φωτισμὸν ἀληθείας
  ἐδίωξας τοῦ ψεύδους τὸ σκότος·

hail, quencher of the furnace of deceit;
hail, illuminator of the initiates of the Trinity;
hail to you who hurled the inhuman tyrant from his dominion;
hail to you who showed forth the Lord Christ, friend of man;
hail to you that free us from the pagan worship;
hail to you that deliver us from deeds foul;
hail to you who put an end to the worship of fire;
hail to you who released us from the flame of passions;
hail, guide of the faithful in righteousness;
hail, joy of all generations;
hail, wedded maiden and virgin.'
The Wise Men became heralds, bearing the message of God, and
returned to Babylon, fulfilling your prophecy. They proclaimed you
the Christ to all men, and abandoned Herod as a fool not knowing
how to sing 'Alleluia.'
By flashing the light of truth in Egypt you banished the darkness of

τὰ γὰρ εἴδωλα ταύτης, σωτήρ,
    μὴ ἐνέγκαντά σου τὴν ἰσχὺν πέπτωκεν·
οἱ τούτων δὲ ῥυσθέντες   ἐβόων πρὸς τὴν θεοτόκον·
‹χαῖρε, ἀνόρθωσις τῶν ἀνθρώπων·
    χαῖρε, κατάπτωσις τῶν δαιμόνων·
χαῖρε, τῆς ἀπάτης τὴν πλάνην πατήσασα·
    χαῖρε, τῶν εἰδώλων τὸν δόλον ἐλέγξασα·
χαῖρε, θάλασσα ποντίσασα   Φαραὼ τὸν νοητόν·
    χαῖρε, πέτρα ἡ ποτίσασα   τοὺς διψῶντας τὴν ζωήν·
χαῖρε, πύρινε στῦλε   ὁδηγῶν τοὺς ἐν σκότει·
    χαῖρε, σκέπη τοῦ κόσμου,   πλατυτέρα νεφέλης·
χαῖρε, τροφὴ τοῦ μάννα διάδοχε·
    χαῖρε, τρυφῆς ἁγίας διάκονε·
χαῖρε, ἡ γῆ τῆς ἐπαγγελίας·
    χαῖρε, ἐξ ἧς ῥέει μέλι καὶ γάλα·
        χαῖρε, νύμφη ἀνύμφευτε.›

Μέλλοντος Συμεῶνος   τοῦ παρόντος αἰῶνος
    μεθίστασθαι τοῦ ἀπατεῶνος,
ἐπεδόθης ὡς βρέφος αὐτῷ,
    ἀλλ' ἐγνώσθης τούτῳ καὶ θεὸς τέλειος·

error; for her idols, Saviour, did not withstand your strength, and fell,
and those who were saved from them cried to the mother of God:
    'Hail, of men the restoration;
    hail, of demons the demolition;
    hail to you who trampled upon the error of deceit;
    hail to you who refuted the lie of idols;
    hail, ocean overwhelming the Pharaoh of the mind;
    hail, rock giving water to those who thirst for life;
    hail, pillar of fire, leading those in darkness;
    hail, shield of the world, broader than the clouds;
    hail sustenance, of manna the successor;
    hail, minister of holy delight;
    hail, promised land;
    hail to you, from whom flow milk and honey;
    hail, wedded maiden and virgin.'
    When Symeon was about to depart from this life of deceit, you were
given to him as an infant, but you were made known to him as a

διόπερ ἐξεπλάγη, σου   τὴν ἄπειρον σοφίαν κράζων·
        ('Αλληλούϊα.)

Νέαν ἔδειξε κτίσιν   ἐμφανίσας ὁ κτίστης
    ἡμῖν τοῖς ὑπ' αὐτοῦ γενομένοις,
ἐξ ἀσπόρου βλαστήσας γαστρὸς
    καὶ φυλάξας ταύτην, ὥσπερ ἦν, ἄφθορον,
ἵνα τὸ θαῦμα βλέποντες   ὑμνήσωμεν αὐτὴν βοῶντες·
⟨χαῖρε, τὸ ἄνθος τῆς ἀφθαρσίας·
    χαῖρε, τὸ στέφος τῆς ἐγκρατείας·
χαῖρε, ἀναστάσεως τύπον ἐκλάμπουσα·
    χαῖρε, τῶν ἀγγέλων τὸν βίον ἐμφαίνουσα·
χαῖρε, δένδρον ἀγλαόκαρπον,   ἐξ οὗ τρέφονται πιστοί·
    χαῖρε, ξύλον εὐσκιόφυλλον,   ὑφ' οὗ σκέπονται πολλοί·
χαῖρε, κυοφοροῦσα   ὁδηγὸν πλανωμένοις·
    χαῖρε, ἀπογεννῶσα   λυτρωτὴν αἰχμαλώτοις·
χαῖρε, κριτοῦ δικαίου δυσώπησις·
    χαῖρε, πολλῶν πταιόντων συγχώρησις·
χαῖρε, στολὴ τῶν γυμνῶν παρρησίας·
    χαῖρε, στοργὴ πάντα πόθον νικῶσα·
        χαῖρε, νύμφη ἀνύμφευτε.⟩

perfect God; and so he was astounded at your limitless wisdom, and
cried 'Alleluia.'

The Creator revealed a new creation, and showed it to us, his crea-
tures. He made it flourish from a womb without seed which he kept
chaste, as it had been before, so that we might see the miracle and sing
her praises, saying:
  'Hail, flower of incorruptibility;
  hail, crown of chastity;
  hail to you who shine forth the pattern of resurrection;
  hail to you who show forth the life of the angels;
  hail, tree of brilliant fruit, from which the faithful are fed;
  hail, branch of fair-shading leaves, under whom many take shelter;
  hail to you who will give birth to the guide of wanderers;
  hail to you who bring into the world the liberator of prisoners;
  hail, conciliation of the upright judge;
  hail, forgiveness of many sinners;
  hail, robe of free intercession given to the naked;
  hail, love that conquers all passion;
  hail, wedded maiden and virgin.'

Ξένον τόκον ἰδόντες   ξενωθῶμεν τοῦ κόσμου
    τὸν νοῦν εἰς οὐρανὸν μεταθέντες·
διὰ τοῦτο γὰρ ὁ ὑψηλὸς θεὸς
    ἐπὶ γῆς ἐφάνη ταπεινὸς ἄνθρωπος,
βουλόμενος ἑλκύσαι πρὸς τὸ ὕψος   τοὺς αὐτῷ βοῶντας·
       ‹ Ἀλληλούϊα.›

Ὅλος ἦν ἐν τοῖς κάτω   καὶ τῶν ἄνω οὐδ' ὅλως
    ἀπῆν ὁ ἀπερίγραπτος Λόγος·
συγκατάβασις γὰρ θεϊκή,
    οὐ μετάβασις δὲ τοπικὴ γέγονε,
καὶ τόκος ἐκ παρθένου   θεολήπτου ἀκουούσης ταῦτα·
‹ χαῖρε, θεοῦ ἀχωρήτου χώρα·
    χαῖρε, σεπτοῦ μυστηρίου θύρα·
χαῖρε, τῶν ἀπίστων ἀμφίβολον ἄκουσμα·
    χαῖρε, τῶν πιστῶν ἀναμφίβολον καύχημα·
χαῖρε, ὄχημα πανάγιον   τοῦ ἐπὶ τῶν Χερουβίμ·
    χαῖρε, οἴκημα πανάριστον   τοῦ ἐπὶ τῶν Σεραφίμ·
χαῖρε, ἡ τἀναντία   εἰς ταὐτὸ ἀγαγοῦσα·
    χαῖρε, ἡ παρθενίαν   καὶ λοχείαν ζευγνῦσα·
χαῖρε, δι' ἧς ἐλύθη παράβασις·
    χαῖρε, δι' ἧς ἠνοίχθη παράδεισος·

And let us, seeing this strange birth, estrange ourselves from the earth, and turn our thoughts to heaven; it was for this that the great God appeared on earth as a humble man; for he wanted to draw to the heights those who cry to him 'Alleluia.'

The unbounded Word was complete among men below, and from Heaven above never absent; this was not merely a journey from place to place, but a divine condescension, the birth of a child by a virgin possessed by God; and she heard the words:

'Hail, container of a God uncontained;
hail, gate of a sacred mystery;
hail, report that brings doubt to unbelievers;
hail, boast that brings freedom from doubt to believers;
hail, all-holy chariot of him who rules the Cherubim;
hail, excellent mansion of him who rules the Seraphim;
hail to you who bring opposites together;
hail, union of virginity and motherhood;
hail to you through whom sin has been abolished;
hail to you through whom paradise has been opened;

χαῖρε, ἡ κλεὶς τῆς Χριστοῦ βασιλείας·
  χαῖρε, ἐλπὶς ἀγαθῶν αἰωνίων·
    χαῖρε, νύμφη ἀνύμφευτε·›

Πᾶσα φύσις ἀγγέλων   κατεπλάγη τὸ μέγα
  τῆς σῆς ἐνανθρωπήσεως ἔργον·
τὸν ἀπρόσιτον γὰρ ὡς θεὸν
  ἐθεώρει πᾶσι προσιτὸν ἄνθρωπον,
ἡμῖν μὲν συνδιάγοντα,   ἀκούοντα δὲ παρὰ πάντων·
          ‹Ἀλληλούϊα.›

Ῥήτορας πολυφθόγγους   ὡς ἰχθύας ἀφώνους
  ὁρῶμεν ἐπὶ σοί, θεοτόκε·
ἀποροῦσι γὰρ λέγειν τό· ‹πῶς
  καὶ παρθένος μένεις καὶ τεκεῖν ἴσχυσας·›
ἡμεῖς δὲ τὸ μυστήριον θαυμάζοντες   πιστῶς βοῶμεν·
‹χαῖρε, σοφίας θεοῦ δοχεῖον·
  χαῖρε, προνοίας αὐτοῦ ταμεῖον·
χαῖρε, φιλοσόφους ἀσόφους δεικνύουσα·
  χαῖρε, τεχνολόγους ἀλόγους ἐλέγχουσα·
χαῖρε, ὅτι ἐμωράνθησαν   οἱ δεινοὶ συζητηταί·
  χαῖρε, ὅτι ἐμαράνθησαν   οἱ τῶν μύθων ποιηταί·

hail, key to the kingdom of Christ;
  hail, hope of eternal happiness;
    hail, wedded maiden and virgin.'
All the orders of the angels were astounded at the great act of your
incarnation; for they saw, as a man approachable by all, him who was
unapproachable as God, living among us and hearing from us all
'Alleluia.'
  Before you, mother of God, we see wordy orators as voiceless as
fish; they are at a loss as they say: 'How is it that you are still a virgin
and yet had the power to give birth?' But let us marvel at the mystery
and cry out in faith:
  'Hail, vessel of the wisdom of God;
  hail, treasury of his holy providence;
  hail to you who show the philosophers to be fools;
  hail to you who prove men of letters to be men of no wisdom;
  hail to you, for able disputers have been shown to be idiots;
  hail to you, for the fashioners of fables have been made to wither;

χαῖρε, τῶν ᾿Αθηναίων   τὰς πλοκὰς διασπῶσα·
   χαῖρε, τῶν ἁλιέων   τὰς σαγήνας πληροῦσα·
χαῖρε, βυθοῦ ἀγνοίας ἐξέλκουσα·
   χαῖρε, πολλοὺς ἐν γνώσει φωτίζουσα·
χαῖρε, ὁλκὰς τῶν θελόντων σωθῆναι·
   χαῖρε, λιμὴν τῶν τοῦ βίου πλωτήρων·
    χαῖρε, νύμφη ἀνύμφευτε.›

Σῶσαι θέλων τὸν κόσμον   ὁ τῶν ὅλων κοσμήτωρ
   πρὸς τοῦτον αὐτεπάγγελτος ἦλθε·
καὶ ποιμὴν ὑπάρχων ὡς θεὸς
   δι᾿ ἡμᾶς ἐφάνη καθ᾿ ἡμᾶς ἄνθρωπος·
ὁμοίῳ γὰρ τὸ ὅμοιον καλέσας   ὡς θεὸς ἀκούει·
      ‹Ἀλληλούϊα.›

Τεῖχος εἶ τῶν παρθένων,   θεοτόκε παρθένε,
   καὶ πάντων τῶν εἰς σὲ προστρεχόντων·
ὁ γὰρ τοῦ οὐρανοῦ καὶ τῆς γῆς
   κατεσκεύασέ σε ποιητής, ἄχραντε,
οἰκήσας ἐν τῇ μήτρᾳ σου   καὶ πάντας σοι προσφωνεῖν
   διδάξας·

hail to you who have torn apart the intricate schemes of the Athenians;
hail to you who have filled the nets of the fishermen;
hail to you who draw forth from the depths of ignorance;
hail to you who illuminate many with knowledge;
hail, boat for those who wish to be saved;
hail, harbour for the sailors of life;
hail, wedded maiden and virgin.'

He who set all things in order came to the world of his own will, wishing to save it. As God he was a shepherd, yet for our sake he came among us, a man like ourselves; and, calling like to like, as a God he heard 'Alleluia.'

Virgin mother of God, you are the defence of virgins, and of all those who run to you for protection. For the Creator of heaven and earth created you, immaculate lady, dwelt in your womb, and taught all men to address you:

‹χαῖρε, ἡ στήλη τῆς παρθενίας·
  χαῖρε, ἡ πύλη τῆς σωτηρίας·
χαῖρε, ἀρχηγὲ νοητῆς ἀναπλάσεως·
  χαῖρε, χορηγὲ θεϊκῆς ἀγαθότητος·
χαῖρε· σὺ γὰρ ἀνεγέννησας   τοὺς συλληφθέντας αἰσχρῶς·
  χαῖρε· σὺ γὰρ ἐνουθέτησας   τοὺς συληθέντας τὸν νοῦν.
χαῖρε, ἡ τὸν φθορέα   τῶν φρενῶν καταργοῦσα·
  χαῖρε, ἡ τὸν σπορέα   τῆς ἁγνείας τεκοῦσα·
χαῖρε, παστὰς ἀσπόρου νυμφεύσεως·
  χαῖρε, πιστοὺς κυρίῳ ἁρμόζουσα·
χαῖρε, καλὴ κουροτρόφε παρθένων·
  χαῖρε, ψυχῶν νυμφοστόλε ἁγίων·
    χαῖρε, νύμφη ἀνύμφευτε.›

Ὕμνος ἅπας ἡττᾶται,   συνεκτείνεσθαι σπεύδων
  τῷ πλήθει τῶν πολλῶν οἰκτιρμῶν σου·
ἰσαρίθμους γὰρ ψάμμῳ ᾠδὰς
  ἂν προσφέρωμέν σοι, βασιλεῦ ἅγιε,
οὐδὲν τελοῦμεν ἄξιον,   ὧν δέδωκας ἡμῖν βοῶσιν·
    ‹Ἀλληλούϊα.›

'Hail, pillar of virginity;
hail, gateway of salvation;
hail, leader of spiritual reformation;
hail, giver of divine goodness;
hail to you, for you have regenerated those who were conceived in
    sin;
hail to you, for you have given reason to those without understand-
    ing;
hail to you, for you have destroyed the corruptor of the mind;
hail to you, for you have borne the sower of purity;
hail, bridal chamber of a union without seed;
hail to you, who unite the faithful with the Lord;
hail, good nurse of maidens;
hail, bridesmaid of saintly souls;
hail, wedded maiden and virgin.'
    All hymns are defeated that attempt to equal the wealth of your
great compassion; for were we to offer you, holy king, as many odes
as there are grains of sand, we would accomplish nothing worthy of
what you have given us, as we sing 'Alleluia.'

Φωτοδόχον λαμπάδα   τοῖς ἐν σκότει φανεῖσαν
   ὁρῶμεν τὴν ἁγίαν παρθένον·
τὸ γὰρ ἄϋλον ἅπτουσα φῶς
   ὁδηγεῖ πρὸς γνῶσιν θεϊκὴν ἅπαντας,
αὐγῇ τὸν νοῦν φωτίζουσα,   κραυγῇ δὲ τιμωμένη ταύτῃ·
‹χαῖρε, ἀκτὶς νοητοῦ ἡλίου·
   χαῖρε, βολὶς τοῦ ἀδύτου φέγγους·
χαῖρε, ἀστραπὴ τὰς ψυχὰς καταλάμπουσα·
   χαῖρε, ὡς βροντὴ τοὺς ἐχθροὺς καταπλήττουσα·
χαῖρε, ὅτι τὸν πολύφωτον   ἀνατέλλεις φωτισμόν·
   χαῖρε, ὅτι τὸν πολύρρυτον   ἀναβλύζεις ποταμόν·
χαῖρε, τῆς κολυμβήθρας   ζωγραφοῦσα τὸν τύπον·
   χαῖρε, τῆς ἁμαρτίας   ἀναιροῦσα τὸν ῥύπον·
χαῖρε, λουτὴρ ἐκπλύνων συνείδησιν·
   χαῖρε, κρατὴρ κιρνῶν ἀγαλλίασιν·
χαῖρε, ὀσμὴ τῆς Χριστοῦ εὐωδίας·
   χαῖρε, ζωὴ μυστικῆς εὐωχίας·
     χαῖρε, νύμφη ἀνύμφευτε.›

Χάριν δοῦναι θελήσας   ὀφλημάτων ἀρχαίων
   ὁ πάντων χρεωλύτης ἀνθρώπων,

We see the holy virgin as a lamp full of light, shining to those in darkness; for by lighting the incorporeal flame she leads everyone towards divine understanding, illuminating the mind with brilliance, and honoured by this cry:
'Hail, ray of the sun of the spirit;
hail, shaft of light that does not set;
hail, soul-illuminating lightning;
hail to you who like thunder stun the foe;
hail to you who kindle the light of many lanterns;
hail to you who make the river of many streams to gush forth;
hail to you who depict the pattern of the font;
hail to you who take away the filth of sin;
hail, basin that washes clean the conscience;
hail, bowl that mixes together delights;
hail, odour of the perfume of Christ;
hail, life of the mystic banquet;
hail, wedded maiden and virgin.'
The Redeemer of all mankind wished to cancel our old debts, and

ANONYMOUS

ἐπεδήμησε δι' ἑαυτοῦ
  πρὸς τοὺς ἀποδήμους τῆς αὐτοῦ χάριτος·
καὶ σχίσας τὸ χειρόγραφον   ἀκούει παρὰ πάντων οὕτως·
      ‹Ἀλληλούϊα.›

Ψάλλοντές σου τὸν τόκον   ἀνυμνοῦμέν σε πάντες
  ὡς ἔμψυχον ναόν, θεοτόκε·
ἐν τῇ σῇ γὰρ οἰκήσας γαστρὶ
  ὁ συνέχων πάντα τῇ χειρὶ κύριος
ἡγίασεν, ἐδόξασεν,   ἐδίδαξε βοᾶν σοι πάντας·
‹χαῖρε, σκηνὴ τοῦ θεοῦ καὶ λόγου·
  χαῖρε, ἁγία ἁγίων μείζων·
χαῖρε, κιβωτὲ χρυσωθεῖσα τῷ πνεύματι·
  χαῖρε, θησαυρὲ τῆς ζωῆς ἀδαπάνητε·
χαῖρε, τίμιον διάδημα   βασιλέων εὐσεβῶν·
  χαῖρε, καύχημα σεβάσμιον   ἱερέων εὐλαβῶν·
χαῖρε, τῆς ἐκκλησίας   ὁ ἀσάλευτος πύργος·
  χαῖρε, τῆς βασιλείας   τὸ ἀπόρθητον τεῖχος·
χαῖρε, δι' ἧς ἐγείρονται τρόπαια·
  χαῖρε, δι' ἧς ἐχθροὶ καταπίπτουσι·

came himself to live with the fugitives from his grace; and having torn up the parchment he hears from them all 'Alleluia.'

We sing your giving birth, and we all celebrate you as a living temple, Mother of God; for the Lord, who holds all in his hand, dwelt in your womb and made you holy, made you glorious, and taught us all to cry out to you:

'Hail, abode of God and Word;
hail, holy one, greater than the saints;
hail, ark, gilded by the Spirit;
hail, inexhaustible treasure of life;
hail, precious diadem of reverent kings;
hail, holy exaltation of dutiful priests;
hail, immovable tower of the church;
hail, impregnable wall of the Kingdom;
hail to you by whom trophies are raised up;
hail to you through whom enemies fall;

388

χαῖρε, χρωτὸς τοῦ ἐμοῦ θεραπεία·
  χαῖρε, ψυχῆς τῆς ἐμῆς σωτηρία·
  χαῖρε, νύμφη ἀνύμφευτε.)

῎Ω πανύμνητε μῆτερ,   ἡ τεκοῦσα τὸν πάντων
  ἁγίων ἁγιώτατον Λόγον,
δεξαμένη τὴν νῦν προσφοράν,
  ἀπὸ πάσης ῥῦσαι συμφορᾶς ἅπαντας
καὶ τῆς μελλούσης λύτρωσαι κολάσεως   τοὺς συμβοῶντας·
  (Ἀλληλούϊα.)

AGATHIAS SCHOLASTICUS
c. 536–82

214. On the Archangel Michael

῎Ασκοπον ἀγγελίαρχον, ἀσώματον εἴδεϊ μορφῆς,
  ᾗ μέγα τολμήεις, κηρὸς ἀπεπλάσσατο.
ἔμπης οὐκ ἀχάριστον, ἐπεὶ βροτὸς εἰκόνα λεύσσων
  θυμὸν ἀπιθύνει κρέσσονι φαντασίῃ·

hail, care of my flesh;
hail, protection of my soul;
hail, wedded maiden and virgin.'

O mother hymned by all, mother who bore the Word, most holy of
all saints: accept this present offering and deliver us from every evil,
and from the punishment that is to come free those who cry together
'Alleluia.'

VERY daring was the wax that shaped the image of the invisible leader
of the angels, incorporeal in the shape of his form. Yet it was not a
worthless task; for a mortal, looking at the image, directs his mind to a
higher concept. No longer has he a confused reverence, but he paints

οὐκέτι ἀλλοπρόσαλλον ἔχει σέβας, ἀλλ' ἐν ἑαυτῷ
τὸν τύπον ἐγγράψας ὡς παρεόντα τρέμει·
ὄμματα δ' ὀτρύνουσι βαθὺν νόον· οἶδε δὲ τέχνη
χρώμασι πορθμεῦσαι τὴν φρενὸς ἱκεσίην.

215. On the Death of a Partridge

Οὐκέτι που, τλῆμον σκοπέλων μετανάστρια πέρδιξ,
πλεκτὸς λεπταλέαις οἶκος ἔχει σε λύγοις,
οὐδ' ὑπὸ μαρμαρυγῇ θαλερώπιδος Ἠριγενείης
ἄκρα παραιθύσσεις θαλπομένων πτερύγων.
σὴν κεφαλὴν αἴλουρος ἀπέθρισε· τἄλλα δὲ πάντα
ἥρπασα, καὶ φθονερὴν οὐκ ἐκόρεσσε γένυν.
νῦν δέ σε μὴ κούφη κρύπτοι κόνις, ἀλλὰ βαρεῖα,
μὴ τὸ τεὸν κείνη λείψανον ἐξερύσῃ.

the image in himself and fears him as though he were present. The eyes command deep thought, for art can convey by colours the prayer of the heart.

No longer, poor partridge, migrant from the rocks, does your plaited house hold you within its delicate willow-twigs; nor in the shimmer of bright-eyed dawn do you shake the tips of your wings as they grow warm. A cat scythed off your head; all the rest of you I seized from her, and she was unable to sate her envious jaws. And now may the dust lie not lightly upon you, but heavily, so that she will not be able to drag out your corpse.

216. On Justinian's Bridge over the River Sangarios

Καὶ σὺ μεθ' Ἑσπερίην ὑψαύχενα καὶ μετὰ Μήδων
ἔθνεα καὶ πᾶσαν βαρβαρικὴν ἀγέλην,
Σαγγάριε, κρατεραῖσι ῥοὰς ἀψῖσι πεδηθεὶς
αὐτὸς ἐδουλώθης κοιρανικῇ παλάμῃ·
ὁ πρὶν γὰρ σκαφέεσσιν ἀνέμβατος, ὁ πρὶν ἀτειρὴς
κεῖσαι λαϊνέῃ σφιγκτὸς ἀλυκτοπέδῃ.

MACEDONIUS
fl. 550

217. On the Morning Star

Φωσφόρε, μὴ τὸν Ἔρωτα βιάζεο μηδὲ διδάσκου,
Ἄρεϊ γειτονέων, νηλεὲς ἦτορ ἔχειν.
ὡς δὲ πάρος Κλυμένης ὁρόων Φαέθοντα μελάθρῳ
οὐ δρόμον ὠκυπόδην εἶχες ἀπ' ἀντολίης,
οὕτω μοι περὶ νύκτα, μόγις ποθέοντι φανεῖσαν,
ἔρχεο δηθύνων ὡς παρὰ Κιμμερίοις.

AND you, Sangarios, after the haughty West and the Persian tribes and the whole barbarian herd, you have had your streams fettered by powerful arches, and you yourself have been enslaved by the hand of the king. You, who formerly were inaccessible to boats, you who formerly were so unyielding, now lie tightly bound by bonds of stone.

MORNING STAR, do not force Love away; and do not follow Ares, your neighbour, in having a pitiless heart. But as once before, when you saw Phaethon [the sun] in the hall of Clymene, you did not come swift-footed from the east, even so, on this night which has appeared to one who painfully longed for it, delay your coming as you do among the Cimmerians.

ROMANOS

fl. 540

218. *Christmas Hymn*

Ἡ παρθένος σήμερον   τὸν ὑπερούσιον τίκτει,
  καὶ ἡ γῆ τὸ σπήλαιον   τῷ ἀπροσίτῳ προσάγει·
ἄγγελοι μετὰ ποιμένων   δοξολογοῦσι,
  μάγοι δὲ μετὰ ἀστέρος   ὁδοιποροῦσι·
δι' ἡμᾶς γὰρ   ἐγεννήθη
  |: παιδίον νέον,   ὁ πρὸ αἰώνων θεός. :|

Τὴν Ἐδὲμ Βηθλεὲμ   ἤνοιξε, δεῦτε ἴδωμεν·
  τὴν τρυφὴν ἐν κρυφῇ   ηὕραμεν, δεῦτε λάβωμεν
  τὰ τοῦ παραδείσου   ἐντὸς τοῦ σπηλαίου·
ἐκεῖ ἐφάνη   ῥίζα ἀπότιστος   βλαστάνουσα ἄφεσιν,
  ἐκεῖ ηὑρέθη   φρέαρ ἀνόρυκτον,
  οὗ πιεῖν Δαβὶδ   πρὶν ἐπεθύμησεν·
ἐκεῖ παρθένος   τεκοῦσα βρέφος
  τὴν δίψαν ἔπαυσεν εὐθὺς   τὴν τοῦ Ἀδὰμ καὶ τοῦ Δαβίδ·
διὰ τοῦτο πρὸς τοῦτο   ἐπειχθῶμεν, ποῦ ἐτέχθη
  |: παιδίον νέον,   ὁ πρὸ αἰώνων θεός. :|

TODAY the Virgin gives birth to him who is beyond substance; and the earth offers a cave to him who is unapproachable. Angels with shepherds give praise, and by a star the Wise Men make their way; for unto us is born a little child, God of all time.

Bethlehem has opened the gates of Eden; come, let us see. In a secret place we have found delight; come, let us partake of paradise within the cave. In it has appeared a root never watered, blossoming forth forgiveness; in it has been found a well never dug, a well from which David once longed to drink. In it a virgin has given birth to a child, and at once has brought an end to the thirst of Adam and of David. Therefore, let us hasten to the place where has been born a little child, God of all time.

'Ο πατὴρ τῆς μητρὸς   γνώμῃ υἱὸς ἐγένετο·
    ὁ σωτὴρ τῶν βρεφῶν   βρέφος ἐν φάτνῃ ἔκειτο·
    ὃν κατανοοῦσα   φησὶν ἡ τεκοῦσα·
‹Εἰπέ μοι, τέκνον,   πῶς ἐνεσπάρης μοι   ἢ πῶς ἐνεφύης
    μοι;
    ὁρῶ σε, σπλάγχνον,   καὶ καταπλήττομαι,
    ὅτι γαλουχῶ   καὶ οὐ νενύμφευμαι·
καὶ σὲ μὲν βλέπω   μετὰ σπαργάνων,
    τὴν παρθενίαν δὲ ἀκμὴν   ἐσφραγισμένην θεωρῶ·
σὺ γὰρ ταύτην φυλάξας   ἐγεννήθης εὐδοκήσας
    |: παιδίον νέον,   ὁ πρὸ αἰώνων θεός. :|

‹Ὑψηλὲ βασιλεῦ,   τί σοὶ καὶ τοῖς πτωχεύσασι;
    ποιητὰ οὐρανοῦ,   τί πρὸς γηΐνους ἤλυθας;
    σπηλαίου ἠράσθης   ἢ φάτνῃ ἐτέρφθης;
'Ιδοὺ οὐκ ἔστι   τόπος τῇ δούλῃ σου   ἐν τῷ καταλύματι·
    οὐ λέγω τόπον,   ἀλλ' οὐδὲ σπήλαιον,
    ὅτι καὶ αὐτὸ   τοῦτο ἀλλότριον·
καὶ τῇ μὲν Σάρρα   τεκούσῃ βρέφος
    ἐδόθη κλῆρος γῆς πολύς,   ἐμοὶ δὲ οὐδὲ φωλεός·
ἐχρησάμην τὸ ἄντρον   ὃ κατῴκησας βουλήσει
    |: παιδίον νέον,   ὁ πρὸ αἰώνων θεός.› :|

The Father, by his will alone, became the Son of the Mother. The Saviour of infants, an infant himself, lay in the manger. When his mother realized this she said: 'Tell me, child, how were you sown in me, and how did you set your roots in me? I see you, my flesh and blood, and am amazed, that I give suck and am not married, that I see you in swaddling bands and yet still see that my virginity is sealed; for it pleased you to preserve it when you were born, a little child, God of all time.

'Great monarch, what have you in common with the poor? Creator of the heavens, why have you come to the people of the earth? Did you desire a cave or take pleasure in a manger? See, there is no room for your handmaiden at the inn; no room, I say, not even a cave, for even that is not mine. And yet to Sarah, when she bore a child, was allotted a wide stretch of land; but to me not even a wild beast's lair. I used the cave which you, of your own will, inhabited, a little child, God of all time.'

Τὰ τοιαῦτα ῥητὰ   ἐν ἀπορρήτῳ λέγουσα
   καὶ τὸν τῶν ἀφανῶν   γνώστην καθικετεύουσα
   ἀκούει τῶν μάγων   τὸ βρέφος ζητούντων·
εὐθὺς δὲ τούτοις·   〈Τίνες ὑπάρχετε;〉   ἡ κόρη ἐβόησεν·
   οἱ δὲ πρὸς ταύτην·   〈Σὺ γὰρ τίς πέφυκας,
   ὅτι τὸν τοιοῦτον ἀπεκύησας;
Τίς ὁ πατήρ σου;   τίς ἡ τεκοῦσα;
   ὅτι ἀπάτορος υἱοῦ   ἐγένου μήτηρ καὶ τροφός,
   οὗ τὸ ἄστρον ἰδόντες   συνήκαμεν ὅτι ὤφθη
   |: παιδίον νέον,   ὁ πρὸ αἰώνων θεός. :|

〈Ἀκριβῶς γὰρ ἡμῖν   ὁ Βαρλαὰμ παρέθετο
   τῶν ῥημάτων τὸν νοῦν   ὧνπερ προεμαντεύσατο,
   εἰπὼν ὅτι μέλλει   ἀστὴρ ἀνατέλλειν,
ἀστὴρ σβεννύων   πάντα μαντεύματα   καὶ τὰ οἰωνίσματα·
   ἀστὴρ ἐκλύων   παραβολὰς σοφῶν
   ῥήσεις τε αὐτῶν   καὶ τὰ αἰνίγματα·
ἀστὴρ ἀστέρος   τοῦ φαινομένου
   ὑπερφαιδρότερος πολὺ   ὡς πάντων ἄστρων   ποιη-
   τής,
περὶ οὗ προεγράφη·   ἐξ Ἰακὼβ ἀνατέλλει
   |: παιδίον νέον,   ὁ πρὸ αἰώνων θεός.〉 :|

As she said these words in secret and entreated him who knows all
secrets, she heard the Wise Men seeking the child; and at once the
maiden cried to them: 'Who are you?' And they said to her: 'And you,
who are you, that you have borne such a son? Who is your father, who
your mother, that you have become the mother and nurse of a father-
less son, whose star we saw, and understood that there has appeared a
little child, God of all time?

'Barlaam set forth for us exactly the meaning of the words which he
foretold, saying that a star should rise, a star that should extinguish all
prophecies and auguries; a star that should solve the parables of sages,
their utterances and their riddles; a star more resplendent than any
star that the eye can see, for it is the creator of all stars; of whom it was
foretold, that from Jacob there should arise a little child, God of all
time.'

Παραδόξων ῥητῶν   ἡ Μαριὰμ ὡς ἤκουσε,
   τῷ ἐκ σπλάγχνων αὐτῆς   κύψασα προσεκύνησε
   καὶ κλαίουσα εἶπε·   ‹ Μεγάλα μοι, τέκνον,
μεγάλα πάντα,   ὅσα ἐποίησας   μετὰ τῆς πτωχείας μου·
   ἰδοὺ γὰρ μάγοι   ἔξω ζητοῦσί σε
   τῶν ἀνατολῶν   οἱ βασιλεύοντες·
τὸ πρόσωπόν σου   ἐπιζητοῦσι
   καὶ λιτανεύουσιν ἰδεῖν   οἱ πλούσιοι τοῦ σοῦ λαοῦ·
ὁ λαός σου γὰρ ὄντως   εἰσὶν οὗτοι, οἷς ἐγνώσθης
   |: παιδίον νέον,   ὁ πρὸ αἰώνων θεός. :|

‹Ἐπειδὴ οὖν λαὸς   σός ἐστι, τέκνον, κέλευσον
   ὑπὸ σκέπην τὴν σὴν   γένωνται, ἵνα ἴδωσι
   πενίαν πλουσίαν,   πτωχείαν τιμίαν·
αὐτόν σε δόξαν   ἔχω καὶ καύχημα·   διὸ οὐκ αἰσχύνομαι·
   αὐτὸς εἶ χάρις   καὶ ἡ εὐπρέπεια
   τῆς σκηνῆς κἀμοῦ·   νεῦσον εἰσέλθωσιν·
οὐδέν μοι μέλει   τῆς εὐτελείας·
   ὡς θησαυρὸν γὰρ σὲ κρατῶ,   ὃν βασιλεῖς ἦλθον ἰδεῖν,
βασιλέων καὶ μάγων   ἐγνωκότων ὅτι ὤφθης
   |: παιδίον νέον,   ὁ πρὸ αἰώνων θεός.› :|

When Mary heard these strange words, she knelt and worshipped
the child of her womb. And weeping she said: 'Great, my child, great
are all the things that you have done to me in my poverty. For see, the
Wise Men outside are looking for you, the kings of the East; the rich
men of your people are seeking you and begging to see your face. For
truly, your people are those to whom you have been made known, a
little child, God of all time.

'Now since the people are yours, my child, bid them come under
your roof, that they may see poverty full of riches, beggary full of
honour. I have you as my glory and pride; therefore I am not ashamed.
You are the grace and dignity of my dwelling and of me; nod now, and
let them come in. I am not ashamed of my humble ways of living, for in
my arms I hold you, a treasure that kings have come to see: for kings
and wise men know that you have been seen, a little child, God of all
time.'

Ἰησοῦς ὁ Χριστὸς   ὄντως καὶ ὁ θεὸς ἡμῶν
τῶν φρενῶν ἀφανῶς   ἥψατο τῆς μητρὸς αὐτοῦ
‹Εἰσάγαγε, λέγων,   οὓς ἤγαγον λόγῳ·
ἐμὸς γὰρ λόγος   τούτοις ἐπέλαμψε   τοῖς ἐπιζητοῦσί με·
ἀστὴρ μὲν ἔστιν   εἰς τὸ φαινόμενον,
δύναμις δέ τις   πρὸς τὸ νοούμενον·
συνῆλθε μάγοις   ὡς λειτουργῶν μοι
καὶ ἔτι ἵσταται πληρῶν   τὴν διακονίαν αὐτοῦ
καὶ ἀκτῖσι δεικνύων   τὸν τόπον ὅπου ἐτέχθη
|: παιδίον νέον,   ὁ πρὸ αἰώνων θεός. :|

‹Νῦν οὖν δέξαι, σεμνή,   δέξαι τοὺς δεξαμένους με·
ἐν αὐτοῖς γὰρ εἰμὶ   ὥσπερ ἐν ταῖς ἀγκάλαις σου·
καὶ σοῦ οὐκ ἀπέστην   κἀκείνοις συνῆλθον.›
Ἡ δὲ ἀνοίγει   θύραν καὶ δέχεται   τῶν μάγων τὸ σύστημα·
ἀνοίγει θύραν   ἡ ἀπαράνοικτος
πύλη, ἣν Χριστὸς   μόνος διώδευσεν·
ἀνοίγει θύραν   ἡ ἀνοιχθεῖσα
καὶ μὴ κλαπεῖσα μηδαμῶς   τὸν τῆς ἁγνείας θησαυρόν·
αὐτὴ ἤνοιξε θύραν,   ἀφ' ἧς ἐγεννήθη θύρα
|: παιδίον νέον,   ὁ πρὸ αἰώνων θεός. :|

And Jesus Christ, who is truly our God, secretly touched his mother's mind saying: 'Bring in the men whom I have brought with my word; for it was my word that shone before these men who are searching for me; to the eyes it is a star, and to the eyes of the mind a power. It journeyed with the Wise Men at my command, and still stands, fulfilling its office, and shows with its rays the place where was born a little child, God of all time.

'Receive now therefore, holy lady, receive those who receive me, I am in them as I am in your arms. Though I have not left you, with them too have I walked.' So she opened the door and received the company of the Wise Men: she opened the door – she, the gate that none had opened, through which Christ alone had passed; she opened the door – she, who had been unsealed, yet never the smallest part stolen of the treasure of her purity. She opened the door, she from whom was born the door [to salvation], a little child, God of all time.

Οἱ δὲ μάγοι εὐθὺς   ὥρμησαν εἰς τὸν θάλαμον
    καὶ ἰδόντες Χριστὸν   ἔφριξαν, ὅτι εἴδοσαν
    τὴν τούτου μητέρα,   τὸν ταύτης μνηστῆρα·
καὶ φόβῳ εἶπον·   ‹Οὗτος υἱός ἐστιν   ἀγενεαλόγητος·
    καὶ πῶς, παρθένε,   τὸν μνηστευσάμενον
    βλέπομεν ἀκμὴν   ἔνδον τοῦ οἴκου σου;
οὐκ ἔσχε μῶμον   ἡ κύησίς σου;
    μὴ ἡ κατοίκησις ψεχθῇ   συνόντος σοι τοῦ Ἰωσήφ;
πλῆθος ἔχεις φθονούντων,   ἐρευνώντων ποῦ ἐτέχθη
    |: παιδίον νέον,   ὁ πρὸ αἰώνων θεός.› :|

‹Ὑπομνήσω ὑμᾶς,   μάγοις Μαρία ἔφησε,
    τίνος χάριν κρατῶ   τὸν Ἰωσὴφ ἐν οἴκῳ μου·
    εἰς ἔλεγχον πάντων   τῶν καταλαλούντων·
αὐτὸς γὰρ λέξει   ἅπερ ἀκήκοε   περὶ τοῦ παιδίου μου·
    ὑπνῶν γὰρ εἶδεν   ἄγγελον ἅγιον
    λέγοντα αὐτῷ,   πόθεν συνέλαβον·
πυρίνη θέα   τὸν ἀκανθώδη
    ἐπληροφόρησε νυκτὸς   περὶ τῶν λυπούντων αὐτόν·
δι' αὐτὸ σύνεστί μοι   Ἰωσὴφ δηλῶν ὡς ἔστι
    |: παιδίον νέον,   ὁ πρὸ αἰώνων θεός. :|

At once the Wise Men hastened into the room, and, seeing Christ,
shuddered as they saw the mother of the child, the betrothed of the
mother. And in awe they said: 'This child is of unknown descent; and
how, Maiden, is it that we still see your betrothed within your house?
Was your conception blameless? Will men find no fault in Joseph
living with you? You have a host of jealous enemies, looking for the
place where was born a little child, God of all time.'

Mary said to the Wise Men: 'I will tell you why I keep Joseph in my
house: it is to refute all those who slander me. He will tell what he
heard about my child; for in his sleep he saw a holy angel who told
him how I had conceived: in the night a fiery vision told him, anxious
as he was, about the things that caused him sorrow. That is why
Joseph is here with me: to show that there is a little child, God of all
time.

‹Ῥητορεύει σαφῶς   ἅπαντα ἅπερ ἤκουσεν·
  ἀπαγγέλλει τρανῶς   ὅσα αὐτὸς ἑώρακεν
  ἐν τοῖς οὐρανίοις   καὶ τοῖς ἐπιγείοις·
τὰ τῶν ποιμένων,   πῶς συνανύμνησαν   πηλίνοις οἱ
  πύρινοι·
  ὑμῶν τῶν μάγων,   ὅτι προέδραμεν
  ἄστρον φωταυγοῦν   καὶ ὁδηγοῦν ὑμᾶς·
διὸ ἀφέντες   τὰ προρρηθέντα
  ἐκδιηγήσασθε ἡμῖν   τὰ νῦν γενόμενα ὑμῖν·
πόθεν ἥκατε, πῶς δὲ   συνήκατε ὅτι ὤφθη
  |: παιδίον νέον,   ὁ πρὸ αἰώνων θεός.) :|

Ὡς δὲ ταῦτα αὐτοῖς   ἡ φαεινὴ ἐλάλησεν,
  οἱ τῆς ἀνατολῆς   λύχνοι πρὸς ταύτην ἔφησαν·
  «Μαθεῖν θέλεις, πόθεν   ἠλύθαμεν ὧδε;
Ἐκ γῆς Χαλδαίων,   ὅθεν οὐ λέγουσι·   •θεὸς θεῶν
  κύριος»,
  ἐκ Βαβυλῶνος,   ὅπου οὐκ οἴδασι
  τίς ὁ ποιητὴς   τούτων ὧν σέβουσιν·
ἐκεῖθεν ἦλθε   καὶ ἦρεν ἡμᾶς
ὁ τοῦ παιδίου σου σπινθὴρ   ἐκ τοῦ πυρὸς τοῦ Περσικοῦ·
πῦρ παμφάγον λιπόντες   πῦρ δροσίζον θεωροῦμεν
  |: παιδίον νέον,   τὸν πρὸ αἰώνων θεόν. :|

'He will tell you clearly all that he heard; he will openly relate all that he saw in Heaven and upon the earth: of the shepherds and how the spirits of fire sang praises together with the men of clay. And how a star went before you, Wise Men, shedding a light and leading the way. Therefore, setting aside all you have said, relate to us what has befallen you, from where you have come, how you understood that there has appeared a little child, God of all time.'

And, when the lady full of light had thus spoken to them, the luminaries of the East said to her: 'Do you want to learn whence we have come here? From the land of the Chaldaeans, where they do not say that God is the Lord of Gods; from Babylon, where they do not know who is the creator of the things they worship; there it came, the spark kindled by your child, and raised us up from the Persian fire; and now that we have left the all-devouring fire, we see the flame that refreshes, a little child, God of all time.

‹Ματαιότης ἐστὶ   ματαιοτήτων ἅπαντα·
   ἀλλ᾽ οὐδεὶς ἐν ἡμῖν   ταῦτα φρονῶν εὑρίσκεται·
   οἱ μὲν γὰρ πλανῶσιν,   οἱ δὲ καὶ πλανῶνται·
διό, παρθένε,   χάρις τῷ τόκῳ σου,   δι᾽ οὗ ἐλυτρώθημεν
   οὐ μόνον πλάνης,   ἀλλὰ καὶ θλίψεως
   τῶν χωρῶν πασῶν   ὧνπερ διήλθομεν,
ἐθνῶν ἀσήμων,   γλωσσῶν ἀγνώστων,
   περιερχόμενοι τὴν γῆν   καὶ ἐξερευνῶντες αὐτὴν
μετὰ λύχνου τοῦ ἄστρου   ἐκζητοῦντες, ποῦ ἐτέχθη
  |: παιδίον νέον,   ὁ πρὸ αἰώνων θεός. :|

‹᾽Αλλ᾽ ὡς ἔτι αὐτὸν   τοῦτον τὸν λύχνον εἴχομεν,
   τὴν ῾Ιερουσαλὴμ   πᾶσαν περιωδεύσαμεν
   πληροῦντες εἰκότως   τὰ τῆς προφητείας·
ἠκούσαμεν γάρ,   ὅτι ἠπείλησε   θεὸς ἐρευνᾶν αὐτήν·
   καὶ μετὰ λύχνου   περιηρχόμεθα
   θέλοντες εὑρεῖν   μέγα δικαίωμα·
ἀλλ᾽ οὐχ εὑρέθη,   ὅτι ἐπήρθη
   ἡ κιβωτὸς αὐτῆς μεθ᾽ ὧν   συνεῖχε πρότερον καλῶν·
τὰ ἀρχαῖα παρῆλθεν·   ἀνεκαίνισε γὰρ πάντα
  |: παιδίον νέον,   ὁ πρὸ αἰώνων θεός.› :|

'All is vanity of vanities; but among us there is none who believes this. Some lead astray, and others are led. Therefore, Virgin, we give thanks to your child, through whom we have been delivered not only from error but also from hardship in all the lands through which we passed, among nations unknown and tongues incomprehensible; wandering over the earth and searching for that land, seeking with the star as our lantern where there has been born a little child, God of all time.

'And while we still had this very lantern, we journeyed through the whole of Jerusalem, fulfilling fitly the words of the prophecy; for we had heard that God had threatened to search her out. And with the lantern we wandered seeking to find the great justification. But it was not found, for her [Jerusalem's] ark had been taken away with all the good things that it had held before. The things of old have passed, for all has been made new by a little child, God of all time.'

‹Ναί, φησί, τοῖς πιστοῖς   μάγοις Μαρία ἔφησε,
      τὴν ᾽Ιερουσαλήμ   πᾶσαν περιωδεύσατε,
      τὴν πόλιν ἐκείνην   τὴν προφητοκτόνον;
καὶ πῶς ἀλύπως,   ταύτην διήλθατε   τὴν πᾶσι βασκαί-
      νουσαν;
      ᾽Ηρώδην πάλιν   πῶς διελάθετε
      τὸν ἀντὶ θεσμῶν   φόνον ἐμπνέοντα;›
Οἱ δὲ πρὸς ταύτην   φησί· ‹Παρθένε,
      οὐ διελάθομεν αὐτόν,   ἀλλ᾽ ἐνεπαίξαμεν αὐτῷ·
συνετύχομεν πᾶσιν   ἐρωτῶντες ποῦ ἐτέχθη
      |: παιδίον νέον,   ὁ πρὸ αἰώνων θεός.) : |

῞Οτε ταῦτα αὐτῶν   ἡ θεοτόκος ἤκουσεν,
      τότε εἶπεν αὐτοῖς·   ‹Τί ὑμᾶς ἐπερώτησεν
      ᾽Ηρώδης ὁ ἄναξ   καὶ οἱ Φαρισαῖοι;›
‹᾽Ηρώδης πρῶτον,   εἶτα, ὡς ἔφησας,   οἱ πρῶτοι τοῦ
      ἔθνους σου
      τὸν χρόνον τούτου   τοῦ φαινομένου νῦν
      ἄστρου παρ᾽ ἡμῶν   ἐξηκριβώσαντο·
καὶ ἐπιγνόντες   ὡς μὴ μαθόντες
      οὐκ ἐπεθύμησαν ἰδεῖν   ὃν ἐξηρεύνησαν μαθεῖν,
ὅτι τοῖς ἐρευνῶσιν   ὀφείλει θεωρηθῆναι
      |: παιδίον νέον,   ὁ πρὸ αἰώνων θεός. : |

Then – so scripture relates – Mary said to the faithful, to the Wise
Men: 'Indeed – have you travelled through the whole of Jerusalem, that
prophet-killing city? Then how did you pass unharmed through the city
malevolent to all? How, too, did you stay hid from Herod, who instead
of justice breathes out murder?' And they said to her: 'We did not
hide from him; we mocked him, and conversed with them all and
asked where there was born a little child, God of all time.'

When the Virgin heard this from them, she said: 'What did King
Herod and the Pharisees ask you?' 'First Herod, and then, as you said,
the leaders of your nation inquired of us exactly the time of this star
that now appears; and when they knew, as though they had not under-
stood, they were not seized by the desire to see him, of whom they had
sought to learn. For by those who seek there must be seen a little child,
God of all time.

‹'Υπενόουν ἡμᾶς   ἄφρονας οἱ ἀνόητοι
   καὶ ἠρώτων, φησί·   «πόθεν καὶ πότε ἥκατε;
   πῶς μὴ φαινομένας   ὡδεύσατε τρίβους;»
Ἡμεῖς δὲ τούτοις,   ὅπερ ἠπίσταντο,   ἀντεπηρωτήσαμεν·
   «ὑμεῖς τὸ πάρος   πῶς διωδεύσατε
   ἔρημον πολλήν,   ἥνπερ διήλθετε;»
Ὁ ὁδηγήσας   τοὺς ἀπ' Αἰγύπτου
   αὐτὸς ὡδήγησε καὶ νῦν   τοὺς ἐκ Χαλδαίων πρὸς αὐτόν,
τότε στύλῳ πυρίνῳ,   νῦν δὲ ἄστρῳ δηλοῦντι
   |: παιδίον νέον,   τὸν πρὸ αἰώνων θεόν. :|

‹Ὁ ἀστὴρ   πανταχοῦ   ἦν ἡμῶν προηγούμενος
   ὡς ὑμῖν ὁ Μωσῆς   ῥάβδον ἐπιφερόμενος,
   τὸ φῶς περιλάμπων   τῆς θεογνωσίας·
ὑμᾶς τὸ μάννα   πάλαι διέθρεψε,   καὶ πέτρα ἐπότισεν·
   ἡμᾶς ἐλπὶς   ἡ τούτου ἐνέπλησε·
   τῇ τούτου χαρᾷ   διατρεφόμενοι
οὐκ ἐν Περσίδι   ἀναποδίσαι
   διὰ τὸ ἄβατον ὁδὸν   ὁδεύειν ἔσχομεν ἐν νῷ
θεωρῆσαι ποθοῦντες,   προσκυνῆσαι καὶ δοξάσαι
   |: παιδίον νέον,   τὸν πρὸ αἰώνων θεόν.› :|

'The fools thought that we were mad and asked us: "Whence did
you come and when? And how did you follow unseen paths?" We in
turn asked of them what they well knew: "In the past how did you
travel through the great desert which you crossed?" He who led those
men from Egypt, now has led the men of the Chaldees to him; then
with a pillar of fire, now with a star that shows a little child, God of all
time.

'Everywhere the star was before us, shining forth the light of the
knowledge of God, just as Moses went before you, holding a staff. Of
old the manna fed you and the rock gave you water: but hope of him
filled us: we were nourished with the joy of him: although the road
that we travelled was impassable, it never came to our minds to retrace
our steps to Persia; for we desired to see, to worship, to celebrate, a
little child, God of all time.'

Ὑπὸ τῶν ἀπλανῶν   μάγων ταῦτα ἐλέγετο·
    ὑπὸ τῆς σεμνῆς   πάντα ἐπεσφραγίζετο
    κυροῦντος τοῦ βρέφους   τὰ τῶν ἀμφοτέρων,
τῆς μὲν ποιοῦντος   μετὰ τὴν κύησιν   τὴν μήτραν ἀμίαντον,
    τῶν δὲ δεικνύντος   μετὰ τὴν ἔλευσιν
    ἄμοχθον τὸν νοῦν   ὥσπερ τὰ βήματα·
οὐδεὶς γὰρ τούτων   ὑπέστη κόπον,
    ὡς οὐκ ἐμόχθησεν ἐλθὼν   ὁ Ἀμβακοὺμ πρὸς Δανιήλ.
ὁ φανεὶς γὰρ προφήταις   ὁ αὐτὸς ἐφάνη μάγοις,
    |: παιδίον νέον,   ὁ πρὸ αἰώνων θεός. :|

Μετὰ πάντα αὐτῶν   ταῦτα τὰ διηγήματα
    δῶρα μάγοι χερσὶν   ἦραν καὶ προσεκύνησαν
    τῷ δώρῳ τῶν δώρων,   τῷ μύρῳ τῶν μύρων·
χρυσὸν καὶ σμύρναν   εἶτα καὶ λίβανον   Χριστῷ προσ-
    εκόμισαν
    βοῶντες· ‹Δέξαι   δώρημα τρίϋλον,
    ὡς τῶν Σεραφὶμ   ὕμνον τρισάγιον·
μὴ ἀποστρέψῃς   ὡς τὰ τοῦ Κάϊν,
    ἀλλ' ἐναγκάλισαι αὐτὰ   ὡς τὴν τοῦ Ἄβελ προσφορὰν
διὰ τῆς σε τεκούσης,   δι' ἧς ἡμῖν ἐγεννήθης
    |: παιδίον νέον,   ὁ πρὸ αἰώνων θεός.› :|

So spoke the Wise Men, who had not been led astray, and the Virgin set a seal of approval on it all, and the child confirmed what both had said. For he had left her womb immaculate after his birth, and had revealed their minds as unwearied after their coming as their steps. Not one of them had suffered, just as Habakkuk had felt no fatigue when he had come to Daniel. For he who had appeared before the prophets was the same who appeared before the Wise Men, a little child, God of all time.

After this narrative of theirs, the Wise Men took the gifts in their hands, and worshipped the gift of gifts, the myrrh of myrrh; then to Christ they gave gold and myrrh and frankincense, and cried: 'Accept our threefold gift, like the thrice-sacred hymn of the Seraphim; do not reject our gifts like those of Cain, but embrace them like the offerings of Abel, through her who gave you birth, and from whom you were born, a little child, God of all time.'

Νέα νῦν καὶ φαιδρὰ   βλέπουσα ἡ ἀμώμητος
   μάγους δῶρα χερσὶ   φέροντας καὶ προσπίπτοντας,
   ἀστέρα δηλοῦντα,   ποιμένας ὑμνοῦντας,
τὸν πάντων τούτων   κτίστην καὶ κύριον   ἱκέτευε λέγουσα·
   ‹Τριάδα δώρων,   τέκνον, δεξάμενος
   τρεῖς αἰτήσεις δὸς   τῇ γεννησάσῃ σε·
ὑπὲρ ἀέρων   παρακαλῶ σε
   καὶ ὑπὲρ τῶν καρπῶν τῆς γῆς   καὶ τῶν οἰκούντων ἐν αὐτῇ·
διαλλάγηθι πᾶσι   δι᾽ ἐμοῦ, ὅτι ἐτέχθης
   |: παιδίον νέον,   ὁ πρὸ αἰώνων θεός. :|

   ‹Οὐχ ἁπλῶς γὰρ εἰμὶ   μήτηρ σου, σῶτερ εὔσπλαγχνε·
   οὐκ εἰκῇ γαλουχῶ   τὸν χορηγὸν τοῦ γάλακτος·
   ἀλλὰ ὑπὲρ πάντων   ἐγὼ δυσωπῶ σε·
ἐποίησάς με   ὅλου τοῦ γένους μου   καὶ στόμα καὶ καύ-
     χημα·
   ἐμὲ γὰρ ἔχει   ἡ οἰκουμένη σου
   σκέπην κραταιάν,   τεῖχος καὶ στήριγμα·
ἐμὲ ὁρῶσιν   οἱ ἐκβληθέντες
   τοῦ παραδείσου τῆς τρυφῆς,   ὅτι ἐπιστρέφω αὐτούς
λαβεῖν αἴσθησιν πάντων   δι᾽ ἐμοῦ τῆς σε τεκούσης
   |: παιδίον νέον,   τὸν πρὸ αἰώνων θεόν. :|

The blameless lady, seeing the new and joyful gifts that the Wise Men brought in their hands as they worshipped, and seeing the guiding star and the shepherds who sang hymns, besought the creator and master of all these things, saying: 'Receive a triad of gifts, my child, and grant your mother three requests: I pray to you on behalf of the winds, and of the fruits of the earth and of those who live on it; be reconciled to all, for my sake, of whom you were born a little child, God of all time.

'I am not only your mother, O merciful Saviour; not in vain do I suckle the giver of milk, but for all men do I supplicate you. You have made me the mouthpiece and the pride of all my race and your creation has me as a firm defence, a wall and a buttress. To me do those men look who were cast from the delight of Paradise. For I shall lead them back, and they shall understand all things through me, who bore you a little child, God of all time.

‹Σῶσον κόσμον, σωτήρ·   τούτου γὰρ χάριν ἤλυθας·
  στῆσον πάντα τὰ σά·   τουτου γὰρ χάριν ἔλαμψας
  ἐμοὶ καὶ τοῖς μάγοις   καὶ πάσῃ τῇ κτίσει·
Ἰδοὺ γὰρ μάγοι,   οἷς ἐνεφάνισας   τὸ φῶς τοῦ προσώπου
  σου,
  προσπίπτοντές σοι   δῶρα προσφέρουσι
  χρήσιμα καλὰ   λίαν ζητούμενα·
αὐτῶν γὰρ χρῄζω,   ἐπειδὴ μέλλω
  ἐπὶ τὴν Αἴγυπτον μολεῖν   καὶ φεύγειν σὺν σοὶ διὰ σέ,
ὁδηγέ μου, υἱέ μου,   ποιητά μου, λυτρωτά μου,
  |: παιδίον νέον,   ὁ πρὸ αἰώνων θεός.› :|

219. Mary at the Cross

Τὸν δι' ἡμᾶς σταυρωθέντα   δεῦτε πάντες ὑμνήσωμεν·
  αὐτὸν γὰρ κατεῖδε Μαρία   ἐπὶ ξύλου καὶ ἔλεγεν·
  ‹Εἰ καὶ σταυρὸν ὑπομένεις,   σὺ ὑπάρχεις
|: ὁ υἱὸς καὶ θεός μου.› :|

'Save the world, O Saviour: it was for this that you came. Make everything in your creation to stand aright. For this you shone forth to me and to the Wise Men and to the whole earth. See the Wise Men, to whom you have shown the light of your face, and who worship you and offer gifts useful, fair, and much sought after. Of these I have need, for I shall go to Egypt and escape, with you and for your sake, my guide, my son, my Creator, my Saviour, little child, God of all time.'

COME, let us all celebrate him who was crucified for us: for Mary looked on him upon the cross and said: 'Though you endure crucifixion, yet you are my son, my God.'

Τὸν ἴδιον ἄρνα   ἀμνὰς θεωροῦσα
  πρὸς σφαγὴν ἑλκόμενον   ἠκολούθει ἡ Μαρία   τρυχομένη
  μεθ᾽ ἑτέρων γυναικῶν   ταῦτα βοῶσα·
‹Ποῦ πορεύῃ, τέκνον;   τίνος χάριν τὸν ταχὺν   δρόμον
  τελέεις;
  μὴ ἕτερος γάμος   πάλιν ἔστιν ἐν Κανᾷ,
  κἀκεῖ νυνὶ σπεύδεις,   ἵν᾽ ἐξ ὕδατος αὐτοῖς οἶνον ποιήσῃς;
  συνέλθω σοι, τέκνον,   ἢ μείνω σε μᾶλλον;
   δός μοι λόγον, Λόγε,   μὴ σιγῶν παρέλθῃς με,
   ὁ ἁγνὴν τηρήσας με,
|: ὁ υἱὸς καὶ θεός μου. :|

‹Οὐκ ἤλπιζον, τέκνον,   ἐν τούτοις ἰδεῖν σε,
  οὐδ᾽ ἐπίστευον ποτέ,   ἕως τούτου τους ἀνόμους   ἐκ-
  μανῆναι
  καὶ ἐκτεῖναι ἐπὶ σέ   χεῖρας ἀδίκως·
ἔτι γὰρ τὰ βρέφη   τούτων κράζουσί σοι τὸ   «εὐλογη-
  μένος»·
  ἀκμὴν δὲ βαΐων   πεπλησμένη ἡ ὁδὸς
  μηνύει τοῖς πᾶσι   τῶν ἀθέσμων τὰς πρὸς σὲ πανευφημίας.
καὶ νῦν, τίνος χάριν   ἐπράχθη τὸ χεῖρον;
  γνῶναι θέλω, οἴμοι,   πῶς τὸ φῶς μου σβέννυται,
  πῶς σταυρῷ προσπήγνυται
|: ὁ υἱὸς καὶ θεός μου. :|

Worn out with grief, Mary, the ewe, seeing her own lamb taken to the slaughter, followed with the other women and cried: 'Where are you going, my child? For whose sake are you finishing this swift race? Is there yet another marriage in Cana, and are you hastening there now to change the water into wine for them? Shall I go with you, child, or shall I rather wait for you? Speak to me, O Word; do not pass me by in silence: for you kept me in my purity, my son, my God.

'I never thought that I would see you, my child, in such necessity nor did I ever believe that the lawless would rage so, and unjustly stretch out their hands against you; for still their infants cry "Hosanna" to you; still the road is strewn with palm-branches proclaiming to all how the lawless had sung your praises. And now a worse deed is done, and for whose sake? Alas; how is my light snuffed out, how to a cross is nailed my son, my God.

‹ Ὑπάγεις, ὦ τέκνον,   πρὸς ἄδικον φόνον,
    καὶ οὐδείς σοι συναλγεῖ·   οὐ συνέρχεταί σοι Πέτρος   ὁ
        εἰπών σοι·
    ‹οὐκ ἀρνοῦμαι σε ποτέ,   κἂν ἀποθνήσκω.›
Ἔλιπέ σε Θώμας   ὁ βοήσας· ‹μετ' αὐτοῦ   θάνωμεν πάντες.›
    οἱ ἄλλοι δὲ πάλιν,   οἱ οἰκεῖοι καὶ γνωστοὶ
    καὶ μέλλοντες κρίνειν   τὰς φυλὰς τοῦ Ἰσραὴλ ποῦ εἰσιν
        ἄρτι;
    οὐδεὶς ἐκ τῶν πάντων,   ἀλλ' εἷς ὑπὲρ πάντων,
    θνήσκει, τέκνον, μόνος,   ἀνθ' ὧν πάντας ἔσωσας,
    ἀνθ' ὧν πᾶσιν ἤρεσας,
    |: ὁ υἱὸς καὶ θεός μου.› :|

Τοιαῦτα Μαρίας   ἐκ λύπης βαρείας
    καὶ ἐκ θλίψεως πολλῆς   κραυγαζούσης καὶ κλαιούσης,
        ἐπεστράφη
    πρὸς αὐτὴν ὁ ἐξ αὐτῆς   οὕτω βοήσας·
‹Τί δακρύεις, μήτηρ;   τί ταῖς ἄλλαις γυναιξὶ   συναπο-
        φέρῃ;
    μὴ πάθω; μὴ θάνω;   πῶς οὖν σώσω τὸν Ἀδάμ;
    μὴ τάφον οἰκήσω;   πῶς ἑλκύσω πρὸς ζωὴν τοὺς ἐν τῷ
        Ἄδῃ;

'You are going to unjust slaughter, my child, and no one is suffering
with you. Peter does not go with you, Peter who said to you: "Never
shall I deny you even though I die." Thomas deserted you, Thomas
who cried: "Let us all die with him." The others too, the friends and
companions who were to judge the tribes of Israel, where are they now?
None of them is here; but one, alone, for the sake of them all, you are
dying, my child; because instead of them you have saved all, because
instead of them you have loved all, my son, my God.'

Mary cried thus, from her heavy grief; and as she wailed and wept
in her very deep sorrow, her son turned to her and said: 'Why,
mother, do you weep? Why do you grieve with the other women?
Lest I suffer? Lest I die? How then should I save Adam? Lest I dwell
in the tomb? How then should I draw to life those in Hades? And yet,

καὶ μήν, καθὼς οἶδας,   ἀδίκως σταυροῦμαι·
  τί οὖν κλαίεις, μῆτερ;   μᾶλλον οὕτω κραύγασον,
  ὅτι θέλων ἔπαθον,
|: ὁ υἱὸς καὶ θεός σου. :|

‹Ἀπόθου, ὦ μῆτερ,   τὴν λύπην ἀπόθου·
  οὐ γὰρ πρέπει σοι θρηνεῖν,   ὅτι κεχαριτωμένη   ὠνο-
    μάσθης·
  τὴν οὖν κλῆσιν τῷ κλαυθμῷ   μὴ συγκαλύψῃς·
μὴ ταῖς ἀσυνέτοις   ὁμοιώσῃς ἑαυτήν,   πάνσοφε κόρη·
  ἐν μέσῳ ὑπάρχεις   τοῦ νυμφῶνος τοῦ ἐμοῦ.
  μὴ οὖν ὥσπερ ἔξω   ἱσταμένη τὴν ψυχὴν καταμαράνῃς.
τοὺς ἐν τῷ νυμφῶνι   ὡς δούλους σου φώνει·
  πᾶς γὰρ τρέχων τρόμῳ   ὑπακούσει σου, σεμνή,
  ὅταν εἴπῃς· «ποῦ ἐστιν
|: ὁ υἱὸς καὶ θεός μου;» :|

‹Πικρὰν τὴν ἡμέραν   τοῦ πάθους μὴ δείξῃς·
  δι' αὐτὴν γὰρ ὁ γλυκὺς   οὐρανόθεν νῦν κατῆλθον   ὡς
    τὸ μάννα,
  οὐκ ἐν ὄρει τῷ Σινᾷ,   ἀλλ' ἐν γαστρί σου.
ἔνδοθεν γὰρ ταύτης   ἐτυρώθην, ὡς Δαυὶδ   προανεφώνει·

as you know, I am crucified most unjustly. Why do you weep, my mother? Rather cry out thus, that willingly I suffered, your son, your God.

'Put aside your grief, mother, put it aside; mourning is not right for you who have been called the All-favoured. Do not conceal the title in weeping; do not liken yourself, wise maid, to those with no understanding. You are in the centre of my bridal chamber; do not consume your soul as though you were standing outside. Address those within the bridal chamber as your servants; for all, when they rush in terror, will hear you, holy one, when you say: "Where is my son, my God?"'

'Do not make the day of my suffering a bitter day; it is for this day that I, the compassionate, (now) descended from heaven as manna, not upon Mount Sinai but in your womb; for within it I was conceived,

τὸ τετυρωμένον   ὄρος νόησον, σεμνή,
ἐγὼ νῦν ὑπάρχω,   ὅτι Λόγος ὢν ἐν σοὶ σάρξ ἐγενόμην·
ἐν ταύτῃ οὖν πάσχω,   ἐν ταύτῃ καὶ σώζω·
μὴ οὖν κλαῖε, μῆτερ·   μᾶλλον τοῦτο βόησον·
«θέλων πάθος δέχεται
|: ὁ υἱὸς καὶ θεός μου.» :|

‹'Ιδού, φησι, τέκνον,   ἐκ τῶν ὀφθαλμῶν μου
    τὸν κλαυθμὸν ἀποσοβῶ·   τὴν καρδίαν μου συντρίβω
        ἐπὶ πλεῖον·
    ἀλλ' οὐ δύναται σιγᾶν   ὁ λογισμός μου.
    τί μοι λέγεις, σπλάγχνον·   «εἰ μὴ θάνω, ὁ 'Αδὰμ   οὐχ ὑγι-
        αίνει»;
    καὶ μὴν ἄνευ πάθους,   ἐθεράπευσας πολλούς·
    λεπρὸν γὰρ καθῆρας   καὶ οὐκ ἤλγησας οὐδέν, ἀλλ' ἠβου-
        λήθης·
    παράλυτον σφίγξας   οὐ κατεπονήθης·
        πῆρον πάλιν λόγῳ   ὀμματώσας, ἀγαθέ.
    ἀπαθὴς μεμένηκας,
|: ὁ υἱὸς καὶ θεός μου. :|

as David once foretold. Recognize, holy one, the "mountain God delighted to dwell in"; I now exist, I, the Word, who in you became flesh. This day I suffer and this day I save; do not therefore weep, mother. Rather cry out in joy: "Willingly he suffered, my son, my God."'

'See, my child,' she said, 'I wipe the tears from my eyes, though my heart I wear down still more; but my thoughts cannot be silent. Why, offspring, do you say to me: "If I do not die, Adam will not be healed"? And yet, without suffering yourself, you have healed many. You made the leper clean and have felt no pain, for so you willed it. You bound the paralytic together, yet you yourself were not undone. Again, when by your word you gave sight to the blind, you yourself, good one, remained unharmed, my son, my God.

‹Νεκροὺς ἀναστήσας   νέκρος οὐκ ἐγένου,
   οὐδ' ἐτέθης ἐν ταφῇ,   υἱέ μου καὶ ζωή μου·   πῶς οὖν
   λέγεις·
  «εἰ μὴ πάθω, ὁ Ἀδάμ   οὐχ ὑγιαίνει»;
κέλευσον, σωτήρ μου,   καὶ ἐγείρεται εὐθὺς   κλίνην βαστά-
   ζων.
  εἰ δὲ καὶ ἐν τάφῳ   κατεχώσθη ὁ Ἀδάμ,
   ὡς Λάζαρον τάφου   ἐξανέστησας φωνῇ, οὕτως καὶ τοῦτον·
δουλεύει σοι πάντα   ὡς πλάστῃ τῶν πάντων.
  τί οὖν τρέχεις, τέκνον;   μὴ ἐπείγου πρὸς σφαγήν·
  μὴ φιλῇς τὸν θάνατον,
|: ὁ υἱὸς καὶ θεός μου.› :|

‹Οὐκ οἶδας, ὦ μῆτερ,   οὐκ οἶδας ὃ λέγω·
   διὸ ἄνοιξον τὸν νοῦν   καὶ εἰσοίκησον τὸ ῥῆμα   ὃ ἀκούεις,
  καὶ αὐτὴ καθ' ἑαυτὴν   νόει, ἅ λέγω·
οὗτος, ὃν προεῖπον,   ὁ ταλαίπωρος Ἀδάμ,   ὁ ἀρρωστήσας
  οὐ μόνον τὸ σῶμα,   ἀλλὰ γὰρ καὶ τὴν ψυχήν,
  ἐνόσησε θέλων·   οὐ γὰρ ἤκουσεν ἐμοῦ καὶ κινδυνεύει.
γνωρίζεις, ὃ λέγω·   μὴ κλαύσῃς οὖν, μῆτερ·
  μᾶλλον τοῦτο κράξον·   ‹τὸν Ἀδάμ ἐλέησον
  καὶ τὴν Εὔαν οἴκτειρον,
|: ὁ υἱὸς καὶ θεός μου.» :|

'You raised the dead but did not yourself die, nor, my son and my
life, were you laid within the grave. How then can you say: "Unless
I suffer Adam will not be healed"? Command, my saviour, and he will
rise at once and take up his bed. And even if Adam is covered by a
tomb, call him forth, as you called Lazarus from the grave; for all
things serve you; you are the creator of all. Why then do you hasten,
my child? Do not rush to the slaughter, do not embrace death, my son,
my God.'

'You do not know, mother, you do not know what I say. Therefore
open your mind and take in the words you hear, and consider on your
own what I say. This miserable Adam, of whom I spoke before, who
is sick not only in body but yet more so in his soul, is sick of his own
will; for he did not obey me, and is in danger. You know what I say —
therefore do not weep, mother; rather cry out: "Take pity on Adam,
and show compassion to Eve, my son, my God."

‹ Ὑπὸ ἀσωτίας,   ὑπ' ἀδηφαγίας

ἀρρωστήσας ὁ Ἀδὰμ   κατηνέχθη ἕως Ἅδου   κατωτάτου,

καὶ ἐκεῖ τὸν τῆς ψυχῆς   πόνον δακρύει.

Εὔα δὲ ἡ τοῦτον   ἐκδιδάξασα ποτὲ   τὴν ἀταξίαν

σὺν τούτῳ στενάζει·   σὺν αὐτῷ γὰρ ἀρρωστεῖ,

ἵνα μάθωσιν ἅμα   τοῦ φυλάττειν ἰατροῦ παραγγελίαν·

συνῆκας κἂν ἄρτι;   ἐπέγνως ἃ εἶπον;

πάλιν, μῆτερ, κρᾶξον·   ‹τῷ Ἀδὰμ εἰ συγχωρεῖς,

καὶ τῇ Εὔᾳ σύγγνωθι,

|: ὁ υἱὸς καὶ θεός μου.›› : |

Ῥημάτων δὲ τούτων   ὡς ἤκουσε τότε

ἡ ἀμώμητος ἀμνάς,   ἀπεκρίθη πρὸς τὸν ἄρνα   ‹Κύριέ μου,

ἔτι ἅπαξ ἂν εἴπω,   μὴ ὀργισθῇς μοι·

λέξω σοι, ὃ ἔχω,   ἵνα μάθω παρὰ σοῦ   πάντως, ὃ θέλω·

ἂν πάθῃς, ἂν θάνῃς,   ἀναλύσεις πρὸς ἐμέ·

ἂν περιοδεύσῃς   σὺν τῇ Εὔᾳ τὸν Ἀδάμ, βλέψω σε πάλιν;

αὐτὸ γὰρ φοβοῦμαι,   μήπως ἐκ τοῦ τάφου

ἄνω δράμῃς, τέκνον,   καὶ ζητοῦσα σὲ ἰδεῖν

κλαύσω, κράξω· ‹ποῦ ἐστιν

|: ὁ υἱὸς καὶ θεός μου;›› : |

'Adam, sick through debauchery, through gluttony, was led down
to deepest Hell, and there he weeps for the suffering of his soul; and
Eve, who once taught him disobedience, grieves with him and lan-
guishes with him, that together they may learn to heed the Healer's
word. Now, do you see? Do you understand what I have said? Cry out
again, mother: "If you forgive Adam, forgive also Eve, my son, my
God."'

And when the blameless ewe heard this, she answered to her lamb:
'My Lord, if I speak yet once more, do not be angry with me. I shall
tell you what is on my mind, so that I may learn from you all I wish to
know. If you suffer, if you die, will you come back to me? If you heal
Adam, and Eve with him, shall I see you again? For my fear is that
from the tomb you may hasten to Heaven, my child; and I, searching
to see you, shall weep and cry out: "Where is my son, my God?"'

Ὡς ἤκουσε ταῦτα   ὁ πάντα γινώσκων
  πρὶν γενέσεως αὐτῶν,   ἀπεκρίθη πρὸς Μαρίαν·   ‹Θάρ-
  σει, μῆτερ,
  ὅτι πρώτη με ὁρᾷς   ἀπὸ τοῦ τάφου·
Ἔρχομαί σοι δεῖξαι   πόσων πόνων τὸν Ἀδὰμ   ἐλυτρω-
  σάμην,
  καὶ πόσους ἱδρῶτας   ἔσχον ἕνεκεν αὐτοῦ·
  δηλώσω τοῖς φίλοις   τὰ τεκμήρια δεικνὺς ἐν ταῖς χερσί μου.
καὶ τότε θεάσῃ   τὴν Εὔαν, ὦ μῆτερ,
  ζῶσαν ὥσπερ πρώην   καὶ βοήσεις ἐν χαρᾷ·
  ‹τοὺς γονεῖς μου ἔσωσεν
|: ὁ υἱὸς καὶ θεός μου.› :|

‹ Μικρὸν οὖν, ὦ μῆτερ,   ἀνάσχου καὶ βλέπεις,
  πῶς καθάπερ ἰατρὸς   ἀποδύομαι καὶ φθάνω   ὅπου
  κεῖνται,
  καὶ ἐκείνων τὰς πληγὰς   περιοδεύω,
τέμνων ἐν τῇ λόγχῃ   τὰ πωρώματα αὐτῶν   καὶ τὴν
  σκληρίαν·
  λαμβάνω καὶ ὄξος,   καὶ ἐπιστύφω τὴν πληγήν·
  τῇ σμίλῃ τῶν ἥλων   ἀνευρύνας τὴν τομὴν χλαίνῃ μοτώσω.
καὶ δὴ τὸν σταυρόν μου   ὡς νάρθηκα ἔχων
  τούτῳ χρῶμαι, μῆτερ,   ἵνα ψάλλῃς συνετῶς·
  ‹πάσχων πάθος ἔλυσεν
|: ὁ υἱὸς καὶ θεός μου.› :|

When he who knows of all things before their birth heard this, he
answered Mary: 'Take courage, mother, for you shall be the first to
see me [risen] from the tomb; and I shall come to show you from what
suffering I liberated Adam and how much I sweated for his sake. I
shall reveal it to my friends and show them the tokens in my hands;
and then, mother, you shall see Eve living as before, and you shall cry
out for joy: "He saved my parents, my son, my God."
    'Endure a little, mother, and you shall see how I, like a healer,
divest myself and come to where they lie, and how I heal their wounds,
cutting their calluses and scabs with the lance; and I shall take the
vinegar and with it bathe their wounds; I shall open the wound with
the chisel [made] of the nails and dress it with the cloak, and my cross
I shall use, mother, as a splint, that you may sing with understanding:
"By suffering he freed us from suffering, my son, my God."

‹’Απόθου οὖν, μῆτερ,   τὴν λύπην ἀπόθου,
  καὶ πορεύου ἐν χαρᾷ·   ἐγὼ γάρ, δι’ ὃ κατῆλθον,   ἤδη σπεύδω
ἐκτελέσαι τὴν βουλὴν   τοῦ πέμψαντός με·
τοῦτο γὰρ ἐκ πρώτης   δεδογμένον ἦν ἐμοὶ   καὶ τῷ πατρί μου,
  καὶ τῷ πνεύματί μου   οὐκ ἀπήρεσε ποτὲ
τὸ ἐνανθρωπῆσαι   καὶ παθεῖν με διὰ τὸν παραπεσόντα.
δραμοῦσα οὖν, μῆτερ,   ἀνάγγειλον πᾶσιν
  ὅτι «πάσχων πλήττει   τὸν μισοῦντα τὸν ’Αδάμ,
καὶ νικήσας ἔρχεται
|: ὁ υἱὸς καὶ θεός μου.» :|

‹Νικῶμαι, ὦ τέκνον,   νικῶμαι τῷ πόθῳ
καὶ οὐ στέγω ἀληθῶς,   ἵν’ ἐγὼ μὲν ἐν θαλάμῳ,   σὺ δ’ ἐν ξύλῳ,
καὶ ἐγὼ μὲν ἐν οἰκίᾳ,   σὺ δ’ ἐν μνημείῳ·
ἄφες οὖν συνέλθω·   θεραπεύει γὰρ ἐμὲ   τὸ θεωρεῖν σε·
κατίδω τὴν τόλμαν   τῶν τιμώντων τὸν Μωσῆν·
αὐτὸν γὰρ ὡς δῆθεν   ἐκδικοῦντες οἱ τυφλοὶ κτεῖναί σε ἦλθον.
Μωσῆς δὲ τοιοῦτο   τῷ ’Ισραὴλ εἶπεν,
  ὅτι «μέλλεις βλέπειν   ἐπὶ ξύλου τὴν ζωήν»
ἡ ζωὴ δὲ τίς ἐστιν;
|: ὁ υἱὸς καὶ θεός μου.› :|

'Put aside your grief, mother, put it aside, and go in joy; for now I hasten to fulfil that for which I came, the will of Him who sent me. For from the first this was resolved by me and by my Father, and it was never displeasing to my spirit: that I become man and suffer for him who had fallen. Hasten then, mother, and announce to all that "By suffering he lays low the hater of Adam, and comes as a conqueror, my son, my God."'

'I am overcome, my child, overcome by love, and truly I cannot bear it, that I am to be in my room while you are on the cross, I within my house, you within the tomb. Therefore let me go with you, for it heals me to look upon you, I shall look upon the outrageous daring of those who honour Moses: for these blind men, pretending to be his avengers, have come here to kill you. But what Moses said to Israel was this: "You will see life hanging on the cross." And what is life? My son and my God.'

‹Οὐκοῦν εἰ συνέρχῃ,   μὴ κλαύσῃς, ὦ μῆτερ,

  μηδὲ πάλιν πτοηθῇς,   ἐὰν ἴδῃς σαλευθέντα   τὰ στοι-
χεῖα·

  τὸ γὰρ τόλμημα δονεῖ   πᾶσαν τὴν κτίσιν·

πόλος ἐκτυφλοῦται   καὶ οὐκ ἀνοίγει ὀφθαλμόν,   ἕως
ἂν εἴπω·

  ἡ γῆ σὺν θαλάσσῃ   τότε σπεύσωσι φυγεῖν·

  ναὸς τὸν χιτῶνα   ῥήξει τότε κατὰ τῶν ταῦτα τολμώντων·

τὰ ὄρη δονοῦνται,   οἱ τάφοι κενοῦνται·

  ὅταν ἴδῃς ταῦτα,   ἐὰν πτήξῃς ὡς γυνή,

  κρᾶζον πρός με· ‹φεῖσαί μου,

|: ὁ υἱὸς καὶ θεός μου.›› :|

Υἱὲ τῆς παρθένου,   θεὲ τῆς παρθένου

  καὶ τοῦ κόσμου ποιητά,   σὸν τὸ πάθος, σὸν τὸ βάθος
τῆς σοφίας·

σὺ ἐπίστασαι, ὃ ἦς   καὶ ὃ ἐγένου·

σὺ παθεῖν θελήσας   κατηξίωσας ἐλθεῖν   ἀνθρώπους σῶσαι·

σὺ τὰς ἁμαρτίας   ἡμῶν ἦρας ὡς ἀμνός·

σὺ ταύτας νεκρώσας   τῇ σφαγῇ σου, ὁ σωτήρ, ἔσωσας
πάντας·

σὺ εἶ ἐν τῷ πάσχειν   καὶ ἐν τῷ μὴ πάσχειν·

'If you come with me, mother, do not weep, and do not tremble if you see the elements shaken. For this outrage will make all creation tremble; the sky will be blinded and not open its eyes until I speak; then the earth and the sea together will hasten to disappear, and the temple will rend its veil against the perpetrators of this outrage. The mountains will be shaken, the graves emptied. If, like a woman, you are seized by fear when you see this, cry out to me: "Spare me, my son, my God."'

Son of the Virgin, God of the Virgin, and creator of the world: yours is the suffering, yours the depths of wisdom. You know what you were and what you became; because you were willing to suffer, you deigned to come and save mankind. Like a lamb you have lifted our sins from us, and you have abolished them by your sacrifice, my Saviour, and saved every man. You exist both in suffering and in not

σὺ εἶ θνῄσκων, σῴζων   σὺ παρέσχες τῇ σεμνῇ
παρρησίαν κράζειν σοι·
|: ‹ὁ υἱός καὶ θεός μου.› :|

220. On the Crucifixion

Ψυχή μου, ψυχή μου,   ἀνάστα·   τί καθεύδεις;
τὸ τέλος ἐγγίζει,   καὶ μέλλεις   θορυβεῖσθαι·
ἀνάνηψον οὖν,   ἵνα φείσηταί σου
Χριστὸς ὁ θεός,
|: ὁ πανταχοῦ τὰ πάντα πληρῶν. :|

221. On the Resurrection

Τὸν πρὸ ἡλίου ἥλιον   δύναντα τότε ἐν τάφῳ
προέφθασαν πρὸς ὄρθρον   ἐκζητοῦσαι ὡς ἡμέραν
μυροφόροι κόραι   καὶ πρὸς ἀλλήλας ἐβόων·
‹Ὦ φίλαι δεῦτε   τοῖς ἀρώμασιν ὑπαλείψωμεν
σῶμα ζωηφόρον   καὶ τεθαμμένον,
σάρκα ἀνιστῶσαν   τὸν παραπεσόντα Ἀδάμ   κειμένην
ἐν τῷ μνήματι·

suffering; by dying you save, and you have given to the holy lady freedom to cry to you: 'My son and my God.'

My soul, my soul, arise; why are you sleeping? The end is drawing near, and you will be in tumult and confusion. Therefore recover your senses and let Christ the God save you, he who everywhere fulfils everything.

Searching as if for the light of day, at dawn the myrrh-bearing maidens reached the sun that existed before the sun was created, the sun which had then set in a tomb; and they cried out to one another: 'Come, friends, let us gently anoint with perfumes the life-bringing body which is buried, the flesh which lies in a tomb and which resurrects fallen Adam. Let us go, let us hurry like the Wise Men, and let us

ἄγωμεν, σπεύσωμεν ὥσπερ οἱ μάγοι
   καὶ προσκυνήσωμεν καὶ προσκομίσωμεν
τὰ μύρα ὡς δῶρα τῷ μὴ ἐν σπαργάνοις
   ἀλλ᾽ ἐν σινδόνι ἐνειλημένῳ·
καὶ κλαύσωμεν καὶ κράξωμεν· ⸱ὦ δέσποτα, ἐξεγέρθητι,
|: ὁ τοῖς πεσοῦσι παρέχων ἀνάστασιν.⸱ :|

· · · · · · · ·

Συναναστήτω σοί, σωτήρ, ἡ νεκρωθεῖσα ψυχή μου·
   μὴ φθείρῃ ταύτην λύπη καὶ λοιπὸν εἰς λήθην ἔλθῃ
   τῶν ᾀσμάτων τούτων τῶν ταύτην ἁγιαζόντων·
ναί, ἐλεήμων, ἱκετεύω, μὴ καταλείπῃς με
   τὸν ταῖς πλημμελείαις κατεστιγμένον·
ἐν γὰρ ἀνομίαις καὶ ἐν ἁμαρτίαις ἐμὲ ἐκίσσησεν
   ἡ μήτηρ μου·
πάτερ μου, ἅγιε καὶ φιλοικτίρμον,
   ἁγιασθήτω σου ἀεὶ τὸ ὄνομα
ἐν τῷ στόματί μου καὶ τοῖς χείλεσί μου,
   ἐν τῇ φωνῇ μου καὶ τῇ ᾠδῇ μου·
δός μοι χάριν κηρύττοντι τοὺς ὕμνους σου, ὅτι
   δύνασαι,
|: ὁ τοῖς πεσοῦσι παρέχων ἀνάστασιν. :|

worship and bring myrrh as a gift to him who is wound not in swad-
dling-bands but in a winding-sheet. And let us weep and cry out:
"Arise, Lord, you who lift up those who have fallen."'

May my deadened soul be raised to life by your resurrection, O Saviour;
may it not be worn down by sorrow and afterwards come to forget
these songs that make it holy. Yes, O Merciful One, I beseech you not
to abandon me, who am tarnished with sins; for in transgressions and in
sins my mother conceived me. My Father, holy and full of compassion,
may your name be held sacred for ever in my mouth and on my lips,
in my voice and in my song. Give me grace as I proclaim your hymns;
this is your power, for you lift up those who have fallen.

222. *On the Forty Martyrs of Sebastia*

Ὑπὲρ ἡλίου αἴγλην   ὑπερβαλλόντως
  ἡ τῶν ἁγίων τούτων   λάμπει φαιδρότης·
  νέφη γὰρ καλύπτουσι   τὴν ἐκείνου, τὴν τούτων δὲ
  οὐδὲ νὺξ διαδέχεται·
ἐκεῖνος ἀνατέλλων   μαρμαρυγὰς ἐκπέμπει
  καὶ δύνων αὖθις ἕλκει   πάσας σὺν αὐτῷ·
τῶν δὲ πανολβίων   τὴν φαεινὴν λαμπηδόνα
  καὶ ἡ ἡμέρα   ἀνακηρύττει,
  καὶ ἡ νὺξ δὲ πάλιν   θαυμάζει ἄγαν,
πῶς διασχίσαι ἴσχυσε   τὴν τῶν πραγμάτων θύελλαν·
  παρέστη γὰρ πολύδοξος   τῷ τοὺς πιστοὺς δοξάζοντι
καὶ ἤκουσε παρ' αὐτοῦ·   ‹Σὺ ἐδόξασας ἐμὲ   ἐπὶ τῶν γη-
    γενῶν·
  ἐν ὑψίστοις οὖν κἀγὼ   ἐν σοὶ ὁμολογῶ
  παρασχών σοι ἀγαθὰ
|: δόξαν ἐκ τῶν οὐρανῶν   καὶ στεφάνων πληθύν.› :|

ANONYMOUS
?6th century

223. *Wash away Your Sins*

Νῖψον ἀνομήματα μὴ μόναν ὄψιν.

MUCH more brilliant than the sun shines forth the brightness of these
saints. For clouds cover the sun's brilliance; but not even night over-
takes the radiance of these martyrs. The sun casts forth flashes in
rising, and in setting he draws them all away with him. But the bril-
liant light shed by the All-Blessed Ones is heralded by the day,
and the night, too, is greatly amazed at it – how it had the power to
penetrate the storm clouds of events. And they stood in great glory
by him who gives glory to the faithful, and they heard him say: 'You
have given me glory among men; therefore I too in the highest will
avow my belief in you by giving you gifts: glory from heaven and a
multitude of crowns.'

WASH [away] your sins, not only your face.

224. *The Lighted Dome will Guide the Sailors*

Μυρία δ' αἰολόμορφον ἀνάκτορον ἐντὸς ἐέργει
ἄλλα πολυγνάμπτοισι μετάρσια φάεα σειραῖς·
καὶ τὰ μὲν αἰθούσῃσιν ἀναίθεται, ἄλλα δὲ μέσσῳ,
ἄλλα δὲ πρὸς φαέθοντα καὶ ἕσπερον, ἄλλα καρήνοις,
ἔκχυτον ἀστράπτοντα πυρὸς φλόγα· νὺξ δὲ φαεινὴ
ἡμάτιον γελόωσα ῥοδόσφυρός ἐστι καὶ αὐτή.
Καὶ τις ἀνὴρ στεφάνοιο χοροστασίῃς τε δοκεύων
δένδρεα φεγγήεντα λιπαλγέα θυμὸν ἰαίνει,
ὃς δὲ πυρισπείρητον ἐπακτρίδα, θέλγεται ἄλλος
εἰσορόων λαμπτῆρα μονάμπυκα, σύμβολον ἄλλος
οὐρανίου Χριστοῖο νόον λαθικηδέα τέρπει.
'Ὡς δ' ὅταν ἀννεφέλοιο δι' ἠέρος ἄνδρες ὁδῖται
ἀστέρας ἄλλοθεν ἄλλος ἀναθρώσκοντας ἰδόντες
ὃς μὲν ἀποσκοπέει γλυκὺν Ἕσπερον, ὃς δ' ἐπὶ Ταύρῳ
θυμὸν ἀποπλάζει, γάνυται δέ τις ἀμφὶ Βοώτην,
ἄλλος ἐπ' Ὠρίωνα καὶ ἄβροχον ὁλκὸν Ἁμάξης
ὄμμα φέρει· πολλοῖς δὲ πεπασμένος ἀστράσιν αἰθὴρ
ἀτραπιτοὺς ὤϊξεν, ἔπεισε δὲ νύκτα γελάσσαι·

THE sparkling building holds within it countless other lights which
hang in the air from richly twisting chains. Some of these are lit in the
colonnades and others in the middle [of the church]; some pour out a
flashing beam of fire to the east, others to the west, and there are more
in the domes. Even night smiles, full of light, rose-ankled like the dawn.
And any man who looks at the glittering grief-curing trees of this
crown and of the stand of the choirs is healed in his heart; and of those
who look upon the small boat which is wrapped in fire, one is de-
lighted to gaze at the single lamp, another rejoices at this symbol of the
heavenly Christ and forgets all his troubles. Just as travellers see from
different places the stars rising in the cloudless sky — one watches the
sweet Evening Star, the thoughts of another wander to the Bull, yet
another delights in Boötes, while others still direct their eyes to Orion
and the unmoistened track of the Wain, and the sky, dappled with
multitudes of stars, opens its paths and persuades the night to smile —

οὕτω καλλιχόροιο κατ' ἔνδια θέλγεται οἴκου
ἀγλαΐης ἀκτῖνι φεραυγέος ἄλλος ἐπ' ἄλλη.
Πᾶσι μὲν εὐφροσύνης ἀναπέπταται εὔδιος αἴθρη
ψυχαίην ἐλάσασα μελαγκρήδεμνον ὀμίχλην·
πάντας ἐπαυγάζει σέλας ἱερόν, εὖτε καὶ αὐτὸς
ναυτίλος οἰήκεσσι θαλασσοπόροισι κελεύων
(εἴτε λιπὼν ἄξεινα μεμηνότος οἴδματα Πόντου
πλαγκτοὺς ἀντιπόρων σκοπιῶν ἀγκῶνας ἑλίσσει,
ἐννύχιον μέγα τάρβος ἔχων γναμπτῇσι κελεύθοις,
εἴτε μετ' Αἰγαίωνα παρ' Ἑλλησπόντιον ὕδωρ
νῆα κατιθύνῃσι ῥοώδεος ἀντία δίνης,
δεχνύμενος προτόνοισι Λιβυστίδος ὄγκον ἀέλλης,)
οὐχ Ἑλίκην, οὐχ ἡδὺ φάος Κυνοσουρίδος ἄρκτου
εἰσορόων οἴηκι φερέσβιον ὁλκάδα πάλλει,
ἀλλὰ τεοῦ νηοῖο θεουδέα λαμπάδα λεύσσων,
φορτίδος εὐτόλμοιο προηγέτιν, οὐχ ὑπὸ μούνοις
φέγγεσιν ἐννυχίοισι (τὸ γὰρ καὶ Πρωτέος ἀκταὶ
ἐν Φαρίῃ τεύχουσι Λιβυστίδος ἐς πόδα γαίης)
ἀλλὰ καὶ εὐδώροισι θεοῦ ζώοντος ἀρωγαῖς.

(*Description of the Church of Santa Sophia*)

even so in the evening men are delighted at the various shafts of light
of the radiant, light-bringing house of resplendent choirs. And the
calm clear sky of joy lies open to all driving away the dark-veiled mist
of the soul. A holy light illuminates all; and even the sailor, as he
guides the seafaring rudder – whether he has left the unfriendly swell
of raging Pontus and is weaving through the twisting reaches of the
opposing rocks filled with a great fear by night for the intricacies of
his course, or whether he is coming from the Aegean through the
waters of the Hellespont and is guiding his ship against the violent
whirlpool and taking upon his forestays the blast of the Libyan storm
– even he does not look at the Great Bear, nor at the sweet light of the
Little Bear as he steers his life-bearing ship, but looks to the godly
torch of your temple to guide his daring vessel. And this is not only
because of the light it casts at night – for this the shores of Proteus do
too, on the island of Pharos just before the land of Libya – but also
because of the generous gift of help that the living God gives.

IV
THE BYZANTINE EMPIRE

GEORGE PISIDIS
fl. c. 630

225. *The Victory of Heraclius over the Persians**

Πρὶν ἢ γὰρ ἡ νὺξ τὴν μέσην τομὴν λάβοι,
πάντας μὲν αὐτῶν τοὺς κεκρυμμένους δόλους
ταῖς σαῖς μερίμναις ἐξ ἔθους ἠπίστασο,
τάξας δὲ θείως τὸν στρατὸν καὶ ῥυθμίσας
πρὸς τὴν μάχην ἐξῆγες αὐτούς, ἡνίκα
τὸ φῶς ἀνίσχων τοὺς ἐναντίους πάλιν
ὁ σεπτὸς αὐτοῖς ἐσκότιζεν ἥλιος.
Καὶ δὴ προπέμπεις εὐαρίθμητον μέρος
τοῦ σοῦ στρατοῦ, κράτιστε, τούτους ὁπλίσας
οὐ τοῖς ὅπλοις τοσοῦτον ὡς εὐβουλίαις.
Ἐπεὶ γὰρ ἐξήλαυνον ὥσπερ εἰς μάχην,
τὸν πλαστὸν αὖθις σχηματίζονται φόβον,
ἐψευσμένως φεύγοντες. Οἱ δὲ βάρβαροι,
τῆς ἐκλογῆς ἐκεῖνο τὸ στερρὸν νέφος,
ἐκ τῶν ἀδήλων ἐκπεσόντες αὐλάκων
ἤλαυνον αὐτοὺς τῷ δοκεῖν πεφευγότας.
Αὐτὸς δὲ τούτοις ἀντεπεξάγεις τάχος
τοὺς σοὺς ἀρίστους, καὶ παρ' ἐλπίδας τότε
ἀπροσδοκήτῳ προσραγέντες συντάσει
τὰ νῶτα τοῖς σοῖς οἰκέταις ἀπέστρεφον.

EVEN before the middle of the night you had, with your usual care, discovered all their secret stratagems. And you arranged and disposed your army with divine inspiration and then led it out to battle when the sun, which the enemy venerates, rose once again and blinded them. Then you sent forward a small part of your army, most powerful monarch, equipping it not so much with weapons as with good instructions. For when your men went out as if to battle they pretended to show fear and feigned flight; and the barbarians, that thick cloud of chosen men, jumped out from their concealed trenches and attacked them as they gave the impression of fleeing. Then, swiftly, you yourself led out against them your best soldiers, and the enemy, crashing against an unexpected force, turned their backs upon your followers.

*A.D. 622.

421

Ὦ νοῦς διαρκὴς καὶ τομωτάτη φύσις
καὶ πῦρ λογισμῶν ἐν βάθει διατρέχον!
Ὅμως τὸ πῦρ μὲν καὶ μελαίνει καὶ φλέγει·
ὁ σὸς δὲ νοῦς, κράτιστε, λευκαίνει τὸ πᾶν,
θάλπει δὲ πάντας τῇ πυρώσει μὴ φλέγων.
Ὁ βάρβαρος δὲ τὸν κεκρυμμένον δόλον
εὑρὼν ἑαυτῷ βόθρον ἐκ τοὐναντίου,
ὅλους προπηδᾶν τοῖς τραπεῖσι συμμάχους
ἐκ τῶν ἑαυτοῦ ταγμάτων ἐπέτρεπεν·
ἐπεὶ δὲ καὐτοὺς εἶδεν ἐπτοημένους,
καὶ συντόνως πίπτοντας ἀσχέτῳ φόβῳ,
πρῶτον μὲν αὐτοῦ δυσσεβεῖ τοὺς προστάτας
καὶ θᾶττον ἠτίμωσε τοὺς τιμωμένους,
ὕδωρ κενώσας καὶ τὸ πῦρ κατασβέσας.
Καπνοῦ δὲ πολλὰς συγχύσεις ποιούμενος
κλέπτει τὸ φεύγειν καὶ σχεδιάζει τὸν γνόφον,
καὶ νύκτα ποιεῖ καινοτομῶν τὴν ἡμέραν.
Εὑρών τε κρημνοὺς καὶ στενὰς διεξόδους
λοξάς τε πετρῶν ἐξοχὰς καὶ δυσβάτους,
ὠθεῖ καλύψας τῷ γνόφῳ τὰ τάγματα
καὶ τὰς ἐκείνων δυστυχεῖς συνοικίας
πρὸς ἄκρον ὕψος καὶ κατάρροπον βάθος.
Ἐντεῦθεν αὐτοῖς συμφορῶν πολυτρόπων

How competent your mind! How very keen your nature! How deep and fiery your thoughts! But fire both blackens and burns, while your mind, most mighty king, whitens everything and warms everyone with a fire that does not burn. Now the barbarians found the secret stratagem turned to a trap against themselves, for it allowed all their allies to break ranks and run before those who were fleeing. And when the barbarians saw their men full of terror and falling in violent and ungovernable panic, they first disobeyed their leaders, and then swiftly dishonoured those they had honoured: they poured out water and extinguished the fire. By creating a vast and confusing mass of smoke they cut off their own escape and made a semblance of darkness changing the day to make night. They found precipices, narrow pathways, crooked unapproachable projections of rock, and, submerged in darkness, pressed forward their ranks and their unfortunate allies towards the steep heights and plunging abysses. Thus danger of all sorts was laid up for them and ruinous evil fate, as they fell off the

συμπτωμάτων τε καὶ φόνων καὶ κλασμάτων
κίνδυνος ηὐτρέπιστο συντριβῆς γέμων.
Καὶ πού τις αὐτῶν ἐξ ἀνάγκης ηὔξατο
ἐλθεῖν κατ’ αὐτοῦ συντομώτερον ξίφος·
ἄλλος δὲ νώτοις ἱππικοῖς ἐφιζάνων
μετέωρος ἤρθη τῇ βίᾳ τοῦ σφίγματος.
Πολλοῖς δὲ τεῖχος τὰς καμηλείους τότε
πλευρὰς κατεσκεύαζεν ἡ περίστασις.
Κρημνούς τε πάντες ἀγρίων αἰγῶν δίκην
φυγῆς ἀνεξίχνευον ἐκπηδήματα.
Ἡ δὲ σὴ πᾶσα τοῦ στρατοῦ συνοικία
βλέποντες εὐφραίνοντο τῇ θείᾳ κρίσει
τὰ τῆς παραδόξου θαύματα στρατηγίας·
βολὴ γὰρ οὐκ ἦν ἐπτερωμένου βέλους
ἐν τῇ μεταξὺ τῶν στρατῶν διαστάσει,
καὶ πᾶς τις ἡμῶν εὐκόλως ἀπέβλεπε
πρὸς τὰς ἐπάλξεις τῶν φαράγγων τὰς νόθους,
ἐν αἷς τὸ πλῆθος ἐκχυθὲν τῶν βαρβάρων
πυκνῶς ἐνεστρέφοντο μὴ κινούμενοι.
Ἀλλ’ οἱ μὲν ἦσαν ἐν τοσαύτῃ φροντίδων
ζάλῃ διαρρέοντες ὡς τὰ κύματα,
ἃ ταῖς ἑαυτῶν ἐκδρομαῖς ὠθούμενα
τὰ μὲν πρὸς ὕψος ἐκ βάθους ἀνέρχεται,
τὰ δὲ προπίπτει καὶ πάλιν κοιλαίνεται·
οὕτως ἐκείνων τῶν ἀτάκτων ταγμάτων

rocks, killed themselves, and broke their limbs. Some of them in these
straits prayed for a sword to come against them, that they might die
more quickly; others mounted their horses and were thrown by the
surge of the pressing crowd. Many found that circumstances made a
wall of the camels’ flanks; and all of them searched like wild goats for
precipices from which to leap off and escape. And all the men of your
army saw the miracle wrought by your incredible manoeuvre and
showed delight at the judgement of heaven; for the armies were not a
feathered arrow’s shot apart, and every one of us could easily see the
false battlements of the ravines where the barbarian multitude had
poured and was whirling in a mass without advancing. Some were
caught in a great giddy tide of troubles and were surging like the waves
which push one another with their own onrush, some rising on high
from the depths, some falling back and becoming hollow again: even
so did these unruly divisions swell like waves among the waterless

ἐν τοῖς ἀνύδροις κυματουμένων λίθοις,
τὰ μὲν πρὸς ὕψος ἐκ βάθους ἀνήρχετο,
τὰ δὲ πρὸς αὐτὰ τῶν κάτω τὰ τέρματα
πίπτοντα πυκνὰς συγχύσεις εἰργάζετο.
Οὕτως ἕκαστος ἀφρόνως ἐδυστύχει,
ὁ δὲ προπίπτων ἦν ἐπίφθονος μόνου·
πᾶς γὰρ παρ' αὐτοῖς εὐτυχὴς ἐκρίνετο,
ὃς πρὸς τὸ θνήσκειν εὑρέθη τομώτερος.
Ἡμῖν δὲ πᾶσα καὶ γαλήνη καὶ χάρις,
τέρψις δὲ μᾶλλον ἢ φόβος προσήρχετο.
Καὶ πᾶς πρὸς ὕψος τῷ θεῷ τῶν κτισμάτων
τὰς χεῖρας ἐξέτεινε σὺν τῇ καρδίᾳ,
καὶ τῷ στρατηγῷ συντόνως ἐπηύχετο.

ANDREW OF CRETE
c. 660–740

226. The Major Kanon

I

Βοηθὸς καὶ σκεπαστὴς   ἐγένετό μοι εἰς σωτηρίαν·
οὗτός μου θεός,   καὶ δοξάζω αὐτόν·
θεὸς τοῦ πατρός μου,   καὶ ὑψώσω αὐτόν·
ἐνδόξως γὰρ δεδόξασται.

stones, some rising from the bottom to the top, while others fell to the very depths below and brought widespread confusion. So all were in senseless misery and only those killed were envied; for every man who found a swift death was considered by them lucky. But over us a broad calm and gratitude came, and delight rather than fear. And we all lifted our hands and our hearts on high to the God of creation, and gave fervent thanks to the general.

I

HE has become the guardian, the protector who leads me to salvation; he is my God and I pay honour to him; he is the God of my father, and I shall exalt him; for in glory he is honoured.

424

Πόθεν ἄρξωμαι θρηνεῖν   τὰς τοῦ ἀθλίου μου βίου πράξεις;
   ποίαν ἀπαρχὴν   ἐπιθήσω, Χριστέ,
τῇ νῦν θρηνῳδίᾳ;   Ἀλλ' ὡς εὔσπλαγχνός μοι δὸς
   παραπτωμάτων ἄφεσιν.

Δεῦρο τάλαινα ψυχή,   σὺν τῇ σαρκί σου τῷ κτίστῃ πάντων
   ἐξομολογοῦ   καὶ ἀπόσχου λοιπὸν
τῆς πρὶν ἀλογίας   καὶ προσάγαγε θεῷ
   ἐν μετανοίᾳ δάκρυα.

Τὸν πρωτόπλαστον Ἀδὰμ   τῇ παραβάσει παραζηλώσας
   ἔγνων ἐμαυτὸν   γυμνωθέντα θεοῦ
καὶ τῆς ἀιδίου   βασιλείας καὶ τρυφῆς
   διὰ τὰς ἁμαρτίας μου.

Οἴμοι τάλαινα ψυχή!   Τί ὡμοιώθης τῇ πρώτῃ Εὔᾳ;
   Εἶδες γὰρ κακῶς   καὶ ἐτρώθης πικρῶς
καὶ ἥψω τοῦ ξύλου   καὶ ἐγεύσω προπετῶς
   τῆς παραλόγου βρώσεως.

Ἀντὶ Εὔας αἰσθητῆς   ἡ νοητή μοι κατέστη Εὔα,
   ὁ ἐν τῇ σαρκὶ   ἐμπαθὴς λογισμός,
δεικνὺς τὰ ἡδέα   καὶ γευόμενος ἀεὶ
   τῆς πικρᾶς καταπόσεως.

From what point shall I begin to weep for the doings of my wretched life? Where shall I start, O Christ, in my present lamentation? Of your mercy forgive my trespasses.

Come, miserable soul, confess with your flesh to the Creator of all, and in future desist from your former indifference; offer tears of repentance to God.

You have vied with Adam, the first created man, in disobedience; I have felt myself stripped of God, of the eternal kingdom, of delight, because of my sins.

Alas, wretched soul, why did you make yourself like the first Eve? Evil was your glance and you were bitterly wounded; you touched the tree and impudently tasted of the deceitful fruit.

Instead of an Eve of the flesh, mine is an Eve of the spirit: the thoughts of the flesh, full of passion, pointing to what is sweet, and always tasting of a mouthful of bitterness.

Ἐπαξίως τῆς Ἐδὲμ   προεξερρίφη ὡς μὴ φυλάξας
  μίαν σου, σωτήρ,   ἐντολὴν ὁ Ἀδάμ·
ἐγὼ δὲ τί πάθω,   ἀθετῶν διὰ παντὸς
  τὰ ζωηρά σου λόγια;

Ὑπερούσιε τριὰς   ἡ ἐν μονάδι προσκυνουμένη,
  ἆρον τὸν κλοιὸν   ἀπ' ἐμοῦ τὸν βαρὺν
τὸν τῆς ἁμαρτίας   καὶ ὡς εὔσπλαγχνός μοι δὸς
  δάκρυα κατανύξεως.

Θεοτόκε, ἡ ἐλπὶς   καὶ προστασία τῶν σὲ ὑμνούντων,
  ἆρον τὸν κλοιὸν   ἀπ' ἐμοῦ τὸν βαρὺν
τὸν τῆς ἁμαρτίας,   καὶ ὡς δέσποινα ἁγνὴ
  μετανοοῦντα δέξαι με.

II

Πρόσεχε,   οὐρανέ, καὶ λαλήσω   καὶ ἀνυμνήσω Χριστὸν
  τὸν ἐκ παρθένου σαρκὶ   ἐπιδημήσαντα.

Πρόσεχε,   οὐρανέ, καὶ λαλήσω·   γῆ, ἐνωτίζου φωνῆς
  μετανοούσης θεῷ   καὶ ἀνυμνούσης αὐτόν.

Adam was deservedly cast out of Eden, since he did not keep one of your commandments, O Saviour. What then shall I suffer? For I have disregarded all your life-giving sayings.

O Trinity, beyond substance, whom we worship as one: lift off from me the heavy collar of sin; of your mercy grant me tears of contrition.

Mother of God, hope and protector of your worshippers, lift off from me the heavy collar of sin; receive me, pure lady, as I repent.

II

Attend, O sky, and I will speak and celebrate Christ who came in flesh from a virgin to live among us.

Attend, O sky, and I will speak on. Earth, lend your ears to a voice which repents before God and sings his praises.

Πρόσχες μοι,   ὁ θεὸς ὁ σωτήρ μου,   ἵλεῳ ὄμματί σου
καὶ δέξαι μου τὴν θερμὴν   ἐξομολόγησιν.

Ἡμάρτηκα   ὑπὲρ πάντας ἀνθρώπους,   μόνος ἡμάρτηκά
σοι·
ἀλλ' οἴκτειρον ὡς θεός,   σῶτερ, τὸ ποίημά σου.

Μορφώσας μου   τὴν τῶν παθῶν ἀμορφίαν   ταῖς φιληδό-
νοις ὁρμαῖς
ἐλυμηνάμην τοῦ νοῦ   τὴν ὡραιότητα.

Ζάλη με   τῶν κακῶν περιέχει,   εὔσπλαγχνε κύριε·
ἀλλ' ὡς τῷ Πέτρῳ κἀμοὶ   τὴν χεῖρα ἔκτεινον.

Ἐσπίλωσα   τὸν τῆς σαρκός μου χιτῶνα,   καὶ κατερρύ-
πωσα
τὸ κατ' εἰκόνα, σωτήρ,   καὶ καθ' ὁμοίωσιν.

Ἡμαύρωσα   τῆς ψυχῆς τὸ ὡραῖον   ταῖς τῶν παθῶν
ἡδοναῖς,
καὶ ὅλως ὅλον τὸν νοῦν   χοῦν ἀπετέλεσα.

Διέρρηξα   νῦν τὴν στολήν μου τὴν πρώτην,   ἣν ἐξυ-
φάνατό μοι
ὁ πλαστουργὸς ἐξ ἀρχῆς,   καὶ ἔνθεν κεῖμαι γυμνός.

Attend to me, my God and Saviour, with eyes of compassion, and receive my impassioned confession.

I have sinned more than any man – I am the only sinner against you; but, Saviour, take compassion as a God, upon your creation.

Pleasure-loving urges moulded my shapeless passions; I outraged the beauty of the spirit.

I am surrounded by a storm of evils, compassionate Lord; but stretch out your hand to me as you did to Peter.

I have befouled the cloak of my flesh and covered your image and likeness in filth, O Saviour.

Through the pleasures of passion I have darkened the beauty of the soul, and altogether turned my entire spirit into earth.

I have torn my first cloak which at the beginning the Creator wove for me; and from that time I have been naked.

Ἐνδέδυμαι διερρηγμένον χιτῶνα, ὃν ἐξυφάνατό μοι
ὁ ὄφις τῇ συμβουλῇ, καὶ καταισχύνομαι.

Τὰ δάκρυα τὰ τῆς πόρνης, οἰκτίρμων, κἀγὼ προβάλλο-
μαι·
ἱλάσθητί μοι, σωτήρ, τῇ εὐσπλαγχνίᾳ σου.

Προσέβλεψα τοῦ φυτοῦ τὸ ὡραῖον καὶ ἠπατήθην τὸν
νοῦν,
καὶ ἄρτι κεῖμαι γυμνὸς καὶ καταισχύνομαι.

Ἐτέκταινον ἐπὶ τὸν νῶτόν μου πάντες οἱ ἀρχηγοὶ τῶν
κακῶν,
μακρύνοντες κατ' ἐμοῦ τὴν ἀνομίαν αὐτῶν.

Ἕνα σε ἐν τρισὶ τοῖς προσώποις θεὸν ἁπάντων ὑμνῶ,
τὸν πατέρα καὶ τὸν υἱὸν καὶ πνεῦμα τὸ ἅγιον.

Ἄχραντε θεοτόκε παρθένε, μόνη πανύμνητε,
ἱκέτευε ἐκτενῶς εἰς τὸ σωθῆναι ἡμᾶς.

I am clothed in a torn shirt, which the serpent wove for me on his suggestion, and I feel deeply ashamed.

I too, compassionate one, offer the tears [as] of the prostitute; of your charity, Saviour, be merciful to me.

I looked upon the beauty of the tree and my mind was deceived; and now I am naked and deeply ashamed.

All the leaders of evil piled [evils] on my back, heaping up their lawlessness against me.

Thee, one God of all in three persons, I celebrate: the Father, the Son and the Holy Ghost.

Immaculate Virgin, Mother of God, the one worthy of every hymn, make continual entreaty for our salvation.

ST JOHN DAMASCENE
fl. c. 730

227. On the Birth of Christ

I

Ἔσωσε λαὸν θαυματουργῶν δεσπότης,
ὑγρὸν θαλάσσης κῦμα χερσώσας πάλαι·
ἑκὼν δὲ τεχθεὶς ἐκ κόρης, τρίβον βατὴν
πόλου τίθησιν ἡμῖν, ὃν κατ' οὐσίαν
ἴσόν τε πατρὶ καὶ βροτοῖς δοξάζομεν.

Ἤνεγκε γαστὴρ ἡγιασμένη Λόγον,
σαφῶς ἀφλέκτῳ ζωγραφουμένη βάτῳ,
μιγέντα μορφῇ τῇ βροτησίᾳ θεόν,
Εὔας τάλαιναν νηδὺν ἄρας τῆς πάλαι
λύοντα πικρᾶς, ὃν βροτοὶ δοξάζομεν.

Ἔδειξεν ἀστὴρ τὸν πρὸ ἡλίου Λόγον,
ἐλθόντα παῦσαι τὴν ἁμαρτίαν, μάγοις,
σαφῶς πενιχρὸν εἰς σπέος, τὸν συμπαθῆ
σὲ σπαργάνοις ἑλικτόν, ὃν γεγηθότες
ἴδον τὸν αὐτὸν καὶ βροτὸν καὶ κύριον.

I

THE Lord saved his people by a miracle in the past, when he turned the wet waves of the sea into dry land. Of his own will he was born of a maiden, and made it possible for us to walk in the path of heaven, he whom we celebrate as equal in substance to his Father and to mortal men.

A holy womb, clearly depicted in the unburnable bush, bore the Word, the God who partook of human shape, who saved the miserable progeny of Eve from the ancient bitter curse, and whom we mortals celebrate.

A star pointed out to the Wise Men the Word who existed before the sun was created, and who came to abolish sin. It pointed out you, who suffered with man, clearly lying in a humble cave, wrapped in swaddling bands, whom in their delight the Wise Men saw both as their Lord and as a mortal.

II

Νεῦσον πρὸς ὕμνους οἰκετῶν, εὐεργέτα,
ἐχθροῦ ταπεινῶν τὴν ἐπηρμένην ὀφρύν,
φέρων τε, παντεπόπτα, τῆς ἁμαρτίας
ὕπερθεν ἀκλόνητον ἐστηριγμένους,
μάκαρ, μελῳδοὺς τῇ βάσει τῆς πίστεως.

Νύμφης πανάγνου τὸν πανόλβιον τόκον
ἰδεῖν ὑπὲρ νοῦν ἠξιωμένος χορὸς
ἄγραυλος ἐκλονεῖτο τῷ ξένῳ τρόπῳ
τάξιν μελῳδοῦσάν τε τῶν ἀσωμάτων
ἄνακτα Χριστόν, ἀσπόρως σαρκούμενον.

Ὕψους ἀνάσσων οὐρανῶν, εὐσπλαγχνίᾳ
τελεῖ καθ᾽ ἡμᾶς ἐξ ἀνυμφεύτου κόρης,
ἄϋλος ὢν τὸ πρόσθεν, ἀλλ᾽ ἐπ᾽ ἐσχάτων
Λόγος παχυνθεὶς σαρκί, τὸν πεπτωκότα
ἵνα πρὸς αὐτὸν ἑλκύσῃ πρωτόπλαστον.

Γένους βροτείου τὴν ἀνάπλασιν πάλαι
ᾄδων προφήτης Ἀββακοὺμ προμηνύει,
ἰδεῖν ἀφράστως ἀξιωθεὶς τὸν τύπον·

II

Accept the hymns of your servants, O Benefactor, and humble the swollen pride of the enemy; lead them, you who see everything, to stand firm and unshaken on the foundation of faith, above sin, chanting, O blessed God.

The band of shepherds, which was deemed worthy of seeing the most blessed infant of the purest bride, a thing beyond the grasp of mortal mind, was seized with wonder at the strange event, at the array of angels chanting to Christ the Lord, as he became flesh through no human seed.

He rules in the highest heavens; he is charitable to us because of the unwedded maiden, he who, incorporeal in the past, recently turned into the flesh-burdened Word to draw to himself fallen Adam.

The prophet Habakkuk had chanted of old, foretelling the rebirth of the human race: he was deemed worthy of seeing, inexpressibly, the

νέον βρέφος γὰρ ἐξ ὄρους τῆς παρθένου
ἐξῆλθε λαῶν εἰς ἀνάπλασιν, Λόγος.

COSMAS OF MAIOUMA
fl. c. 730

228. Kanon on Easter Saturday

I

Κύματι θαλάσσης   τὸν κρύψαντα πάλαι
   διώκτην τύραννον
ὑπὸ γῆν ἔκρυψαν   τῶν σεσωσμένων οἱ παῖδες·
ἀλλ' ἡμεῖς ὡς αἱ νεάνιδες   τῷ κυρίῳ ᾄσωμεν·
   ἐνδόξως γὰρ δεδόξασται.

Κύριε θεέ μου,   ἐξόδιον ὕμνον
   καὶ ἐπιτάφιον
ᾠδήν σοι ᾄσομαι,   τῷ τῇ ταφῇ σου ζωῆς μοι
τὰς εἰσόδους διανοίξαντι   καὶ θανάτῳ θάνατον
   καὶ Ἅιδην θανατώσαντι.

prototype: for a little babe, the Word, emerged from the Virgin, 'the mountain [God delighted to dwell in]', to reshape the human race.

I

HE who of old buried the pursuing tyrant in the waves of the sea was himself buried in the earth by the sons of those he had saved; and let us, like the [ten] maidens, chant to the Lord: for in glory he is honoured.

My Lord, my God, I will chant for you a funereal, a burial chant: for by your burial you opened the gateway of life to me and through death killed Death and Hades.

Ἄνω σε ἐν θρόνῳ   καὶ κάτω ἐν τάφῳ
   τὰ ὑπερκόσμια
καὶ ὑποχθόνια   κατανοοῦντα, σωτήρ μου,
ἐδονεῖτο τῇ νεκρώσει σου·   ὑπὲρ νοῦν ὡράθης γὰρ
   νεκρὸς ζωαρχικώτατος.

Ἵνα σου τῆς δόξης   τὰ πάντα πληρώσῃς,
   καταπεφοίτηκας
ἐν κατωτάτοις τῆς γῆς·   ἀπὸ γάρ σου οὐκ ἐκρύβη
ἡ ὑπόστασίς μου ἡ ἐν ᾿Αδάμ·   καὶ ταφεὶς φθαρέντα με
   καινοποιεῖς, φιλάνθρωπε.

II

Σὲ τὸν ἐπὶ ὑδάτων   κρεμάσαντα
   πᾶσαν τὴν γῆν ἀσχέτως
ἡ κτίσις κατιδοῦσα   ἐν τῷ Κρανίῳ κρεμάμενον,
θαμβητικῶς συνείχετο,   ⟨οὐκ ἔστιν ἅγιος
   πλήν σου, κύριε,⟩ κραυγάζουσα.

Σύμβολα τῆς ταφῆς σου   παρέδειξας,
   τὰς ὁράσεις πληθύνας·

When all things that lie above the earth and below it observed you,
my Saviour, on your throne above and in your tomb below, they were
shaken by your death; for, beyond what the mind could grasp, you
appeared as a dead body having full power over life.

You came down to the depths of the earth to accomplish all your
glory; my presence in Adam was not hidden from you; through your
burial, compassionate Lord, you have brought new life to me when I
was dead.

II

The Universe saw you, who without hindrance hung the whole earth
on the waters, hanging upon Golgotha, and it was filled with wonder
and cried out: 'There is no one holy but you, O Lord.'

By appearing to many you gave proof of your burial; and now, like

νῦν δὲ τὰ κρύφιά σου   θεανδρικῶς διετράνωσας
καὶ τοῖς Ἅιδου, δέσποτα,   ⟨οὐκ ἔστιν ἅγιος
    πλήν σου, κύριε,⟩ κραυγάζουσιν.

Ἥπλωσας τὰς ἀγκάλας   καὶ ἥνωσας
    τὰ τὸ πρὶν διεστῶτα·
καταστολῇ δέ, σῶτερ, τῇ ἐν σινδόνι καὶ μνήματι
πεπεδημένους ἔλυσας,   ⟨οὐκ ἔστιν ἅγιος
    πλήν σου, κύριε,⟩ κραυγάζοντας.

Μνήματι καὶ σφραγῖσιν,   ἀχώρητε,
    συνεσχέθης βουλήσει·
καὶ γὰρ τὴν δύναμίν σου   ταῖς ἐνεργείαις ἐγνώρισας
θεουργικῶς τοῖς μέλπουσιν·   ⟨οὐκ ἔστιν ἅγιος
    πλήν σου, κύριε φιλάνθρωπε.⟩

THEODORE THE STUDITE
759–826

229. On the Attendant of the Sick Monks

Τὸ χρῆμα θεῖον, ἀσθενῶν βάρη φέρειν.
Τούτου λαχὼν πύκτευσον, ὦ μοι τεκνίον,
θερμῶς, προθύμως ἐκτελεῖν σου τὸν δρόμον·

a God and a man, you have clearly shown to those too in Hades your secrets; and they cry out: 'There is no one holy but you, O Lord.'

You have opened your arms and joined together what was before separated. You released those who were held fettered in linen shrouds and under gravestones, and they cried out: 'There is no one holy but you, O Lord.'

You, who cannot be contained, were held in a sealed tomb of your own will; you have clearly made known through your actions your power like a God to those who chant to you: 'There is no one holy but you, compassionate Lord.'

IT is a sacred thing to bear the burden of the sick. If that is your lot, fight fervently, my child, eagerly to fulfil the course of your duty. As

ἕωθεν εὐθὺς τοὺς κλινήρεις σου βλέποις,
ἄλλου πρὸ παντὸς φαρμακεύων τοῖς λόγοις,
εἶτ' αὖ πρεπόντως προσφέροις σίτων δόσεις,
ὡς χρὴ δ' ἑκάστῳ, σὺν διακρίσει λόγου.
Μέλος γάρ ἐστι, μὴ παρέρχου τὸν πέλας.
Οὕτως ὑπηρετοῦντι μισθός σοι μέγας,
φῶς ἀπρόσιτον, οὐρανῶν εὐκληρία.

230. On the Shoemakers

Πεδιλοποιῶν ὡς ἀρίστη ἡ τέχνη!
'Αποστόλου γάρ ἐστι Παύλου τοῦ πάνυ.
Ζηλοῦντες αὐτοῦ τοὺς ἰδρῶτας τῶν κόπων,
δέξασθε θερμῶς τοὺς πόνους καθ' ἡμέραν,
ὡς ἐργάται Χριστοῖο, τῆσδε φροντίδος.
Δέρρεις τε βύρσας τ', ὡς δέον, τετμηκότες,
παλαιὰ καινουργοῦντες, εἶτα καὶ νέα,
μὴ νωθρότητι πρὸς παράχρησιν λόγου
ῥιπτοῦντες, εἴ τι τῶν ῥιφῆς οὐκ ἀξίων,
ἢ τὴν τομὴν φέροντες ἐλλειπῶς ὕπερ.
"Απαντα γὰρ ποιοῦντες ἀξιοχρέως
τῶν μαρτυρούντων ἐξανύσετε δρόμον.

soon as dawn breaks you should see to your bed-ridden sick, administering words to them before offering any other medicine. And then you should fitly offer the portions of food, to each according to his need, discriminating wisely. Do not overlook the man nearest you, for he is part of you. If you offer your services in this way your recompense will be great; light unapproachable and the happy lot of heaven.

How excellent is the shoemaker's craft! It is that of the great apostle Paul. Emulate the sweat of his labours and accept gratefully the daily toils of this duty as workers for Christ. Cut the skins and the hides properly; renew the old ones, then, also, cut the new, not discarding unreasonably, through laziness, what should not be thrown away, nor cutting the skin defectively. And if you do everything as you should, you will complete the course of the martyrs.

CASSIA

fl. c. 840

231. On Mary Magdalene

Κύριε, ἡ ἐν πολλαῖς ἁμαρτίαις περιπεσοῦσα γυνή,
   τὴν σὴν αἰσθομένη θεότητα,
   μυροφόρου ἀναλαβοῦσα τάξιν,
   ὀδυρομένη μύρον σοι   πρὸ τοῦ ἐνταφιασμοῦ κομίζει·
‹οἴμοι! λέγουσα,   ὅτι νύξ μοι ὑπάρχει,
   οἶστρος ἀκολασίας   ζοφώδης τε καὶ ἀσέληνος,
   ἔρως τῆς ἁμαρτίας·
δέξαι μου τὰς πηγὰς τῶν δακρύων
   ὁ νεφέλαις διεξάγων   τῆς θαλάσσης τὸ ὕδωρ·
κάμφθητί μοι   πρὸς τοὺς στεναγμοὺς τῆς καρδίας
   ὁ κλίνας τοὺς οὐρανοὺς   τῇ ἀφράστῳ σου κενώσει·
καταφιλήσω τοὺς ἀχράντους σου πόδας,
   ἀποσμήξω τούτους δὲ πάλιν
      τοῖς τῆς κεφαλῆς μου βοστρύχοις·
ὧν ἐν τῷ παραδείσῳ Εὔα τὸ δειλινὸν
   κρότον τοῖς ὠσὶν ἠχηθεῖσα   τῷ φόβῳ ἐκρύβη·
ἁμαρτιῶν μου τὰ πλήθη   καὶ κριμάτων σου ἀβύσσους
   τίς ἐξιχνιάσει, ψυχοσῶστα σωτήρ μου;
Μή με τὴν σὴν δούλην παρίδῃς
   ὁ ἀμέτρητον ἔχων τὸ ἔλεος.›

LORD, she who fell into many sins has recognized your Godhead and
has joined the myrrh-bearing women; weeping she brings myrrh for
you before your entombment. 'Alas,' she cries, 'what night is upon me,
what a dark and moonless madness of unrestraint, a lust for sin. Accept
my welling tears, you who procure the water of the sea through the
clouds; incline to the grievings of my heart, you who made the sky
bow down by the unutterable abasement [of your incarnation]. Many
times will I kiss your undefiled feet, and then dry them with the hair of
my head; those feet whose footfalls Eve heard at dusk in Paradise and
hid in terror. Who will trace out the multitude of my transgressions,
or the abysses [unpredictability] of your judgements, Saviour of
souls? Do not overlook me, your servant, in your boundless com-
passion.'

JOHN GEOMETRES
fl. 975

232. On the Church of St John of the Studion

Ἄϋλα φῶτα πυρφλόγα πρὸ τῆς πύλης
καὶ λύχνον ἐκλάμποντα φωτὸς κυρίου,
καὶ τοῦ πόλου μίμημα τὸν δόμον βλέπω.
Τὸ πνεῦμα ῥυπῶν, στῆθι τῆς πύλης ἄπο·
τὸν νοῦν δὲ λαμπρός, φαιδρὸς ὢν τὴν καρδίαν,
ἴθι πρόβαινε, φωτὶ φῶς προσλαμβάνων,
πρὸς ναὸν ἁγνόν, ναὸς ἐμψυχωμένος.

233. The Bitter-sweet Arrows are Aimed at Us Again

Οἴμοι, καθ' ἡμῶν καὶ πάλιν τὰ πυρφόρα
πέμπει φλογίζων καρδιῶν ὁ τοξότης
βέλη τὰ πικρὰ καὶ μέλιτος ἡδίω,
βέλη τὰ δεινὰ καὶ ποθεινὰ τῇ νόσῳ.
Ἕστηκα βληθείς, ἐξερύσαι δ' οὐ σθένω,
ὠθῶ καθ' αὑτοῦ τὸ ξίφος, θανεῖν θέλω.
Ποθῶ φλέγεσθαι, τραυματίζεσθαι πλέον.
Ὦ δεινὰ δεινῶν, ποῖον ὕδωρ τὴν φλόγα

I SEE incorporeal lights flaming before the door, a lamp casting forth the light of the Lord, and a building which is the image of the sky. If your spirit is soiled stand away from the door, but if your conscience is shining go forward, a living temple approaching a temple without stain, light drawing light from the light.

ALAS! Yet again the archer of hearts shoots the fire-bearing arrows against us and sets us ablaze – the bitter arrows that are sweeter than honey, the dreadful arrows that our sickness longs for. I stand hit and have not the power to pull them out. I press my sword against myself, I wish to die. I desire to be burnt, to be wounded deeper. O suffering

436

σβέσει; τὸ πικρὸν ποῖον ἑλκύσει βέλος;
Ὕδωρ τὸ σὸν ζῶν, Χριστέ μου, καὶ σὸς λόγος.
Χρῆσαι, λυτρωτά, συντόμως τοῖς φαρμάκοις.

SYMEON THE MYSTIC

c. 949–1022

234. You Alone Can See

Εἰ τοίνυν σὺ ἐνδέδυσαι σαρκός σου τὴν αἰσχύνην
καὶ νοῦν οὐκ ἀπεγύμνωσας, ψυχὴν οὐκ ἀπεδύσω,
τὸ φῶς ἰδεῖν οὐκ ἴσχυσας σκότει κεκαλυμμένος,
ἐγώ σοι τί ποιήσαιμι; τὰ φρικτὰ πῶς σοι δείξω;
πῶς εἰς τὸν οἶκον τοῦ Δαβὶδ εἰσενέγκω σε οἴμοι;
Ἐστὶ καὶ γὰρ ἀπρόσιτος τοῖς κατ᾽ ἐμὲ ῥαθύμοις,
ἐστὶν ὅλος ἀόρατος τυφλοῖς ἐμοὶ ὁμοίοις,
ἐστὶ μακρὰν ἀπίστων τε καὶ ὀκνηρῶν εἰσάπαν,
πονηρῶν πάντων πόρρωθεν, πάντων τῶν φιλοκόσμων·
τῶν κενοδόξων δὲ οὕτως ἀσυγκρίτως ἀπέχει
ὡς ὑπὲρ ὕψος οὐρανοῦ, ὑπὲρ βάθος ἀβύσσου·
καὶ τίς ἢ πῶς εἰς οὐρανὸν ἀναβήσεται ὅλως,
ἢ ὑπὸ γῆν κατέλθοι δὲ ἀνερευνῶν ἀβύσσους

of sufferings, what water can quench the flame? What will pull out the
bitter arrow? The living water which is you, my Christ, and your
word. O my deliverer, swiftly use the remedy.

WHAT can I do for you if you wear the shameful garment of the flesh
and have not laid bare your mind and made naked your soul, if you re-
main covered in darkness and do not have the strength to see the light?
How can I show you things full of terror? Alas, how can I lead you into
the House of David? It is unapproachable to thoughtless people like
myself; no trace of it can be seen by the blind like myself; it lies very
far from the faithless and the indolent, far from all those who are evil,
from the lovers of worldly things. It is as incomparably distant from
the conceited as the heights of the sky or the depths of the abyss. Who
will climb right up to the sky, and how? Or who can reach under the
earth to search the abyss and find a pearl the size of a mustard seed?

καὶ μαργαρίτην ἐκζητῶν ὡς σινάπεως κόκκον
σμικρότατον ὑπάρχοντα πῶς εὑρεῖν ἐξισχύσει;
Ἀλλ', ὦ παῖδες, συνάχθητε, ἀλλ', ὦ γυναῖκες, δεῦτε,
ἀλλ', ὦ πατέρες, φθάσατε πρὶν ἢ τὸ τέλος φθάσει,
καὶ σὺν ἐμοὶ θρηνήσατε καὶ κλαύσατε οἱ πάντες,
ὅτι ἐν τῷ βαπτίσματι μικροὶ θεὸν λαβόντες,
καὶ μᾶλλον δὲ υἱοὶ θεοῦ νήπιοι γεγονότες,
ἔξω οἱ ἁμαρτήσαντες ἐβλήθημεν εὐθέως
ἀπὸ τοῦ οἴκου τοῦ Δαβὶδ (καὶ τοῦτο ἀναισθήτως
πεπόνθαμεν), καὶ δράμωμεν διὰ τῆς μετανοίας·
ἐκεῖθεν γὰρ εἰσέρχονται οἱ ἐκβληθέντες πάντες·
ἄλλως δ' οὐκ ἔνι ἔνδοθεν εἰσελθεῖν (μὴ πλανᾶσθε),
οὐδὲ ἰδεῖν τὰ ἐν αὐτῷ τελεσιουργηθέντα
καὶ νῦν τελετουργούμενα εἰς ἀπείρους αἰῶνας
ἐν τῷ Χριστῷ μου καὶ θεῷ, ᾧ πρέπει πᾶσα δόξα
τιμή τε καὶ προσκύνησις νῦν καὶ εἰς τοὺς αἰῶνας.

235. The Sorrow of Death

Ἤκουσα πρᾶγμα ξένον καὶ πλῆρες θάμβους·
φύσιν ἄυλον τὴν λίθου στερροτέραν
ἴσ' ἀδάμαντος καλουμένου παθοῦσαν,
ὃς μὴ μαλαχθεὶς ἢ πυρὶ ἢ σιδήρῳ

How could anyone have the power to find so small a thing? But come, children, and gather together; hasten, women and fathers, before the end comes; weep, all, and lament with me, because when we were young we received God through baptism, and yet, though as infants we were sons of God, we sinned and were swiftly cast out of the House of David – all this we suffered without realizing it. Now let us go forward repenting. That is the doorway for all who are cast out. Do not be misled – there is no other entrance, no other way of seeing what has been accomplished there and what is now being accomplished for endless centuries in my Christ and God, to whom all glory and honour and worship is due, now and for ever.

I HEARD something strange and full of wonder: that incorporeal nature, which is stronger than stone, suffers the same as that which is called steel; for this, though not softened by fire or by the iron ham-

γέγονεν κηρὸς ἐμπλεχθεὶς τῷ μολύβδῳ·
ἄρτ' ἐπίστευσα μικρὸν ὕδατος ῥεῦμα
πέτρας τὸ στερρὸν ἐγχρονίζον κοιλαίνειν·
καὶ ὄντως οὐδὲν ἄτρεπτον τῶν ἐν βίῳ·
μηδείς μ' ἐκ τοῦ νῦν ἀπατᾶν νομιζέτω·
φεῦ τῷ βλέποντι τὰ φεύγοντα τοῦ βίου
ὡς κρατούμενα, καὶ τερπομένῳ τούτοις·
ταῦτα πείσεται, ἅπερ κἀγὼ ὁ τάλας·
νὺξ μ' ἐχώρισεν ἀδελφοῦ γλυκυτάτου
τὸ ἄτμητον φῶς τῆς ἀγάπης τεμοῦσα.

CHRISTOPHER OF MYTILENE
c. 1000–1050

236. On the Death of his Sister Anastasia

'Ροδοεικέλην γυναῖκα   θάνατος μέλας κατέσχεν,
ἐπὶ τῆς κλίνης δὲ κεῖται   ἀποτμηθὲν ἔρνος οἷα,
ἀρετῆς δ' ἄσυλον ὅρμον   περικειμένη καθεύδει,
ἀνακειμένη δὲ λάμπει,   νενεκρωμένη περ οὖσα.
     Νεφέλαι ὀμβροτόκοι, δάκρυα χεῖτε,
     ὅτι καλλίστη ἄφνω ἔσβετο κούρη.

mer, becomes as wax when it is mixed with lead. Lately I came to believe that a small stream of water can, over a length of time, scoop out a solid stone. For it is certain that nothing that belongs to Life is above change. Let no one think he can deceive me from now. Alas for him who considers permanent the things that leave us in life, and takes delight in them; he will suffer what I have suffered in my misery. The dark night of death has separated me from the sweetest of brothers, and severed the inextinguishable light of love.

BLACK death has claimed a woman, the likeness of a rose. She lies upon the couch like a sapling cut down. Girdled with the inviolate wreath of virtue she sleeps; in spite of death she lies radiant. Clouds that bring rain, pour forth your tears, for the loveliest light of maidens has been suddenly extinguished.

Ἄγε πᾶν φίλοικτον ὄμμα,   δάκρυσον μάλα πρὸ τῆσδε.
Ἄγε πᾶν στόμα, προθύμως   καλά μοι λάλει τὰ ταύτης.
Ἀπὸ καρδίας στενάζω   σὸς ἀδελφός, ὦ γλυκεῖα·
ἀπὸ καρδίας στενάζω,   ἀπὸ καρδίας φιλῶν σε.
    Κυπάριττος καθάπερ ἐνθάδε κεῖσαι,
    κασιγνήτη, μέγ' ἄχος ἄμμι λιποῦσα.

Κινύρας λόγων δονεῖτε,   φιλοϊστόρων τὰ πλήθη,
ὁλολαμπρόχρουν δὲ κούρην   στέφετε κρότοις ἐπαίνων·
δοκέει κλύειν γὰρ ἴδε,   λαλέειν τις εἰ θελήσει,
ἴχνος οὐδὲν ἐν προσώπῳ   θανάτου φέρουσα πάντως.
    Γενεῆς ἡμετέρης ὤλετο κόσμος
    τριακοστῇ Μαΐου, φεῦ μοι, ἰώ μοι.

Μακάρων ὅπου χορεῖαι,   ἀγέλαι ὅπου κροτούντων,
κατάταξον ἣν προείλου,   θεέ μου, ἄναξ ἁπάντων,
μετὰ πνευμάτων ἀμέμπτων,   μετὰ ἀγγέλων ἀΰλων,
μετὰ τῶν σέ, παντεπόπτα,   πεφιληκότων δικαίων.
    Στενάχω, αἰρομένου σκίμποδος ἤδη·
    ἐπὶ γὰρ τύμβον ἄγῃ, εὔχροε κούρη.

Come, all compassionate eyes, weep abundantly for her. Let every mouth eagerly speak her praises. I, your brother, grieve from my heart, sweet child; from my heart I grieve, and from my heart I love you. Here you lie like the cypress-tree, dear sister, leaving us a great sorrow.

Play upon the lyres of language, all you lovers of learning. Crown with the sounds of praise the maiden of all-shining brightness. See; she seems to hear, if one were to speak, and there is not the least trace of death upon her face. Woe, woe is me that on the thirtieth of May perished the jewel of our race.

Where stand the choruses of the blessed and the flocks of those that chant, there, my God, master of all, set her whom you have chosen, among the impeccable spirits, the incorporeal angels; among the righteous who love you, the all-seeing Lord. And now, as they lift your couch, I lament; for they bear you to the tomb, bright-coloured maiden.

237. *The Hours*

Ἡμεῖς ἀδελφαὶ γνήσιαι ψυχῶν δίχα·
ἄλλη μὲν ἄλλης τῷ χρόνῳ πρεσβυτέρα,
ἴσαι δὲ πᾶσαι τοὺς διαύλους τῶν χρόνων·
αἳ καὶ καλοῦμεν οὐκ ἀνοίγουσαι στόμα,
βαδίζομεν δὲ μὴ πόδας κεκτημέναι.
Ἐνταῦθά σοι λαλοῦμεν, ὡς ὁρᾶν ἔχεις,
καὶ πανταχοῦ πάρεσμεν, εἰ σκοπεῖν θέλεις.

JOHN MAVROPOUS
fl. c. 1050

238. *On Plato and Plutarch*

Εἴπερ τινὰς βούλοιο τῶν ἀλλοτρίων
τῆς σῆς ἀπειλῆς ἐξελέσθαι, Χριστέ μου,
Πλάτωνα καὶ Πλούταρχον ἐξέλοιό μοι·
ἄμφω γὰρ εἰσὶ καὶ λόγον καὶ τὸν τρόπον
τοῖς σοῖς νόμοις ἔγγιστα προσπεφυκότες.
Εἰ δ᾽ ἠγνόησαν ὡς θεὸς σὺ τῶν ὅλων,
ἐνταῦθα τῆς σῆς χρηστότητος δεῖ μόνον,
δι᾽ ἣν ἅπαντας δωρεὰν σῴζειν θέλεις.

WE are true sisters without souls. One is older than the other, but in the circling courses of the years we are of equal length. We call out without opening our mouths, and we walk though we have no legs. We speak to you here, as you can see; and we are everywhere present, if you wish to look.

IF you are willing to spare some of the others [those who were not Christians] from your punishment, my Christ, may you choose Plato and Plutarch, for my sake. For both of them clung very closely to your laws in both word and deed. If they did not know you as Lord of all, only your charity is needed here, through which you are willing to save all men and ask for nothing in return.

JOHN MAVROPOUS

239. *The Virgin's Tears*

⟨῏Ω τοῦ πάθους δέσποινα, καὶ σὺ δακρύεις;
καὶ τίς βοηθὸς τῶν παρ' ἡμῖν δακρύων,
εἰ καὶ σὺ πάσχεις ἄξια θρηνῳδίας;
τίς ἐλπὶς ἄλλη; τίς παράκλησις; φράσον.⟩
⟨Καὶ μὴν ἐχρῆν σε μᾶλλον εὐθύμως ἔχειν,
ἄνθρωπε, χρηστοῦ τοῦ τέλους προκειμένου·
ἄλλοις γὰρ ἄλλο φάρμακον σωτηρίας·
ἐμὸν δὲ πένθος κοσμικοῦ πένθους λύσις.⟩

THEODORE PRODROMOS
fl. 1140

240. *Cursed be Learning*

'Ἀπὸ μικρόθεν μ' ἔλεγεν ὁ γέρων ὁ πατήρ μου·
⟨Παιδίν μου, μάθε γράμματα, καὶ ὡσὰν ἐσέναν ἔχει.
Βλέπεις τὸν δεῖνα, τέκνον μου, πεζὸς περιεπάτει,
καὶ τώρα διπλοεντέληνος καὶ παχυμουλαράτος.
Αὐτός, ὅταν ἐμάνθανε, ὑπόδησιν οὐκ εἶχεν,
καὶ τώρα βλέπεις τον φορεῖ τὰ μακρυμύτικά του.
Αὐτός, ὅταν ἐμάνθανε, ποτέ του οὐκ ἐκτενίσθη,
καὶ τώρα καλοκτένιστος καὶ καμαροτριχάρης.

'OH, what suffering, Lady: even you weep? And who will help our tears, if you suffer things which bring you to mourning? What other hope is there? Whom should we entreat? Tell me.' 'Surely, Man, you should rather be of good cheer, now that a good end is before you. For others there are other means of salvation, but my sorrow is freedom from worldly sorrow.'

FROM the time when I was little my old father used to tell me: 'My child, learn letters, for there are others like you. You see so-and-so, my child, he used to go on foot, and now he has a double breast-plate [for his mule] and rides a well-fed mule. When he was studying he had no shoes, and now you see he wears pointed shoes. When he was studying he never combed his hair, and now he is well-groomed and proud of

442

Αὐτός, ὅταν ἐμάνθανε, λουτρόθυραν οὐκ εἶδε,
καὶ τώρα λουτρακίζεται τρίτον τὴν ἑβδομάδα.
Αὐτός, ὁ κόλπος του ἔγεμε φθεῖρας ἀμυγδαλάτας,
καὶ τώρα τὰ ὑπέρπυρα γέμει τὰ μανοηλάτα.
Καὶ πείσθητι γεροντικοῖς καὶ πατρικοῖς μου λόγοις,
καὶ μάθε τὰ γραμματικά, καὶ ὡσὰν ἐσέναν ἔχει.〉
Καὶ ἔμαθον τὰ γράμματα μετὰ πολλοῦ τοῦ κόπου.
Ἀφ᾽ οὗ δὲ τάχα γέγονα γραμματικὸς τεχνίτης,
ἐπιθυμῶ καὶ τὸ ψωμὶν καὶ τοῦ ψωμιοῦ τὴν μάνναν·
ὑβρίζω τὰ γραμματικά, λέγω μετὰ δακρύων·
〈Ἀνάθεμαν τὰ γράμματα, Χριστέ, καὶ ὅπου τὰ θέλει,
ἀνάθεμαν καὶ τὸν καιρὸν καὶ ἐκείνην τὴν ἡμέραν,
καθ᾽ ἥν μὲ παρεδώκασιν εἰς τὸ διδασκαλεῖον,
πρὸς τὸ νὰ μάθω γράμματα, τάχα νὰ ζῶ ἀπ᾽ ἐκεῖνα!〉
Ἐδάρε τότε ἄν μ᾽ ἔποικαν τεχνίτην χρυσοράπτην,
ἀπ᾽ αὐτοὺς ὁπού κάμνουσι τὰ κλαπωτὰ καὶ ζῶσι,
καὶ ἔμαθα τέχνην κλαπωτὴν τὴν περιφρονημένην,
οὐ μὴ ἤνοιγα τὸ ἀρμάριν μου καὶ ηὕρισκα ὅτι γέμει
ψωμίν, κρασὶν πληθυντικὸν καὶ θυννομαγειρίαν,
καὶ παλαμιδοκόμματα καὶ τσίρους καὶ σκουμπρία·
παρ᾽ οὗ ὅτι τώρα ἀνοίγω το, βλέπω τοὺς πάτους ὅλους,
καὶ βλέπω χαρτοσάκουλα γεμάτα μὲ χαρτία.
Ἀνοίγω τὴν ἀρκλίτσαν μου, νὰ εὕρω ψωμὶν κομμάτιν,
καὶ εὑρίσκω χαρτοσάκουλον ἄλλο μικροτερίτσιν.

his coiffure. When he was studying, he never saw the door of a bath-house, and now he takes three baths a week. The fold of his cloak was covered in lice big as almonds, and now it is full of the golden coins of Emperor Manuel. Listen to the words of an old man, your father, learn your grammar, there are others like you.' And I learned my grammar with great pains, and now that I have become, so to speak, a master of letters, I long for bread and for all that goes to make bread, and curse education, and cry out with tears: 'Cursed be learning, my Christ, and cursed those who wish to be educated. Cursed be the time and the day when they handed me over to school to learn how to read and write, as if to make a living from it.' Look, if they had then turned me into an artisan, a tailor of gold-embroidery, one of those who sew gold-embroidered garments to make a living, and, if I had learnt this despised art of sewing gold-embroidered clothes, I would now open my cupboard and find it full of bread, full of much wine and cooked tunny fish, and pieces of tunny, and dried sardines and mackerel.

Ἀπλώνω εἰς τὸ περσίκιν μου, γυρεύω τὸ πουγγίν μου,
διὰ στάμενον τὸ ψηλαφῶ, καὶ αὐτὸ γέμει χαρτία.
Ἀφ' οὗ δὲ τὰς γωνίας μου τὰς ὅλας ψηλαφήσω,
ἵσταμαι τότε κατηφὴς καὶ ἀπομεριμνημένος,
λιποθυμῶ καὶ ὀλιγωρῶ ἐκ τῆς πολλῆς μου πείνας·
καὶ ἀπὸ τὴν πείναν τὴν πολλὴν καὶ τὴν στενοχωρίαν
γραμμάτων καὶ γραμματικῶν τὰ κλαπωτὰ προκρίνω.

?THEODORE PRODROMOS

241. *Promises Are Not to be Kept*

Ἀφῆτέ με, ἐξαφῆτέ με, τώρα ἡ ψυχή μου ἐρράγη·
εἶπα την, καὶ ἀπεστράφη με καὶ ὀργῆς ἰχάδιν ἔχει·
τί ἔνι τὸ φονικοῖχάδιν σου, φονεύτρα, νὰ μὲ πλήξῃς;
‹Εἶπες το κι ἐξαναεῖπες το, κἂν θέλῃς πάλιν εἰπέ το·
ἂν οὐκ ἐλεῆς τὸ στόμαν σου, λάλει καὶ πάλιν λάλει·
δωρεὰν ὀχλεῖσαι, νεώτερε, μετ' ἄλλον ὅρκους ἔχω.›
‹Καὶ οἱ ὅρκοι παραβαίνονται καὶ οἱ λόγοι μεταστρέφουν,

Whereas now I open it and look through all the shelves and see paper-bags full of paper. I open my bread box to find a piece of bread, and find another smaller paper-bag. I stretch my hand into my pocket to find my purse, I search for a coin, and my pocket is full of paper. And then I search through all the corners of my house and stand dejected and full of cares, I faint and feel weak, because I am so hungry; and being hungry and full of worries I declare the occupation of a tailor of gold-embroidered clothes superior to that of a man of learning and grammarians.

LEAVE me, leave me alone, now my heart is broken. I spoke to her and she turned away, and her caress was angry: what is this killing tenderness you inflict on me, murderess? 'You said it once and you said it a second time; if you wish, you may repeat it. If you don't feel pity for your mouth, speak, and go on speaking. The trouble you take is for nothing, young man: my vows are owed to another.' 'Vows can be broken, words spoken can be changed, and love too can pass from

καὶ ἀγάπαι μετατίθενται πρὸς τούτους ἐξ ἐκείνων·
τέως δὲ τοὺς ὅρκους τοῦ ἔρωτος μηδὲ προβάλλεσαί τους,
ἐρώτησε καὶ νὰ σὲ εἰποῦν οὐκ ἔχουν οἱ ὅρκοι κρίμαν.)

MICHAEL ACOMINATOS

c. 1140–1220

242. *Athens in the Middle Ages*

Ἔρως Ἀθηνῶν τῶν πάλαι θρυλουμένων
ἔγραψε ταῦτα ταῖς σκιαῖς προσαθύρων
καὶ τοῦ πόθου τὸ θάλπον ὑπαναψύχων·
Ἐπεὶ γὰρ οὐκ ἦν οὐδαμοῦ φεῦ προσβλέπειν
αὐτὴν ἐκείνην τὴν ἀοίδιμον πόλιν,
τὴν δυσαρίθμου καὶ μακραίωνος χρόνου
λήθης βυθοῖς κρύψαντος ἠφαντωμένην,
ἐρωτολήπτων ἀτεχνῶς πάσχω πάθος,
οἳ τὰς ἀληθεῖς τῶν ποθουμένων θέας
ἀμηχανοῦντες τῶν παρόντων προσβλέπειν
τὰς εἰκόνας ὁρῶντες αὐτῶν, ὡς λόγῳ,
παραμυθοῦνται τῶν ἐρώτων τὴν φλόγα.
Ὡς δυστυχὴς ἔγωγε, καινὸς Ἰξίων,
ἐρῶν Ἀθηνῶν, ὡς ἐκεῖνος τῆς Ἥρας,
εἶτα λαθὼν εἴδωλον ἠγκαλισμένος.
Φεῦ οἷα πάσχω καὶ λέγω τε καὶ γράφω·

one man to another. As for the promises of love: do not bring them as
an excuse. Ask anyone and he will tell you: it is no sin to break such
vows.'

LOVE for Athens, a city once famous, wrote these words, a love that
plays with shadows, that gives a little comfort to burning desire. Alas;
it is impossible to see anything of that city famous in song, which has
disappeared, hidden for long incalculable years in the depths of obli-
vion: and, to speak the truth, I suffer what lovers suffer. For they,
when they cannot see the real shapes of their loves present, console the
flame of longing, so to speak, by looking at their pictures. Thus,
unhappy, I, a new Ixion, in love with Athens as he was with Hera, miss
her and embrace an image. Alas for what I suffer and say and write.

οἰκῶν ᾿Αθήνας οὐκ ᾿Αθήνας που βλέπω,
κόνιν δὲ λυπρὰν καὶ κενὴν μακαρίαν.
Ποῦ σοι τὰ σεμνά, τλημονεστάτη πόλις;
῾Ως φροῦδα πάντα καὶ κατάλληλα μύθοις
δίκαι, δικασταί, βήματα, ψῆφοι, νόμοι,
δημηγορίαι, πειθανάγκη ῥητόρων,
βουλαί, πανηγύρεις τε καὶ στρατηγίαι
τῶν πεζομάχων ἅμα καὶ τῶν ναυμάχων,
ἡ παντοδαπὴς Μοῦσα, τῶν λόγων κράτος.
῏Ολωλε σύμπαν τῶν ᾿Αθηνῶν τὸ κλέος·
γνώρισμα δ᾿ αὐτῶν οὐδ᾿ ἀμυδρόν τις ἴδοι.
Συγγνωστὸς οὐκοῦν, εἴπερ οὐκ ἔχων βλέπειν
τῶν ᾿Αθηναίων τὴν ἀοίδιμον πόλιν,
ἴνδαλμα ταύτης γραφικὸν ἐστησάμην.

MANUEL PHILES

c. 1275–1345

243. On an Ikon of the Virgin

Τί τοῦτο; καὶ πῶς καὶ παρὰ τέχνης τίνος
εἰκὼν ἀμυδρὰ καὶ σκιώδης εὑρέθης ｜
εἰς εὐτελοῦς ὕφασμα ληφθεῖσα κρόκης;
καὶ πῶς ὁ κηρὸς ἐγχεθεὶς ὑπὸ φλόγα,
κἂν εἰς ὕλην εὔπρηστον οὐκ εἶχε φλέγειν,

Though I live in Athens I see Athens nowhere: only sad, empty, and
blessed dust. Most unhappy city, where is your splendour? Everything
has disappeared and is become as if it belonged to a myth: lawsuits,
judges, the orators' stands, ballots, laws, speeches, the persuasive
arguments of orators, councils, festivals, generals to lead your soldiers
and your sailors, all the Muses, the very power of words. The entire
glory of Athens is passed away; not even a dim trace of it can be seen.
So, if I cannot see the city of Athens, famous in song, I must be for-
given for setting up an image of it in writing.

WHAT is this? How, and through what art, did you find yourself, a
faint and shadowy picture, gripped in the weaving of a humble woof?
And how did the wax, melted by the flame, not burn the inflammable

ἔγραψε τὸν σὸν πλαστικῶς τοῦτον τύπον;
Βαβαί, Μαριάμ, ἐξαμείβεις τὰς φύσεις·
καὶ γὰρ σεαυτὴν ἐκ πυρὸς ξένου γράφεις
αὖθις φανεῖσα καὶ πυρὸς κρείσσων βάτος,
οὗ Χριστὸς αὐτὸς πρὸς τὸ πῦρ τῆς λαμπάδος
τὴν μυστικὴν ἄνωθεν ἐκβλύζει δρόσον,
ὡς ἂν ὁ πιστὸς τὴν γραφὴν ταύτην βλέπων
τὴν φασματώδη τῶν παθῶν φεύγῃ φλόγα.

ANONYMOUS
13th century

244. *The Description of Chrysorrhoe*

Ἦν γὰρ ἡ κόρη πάντερπνος ἐρωτοφορουμένη,
ἀσύγκριτος τὰς ἡδονάς, τὸ κάλλος ὑπὲρ λόγον,
τὰς χάριτας ὑπὲρ αὐτὴν τὴν τῶν χαρίτων φύσιν.
Βοστρύχους εἶχεν ποταμούς, ἐρωτικοὺς πλοκάμους·
εἶχεν ὁ βόστρυχος αὐγὴν εἰς κεφαλὴν τῆς κόρης,
ἀπέστιλβε ὑπὲρ χρυσῆν ἀκτῖναν τοῦ ἡλίου.
Σῶμα λευκὸν ὑπὲρ αὐτὴν τὴν τοῦ κρυστάλλου φύσιν
ὑπέκλεπτεν τοὺς ὀφθαλμοὺς τοῦ σώματος ἡ χάρις.
Ἐδόκει γὰρ σὺν τῷ λευκῷ καὶ ῥόδου χάριν ἔχειν.
Ἂν μόνον ἀνενδράνισες, τὸ πρόσωπον ἂν εἶδες,

cloth upon which it fell, but skilfully paint this your image? Ah, Mary, you change the very nature of matter: you who once appeared in the guise of a bush the flames could not consume now depict yourself by means of this strange fire; and here Christ himself pours from above a secret moisture on the flame of the torch so that the believer may look on this picture and escape the ghostly flame of suffering.

THE maiden was wholly delightful, adorned with love and incomparable in sweetness. No words can describe her beauty; her grace was superior to the very nature of the Graces. Her tresses were like rivers, locks full of love: the hair on the maiden's head glowed and flashed brighter than the sun's golden rays. Her body was whiter than the very nature of crystal, and the grace of her form softly enslaved the eyes; for with her whiteness she seemed to have the charm of the rose. If you only cast your eyes on her, if you looked at her face, your whole soul was shaken, your whole heart; you would simply have called the

ἐσείσθης ὅλην τὴν ψυχήν, ὅλην σου τὴν καρδίαν·
ἁπλῶς τὴν κόρην ἄγαλμα τῆς Ἀφροδίτης εἶπες
καὶ πάσης ἄλλης ἡδονῆς ὅσας ὁ νοῦς συμπλέκει.
Τί δὲ πολλὰ πολυλογῶ, τί δὲ πολλὰ καὶ γράφω.
τάχα πρὸς τὸν καλλωπισμὸν τοῦ σώματος τῆς κόρης;
Λόγος μικρὸς ἂν ἐξαρκῆ πρὸς τὸ νά το δηλώσῃ·
ὅσας ὁ κόσμος ἔφερε γυναῖκας εἰς τὸ μέσον
καὶ πρὸ αὐτῆς καὶ μετ’ αὐτὴν καὶ τότε ὅσαι ἦσαν
ὡς πρὸς τὰς χάριτας αὐτῆς μιμῶ πρὸς Ἀφροδίτην.

(*Callimachus and Chrysorrhoe*)

ANONYMOUS
14th-century version

245. Young Digenis after his First Hunt

Εἶχε γὰρ ὁ νεώτερος εὔνοστον ἡλικίαν,
κόμην ξανθήν, ἐπίσγουρον, ὀμμάτια μεγάλα,
πρόσωπον ἄσπρον, ῥοδινόν, κατάμαυρον ὀφρύδιν,
καὶ στῆθος ὥσπερ κρύσταλλον, ὀργυιὰν εἶχε τὸ πλάτος.
Τοῦτον ὁρῶν ἠγάλλετο ὁ πατὴρ αὐτοῦ λίαν,
καὶ χαίρων ἔλεγεν αὐτῷ μεθ’ ἡδονῆς μεγάλης·
ὅτι τὸ καῦμα ἔστι πολύ, ἔνι καὶ μεσημέριν,
καὶ τὰ θηρία κρύβονται ἀπάρτι εἰς τὴν ἕλην·
‹Καὶ δεῦρο ἂς ἀπέλθωμεν εἰς τὸ ψυχρὸν τὸ ὕδωρ,

maiden a statue of Aphrodite, a statue of all the delights that the mind
can combine. There is no need to say much, to write long about the
natural adornments of her body; it is enough to say briefly that all the
women whom the world brought forth before she was born and after
her time, and all who were then living, compared with her charms only
as a monkey to Aphrodite.

THE young man [Digenis] was handsome, with fair curly hair, large
eyes, pink and white cheeks, and very dark brows. His chest was a
fathom wide and shone like crystal. His father looked at him and de-
lighted in him, and joyously told him with great pleasure that the heat
of the day was great and that it was midday, and that at that time the
wild beasts would be hiding in the swamp. 'Now let us leave this
place,' he said, 'and find cool water to wash the steaming sweat from
your face and change the clothes you are wearing; for they are soiled

καὶ νῖψον σου τὸ πρόσωπον ἐκ τῶν πολλῶν ἱδρώτων·
ἀλλάξεις δὲ καὶ τὰ φορεῖς, εἰσὶ γὰρ μεμιασμένα
ἐκ τῶν θηρίων τοὺς ἀφροὺς καὶ λέοντος τὸ αἶμα·
καὶ τρισμακάριστος ἐγὼ ἔχων τοιοῦτον παῖδα,
πλύνω δὲ καὶ τοὺς πόδας σου μὲ τὰς ἰδίας χεῖρας·
ἀπάρτι πᾶσαν μέριμναν ῥίψω ἐκ τὴν ψυχήν μου,
νὰ εἰμὶ καὶ ἀφρόντιστος ἔνθα σε ἀποστείλω,
εἴς τε τὰ κούρση τὰ πολλὰ καὶ πολεμίων βίγλας.›
Καὶ παρευθὺς ἀμφότεροι εἰς τὴν πηγὴν ἀπῆλθον,
ἦν δὲ τὸ ὕδωρ θαυμαστόν, ψυχρὸν ὡς τὸ χιόνιν·
καὶ καθεσθέντες γύρωθεν, οἱ μὲν ἔνιπτον χεῖρας,
οἱ δὲ τὸ πρόσωπον αὐτοῦ, ὁμοίως καὶ τοὺς πόδας·
ἔρρεεν ἔξω τῆς πηγῆς καὶ ἔπινον ἀπλήστως,
ὡς ἂν ἐκ τούτου γένωνται κἀκεῖνοι ἀνδρειωμένοι.
Ἄλλαξε δὲ καὶ τὸ παιδὶν τὴν ἑαυτοῦ ἐσθῆτα,
βάλλει στενὰ μοχλόβια διὰ τὸ καταψυχῆσαι,
τὸ μὲν ἐπάνω κόκκινον μὲ τὰς χρυσᾶς τὰς ῥίζας,
αἱ δὲ ῥίζαι του χυμευταὶ μετὰ μαργαριτάρων,
τὸν τράχηλόν του γεμιστὸν ἄβαρ ὁμοῦ καὶ μόσχον,
τρανὰ μαργαριτάρια εἶχεν ἀντὶ κομβίων,
τὰ δὲ θηλύκια στρεπτὰ ἐκ καθαροῦ χρυσίου,
τουβία ἐφόρει ἐξακουστά, γρύψους ὡραϊσμένους,
τὰ πτερνιστήρια πλεκτὰ μετὰ λίθων τιμίων,
ἐπὶ τῶν ἔργων τῶν χρυσῶν εἶχε λυχνίτας λίθους.
Πάμπολλα δὲ ἐσπούδαζε τὸ εὐγενὲς παιδίον

with the froth from the wild beasts' mouths and the blood of the lion. Thrice blessed am I to have such a son; with my own hands I shall wash your feet. From this time on I shall cast all cares from my heart and will no longer worry where to send you to sack many cities and keep watch for the enemy.' At once they both left for the fountain; its water was marvellous – as cold as snow, and everyone sat around it. Some washed his [Digenis'] hands, others his face and his feet. The water flowed out of the fountain and they drank it avidly, so that by doing so they too might become brave. The young man changed his clothes and put on a short narrow tunic to relax in; it was purple at the top and embroidered in gold and the embroidery had enamel decorations and pearls. He covered his neck with musk and ambergris: he had huge pearls for buttons and the twisted button-holes were of pure gold. He wore splendid trousers decorated with gryphons; his spurs were worked with precious stones and gold inset with red gems. The noble boy was very eager to get back to his mother in case she should be

εἰς τὴν μητέρα ἀπελθεῖν μὴ δι' αὐτὸν λυπῆται,
καὶ ἠνάγκαζεν ἅπαντας εἰς τὸ καβαλλικεῦσαι.
Ἵππον ἐμετεσέλλισεν ἄσπρον ὡς περιστέριν,
πλεκτὸς ἦτον ὁ σγόρδος του μετὰ λίθων τιμίων,
καὶ κωδωνίτζια χρυσᾶ μέσον τῶν λιθαρίων·
πάμπολλα κωδωνίτζια, καὶ ἦχος ἐτελεῖτο
ἐνήδονος καὶ θαυμαστός, πάντας ὑπερεκπλήττων·
πράσινον, ῥόδινον βλαττὶν εἶχεν εἰς τὸ καποῦλιν,
καὶ τὴν σέλλαν ἐσκέπαζε νὰ μὴ κονιορτοῦται·
τὸ σελλοχάλινον πλεκτὸν μετὰ χρυσῶν σβερνίδων,
τὰ ὅλα ἔργα χυμευτὰ μετὰ μαργαριτάρων.
Ἦτον ὁ ἵππος τολμηρὸς καὶ θρασὺς εἰς τὸ παίζειν,
τὸ δὲ παιδίον εὔθιον εἰς τὸ καβαλικεύειν·
πᾶς ὁ βλέπων ἐθαύμαζε τὸν ἄγουρον ἐκεῖνον,
πῶς μὲν ὁ ἵππος ἔπαιζε κατὰ γνώμην τοῦ νέου,
πῶς δὲ αὐτὸς ἐκάθητο ὥσπερ μῆλον εἰς δένδρον.
Καὶ ὥρμησαν τοῦ ἀπελθεῖν εἰς τὸν ἴδιον οἶκον.

(*The Epic of Digenis Akritas*)

246. The Combat between Digenis and Philopappos

Εὐθὺς δὲ ὁ Φιλόπαππος κατέβη ἐκ τοῦ ἵππου
καὶ τὸ σπαθί του ἐσήκωσεν ὁμοῦ καὶ τὸ σκουτάριν,
μεγάλως ἦλθεν πρὸς ἐμὲ νομίζων μὲ φοβίσῃ,
ὡς λέων δὲ ἐφώναζεν, ὡς δράκοντας συρίζων,

worried about him, and he urged them all to mount their horses. He saddled a horse as white as a dove; its mane had gems plaited in it, and there were small golden bells among the precious stones – many little bells, and their sound was sweet and strange, surprising everyone. There was a green and red cloth upon the back of the horse and this covered and protected the saddle from the dust. Into the saddle and the bit were set golden buckles, and the whole fabric was sequinned with pearls. The horse was spirited and playfully eager, and the young man was able in riding it. Everyone who saw the youth admired the way the horse frisked at his command, and how he sat upon it like an apple on an apple-tree. And they set out swiftly for home.

At once Philopappos jumped down from his horse and lifted his sword and his shield. He came mightily towards me thinking he would terrify

εἶχεν καὶ γὰρ ὡς ἀληθῶς ὁρμὴν ἀνδρειοτάτην·
σπαθέαν οὖν μοῦ ἔδωσεν καλὴν εἰς τὸ σκουτάριν,
τοῦ σκουταρίου τὸ κράτημα ἐπόμεινεν στὸ χέρι.
Οἱ δύο ἐξεφώνησαν ἄντικρυς βλέποντάς μας·
‹Καὶ ἄλλην μίαν, Φιλόπαππε, γεροντικήν του δῶσε!›
Ἐκεῖνος τότε ἠθέλησε νὰ σηκώση τὸ σπαθί του,
ἐγὼ ὀπισθαπόδησα, μικρὸν ἀναπηδήσας
μὲ τὸ ραβδὶ τὸν ἔδωσα στὴν κεφαλὴν ἀπάνω,
καὶ εἰ μὴ ταύτην ἔσκεπε διόλου τὸ σκουτάριν,
κόκκαλον δὲν ἀπόμενεν γερὸν ἀπάνω εἰς αὐτήν·
ὅμως ὁ γέρων ζαλισθεὶς ἐτρόμαξε μεγάλως,
καὶ μυκησάμενος ὡς βοῦς ἐπὶ τὴν γῆν ἡπλώθη.

(*The Epic of Digenis Akritas*)

ANONYMOUS
?14th-century version

247. The Soldier's Love

Ἀναστενάζουν τὰ βουνά, πάσχουν δι᾿ ἐμὲν οἱ κάμποι,
θρηνοῦσιν τὰ παράπλαγα, βροντοῦν οἱ λιβαδίες,
καὶ δένδρα τὰ ἐπαρέδραμα καὶ οἱ ραχωτὲς κλεισοῦρες
ἔχουν τοὺς πόνους μου ἀκομὴ καὶ ἀντίς μου ἀναστενάζουν,

me, roaring like a lion and hissing like a snake – truly he rushed forward with great spirit. He struck my shield violently with his sword; only the handle of the shield was left in my hand. His two supporters, looking directly at us, cried out: 'Hit him again, old Philopappos.' He then tried to lift his sword, but I moved back, jumping slightly, and struck him on the head with my club; and if his head had not been completely covered by his shield, not a bone in it would have been left uncracked. Even so, the old man was stunned and greatly terrified; and, lowing like a bull, he fell flat on the ground.

THE mountains sigh and the plains suffer for my sake; the hillsides weep, the meadows moan, and the trees I went by and the rocky passes still possess my grief: they sigh where I sighed, and say: 'Here passed

λέγουν· ‹'Εδιέβην ἀπεδῶ στρατιώτης πονεμένος,
ἄγουρος ποθοφλόγιστος διὰ πόθον ὡραιωμένης·
τὰ δάκρυά του εἶχεν ποταμούς, βροντὰς τοὺς στεναγμούς του,
καπνὸν ἐπάνω εἰς τὰ βουνὰ τὸν πονοανασασμόν του.
Τὸν ἥλιον εἶχε μάρτυραν καὶ εἰς τόπους μετ' ἐκεῖνον
τὰ σύννεφα ἐσκεπάζετον, συνέπασχεν μετ' αὐτόν.
Καὶ πόνος, φίλε Κλιτοβών, ἔδε καρδίας ὀδύνη,
τὸν συμπονοῦσιν τὰ βουνὰ καὶ τὰ ἄψυχα συμπάσχουν.›

(Lybistros and Rhodamne)

ANONYMOUS
15th century

248. *Pity Me, My Love*

Τριαντακλωνοκυπάρισσε μὲ τοὺς χρυσοὺς τοὺς κλώνους
καὶ μὲ τὰ φύλλα τὰ πλατιά, μὲ τὸν πολὺν τὸν ἴσκιον,
καὶ τὸν ἀέρα τὸν γλυκύν, μὲ τὴν πολλὴν δροσίαν,
περιβολίτσιν ἔμορφον τὰ ρόδα φυτεμένον,
γλυκομηλέα μου κόκκινη, τὰ μῆλα φορτωμένη,
ἀπόκλινε τὴν νιότην σου νὰ μείνω στὴν ἰσκιά σου,
νὰ δροσιστῶ στὸν ἴσκιον σου καὶ εἰς τὸ κατάψυχόν σου.

a soldier in distress, a young man burning with desire, in love with a
beautiful girl; his tears were rivers, his groans were like thunder, his
mournful lamenting like smoke upon the mountains. The sun was his
witness; and behind him, in the places where he passed, it covered it-
self with clouds and grieved with him. For when there is pain, friend
Klitophon – oh, anguish of the heart – the mountains share it and in-
animate nature suffers in sympathy.'

CYPRESS-TREE with your thirty branches, your branches of gold, with
your wide leaves and your thick shade, with your sweet breeze and
rich coolness, beautiful garden full of roses, sweet red apple-tree laden
with apples, bend down your young body so that I may stand in your
shade, and enjoy the coolness of your shadow and of your freshness.

249. *The Bird Has Flown*

Ἑβδομηντάθυρον κλουβὶν ἦτον εἰς τὴν αὐλήν μου·
ἀδόνιν εἶχε τὸ κλουβὶν ἥμερον ἐδικόν μου,
γλυκόλαλον, πανέμορφον καὶ ὡραιοπλουμισμένον,
καὶ μετὰ μέρες καὶ καιροὺς ἐφούμισε τ’ ἀδόνιν,
καὶ πιάνει το ἄλλος κυνηγός, γλυκοκαταφιλεῖ το·
καὶ ὄνταν διαβῶ ἐκ τὴν ρύμνην του καὶ ἀπὸ τὴν γειτονιάν του,
καὶ ἀκούσω το καὶ κιλαδεῖ, τὰ μέλη μου τρομάσσουν,
μαραίνεται ἡ καρδία μου, ὑπομονὴν δὲν ἔχω,
ὡς νὰ τὸ στρέψω στὸ κλουβίν, ὡς ἦτον μαθημένο.

250. *The Fountain and the Golden Tree*

Τὸ περιβόλιν ἐκ παντὸς τίς νὰ το ἀνιστορίσῃ;
Ἦτον ὁ τοῖχος του ὑψηλός, ὅλος μετὰ μουσείου,
εἶχεν καὶ πόρτας σιδηρᾶς τινὰς νὰ μὴ φοβῆται,
τὰ κάλλη δέ, τὰς χάριτας τὰς τοῦ περιβολίου,

THERE was a cage with seventy doors in my courtyard, and the cage had a tame nightingale in it that was my own; it sang sweetly, it was most beautiful and had a lovely plumage. After some time the nightingale escaped and another hunter caught it and kissed it sweetly and often. And whenever I go past its street, past that neighbourhood, and hear it singing, my limbs shake, my heart is withered, and I cannot wait to bring it back to the cage it knew.

How can one describe the garden in detail? Its wall was high, covered with mosaics, and it had secure iron doors; but my resources of speech

ἐξαπορεῖ μου ὁ λογισμὸς καὶ ὁ νοῦς μου νά τα γράψω,
καὶ ἀδυνατεῖ ἡ γλῶσσα μου πῶς νά τα ἀφηγῆται·
δένδρα γὰρ εἶχεν θαυμαστά, πάντρεπνα καὶ ὡραῖα,
ὡς ὑπερβαίνουν ἄνωθεν οἱ κορυφὲς τὸν τοῖχον·
εἰς τὸ καθὲν κλωνάριον Ἔρωτες κατοικοῦσιν.
Ἦσαν δὲ καὶ τριαντάφυλλα καὶ ἄνθια ποικιλάτα,
καὶ ποῖος νοῦς νά δυνηθῇ κατὰ λεπτὸν νά γράψῃ;
Βρύσις ἦτον ἐρωτική· τὸν κῆπον κατεβαίνει
ἀπὸ φουσκίνας πάντρεπνου καὶ πλήρης, πανευμόρφου·
τὰ δένδρη δὲ καὶ τὰ φυτὰ ἔρραινε ἡ φουσκίνα·
τῆς δὲ φουσκίνας τὰ λαμπρὰ τίς νά τὰ ἀνιστορήσῃ;
Λιθάριν ἦτον παμφανὲς εἰς βάθος ἐζωσμένη,
γύροθεν ταύτης ἵσταντο καὶ λέοντες καὶ πάρδοι,
ὅλα λιθάρια πάντρεπνα εἰς βάθος ἐζωσμένα,
ἐξ ὧν ἀπάντων ἔτρεχεν ὕδωρ ἐκ τῆς φουσκίνας,
τὸ μὲν ἀπὸ τοῦ στόματος, τὸ δὲ ἄλλον ἐκ τοῦ στήθους,
ἕτερον ἐκ τῆς κεφαλῆς καὶ ἄλλον ἐκ τῶν ὠτίων.
Ἦσαν δὲ γένη πάντρεπνα ἀπλήστως τῶν πουλίων
καὶ ἐκιλαδοῦσαν πάντρεπνα Μαΐου τὰς ἡμέρας,
ὅταν τ᾽ ἀηδόνια κιλαδοῦν καὶ τὰ πουλιὰ στριγγίζουν,
ὅταν τὰ δένδρη ἄνθη ποιοῦν καὶ θάλλουσιν τὰ πάντα,
ὅταν τὸ ποικιλόμορφον καὶ χάριτος λιβάδιν
ἡ καὶ προσφέρειν παρευθὺς μυριοκατακοσμεῖ το.

and thought are at a loss to describe, and my tongue is unable to relate,
the beauty and the grace of the garden. For it had amazing trees, most
beautiful and lovely, and their tops came up over the wall, and on each
branch a cupid had a nest. And there was a great variety of roses and
flowers that no one could write of in detail. There was a lovely spring
of water: it poured down on the garden from a graceful, beautiful
fountain that was full of water, and the fountain sprinkled the trees and
the plants. And how could one describe the splendour of that foun-
tain? Its depths were girded round by bright stones, and round it stood
lions and leopards, all made of beautiful stone, from all of which flowed
the water of the fountain, from the mouth of one, from the breast of
another, from the head of yet another, and from the ears of a fourth.
And there were surpassingly beautiful tribes of birds which sang most
sweetly in the days of May, when the nightingales sing and the other
birds cry, when the trees blossom and everything is flourishing, when
the varied and graceful meadow [?] is richly decorated. Now the

Ἡ μήτηρ δὲ τῆς εὐγενοῦς ἐκείνης τῆς κουρτέσας
χρυσῆν ἐποῖκεν πλάτανον, μέσον τοῦ κήπου σταίνει,
καὶ γένος ἅπαν τῶν πουλιῶν χρυσᾶ κατασκευάζει·
ἐντέχνως ὅλα ἐκάθουντα ἐκεῖνα εἰς τὴν πλατάνην,
ἐπνέασιν οἱ ἄνεμοι καὶ ἐκεῖνα ἐκιλαδοῦσαν,
ἕναν καθέναν τὸ αὐτὸ τὸ μέλος τὸ οἰκεῖον.
Τὸν νοῦν θαυμάζω, ἐξαπορῶ ἐκεῖνον τὸν τεχνίτην,
πῶς ἔστησεν τὴν πλάτανον μέσα εἰς τὸ περιβόλιν,
καὶ πῶς ἐκατεσκεύασεν τοῦ κιλαδεῖν πουλία·
τὸ γὰρ σκευᾶσαι ἀπὸ χρυσὸν ἢ ἐξ ἑτέρας ὕλης
πουλίων γένος, ἑρπετῶν ἢ καὶ τῶν τετραπόδων
εἶδον πολλὰ ὅτι ἐνέτυχον καὶ παλαιὰ καὶ νέα,
τὸ δ' ᾄδειν τε, τὸ κιλαδεῖν χρυσᾶ μυρία μέλη
χρυσῶν ὀρνέων καὶ πουλιῶν, πτηνῶν καὶ τῶν ἑτέρων,
ἐκτὸς σαρκὸς καὶ αἵματος πνοῆς πτερῶν τε δίχου,
τῆς φύσεως ἔστιν θαυμαστόν, πολλὰ ἐξαιρημένον.
Χαρὰ εἰς τὴν χρυσοπλάτανον καὶ ἐκεῖνον τὸν τεχνίτην
ποὺ τὴν ἐτεχνοποίησεν καὶ ἐκατέστησέν την,
πολλὴ χαρὰ εἰς τὴν δέσποιναν ὁποὺ ὥρισε νὰ γένη,
χαρὰ εἰς τὴν θυγατέραν της, ἐκείνην τὴν κουρτέσαν,
ὁποὺ τὰ ἐκατετρέπεντο καὶ ἐκατεχαίρετόν τα.

(*The Achilleïs*)

mother of that noble lady of the court had a golden plane-tree made
and set in the middle of the garden, and had all the tribes of birds
fashioned in gold. They all sat gracefully on the plane-tree; the breezes
blew and they sang, each one its own song. In my heart I wonder, I
marvel how that artist set the plane-tree in the garden, and how he
made birds that could sing. I know that there have been, both in the
past and recently, many tribes of birds, reptiles, and even of other
animals, made of gold, or of some other material; but it is a marvel of
nature, something extraordinary, that wild and tame golden birds,
flying creatures, and other animals, which have no flesh or blood, no
breath or wings, should be able to sing and chirrup endless golden
songs. Joy then to the golden plane-tree and to the artist who fashioned
it and set it up, much joy to the lady who ordered it to be made, and
joy to her daughter, that lady of the court, who took great pleasure and
delight in it.

ANONYMOUS
?early 15th century

251. Lament for Christ

Ὕπτιον ὁρῶσα   ἡ πάναγνός σε, Λόγε,   μητροπρεπῶς
ἐθρήνει·

‹ Ὦ γλυκύ μου ἔαρ,   γλυκύτατόν μου τέκνον,   ποῦ σου
ἔδυ τὸ κάλλος; ›

Θρῆνον συνεκίνει   ἡ πάναγνός σου μήτηρ,   σοῦ, Λόγε,
νεκρωθέντος.

Γύναια σὺν μύροις   ἥκουσι μυρίσαι   Χριστόν, τὸ θεῖον
μύρον.

Θάνατον θανάτῳ   σὺ θανατοῖς, θεέ μου,   θείᾳ σου δυνα-
στείᾳ.

Πεπλάνηται ὁ πλάνος,   ὁ πλανηθεὶς λυτροῦται   σοφίᾳ
σῇ, θεέ μου.

Πρὸς τὸν πυθμένα Ἅιδου   κατήχθη ὁ προδότης   δια-
φθορᾶς εἰς φρέαρ.

THE most pure [Virgin] saw you, Word of God, lying supine, and lamented in words befitting a mother:

'O my sweet springtime, my sweetest child, where has your beauty set?'

Your immaculate mother, Word of God, began a lamentation when death came over you.

Women came with myrrh, my Christ, to anoint you, you, the sacred myrrh.

Death through death you destroyed, my God, with your godly power.

The deceiver of men was deceived, the deceived set free from error, my God, by your wisdom.

The traitor was driven to the bottom of Hades, to the pit of destruction.

Τρίβολοι καὶ παγίδες   ὁδοὶ τοῦ τρισαθλίου   παρά-
φρονος Ἰούδα.

Πάντες συναπολοῦνται   οἱ σταυρωταί σου, Λόγε,   υἱὲ
θεοῦ παντάναξ.

Διαφθορᾶς εἰς φρέαρ   πάντες συναπολοῦνται   οἱ ἄνδρες
τῶν αἱμάτων.

Υἱὲ θεοῦ παντάναξ,   θεέ μου, πλαστουργέ μου,   πῶς πά-
θος κατεδέξω;

Ἡ δάμαλις τὸν μόσχον   ἐν ξύλῳ κρεμασθέντα   ἠλάλαζεν
ὁρῶσα.

Σῶμα τὸ ζωηφόρον   ὁ Ἰωσὴφ κηδεύει   μετὰ τοῦ Νικο-
δήμου.

Ἀνέκραζεν ἡ κόρη,   θερμῶς δακρυρροοῦσα,   τὰ σπλάγ-
χνα κεντουμένη·

‹Ὦ φῶς τῶν ὀφθαλμῶν μου,   γλυκύτατόν μου τέκνον,
πῶς τάφῳ νῦν καλύπτῃ;›

‹Τὸν Ἀδὰμ καὶ τὴν Εὔαν   ἐλευθερῶσαι, μῆτερ,   μὴ
θρήνει, ταῦτα πάσχω.›

Thorns and snares, in the path of thrice-miserable Judas, the insane.

With him shall all those perish who crucified you, Word, Son of God, Lord of all.

With him shall all the bloodstained men perish in the pit of destruction.

Son of God, Lord of all, my God and my creator, how did you condescend to suffer?

Your mother, the heifer, lowed in sorrow as she saw the calf hung upon the cross.

Joseph and Nicodemus gave burial to the body that brings life.

The Virgin, stung at heart, wept fervently and cried out:

‘Light of my eyes, my sweetest child, how is it that a tomb now covers you?’

‘Mother, do not weep; this I suffer to set free Adam and Eve.’

ANONYMOUS

⟨Δοξάζω σου, υἱέ μου,   τὴν ἄκραν εὐσπλαγχνίαν,   ἧς
χάριν ταῦτα πάσχεις.⟩

Τὸ ὄξος ἐποτίσθης   καὶ χολήν, οἰκτίρμον,   τὴν πάλαι
λύων γεῦσιν.

Ἰκρίῳ προσεπάγης,   ὁ πάλαι τὸν λαόν σου   στύλῳ
νεφέλης σκέπων.

Αἱ μυροφόροι, σῶτερ,   τῷ τάφῳ προσελθοῦσαι,   προσέ-
φερόν σοι μύρα.

Ἀνάστηθι, οἰκτίρμον,   ἡμᾶς ἐκ τῶν βαράθρων   ἐξανι-
στῶν τοῦ Ἅιδου.

⟨Ἀνάστα, ζωοδότα⟩   ἡ σὲ τεκοῦσα μήτηρ   δα-
κρυρροοῦσα λέγει.

Σπεῦσον ἐξαναστῆναι,   τὴν λύπην λύων, Λόγε,   τῆς σε
ἁγνῶς τεκούσης.

Οὐράνιαι δυνάμεις   ἐξέστησαν τῷ φόβῳ,   νεκρόν σε
καθορῶσαι.

'My son, I celebrate your great compassion which leads you to this suffering.'

Compassionate Lord, they gave you vinegar and gall to drink, and thus you abolished the taste of the past [the apple Adam ate].

You were nailed to a scaffold, you who in the past protected your people with a pillar of cloud.

Women bearing ointment came to your tomb, O Saviour, and brought you myrrh.

Rise, compassionate Lord, and raise us from the pit of Hades.

'Rise, life-giving Lord,' cries the mother that bore you, and weeps.

Make haste, rise, bring to an end the sorrow of her who bore you, Word of God, in purity.

The heavenly powers were beside themselves with terror when they saw you dead.

458

ANONYMOUS

Τοῖς πόθῳ τε καὶ φόβῳ   τὰ πάθη σου τιμῶσι   δίδου πταισμάτων λύσιν.

῏Ω φρικτὸν καὶ ξένον   θέαμα θεοῦ Λόγε,   πῶς γῆ σε συγκαλύπτει;

Φέρων πάλαι φεύγει,   σῶτερ, Ἰωσήφ σε,   καὶ νῦν σε ἄλλος θάπτει.

Κλαίει καὶ θρηνεῖ σε   ἡ πάναγνός σου μήτηρ,   σωτήρ μου, νεκρωθέντα.

Φρίττουσιν οἱ νόες   τὴν ξένην καὶ φρικτήν σου   ταφὴν τοῦ πάντων κτίστου.

Ἔρραναν εἰς τὸν τάφον   αἱ μυροφόροι μύρα,   λίαν πρωῒ ἐλθοῦσαι.

Εἰρήνην ἐκκλησίᾳ,   λαῷ σου σωτηρίαν   δώρησαι σῇ ἐγέρσει.

Grant forgiveness of sins to those who in love and fear give honour to your sufferings.

What a strange and terrible sight, O Word, O God! How can the earth cover you?

Joseph, who carried you once, now leaves; and another buries you O Saviour.

Your all-holy mother weeps and laments over your dead body, my Saviour.

The mind shudders at your strange and terrible burial, creator of all.

Very early in the morning came myrrh-bearing women with ointment and sprinkled your tomb.

Grant peace to the church and salvation to your people by your resurrection.

V

UNDER FRANKISH AND
TURKISH RULE

ANONYMOUS FOLK-SONGS

18th- and 19th-century versions. The origins of
some go deep into the Byzantine period.

252. The Death of Digenis

I

Ὁ Διγενὴς ψυχομαχεῖ κι ἡ γῆ τόνε τρομάσσει.
Βροντᾶ κι ἀστράφτει ὁ οὐρανὸς καὶ σειέτ' ὁ ἀπάνω κόσμος,
κι ὁ κάτω κόσμος ἄνοιξε καὶ τρίζουν τὰ θεμέλια,
κι ἡ πλάκα τὸν ἀνατριχιᾶ πῶς θὰ τόνε σκεπάση,
πῶς θὰ σκεπάση τὸν ἀϊτὸ τσῆ γῆς τὸν ἀντρειωμένο.
Σπίτι δὲν τὸν ἐσκέπαζε, σπήλιο δὲν τὸν ἐχώρει,
τὰ ὄρη ἐδιασκέλιζε, βουνοῦ κορφὲς ἐπήδα,
χαράκια ἁμαδολόγανε καὶ ριζιμιὰ ξεκούνιε.
Στὸ βίτσιμά 'πιανε πουλιά, στὸ πέταμα γεράκια,
στὸ γλάκιο καὶ στὸ πήδημα τὰ λάφια καὶ τ' ἀγρίμια.

Ζηλεύγει ὁ Χάρος μὲ χωσιά, μακρὰ τόνε βιγλίζει,
καὶ λάβωσέ του τὴν καρδιὰ καὶ τὴν ψυχή του πῆρε.

I

DIGENIS is struggling with death and the earth shudders. The sky is
filled with thunder and lightning, the upper world shakes, the nether
world has opened and its foundations creak. And the trembling tomb-
stone wonders how to cover him, how to cover the brave eagle of the
world. No house could put a roof over his head, no cave could hold
him; he strode across the hills, he leapt over the mountain tops, he
played quoits with boulders, he shook loose deep-rooted rocks; he
jumped so high that he caught the birds, the falcon on the wing; he
jumped and ran faster than the deer or the wild beast.

Death was envious and from a distant ambush watched him, and
wounded him in the heart, snatching away his soul.

II

Τρίτη ἐγεννήθη ὁ Διγενὴς καὶ Τρίτη θὰ πεθάνη.
Πιάνει καλεῖ τοὺς φίλους του κι ὅλους τοὺς ἀντρειωμένους,
νὰ ῥθῆ ὁ Μηνᾶς κι ὁ Μαυραϊλής, νὰ ῥθῆ κι ὁ γιὸς τοῦ Δράκου,
νὰ ῥθῆ κι ὁ Τρεμαντάχειλος, ποὺ τρέμει ἡ γῆ κι ὁ κόσμος.
Καὶ πῆγαν καὶ τὸν ηὖρανε στὸν κάμπο ξαπλωμένο.
Βογγάει, τρέμουν τὰ βουνά· βογγάει, τρέμουν οἱ κάμποι.
‹Σὰν τί νὰ σ’ ηὖρε, Διγενή, καὶ θέλεις νὰ πεθάνης;›
‹Φίλοι, καλῶς ὁρίσατε, φίλοι κι ἀγαπημένοι,
συχάσατε, καθίσατε κι ἐγὼ σᾶς ἀφηγιέμαι·
τῆς Ἀραβίνας τὰ βουνά, τῆς Σύρας τὰ λαγκάδια,
ποὺ κεῖ συνδυὸ δὲν περπατοῦν, συντρεῖς δὲν κουβεντιάζουν,
παρὰ πενήντα κι ἑκατό, καὶ πάλε φόβον ἔχουν,
κι ἐγὼ μονάχος πέρασα πεζὸς κι ἀρματωμένος,
μὲ τετραπίθαμο σπαθί, μὲ τρεῖς ὀργιὲς κοντάρι.
Βουνὰ καὶ κάμπους ἔδειρα, βουνὰ καὶ καταράχια,
νυχτιὲς χωρὶς ἀστροφεγγιά, νυχτιὲς χωρὶς φεγγάρι.
Καὶ τόσα χρόνια ποὺ ’ζησα δῶ στὸν ἀπάνου κόσμο
κανένα δὲ φοβήθηκα ἀπὸ τοὺς ἀντρειωμένους.
Τώρα εἶδα ἕναν ξυπόλυτο καὶ λαμπροφορεμένο
πόχει τοῦ ῥίσου τὰ πλουμιά, τῆς ἀστραπῆς τὰ μάτια·

II

Digenis was born on a Tuesday and on a Tuesday he will die. He called his friends and all the warriors; he asked Menas and Mavrailis, the son of Drakos, to come, and Tremantacheilos, whom the whole world fears. They came and found him lying on the plain, groaning. The mountains trembled; he groaned, and the plains trembled. 'What is the matter, Digenis? Why are you about to die?' 'Welcome, my friends, my dear companions; keep quiet, take a seat and I will tell you. The Arabian mountains, the Syrian valleys, where men fear to cross in twos or to talk together in threes – where they march in fifties and hundreds and, even so, are afraid – these I crossed all alone on foot, armed with my sword, four spans long, and my spear, three fathoms long. I ploughed across mountains and plains, hillsides and hills, through nights with no starlight, nights with no moon. And all the time I have lived in the upper world I have never felt fear for any warrior. But now I see a bare-footed fellow with flashing garments, with the plumage of an eagle and eyes of lightning; and he has called

μὲ κράζει νὰ παλέψωμε σὲ μαρμαρένια ἀλώνια,
κι ὅποιος νικήση ἀπὸ τοὺς δυὸ νὰ παίρνη τὴν ψυχή του.)

Καὶ πῆγαν καὶ παλέψανε στὰ μαρμαρένια ἀλώνια·
κι ὅθε χτυπάει ὁ Διγενὴς τὸ αἷμα αὐλάκι κάνει,
κι ὅθε χτυπάει ὁ Χάροντας τὸ αἷμα τράφο κάνει.

253. Constantine and Arete

Μάνα μὲ τοὺς ἐννιά σου γιοὺς καὶ μὲ τὴ μιά σου κόρη,
τὴν κόρη τὴ μονάκριβη τὴν πολυαγαπημένη,
τὴν εἶχες δώδεκα χρονῶ κι ἥλιος δὲ σοῦ τὴν εἶδε.
Στὰ σκοτινὰ τὴν ἔλουζε στ' ἄφεγγα τὴ χτενίζει
στ' ἄστρι καὶ στὸν αὐγερινὸ ἔπλεκε τὰ μαλλιά της.
Προξενητάδες ἥρθανε ἀπὸ τὴ Βαβυλώνα,
νὰ πάρουνε τὴν 'Αρετὴ πολὺ μακριὰ στὰ ξένα.
Οἱ ὀχτὼ ἀδερφοὶ δὲ θέλουνε κι ὁ Κωσταντῖνος θέλει.
«Μάνα μου, κι ἂς τὴ δώσωμε τὴν 'Αρετὴ στὰ ξένα,
στὰ ξένα κεῖ ποὺ περπατῶ, στὰ ξένα τοῦ πηγαίνω,
ἂν πᾶμ' ἐμεῖς στὴν ξενιτιά, ξένοι νὰ μὴν περνοῦμε.»
«Φρόνιμος εἶσαι, Κωσταντή, μ' ἄσκημα ἀπιλογήθης.

out to me to wrestle with him on the marble threshing-floor, and for
the winner to take the other's soul away.'

And they went and wrestled on the marble threshing-floor: and
where the blows of Digenis fell the blood flowed in a furrow, and where
Death struck the blood opened a moat.

MOTHER, with your nine sons and your single daughter, your only
daughter, dearly loved: she was twelve years old and the sun had not
yet seen her. She washed her hair in the dark; by night she combed it;
in the starlight, when the morning star was shining, she plaited her
tresses. Matchmakers came from Babylon to take Arete very far away,
to foreign lands; eight of her brothers objected, but Constantine would
have it. 'Mother, let us give Arete to marry into a foreign land: for I
march and travel as a soldier in foreign lands, and so, should we go
there, we should not be considered strangers.' 'You are a wise man
Constantine, but what you say is wrong. If I fall ill, my son, if death

Κι ἂ μόρτη, γιέ μου, θάνατος, κι ἂ μόρτη γιέ μου, ἀρρώστια,
κι ἂν τύχη πίκρα γὴ χαρά, ποιὸς πάει νὰ μοῦ τὴ φέρη; ›
‹Βάλλω τὸν οὐρανὸ κριτὴ καὶ τοὺς ἁγιοὺς μαρτύρους,
ἂν τύχη κι ἔρτη θάνατος, ἂν τύχη κι ἔρτη ἀρρώστια,
ἂν τύχη πίκρα γὴ χορά, ἐγω νὰ σοῦ τὴ φέρω.›

Καὶ σὰν τὴν ἐπαντρέψανε τὴν Ἀρετὴ στὰ ξένα,
καὶ μπῆκε χρόνος δίσεχτος καὶ μῆνες ὀργισμένοι
κι ἔπεσε τὸ θανατικό, κι οἱ ἐννιὰ ἀδερφοὶ πεθάναν,
βρέθηκε ἡ μάνα μοναχὴ σὰν καλαμιὰ στὸν κάμπο.
Σ' ὅλα τὰ μνήματα ἔκλαιγε σ' ὅλα μοιρολογιόταν,
στοῦ Κωσταντίνου τὸ μνημιὸ ἀνέσπα τὰ μαλλιά της.
‹Ἀνάθεμά σε, Κωσταντή, καὶ μυριανάθεμά σε,
ὁπού μοῦ τὴν ἐξόριζες τὴν Ἀρετὴ στὰ ξένα.
Τὸ τάξιμο ποὺ μοῦ 'ταξες, πότε θὰ μοῦ τὸ κάμης;
Τὸν οὐρανό 'βαλες κριτὴ καὶ τοὺς ἁγιοὺς μορτύρους,
ἂν τύχη πίκρα γὴ χαρὰ νὰ πᾶς νὰ μοῦ τὴ φέρης.›
Ἀπὸ τὸ μυριανάθεμα καὶ τὴ βαριὰ κατάρα,
ἡ γῆς ἀναταράχτηκε κι ὁ Κωσταντὴς ἐβγῆκε·
κάνει τὸ σύγνεφο ἄλογο καὶ τ' ἄστρο χαλινάρι,
καὶ τὸ φεγγάρι συντροφιὰ καὶ πάει νὰ τῆς τὴ φέρη.
Παίρνει τὰ ὄρη πίσω του καὶ τὰ βουνὰ μπροστά του·

should come my way, if joy or sorrow come, who will go to bring her back to me?' 'As the sky is my judge, and the holy martyrs will testify: should death come your way, should sickness come, sorrow or joy, I will bring her back to you.'

After they had married off Arete into foreign lands, a leap-year came, and angry months: the plague fell upon them and all nine sons died – the mother found herself alone, like stubble on a plain. She wept over all the graves; over all she sang a dirge, but over the grave of Constantine she tore out her hair. 'My curse upon you, Constantine; a thousand curses on you, who sent my Arete away, an exile into foreign lands. When will you keep the promise you gave me, when you swore the sky and the holy martyrs would be your judge, that if joy or sorrow should come you would go and bring her back?' The many heavy curses shook the earth, and Constantine sprang out. He took a cloud for a horse, a star for his harness, the moon for his companion, and set out to bring her back. He left the hills behind him and ran to the mountains facing him, and found his sister combing her hair out-

βρίσκει την καὶ χτενίζουνταν ὄξου στὸ φεγγαράκι.
'Απὸ μακριὰ τὴ χαιρετᾶ κι ἀπὸ κοντὰ τῆς λέγει·
‹ "Αϊντε, ἀδερφή, νὰ φύγωμε στὴ μάνα μας νὰ πᾶμε.›
‹'Αλίμονο, ἀδερφάκι μου, καὶ τί 'ναι τούτη ἡ ὥρα;
"Αν ἴσως κι εἶναι γιὰ χαρὰ νὰ στολιστῶ καὶ νά 'ρθω,
κι ἂν εἶναι πίκρα, πές μου το, νὰ βάλω μαῦρα νά 'ρθω.›
‹"Ελα, 'Αρετή, στὸ σπίτι μας, κι ἂς εἶσαι ὅπως καὶ ἂν εἶσαι.›
Κοντολυγίζει τ' ἄλογο καὶ πίσω τὴν καθίζει.

Στὴ στράτα ποὺ διαβαίνανε πουλάκια κιλαηδοῦσαν,
δὲν κιλαηδοῦσαν σὰν πουλιά, μήτε σὰν χελιδόνια,
μόν' κιλαηδοῦσαν κι ἔλεγαν ἀνθρωπινὴ ὁμιλία·
‹Ποιὸς εἶδε κόρην ὄμορφη νὰ σέρνη ὁ πεθαμένος!›
‹"Ακουσες, Κωσταντῖνέ μου, τί λένε τὰ πουλάκια;›
‹Πουλάκια εἶναι κι ἂς κιλαηδοῦν, πουλάκια εἶναι κι ἂς λένε.›
Καὶ παρεκεῖ ποὺ πάγαιναν κι ἄλλα πουλιὰ τοὺς λένε·
‹Δεν εἶναι κρίμα κι ἄδικο, παράξενο μεγάλο,
νὰ περπατοῦν οἱ ζωντανοὶ μὲ τοὺς ἀπεθαμένους!›
‹"Ακουσες, Κωσταντῖνέ μου, τί λένε τὰ πουλάκια
πῶς περπατοῦν οἱ ζωντανοὶ μὲ τοὺς ἀπεθαμένους;›
‹'Απρίλης εἶναι καὶ λαλοῦν καὶ Μάης καὶ φωλεύουν.›

side her house in the sweet moonlight. From a distance he greeted her and came close and said: 'Come, sister, let us leave and go to our mother.' 'Alas, my brother – what is the occasion of this? If the journey is for a happy event I shall dress gaily and follow you; but if some sorrow is in store, tell me and I shall wear black.' 'Come, Arete, back to our home, no matter what you wear.' He forced his horse down and she sat behind him.

As they rode along there were little birds singing. They were not singing like birds, not like swallows; they were speaking with human voice: 'Who saw a lovely girl ever snatched away by a corpse?' 'Did you hear, my Constantine, what the little birds are saying?' 'They are little birds, let them sing; they are little birds, let them speak.' And further on, as they rode, more birds cried out to them: 'Is it not shameful and wrong and most strange that the living should travel with the dead?' 'Did you hear, my Constantine, what the little birds say: that the living are travelling with the dead?' 'It is April and they sing; it is May and they build their nests.' 'I am afraid of you, my dear brother,

‹Φοβοῦμαι σ', ἀδερφάκι μου, καὶ λιβανιὲς μυρίζεις.›
‹'Εχτὲς βραδὺς ἐπήγαμε πέρα στὸν Ἅη Γιάννη,
καὶ θύμιασέ μας ὁ παπᾶς μὲ περισσὸ λιβάνι.›
Καὶ παρεμπρὸς ποὺ πήγανε, κι ἄλλα πουλιὰ τοὺς λένε·
‹Γιὰ ἰδὲς θάμα κι ἀντίθαμα ποὺ γίνεται στὸν κόσμο,
τέτοια πανώρια λυγερὴ νὰ σέρνη ὁ πεθαμένος!›
Τ' ἄκουσε πάλι ἡ 'Αρετὴ καὶ ράγισε ἡ καρδιά της.
‹Ἄκουσες, Κωσταντάκι μου, τί λένε τὰ πουλάκια;›
‹Ἄφησ', 'Αρέτω, τὰ πουλιὰ κι ὅτι κι ἂ θέλ' ἂς λέγουν.›
‹Πές μου, ποῦ εἶναι τὰ κάλλη σου, καὶ ποῦ εἶν' ἡ λεβεντιὰ σου
καὶ τὰ ξανθά σου τὰ μαλλιὰ καὶ τ' ὄμορφο μουστάκι;›
‹Ἔχω καιρὸ π' ἀρρώστησα καὶ πέσαν τὰ μαλλιά μου.›

Αὐτοῦ σιμά, αὐτοῦ κοντὰ στὴν ἐκκλησιὰ προφτάνουν,
βαριὰ χτυπᾶ τ' ἀλόγου του κι ἀπ' ἐμπροστὰ τῆς χάθη·
κι ἀκούει τὴν πλάκα καὶ βροντᾶ, τὸ χῶμα καὶ βοΐζει.
Κινάει καὶ πάει ἡ 'Αρετὴ στὸ σπίτι μοναχή της,
βλέπει τοὺς κήπους της γυμνοὺς τὰ δέντρα μαραμένα,
βλέπει τὸν μπάλσαμο ξερό, τὸ καρυοφύλλι μαῦρο,
βλέπει μπροστὰ στὴν πόρτα της χορτάρια φυτρωμένα.
Βρίσκει τὴν πόρτα σφαλιστὴ καὶ τὰ κλειδιὰ παρμένα,
καὶ τὰ σπιτοπαράθυρα σφιχτὰ μανταλωμένα.

you smell of incense.' 'Late last night we went to St John's church and the priest used too much incense.' And as they went along, more birds said to them: 'Look at this marvel, this amazing marvel on earth: such a lovely girl being dragged away by a dead man.' Again Arete heard them and her heart was broken: 'My dear Constantine, do you hear what the birds are saying?' 'Let the birds alone, Arete, let them say what they want.' 'Tell me, where is your beauty, where has your manhood vanished, and your fair hair and your handsome moustache?' 'I have been a long time ill and my hair has fallen out.'

Just then they came close by the church: he whipped the horse violently and vanished from her sight. She heard the tombstone thud and the earth rumble. Arete set out for the house alone. She saw her gardens empty, the trees withered, the balsam dry, the gillyflower blackened; she saw grass growing in front of the door. She found the door locked and the keys taken and the windows of the house tightly

Χτυπᾶ τὴν πόρτα δυνατά, τὰ παραθύρια τρίζουν.
‹"Ἂν εἶσαι φίλος διάβαινε, κι ἂν εἶσαι ἐχτρός μου φύγε,
κι ἂν εἶσαι ὁ Πικροχάροντας, ἄλλα παιδιὰ δὲν ἔχω,
κι ἡ δόλια ἡ 'Αρετούλα μου λείπει μακριὰ στὰ ξένα.›
‹Σήκω, μανούλα μου, ἄνοιξε, σήκω γλυκιά μου μάνα.›
‹Ποιὸς εἶν' αὐτὸς ποὺ μοῦ χτυπάει καὶ μὲ φωνάζει μάνα;›
‹"Ανοιξε, μάνα μου, ἄνοιξε, κι ἐγὼ εἶμαι ἡ 'Αρετή σου.›

Κατέβηκε, ἀγκαλιάστησαν κι ἀπέθαναν κι οἱ δύο.

254. The Last Mass in Santa Sophia

Σημαίνει ὁ Θιός, σημαίνει ἡ γῆς, σημαίνουν τὰ ἐπουράνια,
σημαίνει κι ἡ 'Αγιὰ Σοφιά, τὸ μέγα μοναστήρι,
μὲ τετρακόσια σήμαντρα κι ἑξηνταδυὸ καμπάνες,
κάθε καμπάνα καὶ παπάς, κάθε παπὰς καὶ διάκος.
Ψάλλει ζερβὰ ὁ βασιλιάς, δεξιὰ ὁ πατριάρχης,
κι ἀπ' τὴν πολλὴ τὴν ψαλμουδιὰ ἐσειόντανε οἱ κολόνες.
Νὰ μποῦνε στὸ χερουβικὸ καὶ νὰ 'βγη ὁ βασιλέας,
φωνὴ τοὺς ἦρθε ἐξ οὐρανοῦ κι ἀπ' ἀρχαγγέλου στόμα·

closed. She knocked sharply at the door and the windows creaked. 'If
you are a friend, go your way: and if you are my enemy, leave; but if
you are bitter Death, I have no more sons to give you, and my poor
Arete is far away in foreign lands.' 'Rise, sweet mother, open the door;
rise, sweet mother'. 'Who is it that knocks for me and calls me mother?'
'Open, mother, open; it is I, your Arete.'
    She came down, they embraced one another, and they both died.

GOD rings the bells, the earth rings the bells, the sky rings the bells,
and Santa Sophia, the great church, rings the bells: four hundred
sounding boards and sixty-two bells, a priest for each bell and a deacon
for each priest. To the left the emperor was chanting, to the right the
patriarch, and from the volume of the chant the pillars were shaking.
When they were about to sing the hymn of the Cherubim and the
emperor was about to appear, they heard a voice from the sky and
from the mouth of the Archangel: 'Stop the Cherubic hymn, and let

«Πάψετε τὸ χερουβικὸ κι ἂς χαμηλώσουν τ' ἅγια,
παπάδες πᾶρτε τὰ γιερά, καὶ σεῖς κεριὰ σβηστῆτε,
γιατὶ εἶναι θέλημα θεοῦ ἡ Πόλη νὰ τουρκέψη.
Μὸν στεῖλτε λόγο στὴ Φραγκιά, νὰ 'ρτουνε τρία καράβια.
τὸ 'να νὰ πάρη τὸ σταυρὸ καὶ τ' ἄλλο τὸ βαγγέλιο,
τὸ τρίτο, τὸ καλύτερο, τὴν ἁγία τράπεζά μας,
μὴ μᾶς τὴν πάρουν τὰ σκυλιὰ καὶ μᾶς τὴ μαγαρίσουν.»
Ἡ Δέσποινα ταράχτηκε, καὶ δάκρυσαν οἱ εἰκόνες.
«Σώπασε, κυρὰ Δέσποινα, καὶ μὴ πολυδακρύζης,
πάλι μὲ χρόνους, μὲ καιρούς, πάλι δικά σας εἶναι.»

255. The Bridge of Arta

Σαράντα πέντε μάστοροι κι ἐξῆντα μαθητάδες
γιοφύριν ἐθεμέλιωναν στῆς Ἄρτας τὸ ποτάμι.
Ὁλημερὶς τὸ χτίζανε, τὸ βράδυ ἐγκρεμιζόταν.
Μοιριολογοῦν οἱ μάστοροι καὶ κλαῖν οἱ μαθητάδες·
«Ἀλίμονο στοὺς κόπους μας, κρίμα στὶς δούλεψές μας,
ὁλημερὶς νὰ χτίζουμε, τὸ βράδυ νὰ γκρεμιέται.»
Πουλάκι ἐδιάβη κι ἔκατσε ἀντίκρυ στὸ ποτάμι,
δὲν ἐκελάηδε σὰν πουλί, μηδὲ σὰ χιλιδόνι,

the holy elements bow in mourning. The priests must take the sacred vessels away and you candles must be extinguished, for it is the will of God that the City fall to the Turks. But send a message to the West asking for three ships to come; one to take the Cross away, another the Holy Bible, the third, the best of the three, our holy Altar, lest the dogs seize it from us and defile it.' The Virgin was distressed and the holy ikons wept. 'Hush, Lady, do not weep so profusely; after years and after centuries they will be yours again.'

FORTY-FIVE builders and sixty apprentices were setting the foundations of a bridge across the river of Arta. All day long they built it but at night it crumbled away. The builders lamented, the apprentices wept: 'Alas for our labours! Alas for our efforts! To build all day and have it fall at night.' A little bird was passing by and alighted over against the river; it was not singing like a bird, nor like a swallow, but

παρά ἐκελάηδε κι ἔλεγε ἀνθρωπινή λαλίτσα·
⟨"Α δὲ στοιχειώσετε ἄνθρωπο, γιοφύρι δὲ στεριώνει·
καὶ μὴ στοιχειώσετε ὀρφανό, μὴ ξένο, μὴ διαβάτη,
παρά τοῦ πρωτομάστορα τὴν ὄμορφη γυναίκα,
πόρχεται ἀργὰ τ' ἀποταχύ, καὶ πάρωρα τὸ γιόμα.⟩

Τ' ἄκουσ' ὁ πρωτομάστορας καὶ τοῦ θανάτου πέφτει.
Πιάνει, μηνάει τῆς λυ〉ερ〉ῆς μὲ τὸ πουλί τ' ἀηδόνι·
ἀργὰ ντυθῇ, ἀργὰ ἀλλαχτῇ ἀργὰ νὰ πάη τὸ γιόμα,
ἀργὰ νὰ πάη καὶ νὰ διαβῇ τῆς Ἄρτας τὸ γιοφύρι.
Καὶ τὸ πουλὶ παράκουσε, κι ἀλλιῶς ἐπῆγε κι εἶπε·
⟨Γοργὰ ντύσου, γοργὰ ἄλλαξε, γοργὰ νὰ πᾶς τὸ γιόμα,
γοργὰ νὰ πᾶς καὶ νὰ διαβῇς τῆς Ἄρτας τὸ γιοφύρι.⟩

Νὰ τηνε καὶ ξανάφανεν ἀπὸ τὴν ἄσπρη στράτα·
τὴν εἶδ' ὁ πρωτομάστορας, ραγίζεται ἡ καρδιά του.
Ἀπὸ μακριὰ τοὺς χαιρετᾶ κι ἀπὸ κοντὰ τοὺς λέει·
⟨Γειά σας, χαρά σας, μάστοροι καὶ σεῖς οἱ μαθητάδες,
μὰ τί ἔχει ὁ πρωτομάστορας κι εἶναι βαργωμισμένος;⟩
⟨Τὸ δαχτυλίδι τόπεσε στὴν πρώτη τὴν καμάρα,
καὶ ποιὸς νὰ μπῆ καὶ ποιὸς νὰ βγῆ τὸ δαχτυλίδι νὰ 'βρῆ;⟩

it was singing and speaking with a human voice. 'Unless you kill a man and turn him to a ghost, the bridge will never stand firm; but do not do this to an orphan, a foreigner, or a passer-by, but to the master-builder's beautiful wife, who comes here late in the morning and late at dinner-time.'

The master-builder heard this and fell sick to death; he sent a message by a nightingale to his young wife, telling her to dress slowly, to change slowly, to bring dinner slowly, to be late in coming to cross the bridge of Arta. But the bird misunderstood it, and took another message saying: 'Dress quickly, change quickly, bring the dinner quickly, quickly go and cross the bridge of Arta.'

And now she appears on the white path; the master-builder sees her and his heart breaks. From afar she greets them, and coming close she says to them: 'Joy and health to you builders and to you apprentices too. But what is the matter with the master-builder? Why does he look so downcast?' 'His ring has fallen under the first arch, and who can get in and out of the water to find the ring?' 'Master-builder, do not

‹ Μάστορα, μὴν πικραίνεσαι, κι ἐγὼ νὰ πά᾽ σ᾽ τὸ φέρω,
ἐγὼ νὰ μπῶ, κι ἐγὼ νὰ βγῶ τὸ δαχτυλίδι νὰ ᾽βρω.›

Μηδὲ καλὰ κατέβηκε, μηδὲ στὴ μέσ᾽ ἐπῆγε,
‹Τράβα, καλέ μ᾽, τὸν ἄλυσο, τράβα τὴν ἁλυσίδα,
τὶ ὅλον τὸν κόσμο ἀνάγειρα καὶ τίποτες δὲν ηὖρα.›
Ἕνας πιχάει μὲ τὸ μυστρί, κι ἄλλος μὲ τὸν ἀσβέστη,
παίρνει κι ὁ πρωτομάστορας καὶ ρίχνει μέγα λίθο.

‹᾽Αλίμονο στὴ μοῖρα μας, κρίμα στὸ ριζικό μας!
Τρεῖς ἀδερφάδες ἤμαστε, κι οἱ τρεῖς κακογραμμένες,
ἡ μιά ᾽χτισε τὸ Δούναβη, κι ἡ ἄλλη τὸν ᾽Αφράτη
κι ἐγὼ ἡ πιλιὸ στερνότερη τῆς ῎Αρτας τὸ γιοφύρι.
῾Ως τρέμει τὸ καρυόφυλλο, νὰ τρέμη τὸ γιοφύρι,
κι ὡς πέφτουν τὰ δεντρόφυλλα, νὰ πέφτουν οἱ διαβάτες.›
‹Κόρη, τὸ λόγον ἄλλαξε, κι ἄλλη κατάρα δῶσε,
πόχεις μονάκριβο ἀδερφό, μὴ λάχη καὶ περάση.›
Κι αὐτὴ τὸ λόγον ἄλλαξε, κι ἄλλη κατάρα δίνει·
‹῎Αν τρέμουν τ᾽ ἄγρια βουνά, νὰ τρέμη τὸ γιοφύρι,
κι ἂν πέφτουν τ᾽ ἄγρια πουλιά, νὰ πέφτουν οἱ διαβάτες,
τὶ ἔχω ἀδερφὸ στὴν ξενιτιά, μὴ λάχη καὶ περάση.›

be sad: I will go and fetch it for you; I will go in and out of the water
to find the ring.'

She had not fully got down, nor had she yet reached the middle of
the stream: 'Pull up the chain, my dear, pull up the chain, for I have
searched everywhere and found nothing.' One of them was pouring
mortar over her with a trowel, the other lime, and the master-builder
took hold of a huge stone and threw it.

'Alas, such was our fate, our doom! We were three sisters, all three
ill-starred. One of us built the bridge over the Danube, another over
the Euphrates, and I, the youngest of the three, the bridge of Arta.
May this bridge shake like the gillyflower, and may those passing over
it fall like leaves from a tree.' 'Woman, say something else, utter
another curse; for you have only one brother and some day he may
cross this bridge.' And she changed her words and uttered another
wish: 'If the high mountains tremble, then let this bridge shake; if the
wild birds fall to the earth, then let those crossing the bridge fall into
the water, for I have a brother who is in foreign lands, and he may
cross over it.'

256. The Curse of the Deserted Maiden

Φεγγάρι μου, πού 'σαι ψηλά καὶ χαμηλὰ λογιάζεις,
πουλάκια, πού εἶστε στὰ κλαριὰ καὶ στὶς κοντοραχοῦλες,
καὶ σεῖς περιβολάκια μου μὲ τὸ πολὺ τὸ ἄνθι,
μὴν εἴδατε τὸν ἀρνηστή, τὸν ψεύτη τῆς ἀγάπης,
ὁπού μὲ φίλιε κι ὅμονε, ποτὲ δέν μ' ἀπαρνιέται,
καὶ τώρα μ' ἀπαράτησε σὰν καλαμιὰ στὸν κάμπο;
σπέρνουν, θερίζουν τὸν καρπό κι ἡ καλαμιὰ ἀπομένει,
βάνουν φωτιὰ στὴν καλαμιὰ κι ἀπομαυρίζει ὁ κάμπος.
Ἔτσι εἶναι κι ἡ καρδούλα μου μαύρη, σκοτεινιασμένη.

Θέλω νὰ τὸν καταραστῶ καὶ τὸν πονεῖ ἡ ψυχή μου,
μὰ πάλι ἂς τὸν καταραστῶ κι ὅτι τοῦ μέλλει ἂς πάθη.
Σὲ κυπαρίσσι ν' ἀνεβῆ, νὰ μάση τὸν καρπό του,
τὸ κυπαρίσσι νὰ εἶν' ψηλὸ νὰ λυγιστῆ νὰ πέση.
Σὰν τὸ γυαλὶ νὰ ῥαγιστῆ, σὰν τὸ κερὶ νὰ λιώση·
νὰ πέση εἰς τούρικικα σπαθιά, εἰς φράγκικα μαχαίρια.
Πέντε γιατροὶ νὰ τὸν κρατοῦν καὶ δέκα μαθητάδες,
καὶ δεκοχτὼ γραμματικοὶ τὰ πάθη του νὰ γράφουν.
Κι ἐγὼ διαβάτρα νὰ γενῶ καὶ νὰ τούς χαιρετήσω.
‹Καλῶς τὰ κάνετε, γιατροί, καλῶς τὰ πολεμᾶτε,

My moon, you who, high above, look upon things below; little birds
on the branches or on the low hills, and you, my sweet gardens with
your rich blossom, have you perhaps seen the man who abandoned
me the deceiver of love, the man who kissed me and swore he would
never forsake me, but who has now left me like stubble on the plain?
They sow, they reap the crop, but the stubble is left there; they set fire
to the stubble, and the plain turns fully black. So is my poor heart
black, covered in darkness.

I want to curse him, but my heart pities him. Still, let me curse him,
and let him suffer what he must. May he climb a cypress-tree to gather
its fruit, and may the cypress-tree be tall and bend, and he fall down;
may he crack like glass, melt like wax; may he fall to the swords of the
Turks, the knives of the Franks. May five doctors get hold of him and
ten of their assistants, and may eighteen scribes write out what he
suffered. And may I be passing by and greet them: 'Doctors, you are
doing well, you are managing well. If your scissors are sharp, do not

ἂν κόβουν τὰ ψαλίδια σας, κορμὶ μὴ λυπηθῆτε,
ἔχω κι ἐγὼ λινὸ πανὶ σαρανταπέντε πῆχες,
ὅλο μουρτάρια καὶ ξαντὰ στοῦ δίγνωμου τὴ σάρκα·
κι ἂ δὲ σᾶς φτάσουνε κι αὐτὰ κόβω καὶ τὴν ποδιά μου,
πουλῶ καὶ τὰ μεταξωτὰ τὰ ρημοσκοτεινά μου,
κι ἂ θέλη γαῖμα γιατρικό, πάρετε ὀχ τὴν καρδιά μου.)

257. Love Song

Ὁ αὐγερινὸς κι ἡ πούλια, τ' ἄστρα τῆς αὐγῆς,
καὶ τὸ λαμπρὸ φεγγάρι μὲ ξεπλάνεψαν,
κι ὅταν ἐβγῆκε ὁ ἥλιος μὲ ξεγνάντεψε
εἰς τὸ πλευρὸ τῆς κόρης ποὺ ξενύχτησα.
Γυρνῶ, τὴν κόρη βλέπω ποὺ κοιμόντανε·
στέκω καὶ διαλογοῦμαι πῶς νὰ τῆς τὸ εἰπῶ,
πῶς νὰ τὴν ἐξυπνήσω, τὴν πολυαγαπῶ.
‹Ξύπνα, σηκώσου, μῆλο, τρυφερὴ μηλιά,
ἄνοιξ' τὰ δυό σου μάτια, ἄνοιξ' τα νὰ ἰδῆς
ποὺ μ' ἔκλεισεν ὁ ἥλιος μέσα στὸ κλουβί.›
‹Ἐμένα δέ με λένε μῆλο καὶ μηλιά,
μὲ λένε γλυκὸ ρόδο καὶ ροδοσταμιά,
κι' ἂ σ' ἔκλεισεν ὁ ἥλιος, φεύγεις τὸ βραδύ.›

spare the flesh. I have a piece of linen cloth thirty yards long, all un-
woven threads, undone for the deceiver's flesh. Should that not be
enough, I will tear up my apron and sell my silken clothes, my unlucky
and useless dowry — and if you need blood to cure him, take it from
my heart.'

THE Morning Star and the Pleiades, the stars of dawn and the bright
moon led me astray, and when the sun arose he saw me beside the girl
with whom I spent the night. I turned my head and looked at the sleep-
ing girl; I paused and debated how to tell her, whom I love so much,
how to wake her up: 'Wake, rise, my apple, my tender apple-tree;
open your two eyes, open them and see how the sun has locked me in a
cage.' 'I am not called an apple nor an apple-tree; my name is sweet
rose and rose-water; and if the sun has imprisoned you, you can escape
when night falls.'

258. The Red Lips

Κόκκιν' ἀχείλι ἐφίλησα κι ἔβαψε τὸ δικό μου,
καὶ στὸ μαντήλι τό 'συρα κι ἔβαψε τὸ μαντήλι,
καὶ στὸ ποτάμι τό 'πλυνα κι ἔβαψε τὸ ποτάμι,
κι ἔβαψε ἡ ἄκρη τοῦ γιαλοῦ κι ἡ μέση τοῦ πελάγου.
Κατέβη ὁ ἀιτὸς νὰ πιῆ νερό, κι ἔβαψαν τὰ φτερά του,
κι ἔβαψε ὁ ἥλιος ὁ μισὸς καὶ τὸ φεγγάρι ἀκέριο.

259. Black Swallows from the Desert

Μαῦρα μου χελιδόνια ἀπ' τὴν ἔρημο,
κι ἄσπρα μου περιστέρια τῆς ἀκρογιαλιᾶς,
αὐτοῦ ψηλὰ ποὺ πᾶτε κατ' τὸν τόπο μου,
μηλιά 'χω στὴν αὐλή μου καὶ κονέψετε,
καὶ πῆτε τῆς καλῆς μου, τῆς γυναίκας μου:
θέλει καλόγρια ἂς γίνη, θέλει ἂς παντρευτῆ,
θέλει τὰ ροῦχα ἂς βάψη, μαῦρα νὰ ντυθῆ,
νὰ μή με παντυχαίνη, μή με καρτερῆ.
Τί ἐμένα μὲ παντρέψαν δῶ στὴν Ἀρμενιά,
καὶ πῆρα Ἀρμενοπούλα, μάγισσας παιδί,
ὅπου μαγεύει τ' ἄστρη καὶ τὸν οὐρανό,

I KISSED a red lip and it dyed my own, and I wiped my lip on a hand-
kerchief and it dyed the handkerchief; and I washed it in the river and
the river was stained, and the edge of the shore and the middle of the
sea were painted red. The eagle flew down to drink water, and he dyed
his wings, and half the sun was painted and the whole moon.

MY black swallows from the desert, and my white doves of the beach,
you who are flying high above, heading for my homeland, I have an
apple-tree in my yard; alight there, and say to my love, my wife: she
may become a nun if she so wishes; she may marry again if that be her
wish; she may dye her clothes black, wear mourning, but she must not
wait for me, not expect me to return. For they have married me here in
Armenia, and I have taken for a wife a young Armenian girl, the
daughter of a witch. She casts a spell upon the stars and upon the sky;

μαγεύει τὰ πουλάκια καὶ δὲν ἀπετοῦν,
μαγεύει τὰ ποτάμια καὶ δὲν τρέχουνε,
τὴ θάλασσα μαγεύει καὶ δὲν κυματεῖ,
μαγεύει τὰ καράβια καὶ δὲν ἀρμενοῦν,
μαγεύει με κι ἐμένα καὶ δὲν ἔρχομαι.
Ὄντας κινάω γιὰ νὰ 'ρθω, χιόνια καὶ βροχές,
κι ὄντας γυρίζω πίσω, ἥλιος ξαστεριά.
Σελώνω τ' ἄλογό μου, ξεσελώνεται,
ζώνομαι τὸ σπαθί μου καὶ ξεζώνεται,
πιάνω γραφὴ νὰ γράψω καὶ ξεγράφεται.

260. *Love and Friendship are Transitory*

Ἀλησμονιόνται κι οἱ φιλιές, ξεχνιόνται κι οἱ ἀγάπες,
στὸ δρόμον ἀνταμώνονται σὰν ξένοι, σὰ διαβάτες.

261. *A Lullaby*

Κοιμήσου ἀστρί, κοιμήσου αὐγή, κοιμήσου νιὸ φεγγάρι,
κοιμήσου ποὺ νὰ σὲ χαρῆ ὁ νιὸς ποὺ θὰ σε πάρη.
Κοιμήσου ποὺ παράγγειλα στὴν Πόλη τὰ χρυσά σου,
στὴ Βενετιὰ τὰ ροῦχα σου καὶ τὰ διαμαντικά σου.

she casts a spell upon the little birds and they fly no more; she casts a spell upon the rivers and they flow no more; she casts a spell upon the sea and there are no more waves; she casts a spell upon the ships and they cannot sail; she casts a spell upon me, and I can return no more. Whenever I set out to come back home, there is snow and rain; but when I return to her there is sunshine and starlight in the sky. I saddle my horse, and the saddle is thrown off; I gird on my sword and it comes undone; I take ink to write, and it is washed away.

FRIENDS are forgotten, and lovers are forgotten; they meet in the street like strangers, like passers-by.

SLEEP little star, sleep dawn, sleep new moon; sleep, and may the young man who marries you delight in you. Sleep; I have ordered the golden vessel for your dowry in Constantinople, and in Venice your clothes and your jewellery. Sleep; for they are sewing your quilt in

Κοιμήσου, ποὺ σοῦ ῥάβουνε τὸ πάπλωμα στὴν Πόλη,
καὶ σοῦ το τελειώνουνε σαρανταδυὸ μαστόροι·
στὴ μέση βάνουν τὸν ἀετό, στὴν ἄκρη τὸ παγόνι·
νάνι τοῦ ῥήγα τὸ παιδί, τοῦ βασιλιᾶ τ' ἀγγόνι.
Κοιμήσου καὶ παράγγειλα παπούτσια στὸν τσαγγάρη,
νὰ σοῦ τὰ κάνη κόκκινα μὲ τὸ μαργαριτάρι.
Κοιμήσου μὲς στὴν κούνια σου καὶ στὰ παχιὰ πανιά σου,
ἡ Παναγιὰ ἡ δέσποινα νὰ εἶναι συντροφιά σου.

262. The Maiden in the Underworld

Καλὰ τό 'χουνε τὰ βουνά, καλόμοιρ' εἶν' οἱ κάμποι,
ποὺ Χάρο δὲν παντέχουνε, Χάρο δὲν καρτεροῦνε,
τὸ καλοκαίρι πρόβατα καὶ τὸ χειμώνα χιόνια.

Τρεῖς ἀντρειωμένοι βούλονται νὰ βγοῦν ἀπὸ τὸν Ἄδη.
Ὁ ἕνας νὰ βγῆ τὴν ἄνοιξη, κι ὁ ἄλλος τὸ καλοκαίρι,
κι ὁ τρίτος τὸ χινόπωρο, ὁπού εἶναι τὰ σταφύλια.
Μιὰ κόρη τοὺς παρακαλεῖ, τὰ χέρια σταυρωμένα·
«Γιὰ πᾶρτε με, λεβέντες μου, γιὰ τὸν ἀπάνου κόσμο.»
«Δὲν ἠμποροῦμε, λυγερή, δὲν ἠμποροῦμε, κόρη.
Βροντομαχοῦν τὰ ροῦχα σου κι ἀστράφτουν τὰ μαλλιά σου,

Constantinople and forty-two craftsmen are putting on the final touches; in the middle they set an eagle and at the end a peacock. Sleep, royal child, grandchild of a king. Sleep, I have ordered your shoes; the shoemaker will make them purple with pearls. Sleep in your cradle, in your thick soft covers, and may the Virgin, our Lady, be with you.

How lucky the mountains are, how lucky the plains that they never expect Death, never wait for him to come, but in summer expect the sheep, and in winter the snow.

Three fine men wanted to escape from Hades: one to escape in spring, another in summer, the third in autumn, when the grapes are ripe. A young girl, her arms crossed over her breast, besought them. 'My fine young men, take me with you on your journey to the upper world.' 'Young slender girl, we cannot. Your clothes rustle loudly and your hair flashes like lightning; your cork-soled shoes make a noise

χτυπάει τὸ φελλοκάλιγο καὶ μᾶς ἀκούει ὁ Χάρος.〉
〈 Μὰ γὼ τὰ ροῦχα βγάνω τα καὶ δένω τὰ μαλλιά μου,
κι αὐτὸ τὸ φελλοκάλιγο μὲς στὴ φωτιὰ τὸ ρίχνω.
Πᾶρτε με, ἀντρειωμένοι μου, νὰ βγῶ στὸν πάνω κόσμο,
νὰ πάω νὰ ἰδῶ τὴ μάνα μου πῶς χλίβεται γιὰ μένα.〉
〈 Κόρη μου, ἐσένα ἡ μάνα σου στὴ ρούγα κουβεντιάζει.〉
〈 Νὰ ἰδῶ καὶ τὸν πατέρα μου πῶς χλίβεται γιὰ μένα.〉
〈 Κόρη μου, κι ὁ πατέρας σου στὸ καπελιὸ εἶν' καὶ πίνει.〉
〈 Νὰ πάω νὰ ἰδῶ τ' ἀδέρφια μου πῶς χλίβονται γιὰ μένα.〉
〈 Κόρη μου, ἐσέν' τ' ἀδέρφια σου ρίχτουνε τὸ λιθάρι.〉
〈 Νὰ ἰδῶ καὶ τὰ ξαδέρφια μου πῶς χλίβονται γιὰ μένα.〉
〈 Κόρη μου, τὰ ξαδέρφια σου μὲς στὸ χορὸ χορεύουν.〉

263. The Ship of Death

῎Ενα καράβι στὸ γιαλὸ λεβέντες φορτωμένο,
στὴν πρύμη κάθοντ' οἱ ἄρρωστοι, στὴν πλώρ' οἱ λαβωμένοι,
καταμεσὶς τοῦ καραβιοῦ οἱ θαλασσοπνιγμένοι.
Ντελάλης τὸ διαλάλησε, κι ὁλοῦθε τὸ ἀγρικῆσαν·
〈 Μανάδες, ποὺ ἔχετε παιδιά, γυναῖκες, ποὺ ἔχετ' ἄντρες,
καὶ σεῖς θλιμμένες ἀδερφὲς πουλιόνται οἱ ἀδερφοί σας.〉
Τρέξαν οἱ μάνες μὲ φλουριὰ κι οἱ ἀδερφὲς μὲ γρόσια,
τρέξανε κι οἱ μαυρόχηρες τὰ δῶρα φορτωμένες,

and Death will hear us.' 'But I can take off my clothes, and tie up my hair, and throw those shoes in the fire. Take me with you, my brave young men, to reach the upper world, to see my mother who mourns for me.' 'My girl, your mother is gossiping in the street.' 'To see my father, who mourns for me.' 'My girl, your father is in the tavern, drinking.' 'To see my brothers who mourn for me.' 'My girl, your brothers are playing quoits.' 'To see my cousins who mourn for me.' 'Your cousins, my girl, have joined the dance.'

A SHIP near the shore was full of young men; on the stern sat the sick, on the prow the wounded, and in the middle of the ship those drowned in the sea. A crier cried out, and all around they heard him: 'Mothers, who have children, wives who have husbands, and you sad sisters, your brothers are for sale.' The mothers ran bringing gold coins, the sisters bringing silver, and the black-clad widows ran laden with gifts; but

μὰ ὅσο νὰ φτάσουν στὸ γιαλὸ μίσεψε τὸ καράβι.
Παίρνουν μανάδες τὰ βουνὰ κι οἱ ἀδερφὲς τοὺς κάμπους,
κι οἱ χῆρες οἱ μαυρόχηρες τὴ μέση τοῦ πελάγου.

264. The Passing of Death

Γιατὶ εἶναι μαῦρα τὰ βουνὰ καὶ στέκουν βουρκωμένα;
μὴν ἄνεμος τὰ πολεμᾶ, μήνα βροχὴ τὰ δέρνει;
Κι οὐδ' ἄνεμος τὰ πολεμᾶ κι οὐδὲ βροχὴ τὰ δέρνει,
μόνε διαβαίνει ὁ Χάροντας μὲ τοὺς ἀποθαμένους.
Σέρνει τοὺς νιοὺς ἀπὸ μπροστά, τοὺς γέροντες κατόπι,
τὰ τρυφερὰ παιδόπουλα στὴ σέλα ἀραδιασμένα.
Παρακαλοῦν οἱ γέροντες, κι οἱ νέοι γονατίζουν,
καὶ τὰ μικρὰ παιδόπουλα τὰ χέρια σταυρωμένα·
‹Χάρε μου, διάβ' ἀπὸ χωριό, κάτσε σὲ κρύα βρύση,
νὰ πιοῦν οἱ γέροντες νερό, κι οἱ νιοὶ νὰ λιθαρίσουν,
καὶ τὰ μικρὰ παιδόπουλα λουλούδια νὰ μαζώξουν.›
‹Ἀνὶ διαβῶν ἀπὸ χωριό, ἂν ἀπὸ κρύα βρύση,
ἔρχονται οἱ μάνες γιὰ νερό, γνωρίζουν τὰ παιδιά τους,
γνωρίζονται τ' ἀντρόγενα καὶ χωρισμὸ δὲν ἔχουν.›

before they reached the shore the ship had left. The mothers took to
the mountains, the sisters to the plains and the widows, the miserable
widows, to the middle of the sea.

WHY are the mountains black? Why do they stand covered in cloud?
Is the wind fighting with them? Is the rain beating on them? Neither
does the wind fight with them, nor does the rain beat upon them; it is
Death who strides across them carrying away the dead. He drags the
young in front of him, the old people behind, and the little tender
children he carries in a row in his saddle. The old implore him, the
young kneel before him, and the little children, with crossed arms, cry:
'Death, pass through a village, stop at a cool fountain for the old
to drink water, the young to play quoits, and the little children to
gather flowers.' 'Should I go past a village, or by a cool fountain, the
mothers come to fetch water and they will recognize their children;
husbands and wives will recognize one another and it is hard to part
them.'

265. The Battle of the Mountains

Ὁ Ὄλυμπος κι ὁ Κίσαβος, τὰ δυὸ βουνὰ μαλώνουν,
τὸ ποιὸ νὰ ῥίξῃ τὴ βροχή, τὸ ποιὸ νὰ ῥίξῃ χιόνι.
Ὁ Κίσαβος ῥίχνει βροχὴ κι ὁ Ὄλυμπος τὸ χιόνι.
Γυρίζει τότ᾽ ὁ Ὄλυμπος καὶ λέγει τοῦ Κισάβου·
« Μὴ μὲ μαλώνῃς, Κίσαβε, μπρὲ τουρκοπατημένε,
ποὺ σὲ πατάει ἡ Κονιαριὰ κι οἱ Λαρσινοὶ ἀγάδες.
Ἐγὼ εἶμ᾽ ὁ γέρος Ὄλυμπος στὸν κόσμο ξακουσμένος,
ἔχω σαράντα δυὸ κορφὲς κι ἐξήντα δυὸ βρυσοῦλες,
κάθε κορφὴ καὶ φλάμπουρο, κάθε κλαδὶ καὶ κλέφτης.
Κι ὅταν τὸ παίρν᾽ ἡ ἄνοιξη κι ἀνοίγουν τὰ κλαδάκια,
γεμίζουν τὰ βουνὰ κλεφτιὰ καὶ τὰ λαγκάδια σκλάβους.
Ἔχω καὶ τὸ χρυσὸν ἀϊτό, τὸ χρυσοπλουμισμένο,
πάνω στὴν πέτρα κάθεται καὶ μὲ τὸν ἥλιο λέγει·
« ἥλιε μ᾽, δὲν κροῦς τ᾽ ἀποταχύ, μόν᾽ κροῦς τὸ μεσημέρι,
νὰ ζεσταθοῦν τὰ νύχια μου, τὰ νυχοπόδαρά μου; »»

OLYMPUS and Kisavos, the two mountains, are quarrelling: which of them is to pour down rain and which to send snow. Kisavos pours rain and Olympus sends snow; Olympus then turns to Kisavos and says to him: 'Do not abuse me, Kisavos. You are under the heel of the Turks, you are trampled by the hordes from Iconium, the lords of Larisa. I am ancient Olympus, famous throughout the world; I have forty-two peaks and sixty-two sweet springs. On every peak a flag flies; behind each branch stands a klepht.* When spring comes and the young branches bloom, the mountains fill with klephts, but the valleys are filled with slaves. And mine is the golden eagle, the bird of golden plumage; he sits upon a rock and cries out to the sun: "My sun, your shafts do not hit me at dawn: they only reach me at noon, to warm my claws, to warm my taloned feet."'

*Guerrilla brigand.

266. Kolokotronis' Band

Λάμπουν τὰ χιόνια στὰ βουνὰ κι ὁ ἥλιος στὰ λαγκάδια,
λάμπουν καὶ τ' ἀλαφρὰ σπαθιὰ τῶν Κολοκοτρωναίων,
πόχουν τ' ἀσήμια τὰ πολλά, τὶς ἀσημένιες πάλες,
τὶς πέντε ἀράδες τὰ κουμπιά, τὶς ἕξι τὰ τσαπράζια,
ὁπού δὲν καταδέχονται τὴ γῆς νὰ τὴν πατήσουν.
Καβάλα τρῶνε τὸ ψωμί, καβάλα πολεμᾶνε,
καβάλα πᾶν στὴν ἐκκλησιά, καβάλα προσκυνᾶνε,
καβάλα παίρν' ἀντίδερο ἀπ' τοῦ παπᾶ τὸ χέρι.
Φλωριὰ ρίχνουν στὴν Παναγιά, φλωριὰ ρίχνουν στοὺς ἅγιους,
καὶ στὸν ἀφέντη τὸ Χριστὸ τὶς ἀσημένιες πάλες.
‹Χριστέ μας, βλόγα τὰ σπαθιά, βλόγα μας καὶ τὰ χέρια.›
Κι ὁ Θοδωράκης μίλησε, κι ὁ Θοδωράκης λέει·
‹τοῦτ' οἱ χαρὲς ποὺ κάνουμε σὲ λύπη θὰ μᾶς βγάλουν.
'Απόψ' εἶδα στὸν ὕπνο μου, στὴν ὑπνοφαντασιά μου,
θολὸ ποτάμι πέρναγα καὶ πέρα δὲν ἐβγῆκα.
'Ελᾶτε νὰ σκορπίσουμε, μπουλούκια νὰ γενοῦμε.
Σύρε, Γιῶργο μ', στὸν τόπο σου, Νικήτα, στὸ Λοντάρι·
ἐγὼ πάου στὴν Καρύταινα, πάου στοὺς ἐδικούς μου,
ν' ἀφήκω τὴ διαθήκη μου καὶ τὶς παραγγολές μου,
τὶ θὰ περάσω θάλασσα, στὴ Ζάκυνθο θὰ πάω.›

SNOW flashes on the hills, sunshine in the valleys, and the swift swords of the men of Kolokotronis flash. They have much silver, and bullets made of silver; they wear five rows of [silver] buttons, and six of silver decorations, they never deign to tread the earth. Mounted upon their horses they eat their food, mounted they fight, mounted they go to church; mounted they worship, and mounted they take the holy bread from the priest's hand. They offer gold coins to our Lady, gold coins to the saints, and to Christ, our Lord, silver bullets. 'Christ bless our swords, and bless our hands.' And Theodore spoke, and Theodore said: 'This feast we hold will lead to sorrow. Last night I saw in my sleep, in my dream, that I was trying to cross a muddy stream and did not get across. Come, let us disperse, let us break into different bands. George, you go to your homeland, and you, Niketas, to Leontari; I am going to Karytena, to my people, to make my will and give my orders, for I shall cross the sea and go to Zante.'

? VIZENTZOS CORNAROS

16th–17th century

267. The Sacrifice of Abraham

ΣΑΡΡΑ, ΑΒΡΑΑΜ

Σα. Δὲν ἔχω πλιό μου νάκαρα, ἡ δύναμή μου χάθη,
ἐτοῦτο φέρνουν οἱ καημοί, τῶν σωθικῶν τὰ πάθη·
δὲν ἔχω πόδια νὰ σταθῶ, ζαλίζομαι νὰ πέσω,
δὲν ἔχω νοῦ νὰ δέωμαι καὶ νὰ παρακαλέσω.

Αβ. Ἠγαπημένη μου γυνή, μὴν κάνης σὰν κοπέλι·
τοῦτο ποὺ θὲ νὰ πάθωμεν ἀφέντης μας τὸ θέλει.
Σίμωσε, κάτσε μετὰ μέ, μὴν κλαίγης, μὴ θρηνᾶσαι,
μὲ κλάηματα καὶ μὲ δαρμούς, καημένη, δὲ φελᾶσαι·
τὸ τέκνον ποὺ ἐκάμαμεν δὲν εἶν' δική μας χάρη,
ὁ πλάστης μᾶς τὸ χάρισε, τώρα θὲ νὰ τὸ πάρη.
Τί θέλεις, ὦ βαριόμοιρη, νὰ κλαίγης, νὰ θρηνᾶσαι,
καὶ τυραννᾶς με, τὸν πτωχόν, καὶ σὺ δὲν ὠφελᾶσαι;
Δὲν εἶν' καιρος γιὰ κλάηματα, Σάρρα μου θυγατέρα,
εἶναι καιρὸς παρηγοριᾶς, ἀπομονῆς ἡμέρα.

Σα. Ὄφου μυστήριον φρικτόν! ὄφου καημὸς καὶ πάθος,
ὅταν μοῦ ποῦσι, τέκνον μου, τὸ πῶς ἐγίνης ἄθος.

SARAH: I have no strength left; all my vigour has gone. That is what sorrow brings, the suffering of the heart. My legs do not hold me, I feel as if I were going to faint to the ground. I have no mind to pray to God and to supplicate him.

ABRAHAM: My dear wife, do not behave like a child; what we must suffer is the will of the Lord. Come close, sit next to me, do not weep or lament. Weeping and beating your breast, poor wife, will not help you. The child we had was not a favour we did to ourselves: the Creator gave it as a gift to us and now he will take it back. Why cry, unlucky woman, why lament? You only torture me, and you reap no advantage. This is no time for lamentation, Sarah my daughter: it is a time for consolation, a day of patience.

SARAH: Oh, what a fearful mystery; what suffering, what woe, when they tell me, my child, that you have turned into a flower. Alas, how

Ὄφου! μὲ ποιὰν ἀποκοτιὰν νὰ δυνηθῆς νὰ σφάξῃς
τέτοιο κορμὶ ἀκριμάτιστον καὶ νὰ μηδὲν τρομάξῃς;
Θέλεις το νὰ σκοτεινιαστοῦν τὰ μάτια σου, τὸ φῶς σου,
καὶ νὰ νεκρώσῃ τὸ παιδί, νὰ ξεψυχῆσ' ὀμπρός σου;
Μὲ ποιᾶς καρδιᾶς ἀπομονὴ ν' ἀκούσῃς τῆ φωνήν του,
ὅταν ταράξῃ ὡσὰν ἀρνὶ ὀμπρός σου τὸ κορμίν του;
Ὄφου, παιδί τσ' ὑπακοῆς, ποὺ μέλλεις νὰ στρατέψῃς;
σ' ποιὸν τόπον σὲ καλέσασι νὰ πᾶς νὰ ταξιδέψῃς;
Καὶ πότες νὰ σὲ καρτερῆ ὁ κύρης κι ἡ μητέρα,
ποιὰν ἑβδομάδα, ποιὸν καιρό, ποιὸ μῆνα, ποιὰν ἡμέρα;
Ὄφου τὰ φύλλα τσῆ καρδιᾶς καὶ πῶς νὰ μὴν τρομάσσου,
ὅταν εἰς ἀλλουνοῦ παιδιοῦ γρικήσω τ' ὄνομά σου;
Τέκνο μου, πῶς νὰ δυνηθῶ τὴν ἀποχώρισή σου,
πῶς νὰ γρικήσω ἄλλου φωνή, ὄχι τὴν ἐδική σου;
Τέκνο μου, καὶ γιατ' ἤθελες νὰ λείψῃς ἀπὸ μένα,
ἐγίνης τόσα φρόνιμο παρὰ παιδὶ κανένα;
Τάσσω σου, ὑγιέ μου, τὸν καιρὸ ποὺ θέλω ἀκόμη ζήσει,
νὰ μὴν ἀφήσω κοπελιοῦ γλώσσα νὰ μοῦ μιλήσῃ,
καὶ νὰ θωροῦν τὰ μάτια μου πάντα τσῆ γῆς τὸν πάτο,
καὶ νὰ θυμοῦμαι πάντοτε τὸ σημερνὸ μαντάτο.

Αβ. Σάρρα, μὴ δίδῃς πλιὰ καημὸν καὶ πάθη στὴν καρδιά μου,
καὶ κάμῃς με ἀνυπόληφτον δοῦλον στὰ γερατιά μου·

will you have the heart to kill that sinless body? Will not horror
seize you? Do you wish to see the light of your eyes, your very eye-
sight, go dark? To see the child expire and die in your presence?
How will your heart have the strength to hear his voice when like a
lamb his body writhes before you? Alas, obedient child, what has this
journey in store for you? To what place do they bid you travel?
When can your father and your mother expect you to return?
What week, what time, what month, what day? Ah, how will my
heart, the depths of my heart, have the strength not to tremble when
I hear another child called by your name? My child, how will I
suffer to be separated from you, how will I hear another's voice, and
not your own? My child, was it because you were to be taken away
from me that you became so much more obedient than any other
child? I promise you, my son, not to let another boy speak to me as
long as I live, and always to keep my eyes turned to the ground and
ever to remember the message of this day.

ABRAHAM: Sarah, add no more pain and suffering to my heart; do not
turn me into a dishonoured slave in my old age. Do not frighten me

μὴ μοῦ δειλιᾶς τὴν ὄρεξη, νὰ μὴ γιαγείρω ὀπίσω
καὶ πιάσω ἄρμα καὶ σφαγῶ καὶ κακοθανατίσω·
τὸ λογισμὸ συνήφερε, τὰ σφάλματά σου φτιάσε,
καὶ δὲν ἀρέσουν τοῦ θεοῦ ἐτοῦτα ποὺ δηγᾶσαι.
Καὶ τίνος ἀντιστένεσαι, κλαίγεις καὶ δὲν ἀρνεύγεις,
καὶ τοῦ θεοῦ τοὺς ὁρισμοὺς κάθεσαι καὶ γυρεύγεις;
Τὸ τέκνο μας καὶ τὸ κορμί, ψυχὴ καὶ τὰ καλά μας,
ὅλα 'ν' τοῦ πλάστη μας θεοῦ, δὲν εἶναι ἐδικά μας.
Μόνο νὰ πέψ' ἡ χάρη του, σὰν πά 'στὸ πρόσωπό του,
τούτη ἡ θυσία ποὺ μελετῶ, νὰ πάψη τὸ θυμό του·
δὲ θέλω πλιὸ νὰ καρτερῶ, δὲ θέλω ν' ἀνιμένω,
πά' νὰ ξυπνήσω τὸ παιδί, νὰ σηκωθῆ νὰ πηαίνω.
Σα. Ἐννιὰ μῆνες σ' ἐβάσταξα, τέκνο μου, κανακάρη,
σ' τοῦτο τὸ κακορίζικο καὶ σκοτεινὸ κουφάρι·
τρεῖς χρόνους, γιέ μου, σοῦ 'διδα τὸ γάλα τῶ βυζιῶ μου,
καὶ σύ 'σουνε τὰ μάτια μου, καὶ σύ 'σουνε τὸ φῶς μου.
Ἐθώρουν κι ἐμεγάλωνες ὡσὰ δεντροῦ κλωνάρι,
κι ἐπλήθαινες στὴν ἀρετή, στὴ γνώμη, κι εἰς τὴ χάρη·
καὶ τώρα πέ μου ποιὰ χαρὰ βούλεσαι νὰ μοῦ δώσης;
ὡσὰν βροντή, σὰν ἀστραπή, θὲ νὰ χαθῆς νὰ λιώσης.
Κι ἐγὼ πῶς εἶναι μπορετὸ δίχως σου πλιὸ νὰ ζήσω;

away from my purpose lest I turn back, seize a weapon, and kill my-
self and so find an evil end. Collect your wits, correct your mis-
takes; what you say is not pleasing to God. Whom do you think
you are fighting? Why this ceaseless weeping? Why do you ques-
tion the will of God? Our child, our bodies, our souls, and our for-
tune all belong to God the Creator; they are not our own. May he
only send his grace when this sacrifice I am going to offer comes
before him; may he stay his anger. I do not wish to wait any longer,
I will linger no more; I will go and wake up the child, rouse him, and
set out.

SARAH: Nine months I bore you, my dearest child, in this unlucky
black-fated body of mine. For three years, my son, I gave you the milk
of my breasts, and you were my eyes, my very eyesight. I watched
you grow like the young branch of a tree, and your virtue grew with
you and your wisdom and grace. And now, tell me, what is this joy
you are about to give me? You will vanish, melt away, like a peal of
thunder, like lightning. And how will it be possible for me to live

ποιὸ θάρρος ἔχω, ποιὰ δροσιὰ στὰ γέρα μου τὰ πίσω;
Πόση χαρὰ τ' ἀντρόγυνον ἐπήραμεν ἀντάμι,
ὄντα μᾶς εἶπεν ὁ θεὸς τὸ πῶς σὲ θέλω κάμει!
Καημένο σπίτι τ' Ἀβραάμ, πόσες χαρὲς ἐξώθης,
παιδάκι μ' ὄντας ἔπεσες στὴ γῆ κι ἐφανερώθης!
Πῶς ἐγυρίσαν οἱ χαρὲς σὲ θλίψες μιὰν ἡμέρα;
πῶς ἐσκορπίσαν τὰ καλὰ σὰ νέφη στὸν ἀέρα;

Αβ. Μὴ τὰ λογιάζωμεν αὐτά, μέλλει του ν' ἀποθάνη,
οὐδ' ὄφελος, οὐδὲ καλὸ τὸ κλάημα σου τοῦ κάνει,
μόνο βαραίνεις τὸ θεό, καὶ χάρη δὲ μᾶς ἔχει
εἰς τὴ θυσία, τὴν κάνομε, γιατὶ ὅλα τὰ κατέχει.
Ζύγωξε τσὶ ἀναστενασμούς, ζύγωξε καὶ τὴν πρίκα,
τὸν πλάστην εὐχαρίστησε εἰς ὅ τι μᾶς εὑρῆκα.

Σα. Ἄγωμε, νοικοκύρη μου, 'πειδὴ θεὸς τὸ θέλει,
ἄμε, καὶ νά 'ν' ἡ στράτα σας γάλα, δροσὲς καὶ μέλι·
ἄμε, ποὺ νὰ σὲ λυπηθῇ ὁ θεὸς νά σ' ἀπακούση,
γλυκιὰ φωνὴ εἰς τὸ βουνὶ σήμερο νὰ σοῦ ποῦσι.
Καὶ ἂς τάξω δὲν τὸ γέννησα, μηδ' εἶδα το ποτέ μου,
μά 'ναν κερὶν ἀφτούμενο ἐκράτουν κι ἤσβησέ μου.

Αβ. Κάμε καὶ μὴ πικραίνεσαι, σπούδαξε νὰ τὸ ντύσης,
καὶ φίλησε τὰ χείλη του, νά τ' ἀποχαιρετήσης·

without you? What courage, what pleasure is left for me when old age comes? What joy we both felt when God told us that I would give birth to you. Poor house of Abraham, what joy was given you when you, my child, appeared in the world. How did joy turn to sorrow within one day? How did all blessings vanish in the air like a cloud?

ABRAHAM: Let us not think about this; he is doomed to die and your weeping does not do him any good or help him at all. You only anger God and he will not be thankful for our sacrifice: for he knows everything. Banish your sighs and your bitterness and thank the Creator for what has been given us.

SARAH: Come then, my master, since it is the will of God. Go, and may your journey be milk, dew, and honey. Go, and may God take pity on you and hear you, and may they give you a sweet message today upon the hill. And let me say that I never gave him birth, that I never saw him, but that I held in my hands a burning candle, and it was put out.

ABRAHAM: Hasten, and stop worrying, hasten to dress him and kiss him on the lips to bid him farewell. Prepare him quickly, dress

ὀρδίνιασέ το γλήγορα, ντύσε το νὰ κινήση,
κι ἐκεῖνος ὁπού τ' ὅρισε νὰ σὲ παρηγορήση.

Σα. Ἐπὰ τὸ φῶς ὁπού 'βλεπα, ἐπὰ ἡ γλυκιά μου ζήση,
τὰ μάτια, τὰ δὲν ὅρισεν ὁ πλάστης νά μ' ἀφήση·
ἐπὰ 'ν' ἀφτούμενον κερί, πού μελετᾶς νὰ σβήσης,
καὶ τὸ κορμὶ ὁπού ζητᾶς νὰ κακοθανατίσης·
ὡσὰν ἀρνάκι κείτεται, κι ὡσὰν πουλὶ κοιμᾶται,
κι εἰς τοῦ κυροῦ τὴν ἀπονιὰ πολλὰ παραπονᾶται.
Θωρεῖς τὸ τέκνο τὸ γλυκύ, τὸ τέκνο τὸ καημένο,
τὸ πῶς ἐδᾶ παρὰ ποτὲ εἶν' ἀποχλωμνιασμένο;
Ἰδὲ τὴν ταπεινότητα, ἰδὲ τὸ πρόσωπό του,
πῶς φαίνεταί σου καὶ γρικᾶ καὶ βλέπει τὸ σφαμό του.
Παιδάκι μου, καὶ νὰ θωρῆς ὄνειρο πρικαμένο;
γιὰ κεῖνο κείτεσαι κλιτὸ καὶ παραπονεμένο;
Ὁλόχαρον ἐψὲς ἀργὰ σ' ἥθεκα, καλογιέ μου,
καὶ μὲ χαιράμενην καρδιὰ ἥμουν παρὰ ποτέ μου·
ἥστεκα κι ἐκαμάρωνα τοῦ ὕπνου σου τὴ ζάλη
κι ἐρέγουμου νὰ σὲ θωρῶ, κι εἶχα χαρὰ μεγάλη.
Ἐποκοιμούσουν, τέκνο μου, παίζοντας μετὰ μένα,
σ' πολλὴ χαρὰ εὑρίσκουμου παρ' ἄνθρωπο κανένα·
καὶ τώρα ποιά 'ν' ἡ ἀφορμὴ καὶ θέλεις νά μ' ἀφήσης
ὁλότυφλη καὶ σκοτεινή, τοῦ πόνου καὶ τσῆ κρίσης;

Αβ. Μὴ θέλης μὲ τὸ κλάημα σου νὰ τοῦ ξεφανερώσης

him up to start the journey, and may he who ordained this console you.

SARAH: This is the light I looked upon, this was my sweet life, the eyes the Creator was unwilling to spare for me. This is the lighted candle you are preparing to darken, the body you wish cruelly to destroy. He lies like a lamb, he sleeps like a bird, and complains bitterly about his father's cruelty. You see the sweet child, the poor child, how pale he looks, now more than ever. Look at his meekness, look at his face: it is as if he hears and sees his slaughter. My sweet child, is it a bitter dream that you see? Is that why you are lying hunched up and full of complaint? Late last night I put you to sleep brimming with joy, my dear son, and my heart was lighter than ever. I stood over you admiring the drift of your sleep, and I took delight in watching you; I was full of joy. You fell asleep, my child, playing with me, and I was happier than anyone. Why is it that you are now going to leave me blind, in darkness, full of suffering and torment?

ABRAHAM: Your tears must not show him so dreadful a secret: it will

τέτοιο μυστήριο φοβερό καὶ νὰ τὸ θανατώσης·
μὰ σιγανά το ξύπνησε, τὸ κλάημα σκόλασέ το
μὲ τὰ κανάκια ντύσε το κι ἀποχαιρέτισέ το.

Σα. Ποιὸ πρόσωπο καὶ ποιά καρδιὰ νὰ δυνηθῆ νὰ χώση
τέτοιο μυστήριο φρικτό, νὰ μὴν τὸ φανερώση;
Ξύπνησε, κανακάρικο καὶ ἀκριβαναθρεμμένο,
νὰ πᾶς εἰς τὴν ξεφάντωση, πού σ᾽ ἔχουν καλεσμένο.
Ντύσου, νὰ βάλης σκολινά, ῥοῦχα τοῦ μισεμοῦ σου,
καὶ ν᾽ ἀκλουθᾶς τοῦ Χάρου σου, ἀμ᾽ ὄχι τοῦ κυροῦ σου.
Τέκνο τοῦ θελημάτου μου, πού νὰ ᾽χης τὴν εὐκή μου,
ὁ θάνατός σου φέρνει μου εἰς τέλος τὴ ζωή μου·
ἡ εὐκή τσ᾽ εὐκῆς μου, καλογιέ, εἰς τὰ στρατέματά σου,
καὶ νά ᾽ν᾽ ὀμπρὸς καὶ ὀπίσω σου κι εἰς τὰ ποδόζαλά σου.

Αβ. Σώπα, μὴν κλαίγης, μὴ μιλῆς, Σάρρα, παρακαλῶ σε,
κι ἄγωμε, μίσεψ᾽ ἀπὸ δῶ, καὶ τόπο μας ἐδῶσε.
Μὴ τὸ ξυπνήσης τὸ παιδὶ μὲ πικραμένα λόγια,
μὰ κάμε σιδερὴν καρδιὰ κι ἄφης τὰ μοιρολόγια.

Σα. Σωπαίνω, καὶ ἄφης με, ᾽Αβραάμ, κι ἐγὼ νὰ τὸ ξυπνήσω,
νὰ τὸ στολίσω τὸ φτωχό, καὶ νά τ᾽ ὀμορφοντύσω.
Κάλεσμα τό ᾽χου σήμερο καὶ γάμον εἰς τὸν ᾽Αδη,
κι ἄφης νὰ καταρδινιαστῆ, νὰ μὴ τοῦ βροῦν ψεγάδι.

kill him. Wake him up gently; stop crying, dress him with tender-
ness and bid him farewell.

SARAH: What face, what heart can conceal such a dreadful secret and
not reveal it? Wake up, my darling, my child, so carefully brought
up: go to the feast where you are invited. Dress, put on your best
clothes, the clothes for your departure: follow your Death and not
your father. My child. you have always obeyed me: take my bless-
ing. Your death brings my life to its end. My good son, my full
blessing be with you on your journey, before you and behind you,
leading your footsteps.

ABRAHAM: Hush, do not weep, do not speak, Sarah, I beg you. Let us
go: leave, make room for us. Do not wake the child with such bitter
words: steel your heart and leave off your lamenting.

SARAH: I will be silent, Abraham; let me wake him up and dress him
properly, the poor boy, and make him look as beautiful as possible.
Today he is invited to a wedding in Hades: let him be beautifully
dressed, so that no one can find fault with him.

487

GEORGE CHORTATZIS

fl. c. 1590

268. *The Nurse's Lament for Erophile*

NENA

'Οϊμένα, 'Ερωφίλη μου, κι ὀγιάντα δὲ μποροῦσι
τ' ἀμάτια μου τὰ σκοτεινὰ δυὸ βρύσες νὰ γενοῦσι,
νὰ σοῦ ξεπλύνου τὴν καρδιὰ τὴν καταματωμένη,
κι ὕστερα μὲ τὴ χέρα μου κι ἐγώ, καθὼς τυχαίνει,
τὴν ἐδική μ' ἀλύπητα κι ἄπονα νὰ πληγώσω,
κι ὡσὰν ἐσένα θάνατο κακὸ κι ἐγὼ νὰ δώσω!
'Οϊμένα, 'Ερωφίλη μου, καὶ πῶς νὰ κατεβοῦσι
στὸν "Αδη τόσες ὀμορφιὲς καὶ χῶμα νὰ γενοῦσι;
Πῶς νὰ μαδήσουν τὰ μαλλιὰ τὰ παραχρουσωμένα,
πῶς νὰ λυθοῦν τ' ἀμάτια σου στὴ γῆ τὰ ζαφειρένια;
Πῶς τ' ὀμορφό σου πρόσωπο κι ἡ μαραμαρένια χέρα
θροφὴ σκουλήκω νὰ γενῆ, χρουσή μου θυγατέρα;
'Οϊμένα, 'Ερωφίλη μου, τὸν "Αδη πῶς πλουταίνεις
μὲ το' ὀμορφιές σου τσὶ πολλὲς κι ὅλη τὴ γῆ φτωχαίνεις!
Τὸν ἥλιο ἀφήνεις δίχως σου σβηστὸ καὶ θαμπωμένο,
κι ὅλο τὸν κόσμο σκοτεινὸ καὶ παραπονεμένο.
Τσὶ χάρες ἐθανάτωσες καὶ μετὰ σέν' ὁμάδι
σήμερον, 'Ερωφίλη μου, το' ἐπῆρες εἰς τὸν "Αδη.

NENA: Alas, my Erophile, why cannot my darkened eyes become two springs and wash away the thick blood on your heart? And why cannot I, too, with my own hand, just as it is, strike my own heart mercilessly and insensibly and find a miserable death, as you did? Alas, my Erophile, how can such beauty go down to Hades, perish and turn to earth? How can your bright gold hair wither and your sapphire eyes vanish in dust? How can your lovely face, your marble hands, become the food of worms, my golden daughter? Alas, my Erophile, how rich you make Hades with your great beauty, how poor the earth. Without you the sun is left dim and dark, the whole world black and sad. You have today killed all the graces and taken them with you to Hades, my

'Οϊμένα ἡ βαριόμοιρη κι ἡ πολυπρικαμένη
  πῶς βρίσκομαι στὸ θάρρος σου σφαλτὴ καὶ κομπωμένη!
Στὴν κεφαλή σου ἐλόγιασα στεφάνι νὰ φιλήσω,
  κι ἐδᾶ σφαμένη σὲ θωρῶ καὶ τρέμω νὰ σοῦ 'γγίσω.
Παιδάκι σου ἐλογάριαζα τὰ χέρια μου νὰ πιάσου,
  νά τ' ἀναθρέψου σπλαχνικά, νὰ δῶ κλερονομιά σου,
κι ἐγὼ σὲ θάφτω σήμερο, κι ὁμάδι μετὰ σένα
  τὰ μέλη μ' ἐθανάτωσες τὰ πολυπρικαμένα.
Ὄφου, καὶ πῶς τὸ κόβγουσου, πῶς τό 'βανες στὸ νοῦ σου,
  πῶς τ' ὄνειρό σου τὸ πρικὺ σήμερον ἐφοβούσου!
Πῶς τό 'ξευρες, ἀφέντρα μου, κι ἀποχαιρέτισές με,
  καὶ σπλαχνικὰ στὸ πρόσωπο σὰ μάνα φιλησές με.
Μὰ νά 'ρθω τάσσω σου κι ἐγὼ στὸν Ἅδη μετὰ σένα,
  δούλη σου πάλι νά 'μ' ἐκεῖ κι ἀγαπημένη νένα,
σὰ θάψω τοῦ Πανάρετου τοῦτα τα λίγα μέλη
  μὲ τὸ κορμί σ', ἀφέντρα μου, καθὼς ἡ τύχη θέλει.

Erophile. Alas, how miserable I am, how overwhelmed with sorrow.
I have lost my support and been tricked out of it. I had hoped to kiss a
wedding crown upon your head, and now I see you dead and tremble
to touch you. I had hoped my hands would hold a child of yours and
bring it up with love, see a child that would be your heir; but today I
bury you. When you killed yourself you killed my sorrow-burdened
body too. Ah, how did it cross your mind, how did you know? How
you feared today your bitter dream! How you knew, my mistress, and
bade me good-bye, and kissed me tenderly on the cheek, as if I were
your mother. But I promise to come with you to Hades, to be there
again your servant, your dear nurse, when I have buried these few
limbs of Panaretos together with your body, my mistress, as Fate in-
tended.

VIZENTZOS CORNAROS

16th–17th century

269. The Terrible Caramanite

'Επρόβαλεν ὠσὰ θεριὸ ἕνας Καραμανίτης,
ὁπού 'χεν ὅχθριτα πολλὴ μὲ τὸ νησὶ τῆς Κρήτης.
῏Ητον ἀφέντης δυνατὸς καὶ πλούσιος καὶ μεγάλος,
σ' κεῖνα τὰ μέρη σὰν αὐτὸ δὲν ἐγεννήθη ἄλλος·
δὲν ἐπροσκύναν οὐρανό, ἄστρα μηδὲ σελήνη,
τὸν κόσμο ἐφοβέριζε μὲ τὴ θωριὰν ἐκείνη·
εἰς τὸ σπαθί του πίστευγε, κι ἐκεῖνον ἐπροσκύνα,
πάντα πολέμους κι ὅχθριτες πάντα μαλιὲς ἐκίνα.
῏Ητονε κακοσύβαστος καὶ δύσκολος περίσσα,
εἰς τὴ μαλιὰν ἐχαίρετο καὶ τὴν ἀγάπ' ἐμίσα.
Σπιδόλιοντας ἐκράζετο, κι ὡς ἦρθεν εἰς τὸ 'Ρήγα,
μὲ γρίνιες ἐχαιρέτισε καὶ μίλησε καὶ λίγα.
Ποτέ ντου δὲν ἐγέλασε, μὰ πάντα ντου λογιάζει,
κι εἶν ἡ λαλιάν του ἡ σιγανὴ σὰν ἄλλου ὀντὲ φωνιάζει·
μιλώντας ἐφοβέριζε, μὲ τὴ θωριάν του βλάφτει,
καὶ μιὰ πλεξούδα κρέμουντον εἰς τό 'να του ριζαύτι.
'Εκαβαλίκευγε ἕνα ζῶ ἀγριότατο περίσσα,
ὁπού τὸ φοβηθήκασι στὸ φόρο ὅσοι κι ἂν ἦσα·

LIKE a wild beast, a man from Caramania appeared; a man who felt
violent hate for the island of Crete. He was a powerful lord, rich and
great, and there was no one else like him in that part of the world. He
did not worship the sky, the stars, or the moon, but scared the world
with that look of his. He trusted in his sword and worshipped it, and
was always involved in wars, quarrels and enmities. He was difficult
to deal with, most difficult: he delighted in strife and hated friendship.
He was called Spidoliontas, and as he approached the king he saluted
him angrily and spoke but few words. He never laughed; he was always
deep in thought, and his voice when low was like another man's
screaming. He frightened you when he talked and his glance was
dangerous, and he had a plaited lock which hung down from the base of
his ear. He rode the wildest horse: everyone in the market-place was

ὁρά 'χε σὰν κατόπαρδος καὶ πόδια σὰ βουβάλι,
  καὶ μάτια σὰν ἀγριόκατος κι ἡ γλῶσσα ντου μεγάλη·
ἦτον ἡ τρίχα ντου ψαρὴ μπαλώματα γεμάτη
  κόκκινα, μαῦρα, μούρτζινα σ' ὅλον του τὸ δερμάτι.
Ἦτο λυγνὸ κι ἐλεύτερο, στὸ γλάκι δὲν τὸ σώνει,
  νά 'ν' κι ἀπὸ χέρα δυνατή, σαΐτα οὐδὲ βελτόνι·
συχνιά, συχνιά 'σερνε φωνές μὰ δὲ χιλμιντρίζει,
  ἀμ' εἶχεν ἄγρια τὴ φωνή, καὶ σὰ θεριὸ μουγκρίζει.
Ὡσὰν ἐγράφτη στοῦ Ρηγός, καὶ τ' ὄνομά ντου λέγει,
  γιὰ νὰ σταθῇ τόπο πολύ, μεγάλη ἀδειὰ γυρεύγει·
οἱ κάμποι δὲν τ' ἀρέσουσι, κι ὁ τόπος δὲν τὸν παίρνει,
  κι ἐπὰ κι ἐκεῖ μὲ τὸ φαρὶ συχνοπηαινογέρνει.
Εἶχεν κι ἀπάνω στ' ἄρματα βαλμένο 'να δερμάτι
  'νοὺς λεονταριοῦ, ποὺ σκότωσε στὰ δάση ποὺ πορπάτει,
κι ἐκρέμουνταν τοῦ λιονταριοῦ τὰ πόδια ὀμπρὸς στὰ στήθη,
  πολλά 'χε δυνατὴ καρδιὰ ποὺ δὲν τὸν ἐφοβήθη.
Συχνιὰ συχνιὰ τοῦ λιονταριοῦ τὰ πόδια ἔτσι σαλεῦγα,
  ποὺ φαίνετο πὼς ἄνθρωπο ν' ἁρπάξουν ἐγυρεῦγα.
Καὶ δίχως νὰ στραφῇ νὰ δῇ τσ' ἄλλους νὰ χαιρετίση,
  καὶ δίχως νὰ συγκατεβῇ ἀνθρώπου νὰ μιλήση,
ἐγρίνια πρὸς τὸν οὐρανό, ἐγρίνια στὸν ἀέρα,
  ἡ ὄψη ντου φανέρωνε τὰ κανε μὲ τὴ χέρα.

afraid of it. It had the tail of a leopard, and the legs of a buffalo, the eyes of a wild cat, and a long tongue. Its hair was grey and it had many patches – red, black, and purple – all over its skin. It was thin and free in its movements, and could jump farther than an arrow or a bowshot cast by a strong arm. Often, very often, it bellowed, but it did not neigh: it had a savage cry and roared like a wild beast. When he enrolled for the king's tournament and gave his name he looked for a wide space to stand in, a big open area. He did not like the plains; in fact the space was not wide enough for him, and all the time he paced up and down there with his horse. And over his armour he wore the skin of a lion he had killed in the forests he frequented. The lion's paws hung in front over his breast: whoever saw it and was not scared had to have a very stout heart. Often the paws of the lion moved as if they were searching for a man to seize. And without turning to look and salute the others, without deigning to speak to anyone he scowled at the sky and scowled at the wind: his face betrayed what his hands per-

Ἡ φορεσά ντου κι ἡ θωριά καὶ τὸ φαρὶν ὁμάδι
ἐδεῖχναν πὼς εἴν δαίμονας κι ἐβγῆκ' ἀπὸ τὸν Ἅδη.
Στὴν κεφαλή 'χε ὁλόμαυρο τὸ Χάρο μὲ δραπάνι,
καὶ μὲ τὸ αἷμα γράμματα κι ὄχι μὲ τὸ μελάνι,
κι ἐλέγα· ‹Ὅποιος μὲ θωρεῖ, ἄς τρέμη κι ἄς φοβᾶται,
καὶ τὸ σπαθὶ ὁπού βαστῶ κιανένα δὲ λυπᾶται.›

(Erotocritos)

270. The Power of Words

Κι ὁπού κατέχει νὰ μιλῆ μὲ γνώση καὶ μὲ τρόπο,
κάνει καὶ κλαίσιν καὶ γελοῦ τὰ μάτια τῶν ἀνθρώπω.

(Erotocritos)

271. The Parting of Arete and Erotocritos

Ἐμίλειε κείνη σ' μιὰ μερά, ἐμίλειε αὐτὸς στὴν ἄλλη,
μιὰ παίδα τοὺς ἐπαίδευγε, ἕνας καημός, μιὰ ζάλη.
Δὲν ἔχουν μπλιὸ κι οἱ δυὸ καιρὸ τὰ πάθη νὰ μιλοῦσι,
ἦρθεν ἡ ὥρα ἡ σκοτεινή, ποὺ θὲ νὰ χωριστοῦσι.

formed. His clothes, his looks, and his horse showed that he was a demon, that he had come from Hades. On his head he had a black figure of Death carrying a scythe, and letters, written with blood and not with ink, which said: 'Let the man who looks at me shudder and fear: for the sword I hold spares no one.'

WHOEVER knows how to speak with wisdom and with style makes the eyes of men weep and laugh.

SHE was speaking on one side [of the window], he on the other; the same suffering gripped them both, one pain, one storm. No longer had they time to speak of their misfortune; the dark moment came when they had to part. Lightning flashed in the east and thunder rolled in

Ἤστραψεν ἡ Ἀνατολὴ καὶ βρόντηξεν ἡ Δύση,
  ὅντε τὰ χείλη ντοῦ 'νοιξε γιὰ ν' ἀποχαιρετίση,
καὶ τὸ παλάτι σείστηκε 'κ τὸν πόνο ποὺ ἐγρίκα,
  ὅντε τὰ χέρια πιάσασι κι ἀποχαιρετιστῆκα.
Καὶ τίς μπορεῖ νὰ διηγηθῆ ὀγιὰ τὴν ὥρα κείνη,
  ἡ κόρη πῶς ἐπόμεινε, κι ἄγουρος πῶς ἐγίνη;
Δὲν ἔχου γλώσσα νὰ τὸ ποῦ, χείλη νὰ τὸ μιλήσου,
  καὶ μηδὲ μάτια νὰ τὸ δοῦ, κι αὐτιὰ νὰ τοῦ γρικήσου.
Ποῦρι ἥβιαζέν τους ὁ καιρός, καὶ σίμωνεν ἡ μέρα,
  κι ὁ γεῖς τ' ἄλλοῦ ντως σπλαχνικὰ ἐσφίξασι τὴ χέρα·
κι ἕνα μεγάλο θάμασμα στὸ παραθύρι γίνη,
  οἱ πέτρες καὶ τὰ σίδερα κλαίσι τὴν ὥρα κείνη,
κι ἐπέφταν οἱ σταλαματιὲς τσῆ πέτρας, τοῦ σιδέρου,
  κι ἡ Ἀρετούσα τσ' ηὗρεν κεῖ, κι ἦσαν αἷμα ταχυτέρου.
Ἐμίσεψ' ὁ Ρωτόκριτος, καὶ βιάζει τον ἡ ὥρα
  μ' ἕναν πρικὺ ἀναστεναμό, ποὺ σείστηκεν ἡ χώρα.
Ἐπόμεινεν ἡ Ἀρετὴ μόνο μὲ τὴ Φροσύνη,
  πρᾶμα μεγάλο γίνηκε σ' αὐτὴ τὴν ὥρα κείνη.
Εἰς τὴν ποδιὰ τῆς νένας τση ἤπεσε καὶ λιγώθη,
  γὴ πόθανε γὴ ζωντανὴ ἂν εἶναι, δὲν τὸ γνώθει.

(*Erotocritos*)

the west when he opened his lips to say good-bye, and the palace shook from the pain it felt when they held hands and said good-bye. Who can describe how the young girl stood there dazed at that moment and how the young man looked? They had no mouth, no lips to say good-bye, no eyes to see nor ears to hear. But time was pressing; the day had come, and full of passion they pressed each other's hand. And a great marvel happened to that window: the stones and the iron bars wept at that moment, tear-drops rolled down from the stone and the iron; Aretousa found them there and they were warmer than blood. But time was pressing; Erotocritos left with a bitter sigh that shook the land. Arete was left alone with Phrosyne and then a dreadful thing happened: she fell and swooned on the lap of her nurse, not knowing if she were dead or living.

272. Time Heals All Wounds

"Αφης τσὶ μέρες νὰ διαβοῦ, τὸ χρόνο νὰ περάση·
  τ' ἄγρια θεριὰ μερώνουσι μὲ τὸν καιρὸ στὰ δάση·
μὲ τὸν καιρὸ τὰ δύσκολα καὶ τὰ βαρὰ λαφραίνου,
  οἱ ἀνάγκες, πάθη κι ἀρρωστιὲς γιατρεύγουνται καὶ
  γιαίνου.
Μὲ τὸν καιρὸ οἱ ἀνεμικὲς κι οἱ ταραχὲς σκολάζου,
  καὶ τὰ ζεστὰ κρυγαίνουσι, τὰ μαργωμένα βράζου·
μὲ τὸν καιρὸν οἱ συννεφιὲς παύγουσι κι οἱ ἀντάρες,
  κι εὐκὲς μεγάλες γίνουνται μὲ τὸν καιρὸ οἱ κατάρες.

(Erotocritos)

273. Glory is Transitory

"Οποιος τσὶ μεγαλότητες ζητᾶ τουνοῦ τοῦ κόσμου,
  καὶ δὲν γνωρίζει πὼς ἐπὰ διαβάτης εἶν τοῦ δρόμου,
μὰ ρέμπεται στὶς ἀφεντιές, στὰ πλούτη ντου καυκᾶται,
  ἐγὼ ἄγνωστο τόνε κρατῶ, καὶ πελελὸς λογᾶται·
τοῦτά 'ν ἀθοὶ καὶ λούλουδα, διαβαίνουν καὶ περνοῦσι,
  καὶ μεταλλάσσουν τα οἱ καιροί, συχνιὰ τὰ καταλοῦσι,
σὰν τυ γυαλὶ ραΐζουσι, σὰν τὸν καπνὸ διαβαίνου,
  ποτὲ δὲ στέκου ἀσάλευτα, μὰ πιλαλοῦν καὶ πηαίνου·

LET days go by, let time pass. Wild beasts in the forests become tame with the passage of time; difficulties and griefs grow light as time goes by; necessity, passions and sickness are cured; and you are healthy again. Storms and gales calm down with the passage of time; what is hot becomes cool, what is icy begins to boil. In time clouds and storms move away, and curses turn into great blessings.

WHOEVER seeks the glories of this world, and does not know that he is a mere passer-by in a street but wishes to be powerful and boasts of his wealth, is worth nothing in my opinion and should be considered mad. These are but flowers and blossoms; they pass away, they wither; time changes them and often destroys them; they break like glass, blow away like smoke; they are never permanent, but run swiftly away.

κι ὅσο πλιὰ ἡ μοῖρα στὰ ψηλὰ τὸν ἄνθρωπο καθίζει,
τόσο καὶ πλιότερα πονεῖ, ὅντε τόνε γκρεμνίζει·
κι ἐκεῖνα ποὺ τὸν κάνουσι συχνιὰ ν' ἀναγαλλιάση,
μεγάλοι ὀχθροί ντου γίνουνται τὴν ὥρα ποὺ τὰ χάση·
κι ὅσο πλιὰ ἀφέντης κράζεται καὶ βασιλιὸς λογᾶται,
τόσο πλιὰ πρέπει νὰ δειλιᾶ, πλιότερα νὰ φοβᾶται·
γιατὶ ἔτσι τό 'χει φυσικὸ τσῆ μοίρας τὸ παιγνίδι,
νὰ παίρνη ἀπὸ τὴ μιὰ μερὰ στὴν ἄλλη νὰ τὰ δίδη.

(*Erotocritos*)

274. The Death of Aristos

Ὡσὰν ἀθὸς καὶ λούλουδο, πόχει ὀμορφιὰ καὶ κάλλη
κι εἶναι στὸν κάμπο δροσερὸ μὲ μυρωδιὰ μεγάλη,
κι ἔρθη τ' ἀλέτρι ἀλύπητα βαθιὰ τὸ ξεριζώση,
ψυγῆ ζιμιὸ καὶ μαραθῆ, κι ἡ ὀμορφιά ντου λιώση,
χλωμαίνει, ἂν εἶναι κόκκινο, κι ἂν εἶν ἄσπρο, μαυρίζει,
καὶ μπλάβο ἂν εἶναι, λιώνεται ζιμιὸ καὶ κιτρινίζει,
χάνει ὀμορφιὰ καὶ μυρωδιά, κάλλη καὶ δροσερότη,
γερᾶ ζιμιὸ καὶ ψύγεται, καὶ μπλιὸ δὲν ἔχει νιότη,
ἔτσι ἦτον κι εἰς τὸν Ἄριστο, ὄντεν ἡ ψή ντου βγῆκε,
μὲ δίχως αἷμα ἄσπρο, χλωμό, ψυμένο τὸν ἀφῆκε.

(*Erotocritos*)

And the higher that Fate places man, the more pain he feels when she
throws him down; the things that so often give him delight become his
great enemies the moment he loses them. The more he is considered a
master and a king, the more he should be afraid, the more he should
feel uneasy, because such is the game Fate plays: she takes from the
one side to give to the other.

LIKE a flower and a blossom that has beauty and splendour and grows
fresh and most fragrant in the fields, and that the plough heartlessly
roots up from its depths; and swiftly it shrivels, grows cold, and its
beauty melts away. It grows pale if it was red, and black if it was white,
and if it was blue it swiftly melts into yellow. It loses its beauty and
perfume, its freshness and splendour, and quickly grows old and icy
and has youth no longer. So it was with Aristos when the soul left his
body: white, bloodless, pale, cold it left him.

275. The Soul Leaves the Hero's Body

Κι ὄντεν ἐμίσεψ' ἡ ψυχή, καὶ τὸ κορμὶν ἀφῆκε,
ἕνας μεγάλος βροντισμὸς στὸν οὐρανὸν ἐβγῆκε,
κι ἕναν ἀνεμοστρόβιλο θωροῦ σκοτεινιασμένο,
καὶ τριγυρίζει τὸ κορμὶ τοῦ νιοῦ τ' ἀποθαμένο.

(Erotocritos)

276. The Happy End

Ἦρθεν ἡ ὥρα κι ὁ καιρὸς κι ἡ μέρα ξημερώνει,
νὰ φανερώση ὁ 'Ρώκριτος τὸ πρόσωπο ποὺ χώνει.
Ἐφάνη ὁλόχαρη ἡ αὐγή, καὶ τὴ δροσούλα ρίχνει,
σημάδια τῆς ξεφάντωσης κείνη τὴν ὥρα δείχνει.
Χορτάρια βγήκασι στὴ γῆς, τὰ δεντρουλάκια ἀθίσα,
κι ἀπὸ τσ' ἀγκάλες τ' οὐρανοῦ γλυκὺς βορρᾶς ἐφύσα,
τὰ περιγιάλια λάμπασι, κι ἡ θάλασσα κοιμᾶτο,
γλυκὺς σκοπὸς εἰς τὰ δεντρὰ κι εἰς τὰ νερὰ γρικᾶτο·
ὁλόχαρη καὶ λαμπιρὴ ἡ μέρα ξημερώνει,
ἐγέλαν ἡ 'Ανατολή, κι ἡ Δύση καμαρώνει.
Ὁ ἥλιος τὶς ἀκτῖνες του παρὰ ποτὲ στολίζει
μὲ λάψη, κι ὅλα τὰ βουνιὰ καὶ κάμπους ὀμορφίζει.

AND when the soul left the body and moved away, a loud thunderclap was heard in the sky; and they saw a dark whirlwind circling round the body of the young man who was dead.

THE time and the moment came; the day dawned for Erotocritos to show the face that he had been hiding. Dawn came up full of joy, showering dew, giving them a foretaste of the celebration to follow. Grass grew on the earth, the young trees blossomed, and from the sky's embrace a sweet north wind was blowing; the shores glittered and the sea slept and a sweet music was heard from the trees and the fountains. Brilliant and full of joy the day dawned: the east laughed and the west watched in admiration. The sun adorned his rays with more brilliance than ever and made all the hills and the plains look beautiful. The birds,

Χαμοπετώντας τὰ πουλιὰ ἐγλυκοκιλαηδοῦσα,
  στὰ κλωναράκια τῶ δεντρῶ ἐσμίγαν καὶ φιλοῦσα,
δυὸ δυὸ ἐζευγαρώνασι, ζεστὸς καιρὸς ἐκίνα,
  ἔσμιξες, γάμους καὶ χαρὲς ἐδείχνασιν κι ἐκεῖνα·
ἐσκόρπισεν ἡ συννεφιά, οἱ ἀντάρες ἐχαθῆκα,
  πολλὰ σημάδια τσῆ χαρᾶς στὸν οὐρανὸ φανῆκα·
παρὰ ποτέ ντως λαμπιρὰ τριγύρου στολισμένα
  στὸν οὐρανό 'ν τὰ νέφαλα σὰν παραχρυσωμένα.
Τὰ πάθη μπλιὸ δὲ κιλαηδεῖ τὸ πρικαμένο ἀηδόνι,
  ἀμὴ πετᾶ πασίχαρό μ' ἄλλα πουλιὰ σιμώνει.
Γελοῦν τσῆ χώρας τὰ στενά, κι οἱ στράτες καμαρώνου,
  ὅλα γρικοῦν κουρφὲς χαρές, κι ὅλα τσὶ φανερώνου,
καὶ μὲς στὴ σκοτεινὴ φλακή, πού 'τον ἡ Ἀρετοῦσα,
  ἐμπῆκα δυὸ ὄμορφα πουλιὰ καὶ γλυκοκιλαηδοῦσα·
στὴν κεφαλὴ τῆς Ἀρετῆς συχνιὰ χαμοπετοῦσι,
  καὶ φαίνεταί σου καὶ χαρὲς μεγάλες προμηνοῦσι·
πάλι μὲ τὸν κελαηδισμὸν ἐκ τῆ φλακὴν ἐφύγα,
  ἀγκαλιαστά, περιμπλεκτὰ τσὶ μοῦρες τως ἐσμίγα.

(*Erotocritos*)

flying low, sang sweetly; they met on the young branches of the trees
and kissed one another. In pairs they sat and the warm weather glowed,
and the birds gave signs of unions and marriage and happiness. The
clouds dispersed and the darkness disappeared and many signs of de-
light filled the sky. The clouds in the sky, brighter than ever, were
decorated all around and looked richly gilded. The sad nightingale no
longer sang her misfortunes, but flew full of joy and mingled with the
other birds. The valleys of the earth were laughing, and the footpaths
watched them with admiration; everything felt a secret joy, and every-
thing showed it. And two lovely birds entered the dark prison where
Arete was living and sang sweetly: many times they flew down near
Arete's head as though bringing a message of great joy. Then once
more they left the prison in each other's embrace, singing, their faces
close to each other.

RHIGAS PHERRHAIOS
1759–98

277. The War-hymn

'Ως πότε, παλικάρια, νὰ ζοῦμεν στὰ στενά,
μονάχοι, σὰν λεοντάρια, στὲς ράχες, στὰ βουνά,
σπηλιὲς νὰ κατοικοῦμεν, νὰ βλέπωμεν κλαδιά;
Νὰ φεύγωμεν τὸν κόσμον γιὰ τὴν πικρὴν σκλαβιά,
ν' ἀφήνωμεν ἀδέλφια, πατρίδα καὶ γονεῖς
τοὺς φίλους, τὰ παιδιά μας κι ὅλους τοὺς συγγενεῖς;
Καλύτερα μιᾶς ὥρας ἐλεύθερη ζωή,
παρὰ σαράντα χρόνων σκλαβιὰ καὶ φυλακή.

Τί σ' ὠφελεῖ, ἂν ζήσης, καὶ εἶσαι στὴν σκλαβιά;
Στοχάσου πῶς σὲ ψένουν καθ' ὥραν στὴν φωτιά·
βεζίρης, δραγουμάνος, αὐθέντης κι ἂν γενῆς,
ὁ τύραννος ἀδίκως σὲ κάμνει νὰ χαθῆς.
Δουλεύεις ὅλ' ἡμέρα εἰς ὅ τι κι ἂν σ' εἰπῆ,
κι αὐτὸς κοιτάζει πάλιν τὸ αἷμα σου νὰ πιῆ.
Ὁ Σοῦτσος, ὁ Μουρούζης, Πετράκης, Σκαναβής,
Γκίκας καὶ Μαυρογένης καθρέπτης εἶν' νὰ ἰδῆς.

YOUNG men, how long must we live in mountain passes, lonely like lions, on mountain ridges, in the hills, inhabiting caves and watching the branches of the trees? How long must we stay away from the world because of bitter servitude, leaving brothers, homeland, and parents, friends, our children, and all our relatives? One hour of freedom is worth forty years of slavery, of life in prison.

What is the good of living, if you are a slave? Think how, hour by hour, they roast you on the fire; and even if you become a vizier or dragoman or ruler, the tyrant sees that you find an unjust end: you work all day at his command and he seeks to drink your blood in return. Men like Soutsos, Mourouzis, Petrakis, Skanavis, Gikas and Mavrogenis are mirrors where you can see all this.

VI
MODERN GREECE

DIONYSIOS SOLOMOS
1798–1857

278. Ode to Liberty

Σὲ γνωρίζω ἀπὸ τὴν κόψη
τοῦ σπαθιοῦ τὴν τρομερή,
σὲ γνωρίζω ἀπὸ τὴν ὄψη
ποὺ μὲ βία μετράει τὴ γῆ.

Ἀπ' τὰ κόκκαλα βγαλμένη
τῶν Ἑλλήνων τὰ ἱερά,
καὶ σὰν πρῶτα ἀνδρειωμένη
χαῖρε, ὢ χαῖρε, Ἐλευθεριά!

Ἐκεῖ μέσα ἐκατοικοῦσες
πικραμένη, ἐντροπαλή,
κι ἕνα στόμα ἐκαρτεροῦσες,
‹ἔλα πάλι›, νὰ σοῦ πῆ.

Ἄργιε νὰ 'λθη ἐκείνη ἡ μέρα,
καὶ ἦταν ὅλα σιωπηλά,
γιατὶ τὰ 'σκιαζε ἡ φοβέρα,
καὶ τὰ πλάκωνε ἡ σκλαβιά.

I RECOGNIZE you by the fierce edge of your sword; I recognize you by the look that measures the earth.

Liberty, who sprang out of the sacred bones of the Greeks brave as in the past, I greet you, I greet you.

Therein you lived, grieving and timid, waiting for a mouth to tell you: 'Come again.'

That day took long to come, and everything was silent, because it was overshadowed by fear and crushed by slavery.

279. On Psara

Στῶν Ψαρῶν τὴν ὁλόμαυρη ῥάχη
περπατώντας ἡ Δόξα μονάχη
μελετᾶ τὰ λαμπρὰ παλικάρια
καὶ στὴν κόμη στεφάνι φορεῖ
γεναμένο ἀπὸ λίγα χορτάρια,
ποὺ εἶχαν μείνει στὴν ἔρημη γῆ.

280. Easter Day

Καθαρότατον ἥλιο ἐπρομηνοῦσε
τῆς αὐγῆς τὸ δροσάτο ὕστερο ἀστέρι,
σύγνεφο, καταχνιά, δὲν ἀπερνοῦσε
τ᾿ οὐρανοῦ σὲ κανένα ἀπὸ τὰ μέρη·
καὶ ἀπὸ κεῖ κινημένο ἀργοφυσοῦσε
τόσο γλυκὸ στὸ πρόσωπο τ᾿ ἀέρι,
ποὺ λὲς καὶ λέει μὲς στῆς καρδιᾶς τὰ φύλλα·
‹γλυκιὰ ἡ ζωὴ καὶ ὁ θάνατος μαυρίλα.›

‹Χριστὸς ἀνέστη !› Νέοι, γέροι καὶ κόρες,
ὅλοι, μικροὶ μεγάλοι, ἑτοιμαστῆτε·
μέσα στὲς ἐκκλησίες τὲς δαφνοφόρες
μὲ τὸ φῶς τῆς χαρᾶς συμμαζωχτῆτε·

ON the coal-black ridge of Psara, Glory walks in solitude; she muses on those excellent heroes, and upon her head she wears a crown made from the few blades of grass that were left on that desolate land.

THE last cool star of dawn was foretelling the brightest sunshine; no cloud, no drift of mist was travelling across any part of the sky. Coming from there, the breeze blew so sweetly across the face, so gently, that it seemed to say to the depths of the heart: 'Life is sweet and death is darkness.'
    'Christ is risen!' Young and old, maidens, everyone, little and great, be prepared; gather with the light of joy in the bay-covered churches;

ἀνοίξετε ἀγκαλιὲς εἰρηνοφόρες
ὀμπροστὰ στοὺς ἁγίους καὶ φιληθῆτε·
φιληθῆτε γλυκὰ χείλη μὲ χείλη,
πέστε· ‹Χριστὸς ἀνέστη›, ἐχθροὶ καὶ φίλοι.

Δάφνες εἰς κάθε πλάκα ἔχουν οἱ τάφοι,
καὶ βρέφη ὡραῖα στὴν ἀγκαλιὰ οἱ μανάδες·
γλυκόφωνα, κοιτώντας τὲς ζωγραφι-
σμένες εἰκόνες, ψάλλουνε οἱ ψαλτάδες·
λάμπει τὸ ἀσήμι, λάμπει τὸ χρυσάφι
ἀπὸ τὸ φῶς ποὺ χύνουνε οἱ λαμπάδες·
κάθε πρόσωπο λάμπει ἀπ' τ' ἁγιοκέρι
ὁποὺ κρατοῦνε οἱ Χριστιανοὶ στὸ χέρι.

(*Lambros*)

281. *April and Love*

I

'Ο 'Απρίλης μὲ τὸν Ἔρωτα χορεύουν καὶ γελοῦνε,
κι ὅσ' ἄνθια βγαίνουν καὶ καρποὶ τόσ' ἄρματα σὲ κλειοῦνε.

Λευκὸ βουνάκι πρόβατα κινούμενο βελάζει,
καὶ μὲς στὴ θάλασσα βαθιὰ ξαναπετιέται πάλι,
κι ὁλόλευκο ἐσύσμιξε μὲ τ' οὐρανοῦ τὰ κάλλη.

open peace-offering arms before the ikons of the saints, and embrace
one another. Lips with lips kiss sweetly, and say: 'Christ is risen' —
enemies and foes.

Bay-leaves are strewn on all the tombs, the mothers hold beautiful
babies in their arms; the choristers, looking at the painted ikons, chant
sweetly. Silver flashes, gold gleams in the light shed by candles;
candles the faithful hold in their hands make every face shine.

I

APRIL is dancing and laughing with love, but as many flowers and
fruits come up, so many are the arms that besiege you!

A hill, white with sheep, shifts and bleats, and is reflected again deep
in the water; snow-white it has fused with the beauty of the sky. And

Καὶ μὲς στῆς λίμνης τὰ νερά, ὅπ' ἔφθασε μ' ἀσπούδα,
ἔπαιξε μὲ τὸν ἴσκιο της γαλάζια πεταλούδα,
ποὺ εὐώδιασε τὸν ὕπνο της μέσα στὸν ἄγριο κρίνο·
τὸ σκουληκάκι βρίσκεται σ' ὥρα γλυκιὰ κι ἐκεῖνο.
Μάγεμα ἡ φύσις κι ὄνειρο στὴν ὀμορφιὰ καὶ χάρη,
ἡ μαύρη πέτρα ὁλόχρυση καὶ τὸ ξερὸ χορτάρι.
Μὲ χίλιες βρύσες χύνεται, μὲ χίλιες γλῶσσες κραίνει·
‹ὅποιος πεθάνη σήμερα χίλιας φορὲς πεθαίνει.›

Τρέμ' ἡ ψυχὴ καὶ ξαστοχᾶ γλυκὰ τὸν ἑαυτό της.

II

Πάντ' ἀνοιχτά, πάντ' ἄγρυπνα τὰ μάτια τῆς ψυχῆς μου.

(The Free Besieged)

282. Temptation

῎Εστησ' ὁ ῎Ερωτας χορὸ μὲ τὸν ξανθὸν ᾽Απρίλη,
κι ἡ φύσις ηὗρε τὴν καλὴ καὶ τὴ γλυκιά της ὥρα,
καὶ μὲς στὴ σκιὰ ποὺ φούντωσε καὶ κλεῖ δροσιὲς καὶ μόσχους
ἀνάκουστος κιλαηδισμὸς καὶ λιποθυμισμένος.

the blue butterfly came hurrying to play with her shadow on the waters of the lake, after she had breathed the perfume of the wild lily she had slept in; the very worm is happy at this hour. Nature is like a spell, a dream of beauty and grace; the black stones flash golden and the dry grass too. A thousand fountains pour it out, a thousand voices cry: 'He who must die today shall die a thousand deaths.'
The soul shivers, and sweetly forgets itself.

II

Always open, always sleepless are the eyes of my soul.

LOVE is dancing with fair-haired April; the good, sweet time of the year has come, and the shadows that blossomed out full with coolness and perfume are haunted by the strange, gentle song of birds. Sweet,

Νερὰ καθάρια καὶ γλυκά, νερὰ χαριτωμένα,
χύνονται μὲς στὴν ἄβυσσο τὴ μοσχοβολισμένη,
καὶ παίρνουνε τὸ μόσχο της, ι:ι ἀφήνουν τὴ δροσιά τους,
κι οὖλα στὸν ἥλιο δείχνοντας τὰ πλούτια τῆς πηγῆς τους,
τρέχουν ἐδῶ, τρέχουν ἐκεῖ, καὶ κάνουν σὰν ἀηδόνια.
Ἔξ' ἀναβρύζει κι ἡ ζωὴ σ' γῆ, σ' οὐρανό, σὲ κύμα·
ἀλλὰ στῆς λίμνης τὸ νερό, π' ἀκίνητό 'ναι κι ἄσπρο,
ἀκίνητ' ὅπου κι ἂν ἰδῇς, καὶ κάτασπρ' ὡς τὸν πάτο,
μὲ μικρὸν ἴσκιον ἄγνωρον ἔπαιξ' ἡ πεταλούδα,
πού 'χ' εὐωδίσει τς ὕπνους της μέσα στὸν ἄγριο κρίνο.
‹'Αλαφροΐσκιωτε καλέ, γιὰ πὲς ἀπόψε τί 'δες;›
‹Νύχτα γιομάτη θαύματα, νύχτα σπαρμένη μάγια!
Χωρὶς ποσῶς γῆς, οὐρανὸς καὶ θάλασσα νὰ πνένε,
οὐδ' ὅσο κάν' ἡ μέλισσα κοντὰ στὸ λουλουδάκι,
γύρου σὲ κάτι ἀτάραχο π' ἀσπρίζει μὲς στὴ λίμνη,
μονάχο ἀνακατώθηκε τὸ στρογγυλὸ φεγγάρι,
κι ὅμορφη βγαίνει κορασιὰ ντυμένη μὲ τὸ φῶς του.›

(*The Free Besieged*)

pure waters flow gracefully in the fragrant deep; they lend it their cool-
ness and take on its perfume; they flow in all directions and show the
riches of their fountainhead to the sun, singing like nightingales.
Beyond them, life springs up on earth, sky and sea. But on the waters
of the lake which lie motionless and white – totally motionless, white
to the bottom – a butterfly played with a little unknown shadow, after
she had breathed the perfume of the wild lily in which she had slept.
'Tell me, prophetic friend, what have you seen tonight?' 'A night full
of wonders, a night sown with magic. Earth, sky and sea without a
breath of wind, not even as much as a bee would stir hovering round
a little flower; only the circle of the moon melts in the lake round
something motionless looking white, and a lovely maiden emerges
dressed in its light.'

ANDREAS KALVOS

1792–1869

283. Zante

Ὦ φιλτάτη πατρίς,
ὦ θαυμασία νῆσος,
Ζάκυνθε· σὺ μοῦ ἔδωκας
τὴν πνοὴν καὶ τοῦ Ἀπόλλωνος
τὰ χρυσᾶ δῶρα!

Καὶ σὺ τὸν ὕμνον δέξου·
ἐχθαίρουσιν οἱ ἀθάνατοι
τὴν ψυχήν, καὶ βροντάουσιν
ἐπὶ τὰς κεφαλὰς
τῶν ἀχαρίστων.

Ποτὲ δὲν σὲ ἐλησμόνησα,
ποτέ· καὶ ἡ τύχη μ' ἔρριψε
μακρὰ ἀπὸ σέ· μὲ εἶδε
τὸ πέμπτον τοῦ αἰῶνος
εἰς ξένα ἔθνη.

Ἀλλὰ εὐτυχὴς ἢ δύστηνος,
ὅταν τὸ φῶς ἐπλούτει
τὰ βουνὰ καὶ τὰ κύματα,
σὲ ἐμπρὸς τῶν ὀφθαλμῶν μου
πάντοτες εἶχον.

O, MY most beloved homeland, marvellous island, Zante! From you I took my life, from you the gold gifts of Apollo.

And you, accept my hymn. The immortal gods detest souls without gratitude, and cast on such heads their thunder.

I have never forgotten you, never, though Fate threw me far away from you. A fifth of a century I have spent among foreigners.

But, happy or unhappy, I held you always before my eyes, when the light cast its riches on your hills and on your waves;

Σύ, ὅταν τὰ οὐράνια
ρόδα μὲ τὸν ἀμαυρότατον
πέπλον σκεπάζῃ ἡ νύκτα,
σὺ εἶσαι τῶν ὀνείρων μου
    ἡ χαρὰ μόνη.

Τὰ βήματά μου ἐφώτισέ
ποτε εἰς τὴν Αὐσονίαν,
γῆ μακαρία, ὁ ἥλιος·
κεῖ καθαρὸς ὁ ἀέρας
    πάντα γελάει.

Ἐκεῖ ὁ λαὸς ηὐτύχησεν·
ἐκεῖ οἱ Παρνάσιαι κόραι
χορεύουν, καὶ τὸ λύσιον
φύλλον αὐτῶν τὴν λύραν
    κεῖ στεφανώνει.

Ἄγρια, μεγάλα τρέχουσι
τὰ νερὰ τῆς θαλάσσης,
καὶ ρίπτονται, καὶ σχίζονται
βίαια ἐπὶ τοὺς βράχους
    Ἀλβιωνίους.

Ἀδειάζει ἐπὶ τὰς ὄχθας
τοῦ κλεινοῦ Ταμησσοῦ
καὶ δύναμιν, καὶ δόξαν,
καὶ πλοῦτον ἀναρίθμητον
    τὸ ἀμαλθεῖον.

You, when night casts over the roses of the sky her darkest veil, you are the only joy in my dreams.

The sun once lit my footsteps in Ausonia's blessed land; there the air always smiles clear and bright.

The people there are happy; there the daughters of Parnassus dance, and pleasant leaves crown their lyre.

Violent and vast run the waves of the sea; they fling and tear themselves wildly upon the rocky headlands of Albion.

On the banks of the famous Thames the Horn of Plenty pours power, glory and endless riches.

Ἐκεῖ τὸ αἰόλιον φύσημα
μ' ἔφερεν· οἱ ἀκτῖνες
μ' ἔθρεψαν, μ' ἐθεράπευσαν
τῆς ὑπεργλυκυτάτης
ἐλευθερίας.

Καὶ τοὺς ναούς σου ἐθαύμασα
τῶν Κελτῶν ἱερὰ
πόλις· τοῦ λόγου ποία,
ποία εἰς ἐσὲ τοῦ πνεύματος
λείπει Ἀφροδίτη;

Χαῖρε Αὐσονία, χαῖρε
καὶ σὺ Ἀλβιών, χαιρέτωσαν
τὰ ἔνδοξα Παρίσια·
ὡραία καὶ μόνη ἡ Ζάκυνθος
μὲ κυριεύει.

Τῆς Ζακύνθου τὰ δάση
καὶ τὰ βουνὰ σκιώδη
ἤκουόν ποτε σημαίνοντα
τὰ θεῖα τῆς Ἀρτέμιδος
ἀργυρᾶ τόξα.

Καὶ σήμερον τὰ δένδρα,
καὶ τὰς πηγὰς σεβάζονται
δροσερὰς οἱ ποιμένες·
αὐτοῦ πλανῶνται ἀκόμα
οἱ Νηρηίδες.

The breath of Aeolus brought me there; the rays of sweetest liberty warmed me and nurtured me there.

And I admired your temples, sacred city of the Celts; no Aphrodite of the word or of the spirit is absent from you.

But farewell Albion, and you Ausonia, farewell; farewell glorious Paris; beautiful Zante is my only mistress.

The forests and shady hills of Zante once heard the message of goddess Artemis' silver bow.

And today the shepherds honour the trees and the cool fountains; the Nereids still wander there.

Τὸ κῦμα 'Ιόνιον πρῶτον
ἐφίλησε τὸ σῶμα,
πρῶτοι οἱ 'Ιόνιοι Ζέφυροι
ἐχάιδευσαν τὸ στῆθος
   τῆς Κυθερείας.

Καὶ ὅταν τὸ ἐσπέριον ἄστρον
ὁ οὐρανὸς ἀνάπτῃ,
καὶ πλέωσι γέμοντα ἔρωτος
καὶ φωνῶν μουσικῶν
   θαλάσσια ξύλα,

φιλεῖ τὸ ἴδιον κῦμα,
οἱ αὐτοὶ χαϊδεύουν Ζέφυροι,
τὸ σῶμα καὶ τὸ στῆθος
τῶν λαμπρῶν Ζακυνθίων
   ἄνθος παρθένων.

Μοσχοβολάει τὸ κλῖμά σου,
ὦ φιλτάτη πατρίς μου,
καὶ πλουτίζει τὸ πέλαγος
ἀπὸ τὴν μυρωδίαν
   τῶν χρυσῶν κίτρων.

Σταφυλοφόρους ῥίζας,
ἐλαφρά, καθαρά,
διαφανῆ τὰ σύννεφα
ὁ βασιλεὺς σοῦ ἐχάρισε
   τῶν ἀθανάτων.

The Ionian wave first kissed the body of Cythereia, and Ionian
Zephyrs first caressed her breast.

And when the sky kindles the Evening Star, and wooden barks sail
laden with love and with the voices of music,

The same wave kisses, the same Zephyrs caress the bodies and
breasts of the bright maidens of Zante, the flower of maidenhood.

Your air is perfumed, my dearest homeland, and enriches the sea
with the scent of golden lemons.

The king of the immortals has endowed you with heavy-laden
vines, and light pure, transparent clouds.

Ἡ λαμπὰς ἡ αἰώνιος
σοῦ βρέχει τὴν ἡμέραν
τοὺς καρπούς, καὶ τὰ δάκρυα
γίνονται τῆς νυκτὸς
εἰς ἐσὲ κρίνοι.

Δὲν ἔμεινεν, ἐὰν ἔπεσε,
ποτὲ εἰς τὸ πρόσωπόν σου
ἡ χιών· δὲν ἐμάρανε
ποτὲ ὁ θερμὸς Κύων,
τὰ σμάραγδά σου.

Εἶσαι εὐτυχής· καὶ πλέον
σὲ λέγω εὐτυχεστέραν,
ὅτι σὺ δὲν ἐγνώρισας
ποτὲ τὴν σκληρὰν μάστιγα
ἐχθρῶν, τυράννων.

Ἂς μὴ μοῦ δώσῃ ἡ μοῖρά μου
εἰς ξένην γῆν τὸν τάφον·
εἶναι γλυκὺς ὁ θάνατος
μόνον ὅταν κοιμώμεθα
εἰς τὴν πατρίδα.

The eternal lamp of the sun pours its light by day on your fruits, and the tears of night become your lilies.

Snow has never fallen or rested on your face, the fiery dog-star never dulled your emeralds.

You are happy; and I call you still happier, because you have not known the hard whip of the enemy, the tyrant.

May Fate not give me a foreign grave, for death is sweet only to him who sleeps in his homeland.

ALEXANDER SOUTSOS
1803–63

284. The Roumeliote Veteran

Εἰς τὸν γέρον Ὄλυμπόν μας, κοντὰ σ' ἕνα κυπαρίσσι
    ἕνας γέρος Ῥουμελιώτης
μὲ τοὺς φίλους του τὸ βράδυ κάθισε νὰ τραγουδήση.
    Τῆς πατρίδος στρατιώτης,
‹ἑπτά, ἔλεγ', ἑπτὰ χρόνους μὲ καρδιὰ πάντοτε νέα
βάσταξα καὶ στὸ δερβένι καὶ στὸν κάμπο τὴν σημαία.
'Ενθυμᾶσθε, σύντροφοί μου, ἐνθυμᾶσθε τοὺς καλούς μας,
    τοὺς ἡρωϊκοὺς καιρούς μας;

‹'Ενθυμᾶσθε, τοῦ Χουρσίτη αἱ τριάντα χιλιάδες,
    μιὰ μιὰ ὅλες διαλεκτές,
ὅταν γέμισαν τοῦ Ἄργους τὲς μεγάλες πεδιάδες
    μ' ἀστραπὲς καὶ μὲ βροντές;
ἐνθυμᾶσθε μὲ τί θάρρος ἐπιασθήκαμε στὰ χέρια
μὲ δρεπάνια, μὲ κοντάρια καὶ μὲ ξύλ' ἀντὶς μαχαίρια;
'Ενθυμᾶσθε, σύντροφοί μου, ἐνθυμᾶσθε τοὺς καλούς μας,
    τοὺς ἡρωϊκοὺς καιρούς μας;

‹'Ενθυμᾶσθε τῶν Σκοδριάνων σὰν μᾶς πλάκωσε τὸ πλῆθος,
    πὼς εὐθὺς στὸ Καρπενήσι
ἔτρεξεν ὁ Μπότζαρής μας, καὶ μὲ τ' ἄφοβό του στῆθος
    πρόφθασε νὰ τοὺς σκορπίση;

NEAR our ancient Mount Olympus by a cypress-tree an old man from
Roumeli sat down at dusk with his friends to sing. A soldier of the
fatherland, he said: 'For seven years with a youthful heart I held the
flag in valley and plain. Do you remember, my comrades, our good,
heroic years?

'Do you remember the thirty thousand men of Hoursit Pasha, every
one a chosen man, when they filled the wide plains of Arta with lightning
and thunder? Do you remember how bravely we joined battle with
scythes and poles and pieces of wood instead of swords? Do you re-
member, my comrades, our good, heroic years?

'Do you remember when the crowd from Skorda fell upon us, how
at Karpenesi Botzaris ran at once to help, and quickly and fearlessly

'Ενθυμᾶσθε τῆς πληγῆς του πῶς μᾶς ἔκρυφτε τὸ αἷμα;
τί καρδιά μας ἔδιδ' ὅλους μὲ τὸ ὑστερό του βλέμμα;
'Ενθυμᾶσθε, συντροφοί μου, ἐνθυμᾶσθε τοὺς καλούς μας,
    τοὺς ἡρωϊκοὺς καιρούς μας;

‹'Ενθυμᾶσθε ἀπ' τοὺς Τούρκους σὰν σκεπάσθηκαν οἱ λόγγοι
    τῆς ἀνδρείας 'Ρούμελῆς μας,
καὶ βαστοῦσε ὁ 'Αράπης σφαλιστοὺς στὸ Μισολόγγι
    τὰ παιδιά μας, τοὺς γονεῖς μας;
ἐνθυμᾶσθε μὲς στὰ μάτια τῆς σκληρῆς Εὐρώπης ὅλης
πῶς ἀνέβηκεν ὣς τ' ἄστρα τοῦ Μισολογγιοῦ ἡ πόλις;
'Ενθυμᾶσθε, συντροφοί μου, ἐνθυμᾶσθε τοὺς καλούς μας,
    τοὺς ἡρωϊκοὺς καιρούς μας;

‹'Ενθυμᾶσθ' ὁ Καραΐσκος μὲ τριακόσιους διαλεχτούς του,
    ὅταν ἦλθε στὰς 'Αθήνας,
πῶς τοῦ Κιουταχῆ ἐχάθη κι ἡ ἀνδρεία του κι ὁ νοῦς του;
    Δὲν ἐπέρασ' ἕνας μήνας,
καὶ ἡ 'Ρούμελη σηκώθη, κι ἔγιν' ὅλη ἕνα σῶμα,
καὶ κοκκίνισ' ἀπὸ αἷμα τῆς 'Αράχοβας τὸ χῶμα.
'Ενθυμᾶσθε, συντροφοί μου, ἐνθυμᾶσθε τοὺς καλούς μας,
    τοὺς ἡρωϊκοὺς καιρούς μας;

‹Χωρὶς πόλεις, χωρὶς κάστρα, ξεσχισμένοι, πεινασμένοι
    καὶ μὲ διψασμένο στόμα,

scattered them? Do you remember how he hid the blood of his wound from our eyes, the courage he gave us all with his final glance? Do you remember, my comrades, our good, heroic years?

'Do you remember when the valleys of our brave Roumeli were covered with Turks, and the Arab held our children and our parents under siege in Missolonghi? Do you remember how in the eyes of the whole of hard-hearted Europe the town of Missolonghi soared up to the stars? Do you remember, my comrades, our good, heroic years?

'Do you remember when Karaiskakis came to Athens with his chosen three hundred, how Kioutahi Pasha lost his courage and his wits? In less than a month's time Roumeli was afoot, became a single body, and the soil of Arachova was stained red with blood. Do you remember, my comrades, our good, heroic years?

'With no cities and no fortresses, ragged, hungry and with thirsty

νεκρωμένοι ἀπὸ τὸν τύφο, ἀπ' τὰ βόλια πληγωμένοι
 καὶ χλωμοὶ ὡσὰν τὸ χῶμα,
εἰς τὸν οὐρανὸν τὰ μάτια εἴχαμ' ὅλοι γυρισμένα,
πλὴν ποτὲ εἰς τοὺς τυράννους δὲν ἐκλίναμεν αὐχένα.
Ἐνθυμᾶσθε, σύντροφοί μου, ἐνθυμᾶσθε τοὺς καλούς μας,
 τοὺς ἡρωϊκοὺς καιρούς μας; ›

GEORGE ZALOKOSTAS
1805-58

285. The Cold North Wind

Ἦτον νύχτα, εἰς τὴν στέγη ἐβογγοῦσε
ὁ βοριάς, καὶ ψιλὸ ἔπεφτε χιόνι·
τί μεγάλο κακὸ νὰ ἐμηνοῦσε
ὁ βοριὰς ποὺ τ' ἀρνάκια παγώνει;

Μὲς στὸ σπίτι μιὰ χαροκαμένη,
μιὰ μητέρα ἀπὸ πόνους γεμάτη,
στοῦ παιδιοῦ της τὴν κούνια σκυμμένη
δέκα νύχτες δὲν ἔκλειε μάτι.

Εἶχε τρία παιδιὰ πεθαμένα,
ἀγγελούδια λευκὰ σὰν τὸν κρίνο·
κι ἕνα μόνο τῆς ἔμενεν, ἕνα,
καὶ στὸν τάφο κοντὰ ἦτον κι ἐκεῖνο.

mouths, dying of typhoid fever, wounded by bullets and pale as clay,
we kept our eyes turned to the sky, but never bent our necks before
the tyrants? Do you remember, my comrades, our good, heroic years?'

IT was night; on the roof the north wind was moaning, and thin
snow was falling; what was the terrible message the north wind was
bringing, the north wind that freezes the little lambs?

In the house a suffering mother, who had lost many dear ones, had
not closed an eye for ten nights, bent over her child's cradle.

Three of her children had died, little angels white like lilies; only one
was left, and that one close to the grave.

Τὸ παιδί της μὲ κλάμα ἐβογγοῦσε
ὡς νὰ ἐζήτᾳε τὸ δόλιο βοήθεια,
κι ἡ μητέρα σιμά του ἐθρηνοῦσε
μὲ λαχτάρα χτυπώντας τὰ στήθια.

Τὰ γογγύσματα ἐκεῖνα κι οἱ θρῆνοι
ἐπληγῶναν βαθιὰ τὴν ψυχή μου·
σύντροφός μου ἡ ταλαίπωρη ἐκείνη,
ἄχ! καὶ τ' ἄρρωστο ἦτον παιδί μου.

Στοῦ σπιτιοῦ μου τὴ στέγη ἐβογγοῦσε
ὁ βοριάς, καὶ ψιλὸ ἔπεφτε χιόνι.
Ἄχ! μεγάλο κακὸ μοῦ ἐμηνοῦσε
ὁ βοριὰς ποὺ τ' ἀρνάκια παγώνει.

Τὸν γιατρὸ καθὼς εἶδε, ἐσηκώθη
σὰν τρελλή. Ὅλοι γύρω ἐσωπαῖναν·
φλογεροὶ τῆς ψυχῆς της οἱ πόθοι
μὲ τὰ λόγια ἀπ' τὸ στόμα της βγαῖναν·

‹Ὤ, κακὸ ποὺ μὲ βρῆκε μεγάλο!
Τὸ παιδί μου, γιατρέ, τὸ παιδί μου ...
Ἕνα τό 'χω δὲν μ' ἔμεινεν ἄλλο·
σῶσε μού το, καὶ πάρ' τὴν ψυχή μου.›

Her child was tearfully moaning, as though, poor thing, it were asking for help; and the mother beside it was weeping, beating her breast with fear.

That moaning and those tears deeply wounded my heart, for that poor woman was my wife, and oh! the sick child, my child.

On the roof of my house the north wind was howling, and thin snow was falling. Oh, what a terrible message the north wind was bringing, the north wind that freezes the little lambs.

Like a mad woman she rose, when she saw the doctor; everyone round her was silent. From her mouth the burning desire of her heart poured out with these words:

'Oh, what a terrible calamity has come upon me! My child, doctor, my child! I have only one, no other has been left, save it and take my life away.'

GEORGE ZALOKOSTAS

Κι ὁ γιατρὸς μὲ τὰ μάτια σκυμμένα
πολλὴν ὥρα δὲν ἄνοιξε στόμα.
Τέλος πάντων — ἄχ ! λόγια χαμένα —
‹ Μὴ φοβᾶσαι, τῆς εἶπεν, ἀκόμα.›

Κι ἐκαμώθη πὼς θέλει νὰ σκύψη
στὸ παιδί, καὶ νὰ ἰδῆ τὸ σφυγμό του.
Ἕνα δάκρυ ἐπροσπάθαε νὰ κρύψη
ποὺ κατέβ᾽ εἰς τ᾽ ὠχρὸ πρόσωπό του.

Στοῦ σπιτιοῦ μας τὴ στέγη ἐβογγοῦσε
ὁ βοριάς, καὶ ψιλὸ ἔπεφτε χιόνι.
Ἄχ ! μεγάλο κακὸ μᾶς μηνοῦσε
ὁ βοριὰς ποὺ τ᾽ ἀρνάκια παγώνει.

Ἡ μητέρα ποτὲ δακρυσμένο
τοῦ γιατροῦ νὰ μὴ νιώση τὸ μάτι,
ὅταν ἔχη βαριὰ ξαπλωμένο
τὸ παιδί της σὲ πόνου κρεβάτι.

And the doctor with downcast eyes kept silent for long, and finally —
oh, useless words — 'Do not be frightened yet,' he told her.

And he pretended to stoop over the child and feel its pulse; he was
trying to hide a tear that came rolling down his pale face.

On the roof of our house the north wind was moaning, and thin
snow was falling. Oh, what a terrible message the north wind was
bringing, the north wind that freezes the little lambs.

May a mother never see tears in a doctor's eyes, when she has a child
seriously ill, lying in the bed of pain.

ALEXANDER RIZOS RANGAVIS
1809–92

286. The Voyage of Dionysus

I

Τῶν δροσερῶν της παρειῶν
  ὡμοίαζον τὰ κάλλη
τὸ ῥόδον τὸ ἐρυθριῶν,
  ὅταν στοιβάζηται χιὼν
  κ' εἰς τὴν χιόνα θάλλη.

'Επὶ τοὺς ὤμους της χυτὴ
  κατέρρεεν ἡ κόμη·
ὡς ἡ σελήνη δ' ὁρατὴ
  εἰς χρυσᾶ νέφη, ἐν αὐτῇ
  ὑπέλαμπον οἱ ὦμοι.

Πλούσιαι πόρπαι πρὸς στολὴν
  διάλιθοι συνεῖχον
τῆς κόρης τὴν ἀναβολήν,
  κ' εἰς τὴν χρυσῆν της κεφαλὴν
  τὸν πλοῦτον τῶν βοστρύχων.

Οἱ εὔγλωττοί της ὀφθαλμοὶ
  ὅταν χαρὰν ἐδήλουν,
ἀπήντων καρδιῶν παλμοί,
  καὶ ἦσαν ἔρωτος ψαλμοὶ
  ἐκεῖνα ποὺ ὡμίλουν.

I

THE beauty of her fresh cheeks looked like the blushing rose when snow is piling high, and it flourishes in the snow.

On her shoulders fell the flowing hair, and as the moon can be seen through golden clouds, so her shoulders faintly shone.

Rich clasps with many gems held the maiden's garment and the wealth of her tresses on her golden head.

When her eloquent eyes betrayed joy, beating hearts answered it, and what they uttered were songs of love.

Τ' ἁπαλὰ χείλη της, καλὰ
ὡς κάλυξ ἀνεμώνης,
μικρὸν προεῖχον τρυφηλά,
καί, ὅτ' ἐγέλων, πῶς γελᾷ
ὁ οὐρανὸς ἐφρόνεις.

II

Νὺξ ἦλθε μέλαινα. Περᾷ
ἡ ἀστραπὴ τὸ σκότος,
κ' εἰς τὰ πυργούμενα νερὰ
κατὰ λυσσῶντος τοῦ βορρᾶ
λυσσῶν παλαίει νότος.

Ὡς ὠρυόμεναι κυνῶν
ἠκούντο ἀγέλαι
εἰς τὸν εὐρὺν ὠκεανόν,
καὶ πελιδναὶ τὸν οὐρανὸν
διέτρεχον νεφέλαι.

Τὸ πνεῦμα τῶν τρικυμιῶν
τὸ πλοῖον ἀναπνέει,
καὶ καθὼς ἔμψυχόν τι ὄν,
ὀρθοῦται, πίπτει πνευστιῶν,
γογγύζει καὶ παλαίει.

Her tender lips, beautiful like anemone petals, protruded slightly,
sensuously, and when they laughed you thought the sky was laughing.

II

Black came the night; lightning pierced the darkness, and on the
towering waters a rabid south was wrestling with a mad north wind.

You could hear them on the wide ocean howling like packs of mad
dogs, and pale clouds ran across the sky.

The ship inhaled the wind of the storm, and like a living thing rose,
then panting fell, and sighing battled on.

JULIUS TYPALDOS
1814–83

287. Escape

‹Ξύπνα, γλυκιά μου ἀγάπη, κι ἡ νύχτα εἶναι βαθιά,
ὅλη κοιμᾶται ἡ φύσις, εἶναι ὅλα σιωπηλά.
Μόνον τ' ἀχνὸ φεγγάρι, ποὺ σὰν ἐμὲ ἀγρυπνᾶ,
μὲς τ' οὐρανοῦ ἀρμενίζει τὴν ἥσυχη ἐρημιά.

‹"Ἂν μᾶς χωρίζῃ τώρα μιὰ θέληση σκληρή,
μιὰν ἄκρη γῆς θὰ βροῦμε νὰ ζήσουμε μαζί.
Ξύπνα, γλυκιά μου ἀγάπη, κι ἡ νύχτα εἶναι βαθιά,
μᾶς καρτερεῖ ἡ βαρκούλα στὴν ἔρμη ἀκρογιαλιά.›

‹Ἀκόμη τὸ φεγγάρι ἔλαμπε σπλαχνικό,
μὲ μάτια δακρυσμένα τὸ κοίταζαν κι οἱ δυό.
‹Λάμνε, γλυκέ μου, λάμνε νὰ φύγουμε μακριά,
ὅσο σιγάει τ' ἀέρι στὰ ὁλόστρωτα νερά.›

Καὶ κάθε ποὺ στὸ κύμα βουτήξῃ τὸ κουπί,
στὸ μέτωπο τοῦ δίνει ἡ κόρη ἕνα φιλί.
‹Λάμνε, γλυκέ μου, λάμνε νὰ φύγουμε μακριά,
ὅσο σιγάει τ' ἀέρι στὰ ὁλόστρωτα νερά.›

'WAKE, my sweet love, the night is deep; all nature is sleeping, everything is silent. Only the hazy moon, that is awake as I, sails across the still wilderness of the sky.

'Though a cruel will now keeps us apart, we shall find a corner of the world where we shall live together. Wake, my sweet love, the night is deep, the little boat waits for us on the lonely beach.'

The compassionate moon was still shining, and both watched it with eyes full of tears. 'Row, my sweet love, row, and take us far away, as long as the wind is silent on the still water.'

And every time he dipped the oar in the wave, the girl gave him a kiss on the forehead. 'Row, my sweet love, row and take us far away, as long as the wind is silent on the still water.'

Κοιτάει τὴ γῆ ποὺ φεύγει σὰ σύγνεφο θολό,
τὴν ἀποχαιρετάει μ' ἕνα ἀναστεναγμό.
‹"Εχετε γειὰ λαγκάδια, βρυσοῦλες, κρύα νερά,
γλυκὲς αὐγές, πουλάκια, γιὰ πάντα ἔχετε γειά.

‹Μάνα, μακριὰ μὲ σπρώχνει εἰς ἄλλην ξένη γῆ,
μακριὰ ἀπὸ σὲ μιὰ ἀγάπη ἀνίκητη, θερμή.
Λάμνε, γλυκέ μου, λάμνε νὰ φύγουμε μακριά,
ὅσο σιγάει τ' ἀέρι, κι ἡ νύχτα εἶναι βαθιά.›

Προβαίνει τὸ φεγγάρι, κρυφὴ παρηγοριὰ
νὰ φέρη εἰς μύρια πάθη ἀγνώριστα, κρυφά.
Κι οἱ δύο μακριὰ στὰ ξένα τὸ κοίταζαν μαζί,
κι εἶχαν στὴν ἀγκαλιά τους παράδεισο καὶ γῆ.

JOHN KARASOUTSAS
1824-73

288. Nostalgia

Τίς τὴν ψυχήν μου θὰ ἡμερώση,
τίς εἰς τὸν πόθον μου θέλει δώσει
    πτερὰ ζεφύρου;
τίς εἰς τοὺς τόπους θενὰ μὲ φέρη,
ὅπου ὁ Μέλης στιλπνὸς μαρμαίρει
    ὡς πλὰξ ἀργύρου;

She looks at the land that fades away like a dim cloud, and bids it good-bye with a sigh: 'Good-bye, valleys, fountains, fresh streams, sweet dawns, little birds; for ever farewell.

'Mother, a love that burns invincible drags me far from you to a foreign land. Row, my dear love, row, and take us far away, as long as the wind is silent and the night is deep.'

The moon appears, bringing secret consolation to a thousand unknown, hidden pains. And the two of them, in a foreign land, looked at it together, holding in their arms paradise and earth.

WHO will calm my heart, who will give to my longing the wings of a Zephyr? Who will bring me to the land where Meles flashes, bright as a slab of silver?

Ἐκεῖ γλυκεῖαι πνέουσιν αὖραι,
καὶ εἰς τὸ κῦμα δονοῦνται μαῦραι
    σκιαὶ πλατάνων·
ἐκεῖ εὐώδης θάλλει μυρσίνη,
καὶ ὅλα εἶναι τέρψις, γαλήνη,
    πλὴν τῶν τυράννων.

Οὗτοι τὴν φρίκην παντοῦ ἐνσπείρουν,
καὶ τῆς ὡραίας φύσεως φθείρουν
    τὴν ἁρμονίαν·
οὗτοι μαραίνουν τὰ κάλλιστ' ἄνθη,
καὶ ἡ πνοή των κατελυμάνθη
    τὴν Ἰωνίαν.

Ἀλλ' ἂν τὰ κάλλη της λαῖλαψ τύπτῃ,
ὑπὸ τὸ βάρος της ἀνακύπτει
    πλέον ὡραία,
κ' εἰς τὴν γλυκεῖαν μορφήν της ἔτι
τὸ δουλικόν της πένθος προσθέτει
    θέλγητρα νέα.

Οὕτως εἰς ῥόδον πίπτει βαρεῖα
ἡ ὀλολύζουσα τρικυμία
    μὲ ὄμβρου σάλον,
πλὴν εἰς τὴν τόσην ἀνεμοζάλην
ὑπερηφάνως ἐγείρει πάλιν
    μέτωπον θάλλον.

Sweet breezes blow there, and the black shadows of plane-trees sway on the wave; there blooms the fragrant myrtle-bush, and all is pleasure and peace, but for the tyrants.

They sow horror everywhere, and ruin the harmony of the beautiful landscape. They wither the loveliest flowers, and their breath has stained Ionia.

But, though a storm beats on her beauty, more lovely she emerges from its rage, and the sorrow of servitude adds new charms to her sweet face.

So the howling tempest with whirling rain falls heavily upon a rose, but proudly it lifts once more, from the great windy storm, a flourishing brow.

GERASIMOS MARKORAS
1826–1911

289. *The Dead Maiden's Lament*

Κόσμε ὡραῖε, μὲ πόση λάβρα
σ' ἔχω τώρα στὴν καρδιά!
Τ' Ἀπριλιοῦ σου ἀκούω τὴν αὔρα
καὶ στὸ λάκκο μου βαθιά.

Μ' ὅσα ὁλοῦθε ἡ γῆ φυτρώνει,
νά 'ταν, θέ μου, βολετό,
ἀπ' τὸ χῶμα ποὺ μὲ ζώνει
σὰ τριαντάφυλλο νὰ βγῶ!

Πρὶν ὁ θάνατος μὲ σύρη
σὲ ἀλουλούδιαστες ἐρμιές,
εἶδα τέτοιο πανηγύρι
δεκατέσσερες φορές.

Μόλις εἶχα ἡ μαύρη ἀρχίσει
ἀνταπόκριση γλυκιὰ
μὲ τ' ἀέρι, μὲ τὴ βρύση,
μὲ τὰ πράσινα κλαριά.

Τὰ λουλούδια, ἡ χλόη, τὸ πλῆθος
ἀπὸ τ' ἄστρα τ' οὐρανοῦ
κάτι μόλεγαν στὸ στῆθος,
ποὺ δὲν ἔφτανε στὸ νοῦ.

BEAUTIFUL world, how passionately now I clasp you to my heart; I can hear your April's breeze even in the depths of my grave.

When the earth puts forth her shoots all around, would that I could emerge, my God, like a rose from the soil that embraces me.

I had seen this festival fourteen times before death dragged me to a flowerless wilderness.

I had just started – oh misery – a sweet contact with the breeze and the fountain and the green branches of the trees.

The flowers, the grass, the many stars of the sky were telling my heart something that did not reach my mind.

Νέα στὰ μάτια μου εἶχαν πάρει
  τὰ χαράματα ὀμορφιά,
  καὶ μοῦ ξύπναε τὸ φεγγάρι
  χίλια αἰσθήματα κρυφά.

Σ' ἀνθισμένα ἢ σ' ἄγρια μέρη
  περπατώντας μοναχή,
  ποιός, ἐρώτουνα, ποιός ξέρει
  τὸ τί αἰσθάνομαι νὰ πῆ;

Σὲ θωριὰ χαριτωμένη,
  σ' ἕνα μάτι ἀγγελικὸ
  τὴν ἀπόκριση γραμμένη
  κάπως ἔφτασα νὰ ἰδῶ.

Προτοῦ ξάστερα, μὲ θάρρος
  μοῦ τὴ δώση κι ἡ φωνή,
  σὰ γεράκι ἐχύθη ὁ Χάρος
  κι ἐδῶ μ' ἔριξε νεκρή.

Μνήμη τέτοια μὲ πλακώνει
  σὰν τὸ χῶμα μου βαριά.
  Τ' ἄλλου κόσμου χελιδόνι
  θὲ νὰ πάω κι ἐγὼ ψηλά!

Ὦ, Χριστέ μου, ἂς ξαναζήσω
  μόνον ὅσο εἶν' ἀρκετὸ
  τῆς καρδιᾶς μου νὰ γνωρίσω
  τὸ μεγάλο μυστικό!

Dawn appeared to my eyes with a new beauty, and the moon awoke
within me a thousand secret feelings.

Walking alone among flowers or in rugged places, who, I asked,
who knows, and who can tell what I feel?

In a beautiful shape, in an angel's eyes, I somehow reached the sight
of the answer, written.

Before the voice had given me a clear and straightforward answer,
Death swooped like a hawk and cast me here, dead.

Memory presses upon me as heavy as the earth of my tomb; the
swallow of another world, I too will fly high up.

O my Christ, may I live again only long enough to find out the
great secret of my heart.

ACHILLES PARASCHOS
1838–95

290. *The Laurel*

Μή με ζηλεύετε· κανείς τή δάφνη μή ζηλεύη·
μ' αἷμα καί δάκρυ πύρινο τή ρίζα μου ποτίζουν.
Καλότυχος ὅποιος ποτέ τή δάφνη δέν γυρεύει,
καί μόνον τά τριαντάφυλλα τό στῆθός του στολίζουν.
Κοινό στεφάνι μ' ἔχουνε ή δόξα καί ό πόνος,
καί τά θλιμμέν' ἀπόπαιδα τῆς μοίρας μ' ἔχουν μόνο.
Κάθε μου φύλλο ἄδοξος τό φαρμακεύει φθόνος·
γιά τοῦτο μόνο ποιητάς στόν κόσμο στεφανώνω.

291. *Rest, O My Eyes*

Κλεισθῆτε, μάτια μου, κλεισθῆτε
εἰς τό σκοτάδι·
χέρια, στό στῆθος σταυρωθῆτε,
ξεκουρασθῆτε·
ἦλθε τό βράδυ!

Σταθῆτε, πόδια κουρασμένα,
τό μνῆμα ἐφάνη·
ξαπλώσετε σαβανωμένα·
δυστυχισμένα,
ό δρόμος φθάνει. . .

Do not envy me. Let no one envy the laurel-tree. They water my root
with blood and burning tears. Lucky the man who never seeks laurels,
whose breast only roses adorn. Glory and pain have me as their com-
mon crown; only the sad outcasts of fortune carry me. Ignoble envy
poisons every one of my leaves; that is the only reason why I crown
the poets of the world.

CLOSE, close, my eyes, in the darkness. Arms, lie crossed upon my
breast; rest, the night has come.

Exhausted legs, be still; the tomb is in sight; lie shrouded, unhappy
limbs, you have wandered enough.

Ὕπνο καρδιά· καρδιά, κοιμήσου
στῆς γῆς τὰ στήθη·
στὴ γῆ θὰ παύσουν οἱ παλμοί σου
κι οἱ γογγυσμοί σου.
Χόρτασε λήθη!

DEMETRIOS PAPARRHEGOPOULOS
1843–73

292. *The Lantern of the Cemetery of Athens*

Ἐν μέσῳ πένθους οἱονεὶ γλυκείας εὐτυχίας,
φάροι τὸν νοῦν εὐθύνοντες πρὸς τὴν ἀθανασίαν,
διάδημα ἐπικοσμοῦν τὸ φάσμα τῆς σκοτίας,
τὰ ἄστρα, τὴν ἀτέρμονα βαδίζουσι πορείαν.

Ἀλλὰ ἰδέ, ἐκεῖ μακράν, εἰς τὸ νεκροταφεῖον,
φανὸν μὲ τοῦ ὁρίζοντος συμπίπτοντα τὸ πέρας·
δὲν εἶναι μέγας ὡς ἀστὴρ καὶ πλήρης μυστηρίων,
ἀλλ' ἔχει τὰς ἀκτῖνάς του πολὺ συμπαθεστέρας.

Φανέ, φυλάσσων τοὺς νεκρούς, τὸν θάνατον φωτίζων,
σέ, φῶς, ζωήν, τίς ἔρριψεν ἐντὸς κοιμητηρίου;
Δὲν εἶσαι ὡς μειδίαμα χεῖλος νεκροῦ στολίζον;
Σὲ βλέπουν οἱ ὑπνώττοντες κάτωθεν τοῦ φορείου;

My heart, sleep; sleep, my heart, on the earth's bosom. In the earth you will cease to beat and to sigh. Drink oblivion to satiety!

THE stars move on in their endless journey in sorrow, as if in the midst of sweet happiness; lights directing the mind to eternity, a diadem adorning a ghost of darkness.

But look, there at a distance, in the cemetery, a lantern hangs against the skyline; it is not as big as a star, nor full of mystery, but the rays it sheds are far more friendly.

Lantern, keeping guard over the dead, shedding light on death, who set you — life and light — in a cemetery? Are you not like a smile on the lips of a corpse? Do those who sleep in their coffins see you?

Σχίζε τὸ σκότος τῆς νυκτὸς καί, ἀπειλῶν τοὺς ζῶντας,
ῥίπτε τὸ φῶς σου ὅπου χοῦς ὑπάρχει καὶ σκοτία,
μέτρει τοὺς λίθους τῶν νεκρῶν καὶ τοὺς ἀποθανόντας·
ὤ! πόσοι εἶναι! φρικιᾷ καὶ τρέμει ἡ καρδία.

Μή, ἂν μετρῆται ἡ ζωή, ὁ θάνατος μετρεῖται;
Στιγμὴ εἰς τὸν ὠκεανὸν ῥιφθεῖσα τῶν αἰώνων,
πρὶν κἂν ὑπάρξῃ σβέννυται, πρὶν πέσῃ λησμονεῖται.
Ὁ χρόνος πρὸς τὸν θάνατον καταμετρεῖται μόνον.

Ζῆς ὡς ἀνάμνησις ἐκεῖ, φανέ, μεμονωμένη,
διπλῆν φωτίζων νέκρωσιν· τοὺς τάφους τῶν θανόντων,
τὴν λήθην, ἄλλον θάνατον, ὅστις αὐτοὺς προσμένει,
τὴν λήθην, κοιμητήριον ἐν τῇ ψυχῇ τῶν ζώντων.

Ναί! λησμονοῦσι· καὶ αὐτοὺς τοὺς ζῶντας λησμονοῦσι,
τὸ παρελθὸν ὡς σάβανον ἡ λήθη περιβάλλει.
Οἱ ἐπιζῶντες τοὺς νεκροὺς ἐπὶ μακρὸν θρηνοῦσι,
καὶ μόνη ἡ κυπάρισσος ἐπὶ τῶν τάφων θάλλει.

Ὦ φῶς, ὦ φῶς ταλαίπωρον! Ἐνῶ οἱ ἀδελφοί σου
φωτίζουσι συμπόσια χαρᾶς καὶ εὐθυμίας,
ἀλλ᾽ ἔρημος διέρχεται εἰς τάφους ἡ ἀκτίς σου
φωτίζουσα τοῦ Χάρωνος ὠχρὰς τὰς εὐωχίας.

Rend the darkness of the night and threaten the living; cast your brightness over ashes and blackness wherever they be. Count the tombstones and the dead; oh, how many they are – the heart shudders!

If life can be measured, can death be also measured? A moment cast in the ocean of centuries, extinguished even before it is born, forgotten before it drops in, time is measured only in relation to death.

There you live, lantern, like a solitary memory, lighting a double death: the tombs of the dead, and forgetfulness, oblivion, another death that awaits them: the graveyard in the heart of the living.

Yes, they forget; they forget, even the living. Oblivion covers the past like a winding-sheet; the living lament for long over the dead; then only the cypress-tree blooms over the graves.

Light, O poor light! Though your brothers shine over revelries and happy drinking-bouts, your lonely rays fall on the graves, lighting the pale feasts of Charon.

Παράδοξον συμπόσιον! Άπλοῦνται ἐσπαρμέναι
αἱ τράπεζαι μαρμάρινοι καὶ ὁ σταυρὸς πλησίον,
ἐπιγραφαὶ δεικνύονται ἐπάνω ἐστρωμέναι,
κιρνᾷ τὴν λήθην ἡ σιγὴ εἰς τὸ νεκροταφεῖον.

Τὸ φῶς σου πίπτει ἐπ' αὐτῶν ὡς νεκρικὴ ὠχρότης·
τίς ἐφαντάσθη ἑορτὴν μὲ τόσην ἠρεμίαν;
Καὶ ποῦ καὶ ποῦ ἐγείρεται μαρμάρινος συμπότης·
ὤ! πάντες θὰ καθίσωμεν εἰς τράπεζαν ὁμοίαν.

Θώπευε, θώπευε, φανέ, τὴν πλάκα τῶν θανόντων·
ὁπόσοι ἐκοιμήθησαν χωρίς τινος θωπείας,
πόσοι θὰ ἦσαν σήμερον ἐδῶ ἐν μέσῳ ζώντων,
ἐὰν ἐθώπευεν αὐτοὺς ἓν βλέμμα συμπαθείας!

Ἀστὴρ τῶν τάφων θλιβερός, τὸ φῶς ἐκεῖνο, τρέμον
φωτίζει τὴν ὑστερινὴν ὁδὸν τοῦ διαβάτου,
καὶ πνευστιᾷ εἰς τὴν πνοὴν τὴν κρύαν τῶν ἀνέμων.
Ὦ φῶς, τί μὲ παρατηρεῖς ὡς ὀφθαλμὸς θανάτου;

Δὲν τὸν φοβοῦμαι· ὄρθιος πρὸ τοῦ θανάτου βαίνω·
δὲν ψάλλω τὴν ἰσχὺν αὐτοῦ αἰτῶν ἀθανασίαν,
τὸ φίλημά του τὸ ψυχρὸν ἀτάραχος προσμένω·
τίς τὴν γαλήνην δὲν ποθεῖ μετὰ τὴν τρικυμίαν;

Strange drinking-party! The marble tables are scattered around, and the cross is beside them, and on them inscriptions are laid; in the cemetery silence pours out the drink of oblivion.

Your light falls upon them like a dead man's pallor. Who ever imagined a feast with such peace? And here and there you see a marble guest stand up – alas, we shall all sit at such a table!

Caress, lantern, caress the grave-stones of the dead; how many fell asleep with no caress; how many would be here among the living if a glance of sympathy had touched them?

The sad star of the tombs, that trembling flame lights the last journey of those who pass by it and gasps at the cold blasts of the wind. Light, why are you looking at me like the eye of death?

I do not fear it; I stand upright and walk facing death. I do not beg for immortality by singing his power; unperturbed, I wait for his cold kiss. Who does not long for peace after the storm?

Πόσον ὡραία μηδειᾷ ἡ ὄψις τῆς πρωίας·
εἶναι γλυκὺς ὁ ἥλιος τὸ πρῶτον φῶς του στέλλων.
Ἄ! πανταχοῦ ἀπήντησα ἐν φάσμα εὐτυχίας,
τὴν εὐτυχίαν οὐδαμοῦ· οὐδ' εἰς αὐτὸ τὸ μέλλον.

Μέλλον, τῆς τύχης παίγνιον, τοῦ βίου εἰρωνεία,
λέξις οὐδὲν σημαίνουσα ἢ πάροδον τοῦ χρόνου
καὶ φάρμακον, ὅπερ ῥοφᾷ, παροῦσα ἡ πικρία,
ὅπως ἐπέλθῃ αὔριον μετὰ ὁμοίου πόνου.

Μέλλον, λέξις σημαίνουσα τὴν ἔλλειψιν παρόντος,
ἠχὼ τῶν πόθων, οἵτινες βλαστάνουσι λαθραίως,
πολλάκις ἀντανάκλασις ὠχρὰ τοῦ παρελθόντος,
πλὴν πάντοτε κατοπτρισμὸς δεικνύμενος ματαίως.

Μέλλον, καθὼς ἡ ἀστραπὴ τὸ σκότος ἐπεκτεῖνον,
τῆς συμφορᾶς ὁ ἐμπαιγμός, ἰσχὺς ἀδυναμίας,
τὸ σκοτεινόν του πρόσωπον ἐπὶ τοῦ τάφου κλῖνον,
κ' ἐκεῖθεν θάλλον ὡς ἐλπὶς κενὴ ἀθανασίας.

Ἰδοὺ τὸ μέλλον· ἡ ῥυτίς, θωπεία τοῦ θανάτου·
ἐν δάκρυ σπεῖρον ἕτερον· κραυγὴ ἀπελπισίας·
ἕως οὗ ἔπειτα ἐντὸς μακροῦ νεκροκραββάτου,
σταυρώσῃς τοὺς βραχίονας ἐπὶ νεκρᾶς καρδίας.

How beautiful the smile on the morning's face. The sun is sweet as
it sheds its first light. Alas, everywhere I have only met the ghost of
happiness, but happiness nowhere, not even in the future.

The future: a toy in the hands of fortune, the irony of life, a word
meaning nothing beyond the passage of time, a medicine that present
bitterness drinks so that tomorrow she may come with similar pain.

The future: a word meaning there is no present, the echo of longings
which secretly branch out; often the pale reflection of the past, always
an image set before us for nothing.

The future that, like lightning, makes darkness look deeper, the
derision of calamity, the power of weakness, bows its sombre face
over the tomb, and blossoms out of it like the empty hope of im-
mortality.

This is the future: wrinkles, death's caress, a tear sowing more tears,
a cry of despair, until, stretched out on a long deathbed, you cross your
arms over a dead heart.

Μόνος, καθὼς αὐτὸ τὸ φῶς εἰς τὸ νεκροταφεῖον,
φωτίζον πόθων μνήματα καὶ πτώματα ὀνείρων,
ἀγνώστου πόνου ἕρμαιον, διέρχομαι τὸν βίον
τὰ ῥάκη σύρων τῆς ζωῆς, τὸ παρελθόν μου σύρων.

Φανέ, ὅταν τὸ ἔλαιον σὲ λείψῃ, τί θὰ γίνῃς;
Τί; θὰ σβεσθῇς. Καλύτερον. Ἀφοῦ ἡ μοῖρ' ἀγρίως
προώρισε τὴν λάμψιν σου ἐπὶ σποδοῦ νὰ χύνῃς,
τί ὠφελεῖ εἰς σὲ τὸ φῶς καὶ εἰς ἐμὲ ὁ βίος;

G. VIZYENOS
1848–94

293. The Dream

Ἐψὲς΄ εἶδα στὸν ὕπνο μου
ἕνα βαθὺ ποτάμι,
— θεὸς νὰ μὴν το κάμη
νὰ γίνη ἀληθινό! —
Στὴν ὄχθη του στεκότανε
γνωστό μου παλληκάρι,
χλωμὸ σὰν τὸ φεγγάρι,
σὰ νύχτα σιγανό.

I spend my life alone like that light at the cemetery, lighting the tombs of my desires, the corpses of my dreams; plaything of an unknown pain, I pass my days dragging along the rags of my life; I drag along my past.

When your oil has finished, lantern, what will become of you? What? You will go out. Better so, since Fate cruelly ordered that your light should fall on ashes; of what use is light to you or life to me?

LAST night in my sleep I saw a deep river — may God never make it come true. A young man I knew, pale as the moon, silent as the night, was standing on its bank.

'Αγέρας τὸ παράσπρωχνε
μὲ δύναμη μεγάλη,
   σὰ νὰ θε νὰ τὸ βγάλη
   ἀπ' τῆς ζωῆς τὴ μέση.
Καὶ τὸ νερό, που ἀχόρταγα
τὰ πόδια του φιλοῦσε,
   θαρρεῖς τὸ προσκαλοῦσε
   στ' ἀγκάλια του νὰ πέση.

— Δὲν εἶν' ἀγέρας σκέφθηκα
καὶ σένα ποὺ σὲ δέρνει·
   ἡ ἀπελπισιὰ σὲ παίρνει
   κι ἡ ἀπονιὰ τοῦ κόσμου.
Κι ἐχύθηκα ἀπ' τὸ θάνατο
τὸν δύστυχο ν' ἀρπάξω . . .
   'Ωιμέ! Πρίν ἢ προφθάξω,
   ἐχάθηκε ἀπ' ἐμπρός μου.

Στὰ ρέματα παράσκυψα,
νὰ τὸν εὑρῶ γυρεύω.
   Στὰ ρέματα ἀγναντεύω —
   τὸ λείψανό μ' ἀχνό . . .
'Εψὲς εἶδα στὸν ὕπνο μου
ἕνα βαθὺ ποτάμι
   — θεὸς νὰ μὴν το κάμη
   νὰ γίνη ἀληθινό!

The wind was beating at him wildly, as if it wanted to drive him
from among the living. And it looked as though the water that was
avidly kissing his feet was inviting him to fall into its arms.

This is not the wind, I thought, that beats upon you too. You must
be overwhelmed by despair, and by the heartless world. And I rushed
to wrest the poor young man from death. Alas, I was not in time; he
vanished from my sight.

I stooped over the stream searching to find him and in the currents I
saw — my own pale corpse. Last night in my sleep I saw a deep river —
may God never make it come true.

ARISTOTLE VALAORITIS
1824–79

294. The Rock and the Wave

‹ Μέριασε, βράχε, νὰ διαβῶ !› τὸ κύμ' ἀνδρειωμένο
λέγει στὴν πέτρα τοῦ γιαλοῦ θολό, μελανιασμένο·
‹μέριασε, μὲς στὰ στήθη μου, ποὺ 'σαν νεκρὰ καὶ κρύα,
μαῦρος βοριὰς ἐφώλιασε καὶ μαύρη τρικυμία.
'Αφροὺς δὲν ἔχω γι' ἄρματα, κούφια βοὴ γι' ἀντάρα,
ἔχω ποτάμι αἵματα, μὲ θέριεψε ἡ κατάρα
τοῦ κόσμου ποὺ βαρέθηκε, τοῦ κόσμου ποὺ 'πε τώρα,
‹βράχε, θὰ πέσῃς, ἔφτασεν ἡ φοβερή σου ἡ ὥρα.›
῝Οταν ἐρχόμουννα σιγά, δειλό, παραδαρμένο,
καὶ σόγλυφα καὶ σόπλενα τὰ πόδια δουλωμένο,
περήφανα μὲ κοίταζες, καὶ φώναζες τοῦ κόσμου
νὰ ἰδῆ τὴν καταφρόνεση, ποὺ πάθαινε ὁ ἀφρός μου.
Κι ἀντὶς ἐγὼ κρυφὰ κρυφά, ἐκεῖ ποὺ σὲ φιλοῦσα
μέρα καὶ νύχτα σ' ἔσκαφτα, τὴ σάρκα σου ἐδαγκοῦσα,
καὶ τὴν πληγὴ ποὺ σ' ἄνοιγα, τὸ λάκκο ποὺ θὲ κάμω,
μὲ φύκι τὸν ἐπλάκωνα, τὸν ἔκρυβα στὸν ἄμμο.
Σκύψε νὰ ἰδῆς τὴ ρίζα σου στῆς θάλασσας τὰ βύθη,
τὰ θέμελά σου τὰ 'φαγα, σ' ἔκαμα κουφολίθι.

'MAKE way, rock, for me to pass,' cries the dark seething wave, full of courage, to the rock on the shore. 'Make way, for in my breast, once dead and cold, the black north wind has made his nest, and a black storm! My foam is not my weapon, nor empty noise my war-cry; I carry rivers of blood, the curse of a world that had enough has made me rear gigantic, a world that said: "Rock, now you will fall, the hour you dreaded has come!" When I came gently, timidly, brow-beaten, and washed and licked your feet enslaved, you looked proudly at me and cried to the world to see the contempt with which my spray was treated. And I, day and night, as I kissed you, secretly dug up your roots and bit your flesh; and the wound I opened, the grave I dug, I covered with seaweed, I hid it under the sand. Stoop and look at your roots in the depths of the sea. I have eaten away your foundations, I have turned you into a pumice-stone. Make way for me to pass, rock!

Μέριασε, βράχε, νά διαβῶ! Τοῦ δούλου τό ποδάρι
θά σέ πατήση στό λαιμό. . . . Ἐξύπνησα λιοντάρι . . .›

Ὁ βράχος ἐκοιμότουνε. Στήν καταχνιά κρυμμένος,
ἀναίσθητος σοῦ φαίνεται, νεκρός, σαβανωμένος.
Τοῦ φώτιζαν τό μέτωπο, σχισμένο ἀπό ρυτίδες,
τοῦ φεγγαριοῦ, πού 'ταν χλωμό, μισόσβυστες ἀχτίδες.
Ὁλόγυρά του ὀνείρατα, κατάρες ἀνεμίζουν,
καί στόν ἀνεμοστρόβιλο φαντάσματα ἀρμενίζουν,
καθώς ἀνεμοδέρνουνε καί φτεροθορυβοῦνε
τή δυσωδία τοῦ νεκροῦ τά ὄρνια ἄν μυριστοῦνε.

Τό μούγκρισμα τοῦ κύματος, τήν ἄσπλαχνη φορβέρα
χίλιες φορές τήν ἄκουσεν ὁ βράχος στόν ἀθέρα
ν' ἀντιβοᾶ τρομαχτικά χωρίς κάν νά ξυπνήση·
καί σήμερ' ἀνατρίχιασε λές θά λιγοψυχήση.

‹Κύμα, τί θέλεις ἀπό μέ καί τί μέ φοβερίζεις;
Ποιός εἶσαι σύ κι ἐτόλμησες, ἀντί νά μέ δροσίζης,
ἀντί μέ τό τραγούδι σου τόν ὕπνο μου νά εὐφραίνης
καί μέ τά κρύα σου νερά τή φτέρνα μου νά πλένης,
ἐμπρός μου στέκεις φοβερό, μ' ἀφρούς στεφανωμένο;
Ὅποιος κι ἄν εἶσαι, μάθε το, εὔκολα δέν πεθαίνω.›

The foot of the slave will tread on your neck. . . . I have awakened like
a lion . . .'

The rock was sleeping. Hidden in the mist, he looked as though he
were numb, dead and shrouded. His brow, ploughed by wrinkles, was
lit by the half-dead rays of the pale moon. Around him hovered
dreams and curses, ghosts that floated like a whirlwind, like birds of
prey that beat the wind with noisy wings when they sense the smell of
a corpse.

The rock had heard a thousand times the growl of the wave, its
heartless menace resounding frightfully in the wind, but had not
even awakened. Yet today he felt a shiver, almost as if he were going to
lose courage.

'Wave, what do you want from me? Why are you threatening me?
Who are you, that you dare instead of refreshing me, instead of sooth-
ing my sleep with your song and washing my feet with your water, to
stand menacing before me, crowned with foam? Whoever you be,
know that I will not die easily.'

‹ Βράχε, μὲ λένε ἐκδίκηση. Μὲ πότισεν ὁ χρόνος
χολὴ καὶ καταφρόνεση· μ' ἀνάθρεψεν ὁ πόνος.
Ἤμουνα δάκρυ μιὰ φορά, καὶ τώρα, κοίταξέ με,
ἔγινα θάλασσα πλατιά, πέσε, προσκύνησέ με.
Ἐδῶ μέσα στὰ σπλάχνα μου, βλέπεις, δὲν ἔχω φύκη,
σέρνω ἕνα σύγνεφο ψυχές, ἐρμιὰ καὶ καταδίκη.
Ξύπνησε τώρα, σὲ ζητοῦν τοῦ Ἅδη μου τ' ἀχνάρια...
Μ' ἔκαμες ξυλοκρέβατο. ... Μὲ φόρτωσες κουφάρια...
Σὲ ξένους μ' ἔριξες γιαλούς. ... Τὸ ψυχομάχημά μου
τὸ περιγέλασαν πολλοί, καὶ τὰ παθήματά μου
τὰ φαρμακέψανε κρυφὰ μὲ τὴν ἐλεημοσύνη.
Μέριασε, βράχε, νὰ διαβῶ, ἐπέρασε ἡ γαλήνη,
καταποτήρας εἶμ' ἐγώ, ὁ ἄσπονδος ἐχθρός σου,
      γίγαντας στέκω ἐμπρός σου! ›

Ὁ βράχος ἐβουβάθηκε. Τὸ κύμα στὴν ὁρμή του
ἐκαταπόντισε μὲ μιᾶς τὸ κούφιο τὸ κορμί του.
Χάνεται μὲς στὴν ἄβυσσο, τρίβεται, σβυέται, λειώνει
      σὰν νά 'ταν ἀπὸ χιόνι.
Ἐπάνωθέ του ἐβρόγγιξε γιὰ λίγο ἀγριωμένη
ἡ θάλασσα κι ἐκλείστηκε. Τώρα δὲν ἀπομένει
στὸν τόπο πού 'ταν τὸ στοιχειὸ κανεὶς παρὰ τὸ κύμα,
ποὺ παίζει γαλανόλευκο ἐπάνω ἀπὸ τὸ μνῆμα.

'Rock, I am called revenge. Time has fed me with gall and contempt.
Pain has reared me. I was a tear once, and now look at me: I have be-
come a wide sea. Fall at my feet and worship me. Look, here in my
heart I do not carry seaweed, I carry a cloud of souls, solitude and
condemnation. Wake up, now the footfalls of my Hades are after
you.... You turned me into a deathbed ... you piled upon me
corpses ... you sent me away to foreign shores.... Many laughed at
my death agony, and secretly poisoned my suffering with almsgiving.
Make way for me to pass, rock; the calm weather is over; I am the
drowning wave, your implacable enemy, standing like a giant before
you!'
The rock was stunned into silence. The rushing wave swiftly
covered the rotten body. It was lost in the abyss, crumbled, quenched,
melted as if it had been made of snow. The wild sea growled for a
while above him and then closed over him. There, where that ghost
stood, nothing remains, only the wave that, white and blue, plays
over the grave.

GEORGE DROSINIS
1859–1951

295. *The Soil of Greece*

Τώρα ποὺ θὰ φύγω καὶ θὰ πάω στὰ ξένα,
καὶ θὰ ζοῦμε μῆνες, χρόνους χωρισμένοι,
ἄφησε νὰ πάρω κάτι κι ἀπὸ σένα,
γαλανὴ πατρίδα, πολυαγαπημένη·
ἄφησε μαζί μου φυλαχτὸ νὰ πάρω
γιὰ τὴν κάθε λύπη, κάθε τι κακό,
φυλαχτὸ ἀπ' ἀρρώστια, φυλαχτὸ ἀπὸ Χάρο,
μόνο λίγο χῶμα, χῶμα Ἑλληνικό.

Χῶμα δροσισμένο μὲ νυχτιᾶς ἀγέρι,
χῶμα βαφτισμένο μὲ βροχὴ τοῦ Μάη,
χῶμα μυρισμένο ἀπ' τὸ καλοκαίρι,
χῶμα εὐλογημένο, χῶμα ποὺ γεννάει
μόνο μὲ τῆς Πούλιας τὴν οὐράνια χάρη,
μόνο μὲ ἥλιου τὰ θερμὰ φιλιὰ
τὸ μοσχάτο κλῆμα, τὸ ξανθὸ σιτάρι,
τὴ χλωρὴ τὴ δάφνη, τὴν πικρὴν ἐλιά.

Χῶμα τιμημένο, πόχουν ἀνασκάψει
γιὰ νὰ θεμελιώσουν ἕνα Παρθενώνα,

Now that I am leaving and shall go to foreign lands, and we shall live apart for months and years, let me take with me something from you too, my blue beloved homeland. Let me take an amulet to protect me from all sorrow, from every evil, an amulet against sickness and death, a little, only a little of the soil of Greece.

Soil that the night-breeze cooled, the rain of May moistened; summer gave it fragrance; blessed earth that, if only touched by the heavenly grace of the Pleiades and the warm kisses of the sun, yields the fragrant vine, the golden corn, the green laurel and the bitter olive.

Honoured soil, which was dug for the foundations of a Parthenon;

χῶμα δοξασμένο, πόχουν ῥοδοβάψει
αἵματα στὸ Σούλι καὶ στὸ Μαραθώνα·
χῶμα πόχει θάψει λείψαν' ἁγιασμένα
ἀπ' τὸ Μεσολόγγι κι ἀπὸ τὰ Ψαρά,
χῶμα ποὺ θὰ φέρνη στὸν μικρὸν ἐμένα
θάρρος, περηφάνια, δόξα καὶ χαρά.

Θὲ νὰ σὲ κρεμάσω φυλαχτὸ στὰ στήθια,
κι ὅταν ἡ καρδιά μου φυλαχτὸ σὲ βάλη
ἀπὸ σὲ θὰ παίρνη δύναμη, βοήθεια,
μὴν τὴν ξεπλανέσουν ἄλλα, ξένα κάλλη.
Ἡ δική σου χάρη θὰ μὲ δυναμώνη,
κι ὅπου κι ἂν γυρίσω κι ὅπου κι ἂν σταθῶ,
σὺ θὲ νὰ μοῦ δίνης μιὰ λαχτάρα μόνη,
πότε στὴν Ἑλλάδα πίσω θὲ νὰ 'ρθῶ.

Κι ἂν τὸ ριζικό μου — ἔρημο καὶ μαῦρο —
μοῦ 'γραψε νὰ φύγω καὶ νὰ μὴ γυρίσω,
τὸ στερνὸ συχώριο εἰς ἐσένα θὰ 'βρω,
τὸ στερνὸ φιλί μου θὲ νὰ σοῦ χαρίσω.
Ἔτσι, κι ἂν σὲ ξένα χώματα πεθάνω,
καὶ τὸ ξένο μνῆμα θὰ 'ναι πιὸ γλυκό,
σὰ θαφτῆς μαζί μου στὴν καρδιά μου ἀπάνω,
χῶμα ἀγαπημένο, χῶμα Ἑλληνικό.

glorious soil, dyed red by the blood of Souli and of Marathon; soil that
buried holy relics from Missolonghi and Psara, soil that will give me,
a young boy, courage, pride, glory and joy.

I will hang you as an amulet on my breast, and when my heart wears
you as an amulet she will take courage, be helped by you, and will not
be bewitched by other foreign beauties. Your grace will give me
strength; wherever I turn, wherever I stand, you will kindle in me only
one desire: to return to Greece.

And should it be my fate – a black desolate fate – to leave and never
to return, I will finally ask you to forgive me, and give you my last
kiss. So, if I die in foreign lands, the foreign tomb will be sweeter if
you will be buried with me on my heart, beloved soil, soil of Greece.

296. Evensong

Στὸ ῥημαγμένο παρακκλήσι
τῆς ἄνοιξης τὸ θεῖο κοντύλι
εἰκόνες ἔχει ζωγραφίσει
μὲ τ' ἀγριολούλουδα τ' 'Απρίλη.

'Ο ἥλιος, γέρνοντας στὴ δύση,
μπροστὰ στοῦ ἱεροῦ τὴν πύλη
μπαίνει δειλὰ νὰ προσκυνήση,
κι ἀνάφτει ὑπέρλαμπρο καντήλι.

Σκορπάει γλυκιὰ μοσκοβολιὰ
δάφνη στὸν τοῖχο ριζωμένη
— θυμίαμα ποὺ καίει ἡ πίστις —

καὶ μιὰ χελιδονοφωλιὰ
ψηλὰ στὸ νάρθηκα χτισμένη
ψάλλει τὸ ‹Δόξα ἐν 'Υψίστοις›.

THE divine brush of springtime has painted ikons with the wild flowers of April in the ruined chapel.

The sun, dipping to the west, enters timidly to worship before the altar's door and lights a brilliant lamp.

A laurel, rooted in the wall, spreads sweet fragrance — incense the faithful burn —

And a swallow's nest, built high up in the narthex, chants: 'Glory to God in the highest.'

KOSTIS PALAMAS
1859–1943

297. *Digenis Akritas*

I

Καβάλα πάει ὁ Χάροντας
τὸ Διγενὴ στὸν Ἅδη,
κι ἄλλους μαζί. . . . Κλαίει, δέρνεται
τ' ἀνθρώπινο κοπάδι.

Καὶ τοὺς κρατεῖ στοῦ ἀλόγου του
δεμένους τὰ καπούλια
τῆς λεβεντιᾶς τὸν ἄνεμο,
τῆς ὀμορφιᾶς τὴν πούλια.

Καὶ σὰ νὰ μὴν τὸν πάτησε
τοῦ Χάρου τὸ ποδάρι,
ὁ Ἀκρίτας μόνο ἀτάραχα
κοιτάει τὸν καβαλάρη.

II

«Ὁ Ἀκρίτας εἶμαι, Χάροντα,
δὲν περνῶ μὲ τὰ χρόνια,
μ' ἄγγιξες καὶ δὲ μ' ἔνιωσες
στὰ μαρμαρένια ἀλώνια;

I

DEATH takes Digenis to Hades on his horse, and many more. . . . The herd of mortals beat their breast and lament.

He has tied behind the saddle of his horse the breath of manhood, the Pleiades of beauty.

But only Akritas, as though the foot of Death had not stepped upon him, stares calmly at the horseman.

II

'I am Akritas, Death, I do not pass with the years; how is it that you touched me, but did not realize who I was, on the marble threshing-floor?

536

‹Εἶμ' ἐγὼ ἡ ἀκατάλυτη
ψυχὴ τῶν Σαλαμίνων·
στὴν Ἑφτάλοφην ἔφερα
τὸ σπαθὶ τῶν Ἑλλήνων.

‹Δὲ χάνομαι στὰ Τάρταρα,
μονάχα ξαποσταίνω·
στὴ ζωὴ ξαναφαίνομαι
καὶ λαοὺς ἀνασταίνω!›

298. Eternal Greece

Ἡ γῆ μας γῆ τῶν ἄφθαρτων
ἀερικῶν καὶ εἰδώλων,
πασίχαρος καὶ ὑπέρτατος
θεός μας εἶν' ὁ Ἀπόλλων.

Στὰ ἐντάφια λευκὰ σάβανα
γυρτὸς ὁ Ἐσταυρωμένος
εἶν' ὁλόμορφος Ἄδωνης
ῥοδοπεριχυμένος.

Ἡ ἀρχαία ψυχὴ ζῆ μέσα μας
ἀθέλητα κρυμμένη·
ὁ Μέγας Πὰν δὲν πέθανεν,
ὄχι· ὁ Πὰν δὲν πεθαίνει!

'I am the undying soul of Salamis, I have brought the sword of the Greeks to the gates of the seven-hilled city [Constantinople].

'I do not perish in Tartarus, I only rest a little; I reappear in life, and resurrect nations.'

OUR land is the land of immortal spirits and idols; Apollo, full of joy and supreme, is our god.

Christ crucified, lying in his white winding-sheet, is beautiful Adonis covered with roses.

The soul of ancient Greece lives hidden unwillingly within us. Great Pan is not dead, no, great Pan does not die!

299. The Grave

Στὸ ταξίδι ποὺ σὲ πάει
ὁ μαῦρος καβαλάρης,
κοίτα ἀπὸ τὸ χέρι του
τίποτε νὰ μὴν πάρης·

κι ἂ διψάσης, μὴν τὸ πιῆς
ἀπὸ τὸν κάτου κόσμο
τὸ νερὸ τῆς ἀρνησιᾶς,
φτωχὸ κομμένο δυόσμο!

Μὴν τὸ πιῆς, κι ὁλότελα
κι αἰώνια μᾶς ξεχάσης·
βάλε τὰ σημάδια σου
τὸ δρόμο νὰ μὴ χάσης,

κι ὅπως εἶσαι ἀνάλαφρο,
μικρό, σὰ χελιδόνι,
κι ἄρματα δὲ σοῦ βροντᾶν
παλικαριοῦ στὴ ζώνη,

κοίταξε καὶ γέλασε
τῆς νύχτας τὸ σουλτάνο,
γλίστρησε σιγὰ κρυφὰ
καὶ πέταξ' ἐδῶ πάνω,

On the journey on which the Black Horseman takes you, be careful not to accept anything from his hand;

And, if you feel thirsty, do not drink the water of oblivion in the world below, my poor plucked spearmint!

Do not drink, lest you forget us fully, forever; leave marks so as not to lose the way,

And, being light and small like a swallow, with no warrior's weapons clashing round your waist,

See how you can trick the Sultan of the Night; slip away gently, secretly, and fly to us up here;

καὶ στὸ σπίτι τ' ἀραχνο
γυρνώντας, ὦ ἀκριβέ μας,
γίνε ἀεροφύσημα,
καὶ γλυκοφίλησέ μας.

300. Athens

Ἐδῶ οὐρανὸς παντοῦ κι ὁλοῦθε ἥλιου ἀχτίνα,
καὶ κάτι ὁλόγυρα σὰν τοῦ Ὑμηττοῦ τὸ μέλι,
βγαίνουν ἀμάραντ' ἀπὸ μάρμαρο τὰ κρίνα,
λάμπει γεννήτρα ἑνὸς Ὀλύμπου ἡ θεία Πεντέλη.

Στὴν Ὀμορφιὰ σκοντάβει σκάφτοντας ἡ ἀξίνα,
στὰ σπλάχνα ἀντὶ θνητοὺς θεοὺς κρατᾶ ἡ Κυβέλη,
μενεξεδένιο αἷμα γοργοστάζ' ἡ Ἀθήνα
κάθε ποὺ τῆ χτυπᾶν τοῦ δειλινοῦ τὰ βέλη.

Τῆς ἱερῆς Ἐλιᾶς ἐδῶ ναοὶ καὶ κάμποι·
ἀνάμεσα στὸν ὄχλο ἐδῶ ποὺ ἀργοσαλεύει,
καθὼς ἀπάνου σ' ἀσπρολούλουδο μιὰ κάμπη,

ὁ λαὸς τῶν λειψάνων ζῆ καὶ βασιλεύει
χιλιόψυχος· τὸ πνεῦμα καὶ στὸ χῶμα λάμπει·
τὸ νιώθω· μὲ σκοτάδια μέσα μου παλεύει.

Come back to this empty house, O our precious boy; turn into a breath of wind, and give us a sweet kiss.

HERE the sky is everywhere, on all sides shines the sun, and something like the honey of Hymettus is all around; out of the marble grow lilies unwithering; divine Mount Pentelicon flashes, begetter of an Olympus.

The digging axe stumbles on beauty; in her bosom Cybele holds gods, not mortals; when the shafts of twilight strike her, Athens gushes violet blood.

Here are the temples and the groves of the sacred olive, and in the slowly shifting crowd, like a caterpillar on a white flower,

A host of deathless relics live and reign with myriad souls; the spirit flashes even in the earth; I feel it wrestling with the darkness in me.

301. The Dead Boy

Μέσα ἐδῶ τὴν ψυχὴ κάποιου νεκροῦ ἀναπνέω,
καὶ εἶν' ὁ νεκρὸς ξανθός, ἀγένειο παλικάρι,
καὶ φέγγος νέο ξανθὸ σαλεύει καὶ στὸ σπίτι,
καὶ φεύγουν μέρες καὶ στιγμές, καιροὶ καὶ χρόνια,
καὶ εἶν' ἡ ψυχὴ τοῦ ἑνὸς νεκροῦ σ' αὐτὸ τὸ σπίτι
σὰν τὴν πικρὴ γαλήνη γύρω στὸ καράβι
ποῦ δρόμους λαχταρεῖ κι ὀνειρεύεται μπόρες.
Καὶ εἶναι τὰ πρόσωπα ὅλων πρόσωπα ἀχνισμένα
σὰν ἀπὸ νεκροκέρια, καὶ τὰ μάτια εἶν' ὅλων
μάτια σὲ φέρετρο ἴσα ἀπάνου στυλωμένα,
καὶ σιγοτρέμουν πικροστάζοντας τὰ χείλη
τῇ φαρμακίλα τοῦ ἀσπασμοῦ τοῦ τελευταίου.
Σάμπως γιὰ προσευχὴ νὰ ὑψώνουνται τὰ χέρια,
καὶ τὰ πόδια πηγαίνουν σὰ νὰ συνοδεύουν
ἕνα νεκρό· κ' ἡ γύμνια ἡ κάτασπρη τῶν τοίχων,
καὶ ὁ πλοῦτος ὁ κατάμαυρος τῶν φορεμάτων,
μιὰ μουσικὴ ἀπὸ χωριστὰ λαλούμενα εἶναι.
Καὶ τὰ παιδιὰ ἀλαφροπατοῦν, σὰ νὰ μὴ θέλουν
νὰ ταράξουν τὸν ὕπνο ἑνὸς νεκροῦ, καὶ οἱ γέροι
πάντα σκυμμένοι σὰ στὴν ἄκρη κάποιου λάκκου,

HERE I breathe the soul of a dead man, and the dead man is a fair-haired beardless youth, and a golden light moves in the house; and days, time, moments, years go by, and the soul of the dead man is round the house like the bitter calm round a ship that longs to sail and dreams of storms. And the faces of all are wrapped in a haze as though lit by candles round a deathbed, and all eyes are as though fixed on a coffin, and lips silently tremble as though dripping the poison of the last kiss; hands rise as if to pray, and legs move as though escorting a dead body. And the white nakedness of the walls, and the rich blackness of the clothes, are a music of extraordinary instruments. And the children walk gently, as though careful not to disturb the sleep of a corpse, and the old people are hunched, as if always looking into a

στούς ὤμους τῶν παρθένων ἀκκουμποῦν, καὶ κεῖνες
μοῖρες καλοπροαίρετες παρηγορῆτρες,
καὶ οἱ νέοι σ' ἀτέλειωτα διαβάσματα ζητοῦνε
τὸ λησμοβότανο ἀπὸ τὰ χέρια τῆς σοφίας.
Καὶ στὰ πορτοπαράθυρα τὰ σφαλισμένα
τῆς γάστρας τᾶνθη σὰ νεκροστολίσματα εἶναι,
κ' ἡ ἀχτίδα ποῦ γλιστράει ἀπὸ τὴ χαραμάδα
ψυχοσαββάτου γίνεται κερὶ ἐδῶ μέσα,
καὶ τὸ καντήλι στὴν εἰκόνα τρεμοσβύνει,
κ' εἶναι σὰ χαροπάλαιμα τὸ τρίξιμό του,
καὶ κάπου κάπου πλουμισμένη πεταλοῦδα
ξεπέφτοντας ἐδῶ, στὴ σάρκα ἀνάερα δείχνει
τὸ ‹χαῖρε› τῆς ψυχῆς ποῦ μάγεψε τὸ σπίτι . . .
'Αλλὰ καὶ πῶς τὸν ἀγαπάει, πῶς τόνε θέλει
τὸν πεθαμένο, τὸ ξανθὸ τὸ παλικάρι,
τὸ δικό του νεκρό, τὸ νεκρόχαρο σπίτι!
Καὶ πλανεύοντας, πάντα γιὰ νὰ τὸν κρατάη,
πάντα μέσα ἀμετάνιωτο τὸν ἀκριβό του,
μπόρεσε κι ἄλλαξε, ἔγινε ἀπὸ σπίτι, μνῆμα.

grave; they lean on the young girls' shoulders, who look like kind
consoling Fates, and through endless study the young seek the herb of
oblivion from the hands of wisdom. And at the closed doors and win-
dows the flowers in the flower-pots are like funeral flowers, and the ray
of light, that slips through a crack, here becomes a candle lit on the
Sabbath of the Dead. And the lamp trembles before the ikon, and its
spluttering is like a death agony; and from time to time a painted
butterfly that strayed in here brings to the living the air-borne 'Fare-
well' of the soul that cast a spell upon the house. . . . But that death-
delighting house, how it loves him, longs for him, the fair-haired
youth, its own dead man! Remorselessly it deceives the living to keep
its dear one within; it has changed from a house to a tomb.

302. The Bronze Age

Κι ὕστερα φύτρωσα στὴ χαλκόβλαστη τραχιὰ πλάση·
νά, τῶν πολέμων καὶ τῶν ὀλέθρων οἱ λειτουργοί!
Ῥουφᾶν αἱμάτων κρασὶ σὲ χάλκινο μέγα τάσι
ἡ Βία κι ἡ Ἔχτρα μὲ τὴν Ὀργή.

Χάλκινη γνώμη, χάλκινα σπίτια, χάλκινα κάστρα,
χάλκινα ὅπλα, χάλκινα στήθια, καὶ μιὰν ὁρμή,
ποὺ πάντα ὁρμάει καὶ πάντα φόνισσα καὶ χαλάστρα,
σπρώχνει τὸ χέρι πρὸς τὸ κορμί.

Κι ἐμὲ ἡ ψυχή μου, τοῦ χαϊδεμένου ῥυθμοῦ δουλεύτρα,
κι ἐμὲ ἡ ψυχή μου, κόρη τῆς αὔρας καὶ τοῦ βοριᾶ,
πρὸς τὸν αἰθέρα λυγεροκάμωτη ταξιδεύτρα,
κι ἐμὲ ἡ ψυχή μου μὲς στὰ βαριά,

στὰ σκληρὰ μέσα, στ᾽ ἄκαρδα μέσα, μέσα στὰ γαῦρα,
(στ᾽ ἀμόνι κόσμος πελεκημένος μὲ τὸ σφυρί),
πιάστηκε, δάρθηκε στῆς χαλκόφλογας τὴν ἀνάβρα,
σὰν πεταλούδα μαυριδερή.

Κι ὅταν ἡ μάνητα τῶν Τυφώνων καὶ τῶν Κυκλώπων,
θυμοὶ καὶ φόνοι, καὶ πρὶν ἀκόμα τὸ στοχαστῆς,
τὸ γένος δάμασαν τῶν ἀδάμαστων τῶν ἀνθρώπων,
κι ἦρθε κι ὁ Χάρος ἀφανιστής,

AND then I grew in the rough, bronze-rooted world. Look! The agents
of war and destruction! Force, Hatred and Anger drinking the wine of
blood from a wide cup of brass!

A brazen will, brazen houses, brazen castles, brazen armour, brazen
breasts, and a wild urge always rushing forth to ruin and kill, driving
the hand against the flesh.

And my heart, servant of pampered Rhythm, my heart, daughter of
summer's breeze and of the north wind, slender traveller to purest air,
my heart was trapped amid heaviness,

Harshness, heartlessness and arrogance – a world beaten on the anvil
by the hammer – and it was seized and beaten like a dark butterfly
against the seething brazen flame.

And when the fury of the Tryphons and the Cyclopes – anger and
killing – overpowered the race of indomitable men, before you could
realize it, and Death the destroyer had come,

ἐκεῖ ποὺ ζήσανε, τὸ σιτάρι δὲν παραστέκει,
δὲν πάει τὸ ρόδο, κισσὸς δὲν ἔρχεται νὰ πλεχτῆ.
Χάλκινη γύμνια καὶ λάμψη γύρω, κι ἀστροπελέκι
ποὺ φοβερίζει νὰ τιναχτῆ.
Καὶ χαλκοπράσινη μιὰ σκληράδα μονάχα νιώθω
τὰ φυλλοκάρδια μου νά τα σφίγγη καμιὰ φορά,
κι ἀκούγω κάθε ποὺ λαχταρίζω πρὸς κάποιο πόθο,
κάτι σὰ φλόγα ποὺ καίει φτερά.

(*Askraeos*)

303. The Cypress-tree

'Αγνάντια τὸ παράθυρο· στὸ βάθος
ὁ οὐρανός, ὅλο οὐρανὸς καὶ τίποτ' ἄλλο·
κι ἀνάμεσα, οὐρανόζωστον ὁλόκληρο,
ψηλόλιγνο ἕνα κυπαρίσσι· τίποτ' ἄλλο.
Καὶ ἡ ξάστερος ὁ οὐρανὸς ἢ μαῦρος εἶναι;
στὴ χαρὰ τοῦ γλαυκοῦ, στῆς τρικυμιᾶς τὸ σάλο,
ὅμοια καὶ πάντα ἀργολυγάει τὸ κυπαρίσσι,
ἥσυχο, ὡραῖο, ἀπελπισμένο. Τίποτ' ἄλλο.

(*Hundred Voices*)

There, where they had lived, wheat never grows, the rose never appears, ivy will never weave its leaves. A bronze nakedness, a bronze glare flashes, and a thunderbolt is always threatening to fall.

And I can only feel a green-bronze hardness choking my inner heart from time to time, and hear, whenever I long after something, a sound like a flame that puts wings to fire.

I FACE the window. Far away the sky, only sky, nothing more; and in the middle, all sky-girt, slender and tall a cypress-tree; nothing else. And whether the sky is clear or black, in the joy of the blue or the swell of the storm, always the same, that cypress-tree gently sways, calm, beautiful, hopeless. Nothing more.

304. *The Gypsy's Freedom*

Οὔτε σπίτια, οὔτε καλύβια
δὲ σοῦ πόδισαν ποτέ,
δὲ σοῦ κάρφωσαν τὸ δρόμο
τὸν παντοτινό, τὸν ἀνεμπόδιστο,
Γύφτε, ἀταίριαστε λαέ.
Τῆς στεριᾶς τὰ τρεχαντήρια,
νὰ τ' ἀδάμαστα μουλάρια!
Τ'ἄρμενά τους εἶναι τὰ τσαντήρια·
νὰ παλάτια, ἰδὲς ναοί!
Σ' ἕνα παίξιμο ματιῶν ἐδῶ καὶ ἐκεῖ
χτίζονται καὶ ὑψώνονται καὶ πᾶνε
καὶ γκρεμίζονται, ὅπως πᾶνε,
ὕστερ' ἀπ' τὸ χτίσμα κι ἀπ' τὸν ὑψωμό,
ὅσα πλάθει ὁ λογισμός μας κάτου ἐδῶ.
Καὶ δὲν εἶναι ὁ γύφτος τοῦ σπιτιοῦ ραγιές,
καὶ τὸ σπίτι ἔχει φτερούγια σὰν ἐμᾶς,
καὶ τὸ σπίτι ἀκολουθάει,
καὶ εἶν' αὐτὸ πιστὸ
στὸν ἀφέντη, ὄχι ἐκεῖνος πρὸς αὐτό. . .
Κι ἐγὼ λέω σὲ σᾶς ἀνάμεσα,
στοὺς ξεχωριστοὺς ξεχωριστός·
‹Οὔτε σπίτια, οὔτε καλύβια, οὔτε τσαντήρια·
στὸ μεγάλο ἀφεντοπάλατο τῆς πλάσης
μιὰ μονάκριβη σκεπή μου, ὁ οὐρανός!

NEITHER houses nor huts ever shackled, ever nailed down your feet in your eternal unhindered journey, Gypsies, incomparable race! Look, there are the indomitable mules, ships of the land! Tents are their rigging — see, they are palaces, temples! And in the wink of an eye they are built here and there and grow tall, and are pulled down and pass away, as passes, after the building and raising up, all that our intellect fashions here below. And the gypsy is not bond-slave to the house: the house has wings like us; the house follows us and is true to its master, not he to it. . . . And I, a chosen man, say to you, a people set apart, 'I have no need of houses, huts or tents. In the great royal palace of Nature I have only one roof, the sky! And the hollow of some

Καὶ μοῦ φτάνει γιὰ ξενύχτι
κάποιου ἀρχαίου δεντροῦ κουφάλα,
πάντα φτάνει ὁ τοῖχος κάποιου βράχου
γιὰ ν' ἀποκουμπήσω τὴν πηλάλα
τῆς ζωῆς μου μιὰ στιγμή.

Κι ἕνα χάλασμα μοῦ φτάνει
γιὰ νὰ γύρω χρυσοπλέκοντας
τῶν ὀνείρων τὸ στεφάνι·
καὶ μιὰ γούβα ὁλοβαθιὰ σκαφτὴ στὴ γῆ,
καὶ μιὰ γούβα εἶν' ἀρκετὴ
γιὰ νὰ πέσω καὶ ὕπνο νὰ 'βρω
καὶ δροσούλα ἢ ζεστασιά,
καὶ νὰ ἰδῶ τὴν ὄψη τῆς αὐγῆς
μὲ μιὰ θείαν ἀφροντισιά,
καὶ νὰ τρανοχαιρετήσω
καλοκαίρια μεσημέρια,
τζίτζηκας τραγουδιστής!»

(*The Twelve Lays of the Gypsy*)

305. The Lake

Καὶ μιὰ μέρα μόνος βρέθηκα,
ἔξω ἀπὸ τὸ βούισμα τοῦ κόσμου·
σὲ μιᾶς λίμνης ἄκρη, ἐγώ, ἀσυντρόφευτος,
μόνος, ἐγὼ κι ὁ ἑαυτός μου·

ancient tree is enough for a night's rest, and the wall of some rock suffices me to rest for a moment from the onward journey of my life. And a ruin is enough for me to rest my head on and weave the golden crown of my dreams. And a deep hollow scooped in the earth, a hollow is enough for me to lie in and find sleep, warmth or coolness to see the face of the dawn with divine unconcern, and to greet triumphantly, like a singing cicada, the summer noon.'

AND one day I found myself alone, out of the bustle of the world, on the shore of a lake; I without a companion, I and myself. And I was

κι ἔβλεπα τὰ ὁλόστρωτα νερά,
καὶ μαζὶ τὰ βάθια τὰ δικά μου,
κι ἄνθιζε ἄνθος μέσα στὴν καρδιά μου
πιὸ ἁπαλὸ γιὰ νὰ τὸ πῶ καημό,
πιὸ βαθὺ γιὰ νὰ τὸ κράξω ἔννοια·
καὶ τριγύρω ἀχνὸ τὸ δειλινὸ
τὴν παιδούλαν ὥρα κοίμιζε
σὲ ἀγκαλιὰ μενεξεδένια.
Καὶ ἦταν ὅλα ἀσάλευτα·
καὶ οἱ λευκοὶ λωτοὶ οἱ ἀπανωτοὶ
καὶ ὁ ψηλόλιγνος ὁ καλαμιώνας,
ἄνθια, πολυτρίχια, καὶ ὅλα
μὲς στὰ βάθη σὰ νὰ τά ᾽βλεπες
μιᾶς λιγνοζωγράφιστης εἰκόνας.
Καὶ ὅλα σώπαιναν ὁλότελα,
καὶ ἦταν ἡ μεγάλη ἡ σιωπὴ
τῆς μεγάλης πλάσης ποὺ ἔσκυψε
κι ἔβαλε τ᾽ αὐτὶ
γιὰ ν᾽ ἀκούση τὸ μεγάλο μυστικὸ
ποὺ δὲν ἔχει ὡς τώρα γρικηθῆ.
Κι ἔξαφνα μὲ σπρώχνει ὁ πειρασμὸς
τὰ ἱερώτατα νὰ βρίσω,
καὶ τὸ σκούξιμο τοῦ γύφτικου ζουρνᾶ,
μέσα του φυσώντας, νὰ ξυπνήσω.
Καὶ τὴ σκότωσα τὴν ἅγια σιωπή,
καὶ τὸ μέγα μυστικό της πάει καὶ πάει,

looking at the calm flat water, and at the same time into my own depths;
and a flower blossomed in my heart, gentler than what I could call pain,
deeper than what I could call care. And all around me the dim twilight
was lulling the young evening to sleep in a violet embrace. And every-
thing was motionless: the dense white lotuses, the slender reeds, the
flowers, Venus-hair, and everything was as if you saw it in the depths of
a delicately painted picture. And there was utter silence, the great
silence of the great universe as it leant forward and set its ear to hear
the great secret which had never till then been heard. And suddenly
temptation drove me to insult this great holiness, and, blowing into it,
to awaken the peal of the Gypsy trumpet. And I killed the holy silence;
and her great secret was lost forever; and the lake shuddered, and every-

κι ἀνατρίχιασε κι ἡ λίμνη, καὶ ὅλα
γύρω μου καὶ πλάι,
κι ὁ ἦχος χύμησε σὰ δράκοντας
λάγνος πρὸς τὴν πλάση τὴν παρθένα.
᾽Αλλὰ ἐκεῖ ποὺ κακουργοῦσα μὲ τὸ στόμα μου,
μέσα μου ἡ ψυχή μου ἐμένα
λαβωμένη βόγγηξεν, ὀιμένα!
Κι ὁ ἀνθὸς ποὺ ἀνθοῦσε στὴν καρδιά μου
σάλεψε τὰ φύλλα τὰ γεράνια
σὲ ὑστερνὴ καὶ δυνατὴ καὶ μυστικὴ
ἀπὸ δέηση μυρουδιὰ καὶ ἀπὸ μετάνοια.
Κι ἐνῶ ἀκόμα καὶ ὁ στριγγόλαλος ζουρνὰς
ξεπαρθένευε ξεσπώντας καὶ χαλοῦσε,
ἔγειρα τὴν ὄψη πρὸς τὴ λίμνη
ποὺ θλιμμένα μοῦ χαμογελοῦσε·
καὶ εἶδα μέσα της τὸ πρόσωπο τοῦ γύφτου
λαλητῆ
ἀλλασμένο καὶ ὀγκωμένο καὶ πλατὺ
καὶ πανάθλιο κι ἀπὸ τὴν ἀσκήμια,
καὶ ἤτανε λαχάνιασμα καὶ ἀγώνας
καὶ ἄμοιαστη φοβέρα,
καὶ δὲν εἶχε ἀγαλματένιο τὸν ἀτάραχο,
καὶ δὲν εἶχε τὸ δικό του τὸν ἀέρα.
Τὸ ζουρνὰ τὸν ἔκαμα συντρίμμια,
καὶ τὸν πέταξα στὸ δρόμο.
Καὶ ὕστερα μὲ εἶδαν οἰκοδόμο.

(*The Twelve Lays of the Gypsy*)

thing around and near me. And the sound leapt out, a lustful dragon
on the virgin creation. But as I was committing this desecration with
my mouth, my wounded soul, alas, groaned deep within me. And the
flower which blossomed in my heart moved its blue leaves in a last per-
fume, strong and secret, full of prayer and penitence. And while the
shrill-shrieking trumpet still pealed, ravishing and rending, I stooped
over the lake, which was smiling sadly at me; and I saw in it the face of
the Gypsy musician, changed and swollen and flat, and most vile in its
ugliness. And it was as though panting and struggling in unparalleled
terror. It did not have its statuesque calm, and it did not have its own
expression. I smashed the trumpet and threw the fragments on the road.
After that they saw me a builder.

306. Love

Περδικόστηθη Τσιγγάνα,
ὦ μαγεύτρα, ποὺ μιλεῖς
τὰ μεσάνυχτα πρὸς τ᾽ ἄστρα
γλώσσα προσταγῆς,

ποὺ μιλώντας γιγαντεύεις
καὶ τοὺς κόσμους ξεπερνᾶς
καὶ τ᾽ ἀστέρια σοῦ φοροῦνε
μιὰ κορώνα ξωτικιᾶς !

Σφίξε γύρω μου τὴ ζώνη
τῶν ἀντρίκειω σου χεριῶν·
εἶμ᾽ ὁ μάγος τῆς ἀγάπης,
μάγισσα τῶν ἀστεριῶν.

Μάθε με πῶς νὰ κατέχω
τὰ γραφτὰ θνητῶν κι ἐθνῶν,
πῶς τ᾽ ἀπόκρυφα τῶν κύκλων
καὶ τῶν οὐρανῶν·

πῶς νὰ φέρνω ἀναστημένους
σὲ καθρέφτες μαγικούς
τὶς πεντάμορφες τοῦ κόσμου
κι ὅλους τοὺς καιρούς·

PARTRIDGE-BREASTED Gypsy woman, witch, you who speak at midnight to the stars a language of command,

You who, as you speak, assume huge dimensions, greater than the world, and the stars put on your head the crown of a fairy,

Close tightly round me the girdle of your manly arms, witch of the stars; I am the wizard of love;

Teach me how to know the destiny of men and nations, the secret of the cycles and of the heavens,

How to bring back to life in magic mirrors the most beautiful women of the world and all the bygone centuries,

πῶς, ὑπάκουους τοὺς δαιμόνους,
τοὺς λαοὺς τῶν ξωτικῶν
στοὺς χρυσοὺς νὰ δένω γύρους
τῶν δαχτυλιδιῶν,

καθὼς δένω καὶ τὸ λόγο,
δαίμονα καὶ ξωτικό,
στὸ χρυσὸ τὸ δαχτυλίδι,
στὸ ρυθμό.

(The Twelve Lays of the Gypsy)

307. Resurrection

Καὶ θὰ φύγης κι ἀπ' τὸ σάπιο τὸ κορμί,
ὦ Ψυχὴ παραδαρμένη ἀπὸ τὸ κρίμα,
καὶ δὲ θά 'βρη τὸ κορμὶ μιὰ σπιθαμὴ
μὲς στὴ γῆ γιὰ νὰ τὴν κάμη μνῆμα,
κι ἄθαφτο θὰ μείνη τὸ ψοφήμι
νὰ τὸ φᾶνε τὰ σκυλιὰ καὶ τὰ ἑρπετά,
κι ὁ Καιρὸς μέσα στοὺς γύρους του τὴ μνήμη
κάποιου σκέλεθρου πανάθλιου θὰ βαστᾶ.

Ὅσο νὰ σὲ λυπηθῆ
τῆς ἀγάπης ὁ Θεός,
καὶ νὰ ξημερώση μιὰν αὐγή,
καὶ νὰ σὲ καλέση ὁ λυτρωμός,
ὦ Ψυχὴ παραδαρμένη ἀπὸ τὸ κρίμα!

How to bind in the golden circle of a ring the demons and the droves
of ghostly beings and make them submissive

As I tie together the Word, a demon and a ghost, in the golden ring
of Rhythm.

AND you will abandon the rotting body, O Soul hounded by sin, and
the body will not find a span of earth to be buried in; and the corpse
will be left uncovered, for the dogs and creeping things to eat, and
Time in her circles will remember a wretched skeleton;

Until the God of Love takes pity upon you, and a dawn breaks, and
freedom calls you, O Soul hounded by sin! And you will hear the

Καὶ θ' ἀκούσῃς τὴ φωνὴ τοῦ λυτρωτῆ,
θὰ γδυθῆς τῆς ἁμαρτίας τὸ ντύμα,
καὶ ξανὰ κυβερνημένη κι ἀλαφρὴ
θὰ σαλέψῃς σὰν τὴ χλόη, σὰν τὸ πουλί,
σὰν τὸ κόλπο τὸ γυναίκειο, σὰν τὸ κύμα,
καὶ μὴν ἔχοντας πιὸ κάτου ἄλλο σκαλὶ
νὰ κατρακυλίσῃς πιὸ βαθιὰ
στοῦ Κακοῦ τὴ σκάλα,
γιὰ τ' ἀνέβασμα ξανὰ ποὺ σὲ καλεῖ
θὰ αἰστανθῆς νὰ σοῦ φυτρώσουν, ὦ χαρά!
τὰ φτερά,
τὰ φτερὰ τὰ πρωτινά σου τὰ μεγάλα!

(The Twelve Lays of the Gypsy)

308. *The Empress Theophano*

Νά την ἡ Αὐγούστα Θεοφανώ! Πούλια καὶ Φούρια: Κοίτα.
Βέργα κρατᾶ, λιγνόβεργα, καὶ στὴν κορφὴ τῆς βέργας
ἀσάλευτος ὁ τρίφυλλος λωτός, μαλαματένιος.
Καὶ εἶν' ὁ λωτὸς ποὺ δὲν τὸν τρῶς, τὸ στριγλοβότανο εἶναι,
ποὺ μὲ τὸ θώρι σὲ χαλᾶ, μὲ τ' ἄγγισμα σὲ λιώνει,
κι ὅποιος κι ἂν εἶσαι, ἀσκητευτὴς ἢ χαροκόπος, ὅ τι,
τὰ ξεχνᾶς ὅλα· τὴ ζωή, τὴ δύναμη, τὴ νιότη,

voice of the redeemer, and will cast away the garment of your sins, and, once again light and purposeful, you will move like the leaves of grass, like a bird, like a woman's bosom, like a wave; and having no lower rung to fall down the Ladder of Evil, for the upward course which is calling you, you will feel your wings growing – what joy – your wide-spreading wings of old.

HERE comes the Empress Theophano! Pleiad, Fury, look! She holds a wand, a slender wand, and at the top, unmoving, stands the three-leaved lotus of gold. This is the lotus you must not eat; it is the witches' herb; it ruins you at a look, dissolves you at a touch; and whoever you are, a monk or a merry-maker, you forget all: life, strength, youth; if

κι ἂν εἶσαι τίμιος, τὴν τιμή, τὸ θρόνο, ἂν εἶσαι ῥήγας,
θησαυριστής, καὶ γίνεσαι ζητιάνος κι ἑρμοσπίτης,
παιδὶ γιὰ τὴν ἀγάπη της, φονιὰς γιὰ τὸ φιλί της.
Καὶ μὲ τὴ βέργα κυβερνᾶ καὶ δένει πολεμάρχους,
τοὺς λογισμοὺς καὶ τὶς καρδιές, τὶς χῶρες καὶ τοὺς κόσμους,
αὐτοκρατόρους Ῥωμανούς, Φωκάδες, Τσιμισκῆδες,
κι ὅσα γιὰ νὰ κυβερνηθοῦν, κι ὅσα γιὰ νὰ δεθοῦνε
στοῦ πέλαου τὰ πλεούμενα καὶ στοῦ ντουνιᾶ τὰ κάστρα
ταράζουν τὰ γυμνὰ σπαθιὰ καὶ τ' ἄξια παλικάρια,
καὶ τὴν ὀγρὴ φωτιὰ ποὺ καίει, δὲ σβήνει, καὶ ρημάζει.
Κι ὅπως δὲ σβήν' ἡ ὀγρὴ φωτιὰ μηδὲ στὸ πέλαο μέσα,
καὶ καταλύτρα καὶ στὴ γῆ καὶ στὸ νερὸ ἐκδικήτρα,
νά την ἡ Αὐγούστα Θεοφανώ, παντοῦ καὶ πάντα ἀφέντρα,
γιὰ βασιλεύει στὴν καρδιά, γιὰ κυβερνᾶ στὴν Πόλη.
Σὰν τὸ δοξάρι τοῦ οὐρανοῦ τοῦ κόρφου της οἱ ῥόγες
λάμπουν, καὶ τὶς βυζαίνουνε καὶ τρεμοκοκαλιάζουν
τὸ χαῦνο βασιλόπουλο τὸ γυναικοδοσμένο
κι ὁ νικητὴς ὁ ἀσύντριφτος τῶν ἀμηράδων, ὅμοια·
καὶ λάμπει, βίγλα ἀγγελικὴ σὲ οὐρανικὴ μιὰ πύλη,
τὸ μουσικὸ χαμόγελο στὰ πλαστικά της χείλη.
Νά την ἡ Αὐγούστα Θεοφανώ! Γλυκοτηρᾶ καὶ σφάζει·
στὴν ἄκρη ἀπὸ τὴ βέργα της πῶς κρέμεστε, σφαγάρια!

you are honest your honour, if a king your throne, if a miser you turn
into a homeless beggar; you turn into a child to win her love, into a
killer to win her kiss. She rules with her wand and shackles mighty
warriors, thoughts and hearts, lands and worlds, emperors – Romanos,
Phocas, Tsimiskis – and all that to be seized and ruled excites un-
sheathed swords and worthy fighters in the ships of the sea and castles
of the world, and the liquid fire which burns and ruins but cannot be
quenched. And as the liquid fire, ruiner on land and avenger on water,
cannot be quenched even in the wide sea, so comes the Empress
Theophano, queen always and everywhere, whether she reigns in the
heart or rules in the Imperial City. The nipples of her breasts glow like
the bow of heaven; the languid prince given to lust and the uncon-
quered conqueror of Emirs alike suck them, and shudder to the bone.
The music of her smile flashes on her shapely lips like a guard of
angels before a gate of heaven. Here comes the Empress Theophano!
With one sweet glance she kills; how the victims hang from the tip of

Καὶ νὰ κι ἡ Αὐγούστα Θεοφανώ! γλυκογελᾶ καὶ στάζει
τὸ φόνο καὶ τὸ χαλασμό, καθὼς ἡ αὐγὴ σταλάζει
μέσ' ἀπὸ τὰ ῥοδόχερα δροσομαργαριτάρια.
Τοῦ νιοῦ τὸ θρασομάνημα, τοῦ γέρου ἡ ξελογιάστρα,
λυγίζει τοὺς ἀλύγιστους, τὰ κατεβάζει τ' ἄστρα·
μὲ τὴν εἰδή της ἡ ὀμορφιὰ σὰν τὸ χρυσὸ δρεπάνι,
σὰν τὴν ἀράχνη ἡ σκέψη της, ἡ ἀγάπη της ἀφιόνι.
Λύσσα καὶ σφίγγα, σάρκα ἐσύ, δρακόντισσα, 'Αφροδίτη!

(The King's Flute)

309. Morning Light

Πρωΐ, καὶ λιοπερίχυτη καὶ λιόκαλ' εἶναι ἡ μέρα,
κι ἡ 'Αθήνα ζαφειρόπετρα στῆς γῆς τὸ δαχτυλίδι.
Τὸ φῶς παντοῦ, κι ὅλο τὸ φῶς, κι ὅλα τὸ φῶς τὰ δείχνει
καὶ στρογγυλὰ καὶ σταλωμένα, κοίτα, δὲν ἀφίνει
τίποτε θαμποχάραγο, νὰ μὴν τὸ ξεδιαλύνη
ὄνειρο ἂν εἶναι, ἢ κι ἂν ἀχνός, ἢ ἂν εἶναι κρουστὸ κάτι.
Περήφανα καὶ ταπεινά, κι ὅλα φαντάζουν ἴδια.
Καὶ τῆς Πεντέλης ἡ κορφὴ καὶ τ' ἀχαμνὸ σπερδούκλι,
κι ὁ λαμπρομέτωπος ναὸς καὶ μιὰ χλωμὴ ἀνεμώνη,

her wand! Here comes the Empress Theophano! From her sweet smile
drops death and ruin, just as dawn showers dew-pearls from her rosy
hands. She is the young man's reckless madness, the deceiver of the
old; she bends the unbending, brings down the stars. If glanced at, her
beauty is like a golden scythe; her thoughts are like a spider's web, her
love, opium. Fury and sphinx, you are the flesh, a serpent, Aphrodite!

MORNING, sun-flooded, sun-lovely, the day; Athens, a sapphire in the
ring of earth. Light everywhere, full light; the light shows everything
globed like a dew-drop; look, it does not leave anything blurred, un-
clearly seen, be it a dream, a mist, a concrete form. The proud, the
lowly, all things appear the same: the peak of Pentelicon, the lean
asphodel, the shining-fronted temple, a pale anemone; all in creation's

τὰ πάντα, ὅμοια βαραίνουνε στὴ ζυγαριὰ τῆς πλάσης.
Κι ὅλα σιμὰ τὰ φέρνεις, φῶς, κι ὅλα τὸ φῶς τὰ δείχνει
μὲ μοῖρα σὰν ξεχωριστή. Τῆς Αἴγινας ὁ κόρφος
ἀσπρογαλιάζει ὁλόχυτος, λαμποκοπᾶ' τὸν πάει
σιμὰ πρὸς τοὺς κυματιστοὺς καὶ σὰ γραμμένους λόφους·
καὶ τὸ βαθὺ ἀκροούρανο σημαδεμένο μόνο
ἀπὸ τὸ μαῦρο ἑνὸς πουλιοῦ καὶ τ' ἄσπρο ἑνοῦ συγνέφου
τὰ πάει πρὸς τὸ βουνόπλαγο, καὶ τοῦ βουνοῦ τὴ ράχη
τὴν πάει σιμὰ στὸ λιόφυτο τοῦ κάμπου, καὶ τὸν κάμπο
τόνε σιμώνει στὸ γιαλό, καὶ τοῦ γιαλοῦ καὶ οἱ βάρκες
στὰ σπιτικὰ κατώφλια ὀμπρὸς τραβᾶν κατὰ τὴ χώρα
ἥσυχα γιὰ ν' ἀράξουνε. Κι ὅλα τὸ φῶς τὰ δείχνει
ἀεροφερμένα πιὸ κοντὰ σάμπως καημὸ νὰ τό 'χη
νὰ τὰ ὁρμηνέψη νὰ πιαστοῦν κ' ἕνα χορὸ νὰ στήσουν,
ὅσο ποὺ τόνα στ' ἄλλουνοῦ τὴν ἀγκαλιὰ νὰ πέση.

(*The King's Flute*)

310. The Naked Song

Ὅλα γυμνὰ τριγύρω μας,
ὅλα γυμνὰ ἐδῶ πέρα,
κάμποι, βουνά, ἀκροούρανα,
ἀκράταγ' εἶναι ἡ μέρα.

balance weigh alike. Light, you bring all near; and the light shows
everything as if it were fated to be unique. Aegina's bay gleams blue
and white, liquid, burns bright. Light brings it close to the un-
dulating pencilled hills; it brings towards the hillside the deep ends
of heaven printed only with the black fleck of a bird, the white of a
cloud; the hill's spine it brings near to the olive-sown plain, the plain
near to the beaches; and the boats on the beach move through the land
to anchor quietly at the thresholds of the houses. The light shows all
things afloat on air, drawn close, as though it longs to teach them to
take hands and tread a dance to the point where each may drop into
the other's arms.

EVERYTHING is naked around us; here everything is naked, the plains,
the mountains, the skyline; the daylight is beyond control. Creation

Διάφαν' ἡ πλάση, ὁλάνοιχτα
τὰ ὁλόβαθα παλάτια·
τὸ φῶς χορτάστε, μάτια,
κιθάρες, τὸ ῥυθμό.

'Εδῶ εἶν' ἀριὰ κι ἀταίριαστα
λεκιάσματα τὰ δέντρα,
κρασὶ εἶν' ὁ κόσμος ἄκρατο,
ἐδῶ εἶν' ἡ γύμνια ἀφέντρα.
'Εδῶ εἶν' ὁ ἴσκιος ὄνειρο,
ἐδῶ χαράζει ἀκόμα
στῆς νύχτας τ' ἀχνὸ στόμα
χαμόγελο ξανθό.

'Εδῶ τὰ πάντα ξέστηθα
κι ἀδιάντροπα λυσσᾶνε·
ἀστέρι εἶν' ὁ ξερόβραχος,
καὶ τὸ κορμὶ φωτιά 'ναι.
'Ρουμπίνια ἐδῶ, μαλάματα,
μαργαριτάρια, ἀσήμια
μοιράζει ἡ θεία σου γύμνια,
τρισεύγενη 'Αττική!

'Εδῶ ὁ λεβέντης μάγεμα,
ἡ σάρκα ἀποθεώθη,
οἱ παρθενιές, 'Αρτέμιδες,
'Ερμῆδες εἶναι οἱ πόθοι.
'Εδῶ κάθε ὥρα ὁλόγυμνη,
θάμα στὰ ὑγρόζωα κήτη,

is transparent; the deep palaces are wide open. Eyes, quench your
hunger for light, guitars, your hunger for rhythm.

Here the trees grow wide apart, incongruous patches; the world is
unmixed wine, nakedness is queen. The shadows are like dreams; here
even on the dim mouth of Night a golden smile dawns.

Here everything riots with naked breast, unashamed. The dry rock
is a star, the body a flame. Your divine nakedness, most noble Attica,
is strewing rubies, gold, pearls and silver.

Here the young man is a magic spell, the flesh deified; virginity is
Artemis, desire Hermes. Here every moment, startling the monsters of

πετιέται κι ἡ Ἀφροδίτη
καὶ χύνεται παντοῦ.

‹Παράτησε τὸ φόρεμα,
καὶ μὲ τὴ γύμνια ντύσου,
Ψυχή, τῆς γύμνιας ἱέρισσα,
ναὸς εἶναι τὸ κορμί σου.
Μαγνήτεψε τὰ χέρια μου,
τῆς σάρκας κεχριμπάρι,
τ᾽ Ὀλύμπιο τὸ νεχτάρι
τῆς γύμνιας δὸς νὰ πιῶ.

‹Σκίσε τὸν πέπλο, πέταξε
τὸν ἄμοιαστο χιτώνα
καὶ μὲ τὴ φύση ταίριασε
τὴν πλαστική σου εἰκόνα.
Λύσε τὴ ζώνη, σταύρωσε
τὰ χέρια στὴν καρδιά σου·
πορφύρα τὰ μαλλιά σου,
μακρόσυρτη στολή.

‹Καὶ γίνε ἀτάραχο ἄγαλμα,
καὶ τὸ κορμί σου ἂς πάρη
τῆς τέχνης τὴν ἐντέλεια
ποὺ λάμπει στὸ λιθάρι·
καὶ παῖξε καὶ παράστησε
μὲ τῆς ἰδέας τὴ γύμνια
τὰ λυγερὰ τ᾽ ἀγρίμια,
τὰ φίδια, τὰ πουλιά.

the sea, naked Aphrodite surges forward and flows over everything.

'Cast off your clothes and put on nakedness, my soul, priestess of nakedness; your body is a temple. Amber of the flesh, draw my arms like a magnet; give me to drink the Olympian nectar of nakedness.

'Tear the veil, throw away the unbecoming tunic, blend your statue-like form with nature. Undo your girdle, cross your arms over your heart; your hair is a royal garment, a long-trailing gown.

'Become a calm statue and let your body assume the perfection of art that flashes in stone. Play and act with naked thought like lithe wild animals, snakes, birds.

‹Καὶ παῖξε καὶ παράστησε
τὰ ἡδονικά, τὰ ὡραῖα,
λαγάρισε τὴ γύμνια σου
καὶ κάμε τὴν ἰδέα.
Τὰ στρογγυλά, τὰ ὁλόισα,
χνούδια, γραμμές, καμπύλες,
ὦ θεῖες ἀνατριχίλες,
χωρεῦτε ἕνα χορό.

‹Μέτωπο, μάτια, κύματα
μαλλιά, γλουτοί, λαγόνες,
κρυφὰ λαγκάδια, τοῦ Ἔρωτα
ρόδα, μυρτιές, κρυψῶνες,
πόδια ποὺ ἁλυσοδένετε,
βρύσες τοῦ χάιδιου, ὦ χέρια,
τοῦ πόθου περιστέρια,
γεράκια τοῦ χαμοῦ!

‹Καὶ ὁλόκαρδα, κι ἀμπόδιστα
λογάκια, ὦ στόμα, ὦ στόμα,
σὰν τὸ κερὶ τῆς μέλισσας,
σὰν τοῦ ῥοδιοῦ τὸ χρῶμα.
Τὰ κρίνα τ’ ἀλαβάστρινα,
τοῦ Ἀπρίλη θυμιατήρια,
ζηλεύουν τὰ ποτήρια
τοῦ κόρφου σου. Ὦ! νὰ πιῶ,

‘Play, and act like all voluptuous things, all that is beautiful; purify
your nakedness and turn it into spirit. Let the rounded, the fully
straight, soft down, lines, curves, O divine tremors, dance a dance.

‘Forehead, eyes, waves, hair, thighs, loins, secret valleys, roses of
love, myrtle, hiding-places, legs that shackle, fountains of caresses,
hands, doves of desire, hawks of destruction!

‘Speak full-hearted, unhindered sweet words, O mouth, mouth, like
the bee's wax, coloured like a pomegranate. The lilies of alabaster, the
thuribles of April, are envious of the cups of your breast – O for a
drink;

‹νὰ πιῶ στὰ ῥοδοχάραγα,
στὰ ὀρθά, στὰ σμαλτωμένα,
τὸ γάλα ποὺ ὀνειρεύτηκα
τῆς εὐτυχίας, ἐσένα.
Ἐγὼ εἶμαι ἱεροφάντης σου,
βωμοὶ τὰ γόνατά σου,
στὴν πύρινη ἀγκαλιά σου
θεοὶ θαματουργοῦν.

‹ Μακριὰ μας ὅσα ἀταίριαστα,
ντυμένα καὶ κρυμμένα,
τὰ μισερὰ καὶ τ' ἄσκημα
καὶ ἀκάθαρτα καὶ ξένα.
Ὀρθὰ ὅλα· ξέσκεπα, ἄδολα,
γῆ, αἰθέρες, κορμιά, στήθια.
Γύμνια εἶναι κι ἡ ἀλήθεια,
καὶ γύμνια κι ἡ ὀμορφιά.

‹Στὴ γύμνια τὴν ἡλιόκαλη
τῆς Ἀθηναίας ἡμέρας
κι ἀνίσως καὶ φαντάξη σου
κάτι ἄντυτο σὰν τέρας,
κάτι σὰ δέντρο ἀφύλλιαστο
καὶ δίχως ἴσκιου χάρη,
ἀδούλευτο λιθάρι,
ξερακιανὸ κορμί,

'To drink from the rose-carved, the rising, enamelled breasts the milk of my dreams of happiness – you. I am your hierophant; your knees are altars; gods perform miracles in your flaming embrace.

'Away from us all that is unseemly, all that is dressed and hidden: the warped, the ugly, the impure, the foreign. Everything upright, un-covered, guileless – earth, aether, bodies, breasts. Truth is nakedness and beauty is nakedness.

'In the sun-splendid nakedness of the Athenian day, if to you some-thing looks like a naked monster, like a leafless tree, without the grace of a shade, like a rough stone, a thin dry body,

‹κάτι γυμνὸ καὶ ξέσκεπο
στὰ ὁλανοιγμένα πλάτια,
ποὺ ζωντανὸ θὰ τό 'δειχναν
μόνο δύο φλόγες μάτια,
κάτι ποὺ ἀπὸ τοὺς σάτυρους
κρατιέται, καὶ εἴν' ἀγρίμι,
καὶ εἴν' ἡ φωνή του ἀσήμι,
μὴ φύγης· εἴμ' ἐγώ,

‹ὁ Σάτυρος. Καὶ ρίζωσα
σὰν τὴν ἐλιὰ ἐδῶ πέρα,
λιγώνω τοὺς ἀγέρηδες
μὲ τὴ βαθιὰ φλογέρα.
Καὶ παίζω καὶ παντρεύονται,
λατρεύονται, λατρεύουν,
καὶ παίζω καὶ χορεύουν
ἄνθρωποι, ζά, στοιχειά.›

311. The East

Γιαννιώτικα, Σμυρνιώτικα, Πολίτικα,
μακρόσυρτα τραγούδια ἀνατολίτικα,
λυπητερά,
πῶς ἡ ψυχή μου σέρνεται μαζί σας!
Εἶναι χυμένη ἀπὸ τὴ μουσική σας,
καὶ πάει μὲ τὰ δικά σας τὰ φτερά.

'Something undressed, uncovered in the open, with only two burn-
ing eyes to show that it is living, an offspring of the satyrs, a wild
animal with a silver voice, do not run away; it is I,

'I am the satyr. I have cast roots here like the olive-tree, and I make
the winds languish with my deep-sounding pipe. I play; and men,
animals, ghosts mate, worship and are worshipped; I play and they
dance.'

LONG-DRAWN, sad, eastern songs of Iannina, Smyrna and Istanbul,
how my heart is dragged along with you; it is moulded by your music,
and flies with the movement of your wings.

Σᾶς γέννησε καὶ μέσα σας μιλάει
καὶ βογγάει καὶ βαριὰ μοσκοβολάει
μιὰ μάνα· καίει τὸ λάγνο της φιλί,
κι εἶναι τῆς Μοίρας λάτρισσα καὶ τρέμει,
ψυχὴ ὅλη σάρκα, σκλάβα σὲ χαρέμι,
ἡ λαγγεμένη ᾽Ανατολή.

Μέσα σας κλαίει τὸ μαῦρο φτωχολόι,
κι ὅλα σας, κι ἡ χαρά σας, μοιρολόι
πικρὸ κι ἀργό·
μαῦρος, φτωχὸς καὶ σκλάβος καὶ ἀκαμάτης,
στενόκαρδος, ἀδούλευτος, διαβάτης
μ᾽ ἐσᾶς κι ἐγώ.

Στὸ γιαλὸ ποὺ τοῦ φύγαν τὰ καΐκια,
καὶ τοῦ μεῖναν τὰ κρίνα καὶ τὰ φύκια,
στ᾽ ὄνειρο τοῦ πελάου καὶ τ᾽ οὐρανοῦ,
ἄνεργη τὴ ζωὴ νὰ ζοῦσα κι ἔρμη,
βουβός, χωρὶς καμιᾶς φροντίδας θέρμη,
μὲ τόσο νοῦ,

ὅσος φτάνει σὰ δέντρο γιὰ νὰ στέκω
καὶ καπνιστὴς μὲ τὸν καπνὸ νὰ πλέκω
δαχτυλιδάκια γαλανά·
καὶ κάποτε τὸ στόμα νὰ σαλεύω
κι ἀπάνω του νὰ ξαναζωντανεύω
τὸν καημὸ ποὺ βαριὰ σᾶς τυραννᾶ

A mother gave you birth; she speaks and groans and sheds heavy perfume on you; her lustful kiss burns. She trembles, worshipping Fate, a soul of the flesh, a slave in a harem: the love-weary East.

In you, black poverty is weeping; everything, even your joy, is a bitter slow dirge. Wretched, poor, a slave, lazy, narrow-hearted, unemployed, I too am a passer-by with you.

On the beach abandoned by its ships, where only seaweed and sealilies grow, in the dream of the sea and of the sky, to live my life forlorn, inactive, dumb, with no single care to warm me, with such thoughts only

As suffice to stand like a tree, like a smoker weaving small blue circles of smoke in the air, and, from time to time, moving my lips to revive the sorrow that crushes heavily upon you,

κι ὅλο ἀρχίζει, γυρίζει, δὲν τελειώνει.
Καὶ μιὰ φυλὴ ξῆ μέσα οας καὶ λιώνει,
καὶ μιὰ ζωὴ δεμένη σπαρταρᾷ,
Γιαννιώτικα, Σμυρνιώτικα, Πολίτικα,
μακρόσυρτα τραγούδια ἀνατολίτικα,
λυπητερά.

JOHN POLEMIS
1862–1925

312. The Old Violin

'Άκουσε τ' ἀπόκοσμο, τὸ παλιὸ βιολὶ
μέσα στὴ νυχτερινὴ σιγαλιὰ τοῦ 'Απρίλη·
στὸ παλιὸ κουφάρι του μιὰ ψυχὴ λαλεῖ
μὲ τ' ἀχνὰ κι ἀπάρθενα τῆς ἀγάπης χείλη.

Καὶ τ' ἀηδόνι τ' ἄγρυπνο καὶ τὸ ζηλευτὸ
ζήλεψε κι ἐσώπασε κι ἔσκυψε κι ἐστάθη,
γιὰ νὰ δῆ περήφανο τί πουλὶ εἶν' αὐτὸ
ποὺ τὰ λέει γλυκύτερα τῆς καρδιᾶς τὰ πάθη.

'Ως κι ὁ γκιώνης τ' ἄχαρο, τὸ δειλὸ πουλί,
μὲ λαχτάρ' ἀπόκρυφη τὰ φτερὰ τινάζει

That is always starting, circling, and that never ends. A people live
in you and wither; shackled lives that writhe; long-drawn, sad eastern
songs of Iannina, Smyrna and Istanbul.

LISTEN to the lonely, the old violin playing in the stillness of the April
night; in its ancient body a heart is speaking with the pale and pure lips
of love.
And the sleepless, much-admired nightingale was jealous and kept
silent; proudly she stopped and bent to see which bird could speak
more sweetly of the pain of the heart.
Even the screech-owl, that graceless cowardly bird, shook its wings

καὶ σωπαίνει ἀκούοντας τὸ παλιὸ βιολί,
γιὰ νὰ μάθη ὁ δύστυχος πῶς ν' ἀναστενάζη.

Τί κι ἂν τρώη τὸ ξύλο του τὸ σαράκι; τί
κι ἂν περνοῦν ἀγύριστοι χρόνοι κι ἄλλοι χρόνοι;
Πιὸ γλυκιὰ καὶ πιὸ ὅμορφη καὶ πιὸ δυνατὴ
ἡ φωνή του γίνεται, ὅσο αὐτὸ παλιώνει.

Εἶμ' ἐγὼ τ' ἀπόκοσμο, τὸ παλιὸ βιολὶ
μέσα στὴ νυχτερινὴ σιγαλιὰ τοῦ 'Απρίλη·
στὸ παλιὸ κουφάρι μου μιὰ ψυχὴ λαλεῖ
μὲ τῆς πρώτης νιότης μου τὰ δροσάτα χείλη.

Τί κι ἂν τρώη τὰ σπλάχνα μου τὸ σαράκι; τί
κι ἂν βαδίζω ἀγύριστα χρόνο μὲ τὸ χρόνο;
Πιὸ γλυκιὰ πιὸ ὅμορφη καὶ πιὸ δυνατὴ
γίνεται ἡ ἀγάπη μου, ὅσο ἐγὼ παλιώνω.

with secret longing and silently listened to the old violin to learn, poor
thing, how to sigh.

What if the worm eats the wood, if years roll by that never return,
years on years? Sweeter, more beautiful and stronger grows its voice,
as it grows older.

I am the lonely, the old violin in the silence of the April night. In my
ancient body a soul is speaking with the fresh lips of my first youth.

What if the worm eats my heart, if year by year I move away, never
to return? Sweeter, more beautiful and stronger grows my love, as I
grow older.

K. KRYSTALLIS

1868-94

313. The Sunset

Πίσω ἀπὸ μακρινὲς κορφὲς ὁ ἥλιος βασιλεύει
καὶ τ' οὐρανοῦ τὰ σύνορα χίλιες βαφὲς ἀλλάζουν,
πράσινες, κόκκινες, ξανθές, ὁλόχρυσες, γαλάζες,
κι ἀνάμεσά τους σκάει λαμπρὸς λαμπρὸς ὁ ἀποσπερίτης.
Τὴν πύρη τοῦ καλοκαιριοῦ τὴν σβεῖ γλυκὸ ἀγεράκι,
ποὺ κατεβάζουν τὰ βουνὰ καὶ φέρνουν τ' ἀκρογιάλια.
'Ανάρια τὰ κλωνάρια του κουνάει ὁ γέρο πεῦκος,
καὶ πίνει καὶ ρουφάει δροσιὰ κι ἀχολογάει καὶ τρίζει·
ἡ βρύση ἡ χορταρόστρωτη δροσίζει τὰ λουλούδια
καὶ μ' ἀλαφρὸ μουρμουρητὸ γλυκὰ τὰ νανουρίζει·
θολώνει πέρα ἡ θάλασσα, τὰ ριζοβούνια ἰσκιώνουν,
τὰ ζάλογγα μαυρολογοῦν, σκύβουν τὰ φρύδια οἱ βράχοι,
κι οἱ κάμποι γύρω οἱ ἀπλωτοὶ πράσινο πέλαο μοιάζουν.

'Απ' ὄξω, ἀπ' τὰ ὀργώματα, γυρνοῦνε οἱ ζευγολάτες
ἡλιοκαμένοι, ξέκοποι, βουβοί, ἀποκαρωμένοι,
μὲ τοὺς ζυγούς, μὲ τὰ βαριὰ τ' ἀλέτρια φορτωμένοι,
καὶ σαλαγοῦν ἀπὸ μπροστὰ τὰ δυὸ καματερά τους·
τρανά, στεφανοκέρατα, κοιλάτα, τραχηλάτα,
⟨'Οώ! φωνάζοντας, ὀώ! Μελισσινέ, Λαμπίρη·⟩
κι ἀργὰ τὰ βόιδια περπατοῦν καὶ ποῦ καὶ ποῦ μουγγρίζουν.

BEHIND the distant mountain peaks the sun is setting, and the skyline
changes through a thousand colours – green, red, yellow, golden, blue;
brilliantly the evening star breaks out through them. A sweet breeze,
coming from the hills and the shores, quenches the summer heat. The
old pine gently sways his branches; drinking, sucking in the coolness,
he murmurs and creaks. The weed-encircled fountain refreshes the
flowers and murmurs a gentle lullaby to them. The colour of the distant
sea becomes misty, and shadows fall on the foothills; the headlands
grow dark, the rocks knit their eyebrows, and the wide plain all round
looks like a green sea.

The teamsters return from the ploughed fields, sunburnt, exhausted,
silent, parched, carrying the yokes and the heavy ploughshares, calling
out to their pairs of oxen that move in front of them, great animals,
crowned with horns, big-bellied, and heavy-necked. They cry out
'Hoo, Hoo, Melissinos, Lambiris,' and the oxen move slowly along,

Γυρνοῦνε ἀπὸ τὰ ἔργα τους οἱ λυγερές, γυρνοῦνε
μὲ τὰ ζαλίκια ἀχ' τὴ λογγιά, μέ τὰ σκουτιὰ ἀχ' τὸ πλύμα,
μὲ τὲς πλατιές των τὲς ποδιὲς σφογγίζοντας τὸν ἴδρω·
καὶ σ' ὅποιο δέντρο κι ἂν σταθοῦν, σ' ὅποιο κοντρὶ ἀκουμπή-
    σουν,
εἰς τὸ μουρμούρι τοῦ κλαριοῦ, εἰς τὴν θωριὰ τοῦ βράχου
γλυκὸ γλυκὸ καὶ πρόσχαρο χαιρετισμὸ ξανοίγουν·
‹Γειὰ καὶ χαρὰ στὸν κόσμο μας, στὸν ὄμορφό μας κόσμο!›

Σὰν τὸ ζαρκάδι ὁ νιὸς βοσκὸς ξετρέχει τὴν κοπή του·
σουρίζει, σαλαγάει ‹δι, δι,› καὶ τήνε ροβολάει
ἀπὸ τὰ πλάγια στὸ μαντρί, στὴν στρούγγα γιὰ ν' ἀρμέξῃ.
'Απὸ στεφάνι, ἀπὸ γκρεμόν, ἀπὸ ῥαϊδιὸ καὶ λόγγο
καὶ τοῦ γιδάρη ἡ σαλαγὴ στριγγιὰ στριγγιὰ γρικιέται
τ' ἀνάποδο κοπάδι του ‹τσάπ, τσάπ! ἔι, ἔι!› βαρώντας.
Κι ἀχολογοῦν βελάσματα, κι ἀχολογοῦν κουδούνια.
'Απὸ μακριά, ἀχ' τὸ βουκουλιό, ἀκούγεται φλογέρα.
Κάπου βροντάει μιὰ τουφεκιὰ ἢ κυνηγοῦ ἢ δραγάτη,
καὶ κάπου κάπου ὁ ἀντίλαλος βραχνὸ τραγούδι φέρνει
τοῦ ἀλογολάτη, τοῦ βαλμᾶ, ὅπου γυρνάει κι ἐκεῖνος.
Τοῦ κάμπου τ' ἄγρια τὰ πουλιὰ γυρνοῦν ἀχ' τὲς βοσκές τους
καὶ μ' ἄμετρους κελαηδισμοὺς μὲς στὰ δεντρὰ κουρνιάζουν·
σκαλώνει ὁ γκιώνης στὸ κλαρὶ καὶ κλαίει τὸν ἀδερφό του·
στὰ ῥέπια, στὰ χαλάσματα, ἡ κουκουβάγια σκούζει·

and low from time to time. The young girls return from their work, carrying loads of wood from the thicket, or clothes from washing, wiping the sweat away with their wide aprons; and wherever they stop, by a tree or against a rock, where the branches murmur or the stone stares, they greet the world with a sweet and happy greeting: 'Health and joy to all, to our beautiful world.'

The young shepherd outruns his flock like a fawn; he whistles and calls 'Oi, oi,' and brings it helter-skelter down from the hillside to the fold, and to the stalls to milk the sheep. The sharp cry of the goatherd is also heard resounding from crowning rock, precipice, gorge, and valley: 'Tsap, tsap, ei, ei,' driving his unruly flock; and the bleating of sheep resounds, and the noise of bells. The sound of a pipe is heard at a distance coming from a cowshed; from time to time you hear a gunshot, fired by a hunter or a watchman, and now and again the echoes carry the throaty song of the horse-driver, the horse-breeder who is also returning home. The wild birds of the plains come back from their pastures and nestle in the trees with endless twittering. The

μέσα σὲ αὐλάκι, σὲ βαρκό, λαλεῖ ἡ νεροχελώνα,
τ' ἀηδόνι κρύβεται βαθιὰ στ' ἀγγαθερὰ τὰ βάτα
καὶ τὴν ἀγάπη τραγουδάει μὲ τὸν γλυκὸ σκοπό του·
κι ἡ νυχτερίδα ἡ μάγισσα, μὲ τὸ φτερούγισμά της
τὸ γλήγορο καὶ τὸ τρελλό, σχίζει τὰ σκότα ἀπάνου
καὶ μὲ τὰ ὁλόχαρα παιδιὰ τοῦ ζευγολάτη παίζει.

Καλότυχοί μου χωριανοί, ζηλεύω τὴ ζωή σας,
τὴν ἀπλοϊκή σας τὴ ζωή, πόχει περίσσιες χάρες.
Μὰ πιὸ πολὺ τὸν μαγικὸ ζηλεύω γυρισμό σας,
ὅντας ἡ μέρα σώνεται καὶ βασιλεύει ὁ ἥλιος.

LORENTZOS MAVILIS
1860–1912·

314. Forgetfulness

Καλότυχοι οἱ νεκροὶ ποὺ λησμονᾶνε
τὴν πίκρια τῆς ζωῆς. Ὅντας βυθήση
ὁ ἥλιος καὶ τὸ σούρουπο ἀκλουθήση,
μὴν τοὺς κλαῖς, ὁ καημός σου ὅσος καὶ νά 'ναι.

screech-owl sits on the branch and weeps over his brother; over the
ruins, the derelict places, the owl is hooting. In the water-ditches, in the
marshes, the turtle cries; the nightingale hides deep in the thorny
bushes, and sings of love with sweet music. And the bat, the witch,
tears the darkness with her swift mad flight, playing with the plough-
man's happy children.

Happy countrymen of mine, I envy your life, your simple life with
its many joys. But most of all I envy your enchanting homecoming,
when the day ends and the sun sets.

THE dead are lucky; they forget the bitterness of life. When the sun
sets and twilight follows, do not weep for them, no matter how great
your sorrow,

Τέτοιαν ὥρα οἱ ψυχὲς διψοῦν καὶ πᾶνε
στῆς λησμονιᾶς τὴν κρουσταλλένια βρύση·
μὰ βοῦρκος τὸ νεράκι θὰ μαυρίση,
ἃ στάξη γι᾽ αὐτὲς δάκρυ ὅθε ἀγαπᾶνε.

Κι ἂν πιοῦν θολὸ νερὸ ξαναθυμοῦνται,
διαβαίνοντας λιβάδια ἀπὸ ἀσφοδίλι,
πόνους παλιούς, ποὺ μέσα τους κοιμοῦνται.

Ἃ δὲ μπορῆς παρὰ νὰ κλαῖς τὸ δείλι,
τοὺς ζωντανοὺς τὰ μάτια σου ἂς θρηνήσουν·
θέλουν, μὰ δὲ βολεῖ νὰ λησμονήσουν.

315. The Olive-tree

Στὴν κουφάλα σου ἐφώλιασε μελίσσι,
γέρικη ἐλιά, ποὺ γέρνεις μὲ τὴ λίγη
πρασινάδα ποὺ ἀκόμα σὲ τυλίγει
σὰ νά 'θελε νὰ σὲ νεκροστολίση.

Καὶ τὸ κάθε πουλάκι στὸ μεθύσι
τῆς ἀγάπης πιπίζοντας ἀνοίγει
στὸ κλαρί σου ἐρωτάρικο κυνήγι,
στὸ κλαρί σου ποὺ δὲ θὰ ξανανθίση.

For it is then the souls feel thirsty and go to the crystal Spring of Oblivion; but, if a tear drops from those they love, the water darkens into mire.

And if they drink clouded water, they remember, as they cross the fields of asphodel, the old suffering that slumbers in them.

If you must weep when twilight falls, let your eyes weep for the living: they try to, but cannot, forget.

A SWARM of bees has hived in your hollow trunk, old olive-tree, you who bend beneath the scanty green that still clings around you, as if to adorn your corpse.

And every little bird, drunk with love, twitters and starts an amorous chase in your boughs, boughs that will never blossom again.

Ὦ πόσο στὴ θανὴ θὰ σὲ γλυκάνουν,
μὲ τὴ μαγευτικιὰ βοὴ ποὺ κάνουν,
ὁλοζώντανης νιότης ὁμορφάδες,

ποὺ σὰ θύμησες μέσα σου πληθαίνουν.
Ὦ, νὰ μποροῦσαν ἔτσι νὰ πεθαίνουν
καὶ ἄλλες ψυχές, τῆς ψυχῆς σου ἀδερφάδες.

LAMBROS PORPHYRAS
1879–1932

316. The Journey

Ὄνειρο ἀπίστευτο ἡ λιόχαρη μέρα! Κι ἐγὼ κι ἡ Ἀννούλα
λίγοι παλιοὶ σύντροφοί μου καὶ κάποιες κοπέλες μαζί,
μπήκαμε μέσα σὲ μιὰ γαλανή, μεθυσμένη βαρκούλα,
μπήκαμε μέσα καὶ πᾶμε μακριὰ στῆς Χαρᾶς τὸ νησί.

Οὔτ' ἕνα σύννεφο κι οὔτ' ἕνας μαῦρος καπνὸς στὸν ἀγέρα·
πλάι μας στήθη ἐρωτιάρικα κι ἄσπροι χιονάτοι λαιμοί,
φῶς στὰ μαλλιὰ τὰ ξανθά, φῶς στὸ πέλαγο, φῶς πέρα ὡς πέρα·
μὰ ποιὸς ἐπῆγε ποτέ του μακριὰ στῆς Χαρᾶς τὸ νησί;

As you die, ah, how you must be gladdened by these lively delights
of youth which make their enchanting sounds
  And multiply like memories in your heart. Ah, if only other souls
could die as you do, sister-souls of you!

THE sun-flooded day is an unbelievable dream! Annie and I, together
with a few old friends of mine and some girls, got into a blue, drunken
boat; we got in and off we went, away to the Island of Joy.
  Not a cloud, not a trace of black smoke in the air; beside us breasts
full of love, and snow-white throats; light on golden hair, light on the
sea, light everywhere. But who ever got to the distant Island of Joy?

"Ω! τί με νοιάζει κι ἄν πᾶμε ὡς ἐκεῖ; τί με νοιάζει; Γελάει
ὅλ' ἡ γλυκιά συντροφιά μου, γελᾶ ἡ θλιμμένη ζωή,
στ' ἄπειρο μέσα κυλᾶμε· κι ἡ 'Αννούλα τρελλά τραγουδάει·
ὅπου καὶ νά 'ναι μακριὰ θὰ φανῆ τῆς Χαρᾶς τὸ νησί...

317. The Last Fairy-tale

Πῆραν στρατὶ στρατὶ τὸ μονοπάτι
βασιλοποῦλες καὶ καλοκυράδες,
ἀπὸ τὶς ξένες χῶρες βασιλιάδες
καὶ καβαλάρηδες ἀπάνω στ' ἄτι.

Καὶ γύρω στῆς γιαγιᾶς μου τὸ κρεβάτι,
ἀνάμεσ' ἀπὸ δυὸ χλωμὲς λαμπάδες,
περνούσανε καὶ σὰν τραγουδιστάδες
τῆς τραγουδοῦσαν — ποιὸς τὸ ξέρει; — κάτι.

Κανεὶς γιὰ τῆς γιαγιᾶς μου τὴν ἀγάπη
δὲ σκότωσε τὸ Δράκο ἢ τὸν 'Αράπη,
καὶ νὰ τῆς φέρη ἀθάνατο νερό.

'Η μάνα μου εἶχε γονατίσει κάτου·
μ' ἀπάνω — μιὰ φορὰ κι ἕναν καιρὸ —
ὁ 'Αρχάγγελος χτυποῦσε τὰ φτερά του.

Oh, what does it matter to me whether we get there or not? What do I care? All our sweet company is laughing, sad life is laughing; we are rolling in infinity, and Annie is singing with wild joy. Wherever it may be, the Island of Joy will show in the distance.

PRINCESSES and mermaids, kings from faraway lands and horsemen on their horses slowly took the path;

And around my grandmother's bed, between two dim tapers, they passed; and like singers they chanted to her — who knows what? — something.

Yet nobody killed the ogre or the black bogey-man for love of my grandmother, to bring her water of immortality.

My mother had knelt down; but above — once upon a time — the archangel was beating his wings.

318. Stand Death a Drink

Πιὲ στοῦ γιαλοῦ τὴ σκοτεινὴ ταβέρνα τὸ κρασί σου,
σὲ μι' ἄκρη, τώρα π' ἄρχισαν ξανὰ τὰ πρωτοβρόχια,
πιέ το μὲ ναῦτες καὶ σκυφτοὺς ψαράδες ἀντικρύ σου,
μ' ἀνθρώπους ποὺ βασάνισε κι ἡ θάλασσα κι ἡ φτώχεια.

Πιὲ το, ἡ ψυχή σου ἀξένοιαστη τόσο πολὺ νὰ γίνη,
ποὺ ἂν ἔρθ' ἡ Μοίρα σου ἡ κακιὰ νὰ τῆς χαμογελάσης,
καημοὶ καινούργιοι ἂν ἔρθουνε, μαζί σου ἂς πιοῦν κι ἐκεῖνοι,
κι ἂν ἔρθη ὁ Χάρος, ἥσυχα κι αὐτὸν νὰ τὸν κεράσης.

CONSTANTINE HATZOPOULOS
1871–1920

319. The Dance of the Shades

Μὴν ἀκοῦς ἀπάνω
τὴν ἀστροφεγγιά,
μὴν ἀκοῦς τί νεύει·
μὰ ἔλα δῶ κοντά μας,
ἔλα μὴν ἀργῆς,
στὴ συντροφιά μας.

DRINK your wine in the dark seaside tavern, in a corner, now the first rains of autumn have started again; drink facing the sailors and the hunched fishermen, men tortured by poverty and the sea.

Drink for the heart to become so carefree that if evil Fate came in, you would smile at her; if new sufferings came, you would drink with them, and if Death were to come, you would calmly stand even him a drink.

GIVE no heed to the starlight above, give no heed to its beckoning; but come here to us – do not delay – come to join our band.

CONSTANTINE HATZOPOULOS

Μὴν ἀκοῦς τριγύρου
ἡ λευκὴ νυχτιά
μὴ σὲ ξεπλανεύη·
μὰ ἔλα δῶ κοντά μας,
ἔλα μὴν ἀργῆς,
στὴ βαθιὰ σπηλιά μας.

Εἶναι ἀπάνω τ' ἄστρα
πνεύματα κακά,
λάμιες τῆς ψυχῆς·
ἔλα ἐδῶ κοντά μας,
ἔλα μὴν ἀργῆς,
στὸ ξεφάντωμά μας.

Κι ἔχει τὸ φεγγάρι
σπείρει στὶς ὀχτιὲς
μάγισσες ξωθιές·
ἔλα ἀνάμεσό μας,
ἔλα μὴν ἀργῆς,
στὸν παλιὸ χορό μας.

Σοῦ 'στησαν στὰ κλώνια
γήτεμα γλυκὸ
οἱ κακὲς τ' ἀηδόνια·
μὰ γιὰ μᾶς μιὰ γλαύκα
ἀπ' τὰ ἐρείπια ἐκεῖ,
μὴν ἀνατριχιάζης,
παίζει μουσικὴ

Do not listen to the sounds all around, do not let the white night
lead you astray, but come here to us; do not delay – come to our deep
cave.

The stars above are evil spirits, witches of the soul; come here to
us; do not delay – come to join our revels.

For the moon has sown the river-banks with bewitching fairies.
Come here among us; do not delay – come and join our ancient dance.

Evil spirits, the nightingales, have set on the branches a sweet spell
to enchant you; but for us the owl plays from yonder ruins (do not

πιὸ νοσταλγική·
σέρνει τὸ ρυθμό μας
στὸν ἀργὸ χορό μας.

Μὴν ἀνατριχιάζῃς!
Ἔλα δῶ μὲ μᾶς,
θὰ σὲ νανουρίσωμε
ποὺ νὰ μὴν ξυπνᾶς·
Ἔλα, θὰ σὲ πάρωμε
πάντα σύντροφό μας
στὸ μακρὺ καὶ ἀτέλειωτο,
στὸν ἀργὸ χορό μας.

PAUL NIRVANAS
1866–1937

320. Hellenic Dawn

Παρθενικὸ ξημέρωμα
στοῦ Αἰγαίου τὴ γαλήνη. . .
Ἡ πλάση ἡ νεογέννητη
πλέει σὲ θεῖον αἰθέρα·
ἀπὸ τὰ ὄργια τῆς νυκτὸς
λιπόθυμη ἡ Σελήνη,
χαρὰ θεῶν, ἡ Ἑλληνικὴ
ροδοχαράζει ἡμέρα.

shudder!) a more nostalgic music, and beats the time for our slow dance.

Do not shudder: come here with us, and we shall sing you a lullaby from which you will never wake. Come, we shall take you with us, a companion for ever in our long and endless, in our slow dance.

O PUREST dawn over the calm Aegean sea! The newly-born world sails in the holy air; the moon is faint from the orgies of the night; joy of the gods, the Hellenic day breaks in roses.

MILTIADES MALAKASIS
1870–1943

321. *Spring Shower*

Βαριές, πλατιὲς οἱ στάλες
πέφτουν οἱ μεγάλες
τῆς βροχῆς,
κι ἀριές·
κλάμα βουβό, καὶ πῶς ἀχεῖς!
πῶς ἀντηχεῖς
μὲς στὶς θλιμμένες τὶς καρδιές!
ἀντάμα με σπασμένες δοξαριές·
κακὲς πού 'ν' οἱ παλιὲς πληγὲς
καὶ τῆς φτωχῆς
ἀπαντοχῆς
οἱ ἀπελπισιές!...

Διές,
ἥλιος τοῦ Μαρτιοῦ μαζὶ
μὲ τὸ χαλάζι τὸ σκληρὸ
σὰν τ' ἄστρα·
ὦ ἔννοια, ζῆ
μὲς στ' ἄλλα
πόχ' ἡ μπόρα,
ζῆ κι ἡ στάλα
ἀκόμα τὸ νερό,
ἀφοῦ
στάζ' ἔτσι τώρα
μὲς στὴ φαρφου-
ρένια
γλάστρα.

HEAVY, flat, the big drops of rain fall one by one; dumb lamentation, yet how loud! How you re-echo in the sad hearts! You mingle with the broken sound of violins. How evil old memories are, and the despair of sad expectation.

Look! the March sun and the hard hail; like stars! O worries, even the drop of water lives together with all else the storm carries, for now it drops in the china flower-pot.

'Απόψ' άλί!
απόψ' άλυ-
σοδέθηκε όλη μου ή ζωή
μ' ό τι θροεῖ, φυλλορροεῖ,
σπάζει, σπαράζει,
κι εἶναι τοῦ πόνου μου ἀδερφός·
απόψ' ὁ ἥλιος ποὺ κρυφὸς
ἀσπρογαλιάζει
καὶ πνίγετ' ἔτσι δίχως φῶς,
σὰν τὴ χαμένη μου ψυχή,
μέσα στὸ βρόχι σου, ὦ βροχή!
καὶ στὸ χαλάζι
τὸ μαράζι...

JOHN GRYPARIS
1871–1942

322. *Death*

Καλῶς νὰ 'ρθῆ σὰν ἔρθ' ἡ στερνὴ ὥρα
τὰ μάτια μου γιὰ πάντα νὰ μοῦ κλείση,
κι ὅποτα νὰ 'ναι, ἢ τώρα ἢ ἀργήση,
φτάνει νὰ μὴν ἐρθῆ σὰν ἄγρια μπόρα.

Today alas, today my whole life is chained to all that murmurs, that
casts its leaves, breaks and suffers: the brothers of my pain. Today the
sun that secretly shines white is choked with no light, like my lost
soul in your noose, rain; and in the hail, pining ...

He will be welcome when the last moments come to close my eyes for-
ever, whenever that may be, now or later, provided he does not come
like a wild storm.

Ανοιξη βέβαια νά 'ναι, σάν καί τώρα,
κι ἀκόμα μιά γλυκιά γλυκούλα δύση,
κι ἔτσι νά πάρη μιά αὖρα νά φυσήση
καί νά πέση ἡ ψυχούλα ἡ λευκοφόρα

σάν ἄνθι τῆς μηλιᾶς· κι ὅπου τό βγάλη
ἡ ἀγνή νεροσυρμή πού ῥέει ἀγάλι
σὲ δεντρόκηπους μέσα καί βραγιές,

κι ὅπου τό πάη κι ὅπου ἀκόμα μείνη
ἀπ' τὶς παλιὲς μονάχα τὶς φωνὲς
ν' ἀκούη τό ‹χαῖρε› πού θά κλαίη ἡ Κρήνη.

323. Sleep

Ἔλα, ὕπνε, καί πάρε με· στήν κλίνη
πού σῶμα καί ψυχή σοῦ παραδίνω
κάμε, παρηγοριά μου, ν' ἀπαλύνη
ὁ μαῦρος πόνος πού στά στήθη κλείνω.

Μὲς στή βαθιὰ πού σοῦ ζητῶ γαλήνη
σά νά μὲ πῆρε ὁ ἀδερφός σου ἃς γίνω,
κι ἀπ' τή ζωή, πού λαχταράω, ἃς μοῦ μείνη
τόση, ὅση ἀνασαίνει σ' ἕναν κρίνο.

It should be spring, of course, like now, and moreover a sweet, a
gentle sunset; and let a breeze blow that the little white-clad soul may
drop
Like apple-blossom. And wherever the pure, gently-flowing stream
takes it, among orchards and gardens,
No matter where it goes or stops, from the old voices let it hear only
that farewell which the weeping fountain will bid.

COME, Sleep, take me away; you, my consolation, make the black
pain that I close in my breast grow softer on this bed, where I sur-
render my soul and body to you.
Let me feel, in this deep calm that I am asking from you, as if your
brother took me away; and from the life I love let as much be left for
me as breathes in a lily.

Σ' ἕναν κρίνο λευκὸ σὰν τὸ χαλάζι,
ποῦ ὅταν στὸ νέο τὸ φῶς, π' ἀσπροχαράζει,
ἀναγαλιάζει ὁ οὐρανὸς κι ἡ γῆ,

μιὰ ψυχούλα θὰ 'ρθῆ τὰ πέταλά του
φιλώντας νὰ τοῦ ἀνοίξη τὴν αὐγὴ
μ' ἕνα κόμπο δροσιᾶς μὲς στὴν καρδιά του.

CONSTANTINE KARYOTAKIS
1896–1928

324. Sleep

Θὰ μᾶς δοθῆ τὸ χάρισμα καὶ ἡ μοίρα
νὰ πᾶμε νὰ πεθάνουμε μιὰ νύχτα
στὸ πράσινο ἀκρογιάλι τῆς πατρίδας;
Γλυκὰ θὰ κοιμηθοῦμε σὰν παιδάκια
γλυκά. Κι ἀπάνωθέ μας θὲ νὰ φεύγουν,
στὸν οὐρανό, τ' ἀστέρια καὶ τὰ ἐγκόσμια.
Θὰ μᾶς χαϊδεύη ὡς ὄνειρο τὸ κῦμα.
Καὶ γαλανὸ σὰν κῦμα τ' ὄνειρό μας
θὰ μᾶς τραβάη σὲ χῶρες ποὺ δὲν εἶναι.
'Αγάπες θὰ 'ναι στὰ μαλλιά μας οἱ αὔρες,
ἡ ἀνάσα τῶν φυκιῶν θὰ μᾶς μυρώνη;

In a lily white as hail, whose petals a small butterfly will come at dawn to open with a kiss when sky and earth delight in the new light that is breaking in whiteness, a lily with a drop of cool dew in its heart.

WILL we be given that gift, will we be fated to reach the green shore of our native land, and there to die one night? Sweetly we shall sleep, like children, sweetly; and above us into the sky the stars and all worldly things will drift away. The waves will caress us like a dream; and our dreams, blue like the waves, will lead us away to lands that do not exist. The breeze will touch our hair like love; the breath of sea-

καὶ κάτου ἀπ' τὰ μεγάλα βλεφαρά μας,
χωρὶς νὰν τὸ γρικοῦμε, θὰ γελᾶμε.
Τὰ ῥόδα θὰ κινήσουν ἀπ' τοὺς φράχτες
καὶ θὰ 'ρθουν νὰ μᾶς γίνουν προσκεφάλι.
Γιὰ νὰ μᾶς κάνουν ἁρμονία τὸν ὕπνο,
θ' ἀφήσουνε τὸν ὕπνο τους τ' ἀηδόνια.
Γλυκὰ θὰ κοιμηθοῦμε σὰν παιδάκια
γλυκά. Καὶ τὰ κορίτσια τοῦ χωριοῦ μας,
ἀγριαπιδιές, θὰ στέκουνε τριγύρω
καί, σκύβοντας, κρυφὰ θὰ μᾶς μιλοῦνε
γιὰ τὰ χρυσὰ καλύβια, γιὰ τὸν ἥλιο
τῆς Κυριακῆς, γιὰ τὶς ὁλάσπρες γάστρες,
γιὰ τὰ καλὰ τὰ χρόνια μας ποὺ πᾶνε.
Τὸ χέρι μας κρατώντας ἡ κυρούλα,
κι ὅπως ἀργὰ θὰ κλείνουμε τὰ μάτια,
θὰ μᾶς διηγιέται, ὠχρή, σὰν παραμύθι
τὴν πίκρα τῆς ζωῆς. Καὶ τὸ φεγγάρι
θὰ κατεβῆ στὰ πόδια μας λαμπάδα,
τὴν ὥρα ποὺ στερνὰ θὰ κοιμηθοῦμε
στὸ πράσινο ἀκρογιάλι τῆς πατρίδας.
Γλυκὰ θὰ κοιμηθοῦμε σὰν παιδάκια,
ποὺ ὅλη τὴ μέρα ἔκλαψαν καὶ ἀποστάσαν.

weed will anoint us, and under our long lashes, without realizing it, we shall smile. The roses will move from the hedges and come to be our pillows; the nightingales will leave their sleep to turn our sleep to music. Sweetly we shall sleep like children, sweetly. And the girls of our village, wild pear-trees, will be standing round us, and bending down will gently whisper of the golden cottages, the Sunday sunshine, the snow-white flower-pots, about the good years now gone; and as at length we close our eyes, a little old woman will hold our hand and tell us, pale-faced, of the bitterness of life, as if it were a fairy-tale. And the moon will come down and stand, a candle, at our feet, when for the last time we fall asleep on the green shore of our native land. Sweetly we shall sleep, like children that had wept all day until they were exhausted and ceased.

MARIA POLYDOURE
1905–30

325. Because You Loved Me

Δὲν τραγουδῶ παρὰ γιατὶ μ' ἀγάπησες
στὰ περασμένα χρόνια·
καὶ σὲ ἥλιο, σὲ καλοκαιριοῦ προμάντεμα
καὶ σὲ βροχή, σὲ χιόνια,
δὲν τραγουδῶ παρὰ γιατὶ μ' ἀγάπησες.

Μόνο γιατὶ μὲ κράτησες στὰ χέρια σου
μιὰ νύχτα καὶ μὲ φίλησες στὸ στόμα,
μόνο γι' αὐτὸ εἶμαι ὡραία σὰν κρίνο ὁλάνοιχτο
κι ἔχω ἕνα ρίγος στὴν ψυχή μου ἀκόμα,
μόνο γιατὶ μὲ κράτησες στὰ χέρια σου.

Μόνο γιατὶ τὰ μάτια σου μὲ κοίταξαν
μὲ τὴν ψυχὴ στὸ βλέμμα,
περήφανα στολίστηκα τὸ ὑπέρτατο
τῆς ὑπαρξῆς μου στέμμα,
μόνο γιατὶ τὰ μάτια σου μὲ κοίταξαν.

Μόνο γιατὶ ὅπως πέρναα μὲ καμάρωσες
καὶ στὴ ματιά σου νὰ περνάῃ

I SING, only because you loved me in years gone by; only because you
loved me, I sing when the sun shines, when the message of summer
comes, when it rains and when it snows.

Only because you held me in your arms one night and kissed my
mouth, only because of that am I as beautiful as a wide-open lily, and
still feel a shiver in my heart; only because you held me in your arms.

Only because your eyes looked at me and your soul was in their
gaze did I proudly adorn myself with the supreme diadem of my
existence; only because your eyes looked at me.

Only because you admired me as I was walking by, and I saw in your

εἶδα τὴ λυγερὴ σκιά μου, ὡς ὄνειρο
νὰ παίζῃ, νὰ πονάῃ,
μόνο γιατὶ ὅπως πέρναα μὲ καμάρωσες,

γιατὶ δισταχτικὰ σὰ νὰ μὲ φώναξες
καὶ μοῦ ἅπλωσες τὰ χέρια
κι εἶχες μέσα στὰ μάτια σου τὸ θάμπωμα,
μιὰ ἀγάπη πλέρια,
γιατὶ δισταχτικὰ σὰ νὰ μὲ φώναξες,

γιατί, μόνο γιατὶ σὲ σέναν ἄρεσε,
γι᾽ αὐτὸ ἔμεινεν ὡραῖο τὸ πέρασμά μου·
σὰ νὰ μ᾽ ἀκολουθοῦσες ὅπου πήγαινα,
σὰ νὰ περνοῦσες κάπου ἐκεῖ σιμά μου·
γιατί, μόνο γιατὶ σὲ σέναν ἄρεσε.

Μόνο γιατὶ μ᾽ ἀγάπησες γεννήθηκα,
γι᾽ αὐτὸ ἡ ζωὴ μοῦ ἐδόθη.
Στὴν ἄχαρη ζωὴ τὴν ἀνεκπλήρωτη
μένα ἡ ζωὴ πληρώθη.
Μόνο γιατὶ μ᾽ ἀγάπησες γεννήθηκα.

Μονάχα γιὰ τὴ διαλεχτὴν ἀγάπη σου
μοῦ χάρισε ἡ αὐγὴ ρόδα στὰ χέρια.

eyes my slender shadow move, play like a dream, ache, only because
you admired me as I was walking by;

Because reluctantly you seemed to call me, and you stretched out
your arms, and there was a haze of wonder in your glance, a love
complete, because reluctantly you seemed to call me;

Because, only because, it pleased you, was my passing-by beautiful.
It looked as though you followed me wherever I went, as though you
were walking by me somewhere near, because, only because, it pleased
you;

Only because you loved me was I born, only for that my life was
given me; in this thankless life that never knows fulfilment, my life has
been fulfilled. Only because you loved me was I born.

Only because of your exquisite love, the dawn put roses in my

Γιὰ νὰ φωτίσω μιὰ στιγμὴ τὸ δρόμο σου
μοῦ γέμισε τὰ μάτια ἡ νύχτα ἀστέρια,
μονάχα γιὰ τὴ διαλεχτὴν ἀγάπη σου.

Μονάχα γιατὶ τόσο ὡραῖα μ' ἀγάπησες
ἔζησα, νὰ πληθαίνω
τὰ ὀνείρατά σου, ὡραῖε, ποὺ βασίλεψες,
κι ἔτσι γλυκὰ πεθαίνω,
μονάχα γιατὶ τόσο ὡραῖα μ' ἀγάπησες.

MYRTIOTISSA
1883–1967

326. I Love You

Σ' ἀγαπῶ· δὲν μπορῶ
τίποτ' ἄλλο νὰ πῶ
πιὸ βαθύ, πιὸ ἁπλό,
πιὸ μεγάλο!

Μπρὸς στὰ πόδια σου ἐδῶ
μὲ λαχτάρα σκορπῶ
τὸν πολύφυλλο ἀνθὸ
τῆς ζωῆς μου.

hands, the night filled my eyes with stars to light your path for a moment, only because of your exquisite love.

I lived only because you loved me so beautifully, to feed your dreams, my handsome lover that set like the sun, and so I sweetly die, only because you loved me so beautifully.

I LOVE you. I can say nothing deeper, more simple or greater.

Here, before your feet, I scatter, full of longing, the rich-petalled blossom of my life.

"Ω! μελίσσι μου! πιὲς
ἀπ' αὐτὸν τὶς γλυκιές,
τὶς ἀγνὲς εὐωδιὲς
τῆς ψυχῆς μου!

Τὰ δυὸ χέρια μου, νά!
στὰ προσφέρω δετὰ
γιὰ νὰ γύρης γλυκὰ
τὸ κεφάλι.

Κι ἡ καρδιά μου σκιρτᾶ,
κι ὅλη ζήλια ζητᾶ
νὰ σοῦ γίνη ὡς αὐτὰ
προσκεφάλι!

Καὶ γιὰ στρῶμα, καλέ,
πᾶρε ὅλην ἐμέ,
σβῆσ' τὴ φλόγα σὲ μὲ
τῆς φωτιᾶς σου,

ἐνῶ δίπλα σου ἐγὼ
τὴ ζωὴ θ' ἀγρικῶ
νὰ κυλάη στὸ ρυθμὸ
τῆς καρδιᾶς σου...

O, my swarm of bees! Suck from it the sweet, the pure perfume of my heart!

See, I offer you my two hands, clasped for you to lean your head softly upon.

And my heart is dancing, is all envy, and begs to be, like them, a pillow for your head.

And for a bed, my love, take the whole of me, extinguish upon me the flame of your fire,

While I, close to you, hear life flowing away to the beat of your heart...

MYRTIOTISSA

Σ' ἀγαπῶ· τί μπορῶ,
ἀκριβέ, νά σοῦ πῶ
πιὸ βαθύ, πιὸ ἁπλό,
πιὸ μεγάλο;

EMILY S. DAPHNE
1887–1941

327. *Attic Nights*

'Απόψε λάμπει ὁ οὐρανὸς μὲ τ' ἄστρα πλουμισμένος
καθὼς γιγάντιου παγωνιοῦ ἡ χρυσομάτα οὐρά·
ὁ Σαπφικὸς κελαηδισμὸς ζῆ κάπου ἐδῶ κρυμμένος
στὰ φύλλα, στὰ νερά.

Σὲ ποιὰ 'Ελευσίνια προσφορὰ τὸ κάνιστρό σου φέρνεις,
νύχτα 'Αθηναία, γεμάτο ἀνθοὺς ὀνείρων, παρθενιᾶς,
καθὼς περνᾶς καὶ γύρω σου δροσιᾶς διαμάντια σπέρνεις,
καθὼς μέσα στὰ κύπελλα τῶν κρίνων τὴν κερνᾶς;

Στὰ 'Ελληνικὰ τὰ μάτια σου ἴσκοι περνοῦν οἱ πόθοι·
κάτου ἀπ' τὸ φέγγος σου οἱ καρδιὲς τρεμίζουν καὶ τὰ χείλη.
Κι ὁ ποιητὴς κοιτάζοντας τὴν ὀμορφία σου νιώθει
τὸ λυρικό σου τ' ἄγγιγμα, νύχτα γλυκιὰ τοῦ 'Απρίλη!

I love you. What more, my precious love, can I tell you that is
deeper, more simple, or greater?

Tonight the star-embroidered sky flashes like a huge peacock's gold-
eyed tail. Sappho's song lives somewhere here, hidden in the leaves,
the water.

Athenian night, to what Eleusinian offering are you bringing your
basket full of the blossom of dreams, full of virginity; as you move past
me, scattering dew-diamonds about you and filling the cups of the
lilies?

In your Greek eyes desires flash like shadows; in your shimmering
light, hearts and lips shiver; and the poet, looking at your beauty, feels
your lyrical touch, sweet April night.

C. KAVAFIS
1863–1933

328. Desires

Σὰν σώματα ὡραῖα νεκρῶν ποὺ δὲν ἐγέρασαν
καὶ τά 'κλεισαν, μὲ δάκρυα, σὲ μαυσωλεῖο λαμπρό,
μὲ ρόδα στὸ κεφάλι καὶ στὰ πόδια γιασεμιά —
ἔτσ' οἱ ἐπιθυμίες μοιάζουν ποὺ ἐπέρασαν
χωρὶς νὰ ἐκπληρωθοῦν· χωρὶς ν' ἀξιωθῆ καμιὰ
τῆς ἡδονῆς μιὰ νύχτα ἢ ἕνα πρωί της φεγγερό.

329. Monotony

Τὴν μιὰ μονότονην ἡμέραν ἄλλη
μονότονη, ἀπαράλλακτη ἀκολουθεῖ. Θὰ γίνουν
τὰ ἴδια πράγματα, θὰ ξαναγίνουν πάλι —
οἱ ὅμοιες στιγμὲς μᾶς βρίσκουνε καὶ μᾶς ἀφίνουν.

Μῆνας περνᾶ καὶ φέρνει ἄλλον μῆνα.
Αὐτὰ ποὺ ἔρχονται κανεὶς εὔκολα τὰ εἰκάζει·
εἶναι τὰ χθεσινὰ τὰ βαρετὰ ἐκεῖνα.
Καὶ καταντᾶ τὸ αὔριο σὰν αὔριο νὰ μὴ μοιάζη.

LIKE beautiful dead bodies which never grow old but are enclosed with
tears in a splendid tomb, roses around their foreheads, and jasmine at
their feet – so look desires that passed without fulfilment, without the
blessing of a single night of pleasure, or one of her light-rich mornings.

ONE monotonous day is followed by another monotonous day, exactly
the same. The same things will be done, and done again – the identical
moments find us and leave us.

One month brings another. What is to come is easily guessed: those
same boring things as yesterday. So it comes about that tomorrow does
not look like tomorrow.

330. Thermopylae

Τιμή σ' ἐκείνους ὅπου στὴν ζωήν των
ὅρισαν καὶ φυλάγουν Θερμοπύλες.
Ποτὲ ἀπὸ τὸ χρέος μὴ κινοῦντες·
δίκαιοι κι ἴσιοι σ' ὅλες των τὲς πράξεις,
ἀλλὰ μὲ λύπη κιόλας κι εὐσπλαχνία·
γενναῖοι ὁσάκις εἶναι πλούσιοι, κι ὅταν
εἶναι πτωχοὶ πάλ' εἰς μικρὸν γενναῖοι,
πάλι συντρέχοντες ὅσο μποροῦνε·
πάντοτε τὴν ἀλήθειαν ὁμιλοῦντες,
πλὴν χωρὶς μίσος γιὰ τοὺς ψευδομένους.
Καὶ περισσότερη τιμή τοὺς πρέπει
ὅταν προβλέπουν (καὶ πολλοὶ προβλέπουν)
πὼς ὁ Ἐφιάλτης θὰ φανῇ στὸ τέλος,
κι οἱ Μῆδοι ἐπὶ τέλους θὰ διαβοῦνε.

331. The God Abandons Antony

Σὰν ἔξαφνα ὥρα μεσάνυχτ' ἀκουσθῇ
ἀόρατος θίασος νὰ περνᾶ
μὲ μουσικὲς ἐξαίσιες, μὲ φωνές —
τὴν τύχη σου ποὺ ἐνδίδει πιά, τὰ ἔργα σου
ποὺ ἀπέτυχαν, τὰ σχέδια τῆς ζωῆς σου

HONOUR to those who in their lives have set themselves to guard
Thermopylae, never moving from their duty. Just and straightforward
in all they do, but also with pity and compassion. Generous when they
are rich; and again, when poor, in smaller measure generous, helping
as much as they can; always speaking the truth, but without hatred for
those who lie. And greater honour is due to those who foresee – and
many foresee – that Ephialtes will appear in the end, and the Persians
will finally get through.

WHEN suddenly at the midnight hour an invisible Bacchic revel is
heard passing, with exquisite music, with voices – do not lament,
pointlessly, your luck that finally gives out, your work that has failed,

ποὺ βγῆκαν ὅλα πλάνες μὴ ἀνωφέλετα θρηνήσῃς.
Σὰν ἕτοιμος ἀπὸ καιρό, σὰ θαρραλέος,
ἀποχαιρέτα την, τὴν Ἀλεξάνδρεια ποὺ φεύγει.
Πρὸ πάντων νὰ μὴ γελασθῇς, μὴν πῇς πὼς ἦταν
ἕνα ὄνειρο, πὼς ἀπατήθηκεν ἡ ἀκοή σου·
μάταιες ἐλπίδες τέτοιες μὴν καταδεχθῇς.
Σὰν ἕτοιμος ἀπὸ καιρό, σὰ θαρραλέος,
σὰν ποὺ ταιριάζει σε ποὺ ἀξιώθηκες μιὰ τέτοια πόλη,
πλησίασε σταθερὰ πρὸς τὸ παράθυρο
κι ἄκουσε μὲ συγκίνησιν, ἀλλ᾽ ὄχι
μὲ τῶν δειλῶν τὰ παρακάλια καὶ παράπονα,
ὡς τελευταίαν ἀπόλαυσιν, τοὺς ἤχους,
τὰ ἐξαίσια ὄργανα τοῦ μυστικοῦ θιάσου,
κι ἀποχαιρέτα την, τὴν Ἀλεξάνδρεια ποὺ χάνεις.

332. *Waiting for the Barbarians*

‹Τί περιμένουμε στὴν ἀγορὰ συναθροισμένοι;›
‹Εἶναι οἱ βάρβαροι νὰ φθάσουν σήμερα.›
‹Γιατί μέσα στὴ Σύγκλητο μιὰ τέτοια ἀπραξία;
τί κάθονται οἱ συγκλητικοὶ καὶ δὲν νομοθετοῦνε;›

all you had planned in your life that proved to be false. Like one for long prepared, like a courageous man, say good-bye to her, to the Alexandria who is leaving. Above all do not deceive yourself, do not say it was a dream, that your hearing was mistaken; do not stoop to such vain hopes as these. Like one for long prepared, like a courageous man, as it becomes you who were considered worthy of such a city, go steadily to the window, and listen with emotion, but without the prayers or complaints of a coward, listen as a final delight to that sound, to the exquisite instruments of the secret Bacchic band, and say good-bye to her, the Alexandria you are losing.

'WHAT are we waiting for, gathered in the market-place?' 'The barbarians will come today.' 'Why is there no activity in the senate? Why are the senators seated without legislating?' 'Because the barbarians

‹Γιατὶ οἱ βάρβαροι θὰ φθάσουν σήμερα·
τί νόμους πιὰ νὰ κάμουν οἱ συγκλητικοί;
οἱ βάρβαροι, σὰν ἔρθουν, θὰ νομοθετήσουν.›
‹Γιατὶ ὁ αὐτοκράτωρ μας τόσο πρωὶ σηκώθη
καὶ κάθεται στῆς πόλεως τὴν πιὸ μεγάλη πύλη,
στὸ θρόνο ἐπάνω, ἐπίσημος, φορώντας τὴν κορόνα;›
‹Γιατὶ οἱ βάρβαροι θὰ φθάσουν σήμερα,
κι ὁ αὐτοκράτωρ περιμένει νὰ δεχθῆ
τὸν ἀρχηγό τους. Μάλιστα ἑτοίμασε
γιὰ νὰ τὸν δώση μιὰ περγαμηνή. Ἐκεῖ
τὸν ἔγραψε τίτλους πολλοὺς κι ὀνόματα.›
‹Γιατὶ οἱ δυό μας ὕπατοι καὶ πραίτορες ἐβγῆκαν
σήμερα μὲ τὲς κόκκινες τὲς κεντημένες τόγιες;
γιατὶ βραχιόλια φόρεσαν μὲ τόσους ἀμεθύστους
καὶ δαχτυλίδια μὲ λαμπρὰ γυαλιστερὰ σμαράγδια;
γιατί νὰ πιάσουν σήμερα πολύτιμα μπαστούνια
μ᾿ ἀσήμια καὶ μαλάματα ἔκτακτα σκαλιγμένα;›
‹Γιατὶ οἱ βάρβαροι θὰ φθάσουν σήμερα·
καὶ τέτοια πράγματα θαμπώνουν τοὺς βαρβάρους.›
‹Γιατὶ κι οἱ ἄξιοι ῥήτορες δὲν ἔρχονται σὰν πάντα
νὰ βγάλουνε τοὺς λόγους τους, νὰ ποῦνε τὰ δικά τους;›
‹Γιατὶ οἱ βάρβαροι θὰ φθάσουν σήμερα
κι αὐτοὶ βαριοῦνται εὐφράδειες καὶ δημηγορίες.›

will come today; what laws can the senators pass now? The barbarians, when they come, will make the laws.' 'Why has our emperor risen so early, and is seated at the greatest gate of the city on the throne, in state, wearing the crown?' 'Because the barbarians will come today, and the emperor is waiting to receive their leader. He has even prepared a parchment to give him. There he has written out for him many titles and names.' 'Why did our two consuls and our praetors come out today in the scarlet, the embroidered togas? Why did they put on bracelets with so many amethysts, and rings with bright flashing emeralds? Why did they get hold of the precious staves splendidly wrought with silver and gold?' 'Because the barbarians will come today; and such things dazzle barbarians.' 'And why don't the worthy orators come as always to deliver their speeches, and say what they usually say?' 'Because the barbarians will arrive today, and they are bored with eloquence and public speaking.' 'Why has this uneasiness

‹Γιατὶ ν' ἀρχίση μονομιᾶς αὐτὴ ἡ ἀνησυχία
κι ἡ σύγχυσις· (τὰ πρόσωπα τί σοβαρὰ ποὺ ἐγίναν!);
Γιατὶ ἀδειάζουν γρήγορα οἱ δρόμοι κι οἱ πλατέες,
κι ὅλοι γυρνοῦν στὰ σπίτια τους πολὺ συλλογισμένοι;›
    ‹Γιατὶ ἐνύχτωσε κι οἱ βάρβαροι δὲν ἦλθαν·
    καὶ μερικοὶ ἔφθασαν ἀπ' τὰ σύνορα
    καὶ εἶπανε πὼς βάρβαροι πιὰ δὲν ὑπάρχουν.›
Καὶ τώρα τί θὰ γένουμε χωρὶς βαρβάρους;
Οἱ ἄνθρωποι αὐτοὶ ἦσαν μιὰ κάποια λύσις.

333. Ithaca

Σὰ βγῆς στὸν πηγαιμὸ γιὰ τὴν Ἰθάκη,
νὰ εὔχεσαι νά 'ναι μακρὺς ὁ δρόμος,
γεμάτος περιπέτειες, γεμάτος γνώσεις.
Τοὺς Λαιστρυγόνας καὶ τοὺς Κύκλωπας,
τὸν θυμωμένο Ποσειδῶνα, μὴ φοβᾶσαι,
τέτοια στὸ δρόμο σου ποτέ σου δὲν θὰ βρῆς,
ἂν μέν' ἡ σκέψη σου ὑψηλή, ἂν ἐκλεκτὴ
συγκίνησις τὸ πνεῦμα καὶ τὸ σῶμα σου ἀγγίζη.
Τοὺς Λαιστρυγόνας καὶ τοὺς Κύκλωπας,
τὸν ἄγριο Ποσειδῶνα δὲν θὰ συναντήσης,

suddenly started, this confusion? How grave the faces have become! Why are the streets and squares quickly emptying, and why is everyone going back home so very concerned?' 'Because night has fallen, and the barbarians have not come. And some men have arrived from the frontiers and they said that there are no barbarians any more.' And now, what will become of us without barbarians? Those people were a kind of solution.

WHEN you set out for Ithaca, ask that the journey be long, full of adventures, full of things to learn. The Laestrygonians and the Cyclopes, angry Poseidon – do not fear them. Such as these you will never find on your way, if you have elevated thoughts, if choice emotions touch your spirit and your flesh. The Laestrygonians and the

ἂν δὲν τοὺς κουβανῆς μὲς στὴν ψυχή σου,
ἂν ἡ ψυχή σου δὲν τοὺς στήνη ἐμπρός σου.

Νὰ εὔχεσαι νὰ 'ναι μακρὺς ὁ δρόμος.
Πολλὰ τὰ καλοκαιρινὰ πρωϊὰ νὰ εἶναι
ποὺ μὲ τί εὐχαρίστηση, μὲ τί χαρὰ
θὰ μπαίνης σὲ λιμένες πρωτοειδωμένους·
νὰ σταματήσης σ' ἐμπορεῖα Φοινικικά,
καὶ τὲς καλὲς πραμάτειες ν' ἀποκτήσης,
σεντέφια καὶ κοράλλια, κεχριμπάρια κι ἔβενους,
καὶ ἡδονικὰ μυρωδικὰ κάθε λογῆς,
ὅσο μπορεῖς πιὸ ἄφθονα ἡδονικὰ μυρωδικά·
σὲ πόλεις Αἰγυπτιακὲς πολλὲς νὰ πᾶς,
νὰ μάθης καὶ νὰ μάθης ἀπ' τοὺς σπουδασμένους.

Πάντα στὸ νοῦ σου νὰ 'χης τὴν Ἰθάκη.
Τὸ φθάσιμον ἐκεῖ εἶν' ὁ προορισμός σου.
Ἀλλὰ μὴ βιάζης τὸ ταξίδι διόλου.
Καλύτερα χρόνια πολλὰ νὰ διαρκέση·
καὶ γέρος πιὰ ν' ἀράξης στὸ νησί,
πλούσιος μὲ ὅσα κέρδισες στὸν δρόμο,
μὴ προσδοκώντας πλούτη νὰ σε δώση ἡ Ἰθάκη.

Ἡ Ἰθάκη σ' ἔδωσε τ' ὡραῖο ταξίδι.
Χωρὶς αὐτὴν δὲ θά βγαινες στὸν δρόμο.
Ἄλλα δὲν ἔχει νὰ σὲ δώση πιά.

Cyclopes and fierce Poseidon you will not meet, unless you carry them in your heart, unless your heart sets them in your path.

Pray that your journey be long; that there may be many summer mornings when with what joy, what delight, you will enter harbours you have not seen before; and will stop at Phoenician trading-ports, acquire beautiful merchandise, mother-of-pearl and coral, amber and ebony, and sensuous perfumes of all kinds – as many sensuous perfumes as you can. Visit many Egyptian cities, to gather stores of knowledge from the learned.

Have Ithaca always in your mind. Your destination is to arrive there; but do not hurry your journey in the least. Better that it may last for many years, that you cast anchor at that island when you are old, rich with all you have gained on the way, not expecting that Ithaca will give you wealth; Ithaca gave you that splendid journey. Without her you would not have set out. She has nothing more to offer.

Κι ἂν πτωχικὴ τὴν βρῇς, ἡ Ἰθάκη δὲν·σὲ γέλασε.
Ἔτσι σοφὸς ποὺ ἔγινες, μὲ τόση πεῖρα,
ἤδη θὰ τὸ κατάλαβες ἡ Ἰθάκες τί σημαίνουν.

334. The City

Εἶπες· ‹θὰ πάγω σ᾽ ἄλλη γῆ, θὰ πάγω σ᾽ ἄλλη θάλασσα.
Μιὰ πόλις ἄλλη θὰ βρεθῇ καλύτερη ἀπ᾽ αὐτή.
Κάθε προσπάθειά μου μιὰ καταδίκη εἶναι γραφτή,
κι εἶν᾽ ἡ καρδιά μου, σὰν νεκρός, θαμμένη.
Ὁ νοῦς μου ὡς πότε μὲς στὸν μαρασμὸν αὐτὸν θὰ μένη;
Ὅπου τὸ μάτι μου γυρίσω, ὅπου κι ἂν δῶ,
ἐρείπια μαῦρα τῆς ζωῆς μου βλέπω ἐδῶ,
ποὺ τόσα χρόνια πέρασα καὶ ρήμαξα καὶ χάλασα.›

Καινούριους τόπους δὲν θὰ βρῇς, δὲν θὰ βρῇς ἄλλες θάλασσες.
Ἡ πόλις θὰ σὲ ἀκολουθῇ. Στοὺς δρόμους θὰ γερνᾶς
τοὺς ἴδιους, καὶ στὲς γειτονιὲς τὲς ἴδιες θὰ γερνᾶς,
καὶ μὲς στὰ ἴδια σπίτια αὐτὰ θ᾽ ἀσπρίζης.

And if you find her poor, Ithaca has not deceived you. You have acquired such wisdom, so much experience, that you will have already realized what these Ithacas mean.

You said: 'I shall go to another land, I shall go to another sea. Another city shall be found better than this. All I have ever tried to do was doomed to fail, and my heart is like a body dead and buried. For how long will my thoughts stay in this state of desolation? Wherever I turn my eyes, no matter where I look, I see the black ruins of my life, here, where I have spent so many years and wasted and ruined them.'

You will not find new places, you will not find other seas. The city will follow you. And you will grow old in the same streets, in the same neighbourhoods; in these same houses your hair will grow white.

Πάντα στὴν πόλη αὐτὴ θὰ φτάνης. Γιὰ τὰ ἀλλοῦ — μὴ
    ἐλπίζης, —
δὲν ἔχει πλοῖο γιὰ σέ, δὲν ἔχει ὁδό.
Ἔτσι ποὺ τὴ ζωή σου ρήμαξες ἐδῶ
στὴ κόχη τούτη τὴ μικρή, σ᾿ ὅλη τὴ γῆ τὴ χάλασες.

335. On a Ship

Τὸν μοιάζει βέβαια ἡ μικρὴ αὐτὴ
μὲ τὸ μολύβι ἀπεικόνισίς του.

Γρήγορα καμωμένη, στὸ κατάστρωμα τοῦ πλοίου,
ἕνα μαγευτικο ἀπόγευμα.
Τὸ Ἰόνιον πέλαγος ὁλόγυρά μας.

Τὸν μοιάζει. Ὅμως τὸν θυμοῦμαι σὰν πιὸ ἔμορφο.
Μέχρι παθήσεως ἦταν αἰσθητικός,
κι αὐτὸ ἐφώτιζε τὴν ἔκφρασή του.
Πιὸ ἔμορφος μὲ φανερώνεται,
τώρα ποὺ ἡ ψυχή μου τὸν ἀνακαλεῖ ἀπ᾿ τὸν καιρό.

Ἀπ᾿ τὸν καιρό. Εἶν᾿ ὅλ᾿ αὐτὰ τὰ πράγματα πολὺ παλιά —
τὸ σκίτσο καὶ τὸ πλοῖο καὶ τὸ ἀπόγευμα.

It is always this city that you will reach. Do not hope that you will ever
get anywhere else; for you there is no ship, no road. As you have
ruined your life here in this small corner, so you have ruined it in the
whole world.

THIS small pencilled sketch certainly looks like him.
    Swiftly done on the deck of a ship one enchanting afternoon, the
Ionian sea all round us.
    It looks like him. Yet, I remember him more handsome. He was
sensuous to the last degree, and that lit up his expression. He looks
handsomer now that my heart calls him back from so long ago.
    So long ago. All these things are very old – the sketch, and the ship
and the afternoon.

ANGELOS SIKELIANOS
1884–1951

336. *Thalero*

Φλογάτη, γελαστή, ζεστὴ ἀπὸ τ' ἀμπέλια ἀπάνωθεν
   ἐκοίταγε ἡ σελήνη,
κι ἀκόμα ὁ ἥλιος πύρωνε τὰ θάμνα, βασιλεύοντας
   μὲς σὲ διπλὴ γαλήνη·
βαριὰ τὰ χόρτα ἱδρώνανε στὴν ἀψηλὴν ἀπανεμιὰ
   τὸ θυμωμένο γάλα,
κι ἀπὸ τὰ κλήματα τὰ νιά, ποὺ τῆς πλαγιᾶς ἀνέβαιναν
   μακριὰ πλατιὰ τὴ σκάλα,
σουρίζανε οἱ ἀμπελουργοί, φτερίζοντας, ἐσειόντανε
   στὸν ὄχτο οἱ καλογιάνοι,
κι ἅπλων' ἀπάνω στὸ φεγγάρι ἡ ζέστη ἀραχνοΰφαντο
   κεφαλοπάνι·
στὸ σύρμα, μὲς στὸ γέννημα, μονάχα τρία καματερά,
   τό 'να ἀπὸ τ' ἄλλο πίσω,
τὴν κρεμαστὴ τους τραχηλιὰ κουνώντας, τὸν ἀνήφορο
   ξεκόβαν τὸ βουνίσο.
σκυφτὸ τὴ γῆς μυρίζοντας καὶ τὸ λιγνὸ λαγωνικὸ
   μὲ τὰ γοργὰ ποδάρια,
στοῦ δειλινοῦ τὴ σιγαλιά, βράχο τὸ βράχο ἐπήδαγε,
   ζητώντας μου τὰ χνάρια·

BLAZING, laughing, warm, the moon watched over the vineyards, and the sun was still parching the bushes, as it set in the dead calmness. The angry grass was heavily sweating milk in the warm stillness; and you could hear the grape-pickers whistle among the young vines that climbed up the many wide steps of the hillside; the robins were shaking their wings on the river's banks; the heat-haze spread over the moon a spider-web kerchief. On the path through the corn, in line, one behind the other, three oxen alone swayed their drooping dewlaps, climbing the mountain slope. The thin swift-legged hound, head down, sniffing the earth, leapt from rock to rock, searching for my tracks in the evening stillness. And in the house you could clearly see, under the

καὶ κάτω ἀπ' τὴν κληματαριὰ τὴν ἄγουρη μ' ἐπρόσμενε,
  στὸ ξάγναντο τὸ σπίτι,
στρωτὸ τραπέζι, πόφεγγε λυχνάρι ὀμπρός του κρεμαστὸ
  τὸ φῶς τοῦ ἀποσπερίτη·
ἐκεῖ κερήθρα μόφερε, ψωμὶ σταρένιο κρύο νερὸ
  ἡ ἀρχοντοθυγατέρα,
ὁπού 'χε ἀπὸ τὴ δύναμη στὸν πετρωτό της τὸ λαιμὸ
  χαράκι ὡς περιστέρα·
ποὺ ἡ ὄψη της, σὰν τῆς βραδιᾶς τὸ λάμπο, ἔδειχνε διάφωτη
  τῆς παρθενιᾶς τὴ φλόγα,
κι ἀπ' τὴ σφιχτή της ντυμασιὰ στὰ στήθια της τ' ἀμάλαγα
  χώριζ' ὁλόρτη ἡ ρόγα·
ποὺ ὀμπρὸς ἀπὸ τὸ μέτωπο σὲ δυὸ πλεξοῦδες τὰ μαλλιὰ
  πλεμένα εἶχε σηκώσει,
σὰν τὰ σκοινιὰ τοῦ καραβιοῦ ποὺ δὲ θὰ μπόριε ἡ φούχτα μου
  νὰν τῆς τὰ χερακώση.
Λαχανιασμένος στάθη ἐκεῖ κι ὁ σκύλος, π' ἀγανάχτησε
  στὰ ὀρτὰ τὰ μονοπάτια,
κι ἀσάλευτος στὰ μπροστινὰ μ' ἐκοίταγε, προσμένοντας
  μιὰ σφήνα, μὲς στὰ μάτια·
ἐκεῖ τ' ἀηδόνια ὡς ἄκουγα τριγύρα μου καὶ τοὺς καρποὺς
  γευόμουν ἀπ' τὸ δίσκο,
εἶχα τὴ γέψη τοῦ σταριοῦ, τοῦ τραγουδιοῦ καὶ τοῦ μελιοῦ
  βαθιὰ στὸν οὐρανίσκο·

unripe vine, a table was waiting for me, lit by the light of the evening
star which hung over it. There the stately daughter of the house
brought me wheaten bread, cold water and honeycomb; her vigour
shaped round her marble neck a groove like that on a dove; her
appearance clearly showed the glowing flame of virginity, like the
evening light; through the tight dress that covered her firm breasts the
nipples stood out sharply. Her plaited hair was lifted in two braids over
her forehead, thick like a ship's cable – I could not have clasped them
in my hand. The hound, which had been vexed by the steep footpaths,
stood there panting, and, motionless on his front legs, staring sharply
in my eyes in expectation. There, as I heard the nightingales and ate
fruit from the dish before me, deep in my palate I had the taste of
wheat, honey and song. As in a glass hive my soul moved within me, a

σὰ σὲ κυβέρτι γυάλινο μέσα μου σάλευε ἡ ψυχή,
　　πασίχαρο μελίσσι,
ποὺ ὅλο κρυφὰ πληθαίνοντας γυρεύει σμάρια ὡσὰν τσαμπιὰ
　　στὰ δένδρα ν' ἀμολήσῃ·
κι ἔνιωθα κρούσταλλο τὴ γῆ στὰ πόδια μου ἀποκάτωθε
　　καὶ διάφανο τὸ χῶμα,
γιατὶ πλατάνια τριέτικα τριγύρα μου ὑψωνόντανε
　　μ' ἀδρὸ γαλήνιο σῶμα.
Ἐκεῖ μοῦ ἀνοίξαν τὸ παλιὸ κρασὶ ποὺ πλέριο εὐώδισε
　　μὲς στὴν ἰδρένια στάμνα,
σὰν τῇ βουνίσα μυρουδιά, σύντας βαρῇ κατάψυχρη
　　νύχτια δροσιὰ τὰ θάμνα.
Φλογάτη, γελαστή, ζεστὴ ἐκεῖ ἡ καρδιά μου ἐδέχτηκε
　　ν' ἀναπαυτῇ λιγάκι
πὰ σὲ σεντόνια εὐώδερα ἀπὸ βότανα καὶ γαλανὰ
　　στὴ βάψη ἀπὸ λουλάκι.

337. Pan

Στὰ βράχια τοῦ ἔρμου ἀκρογιαλιοῦ καὶ στῆς τραχιᾶς χαλικω-
　　σιᾶς τὴ λαύρα,
τὸ μεσημέρι, ὅμοιο πηγή, δίπλα ἀπὸ κύμα σμάραγδο, τρέ-
　　μοντας ὅλο ἀνάβρα.

happy bee-swarm that secretly growing larger seeks to send out to the
trees its clusters like bunches of grapes. I felt under my feet the earth
was crystal cool, the soil transparent, for three-year-old plane-trees
lifted about me their rough, calm bodies. There they opened the old
wine for me that was fully fragrant in the sweating pitcher, like moun-
tain scents when the coolest night-dew falls on the bushes. Blazing,
laughing, warm, my heart agreed to rest there for a while on sheets
made fragrant by herbs, azure by washing-blue.

MIDDAY, like a fountain near the emerald sea, was shimmering and
seething on the rocks of the empty beach and the heat of the rough
shingle.

Γαλάζια τριήρη στὸ βυθόν, ἀνάμεσα σ' ἐαρινοὺς ἀφροὺς ἡ
    Σαλαμίνα,
καὶ τῆς Κινέτας, μέσα μου κατάβαθος ἀνασασμός, πεῦκα καὶ
    σκοῖνα.

Τὸ πέλαγο ἔσκαγ' ὅλο ἀφροὺς καὶ τιναχτὸ στὸν ἄνεμο ἀσπρο-
    βόλα,
τὴν ὥρα ποὺ τ' ἀρίφνητο κοπάδι τῶν σιδέρικων γιδιῶν
    ροβόλα.

Μὲ δυὸ σουρίγματα τραχιά, ποὺ κάτουθε τὸ δάχτυλο ἀπ' τὴ
    γλώσσα
βάνοντας βούιξ' ὁ μπιστικός, τὰ μάζωξ' ὅλα στὸ γιαλό, κι ἂς
    ἦταν πεντακόσα!

Κι ὅλα ἐσταλιάσανε σφιχτὰ τριγύρ' ἀπ' τὰ κοντόθαμνα κι ἀπ'
    τὸ θυμάρι,
κι ὡς ἐσταλιάσανε, γοργὰ τὰ γίδια καὶ τὸν ἄνθρωπο τὸ
    κάρωμα εἶχε πάρει.

Καὶ πιά, στὶς πέτρες τοῦ γιαλοῦ κι ἀπάνου ἀπ' τῶν σιδέρικων
    γιδιῶν τὴ λαύρα,
σιγή· κι ὡς ἀπὸ στρίποδα, μὲς ἀπ' τὰ κέρατα, γοργὸς ὁ ἥλιος
    καπνὸς ἀνάβρα.

Salamis looked like a blue trireme on the horizon through the spring-
time spray, and I breathed deeply the smell of the pines and the rushes
of Kineta.

The whole sea, bursting in froth and shaking in the wind, looked
white when the huge flock of rust-coloured goats came running down
the hill.

The shepherd put his finger under his tongue, whistled twice,
roughly, and gathered them all near the beach – they could have been
five hundred!

And, close to one another, they all stood still round the low bushes
and the thyme, and as they stood the heat-daze seized goats and man.

Silence fell on the stones of the beach and on the heat of the rust-
coloured goats; and the sun like smoke whirled swiftly up between the
horns, as from tripods.

Τότε εἴδαμε — ἄρχος καὶ ταγός — ὁ τράγος νὰ σηκώνεται μονά-
χος,
βαρὺς στὸ πάτημα κι ἀργός, νὰ ξεχωρίση κόβοντας, καὶ κεῖ
ὅπου βράχος,

σφήνα στὸ κύμα μπαίνοντας, στέκει λαμπρὸ γιὰ ξάγναντο
ἀκρωτήρι,
στὴν ἄκρη ἀπάνου νὰ σταθῆ, ποὺ ἡ ἄχνη διασκορπᾶ τ'
ἀφροῦ, κι ἀσάλευτος νὰ γύρη,

μ' ἀνασκωμένο, ἀφήνοντας νὰ λάμπουνε τὰ δόντια του, τ'
ἀπάνω χείλι,
μέγας καὶ ὀρτός, μυρίζοντας τὸ πέλαγο τὸ ἀφρόκοπο, ὡς τὸ
δείλι!

338. *Pantarkes*

Βαθιὰ ἡ κοιλάδα ἡ μυστική, κι ὀγρὸ τὸ Κρόνιο τὸ δασιὸ εἶχε
πάρει
Ἴσκιους θαμπούς καὶ ξάστερους, ἀπὸ ἄνεμο μανὸν ἀποβροχάρη.

Καὶ στὰ καταχυτὰ τῶν ναῶν, ποὺ ἐτρέχανε οἱ ρονιὲς ἀηδόνια,
μαῦρος συρτὸς μαζώνονταν τοῦ μάκρου, ἀραδαριὰ τὰ χελι-
δόνια.

Then we saw the he-goat – the leader and the king – rise alone, and
with a slow and heavy step move off and away to where a rock,
  Wedged in the sea, stood like a bright and clear headland; he stood
on the top where the froth sprayed and only bowed his head;
  His upper lip pulled back, so that the teeth flashed, tall and erect he
stood, sniffing the foaming sea, till sundown.

THE mystic valley was deep, and the damp, wooded Cronion had taken
on dim and clear shadows from a moist wind that blew after the rain.
  And on the temples' colonnades, where gushing streams sang like
nightingales, the swallows, a black string of dancers, were gathered in
a line.

Μελιοῦ εὐωδιὰν ἀνάδινε, ποὺ τὰ ρουθούνια ἐτέντωνε, ἡ
    κουφάλα,
καὶ τὰ ξερὰ πευκόφυλλα, τοὺ ἐκρέμονταν ἀπ᾽ τὰ κλαριὰ
    διχάλα.

Γοργὴ ριπὴ τὰ μάζωνε, κι ἄλλη ριπὴ τὰ σκόρπαγε, τὰ μύρα,
    φτεροπόδα,
κι ἀπ᾽ τὸ ἀξεχώριστο ἀγαθὸ τῶν ἄφαντων ἀνθῶν ἡ γῆς σὰν
    ἕνα στόμα εὐώδα.

᾽Ατέλειωτον, ἐδῶ καὶ κεῖ, μακρὺ συμπόσιο μυστικὸν ἐκέρνα,
καθὼς τῆς ἐκυκλόφερνε μὲ πλούσια χάρη κι ἄφαντην ἡ φτέρνα.

Ἔτσι κι ὁ κόρφος κι ὁ λαιμὸς ἀποβροχάρης πάγωσε κι
    εὐφράνθη
τοῦ ἐφήβου, ὅπου τὰ δόντια του στὴν πλέρια ἀνάσα ἐφέγγανε
    σὰ νερατζάνθι·

κι ὡς τὰ χλωρὰ τὰ μύγδαλα στὰ σφιχτὰ γούλια τὰ ᾽νιωθε
    δεμένα,
τὶ ἦταν ὡς μέσα, ἀπ᾽ τὸ δροσιό, τὰ φρένα τὰ παρθενικὰ συν-
    επαρμένα.

᾽Αργά, σὰν ἁπλωθήκανε βαθιὰ τὰ δροσερὰ σκοτάδια,
ἀμολητὴ βουβὴ ἀστραπὴ ἄναψ᾽ ὁλοῦθε, ὡσὰν ξερὰ ἀπο-
    κλάδια,

From the hollow trunk, and the dry cleft pine-needles that hung
from the branches, there rose a smell of honey that dilated the nostrils.
  One swift, wing-footed blast gathered, and another scattered the
perfumes, and Earth, like a mouth, breathed fragrance from the tangled
unseen flowers;
  She was offering everywhere a long and mystic symposium, as the
foot walked over her with rich silent grace.
  So too, the throat and the breast of the young man felt cool and re-
joiced after the rain, the young man whose teeth shone like bitter-
orange blossoms, as he breathed in deeply;
  And he felt them like fresh almonds clasped by his firm gums, now
the freshness and the rain had conquered to the depths his virgin heart.
  And slowly, when the deep cool darkness spread, a dumb lightning
was cast, and it flashed far away, like dry branches burning,

κι ἀπ' τὸ ρετσίνι τοῦ δεντροῦ τοῦ νοτισμένου ἀνάπνεεν
   εὐωδία,
σὰ νὰ κρεμόνταν πρὸς τὴ γῆς μ' ἔρωτα γνώμη οἱ βόστρυχοι
   τοῦ Δία.

Περίδροσα τὰ βλέφαρα διάπλατα ἐκράτει ὁ στοχασμὸς καὶ δὲν
   τὰ ζύγωνε ὕπνος·
τόσο ἤτανε ποτιστικὸς τῶν ἀρωμάτων καὶ γλυκὸς ὁ δεῖπνος.

Ὁ λυχνοστάτης τρίφλογος, στὸ τρίποδο στητὸς μὲς στ'
   ἀργαστήρι,
ἐφώταε τὸ συλλογισμὸ τ' ἀντρός, ποὺ στὴν παλάμη του εἶχε
   γύρει.

Κι ὁ ἐφηβικὸς πενταθλητὴς ἐδιάνευεν ἀργὸς στ' Ὀλύμπιο
   μάτι,
ἀνάμεσα στὰ σύνεργα, γυμνός, μπροστὰ ἀπ' τὸ τρίφλογο τοῦ
   λυχνοστάτη.

Μὲ τὴ γαλήνη καὶ τὴ θεία νοτιὰ ὁ τεχνίτης ἔμενε κι ἀγρύπνα,
στὰ μυστικὰ συμπόσια συνηθισμένος μὲ τοὺς θεοὺς ποὺ
   ἐδεῖπνα.

Καὶ μὲς στὸ νοῦ του τὸ λαμπρό, π' ὡς ὁ Ἀλφειὸς ἀβόγγητα
   κυλοῦσε,
τοῦ ἐλέφαντα καὶ τοῦ χρυσοῦ μπροστά του ὁ θησαυρὸς
   ἀναρροοῦσε,

And the resin of the damp trees breathed fragrance, as though the
locks of Zeus were hanging over the earth with thoughts of love.
   Reflection kept the cool eyelids wide open; no sleep came near, so
sweet and dewy was that feast of perfumes.
   The three-flamed lampstand on the tripod in the workshop was
lighting the meditation of the man who rested his head on the palm of
his hand.
   And the youth, the pentathlon winner, was moving slowly through
the Olympian eye, between sculptor's tools, naked in front of the three
flames of the lampstand.
   Peaceful, in the divine coolness, the artist kept awake, accustomed as
he was to secret symposia with the gods, where he feasted.
   And in the brightness of his mind that flowed silent as the Alpheus,
the treasures of ivory and gold were rolling before him;

κι ὡς τὸν ἀνθὸ τοῦ λιναριοῦ ἢ τ' ἀγανὰ τοῦ λουλακιοῦ
    ζαφείρια,
κρύα τὰ πετράδια ἐλάμπανε, βαθιά του, μυστικὰ καὶ μύρια,

νὰ ξεδιαλέξῃ ἀνάμεσα κι ἀπὸ τὰ γαλανότερα διαμάντια
τὴ γύμνια τὴν ἀνείπωτη τῶν Ὀλύμπιων ματιῶν στὴ Φύση
    ἀγνάντια.

Κι ὡς στὰ κλεισμένα βλέφαρα μύρια λουλούδια ὑφαίνουνε
    χιλιόχροα τὰ σκοτίδια,
τοῦ ἐβένου ἐστοχαζόντανε στὸ θρόνο νὰ λαμπίζουνε τ'
    ἀκροπρεπίδια,

κι ὅλο τὸ πλούσιο ἀστέρωμα, ὁποὺ ἀναπνέει τὴν τρίσβαθη
    γαλήνη,
σὰν τὴν ὀρὰ τοῦ παγονιοῦ στὰ πόδια του γυρίζοντας νὰ
    κλείνῃ.

Ἔτσι τοῦ ἀνάφανε ὁ θεός, ὁ Κατεβάτης αἰώνια κάθε νιότης,
κι ὁ νοῦς του στὸ χαμόγελο λουζόντανε, ὡς τῆς Αἴγινας
    τοξότης,

ποὺ ἀγάλλεται γονατιστὸς πιθώνοντας στὸ τόξο του τὸ χέρι,
σὰ νὰ εἶναι λύρας ἡ νευρή, κι ἡ ζωὴ κι ὁ θάνατος διπλὸν
    ἀστέρι.

And like the flowers of flax, or the loose sapphires of indigo, the gems were flashing, cold, secret, endless in his deepest thoughts,

For him to choose among the bluest diamonds the inexpressible nakedness of the Olympian eyes that face the world.

And as the darkness weaves under closed eyelids a thousand many-coloured flowers, so he was thinking of the decorations flashing on the ebony border of the throne,

And of all the many constellations that breathe in threefold peace, like a peacock's tail curling and bowing at his feet.

So the god appeared to him, the thunder-hurler, giver of all youth, and his thoughts were bathed in a smile, like that of an archer of Aegina,

Who delights as he kneels and rests his bow on his knee, as though the string were a lyre's, and life and death a double star.

Κι ὅπως τὰ μάτια ἐσήκωσε κι εἶδε ψυχὴ τὸν ἔφηβο χορτάτη
ἀπ' τὴν Ὀλύμπια σιγαλιὰ καὶ τὴ νυχτιὰν ὁπόσβυε μυρω-
δάτη,

τὸ βλέμμα, ὁπού τῆς ἡδονῆς συνήθισε ὡς ἀιτός τὸ δρόμο,
κατέβασε στὰ στήθη του, στὰ χέρια, στοὺς λαγόνες του, στὸν
ὦμο,

κι ἀναλογίστη· Ὀλύμπιον, ὦ Δία, ἂν ἀναστήσω σε, δική μου
ἂς εἶναι ἡ χάρη,
νὰ γράψω μόνο στοῦ ποδιοῦ σου μιὰ γωνιάν· ‹εἶν' ὅμορφο ὁ
Παντάρκης παλικάρι.›

339. The Sacred Roaa

Ἀπὸ τὴ νέα πληγὴ ποὺ μ' ἄνοιξεν ἡ μοίρα
ἔμπαιν' ὁ ἥλιος, θαρρούσα, στὴν καρδιά μου,
μὲ τόση ὁρμή, καθὼς βασίλευε, ὅπως
ἀπὸ ραγισματιὰν αἰφνίδια μπαίνει
τὸ κύμα σὲ καράβι π' ὁλοένα
βουλιάζει.
              Γιατὶ ἐκεῖνο πιὰ τὸ δείλι,
σὰν ἄρρωστος καιρό, ποὺ πρωτοβγαίνει
ν' ἀρμέξη ζωὴ ἀπ' τὸν ἔξω κόσμον, ἤμουν

And, as he lifted his eyes, and his soul saw the youth, his soul filled
with Olympian silence and the fragrant dying night,
    His eagle glance that knew so well the paths of sensuous delight,
moved down to the breast, the hands, the thighs, the shoulders, and
he thought:
    If I bring you back to life, Olympian Zeus, grant me one favour only:
to write on a corner of your foot: 'Pantarkes is a beautiful young man.'

I FELT as if the setting sun poured into my heart, through the new
wound Fate had opened in me, with as much violence as waves pouring
through a sudden rent into a sinking ship. For I, that evening, like a
man long sick and now for the first time come out to wrest life from
the outside world, was a solitary walker on the road that leads out of

περπατητὴς μοναχικὸς στὸ δρόμο
ποὺ ξεκινᾶ ἀπὸ τὴν Ἀθήνα κι ἔχει
σημάδι του ἱερὸ τὴν Ἐλευσίνα.
Τὶ ἦταν γιὰ μένα αὐτὸς ὁ δρόμος πάντα
σὰ δρόμος τῆς ψυχῆς.
                            — Φανερωμένος
μεγάλος ποταμὸς κυλοῦσε ἐδῶθε
ἀργὰ συρμένα ἀπὸ τὰ βόδια ἁμάξια
γεμάτα ἀθεμωνιὲς ἢ ξύλα, κι ἄλλα
ἁμάξια γοργά, ποὺ προσπερνοῦσαν
μὲ τοὺς ἀνθρώπους μέσα τους σὰν ἴσκιους.

Μὰ παραπέρα σὰ νὰ χάθη ὁ κόσμος
κι ἔμειν' ἡ φύση μόνη, ὥρα κι ὥρα
μιὰν ἡσυχία βασίλεψε. Κι ἡ πέτρα
π' ἀντίκρισα σὲ μιὰ ἄκρη ριζωμένη,
θρονὶ μοῦ φάνη μοιραμένο μου ἦταν
ἀπ' τοὺς αἰῶνες. Κι ἔπλεξα τὰ χέρια,
σὰν κάθησα, στὰ γόνατα, ξεχνώντας
ἂν κίνησα τὴ μέρα αὐτὴ ἢ ἂν πῆρα
αἰῶνες πίσω αὐτὸ τὸν ἴδιο δρόμο.
Μὰ νά, στὴν ἡσυχία αὐτή, ἀπ' τὸ γύρο
τὸν κοντινὸ προβάλανε τρεῖς ἴσκιοι.
Ἕνας Ἀτσίγγανος ἀγνάντια ἐρχόνταν
καὶ πίσωθέ του ἀκλούθααν, μ' ἀλυσίδες
συρμένες, δυὸ ἀργοβάδιστες ἀρκοῦδες.

Athens and has as its sacred goal Eleusis. Because that road was always
for me like a road of the soul. There approached a great river — carts
slowly drawn by oxen, and filled with sheaves of corn or with wood,
and other, faster carriages that passed with people inside them, like
shadows.

But farther on, as if the world were lost, and nature alone remained,
hour after hour a peace reigned. And the rock which I came across,
rooted on one side, looked like a throne destined for me from long ago.
And sitting on it, I clasped my hands on my knees, forgetting whether
it was today that I had started out, or whether I had taken this same
road centuries ago. But there, in that quietness, three shadows ap-
peared from the near corner. A gypsy came towards me, and behind
him, dragged on by chains, two bears followed, shuffling.

Καὶ νά, ὡς σὲ λίγο ζύγωσαν μπροστά μου
καὶ μ' εἶδε ὁ Γύφτος, πρὶν καλὰ προφτάσω
νὰ τὸν κοιτάξω, τράβηξε ἀπ' τὸν ὦμο
τὸ ντέφι, καὶ χτυπώντας το μὲ τό 'να
χέρι, μὲ τ' ἄλλον ἔσυρε μὲ βία
τὶς ἀλυσίδες. Κι οἱ δυὸ ἀρκοῦδες τότε
στὰ δυό τους σκώθηκαν βαριά.

                        Ἡ μία
(ἤτανε ἡ μάνα φανερά), ἡ μεγάλη,
μὲ πλεχτὲς χάντρες ὅλο στολισμένο
τὸ μέτωπο γαλάζιες, κι ἀπὸ πάνω
μιὰν ἄσπρη ἀβασκαντήρα, ἀνασηκώθη
ξάφνου τρανή, σὰν προσαιώνιο νά 'ταν
ξόανο Μεγάλης Θεᾶς, τῆς αἰώνιας Μάνας,
αὐτῆς τῆς ἴδιας ποὺ ἱερὰ θλιμμένη,
μὲ τὸν καιρὸν ὡς πῆρε ἀνθρώπινη ὄψη,
γιὰ τὸν καημὸ τῆς κόρης της λεγόνταν
Δήμητρα ἐδῶ, γιὰ τὸν καημὸ τοῦ γιοῦ της
πιὸ πέρα ἦταν Ἀλκμήνη ἢ Παναγία·
καὶ τὸ μικρὸ στὸ πλάγι της ἀρκούδι,
σὰ μεγάλο παιχνίδι, σὰν ἀνίδεο
μικρὸ παιδί, ἀνασκώθηκε καὶ κεῖνο,
ὑπάκοο, μὴ μαντεύοντας ἀκόμα
τοῦ πόνου του τὸ μάκρος καὶ τὴν πίκρα

And then, when in a little while they came right up to me and the
gypsy saw me — before I had properly seen him — he pulled his
tambourine from his shoulder, and beating it with one hand, with the
other he tugged roughly at the chains. And at that the two bears rose
heavily on their hind legs. The larger one — she was plainly the mother
— her forehead decorated with blue beads, and on top a white talisman,
suddenly stood up tall, as if she were a primeval image of the Great
Goddess, of the Eternal Mother; that same mother who in her divine
sadness — as with the passage of ages she took human form — was called
Demeter in this place when she grieved for her daughter, and elsewhere,
in her grief for her son, Alcmene or the Virgin Mary. And the small
bear at her side, like a great toy, like an unsuspecting child, rose up in
its turn, submissively, not yet guessing the length of its suffering and

τῆς σκλαβιᾶς ποὺ καθρέφτιζεν ἡ μάνα
στὰ δυὸ πυρρά της ποὺ τὸ κοίτααν μάτια!

'Αλλ' ὡς ἀπὸ τὸν κάματον ἐκείνη
ὀκνοῦσε νὰ χορέψῃ, ὁ Γύφτος, μ' ἕνα
πιδέξιο τράβηγμα τῆς ἀλυσίδας
στοῦ μικροῦ τὸ ῥουθούνι, ματωμένο
ἀκόμα ἀπ' τὸ χαλκὰ ποὺ λίγες μέρες
φαινόνταν πὼς τοῦ τρύπησεν, αἰφνίδια
τὴν ἔκανε μουγκρίζοντας μὲ πόνο
νὰ ὀρθώνεται ψηλά, πρὸς τὸ παιδί της
γυρνώντας τὸ κεφάλι, καὶ νὰ ὀρχιέται
ζωηρά.
            Κι ἐγώ, ὡς ἐκοίταζα, τραβοῦσα
ἔξω ἀπ' τὸ χρόνο, μακριὰ ἀπ' τὸ χρόνο,
ἐλεύτερος ἀπο μορφὲς κλεισμένες
στὸν καιρό, ἀπὸ ἀγάλματα κι εἰκόνες,
ἤμουν ἔξω, ἤμουν ἔξω ἀπὸ τὸ χρόνο.
Μὰ μπροστά μου, ὀρθωμένη ἀπὸ τὴ βία
τοῦ χαλκᾶ καὶ τῆς ἄμοιρης στοργῆς της,
δὲν ἔβλεπα ἄλλο ἀπ' τὴν τρανὴν ἀρκούδα
μὲ τὶς γαλάζιες χάντρες στὸ κεφάλι,
μαρτυρικὸ τεράστιο σύμβολο ὅλου
τοῦ κόσμου, τωρινοῦ καὶ περασμένου,

the bitterness of slavery mirrored in its mother's flame-red eyes that gazed upon it.

But as from weariness she was reluctant to dance, the gypsy, with one deft pull on the chain attached to the young bear's nostril – still bloody from the ring for which it had been pierced apparently only a few days ago – made her suddenly growl with pain and stand upright, turning her head towards her child and dancing vigorously. And I, as I watched, withdrew outside time, far from time; I was free from forms enclosed in time, from statues and images; I stood outside time. But in front of me I saw nothing but that enormous bear, with the blue beads on its head, raised up by the tug of the ring, and by her wretched love, a gigantic symbol witnessing to the whole world, past and present, a

μαρτυρικὸ τεράστιο σύμβολο ὅλου
τοῦ πόνου τοῦ πανάρχαιου, ὁπ' ἀκόμα
δὲν τοῦ πληρώθη ἀπ' τοὺς θνητοὺς αἰῶνες
ὁ φόρος τῆς ψυχῆς.

                    Τί ἐτούτη ἀκόμα
ἦταν κι εἶναι στὸν Ἅδη.

                         Καὶ σκυμμένο
τὸ κεφάλι μου κράτησα ὁλοένα,
καθὼς στὸ ντέφι μέσα ἔριχνα, σκλάβος
κι ἐγὼ τοῦ κόσμου, μιὰ δραχμή.

                              Μὰ ὡς τέλος
ὁ Ἀτσίγγανος ξεμάκρυνε τραβώντας
ξανὰ τὶς δυὸ ἀργοβάδιστες ἀρκοῦδες
καὶ χάθηκε στὸ μούχρωμα, ἡ καρδιά μου
μὲ σήκωσε νὰ ξαναπάρω πάλι
τὸ δρόμον ὁποὺ τέλειωνε στὰ ρείπια
τοῦ Ἱεροῦ τῆς Ψυχῆς, στὴν Ἐλευσίνα.
Κι ἡ καρδιά μου, ὡς ἐβάδιζα, βογγοῦσε·
‹Θά 'ρτη τάχα ποτέ, θανά 'ρτη ἡ ὥρα,
ποὺ ἡ ψυχὴ τῆς ἀρκούδας καὶ τοῦ Γύφτου
κι ἡ ψυχή μου, ποὺ μυημένη τήνε κράζω,
θὰ γιορτάσουν μαζί;›

                    Κι ὡς προχωροῦσα
κι ἐβράδιαζε, ξανάνιωσα ἀπ' τὴν ἴδια
πληγή, ποὺ ἡ μοίρα μ' ἄνοιξε, τὸ σκότος
νὰ μπαίνη ὁρμητικὰ μὲς στὴν καρδιά μου,

gigantic symbol witnessing all primeval suffering; for still, through all
the ages of man, the tax of the soul has not been paid.

For the soul still is, as it was, in Hades. And I kept my head bent as I,
also a slave of the world, dropped a coin into the tambourine. But as
the gypsy finally moved away, once more dragging along his two
shuffling bears, and was lost in the twilight, my heart roused me to take
once more the road which ends at the ruins of the Temple of the Soul,
at Eleusis. And as I walked on, my heart groaned: 'Will the time ever
come when the souls of the bear and the gypsy, and my soul, which I
call initiated, will rejoice together?' And as I walked along, and the
twilight fell, I felt again as if, through the same wound that Fate
opened in me, the darkness was pouring violently into my heart, as the

καθὼς ἀπὸ ραγισματιὰν αἰφνίδια μπαίνει
τὸ κύμα σὲ καράβι ποὺ ὁλοένα
βουλιάζει. Κι ὅμως τέτοια ὡς νὰ διψοῦσε
πλημμύραν ἡ καρδιά μου, σὰ βυθίστη
ὡς νὰ πνίγηκε ἀκέρια στὰ σκοτάδια,
σὰ βυθίστηκε ἀκέρια στὰ σκοτάδια,
ἕνα μούρμουρο ἁπλώθη ἀπάνωθέ μου,
ἕνα μούρμουρο, κι ἔμοιαζ' ἔλεε·

⟨Θὰ 'ρτη.⟩

340. *The Suicide of Atzesivano*

'Ανεπίληπτα ἐπῆρε τὸ μαχαίρι
ὁ 'Ατζεσιβάνο. Κ' ἤτανε ἡ ψυχή του
τὴν ὥρα ἐκείνη ὁλάσπρο περιστέρι.
Κι ὅπως κυλᾶ ἀπὸ τ' ἄδυτα τοῦ ἀδύτου
τῶν οὐρανῶν μέσ' στὴ νυχτιὰ ἕν' ἀστέρι,
ἤ, ὡς πέφτει ἀνθὸς μηλιᾶς μὲ πράο ἀγέρι,
ἔτσι ἀπ' τὰ στήθη πέταξε ἡ πνοή του.
Χαμένοι τέτοιοι θάνατοι δὲν πᾶνε.
Γιατὶ μονάχα ἐκεῖνοι π' ἀγαπᾶνε
τὴ ζωὴ στὴ μυστική της πρώτη ἀξία,
μποροῦν καὶ νὰ θερίσουνε μονάχοι

waves pour through a sudden rent into a sinking ship. Yet, as if my heart was athirst for such a flood, when it had sunk, as though completely drowned in the darkness, when it had fully sunk into the blackness, a murmur spread above me, a murmur which seemed to say: 'It will come.'

IRREPROACHABLY Atzesivano took the knife; and his soul was at that moment a snow-white dove. And as a star rolls from the deepest sky into the night, or as apple-blossom falls, when a gentle breeze is blowing, so flew the last breath from his breast. Such deaths are not for nothing; for only those who love life in its first secret value can reap

τῆς ὕπαρξής τους τὸ μεγάλο ἀστάχυ,
ποὺ γέρνει πιά, μὲ θεία ἀταραξία!

341. At St Luke's Monastery

Στ' Ὅσιου Λουκᾶ τὸ μοναστήρι, ἀπ' ὅσες
γυναῖκες τοῦ Στειριοῦ συμμαζευτῆκαν
τὸν Ἐπιτάφιο νὰ στολίσουν, κι' ὅσες,
μοιρολογῆτρες, ὡς μὲ τοῦ Μεγάλου
Σαβάτου τὸ ξημέρωμα ἀγρυπνῆσαν,
ποιὰ νὰ στοχάστη — ἔτσι γλυκὰ θρηνοῦσαν! —
πώς, κάτου ἀπ' τοὺς ἀνθούς, τ' ὁλόαχνο σμάλτο
τοῦ πεθαμένου τοῦ Ἄδωνη ἦταν σάρκα
ποὺ πόνεσε βαθιά;
             Γιατὶ κι' ὁ πόνος
στὰ ρόδα μέσα, κι' ὁ ἐπιτάφιος θρῆνος,
κ' οἱ ἀναπνοὲς τῆς ἄνοιξης ποὺ μπαῖναν
ἀπ' τοῦ ναοῦ τὴ θύρα, ἀναφτερῶναν
τὸ νοῦ τους στῆς Ἀνάστασης τὸ θάμα,
καὶ τοῦ Χριστοῦ οἱ πληγὲς σὰν ἀνεμῶνες
τοὺς φάνταζαν στὰ χέρια καὶ στὰ πόδια,
τὶ πολλὰ τὸν σκεπάζανε λουλούδια,
ποὺ ἔτσι τρανά, ἔτσι βαθιὰ εὐωδοῦσαν!

alone the tall corn-stalk of their existence, which stoops at last, with divine tranquillity.

In St Luke's monastery, of all the women of Steiri who had gathered to decorate the Epitaphios, the 'Burial of Christ', and of all the mourners who had kept vigil till Holy Saturday's dawn, was there any who had thought – so sweetly they mourned – that under the blossoms, the dim enamel of dead Adonis, was flesh that had suffered deeply? Because pain amid the roses, the lament for his burial, and the breath of spring that floated in from the church's door lifted their hearts to the miracle of the Resurrection; and the wounds of Christ looked to them like anemones on his hands and on his feet, covered under the many flowers whose perfume was so strong, so deep.

'Αλλά τὸ βράδυ τὸ ἴδιο τοῦ Σαβάτου,
τὴν ὥρα π' ἀπ' τὴν Ἅγια Πύλη τὸ ἕνα
κερὶ ἐπροσάναψε ὅλα τ' ἄλλα ὡς κάτου,
κι' ἀπ' τ' Ἅγιο Βῆμα σάμπως κύμα ἀπλώθη
τὸ φῶς ὡς μὲ τὴν ξώπορτα, ὅλοι κι' ὅλες
ἀνατριχιάξαν π' ἄκουσαν στὴ μέση
ἀπ' τὰ ⟨Χριστὸς Ἀνέστη⟩ μιὰν αἰφνίδια
φωνὴ νὰ σκούξη: ⟨Γιώργαινα, ὁ Βαγγέλης!⟩

Καὶ νά, ὁ λεβέντης τοῦ χωριοῦ, ὁ Βαγγέλης,
τῶν κοριτσιῶν τὸ λάμπασμα, ὁ Βαγγέλης,
ποὺ τὸν λογιάζαν ὅλοι γιὰ χαμένο
στὸν πόλεμο — καὶ στέκονταν ὁλόρτος
στῆς ἐκκλησιᾶς τὴ θύρα, μὲ ποδάρι
ξύλινο, καὶ δὲ διάβαινε τὴ θύρα
τῆς ἐκκλησιᾶς, τί τὸν κοιτάζαν ὅλοι
μὲ τὰ κεριὰ στὸ χέρι, τὸν κοιτάζαν
τὸ χορευτὴ ποὺ τράνταζε τ' ἀλώνι
τοῦ Στειριοῦ, μιὰ στὴν ὄψη, μιὰ στὸ πόδι,
ποὺ ὡς νὰ τὸ κάρφωσε ἦταν στὸ κατώφλι
τῆς θύρας, καὶ δὲν ἔμπαινε πιὸ μέσα!

But in the night of that same Saturday, the moment that one candle
had kindled all the others right down the church, and the light spread
like a wave from the sanctuary to the door, all, men and women,
shuddered, when they heard, among the cries of 'Christ is risen', a
voice suddenly cry, 'Mrs George, there's Vangelis!'

And Vangelis, the young blood of the village, the light in the eyes of
the girls, Vangelis, whom all considered lost in the war, was standing
there at the church door with a wooden leg, and did not cross the
threshold; for all were staring at him with the candles in their hands;
they were staring at the dancer, who had shaken the threshing-floor of
Steiri, looking once at his face and once at his leg, which seemed nailed
to the threshold, and would not come in.

Καὶ τότε — μάρτυράς μου νὰ 'ναι ὁ στίχος
ὁ ἁπλὸς κι' ἀληθινὸς ἐτοῦτος στίχος, —
ἀπ' τὸ στασίδι πούμουνα στημένος
ξαντίκρυσα τὴ μάνα, ἀπ' τὸ κεφάλι
πετώντας τὸ μαντήλι, νὰ χιμήξη
σκυφτὴ καὶ ν' ἀγκαλιάση τὸ ποδάρι,
τὸ ξύλινο ποδάρι τοῦ στρατιώτη,
(ἔτσι ὅπως τόειδα ὁ στίχος μου τὸ γράφει,
ὁ ἁπλὸς κι' ἀληθινὸς ἐτοῦτος στίχος),
καὶ νὰ σύρη ἀπ' τὰ βάθη τῆς καρδιᾶς της
ἕνα σκούξιμο: «Μάτια μου, Βαγγέλη!»

Κι' ἀκόμα — μάρτυράς μου νὰ 'ναι ὁ στίχος,
ὁ ἁπλὸς κι' ἀληθινὸς ἐτοῦτος στίχος —
ξωπίσωθέ της, ὅσες μαζευτῆκαν
ἀπὸ τὸ βράδυ τῆς Μεγάλης Πέφτης,
νανουριστά, θαμπὰ γιὰ νὰ θρηνήσουν
τὸν πεθαμένον Ἄδωνη, κρυμμένο
μέσ' στὰ λουλούδια, τώρα νὰ ξεσπάσουν
μαζὶ τὴν ἀξεθύμαστη τοῦ τρόμου
κραυγή — πού, ὡς στὸ στασίδι μου κρατιόμουν,
ἕνας πέπλος μοῦ σκέπασε τὰ μάτια!...

And then – let this verse, this simple and true verse be my witness –.
from the pew where I was standing I saw his mother throw the black
kerchief from her head, and, bending low, rush and embrace the leg,
the wooden leg of the soldier – my verse writes this just as I saw it,
this simple and true verse – with a cry from the bottom of her heart:
'Vangelis, dearer than my eyes.'

And after her – let this verse, this simple and true verse be my wit-
ness – all those who had gathered from Maundy Thursday night to
mourn with a dim lullaby Adonis dead under his many flowers, burst
out into a stifled scream of terror – and as I clutched my seat, a mist
clouded my eyes . . .

GEORGE SEFERIS

1900–1971

342. The Song of Love

Τὰ μυστικὰ τῆς θάλασσας ξεχνιοῦνται στ' ἀκρογιάλια,
ἡ σκοτεινάγρα τοῦ βυθοῦ ξεχνιέται στὸν ἀφρό·
λάμπουνε ξάφνου πορφυρὰ τῆς μνήμης τὰ κοράλια...
ὦ μὴν ταράξῃς... πρόσεξε ν' ἀκούσῃς τ' ἀλαφρὸ

ξεκίνημά της... τ' ἄγγιξες τὸ δέντρο μὲ τὰ μῆλα,
τὸ χέρι ἁπλώθη κι ἡ κλωστὴ δείχνει καὶ σὲ ὁδηγεῖ...
ὦ σκοτεινὸ ἀνατρίχιασμα στὴ ῥίζα καὶ στὰ φύλλα
νὰ 'σουν ἐσὺ ποὺ θά 'φερνες τὴν ξεχασμένη αὐγή!

Στὸν κάμπο τοῦ ἀποχωρισμοῦ νὰ ξανανθίζουν κρίνα,
μέρες ν' ἀνοίγουνται ὥριμες, οἱ ἀγκάλες τ' οὐρανοῦ,
νὰ φέγγουν στὸ ἀντιλάρισμα τὰ μάτια μόνο ἐκεῖνα,
ἀγνὴ ἡ ψυχὴ νὰ γράφεται σὰν τὸ τραγούδι αὐλοῦ...

Ἡ νύχτα νά 'ταν ποὺ ἔκλεισε τὰ μάτια; Μένει ἀθάλη,
σὰν ἀπὸ δοξαριοῦ νευρὰ μένει πνιχτὸ βουητό,
μιὰ στάχτη κι ἕνας ἴλιγγος στὸ μαῦρο γυρογιάλι,
κι ἕνα πυκνὸ φτερούγισμα στὴν εἰκασία κλειστό.

THE secrets of the sea are forgotten on the beach, the darkness of the
deep is forgotten in the foam, the corals of memory suddenly flash
purple.... O, do not move, listen to the gentle beginning...

You touched the tree with the apples, the hand stretched out, and
the thread points the way.... O, dark shivering in the root and in the
leaves, if you could only bring back that forgotten dawn!

For lilies to blossom again on the plain where we parted, for days to
open ripe, the sky's embrace, for those eyes only to shine in the
trembling light, for the soul to appear as pure as the song of a flute...

Was it the night that closed the eyes? The embers remain. A
drowned noise lingers as from the twang of a bow, ashes and dizziness
in the black glass, a rich flutter of wings no one can guess at.

'Ρόδο τοῦ ἀνέμου, γνώριζες μὰ ἀνέγνωρους μᾶς πῆρες
τὴν ὥρα ποὺ θεμέλιωνε γιοφύρια ὁ λογισμός,
νὰ πλέξουνε τὰ δάχτυλα καὶ νὰ διαβοῦν δυὸ μοῖρες
καὶ νὰ χυθοῦν στὸ χαμηλὸ κι ἀναπαμένο φῶς.

343. The Argonauts

Καὶ ψυχή,
εἰ μέλλει γνώσεσθαι αὐτήν,
εἰς ψυχὴν
αὐτῇ βλεπτέον·
τὸν ξένο καὶ τὸν ἐχθρὸ τὸν εἴδαμε στὸν καθρέφτη.

Εἴτανε καλὰ παιδιὰ οἱ σύντροφοι· δὲ φώναζαν
οὔτε ἀπὸ τὸν κάματο, οὔτε ἀπὸ τὴ δίψα, οὔτε ἀπὸ τὴν
    παγωνιὰ·
εἴχανε τὸ φέρσιμο τῶν δένδρων καὶ τῶν κυμάτων,
ποὺ δέχουνται τὸν ἄνεμο καὶ τὴ βροχή,
δέχουνται τὴ νύχτα καὶ τὸν ἥλιο,
χωρὶς ν' ἀλλάζουν μέσα στὴν ἀλλαγή.
Εἴτανε καλὰ παιδιά, μέρες ὁλόκληρες
ἵδρωναν στὸ κουπὶ μὲ χαμηλωμένα μάτια
ἀνασαίνοντας μὲ ρυθμό,
καὶ τὸ αἷμα τους κοκκίνιζε ἕνα δέρμα ὑποταγμένο.

Rose of the wind, you knew, but snatched us, the unknowing, while
our thoughts were building a bridge for fingers to mingle and two
destinies to cross, and pour out in the low, unwearied light.

AND the soul, if it is to know itself, must look into a soul. The
stranger and the enemy, we saw him in the mirror.

They were good lads, the comrades. They did not grumble because
of fatigue, or because of thirst, or because of frost. They had the manner
of trees and of waves that accept the wind and the rain, accept the night
and the sun, and in the midst of change do not change. They were
good lads; for whole days with downcast eyes they sweated at the oar,
breathing rhythmically, and their blood flushed an obedient skin. Once

Κάποτε τραγούδησαν μὲ χαμηλωμένα μάτια,
ὅταν περάσαμε τὸ ἐρημόνησο μὲ τὶς ἀραποσυκιὲς
κατὰ τὴ δύση, πέρα ἀπὸ τὸν κάβο τῶν σκύλων
ποὺ γαυγίζουν.

Εἰ μέλλει γνώσεσθαι αὑτήν, ἔλεγαν,
εἰς ψυχὴν βλεπτέον, ἔλεγαν,
καὶ τὰ κουπιὰ χτυποῦσαν τὸ χρυσάφι τοῦ πελάγου
μέσα στὸ ἡλιόγερμα.
Περάσαμε κάβους πολλούς, πολλὰ νησιά, τὴ θάλασσα
ποὺ φέρνει τὴν ἄλλη θάλασσα, γλάρους καὶ φώκιες.
Δυστυχισμένες γυναῖκες κάποτε μὲ ὀλολυγμοὺς
κλαίγανε τὰ χαμένα τους παιδιά,
κι ἄλλες ἀγριεμένες γύρευαν τὸ Μεγαλέξαντρο
καὶ δόξες βυθισμένες στὰ βάθη τῆς Ἀσίας.
Ἀράξαμε σ' ἀκρογιαλιὲς γεμάτες ἀρώματα νυχτερινά,
μὲ κελαηδίσματα πουλιῶν, νερὰ ποὺ ἀφήνανε στὰ χέρια
τὴ μνήμη μιᾶς μεγάλης εὐτυχίας,
μὰ δὲν τελειώναν τὰ ταξίδια.
Οἱ ψυχές τους ἔγιναν ἕνα μὲ τὰ κουπιὰ καὶ τοὺς σκαρμούς,
μὲ τὸ σοβαρὸ πρόσωπο τῆς πλώρης,
μὲ τ' αὐλάκι τοῦ τιμονιοῦ,
μὲ τὸ νερὸ ποὺ ἔσπαζε τὴ μορφή τους.
Οἱ σύντροφοι τέλειωσαν μὲ τὴ σειρά,

they sang with downcast eyes, when we passed the desert island with the Arabian figs, towards the setting of the sun, beyond the cape of dogs that howl.

If it is to know itself, they used to say, it is into the soul that it must look, they used to say, and the oars beat on the gold of the sea as the sun was setting. We passed many capes, many islands, the sea which leads to the other sea, sea-gulls and seals. There were times when unfortunate women cried out lamenting their dead children, and others searched wildly for Alexander the Great, and glories sunken in the depths of Asia. We anchored by shores full of night perfumes, among the singing of birds, waters that left on the hands the recollection of a great happiness. But there was never an end to our journeys. Their souls became one with the oars and the rowlocks, with the grave figurehead at the prow, with the wake of the rudder, with the water

μὲ χαμηλωμένα μάτια. Τὰ κουπιά τους
δείχνουν τὸ μέρος ποὺ κοιμοῦνται στ' ἀκρογιάλι.

Κανεὶς δὲν τοὺς θυμᾶται. Δικαιοσύνη.

344. Sleep

Quid πλατανῶν opacissimus?

'Ο ὕπνος σὲ τύλιξε, σὰν ἕνα δέντρο, μὲ πράσινα φύλλα
ἀνάσαινες, σὰν ἕνα δέντρο, μέσα στὸ ἥσυχο φῶς
μέσα στὴ διάφανη πηγὴ κοίταξα τὴ μορφή σου·
κλεισμένα βλέφαρα καὶ τὰ ματόκλαδα χάραζαν τὸ νερό.
Τὰ δάχτυλά μου στὸ μαλακὸ χορτάρι, βρῆκαν τὰ δάχτυλά σου
κράτησα τὸ σφυγμό σου μιὰ στιγμὴ
κι' ἔνιωσα ἀλλοῦ τὸν πόνο τῆς καρδιᾶς σου.

Κάτω ἀπὸ τὸ πλατάνι, κοντὰ στὸ νερό, μέσα στὶς δάφνες
ὁ ὕπνος σὲ μετακινοῦσε καὶ σὲ κομμάτιαζε
γύρω μου, κοντά μου, χωρὶς νὰ μπορῶ νὰ σ' ἀγγίξω ὁλό-
κληρη,
ἐνωμένη μὲ τὴ σιωπή σου·

that fractured their images. One after another the comrades passed
away with downcast eyes. Their oars show the place where they sleep
on the shore.

No one remembers them. Justice.

SLEEP enfolded you, like a tree, in green leaves you breathe, like a
tree, in the calm light, in the translucent fountain I saw your image;
eyelids closed, eyelashes sweeping the water. My fingers found your
fingers in the soft grass, I held your pulse for a moment, and felt else-
where the pain of your heart.

Under the plane-tree, near the water, among the laurels, sleep moved
you about and scattered you round me, near me, though I was not able
to touch the whole of you, joined as you were with your silence;

βλέποντας τὸν ἴσκιο σου νὰ μεγαλώνη καὶ νὰ μικραίνη,
νὰ χάνεται στοὺς ἄλλους ἴσκιους, μέσα στὸν ἄλλο
κόσμο ποὺ σ' ἄφηνε καὶ σὲ κρατοῦσε.

Τὴ ζωὴ ποὺ μᾶς ἔδωσαν νὰ ζήσουμε, τὴ ζήσαμε.
Λυπήσου ἐκείνους ποὺ περιμένουν μὲ τόση ὑπομονὴ
χαμένοι μέσα στὶς μαῦρες δάφνες κάτω ἀπὸ τὰ βαριὰ πλα-
   τάνια
κι ὅσους μονάχοι τους μιλοῦν σὲ στέρνες καὶ σὲ πηγάδια
καὶ πνίγουνται μέσα στοὺς κύκλους τῆς φωνῆς.
Λυπήσου τὸ σύντροφο ποὺ μοιράστηκε τὴ στέρησή μας καὶ
   τὸν ἱδρῶτα
καὶ βύθισε μέσα στὸν ἥλιο σὰν κοράκι πέρα ἀπ' τὰ μάρμαρα,
χωρὶς ἐλπίδα νὰ χαρῇ τὴν ἀμοιβή μας.

Δῶσε μας, ἔξω ἀπὸ τὸν ὕπνο, τὴ γαλήνη.

345. The King of Asine

Κοιτάξαμε ὅλο τὸ πρωὶ γύρω γύρω τὸ κάστρο
ἀρχίζοντας ἀπὸ τὸ μέρος τοῦ ἴσκιου, ἐκεῖ ποὺ ἡ θάλασσα
πράσινη καὶ χωρὶς ἀναλαμπή, τὸ στῆθος σκοτωμένου παγο-
   νιοῦ,
μᾶς δέχτηκε ὅπως ὁ καιρὸς χωρὶς κανένα χάσμα.

watching your shadow grow and dwindle, lose itself among the other shadows, in that other world that was holding and letting you go.

We lived the life they gave us to live. Pity those who so patiently wait, lost in the black laurels under the heavy plane-trees, and those who speak to cisterns and to wells in their loneliness and drown in the circles of their voice. Pity the companion who shared our privations and our sweat, and sank into the sun like a crow beyond the marble ruins, never hoping to enjoy our reward.

Give us, beyond sleep, serenity.

WE spent all the morning looking round the castle, beginning from the side of the shadow, where the sea, green and unshining – breast of a dead peacock – received us like time without a break. The veins of the

Οἱ φλέβες τοῦ βράχου κατέβαιναν ἀπὸ ψηλὰ
στριμμένα κλήματα γυμνὰ πολύκλωνα, ζωντανεύοντας
στ' ἄγγιγμα τοῦ νεροῦ, καθὼς τὸ μάτι ἀκολουθώντας τις
πάλευε νὰ ξεφύγη τὸ κουραστικὸ λίκνισμα
χάνοντας δύναμη ὁλοένα.

'Απὸ τὸ μέρος τοῦ ἥλιου ἕνας μακρὺς γιαλὸς ὁλάνοιχτος
καὶ τὸ φῶς τρίβοντας διαμαντικὰ στὰ μεγάλα τείχη.
Κανένα πλάσμα ζωντανό, τ' ἀγριοπερίστερα φευγάτα,
κι ὁ βασιλιὰς τῆς 'Ασίνης, ποὺ τὸν γυρεύουμε δυὸ χρόνια
    τώρα,
ἄγνωστος, λησμονημένος ἀπ' ὅλους κι ἀπὸ τὸν "Ομηρο,
μόνο μιὰ λέξη στὴν 'Ιλιάδα, κι ἐκείνη ἀβέβαιη,
ριγμένη ἐδῶ σὰν τὴν ἐντάφια χρυσὴ προσωπίδα.
Τὴν ἄγγιξες; θυμᾶσαι τὸν ἦχο της; κούφιο μέσα στὸ φῶς
σὰν τὸ στεγνὸ πιθάρι στὸ σκαμμένο χῶμα·
κι ὁ ἴδιος ἦχος μὲς στὴ θάλασσα μὲ τὰ κουπιά μας.
'Ο βασιλιὰς τῆς 'Ασίνης ἕνα κενὸ κάτω ἀπ' τὴν προσωπίδα
παντοῦ μαζί μας παντοῦ μαζί μας, κάτω ἀπὸ ἕνα ὄνομα:
‹'Ασίνην τε . . . 'Ασίνην τε . . .›,
                                    καὶ τὰ παιδιά του ἀγάλματα,
κι οἱ πόθοι του φτερουγίσματα πουλιῶν, κι ὁ ἀγέρας

rock came down from high, twisted vine-stocks bare with many
branches, living at the touch of the water, so that the eye as it followed
them struggled to escape from the wearisome rolling, continually
losing strength.

From the sunny side a long wide-open shore, and the light, polishing
gems on the great walls. Not a living thing, the wild doves fled, and
the king of Asine whom we have been seeking two years now, un-
known, forgotten by all, even by Homer – one word only in the Iliad
and that not certain, thrown there like the gold burial-mask. You
touched it? Remember its sound? Hollow in the midst of the light, like
a dry jar on the excavated earth; and our oars in the sea that made the
same sound. The king of Asine a void beneath the mask, everywhere
with us, beneath a name: 'Asine too . . . Asine too . . .', and his children
statues, and his longings the flutter of birds' wings, and the wind in the

στά διαστήματα τῶν στοχασμῶν του, καὶ τὰ καράβια του
ἀραγμένα σ' ἄφαντο λιμάνι·
κάτω ἀπὸ μιὰ προσωπίδα ἕνα κενό.

Πίσω ἀπὸ τὰ μεγάλα μάτια, τὰ καμπύλα χείλια, τοὺς βοστρύ-
χους,
ἀνάγλυφα στὸ μαλαματένιο σκέπασμα τῆς ὕπαρξῆς μας,
ἕνα σημεῖο σκοτεινὸ ποὺ ταξιδεύει σὰν τὸ ψάρι
μέσα στὴν αὐγινὴ γαλήνη τοῦ πελάγου καὶ τὸ βλέπεις·
ἕνα κενὸ παντοῦ μαζί μας.
Καὶ τὸ πουλὶ ποὺ πέταξε τὸν ἄλλο χειμώνα
μὲ σπασμένη φτερούγα,
σκήνωμα ζωῆς,
κι ἡ νέα γυναίκα ποὺ ἔφυγε νὰ παίξη
μέ τὰ σκυλόδοντα τοῦ καλοκαιριοῦ,
κι ἡ ψυχὴ ποὺ γύρεψε τσιρίζοντας τὸν κάτω κόσμο,
κι ὁ τόπος σὰν τὸ μεγάλο πλατανόφυλλο ποὺ παρασέρνει ὁ
χείμαρρος τοῦ ἥλιου
μὲ τ' ἀρχαῖα μνημεῖα καὶ τὴ σύγχρονη θλίψη.

Κι ὁ ποιητὴς ἀργοπορεῖ κοιτάζοντας τὶς πέτρες κι ἀναρωτι-
έται·
ὑπάρχουν ἄραγε
ἀνάμεσα στὶς χαλασμένες τοῦτες γραμμές, τὶς ἀκμές, τὶς αἰχμές,
τὰ κοῖλα καὶ τὶς καμπύλες,

space between his thoughts, and his ships at anchor in a vanished har-
bour; beneath a mask a void.

Behind the big eyes, the curls of hair embossed in the golden cover
of our existence, a shadowy mark that travels like a fish in the calm of
the sea at dawn, and you can see it; a void everywhere with us. And
the bird that flew away last winter with broken wing, lodging of life,
and the young girl that went off to play with the dog-teeth of summer,
and the soul that shrieking sought the nether world, and the place like
a great plane-leaf that the sun's torrent carries away with the ancient
memorials and the present sorrow.

And the poet lingers looking at the stones, and asks himself: Do
there then exist within these broken lines, points, edges, hollows and
curves, do there then exist here where the passage of rain, wind and

ὑπάρχουν ἄραγε
ἐδῶ ποὺ συναντιέται τὸ πέρασμα τῆς βροχῆς, τοῦ ἀγέρα καὶ
	τῆς φθορᾶς,
ὑπάρχουν, ἡ κίνηση τοῦ προσώπου, τὸ σχῆμα τῆς στοργῆς
ἐκείνων ποὺ λιγόστεψαν τόσο παράξενα μὲς στὴ ζωή μας,
αὐτῶν ποὺ ἀπόμειναν σκιὲς κυμάτων καὶ στοχασμοὶ μὲ τὴν
ἀπεραντωσύνη τοῦ πελάγου;
ἢ μήπως ὄχι δὲν ἀπομένει τίποτε παρὰ μόνο τὸ βάρος,
ἡ νοσταλγία τοῦ βάρους μιᾶς ὕπαρξης ζωντανῆς,
ἐκεῖ ποὺ μένουμε τώρα ἀνυπόστατοι λυγίζοντας
σὰν τὰ κλωνάρια τῆς φριχτῆς Ἰτιᾶς σωριασμένα μέσα στὴ
	διάρκεια τῆς ἀπελπισίας
ἐνῶ τὸ ρέμα κίτρινο κατεβάζει ἀργὰ βοῦρλα ξεριζωμένα μὲς
	στὸ βοῦρκο
εἰκόνα μορφῆς ποὺ μαρμάρωσε μὲ τὴν ἀπόφαση μιᾶς πίκρας
	παντοτινῆς.
Ὁ ποιητὴς ἕνα κενό.

Ἀσπιδοφόρος ὁ ἥλιος ἀνέβαινε πολεμώντας,
κι ἀπὸ τὸ βάθος τῆς σπηλιᾶς μιὰ νυχτερίδα τρομαγμένη
χτύπησε πάνω στὸ φῶς σὰν τὴ σαΐτα πάνω στὸ σκουτάρι:
‹Ἀσίνην τε . . . Ἀσίνην τε. . . › . Νά ᾽ταν αὐτὴ ὁ βασιλιὰς τῆς
	Ἀσίνης
ποὺ τὸν γυρεύουμε τόσο προσεχτικὰ σὲ τούτη τὴν ἀκρόπολη
᾽γγίζοντας κάποτε μὲ τὰ δάχτυλά μας τὴν ἀφή του πάνω
στὶς πέτρες.

decay meet, do there exist the movement of the face, the shape of the
love of those who have shrunk so strangely within our life, of those
who have remained as shadows of waves, thoughts limitless as the sea;
or no, perhaps nothing remains, but the burden alone, the nostalgia
for the burden of a living existence, where we are left now, unsup-
ported, bending like the boughs of the terrible willow, heaped in the
duration of despair while the yellow stream slowly bears down rushes
uprooted in the swamp, image of a form turned to marble by the sen-
tence of an unending bitterness; the poet a void.

Shield on arm, the sun was rising for battle, and from the depth of
the cave a frightened bat struck on the light like an arrow on a shield;
'Asine too . . . Asine too. . .'. Suppose that were the king of Asine
whom we are seeking so carefully in this citadel, feeling sometimes
with our fingers his touch on the stones.

ODYSSEUS ELYTIS

b. 1911

346. Anniversary

Ἔφερα τὴ ζωή μου ὡς ἐδῶ,
στὸ σημάδι ἐτοῦτο ποὺ παλεύει
πάντα κοντὰ στὴ θάλασσα,
νιάτα στὰ βράχια ἐπάνω, στῆθος
μὲ στῆθος πρὸς τὸν ἄνεμο
ποὺ νὰ πηγαίνη ἕνας ἄνθρωπος
ποὺ δὲν εἶναι ἄλλο ἀπὸ ἄνθρωπος,
λογαριάζοντας μὲ τὶς δροσιὲς τὶς πράσινες
στιγμές του, μὲ νερὰ τὰ ὁράματα
τῆς ἀκοῆς του, μὲ φτερὰ τὶς τύψεις του.
Ἄ, ζωὴ
παιδιοῦ ποὺ γίνεται ἄντρας
πάντα κοντὰ στὴ θάλασσα, ὅταν ὁ ἥλιος
τὸν μαθαίνει ν' ἀνασαίνη κατὰ κεῖ ποὺ σβήνεται
ἡ σκιὰ ἑνὸς γλάρου.

Ἔφερα τὴ ζωή μου ὡς ἐδῶ,
ἄσπρο μέτρημα, μελανὸ ἄθροισμα,
λίγα δέντρα καὶ λίγα
βρεμένα χαλίκια,
δάχτυλα ἐλαφρὰ γιὰ νὰ χαϊδέψουν ἕνα μέτωπο·
ποιὸ μέτωπο;
Κλάψαν ὅλη τὴ νύχτα οἱ προσδοκίες καὶ δὲν εἶναι πιὰ
κανείς, δέν εἶναι

HAVE brought my life as far as this, to this point where youth,
on the rocks, ever wrestles by the sea, breast-to-breast with the wind,
where there comes a man, who is nothing else but a man, reckoning
in dews his green moments, in waters the visions of his hearing, in
wings his pangs of remorse. Oh, life of the child that becomes a man,
ever by the sea, when the sun teaches him to take breath there, where
vanishes the seagull's shadow.

I have brought my life as far as this, white computation, black total,
a few trees, a few wet pebbles, light fingers to caress a forehead; what
forehead? They wept all night, my expectations, there is no one any

614

ν' ἀκουστῆ ἕνα βῆμα ἐλεύθερο,
ν' ἀνατείλη μιὰ φωνὴ ξεκούραστη,
στὸ μουράγιο οἱ πρύμνες νὰ παφλάσουν, γράφοντας
ὄνομα πιὸ γλαυκὸ μὲς στὸν ὁρίζοντά τους·
λίγα χρόνια, λίγα κύματα,
κωπηλασία εὐαίσθητη
στοὺς ὅρμους γύρω ἀπ' τὴν ἀγάπη.

Ἔφερα τὴ ζωή μου ὡς ἐδῶ,
χαρακιὰ πικρὴ στὴν ἄμμο ποὺ θὰ σβύση
— ὅποιος εἶδε δυὸ μάτια ν' ἀγγίζουν τὴ σιωπή του,
κι ἔσμιξε τὴ λιακάδα τους κλείνοντας χίλιους κόσμους,
ἂς θυμίση τὸ αἷμα του στοὺς ἄλλους ἥλιους,
πιὸ κοντὰ στὸ φῶς
ὑπάρχει ἕνα χαμόγελο ποὺ πληρώνει τὴ φλόγα —
μὰ ἐδῶ στὸ ἀνήξερο τοπεῖο ποὺ χάνεται,
σὲ μιὰ θάλασσα ἀνοιχτὴ κι ἀνέλεη,
μαδᾶ ἡ ἐπιτυχία,
στρόβιλοι φτερῶν
καὶ στιγμῶν ποὺ δέθηκαν στὸ χῶμα,
χῶμα σκληρὸ κάτω ἀπὸ τ' ἀνυπόμονα
πέλματα, χῶμα καμωμένο γιὰ ἴλιγγο,
ἡφαίστιο νεκρό.

Ἔφερα τὴ ζωή μου ὡς ἐδῶ,
πέτρα ταμένη στὸ ὑγρὸ στοιχεῖο,

longer, there is no free step to be heard, no voice may dawn re-
freshed, for the prows to plash at the mole, writing a bluer name within
their horizon; a few years, a few waves, sensitive motion of oars in the
bays round love.

I have brought my life as far as this, bitter groove on the sand which
will be erased – he who has seen two eyes touch his silence, and mingled
in their sunlight, closing in a thousand worlds, let him remind his
blood of the other suns; nearer to the light there is a smile which pays
or the flame – but here in this ignorant, sinking landscape, in an open
and pitiless sea, success withers; flurries of feathers and of moments
bound to the earth, earth hard under impatient feet, earth made for
dizziness, dead volcano.

I have brought my life as far as this, stone vowed to the liquid ele-

πιὸ πέρ' ἀπ' τὰ νησιά,
πιὸ χαμηλὰ ἀπ' τὸ κύμα,
γειτονιὰ στὶς ἄγκυρες.
— Ὅταν περνᾶν καρίνες σκίζοντας μὲ πάθος
ἕνα καινούργιο ἐμπόδιο καὶ τὸ νικᾶνε,
καὶ μ' ὅλα τὰ δελφίνια της αὐγάζ' ἡ ἐλπίδα,
κέρδος τοῦ ἥλιου σὲ μι' ἀνθρώπινη καρδιά —
τὰ δίχτυα τῆς ἀμφιβολίας τραβᾶνε
μιὰ μορφὴ ἀπὸ ἀλάτι,
λαξεμένη μὲ κόπο,
ἀδιάφορη, ἄσπρη,
ποὺ γυρνάει πρὸς τὸ πέλαγος τὰ κενὰ τῶν ματιῶν της
στηρίζοντας τὸ ἄπειρο.

347. The Mad Pomegranate Tree

Πρωινὸ ἐρωτηματικὸ κέφι à perdre haleine.

Σ' αὐτὲς τὶς κάτασπρες αὐλὲς ὅπου φυσᾶ ὁ νοτιᾶς
σφυρίζοντας σὲ θολωτὲς καμάρες, πέστε μου εἶναι ἡ τρελλὴ
      ῥοδιὰ
ποὺ σκιρτάει στὸ φῶς σκορπίζοντας τὸ καρποφόρο γέλοιο της
μὲ ἀνέμου πείσματα καὶ ψιθυρίσματα, πέστε μου εἶναι ἡ τρελλὴ
      ῥοδιὰ
ποὺ σπαρταράει μὲ φυλλωσιὲς νιογέννητες τὸν ὄρθρο
ἀνοίγοντας ὅλα τὰ χρώματα ψηλὰ μὲ ρῖγος θριάμβου;

ment, further off than the islands, lower than the waves, neighbour to
the anchors. When keels pass a new obstacle and tear it with passion
and conquer it, and hope with all her dolphins dawns, gain of the sun
in a man's heart — the nets of doubt draw in a figure of salt painfully
chiselled, indifferent, white, turning to the sea the void of its eyes,
sustaining the infinite.

IN these all-white courtyards where the south wind blows whistling
through vaulted arches, tell me, is it the mad pomegranate tree that
jumps in the light, scattering its fruitful laughter with windy obstinacy
and rustlings – tell me, is it the mad pomegranate tree that quivers with
foliage newly born at dawn opening high up all its colours in a shiver
of triumph?

*Όταν στούς κάμπους πού ξυπνοῦν τά ὁλόγυμνα κορίτσια
θερίζουνε μέ τά ξανθά τους χέρια τά τριφύλλια
γυρίζοντας τά πέρατα τῶν ὕπνων τους, πέστε μου εἶναι ἡ
    τρελλή ροδιά
πού βάζει ἀνύποπτη μές' τά χλωρά πανέρια τους τά φῶτα
πού ξεχειλίζει ἀπό κελαϊδισμούς τά ὀνόματά τους, πέστε μου
εἶναι ἡ τρελλή ροδιά πού μάχεται τή συννεφιά τοῦ κόσμου;

Στή μέρα πού ἀπ' τή ζήλεια της στολίζεται μ' ἐφτά λογιῶ
    φτερά
ζώνοντας τόν αἰώνιον ἥλιο μέ χιλιάδες πρίσματα
ἐκτυφλωτικά, πέστε μου εἶναι ἡ τρελλή ροδιά
πού ἁρπάει μιά χαίτη μ' ἑκατό βιτσιές στό τρέξιμό της
ποτέ θλιμμένη καί ποτέ γκρινιάρα, πέστε μου εἶναι ἡ τρελλή
    ροδιά
πού ξεφωνίζει τήν καινούρια ἐλπίδα πού ἀνατέλλει;

Πέστε μου εἶναι ἡ τρελλή ροδιά πού χαιρετάει στά μάκρη
τινάζοντας ἕνα μαντύλι φύλλων ἀπό δροσερή φωτιά
μιά θάλασσα ἑτοιμόγεννη μέ χίλια δυό καράβια
μέ κύματα πού χίλιες δυό φορές κινᾶν καί πᾶνε
σ' ἀμύριστες ἀκρογιαλιές, πέστε μου εἶναι ἡ τρελλή ροδιά
πού τρίζει τ' ἄρμενα ψηλά στό διάφανον αἰθέρα;

On plains where the naked girls wake, harvesting clover with their
light yellow arms, wandering on the borders of their dreams – tell me,
is it the mad pomegranate tree, unsuspecting, that puts the lights in
their fresh green baskets, that floods their names with the singing of
birds – tell me, is it the mad pomegranate tree that fights the cloudy
skies of the world?
    On the day that it adorns itself jealously with seven kinds of feathers,
binding the eternal sun with a thousand blinding prisms – tell me, is it
the mad pomegranate tree that seizes on the run a horse's mane with a
hundred lashes, never sad, and never grumbling – tell me, is it the mad
pomegranate tree that cries out the new hope now dawning?
    Tell me, is that the mad pomegranate tree delighting in distance,
fluttering a handkerchief of leaves made of cool flame, a sea near birth
with numberless ships, with waves that a thousand times and more set
out and go to unscented shores – tell me, is it the mad pomegranate
tree that causes the rigging to creak high up in the transparent air?

Πανύψηλα μὲ τὸ γλαυκὸ τσαμπὶ ποὺ ἀνάβει κι' ἑορτάζει
ἀγέρωχο, γεμάτο κίνδυνο, πέστε μου εἶναι ἡ τρελλὴ ροδιὰ
ποὺ σπάει μὲ φῶς καταμεσὶς τοῦ κόσμου τὶς κακοκαιριὲς τοῦ
    δαίμονα
ποὺ πέρα ὡς πέρα τὴν κροκάτη ἁπλώνει τραχηλιὰ τῆς μέρας
τὴν πολυκεντημένη ἀπὸ σπαρτὰ τραγούδια, πέστε μου εἶναι
ἡ τρελλὴ ροδιὰ
ποὺ βιαστικὰ ξεθηλυκώνει τὰ μεταξωτὰ τῆς μέρας;

Σὲ μεσοφούστανα πρωταπριλιᾶς καὶ σὲ τζιτζίκια δεκαπενταυ-
    γούστου
πέστε μου, αὐτὴ ποὺ παίζει, αὐτὴ ποὺ ὀργίζεται, αὐτὴ ποὺ
    ξελογιάζει
τινάζοντας ἀπ' τὴ φοβέρα τὰ κακὰ μαῦρα σκοτάδια της
ξεχύνοντας στοὺς κόρφους τοῦ ἥλιου τὰ μεθυστικὰ πουλιὰ
πέστε μου αὐτὴ ποὺ ἀνοίγει τὰ φτερὰ στὸ στῆθος τῶν πραγ-
    μάτων
στὸ στῆθος τῶν βαθιῶν ὀνείρων μας εἶναι ἡ τρελλὴ ροδιά;

Very high up with the blue bunch of grapes that flares and cele-
brates, arrogant, full of danger — tell me, is it the mad pomegranate
tree that shatters with light the demon's storm in the middle of the
world, that spreads far as can be the saffron ruffle of day richly em-
broidered with scattered songs — tell me, is it the mad pomegranate
tree that unfastens in a hurry the silk of the day?

In petticoats of April the first and cicadas of the mid-August feast —
tell me, that which plays, that which rages, that which leads astray,
shaking out of fear its evil black darkness, spilling in the sun's bosom
intoxicating birds — tell me, that which opens its wings on the breast of
things, on the breast of our deep dreams, is that the mad pomegranate
tree?

REFERENCES

Figures refer to the numbers of the pieces

1. *Homeri Opera*, ed. T. W. Allen, vol. I, *Ilias*, I, 1–311.
2. ibid., vol. I, *Ilias*, VI, 440–96.
3. ibid., vol. II, *Ilias*, XIII, 10–31.
4. ibid., vol. II, *Ilias*, XVII, 424–458.
5. ibid., vol. II, *Ilias*, XVIII, 478–608.
6. ibid., vol. II, *Ilias*, XXII, 21–375.
7. ibid., vol. II, *Ilias*, XXIII, 1–110, 161–261.
8. ibid., vol. II, *Ilias*, XXIV, 468–676.
9. ibid., vol. III, *Odysseia*, I, 1–21.
10. ibid., vol. III, *Odysseia*, V, 51–83.
11. ibid., vol. III, *Odysseia*, V, 388–493.
12. ibid., vol. III, *Odysseia*, VI, 85–185.
13. ibid., vol. III, *Odysseia*, IX, 353–414.
14. ibid., vol. III, *Odysseia*, X, 210–43.
15. ibid., vol. III, *Odysseia*, XI, 541–64.
16. ibid., vol. III, *Odysseia*, XII, 165–200.
17. ibid., vol. III, *Odysseia*, XII, 234–59.
18. ibid., vol. IV, *Odysseia*, XIII, 93–119.
19. ibid., vol. IV, *Odysseia*, XVII, 290–327.
20. ibid., vol. IV, *Odysseia*, XXI, 388–XXII, 8; XXII, 381–9.
21. ibid., vol. IV, *Odysseia*, XXIII, 205–40.
22. ibid., vol. IV, *Odysseia*, XXIV, 1–14.
23. *Hesiod*, ed. H. G. Evelyn-White, *Opera et Dies*, 42–104.
24. ibid., *Opera et Dies*, 174–201.
25. ibid., *Opera et Dies*, 202–14, 248–55, 265–6.
26. ibid., *Opera et Dies*, 448–92.
27. ibid., *Opera et Dies*, 504–53.
28. ibid., *Opera et Dies*, 663–94.
29. ibid., *Theogonia*, 1–4, 22–35, 81–103.
30. ibid., *Theogonia*, 687–719.
31. *Homeri Opera*, ed. T. W. Allen, vol. V, *Hymni Homerici*, II, 1–23.
32. ibid., vol. V, *Hymni Homerici*, II, 169–91.
33. ibid., vol. V, *Hymni Homerici*, III, 146–78.
34. ibid., vol. V, *Hymni Homerici*, IV, 212–80.
35. *Certamen Homeri et Hesiodi*, ll. 265–70; *Homeri Opera*, ed. T. W. Allen, vol. V, p. 235.
36. *Anthologia Lyrica Graeca*, ed. E. Diehl (3rd ed.), vol. I (fasc. I), pp. 11–12, nos. 6 and 7.
37. ibid., vol. I (fasc. I), p. 1, no. 1.
38. ibid., vol. I (fasc. II), p. 2, no. 2.
39. ibid., vol. I (fasc. II), p. 4, no. 6.
40. ibid., vol. I (fasc. II), p. 27, no. 60.
41. ibid., vol. I (fasc. II), p. 31, no. 74.
42. *Poetae Melici Graeci*, ed. D. L. Page, p. 3, no. 1.

43. ibid., p. 62, no. 89.

44. *Anthologia Lyrica Graeca*, ed. E. Diehl (3rd ed.), vol. I (fasc. 1), p. 48, no. 1.

45. ibid., vol. I (fasc. 1), p. 49, no. 2.

46. ibid., vol. I (fasc. III), p. 62, no. 29.

47. *Poetae Melici Graeci*, ed. D. L. Page, p. 450, no. 848. Line 17 is emended.

48. *Poetarum Lesbiorum Fragmenta*, ed. E. Lobel et D. L. Page, p. 274, no. 357.

49 (I). ibid., p. 265, no. 326.

49 (II). ibid., p. 116, no. 6. The final words from l. 3 ff. are conjectural.

50 (I). ibid., p. 267, no. 338.

50 (II). ibid., p. 270, no. 347. The end of line 4 is conjectural.

50 (III). ibid., p. 269, no. 346.

51. ibid., p. 128, no. 38. The last words of the lines are conjectural.

52. ibid., p. 131, no. 42. The last words of most lines are conjectural.

53. ibid., p. 125, no. 34. Conjectures in ll. 1–3 and 11.

54. ibid., p. 2, no. 1.

55. ibid., p. 32, no. 31. Conjectures in ll. 9 and 13.

56. ibid., p. 33, no. 34. The last words of the last line are conjectural.

57. ibid., p. 78, no. 96. Lines 1–5, 8 and 17 contain conjectures.

58. ibid., p. 86, no. 104 (a).

59. ibid., p. 75, no. 94. Lines 3, 10–14 and 17–19 contain conjectures.

60 (I). ibid., p. 86, no. 105 (a).

60 (II). ibid., p. 87, no. 105 (c).

61. ibid., p. 92, no. 130.

62. Σαπφοῦς Μέλη, ed. E. Lobel, Inc. Auct. 6, p. 72.

63. *Poetarum Lesbiorum Fragmenta*, ed. E. Lobel et D. L. Page, p. 38, no. 47.

64. ibid., p. 14, no. 16. Lines 8 and 12 include conjectures.

65. ibid., p. 36, no. 44. Lines 2, 6–7, 12–15 and 16–19 contain conjectures.

66. *Anthologia Lyrica Graeca*, ed. E. Diehl (3rd ed.), vol. I (fasc. 1), p. 23, no. 1, ll. 43–60.

67. *Poetae Melici Graeci*, ed. D. L. Page, p. 100, no. 185.

68. ibid., p. 149, no. 286.

69. ibid., p. 150, no. 287.

70. *Anthologia Lyrica Graeca*, ed. E. Diehl (3rd ed.), vol. I (fasc. 1), p. 57, no. 1.

71. *Poetae Melici Graeci*, ed. D. L. Page, p. 177, no. 348.

72. ibid., p. 183, no. 357.

73. ibid., p. 183, no. 358.

74. ibid., p. 198, no. 395.

75 (I). ibid., p. 198, no. 396.

75 (II). ibid., p. 181, no. 356 (a). Line 5 contains emendation.

75 (III). ibid., p. 181, no. 356 (b).

76. ibid., p. 207, no. 417.

77. *Carmina Anacreonta*, ed. C. Preisedanz, p. 26, no. 33.

78. ibid., p. 28, no. 34.

79. *Anthologia Lyrica Graeca*, ed. E. Diehl, 3rd ed., vol. I (fasc. II), p. 17, 237–54.

80. *Poetae Melici Graeci*, ed. D. L. Page, p. 276, no. 531.

81. ibid., p. 284, no. 543. The division into lines and strophes is uncertain.

82. *Anthologia Lyrica Graeca*, ed. E. Diehl, 2nd ed., vol. II, p. 94, no. 92.

83. ibid., p. 90, no. 83.

84. ibid., p. 102, no. 105.

85. ibid., p. 107, no. 121.

86. ibid., p. 108, no. 122.

87. ibid., p. 97, no. 99.

88. *Poetae Melici Graeci*, ed. D. L. Page, pp. 274–5, nos. 893–6.

89. *Aeschyli Tragoediae*, ed. G. Murray, *Persae*, 353–432.

90. ibid., *Prometheus Vinctus*, 87–113.

91. ibid., *Agamemnon*, 160–254.

92. ibid., *Agamemnon*, 281–314.

93. ibid., *Choephoroe*, 973–1062.

94. *Anthologia Lyrica Graeca*, ed. E. Diehl (3rd ed.), vol. I (fasc. 1), p. 79, no. 3.

95. Pindarus, *Carmina*, ed. O. Schroeder, *Olympia I*, 67–93.

96. ibid., *Olympia VI*, 29–70.

97. ibid., *Pythia I*.

98. ibid., frag. 76.

99. ibid., frag. 123.

100. *Bacchylidis Carmina*, ed. B. Snell, III, 15–62.

101. *Sophoclis Fabulae*, ed. A. C. Pearson, *Ajax*, 646–84.

102. ibid., *Antigone*, 332–75.

103. ibid., *Antigone*, 781–801.

104. ibid., *Electra*, 681–763.

105. ibid., *Oedipus Tyrannus*, 151–215.

106. ibid., *Oedipus Tyrannus*, 950–1185.

107. ibid., *Oedipus Coloneus*, 668–719.

108. ibid., *Oedipus Coloneus*, 1211–48.

109. ibid., *Oedipus Coloneus*, 1587–1666.

110. *Euripidis Fabulae*, ed. G. Murray, vol. I, *Cyclops*, 316–346.

111. ibid., vol. I, *Alcestis*, 435–465.

112. ibid., vol. I, *Medea*, 764–810.

113. ibid., vol. I, *Hippolytus*, 732–51.

114. ibid., vol. I, *Hecuba*, 444–65.

115. ibid., vol. II, *Hercules Furens*, 637–700.

116. ibid., vol. II, *Ion*, 82–111.

117. ibid., vol. II, *Iphigenia Taurica*, 1089–1151.

118. ibid., vol. III, *Orestes*, 316–347.

119. ibid., vol. III, *Bacchae*, 677–774.

120. ibid., vol. III, *Bacchae*, 863–876, 897–911.

121. *Tragicorum Graecorum Fragmenta*, ed. A. Nauck, p. 474, no. 76.

122. ibid., p. 602, no. 773.

123. *Aristophanis Comoediae*, ed. F. W. Hall et W. M. Geldart, vol. I, *Acharnenses*, 496–556.

124. ibid., vol. I, *Equites*, 40–70.

125. ibid., vol. I, *Nubes*, 275–90, 299–313.

126. ibid., vol. I, *Aves*, 209–22, 227–54.

127. ibid., vol. I, *Aves*, 1058–1070, 1088–1100.

128. ibid., vol. II, *Lysistrata*, 565–97.

129. ibid., vol. II, *Lysistrata*, 1279–94, 1296–1321.

130. ibid., vol. II, *Ranae*, 814–29.

131. ibid., vol. II, *Plutus*, 535–47.

132. *Poetae Melici Graeci*, ed. D. L. Page, p. 407 (Timotheus, *Persae*, 64–97).

133. *Anthologia Lyrica Graeca*, ed. E. Diehl (3rd ed.), vol. I (fasc. 1), p. 102, no. 1.

134. ibid., p. 103, no. 5.

135. ibid., p. 103, no. 6.

136. ibid., p. 105, no. 10.

137. *Poetae Melici Graeci*, ed. D. L. Page, p. 444, no. 842.

138. *Comicorum Graecorum Fragmenta*, ed. T. Kock, vol. III, p. 36, no. 125.

139. ibid., p. 138, no. 481.

140. ibid., p. 161, no. 538.

141. ibid., p. 162, no. 540.

142. Menander, *Reliquiae*, ed. A. Körte, p. 108, no. 2.

143. *Collectanea Alexandrina*, ed. J. U. Powell, p. 93, no. 11.

144. *Anthologia Palatina*, vol. VI, no. 312.

145. ibid., vol. VII, no. 190.

146. ibid., vol. VII, no. 208.

147. *Bucolici Graeci*, ed. A. S. F. Gow, Theocritus, *Carmen I*, 29–56.

148. ibid., Theocritus, *Carmen I*, 123–42.

149. ibid., Theocritus, *Carmen II*, 64–166.

150. ibid., Theocritus, *Carmen VII*.

151. ibid., Theocritus, *Carmen X*, 24–37.

152. ibid., Theocritus, *Carmen XV*, 1–43.

153. ibid., Theocritus, *Carmen XXVIII*.

154. *Aratus*, ed. G. R. Mair, *Phaenomena*, 1–18.

155. *Callimachus*, ed. R. Pfeiffer, vol. I, *Aetia*, frag. 1, 1–2, 17–38.

156. ibid., vol. I, *Aetia*, frag. XLIII, 12–17.

157. ibid., vol. I, *Aetia*, fragg. LXVII et LXXV.

158. ibid., vol. I, *Iambus IV*, frag. CXCIV, 1, 6–9, 22–84, 93–106.

159. ibid., vol. I, *Hecala*, frag. CCLX, 62–9.

160. ibid., vol. II, *Hymnus II*, 1–24.

161. ibid., vol. II, *Hymnus III*, 46–71.

162. ibid., vol. II, *Epigramma XIX*.

163. ibid., vol. II, *Epigramma II*.

164. ibid., vol. II, *Epigramma XXVIII*.

165. *Anthologia Palatina*, vol. V, no. 64.

166. ibid., vol. V, no. 153.

167. ibid., vol. V, no. 185.

168. ibid., vol. XII, no. 47.

169. ibid., vol. XII, no. 135.

170. ibid., vol. VII, no. 170.

171. ibid., vol. V, no. 135.

172. ibid. (ed. E. Cougny, vol. III, ch. iv, no. 26).

173. *Apollonii Rhodii Argonautica*, ed. H. Fränkel, I, 536–58.

174. ibid., III, 111–36.

175. ibid., III, 744–824.

176. ibid., III, 1008–24.

177. ibid., IV, 930–67.

178. *Anthologia Palatina*, vol. X, no. 1.

179. ibid., vol. IX, no. 99.

180. ibid., vol. VI, no. 4.

181. ibid., vol. VII, no. 715.

182. *Herodas*, ed. A. D. Knox, *Mimiambus II*, 16–40.

183. *Anthologia Palatina*, vol. VII, no. 247.

184. ibid. (Appendix Planudea), vol. XVI, no. 26b.

185. *Anthologia Palatina*, vol. VII, no. 178.

186. *Bucolici Graeci*, ed. U. von Wilamowitz-Moellendorff, Moschus, *Carmen II*, 108–30.

187. ibid., Bion, *Carmen 1*, 1–63.

188. ibid., *Epitaphius Bionis*, 98–104.

189. *Anthologia Palatina*, vol. VII, no. 8.

190. ibid., vol. V, no. 143.

191. ibid., vol. V, no. 136.

192. ibid., vol. V, no. 147.

193. ibid., vol. VII, no. 196.

194. ibid., vol. IX, no. 546.

195. ibid., vol, IX, no. 28.

196. *Collectanea Alexandrina*, ed. J. U. Powell, p. 199, no. 37, ll. 5–19.

197. *Anthologia Palatina*, vol. XIV, no. 153.

198. *Quinti Smyrnaei Posthomerica*, ed. A. Zimmermann, XIV, 505–29.

199. *Anthologia Palatina*, vol. III, ch. vi, no. 122.

200. *Musaei De Herone et Leandro*, ed. A. Ludwich, 309–43.

201. *Patrologia Graeca*, ed. Migne, vol. XXXVII, col. 993. (Gregorius Nazianzen, *De Seipso*, 1, 305–21.)

202. *Anthologia Palatina*, vol. VIII, no. 80.

203. *Anthologia Graeca Carminum Christianorum*, ed. W. Christ et M. Paranikas, p. 40.

204. *Medieval and Modern Greek Poetry*, ed. C. A. Trypanis, p. 3, no. 3.

205. *Synesii Cyrenensis Hymni*, ed. N. Terzaghi, p. 53, VIII (= IX), 31–71.

206. *Anthologia Palatina*, vol. I, no. 99.

207. *Nonni Panopolitani Dionysiaca*, ed. R. Keydell, XXXV, 184–215.

208. *Anthologia Palatina*, vol. VII, no. 346.

209. *Epigrammata Graeca ex Lapidibus Collecta*, ed. G. Kaibel, p. 222, no. 548.

210. *Frühbyzantinische Kirchenpoesie*, ed. P. Maas, p. 4, no. 1.

211. ibid., p. 16, no. 2.

212. *Greek Literary Papyri* (Loeb), ed. D. L. Page, vol. I, p. 560, no. 140, ll. 7–23, 49–70, 135–50.

213. *Anthologia Graeca Carminum Christianorum*, ed. W. Christ et M. Paranikas, p. 140.

214. *Anthologia Palatina*, vol. I, no. 34.

215. ibid., vol. VII, no. 204.

216. ibid., vol. IX, no. 641.

217. ibid., vol. V, no. 223.

218. *Sancti Romani Melodi Cantrica*, ed. P. Maas et C. A. Trypanis, p. 1, no. 1.

219. ibid., p. 142, no. 19.

220. ibid., p. 157, no. 21, ll. 1–5.

221. ibid., p. 223, no. 29, strophes 1 and 24.

222. ibid., p. 497, no. 58, strophe 3.

223. *Anthologia Palatina* (Appendix Planudea), vol. XVI, no. 387.

224. *Johannes von Gaza u. Paulus Silentiarius*, ed. P. Friedländer, *Ecphrasis*, ll. 884–917.

225. *Georgii Pisidae Expeditio Persica*, ed. Imm. Bekkerus, III, ll. 200–80.

226. *Anthologia Graeca Carminum Christianorum*, ed. W. Christ et M. Paranikas, p. 147, ll. 1–66.

227. ibid., p. 205, ll. 1–35.

228. ibid., p. 196, ll. 1–40.

229. *Patrologia Graeca*, ed. Migne, vol. XCIX, col. 1785, no. XVII.

230. ibid., col. 1788, no. XIX.

231. *Anthologia Graeca Carminum Christianorum*, ed. W. Christ et M. Paranikas, p. 104.

232. *Anecdota Graeca*, ed. J. A. Cramer, vol. IV, p. 306.

233. ibid., vol. IV, p. 316.

234. *Aus der Poesie des Mystikers Symeon*, ed. P. Maas (Festgabe für A. Ehrhard), p. 339, ll. 236–66.

235. ibid., p. 335.

236. *Die Gedichte d. Christophoros Mytilenaios*, ed. E. Kurz, no. 75.

237. ibid., no. 56.

238. *Iohannis Euchaitorum metropolitae, quae in codice Vaticano Gr. 676 supersunt*, ed. P. de Lagarde (Abh. d. hist.-phil. Klasse d. k. Gesellschaft d. Wiss. zu Göttingen, XXVIII, 1881), no. 43.

239. ibid., no. 20.

240. *Poèmes Prodromiques*, ed. D. C. Hesseling et H. Pernot, IV, 1–39.

241. *Bibliothèque Grècque Vulgaire*, ed. E. Legrand, vol. I, p. 17.

242. *Intorno alla elegia di Michele Acominato sulla decadenza della cita di Atene*, ed. S. G. Mercati (Εἰς Μνήμην Σ. Λάμπρου, Athens, 1935), p. 423.

243. *Manuelis Philae Carmina Inedita*, ed. E. Martini, No. 26.

244. *Collection de Romans grecs* ed. S. Lambros, Καλλίμαχος καὶ Χρυσορρόη, ll. 808–26.

245. *Les Exploits de Basile Digenis Acritas*, ed. E. Legrand (2nd ed.), IV, 196–254.

246. Βασίλειος Διγενῆς Ἀκρίτας, ed. P. Kalonaros, vol. I, 1, ll. 3140–55.

247. *Le Roman de Libistros et Rhodamne*, ed. J. A. Lambert, ll. 2631–42.

248. Ἐρωτοπαίγνια, ed. D. C. Hesseling et H. Pernot, p. 24.

249. ibid., p. 26.

250. *L'Achilléide Byzantine*, ed. D. C. Hesseling, ll. 712–759.

251. Ὀρθόδοξος Ἱερὰ Σύνοψις, ed. J. Nikolaidis, p. 506 f.

252. (I) Ἐκλογαὶ ἀπὸ τὰ Τραγούδια τοῦ Ἑλλ. Λαοῦ, ed. N. G. Politis (3rd ed.), no. 78.

252 (II). ibid., no. 78b.

253. ibid., no. 92.

254. ibid., no. 2.

255. ibid., no. 89.

256. ibid., no. 128a.

257. ibid., no. 117.

258. ibid., no. 126.

259. ibid., no. 172.

260. ibid., no. 135.

261. ibid., no. 153.

262. ibid., no. 222.

263. ibid., no. 184.

264. ibid., no. 218.

265. ibid., no. 23.

266. ibid., no. 64.

267. Ἡ Θυσία τοῦ Ἀβραάμ, ed. G. Megas, ll. 325–448.

268. Ἐρωφίλη, ed. S. Xanthoudidis, vol. V, ll. 561–94.

REFERENCES

269. Ἐρωτόκριτος, ed. S. Xanthoudidis, vol. II, ll. 319–364.
270. ibid., vol. I, ll. 887–8.
271. ibid., vol. III, ll. 1553–76.
272. ibid., vol. III, ll. 1629–36.
273. ibid., vol. IV, ll. 601–16.
274. ibid., vol. IV, ll. 1889–98.
275. ibid., vol. IV, ll. 1915–18.
276. ibid., vol. V, ll. 767–96.
277. Chants populaires de la Grèce Moderne, ed. C. Fauriel, vol. II, p. 20, ll 1–16.
278. Διονυσίου Σολωμοῦ Ποιήματα, ed. L. Politis, vol. I, p. 71, ll. 1–16.
279. ibid., p. 139.
280. ibid., p. 185, no. 21.
281 (I). ibid., p. 217, ll. 1–14.
281 (II). ibid., p. 32, frag. 36.
282. ibid., p. 243, ll. 1–21.
283. Λύρα, A. Kalvos (Athens, 1927), p. 37.
284. Ἅπαντα, A. Soutsos (Athens, 1916), p. 42.
285. Τὰ Ἅπαντα, G. Zalokostas (Athens, 1873), p. 288.
286. Ἅπαντα τὰ Φιλολογικά, A. Rizos-Rangavis, vol. II, Διονύσου Πλοῦς ll. 76–100.
286. ibid., ll. 236–50.
287. Ποιήματα, J. Typaldos (Athens, 1916), p. 39.
288. Ἡ Βάρβιτος, J. Karasoutsas (Athens, 1866), p. 11.
289. Ἔργα, G. Marcoras (Corfu, 1890), p. 263.
290. Ποιήματα, A. Paraschos (Athens, 1881), vol. III, p. 145.
291. ibid., p. 320.
292. Ἅπαντα, D. Paparrhegopoulos (Athens, 1915), p. 11.
293. Τὰ Ποιήματα, G. Vizyenos (Athens, 1916), p. 56.
294. Ποιήματα, A. Valaoritis (Athens, 1891), vol. I, p. 176.
295. Ἀμάραντα, G. Drosinis (Athens, 1890), p. 119.
296. Γαλήνη, G. Drosinis (Athens, 1902), p. 27.
297 (I). Ἴαμβοι καὶ Ἀνάπαιστοι, K. Palamas (Athens, 1920, 2nd ed.), no. 17.
297 (II). ibid., no. 18.
298. ibid., no. 37.
299. Ὁ Τάφος, K. Palamas, (Athens, 1928, 4th ed.), p. 27.
300. Ἡ Ἀσάλευτη Ζωή, K. Palamas (Athens, 1926, 3rd ed.), p. 10.
301. ibid., p. 40.
302. ibid., p. 170.
303. ibid., p. 107.
304. Ὁ Δωδεκάλογος τοῦ Γύφτου, K. Palamas (Athens, no date, 3rd ed.), p. 39.
305. ibid., p. 53.
306. ibid., p. 59.
307. ibid., p. 139.
308. Ἡ Φλογέρα τοῦ Βασιλιᾶ μέ τὴν Ἡρωικὴ Τριλογία, K. Palamas (Athens, 1920, 2nd ed.), p. 36.
309. ibid., p. 82.
310. Ἡ Πολιτεία καὶ ἡ Μοναξιά, K. Palamas (Athens, no date, 2nd ed.), p. 131.
311. Οἱ Καημοὶ τῆς Λιμνοθάλασσας, K. Palamas (Athens, 1925, 2nd ed.), p. 47.
312. Τὸ Παλιὸ Βιολί, J. Polemis (Athens, 1931, 3rd ed.), p. 7.
313. Ἔργα, K. Krystallis (Athens, 1912), vol. II, p. 14.

314. *Τὰ Ἔργα*, L. Mavilis (Alexandria, 1928, 2nd ed.), p. 34.
315. ibid., p. 46.
316. *Σκιές*, L. Porphyras (Athens, 1920), p. 125.
317. ibid., p. 31.
318. *Οἱ Μουσικὲς Φωνές*, L. Porphyras (Athens, 1934), p. 17.
319. *Βραδυνοὶ Θρύλοι*, K. Chatzopoulos (Athens, 1927), p. 27.
320. *Παγὰ Λαλέουνα*, P. Nirvanas (Athens, 1921, 2nd ed.), p. 49.
321. *Ἀσφόδελοι*, M. Malakasis (Athens, no date, 2nd ed.), p. 62.
322. *Σκαραβαῖοι καὶ Τερρακόττες*, J. Gryparis (Athens, no date), p. 41.
323. ibid., p. 40.
324. *Ἅπαντα*, K. Karyotakis (Athens, 1938), p. 70.
325. *Οἱ Τρίλλιες ποὺ Σβύνουν*, M. Polydoure (Athens, 1928), p. 77.
326. *Κίτρινες Φλόγες*, Myrtiotissa (Athens, no date), p. 53.

327. *Τὰ Χρυσᾶ Κύπελλα*, E. Daphne (Athens, 1933), p. 34.
328. *Ποιήματα*, K. Kavafis (Athens, 1948, 2nd ed.), p. 7.
329. ibid., p. 20.
330. ibid., p. 13.
331. ibid., p. 35.
332. ibid., p. 22.
333. ibid., p. 42.
334. ibid., p. 32.
335. ibid., p. 105.
336. *Λυρικὸς Βίος*, A. Sikelianos (Athens, no date), vol. I, p. 229.
337. ibid., vol. I, p. 227.
338. ibid., vol. I, p. 232.
339. ibid., vol. III, p. 204.
340. ibid., vol. III, p. 203.
341. ibid., vol. III, p. 211.
342. *Ποιήματα*, G. Seferis (Athens, 1950), p. 33.
343. ibid., p. 52.
344. ibid., p. 66.
345. ibid., p. 189.
346. Elytis, *Poèmes*, ed. R. Levesques (Athens, 1945), p. 14.
347. ibid., p. 52.

SELECT BIBLIOGRAPHY

ANCIENT GREEK POETRY

SCHMID, W., STÄHLIN, O., *Geschichte der griechischen Literatur I, II* (seven volumes Munich, 1920–48;=*Handbuch der Altertumswissenschaft VII*, ed. W. Otto)

BOWRA, C. M., *Ancient Greek Literature*, London, 1933

BOWRA, C. M., *Landmarks in Greek Literature*, Harmondsworth, 1968

LESKY, A., *A History of Greek Literature* (English translation by J. Willis and C. de Heer), London, 1966

KRANZ, W., *Geschichte der griechischen Literatur*, Bremen, no date (4th ed.)

MURRAY, G., *Ancient Greek Literature*, Oxford, 1907 (4th ed.)

ROSE, H. J., *A Handbook of Greek Literature*, London, 1961 (4th ed.)

WRIGHT, F. A., *A History of Later Greek Literature*, New York, 1932

MEDIEVAL GREEK POETRY

KRUMBACHER, K., *Geschichte der byzantinischen Literatur*, Munich, 1897 (2nd ed.); (=*Handbuch der Altertumswissenschaft, IX,1*)

KRUMBACHER, K., 'Greek Literature: Byzantine', *Encyclopaedia Britannica* (11th ed.)

BECK, H. G., *Kirche und theologische Literatur im byzantinischen Reich*, Munich, 1959; (=*Handbuch der Altertumswissenschaft XII,2.1*)

DÖLGER, F., *Die byzantinische Dichtung in der Reinsprache*, in Εὐχαριστήριον *Franz Dölger zum 70. Geburtstage*, Thessaloniki, 1961 (2nd ed.)

HUSSEY, J. M., *Church and Learning in the Byzantine Empire*, Oxford, 1937

HUNGER, H., *Byzantinische Geisteswelt von Konstantin dem Grossen bis zum Fall Konstantinopels*, Baden-Baden, 1958

IMPELLIZZERI, S., *La letteratura bizantina da Costantino agli iconoclasti*, Bari, 1965

BAYNES, N. H., MOSS, H. ST. L. B., *Byzantium*, Oxford, 1949 (2nd ed.), the chapters on Byzantine literature by F. H. Marshall and J. Mavrogordato

RUNCIMAN, S., *Byzantine Civilization*, London, 1948 (3rd ed.)

MODERN GREEK POETRY

DEMARAS, K. T., Ἱστορία τῆς Νεοελληνικῆς Λογοτεχνίας, Athens, 1968 (4th ed.); French translation by the author, no date

BOUTIERIDES, E., Ἱστορία τῆς Νεοελληνικῆς Λογοτεχνίας, Athens, 1965 (2nd ed.)

KNÖS, B., *L'Histoire de la littérature néo-hellénique*, Göteborg-Uppsala, 1962

LAVAGNINI, B., *Storia della letteratura neoellenica*, Milan, 1955

MANOUSSAKAS, M. J., Ἡ Κρητικὴ Λογοτεχνία κατὰ τὴν ἐποχὴν τῆς Βενετοκρατίας, Thessaloniki, 1965; the same study in French in *L'Hellénisme contemporain*, IX (1955), pp. 95f.

MIRAMBEL, A., *La Littérature grecque moderne*, Paris, 1953

KARANDONIS, A., Εἰσαγωγὴ στὴ Νεώτερη Ποίηση, Athens, 1955

TRYPANIS, C. A., 'Greek Literature: Modern', *Encyclopaedia Britannica* (1970)
— Διαλέξεις Φιλολογικοῦ Συλλόγου Παρνασσοῦ περὶ Ἑλλήνων Ποιητῶν τοῦ ιθ' Αἰῶνος, vols. I–II, Athens, 1925

INDEX OF POETS

Numbers refer to pages

READ MORE IN PENGUIN

In every corner of the world, on every subject under the sun, Penguin represents quality and variety – the very best in publishing today.

For complete information about books available from Penguin – including Puffins, Penguin Classics and Arkana – and how to order them, write to us at the appropriate address below. Please note that for copyright reasons the selection of books varies from country to country.

In the United Kingdom: Please write to *Dept. JC, Penguin Books Ltd, FREEPOST, West Drayton, Middlesex UB7 0BR*

If you have any difficulty in obtaining a title, please send your order with the correct money, plus ten per cent for postage and packaging, to *PO Box No. 11, West Drayton, Middlesex UB7 0BR*

In the United States: Please write to *Penguin USA Inc., 375 Hudson Street, New York, NY 10014*

In Canada: Please write to *Penguin Books Canada Ltd, 10 Alcorn Avenue, Suite 300, Tororto, Ontario M4V 3B2*

In Australia: Please write to *Penguin Books Australia Ltd, 487 Maroondah Highway, Ringwood, Victoria 3134*

In New Zealand: Please write to *Penguin Books (NZ) Ltd,182–190 Wairau Road, Private Bag, Takapuna, Auckland 9*

In India: Please write to *Penguin Books India Pvt Ltd, 706 Eros Apartments, 56 Nehru Place, New Delhi 110 019*

In the Netherlands: Please write to *Penguin Books Netherlands B.V., Keizersgracht 231 NL–1016 DV Amsterdam*

In Germany: Please write to *Penguin Books Deutschland GmbH, Friedrichstrasse 10–12, W–6000 Frankfurt/Main 1*

In Spain: Please write to *Penguin Books S. A., C. San Bernardo 117–6° E–28015 Madrid*

In Italy: Please write to *Penguin Italia s.r.l., Via Felice Casati 20, I–20124 Milano*

In France: Please write to *Penguin France S. A., 17 rue Lejeune, F–31000 Toulouse*

In Japan: Please write to *Penguin Books Japan, Ishikiribashi Building, 2–5–4, Suido, Tokyo 112*

In Greece: Please write to *Penguin Hellas Ltd, Dimocritou 3, GR–106 71 Athens*

In South Africa: Please write to *Longman Penguin Southern Africa (Pty) Ltd, Private Bag X08, Bertsham 2013*

READ MORE IN PENGUIN

PENGUIN BOOKS OF POETRY

American Verse
Ballads
British Poetry Since 1945
Caribbean Verse
A Choice of Comic and Curious Verse
Contemporary American Poetry
Contemporary British Poetry
Eighteenth-Century Verse
Elizabethan Verse
English Poetry 1918–60
English Romantic Verse
English Verse
First World War Poetry
Georgian Poetry
Irish Verse
Light Verse
London in Verse
Love Poetry
The Metaphysical Poets
Modern African Poetry
Modern Arab Poetry
New Poetry
Poems of Science
Poetry of the Thirties
Post-War Russian Poetry
Spanish Civil War Verse
Unrespectable Verse
Urdu Poetry
Victorian Verse
Women Poets

READ MORE IN PENGUIN

PENGUIN CLASSICS

Netochka Nezvanova   Fyodor Dostoyevsky

Dostoyevsky's first book tells the story of 'Nameless Nobody' and introduces many of the themes and issues which will dominate his great masterpieces.

Selections from the Carmina Burana   A verse translation by David Parlett

The famous songs from the *Carmina Burana* (made into an oratorio by Carl Orff) tell of lecherous monks and corrupt clerics, drinkers and gamblers, and the fleeting pleasures of youth.

Fear and Trembling   Søren Kierkegaard

A profound meditation on the nature of faith and submission to God's will which examines with startling originality the story of Abraham and Isaac.

Selected Prose   Charles Lamb

Lamb's famous essays (under the strange pseudonym of Elia) on anything and everything have long been celebrated for their apparently innocent charm; this major new edition allows readers to discover the darker and more interesting aspects of Lamb.

The Picture of Dorian Gray   Oscar Wilde

Wilde's superb and macabre novella, one of his supreme works, is reprinted here with a masterly Introduction and valuable Notes by Peter Ackroyd.

A Treatise of Human Nature   David Hume

A universally acknowledged masterpiece by 'the greatest of all British Philosophers' – A. J. Ayer

READ MORE IN PENGUIN

PENGUIN CLASSICS

A Passage to India   E. M. Forster

Centred on the unresolved mystery in the Marabar Caves, Forster's great work provides the definitive evocation of the British Raj.

The Republic   Plato

The best-known of Plato's dialogues, *The Republic* is also one of the supreme masterpieces of Western philosophy whose influence cannot be overestimated.

The Life of Johnson   James Boswell

Perhaps the finest 'life' ever written, Boswell's *Johnson* captures for all time one of the most colourful and talented figures in English literary history.

Remembrance of Things Past (3 volumes)   Marcel Proust

This revised version by Terence Kilmartin of C. K. Scott Moncrieff's original translation has been universally acclaimed – available for the first time in paperback.

Metamorphoses   Ovid

A golden treasury of myths and legends which has proved a major influence on Western literature.

A Nietzsche Reader   Friedrich Nietzsche

A superb selection from all the major works of one of the greatest thinkers and writers in world literature, translated into clear, modern English.

PENGUIN CLASSICS

Aeschylus	**The Oresteia** **(Agamemnon/Choephori/Eumenides)** **Prometheus Bound/The Suppliants/Seven** **Against Thebes/The Persians**
Aesop	**Fables**
Apollonius of Rhodes	**The Voyage of Argo**
Apuleius	**The Golden Ass**
Aristophanes	**The Knights/Peace/The Birds/The Assembly** **Women/Wealth** **Lysistrata/The Acharnians/The Clouds/** **The Wasps/The Poet and the Women/The Frogs**
Aristotle	**The Athenian Constitution** **The Ethics** **The Politics**
Aristotle/Horace/ Longinus	**Classical Literary Criticism**
Arrian	**The Campaigns of Alexander**
Saint Augustine	**City of God** **Confessions**
Boethius	**The Consolation of Philosophy**
Caesar	**The Civil War** **The Conquest of Gaul**
Catullus	**Poems**
Cicero	**The Murder Trials** **The Nature of the Gods** **On the Good Life** **Selected Letters** **Selected Political Speeches** **Selected Works**
Euripides	**Alcestis/Iphigenia in Tauris/Hippolytus/The** **Bacchae/Ion/The Women of Troy/Helen** **Medea/Hecabe/Electra/Heracles** **Orestes/The Children of Heracles/** **Andromache/The Suppliant Woman/** **The Phoenician Women/Iphigenia in Aulis**

READ MORE IN PENGUIN

PENGUIN CLASSICS

READ MORE IN PENGUIN

PENGUIN CLASSICS

NO MORE TOMORROWS

THE COMPELLING TRUE STORY OF AN INNOCENT WOMAN SENTENCED TO TWENTY YEARS IN A HELLHOLE BALI PRISON

Schapelle Corby
with *Kathryn Bonella*

MAINSTREAM
PUBLISHING

EDINBURGH AND LONDON

Copyright © Mercedes Corby and Kathryn Bonella, 2006
All rights reserved
The moral rights of the authors have been asserted

First published 2006 in Australia by Pan Macmillan Australia Pty Ltd,
1 Market Street, Sydney

First published in Great Britain in 2008 by
MAINSTREAM PUBLISHING COMPANY
(EDINBURGH) LTD
7 Albany Street
Edinburgh EH1 3UG

10

ISBN 9781845963866

This book is a work of non-fiction based on the life, experiences and
recollections of the author. In some instances, names of people have
been changed to protect the privacy of others. The author has stated to
the publishers that, except in such respects, not affecting the substantial
accuracy of the work, the contents of this book are true.

A catalogue record for this book is available
from the British Library

Typeset in Caslon and Granjon

Printed and bound in Great Britain by Clays Ltd, Elcograf S.p.A.

I dedicate this book to all those living in a waking nightmare.
There is a light at the end of the tunnel . . . just have
to wait for it . . . Bloody long tunnel.

Contents

1

Surviving Today

I T'S AMAZING WHAT THE HUMAN SPIRIT CAN ENDURE AND adapt to. If someone had told me four years ago that I would be sleeping alongside rats, feral cats and fifteen girls in a tiny, stinking-hot cell that partly floods with human waste whenever the Balinese hole-in-the-ground toilet blocks – which is fairly often – I would have said there was no way I could survive that.

If someone had told me that I'd be sentenced to this life for the next twenty years, I would have laughed at such a ridiculous notion.

Yet here I am, living in a filthy jail, sentenced to twenty years. Life is not easy – it's very, very hard. It takes a hell of a lot of energy not to collapse into a big black hole of despair, and it's happened a few times, where I struggle badly for days: I can't get out of bed, I cry all day and think about starving myself to death to escape.

But I refuse to let this place break my spirit. I use all my energy and willpower to pull myself back together. I forcibly replace negative thoughts with positive ones. Staying sane really does take a lot of energy, but I have to, out of respect for those who love me.

When I flew to Bali on 8 October 2004 with my brother James and two friends, I imagined my biggest problem was going to be deciding which sarong to wear with which bikini. I was so happy and excited to be going on this holiday – two weeks of surfing, and celebrating my sister's thirtieth birthday – especially as I'd been caring for my sick dad for a while and needed some fun. And I hadn't seen my sister, Mercedes, and her two kids for almost three months and was really missing them.

So, as I happily stepped off the plane that Friday afternoon, looking forward to a poolside beer and some cuddles from my niece and nephew, I didn't in my worst nightmares imagine the appalling turn my life was about to take.

Each day now I wake in jail with the same unbelievably intense burden of pain in my chest. It's always the same, the reality of where I am. Sometimes I wake from a nice dream thinking I'm anywhere else. But too quickly the stench, the heat, the mosquitoes, the rats and the noise tell me where I am, tell me that this disgusting, stinking prison is my world . . . for now.

I know it could be years before I taste freedom again. This is the monstrously heavy weight I wear around my heart. How long will my life continue to pass in a jail full of killers, paedophiles and terrorists who all know my name – even the Bali bomber Amrozi, the Smiling Assassin, knew it. It sent shivers down my spine when he intentionally tried to brush my shoulder as he walked past me once while I was collecting my mail. I hadn't recognised him until he'd looked into my eyes, smiled that smile at me and said, 'Corrrrby . . .'

Every day I have to walk past the prison mosque, where the Muslims taunt me, laughing at me while saying in their creepy voices, 'Ha, ha Corby, you got twenty years . . . you die in heeere.' They say it over and over, laughing away like evil clowns. It takes all my self-control not to react, and sometimes I'm so tired that I give in and scream back. I hate doing that, because I know it's exactly the reaction they're after.

Long gone are the days when I'd kick off my shoes, lie on the couch and flick on the TV to watch my favourite soap opera. There are no chairs or tables in here and only very thin camping mattresses to sleep on, if you're lucky. Some girls make do with a sarong on the concrete floor, as I did in the weeks after I was first arrested, when the guards refused to allow my sister to give me a mattress.

There is obvious sexual discrimination. If the men can afford to sling the guards some cash, they're allowed to have pretty much anything in their cells. Some men have colour TV sets, blenders, vacuum cleaners and proper bed bases and mattresses. They can also play tennis, work out at a makeshift outdoor gym and come and go from their cells pretty freely.

We women live like caged animals, locked up in our little cells for fifteen hours a day. We don't even have the simple luxury of darkness to sleep in, as the bright fluorescent cell lights are left on all night. It is so hot and cramped that I wake up every night with sweaty limbs on top of me; I get bitten by big red ants, which leave welts across my stomach and then scars. We usually have at least one rat in our cell, which skims across sleeping bodies and even around our faces. It is always stinking hot and humid, the moist tropical air perfect for breeding germs. It's no wonder we are constantly sick.

Already this place has taken a toll on my body. I don't know what diseases I might have picked up, but this place is riddled with AIDS and hepatitis, though I haven't done anything to be exposed to those. I had diarrhoea for the first two years, and I still vomit often; I suffer regularly from severe eye and ear infections, and my hair has gone prematurely grey. It's also shorter now, after I chopped my beloved waist-length hair to an inch all over a while ago – a drastic move as I'd always had long hair. But washing it in putrid jail water contributed to my constant, painful ear infections.

I don't have a full-length mirror, so I haven't seen whether I have hail damage, or cellulite, on the back of my legs, but I've noticed that most young girls in here do. I assume it's due to lack of circulation, given that we're not permitted to walk around, and we sit all day, barely moving.

Despite living in this dump, I still take pride in my appearance. Looking my best, or at least passable, has always been important to me, and I don't enjoy looking like crap even if I feel like it most of the time. I still pluck my eyebrows, I put conditioning treatments in my hair and dye it as soon as the grey roots come through. Most mornings I apply Natural Glow bronzing powder and waterproof mascara – for all the tears – and am constantly applying cherry lip gloss. I always make sure my clothes are clean and still enjoy wearing new outfits, though I'm a bit worried about losing my fashion sense. When I first cut my hair, I accessorised with hats and scarves to stop sneaky photographers taking shots of my short hair. I occasionally wear jewellery or spray on a little Gucci perfume to lift my spirits.

Making an effort with my appearance also gives me a bit of dignity in a place where that is something you really have to fight for. Just when you think you've endured every humiliation possible, something else happens, something so gross you will never forget it. There's one girl in my cell who really lives up to the expression 'appearances can be deceptive'. She's very pretty and takes great pride in doing her hair and make-up, but she is the biggest, most disgusting pig. One morning, I used the bathroom just after she'd spent her usual two hours showering and came across one of the most revolting sights I've ever seen. Her bloody sanitary pad was draped across my toothbrush, which was sitting in a cup up on a ledge.

I dry retched for a few seconds, thinking about the number of times I'd brushed my teeth without ever knowing this had been happening, and then went out to confront her.

'Ah, OK, you! Can you go and get that off my toothbrush, please?'

'Oh, I'm sorry, I forgot,' she whined.

'Yeah, thank you for forgetting today, because now at least I know to change my toothbrush. Did you do it yesterday, too, and the day before? You're a disgusting person. Get rid of it.' My mum has since bought me a toothbrush with a cover.

I've seen horrors in here that are sickening beyond belief: prisoners beaten to a pulp, kicked in the face until it's just blood and bone, girls attacking each other with broken glass bottles, a woman miscarrying in my cell and people trying to kill themselves. I've seen prisoners having sex and female guards passionately kissing female prisoners.

I shared a cell with two heroin addicts who were regularly shooting up next to me. One girl would often kneel beside me, injecting herself as I chopped up vegetables to cook on my little gas cooker. She'd spend five minutes pumping the blood in and out of the syringe to intensify the hit, while I concentrated on making my vegetable curry. It got worse. One of the girls later told me this girl often used my spoon to mix the heroin, no doubt also spilling blood onto it, then would give it a quick wipe and put it back with my things. I used it many times without knowing. Merc quickly organised a doctor to come in and give me hepatitis shots when we found out.

I've seen several suicide attempts, usually women drinking a bottle of bleach, then foaming at the mouth and twitching for the next twenty-four hours. Someone always forces coconut milk down their throats, and no female has actually died while I've been here. But men have. I found a guy hanging from the rafters in the hall with a noose around his neck early one morning. He was a guy I used to speak to often. He looked in peace, like he was sleeping, as he hung there. I felt strangely calm.

Though I haven't lived a totally sheltered life, nothing could ever have prepared me for this new one. I never know what I'll see next, but I do know that in my future there'll be many more grim, disgusting sights I can't yet even imagine. That's my reality, that's just the world I live in now.

It's impossible not to get involved in this little society, because unbelievably I'm part of it. I don't want to be here, but I don't have a choice, so I have to adapt. Though I'm spending more and more time vanishing into a daze, alone and lonely, I do still need human contact, to talk to people and interact, because I can't just shut myself down and turn off completely. I would go insane. Life goes on wherever you are.

I help other prisoners when I can and talk to them about their crimes and their sentences, which is unsurprisingly a big part of prison conversation. There's nothing else to talk about; we don't exactly have lives. I've become friends with a few people, but it's very different to my old life where friends stayed friends. In here, you're friends for a while until people show their true colours, reminding you exactly where you are and who you're living with.

It's happened many times, where I've been hurt, let down, lied to. I don't trust anyone totally, and I can't completely relax and let my guard down. I live constantly on edge. I've had a couple of nasty fights, but I've never been badly physically hurt.

My heart hurts almost non-stop. A black heaviness lives inside me, but I snatch moments of joy whenever I can to keep my spirits up. Fleetingly, I can get swept away having a good laugh or conversation with a family member or friend when they visit and can almost forget where I am. I've always had a pretty wicked sense of humour and enjoyed a naughty laugh. I still do.

I was friends for a while with another Australian girl, Renae Lawrence, who'd been caught at Denpasar airport with heroin strapped to her thighs. Stuck in this hellhole together, we sometimes created a bit of fun. In her first few months in here, she regularly made me laugh with her dramatic reactions to new horrific sights that I'd already become numb to. We share that black humour where we find someone slipping on a banana peel pretty funny. We used to joke about going to the jail canteen in our wheelchairs when we're really old – not that funny really.

One morning, I woke to find that a rat had given birth in a pair of my shoes, the pretty ones Mum had bought for me to wear to court. There were five tiny pink rats with their eyes still closed. Disgusting. But I ran to Renae's cell excitedly calling out, 'Hey, Renae, come and take a look at this. I've got something for you to see, come on.' We raced off to my cell, and Renae spun on her heel as soon as she saw them, dry retching all the way back down the path.

I also get a laugh from all the 'Schapelle' jokes that circulated after my arrest and then trial. I think I've heard most of them, as Mercedes would download the latest and bring it in for me to read. My favourites were 'the schapadlock – guaranteed for twenty years', the perfume advertisement 'Conviction . . . for the girl who's lost her appeal', and the sign on my beauty salon door: 'Back in 20!'

It might seem strange that these jokes made me laugh, but I have to make light of all this sometimes or I'd go crazy. I still can't comprehend twenty years. I won't believe it; I can't believe it. The idea of spending the next twenty years locked in a little cell is unfathomable – never to get married, never to have a baby. How can I imagine twenty years? It's nearly as long as I've been living!

Perhaps the very, very worst thing about all this is that I'm innocent. I didn't do it. I have to live this life knowing that I don't deserve to be here for one night, one hour or minute – let alone twenty years. I'm being punished for someone else's crime.

But I've been turned into a drug smuggler. I've heard all the rumours and theories. I know many people believe that I packed a transparent, pillow-sized plastic bag of marijuana into my boogie-board bag. Well . . . I didn't hide it. I didn't lock the bag, but I did put my name, address and phone number clearly on it. Then I checked it in and brazenly boarded a flight that went via two major Australian airports . . . I wasn't content to risk one airport, with a direct flight from Brisbane to Denpasar, but chose two – Brisbane and Sydney, with all their security checks. Then I willingly claimed the bag as my own when an Indonesian customs officer asked to inspect it. I don't know anything about international drug smuggling, but I guess if criminals went about it like that, they'd be pretty bloody stupid.

I was visiting Bali for a holiday and to see my sister Mercedes, her husband Wayan and their two little children. They lived in Australia but had been over there for almost three months to give the kids a taste of their dad's culture before starting school at home. Since my conviction, they've been painted as drug dealers. Rumours flew that they owned a surf shop and sold drugs there. It was ridiculous. They didn't own a surf shop, and they certainly don't have anything to do with drugs. The Bali police didn't even bother to interview either of them at any stage.

It was a situation where each bit of mud that was slung seemed to attract more mud, more innuendo, more rumour, until suddenly people thought it was all true. I used to think that innocence speaks for itself, that just by looking at me, people would see into my heart and know that I was innocent. But I've learnt a lot about people in the last four years. Now I know that to many people I'm guilty until I prove I'm innocent. And I've found that trying to prove your innocence in a foreign country, to a foreign court, with foreign lawyers and a foreign language, is not easy.

My once happy life is now a living hell. But it could soon get even worse. I live in fear that any day I could be plucked from my cell in the dead of night and taken to another prison in a remote part of Indonesia. The guards do it sporadically, without warning, without alerting family or consulates. Merc might just come in one day to find her little sister gone. It terrifies us both. It's hard to fathom, but I actually fear being taken away from Kerobokan Prison.

Some of the guards relish threatening me with being moved from here, making it part of their ongoing campaign of mental abuse. They'll often say, 'White monkey, we move you tonight.'

It frightens me that, as time passes, my real world outside these walls is fading. Not my family, they are as strong and vivid as ever. They are my rock and my lifeline. Sometimes they might say and do things that I'd rather they didn't, but I know they are trying to help, and I love them very much.

When my brother James was arrested for breaking and entering, and stealing marijuana, I guess a lot of people thought, *Well, that's it – if he's involved with drugs, then so was she.* How can you help what your family does? James was an idiot. I don't approve of what he did but I love him. And I'm certain that whatever he's done since I've been in here, as a sixteen-year-old kid going on holiday with me in 2004, he did not put that marijuana in my boogie-board bag. I was the last one to see inside it. But mud sticks.

There have been a few people who've flung mud, creating bullshit stories that are splashed as newspaper headlines, becoming often-repeated fact. I can do very little to defend myself against the lies from in here and have to rely on my family to fight the battles for me. But I get tired of repeating again and again that I'm innocent to a world that doesn't want to listen.

My beautiful sister Mercedes is incredible, and I can't believe how lucky I am to have her. I sometimes wonder if the situation were reversed, could I and would I do the same for her? I hope so. She's put her own life on hold for me, visiting most days with food and anything else I need or want, within reason.

She brings me everything from toilet paper, hair dye and chocolate – a much-needed substitute – to non-essentials like eyelash curlers and a little blow-up swimming pool. I always knew my family loved me, but if there is one positive in all of this, it is to see how loved I am.

But outside my family, I'm forgetting my life before this, and it's sad and scary. Despite mythical sightings of Schapelle Corby reported in the media, I do not get days out surfing or nightclubbing. My whole existence is within this seedy little world. The beautiful world outside is becoming just a blur.

I forget what the beach looks like, I can't remember what the water feels like when I dive in, I can't remember surfing, I can't remember the names of my close friends, I can't remember anything, I can't feel anything. I've stuck photos of the Gold Coast on my cell wall and I usually feel nothing when I look at them: no nostalgic longing for home, nothing. I'm completely numb. I'm not trying to shut things out, it's just happening. Maybe it's like when a child loses a parent and they start to forget what their mum or dad was like, what they looked like, smelt like, felt like.

It's frightening, but I think it must be a survival mechanism of the brain to keep you going day by day, a tactic to say: 'OK, this is a traumatic experience. Forget your life before this, you've got to survive today.'

2

Little S

BE CAREFUL WHAT YOU WISH FOR. LIKE LOTS OF starry-eyed kids, I grew up wanting to be famous. I imagined a glamorous and exciting world of pretty dresses and parties, of being feted and adored and pampered like a princess. Well, whoever waved the magic wand did a lousy job. Being known around the world as a notorious international drug smuggler wasn't quite what I had in mind.

There are no upsides to my dubious fame, and certainly no glamorous parties or pretty dresses. And the most pampering I've had in here is when someone rubs my back as I lean over the squat toilet throwing up from stress or food poisoning, or both.

I admit that seeing a nice photo of myself in a magazine does sometimes give me a buzz, but I can't ever forget why it's there. Being on *FHM* magazine's Sexy 100 list or *Who*'s Most Intriguing People list might be flattering for a millisecond, but little good it does me in here. If I could turn back the clock and live a life of quiet obscurity, I'd do it faster than you could say 'boogie board'.

I was born on 10 July 1977 in a hospital in Brisbane and named just before I took my first breath. My mum actually made it up. She heard a French woman in the next bed saying, '*Schapelle, schapelle.*' Between contractions, Mum thought, *Mmm, that's a nice name.* I joke with her that the French woman was probably saying something like 'Let's christen the new baby at the chapel', but in her accent it sounded like 'Schapelle'.

There are pros and cons to growing up with a name that your mum made up. No one else has it, and you don't get confused with anyone else when the teacher calls it. But you are burdened with nearly always having to repeat it.

'Michelle?'

'No, *Schapelle*.'

'Ah . . . how do you spell that?'

It was a name unique to me, thanks to Mum's creativity. But she recalls that when I started grade one she had a ridiculous dispute with my teacher over how to spell it. At the start of the year, Mum wrote 'Schapelle' on my new school books, but the teacher Tipp-Exed it out and wrote 'Schappelle'. Mum wasn't happy and a war of words raged for a few weeks as the books went back and forth between home and school. Finally, one of them gave up, and it certainly wasn't Mum, because she's doggedly determined when it comes to her kids. And this really was a fight she was entitled to win.

But the name is no longer mine alone. There is the yacht *Schapelle*, the racehorse Schapelle, and a few people have even named their babies Schapelle. Then there are the dogs, cats, birds and goldfish called Schapelle! I know about these because people have written to tell me. It's a very strange feeling to get letters from people saying they've named their goldfish after you.

I guess when I finally do go home I won't have to say my name twice or spell it out any more when I first meet someone. But sadly I know that's only because they'll know my name before I even say it; they'll know my face, know me as convicted drug smuggler Schapelle Corby. It feels so demeaning to have that title connected to my name.

It's certainly not the sort of fame I imagined as a kid, when Mercedes, our brother Michael and I held concerts in our suburban driveway. These were a highlight of my happy childhood. Merc and I were forever singing and dancing around the house, and we spent days choreographing new dances and composing songs. When we were ready, we'd teach Michael his moves and sell tickets to all our neighbours for twenty cents.

From about the time we could walk, Mum had taken Merc and me to modern, tap, jazz and classical ballet classes, which we continued for about ten years. Although I've always been a little shy, I had no qualms about dressing up in my ballet costumes and dancing and singing my heart out.

Merc, Michael and I were and still are very close, as there's just a one-year gap between each of us, descending in that order. Typically, as the baby of Mum's first batch, I learnt early on to stick up for myself – which I guess has stood me in good stead for life in this place, where guards and prisoners are always trying to push you around and mess with your head.

I can recall one night when I was about eight years old, Mercedes decided to have some fun terrifying me. We were going to sleep in our bunk beds when I heard tapping on the window and Merc saying, 'Schapelle, who's out there? Listen, Schapelle, someone's out there . . .' I was scared to death until it hit me that it was *her* tapping the window with her foot. I leapt angrily up onto her bunk, grabbed her arm and pinched it hard until, she reckons, it went numb. She was laughing a lot, saying, 'Let go, Schapelle . . . I won't do it again.' She didn't.

I had to stick up for my rights, too. Like when we did the dishes each night, Merc and Michael always got to stand on chairs to wash and dry while I was left down on the floor to put things away. I had to fight pretty hard with them sometimes to make them switch with me, because putting away was regarded as the lowliest job.

Although I'm writing about my life now, it really goes against my nature. I'm doing it to clarify a lot of the misinformation that's been written about me. To have my life trawled over has been hard, but to have so many lies reported about me has been painful and humiliating. I'm cut off from the world and only find out about things if someone tells me, so I probably haven't heard all the bad stuff. Two of the most humiliating lies were that I worked as a prostitute in Japan and that I got pregnant in jail. If you choose a life in the spotlight, I guess you also choose to accept a level of personal invasion. I didn't choose the spotlight; it chose me.

I'm essentially a private person and have never been a big fan of talking about myself or even just talking for the sake of it. In fact, one of the things I can't stand is when you meet someone and they talk and talk and talk a lot of crap and don't shut up! It irritates me. You may not even seem interested, but they still keep talking at you. I prefer to say what I have to say and then finish.

I'm a people watcher and will often just stand aside, observing, tending to look and listen more than talk. I can sit for hours lost in my thoughts as I watch the world twirl around me. I often did that in court, to pass the hours in the sweltering heat as the judges or prosecutors droned on in Indonesian and the media surrounded me like hunters ready to pounce. There was always plenty of colourful people-watching to do. It made me laugh to hear that a couple of cameramen thought I had the hots for them because I was apparently always looking at them!

But I don't want to give the impression that I'm a loner. I also love having fun and spending time with my friends and my family. Growing up in a house with six kids meant that I didn't get the chance to spend much time alone, anyway.

I was the baby for five years, until Clinton was born. By this time my parents had separated and Mum was married to Clinton's dad, Mick. My dad, Michael, left when I was about two, so I have no memory of life being any other way than Dad living up in the coalmines in central Queensland and Merc, Michael and me visiting him during school holidays. I never felt a loss or longing for my dad to be living with us, because it just seemed normal. And the split between him and my mum had been so amicable that he spent Christmases with us at Mum's and often just dropped in for a few days on a surprise visit. He'd spontaneously appear at breakfast some mornings after driving down through the night. We were always so excited to see him, and he loved to spoil us.

I can remember when I was about four years old, Merc and Michael were already at school, and I'd get Dad all to myself. I loved those days – just the two of us. We were like best mates. He'd take me to Sea World on the Gold Coast, south of Brisbane, and as soon as we'd paid the entry fee, I'd drag him by the hand over to the swinging ship ride. I loved that ride. He'd sit on it with me for two straight rides, then get off and go and stand next to the ride operator, chatting and watching me swing backwards and forwards for almost the whole day.

As we were leaving, I'd go to the shops to buy the three of us kids a big, round, rainbow-coloured lollipop each. We always got home just before Merc and Michael returned from school.

On the weekends, Dad would take all of us to Sea World, so Merc and Michael could join in, too. I'd sit on the swinging ship for most of the day again.

We always had a great time at Dad's place, too, as it was an adventure to camp on the floor of his room in the coalminers' living quarters. There was a smorgasbord restaurant that was the best in town, and as Dad worked at the mine as an auto-electrician, we could eat there for free every night. Having a sweet tooth, it was heaven for me to be able to have two desserts, even for breakfast, if I felt like it.

Dad would usually take his holidays to coincide with ours, so we could go down and hang out on his property, about three hours away at Sarina. It had its own private beach, and Merc and Michael would drive around on it endlessly in a beach buggy that Dad had built for us from old car parts. I had no interest in sitting up front, preferring instead to enjoy the ride in the back seat with my dolls and my handbag. The four of us would also go on bushwalks for hours across Dad's land.

Although he lived hundreds of kilometres away, somehow Dad knew every single thing that went on with us. Even when we got in trouble, he knew. If he'd been a fly on our wall, he couldn't have known more. We'd ask him, 'Dad, how do you know that?' He'd always answer the same: 'I've got spies, spies everywhere!' I guess Mum must have filled him in, because he never missed a trick.

We were always the centre of Dad's life, and he never left us in any shadow of a doubt that he loved us deeply and that we were very precious to him. Seeing me in here broke his heart; I saw that in his eyes every time he came to visit. I cannot accept he is now gone, it is too unbearably painful. I didn't even get a chance to say goodbye before he died in January 2008. I loved my dad so much and I guess I always stayed his baby, as he didn't have any more kids.

Mum calls me her baby, too, although she went on to have three more. Her fourth, Clinton, has always been difficult, and, as has been widely reported, he's spent time in and out of jail. He has a problem: he's a kleptomaniac. My family still tries to look after Clinton, because we love him and we're always hoping that one day he'll learn and change. Life works in mysterious ways, and I think maybe what's happened to me is giving him the will to change. He's got a job, and liking the rewards of earning his own money and buying his own things *legally*. We're proud of him and I love him.

James and Mele are numbers five and six, to Mum's third partner, whom we call 'Big James'. Little James was always a good kid, very quiet and law-abiding. He even made school captain. Mele is the true baby of the family and was like my baby doll, whom I dressed up and pampered, as I was twelve when she was born. We were very close, and it hurts that I have not been around to help her grow, to answer her questions about teenage life and just be there for her any time she needed me.

Growing up with so many brothers and sisters was great fun, and we did a lot together – like bike riding or camping at the beach most summer weekends, squeezing into our little tents. Mum never showed any favouritism; she shared her love, her time and her affections evenly with all of us. And none of us ever classed each other as a half-brother or half-sister – we're all the same. It wasn't until my story hit the headlines that the media started differentiating between us, using the terms 'half-brother' and 'half-sister' and talking about the fact that we had three different fathers.

The media made my family life look like a disgrace, as if we'd had some desperately deprived childhood – which is so far from the truth. We were not rich, but we were certainly loved and never went without. We almost always got what we asked for; we'd just have to wait until Mum had saved up for it. She worked several factory jobs and deprived herself of things so she could give more to us. If I wanted a $100 pair of shoes, Mum would buy them for me when she was able to. She did the best she possibly could for us and gave us all she could. She still does. Other kids in our neighbourhood and at school said that we were spoilt.

And growing up with three different male figures in the house had no effect on me at all. I only had one dad and I saw a lot of him. Getting used to the other two didn't bother me or seem at all strange. I just went with the flow. We always had a lot of love in our house and a very strong sense of family and of security.

I guess I've always had Merc, as well. I can't really talk about my life without talking about my sister in the same breath, because she's played such a defining role in it. All my life, she's looked after me with such love and devotion. She's always been there for me, encouraging me, teaching me and protecting me. I guess I thought that's what big sisters were invented for, although I never imagined I'd end up depending on her for almost every basic essential in life.

As kids, if Mum wasn't home (usually because she was working late), Merc would snap into the role. She'd cook us dinner, prepare our school lunches and generally make sure we were OK. She was and still is my best friend. If I ever needed to talk to someone, I talked to Merc, and do now. We've always done everything together and shared everything; we shared a bedroom, we shared clothes, we shared friends, we shared secrets.

Back when we were kids, we'd spend hours sitting together in the backyard making clover-chain necklaces or picking Mum's best flowers, crushing them and then squeezing them into little bottles to make perfume. Mum's dressing table was always covered in these bottles of our stinky 'flower perfume'. We also sold them to our good-sport neighbours for twenty cents a bottle. Merc and I would go bike riding together, take dancing classes together, play with our dolls together, watch TV together and just hang out. We were virtually inseparable.

Mum used to dress us in matching outfits, as if we were her little blonde and brunette twins, but our personalities were as different as our hair colour. For instance, I like things to be neat and perfectly ordered, while Merc is the untidiest person I know – although Mum comes close. Merc's messiness used to annoy me so much that when we shared a bedroom I placed an imaginary line down the centre of the room, and the deal was that she had to keep her junk on her side of the line. As a result, our dressing table had one side almost bare and the other like an overflowing tip. My invisible line usually ended up becoming pretty visible. Thankfully, we did have separate wardrobes, because no invisible line could have survived that chaos. The bottom of her wardrobe was piled so high with shoes and clothes that it would meet the clothes of hers that were hanging – although there were usually few of those.

I must admit, though, that even with all her big messy piles of school papers and hoarded junk sprawled across her side of the room, Merc could always instantly lay her hands on anything she wanted. I, on the other hand, had a place for everything and didn't hoard a thing but could never find what I wanted, except a use for something that I'd thrown out a week ago.

Apart from being a lot neater, I was also more reserved. I find it uncomfortable sparking up conversations with people I don't know – though I've been forced to do so lately – and instinctively tend to hold back before trusting anyone. Merc, on the other hand, is a born extrovert who loves to talk to everyone, from the person next to her in the supermarket queue to the Queen of Sheba. She always sees the best in people, tending to trust them instantly. It's a beautiful trait and one of the reasons why she's so special, but it can also be very dangerous when you're thrown into deep trouble like this, with all kinds of people crawling out of the woodwork to 'help'. Her open and trusting nature has taken a battering over the last few years, as we've both been burnt by people we'd put our trust in.

A lot of the things I've done in my life have been as a result of being swept along in Merc's current. I can happily just drift, quietly whiling away the hours daydreaming, drawing or watching TV. A day like that would send Merc crazy. She knows how to use time wisely and likes to get the maximum out of each day. She's dynamic, always on the go, creating things to do and encouraging me along with her.

I should stress here that I'd often go with the flow but would never do anything I didn't actually want to do. I was always good at digging my heels in and not budging. I can be stubborn. Nobody, for instance, could have convinced me to put that marijuana in my boogie-board bag.

After Merc and I quit our ballet lessons, she booked us into taekwondo classes. Then, when I was about fifteen, I followed Merc and Michael into the local surf club, which is where I fatefully discovered my love for boogie-boarding.

To me, boogie-boarding was the perfect compromise between the thrill of riding the waves and the danger of being slashed by a sharp surfboard fin: it was still challenging and fun, but not too scary. Merc was into surfboarding, though, and was totally fearless; often her feet didn't even touch the board – she'd catch a wave so fierce that she'd be wiped out. The three of us also trained as lifeguards, and every weekend we'd put on our uniforms and patrol the beaches. I didn't rescue anyone, but Michael, who became a full-time council lifeguard, saved a man and his son from drowning after they were dragged far out to sea in a rip.

I've always had a passion for sport and at school was much more successful outside the classroom than in it. Despite my projects being beautifully presented, I wasn't exactly a straight-A student. But on the sports field, it was blue ribbons all the way. All through my school years, I could outrun the wind.

During my first-ever race day, in grade one, I flew past the finish line so many lengths ahead of the other girls that I was put in the boys' race and won that, too. The excited sports teacher, who was keen to test my limits, then raced me against girls a year older, followed by the boys from the same age group. I kept winning. My limit was finally reached when I was narrowly beaten by a boy two years older than me. My mum was cheering from the sidelines and says that it was one of the proudest days of her life. I was invited to join Little Athletics when I was a bit older, but didn't. I also really loved touch football and was team captain every year in high school.

I was placid, easy-going and usually laughing at something, so much so that in primary school, teachers nicknamed me 'Giggling Gertie'. I've always found little things in daily life funny, although it's getting harder to see them these days. One of my primary school teachers wrote to me recently, saying I was the student she least expected to ever get into trouble.

I was good, but I wasn't perfect. In high school, for instance, I did have the occasional puff on a cigarette and the occasional beer, although Mum was strictly against me doing either. And though it may now hold significance in some people's minds, like many teenagers I tried smoking marijuana. It's hard for me to write about this because of what marijuana has done to my life and the judgements some people will make, but I feel I shouldn't have to hide it. A bit of teenage experimentation doesn't make me guilty of smuggling marijuana ten or so years later. I've got absolutely nothing to hide, and from the very start of all this, in an interview with *60 Minutes* just a couple of weeks after I was arrested, I readily admitted to having experimented with marijuana.

I first tried it when I was about fourteen years old and had gone down to the Gold Coast for the weekend with a group of friends from the surf club. There were around eight of us and everyone wanted to try it, so we each chipped in $5. On the Saturday afternoon, we walked down to the beach, sat in a circle between the rocks, for a windbreak, and prepared to smoke the dope through a Coke can. As we talked and laughed, we started taking turns and passing it on, usually with a lot of coughing and spluttering. I was feeling pretty curious but also awkward and shy because I didn't know how to do it. I watched carefully as the can was passed around, so when it was my turn, I just put my mouth over the can and drew back. It was harder than it looked, and the thick smoke sent me into a coughing fit. I tried a couple more times and soon my coughing fits were followed by fits of uncontrollable laughter.

When everyone had had a couple of turns, we packed up and walked up the hill, still laughing away at absolutely anything. That night I had a great sleep. We tried it a couple more times the following day, but I didn't seem to laugh as much as before. Instead,

I just felt lazy and extremely hungry, and each time I'd end up in a takeaway shop.

I was bored with it and after that weekend didn't try it again until I was eighteen. I had maybe one or two puffs at a couple of parties, but I soon learnt that dope wasn't good for me. It had such a weird effect on my mind. It made me feel so paranoid that I wouldn't even speak to my friends, and afterwards I'd lock myself in my room, not wanting to answer the phone or the door. I was left with a horrible feeling of self-loathing and a depressing, distorted way of looking at the world.

I've known since then that I can't smoke pot, because it doesn't agree with the chemicals in my brain. I didn't touch it again after I was eighteen, and became quite anti marijuana-smoking. I refused to even talk to anyone who was stoned, because they would usually be so out of it, with those sad red eyes.

Although I did like school, I decided to quit when I was sixteen so I could earn my own money. I can now see that that was a big mistake, as I've come to understand the importance of education and will urge my kids – because I will have some one way or another – to finish school. But at the time, Mum didn't fight with me, as she thought I'd want to return to school as soon as I'd discovered work wasn't that much fun. She just said, 'OK, darl, what do you want to do?' I didn't really know what I wanted to do at that stage, so I just started working at the local supermarket as a checkout girl.

Not long after this I had a bit of a teenage identity crisis. I gave up wearing my usual colourful dresses and skirts and started wearing a lot of black. There was no specific reason for my radical style change, and my attitude and personality didn't alter with it, but it worried Mum enough for her to send me to live with Dad at Middle Mount, the coalmining town where he was based.

Wow, it was boring . . . even for me, who rarely feels bored. There's nothing in Middle Mount but mines, and living there would make living inside a cardboard box seem interesting. Everyone who lives there works in the mines. The whole town is owned by the mines, and it looks a bit like Lego Land, because there are only three styles of house. You could only tell the difference between them by the car in the driveway or the kids on the dry front lawn.

For all the years that Dad had worked there, he'd lived in his single room in the men's quarters. But now he had a daughter moving in, so he was allowed to rent one of the houses; and out of a selection of three identical vacant homes, he made his choice by the distinguishing feature of kids. We moved into a house that was across the road from a family with a daughter about my age. They'd also just moved up to Middle Mount from civilisation. Jay and I got along really well, and it was good to have another outsider with me, although I vaguely knew some of the local teenagers from our school-holiday sojourns, and they were very welcoming.

But there was just so little to do. It's hard to describe the nothingness of that town. It's so small that if you wanted to shop for anything other than basic groceries, you had to make a day of it and drive 500 kilometres to the next town of Emerald, which was only slightly better. And if you wanted a swim to escape the oppressive heat, it was a three-hour drive to the closest crocodile-infested mangrove.

I would hang out with Jay, go for walks, do a bit of gardening and watch the one TV channel we could pick up, but I was so bored. I made a few bus trips back to Brisbane because I also missed home.

Despite all this, most of the time I didn't mind Middle Mount. It gave me the chance to spend time with my dad, just the two of us. Some nights we'd drive along the straight road out of town until there was nothing but bush and wildlife surrounding us. He'd stop the car and turn the headlights off, and I'd sit up on the bonnet as we gazed up at the night sky. The stars were magnificent from that spot: no city lights, no streetlights, no lights at all to interrupt their brightness.

I could see every star; the entire sky was covered with twinkling diamonds. I miss that sky. I would always pick out the brightest star of the night and think of Grandpa, my dad's dad, who died when I was very young. I've always believed he's the brightest star shining down, looking over me. I remember having a hard time understanding why Grandpa had to die, and Mum took us kids outside when we were all upset and crying and pointed up to that brightest star and said, 'There's Grandpa.' On some nights now I can just catch a glimpse of the stars through the bars of my little cell window, and I still look up for the brightest star, to see if Grandpa is there. It's nice for me to feel he's here, and it keeps his spirit going.

I liked those nights with just Dad and me. On his days off, we'd also go driving along the open roads with the windows down, listening and singing along to his favourite songs. We'd drive into other towns and down to his beach property at Sarina. I had my learner's permit by this time, and sometimes Dad would pull over and we'd swap seats for a bit, but soon enough I'd be asking him to drive again. Our drives were just something to do, and I really loved hanging out with my dad.

One day out of the blue, I got a call from Merc, asking if I wanted to take a holiday with her and Michael in Bali. She was living in Japan at this point, on a working-holiday visa, and was returning to Japan from a break at home. Bali was a stopover from Australia to Tokyo on Garuda Airlines. I'd never been overseas before, and Merc thought it would be fun for me – and a break from Middle Mount. I jumped at the chance, never imagining that in just a matter of years this little island paradise would grant me my childhood wish in the most hellish of ways.

3

Travel

THE MERE THOUGHT OF GETTING ON AN AEROPLANE now makes my hands tremble and my eyes fill with tears. I've got such an acute fear of flying that I'm pretty sure when I do finally go home, I'll be sailing back. My last flight ripped apart my life and is still causing me so much grief and pain that the simple travel routine of packing bags, driving to the airport and checking in petrifies me. Although I may not have to worry for a while, I can't imagine ever doing it again. I guess it's like falling off a horse: you've got to jump straight back on before the fear becomes part of you. For me, it's already been too long.

But rewinding to my first-ever plane flight, back in 1995, a flight that took me to the same place as my last, I had no such fears. Quite the opposite. I was relaxed, carefree and excited as I stepped onto the plane for my first overseas holiday. It's ironic that the country I picked for my initial taste of freedom and independence was the country that would ultimately slam the cell door shut on those two precious things.

I didn't fall in love with Bali; in fact, I was pretty unimpressed. It was dirty, with stinky open sewers along the sides of the roads, and we were constantly hassled by hawkers crooning, 'Plait your hair, me plait your hair', or trying to sell us fake Gucci sunglasses.

The tourist hot spots were so full of poverty – crammed with beggars, homeless children, hairless skinny dogs and cigarette-smoking monkeys. We drove out of the hustle and bustle to lots of remote beaches, and those beaches, in my opinion, were its only saving grace. I loved tracking single file through the jungle, with our boards under our arms, until the wilderness opened up to reveal crystal-clear waters as far as the eye could see. But I didn't imagine that after that holiday Bali would make any further imprint on my life.

On that first visit, I took my boogie board, as I was already pretty serious about surfing. Merc had won it in a motorised surfboard competition in a Gold Coast bar, as part of the bigger prize of a trip to Bali. That was her first trip to the island, in 1992. She was seventeen at the time, and it blazed the way for her and consequently my connections with Bali and Asia.

I waved goodbye to Merc after our holiday together, not knowing when I'd see her again, as she was flying back to Japan. She'd moved there on an eighteen-month working-holiday visa to experience another language and culture, as she's always hungry to taste life. Michael and I had another week of surfing before he flew back to Brisbane and I went home to Lego Land.

Life in Middle Mount didn't change much when you were there, but it had changed a little while I was away – it seemed to have become duller! I guess Bali's strong colours and culture really highlighted Middle Mount's lack of both. Although I'd spent just six months in the town, it felt much longer, and my life was really going nowhere. So when Merc phoned about two months after I'd returned from Bali and invited me to go to live with her in Japan for a couple of months, it was great news.

'Oh, really?'

'Yeah, get your passport and come.' Merc thought it would be good for me and she even paid for my flight. I was seventeen.

I guess we rarely know what huge impact a little step in the short term might have on our life in the long term – that one small step can change the whole direction of our life. Going to Japan for two months was the catalyst for a whole new chapter in my life: my 'secret life', as one of the women's magazines bizarrely headlined it. But it was no secret to anyone who knew me.

Merc was excitedly waiting for me at Tokyo's Narita International Airport, and it wasn't hard to spot her blonde head among the dark-haired crowd as I went through customs. She was living about 600 kilometres away, in a seaside town called Toyama, and had taken an overnight train in order to meet me. After hugs and tears, we took a taxi to a city hotel she'd booked, where we shared a very small but expensive room and bed for the night. It was nice but so small that there was only just enough space to walk around the bed sideways breathing in. I guess in a city with 22 million people, space is an expensive luxury. Early the next morning, we took a cab back to Narita and flew to Toyama.

I've got a crystal-clear memory of that flight. We must have gone too high too fast for my body to adjust to the altitude, and I seized up. I literally couldn't move. My head was cocked at a weird angle. Merc was sleeping soundly beside me, and despite my desperate attempts for almost the entire one-and-a-half-hour flight, I failed to wake her. My body freed up just as we started descending and naturally just as Merc woke up, stretching like a contented cat and purring about what a great sleep she'd had. I was an exhausted wreck. She was oblivious.

The ten weeks in Toyama passed quickly. Just as I'd done as a kid, I followed Merc around like a shadow. We took judo classes and a Japanese language course together, although Merc had been there for almost six months by then and was close to fluent. She was working several casual jobs, including serving in a noodle bar, hostessing in a restaurant and teaching English conversation to old Japanese women in a combined language–cooking class. It was amusing to watch. Merc would simply describe in English what the cooking teacher was doing, like, 'Crack the egg and put it in the bowl.'

Some days Merc's Japanese friends would take me sightseeing when she went to work. Japan was an eye-opening, awesome experience and a wonderful place to visit but, as I discovered a few years later, not to live in.

I returned to Australia and moved to the Gold Coast, unsure of what I'd do next and unaware that my connection with Japan was about to intensify. I'd been home for about two months when I spotted a cute Japanese boy standing in front of a huge triangular stack of oranges in the fruit section of the supermarket at Pacific Fair. If I hadn't have just been to Japan I wouldn't have given him a second glance, as I'd never found Japanese guys attractive before. But I thought, *Mmm, he's cute . . . Cool, I'll go and speak some Japanese.* During the whole ten weeks I really only learnt to say 'Hi, my name is Schapelle. How are you?' and '123456789', but I still thought I was pretty smart.

So I went up to this guy and said in Japanese, 'Hi, how are you?'

'Ah, who . . . is it me you talk to?' he replied, pointing at his nose.

I just thought, *Oh, my God, that's so Japanese . . . Of course I'm talking to you, but I'm not sure I want to any more!*

I said goodbye, and as I turned to walk away, I saw him pull an orange from the very bottom of the stack. My first thought was *Noooo!* – but it was too late and he sent them flying, like a scene straight out of a Ben Stiller movie.

I confess I didn't help him pick them up, because by this point I was thinking, *What an idiot.* I walked off to finish my shopping. But as I stood in line to pay, he approached me, wanting to continue our abruptly ended conversation. His name was Kimi and, incredibly, he came from Toyama. He'd spent just one month in Australia on a twelve-month working-holiday visa.

He seemed nice enough, but after I'd paid for my groceries I said goodbye again and went to catch my bus. A few minutes later as I was about to board, he came running over and asked for my phone number. As I'm not used to saying 'no' and still thought he was kind of cute-looking, I gave it to him.

When he called me two weeks later, I invited him to come to my eighteenth birthday party the following night. After that, he shadowed me almost everywhere, every day, just as I used to do to Merc. I liked him and really enjoyed his constant company, but it took almost six months before we became boyfriend and girlfriend. By the time his visa ran out a few months later, we were in love.

He was my first love and I guess my first real boyfriend. I'd had a boyfriend in high school, but we didn't actually even kiss because I had braces on my teeth.

Kimi and I decided that the simplest solution to his visa expiring was for both of us to move to Japan. Being so young and in love, I had no doubts, and I knew Australia would always be home and I could always come back. As it turned out, I could only get a maximum three-month holiday visa, so we regularly returned home to allow me to renew it. By this stage, Merc was no longer living in Japan; she'd moved to Bali with her Balinese boyfriend, Wayan.

Kimi and I moved to an old fishing village called Omaezaki, which is about four hours south of Tokyo by car. The village gets very strong winds and, as a result, is renowned for its windsurfing. It's even on the pro circuit. Each year during the pro event, the town would transform into an international hot spot, and in the years I was there, I was given the prestigious job of timekeeper: holding the stopwatch, giving the countdown and blowing the horn as I sat with the judges. The honour had been passed on to me from an English friend who'd had a baby.

Omaezaki is also well known for its energy windmills and, unfortunately, its nuclear plant. Once a year, we'd get a knock on the front door from the plant's reps, giving us a thank-you card with 50,000 yen (about $60) inside. Every home in the town got the cash and card as a little goodwill token/bribe, to say thanks for not protesting. But we should have protested. It wasn't healthy. I'll never forget the day when I was surfing with Kimi and some friends on a popular little break just in front of the nuclear plant. I had an appalling reaction to what must have been chemicals in the water. Within minutes of being in the surf, my face blew up like a puffer fish, turning my eyes to slits. I was sneezing uncontrollably and the pain in my sinuses was so excruciating I thought they'd explode. I got out fast, refusing to ever surf there again.

We lived a simple life in a very old and traditional Japanese house, which we shared with a couple of Kimi's windsurfer mates. The amenities were so basic that they were remarkably similar to the ones here in Kerobokan, but the big difference is I kept them pristine and we didn't have to share with fifteen others. We had an old squat toilet and used a bucket and ladle for showering, just like I do now. It's almost like I had training.

Though it was basic, Kimi and I loved our little house and enjoyed making it into our home. We had two rooms in the attic, which we spent weeks doing up, one as our bedroom and the other as a TV and living room. Being completely immersed in another culture, I felt free and creative and spent a lot of time painting. Kimi would drive me to Tokyo to buy canvases and paints to do oil paintings. I was also into painting glass bottles and asked every guest to our home to take a seat and paint a glass bottle, too. I had a big collection, which I displayed in the toilet in an optimistic attempt to distract from the toilet itself. The house was so decrepit that as soon as we moved out it was demolished.

Kimi worked as a seasonal tea farmer and also as a surfboard-shaper in his mate Mitchi's surfboard factory and shop. We all spent a lot of time hanging out there, usually before and after a surf. We lived to surf in those days, and I became pretty good at it, easily dropping to one knee, doing 360s and catching the big powerful waves that came through during the cyclone season. I'd come to really love my boogie-boarding.

At first I couldn't get any work and spent the days cooking Kimi lunch and hanging out at the surf shop with him. I had two Western girlfriends who lived in the town, one from England, who was married to a pro windsurfer, and the other from Canada, who taught English. But generally it was a bit boring.

Eventually I found a job at the town's hotel. It was gruelling, as I started at dawn preparing breakfast and rolling up the futons, then cycled home for a quick lunch, before returning to help prepare dinner and roll out the futons. I also got some work doing seasonal farming for small farmers of strawberries, melons and tobacco. Kimi and I would spend days out in a field working with a team of really old, hunchback Japanese women.

We lived frugally. Our rent was only $80 a month and surfing costs nothing, but we were always struggling to save enough money for air tickets back to Australia. Within the first two years of living in Japan, we came home about six times to renew my visa and see my family. We'd sometimes stay in Australia for a couple of months so I could spend time with my family, and I'd get a casual job. During these trips, we'd often drive down the coast for a week or two, just camping and surfing. Merc was still living in Bali during this time, so we sometimes took advantage of the Garuda stopover to drop in to see her.

But immigration both in Australia and Japan were starting to give us a hard time when it came to obtaining our visas, and we were also getting tired of the constant expense. So it reached a point where it was either split up or get married. I hate saying it like that, because it sounds like we got married just for a visa, but the truth is we were really in love and neither of us wanted to let go.

Kimi was five years older than me and had often said 'Let's get married' during our first two years together. I was a bit daunted by the idea and kept stalling, saying, 'Yeah, OK, one day . . . later.' I clearly recall the night I finally agreed. There was no diamonds-and-champagne proposal and big 'Oh, I will! I will!' reaction. We were in our TV room, talking about our future, and he said, 'Ah . . . maybe we'll get married now?' This time it was do or die, so I said, 'I'll just call my mum and my sister.' It was important to me that they thought it was a good idea. I might have seen Mum marry and divorce, but for me marriage was for ever. And I really believed Kimi was 'the one', which was a bit naive, I guess, given that he was my first boyfriend and I was only twenty.

I phoned Mum and Merc, and they both just excitedly said, 'Congratulations.' So it was as low key as putting the phone down and saying, 'OK, let's get married.' And that was that.

We started making plans, but then things began to unravel. Though we hadn't set a date yet, I got quite excited about our wedding day and went and bought a pretty mauve silk slip dress with a chiffon cover and ordered some wedding invitations. I thought we'd have a small wedding party in Japan and then a bigger one in

Australia with all my friends and family: after all, I was the bride. But Kimi had other ideas, which was the first sign that the two of us wouldn't work out. He'd been brought up in a culture where men controlled and women obeyed, especially once they're married.

One morning, a couple of weeks after we'd agreed to marry, we were enjoying our usual early surf when Kimi abruptly said to me, 'Let's go.' I assumed he needed to get to work early, so we paddled in, loaded the gear in the car and drove off. We weren't heading home, but he refused to tell me where we were going, which he had started to do a bit and which annoyed the hell out of me. He pulled up at Omaezaki's town hall and leapt out of the car, calling back, 'Aren't you coming?'

So with my hair still soaking wet, and dressed in my board shorts and bikini top, I traipsed behind him into an office and unwittingly signed our marriage certificate. I didn't know what I was signing and just assumed it was some bank document. As we got back into the car, he said, 'We're married.' My jaw dropped and tears sprang to my eyes as I looked at him. We drove home in silence, and I refused to talk to him for the next two weeks. His best friend saw how hurt I was and gave me a beautiful bunch of flowers, saying, 'Congratulations.'

I guess the only way to explain it is to say that it was very Japanese.

Things went downhill from there. Once I was his wife, Kimi became more controlling, always wanting to know where I was. The cultural and language differences were becoming more of a problem rather than less. And combined with the nagging loneliness I felt, and homesickness, little things started to annoy me, like having to explain a simple joke.

It wasn't all bad. We still had some good times together – otherwise we'd never have stayed together for another two years.

I tried to teach him not to control me so much, and he tried. He was also sensitive to my loneliness; he's a nice guy and did want to help me feel less homesick, taking me camping in the Japanese countryside or on a surfing trip for a few days. We still really enjoyed each other's company most of the time.

Looking back, I think most of Kimi's friends could see how homesick I was, even more than I realised myself. They always tried their best to speak with me and help me to feel comfortable, although we struggled to understand each other. I spoke a decent amount of Japanese by this stage, but most of Kimi's friends weren't Omaezaki natives and spoke different dialects, which were often like another language.

But in the end, the loneliness, the language barrier and homesickness got the better of me. I didn't want to feel so lonely for the rest of my life, which at that time I had the feeling I might, especially if I got stuck there with kids. I missed my mum and I missed Australia, and I just wanted to go home. We decided it was best if I did; it was a mutual thing. Kimi and I had stayed married for two years, although if there hadn't been a piece of paper involved, I might have left earlier. My belief in marriage as a lifelong commitment had kept me holding on, but eventually I realised I was young and unhappy and I didn't have to stay. I'm just grateful we didn't have babies.

It was late June 2000, just two weeks before my twenty-third birthday, when I called Mum and told her the news, and asked if she'd meet me in Bali for a break on my way home. My devoted mum didn't hesitate to jump on a plane, and we spent two happy weeks together enjoying each other's company, snorkelling and dolphin watching. It was so good to see her and, rather than being sad, I was simply relieved to be going home.

I had packed up my life fairly neatly, taking with me just a suitcase full of clothes and my bag with my new $400 yellow boogie board, which I'd bought in Japan, and my flippers. I used the board to surf in Bali while Mum sat on the beach watching and having her nails painted. The next trip I made to Bali was four years later, with the same boogie board, same bag and same flippers.

This time, though, the board wouldn't make it into the water. It was incinerated instead.

Although Kimi and I stayed in touch for a year or so, sending Christmas cards and birthday presents and talking on the phone sometimes, all contact gradually died off as we both moved on with our lives. I haven't heard from him while I've been in Kerobokan, nor do I expect to. It's been eight years since I left Japan and he's got a new life with a new wife and kids. The first he knew about me being in jail would most likely have been when one of the women's magazines tracked him down to get the story of my 'secret life'. According to the article, we were married for just three months.

By the time I arrived back in Queensland, Merc was living there again with her new husband Wayan. After being together for five years, they'd decided to get married when Merc learnt she was pregnant. Kimi and I had gone to the wedding, which took place in Bali in March 1999, along with all of my other siblings, Mum and Dad, and various aunties, uncles and cousins. It was a huge event, and in marked contrast to mine. Merc and Wayan were already living in Australia by the time they were married and flew back to Bali for the ceremony. It was a Hindu wedding, lasting a month, as Merc had decided to convert to Wayan's religion.

Back in Australia, Dad had bought a two-storey duplex on the Gold Coast as an investment, and I moved in upstairs with my brother Michael. Merc, Wayan and their two little kids, Wayan and Nyeleigh, lived downstairs. So, just like old times, we were all together again, which put me back in my comfort zone after Japan.

Life moved along happily. I was working a couple of jobs – one in the ANA Hotel galleria and another tour-guiding Japanese people – and after about a year I had a new boyfriend, Shannon. He's had his share of unwanted publicity since my arrest, with a couple of photos of us stirring debate. I know about this because Merc brought in the articles, which showed what people said looked like a joint in an ashtray. It was a Marlboro Light. Although I'm anti dope-smoking, I do smoke cigarettes occasionally, and it was my cigarette in that ashtray.

Our relationship lasted about two years, before Shannon and I both realised it wasn't quite right. I was single for eighteen months before coming to Bali.

Growing up, I always loved playing with make-up, doing facials and all those girly things. So, as I was still just doing odd jobs at this point, Mum suggested that maybe I should study to become a beautician. I agreed and began a year-long course in 2003. I had one unit to finish when Dad was diagnosed with prostate cancer.

For ages he'd complained of lower-back pain, and he'd been told by his doctor to take a course of antibiotics and stop drinking beer for a week or two. The doctor diagnosed it as a urinary tract infection. When they finally gave him the proper tests, Dad was told he had six months to live, as not only did he have prostate cancer but it had also spread to his bones. He got a second opinion and that doctor was more optimistic, telling him he could maybe go on for a few more years.

At first, Merc and the kids moved in with Dad, on his land up north, but it got too difficult for her and she was spending too much time away from Wayan. We organised a nurse to check on Dad every couple of days, but one day she found him collapsed at home. I decided that it was time for me to look after my dad, just like he'd always looked after me. I drove up in my old Toyota Corolla and brought him back to the Gold Coast to live with me in 2004.

Merc's father-in-law had also had cancer and had died recently in Bali. So in July of that fateful year, she and Wayan went to Bali for five months, planning to be home by Christmas. It meant that Wayan could spend some time with his little brother and that their kids could get a taste of Balinese culture before little Wayan started school in Australia the following year.

Merc was determined that her kids would have a good education and wanted them to be schooled in Australia. Merc and Wayan had argued over it, as both wanted to live in their own country – the age-old problem with international relationships – but eventually they agreed it would be Australia.

The idea for a group of us to go to Bali that October to help

Merc celebrate turning thirty wasn't a spontaneous hit. She was a bit depressed by the whole idea of leaving her twenties behind, but, as a few friends talked about coming over for a party, she gradually warmed to the idea. In the end, about sixteen of us were going to be there for the big night. It would turn out to be a bigger night than any of us had expected.

4

Bali Bound

LIFE DIDN'T GIVE ME ANY WARNING THAT IT WAS ABOUT to take a radical turn. The normality of my existence gave me no clue as to what lay ahead. Now those simple happy days are just a relic of another life: a surreal memory.

Two nights before I flew to Bali, I was sitting and talking with Dad, enjoying a beer as I glued the ripped plastic on the top of my boogie board. I'd spent the day cleaning the house and stocking the fridge so that Dad would be OK for the two weeks I'd be gone.

The night before I flew to Bali was just as normal. I slept in a bed with my little sister Mele, while my travelling buddies Katrina, Ally and brother James were in the other beds. We were all staying at Mum's, as she was just twenty-five minutes from the airport and we had a 6 a.m. flight.

'I believe the seven months I have been in prison is severe enough punishment for not putting locks on my bags,' I said to the judges at my trial. It wasn't a crime, but it was dangerously foolish not to lock my bags. I sure know that now, but it's a bit late. I can't believe that on the morning of the flight, I actually mocked Katrina for putting locks on her bag.

It was the joke of the morning when we noticed Katrina, the virgin traveller, had carefully put locks on her suitcase but had already lost her key. We thought it was hysterical – our nervous little travelling mate. I was the one making a big deal. 'What are you doing?' I teased. 'You don't need to lock your bag; you're only going to Bali! And you've lost your key anyway! Ha ha ha!'

How I've eaten those words.

At the airport, Ally, Katrina and I checked our bags in under my name, as I'd booked our flights. We were told to take the boogie board up to the oversized-luggage counter. Meanwhile, James was checking in at another desk with Mum, as she'd bought his ticket separately after he decided to come along at the last minute.

We all went together to check in the boogie board. Then Mum said, 'Quick, quick, a photo!' and took a snap of the four of us, right beside the counter where my fate had just been sealed. I had no idea this snap would come to represent my last hours of freedom, my last hours as a carefree young girl. I felt so relaxed and happy. It was easy to smile for the camera.

I hadn't wanted to fly via Sydney, but all the direct flights had been fully booked. I'd waited until the last minute to confirm our flight, hoping that seats on a direct one would come up, but none did. If it annoyed me at the time that we each had to pay an extra couple of hundred dollars for the privilege of wasting three and a half hours in transit, now it really pisses me off. I believe that if I'd flown direct, I probably wouldn't be where I am today.

During the flight from Sydney, I sat next to Ally, and we were pretty merry after having a couple of beers in the international terminal and then a few more on the plane. Feeling tipsy, I think we spent most of the six-hour flight laughing at nothing. I hadn't been to Bali since meeting up with Mum there in mid-2000 on my way back from Japan, and I'd never flown overseas with my good friends before. I was well into the holiday spirit.

So as we got off the plane at Ngurah Rai Airport at about 3.30 p.m., I had no sense of foreboding that within minutes my life as I knew it would be finished, for good.

I walked over to the baggage carousel and collected my suitcase but couldn't see my boogie-board bag. A second or two later, I spotted it on the ground several metres away and went to pick it up. The little handle I normally used to carry it had been cut. *Nasty people, who'd do that?* I wondered, grabbing it by a shoulder strap on the other side. Ally saw me struggling with all my bags – my boogie board, my suitcase and my little blue carry-on bag – and sang out to James, 'Go help your sister!' He did, dragging the boogie board along with his own stuff to the customs counter. Ally and Katrina had already gone through without having their bags checked and were waiting for us.

James put his suitcase up onto the counter first and opened it for inspection. The customs officer might have been a bit shocked to see that James's case was crammed full of tuna tins. He's super-healthy and into body sculpting, and he never leaves home without a supply of protein-filled tuna. But the officer just zipped it back up. He then pointed to the boogie-board bag and asked James, 'Is that yours?'

I was in high spirits, oblivious to being seconds away from my life turning to hell. I cheerfully picked the bag up off the floor and placed it on the counter, saying, 'No, no, it's mine. Here you go . . .' Almost in the same movement I went to unzip the bag. He didn't ask me to; I just did it. It all happened fast, as I had nothing to hide.

I noticed that the two zips were done up in the middle, which surprised me, because I always did them up to the left side. Any bag with two zippers I always did up to the side, never in the middle. Pedantic, but that's me. So I thought, *Oh, that's strange*. But like all the slightly odd things that happened, I didn't think too much about it at the time. After all, this bag only had my flippers and boogie board in it. It didn't even cross my mind that someone might have actually put something *into* the bag.

I may have paused momentarily when I noticed the zips, but things were still moving quickly. Then time stopped dead.

As I opened my boogie-board bag, I was struck by the sight of something I knew I hadn't put in there. *Whoa!* I reeled back slightly. My heart stopped. I knew what it looked like but wasn't sure. I shot a look at the customs officer to see if he'd seen it, too. I couldn't tell. In a panic, in shock, I shut it fast. The unmistakable smell of marijuana flew up and hit me in the face. My hands started to tremble; I couldn't breathe. What was happening? I knew it wasn't mine, but I also knew it was now my problem. It flashed through my mind that this was just like a scene from a movie: a bad movie.

I looked at the customs officer again. His smile was unreadable. I still didn't know if he'd seen it or smelt it. Either way, I knew I was in trouble: this stuff was not mine and if I did get through customs, whoever owned the drugs would be coming to get them from me somehow. My heart was pounding; my head was feeling light. I couldn't understand it. I didn't know what was going on.

A man in a uniform suddenly appeared very close beside me. He exchanged smirks with the customs officer and then just murmured, 'Ahhhh.'

I felt like I was going to faint. Everything had become surreal. The room was spinning.

Still smirking, the customs officer went to open my bag. I was petrified. I'd seen it, it wasn't mine, but who the hell was going to believe me now?

Panicking, I watched the customs officer move to our side of the counter. He pointed at the bag and said to James, 'You carry this to the office.'

James looked lost and confused.

I felt like throwing up, but I instinctively wanted to keep my little brother out of it. I knew it had nothing to do with him. I had just told these people that it was my bag. It was my bag, so my problem. I'd also had a lot of experience communicating with people whose English was poor and could usually get the drift of what they were trying to say, whereas I knew James would struggle. So I said, 'This is *my* boogie-board bag – I'll carry it. Why does my brother have to carry it?'

'He carry it, not you, you stay here.'

It was the first of many fights I've lost . . . and keep losing.

They made James carry it to the customs office, even though they knew it was mine. I had just claimed ownership of it, I had just opened it, and my name was clearly written on the tag hanging off the side of the bag. They didn't even ask me to follow. I was free to go. Standing there alone with my suitcase, with no customs officers around me, I was free to follow the Exit signs and walk out the front door. I'd been dismissed. I could very easily have gone outside to Ally and Katrina and taken our hotel pick-up bus and left.

But I didn't. I didn't even think to leave. They had my little brother, and whatever was in that bag, whatever had happened, whatever was going on, it had nothing to do with James or me. I figured I'd just have to go into that room, make it clear to the officers that the dope wasn't ours, and then James, Ally, Katrina and I could leave in the hotel bus together.

By this time, my two friends were outside in the Bali heat. I spotted Katrina through a glass wall, patiently sitting on her suitcase, waiting to start her holiday. I then found Ally and, through my tears, told her the news and asked her to wait. She went to pick up James's and my suitcases to take them outside. They'd been left sitting at the customs counter and, bizarrely, mine hadn't even been searched.

Then I ran to the room where James was being held and froze in the doorway. I couldn't believe my eyes.

My boogie board lay on a table and on top was the now infamous clear plastic bag. It was unbelievable. The bag was as big as my board and as thick as a pillow. This wasn't happening. I felt faint and leant on the doorframe for support.

Tears slid down my cheeks as I silently watched the frantic activity inside the room. I felt detached from the world around me. It was chaos. People were racing in and out, touching, looking, smelling, pointing and laughing. The room was electric. People were talking loudly and animatedly on their mobile phones, looking at me and laughing, looking at James and laughing. Lots of them were coming in with little black plastic bags and taking chunks of it. It was a feeding frenzy. There was a lot of loud, excited chatter, and it appeared almost like they were having a party. It was obviously a very happy afternoon for these people.

James and I were the only people not moving. We were like bewildered statues, frozen by shock and fear in the middle of this crazed activity. He was sitting on a chair. I was standing near the door. Occasionally, we exchanged looks but didn't say a word. We were too shocked for words.

But it was as if we weren't there. No one said anything to us. No one questioned us or interrogated us. The only reason I was sure

I wasn't invisible was because people kept laughing in my face.

Then I noticed some men who weren't in uniform come in a side door, cameras in hand, and start snapping away.

'Who are these people? Close the door! Close the door!' I wailed at an officer, opening my mouth for the first time. One of the officers did actually close the door.

Ally had grown impatient waiting for us and now walked back in through the airport's sliding glass doors and up to the little customs office to find out why we were taking so long. Instantly, she saw why and gasped, 'Oh, my God . . .'

At least an hour or so passed before anyone said anything to me, although time had become meaningless. A man in a suit walked up to me and pointed to the plastic bag, saying, 'This is yours?'

'No!'

'What is it?' he asked me.

I didn't want to be tricked into anything so I said, 'I don't know what it is.'

Again he asked, 'Is it yours?'

Pointing to the bag of marijuana, I told him: 'That's not mine. The *boogie board*'s mine, the boogie-board *bag* is mine, but *that* is not mine.' He walked off.

In court, this man claimed that I said the bag of marijuana was mine. It was my word against his. But why would anyone in my situation claim it as their own, whether it was or not?

He came back a while later to do a narcotics test on the marijuana. He put some liquid in a small plastic bag to mix with a tiny sample from the big plastic bag in the centre of the room. If it turned purple, it was a narcotic. It did, proving that it was marijuana.

He didn't feel any need to prove that it actually belonged to me. No fingerprinting was done, because the bag had already been touched by so many hands. James had even been forced to pick it up to put it on the scales. 'James, don't touch the bag, don't touch it,' I told him. But they made him. It weighed 4.2 kilograms. Officially, it was listed as 4.1, after 100 grams was taken out for testing, although I'm sure more than a point left the room that afternoon. Later, when Merc arrived and demanded finger-printing of the bag, the police just laughed. 'Too many people touch.'

'Well, stop touching it now. Just stop touching it!' Merc yelled.

The marijuana was mine because it was in my bag. Case closed. Looking back, I never stood a chance.

But I didn't yet understand how bad things were. I'd seen all the 'Death penalty to drug smugglers' signs around the airport, but I wasn't a drug smuggler and these weren't my drugs, so I wasn't too worried about long-term consequences. It was too ridiculous. I hadn't even been interrogated, so how serious could it be? *Please . . . just let me go and start my holiday*, I thought. I knew things weren't good, but I sure didn't think this spelt the end of my freedom for twenty years.

Back when we'd first arrived, Merc was relaxing poolside with some friends and their kids at a villa she'd rented for her birthday. She was happily looking forward to seeing us. But as time ticked by, she started to get pissed off with me. She'd sent Wayan to pick the four of us up from our hotel and he was told, 'No Corby here.' She then rang the hotel and was told the same.

Merc guiltily recalls saying to her friends: 'Bloody Schapelle, she's given me the name of the wrong hotel! God, I can't believe this, I'll just have to wait for her to call me.'

Then she got a call. It was Katrina. 'Merc, you've got to come quickly. They're saying that Schapelle's been found with drugs – marijuana.'

Merc thought she was joking. 'Yeah, right! Where are you? Which hotel?'

Katrina broke down sobbing, and the shock and fright in her voice told Merc that this was for real. Katrina was in a police car being driven to a customs office outside the airport and had the sense to borrow the policeman's mobile phone. Merc asked to speak to the policeman and was left in no doubt: this wasn't a joke.

Merc, who rarely swears, apparently got off the phone and said, 'Fuck, fuck, fuck . . . ! What am I going to do?' Wayan had gone with the kids to the beach for a swim and hadn't taken his phone. Merc thought it must just be a mistake or that somebody had left half a joint or a tiny speck or something in my bag. She knew I loathed dope and didn't smoke it, but also realised that everyone knew someone who did.

She changed out of her bikini into jeans and a shirt, and jumped on her motorbike. First she went to Wayan's family home, hoping to find someone to take with her. But only a sick old uncle was there. So Merc zoomed off scared and alone.

I was slumped in a chair, leaning my elbow on a desk so I could prop up my heavy head in my hand, and James, Ally and Katrina were huddled together on the couch. Although I have no memory of it, we'd been driven from the airport to the main customs office just outside. I recall stumbling up five small steps in the dark. I think the shock had really hit me.

This room had become the new party zone and was alive with frenetic activity when Merc walked in. She looked at us and asked, 'Are you guys OK?'

No one spoke. We just gave her shocked, useless looks.

She walked out of the room. She hadn't yet seen the marijuana on the floor, as she'd been too worried and focused on us. In these moments, she still thought it was probably a tiny speck and that she could fix this.

Just outside the door were a couple of guys sitting relaxed at a table, and Merc asked them what the hell was going on. She noticed a bowl on the table, filled with finely chopped marijuana. The men didn't say a word. They just smiled at her and pointed back into the room, towards the floor.

Poor Merc turned around and screamed. As I looked up I saw her legs collapse. Her hand flew up to her face as she fell stumbling through the doorway again and over to the couch. It was the last thing she'd ever imagined seeing.

The huge bag was open, with bits of marijuana on the floor and sticking out everywhere, where it had been pulled apart earlier by grasping hands. No one needed to tell her what it was. She just thought, *Shit, what is going on?*

It wasn't blind faith, but not for a second did she think the drugs were mine. Not once has she asked me. She knows me well enough to know I wouldn't be so bloody stupid.

There were now five of us sitting silently, dazed and shocked in that horrible room. But things were about to get worse. The many windows surrounding us were starting to fill with local photographers and reporters. News had travelled fast: 'white girl with marijuana'. They were poking their cameras right through the open glass louvres and into the room, clicking frantically. More and more appeared until the windows were completely filled with people and cameras. Their flashes were going off like crazed lightning. I'd never seen anything like it. I felt like a caged animal on display at the zoo. I didn't have a chance of keeping my story out of the headlines.

I made futile attempts to hide, trying to find places around the room where the cameras couldn't get a clear view of me. But every corner I crouched in, they seemed to find an angle to snap me. I kept my hands over my face, or my hair, blankets, anything, to hide from them. The others were desperately trying to help me too, standing in front of me and shutting the curtains.

But the photographers just became more frantic to get their pictures and started aggressively tearing aside the curtains and reaching their cameras well into the room. Suddenly, they were touching me, too. I became hysterical as hands came snaking in, grabbing my shoulder, touching my face. I leapt up screaming, 'Leave me alone, leave me alone!', desperately fighting off their clawing hands.

Not one of the officials in the room did anything to help. In fact, a policewoman was taking photos with her mobile phone and had been all day. Merc angrily asked her what she was up to. Paperwork, she said. But she was clearly taking shots of me and the marijuana, and we saw her send them. No doubt she was being paid, as the next day her shots were in the local newspaper and ended up in the Australian papers. We knew they were hers because no one else had that angle.

I was sobbing and gasping for breath when even more humiliation was dumped on me. With the cameras still clicking away and the hands still clawing, about ten men walked in and started circling me, saying, 'Strip. Take your clothes off now and strip.'

I shot a panicked look at Merc and we both just lost it. 'What? *What?*'

'Take your clothes off . . . strip . . . strip search.'

I just thought, *Strip – in front of my brother? In front of all these cameras, and these men? No way.*

Merc was crying and asking them, 'Please, please, can't she have a woman with her? You can't do this. Please!'

God only knows how, but miraculously she got them to leave. They sent in a woman ten minutes later.

She took me to a disgusting, dirty, covered-in-shit toilet and told me to strip. So, in that stinky place, I stripped naked in front of her.

How humans could actually breathe in that sickening stench, let alone strip off completely naked, was beyond me. I had never been so humiliated. I felt so small, so vulnerable. Everything was totally out of my control. I could do nothing to help myself. Nothing! I put my clothes back on and, feeling ashamed and dirty, walked back into the room to more flashbulbs. I was exhausted. What the hell *was* going on?

By now, I'd been frightened, upset, shocked and horrified for nearly eight hours, but it wasn't until the next moment that I became truly scared for my life. A big important-looking man walked in holding a couple of papers, which he shoved at me, saying, 'Sign.' A bunch of policemen and plain-clothed men also gathered around, saying, 'Sign, sign.'

I looked down at the papers in my hands and my whole body began to shake. Everything was in Indonesian, and I didn't have a clue what it said. Merc came over to sit beside me and began trying to translate, as she speaks Indonesian. But this was all tricky legal jargon.

It was right around this time the reality hit me that those signs at the airport declaring 'Death penalty to drug smugglers' could actually apply to me, to my life. I knew I was in big, big trouble. I needed a lawyer.

Merc worked out pretty quickly that it was a confession. A couple of the men were trying to translate it for me in their broken English, but Merc told me they weren't being truthful. I had to get a lawyer.

We both started saying, 'We should have a lawyer – we would like a lawyer.' But they kept responding: 'No, no, tomorrow. Just sign. It will be harder for you if you don't sign.' They pushed hard. I didn't have a clue what my rights were but had seen enough movies to know that you don't sign anything without your lawyer present. That just kept going through my head: *Don't sign anything, don't sign anything, don't sign anything* . . .

They finally gave up when they realised I wasn't dumb enough to just sign it. I would love to know what those papers actually said, but I haven't seen them since, and they were never shown to my lawyers.

The fireworks were nearly finished but not quite. It was around 11 p.m., and they were planning to take the four of us to the police station for the night, though Merc convinced them to release Ally and Katrina.

All of our suitcases were still sitting in the back of a police car and, despite the fact that they were ticketed in my name, Ally's and Katrina's were never searched and mine still hadn't even been opened; I don't know if it ever was. The suitcases weren't kept as evidence, as Ally and Katrina took theirs with them that night. If they'd been kept, everything in my name could have been weighed, which would have instantly proved that I didn't do it. It was a devastating blow when we later learned that Qantas only kept total baggage weights. But we didn't know things like that at this point.

They brought my case inside so I could grab a few things to keep me going. I took my toothbrush, toothpaste, change of underwear and my make-up. I gave Merc my $1,000 spending money, still hoping that in a day or so I'd be spending it myself, and I handed my mobile phone and address book to the police.

We all walked outside together, and a dozen or so photographers went berserk. It was dark, but their flashes brightly lit our path. It was just a taste of what was to come, and it was truly frightening. Officers were standing on either side of me, holding my arms and dragging me through the media throng. They'd put my large blue scarf over my head, causing the photographers to shove their cameras underneath it and blind me with their flashes. I was pushed down into the back seat of the police car, as a photographer leapt in next to me, taking more shots, before leaping back out. James was put in on the other side of the car.

I heard Merc wailing and screaming out, 'Leave them alone' as the car door slammed shut. It hurt to hear her pain. I shut my eyes for a second and tears streamed down my face. What a shit day.

I turned to look out the rear window and saw poor Merc sitting helplessly on her bike sobbing, just watching us pull away. I'd forgotten to wish her a happy birthday, though there was nothing happy about it.

The photographers were running alongside the car, still yelling and screaming and snapping wildly. As we sped up, they fell behind, eventually growing smaller and disappearing in the distance. Relentless, some of them were soon alongside us again, on motorbikes. My new life had just begun.

5

Waiting For Monday

IT FELT LIKE SOMEONE WAS PLAYING A MADLY DEPRAVED
trick on me. Maybe I was being punked? *How* could this be
happening? My head was spinning. I just couldn't believe this was
real.

The first night James and I spent at the police station, I
optimistically thought that in forty-eight hours I'd be free. The
Australian airport offices would open on Monday morning to
provide proof of my innocence, surely: CCTV footage, baggage
X-rays and/or recorded weight. Simple! Open and shut. I'd be
off the hook. 'Sorry, Schapelle, it's all been a big mistake. Go and
enjoy your holiday!' I'd be off to surf and soak up the rays on a
sun-kissed Bali beach like I'd planned. Yep, I could handle two
days. No problem.

That's what I kept telling myself as I lay scared and crying on a
couch upstairs at the police headquarters, known locally as Polda, in
Denpasar. James and I each had an old green couch. He didn't sleep
at all, as he wanted to protect me and make sure I was OK. I slept
fitfully. Apart from the stress, it was freezing cold. An air conditioner
blasted cold air all night and, with no blankets, I started to feel fluey
and got up a few times to search for the 'off' button. I also badly
needed to use the toilet but was too scared to wake one of the two
sleeping policemen sprawled out in cane chairs next to us.

In the morning, I felt dazed and numb. This was unbelievable. I
still couldn't comprehend what was happening. Instead of getting
up for an early surf at the beach, I was at the police station meeting
my new lawyer and a guy from the Australian Consulate.

Merc arrived way before everyone else, of course – my beautiful protective big sister. She was looking drawn and upset and hadn't slept a wink but raced straight over to check on us. I was quiet, still in shock and disbelief, as was James. Merc sprang into action, trying to convince the police to at least let James go: he was only sixteen years old and they knew the boogie-board bag wasn't his.

Merc always seems the strong one. But the night before, she had ridden home on her bike, scared and crying helplessly the whole way, thinking, *Oh, my God . . . what is going on? What am I going to do?* Katrina and Ally were following her in a taxi. When they got home, Merc pulled herself together to look after the girls, then hit the phone to find me a lawyer. She first rang a good friend of hers who worked at the Australian Consulate. She gave her the vice-consul's mobile number.

He arrived at about 8 a.m. on Saturday, shook my hand and introduced himself as Brian. He didn't say much except that I'd soon be put in a little cell downstairs, where there was already an Australian guy being held on drugs charges.

'How long has he been there?'

'Oh, a month and a half.'

'Whoa, what does he look like . . . scary?' I asked, visualising an emaciated, hollow-eyed man with a filthy, unshaven face.

Then I met the lawyer, Lily Lubis. At about midnight the night before, Brian had given Merc a list of consulate-approved lawyers. 'Sorry, please call back on Monday' was the standard answering-machine response until Merc finally got through to a woman. She couldn't take the case, or didn't want to touch it, but said her sister Lily could and would phone straight back. She did. It hit us much later that Lily wasn't on the approved list.

After first meeting Lily that Saturday morning, Merc and I had doubts, thinking she was a little too *nice*, too quiet, to be of real help.

But then we watched her take a call and almost yell down the phone, not hysterically but in a firm, 'Do what I say' tone. We signed her up.

Feeling a bit happier now that I at least had a lawyer, I asked her, 'What happens if you can't prove I didn't do this?'

Blankly she stated, 'It's the death penalty, Schapelle.'

I just looked at her and bawled; I just cried and cried unstoppably. It was now an indisputable fact: those signs at the airport really did apply to me. It hit hard.

Calm, calm, calm, I chanted silently to myself. *The evidence will be there.* After all, aren't Australian airports the best, the safest, the most secure in the world? Of course they are! And of course they'd have X-ray scans, recorded baggage weight and CCTV footage.

For the next couple of hours, Merc, James and I were left expectantly hanging around. There were no questions, no interrogation, nothing. *This is ridiculous,* I thought. *It's nothing like the movies. Isn't someone supposed to take me into an interrogation room and sit me down in front of a little tape recorder to ask me lots of questions?* Movies were my only reference to this situation I'd crashed into.

I *wanted* to be questioned. I had nothing to hide, and I wanted to tell these people that I didn't do this and it was all a terrible mistake. I wanted them to see how damn ridiculous it was. But I had no control over my life any more, no free will. I couldn't make things happen when I wanted them to. I wouldn't be in charge of my day again for . . . well, I don't know how long.

I wasn't interrogated for three more days.

Later that day, they let James go, conceding the boogie-board bag was not his. I was taken down to my cell. I won't ever forget first stepping into it. Initially I froze at the door, just sobbing and shaking. Everything was so unreal. Everything was so wrong. *Why was this happening?* The guard gently nudged me through, locking the scary-looking door behind me. With tears streaming down my face, I turned back to look at him through the thick steel bars of the door. I had a strange impulse to reach out and touch it but thought it might make me throw up.

I'd never before felt such fright and gut-wrenching loneliness. It cut through my soul. It was agonising. I collapsed to the floor and cried my eyes out. I cried and cried and cried, like a baby. My chest was heaving with sobs. I wanted my mum. I was venting twenty-four hours of primal fear and anguish.

Slowly it started to pass. *Calm, calm, calm,* the voice in my head started to again say. *It will be OK on Monday . . . Just two days and it will be OK.* I had to believe it.

I slowly turned to gaze around my little cell and take it all in. It was gross. I was surrounded by four faded, yellow cement walls, stained with thick layers of dirt, grime and graffiti. They were covered in drawings of naked girls and scrawled writing in many different languages, most notably Arabic. Later, I was to learn that some of it was done in pen and some, revoltingly, in human shit.

A paper-thin, old green and red carpet covered the cement floor. It was filthy with a musty stench and God-knows-what gross diseases living in it. For sure, no carpet shampoo or vacuum cleaner had ever touched it. In the far corner was my very own covered-in-shit squat toilet with complementary bucket and ladle, and a basin. That was it; there was nothing else.

I don't know how many stars I'd give it but definitely not five! I wasn't going to be slipping on a fresh towelling bathrobe and lathering myself in free bottles of sweet-smelling bath oils in this place. I'd sure taken the wrong hotel pick-up bus for that. There was no luxury here, no mattress, no blanket, no table or chair, nothing to sit on, nothing to sleep on, nothing to eat off. My pale-blue sarong became my furniture; I sat on it and slept on it. It didn't create physical comfort, but it provided a psychological barrier between me and the infested carpet, me and my new life. I needed that.

That afternoon, I deeply felt the pain of my lost freedom. Merc and our brother Michael came to see me. Michael had arrived in Bali with his girlfriend on the Friday afternoon, too, flying in from Perth, where they'd spent a few days visiting her family. This was my first chance to see him.

But the bastard guards wouldn't let them in or me out, though they easily could have if they'd felt like it. I stood at my cage door looking out. Merc and Michael stood outside looking in. They were both crying. From either viewpoint, looking at someone you love in that situation is brutally painful. 'We'll come back tomorrow, Schapelle. You'll be OK – we'll come back tomorrow.'

I stood there holding the bars of my cell door, desperately fighting back tears. I refused to hurt them more than they were already hurting. I loved them too much to let them know that I was so upset and traumatised.

'Yeah, I'm OK, I'm OK . . . It's all right,' I told them.

It's so hard not to cry. I'm trying so hard to keep a strong spirit in front of everyone when they visit. So they can leave and know that I'm handling this OK.

I feel so awful. Although this happened, I know all my friends and family know I didn't do it. Still, it's all me: everyone's been so excited and saving so hard for this holiday, and now everyone's sitting around crying, worried sick, not drinking, not eating, not surfing, not partying – just worrying.

Diary entry, 12 October 2004

When Merc and Michael left, I decided to try to brush my teeth, because I hadn't cleaned them since Friday morning at Mum's house and now it was Saturday afternoon. I knew I was fragile but thought I could handle it. I was fooling myself. Putting the toothbrush in my mouth just forced me to lean over the disgusting toilet and vomit.

In the cell behind mine were about eighteen guys, including the Aussie who Brian had mentioned, Chris Currall, who was arrested with 60,000 ephedrine tablets and 1.5 kilograms of ephedrine powder. I'd seen these guys when I was led down to my cell and could easily hear them through the cell wall. A Balinese guy called out, 'You OK?' after he heard me vomiting. He told the guards I needed a drink, and after I gave them some money that I still had in my pocket they brought me a clear plastic bag filled with Fanta.

Later in the afternoon, the guards let Chris out of his cell to talk to me for two minutes. He stood at my cage door – a very strange feeling.

That first night in the cells at Polda, I threw up for three and a half hours straight: 11 p.m. to 2.30 a.m. I know because I marked it in my diary:

I vomited pretty bad last night, I was actually in pain. The head policeman came to see me for a bit – he told me to let him know if I need to go to hospital. I don't need a hospital; I need to get out of here.

Diary entry, 10 October 2004

I couldn't sleep that night, like most of the nights that followed. Sleep suddenly became a luxury. Lying down on a soft mattress, with a fluffy pillow and fresh, clean sheets, had been a given only two nights before; now it was a fantasy that I longed for. And still do.

It was hell. Almost everything seemed to conspire against me sleeping. The ants and mosquitoes drove me crazy, and the guards sitting just outside my door didn't stop talking all night. Despite trying, I'm now sure you can never adapt to sleeping on a thinly carpeted concrete floor. I did eventually sleep on the concrete, but only when the pain of sleep deprivation became worse than the pain of bruises and swelling and sharp pins-and-needles caused by the hard floor. It's definitely not by chance that sleep deprivation is used as a method of torture.

I have to move my body every five minutes or so. I've not yet become accustomed to sleeping on the HARD floor; my body is in more pain now than the first week. The first week my bones – back bone, hip bones, shoulder, ankle bones – were bruised. Now they've become swollen, especially my tail bone – it's the most painful.

Diary entry, 6 November 2004

Merc often tried to give me a mattress, but the police and guards point-blank refused to allow it. I have no idea why, as some of the guys were allowed mattresses.

On the Sunday, Lily came to see me, and I met Vasu Rasiah for the first time. I wasn't told how Vasu fitted in, and I didn't think to ask. I just assumed he was a lawyer at the same firm as Lily – and I think he was happy for me to assume that. He never corrected anyone when they called him a lawyer.

The Australian media called him a lawyer for months, until he became known as a 'case coordinator'. It took Merc and me a few weeks to realise he was actually a developer/designer/contractor/construction manager and 'case coordinator'. At least that's what it said on the various business cards he handed out.

Two days of hell had passed, and I still had high hopes of getting out on Monday.

6

The 'Celebrity' Prisoner

'**Y**OU'RE FREE TO GO. HAVE A NICE HOLIDAY!' AS THE cell door swings open, I happily step out into the brilliant sunshine with a matching brilliant smile. Tears of joy wash down my cheeks and the darkness clutching at my heart vanishes, along with the deep pain and fear. *Thank God it's over!* Now my biggest problem is deciding between a relaxing poolside beer and the revitalising surf . . .

That's the way I pictured Monday. I'd seen it, dreamt it and convinced myself of it during the past forty-eight hours. This surreal, crazy madness would stop. My spinning world would be set back on its axis. They weren't my drugs, I didn't put them in my bag, *I didn't do this.* Just a quickly faxed X-ray or boogie-board weight would prove it beyond all doubt. The police would say, 'Yeah, look, it's crazy, let her go. Let her go to her sister's birthday.'

So that first Monday I sat anxiously waiting for the guards to come and unlock the cell to release me back to my normal, happy life. The moment I heard the guard's keys jingling I leapt up, almost smiling with excitement. My pulse was pumping as I stood expectantly at the cell door. *Please let it be over – please!*

But Monday reality was harsh. As the guard unlocked the cell, he murmured that he was just moving me to another cell. My gut twisted as it took the kick.

This was the start of my white-knuckle, rollercoaster ride of hope and despair. I'm still on it. I get so hopeful that I might get out, then *bang*, bad news arrives, plunging me into despair. It hurts. The ride's a bit flatter these days: no high expectations, no devastation.

That first Monday, my spirits took quite a plunge. No evidence had been faxed by anyone from the Australian airports. My panic and fear flew back with the terrifying thoughts: *What if they don't actually have the evidence? What if we can't prove the drugs aren't mine?*

> *What happens if they can't prove I didn't do this, then what . . . I stay here? That would kill my mum. It would be all my fault, even though I didn't do it. This is all way too much, and it's because of me! How can I say I'm sorry, how do I start to say I'm sorry? I'm here. Why? Why am I here? It's not me. I shouldn't be here. And I'm sorry. Sorry for what? I didn't do anything.*
>
> *This is so surreal. A nightmare, not just for me, but for everyone who knows and loves me.*
>
> Diary entry, 15 October 2004

I felt sick as the guard hustled me out of the cell. I kept biting my quivering bottom lip to stop the sobs, and my heart felt even more tightly screwed with pain and a heavy blackness.

I started to take deep breaths, soothing myself by forcing new thoughts: *Just a bit longer . . . Maybe tomorrow, maybe a day or two more.* But I'd lost confidence in getting the evidence quickly, as shouldn't it have come today? I was scared as the police marched me across the courtyard, past some pushy reporters and photographers and into a long cement passage to another cell.

Things were about to get worse.

The cell was a dungeon unfit for human life, with no windows, no daylight and no chance of a breeze. It was like a red-hot sauna and my clothes were quickly soaking wet. In the corner was a filthy squat toilet, so vile that it made the covered-in-shit toilet in the other cell seem not so bad.

Even worse than the cell itself were the people who came with it: two sicko, weirdo guards and a fat Balinese prostitute. The guards sat just outside the cage door, creepily staring at me and occasionally saying a slimy 'Wow, sexy body.' I was on display for these creeps, with nowhere to hide. I was very scared. And those sleazy guards were definitely interested in playing more than just mind games.

Sitting on a sarong inside was my first ever cellmate, Agung. At first, when she greeted me with a wide toothy grin, she seemed friendly enough. But after a bit of small talk, she was scarily friendly and just as creepy as those guards.

'My name Agung, what your name?'

'I'm Schapelle.'

For a second she looked at me, shocked; then she jumped up, laughing, as she ran to a pile of stuff. She pulled out a newspaper, pointing to a front-page headline that screamed 'SCHAPELLE' above my photo.

'Ha, ha, Saphel, Saphel!' she kept repeating, and pointing.

It was day three, and already I was a 'celebrity' prisoner – not an asset in a place full of criminals and petty guards. To Agung, it elevated me to a status worthy of adoration.

She's making me feel super self-conscious. Keeps looking at me, lovingly. I try to read my book as much as possible. Keeps asking if 'You like boy? You like big banana? Not banana. Not good.' A couple of times she's touched my breast and stroked my upper arm while she's looking at me and not speaking. She made our beds up together. I was reading and she was lying on her side playing with my arm – staring. Yes, I'm scared!

Help! Get me out of here! I'm so paranoid now and she's still saying, 'Shower, you shower.' I think she's trying to get me naked. If anything happened, I can't help but feel that help wouldn't come. So I read my book until late, with her watching me, and pretend to fall asleep reading so I don't have a shower.

Diary entry, 11 October 2004

The hours in 'the Agung cell', as I called it, were sheer hell. I felt so trapped and helpless. I'd expected to get back control of my life that day, but instead it just kept spinning further out of control: it was stinking hot, Agung didn't shut up or stop touching me, the guards kept leering, Merc had been refused a visit and my lawyer hadn't come. When I asked for permission to call her, it was denied.

I wanted to scream. I wanted to rip that cage door down and go crazy. I wanted to shut that mouth that kept saying, 'Shower, you shower.' What the hell was I doing here? I wanted to lash out. I'd had enough, enough pain, enough indignity, enough disappointment and frustration, enough of these pathetic little guards trying to make my life even more of a misery. Now they were even denying me my basic right to phone my lawyer.

I was losing it. I was shaking with rage. I had so much anger in me at that point. But there was absolutely nothing I could do to release it. I had to try to calm down. It was all I could do. I tried putting my hands on my hips and pacing back and forth, five steps forward and five steps back. *Breathe, breathe!* I kept telling myself. I was blowing hard in and out. *Be positive, be positive.* I was feeling like a trapped tiger in a cage. It took so much energy to calm myself down. What had happened to my life?

A lighter moment in that black day was opening a plastic bag Merc had dropped off and finding she'd slipped in a slice of her thirtieth birthday cake. Tears sprang to my eyes. It was a slice of my real life. I missed it so much. I shut my eyes, pictured Merc and sang her 'Happy Birthday' in my head. *I love you, Merc. I'll be out soon and we can have another party.*

A few hours later, I was lying down with a book flat across my face, pretending to sleep, when I heard Agung get up and walk over to the cage door, towards the guards. Then I heard an unmistakable sound. An unmistakable *sucking* noise. This couldn't be happening, surely . . .

I didn't dare breathe. I didn't dare move. This was too sick, too disgusting. I tried to tell myself it *wasn't* happening: *You're just being paranoid, Schapelle. She wouldn't . . . No way. This doesn't happen!*

A loud groan broke my thoughts. Then I heard Agung run to the toilet and spit.

For what seemed like the millionth time in three days, I asked myself what the hell had happened to my life. She'd done it through the bars in the cell door!

I woke to the sound of my name being called by one of the big police. 'Corby, Corby . . . your sister.' I start to get up and, well, what do you know, Agung rolls over and says, 'Shower.' Does she ever give up? I had to laugh.

Quickly I poured buckets of water on me, dried myself and tried to dress with my towel wrapped round me. Careful not to show anything to those eyes that sit ever so close to where I'm dressing, staring with what I take as love and wonder.

Quick . . . let's go. Get me out of here!

Diary entry, 12 October 2004

It wasn't yet even 7 a.m., but the moment I stepped outside, I was hit by the bright daylight and a media scrum.

'Schapelle, how are you feeling today?'

'Schapelle, are you being treated all right?'

'Schapelle, did you eat yesterday?'

I tried to politely answer a couple of questions as the police yanked me through.

The guards were moving me early to try to outsmart the media, but they hadn't reckoned on quite how obsessive they were. Apparently, while I was in Agung's cell, they'd spent the entire day in the Polda car park waiting to catch a glimpse of me.

It was four days since my arrest, and I was finally being taken to my interrogation. I was really nervous, as my life would depend on me recalling every moment of the trip. And that was hard. I had nothing to cover up, but who clocks every tiny detail of such a casually good time as the start of a holiday, when you're with your mates, drinking beer, joking around and laughing? Now it was vital to my freedom . . . or so I thought.

I did my absolute best, although in the end it didn't seem to matter what I said.

When Lily and I were going through the interrogation transcript a couple of days later, she spotted a fatal, sneaky line just before I signed it: 'Yes, the board cover, body board, fins and the plastic bag do all belong to me.' There was zero chance it was just a typing error. It was the second time the police had tried to fool me into signing a confession. They'd clearly thought that among so many papers, it would slip our eyes. Despite popular belief, the marijuana just being in my bag wasn't enough to convict me. They needed two bits of evidence. A signed confession would have made things perfectly simple.

I quickly learnt not to trust the police but to trust my instincts. During the interrogation, I suspected a policewoman was secretly taking photos of me with her mobile phone. I told Lily, but she said I was being silly. So I tested the woman by walking across the room. Her phone followed. I moved around a bit more to be sure. Now I was sure.

I told Lily again, and the policewoman angrily denied it when Lily asked her to stop. But sure enough, her photos were splashed on the front page of the local papers the next day. This was the start of an ugly and distressing invasion of my privacy by sneaky, snapping fortune-hunters wanting to fill their pockets.

There was nothing hidden about the media pack downstairs that day. We could hear their loud banter from the upstairs office. I peeked out the window and saw at least twenty photographers and reporters milling around. I braced myself to face them as the police got ready at the top of the stairs to take me back to the cell. *Which one? Please, please, not the Agung cell!*

I'd been begging Lily to have me moved back to the first cell. *Please, I can't bear another night in there with that woman.*

I don't know what to expect when I hit outside. The media crowd see me coming down the stairs, and I have police on either side on me, holding my arms and directing me. I get to the bottom step and there's so many people, TV cameras and tape recorders in this huge semi-circle in front of me, everyone asking questions. It's taking a long time to get where we are going.

I see a Western guy with his hat on backwards. He asks me softly, 'Are you OK?' I nod and ask if he's Australian; and 'yes' he is. I also notice a camera guy to the left of me and he has a really nice light-brown eye. He has a camera covering the other one. Thinking that he's a bit of a cutie distracts me for a moment and I just continue walking. Must have gone to fairyland.

I'm brought back to earth by a reporter asking, 'Is there anything you want to say to the Australian public?'

I turn and say: 'Help me! Help me!'

What? How dumb! Why do I say that – why can't I say something positive like: 'I'm innocent, my lawyer's doing everything she can, be patient and I love my family'? That would be better. I could kick myself!

I can't see where we are going, with so much happening around me. I'm in the middle, being pushed and pulled. We come to some stairs and they get me inside. Suddenly the noise stops.

'Where am I, where am I?' Yes, I'm back in the 'nice' cell – thankfully.

Soon after, Merc comes over and a Channel 9 crew is following her. Guess who their camera guy is? He comes up to the cage and is reassuring me to stay strong. Cool, now I have a cute face in my memory.

As I'm writing this I'm feeling, like . . . gross! Here, cute guy; there, girl behind cage. Makes me feel sick. How could I think someone's cute from where I'm standing – the state of my life? What! Who am I?

Diary entry, 12 October 2004

Being suddenly thrown into a hot media spotlight added to the surreal nature of my new life. It's very bizarre to have cameramen waiting an entire day just to catch a glimpse of you. In fleeting moments, it seemed exciting, but mostly I didn't like it. I hated my name being known for this, I hated looking bad, being filmed with red teary eyes and in sweaty clothes that I'd slept in. I'd never liked being on camera and always used to dodge Mum's home video because I thought my voice sounded weird and I looked like I weighed triple my actual weight.

This is a nightmare, not just mine but everyone who knows and loves me. Friends from home are calling Merc and saying that everyone, everywhere is talking about 'that girl in the Bali prison', and out in the surf here in Bali my brother and friends hear people talking about it. Everywhere, everyone knows my name. Might be different if my name was something like Lisa or Suzy. In a couple of years, everyone would forget about this. But no . . . my name is Schapelle.

Diary entry, 15 October 2004

It was hard to believe how big my story had become. People assured me it was a lot bigger than the image I had in my head. Any time I was taken out of my cell, the media clamoured. Police on either side of me would practically drag me across the car park, fighting through a scrum of media people walking backwards, tripping over things, stumbling in potholes, jostling each other, anything to get their shots.

They were desperate with their questions. They'd fire anything at me: 'How do you feel, Schapelle?', 'How are you holding up?', 'Are you getting anything to eat?', 'Are you a drug smuggler?', 'Are you innocent?' Sometimes I'd answer them and sometimes the questions were so stupid that I didn't bother.

One guy stuck a microphone right in my face, yelling, 'So how does it feel to be a drug smuggler, Schapelle?' That question hurt. It stabbed me hard in the chest. I just cast my eyes down, trying to hide new tears and thinking that only an extremely cold, heartless being would ask such a question. Did he really expect me to reply, or was he just there to hurt me and get a reaction?

They were relentless. They'd run into the upstairs office while I was having a visit, snap a shot and run out before the police even realised what was going on. When friends and family came to visit, we'd usually have to talk through the bars and the cameramen would stand close, catching every single word.

All the guards were running around shooing the reporters away from the cages, telling me to stand in the corner of my cell so no reporters could see me. I know some reporters are trying to help, but the majority of them will do anything for a story. They don't realise that when I get a visitor, that's the only time I'm allowed out of my cell. Yesterday I got out for three minutes. I won't get out today either, even if Lily does come they won't walk me to the police room. I wouldn't want to anyway, as it's so awful with the press running around you, knowing they'll soon be writing about you. Makes my time so much harder. It would be very easy to go insane.

Diary entry, 31 October 2004

I quickly discovered that if the reporters didn't get a new story, it didn't stop them writing one. The Bali press were the worst, making up pungent and ridiculous lies. Three big ones in the first week were: I had a drug factory in Bali that converted marijuana to heroin; I'd claimed in my interrogation that we fed marijuana to cattle in Australia; and I was known as 'the Ganja Queen' and used the codeword 'lemon juice'.

Merc didn't tell me at the time, but she was being hassled twenty-four hours a day. She was followed, chased and telephoned incessantly. Day and night she got calls. At 4 a.m. or 11 p.m. radio stations called for live interviews; endlessly throughout the day, the press called. But she didn't turn her phone off in case it was Mum ringing or some important news about my case. When she came to Polda, the media were literally on top of her from the moment they spotted her. She lost five kilograms in the first week, and I'm sure half of it was media strain. It was suffocating and often annoyed the hell out of us.

The media also started squabbling over me. I agreed to do a telephone interview with *A Current Affair*, to let my family and friends know I was holding up OK, and was told not to talk to the other media guys. I felt rude, walking through the scrum, refusing to answer anyone's questions. So when a cameraman later came to my cell asking if I had anything to say to Australia, I simply said,

'I love my mum.' Someone from *ACA* later came to my cell and told me off through the bars. I couldn't believe it.

I was especially distressed to hear that Dad was being hassled at home by media camping outside his front and back yards. He was changing his cancer medications, so it was the worst possible time for him to be stressed at all.

The guards didn't like the media either, so I was refused many visits while they camped outside my cell, to stop them getting their shots. One guard tried to outwit the pack by sneaking me down a long back corridor to a side door. Great plan – shame he forgot the key! I had to laugh. The guard at first looked angry but then turned and laughed with me, and he still somehow managed to get me back to safety before the media realised what had happened.

Merc, my lawyers – that is, Lily and Vasu – and I thought it would be a good idea to talk to the media, to protest my innocence, to get the true facts out there and put pressure on the airports and Qantas (the airline I'd flown with) to deliver the evidence. That is why I decided to do an interview with *60 Minutes*. Although I had concerns about attracting too much attention, and maybe too much influence, from Australia and pissing off the Indonesians, I was desperate for help from the authorities.

The day that the interview was filmed had been one of my worst. I'd only been out of my cell once, briefly, in three days; the particularly nasty guards were on duty and had refused to let me see a friend who tried to visit. I'd spent the whole miserable day crying.

I tried putting on make-up to cover my tear-stained face, but I knew I still looked really bad when the guard came at about 6 p.m. to take me up to the office. As far as he and the rest of the police knew, I was going to have a visit with my lawyers.

It was a cloak-and-dagger affair. Being a Saturday evening, there weren't too many people around, and Lily had lured the sole policeman watching me into another office. I was introduced to the reporter and the cameraman, and after we sat down, he nervously pulled out a little camera hidden in his backpack. The interview abruptly stopped and started many times, as he quickly stashed his camera back in the bag whenever Merc gave a warning cough that a policeman was wandering by. We all knew that getting caught wouldn't be good.

> *We did a quick interview, but I couldn't get my words together because I was having such a bad day and was also still very teary. Everyone was very easy to talk to. I was not nervous at all. Just a bad day for me. I'm a bit worried for my family and friends to see the interview because of the mental state I was in, fumbling to find words, in tears and the stressed state of me. I know that would surely make them worry more than they already are.*

Diary entry, 6 November 2004

7

Dark Days at Polda

It really sux being in here. I've been here for eighteen days. I thought I had no more tears left. I was wrong. I haven't yet made it to twenty days. I want to know HOW I'm supposed to make it through ten or twenty years. Twenty years I wouldn't even contemplate surviving. Ten years . . . oh, I can't think about it. I wonder if someone out there is feeling even a little guilt. I may never know.

Diary entry, 26 October 2004

I SPENT THE FIRST FIVE WEEKS LOCKED UP ALONE IN A tiny, windowless, airless, soulless concrete cell, with a barred door that looked into another cell. Some natural light came through the bars but was outshone by bright fluorescent lights burning around the clock. The air was musty and stinking hot, making it sometimes hard to breathe.

My cell door often went unopened for three or four days straight. I could pace out the room, and occasionally did, for exercise, three steps wide and five steps long. I also spent a lot of time uselessly crying, as there wasn't much else to do. Most animals are treated better; animal protection groups would riot if they weren't. Some days I did have the anger of a captive tiger. It nearly sent me crazy.

Those weeks stressed me way beyond my limits. I didn't eat; I just vomited endlessly. When there was nothing in my stomach, I vomited water or dry retched until my body shook violently. I spent weeks constipated and badly bloated, until I got a severe case of the opposite problem, which has lasted to this day.

As the days passed and still no evidence came through, I became very scared for my future. My whole body trembled when I thought about worst-case scenarios. I tried to block out thoughts of the death penalty and couldn't imagine being locked up for twenty years, never having a baby or getting married. But I had to accept that there was fat chance of my going anywhere pleasant soon. Chris Currall had just found out that his time in the police cells had been extended by sixty days. I would have to wait to go to court and prove my innocence to the judge.

Lily came to see me this afternoon, so I got to go up to the police room for a couple of hours. The case isn't looking too strong. Not surprising. They don't have much to work with. I trust Lily and Vasu. There is still a lot of evidence to be rounded up; that all takes time. Be strong, be strong, be strong.

Lily talks to Mercedes mostly and I like it that way. Less stress, I can keep my energy – put it to better use. Sit-ups, squats, dreaming of boys. No, I figure the less I know the better for me, to keep level-headed.

Usually I'm a very positive person, that's 'usually' as in Schapelle pre-8 October days. I rarely if ever got angry, upset. When I felt my blood beginning to boil, I'd breathe deeply, smile, tell myself it's OK. It's so not worth sweating the small stuff; all you'll ever gain from that is deep frown lines on the forehead and above your nose between your eyes, and wrinkles on the upper lip. But you know I was positive as in encouraging myself, my friends, encouraging others, people I don't know; being honest; walking around with a smile, a true smile that can make someone's shitty day completely turn around. That kind of positive doesn't take any energy at all. But I am finding positive thinking in these post-8 October days very draining. I am innocent, I will keep positive, I will get through this, I will be going home.

Diary entry, 26 October 2004

I knew I had to stay strong and adapt as best I could to living in a little cell – for a while at least. I had no choice, so I might as well try to make the best of it. I survived by refusing to let myself go, working hard to keep my spirits up, keeping the positive energies flowing, exercising, reading, writing and keeping my mind occupied as much as possible. I wanted to remain the healthiest I could, because I knew my life depended on it.

I am determined to keep mind, body and soul healthy. I don't know how long I'll be waiting for my day in court but I will not cause more anxiety, stress and pain to the people who love me and are doing everything they can to help me. I will never be able to repay or thank them enough, so I'll start with respect. RESPECT.

Diary entry, 4 November 2004

I got down on my knees and scrubbed clean the filthy toilet. I did some exercises. I finally managed to eat, and I spent days reading positive affirmations and escaping into good books. I'd probably only ever finished a couple of books in my whole life; now I was getting through one a day. I also started teaching myself some Indonesian words from a dictionary that Lily had given to me.

Occasionally, there were light moments in the long dark hours, and I always tried to squeeze the most out of them. I began to see washing my hair as a treat, saving it up to spoil myself. It had taken a while to get used to washing in cold water with a bucket and scoop, but when I did I would feel 100 per cent after washing my hair.

The guys in the cell behind mine often helped to lift my spirits. When they heard me cry, they'd sing to me. We'd talk and sing to each other through the walls. I was even teaching one of them a bit of Japanese. If they heard me crying, they'd yell out: 'Corby, you OK, Corby? You want a cup of tea, Corby?'

They were always looking after me, making sure I was all right. Most days when they were released into the communal area outside my cell for five minutes, they'd stand at my cell door talking to me and laughing. It was so good to have human contact, and we'd pretty much laugh for the whole five minutes. If a nasty guard was on duty, however, they were not allowed to talk to me, and I'd be told to sit out of sight in the far corner of my cell. The rare times when I was also allowed out made me feel so happy – almost like one step closer to freedom.

Many of the guys didn't get outside help from family like I did, so I used to share the food and drinks that my family and friends brought in for me. The guys thought it was like Valentine's Day when I returned from a visit one day with a gigantic melted Toblerone. Everyone grabbed a spoon and we ate the lot.

I saw a bit of Chris Currall because he used to get severe claustrophobia and was regularly allowed out to the communal area. He'd sit near my cell with a cup of tea and a cigarette, each time looking thinner and sicker. I felt bad, as I wasn't allowed to give him anything. In the first few days, Merc brought him food and eye drops, but the lawyers told us to stop, as the police might try to implicate us in a drug syndicate.

Though we were never allowed outside for exercise, the police organised a little Polda PR one day to make it look like we were. After being told to put on our dark-blue Polda T-shirts and shorts, we were hauled out of our cells and made to stand in a line and strike three poses for photos: 1. hands together above our head to look like the end of a star jump; 2. hands straight out to the sides to look like the start of a star jump; and 3. down on the ground as if we were doing a push-up. As soon as the three pictures were taken, we were slammed back into our cells. The guys called them 'the bullshit shots'. It was quite amazing.

I stole some moments of joy late one night when I was released with one of the guys to drain water from outside my cell during heavy rains. Our cells were inches away from being flooded. I grabbed my shower bucket and started scooping up water and throwing it through the cage bars where the guards usually sat.

Within seconds I was soaking wet. It was such a great feeling, as I love the rain and it had been so long since I'd felt it. All the guys in the back cell were watching me and laughing. They thought I was crazy, as I'm sure they'd never seen a girl standing in the rain before. They were going wild, like it was showtime at a boys' high school. We were all laughing hysterically, especially when a guard came around the corner at the exact moment I threw a bucket of water out. He was soaking wet. Whoops!

He looked at me, shocked for a second, and then started laughing, too.

Very early one morning, a guard came and unlocked my cell door. I warily jumped up and stood in the middle of my cell, confused, wondering what he wanted. I let out a wary 'Hello'. Then he said, 'Come, come look at the sky.' He was pointing to the cage door that led to the outside world. I jumped at the chance and dashed over with a huge smile on my face.

It gave me such a calm feeling to look up at the vast blue sky. How nice of the guard to offer me this. It was beautiful.

As I walked back to my cell, tears were streaming down my face. I hadn't seen the stars and moon for so long, but it was amazing to see the early-morning sky. Little things became so precious.

The pain of my situation never went away, though, no matter how hard I fought. Living with fear, hurt, anger and devastation, along with my physical aches and pains, became as natural as breathing.

> *How could this be happening? I don't know what's my real reality.*
> *I have this painfully sick numbness in me, though I think I'm in a daze, I don't really know.*
>
> Diary entry, 30 October 2004

Most of the guards weren't nice, they were creeps who enjoyed making life harder: laughing at me, refusing me visits, mocking me and taunting me. They'd do little things to upset me: for instance, a guard once opened a bag of food Merc had brought me, knowing ants would quickly ruin it. After a few minutes, he gave me a cheesy smile, singing out, 'Angry Corby!'

I couldn't help exploding 'YES!' as I stared back at this pathetic little man.

He spent the rest of the day saying 'Yes! Yes!' in a voice mimicking mine. I just had to sit there and take it.

Another time, I stood at the cage door trying to catch a slight breeze when one of the guards started screaming out, '*Tidur, tidur!*' (Sleep, sleep!), flinging his arms wildly to tell me to 'move over to your corner' like I was some kind of animal he had locked up. That sort of thing happened all the time. They were horrible, spiteful creeps who enjoyed abusing their little bit of power.

Sometimes they'd unlock my cell in the middle of the night, come in and just stand there looking at me. I always pretended to be asleep, but it terrified me, because if they tried something, the guys were locked up in the cell behind, so there was no one to help me.

The creepy guards also made me paranoid about using the toilet. Because the bottom of the cell door was quite high off the ground, I'd hold up a sarong just in case the sleazy guards bent down to watch.

I hit a low point when I was told the disturbing news that Amrozi, the Smiling Assassin, had lived in the same cell as me for five months. I felt sick knowing that I was using the exact same hand-held bucket to shower that he did and sleeping in the exact same spot. What had my life come to? One of Merc's best friends had lost her husband to his bombs, which exploded in two busy nightclubs in Kuta. His bombs killed 202 innocent people. I scrubbed everything in the bathroom because I didn't want to touch anything that monster had touched. And I changed my sleeping position.

It was such an eerie, horrible feeling to know the terrorist had been in the cell, and I felt like he still had a presence; I suppose he did: his DNA was on the wall. 'Cobra' was written on the wall in what looked like human shit – the guards told me that he'd written it. I was so haunted by his writing that it had a strange pull on my attention. I would just stare at it, and I started obsessing over what he'd really written it with. It could have been dried mud, but how did he get his hands on mud? I didn't want to believe it was shit, but in the end I just had to find out, so got up close and smelt it. It still stank.

I took out my diary and wrote down every single thing that was written on the walls inside that cell, exactly how it was written, just in case there was a hidden code or secret message from the bombers. I also took photos of the writing.

Scrawled right next to where I put my head to sleep were the words 'Sumudra, Freedom fighter'. I pulled up all the carpet, thinking maybe they'd hidden something, a little note, but I couldn't find anything. If my obsession with the prison-wall graffiti seems a bit strange, I did have a lot of time on my hands!

After thirty-six days of living in that little Polda cell, I was moved to Kerobokan Prison. I knew by then that there were no 'Get out of Jail Free' cards coming my way, no quickly faxed evidence from Australia. But my lawyers were fighting to obtain it, and they had to win. They had to, so I could get back my normal happy life.

8

Evidence!

I OFTEN WONDER WHAT I MUST HAVE DONE IN A PAST LIFE to suddenly become so unlucky in this one. Since 'Black Friday', nothing – absolutely nothing – has gone my way.

None of it made any sense from the start. I spent endless hours lying on my hard cell floor, trying to get my head around it, trying to think of something I'd missed and firing impossible questions at the cell walls: who, when, where, why? Why was the stuff in my bag? Why had my bag handle been cut? Why were the zips done up differently? *Why?*

My mind spun wildly with imaginative conspiracy theories, as I tried desperately to make sense of this insanity. But still nothing made sense and no answers bounced back from the dirty yellow walls. I just had to hope that, outside, my lawyers were having more luck.

I needed them to try to find evidence to back my story, to tell the truth, to counter the dynamite evidence against me, of the drugs being found in my bag. There had to be something, some piece of evidence to indisputably prove that I did not do this. Even if we didn't find out the whole story – the who, when and where – that didn't matter as long as we had the crucial bit: that I did *not* put them in.

But my luck was running the wrong way.

From day one, Lily and Vasu struggled to get direct answers to direct questions about possible evidence. 'Is there a baggage X-ray scan?' 'Do you have a recorded weight?' 'Is there CCTV footage?' They were simple questions. Yes or no? But my lawyers just smacked up against a matrix of confusion. Trying to figure out the lines of responsibility was like taking a non-stop ride on the Sea World Corkscrew.

'Sorry, we can't help. Please call this person – please call that person – call Qantas – call the Airport Authority – call Customs . . . Sorry, that's carried out by "other agencies".'

My lawyers were infuriated that they couldn't get any answers, and it became obvious that security at Australian airports was definitely not a synchronised, smooth-running, well-oiled machine. We discovered there was not one but many 'agencies' involved in airport security, and clearly there was no streamlined approach to either security or the handling of a crisis.

It was a PR crisis for the airports and the airline because of the one undisputable fact that a whopping 4.2-kilogram bag of marijuana had sailed undetected through not one but two 'high-security' Australian airports. And it was already big news by the time these people were scrambling for their non-answers.

'The CCTV vision did exist, but, sorry, it's been wiped. No, sorry, the CCTV vision *never* existed, the camera was switched off.'

'The X-ray machine was switched off . . . Oh, in fact, it *was* switched on, but it only scans for explosives.'

'The images are stored for seven days . . . no, thirty days . . . no, just seventy-two hours.'

I needed answers fast – very fast – while the evidence might still exist. My life was at stake; I could get shot dead or locked up for twenty years for this. But as I optimistically waited in my cell for answers, everyone back home was scurrying for cover. It took weeks of endless phone calls to ultimately get nowhere, while any evidence just vanished in the Bermuda Triangle of butt-covering and spin-doctoring.

I know that at least one piece of possibly life-saving evidence went that way. One answer that came too late. It was brutal. Qantas admitted that almost a month after my arrest – a month after we'd first started asking for it – evidence was destroyed. A Qantas lawyer gave us the news in an email nearly two months after my arrest, saying that vision recorded at Brisbane Domestic Airport in

October 2004 that might have had shots of me checking in was destroyed about twenty-five days after my arrest.

> Qantas uses digital video recording equipment to record images from the cameras installed at Brisbane Domestic Terminal. Images are stored in these for a limited period before being overwritten. The retention time is typically about one month.
>
> Unfortunately, during October, the recording equipment at Brisbane had been suffering from an intermittent fault and on or about 2nd November the unit underwent substantial repairs which appear to have resulted in the loss of the data pertaining to the period of interest.
>
> Qantas email, 1 December 2004

Unfortunately. This was my life! What the hell was the problem with these people? Aren't Qantas supposed to *help* their passengers? Not only had my lawyers been screaming out for this evidence from day one but my mum had driven to Brisbane airport four times, begging to see any videotape from that day. She begged them – *begged them* – but no one could even tell her whether it existed or not.

Each time, she got a different story. First it was: 'Yeah, we have it, but we're too busy to look through it.' Too busy? Wasn't this situation exactly the reason why they had multi-million-dollar visual security? Apart from assisting one of their passengers, it might also have helped them discover how 4.2 kilograms of marijuana had got by their airport security.

Mum asked if *she* could look at the tape. 'I'll make the time,' she told them. '*I'll* look at it – please . . . please!' But: 'No, sorry, it's against the Privacy Act.' So while I was locked up in my filthy Polda cell like a caged animal, sure that Qantas would be doing everything possible to help me gather evidence, they were too busy to even look at some footage.

Mum didn't let it rest. But all of a sudden, she was being told different stories: 'The tape never existed'; 'It had existed but it had been wiped.' This was within the first few weeks, before Qantas officially claimed that it was destroyed. Why was it so hard to get an answer? What were they hiding? My lawyers couldn't find out whether it existed either. To then be told in that December email that yes, it had really existed but no more, was gut-wrenching. No one from Qantas had even bothered to view the tape.

We'll never know what was on it. Maybe it showed the size and shape of my boogie board, or perhaps it just showed me looking happy and relaxed as I checked in. It may or may not have been the killer blow we needed, but now we will never ever know.

Qantas did send its international security manager to Bali about a week after my arrest, but he simply talked about how the baggage-handling procedures worked. He told Lily that no 'unauthorised' people had access to the bags during the time that they were transferred from domestic to international terminals. With what we later found out regarding certain 'authorised' airport workers in Sydney, this wasn't much of an assurance.

We did eventually get one piece of evidence from Qantas: the total baggage weight of all four bags checked in under my name – sixty-five kilograms. But unfortunately it was not a legal requirement for Qantas to weigh bags individually, and the total weight was useless because of bad police work in Denpasar, where they didn't bother to search, weigh or keep as evidence the other three bags checked in under my name – those belonging to Katrina and Ally, as well as my suitcase.

It took weeks of phone calls, emails and fob-offs to find out that my bag was definitely *not* scanned at Brisbane airport.

> The baggage checked-in under Ms Corby's name was not X-rayed in Brisbane Domestic Airport when Ms Corby checked-in for the QF 501. At this point in time, the Australian Government does not require X-ray screening of baggage destined for domestic aircraft.
>
> Qantas email, 1 December 2004

The full truth on the X-ray issue only came out when my trial was well under way, when we discovered that Brisbane Domestic Airport did not even have an X-ray machine. Maybe this was why it had been so hard to get an answer. It wasn't exactly a good look in these times of international terrorism. Great for domestic drug traffickers, though!

Qantas told us that luggage on its flight to Indonesia on 8 October had been passed to the Sydney Airport Corporation for screening. 'Sorry, no images, can't help' was the gist of the Corporation's lawyer's eventual abrupt response.

If bags were scanned, how did a 4.2-kilogram bag of marijuana – about the size of a fluffy pillow – get through? What if it had been a bag of anthrax? Would that have sailed through as well? Was it actually ever scanned?

How dangerously insecure were Australia's airports? How could a 4.2-kilogram bag of drugs get through two major airports? What became of those millions of taxpayers' dollars spent on aviation security after the 11 September attacks? Wasn't it an open invitation to terrorists? 'Come on Down Under!'

But I know that the average person watching my story unfold on TV and in the newspapers and magazines was not as scared or captivated by how the drugs slipped through airport security as they were by the idea that I might be innocent. If I really was just a happy girl going on a carefree holiday and ended up facing the death penalty because someone else had put drugs in my bag, that was spine-tinglingly scary. It shook people up. I know, because hundreds of people wrote to tell me, many saying they were now afraid to fly. I guess that's why the airport bubble-wrap business went boom. If it could happen to me, it could happen to them. And this wasn't a Nicole Kidman movie; it was real life.

And there was an even bigger shock to come. The Australian Federal Police (AFP), Qantas and Sydney airport knew almost from day one that they had strong, compelling information that might help to back up my story. But they also realised that this piece of information was far more sinister and frightening than the issue of lax security. So they kept it quiet while feeding the media the line that they were doing all they could to help me. They knew they were sitting on dynamite. They knew that on the very same day I travelled, within minutes of my flight, airport staff had been involved in evading security in order to help move a large amount of cocaine through Sydney airport. The authorities knew that some of those airport workers we trust with our bags – and our lives – were criminals.

It didn't prove my innocence but it backed up my story, because it offered a highly plausible alternative scenario. But it took Qantas, the AFP and the airport months to even admit there was any problem with crime among airport workers, and only then because it came out in a Sydney court during a bail hearing. It would have been so much easier for them if I'd gone down quietly as just another guilty drug smuggler who got lucky by getting her drugs through their security. That was a lot less difficult for the public to swallow.

> Every courier, whether they are coming into Australia or whether they are going into Vietnam, going into Thailand, will say the drugs are not mine. It's the universal excuse . . . If Schapelle Corby wasn't a very attractive lady, the reaction might have been quite different.
>
> Mick Keelty, Federal Police Commissioner,
> *Sydney Morning Herald*, 12 May 2005

Well, thanks for the compliment, Mr Keelty!

From early on, Commissioner Keelty threw regular comments to the press about my case. Usually his comments were damaging, often wrong, and never helpful.

I was a fly in the ointment. Apart from scaring people with my story, I was putting Australia's busiest international airport in the firing line. Sydney's Kingsford Smith Airport had managed to keep its serious level of crime quiet until my boogie-board story hit the news, as there had never been much interest in it before. But suddenly it was dinner-party conversation – or so thousands of people who've written and visited me have said. It's been a while since I was at a dinner party myself.

I know that plenty of news about crime at Sydney airport has come out since – people send me clippings all the time. One showed just how bad the situation had become: a New South Wales Government report was written in early 2003 by a high-ranking NSW policeman, but it was kept secret for two years. It found its way into the press a month after my case had been heard.

> The underlying theme of this paper is reflected in my knowledge that our airport in Sydney has been infiltrated by organised criminals, is susceptible to terrorist activity and is a haven for criminals, criminal networks and global organised crime. I know this because every police agency directly involved in airport policing I have visited over the past four years accepts it as fact.
>
> This document will demonstrate that we have closed our eyes and crossed our fingers. To date we have either been lucky or don't even know what is going on.
>
> Detective Chief Inspector Jason Breton,
> report to the NSW Premier's Department, 2003

There were bigger agendas than mine at stake from the start.

My luck was running no better in Bali. They'd caught a drug smuggler red-handed, and the Balinese police were not interested in any further investigation. The drugs were in my bag: case closed. They would connive to get the second piece of evidence they required to convict me, but it wouldn't involve any investigation.

There was no lab testing for fingerprints. No testing for the origin of the marijuana or its THC level, which, I found out, is how you tell its strength and therefore how valuable it is. There'd been no checking of the other bags in my name for evidence, and there was no questioning of Merc and Wayan – who were supposedly going to sell the marijuana for me. There was no search of their house or car, no search of my house in Australia either. They had obviously never watched *CSI*.

There was no investigation into the fact that the plastic bag had been cleanly sliced open by the time it reached the customs counter with me (which is why I could smell the stuff soon after opening my boogie-board bag). In fact, the marijuana was in *two* bags, one containing the other, each with blue zips at one end. It was packed so that the zips were at opposite ends, and so for the marijuana to be exposed at one end of the double covering, the zip of the outer bag was open and the inside bag had to have been cut.

Lily and Vasu didn't tell me about there being a second bag until sometime in December. 'Well, let's fingerprint that!' was my shocked response. They realised there were two bags after they'd been to Australia to search for space bags with two vacuum plugs but could only find them with one.

Why hadn't I been told this earlier? Why hadn't anyone pushed for fingerprints? Any chance of having the first bag fingerprinted had vanished that Friday night when everyone had frantically touched it. Now there was a second chance, as it was highly likely that none of the prying hands had actually touched the outside surface of this inner bag. We pushed and pushed for them to fingerprint, but the police refused.

It was up to me to formally request that the Indonesian Police test the marijuana for its origin and THC content and, although I was a bit worried about whether they would be done properly and accurately, I confirmed to the Australian Consulate on 3 December 2004 that I would like the tests done. I had been told that the AFP couldn't get involved in the testing without a formal request coming through the Indonesian authorities. I had no idea what the tests would discover, but I was innocent and so I had to try everything. I signed a piece of paper to give my permission, but it didn't happen, because the Bali police refused to do it.

Vasu was so outraged that he illegally acquired a sample of the marijuana to try to get it independently tested. I was a bit pissed off when I found out, as being accused of stealing evidence was the last thing I needed, and any test results would not have been accepted in court anyway. Of course, he didn't find anyone of any authority in Australia prepared to carry out tests on a stolen sample, even though he'd been prepared to risk flying into Australia with it – or so he told a couple of journalists.

Despite Lily's requests, we were never shown any CCTV vision from cameras directly above the customs counter at Denpasar airport, which could have proven that I willingly opened my bag.

Mum received a phone call at home from the AFP, asking her about the mobile phone I'd given to the Bali police on that first night. It was registered in the name of Rosleigh Rose. They must have thought they'd cottoned on to something – maybe she was my drug supplier?

'Rosleigh Rose?' they asked Mum when she picked up the phone.

'Yes.'

'Why did you give Schapelle Corby a phone?'

'Well, because I'm her mum. I'm allowed to give her a bloody phone!'

After a surprisingly long wait, I'd had blood and urine tests – which came out clear, of course – and I got a certificate from the Australian Police stating that I did not have a criminal record.

So, with no positive test results, no signed confession and no known association with drugs, the Bali police did not have any quick hit of secondary evidence on me. And as they had no interest in putting any effort into a real investigation, they had another shot at setting me up instead.

In early November, almost four weeks after I was arrested, a friend, her two little kids, Mum, Merc and Lily were visiting me in the upstairs office at Polda. When three of them left the room to talk to the head of police, leaving my friend and the kids with me, something sinister happened that gave me nightmares for weeks.

'Mummy, what's this?' The little boy was holding up a small plastic bag filled with white powder and some pills.

My friend leapt up, furiously hitting it out of the boy's hands and flinging it underneath a table. It was scary and very weird.

We sat there for a moment in shock, not knowing what the hell to do. I thought, *Oh no, they're trying to set us up for something else.*

As the bag sat on the floor where it had been flung, I noticed the policeman sitting at his computer across from us quietly taking it all in, occasionally smirking and giving us sly looks.

We were trembling in fright, shocked and unsure what to do. It suddenly struck me that Mum had been sitting on the chair where the bag had been found, so they could have been trying to set her up, to make it look like she was bringing her drug-addict daughter some supplies.

When Merc walked back in, we probably looked like ghosts. 'What's going on?' she asked us both.

In frantic whispers, we told her what had just happened, and she went back out to get Lily. Soon, they were both on their hands and knees searching for the packet of drugs as the room started to fill up with policemen. Bingo, Lily found it. She stood up. Then, holding up the incriminating little bag, she let them have it, yelling furiously in Indonesian, though the words of her tirade were lost on the rest of us.

The room erupted. The police were arguing among themselves, pointing at the bag, pointing at each other.

After a minute or two, the policeman who had been sitting behind his computer arrogantly pushed his chair back and stood up slowly, saying, 'Oh yeah, yeah, yeah!' He took the bag from Lily, mumbling that it had fallen from 'the evidence cupboard', which was on the other side of the room from where it was found. He then simply popped it up into the cupboard and sat back down – none of the police bothered asking us any questions. Their little stunt hadn't worked, but it had scared the hell out of us.

We all became a little bit paranoid after that, as it showed that these people really did want to send me to jail and would clearly do whatever it took. Merc and Wayan were even warned by a policeman who was a friend of Wayan's family to be careful of drugs being planted in their car. They lived in fear of it for months, parking their vehicle well away from their house and rarely using it, but always searching it first when they did.

Merc and Wayan lived with hurtful rumours from day one – that they were drug dealers who were going to sell the marijuana through

Wayan's surf shop. To find drugs on them would have been perfect secondary evidence for the police. Merc, Wayan and his two younger sisters were the only people I knew in Bali, so I guess that's why the rumours started. But Bali is a small island, and the police knew who dealt drugs and who didn't; and they definitely knew my sister and her sweet-natured, quiet husband were not drug dealers. Neither of them was ever questioned, not once. Wayan didn't even have a surf shop, and they had not lived in Bali for six years. To anyone who knows my sister and her husband, the idea of them being drug dealers would be laughable if it wasn't so disgusting and hurtful.

Absolutely nothing was going my way. And Merc and I started having doubts about Lily and Vasu, too. They were fighting hard for evidence, but we'd realised by now that Lily wasn't on the consulate list of recommended lawyers, she'd never fought a drug case in court or been lead counsel in court. As for Vasu, he wasn't actually a lawyer at all. He and Lily had been very good friends for years, even wearing matching rings, but he had never worked on a legal case with her before this. But we'd already paid them an advance of US$6,000, which we'd scrambled to pull together from everyone's spending money, so we couldn't afford to switch to a new legal team.

Apart from being disappointed that her credentials were hopeless, I was upset to find out that Lily had stalled the police on doing my blood and urine tests. Thinking it should have been done on or close to the day of my arrest, I asked her in the car when we were finally en route to Polda's police hospital: 'Why have they taken so long to do this, Lily?'

'I waited to be sure your blood is clean.'

'What are you talking about? Of *course* it is!' I was furious with her. Of course I was clean, but even my own lawyer was doubting me.

Lily also started crying regularly, which worried me. She was meant to be my tough lawyer. The first time was about a week after I signed her up, when I sadly joked that I'd been picked up by the wrong airport bus. She also told me that she cried whenever she was out having a cup of coffee in a café, watching foreigners on holiday – young women my age out shopping, carefree, with friends, doing normal things. She'd imagine where I was and what was happening, and start to cry, thinking Schapelle should've been out in the mall just like them. She'd tell me this with a tear in her eye and I'd reply, 'Well, you'd better work hard so I can!' She cried so often that I regularly ended up comforting her and giving her a hug, but at the same time thinking to myself, *Just do your goddamn job.*

Vasu, on the other hand, was becoming increasingly rude and belligerent, often yelling at Merc and me. Many times when I hesitated to make a decision about something, or questioned him, he would say, 'I'll wash my hands of you, Schapelle, I'll wash my hands.' I promised myself that the next time he said this, I would hand him a bar of soap.

Vasu repeatedly asked Merc for dollars to organise someone to help test the marijuana for the Bali police. The day after she gave him the money, the decision not to test it was made by the police, but despite her requests the money was never returned to her.

Merc and I felt alone and frightened, not sure who to trust or turn to. I needed to get out of here and go home to my life. I needed my luck to change. I needed evidence. Without evidence to fight my case, my lawyers only had doubt to fire at the court. It was strong doubt, admittedly, because if you just scratched the surface, it was perfectly and logically obvious I did not do this.

First, I'd assumed that security at our airports was watertight, all bags were scanned, cameras kept an eye out twenty-four/seven, and brilliant, sophisticated technology lurked everywhere. So why would I even think of trying my luck at moving 4.2 kilograms of drugs past such security? Apart from the fact that I respect the law, I would never risk it. Who the hell would?

And if I *had* been stupid enough to risk it, surely I would have at least flown directly from Brisbane to Bali to minimise that risk?

Not only that, but I'd hardly have put the dope in see-through plastic bags sitting blatantly on top of my boogie board, with my name and address written clearly on the outside, without at least bothering to put a lock on the whole package. If I had taken this crazy, stupid risk, why wouldn't I have put it deep inside my suitcase among my clothes, in an attempt to hide it? It would easily have fitted, as the bag would have been significantly smaller before the vacuum seal had been broken. It would have been a perfect fit in any bag.

Also, I would have known that the death penalty lurked at the other end of the flight. And all this risk for what? What the hell was my motive?

I don't know the true value of the dope here or in Australia. No one does, as the THC was never tested. Some say it's worth more in Bali, while others argue the opposite. But even if it was worth more in Bali, it would have been a marginal profit. So why would I risk death or life in jail? Why?

And where and how was I going to sell it? The only people I knew well on the island were certainly no drug dealers – the cops would've been banging on their door immediately if they were.

My lawyers and my mum were trying every avenue and beating down all doors in search of evidence. This evidence could indisputably prove my guilt or my innocence. I knew which one it would be. Why else did I fight so hard to find it? If I was guilty, the discovery of that evidence would have meant I was signing my own death warrant or kissing years of my life goodbye. Yet there I was, wanting to find that evidence more than anything else in the whole world.

The Bali police did not find anything to supplement the dope being found in my bag – not that they really looked. But no one could have found evidence to prove the marijuana in the bag was mine ... because that evidence simply doesn't exist. I have never had anything to do with drugs. I had clean blood tests, clean urine tests and a clean criminal record. The most trouble I'd ever been in was getting a ticket for going eight kilometres over the speed limit.

I lived in hope that my luck would change, that something stronger than doubt would be found. Maybe someone who knew the truth and just couldn't sleep in bed at night would finally speak out.

'I do not fear the future. I am an optimist. Whatever happens will be for the best.' I read this quote in a magazine interview with Imran Khan while I sat in my cell at Polda. It resonated with me and I wrote it down because I had to believe it, too. There was no other way.

9

Hotel Kerobokan

CHECKING IN TO KEROBOKAN PRISON WAS LIKE CHECKING in to a very bad hotel – a hotel where the doorman might be a killer, the smiling hosts heroin addicts and the guests anything from illegal card players to bloodthirsty, mass-murdering terrorists.

But tragically, I was looking forward to it. That's how low my life had sunk. Merc had even been pushing for it. My aching limbs were screaming to be stretched, and I badly needed fresh air and sunlight to revive my spirit. Thirty-six days cramped in Polda had tortured my body and soul to breaking point. Hotel Kerobokan had grass, palm trees and even a tennis court: that part would read OK in a cheap holiday brochure!

First impressions weren't too bad. There was a shabby courtyard just inside the front door, with a few trees, bits of scruffy grass and a murky pond. Its backdrop was an ugly but colourfully painted cement wall. Beyond that, the grounds looked huge. It was no luxury resort but definitely a star up from a concrete box.

Checking in was quick, but the process was shattering. Being made a prisoner in a third-world maximum-security jail was scary and degrading. And for what? What? I was doing time for someone else's crime. It was so unfair. I was starting to feel gut-wrenching anger. I should've been checking in to a hotel for tourists, not terrorists. I wanted my old life back. But I had no control. None at all.

I stood limp and compliant as a guard snapped my mug shot, took my fingerprints, height, weight, and for some strange reason measured my breasts. He then searched my bags. I watched keenly to make sure drugs weren't planted. A second guard asked me a few questions, slipping in a few sleazy ones of his own. 'You got boyfriend? You beautiful – you married?'

I just said, 'Thank you', and politely answered his questions.

It felt like a twisted version of being dropped off at a school camp when my beautiful mum, Merc and Wayan arrived to see me safely into jail. Mum held my hand. Her eyes were full of pain. Poor Merc looked sick. She was ghostly white and skinny. She'd now lost ten kilograms since my arrest. None of us could comprehend any of this. Didn't this only happen in the movies?

The good news was that, like at any hotel, we'd been able to buy a room upgrade. I'd get a spot in the best cell: clean, with no drug addicts, no lesbians and just four other prisoners. It was a relief, as the Polda guards had loved freaking me out with stories of lesbians attacking new girls. The cash price for the upgrade was $100. As we quickly learnt, Hotel Kerobokan is a thriving little business. Nothing is free. The prisoners even have to pay for the septic tank to be emptied.

It was time for the others to go: time for me to get locked up. I was terrified. We were all upset and scared. In those moments, we didn't speak, but we knew we were all thinking the same. What would happen to me in jail? What horror was around the next corner? What sick, twisted thing was next? I trembled as Mum hugged me goodbye. But I had to be brave. 'I'll be OK, I'll be OK,' I whispered.

As I was led away, I heard Mum's and Merc's pained voices fading in the distance: 'Love you, Schapelle! Love you! Love you!' Tears streamed down my cheeks. This was hurting us all way too much.

As I walked down a neatly trimmed pathway through grounds with grass, trees, a basketball hoop and a tennis court, I felt my heart brighten a little. *Yeah, this is OK. I can cope with this until my trial . . .*

It was definitely better than staring at stinky concrete walls. People were playing tennis, freely walking about, and scattered on the grass eating lunch. They all stared as we walked past, many whistling, waving and yelling: 'Hi, Corby! Welcome, Corby!' So much for my plans of keeping a low profile. Hotel Kerobokan obviously had a local paper boy.

The women's section was just beyond the tennis court but isolated behind concrete walls. The only way in and out was through an old metal door. As I stepped through, I got a nasty shock. It was nothing like I'd pictured, nothing like the rest of the jail. It was stinky, muddy and gross. It looked like a section penned off for farm animals. A pen for pigs. I knew this was a third-world prison, but did they really expect human beings to live like this?

I felt sick as I walked down a muddy path between the cells, clinging to my two little bags. All eyes were on me, and I felt like the loneliest girl in the world. How had my life come to this? I wanted to turn and run for it, but I knew it would be useless. I took a couple of breaths and steeled myself to step one foot in front of the other towards the guards' table.

'Name?'

'Schapelle Corby.'

As the guards asked me a few more questions, I was quickly surrounded by a bunch of female prisoners zeroing in for a close-up. In no time, they were rifling through my bags. I just watched in dazed disbelief as they pulled out each item, held it up, looked at it, fingered it then passed it on in noisy, screechy excitement. It was like a scene at a flea market.

I had a hazy, blurry feeling that I'd started getting a lot. I would just stare into space, vanish for a few seconds and then come back with my face flushed with hot tears. I was jolted back to reality by a loud-voiced girl shouting at me. 'Hi, I'm Sonia from Timor!' Sonia instantly appointed herself as my new best friend, though I quickly found out she was very bad news. She grabbed my bags and took me to my new cell.

My heart dropped. It was the same old concrete box as at Polda but slightly bigger. But this time five of us had to live in it – literally *live* in it. We would cook, eat, wash, use the toilet and sleep in this cell that was not much bigger than a Qantas cockpit. We would be cooped up like chickens for fifteen hours a day.

It had no running water, no power and a barred door and window,

ABOVE LEFT: Ballet days – Merc and me with Michael and pug puppy Mugsie. I'm five years old.

ABOVE RIGHT: Dad, Merc, Michael and me.

RIGHT: Ready to go on stage for a ballet concert. I'm three years old (at far left of photo), Merc is six. Always holding on to my big sister, and still do!

BELOW: Michael driving the beach buggy that Dad made. Clinton and I are holding on tight in the back.

No 'secret life' – Kimi and I out to dinner with Mum and Greg (Mum's partner) and a very young James and Mele.

Merc and I looking like dorks walking on the beach path after surfing at Kuta beach. Many moons ago.

Long ago with Kimi in Bali.

24 March 1999. Wayan and Mercedes' Balinese wedding. The two of them are pictured here with Kimi, Mum and me. The ceremony went on for a month and over 500 guests attended their actual wedding day. The headpiece that Merc's wearing was so heavy, as it was made of real gold. She looks gorgeous.

This shot was taken after I broke up with Kimi. I called Mum from Japan and asked her to meet me in Bali. Here we are on the Bali Hai cruise. I'll always remember those two weeks with Mum. This woman is *amazing*.

On Kuta beach with my then troublesss friend, my
'yellow boogie board' and flippers. July 2000.

Going for a surf at Halfway-Kuta beach. Not much surf,
but, hey, it's fun to be out there anyway.

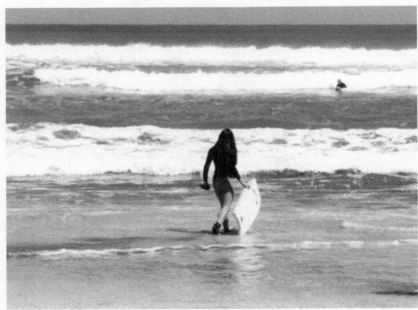

Mum and I suit
up to jet ski at
Nusa Dua, Bali.
Look at Mum,
she's so cute!

Happy days, back at home in 2002.

Hanging out with Dad on the
Broadwater Main beach, Gold Coast,
one week before I flew to Bali.

My last hours of freedom captured in a photograph. Mum took this just after our luggage was checked in and just minutes before we boarded our flight from Brisbane. Katrina, me, Ally, James. 8 October 2004.

The evidence – 4.2 kilograms of marijuana in clear plastic, almost larger than my boogie board, along with my boogie-board bag on the floor of the customs office room. Mercedes snapped this photo. It would have been much smaller when the plastic bags were vacuum-sealed, and fitted in any suitcase. But how is it possible that this got through two major Australian airports?

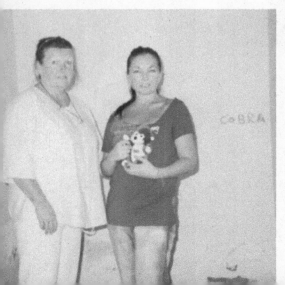

The guards were OK that day, letting Mum in to see my cell. On the wall to the left of Mum is Arabic, written in pen; to the right of me is 'Cobra', written in excrement. Both were written by Amrozi. I slept on the floor with my head positioned in the right-hand corner (where I have my underwear drying on the floor after doing my washing). As I lay down to sleep, if I looked at the wall at eye level I could see a message written by Samudra: 'Imam Samudra, Freedom Fighter'.

This shot says a lot. In the Polda cell, this is what my life had become. Wearing a prison shirt, with my boogie board and the marijuana on the front page of the local paper, and standing beside Amrozi's handwriting done in his own shit. I know it's shit because I smelt it. I had a lot of spare time!

Merc's children, my niece and nephew, Wayan and Nyeleigh. I'd been at Polda for two weeks, but we didn't want the kids to see me caged, so Mercedes somehow organised with the guards to let me out for an hour into the upstairs office. The kids came in to see me, believing that 'this is where Aunty Pelle is working'. I had to stay at work – that's why Aunty Pelle can't come to the hotel and swim with them. It was a very beautiful and very sad time.

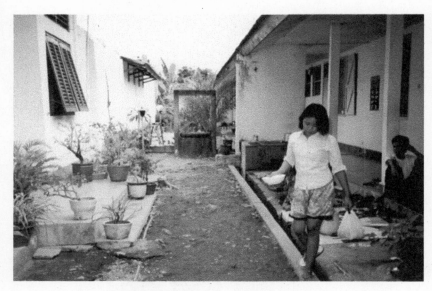

Blok W – women's block. The view from my cell, number seven. The TV room is on the left, though there's rarely ever a TV in there. The sentenced row of six cells is on the right. The well is in the centre.

Cell number seven. I was in this cell for one and a half years. This was the sleeping arrangement for six inmates. We were later crammed in with fifteen inmates, a nightmare where we were literally sleeping on top of each other.

which gave easy access to feral animals including rats, cats, snakes and toads. The floor was of broken and uneven concrete, and there was a very, very high tin ceiling, which I discovered was to prevent hangings. There were four of these primitive cells reserved for prisoners not yet sentenced, who were regarded as the highest suicide risk. I quickly learnt that suicides, or attempted suicides, weren't so rare.

There were six more cells that were slightly bigger and better concrete boxes, with electricity, running water and the greatest luxury of all: a switch to turn off the fluorescent lights at night. But the mod cons were offset by a not-so-modern open septic tank at the back. The foul stench in the cells was stomach-turning by lunchtime, when the hot sun had steamed up the raw sewage. These cells were reserved for the girls who had been sentenced.

My first night in jail, we were locked up at what turned out to be the usual time of 4.30 p.m. I ate some pasta Mum had given me and got to know my four cellmates. They were all Indonesian, but one girl, Puspa, spoke perfect English as she'd grown up in Adelaide. She was a lawyer, jailed for stealing money from her clients. We mostly talked about home and laughed at an older woman, who kept trying to speak to me in English.

I'm very lucky to have been put with these four women. Tomorrow's another day.

Diary entry, 12 November 2004

That night I got my first full night's sleep since smacking head-first into this nightmare. After five weeks of sleeping on my worn-out blue sarong, I was finally allowed the luxury of a thin mattress and pillow. And I knew that Lily was flying out to Australia to meet up with Vasu, who had made a date to see the Foreign Affairs Minister and his Labor counterpart.

Please get something so I can live a normal life, please!

Diary entry, 12 November 2004

I started struggling through the days by clinging to the hope that I would soon be going home. I believed Qantas and the Australian airports would be doing their best to try to find evidence and that something would soon surface to prove my innocence. I just had to wait and be patient, but I really hoped that I'd be home by early January for Mum's birthday.

Adapting to the depressing daily drill was very hard for me. We had no freedom, despite the initial appearances, as the tennis court and grounds outside were almost exclusively for men. Women lived behind the walls within the walls, penned in like animals. The only times we were permitted outside were for twice-daily visits between 10 a.m. and 12 p.m., and 1 p.m. and 3 p.m., and to collect mail or go to church.

Our short days outside the cages were not our own. Three times a day, we had to line up for roll call to ensure no one had escaped. We were unlocked and had roll call at 7.30 a.m., then roll call again at 12 p.m. and 4.30 p.m., just before being put back into our little cages. We really were like chickens. These roll-call times were strict. Being late was punishable by some vile chore, like getting into and cleaning out the slimy, disease-infected pond. That's one I've had to do. I was late due to being stuck on the toilet with diarrhoea. My punishment left me vomiting for the next twenty-four hours.

Life was hard, and the guards seemed to enjoy making it harder. For instance, one day Mum came to visit me and was left waiting for nearly two hours.

Mum should have been here at 1 p.m. It's now 2.30 p.m. so am feeling even more low. I can't even go out to the hall unless I have a visitor. I can't hold back my tears any longer.

... At 2.40 p.m. I pushed open the heavy steel door and walked straight over to the hall — what's the guard going to do? Yell at me in another language I don't understand? Five minutes after I went outside, a prison guy who sells drinks came and said my mum was here. She'd been trying to see me since 1 p.m.

Diary entry, 21 November 2004

We'd been sitting less than twenty metres apart on opposite sides of a wall, both waiting, both worried. I was called fifteen minutes before the end of visiting time. It happened a lot. Late calls were just sport to the guards.

And they enjoyed another cruel sport. They'd dangle a carrot, then snatch it back, laughing. 'Yes, you can play tennis, Corby,' they told me once. I was so excited. I wasn't a great player, but at least I could run around and have a bit of fun. Mum raced off to buy me a racquet. Then nothing. Every day I begged: 'Please can I play today?' But the guards just kept saying, 'Tomorrow, tomorrow, tomorrow!'

Being constantly told what I couldn't do started to provoke a fury inside me. When it wasn't the guards telling me what not to do, it was the other prisoners. 'No, Skepel, no, no, no!' No walking, no tennis, no talking to the boys, no wearing a sarong, no tight jeans. 'No' to even peeking outside the steel door to look longingly at those people lucky enough to be walking around: such a little privilege now seemed enormous.

I was even hassled about sitting in the sun. 'No, Skepel!' On my first day, I grabbed my Walkman and went to sit on the concrete in the sunshine to get a bit of colour on my ghostly white body. I hadn't been so white since living in the Japanese snow for three months. But the Indonesian girls all avoid the sun – it's a status symbol to be light-skinned – and they thought I should avoid it, too. 'No, no, Skepel!' They screamed at me for the whole twenty minutes I sat there. I blasted my Walkman headphones with music to try to block them out and fought to control my temper.

Sonia from Timor was one of the worst. She provoked me so hard on my second day that I lost it. She gripped my arm, pulling and pulling at it and yelling at me to stop talking to a Western guy playing tennis. I'd paused on my way to a visit. I don't usually swear at people, but I screamed 'Fuck off!' in her face.

I hated this place. Who were these people to tell me what to do? I did not belong in this hellhole. I was not a criminal. I was sick of being told what to do, sick of being locked up like a pathetic animal. Sick of the injustice of paying for someone else's crime. When would this end?

I was edgy and angry. Sometimes I screamed at guards and prisoners. Mostly I saved my temper for the walls, crying and screaming, 'Fuuuck! Let me out of here!' while smashing my bag furiously over and over and over against the concrete walls.

I'd never before felt such pain, such fury, such injustice. I'm not a naturally angry person, but with no personal space, no privacy and nowhere to go, this was the only way I could find to release it. I wasn't allowed to do anything else; I couldn't even slam away at a tennis ball. In my old life, if I started to feel upset, I'd just walk across to the beach, sit down alone, stare at the horizon and listen to the beauty of crashing waves. In this soul-sucking dump, the sound was screaming and fighting, the horizon a concrete wall and personal space did not exist.

I'm having a bad day. My body's heavy. It's 10.10 am and I haven't spoken a word since the time I got up at 6 am. I want to sit in a dark corner and break down. I could do that any time I needed to at Polda. I'll have to wait until everyone goes to sleep tonight till I can let go. Otherwise I would be the subject of talk of the day. It would be impossible for them to leave me be. Everyone needs to know everyone else's business.

Diary entry, 21 November 2004

It was a seedy little world. A world full of criminals. A world full of society's worst. I lived on edge. I could never let my guard down, never just kick back and relax without keeping one eye out for trouble – big trouble. Within the first few days I saw fights, a beating, girls taking drugs, a prisoner giving a blowjob to another prisoner, and a suicide attempt.

Today a female prisoner went down on a male prisoner outside the Aula. People were sitting around the corner and walking to and from the female cell section. They were not hidden, they were in full view of anyone who could see and did see. How romantic! . . .

I seriously cannot understand these people. It's now 8 p.m. and someone in my cell is smoking crystal meth. She's leaving in two days. She'd never had any form of drugs on the outside, never smoked cigarettes either. Now she does both and she hasn't even been here long.

Diary entry, 20 November 2004

Sonia came running up to me yelling: 'She's dead, dead – she did suicide. She drank poison, so stupid. Cell number 10!' What? I noticed it was quieter than usual, not many girls sitting around. I went straight to my room in shock. Some time later I heard loud, painful vomiting. I realised at that point that she wasn't dead. Once again, no doctor. Even the guards didn't care. They didn't even go in the cell to check. I gave my teddy to her.

Diary entry, 2 December 2004

The girl in cell number 10 finished vomiting this morning and was in roll call this afternoon. The guards were mocking her for drinking poison. She laughed it off as 'stress'. How nasty some of these people are.

Diary entry, 5 December 2004

One of the most common problems in Hotel K was theft. If in the outside world I had to watch my handbag because a thief might be lurking, in here I could be sure of it. Thieves were everywhere. For most it was a profession. Almost everyone stole. Within the first week my make-up, money and some clothes were all pinched. Puspa's mobile phone, not permitted in jail but discreetly kept, was stolen from our cell in my second week, a day before her release. It incited the first of many beatings I've witnessed, and it haunted my soul.

When Puspa realised in the afternoon that her mobile was gone, a huge fight broke out in our cell. Girls were screaming and hitting each other. I escaped to a visit but could still hear the yelling. The finger had been pointed at Sonia, the busiest thief. Puspa was furious. She wanted it back.

Later that night, six male guards burst into the women's section, storming directly into Sonia's cell to search for the stolen phone. I couldn't see what was going on, but I could hear the angry commotion: the banging, the shouting, the tearing apart of the cell. They soon found it, hidden under a blanket. What I heard next froze my heart. Spine-chilling sounds tore into the night. I felt so helpless. The guards whacked and thumped Sonia fiercely. She let out bloodcurdling screams. I stood at my cell door clutching the bars and sobbing. I hated this place. She might be a thief, but no one deserved that.

When Puspa eventually got the phone, it was a different model, different make and different SIM card. But she didn't speak up. Sonia was bashed, humiliated and disgraced. Puspa was released from Kerobokan the next day.

Never could I forget who I was living with – the bad people in this little society. We were all thrown in together, killers and petty thieves. It would have made a compelling *Big Brother* house, guaranteed to keep the audience riveted. I quickly got to know my housemates and their crimes. And often, it was a shock. You really couldn't judge a book by its cover. Killers came in all guises.

Puspa told me about a woman a couple of cells down who could make clothes for me for a small fee. I just had to supply her with the material and draw a pattern. And by the way, she was a murderer.

I first met her to ask about a hem. She was pretty, with long dark hair, in her mid-thirties and very nice. It was impossible for me to believe she was a killer. But she'd admitted it. She'd admitted to slicing up her maid. The maid had been having an affair with her husband for three years. When she found out, she killed her. She took the unsuspecting woman to the markets, as she did each week, and bought some carving knives. On the drive home, she stopped at a secluded beach and stabbed the maid over and over until she was dead. She then went home, cleaned herself up, drove to the police station, confessed and took them to the body. She got five years.

Another woman killed her one-month-old baby. She'd been

having an affair with a married man who already had children. When she fell pregnant and had the baby, the man wanted nothing to do with her or the child. So she made a noose and hanged the poor little innocent baby. She got three years.

Then there was 'the Black Monster', Sonia. Local newspapers had dubbed her that for her crimes. Now even the guards used it. Her crime was poisoning men's drinks at nightclubs, taking them outside and stealing their cash and credit cards. She was apparently a computer whiz and spent a fortune online with their cards. This was her thirteenth time in prison for these crimes, although she'd loudly boasted to Mum, Merc and me in our first visit that she'd murdered an Australian man. We had all gasped in shock. She was a thief and a liar.

Sonia was one person who did fit her profile. She was a nightmare. She annoyed everyone. At night, she'd yell for hours and violently beat the cell door. She'd sing at the top of her lungs all day. She stole from people. She hit people. She ran up and pinched girls hard on the breast, screaming for money or cigarettes. Nothing stopped her. I saw her kicked in the head, punched in the neck and attacked with scissors. But like an irrepressible monster, she'd just bounce back for more.

There were many people on drugs charges. Salma, a thirty-year-old woman from Mexico, was serving seven years for smuggling fifteen kilograms of cocaine to Bali in surfboards. She and her boyfriend both brought them in, though he was serving twenty-eight years. They'd had the boards specially made for the job, with cocaine hidden under a resin surface. They were caught after a tip-off.

Many of the girls were in for minor drugs offences, such as possession of one or two Ecstasy pills, or for other small crimes such as playing cards or petty theft. One woman had stolen 2,000 rupiah (about thirty cents) to buy some rice. She'd been starving. Another was busted for playing an illegal lottery game at home, a monthly event in her village. It was the eve of her daughter's wedding, and she had had a few friends over to play. The police were tipped off by a jealous niece not invited to the wedding, and the house was raided. All the naughty players were arrested. She got three and a half years.

I also got to know some of the male prisoners, who often came up and said hello during the visits. Within the first week, one guy, Agus, came to sit with Merc and me for a chat. His crime was murder. He'd come home to find his girlfriend in bed with another guy. He went to a cabinet, pulled out a gun, walked back to the bedroom and shot the guy in the head. (He admitted to having a bad temper!) He got nine years. His advice to me was to resist the temptation of drugs, no matter how low I got. He'd started taking heroin in jail to help numb the pain of this life. Now he was an addict and he bitterly regretted it.

Another guy was doing five years for murder. He'd broken someone's neck during a fight.

Then there was a dentist and his assistant. They did about 2,000 illegal abortions at the back of his dental surgery, after hours. Two women actually died. The female assistant started coming into our cell to tell us horrific, disgusting stories of how the dentist aborted babies that were eight months old. The butchering dentist would go in with scissors and cut the baby out piece by piece by piece. He got two years. She was out in eight months. I refused to let her anywhere near me.

All prisoners, regardless of their crimes, were thrown together. There was no special pen for the killers. No more civilised lot for the card sharks and petty thieves. The only segregation was the isolation tower. It had four cells with tiny windows and was reserved for all death-row prisoners, including terrorists, and extra punishment. When I arrived, the Bali bombers Imam Samudra, Amrozi and his brother Mukhlas were in the tower.

I happened to see Amrozi on my second day, as I walked to a visit. A guard pointed to the tower and said, 'Amrozi.' My heart jumped up to my throat. There he was, right in front of me, squatting in the grass behind a steel fence. He stared at me as we walked past, the smile no longer on his evil face. I noted that his hair was a lot longer. After just spending weeks in his old Polda cell, it was especially creepy to be seeing him here so soon.

What is it with me and these monsters? Some people I've spoken to have been here seven years and have never seen him. This is my first full day and I have already seen him. Has some higher power turned my life into a nightmare for me to solve or find, unravel some information? What's going on?

Diary entry, 13 November 2004

I took Merc to have a quick look at the tower on her way out from the visit that day, and we saw a guard walk one of the terrorists into isolation – Mukhlas or Samudra, we weren't sure which one. When the guard came back out two minutes later, he looked really shaken up.

'Fuck, I hate it in there,' he said to a back-up guard waiting outside. Merc translated for me.

He was so disturbed by something that the other guard patted his back. Wow, those monsters could even freak out the guards! It was something for a guard to be rattled; they could usually smash someone's face to a pulp without batting an eyelid.

Apart from the monster bombers and the butcher dentist, I tried not to judge people. I refused to think of their crimes; I couldn't allow myself to. As much as I hated it, I had to live within this world, create a life behind these walls, adapt, until I went home – which would hopefully be soon.

10

Five's a Crowd

Sitting outside my cell at 8 a.m., I smelt an awfully strong, pungent stench of sewage lingering in the air, so strong that I had to run to the toilet dry retching. How long will I have to stay here?

Diary entry, 20 November 2004

LIFE DIDN'T EVER JUST CRUISE ALONG IN HOTEL Kerobokan. Nothing was easy. Nothing was safe. Nothing was comfortable. Nothing was clean. Nothing could have prepared me for it.

We were living in a disgusting slum, in the most vile and unhygienic conditions imaginable. It was not fit for human beings. It was not fit for a dog. It was gross. It made me sick. I threw up often, had non-stop diarrhoea and persistent ear infections. I regularly got tinea, skin rashes and a type of Balinese conjunctivitis called red eye, so painful that my eyeballs felt like they were being scratched by razor blades. Often I felt weak and dizzy. Sickness was just a symptom of my new life.

The filth, the tropical heat and too many bodies made our cell the perfect breeding ground for germs and diseases. Rats and skinny runt cats wandered in and out freely through the bars. I often woke up with a rat sitting at the end of my bed. It wouldn't move without lots of yelling, screaming and frantic shooing. But it really was the perfect home for rats.

Often, the toilet in the corner of the cell blocked up, spewing faeces out onto the cement floor. It was disgusting. Some of the women kept using the blocked toilet, so their shit would float onto the floor. For days it would be awash with dirty water and chunks of floating shit. It stank like a pile of dead rats. When I showered, I held my breath, but I usually still threw up. My skin crawled to see some girls just walk on the squelchy mess in their bare feet. I never went without flip-flops. When the floor wasn't covered in this mess, it was still always overflowing with puddles of stinking piss and lots of spit.

Now I understand the real reason our room has a disturbingly strong urine stench. This morning I saw with my own eyes one of the girls squatting on the ground.

Diary entry, 19 February 2005

It was shocking to find out that it was as much the vile habits of some of the women that fouled up our cell as the primitive third-world conditions. I'm sure it wasn't a cultural clash of hygiene standards but just a lack of self-respect and respect for others. Not in twenty years or even a million years could I get used to some of the sick habits. They never failed to slam home where I was and who I was living with.

Some women bled out onto the floor wherever they sat when they got their periods, wiping it up later. I'd offer them pads, but they weren't interested.

A putrid dark-green cesspool festered close to our cell. It had a sickening stench, bred all sorts of diseases and abnormal animals and was brimming with filthy rubbish thrown in by prisoners too lazy to walk to the bin. I hated even passing it to hang out my washing. So it was a disgusting shock to see women washing their clothes in it and washing their hands in it after going to the toilet, just too lazy to go to the tap. It was especially sick given the local custom of using the left hand instead of toilet paper to wipe. No doubt it worked OK in the real world, where people washed their hands well afterwards, but not in here.

Many of the women also scrubbed their clothes with old toilet brushes pulled out of the bin. At least they were trying, I guess.

Others refused to shower, wash or even change their clothes.

The whole women's section stank. Day and night, a foul stench smacked you hard in the face. It was the raw septic tank, the stinky bathroom, the menstrual blood; but perhaps worst of all was the body odour. It was a big problem, especially at night when we were sleeping shoulder to shoulder in the small sauna-like cell.

I usually woke up soaking wet with sweat. We all did. I wore loads of deodorant, but it didn't do much. I also gave cans of it to the poorer girls, though most chose to keep it to give to their families. The stink was always bad, but sometimes it got worse when a new girl would arrive to blow us all away. One girl, Sitti, came about a month after me, refusing to shower, change her clothes or wear underpants. I had never smelt anything like her.

The new cellmate sleeps at the end of my bed and her pale-blue dress was tucked tightly under her knees, and her bottom was in my full view as she slept, foetus-style. I had such a disgusting shock. There was a pale yellow-brown wet patch. Gross. No wonder she stinks so much; and unbelievably she has not yet showered or changed her clothes. We gave her clothes and washing powder, and have over and over told her to shower, change and wash her clothes. Merc's buying her a bucket tomorrow and a couple of clothes. But we girls have already given her some and she will not shower. Come on! Her smell is unbearable, she makes me feel so sick in the stomach and I don't want to touch anything that she's touched. I almost vomited when she sat on the end of my mattress this morning. I'm not being nasty; I'm merely explaining my cellmate.

Diary entry, 16 December 2004

This vile life often made me shudder, but for now this was my home. I had to live here. I had no choice. I just had to make the best of it, be the best person I could be and try to live in this squalor like a dignified human being.

If you can't do it for yourself, you have to do it for your family and friends. You can't go home to people who love you looking like the walking dead.

Diary entry, 2 November 2004

I did whatever I could to try to make life nicer. I tried keeping everything clean, regularly hand-washing my clothes, showering daily, sweeping the cell floor daily and scrubbing the toilet daily. I put bunches of pretty flowers on the barred windowsill, my favourite photos on the wall, and my clothes and books in neat piles. I gave the poorer girls soaps, detergents, deodorants, buckets for water, clothes and even underpants. Merc always raced out to buy the stuff for me.

I also took care of my face and body by eating well, doing twice-daily exercises, twice-daily cleansing and moisturising, plucking my eyebrows, dying my hair and wearing make-up. Like I said earlier, just because I felt like crap it didn't mean I had to *look* like it!

I threw myself into a bit of a routine to help pull me through the days until I went home. Usually I got up around 5.30 a.m. to use the bathroom first, while the girls were still asleep and before the heat of the day stewed up the mess on the floor. It was back to basics: no basin, no shower. I had to spit into a hole in the floor when I brushed my teeth and I took a shower by ladling dirty cold water over myself from a bucket. God only knows exactly what was in the putrid water but it stank and gave me enormous red itchy rashes. Often it was black, full of sooty dirt, or dark-brown with mud. Centipede-type creatures also swam from the tap. Even the Indonesian girls who'd grown up using the local water got skin rashes from this foul jail stuff.

After showering, I'd rub cream into my rashes and then sit on my bed to do my little exercise routine for about forty-five minutes: sit-ups, stretches and weights using two water bottles that I'd filled with pebbles. Then I'd eat a couple of slices of bread spread with jam or peanut butter before the cage was unlocked at 7.30 a.m.

The focus of my morning was to collect a bucket of the filthy water to use during the day to flush the toilet. It was a pretty simple task but it took up to an hour, as we all shared one slow dripping tap. Even if we had two buckets, we were only allowed to fill up one at a time – it was the law of the jungle. I'd queue again in the afternoon to get water for the next morning's shower.

My afternoon exercise routine was pretty similar to my morning one. I'd work out in the cell after lock-up with Sofie, a 26-year-old local girl. We did weights and she'd sit on my feet while I did sit-ups, and vice versa.

It was survival of the fittest. You had to stand up for yourself or you got trampled. Girls would just brazenly steal your clothes or your food right in front of you and rip a water bucket out of your hand or kick it over for the sheer hell of it. In the first few weeks, I was a soft target. I got hit often. I was too scared to react. What would they do to me? Who were these people? I'd seen plenty of girls suddenly turn very nasty. If prisoners or guards asked me for something, I'd give it to them. But often they'd just take it. My bucket of water frequently got snatched as I filled it up. A girl would tip the water into her own bucket and hurl mine back empty. I'd timidly start filling again, thinking, *Grrrr . . . I hate this place.* It only stopped when I finally had the guts to scream, 'No!' But I couldn't stop girls in my cell from sneaking water during the night. Those too lazy to collect their own just stole. I regularly woke up to find no water left to shower. Very annoying.

The most important part of my routine were my visits. They were vital. They were my lifeline. They brightened my soul. They helped me to keep a grip on my sanity by giving me a line to the people I loved and to the life I loved. Without those visits, I would have crumpled in a sad lost heap.

Merc, big Wayan, little Wayan and Nyeleigh surprised me with a visit. I had such a great day, Wayan and Nyeleigh both drew picture collages for me. They are so cute. I said to Wayan, 'Do you know where you are?' His reply: 'The police station.' Afterwards when we were saying goodbye he asked me, 'Do you sleep in the cages like the tigers do at the zoo, Auntie Pelle?' And that's exactly how I feel!

Diary entry, 5 December 2004

Merc visited me every day, bringing food, toilet paper, cleaning products and anything else I needed, including updates on my case. Poor Merc had lost her old life, too. She'd planned to return to Australia at Christmas so little Wayan could start school in Queensland, where he was enrolled. I'd assumed they'd still go, but Merc refused to leave without me. She'd stay to look after me, like she'd always done, until I could go home, too. My beautiful devoted sister was going to do this sentence with me, negotiating the essentials of her own life – her kids and Wayan – around her daily jail visits, dealing with the lawyers and fending off lots of harassing journalists.

I tried not to burden Merc unnecessarily with my pain and fears. She was stressing and hurting enough; she'd already spent a week bedridden from stress. But my pain was her pain. If I hurt, she hurt. If tears uncontrollably poured down my face, it shattered Merc. I saw it in her eyes. It tore her apart to see me upset. But she'd always fight to stay perky and positive. 'It's OK, Schapelle, we'll get you home. It's OK.' She held a vice-like grip on her own tears and fears in front of me, but I knew she often went home and threw up.

I couldn't ask for a more perfect sister.

My mum also came every day when she was in Bali, usually bringing half the local supermarket with her. She felt helpless, so feeding me was at least something she could do. Often we didn't say a lot; she'd just hold me or clasp my hand. She didn't ask if I was OK – we both knew I had to be – and she could always tell just by looking at me. She was my mum; she knew me. When I came out shaking or crying, she never asked what was wrong. It hurt us both too much. She knew I didn't like to burden her with everything I had to put up with in here. It was breaking her heart that she couldn't fix this for her baby girl. She couldn't put a plaster on it and kiss it better like she used to do. I love my mum so much. It broke my heart to see her hurting so badly.

Other family and close friends regularly flew in to see me, too. As the weeks passed, I even started to get visits from supportive strangers. It helped to heal my aching heart.

In the jail, we all had little ways of trying to make life a bit more bearable.

> *One of the girls is really funny. She's twenty-four years old and each night she gets all dressed up, complete with the full face of make-up, and says, 'See you, I'm going to a bar in Kuta. I'll be back at 5 a.m.' Then she takes her make-up off and that's about as much English as she knows.*
>
> Diary entry, 16 December 2004

I wasn't the only one dying to get out of this hellhole; we all were. But while we couldn't escape in reality, we could in fantasy. I sometimes did. I'd throw on my bikini and sarong and sing out to the girls in my cell, 'Bye! I'm going to Turtle Island today. I'll keep an eye out for cute boys. See you tonight!' Then I'd walk down the muddy pebbled path to my little blow-up kiddies' pool at the end. It had been an inspired gift from Mum's brother, Uncle Shun, who knew I was a water baby.

> *Went down near Salma's room to fill my bucket this morning, and the pool was already out on her grass. She'd blown it up last night. How exciting. We're trying to fill it up with the hose bit by bit in between people's buckets being filled.*
>
> Diary entry, 22 November 2004

I shared my pool with Salma, the Mexican girl, who was the only other foreign female prisoner and someone I'd become friends with. We started to spend some afternoons together, hanging out by the pool, drinking cans of soft drink and snacking on her homemade popcorn.

In her three and a half years in Hotel K, Salma had made life as comfortable for herself as possible. She kept to herself, obeyed all the rules and had slung the guards some cash to get the best-located cell at the very end of the path. No one walked past, so she had the luxury of privacy. She'd also transformed her cell, painting it white with blue trim, putting tiles down and shelves up. She'd furnished it nicely and planted her own little garden out the front. But most enviably she had some say in who shared with her. Usually, it was no more than two others, but sadly I had to stay in the pre-sentencing cells. I didn't ask how much she'd paid for her upgrade.

Trying to create a bit of light-hearted fun whenever I could was vital to me. I knew I needed it to stay sane. I didn't want to be sad or angry all the time. Most days I tried to spend a bit of time in my little pool, lying back, soaking up the rays, reading a book and listening to my iPod. I also spent time playing badminton, chatting to the girls, plucking their eyebrows and my own, cutting their hair and enjoying pampering sessions with the girls in my cell – doing face masks, hair treatments and massages.

The other girls had their own tricks to lift their spirits. Every Saturday night, Puspa went to another cell for 'party night', some girls had regular sleepovers in other cells or spent afternoons drinking arak, the local brew, and playing cards. Quite a few of the girls just got out of it smoking drugs. Naturally, I steered clear of them.

Sonia found her own unique ways of filling in her time, usually annoying the hell out of everyone else.

All the grounds of the girls' block were so flooded, idiot Sonia went swimming and doing backstroke!

Diary entry, 20 January 2005

6.30 a.m. woke up to Sonia singing at the top of her lungs. By 10.30 a.m. I had just about had enough of her singing the one verse, 'One day at a time, sweet Jesus – that's all I'm asking from you.' I went to her, asking if she could please stop or sing a different song. She does not understand how irritating she is! She thought for a bit then said to me, 'Oh, these words, same like in jail, yeah? One day at a time!' She sang a different song, still at the top of her lungs, but came back to the first song about ten minutes later. Luckily Merc came at 11 a.m. and saved me. When I returned at 12 she was still at it.

Diary entry, 6 December 2004

Being continually stuck with all these women often did my head in. I was never left alone. I never had any personal space. I was endlessly fascinating, with my blue eyes and white skin. They'd sit on my bed, stroke my arms, offer to wash my clothes, massage my feet and ask incessantly, 'Skepel, you shower, you eat? You have shower, you eat?' If I cried, it got worse. 'What wrong, Skepel? What wrong?' Sometimes I just wanted to strangle them. I wanted to scream out: 'Leave me alone . . . *Fuck off!*' But I didn't. I knew afterwards I'd feel too bad. I'd just breathe and walk outside, sometimes down to Salma's cell, sometimes to my little pool.

> *Sat in my pool for an hour. That's the only place I can be alone because it's in the sun and I lie down and pretend to be asleep, so I don't have to answer them when they yell out, asking if I'm hot, telling me, 'It too hot', or telling me to get out of the sun, asking if I'm showering.*
>
> Diary entry, 6 December 2004

I also started going to church, as an escape from the women's section and a place to cry. Church and visits were the only times we were regularly allowed out. Initially at least, church gave me a bit of privacy.

> *I cried throughout the whole service: two hours. I found myself staring at Jesus – whether sitting or standing, my eyes never left the painting, as if he were drawing out all my pain and fear. Halfway through the service Chris Currall and an Indonesian prisoner joined me in the back row. Chris patted me on my back and let me be. After the service I met three of the African prisoners, one had already been sentenced to death.*
>
> Diary entry, 3 December 2004

Church and visits were the only time the sexes mixed, though prisoners did find ways around that rule. Talking to men was a good change, a nice rebalancing. I grew close to one guy, Eddie, who was in here for possession of eight Ecstasy tablets. I first met him at Polda. He was an Indonesian Buddhist but converted to Christianity. We could meet at church. He had a miraculous effect on me, always instantly turning my tears into a smile. I started to lean on him emotionally. On my black days when I cried inconsolably for hours, the guards would bring him to the women's block to calm me down.

I started having more black days: more days when I couldn't get out of bed or stop crying. I just wanted to go home. This was so, so unfair. It was not my crime. I was trying so hard to be patient and positive, trying so hard to do my best. But I was teetering on the brink. I couldn't hold my tears back. I cried for whole days. I got exhausted and dizzy. My heart ached. I had to get out; I had to prove my innocence. I had held on tightly to hope, but as the weeks passed, my grip started to slip.

This is my life. I know I'm innocent – so hard to prove. Really we are guilty until proven innocent, which hurts so deeply.

Diary entry, 30 November 2004

Lily and Vasu had returned from Australia, from all their meetings with Qantas, the airports and politicians, with zilch. My case was going nowhere. I knew I wouldn't get home for Mum's birthday in January. I had no idea when I would be going home. I just *had* to prove my innocence in court.

Had first visit with Lily and Vasu since they came back from Australia. I was disappointed and felt a lot of fear for my future.
Cried a lot. I couldn't stop.

Diary entry, 27 November 2004

Just after Lily got back, the Polda police asked to see me again for further questioning. 'Why did you cry when you were arrested?' was their question of interest. It was so ridiculous that Lily became fearful it might just be a ruse to give them one last chance to get me to unwittingly sign a confession. The police were running out of time to find their second bit of evidence, as it was just days before their deadline to pass the case over to the prosecutors.

I simply couldn't trust anyone. Not the police, not the guards and definitely not the other prisoners. I had to watch my back all the time. People were still always trying to snap photos of me, and snippets about me and my case regularly made it into the newspapers. There were spies everywhere, all ready to earn cash.

Lily, Vasu, Merc and I had a meeting in the Kerobokan office discussing important details of my case. There is no privacy. Prisoners and guards walking in and out of the office. Lily was trying to get them out. There are still so many spies; they like to make up stories and sell them to the newspapers. Come on! This is my life we are trying to talk about.

Diary entry, 30 November 2004

So many lies were still being reported in the local media that Merc and Lily held a press conference to set a few things straight: I did not visit Bali in January 2004, Merc and Wayan did not live in Bali permanently, I was not part of a drug syndicate here or anywhere else, and I did not own a drug factory that converts marijuana into heroin!

I felt so exasperated. No one was helping me or my lawyers. Not in Australia and not in Bali. I'd consented to the testing of the marijuana, but the Bali police had said 'no'. I had asked for fingerprinting of the inner bag, but the Bali police said 'no need'. What the hell sort of investigation were they running? I pushed my lawyers to keep pushing. This was my life. My life!

Of course the police knew I wasn't a drug dealer. Why else were they refusing to do any investigation? They had a strong case. It was in my bag. No point digging for evidence that might actually weaken their case, especially one that was so high-profile. I presented a chance for them to make an explosive example of what Bali did to Western drug traffickers.

I was taken to the prosecutors' office on the day the brief was handed over. While being held in a cell, I met the Australian yachtsman Chris Packer, who'd been charged with failing to declare six guns on his boat. He was about to be transferred from Polda to Kerobokan. We were like two animals in a cage, the media snapping away wildly. We both tried uselessly to hide until Merc cut a deal: we'd pose for a couple of shots then they'd go away. Done.

Once inside the office, it was my chance to personally plead with the chief prosecutor. 'Please, please, *fingerprint the inside bag*. PLEASE!'

He pretty much ignored me. 'Ask the judge!'

What I'd thought was an important meeting was just a media show. In front of the photographers, I was made to repack my boogie-board bag. The prosecutor also pulled out the bag of marijuana for the photographers to snap away at, with me in the background. He even gave them my passport to look through and photograph. I could trust no one. No one!

It was exhausting. The stress was endless. Nothing was OK. Just when I thought a day was passing bearably, some sick new drama would break and shock the hell out of me. I've discovered that no matter how many times you see it, you never get used to watching another human being get kicked in the face or brutally beaten.

The first time I saw prisoners attacked by guards was about three weeks after I'd arrived at Hotel K. By chance, I was in the office when the guards laid into them and was shocked at how fierce they were in full public view.

> *About eight new prisoners were brought in – Chris Currall being one of them. He was very skinny, shaking and extremely nervous and scared. I told him he'll be OK, gave him a packet of my ciggies and a bit of money. They had to do a bunch of push-ups, take their shirts off and the guard punched them in the stomach quite fiercely three or four times. Some of the Indonesian guys had their hair chopped with a blunt carving knife, even though they already had short-back-and-side cuts.*

Diary entry, 2 December 2004

Merc was not going to come today, but because Chris had arrived
at Kerobokan and has no one here to bring him anything, she
decided to do some shopping to pick him up some things; also she
bought both of us a nice salad roll.

Diary entry, 3 December 2004

A week later, I saw real bloody, brutal violence for the first time.
Gabriel, the American guy I'd briefly spoken to while he was playing
tennis, was beaten almost to death. I'd been having a good day and
was sitting in the visiting hall chatting to a few girls on holiday
from Perth when action broke out, suddenly turning the lazy, hot
afternoon fast and furious. There was movement everywhere, people
everywhere, all running, all sprinting towards the front jail doors.
We leapt up to see what was going on. Through the windows, we
saw Gabriel being shoved, pushed, punched and beaten up badly
by the guards.

We watched in shock for a little while until I had to go back
for roll call. The girls had to stay for nearly two hours until they
were finally allowed to leave. They passed the wide-open door to
the room where Gabriel lay and saw his legs splayed out on the
floor. The guards were still attacking him.

It turned out that Gabriel had tried to escape over the fence.
He'd only had a few months to go but was drunk. He reached the
street outside and started running down it until he hailed a passing
cab. But that's where his luck ran out. As he was climbing in, the
driver suddenly saw prison guards yelling and running towards him,
so he accelerated, knocking Gabriel out and running over his leg
before speeding off.

The guards caught Gabriel on the road while he was down, kicking
and attacking him before dragging him back into Kerobokan, where
more guards fiercely laid into him with iron bars. Even when he
was lying in a pool of blood, almost unconscious, with deep gashes
to his head and neck, they kept kicking and punching him. He was
almost out, and they still didn't stop the attack.

Later that afternoon, I convinced the guards to let me out to buy
a bottle of Fanta. I snuck a peek at what was going on in the office.

There was still a lot of commotion and yelling, but poor Gabriel was unconscious on the floor. A guy from the American Embassy was being pushed around. He was fighting to get Gabriel to a hospital. He was in dire need of it. But the guards refused and kept yelling and shoving him against the wall. I felt panic. Gabriel might die. I wanted to help. I wanted to scream, 'Get him to a hospital, you monsters!' But I didn't. It knew it wouldn't do any good. It would just put me in the firing line.

> *This American embassy guy is getting nowhere; they won't let Gabriel go to a hospital. The guy needs help. I went back to my section and paid the guard to use her mobile – with a friendly smile I told her I was calling my sister. I quickly told Merc what was happening and to call the Australian Consulate and the Red Cross. The conversation was over in seconds.*
>
> *Couldn't get back out as we were all locked away early. Couldn't sleep at all, spent the night crying and praying. The next morning I found out that Gabriel had stitches. He's now in isolation – the tower of the bombers. I went to church. Walking past the tower I yelled out, 'Thinking about you and praying for you.'*
>
> Diary entry, 13 December 2004

The next day, I put together a bag of antiseptic soap, toothbrush, toothpaste, water, mosquito repellent, pack of cigarettes and lighter, some nibbly food and a magazine. I wrote a little something inside the cover to let him know we were thinking of him. I gave it to my guard helper-friend, Willy, when he came into the women's section, and he assured me he'd take it straight up to Gabriel.

> *At 9 a.m. walking past the tower on my way to church I slowed down to the back of the line, so the guards were way in front and I was able to let everyone go on without me. I stood still with my ears pricked.*
>
> *I could hear Gabriel trying to yell out for help – faintly could hear the moans, 'Help, help me . . . please, help me.' There was*

nothing I could do; I had to keep walking to the church now as male prisoners began walking up behind me.

After church, as I walked back past Gabriel in the tower, he was quiet. I looked at the ground and with a loud voice I said, 'If you can hear me, I'm trying to get help, I'm trying.'

Later I saw Willy. He had taken the bag in to Gabriel; said he looks really bad – both eyes big, black and puffed up, fat lips, broken leg, no cast, extreme pain in his spine, his head's been shaved and has stitches, most of his body is bruised, he's on the floor with no bedding and he's been asking for painkillers. I cannot believe this place; they will not give him painkillers. When he was caught, he had a huge amount of American notes on him to organise his freedom. He'll never be seeing that again.

Diary entry, 13 December 2004

Walking past the tower I saw Gabriel standing, trying to look out of a little square window. I stopped for a second and from what I could see his face was still swollen; I could only see his eyes and nose, and his hairline, which has been shaved. Good to know he's on the way to physically getting better. I told him I'll be going to church each day this week so when he hears us girls, to yell out to me anything he needs and I'll do my best to get it for him.

Diary entry, 14 December 2004

We might have been prisoners, but we were still people. We were human beings, but in Hotel K we were treated worse than animals. We had no human rights. They did not exist. Prisoners were regularly assaulted by the guards, and Christmas Day was no exception.

Must have been around 2.30 or 3 p.m. I heard a male voice screaming in deep pain from a room just off the visitors' room. There were visitors at the time and everyone could hear. We all had the same sad, concerned expression. I asked the drinks guy if a prisoner was in there and he nodded with the same expression as ours.

Apparently the police are torturing a prisoner to find out how the drugs are getting in. His torture had started around 9 a.m. He'd already had two of his fingernails ripped off. So I dread to imagine what else has happened to him by now.

Diary entry, 25 December 2004

The prison didn't provide any medicine. Prisoners had to buy it. If you were poor, you suffered. Merc was regularly buying eye drops and antibiotics for girls in my cell, so their infections didn't endlessly circulate among us. Unbelievably, the prison didn't even give us anything to sleep on or sit on. Those who couldn't afford to buy a mattress slept on the bare concrete floor.

But the most frighteningly inhumane thing was that at night in the women's block we were trapped in our cages, with no chance of getting out in an emergency. There was no key. After the guards locked us in at 4.30 p.m., they went home *with* the key. If there was a fire, we'd die. We'd be trapped like useless monkeys in our cages. We'd be left for dead. We couldn't get out, and no one could get in. We were locked in cages, penned in behind concrete walls with no guard. The only way to get help was by yelling, screaming and banging like crazy. But even if someone heard us, it'd be hours before the key turned up.

One night I thought my cellmate was going to die. We could not get help.

Watini arrived a few weeks after me, bringing knife-edge drama to the cell. I found out she was just over a month pregnant, after conceiving while in a police holding cell. I didn't ask her whether the father was a guard or another prisoner. I didn't want to know. But we spent days talking about this little baby with Watini in tears, not sure whether to have an abortion or have the child and adopt it out.

'It's OK if you want to have the baby,' I told her. 'I'm going home soon, I'll take care of it for you. Or my mum would love to look after your little baby. We'll do that for you, if you want to have the baby.' She said thank you.

A few days later she came out of the bathroom saying, 'I'm clean!'

'What are you talking about?' I asked.

She'd just miscarried her baby. She didn't seem upset or in pain. I felt so sad for her. That night I cried for her and for the lost life. But in the morning, the girls in my cell told me not to be upset, explaining to me that she'd secretly been doing rough stomach massages to help abort it. I felt sick. We'd talked about this little baby. Yeah, she was in jail, but it was a *baby*. They said it was something they all did as a form of contraception. I felt disgust.

Tonight the new cellmate had a miscarriage. We have no guards in our section during the night, as they leave after we're locked in at 4.30 p.m. – no doctor, no help. If something happens, they have to go outside the jail to get the keys. Not quick.

Diary entry, 2 December 2004

The drama wasn't over. Watini was a twenty-two-year-old prostitute who'd forced her poor young body to endure fifteen massaged miscarriages, which had shredded her insides, and a few nights later I woke to her blood-curdling screams of agony. I didn't know what was going on. Fortunately, some of the other girls did. Her insides were falling out. Someone spread her legs, held her ankles for grip and then forcefully put her heel to Watini's groin to push her insides back in. The first time I saw this, I thought she was going to die. I couldn't believe we could not get outside help.

Watini had six or seven more excruciating episodes. She'd just start screaming and screaming and the girls would run in, take her jeans off and put their heels into her. I'd gently stroke her forehead to try to soothe her.

She was in bad shape. She needed to go to hospital. But the prison refused, despite Merc offering to pay the bill. It was ridiculous red tape. Watini's release papers had to come from the police station, as she hadn't yet been sentenced, so she wasn't yet the jail's problem. Eventually, the prison doctor suggested that she get a girdle to help keep her insides nice and tight. She did, and it seemed to work.

Another big drama in our cell was when Sitti, the stinky lady, got possessed by a ghost. It scared the hell out of me. She came from a little village and had been sentenced to six months for stealing a bag of prawn crackers from her local market. As well as not showering, she didn't brush her teeth and had bright-red infected gums with big yellow buck teeth. I'd never seen anything like it before – the teeth stuck out at a ninety-degree angle.

The first night she was possessed, she was lying on the floor at the end of my bed, eating a banana. Suddenly she dropped the banana, closed her eyes and started speaking fast and loud in a weird voice. I leapt up away from her. All the other girls did, too, and we huddled together, crying. We were all freaked out. It went on for about five minutes. One girl got her Bible out and started praying for her. Suddenly Sitti snapped out of it. She stood up, said, 'Where's my banana?' then picked it up and casually started eating it again, oblivious to the group of us huddled hysterically on the bed.

It was terrifying. I really believed she'd been possessed. I didn't sleep at all that night, scared it would happen again.

The next morning it got worse. I was carrying a bucket of water to the cell when Sitti ran up and started carrying it with me. When we were putting the bucket down, water spilt and Sitti slipped. Suddenly she was spread-eagled beneath me, wearing no underpants. She started wildly clutching at my legs like a crazy woman, clawing at me. My pulse was racing, my heart slamming into my chest. 'Let go! Don't touch me, don't touch me!'

We were alone – no one to help. Things were a blur: her bright-red gums and yellow buck teeth fully exposed by her big monkey grin, still clutching, still clawing. I kicked and screamed and finally broke her grip. I ran like hell. The next day Merc bought her some underpants.

She really terrified me and everyone else in the cell, especially when we started to find rocks hidden throughout the cell each night. We all feared she was crazy enough to bash our heads with them while we slept, so each night for weeks one of us would stay awake all night watching her.

Eventually, however, Sitti and I became friends. Things changed one day after she'd been possessed for nearly twenty-four hours straight.

I grabbed a bucket of water, walked over to her and pointed my finger, telling her to 'stop it'. She didn't. Then, as I was about to throw the water over her, other girls stopped me. But it snapped Sitti out of it. When I tried to get her moved to a cell *without* a ghost, she begged me on her hands and knees to let her stay with me. I gave her one last chance, and she didn't get possessed again. I realised that she'd put on this crazy-lady act to scare off the girls who worked her like a slave because she was a poor peasant. Sitti had developed a wary fascination with me, as I was the only real-life Westerner she'd ever seen. But she'd seen white people on TV before and remembered an actress called Veronica. So, after we were friends, she called me Veronica.

If I'd seen my fate in a crystal ball, I would have laughed. No one could live like that! But I was. I was living this hell, day and night. Even sleep was no escape. I had nightmares about the nightmares. I often woke up crying. But I was clinging to hope. This would be set right. It had to be! I was innocent. The judge had to see it, had to see it was *not* my crime. I couldn't lose my life for a crime I didn't commit. I had to convince the judge to let me go home. I *had* to!

By the time I finally started court, I'd been living this dark hell for almost four months.

11

Chaos in the Courtroom

*I'm trying to get an image of the day in my head so I hopefully
don't become overwhelmed with emotion and fear – don't want
to be resembling a puffy-eyed, sweating beetroot when the judge
first sees me.*

Diary entry, 25 January 2005

MY FIRST DAY IN COURT LOOMED LIKE A SEA OF
terrifying dark shadows. I had no clue what was lurking,
no idea what to expect. My lawyers had told me nothing. Everything
terrified me: the court bus, the holding cell, the reporters and the
cameras. But there was really one thing eclipsing all this, one thing
freezing my heart: the bitter fight for my life.

I'd been refusing to think of the gruesome possibilities of death
by firing squad, or a lifetime or a long time in jail. I'd suppressed
thoughts and fears of it. I'd denied it. But it was always there. It
cast an unshakable dark shadow over every moment. It burdened my
heart – always. Starting court just stirred it all up. It made me face
the reality that my future might be grim, and provoked terrifying
thoughts about the gritty details of being shot.

It became a sort of morbid fascination. I thought about it; I asked
other prisoners about it. Did they take you to a beach, draw a cross
on your heart and shoot? Or did they just line you up against a
wall and fire at you, like target practice at a shooting gallery? Did
they cover your eyes with a blindfold or put a bag over your head,
or turn you around to shoot you in the back? No one really seemed
to know. It was often on my mind.

I also thought about being locked up for years, losing my youth and growing old in prison, never having a normal life, never having a baby, never getting married. I wondered how old Mum would be when I got out. Would my dad still be alive?

It all put terror in my heart. I often shook violently, curled up in my cell. I spent most of the night before my first day in court crying, shaking and endlessly putting on layers and layers of make-up. It was not out of vanity but out of fear. It was my nervous habit, my nod to nail-biting. For hours I sat transfixed. I stared into a little mirror and kept applying and re-applying my make-up, waiting for the scary day to break.

Despite the fear, I was relieved that my case was finally being heard after months of just waiting and waiting and waiting. Every single day. I'd had a little glimmer of hope in my heart that I might be released that day, I might get to go home. But nothing changed: I was stuck in hell. Now at least there was action, and deep in my soul I believed I'd be OK. I'd always been taught that if you were good in life, life would be good to you. I was innocent. I wouldn't get shot. I wouldn't get slammed behind bars for years. It wouldn't happen. Somehow I'd be OK. I'd get to go home. Something would break to back my story. Something would turn up. We were still pushing hard. We still had time.

But on my first day in court, all I had was a chance to make a good impression on the judges. A chance to make them see I was not a drug addict, not a drug smuggler or dealer, but just a nice girl who came here on a holiday. I dressed in a pale-blue shirt and brown skirt that Mum had bought for me. I'd pressed them by putting them under my mattress and sitting on it – a useful trick all the girls in my cell used. I skipped breakfast, as I had no hope of keeping it down, and by 9.30 a.m., when my name was called, I was ready to start the grim day.

'You'll be OK, love. Be strong, it will be OK.' Mum surprised me with a quick visit before court to help boost my spirits. She'd flown in the night before. We had ten precious minutes together talking through chicken wire before I was dragged away to get fingerprinted and handcuffed with nineteen other prisoners. It was so degrading and awful. I was cuffed to an old woman on heroin charges. We stood waiting in lines like a dysfunctional school class on a day's excursion before we were filed out in cuffed couples to a waiting bus and a clamouring pack of photographers yelling, 'Schapelle, Schapelle!' I hated being singled out. I didn't respond. I had to focus on getting on the bus. I had to hold it together. I didn't want to cry any more.

The whole day was startling. Nothing was like I'd expected or imagined. I got shock after shock after shock. Even the bus trip to court was hell. The driver was a maniac. He thought he was Michael Schumacher, speeding around the third-world roads like it was his final lap on a Formula 1 track. In the back, we were flung about like rag dolls. Most of us stood clinging to a handrail, and every time the crazy lunatic flew around a corner, we slammed hard into each other. Luckily, but quite bizarrely, we could slip our handcuffs off, which saved our wrists from being cut to shreds. By the time the maniac slammed the brakes on at the court, we all looked like we'd done a round in the ring: our shirts dripping wet with sweat and everyone's hair in a wild mess.

But things were about to get worse. As I stepped off the bus, photographers, cameramen and reporters were all jostling, pushing and shoving to get their shots. They circled tightly around me, some only inches away, pushing microphones in my face and hurling questions.

'You all right, Schapelle?'

'How're you feeling, Schapelle?'

A guard kept pulling me along by yanking hard on my right arm. The scrum moved with me. Suddenly my left arm was jerked towards the ground. It hurt like hell. The cuff cut into my wrist. Then it hit me. I'd forgotten the poor old woman I was cuffed to. I quickly looked down and to my horror she was on the ground, looking up at me with such pain in her eyes. She was being dragged along and trampled by reporters. Her arm was awkwardly up in the air, connected to me. It was like she didn't exist.

As soon as we got to the holding cell behind the court, the guards undid our cuffs and she ran to the toilet. I went in to her.

She was sobbing as she feebly dusted the dirt and footprints off the side of her body with her shaking, bleeding hands. I couldn't say sorry enough. She just kept crying, covering her face with her hands and saying, '*Malu, malu*' (I'm shy, I'm shy). Her wrists had deep cuff cuts, she was covered in scratches and her hair stood up on end. I felt devastated.

The day kept going downhill. I was the first of twenty to be called into court. It was a shambles. There were people everywhere, cameras everywhere, reporters everywhere; people talking loudly on mobile phones, people eating, laughing, smoking and chatting; and people who looked like they'd just walked in off the beach. It was madness. It was nothing like I'd imagined. When I sat, reporters perched right at my feet, nearly on my feet, holding microphones so close that later when I was giving evidence I kept accidentally hitting them with my hands.

It got worse still when the chief judge and his two assistant judges came in and called for the proceedings to start. The microphones came in closer, people in the public area were loudly getting translations, and all eyes were on me. It was hot, noisy chaos. It was hard to focus or to hear anything. I kept wanting the head judge to bang his hammer and shout 'Order in the court!' But he didn't. He didn't even move the bunch of cameramen standing right behind him, or ask people to stop talking on their mobile phones or put out their cigarettes. He didn't stop all the people casually walking in and out the doors or hanging through the windows for a bit of a look. It was wild. It was a circus. Even Lily was still chatting away on her mobile phone.

It hardly seemed like the right kind of atmosphere to be fighting for my life. I felt shaky and upset and kept biting my lip, fighting to hold it together.

I looked anxiously around at Mum and Merc, who were sitting behind me, in the front row. They knew exactly how I was feeling; this was their life, too. Mum blew me a kiss. Just seeing them, their loving looks, their smiles saying 'It's OK', helped me to relax a little. But even before it had all begun, tears were pouring down my face. It all hurt so much.

I am so relieved to finally have it starting; the Indonesian courts
never find anyone innocent because they can be sued, so I'm
mentally preparing myself for a stay here: depressing.

Diary entry, 27 January 2005

I still couldn't quite comprehend the bitter twist in my fate.
Someone out there knew I was enduring this hell instead of them.
How did they sleep? Didn't they feel the guilt? Would they ever
come forward? I wasn't so naive as to believe they would, but I
fantasised and even dreamt about it sometimes. But the reality was,
I was in the hot seat taking the rap.

It felt like a bad omen when my translator didn't show up. Vasu
suggested that we could use his secretary, Eka, who happened to be
with him in court and who spoke English pretty well. She wasn't a
professionally trained translator, but the judges swore her in anyway
just so we could start. It was another mistake.

The next thirty minutes were tough. Tears just kept pouring
down my face as I sat shocked and helplessly listening to the lies
– lies that could help take away my life. In his indictment, the chief
prosecutor claimed I'd acted suspiciously when I walked over to pick
up my bag, that I'd refused to open it when I first got to customs
and that I'd claimed the marijuana was mine. None of it was true.
Not for the first time, I was left in no doubt the police would do
whatever it took to send me down. They hadn't managed to trick
me into a signed confession, their stunt in the Polda visitors' room
had failed, so now they were just going to make it up.

This was insane. How could they lie? My head was spinning. I
felt sick and dizzy. This was my life. I could feel the cameras and
microphones closing in on me, everyone staring at me, scrutinising
me, waiting for my reaction. I felt like collapsing in tears or
running to my mum for a hug. But I sat still and took some deep
breaths as I desperately tried to stay in control. I focused straight
ahead, clasped my hands and prayed. When the judge asked if
I understood, I answered, 'I understand, but it's not true.' It was
bullshit and a bitter taste of what would come.

The prosecutor told the court I'd been charged with possession, which could lead to ten years in jail, and drug trafficking, which carried the death sentence. My heart squeezed even tighter.

When the devastating thirty minutes were over, I didn't want to stand up. I was full of terror and fighting for my life, but in this moment it was sweat marks down my bum that panicked me. It was so hot. I could feel my shirt completely glued to my soaking back and beads of sweat dripping from the bend in my knees. What if my dark brown skirt was covered in sweaty patches from the little plastic chair? There were so many people right behind me who'd see! I finally stood up when the perplexed guards became impatient. Every week after that, Merc put a towel down on the chair for me before I arrived.

I was taken back to the tiny holding cell around the back. All twenty of us were crammed in like monkeys, with people crouched down on the concrete floor or leaning up against the bars or walls. The air was hot and sticky with a hazy blue hue from all the cigarette smoke. Everyone was smoking. It was hard to breathe and my eyes were badly irritated, red and sore. In the corner was the dirty, stinky cell toilet, which became my hideout from prying cameras in the weeks ahead. I ended up spending so much time shut in there that Mum started coming in early and scrubbing it clean for me.

It would be another week before I went to court again, as my case was heard on only one day a week. This meant it would drag on for months, but at least it would give us more time to get evidence.

So hard to concentrate: the courtroom is covered with cameras, reporters, TV cameras sitting on the floor in the middle of the court, and when I speak all these microphones are placed down on the table in front of me, and there's a window behind me with people speaking in Indonesian. Cameramen calling 'Corby, Corby' in my ear; as I turn, they snap the camera. Couldn't they have a little respect? I have to be completely aware and with no distractions: I am on trial for my life! Don't they understand?

Diary entry, 3 February 2005

For the next two weeks, the prosecution witnesses backed up the lies in the indictment with their own lies. It was shattering. If they'd done their jobs properly in the first place, I wouldn't have been fighting for my life. But it was obvious that with no secondary evidence from the police's botched non-investigation, their lying testimonies were going to be used instead.

First up was Gusti Winata, who was the customs officer who'd originally asked James whether the bag was his. He testified that he'd asked me to open my boogie-board bag but I'd refused and said, 'Nothing in there.'

'She was nervous, then I opened it myself. My hand was stopped and she said, "No." When I opened it a bit, she yelled, "No!"

'I asked, "Why?"

'She said, "I have some . . ." and looked confused. I asked the suspect what was in the plastic bags. She said, "That's marijuana."

'I asked her, "How do you know?"

'She said, "I smelt it when you opened the bag."'

I was trembling with fury and shook my head in utter disbelief. I focused ahead and clasped my shaky hands tightly in my lap. When the judge asked if I agreed, I said, 'No, he's lying.'

He then asked me to point out what was untrue.

'Well, firstly he didn't ask me to open the bag. He just asked whose bag it was. I opened the bag, and I don't remember saying anything or hitting anyone's hand. I opened the bag and then I closed it. I was scared. I didn't know what it was. Then when I closed my boogie-board bag up, a strong smell came out. I was very scared; I didn't know what was going on.'

The second customs officer, Komang Gelgel, said I looked suspicious as I went to collect my bag, and then gave the incredible and damning evidence that I had admitted owning the marijuana. 'She said, "This is mine, I own it."'

My response to this was: 'I was not suspicious-looking or acting restless. I was happy because I was on a holiday and I love Bali. I open it, I lift it up, and I'm surprised: there's a plastic bag half-open . . . And I close it up; I can smell it. I never at any stage stated that that marijuana belonged to me. Never, ever, have I stated that.'

It was my word against theirs. But there was one bit of evidence I thought might speak louder than words. When I had arrived at customs, the inner plastic bag had been slashed, exposing the marijuana through the unzipped outer bag. Bits of it were even sticking out. This was proof that the bag had been tampered with. Surely the judges' legal brains could plainly see that. I would not have cut it open, whether I put it in or not. Someone had tampered with the bag.

But there was no explanation and, unsurprisingly, no further investigation. When the judge asked the customs officers if they'd slashed it, they said 'No', and added that no one else at customs had touched it either. The judge did not ask any further questions about it. It was just another thing the judges had no interest in chasing up.

My lawyer's theory was that a customs officer had cut it after spotting it on the X-ray machine out the back. Mr Winata testified that he had seen something suspicious in the boogie-board bag when it went through the machine but did not put a blue chalk cross on it, as they routinely did when a suspicious bag went through, because he thought no one would pick it up. I suspect he thought no one would pick it up if it had a blue cross on it because he knew exactly what was inside it. He'd already seen and smelt it. This didn't make me innocent, but it added to their rule-breaking bungling of my case.

The outer bag had not been fingerprinted because it was 'contaminated' by the very people now giving evidence against me. They broke the rules: they didn't wear gloves. But now it seemed very likely that the inner bag had also been touched. Was that why the police and prosecutors had refused to fingerprint it, despite our continual pleas to do so? We had pleaded for months for it to be fingerprinted. The fact is they refused. Why?

Can't help but break down when I see that plastic bag. It has destroyed my life.

Diary entry, 3 February 2005

When the judge called for the bag of marijuana to be put on his bench, it was not treated like evidence but like an old bale of hay. Bits of it were being pulled out and falling everywhere. When a bit fell on the floor, the judge just casually bent down, picked it up and put it back. The smell was so strong that the judge even put a tissue over his nose – proving that it was one hell of a smell for check-in staff or sniffer dogs to have missed if it had been in my bag and cut open when I had checked in.

But the most shocking thing was that everyone – the judges, the prosecutors and the customs officers – started touching the 'uncontaminated' inner bag. My blood went cold. How could this be happening? The judge was not only letting it happen but also taking part in ruining evidence. Right up until this point we had been pleading with the judge to have that inner bag fingerprinted. It would at least be something – proof my fingerprints were not on it. But right before our eyes, my last hopes of forensic evidence were dashed.

The most sinister moment came when Winata handled the inner bag. To my mind, there was no mistaking his clear intention to touch it. It was a deliberate action. He put his hand inside the outer bag, then tugged at the inner bag. It was such a bizarre and unnecessary thing to do. Mum has a videotape of that extraordinary moment. Why did he need to put his hand in and touch the inner bag? Was he concerned that the judge might finally agree to have it fingerprinted?

As all hands kept grasping at the marijuana, Merc yelled out to Lily and Erwin (another lawyer Lily had brought in to help her) to make them stop. Erwin replied that this would be good for my defence, as they were breaking more rules. But it turned out to be just another bit of lost evidence.

Today we were taken to the court in a smaller police van that seats four in the back. They decided to take a different route, which was a very bumpy and dangerous ride along a road/rocky track. The driver was on a power trip: almost had so many head-ons,

and at one stage a motorbike crashed into the back of us as we
came to a sudden stop.

Diary entry, 11 February 2005

My third day in court started with just the same craziness. The mad drive, the media scrum and then the insane lack of order in the courtroom. The laidback judge didn't seem to give a damn about it.

As the first anti-drug squad officer sat down to give evidence, he casually placed his gun between his feet. There was no objection from the judge, but it was a little indelicate, given the penalty I was facing, and I urged Lily to tell him to put it somewhere else. He did. He simply picked it up and placed it on the edge of the prosecutors' table, where it was well within the reach of all the people constantly walking in and out of the busy side door. Anyone could have snatched it and fired.

There were two officers helping to make the prosecution case against me by telling more lies. It seemed like they'd been told to strengthen it a bit. Not only did they confirm what the first two customs officers had said, but they claimed my reactions at the customs desk had been even more dramatic. This was despite the fact they'd been standing fifteen metres away from the desk. Both also claimed that I'd said the plastic bag of marijuana belonged to me. Neither spoke English.

More lies, more lies! I'm so tired of listening to the same shit over
and over.

Diary entry, 11 February 2005

Both officers demonstrated, with sweeping hand gestures, how I supposedly stopped Winata opening my bag. Police officer Gusti Astawa said: 'The hand of Gusti Winata was stopped and pressed by Corby when he started to open the bag. She said, "No! No! I have something."'

My heart was slamming against my chest. I couldn't stop my tears. How could this be happening? This was such bullshit. These people were lying, just telling straight-out *lies*. But again, it was my word against theirs. There had to be something to *prove* I was telling the truth.

I put it to the judge: 'Do they have a security camera to prove I opened it myself? Isn't there a camera to say that . . . to help me save my life? If it's the death sentence, don't they have something to help me here?'

Erwin also asked if the existence of security camera vision could be investigated, saying that after all his client was on trial for her life.

The judge initially agreed that enquiries should be made but later said, 'We'll get it if we need to'! He obviously never felt the need. Why? Would it prove my story by showing that I had happily collected my bag and in one swift movement willingly flung it up on the customs desk and unzipped it? Yes! Yes, it would!

> They give the death sentence to drug traffickers but it's the customs officers' and the police officers' words against mine. Me, a mere traveller . . . the death sentence. These customs officers and police officers are obviously not given any training; they do not wear gloves, they do not take fingerprints, no interrogation questions, nothing. No tape recorders, surveillance cameras, nothing to back me up. My word against theirs. You'd think that if a country gives out the death sentence they'll be equipped to give the accused a fair trial for their life!
>
> Diary entry, 11 February 2005

When the judge asked Mr Astawa whether fingerprints were necessary in the Corby case, he said, 'No.' When he asked the second officer, Wayan Suwita, why no fingerprints had been taken, he answered, 'In this case, the criminal perpetrator was caught red-handed by the customs officers at the airport. We knew it was marijuana, so it wasn't necessary.' The judge must have agreed, as he denied our continued requests to have the inner bag fingerprinted, though by now it was contaminated anyway. He also turned down our requests to have the marijuana DNA tested to find out its origin.

I couldn't understand how a judge would not want a full investigation when a life was at stake. Didn't they want every bit of information possible before giving their verdict? Before deciding on someone's life? And wasn't I entitled to a fair trial to fight for my life? I could see as clearly as everyone else that the evidence against me was strong. It was in my bag. But didn't I have the right to a proper investigation just in case I was telling the truth? This court could impose a death sentence. Surely taking fingerprints or looking at CCTV footage wasn't asking too much. Wouldn't it have been standard procedure in any other court in the world?

It was all so Mickey Mouse, the whole process – from the bungled non-investigation by the police and the prosecutors to the judges' lack of interest in the lack of investigation, to the disruptive chaos in the courtroom. It was an ironic twist that this casual, disruptive, laidback court, which appeared to be far less imposing than the usual sterile courtroom with its wigs, gowns and mahogany benches, was far deadlier. Its sentences were the harshest in the world. I felt this every single second that I sat there. But it felt like no one else got it. It felt like there was no respect for the fact I was on trial for my life.

It had been a particularly gruelling and infuriating day, and I really didn't want to go back to Kerobokan. I'd simply had enough, enough of this hell and enough of this bullshit justice system. I was tired of helplessly watching these people bang nails into my coffin with their lies, their destruction of evidence and their lack of investigation. I didn't need any more proof of this unfair, unjust system, but I got it on the way home when a guy sitting next to me told me he'd just been sentenced to nine years for murder. With remissions, he'd be out in five!

I am so tired of this place; I didn't want to get locked up behind that cement wall again with the only thing to pass time being walking down the muddy rocky path to collect my water. I needed to release some anger, so, silly me, I punched the inside door of the police van. The guard in front yelled to me, 'You got a problem?'

My reply: 'Yeah, I've got a problem – fuck you!' He was really angry and kept yelling repeatedly, 'You got a problem with me?'

My reply again was 'Fuck you.'

The van stopped, he slammed open our cage door and was still yelling at me. I sat there for a bit to calm down, then I said sorry and got out, the other prisoners getting out after me. Once back inside the prison I told the guard, 'I'm so sorry.' He accepted it and patted me on the back and held my hand.

I need to invest in a boxing bag. Keep me out of trouble.

Diary entry, 11 February 2005

The stress of life in jail and the pressure of court were really affecting me. I was losing weight, throwing up often and wildly swinging from wall-smashing fury to deep black depression. Some days I simply couldn't get out of bed. But I was still trying as hard as I could to be patient, to be positive, to be hopeful, for my family's sake. They were all as stressed out as me.

I will be coming home. I am strong, I have faith, I have support, I have a lot of love in my heart. I am coming home.

Diary entry, 11 February 2005

I started to spend more time at church and more time with Eddie, the former Buddhist who'd been done for possession of a few tablets of Ecstasy. He was still able to turn my tears into a smile, and church somehow started helping lift the burden a little. I'd always heard that people turned to religion in a crisis, used it as a crutch, and I could see why, as it was really helping to give me a sense that this nightmare was happening for a reason: there was a purpose for it. That was easier to believe than thinking I was now living in hell for no reason other than just plain bad luck. And if there was a God who put me here, He could also get me out!

I feel that God has all this planned and He is in control of my fate/destiny/future. So I am not scared; I'm just really finding it hard to come to grips with the meaning of patience!

Diary entry, 17 February 2005

Ironically, my patience was often tested by Christians coming to the jail church and sneakily taking photos of me. I'd get a sixth sense that someone was taking a shot, turn, and see them frantically trying to stash the camera. Regularly, it was visiting Christians being very un-Christian when they were permitted in on Sundays. People coming to visits were also sneakily snapping pictures to sell and fill their pockets.

But it wasn't always covert and sneaky; sometimes it was blatantly in my face. For instance, one afternoon just after lock-up, the guards escorted a huge bunch of photographers and reporters right into my cell. I'm sure the guards were well paid for their trouble.

At 5.30 p.m., the guards came in with twenty other people – reporters and photographers! All of them were saying, 'Corby, Corby.' They came in, took a few shots of my things, my section of the cell, how I live here – they also told me how to sit on my bed for some shots. How embarrassing! I didn't resist. I did as they said. They hung around for fifteen minutes. I was so embarrassed at all these people shooting their cameras at me. The other girls in the cell were running around trying to hide, but there is nowhere so they covered their faces with anything they could find: towel, bucket, one even put on her Muslim veil! Reporters were asking them questions about me, for example: What's it like to live with Corby? How do you all communicate with Corby? Does she speak Indonesian? The girls were yelling out, 'Corby tidak tau!' (I don't know Corby!) How can I keep a straight face with all these crazies around me?

Diary entry, 16 February 2005

At court the media was intensifying, too, with more cameras in my face every week. It was making my court days more stressful, knowing everything I said or did would be filmed from the moment I stepped off the sardine bus. Some days I'd arrive at court already feeling shaky and upset from something horrific I'd seen at Kerobokan and would then have to face a media scrum firing questions.

This morning as I waited at Kerobokan to be taken to court there was a fight between two guys. One had a plank of wood and was bashing the other guy. The other guy was in bad shape. All his face was cut open and bleeding.

Diary entry, 17 February 2005

As soon as I climbed off the bus, still feeling a bit shaken from the fight, a pack of photographers and reporters tightly circled, pushing, shoving and shouting questions. I was starting to get badly bruised each week and my wrists were torn by the cuffs as I was dragged through the jostling scrum to the holding cell, where I would escape to the toilet. But today there was no escape.

Although the little cell was already crammed with twenty of us prisoners, it was suddenly full to the rafters when a guard let in the pack of reporters and photographers. I ran into the toilet, but they still got shots by holding their cameras up above the door. I couldn't believe it when I looked up and saw all the cameras. A second guard, the one that I'd let my anger out on the week before, came to my rescue. He yelled at all the photographers to get out and was furious at the other guard for letting them in.

In the hot seat that day was the last prosecution witness, the senior customs officer, who answered questions about airport operations. Incredibly, when the prosecutor put the plastic bag on display again, much of the marijuana had vanished.

When the prosecutor opened the boogie-board bag to show the plastic bag, it almost seemed that the evidence was missing. The prosecutor had to dig around to find it . . . the evidence is becoming less and less each time we enter the court. Hopefully by the end of this, on my last trial day, there will be only a few crumbs left, then my lawyers can say, 'Where did you get a figure of 4.2 kilograms from? The scales must have been out!'

Diary entry, 17 February 2005

While we were in court, there was a noisy commotion going on outside. People were holding handmade posters with my name written on them, and instinctively I thought they were supporters. But my translator, Eka, told me, 'No, Schapelle, they're here to support the *death sentence* . . . The signs say *kill* you!' I felt sick. I swung around and saw a sign with blood dripping from an axe in the window behind me. It was chilling.

It was the first day the Indonesian anti-drug protest group GRANAT had turned up, and Mum was upset and furious. 'You have already found my daughter guilty, and she is *innocent!*' she screamed. 'Why can't you be saying try to find evidence? No one seems to be trying to find who put the bloody stuff in the bag. They don't care!'

The protesters just laughed at my mum, provoking her to throw water on them, but they still refused to go away. As I was being walked back to the holding cell later on, I started panicking as they surrounded me, thinking one of them might have a gun. But once inside the cell, I was quickly distracted from my fear when four men started laying into a guy who'd just been sentenced to five years' jail for being caught with a joint. I didn't know why and didn't ask why they were beating him, but it was pretty sad and pathetic.

The next day in court would be the start of my defence case, and I was scared. We still had nothing. I had no evidence from Australia, no evidence in Bali, and my lawyers were really starting to worry Merc and me. I was never briefed on what would happen in court, never given any idea of a strategy. Lily often cried in court, but rarely stood up to question the prosecution witnesses. *Come on, Lily – help me. Stop crying, do your job!* I often silently willed her. This was my life. We had to fight. I wanted her to leap up and counter their lies, challenge their bullshit. But she rarely did. Most of the time she just sat quietly watching and sending SMS messages on her phone. She was out of her depth. She'd brought Erwin Siregar in to help, but Lily was lead counsel.

Vasu sat on the public bench endlessly scribbling on scraps of paper and passing them to Lily. He'd told me before the first day in court that he couldn't sit on the bench with Lily because he was Sri Lankan – nothing to do with the fact he was an engineer. At that point, I still believed he was a lawyer: most of the Australian papers were calling him a lawyer, and I guess he'd started believing it, too. Vasu was my case coordinator, but he'd never actually worked on any other legal case in court.

I needed help. We were due to start our defence case, and all we had were the testimonies of me and my travel mates. I desperately needed something to break, something to fall from the sky!

12

Ron and Robin –
the Dynamic Duo

When I first heard I had a millionaire 'white knight' about to gallop into town and rescue me from a fate that could be death, I was at first baffled. *Mad Ron? Isn't he the phone guy? How can he help? Oh, I suppose he's rich and has a big-shot lawyer to bring over,* I thought. But why help me, why spend his time and money on me? What did he want in return? I joked to Merc that maybe he wanted me to model phones for him when I got back home . . . Yeah, I could do that!

I don't like thinking bad things about people, but it's hard to recall any of the initial good feelings I had about Ron Bakir and Robin Tampoe. My 'white knight' did indeed become my 'black knight' because of the sorry way his and Robin's involvement unravelled: the deceptions, the contracts we were pressured to sign but publicly deny, the lies they told and the hungry media they loved to feed, often with misinformation and most often without my OK or even my knowledge.

It didn't matter if something wasn't true; they'd still push a line if they felt like it. Like when Ron kept telling the press I was suicidal. Not only was it untrue and sending out the wrong message – why kill myself if I'm innocent? – but it was hurting my family, especially my mum. Merc and I begged him to stop, but he didn't, and Mum got so upset that, despite us assuring her I was OK, she flew over to check for herself.

Rewinding to around the time when Ron first rang Merc saying he wanted to help me, we felt hope and relief. We were scared, desperate for any help, when this millionaire sprang out of nowhere willing to find me the best defence and pay for it. I thanked my lucky stars. I thought he was heaven sent. When the press called him my 'lifeline', I thought he was, too.

So when he flew to Bali with his lawyer, Robin Tampoe, just a week before I started my defence in court, I was excited and hopeful. I'd occasionally spotted Ron in bars on the Gold Coast and had seen him in his Mad Ron TV advertisements brashly selling his mobile phones, but I was nervous about actually meeting him and his hot-shot lawyer. I relaxed as soon as I saw them, though, as Ron looked like I remembered and Robin reminded me of Barney Rubble, as he's only about five foot tall.

They stayed for about ten or fifteen minutes that first visit and seemed like really nice guys. We talked about the case and about my concerns with my Indonesian lawyers, whom they promised to check out the next day. I light-heartedly told Ron that I'd tried to buy a mobile phone in one of his Gold Coast shops just a couple of months before coming to Bali but had been turned down because of a bad credit rating after failing to pay my home phone bill on time. He promised to give me free phones and calls for the next thirty years. I thought that was very nice.

Their visit lifted my spirits. They were so full of energy and determined to ensure I got the best defence possible, with Ron promising to pay whatever it took. But he made it clear on this first day that it wasn't charity and I'd have to repay him whenever I could. I was fine with that, not for a second imagining that in just three months he'd be asking me for half-a-million dollars.

I'm so relieved and thankful for Ron's determination, care, generosity, his honesty and his time. I'm overwhelmed by his care. My thanks go out to my saviour, Mr Ron Bakir.

Diary entry, 24 February 2005

Ron and Robin went to check out our Indonesian legal team, asking us for permission to sack them if they felt it necessary. They told us we could switch to their powerful legal contacts in Jakarta. We were desperate and grateful, so we gave them the power. Merc spent the day stressed out, fully expecting they'd fire them and that she'd get an abusive call from Vasu. Instead, she got a call from Ron, telling her how great Lily and Vasu were. She literally cried in relief that Vasu was not going to call and yell at her.

The four of them got along so well, in fact, that the next day they met for drinks at Ron and Robin's villa. They enjoyed such a wild time together that Vasu slipped and broke his ribs while playing chasey around the pool. It was certainly rather odd that they seemed to hit it off so quickly, with Ron readily singing their praises to the media. But it would make sense later on.

> The Indonesian legal team has done a wonderful job and
> we are ready to provide the best possible legal defence.
> Ron Bakir, 12 March 2005

Ron visited me about three times on that first trip, and it was always good to see him. Everyone else thought so, too. He instantly made himself a very popular guest among all the jailbird hosts by sweeping in and flashing around his cash like a swashbuckling cowboy. Instead of paying the drink boys the usual 6,000 rupiah (about $1) for the drinks and straw mat, he'd flamboyantly peel off 50,000-rupiah notes from a large wad and fling them about. 'Here you go, champion! Here you go, champion! You want one, too, champion?' Perhaps it made him feel good, although most of the disbelieving but grateful recipients would be putting it straight into their arms.

His generosity wasn't great for me, either. I'd say, 'Ron, don't, please don't.'

'That's OK, Schapelle, he'll look after you!'

'Ron, who is he? He's just another prisoner, and he's a heroin addict.'

In Hotel K, where we were paying for every little privilege, even something as simple as being allowed to get to your visits on time, it wasn't smart to flash cash around. If the guards thought I was rich, life got more expensive for me and all my other visitors – there were no fixed prices, not one price for all. But Ron didn't listen. He did it every time.

I guess he liked to be liked. It was frustrating, but I certainly forgave him a bit of flamboyance because, after all, he was just a generous type of person who was here helping me out of the pure kindness of his heart, wasn't he?

My eyes were opened about three weeks after our first meeting, when Vasu returned from a trip to Australia with a contract signed by Ron stating that he (Ron Bakir) would get 50 per cent of any money I earnt from 'all forms of marketing or media worldwide including but not limited to, television, radio, motion picture, written media, internet based media, merchandising and public or private addresses' and that I 'assign irrevocably to Bakir the exclusive rights to the story and all information relating to and surrounding the MATTER including details preceding and subsequent to the MATTER'.

My mind was spinning. I knew my story was getting big, but world rights? It was ridiculous. I was in jail, fighting for my life. In two months, I might be sentenced to death by firing squad. I didn't care about media deals; all I cared about was going home.

Nevertheless, I tried to read the contract. But the words weren't sinking in. I felt anxious. My pulse raced. It didn't feel right, especially with Vasu standing over me, almost shouting in my face, 'Sign, sign, sign!' And he didn't stop. 'Come on, Schapelle, we do *everything* for you, Schapelle. Why can't you just sign it, Schapelle?'

Lily was sitting, just watching as Vasu badgered me, occasionally saying, 'Sign, Schapelle!'

I was exhausted. I felt sick and tired, and with Vasu still blaring in my ears, I signed the damn thing without even properly reading it through.

Ron had drawn up separate contracts for Merc, Wayan and Mum, and all my friends and the rest of my family were also bound by them – thanks to this sentence: 'The rights further extend to include the family and friends of Corby thereby restraining such persons from breaching the rights assigned to Bakir.'

Merc was also treated to Vasu's bullying and stand-over tactics to make her sign. It was odd he was pushing so hard for Ron, not that we thought too much about it at the time. He chose his moment about a week later, just outside the front of the jail. Ron was there, too. Merc was sitting in the back of Vasu's car, comforting Lily, who was crying again. This time a relative had died, apparently, but it seemed that whenever Merc had to sign something or make a big decision, Lily started crying over a new drama.

In the midst of Lily's hysterical sobbing, Vasu handed Merc the contract and told her to sign. She tried to read it, but with all the noise and stress of Lily crying and Vasu yelling 'Sign, Mercedes', nothing sank in. But, like me, she signed it anyway. Merc and I were trying our best, but neither of us had ever been in a situation like this before and weren't adept at standing up for ourselves.

Merc asked Vasu for one of the two copies, but he refused, saying they had to be legalised. He'd given Merc a contract for Mum, however, so she was able to read it later. I let Merc deal with it because I had enough to cope with in here. I didn't want to think about my world rights, I was too busy fighting for my basic human rights, like getting the septic tank emptied.

By this point, Ron and Robin had for some reason become dead certain that they'd get me home. According to them, the absolute worst-case scenario was one year, minus time served, under house arrest in a luxury Balinese villa. 'Don't worry, Schapelle, we'll get you home.' It was a line they kept selling me right up until the day I was sentenced to twenty years. They were very good salesmen, though in my situation, with the death penalty still on the table, I was also a pretty willing buyer. It was much nicer to believe them than to believe the bad stuff. I still felt scared but was clinging tightly to them and to their promises.

Ron flies back to the Gold Coast tonight. I don't like it when Ron flies away, I feel so much more safe and protected when he's in Bali, nearby. I know Ron has a lot to do and he's only six hours away.

Diary entry, 30 March 2005

Merc, meanwhile, started to get people telling her to be careful of Ron – that he'd been bankrupt, that he didn't have all the cash he endlessly talked of, and that his motives probably weren't as pure as he made out. I was also receiving letters from Australians warning me that Ron Bakir might not be the white knight we all thought he was.

Merc was still angry at the way Vasu had muscled us into signing the contracts. Her gut was telling her it was all wrong and that it was time to stop trusting these self-titled 'Team Corby' characters. She'd watched as people tried taking ownership of my name and set up everything from businesses and websites to charities, and felt that I should at least own the rights to my own life story.

She also sought advice from a couple of people, who told her 50 per cent for Ron was a joke. Of course we'd try to pay Ron back as soon as we could, and it clearly stated in the contract the split wouldn't kick in until after he'd recouped all his expenses. Fair enough. But 50 per cent after that just seemed a bit much.

So, after stressing over it for a couple of weeks, Merc went to talk to Vasu. She knew it would be an angry showdown, with Vasu highly likely to lose his temper at her. He was always going off the deep end about something, and it took guts for my sister to confront him.

As soon as she told Vasu she was unhappy with the contracts, he disappeared for a few minutes – she quickly realised to phone Ron, who was back in Bali and who turned up twenty minutes later. Vasu seemed to have Ron's interests at heart. Merc stood her ground and told them both she wanted me to own my rights and that 30 per cent for Ron was enough.

But together they worked her over. She was stressed and on the point of tears when Vasu printed out a new contract on the spot and yelled, 'OK, Mercedes! It's changed . . . now sign, sign!', thumping the table for emphasis. He was seething. Merc was exhausted, worn down, she just wanted to get out of there and go home to her kids. So she signed. But with Ron and Vasu still standing over her, she again didn't properly read it. They were good at this. I guess Ron had learnt his skills selling contracts for mobile phones. Vasu was simply a bully.

With her last bit of fight that afternoon, Merc insisted that she'd take my contract and give it to me herself. Reluctantly, Vasu agreed. It gave her the chance to read and absorb it quietly at home. She did, and was furious at herself for being duped again. My contract still stated that the financial split was 50 per cent. The only change was a tweak in the wording about the rights, which still left Ron with 'exclusive rights' to my story. So, in effect, nothing had been changed.

Merc wanted to scream. She wanted to get rid of these people. Weren't they supposed to be helping us? Weren't we supposed to trust them? It was as if we needed lawyers for our lawyers. But we had nowhere to turn, no one to trust. We'd already spent $80,000 on Lily and Vasu and couldn't afford to change. Besides, would we get anyone better if we did change?

Merc didn't even bother to bring the new contract in to me, and Mum never signed hers.

Right from the start, Ron and Vasu insisted that we publicly deny the existence of any contract. Merc and I both asked why, as surely it wasn't a sin. They gave us some mumbo-jumbo bullshit answer, but we got the gist that Ron was worried about his image and wanted the public to think his motives were purely altruistic; he certainly didn't want his image of being a white knight in shining armour tainted by a dirty little contract.

About a week before my verdict was due, news of a contract with Ron getting 50 per cent of anything I earnt hit the press – after Dad had a few drinks with a reporter. Both Ron and Vasu rang Merc in a panic, telling her exactly what she had to say to journalists. 'There's no agreement with Ron Bakir; we never signed anything,' she was quoted as saying in *The Australian*. The article went on:

> Mr Bakir refused to talk about the arrangements his agents
> had discussed with the Corby family, but said there were
> no negotiations on the table.

The Australian, 21 May 2005

Merc was really upset about having to lie about the contracts and again asked Ron why we couldn't just tell the truth and admit to them. He told her: 'Now is not the time, Mercedes. People will get the wrong idea.'

But the truth was, I was Ron's investment. He talked non-stop about making money and always had plenty of business ideas for me. He and the other three also regularly spoke about suing Qantas.

Ron wanted me to become a singer and asked me to write some songs.

'But, Ron, I'm not a songwriter. I'm not a singer, and I'm in jail!'

'Just do it – try, try, try to write a song, Schapelle.' He was always very persuasive, a good salesman, so I wrote some stuff down to give to him.

He handed it back, saying I needed to write a chorus. He also asked if I had any music to go with it.

'Excuse me? What?' I laughed and laughed and jokingly made some heavy-metal music sounds. But he didn't think it was funny, he was deadly serious.

'No, Schapelle. Something like Delta Goodrem's music – you could be the next Delta Goodrem.'

'Right, Ron. Right, OK, yeah. Well, I'll try to think of some music to go with this, OK, and get back to you!' It was ridiculous; where was he getting all his ideas from?

There were his book deals, Hollywood movie deals, interview deals. He kept telling me I'd never have to work again, kept coming at us with more ideas, more deals, and we just kept saying, 'No, Ron!' He had dollar signs in his eyes and sky-high, over-the-top expectations. I know he was trying to do a deal for an exclusive TV interview but refused offers of $450,000, because I was worth no less than a million. This was, of course, for when he got me out.

We discovered that Ron didn't always tell us the truth about the money being offered, as Merc often spoke directly to the media. They rang her, unsure if Ron had the authority to do deals when supposedly no contract existed. She found out that on at least one occasion Ron was lying about the amount being offered for an interview. He claimed the offer was $20,000 less than it actually was. At this point he also regularly told Merc to change her number and stop talking directly to the media. She refused, as she did not trust him.

My family wasn't particularly interested in media deals; they just wanted to get me home and for it all to be over. But if we could make a bit of money from a magazine or TV interview, great; it would help support me a bit longer and help to continue the legal fight. Because, despite the media hype that Ron was 'bank-rolling' my defence, he wasn't. By the end of April he was already claiming in the media that he'd spent $300,000 on my defence.

> 'Within the first five minutes of talking to this incredible, brave young girl I knew straight away she didn't have a guilty bone in her body. From that moment, my commitment changed – I decided to do everything possible to get her out. I will only stop when my heart stops. Money didn't come into the equation,' says Ron, whose battle for Schapelle's freedom is estimated to have already cost more than $300,000.
>
> *Woman's Day*, 25 April 2005

We had no idea what Ron was supposedly spending his money on. We were using all Dad's superannuation and any other money we could scrape together to pay the lawyers. By the time we learnt the Australian Government would be contributing to my legal costs, we'd already spent a huge amount of money and continued to pay thousands for witnesses to be brought over and other 'incidentals'.

Things started going quite sour between Merc and Ron when she kept saying 'no' to most of his media deals and money-making schemes. I could see Merc getting more and more edgy around both Ron and Robin when they'd come in to visit me. She knew I was struggling, with the verdict so close, so she didn't tell me exactly how much pressure they were putting her under. Ron even hassled her on the day before my verdict to make me write a diary for *New Idea* about the days leading up to my trial. She told him I was in no state to do it.

Ron and Robin were obsessed with the opinion polls in Australia, constantly telling me how they'd boosted my profile – yeah, thanks, but get me out of here – always thinking of ways to win a bit more sympathy, whip up the press, boost their little investment – me! They had become spin doctors who were spinning out of control. I felt completely forgotten as a person in the middle of all this.

One of their craftier ideas was to write a couple of letters just before my verdict was due, one pleading to Prime Minister John Howard and the other to the Indonesian president. I knew nothing of these letters until after they hit the headlines.

> Mr Howard, as a father and as a leader, I plead for your help. I did not do this. I beg for justice. I don't know how much longer I can do this. Please bring me home. Please.

> Dear President Yudhoyono, you hold the key. Please set me free. I have done enough time for this terrible crime.

Unless I had an uncanny ability to write rhyming couplets in my sleep, I didn't write that letter. And neither did I write the first one. The only person I knew who wrote in rhyming couplets was Ron Bakir. In a letter he gave me, he said: 'Don't ever FALL because Australians want you to stand TALL. You have many loved ones, who want you in your DOME, let me promise you one thing we will bring you HOME.'

Robin told reporters the letter to the Indonesian president was 'a plea from the heart' that he would personally deliver to the president. He said: 'I'll see Schapelle today and she'll give that to me. As I understand it, the letter is more about her affection for Indonesia. It talks about her family and her sister and the fact that she would do nothing to bring disrespect to Indonesia.' To this day, I don't know if the letter actually made it to the president or whether it was just given to the press. But I still fret that maybe it damaged my appeals.

The next time I saw Ron, after the letters had found their way to the media, I asked him for copies so at least I'd learn what was in them. He looked me in the eye and said: 'There's no letter, Schapelle, it's been blown out of proportion. There is no letter.'

My faith in the dynamic duo really faltered on the day the prosecutors recommended to the judges that I should spend my life in jail. The day before, Ron had phoned me from Australia, saying, 'Don't worry, Schapelle, you'll be coming home, we'll get you out. Don't worry, you'll be coming home!'

I was totally frustrated that 'Team Corby' was devoting so much more time, energy and effort to the court of public opinion than to the Bali Court of Law – the only court that actually mattered right now, the court where my life was on the line.

13

More Court Daze

I FELT SO SMALL AND FRAGILE, UP AGAINST A SYSTEM THAT seemed determined to get me, to pull me further into this nightmare, so I could never ever escape, never go home. I'd seen how low the prosecutors would stoop to ensure a guilty verdict. If they'd lie and destroy evidence in court to make their case against me even tighter, what else would they do?

It was all starting to play with my mind. I was breathing fear and paranoia. I often huddled up in my cell and shook, hiding from danger and choking on terror. I felt my enemies everywhere. I felt preyed on, watched – dark shadows, spies and cameras lurking everywhere. I felt everyone was out to get me. I felt every new prisoner was an undercover cop sent to spy on me.

My biggest fear was that drugs would be planted in my cell. It would be simple: drugs were rife. That was the irony. I was in a place where drugs flowed more freely than water. People sold drugs in here like hawkers sold fake Gucci on Kuta Beach. It was part of life. I saw it from day one, when prisoners would slip casually into step with me, whispering, 'Corby, you want smoke? Corby, you want drugs?' 'No, thanks.' Everyone just assumed I used drugs, given my charges. But they quickly learnt I didn't, and I quickly learnt that everything from heroin to crack was so widely available that even people from outside came inside to score.

It spooked me. If drugs were found in my things, my life would be finished. It wouldn't matter whether they were deviously planted to set me up or stashed by a girl protecting her own butt. Who would believe me? It wasn't just crazy paranoia. Other girls feared it, too. When guards sprang cell searches on us, all the girls dived into their cells to check their things for drugs before the guards did. The searches were for anything 'illegal' such as drugs, CD players and phones. We'd buy it all back a few weeks later, but not the drugs. Anyone caught with drugs faced new charges. For me, it might mean a firing squad.

I had to protect my life. I was always suspicious and watching my back. I spent hours sitting in my cell, searching everywhere from under my mattress to inside my toothbrush holder. It took nothing more than a girl from another cell lingering in mine to panic me into a full-scale search.

> *I interrupted two girls from another cell who were in my cell smoking crack. I don't care if they want to do that crap, if they have no respect for themselves or their families; I'm not going to stop them. But I'm not facing just one or two years like they are – I'm in the middle of my trial, facing death by firing squad. Please dig up a little respect and smoke in your own cell! If they get caught, the courts would hear about it, and I could kiss my life goodbye. I'm just watching my back so they don't start hiding the goods in my belongings.*
>
> Diary entry, 5 March 2005

I was struggling to hold it together, stay sane, stay positive and hopeful. All the stress, fear and paranoia were breaking me down, making me sicker, weaker and more fragile. I got raging fevers, insanely itchy rashes, stomach cramps and head spins. In the mornings, I often struggled to lift my head off the pillow, and when I did, I spent most days in a light-headed, dizzy haze.

> *Severe stomach pains had me lying on my bed crunched up foetus-style. Later, in a visit, I suddenly became so hot that in an instant my body became completely wet and my hair damp, everything became hazy. Eddie came and got me, sat me down. My head's been feeling dizzy for a while – but not as extreme as today. Also this morning both my legs broke out in a huge itchy rash. This*

afternoon carrying the water I had to keep stopping, putting the
bucket down – no energy – my cellmates carried the water while
I lay down. I can't get sick. I cannot get sick. My legs are on fire.
My stomach has become huge, like an Ethiopian's.

Diary entry, 9 March 2005

I was having a pretty bad teary day, tried to hold back while Merc
was here but let loose in the church. I'm just so down, so heavy this
past week. I need this mood to lift, I need to be strong, I'm back
in court on Thursday . . . need to get my concentration back.

Diary entry, 14 March 2005

As the weeks in court passed, I spent more time praying. It was all I could do to try to help myself from inside these white walls, as I was completely powerless to do anything else.

I was also putting my faith in Ron, clinging to his promises, his endless assurances that he'd get me acquitted, or at worst six months in a luxury villa with a pool and staff. I lapped it up with tears rolling down my cheeks as I listened to him and Robin talk about my bright future. But each time they left, my heart refilled with fear as I was slammed back into my monkey cage. I so desperately wanted to believe them, but I also knew that court wasn't going so great. All I had so far was my word and that of James, Ally and Katrina.

I was still hoping the Australian Government was doing its own investigation, at least to find out how the bag of marijuana got through two major, apparently secure airports. Surely they would be investigating that? I prayed that their inquiry would uncover the truth, prove it wasn't mine, prove the drugs weren't in my bag at check-in, and maybe even find out who did this.

I needed evidence, a witness, something more than just words. I needed it badly. I was begging God for it every day. Then out of the blue, something broke. Merc told me the news before court. A man in Australia had just come forward, telling of three men who put the drugs in my bag. I was in shock. Merc and I clasped hands through the bars, looking at each other with tears pouring down our cheeks. We didn't need to say anything; we knew we were thinking the same. *Could this be it?* Would I go home now?

Lily arrived a bit later to explain it to me through the bars of the cramped holding cell. This man was in jail in Melbourne and had overheard a conversation between jailed baggage handlers about a drug-smuggling mix-up. He had names. I couldn't believe it. I held Lily's hand as more tears washed down my cheeks. I just kept thinking, *Oh, my God! Oh, my God!*

Everything was a hazy blur as photographers and reporters noisily clamoured at the bars, clicking cameras and yelling questions.

'Schapelle, how do you feel?'

'I can't even talk. I feel numb!'

'Are you happy, Schapelle?'

'Of course I'm happy. But I don't want to get my hopes up, just in case.'

> *My head was spinning . . . what does this mean? Do I go home now? Inside the court my lawyer told the judges of the news and they adjourned the court until next Thursday, to get the evidence together. The prosecutor was not happy about the new evidence. I was thinking I'd never find out who had done this to me or maybe find out like twenty years from now, when someone's confessing on their death bed. Although I'm so excited and relieved at the news, I'm not getting my mind set for release. I don't want to be built up to be let down. Just go with the flow of the process, pray a lot, and see what happens.*
>
> Diary entry, 17 March 2005

My lawyers had a week to sort out the red tape to get this man to come and testify. It was a big week ahead, as I was also giving evidence, but I had no time to put my feet up and relax. The weeks between court appearances were as nightmarish as usual, but the unrelenting daily dramas were getting more draining as my fragile and paranoid state increased. Usually I walked from the bright lights of court straight into a sick new drama.

This particular week, I walked into a suicide attempt. Everyone was hysterical. A lesbian girl, Wanda, had just drunk a concoction of poison after being beaten by her jealous girlfriend, who'd caught her smoking drugs with a new bisexual girl. She was in really bad shape. She looked sick, her head hanging uselessly to one side. But the guards refused to call a doctor. They locked up and left as usual. By morning, Wanda couldn't move. She was dribbling and twitching. Finally she was carried out on a stretcher and taken to hospital. She lived. She walked back in that same afternoon and made up with her guilty girlfriend, who'd even sold her mobile phone to pay off Wanda's overdue drugs bill.

That night, a guy escaped. He'd just been sentenced to eleven years for murder and crawled out through a narrow drain near the women's block, dumping his prison clothes on the side of the road where he exited. The next day, the place was full of talk that he'd been caught in the bushes just outside the jail. I doubted it, as I couldn't see or hear anyone being beaten by the guards when I went out for my afternoon visit. It turned out he had successfully escaped. Lucky man!

Then there was the familiar scene of Sonia going crazy. She was kicking, screaming and thrashing wildly as girls struggled to hold her back from attacking another girl, who'd refused to give her a cigarette. I didn't want to get involved. I went to church. But I walked straight back into new hysteria later on.

The concrete outside my cell was covered in blood. I'd just missed a nasty fight. Like a pack of angry dogs, eight male prisoners had charged into the women's block, attacking a male prisoner there. They brutally beat him for five minutes before the guards pulled them off. He was a bloody unconscious mess and had to be taken to hospital. The other prisoners walked away without any trouble, the guards simply dismissing it as 'a personal matter'. We all knew the guards often got prisoners to do their dirty work.

I woke up the next day at 5 a.m. to Sonia screaming and crying hysterically. She was still screaming at 7.30 a.m. when our cells were unlocked, so I stopped to check on her on my way to collect water. There was a huge rock at her feet. She said she'd woken up with her cellmate, Kartini, who has AIDS, attacking her with the rock and threatening to kill her. The skin had been taken off her stomach and the side of her knee, where she'd been hit. Another girl from her cell had been hit, too, and looked shocked. The guards didn't seem to care!

But the one drama affecting me the most was the broken water pump. Water just trickled from the tap, and it was taking me half an hour to fill a bucket. Salma and I were both pleading with the guards to fix it, but nothing was being done. It didn't seem to worry them that soon we'd have no water to flush the toilet, wash our clothes, our hair or ourselves.

Sleep came in a trickle, too. Several times a night I woke up with stomach cramps, urgently running to the toilet with diarrhoea. Most nights I was also kept awake by girls fighting, screaming between cells, banging the cell bars and going hysterical. I usually ended up crying myself to sleep.

Sonia, shut up! Just past 10.30 p.m. and Sonia has started to yell at girls in her cell and girls in another cell. Hey, but what's new!

Diary entry, 22 March 2005

There were a few upbeat moments to lift my spirits, like receiving a gift from a girl in my cell. Her husband bought me three necklaces as a celebration present: one for each of the men who were going to be named by the jailed informant. Many foreign prisoners were also coming up to me in visits, wishing me luck for my case after hearing the news of the new evidence.

I was getting a huge amount of support from people in letters, with more than a hundred a day flooding in from Australia, Indonesia and, unbelievably, as far away as France, Belgium, England, America and Canada. I was also spoilt with gifts of everything from biscuits, face creams, perfumes, clothes and CD players to bunches of beautiful flowers. I was even sent a most precious gift of a certificate making me the adoptive mother of an endangered orang-utan called Mindow, who lives in an Indonesian forest. I sat in my cell each afternoon reading all the letters, regardless of how ill or blue I felt. They usually made me smile, though I got the odd sick one, like the one that read: 'You are a liar, a common whore, slut, tart and an actress who loves the camera.' I tried not to let it upset me but, in my fragile state, it did. I lived in the hope that one day a letter might be my key to getting out of here, revealing the secrets of who did this.

I also got daily visits from strangers, often up to twenty people a day. The guards freely let everyone through the front door, as 'Schapelle tourism' was becoming a very lucrative business for them. They hit people for the equivalent of $20 to visit instead of the usual ninety cents. For small groups, they were charging around $100 – all the cash just filling up their pockets. The prisoners working as hosts to hand out drinks and straw mats also boosted their prices from $1 to anything up to $20. I couldn't believe how much people were paying.

I was very grateful for so much public support, and I tried to see everyone. But at the same time it was draining, speaking to so many strangers every day, answering the same questions over and over again. I was tired and running out of energy. Most people I felt were genuine, but some came just to gawp at me, and they always made me feel like an animal at the zoo. Some would even whisper about me as though I couldn't hear or wasn't there. But generally the huge swell of public support was uplifting and the single positive thing that came from the media mania.

I had a visit from some more guys from the Darwin Football Club. They're coming to see me on Friday, too – might ask them to take their shirts off!!

Diary entry, 22 March 2005

That was my twisted week before I returned to the glare of lights, cameras and action in the chaotic courtroom.

Court tomorrow. I'm scared, I'm tired. I've got to get out of here. I'm here, I'm alive, but I'm just surviving. I'm locked into this

compound, our own little society, I can't get out, I'm just here
— and it draws all your strength, feels like the strength has to go
somewhere. And it feels like it's drawn out and just keeps building
up the strength of those bloody cement walls and green cage bars.
I can't get out.

Diary entry, 23 March 2005

Could not sleep last night as the court hearings come closer to the
end. I'm so frightened of the final outcome. All the girls in my
cell woke at 12 midnight and all prayed for me, which made me
cry even more — was really nice of them.

Diary entry, 24 March 2005

The morning before court, I made the unusual effort to wash my hair. Collecting the dirty cold water from the dribbling tap, then ladling it over my head in a stinky bathroom as girls with diarrhoea screamed to use it was not my idea of a good time. But I'd been to court week after week with the same greasy, untouched bun, and Merc was starting to get mad at me.

So with clean hair and layers of obsessively applied make-up, I went out to meet Ron and criminologist Professor Paul Wilson, who was giving character evidence on me in court. We talked for about fifteen minutes before I was led off to be handcuffed. I was relieved to find I was going to court with just one other prisoner, as thirty-three of us had been squeezed into the sardine bus the week before. He was a university student who'd burnt a flag of the Indonesian president's face, so the police were anticipating a lot of media for us both.

The crazy mobbing at court each week now made me fear for my life. I was terrified. Anyone could come in close, a member of a drug gang or a crazy person, and stab me or shoot me. It would be easy to slip a knife in my side, unseen in the anarchy. They'd just mingle back into the crowd safely undetected, bringing this drugs case to an end.

The media scrum was becoming more desperate, more grasping, more clawing — swooping and banging me around from the second

I put a foot on the ground. Every single time I was pulled through the mob, I feared I would be killed. I was a sitting duck, an easy target. That day was the worst yet. They were all screaming, yelling, pushing and fighting to get their shots. I squealed in agony as someone stomped on my foot, and winced in pain as the handcuffs sliced my wrists.

It was mayhem inside the court, too. It was packed full of reporters, cameramen and cameras, all eyes and lenses pointed at me. I was up last, but the judge told me to sit in the hot seat for the first few minutes, giving the photographers a chance to get their shots. They leapt around like crazed cats. It was unbelievable. It was humiliating and embarrassing. I was fighting for my life, yet I was made to sit there like a trained monkey at show time. I hated it. I tried to block it out, just kept looking ahead, praying and imagining God's heart. Finally, I was told to sit with my lawyers. I walked across the court biting my lip, trying desperately not to cry.

Baggage handler Scott Speed was first up, telling the judges that airport security in Brisbane was so slack it didn't even have a baggage X-ray machine for checked-in bags. It shocked me, as I knew my lawyers had battled for weeks to get an answer on whether Brisbane airport had an X-ray of my bag. Why hadn't they just said 'No' instantly?

He also testified that airport staff had been sacked for failing drugs tests and for rummaging through passengers' luggage, and that it was possible for someone to insert drugs into a bag after check-in. He said that in 95 per cent of cases a baggage handler would notice a boogie-board bag weighing more than the regulation three kilograms and would ask the passenger to open it.

Just after the next witness sat down in the hot seat, I was taken by surprise when the judge asked me to stand up. I was overcome with a sense of stage fright, as all eyes turned to me, scrutinising me.

The judge then asked Professor Wilson, 'Is this the face of a criminal?' I felt so uncomfortable, so awkward, like my arms and hands were too big for my body. They dangled awkwardly by my sides. Standing in front of all those people, all staring, while someone analysed my character, was awful. I thought, *How could this person I just met for fifteen minutes this morning possibly know what kind of person I am?* But this was all we had to resort to; we didn't have anything else.

'Your honour, I cannot look at her face alone. I can listen to her answer my questions, which I have done. I can look at her face and I can speak to people who know her well. Using all of that information, I can honestly say that she did not know there were drugs in her bag.'

He told the court that I didn't fit the profile of a drug mule and I should be allowed to go home. The whole court was clapping, and Lily and I were both crying. He also said I was neither a genius nor dumb, but of average intelligence. Mum, Merc and I all had a bit of a laugh about that.

During the lunch break, I was told that John Ford, the Melbourne prisoner, would be allowed to enter Indonesia to give evidence in my case. My heart skipped a beat.

After the break, I was on the stand. I answered all the questions as best as I could remember. That's all I can do. I'm facing a possible firing squad. I'm scared shitless, out of my head, constant tears flowing. The best I can do is to tell the truth; that's all. And try to stay in control of myself. I thought I was going to lose it when the judge asked me to stand and touch my boogie board. I couldn't do it, couldn't touch it, literally thought I was either going to faint or vomit. I told the judge, 'No! I won't touch it.' He asked why. So I told him, 'Because this thing is destroying my life. If I didn't boogie-board, I would not be here today! Simple as that!'

Diary entry, 24 March 2005

But proving I didn't do it wasn't simple. When the judge asked me if I had any proof that I didn't put the plastic bag inside my boogie-board bag, what could I say? What proof did I have? I wanted to say that, no, I don't have any proof simply because *no one had done their job properly.* They touched the bags and contaminated evidence. They did not fingerprint the bags, did not weigh all the bags, did not DNA-test the marijuana, did not access security-camera vision at the airport and did not investigate where I might sell the drugs.

In Australia, the airports did not give us any security-camera vision either, despite there being hundreds of cameras at both airports. Though Qantas did admit to destroying some footage, they did not give us baggage X-rays or figures for individual baggage weight. So I'd been screwed at both ends, and now all I had was my word. There was so much I wanted to say but couldn't.

Instead, I said: 'I have never been involved with drugs. I don't like drugs. They are not my drugs. I wouldn't even know where to get drugs from. I surrendered my luggage to go on a holiday. I surrendered it at the airport. I had nothing to do with it after that.'

'So if you did not put the plastic bag inside your boogie-board bag and you are not the owner of the bag,' the judge replied, 'what is your alibi? Why and how is that plastic bag in your bag now?'

'That's what we are here to try to find out. I have many theories in my head. It has been six months now. I am still here. We need to find who put it there. There is nothing I can say to prove to you that I didn't do it. *But I did not do it. It is not mine.* I wouldn't threaten my life – I love my family, I love everybody. I would not jeopardise my life like this.'

My family was suffering so deeply, and me expressing my love for them in a public courtroom was heartbreaking. I was biting my lip, trying to hold back my tears, but I couldn't. I loved them all so much. I was trying my best, pouring out my heart, laying myself bare. I so desperately wanted the judges to believe me. I needed these judges to see I was innocent and make it right. I was fighting so hard – for my life.

It was so painful, so hot and so hard to focus with all the microphones and cameras pointed at me. I tried hard to ignore them, but it was physically impossible. The microphones were so close I'd hit them with my hands whenever I spoke, and cameras went off like machine-gun fire whenever I moved a fraction. If I wiped away a tear or moved my leg, the cameras would fire. It was disruptive and embarrassing. So I was trying not to move, trying to sit as still as a statue so I didn't set off another round of rapid-fire *click-click-click-click*. Didn't they get it? My life was on the line – couldn't they show a little respect?

It was chaos. There were at least thirty people around the walls and fifteen more sprawled across the floor between me and the judges. They were squatting under the judges' bench, lying on the floor, hanging through the windows and even standing behind the judges and filming between their heads. One guy held a long boom microphone right across the middle of the courtroom, losing control of it at one point and hitting the ceiling fan. The judge didn't seem to mind any of it. His only rule was that cameras and mikes were held below my face so he could see it – or so all photographers could get a clear shot!

During the long hot hours, I sometimes looked around in a daze, not really acknowledging or seeing anything but blurry shadows. Other times I'd look around and see it all in sharp focus, occasionally even noticing a person on the ground looking really concerned for me and trying to think if I'd seen his photo on top of a little story he'd written about me. But most of the time I was fighting to focus on what was being said, always straining to hear anything in the noisy courtroom.

After all the questioning by the judges, my defence and the prosecutors, the judge took me by complete surprise, asking me, 'This is your last chance to speak. Is there anything you would like to say?'

I was not expecting it, I was so nervous, I didn't know what to say other than the obvious 'Please let me go home.' Then words started to slowly come out.

'I love my family. I wanted a holiday. I don't like drugs, and I know there are big penalties in Indonesia and all over the world if you have drugs. I would never, never jeopardise my life in this situation, and my family's health and everyone that loves me, to do something like this. I love Bali, I love Indonesia. I respect this country. I don't know how this has happened or why this has happened to me.'

Then he told me to address the prosecutor – and what a cold, nasty face he had. He tried to be so intimidating and it worked. I told him pretty much the same thing.

'Please find it in your heart to get all the facts, all the evidence together, and use your own heart and your mind and the evidence that we don't have, to find it in your heart to maybe bring justice to the right people. You have to use your own judgement. I did not do it; please use your own character judgement, please. Please use all your evidence and let me go home. It has been six months. Please!'

Merc and Mum cried. Lily cried. And the woman prosecutor was crying. I then addressed the judges again, pleading with them to let me go home. The reporters, camera guys and pretty much all the people I could see in the courthouse looked emotional. Erwin then asked the judges if it were possible for bail. It was denied.

There was a lot of talk and tears, and all of sudden I had this intense feeling that I was being declared innocent – that I was going home. And no one was telling me. Then the guard and prosecutors came and grabbed both arms and took me to the holding cell.

Back in my cell at Hotel K, all the girls were waiting to hear about my day. They'd made *nasi goreng* as well.

So relieved yesterday is over. Would definitely go down as one of the most intense days of my life so far. Never want to press 'rewind' to be there again.

Diary entry, 25 March 2005

Team Corby was ready to celebrate, with a seemingly successful day in court and the news that John Ford had received permission to come to Bali and testify. They were sure they'd freed me now. I heard they spent the night after court throwing back shots and shouting 'Free Schapelle!' until early morning. The next night, they threw a party at Vasu's beachfront home for the witnesses, the legal team, my family and a few journalists. Ron, Robin and Vasu stood poolside making passionate speeches, singing each other's praises about how hard they'd worked and what a great job they'd done to set me free. Ron held up a glass, shouting, 'Free Schapelle! Free Schapelle!'

It was all very festive, with drinks flowing, food laid on, live music blaring and people dancing on the pool deck. Mum and Merc were trying to have a good time but felt very uncomfortable. I wasn't free yet. Anything was still possible, and they couldn't enjoy a party while I was still locked up in my filthy cage. They rarely even went out any more, as being at a party or restaurant upset them, making them think of me in my cage. Their hearts were sad. There would be nothing to celebrate until I was there, too. But they went to the party because they felt they should, and because they knew I wanted them to go and try to have some fun.

But in the end, the night was a disaster. It wasn't fun for anyone. As the party was in full swing, with Lily, Ron and Vasu all dancing wildly on the pool deck, Robin walked over to take the mike and sing a song. In an instant, he was nearly dead. He was flung off his feet and into the pool. The frayed microphone cord had dipped in a puddle and given him a big electric shock. He was being fried alive, jerking from shocks, unable to let go of the microphone that was sparking wildly in the water.

Ron crouched down at the side of the pool, trying to grab his mate, but kept getting flung back whenever he touched him.

Suddenly all the lights went out and the music stopped. Someone had turned off the electricity. Ron and Merc hauled Robin out of the pool and laid his lifeless body on the deck. It was dark and silent until terrified screams tore into the night. Robin looked dead.

Ron started slapping him hard across the face, shouting, 'Stay with us, mate, don't leave us.' He wasn't breathing. Merc sprang into action, using her lifesaver training to turn him on his side, pull out his tongue to clear the airways and feel for a pulse. Ron began bouncing frantically hard up and down on his chest. Merc felt a faint pulse and started saying, 'No, Ron! Ron, no. He's got a pulse!' – aware Ron could kill him by putting his heartbeat out.

Ron was in complete panic. Merc started calmly explaining to him what she was doing. She put an ear to Robin's mouth to listen for a breath. But in the next instant, they both reeled back sharply in fright as Robin's eyes snapped wide open. Like a scene from *The X-Files*, his eyeballs were rolled right back in his head, giving him a deadly white-eyed stare. He was still unconscious, still in grave danger.

People were screaming, the party atmosphere long gone. They decided to move him inside, to lay him on the couch away from the crowd. Ron kept yelling, 'Stay with us, mate!' as they carried him inside. Lily walked alongside, praying like a mad woman and crying hysterically. Merc pleaded with her to be quiet, to give him some space, aware it might send Robin into deeper shock when he woke up. But Lily refused to leave his side, crouching beside him on the couch, howling Muslim prayers and sobbing as they waited for him to wake up.

He came to about twenty minutes later and within no time was walking around the party with a cigarette, saying, 'Sorry about that!' His eyes were glazed. An ambulance arrived a bit later and took him to hospital for a check-up. Everyone was saying Merc had saved his life.

All Robin suffered was internal bruising and a very, very sore chest, probably as much from Ron's clobbering as from the shock.

I had a comparatively quiet weekend, just endlessly thinking about John Ford, who was flying in to give evidence that week. I knew I might be taking another white-knuckle ride on the roller-coaster, but I was starting to let myself get a little hopeful. Maybe Ron and Robin were right, maybe I really would go home soon.

Yesterday Mr John Ford arrived and is now in Polda. I wonder if he's in the same holding cell I was in. I'll be going to court tomorrow, to listen for the first time to what happened. Tomorrow will be another that goes down with the most important of my life. I'm feeling very light-headed and numb.

Diary entry, 28 March 2005

I didn't sleep the night before court, but I prayed almost non-stop. In the morning, I was on edge, clinging to hope, more fearful than ever as I anticipated what the day would bring. I knew if it went well today, it could spell my freedom.

At court there were so many reporters – the most I'd ever seen. They were hounding me, I was completely surrounded, being pushed, shoved and pulled. My path was blocked, I couldn't walk, I couldn't see, my eyes were full of tears, and I certainly couldn't think.

I eventually got pushed into the holding cell. John Ford was already inside, sitting on the seat I usually used to hide from the reporters. I tried to thank him but couldn't even get close as he had a Polda guard standing in front of him for protection.

All I could do was cry. In an hour or so, I was going to find out how this had happened to me, whose fate I'd been dealt and why. John Ford was my best chance yet to get my life back. The darkness living in my heart might finally lift. It was chillingly scary to be on the edge of this moment. I was shaking, sobbing, I had to try to calm myself down. I usually did that by singing 'You Raise Me Up' in my head, but today it wasn't working. So I went into the gross toilet and sang aloud, very loud. It worked, although I did have to sing quite a lot that day.

At around midday, we were all called into court – me first. I sat on the side with my lawyers and then watched as John Ford entered, looking very clean-cut, dressed in black slacks, white collar and a tie. This was the first time I could actually look at him.

After so many months of endlessly twisting my brain to figure out how the drugs had got into my bag, it was incredible to sit there listening to Ford's testimony. It really made sense, it added up. He told the court he'd heard a conversation between two prisoners about my bag being used to move drugs through domestic airports. These men were apparently even laughing at the misfortune of the guy who actually lost his marijuana and at the innocent person – me – who was now facing death by firing squad. Anger rippled through my body.

What a day! Coming back to Kerobokan, getting handcuffed, the officer said sorry for having to do this to me. Was up all night praying for the protection of Mr Ford and his family.

Diary entry, 29 March 2005

What loomed next was the frightening court day where the prosecutors would make their demand to the judges. It was the end of my sixth month of living this hellish nightmare. It was six months since I'd slept in a proper bed, eaten at a table, used a Western-style toilet, had a running shower or washed my hair in clean warm water. I'd been in Bali for six months and still hadn't seen a beach. I was wondering how much this hellhole had changed me and how easily I'd slip back into my life, back into the real world. I prayed that I'd soon find out.

I'd got my stomach ache back at around 11 a.m. and by the time of my afternoon visit I was in great pain and also vomiting. We went and sat inside, near the office, where it was a little dark. The darkness made me even sicker, and I realised I haven't been in darkness for over six months. I had to leave the room twice out of fear and it literally made me sick. I hate this place.

Locked in our cage early, all girls are going crazy – waiting for a new prisoner to enter. She's been kept at Polda and today is being moved to Kerobokan. She's an informer, has many enemies here. She's put five girls in here, including one that was only yesterday sentenced to five years. Also put around thirty males in here.

Diary entry, 31 March 2005

14

Media Frenzy

Another month starting. Please, judges, listen and do the right thing; do what is right. Please. I cannot take this place any more.

Woke around 4 a.m. to girls yelling, reminding the new girl that she'll be bashed. Our cells were opened at 7.30 a.m., the girls attacked her, then the guards sent the girl to the TV room. Soon after, Sonia followed . . . the guards also followed . . . the girl jumped towards Sonia. The girl had scissors hidden down the front of her pants. Sonia and the girl were then taken to the office, but not before the girl started attacking a woman guard. We were all locked up in our cells again at 8.45 a.m.

At the office, the new girl told the guards that some girls have mobiles, that we have gas camping stoves and that she's going to get a knife and use it. So every cell was checked, everything of danger was taken, the stoves – we can't cook any more, boil water for coffee, noodles: now we only have the rice that comes around in the cart. Thank God I have friends and family here to look after me. The guards took all the spoons, the handles off the buckets, the pots and pans, and of course all the phones and drugs. They also took any money they could find, except the money from my room – they didn't pocket that. We were let out of our cage at 2 p.m. When will all this be over?

Diary entry, 1 April 2005

I WANTED TO WAKE UP FROM THIS NIGHTMARE. MY HEART was hurting. I was so tired, so scared, so alone. I had no one to turn to, no one to talk to. Everything I did, everything I said, was leaked to the press. Any way I turned, people were taking photos of me, selling stories about me. If I simply said 'I didn't sleep well last night', it was printed. Prisoners, guards, doctors, lawyers, church people, all trying to fill their pockets, all trying to take a ride on Schapelle. I could trust no one but my family, and they were all hurting too much for me to burden them with any more. I had to rely on myself. It was lonely.

I was living from moment to moment. I was jumpy, edgy, strung out and waiting for the next drama, the next turn of bad luck, the next killer blow. Why was this happening to me? What had I done in a past life?

I was terrified of my next day in court, when the prosecutors would make their demand: maybe life, maybe death. It was possible that this cruel and bitter twist of fate might mean the end of my old life for ever, and I was petrified.

I'd spent all night sobbing, shaking, curled up on my mattress, waiting for the sun to come up on the day. The prosecutors had come into jail a few times, as I was still under their care until the verdict, and they'd promised to look after me. The two women prosecutors remarked that I'd lost a fair amount of weight. They were crying, telling me not to worry: it would all be OK. But as much as I truly wanted to believe them, I couldn't. I had no idea what the day would bring. I just prayed they'd let me go home.

Pain ripped into my stomach and stress tore at my shoulders as we drove to court in the sardine bus. By the time we reached the court, I was a shaking mess. I spent an hour in the holding cell. Lily came to see me as usual. As usual, she had nothing to say. Every week she came to the holding cell, and every week I told her not to. I begged everyone not to. It set off the cameras. She'd just hold my hand, posing for the cameras, and ask something banal like, 'Did you eat breakfast this morning?' 'No, Lily, I never do!' This morning as always I went over to her, in case it was

important. It wasn't. 'How're you doing, Schapelle?' The cameras
went ballistic. I was her little show pony.

Hiding in the toilet was hard that morning, as Mum had
overdone it with the ammonia. I had to keep leaning out to gasp
for air because the fumes were so strong.

By the time the guards walked me into the court, I was feeling
worse. I was mobbed, cameras right in my face, people blocking my
way. I threw up, just missing someone's foot, and wiped vomit from
my face before I reached the courtroom door. The guards released
both my arms. This was it. I would learn my likely fate. I paused
for a second, lifting my shaky hand to hold the cross around my
neck and saying a quick prayer. 'Lord, fill me with your holy spirit;
set me free, free to be all you've created me to be. Also send your
angels to fill this court with love, light and compassion.'

Then I walked reluctantly, nervously, through the doors. The
cameras again went ballistic. The judge as usual asked me if I was
OK to start. Sharp pains twisted my gut. I couldn't do it; I couldn't
go on. Not today.

'I am really sick,' I told him. It was a struggle to even get the
words out. I was clutching my stomach, trying not to vomit, tears
pouring down my cheeks. What had my life come to?

The judge adjourned court for a week, ordering me to see a doctor.
'Take care of your health; don't be stressed. If you are stressed, you
might get diarrhoea.'

I nodded and was taken outside, the cameras all still clicking
furiously.

All these days I've been vomiting, diarrhoea. Very tired, and sick.
No energy. Constant tears. And Sonia going crazy each night.

Diary entry, 8 April 2005

Still vomiting, keep crying, no energy at all. How long can this
go on for? I cannot stay feeling like this.

Diary entry, 9 April 2005

Still have the runs – my head is throbbing.

Diary entry, 13 April 2005

I couldn't get better. The stress and pain of the looming day were always there. They wouldn't lift. What if the prosecutors asked for death? I'd been living under the shadow of death for six months. Fear churned my stomach, making me throw up all the time. I was tight, tense, an emotional wreck. I had to get out of here. I had to go home. I didn't do this; I didn't deserve this. I didn't understand this. This life was breaking me down.

That week I didn't get to see a doctor, and there were the usual dramas. A guy called Eka escaped, was quickly caught and beaten by the guards. I watched as they dragged him past me in the visiting area and off to the isolation tower. He was so badly beaten that he went to court the next day half-paralysed, with a limp, a twitch and his head hanging to one side.

Then one day while I was sitting on my mattress in my cell, my cross broke. It simply snapped from around my neck. I felt it was a sign . . . a bad sign. I became hysterical. I'd been clinging to my sanity by a thread, but in that instant, I lost it. It undid me. I couldn't speak. I was crying like a baby, making a lot of noise, gulping for air, just staring at my broken little cross. The girls in my cell were fussing around, trying to figure out what had suddenly happened to me. Then they saw the cross and all huddled over a girl as she frantically put it back together. The second it was fastened back around my neck, my hysteria instantly stopped. I didn't understand myself. It was the weirdest and fastest change in extreme emotion I'd ever experienced. I held so much faith in that little cross.

On the day before I went to court again, I got the fright of my life as I looked into the eyes of evil. I trembled for hours afterwards.

Yesterday had to go to the office to re-register – hate doing that.
If I don't sign, does that mean they are holding me here illegally?
Before I entered the main office, two guys were coming out of
another room on cruise control, just lingering outside the door. As

I walked closer, one started to walk towards me. His face looked slightly familiar – could it be . . . ? No, it couldn't be him: he always has his hat on. The guy behind him was taller and thin, glaring strangely at me. He was wearing the hat. Then as the first guy got closer to me, the one in the hat was looking, watching me; he flashed a smile.

My suspicion was confirmed – the man got so close, we would have brushed shoulders if I hadn't moved sideways. He has eyes unlike anyone I've ever seen, and anyone I'd ever want to see again at such close range. They are very dark, but not black-coloured, and kind of hazy, like the colour has smudged into the whites: foggy black. Took me by surprise to see him there. I see him a lot – looking out of the cell window of the isolation tower, occasionally sitting with his visitors in the visitors' room or in the office. To experience him so close and to be looking directly into each other's eyes – it took a moment for my brain to register who he was. As he got just in front of me, an arm's length away, he said, 'Corrrby . . . ' Then he smiled.

Amrozi. He knows my name. He knows what I look like. Amrozi knows who I am. That's a feeling I will never forget and never want to experience again.

Diary entry, 13 April 2005

The night before court I froze in fright as I was listening to the radio news. An anonymous letter had been sent to the Indonesian Consulate in Perth, saying that if I wasn't set free by the prosecutors' request, an Indonesian man who worked at the embassy would be shot dead. 'All Indonesians out now! Go home, you animals.' I was aghast. I felt so little, so powerless, as I was stuck in my cage listening to this. Everything was so out of control; this madness was just swirling crazily around me.

Death threats, and the envelope containing two bullets. This is so full on. How did my life get like this: so much violence and destruction? I'm stuck in the middle of something huge. How did this happen? I pray no Indonesians get angry at the threat and lash out at me. You know, lately I have been surrounded by a lot more police as I step off the sardine van. Before, I was accompanied by two police but lately it's been six or seven. Could it be that someone wants to shoot me ahead of time? So, no sleep for me last night. My eyes are sore and dry; don't even want to think what I'm looking like. Going to collect my water, wash my hair – much needed, well overdue – dress and off to court for the tenth time.

Diary entry, 14 April 2005

OK, I'm ready for the prosecutors' closing. Got black pants, pink top. Let's go. I am strong; I fear no evil.

Diary entry, 14 April 2005

What a dramatic day. I seemed to find new levels of fear with every week. Inside the sardine bus, I sat crying and shaking, more frightened than ever of being shot while walking into court after news of the death threats. I couldn't stop my tears. I was traumatised. I didn't want to get out. The girl I was handcuffed to was calmly telling me not to worry. She had no idea of the terrifying minutes ahead. No idea! When she first saw all the media, she thought it was going to be great, like true celebrity movie-star status. But this was a drug trial, nothing glamorous about it.

As soon as we got out of the bus, she boldly walked in front of me. But it didn't take long for her to yell out for help. She was being pulled along in a media rip, sucked down by the scrum, drowning. There were so many people everywhere, pushing and shoving. She certainly wasn't smiling now. As she fell, my hand went down with her, the cuff cutting my wrist. I was fighting to stay upright. She was being stomped on. I couldn't see ahead, I couldn't even see the ground. Merc pushed her way through, swinging her handbag around blindly, like a crazy woman. But she wasn't, she was my dear, sweet, protective big sister. The girl managed to get back up, walk for a bit but then fainted. It was madness. I was bawling like a big kid. I had never been so fearful, it was making me sick. Guards carried both of us through the mayhem into the holding cell. I didn't even realise I'd been picked up until I was put down.

Soon I was walking back through the anarchy again to enter court. I'd never throughout this whole ordeal seen so many reporters and photographers. Between the judges and my seat there were about three or four long lines of them, all with their cameras flashing wildly. I tried to keep composed, tried to breathe easy, concentrating hard to keep the air moving through my lungs, but my head became very light. I was still concentrating when the light went out – I'd fainted.

I woke to the comforting voices of my translator Eka, Erwin and my sister, and still all the photographers were flashing their cameras. It was a circus. I was so embarrassed. This was my life.

I'm just so completely stressed: fear of the unknown, which gives me the diarrhoea and vomiting I've had for around three weeks now. All I need is something to calm my nerves for Thursdays. It's the stampede of cameras and reporters that my nerves need to be calmed from. I do realise this is their job, they need to do it, without them Australians would be kept in the dark; and without the help and support of Australians, what would happen to me then? But I just wish they'd give me a little room to move, room to breathe. Each time I come back from court I have bruises on my legs and arms, my feet get trampled all over: even my big toenail was lifted up and bleeding.

Diary entry, 14 April 2005

The judge ordered a bench seat to be brought forward for me to lie on. My mum came to hold my hand and stroke my face. She was crying. The pain this was bringing to all the people that I love hurt so much. All around us the room was erupting.

The judge became angry, unable to bring order to his courtroom; the prosecutors yelled for the reporters to back off. I could hear my dad shouting for them to leave: 'On your bike, leave her alone! Clear out!' I asked Merc to tell Dad to be quiet. I didn't want the judge to get even more upset.

The judge was telling me to stop pretending to be sick. When Eka translated, I closed my eyes, feeling exhausted but angry. I thought, *How about you put a little order in your courthouse? Look at this bloody mess, I can't even breathe!*

I was lying, shaking, on the bench, surrounded by media as the doctor was taking my blood pressure. It was sky high. The judge agreed with the court doctor that I should have a full medical check-up, saying, 'Get her to the hospital, get her well for next week. Get her out of here now!' He ordered the media to give me more space the next week and warned me: 'You sit quietly – don't make it up. If you make it up, we will force the court to go on.' I collapsed again while walking out to the car.

My mum and dad were so upset, in so much pain, crying, devastated, sick with worry for me and starting to break down, too. They couldn't bear to see me go through this. I was their baby and I was innocent. My dad cried the whole night and was so drained by it all that he couldn't get out of bed the next day to come to see me. Wild horses couldn't keep him away usually. But Dad was very sick. He'd just finished his hormone injections for bone cancer. He didn't need this.

Merc was hurting deeply, too, sick with worry for me and upset about being splashed all over the news wildly swinging her handbag. It was so unfair. The very people who'd provoked her were turning it into a big news story. The media pack had been trampling all over the woman I was cuffed to, oblivious to her as they blindly, bloodthirstily pursued their prey: me. They just stomped all over her. They didn't care. They had to get their shots. Merc had leapt in to help, to get a bit of space for both of us, trying to fend off the pack. She'd then helped a guard to carry the girl to the holding cell. Merc said she was still out of it when they got there, had sliced and bloody wrists from the cuffs, and footprints all over her black trousers. Both of us had our shoes torn off our feet. It was so typical of my beautiful, caring sister to help.

I waited all the next day to go to hospital, but it was four days before the prosecutors arrived to pick me up. The media knew about it before I did. As the front doors opened, I reeled back. My heart was pounding. *How did they know?*

A huge pack of reporters and cameramen was outside, all scrambling for their cameras, all clamouring towards me. 'Schapelle . . . Schapelle!' I was crying, shaking; I didn't want to go out. But I had no choice. I had to. I was mobbed.

When we finally screamed off in the police van with sirens blaring and photographers chasing us on motorbikes, I felt relieved. I was finally going to hospital.

But I didn't get there. I was slammed into another monkey cage at the prosecutors' office, fully exposed to the media. At least fifteen photographers stood holding their lenses through the cage bars, furiously clicking. I couldn't breathe. What was happening? Why wasn't I at hospital? I hid in the toilet, shaking, crying and refusing to come out. But they got their shots.

New prisoners were slammed in, one of whom asked to use the toilet, forcing me out. The bars were full of lenses and faces. I was trapped. I stood uselessly, sadly, as they clicked away. I felt like a freak show. It was like I wasn't a person, like I had no feelings. I heard one of the photographers say 'Thanks, Bli!' to the prisoner who had forced me out of the toilet, as I scrambled back in. It was a set-up. I suspected he'd been slung some cash for his trouble. When he tried it again later, I refused to come out. 'You'll have to wait!'

Most of the photographers left a little while later to go to a press conference. Nine Australians had just been arrested on drugs charges.

A couple of cameramen hung around, one politely asking if there was anything I'd like to say. I felt a bit lighter, not so under siege, and decided to take the chance to speak.

'I've received quite a few letters and I'll reply to them when I get home,' I told them. 'But it's been fantastic – they've really, really kept me strong. It's absolutely everything: it keeps me going. And I just want to thank them so much for everything. I mean, the strength of a nation, which hopefully should overcome anything, any problem.'

But I didn't get to hospital that day. After four sweaty hours, I climbed back in the police van, wistfully asking, 'Hospital?'

'No, Kerobokan!'

I slumped back in the seat, closed my eyes and sobbed. I was exhausted. The whole day was just a stupid media stunt.

What a day. Are they trying to make me more stressed and tired? I came back to my cell today, my whole body shaking. I had to endure those four hours for nothing. Today I heard news of nine Australians being arrested for trying to smuggle eleven kilograms of heroin out of Bali.

Diary entry, 18 April 2005

It was take two the next day, and the entrance to the hospital was seething with waiting reporters and photographers, all running towards the police van as we pulled in. How the hell did they know? It was ridiculous. Everything was being leaked. Nothing was private.

Many, many reporters huddled around the paddy-van door. The guard called for me to get out, but I refused, so he told the media to give me some room. I finally got out but was completely mobbed. The police hurried me into the doctor's room. Cameras were pressed up against the windows; the curtains were drawn but not enough, the nurses had to tape paper up. But they kept trying from all angles, sticking their lenses in at the window, even trying to poke them through the door as I stripped half-naked, taking off my top and bra. I was so embarrassed, so worried they'd somehow sneak a shot. A nurse held up some more paper. The doctor monitored my heart and did blood and urine tests. Then, strangely, four white-coated psychiatrists walked in to do some tests. I asked the doctors to give me their word that any tests would be kept quiet and not leaked to the press. 'Of course!' But it was a mistake. I couldn't even trust the doctors. I didn't get any test results, but the press did. A story was even headlined: 'Psychiatrist's secret diagnosis of Schapelle'.

A shattered Schapelle Corby is so drained by her drug trial that she sees herself as a desperate figure without a voice to defend herself, her psychiatrist said yesterday. Just three days before her judgment, Dr Conny Pankahila told of how Ms Corby had sketched a person with eyes, a nose and other facial features but no mouth.

'Schapelle said, "Yes that's me, no voice,"' Dr Pankahila said. 'The picture looked like somebody who has lost hope, who has lost the future. Desperate.'

Daily Telegraph (Australia), 24 May 2005

During the hours at the hospital, I did something once so normal and everyday, now so refreshing. I used a Western toilet. It was clean. It was unbelievable. I stood looking into the bowl, watching the water swirl as I flushed it three times. I got overwhelming pleasure from washing my hands in a clean basin with warm running water. It was only a toilet and basin, but it was 'wow'. It represented so much of what I'd lost. It spun me back to a life I was forgetting. It was the first and last time I've used a Western toilet since my arrest.

My new life was thrust back in my face as soon as I left the hospital, struggling through the pack to the police van. I climbed in quickly, but we didn't move. I sat there with camera lenses prying through the windows. I started to shake, my lip quivering. I was just an object to these people. *Come on!* I knew what was happening. The driver couldn't start the van, but I was sure he wasn't turning the key the whole way. My pulse was racing. How much had he been paid?

Back at Hotel K, there was a new drama. A guy called Benny was found hanged from a toilet window. He was three years into a life sentence and had a wife and kids. As usual with suicides, everyone suspected it was murder. Everyone was saying his hands were tied behind his back.

The following morning, I took one of the five tablets the doctor had given me. He'd advised me to take one an hour before court to calm my nerves, but I wanted to find out their effect on me first.

It knocked me out cold.

I went down fast: I swallowed the pill sitting at my cage door and within ten minutes I was crawling on my hands and knees like an uncoordinated baby to my mattress. I didn't quite make it, but I slept solidly for the next four hours on the floor.

I woke up disbelieving. It was so ridiculous. The doctor had given me sleeping tablets. I did not take anything the next day, or any day after that during my court hearings. This was my life. I wanted to be alert, not a zombie and definitely not asleep.

Ron phoned the prison from Australia later to assure me that all would go well in court the following day. I would be acquitted; I would go home. 'Take it easy, it's going to be OK. Everything is going to be fine; it's all under control. You'll be going home. No problem. It's OK.' He was confident.

Robin was in Bali but Ron was stuck in Australia after speaking publicly about Balinese prosecutors asking for bribes. I couldn't believe he'd been so stupid and was angry with him for potentially jeopardising my case. I still wanted to believe he knew what he was talking about, but was losing faith. And Lily didn't inspire much hope.

Lily took me aside and was crying, telling me she's sorry and that she's done all she and the team could possibly do. OK, so tomorrow I won't be having any good news that I'll like. All I can do at this point is pray.

Diary entry, 20 April 2005

I was cuffed to myself on the way to court, as after the crazed drama last time, no one wanted to be attached to me. The media were still all there, but I wasn't so trampled as in the past. I could actually see the ground I was walking on.

It seemed the judge had finally brought some order to his courtroom, too. Instead of being strewn haphazardly across the floor, the media were lined up against the wall and outside at the windows. And my five-minute photo session in the hot seat before the trial started had been cut.

Then, in the stifling heat, I sat for a very difficult two and a half hours as the prosecutors read through all the points of the case. Eka was only translating parts but enough for me to learn that they held practically none of my witnesses' testimony as credible: not that of my brother James, Ally, Katrina, Professor Paul Wilson or my lifeline, the brave John Ford. None of it would be taken into account by the prosecutors.

I prayed almost the whole time I was sitting there. I knew that if the prosecutors weren't listening to any of my defence witnesses, they could surely request the death penalty, and in Bali when death was requested the judge could pretty much only give either life imprisonment or death by firing squad. So I prayed for anything other than death.

As the main prosecutor kept reading, I was sinking. 'We state that the defendant Schapelle Corby is legally and convincingly guilty for having committed crimes . . . importing narcotics. The defendant's actions can ruin the image of Bali as a tourist destination. The defendant's actions can make Bali look like a drug haven and affect young people's lives.'

The judge then told Eka to stop translating for me, for some strange reason. So I sat listening to the prosecutor request his sentence with no idea of what he was saying, except for the clue from the many faces around me in shock and tears, staring at me in sorrow. It definitely was not good news. Even one of the female prosecutors started crying. Then I recognised a word I'd learnt in church: *hidup* – life. That's what the prosecutor had requested. *Life*. In Indonesia, life meant the age you were when arrested. I was twenty-seven years old, so he had requested twenty-seven years' imprisonment.

I felt panic. I couldn't breathe. I couldn't think. I was trembling inside. I was just so scared. The room was spinning. I whispered to Eka, to myself, 'My life is over.'

I felt dazed, weak, light-headed. I felt like I was going to fall. My chest was heaving, I was trying not to scream, not to get hysterical in court. I was gulping back sobs, trying to force back hysteria, with tears pouring down my face. I turned to look at Merc. She looked sick, pale and shocked. I ran across to hug her.

'Merc, it's not fair. It's so unfair, Merc!'

She was hurting, trying not to cry, trying to be brave, to be strong. She hugged me tight. 'It's OK, Schapelle, it's OK.' But she was sobbing.

Nothing was OK. Nothing.

Photographers mobbed me as I was dragged back to the holding cell. I hurt all over. I was convulsing, shaking. I couldn't keep it in. I cried and screamed a high-pitched, blood-curdling scream tearing straight from my broken heart. My life was finished. Cameras were being pushed through the bars, wanting to catch my agony. I didn't care.

Robin Tampoe came to the bars. I didn't want to see him. What did he want? I'd told everyone not to come, no matter what happened.

Then I saw my beautiful cousin Melissa, who'd brought me a bottle of water. She started stroking my face through the bars as tears poured down my face.

I cried hysterically all the way back to Kerobokan. I was so down. I was a mess. In my cell, I screamed, furiously smashing my bag against the walls. I kept screaming and screaming until I collapsed in an exhausted heap onto my mattress and sobbed for all the injustice, for all the pain and hurt this was causing me and my family. It was all such bullshit. It was all so unfair. I should have been able to go home. I had done *nothing wrong*. I was innocent, but I couldn't change this sick, twisted, bitter turn in my life.

The girls in my cell were all a bit scared of me, as I howled like an animal. I didn't tell them how many years the prosecutors had demanded. I couldn't bear to say it. They were all keeping their distance, which was good, as it gave me some space. But they stood looking and whispering. They didn't know what to do. I didn't know what to do either. I couldn't believe it, twenty-seven years, my whole lifetime over again in this shit hole. It might have only been a guideline, but I'd learnt that the judges usually stuck closely to it.

What can I say? He didn't request death, so I'm still alive; the sentence can only get lighter. My world sucks!

Diary entry, 21 April 2005

Later that day a guard came into the women's block and handed me his mobile phone. It was Chris Packer, who was now sailing his boat to South Africa and had followed my day on the Internet. He wanted to advise me to change to his lawyer, who had successfully got him and Chris Currall freed.

Changing lawyers was something Merc and I had talked about often, but we just didn't know how to say 'Piss off, Lily and Vasu' halfway through my trial. We were scared. Would we get better or worse? We'd also given them almost $80,000 and couldn't afford to switch, as despite Ron continually telling the press he was bankrolling my defence – 'whatever it costs, whatever it takes' – he wasn't.

We'd been worried about our legal team for a long time. I now rarely spoke to Vasu, as I found him belligerent and arrogant, and Lily was out of her depth. The two were close, but Lily was under Vasu's bombastic, bullying thumb. She didn't ever brief me on strategy, she didn't advise me on what would happen in court, even on the day I was asked to speak. She knew but didn't bother to tell me. She and Vasu flew to Jakarta for some reason on the day I was due to get the prosecutors' demand.

And the fact is that Lily was lame in court. She often cried but rarely stood up to ask questions. Merc and I were always scribbling notes to her, trying to get her to fire up, challenge a witness, say something, do something. She usually just sat there, often on her phone sending text messages. I was praying the texts were strategies or questions from Vasu or Ron or Robin. But they weren't. I realised how little focus she had when I glimpsed a text message as I sat next to her at the bench. An important witness was up, and I was willing her to get up and fire questions. *Come on, Lily, please. This is my life.* Then the text came through. I saw what appeared to be a flirty message from Ron. I went numb.

I couldn't believe it. I slumped back in my seat, thinking, *You're kidding! This is my life and you're sending fucking lovey-dovey text messages?* She got all hot and bothered and started fanning herself. I just sat there, very scared and very, very alone.

I didn't know what was going on between Ron and Lily, but every time I saw her she'd say to me, 'I think Ron likes you! I think Ron likes you!' It was ridiculous. It was like primary school. I guess she thought I had the hots for him (which I so didn't). I'd say, 'Er noooo . . . he likes *you!*' and she'd laugh and get all flustered. I couldn't believe I was talking about this shit with my lawyer, who was supposed to be saving my life. I would go with the flow, but the flow was just absurd.

My trust in Ron had almost evaporated, too. I was disappointed in him. I no longer believed he knew what he was talking about. His promises of freedom had turned into twenty-seven years. When he called the next day I could barely speak to him. He still kept saying I was going to be acquitted.

It was also clear by now that his focus was to whip up publicity and for me to make money. He was always pushing me to write songs, to write a book, telling me I'd never have to work another day in my life. He'd make me rich. I also knew now that anything I said or wrote to him went straight to the media, despite often asking him to keep it private. I was embarrassed when I copied a poem for him and he gave it to the papers as if I'd written it. When he snapped me on his camera phone, it went in the papers. He kept saying I was suicidal. I kept telling him, 'Ron, I'm not, I would never do that to my family. Never. Never!'

'She is not coping, I am concerned she is going to become suicidal. She just wants to go home. I keep telling her we are going to take her home if it's the last thing we do.'

Ron Bakir, quoted in the
Daily Telegraph (Australia), 15 April 2005

My week continued to get worse after the day of the demand. A girl in my cell had been released and stole all my creams. It was comparatively a tiny, tiny issue but a kick in the teeth, a reminder of who I was living with. Then I was heaped with humiliation. I'd heard so many of the lies written about me, like I was a prostitute and I'd had an affair with Russell Crowe when I was a high-class escort in Japan, and now came the embarrassing, baseless, ridiculous rumour that I was pregnant. It was so humiliating, and unbelievable that this crap was printed in respectable newspapers. I learnt of the story when the prison boss and the doctor came to take me to the jail clinic.

What's going on, have I had some bad test results from last week's urine and blood tests from the hospital, and the Kerobokan doctor has to tell me the bad news? What kind of disease do I have? What else could possibly go wrong in my life? The doctor told me of big news: I'm pregnant.

Come on, give me a break. Two months pregnant, the papers say. This place is disgusting, and in my situation sex is the last thing to cross my mind. I'm not going to say it hasn't crossed my mind, but it is certainly the last thing I would do here. Take someone into the toilet at church or maybe in the court holding-cell toilet? That's just sick. I have morals. I do have respect for myself, and dignity. How could anyone believe I would do that in a place like this?

So I peed into an empty plastic cup after telling the doctor I would not pee in a plastic bag. And the doctor took photos with a digital camera of them doing the pregnancy test and the result – which of course was negative. We all had a laugh about the stupid rumours that get around, but I am quite embarrassed that someone could believe it.

Diary entry, 26 April 2005

We had one last defence day in court, and I had a final chance to speak.

Didn't sleep much. Put a few points down on paper through the night after I finished praying. Tried to put the words together, but I'm not sure exactly how I should do this. I feel I don't want to speak of the points that the prosecutors and I dispute over, as I've said it all before. I'm tired of the broken record going round and round and round. My lawyers will be pointing it all out in their closing statement, anyway. I feel I want to speak from my heart but nothing that I feel, nothing that I can put on paper, seems adequate. I'm only skimming the surface of how I'm feeling.

Each time I dig a little more I tear apart; I can't handle the pain, and when my pain is so deep I can't think. My head gets full of unbearable visions, my mind races, full of thoughts. They all swim around so fast I can't grab hold of even one to concentrate on. What do I do? What can I possibly say?

But I pray for wisdom, strength, courage to get me through yet another day. One day at a time, that's all I can ask.

Pray for the judges' and prosecutors' hearts to open and show compassion. This scares me, as I think nothing I can say can express my innocence.

Diary entry, 28 April 2005

The next day, forty-one of us went to court in the sardine bus. As usual, I let everyone off first so they wouldn't all get caught up in the scrum. Then, as I did the hideous walk to the holding cell, reporters threw a new and humiliating line of questions at me.

'Is it true, Schapelle? Are you pregnant? The papers say you're pregnant, pregnant, pregnant . . .'

I focused on walking. I never answered their questions, as I wanted them out of my face as fast as possible. And I certainly wasn't going to answer their sick questions today. I was so embarrassed. What did people think of me? I don't take sex and pregnancy lightly. It would be nice to have sex, and to be pregnant would have been absolutely wonderful. But in a dump like this? No, thank you. I longed for human affection, but I could wait.

The holding cell was worse than usual. Everyone was smoking, making it difficult to breathe, and the air stung my eyes so badly that I had to sit with them squeezed shut.

It was soon time to go into the courtroom, which was full of placards that Merc, Wayan and his family had made and handed to supporters, saying 'Corby Tidak Bersalah' (Corby is not guilty) and 'Bebaskan Corby' (Free Corby). They'd also tied yellow ribbons everywhere. The anti-drugs group GRANAT were still there with their signs, as Merc had refused to do a deal with them to go away when they approached her for money. Until we paid, they assured her they'd keep turning up with their vicious signs.

The lawyers read for one and a half hours, and then it was my turn. I read out the statement that I had written the previous night.

> I ask for you to find me innocent, to send me home. Firstly, I would like to say to the prosecutors I cannot admit to a crime I did not commit. And to the judges, my life at the moment is in your hands, but I would prefer it if my life was in your heart. And I say to you again, that I have no knowledge of how the marijuana came to be inside my bag.
>
> I believe that the evidence shows that:
>
> - One: there is a problem in Australia with security at airports and baggage-handling procedures;
> - Two: my only mistake was not putting a lock on my luggage;
> - Three: I have never at any stage claimed ownership of the plastic bag and its contents;
> - Four: had the police weighed all of my luggage for the total weight, it would have shown a difference from the total weight checked in at Brisbane airport;
> - Five: the police had the opportunity to fingerprint both plastic bags to prove my innocence, but they chose not to;
> - Six: I am an innocent victim of a tactless drug-smuggling network;

- Seven: I am not a person involved in drugs and I'm not a person who might become involved in a drug-smuggling operation; and

- Eight: I love Bali and would never want to create problems for any of its people.

I believe the seven months which I've already spent in prison is a severe enough punishment for not putting locks on my bags. My heart and my family are painfully burdened by all these accusations and rumours about me, and I don't know how long I can survive here. And I swear, with God as my witness, that I did not know that the marijuana was in my bag. Please look to your God for guidance in your judgment of me, for God only speaks of justice. And, your honour, I ask for you to show compassion, to find me innocent, to send me home. *Saya tidak bersalah* [I am not guilty].

I walked to the bench and handed my statement to the chief judge. The court applauded. Lily and I were both in tears as we hugged.

I didn't know how much impact it would have. One of the judges was picking his nose, another reading a book called *Life Sentence*. Beautiful Merc called out 'See you, Schapelle' as I was leaving. 'Love you, Merc!' I called back.

I don't think I went too well. I couldn't remember what I had to read out; I felt like my head was full of nothing but air, could not hold it together. Today only one prosecutor was there. The main man and the main woman were absent. The judge didn't ask for my statement to be translated for them, even though it was addressed to them. I had to stand, give him the paper I'd just read, then he would give it to the prosecution to read. I feel like I've let everyone down.

Diary entry, 28 April 2005

15

A Test of Faith

Cried so much last night while everyone was sleeping. I cannot imagine living here after my court is finished. Actually can't use 'living' as a word in this dump – more like breathing and walking like a zombie. But I also can't envision the judge saying 'Go home!' What's going to become of me? I swear, I will not stay here after the final verdict. If the judges don't come to my favour, I'm not sure what I'll do, but I swear my body will not stay one minute longer in this place. I will somehow escape. There are many meanings to the word 'escape'. Got to stop thinking about the ifs. Must be patient – sabar. Pray, pray, pray.

Diary entry, 1 May 2005

I HAD BECOME FANATICALLY RELIGIOUS, PRAYING CONSTANTLY, reading the Bible zealously, even replacing grunt rock with tuneless Christian songs on my CD Walkman. I was clinging, clutching, desperately trying to give this hell some meaning, even creating crazy fantasies about why I was here. Maybe God wanted me to be an angel and needed me to find Him fast. This living hell was His way of clicking His fingers to get my attention. Well, He had it! So now He could set me free.

But my new faith didn't keep me on an even keel. I could swing from calm religious understanding to raging fury at this cruel, senseless injustice in a split second. The world would seem dark, evil, scary, and I'd scream, yell and smash things, even once, shamefully, throttling a girl, before swinging back to Godly calm. It was a constant seesawing between religion and reality – and reality sucked.

I was scared, lonely and so utterly exhausted. I wasn't coping. I was crying non-stop. I was terrified of being locked up like a monkey for twenty-seven years. As the verdict got closer, life got worse. My soul trembled. Everything upset me. Anguished thoughts flew through my mind.

Jail life was hell: the new dramas relentless. Before my next court day, a prisoner's face was smashed up in front of me. He was squatting against the wall in the visiting hall, looking lost in his thoughts. I sat opposite. Then, *whack!* A guard walked up and without warning kicked him in the face with a steel-capped boot. He collapsed to the floor. His shaky hands flew up to his broken face, but the guard hit them away for another free kick. I tensed up, disgusted. I couldn't breathe. I sat uselessly watching as the guard kept kicking his face until it was a mangled mess of smashed-up bone and blood. It was sick. I was strangely mesmerised, sickened, appalled, but I couldn't tear my eyes away. I had no idea why this guy was being beaten, but after he was dragged past me to the isolation tower, I had chilling flashbacks of his gruesome, battered face for days.

Beatings were nothing new, but you never got used to them. At least once a week, I'd be walking along and see a guy go up to another guy and punch him viciously in the jaw. His whole face would collapse, covered in blood. Instinctively, I'd want to run and help, but someone would always grab my hand, urgently whispering, 'Keep walking, keep walking.' I'd turn to look, to make sure he was OK. But you had to keep your head down. You couldn't help, or you'd get beaten, too. I felt absolute disgust that people could do this to each other. These incidents always left me traumatised, unable to stop thinking about them for days.

Apart from Sonia's occasional thrashing from the guards, girls didn't usually get beaten like that. Most of the violence in the women's block was between the women, usually Wanda and her lesbian friends, who were always switching girlfriends and then beating each other senseless in a jealous rage. The only violence I'd suffered was when a guy angrily hurled bricks at me in my cell after I refused to sit on his knee. He was in for murder. I didn't get hit, but it scared the hell out of me. Then, two weeks before my verdict, I was attacked by a lesbian who'd been flirting with me for months.

Inexplicably I'd always attracted lesbians in my old life, but they usually backed off when they found out I wasn't into girls; we respected each other's sexual preferences. In Hotel K, that didn't happen. There were many lesbians in our small compound and none were shy of showing their affections. I just ignored their moves, but this one girl was relentless, always stroking my arms, giving me loving looks and asking girls to translate: 'I want to touch Corby! Ask if I can touch Corby!' It was gross. I hated it.

'No. Tell her I like men,' I'd reply. 'I'm not a lesbian!'

It didn't stop her. She kept it up. She made my skin crawl. I'm sure she was unappealing even to other lesbians. She had three-millimetre-thick bright yellow tartar build-up on her teeth and foul-smelling breath.

Then one day she turned. As I was filling my bucket at the tap, she ran up and kicked it over, splashing water everywhere and trying to put her own bucket down. I'd had enough. I didn't need this bullshit. 'You're an idiot!' I screamed before throwing her bucket out of the way. She went berserk. She sprang at me, screeching, scratching and clawing like a wild cat, taking huge chunks of skin off my arms. Other girls leapt up and pulled her off me. She had a crazed look in her eye. I was shaking and in shock. My arms were a bloody, scratched-up mess. I glared at her but swallowed my anger, thinking, *You're pathetic.* I didn't say a word. I didn't want to give her the satisfaction of reacting. I just stood my bucket back up, took the hose and started refilling it. I hated this place. I had to escape it.

I'm off to court tomorrow and haven't been told what's happening – suppose it doesn't really matter, everything's out of my control anyway. The Lord will overpower the strongest lions and the most deadly snakes.

Diary entry, 5 May 2005

❖ ❖ ❖

As I stepped outside Hotel K's front door the next morning, cameras and microphones were thrust in my face. 'John Ford's been stabbed! How do you feel about that, Schapelle? How do you feel?'

I felt complete shock. My legs trembled and went weak. I stumbled towards the paddy wagon, thinking, *He's dead, he's dead* . . . Reporters were still yelling, but I couldn't hear any more words. An indescribably loud noise was roaring in my ears as I vanished into a surreal daze. I couldn't believe it. This man had risked his life to help me and now he was dead. He'd told the court that he and his daughter had already been threatened and that if he named the person who owned the drugs he was 100 per cent sure he'd be killed and I probably would be, too.

Reporters were all still screaming questions as I sat in the police van, trying to cope with my rising hysteria. But I was losing it. I couldn't stop shaking. I was surrounded by cameras thrusting through the windows, all trying to catch my distress. I put my head in my hands, trying to take a moment to absorb the shocking news. The other prisoner in the van was doing his best to help me, pushing the cameras away and slamming the windows shut before we finally tore off to court.

I was crying hysterically. I'd been living in fear of something like this happening for months. Now my fears were real. It wasn't just paranoia. He'd been stabbed. I was petrified of being stabbed, too. I felt blind terror when we got to court and I was pulled through the media scrum. They kept yelling questions. 'How do you feel, Schapelle? How do you feel?' I was stumbling along, almost falling, but being held up by the guards gripping me tightly by the arms as they almost carried me to the holding cell. As soon as I was inside, I threw up.

Merc saw my distress and screamed at the reporters. They all knew there was no way I could have heard the news about Ford yet, but they'd hurled it straight at me, to get a newsworthy reaction. They got it. Merc was so upset, telling them they were cruel and tactless. They didn't splash *that* all over the news. I found out that Mr Ford wasn't dead but had been stabbed in the back with a razor blade and was doing OK.

Schapelle Corby looked stunned yesterday when she was
told the Australian prisoner who gave evidence in her
defence had been attacked in jail. She was on her way to
court in Bali for her latest hearing when she was told rape
suspect John Ford had been slashed by another inmate at
the prison in Victoria.

Daily Telegraph (Australia), 7 May 2005

In court that day, I learnt that John Ford had risked his life for
nothing. The prosecutors were rejecting his evidence and still
demanding I spend my life in jail.

I was terrified – nothing was going my way. But suddenly we
got an explosive break that backed up what I was saying, what
John Ford was saying and what the Australian Federal Police had
been furiously denying. There was a major drug-smuggling problem
at our very secure Australian airports, involving airport staff. On
the same day, almost at the exact same time that I went through
Sydney airport, corrupt baggage handlers were evading security
to intercept a briefcase with 9.9 kilograms of cocaine before it
reached customs.

News of it broke only when one of the men in the drug syndicate
applied for bail in a Sydney court. A police statement given to the
court gave details of 'Operation Mocha'. For the past six months,
the AFP had been using an informant to unravel a drug-smuggling
ring that was using baggage handlers to help smuggle cocaine into
Australia through Sydney airport. The syndicate had brought 200
kilos of cocaine into Australia between June and December 2004,
the dates of each shipment decided according to the roster of the
corrupt baggage handlers.

On the day I flew to Bali, the corrupt handlers were moving
bags, moving my bags and moving 9.9 kilograms of cocaine
through Sydney airport and being paid $300,000 for their criminal
handiwork. It was unbelievable. I'd been saying from day one I didn't
do this. John Ford had been saying he'd overheard a conversation
about baggage handlers using my bag to move drugs, and my
lawyers had been flying with this theory for months. Now we had

a highly plausible explanation of how it could so easily have been done. What was the chance of it being just a lucky coincidence that this new evidence conveniently and perfectly backed my story? The judges could surely see the odds of this being a coincidence were extremely low. Surely they would believe me now?

Surely it was also a much more plausible explanation of how a whopping 4.2-kilo clear plastic bag, casually tossed into a boogie-board bag, had sailed through two Australian airports?

The government, Qantas and the AFP had all known about this for six long months, and despite my lawyers asking for any information on crime and corruption at the airports, they'd denied it even existed and just repeated their mantra: 'We're doing all we can to help.'

I'd been living in desperate hope of news that would prove I didn't do it and get me out of here. I thought this was finally it. I thought it was my big break. I thought it was big enough news for them to know 'OK, this girl didn't do it.' I was excited to hear that the Australian Prime Minister John Howard was going to write a letter to the court, explaining that there was a problem with airport staff being involved in drug smuggling. I got so excited that the courts would finally believe me, finally listen to this evidence.

Poor Merc really believed this was the big break, too, thinking she was going to have her little sister home again at last. Journalists were frantically phoning her for comment, telling her this was it. Ron and Robin were telling her this was it. Sheer relief hit her. She had a breakdown. After being the strongest in the family since day one, carrying the burden of dealing with lawyers and the media and fearing for me daily, she collapsed on the floor at home, shaking and crying hysterically, scrunched up in the foetal position until Wayan came home and found her. She hadn't cried like that since the night of my arrest.

But our hopes were shattered again. We were crushed and angry when the judge said it was too late to submit any new evidence to the court. He asked my lawyers to give him any new information in writing by the following Monday. He might consider it. But the chief prosecutor said it had no legal standing because the trial was effectively over. I couldn't believe it. The government had known about this for six months. How much did they really know? Did they also know exactly who put the marijuana in my bag?

When I got back to Kerobokan that afternoon, my nerves were jangling. I was tense, angry, sick of this life, sick of the bullshit, the cameras, media, the pain, the agony. I was shaking, ready to lose it, ready to explode. It got worse. I had to fight with all my energy not to rip into a girl who started picking on me.

This girl, Niken, had been doing all she could to irritate me for seven months, always taunting, whispering, pointing, spreading nasty rumours. She was a very, very bitchy girl with a sneaky personality. She started picking the moment I got back from court.

She was tipping me over the edge. I felt blind fury. I was desperately fighting against the urge to punch her. I folded my arms and held them tightly into my body, as tight as I could, trying not to hit her. I was standing almost on top of her, seeing visions of kicking her to the ground, bashing her head into the concrete and not stopping. I don't like violence, but those visions horrifyingly satisfied my anger towards her. I felt sick that I could actually see myself doing that. She just stood there smirking, with no idea of the violent pictures I was seeing. I glared back, asking, 'Do you like your face?' She nodded, still smirking. 'Then you'd better protect it. Stay away from me! Stay away from my cell! Don't even look at me!'

She didn't listen. The next day she started picking again. I was still full of rage, but I tried to stay calm. I tried to ignore her. I knew I was only one bitchy comment away from losing it, so I did all I could to avoid her. I kept my distance, quickly moving if she came anywhere near me. But she was pushing me. The next morning I lost it.

This girl was in my cell when I got back from collecting water. I screamed at her, 'Get out, get out', shoving her out of my cell. She started yelling nasty, bitchy comments. That did it. I snapped. I couldn't control myself.

Shaking with fury, I marched into her cell, grabbed her by the throat and started choking her. The other girls were screaming at me to stop. But I couldn't. I threw her onto the mattress, raging with fury. Another girl screamed 'Get off!' from under the blankets, sticking her head out of hiding to show two gruesome black eyes. She'd been beaten up for flirting with another girl's husband. Niken got up. I wasn't finished. I got her by the throat again and threw her back down in another direction. By this time, the cell was full of girls. Some held me back from another attack. I broke their grip and walked out, still mad as hell.

A few minutes later, the guards called us both to their table. They wanted us to shake hands and get over it. I refused point-blank.

'No, I'm not shaking this girl's hand!' I was fuming. 'I don't like her, and I'm not pretending I like her just for you!'

She wasn't smirking now. But suddenly she had even less to smirk about. An older woman from her cell, whom we all called 'Mum', ran up screaming abuse at her. It was a catfight. She was furious. She'd seen how bitchy and awful Niken was to me. She got her claws out and tore big scratches down Niken's face. I hated this girl but instantly felt bad for starting this fight. The guards yelled at them to stop. They told Niken to stay away from my cell and banned us both from church for a week.

I'm so angry at myself for letting her get to me. I've got so much anger inside, I need some stress release. I need a punching bag. So I guess she was it. I am ashamed that I showed such weakness. The next morning I went and apologised, also to the other girls in her cell for barging in with such rage. Took a lot to apologise, hard thing to do. So much easier to lose your temper than to apologise for it. Once it's said and done, you feel so much better and can get on with the day.

Diary entry, 19 May 2005

I was still shaken and upset about it the next time I saw Lily, and I started telling her how ashamed I felt about it. She just looked at me blankly and asked, 'Is she pretty, Schapelle?'

'What?' I was baffled. 'What has that got to do with anything?'

Lily thought I'd attacked this girl out of jealousy because she was pretty. The conversation ended. She didn't get it. Lily's question told me more about her than anything else.

I needed to speak to someone. I needed a psychiatrist who wouldn't run to the press, or a person I could trust to just let loose with and cry and cry and cry and tell them how shit my cell was, how scared I felt, how horrible life was and just release everything. But there was no one. I didn't want to unload on the only people I could trust – my family – as they already had enough stress to deal with. They didn't need to know all the gruesome details of my daily life. I couldn't do that to them. I'd always try to put on a brave face and say, 'No, no, it's OK!' I just had to deal with it all myself. I only had myself and God to rely on. It was lonely. I prayed to Him a lot, releasing through prayer. It helped to temporarily lift the heavy black cloud of despair. But I spent most of the time praying in my cell, as I no longer felt safe at church. I certainly couldn't trust Christians any more than I could trust lawyers, guards, police or anyone else.

Even an Australian pastor who'd baptised me five months earlier stole my trust, touting his story just weeks before the verdict. He'd already run to the press when he first returned from baptising me. Now he was ringing TV programmes and newspapers offering to do interviews, even faxing journalists a personal thank-you note I'd written and given to him. It got printed. I was shattered – now I was being exploited by a pastor! Not long before my verdict, he had the audacity to return to Bali with Channel 7's *Today Tonight*. They'd paid for his airfares and hotel in return for promises of access to me. They didn't get it. I refused to come out. I never ever, ever wanted to see this man again. He'd burnt me. Like so many others, he'd sold his soul to the media and in the process hurt me. If you couldn't trust a pastor, who could you trust?

Not my lawyer. Lily came in asking me questions about my religion: 'Were you religious in Australia?'

'No.'

'What was your baptism name?'

'Abigail.' I started feeling distressed. 'Lily, what's this got to do with my case? Why are you writing all this down, Lily?'

'Oh, no reason!'

'Scribble it out! You're not giving it to reporters, Lily – scribble it out!'

'Oh, I can't do that!'

She finally did, but only after we had a lengthy argument.

Lily also asked me if I'd do an interview with a TV reporter from Jakarta. Merc and I discussed it and decided 'no'. It might not hurt my case, but it wouldn't help it. So why bother? I was sick of being exploited. It would also probably cause me problems with the prison boss. But Lily still tried to persuade me.

'No! Lily, you know I'll get in trouble.' She kept pushing. 'No! Lily, please!'

She came in with the reporter a few days later, regardless. My wishes didn't count. She started again: 'Schapelle . . . just a quick interview . . .' 'No.' They both pushed. 'No.' I was relieved when they finally let it go.

As we walked out of the prison office to sit outside in the visit area, this reporter walked right behind me. When we sat down, I peeled off my dark-blue prison-issue T-shirt as I usually did at visits. Then my instincts kicked in. I started to tremble. Panic ripped through me. It was happening again. He was holding a small leather clutch bag awkwardly near the ground. I looked closely. I saw it. My hands flew to cover up the small lens peephole in his bag. I screamed, 'Noooo! *Turn it off!*' as I waved my hands frantically in front of the bag. I could trust no one.

The journalist calmly turned to give Lily a questioning look. She nodded. He put the bag down. He didn't apologise. Lily just started pushing me once more. 'Come on, Schapelle, I do everything for you!' She even got Vasu on the phone to try to bully me into it.

'Look at all we do for you, Schapelle!'

I was fuming. I refused to be bullied. 'No!' He left without his interview.

Lily and Vasu were furious. They came in a few days after the incident, telling me off for embarrassing Lily in front of a television journalist. Vasu blasted me for upsetting Lily. It was unbelievable. Who the hell were these people?

Later, I saw the story on Indonesian television. It had an interview with Lily and shots of me walking, peeling off my blue T-shirt and then frantically waving my hands over the lens. My lawyer had conspired with him, despite the fact that I'd repeatedly said no, despite knowing how deeply traumatised I was by sneaky cameras, and despite the little detail of her being my lawyer, whom I was trusting with my life.

The betrayals were non-stop. The invasion of me was at its worst. I'd developed a sixth sense for hidden cameras. I was very aware, always alert, always looking out. I saw them everywhere. It wasn't paranoia – everyone was filling their pockets. I saw disposable cameras and camera phones constantly, as guards, prisoners and visitors weren't exactly professional paparazzi, expert at hiding in bushes with long lenses. Usually, they were clumsy and obvious. Girls would blatantly point their camera phones at me. I'd test it by moving and the phone would always move with me. Or a group of male guards would stand with disposable cameras outside the church, all ready to snap me when I came outside. 'No! You're not allowed to use cameras in here. No!' I usually screamed at them before running off in tears.

But the media were hungry and always looking for willing amateurs. A male prisoner told me a journalist had offered him a wad of cash and a disposable camera to get photos of me throughout my day. He refused. He had a heart.

The irony was that every time a sneaky photo of me was in the news, I'd cop the flak. I was regularly called to the boss's office to get yelled at for a picture of me in the press. Twice I had to write apology letters, even though I'd tell him in tears, 'It's your guards taking the photos; it's the people your guards let in here taking the photos. It's not *my* fault!'

One of the most devious and sinister ways of getting shots of me was with 'the Bible camera'. Christians would visit the prison church with a box crafted to look like a Bible with a little camera inside. It was so hypocritical. But nothing surprised me. I was so super-sensitive to sneaky cameras that I'd instantly sniff them out. I'd see a Bible pointed at me with a little peephole. I'd move seats. The Bible would follow me. These people weren't journalists posing as Christians; they were devious Christians keen to fill up their pockets with fast cash. I often ran out of the church, shaking and in tears.

But in jail, the cameras weren't always hidden. Sometimes they were smack-bang in my face. Kerobokan was cashing in and becoming Bali's busiest film lot. Camera crews were endlessly setting up for yet another media stunt, like the beauty-school course and the yoga course. I went gleefully to the first day of both but turned around and walked straight out as soon as I saw cameras. Unsurprisingly, both courses were cancelled instantly.

On Hotel K's birthday, the Governor of Bali and all his men came through with a local TV crew. He made a beeline to my cell with his entourage. He shook my hand for the cameras, patted me on the back and said, 'You go home!'

'Soon?' I asked.

He smiled and walked off. He had his shots. It was all just another media stunt, with the footage broadcast on both Australian and Balinese TV that night. After he walked away, the others shook my hand, two women indiscreetly whispering to each other: 'Oh, she's small, young and pretty. On TV she looks big and old!' What did they think I was . . . a Madam Tussaud's waxwork dummy?

No one could have cared less about my feelings. I felt that no one saw me as a person with a heart. I was just a monkey. Sometimes I'd be sitting in my cell reading a book when a group of Indonesian university students would turn up and walk into my cell, just gawping at me. The visitors' hall was always swarming with Westerners trying to catch a glimpse of me or meet me. I started refusing to come out of my block to visits with strangers, as I was so sick of being stared at like a freak. I was also too exhausted to keep talking to twenty strangers a day. Local drivers would often bring in vanloads of tourists. It was bizarre. This was a notorious maximum-security prison, crammed with murderers, paedophiles and terrorists, yet Australian tourists would arrive in their beachwear with their babies and little kids. This was a jail, not a must-see tourist hot spot! But Hotel K had an open-door policy: anyone could come in to see its most popular wax dummy. The guards were raking in more money in a day than they were paid in a year. It was raining rupiah.

I had to get out of this hellhole, but my hopes were further dashed when I realised I wouldn't get any real help from the Australian Government. I was shattered when the Australian consul came to see me a week before the verdict, bringing a copy of the supposedly crucial letter about the airport crime. I'd been pinning my hopes on it. It was useless.

> Following a joint investigation, which has been conducted over the last six months, the Australian Federal Police and the NSW Police have dismantled a Sydney-based syndicate involved in the trafficking of drugs. Police are currently investigating a number of baggage handlers who work at Sydney International Airport about these drug trafficking activities. The Police believe these baggage handlers were on duty on 8 October 2004, when a shipment of drugs was brought into Sydney International Airport.
>
> Rod Smith, DFAT, 13 May 2005

What could I do but sit and cry? The letter was nothing. I fought with myself not to rip it to shreds. Instead I folded it back up and placed it back inside Brent's shirt pocket. It did not mention my name; it was not addressed to the judges, instead addressed to Lily, my lawyer, and it even spelt her name incorrectly. It was not written by John Howard but someone else. How would the judges even acknowledge or give it a twice-over when they'd had no idea who this person is who wrote it . . . what a waste of paper. John Howard . . . what a lame Joe Blow to have in charge of our country.

Diary entry, 19 May 2005

Everything was out of my control. The pressures were relentless. My world was spinning fast. I kept talking to God, kept praying endlessly. But even praying didn't calm me; I just cried hysterically to God. Everyone wanted a piece of me: staring, stalking, staking me out and harassing me and harassing my family. Photographers were hanging outside my little sister's school, waiting at James's football games, waiting outside Mum and Dad's houses. It was worst for Merc. She had reporters following her in the street and was too scared to go out for dinner in case she got criticised for enjoying herself while her sister rotted in prison.

But Ron and Robin kept whipping up the media, telling me that the Australian opinion polls were now at 92 per cent in my favour. They were excited. The media were going ballistic. They were interviewed on morning shows, afternoon shows, on radio, newspapers, many times every day, giving the media a good thrashing. They were always coming up with ways to get more exposure, saying any publicity was good publicity.

A week before my verdict, Ron rang Merc to ask her all about our brother Clinton, who was in jail in Queensland. It was no state secret. Merc had told Ron and Robin about him in their first meeting, when she was asked if there was anything they should know. Vasu and Lily had also known about him since day one, and a few journalists knew, but incredibly it hadn't hit the press so far. But Ron was suddenly asking for details. 'What's his surname? Which prison is he in? When will he be released?'

A couple of days later, Clinton's story hit the press.

Six weeks before Ms Corby landed in Bali's Ngurah Rai Airport with 4.1 kg of marijuana in her body board bag, her half-brother Clinton Rose was locked up in a Queensland jail. Rose will get out in about four months while Ms Corby will find out in six days whether a Bali court decides to accept the prosecution's recommendation of a life sentence – or worse – or set her free as an unwitting drug mule.

The Australian, 21 May 2005

Ron was in a frenzy about the media, trying desperately to tie up last-minute deals and make some cash. He still wanted me to write songs, write a diary, do interviews. I felt like I owed him. I still naively believed that he was putting a lot of money towards my defence, even though I was hearing that actually he wasn't. I could also feel the friction between Ron and my family building daily. Merc was edgy around him. But he kept telling me he was paying for everything and spending so much money. All he talked about was money.

He was also trying to persuade me to write diary notes on the final four days leading up to the verdict. He'd already clinched a deal with *New Idea*. He pushed and pushed me: 'Just *try*, Schapelle. Just do it.' I couldn't. I was too stressed. He started harassing Merc. 'She's not up to it, Ron!' she'd tell him. He kept pushing right up until the day of the verdict.

Ron was also pushing Merc about doing a book. He'd been pushing her for weeks to sign a deal, but Merc and Mum both felt it wasn't the right time. Ron was furious.

'You're making a big mistake! You'll be sorry! You'll regret it!' he yelled at them in a three-way phone call. He angrily told them how much work he'd put into getting a deal.

Mum got upset and angry, too. It was the last thing on her mind, as all she wanted was her baby safely home. 'No, Ron! *No!*' The phone call abruptly ended.

With Ron trying to stitch up deals all over town, Merc was receiving a lot of questions from journalists about whether she had a contract with him, but Ron kept telling her to lie. He didn't want the truth known. She had to keep spinning the 'Nothing's signed, there is no contract' line. She was stressed. She felt sick.

She couldn't see why the contracts had to be kept secret, but Ron was insistent and she didn't have the energy to fight him. Despite Merc lying for him to protect his shining white-knight image, it was tarnished anyway. He was copping a lot of negative publicity. He'd been exposed as an ex-bankrupt who'd owed his creditors big bucks. He was in crisis control. Robin told Merc to write a press statement saying how great Ron was. He dictated it to her on the phone.

Please never underestimate what Ron Bakir has done for Schapelle and our family. He has not stopped fighting for Schapelle and has been instrumental in bringing up the problems in Australia that directly relate to her case. He's helped make Australia safer.

Mercedes Corby press release, 18 May 2005

Just two days before the verdict, Ron and Robin brought a radio-journalist friend in with them. It was not an interview, I was assured. 'Are you sure?' 'Yes, he just wants to meet you.' So I sat talking with Ron, Robin and their journalist friend for about twenty minutes. He then walked out of Kerobokan, rang his radio station and relayed our conversation on air, recounting how he'd just been in to see me.

The day before I lost my life, panic was ripping through me, I was crying non-stop, I threw up constantly. My body hurt from stress and tension and my mind was spinning with thoughts . . . *Will I go home? Will the judges see I didn't do this? Will I lose my life and be stuck in this hellhole for ever?*

I don't care how long I have to stay in this place, I will not grow old here. I will not have any birthdays; I will stay 27 until the day I'm released.

Diary entry, 21 May 2005

Ron and Robin were still telling me constantly, 'Schapelle, you're going home. You'll be acquitted! You're going home, Schapelle!' They were so sure, so enthusiastic. But Merc would always just sit there looking totally drained and exasperated, telling me, 'Schapelle, you might get three years or even five years.' She was scared about how hard I'd crash if I did get time and hadn't been prepared. She'd been fighting with Ron and Robin endlessly, asking them not to pump me up with false hopes. But they kept it up right until verdict day.

Mr Tampoe said Ms Corby and the defence team were confident of her acquittal. 'She's certainly very optimistic about the result which will happen on Friday,' he said.

But her sister Mercedes told *The Bulletin* that she and their mother, Rosleigh, had prepared Schapelle for the worst as well.

Gold Coast Bulletin, 24 May 2005

I'd heard that the chief judge had never found anyone 'not guilty' in the 500 or so drug cases he'd heard, but I was clinging to hope. Somehow I started to convince myself that I'd be OK, I'd go home, the judge might not find me not guilty but he'd sentence me to time already served and I'd go home with my mum. There was no other way it could go. God wouldn't let this happen to me, not to an innocent person. I couldn't stay locked in hell for something I didn't do. I'd finally wake from this nightmare. Innocent people did not get locked up.

> *I must stay focused this week. All the defence is over; nothing more humanly possible can be done. I pray for the miracle of the heavenly kingdom to take power and lead the way of what He wants to happen. My heart is open to Him. I trust in Him to make my faith stronger. I need a stronger, deeper faith to come into me leading up to the 27th. I feel my faith becoming stronger, and each hour I'm praying a lot, I'm not questioning the word of the Bible as much as I had been. I'm accepting and truly believing without the doubt and criticism that I used to have.*
>
> Diary entry, 22 May 2005

16

The Verdict

AS I SAT ON MY MATTRESS IN MY LITTLE CAGE, I STARTED to picture life beyond these white walls of hell. For the first time, I could see my house on the coast, streets, shops, restaurants, friends, sunsets and stars. It was all in sharp focus. I could see myself having a beer on the beach or lying on the couch watching TV or shopping with my friends. I hadn't been able to recall anything of home for seven months, but in the days before the verdict, familiar little scenes kept popping into my head. I didn't shut them down. I let myself enjoy them, thinking maybe it was a good sign. Maybe my dark days were almost over. Or was I just torturing myself? Whenever I came back from fantasising, reality was as perverse as ever.

The flies are back, as unbearable as before. This time another animal problem: worms, nice big, juicy worms, everywhere – in the toilet, crawling on the floor, up where we sleep – well, six of us sleep up on the ledge while another two, Aje and Putu, are on the floor. Putu hates sleeping next to Aje, as Aje is a lesbian and tries to touch her while she's sleeping. Aje also masturbates a lot in her sleep. We throw cups of water on her! Anyway, Putu has an abnormal fear of worms. Worm phobia! She's quite a big girl – we've nicknamed her 'Giant'.

Yesterday she became so tired of listening to Sonia's voice, which is mostly high-pitched yelling all day, then loud singing until the early hours of the morning, that she calmly walked over to Sonia, held her up by the neck, told her to shut up, walked back into the cell, sat down and continued eating her breakfast. But the irony is she then spent most of today huddled up in the corner of the cell crying, scared of the worms. We other girls have to keep sweeping and disinfecting the floors every couple of hours.

Putu can't shower tonight; the toilet floor is covered in the worms. We're not sure where they're all coming from. I know the septic tank is full. Our cell stinks and takes so much water to flush, and there are often presents left too. So gross! Look on the bright side; this is Saturday 21 May and it could possibly be my last weekend in this zoo!

Diary entry, 21 May 2005

The night before my verdict, I really believed it would be my last locked up in this vile, worm-infested cage. It felt like the end of a bad school camp as I sat talking to the girls in my cell. We were all getting excited and upbeat about me going home, reflecting on some of the crazy things we'd seen and done together, things that weren't funny at the time but that we could look back on and speak of with a smile. We talked about the time each girl checked into Hotel K and was sent to share a cell with 'Schapelle Corby'. We talked about some fights I'd had, and they all told me they could see some good changes in my personality. Maybe that was why God had put me here. All these girls had helped me to grow and to become more patient.

Then I got ready to go home. I put all the things I wanted to keep in a little pile, like my Bible, some clothes, my diary, photos and a knitted doll I'd been sent. I told the girls everything else was theirs to share, which made them even keener for me to go home. Then I prayed. I prayed for the judges, the prosecutors, my lawyers and my family. I prayed to be freed. I also prayed that, if it wasn't God's will that I walked free tomorrow, He would give my family and me the strength to endure the pain and frustration and to remain calm under pressure, to remain calm, dignified and strong in the chaos around us, and for the strength to keep going on with an open heart, not holding hatred or bitterness.

I slept well. In the morning, I felt calm, not vomiting and

Grrr. Cleaning the toilet in cell number seven. The tub on the right we fill with water from the well and use to flush the toilet. The ladle is what we use to scoop the water to flush and shower.

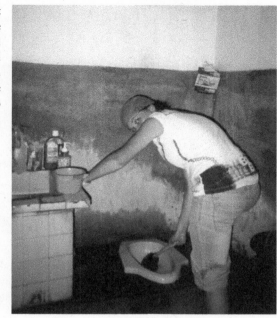

Sonia 'the Black Monster' dressed up for Christmas Day 2004.

Christmas Day 2004. My first Christmas inside jail. I'm standing with Agus. Eighteen months later, I found him hanging from the rafters with a noose around his neck. May you rest in peace, Agus.

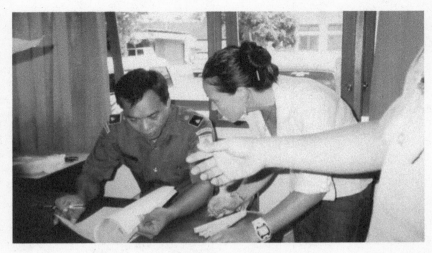

Meeting the prosecutor, Mr Ida Bagus Wiswantanu. Here I'm demanding fingerprints and other forensic tests to be taken. He seems uninterested and tells me, 'Yeah, yeah!' He is flicking through the dossier of the Polda police's so-called investigations.

Leaving the prosecutor's office, heading back to Hotel K – the first ever time I was handcuffed. It was such a shameful and degrading moment that I'd come to experience time and time again.

Cesspool – the mosquito-infected, stinky place where you find snakes with three eyes. Girls actually enter this water and do clothes washing – see the clothes laid out to dry on the grass. I try to avoid this area as much as possible.

The gruelling ritual of filling the water buckets morning and afternoon.
In front of cell number two.

With Ron and Robin in the visiting area of Hotel K.

This looks so much like a Bali holiday tourist shot. This is the isolation tower where Amrozi had the cell window on my left and Samudra had the cell window on my right. Amrozi's brother, Mukhlas, was one cell further around on the left. There are four cells in total in the tower. Nobody goes upstairs, as the stairs are all rotten. A French prisoner walked up there seven years ago and said he could see the beach in the far distance. In the back corner of the fenced area is the tiny tin lot divided into four 1x2-metre isolation cages.

Cooking fried rice for all
the girls in my cell.

Inside cell number seven.
Our water buckets are lined
up against the wall ready
for us to shower. Bottom
right is the kitchen area,
with my gas camper stove.
The door to the right is for
the toilet.

On my mattress as the guards
let the media enter to bombard
me in my cell, hours after the
block was locked up. I was told
to sit and stay while all the girls
did their best to hide. It was
humiliating and a total invasion.
The newspapers then numbered
and named all my belongings.
(Newspix/AFP)

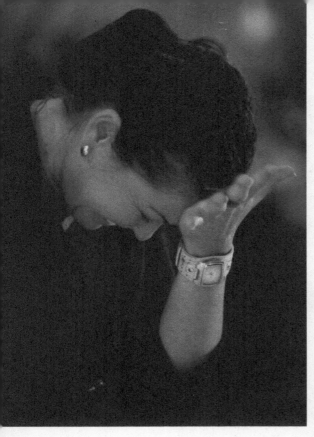

Are words needed . . . On hearing the judges' guilty verdict – being sentenced to twenty years. *(Newspix/AFP)*

Looking and feeling like a German shepherd about to viciously attack. In court, lashing out at the prosecutors after hearing my sentence. *(Newspix/AFP)*

Calm and wrapped in Mum's love. I love this picture. I cry each time I see it. To look at this I feel how much she loves me. *(Newspix/AFP)*

In court
surrounded by
local media. The
judge just let this
happen.

July 2005 – my twenty-
eighth birthday and my
first birthday in Hotel K as
a convicted criminal. I'm
determined not to grow old
in this place, so I choose to
stay twenty-seven till the
day I go home. Pictured
here with my family and
Eddie (sitting behind me)
on the Monday, because
no visits were allowed on
Sunday, my actual birthday.

November 2005 – I love this photo
with my big brother Michael. He
has a habit of coming over for
surprise visits and putting big
smiles on my face.

25 August 2006 – four months after cutting my hair off. In my cell minutes before I place the black scarf over my hair and walk out of the block. I'm heading to my day in court for judicial review.

crying like usual before court, as I got ready to face the day. After showering with my bucket of cold water, I sat wrapped in a towel on my bed while one of the girls put my hair in a bun and I did my make-up, the other girls all sitting around watching. The air was filled with excitement. I dressed in my new outfit that Mum had bought me, and my new pink heels. I filled up the little knitted bag one of the girls had made as a farewell gift with lip gloss, hanky and anything worthy of stealing, put on my Hail Mary pendant necklace, said a prayer and was ready. The girls gave me hugs and wished me good luck. As I stepped outside, more girls came up to give me hugs and best wishes before the guards came to collect me.

I felt a little numb and light-headed but good as we walked through the prison grounds, all quiet apart from the occasional prisoner or guard yelling out 'Good luck, Corby!' and giving me a wave. I waved back, thinking how much this walk had terrified me seven months before. Now it was so familiar: I'd walked it hundreds of times, back and forth at least twice a day to visits. It was the only walking I did. But I felt sure I wouldn't ever walk this way again as I was taken into the office to get fingerprinted and handcuffed. Even the guards were smiling and wishing me good luck. I was smiling, too. Hotel K seemed like a friendly environment for a change.

I was led back outside to the iron-fenced path to wait for the police car, relieved to find out it was picking me up inside the prison. This special door-to-door treatment was only used in extreme cases. It meant we'd avoid the maniacal media mob at the front door, speeding off before they could even shout 'Schapelle, how do you feel?'

I stood waiting in my pretty pink heels, pink slacks, black blouse, hair up in a bun and make-up done, surrounded by six or so larger-than-life Indonesian military men all heavily armed with machine guns. Behind me, Amrozi and Samudra were staring out from separate tiny windows of the isolation tower. It gave me chills. All the guards were hovering, the occasional male prisoner walking past, pointing. Female guards were hassling me for my heels and slacks.

'I want those when you come back. Gimme those,' they screeched, pointing at my shoes.

I was quite calm but occasionally swept by a wave of anxiety. I'd breathe deeply and focus on my breath, realising I'd been forgetting to breathe. Then I'd say a little prayer: *Lord, I know you're with me. Lord, fill me with your holy spirit, set me free to be all you've created me to be. Amen.* I was constantly using this little ritual to help pull me through my darkest moments.

We drove out through an obscure side gate usually reserved for rubbish trucks, but it was anything but a stealthy escape. The photographers and reporters clamouring at the front door saw us, turning sharply towards our screaming sirens. I had to laugh at the looks on their bewildered faces. They were dumbfounded. Their jaws dropped as it sank in they'd missed their shots. They'd been duped. For once, they didn't have the jump on me. Almost in slow motion they started pointing at the car and running after it. But it was futile. They were too late. As we sped off, they were chasing clouds of dust. Even the guards and prosecutors had a bit of a laugh as we watched them vanish into the distance. It was the only light moment in a dark, dark day.

We hurtled through the traffic at top speed with sirens blaring and a trail of police jeeps escorting me, Schapelle Corby, to my most horrific day ever. I sat squeezed between the prosecutor and the men with machine guns. It was like a scene from *The Godfather*. They were all very busy talking on their mobile phones. I just sat quietly, praying, breathing and then praying some more. I was full of naive hope, but felt occasional twinges of doubt in my heart. When the prosecutor finished a call, I turned and asked, 'Will I be going home today?' He smiled but didn't say a word. I had no idea how to take that.

There was a weird calm inside the car. But as soon as we arrived, everything spun into fast motion. Doors flew open, guards leapt out yelling and shouting as people charged towards the car. Within seconds, people were leaning, banging, pushing and crushing around it. I sat frozen in the back seat, the windows filling with cameras, lenses and faces. People were screaming, 'Schapelle, Schapelle,

Schapelle!' Swarming dark figures were moving fast and frenzied. It was terrifying. How the hell had my life come to this? I was suddenly grabbed by the arms and pulled from the car. My feet didn't touch the ground as two guards gripped me tightly at the elbows, lifting me, carrying me through the seething crowd. It was all happening very quickly.

I was surrounded by at least twenty security guards, their sheer force moving us through the ferocious pack. I couldn't breathe. I was numb, scared, disorientated. It was all a blur. I didn't know where I was but could tell I was being taken on a different path from my usual one. There were people everywhere, so many people. It was crazy, madness. We came to a metal detector, like those they have at airports. We barely slowed. I was whisked through, swiftly, smoothly, my feet still not touching the ground, and then through many, many more people. I wasn't thinking, my mind was blank, we were moving so fast. My heart was pounding, my pulse racing, my body shaking furiously as the guards kept pushing me through the crushing mob. Then, everything stopped.

I was suddenly standing alone in the courtroom doorway, the guards gone from my sides. It must have been noisy, because it was suddenly still, quiet – but only for a split second. I stood up straight, looking at the sea of faces. The room was full of standing people. I felt self-conscious. They were all looking at me with what I thought were puzzled half-smiles. I looked down to see my blouse was pulled to one side, revealing half of my white bra. I was so embarrassed. I quickly fitted it on properly and got myself tidy. I looked over to where my family usually sat, to make sure they were there. They were, all giving me looks of love, compassion and anticipation, all beckoning me to come inside. Mum blew me a kiss. The guards were motioning me to come in and sit down. I took a couple of deep breaths and stepped in through the door.

Everything's going to be OK now, I told myself as I walked towards the hot seat, trying to ignore the cameras, which were going ballistic. I was pleased to see Merc had remembered to put a folded towel down on the chair. I took my seat and slowly looked around, not really taking anything in. The whole place, every inch, was covered with people, all the windows darkened by camera lenses. People were clamouring noisily outside every door, every window, there were people absolutely everywhere, with all eyes on me.

Merc later told me the photographers and cameramen had been so desperately keen to get positions that they'd hired Balinese locals to camp outside the windows for at least three days and nights before my verdict, to keep their places. Tents were erected, satellite dishes installed, stages built for the live coverage. So much money had been spent to televise my fate. One dishonest but savvy Balinese guy took advantage of the media's cash-splashing with a devious little plan to fill up his own pockets. He spread the news to all the Western media that they had to buy passes to enter the court area that day. Before anyone caught on to his naughty little scam, he'd vanished into the Balinese sunset with his stash of dirty cash.

My heart was thumping against my chest as I waited for my case to start. Lily and Eka hadn't arrived yet. The judges hadn't entered. I felt scared and alone, sitting in the middle of the room. Then Erwin walked over to sit with me and hold my hand. He was awestruck. He had a look of pure excitement on his face. He turned towards the windows in amazement. 'Schapelle, this is all over the world! This is world news! It's live.' His eyes were shining. 'Never have I ever experienced anything like this. Look at this – look, Schapelle!'

I didn't share his enthusiasm. It might have been incredible to have so much interest, so many reporters, cameras and people, but it was my life on the line. If this didn't go well, the bright lights and cameras would switch off and I'd be going back to a living hell. I knew it was going live on two or three TV stations in Australia, but I didn't think about it. I didn't care. It meant nothing. The only thing on my mind was going home and what the three judges would be saying to me very shortly.

I turned to Erwin and asked, 'Do you think I can go home today?'

He answered, 'I do my best for you. I only ever do my best for you, Schapelle.'

I thought, *So maybe I will be going home today.*

Erwin went back to his seat. I wasn't really feeling anything. I was numb. I just kept glancing around, saying silent prayers with my eyes open, looking into the cameras but not registering that I was gazing down the lenses of live coverage. I turned to look for Merc. I saw her instantly as only Merc, Mum and Dad were in sharp focus, the rest was a blur. Merc's face was glowing. She looked so beautiful, sitting there radiating all of her love and all of her hopes for me. I felt so proud she was my sister. She leant towards me across the wooden barrier between us, whispering, 'Schapelle, do you feel it? Do you feel it?' There was a peaceful energy. 'It's going to be OK, Schapelle! It's over. It's going to be OK.' I smiled and nodded to her. I hoped so.

Lily finally arrived. She'd been stuck in traffic, or something. It didn't surprise me that of all the people to show up late, it was my lawyer. At least she did show up. Vasu wasn't coming at all. My case coordinator was apparently on more pressing, more urgent, more important business in Singapore. Eka rushed in late, sitting down next to me, saying, 'Sorry, sorry.' She'd been stuck on the toilet from nerves. I could sympathise. She went to get miked up for the live TV broadcast of her translations. Then the judges came in, sat down and ordered the start of the most harrowing, most gruelling, most torturous two hours of my life.

At first, I kept calm by saying my silent prayers, but I started losing it when the second assistant judge took over, shouting all the evidence against me into the microphone like a man who yells over the speaker at a horse race. 'Witnesses at the airport have agreed with each other over testimony and found drugs were imported into Indonesia . . . It's clear that importation of a prohibited drug did occur.'

Tears were pouring down my face, blurring my vision, camera flashes firing every time I went to wipe them. I shut my eyes, withdrew into a little prayer and took some breaths, the judge's loud, angry voice blasting across the room and filling my heart with terror. 'It's true that Schapelle Corby has imported marijuana through the customs area at Ngurah Rai Airport, Bali . . . The drug problem is a danger to humanity, therefore it's a very serious offence. Four-point-two kilograms have been imported.'

I felt my world crumbling around me as he shouted out all my witnesses' testimonies that they weren't accepting. They weren't accepting anything: the testimonies of Ally and Katrina were unacceptable because they were my friends; James' because he was my brother. The Brisbane airport worker, the criminologist, the prisoner John Ford – none of their evidence would hold up in court. I shook my head, feeling disgust, thinking, *Yeah, right! This is bullshit. This trial is a sick joke.* I turned to glare at the prosecutors. I felt pure hate. I death-stared them for quite a while just thinking, *You bastards, you lied to me.*

The judge kept shouting away my life. I closed my eyes and mumbled a prayer: '*He says no and gives you something better, He says no and gives you something better.*' My body was shaking furiously.

I was sinking fast as Eka translated: 'None of these testimonies could be used to support the case of the defendant: therefore, the defendant cannot avoid the responsibility for the presence of the marijuana inside the boogie-board bag.'

I couldn't deal with it. I just couldn't deal with it, I was losing it, panicking, my mind screaming: *This is it. I'm over. I'm finished. I'm getting a really big sentence. I'm losing my life. I'm not going home today. They're not accepting anything.* My hands began to cramp up and became extremely painful. I was trying to move my fingers, but I couldn't. I was hot, my heart pounding out of my chest, my eyes and face drenched with tears. *No, no, no, I'm not here, this can't be happening.*

Eka continued: 'The defendant is responsible for the narcotics.'

My teeth were chattering, chin quivering, I was biting on my bottom lip. My leg got the shakes, my heel was tap, tap, tapping on the floor. I was gasping for breath.

Eka stopped me. 'Schapelle, are you OK?'

'Yeah, I'm OK, I'm OK.'

'Slow down, breathe.'

At that point I realised what my body was doing. I turned to look at Eka. She said, 'Calm.' *OK, OK, calm.* I closed my eyes, asked the Lord to fill me with his holy spirit to endure anything that would happen, to give me strength. I calmed down, caught my breath, remembered my family and hoped they hadn't seen me from the back, with my shoulders convulsing as I gasped for air. I didn't want them to know I was crying. I had to be strong. If I could keep it together today in court no matter what, then so could they. *Please be stronger, please keep yourself together. You can do this, Schapelle. Breathe, breathe, breathe.*

The judge was still shouting.

I pulled myself together, turned to Mum, Merc and Dad and gave them a smile, telling them, 'I'm OK, I'm OK.' I knew my family would have seen a little of me losing control, and I didn't want them to be feeling how I was feeling. I didn't want them to start crying for me. I turned back around to the judges, closed my eyes and urgently, desperately kept repeating over and over in my mind: *God answers prayers three ways. One: He says yes and gives you what you want. Two: He says no and gives you something better. Three: He says wait and gives you the best in His own time.* I kept saying it, over and over, until it was time for the verdict.

Suddenly, it was time.

The chief judge told me to stand. My mind was spinning. *This is it, this is the time; this man holds my life in his hands. Please let me go home. I only wanted to have a holiday. I don't know how all this has happened. Please let me go home.* I stood up. Eka didn't stand with me. All of a sudden I felt very alone. I held Eka's hand, tried to pull her up. She didn't get up. I told her to stand up; she didn't. She wasn't allowed to. I felt like fainting, I was so alone. I couldn't feel my legs and thought I was going to fall. I tipped off balance for a second, but caught myself. I had to stand up. *Come on, Schapelle, you can do this. If He says no, then you wait and get something better in His time.*

The judge told Eka to stop translating from this moment on. Eka looked very nervous.

I'd been learning to count to twenty-seven in Indonesian after the prosecutors asked for twenty-seven years a few weeks earlier. I wanted to be able to count just in case I was sentenced to jail time, so I'd know how long the moment the judge said it, without it having to be translated for me. After all, this was my life and I wanted to know everything that was happening to it. I'd also learnt that the Indonesian word for 'years' was *tahun*.

The judge spoke very fast. I didn't understand a word. I felt like the only person there. Everyone else had vanished. It was only me. Then he slowed and I heard, '*Tahun dua pulu tahun.*' I'd been sentenced. I've been sentenced to time. All of a sudden I'd forgotten how to count. *Tahun, tahun . . . does that mean 'months'? Dua pulu . . . two. Oh, I've been sentenced to two months. I'm going home!* I was excited. I gave Eka a big smile. Sitting on her chair with a long face, she shook her head. 'What?' I said.

I heard someone clap at the back of the courtroom. That had to be good. I turned. It wasn't. It was a slightly fat Indonesian man in a black shirt that read 'GRANAT' – the Indonesian anti-narcotics group.

I turned back. '*Dua pulu.* What is it, Eka?' She wasn't allowed to speak. 'Two. Two years? I've got two years? Oh, no.' My heart sank.

'No,' Eka said, shaking her head. 'No.' I was panicking. I couldn't think. I couldn't figure it out, *dua pula, dua, pula, dua, pula.* I got my fingers out, trying desperately to count. What was going on? How could this happen? I didn't do this. I should be going home. 'Ten years? No, not ten years.' Then the noise started.

There was a huge uproar in the courthouse. I heard Mum and Merc yelling out. I turned around to them. 'Mum, it's OK, settle down, it's OK.' I was still unaware of my fate, desperate to figure it out, filled with panicked confusion. Everyone else knew it.

Then Eka said, 'Twenty. Twenty years.'

I froze. A tremor ripped through my soul. I was in shock, motionless, stunned, disbelieving. My heart stopped. Time stopped. The room went hazy. Nothing felt real. I wasn't there. It didn't make sense. I didn't understand. I shook my head, trying to clear the haze. I started breathing hard, blowing in and out. It slowly began to sink in. Then it hit. A cry tore from my soul. '*Nooooooo!*' I hit my forehead. My life was over. I was finished. The room spun fast. The judge and guards were telling me to sit down.

'No!' I screamed. 'I will not sit down.' Eka tried to comfort me. I shoved her hand away. I felt fury. I didn't want comforting. This was so unfair. I didn't do it. I looked at the chief judge with a desperate urge to collapse to my knees and beg him, beg him to let me go home. But I didn't. I just stood helplessly, looking at him, feeling like a terrified child.

The noise of Mum and Merc yelling to the judges brought me back. 'You took the word of a liar! You judges will never sleep.'

No, Mum, you can't, it won't help. It can't make things worse but it won't help. I cried out, 'Try to calm down, Mum. It's OK – stop. Stop it, Mum.'

She was hurting deeply now. I'm her little baby and we thought I'd be going home with them and all the pain and trauma of the past seven heartbreaking, trying months would be over. *Oh, Mum.* My heart broke, seeing the pain in their faces. *Why has this happened? Why?* Mum was still yelling. *Stop, Mum, we can beat this, it's not over, please.* 'I'm OK. Be calm, please, Mum.'

Then I turned and yelled in blind fury at the three bloody prosecutors. I was mainly aiming for the man, Mr Ida Bagus Wiswantanu, and the ugly sour woman to the right of him, as I screamed, '*Permisi, permisi, permisi!*' (Excuse me, excuse me, excuse me!) I didn't think at the time what to say, but that's what happened to come out of my raging mouth. They'd come into jail several times, and this woman had come to me crying, saying she was sorry I was going through all this and that she wanted to help free me. Was it just a twisted game she played on people? Give them a little flutter of hope, only to watch them in desperation in the courtroom, crumbling into a world of nothing thanks to her great work? I could very easily and quite happily have walked over and strangled her with my bare hands. She played me; she lied to me. I hated her. I hated all the prosecutors.

All three needed to do some work training. They had done

nothing on this case, not one bit of investigation. No fingerprints, no baggage-weight checks, nothing. But then again maybe they didn't need training . . . they won, didn't they? They got me twenty years.

At this stage, I suddenly forgot about everything. I just had to get over to my mum; I needed to hug my mum. I brushed off all the guards who were trying to take me away, pushed through them to see Mum, Dad, Merc and Wayan. I leant over the wooden barrier to hold my mumsy. I told her, 'All will be OK. He says no and gives me something better in His own time.' She looked a bit clueless about what I'd just said, as she's not religious, and said sorry for yelling at the judges and told me not to stop fighting, they'd all get me out of there, they'd all get me home. I gave her a hug and then the guards pulled me away.

In what seemed like one second, I was whisked out the door and past a million people. I was surrounded by noise, by more people, by more cameras in my face. My feet again didn't touch the ground as I was lifted, pushed and pulled through a sea of at least a hundred guards in chocolate-brown uniforms, who were opening up the way a little bit for me. At one point, I glimpsed a cameraman trip in the manic scrum, taking a line of them down with him like dominoes. I heard the faint sound of their yelling voices echoing in the distance as they fell.

I quickly found myself sitting in the back of a police van, the door slammed shut and ready to go. A few cameras were held against the windows, the cameramen running beside us as we took off. There were four guards with machine guns in front. The sirens were screaming as we were hurtled back to the place where I really had to start to fight. One of the guards kept staring at me. I was sitting statue-still, completely numb, no tears, no tantrums, nothing. Everyone was silent. No one spoke a word until I looked up at the staring guard and said, 'Twenty years', with zero comprehension of what I'd just said. He nodded with sad eyes. He didn't look at me again.

When we got back to Kerobokan, all the guards swarmed around me, but no one was talking to me like they usually did. They were all just staring as I walked zombie-like back into the prison. Eddie was waiting inside, as he'd heard the sirens. I pushed my way through all the guards to get to him and said, 'Twenty years.' He didn't say anything, just gave me a hug and walked me back to the women's block in silence.

I walked into my cell, put my bag down and said to the girls, 'Hi, how are you?'

They all went quiet. No one wanted to ask the question.

'Do you want to know?'

They nodded. One girl asked, 'Are you going home?'

'No. Twenty years!' I said in a sing-song voice. Their jaws fell open, some burst into tears, all quickly scattered, leaving me alone on my mattress, looking blankly into space. I was a zombie; I was numb. My heart was shut. The only way I could deal with it was by not dealing with it, by turning everything off. I didn't cry again that day. I couldn't comprehend twenty years. I'd only been alive for twenty-seven years. If they'd said five years, I'd have cried, because I could picture that. It was a long time, but I could picture it. Twenty years, though . . . how long was that? There had to be a way out, and we'd find it.

17

Twenty Years in Hell

THERE'S NO MAGIC WAY OF DEALING WITH THE CRUSHING blow of being sentenced to twenty years in a filthy cage for a crime you didn't commit. I was in shock, numb, uncomprehending of the gaping black hole that was, for now, my future. I'd been dealt someone else's dirty destiny, someone who'd probably sat with a beer, watching it all play out as a compelling reality TV show, a reality that should have been theirs. I felt rage burning in my soul.

On that dark Friday afternoon after the verdict, I was called out of my cell to meet with my lawyers. They talked among themselves about my appeal. I didn't listen. I was too tired, still in shock, a zombie, sitting lifeless and limp, slumped in a chair in a faraway world of my own. I needed time alone. I'd asked them not to come if I got jail time. But they'd ignored me.

Lily's sister, Anggia, the lawyer Merc had first called, was there, too, and snapped me out of my daze. She put her hand on my leg, saying, 'Don't worry about it, Schapelle, it's only twenty years, you still have appeals, don't worry about it.' I started trembling. I wanted to scream: 'Fucking shut the fuck up! It's not your fucking life, is it?' I felt my fury flaring. I wanted to leap up, grab her by the throat, strangle her. But I didn't. I just sat there, glaring.

I felt like strangling her sister, too. Lily sat opposite me, crying. I didn't want to speak to her. I didn't want her near me. I didn't even want to look at her any more. I'd started feeling suspicions weeks before that all she was really interested in was keeping the fees rolling in. 'It's OK, Schapelle, we have appeal, we have appeal,' she endlessly repeated.

She'd been totally lame in court and could have done a lot more. I wanted her to stand up, fight, make a case, question witnesses, argue against the bullshit contradictory testimonies of the customs officers. But she didn't. She'd sat almost invisibly, texting or crying, her focus rarely in court. She hadn't even bothered to tell me upfront that I was her first criminal trial, her first drug trial, her test case. I'd put my life in the hands of a novice. Vasu, property developer/engineer, had also never before worked on a criminal case. The only reason they got the case was because Lily's sister was on the consulate list.

Later that afternoon, I got on with life like I usually did: same old roll call, same old lock-up, same old cold dirty-water shower. I was on autopilot, my heart black and tight, my senses seized up. I sat on my mattress reading, before lying down early to sleep. Somehow I slept well, exhausted and in shock.

The next day, Ron, Vasu and Lily came to see me, unsurprisingly still taking no notice of my endless pleas to my lawyers, my family, Ron, Robin, everyone, in the weeks leading up to my verdict: 'Don't come if I get jail time, don't come, don't come, don't come!' I knew I'd desperately need solitude if I got jail time, to think, to wrap my head around it, to cope with my broken heart. I also didn't want to be stared at, photographed, taunted in the visiting area, and I especially didn't want my family to fight through a media scrum at the front door. We'd all been through enough. I would just sit in my cage for a week, maybe go to church. But my pleas didn't stop these three. They were on a mission. They had papers for me to sign.

Vasu, conveniently back from his business in Singapore, took me into a separate room, away from Lily and Ron, held some papers up, handed me a pen and said, 'You sign, Schapelle.' They were legal documents to keep them on as counsel for the appeal. I didn't want them. They'd just got me twenty years. I'd wanted to get rid of silly Lily and bully Vasu for months. The only reason we'd kept them was because Ron and Robin had told us how great they were. Then it got too late to change.

But I signed the stupid documents. The pages were blurry, my head tired, dizzy, confused. It was not by chance they came in on that day. It was a strategic move to get me to sign when my head was in fairyland. I felt exhausted. I was vague, disorientated and totally out of it. I didn't have a chance to talk to Merc. They had to strike fast; they knew we wanted out. They couldn't even wait until the Monday.

Next Ron started telling me a huge sob story about poor Robin. 'He feels he's let you down, Schapelle. He didn't want to come in today because he didn't want to face you.' He told me Robin had been so mortified that he'd spent hours sobbing in the back of the empty courtroom after my verdict. When he finally turned up at their villa, he sat poolside crying into his drink, sad, depressed and drinking himself into oblivion all night long. 'Schapelle, he still hasn't slept, he's still drinking now. He's just drinking and drinking and drinking. He's really down, Schapelle.'

He made me feel sorry for Robin, telling me he'd put his business on hold to run around working on the case, doing interviews, trying to help. Then he revealed his hand.

'Schapelle, Robin thinks you don't want him on the case any more. Please write him a letter telling him how much you want him to stay.'

I flinched. *What? Write?* Every single thing I'd ever given Ron had hit the press. I couldn't trust him. I felt he'd violated my privacy enough, and I wasn't going to write any more letters. 'No, Ron,' I replied. 'I will not write a letter, you can just tell him.'

'Schapelle, you don't understand, he's really, *really* depressed about this.'

Lily sat quietly, watching. Vasu was echoing Ron: 'Schapelle, he needs to know you still want him.'

'No!'

'He's so depressed, Schapelle.'

'No, Ron.'

But Ron didn't let up. He pushed and pushed until he wore me down. 'OK,' I finally relented. 'But promise me it's only for Robin's eyes. Promise me it will not go to the press, Ron.'

He promised. I made them all promise at least five times. I felt so vulnerable, so exposed, nothing was private. Vasu slid a pen and a piece of paper across the table. Ron patted me on the back, smiling and saying, 'You're doing the right thing, Schapelle.'

I should have gone with my instincts. They burned me again. The letter did hit the press, several weeks later. Their egos and reputations were getting a bashing in the press; their motives and abilities were under fire. The letter was their crisis control, their insurance – Schapelle Corby still wants them despite the bad press. I also found out that the day I wrote that letter for my desperately depressed lawyer, he was doing an interview for *60 Minutes*.

> It is now becoming increasingly obvious that Schapelle Corby's legal team was not up to the challenge of securing an acquittal. During her trial, her inexperienced lead lawyer failed to present a credible case and even cried in the courtroom during proceedings.
>
> *Daily Telegraph* (Australia), 30 May 2005

Ron and Robin, my 'dynamic duo', were angry and upset about the backlash they were copping as the truth about their involvement finally leaked out. They reacted to the unravelling truth with their usual fast talking. They fed the press unbelievable and blatant lies, desperately trying to make themselves look and feel better. It was sickening to read.

> Convicted drug smuggler Schapelle Corby has congratulated her legal team despite being sentenced to twenty years in jail. Corby's Australian lawyer, Robin Tampoe, said the 27-year-old was positive about the result considering she could have been sentenced to life. 'She said to us the other day, "Well done, guys, this is a great result. I know what it's like, I know what the system is, I speak to people in jail,"' Mr Tampoe told Macquarie Radio. 'And in fact she sent me a letter asking me to be strong despite the fact she got twenty years.'
>
> *AAP Bulletin*, 30 May 2005

In a prison meeting on Saturday, Corby had to convince the two men (Bakir and Tampoe) to continue standing by her, according to Mr [Vasu] Rasiah. She told them, 'Please stay on and help me. See me through to the end and bring me home.' Mr Rasiah said that a barrage of negative publicity had taken its toll on Mr Bakir and Mr Tampoe. On Friday night, Mr Bakir had said, 'I am very tired, I can't take this shit any more.' The following day, when they visited Corby in jail, the two Australians had offered to stand aside, but Corby had pleaded with them to stay. Mr Bakir had been 'very hurt' by coverage of his background and his motives, Mr Rasiah said.

The Age, 31 May 2005

Ron's motives were clear to us. Hours after my verdict, Merc had been called to an urgent, *urgent* meeting at Vasu's office. She drove forty-five minutes across town. She didn't have a clue what could possibly be so important. They'd kept her in the dark, refusing to tell her over the phone. She found out fast. It was all about Ron.

'When did it start going wrong between us, Mercedes?'

My sister couldn't believe it. She was stressed out and exhausted. She didn't need his shit. 'Ron, it went wrong when you made us sign contracts and then lie about them.'

'Do you still want me, Mercedes?'

The simple answer was no. He'd created more stress for us all. We'd wanted him to be quiet and go away since he'd first made the bribe comment. It had all got out of control. Merc knew how to get rid of him. She told him that all the family wanted to hire an expert to deal with the media.

He went ballistic, furiously yelling at her: 'Why are you listening to your family? What has your family ever done for you, Mercedes? Do *they* give you money?'

Merc wasn't actually planning to hire an expert. She'd ended up handling all the media herself, such as organising family interviews with *60 Minutes* and *Woman's Day* after the verdict. The media kept calling Merc, preferring to deal with her. Ron's angry reaction confirmed what we already knew: he'd been hoping to get rich. But his plan was backfiring.

Ron left Bali on Tuesday after coming in one last time to visit. It was a bad, bad day for me. It was black. I couldn't stop crying, the stress and trauma of the verdict really starting to hit hard as the numbing shock was wearing off. Ron got straight down to business, holding up the contract I'd signed in March.

'Schapelle, do you want me to rip it up?' he asked. 'I'll just rip it up, Schapelle.'

It was a transparent attempt at reverse psychology. I didn't bite. I was so tired, so sick of all the bullshit. I'd just got twenty years! 'It's up to you, Ron. Do whatever you think is best.'

He held the contract in front of my face and started slowly, dramatically, tearing it down the middle like a taunting schoolboy, no doubt hoping I'd stop him. I didn't. Goodbye, Ron!

I needed to be alone, needed to get back to my cage. I was broken, sitting slumped over, with my head in my arms, sobbing, when Lily walked over to us and asked, 'Why are you crying, Schapelle?'

I was incredulous. I glared up at her, thinking, *What the fuck do you think I'm crying about, you silly woman?* But I held back, instead snapping, 'Lily, you have to *ask* why I'm crying?'

She walked off again, my eyes no doubt betraying my angry thoughts.

When Ron was leaving, he got almost to the door, stopped, turned and placed his hand on my shoulder, saying, 'Schapelle, everything that I've spent, you can pay me back. You can pay me back $500,000.'

I shook my head, trying to make it sink in. My mind started spinning with thoughts. *That's a bloody lot of money . . . Where did it go – on your luxury villa, your drunken nights?* It was ridiculous, but I was too tired to ask questions.

'Yeah, OK, Ron. I might be here a while, though,' I mumbled.

He patted me on the shoulder and said, 'When you can, Schapelle.'

So now I had twenty years and a half-million-dollar debt. Great!

As the days in Hotel K passed, my numbness turned to hot anger. I was hurting deeply. It was so unfair. It had taken five months of self-discipline, helplessness, buckets of tears, disbelief, hope and hell to have my life snatched away; five months of being dragged to court each week, being the centre of attention, the topic on everyone's lips, for the judge to take away my everything . . . Twenty years. I hated that judge. How had he suddenly become like God, in total control of my life, my future, my dreams, my freedom? He was able to stop me being a woman, being loved and giving love, and to withhold the most precious gift of having a baby. I wanted to tug him off his throne. He'd dismissed evidence, refused to authorise forensic tests, refused to give me the chance of gathering some real evidence to defend myself. I hoped his halo might slip down and choke him.

I spent endless hours sitting on my little mattress in my cage asking the same questions: how and why did this happen to me? I was getting so tired of trying to make sense of it. How did my life turn in such a way that I'd sat before the same judge who had sentenced the terrorist Amrozi to death? I'd never pretended to be perfect. But I didn't do this, I didn't deserve this. I'd told all I knew in court, I'd told the truth, there was nothing more I could have done or said.

I'm not just a girl; I am Schapelle. I am a human being, with a lot of love inside me and passion for life and living. But now I'm Schapelle the girl locked up for between fifteen and eighteen hours each day, helplessly relying on everyone and challenging my emotions each day, by the hour, a terrified child, without a voice, without a mouth. Help me if you can, help me to understand; I will not disconnect and I will not self-destruct. I am precious and the love for my family is precious.

Diary entry, 5 June 2005

I was surviving from day to day by telling myself it would only be another six months until I won an appeal. I just had to hang on for six more months. But occasionally I let myself think about the alternative: if they didn't give me freedom, what then? What were my options then? Would I stay? And how would I do that? How would my family handle that? It was a possibility. Shit! How would we go about planning for that future? If the appeal didn't turn out well, then it was possible my release would be in 2024. I'd be forty-seven years old – a daunting thought. I should never have done the maths.

But there were always plenty of prisoners in Hotel K who loved to remind me of my fate, constantly yelling, 'Ha ha, Corby, you got twenty years! You *die* in here!' It was like the chorus of a song, and everyone knew the words. Everywhere I went in the prison, people screamed it out. It tore at my heart. It always hurt. It was worst when I walked past the mosque, where at least three or four people would hurl it at me.

In the women's block, it was only Sonia who taunted me. A few nights after my verdict, she started screeching from her cage, 'Corby, you got twenty years! I hope you die in this place!' She kept blurting it out. I was too sad and down to retaliate. I just lay crying in a heap on my mattress.

After about ten minutes, my cellmate, Giant, leapt up and started furiously banging on our cage door, screaming at Sonia: 'Stop it, Black Monster, stop it!' She didn't stop. Giant's temper flared. 'I'll fight you in the morning, Black Monster!'

'OK, Giant!'

They screamed between the cells to arrange the fight and then spent the next two hours shouting abuse at each other.

Giant woke up early, eager to fight. She started to prepare. She was a big girl but as flexible as a Russian gymnast. She threw one leg high up on the wall and did the vertical splits. She threw punches into the air, did crunches and pranced around performing *Rocky*-style exercises. We were all laughing and excited. We plaited her long hair and tied it up to keep it out of the way during the fight.

Then it was time. The cells were unlocked. Giant and Sonia charged like bulls, stopping just short of each other. Giant crouched into the boxing position, her fists clenched and ready, karate-kicking the air with gusto. It was pretty funny but very quickly turned nasty. All of a sudden they were body-hugging each other, falling to the ground, rolling around, tangled up, kicking, punching, scratching and biting. It was a big catfight. It was vicious. The rest of us stood around watching, letting them go for it. No one wanted to get anywhere near them.

Sonia grabbed hold of Giant's plaited hair – it was a killer move. It stopped Giant like kryptonite stops Superman. Giant was stuck on top of Sonia, unable to move without her hair being torn out of her skull.

We were all yelling abuse at Sonia when about eight guards walked over to try to stop the fight. They viciously punched and kicked Sonia to make her let go of Giant's hair. It didn't work. Five minutes later, all these guards still couldn't unlock her monster grip.

Giant was screaming out in pain. I had to do something. This was my fault. Sonia wasn't very big, just very loud and very scary to look at, and she used this to her advantage. I wasn't scared of her. I just went with my instincts. I went up, grabbed her by the hair and started smashing her head hard against the ground. She was glaring into my eyes as I chanted, in a low demonic voice: 'Let her go . . . Let her go . . . Let her go!'

Suddenly she let go. The fight was over. Poor Giant was left sore, with a huge black-and-blue bite mark on her inner thigh. Sonia was all right: she had a hard head. I didn't feel guilty. It was something that had to be done.

But it didn't stop the irrepressible Black Monster. She started screaming abuse at the top of her lungs again a few days later during morning roll call. She was locked in her cage as punishment for her latest sin. We were all in line. She screamed, 'You die in here, Corby! You die, you die!' All the girls turned to look at me. I tensed up.

'You die, Corby!' Sonia kept taunting.

I couldn't believe this girl. Merc brought groceries for her, because she had no one else. This was the thanks she gave. She was sick.

My pulse was racing. I was fuming. I asked the guard, 'Please, please open the cell so I can give her one punch.' I just wanted one shot, to break her nose.

The guard refused – instead doing it herself. She walked into Sonia's cell and hit her hard in the face. It definitely made me feel better. When I calmed down, I was very glad the guard hadn't let me in.

Life got even worse for me when a package possibly containing anthrax was sent to the Indonesian Embassy in Canberra, in retaliation for my verdict. Suddenly, I was being treated with suspicion. I got death stares, all my mail was opened and thoroughly inspected, with the guards often joking, 'Corby anthrax! Corby bomb! Ha ha!' How the hell did I get stuck in the middle of all this?

People are not thinking about their actions. It's not going to help me in any way, but only makes this situation worse for me. Although I have nothing to do with what's happened, it may have devastating effects on my appeal at the High Court. Meanwhile I still have to live in this boxed society. There are so many fanatics. In this small area, over the past week I've had people staring (well, that's usual), but pointing and grinning at me, with knowledge of my sentence. Now, with the anthrax scare, people are 'death-staring' me. I've become completely paranoid, with eyes in the back of my head. My security around the prison has been boosted; I can't do anything without a guard accompanying me. The Oz consulate is on standby in case anything harmful happens to me. Prisoners keep commenting to me about how the Australian public wants to get the money back, their aid to the tsunami appeal. I'm embarrassed. What can I say? We can't take back what we've given and it's not the people of Indonesia's fault, they need our help. It's the government's fault.

Diary entry, 1 June 2005

Being sentenced to twenty years turned me into even more of a freak show. People in church, in visits and around the prison grounds would point, stare, laugh, whisper, try to take sneaky photos. I was the girl locked in for twenty years. I had no escape from it. Church was the worst. Christians would come in from the outside and stare at me. I'd get angry and lose it, often running out in tears. I'd go back to my cell and cry unstoppably. Sometimes the guards got Eddie to come and settle me down. Most of the time, I didn't want to leave my cage. There were eyes and cameras everywhere. It felt even worse than before. Everyone was trying to snap the first shots of me after my verdict. The stalking of me was relentless.

Church today, what a joke. I can't relax there, so many cameras pointing at me, don't think they got a shot: I kept ducking. And the people kept asking other prisoners questions about me. Today guests in the church were a bunch from Jakarta. When they left, the person in charge of the prison church – a prisoner himself – told me that the people today only came to take from me, to get money and to advertise their own church in Jakarta, that he's sorry and next time a bunch like that come, he'll let me know beforehand to warn me.

At the end of today's second service, the priest came to me and said some female reporter had been in contact with him, and that the only reason he comes to services in the jail is because I'm here. I told him, 'You're a priest, and I do not want you to talk to any reporters about me. You are a priest and everything must be confidential – do you understand?' But I think not. I can't believe these people. It does say in the Bible to be wary of false prophets. I'm starting to realise there are many. Very sad.

Diary entry, 5 June 2005

I was still clinging to God but quickly growing even more disillusioned with His followers. I had an Australian priest tell me it was OK for me to kill myself. A husband-and-wife pastor team from Australia came in urging me to take Valium. The Christians who visited the prison often felt they had a God-given right to see me, even though I was turning down around a hundred visits a week, just too tired, stressed and down for polite chit-chat with strangers. I occasionally did come out to meet people, if I was feeling brighter.

One woman was insistent, sending letters through the guards, pleading for me to see her. I was feeling OK, so eventually went to meet her.

She was from a church in New Zealand and had come in to get my mum's home phone number so she could write a book about me. I politely refused. She started rifling through a big white plastic bag. 'Schapelle, I have all these things for you,' she said.

'I'm sorry, I still can't give the phone number to you.'

This woman kept pushing. I kept saying no. She finally handed me the bag and left. I looked inside it once I was back in my cell. It was so insulting. The bag was full of empty shampoo and conditioner bottles, towels covered in stains, half-eaten packets of biscuits and half-empty bottles of drink. Who did she think I was? I flew into a rage, smashing the bag of junk against the concrete ledge again and again and again. Christians!

I just wanted to be left in peace. But it seemed everyone wanted something from me and didn't give a damn how they got it. People would come in and just lie straight to my face about who they were. A woman sidled up to Merc and me one day, posing as a tourist. She looked, sounded and acted like one. I was in a pretty good mood, so had a bit of a chat, opening up more than usual. It was a mistake. This conniving freelance journo went straight to a women's magazine. It was safer to distrust people, always be suspicious. I couldn't afford to relax. I had to rely on my instincts. After months of honing, they were razor-sharp, but it was exhausting to live on high alert.

I picked up on one woman very quickly after a guard stopped me on the way back from collecting my mail. He'd obviously been slung a bit of cash, because he knew I didn't accept visits with strangers but asked me to meet two Australian women. I was feeling a bit blue, but they were right there and I didn't want to be rude. I said hi, instantly recognising the larger woman and asking, 'Do I know you from somewhere? You look familiar.' She quickly answered, 'Well, I'm from the Gold Coast!' She said her brother was a politician and he'd asked her to visit me to find out how he could help. My bullshit radar went off. It was absurd. Why would a politician send his sister? I couldn't get away fast enough. I made an excuse and fled. But it left me with a nagging sense that I knew her. I just couldn't put my finger on it.

I soon found out she was a minor TV and radio personality. She milked our brief chat for her own publicity. She went on a popular TV chat show talking about how she'd met Schapelle Corby. My brother saw the interview. She even had the insensitivity to make a big deal about my pimples. A friend also heard her talking about me on the radio. It was insulting. Why couldn't she have simply been honest with me and said, 'Hi, I'm from *The Panel*, I've just come to see how you are'? Especially as I'd asked her. But she hid the truth. Her brother was a politician, but I'm damn sure he wasn't behind her visit. Did she think I wouldn't find out about her exploits, or did she just not care how I felt?

People clearly believed they had a right to lie to me and bullshit me. It hurt. I felt used. It was like I was no longer a person with a heart and feelings. I was Schapelle Corby: a story, a photograph, a way to make money or gain self-publicity. I was a prisoner, an inferior human being to be taken full advantage of, as I couldn't defend myself in here.

Journalists would even pay the guards to let them come in during a visit, so they could sit and spy on me. My radar was alert to it and when it went off I'd often get so upset that I'd prematurely end a visit and flee back to my cell. The journalists also used their time in Hotel K to quiz other prisoners about me, greasing the palms of anyone who'd talk. It was a total invasion of my privacy. It was worst around the time of my verdict but has never stopped.

Sitting on the edge of an empty fish pond in Kerobokan Jail's main visiting area, she chatted to other inmates . . . Dressed in three-quarter-length Billabong trousers, a crisp white top with her ponytail held in place by a beige peaked cap, she smiled and seemed relaxed, the Marlboro Light cigarettes she smoked the only visible sign of stress. She seemed almost happy the day was nearly upon her, an air of confidence in her walk as she moved around the yard . . . After a visit lasting close to an hour, Corby hugged her father and then her mother, with no sign of the emotion that has been part of her recent court appearances.

The Age, 27 May 2005

It was the endless hounding by people taking sneaky shots of me that affected me the worst. I was on alert, sharply flinching whenever I saw any type of flash. If people openly and politely asked to take a photo with me, I usually agreed – until I was badly burned after being snapped smiling with a guy on drugs charges, who'd asked me politely. It had all caused me to develop an acute phobia of photographers and cameras. As with all phobias, it gave me an irrational terror of them.

A couple of weeks after my retrial was shut down, I was feeling depressed and went to church to try to lift my spirits. It was futile, I just had to put up with more staring. So I walked out but didn't make it back to the block before hell hit.

'Corby, Corby, Corby!!'

I turned and saw a pack of at least thirty photographers and reporters charging towards me. I froze. I felt chilling terror like I'd just seen dark fins circling me in the water. I couldn't breathe. My entire body tensed up tight. Then my flight instincts kicked in. I ran for my life, sprinting along the jail pathway. They were chasing me, snapping at my heels. I flew into a little office, slamming the door shut, locking it quickly and flinging myself under an old wooden desk.

It was like a horror movie. I was curled up and cowering in fright as they started thumping on the door. From under the desk, I could just see the bottom of it vibrating each time they hurled themselves at it. I closed my eyes and started praying: *Please, God, make them go away*. But they weren't giving up. I was terrified. I was shaking like a leaf. They might well have been psychos with axes instead of journos with cameras. I glimpsed their faces pressing into the glass, peering in through the windows, and their hands holding cameras at all angles, desperately trying to fluke a shot of me.

I started to get cramp in my legs. An hour had passed and they were still trying. I felt hopeful I might escape unscathed when I heard a female guard's voice that I recognised. She'd always told me she'd help me. The time to do it was now. But she didn't. Her familiar voice faded and then vanished. Another half an hour passed and they were all still there, staking me out, trying to smoke me out.

My mind was spinning. I had to escape. I knew they'd eventually get a key or smash it open, and I certainly didn't want them to get shots of me hiding under a desk. There was a second door behind me, which no one was banging on. I calculated I could leap up, fling it open and sprint through the courtyard to the boss's office before they'd catch me.

It was at least a plan, so I gulped a few breaths and went for it. But it failed dismally. As I flew across the courtyard, a male prisoner saw me coming and slammed the metal gate shut. He was on duty to make sure no prisoner went past that point. I leapt onto the gate, clinging to the bars and screaming to the prison boss, 'Help me, Pak Bromo, help me!' But it was too late. I was trapped. The photographers came crushing in around me, clicking their cameras like crazy. The guards were suddenly there, too. I went ballistic. 'Fuck off, don't touch me! Fucking don't touch me!' I was hysterically thrashing my arms about, lashing out at their cameras, shoving them out of my face. It was all so unreal. I felt dizzy, but I couldn't stop. I was yelling, unleashing all my pent-up fear and anger. My whole body was shaking.

The guards were trying to pull me off the gate. I knew the cameras were catching it all, but in those moments, I didn't care. I just wanted all these bastards to leave me alone. I had been slammed away for twenty years – why couldn't everyone just leave me alone? I was hyperventilating, sobbing, still fighting and screaming as the guards finally peeled me off the gate and dragged me through the scrum into a room. It wasn't over. The windows were instantly swarming with lenses, as the insatiable media kept trying to get more. It was their lucky day. I was howling loudly, crouching behind a partition in another attempt to hide. I was upset, angry and pissed off. I was in their care, but the guards did nothing to protect me from this. Suddenly two men were standing just two feet away and staring at me. Choking on my sobs, I screamed out, 'What are you looking at? Who are you?'

It was a sick, twisted irony, but the two men were from the Indonesian Human Rights department and had brought the pack of photographers with them. When I got back to my cell, I collapsed onto my mattress in exhaustion. My body was bruised and sore. These people had treated me like a feral animal for so long that they'd turned me into one. The girls in my cell told me that while I'd been at church, the media pack had come in and rifled through all my belongings, taking photographs and asking questions about 'living with Corby'. I hated my life.

It didn't take much to trigger my dark fury these days. I had anger in my heart. I exploded sometimes. I hurt so much because there was nothing more I could do to make people believe me, and I was stuck in here for twenty years. I would often cry with frustration at not being able to get out, not being able to make people believe I was innocent.

Everything irritated me far more than before. I had lost all tolerance. I was angry, aggressive, constantly screaming at people or bursting into tears and collapsing in a broken heap. I'd never sweated the small stuff before, but now I did. Like each afternoon the girls would sing out 'Thanks, Mrs!' when the guards locked us into our stinking monkey cages; they'd done it since day one. But now it enraged me. 'Don't say thank you! Don't *thank* her!' I'd yell at them.

Sometimes I'd completely explode simply because a person looked at me. I'd turn around, screaming, 'Stooop bloody staring at me!' I didn't understand myself and later felt so ashamed and sorry for the poor person who had been looking at me.

Sometimes it was simply running out of drinking water. They

didn't keep any spare containers in the women's block, so Eddie always told us to step outside the block, hold up the empty container and he'd bring a new one across. One time we ran out and I went to give Eddie the signal, but I wasn't allowed to take a single step outside the door. The guard grabbed my arm, yanking me away from it. I screamed into her face, 'We have no bloody water to drink!!' I went crazy. It was a little thing. In that moment, it represented all the basic liberties I'd lost.

It was the minor things like that that really tortured me. All my dark anger at the world would ignite from something so small. The little things brought on the big emotions, and then I'd start to punch the walls and chuck things at them. But I couldn't even do that freely. Everyone would come running, staring at me, and soon I'd have sixty girls in a circle around me. I'd scream, 'Piss off, don't look at me!' And then even more girls would come to see what I was yelling about. There was just no escape. It was all the little things coming together that made me angry at the whole situation. And there was nothing I could do. I felt so angry and frustrated.

When we did our once-weekly exercise programme, I'd often lose it. I'd be fine, doing all the exercises one minute, then the next I'd burst into tears, feeling every cell of my body overcome with black depression. I'd run back to my cell, crying hysterically, the repetitiveness of the exercise disturbing me, representing what my life would be: the same exercises, the same droning music, over and over and over for an hour every week, for months, years, two decades.

I started focusing on this world more than I'd done before, now that I was potentially stuck here for twenty years. I saw it all on a more critical and depressing level. I'd look around with my eyes wide open, see the green bars and collapse into tears, thinking, *How long do I have to stay here?* The dirt and grime that had always covered the walls of my cell suddenly seemed luminous. At times, I'd stand looking at it, frozen in disgust. It seemed the dirt was trying to tell me something, playing games with my mind, reminding me that I was stuck, letting me know its layers had been built up by years of prisoners' hands touching the wall. There were times when I'd become physically sick just by looking at those walls. How long would these walls be around me and how long would I be part of these walls?

I had to get out of this place. But I needed a good legal team. It was stronger than it had been: two Australian QCs had offered to work pro bono for my appeal and had tried to help earlier on by calling Robin's office and leaving messages. It didn't surprise me that they were ignored, but now that I knew about it, I was insistent that they be on the team, despite Vasu being hysterically against it.

The two QCs told us that we needed a Jakarta-based lawyer to help with the appeal and handed Lily and Vasu a list. Vasu wasn't happy, but we left him no option. They chose Hotman Paris Hutapea: flamboyant, over the top, but apparently the best. I couldn't believe all the diamonds on his fingers the day I met him. He was really friendly and dynamic, and Merc and I felt relieved to have him on board. He was also working pro bono.

But we still wanted to get rid of Lily and Vasu. They were completely clueless. We didn't like them or trust them. A week or so after my verdict, Merc had been called to an early-morning meeting. It was with an image consultant from Jakarta, who would be able to groom us all to create a better public image. She'd get Mum and Dad to change their style of clothes, teach us how to speak on camera, how to sit, stand, walk and carry ourselves. It would only cost $5,000. It was absurd.

Merc and I spent a lot of time and stress talking about how we could get rid of Lily and Vasu. We had to be tactical. We'd paid them an extra $50,000 for operations back in March, but they had promised to give most of it back when they claimed it from the government. We didn't want to lose it. We'd already paid them a fortune.

Then the perfect chance to sack them arose when one of the QCs (rather stupidly) stated publicly that Vasu had asked the Australian Government for $500,000 for bribe money. Merc and

I decided: 'This is it, they're gone.' No doubt this was exactly what the comment had been designed to do. But as all the team were working together, we felt we had to sack the lot. It was the start of a very fraught weekend and of a vicious unravelling of our relationship with Lily, Vasu, Ron and Robin.

We had someone lined up to take over. He wasn't a lawyer but apparently had connections, worked closely with the government and promised us he'd have me out in three months. He'd first approached Merc a few days beforehand and knew every detail of my case. We asked him what his fees were. 'Don't worry, pay me back when you're free.' He refused to give us even a ballpark figure, which worried me a lot. But he seemed to have all these strategies worked out, and we were desperate. We didn't know where to turn. We just thought, *Why not?* We had to get rid of what we had. So I signed up with Walter Tonetto on a Friday afternoon. Merc and I felt relieved . . . but not for long.

That afternoon, I called all the old team to let them know of my decision. Their responses were exactly as I'd expected, reflecting who they were. I called Erwin first. He was charming and courteous. 'That's OK, Schapelle, I understand. I'll always support you whether I'm your lawyer or not. Good luck for the future.'

Next I called Hotman. He was very generous. 'OK, OK, I support you, good luck for your future. Sorry I couldn't do more to help.' He didn't sound it, but he was angry and disappointed, yanking his girlfriend out of the Mercedes-Benz showroom when we hung up. He told me later that he'd been out buying her the latest model as a celebration present for getting my case when I called him.

Then I made the last, dreaded call to Lily. She was driving in the car with Vasu. I was polite but direct. 'Thanks for all your help, Lily, but I don't need you as my lawyer any more. I'm sorry, but I've found new lawyers.'

'Sorry, Schapelle, I can't hear you . . . wait . . .' I knew she was putting it on speakerphone so that Vasu could abuse me.

'Schapelle, you can't do this, you can't do this!' he yelled. 'No one can help you but us. We have information, Schapelle. We will let that information come out, and you'll stay there, you won't ever get out.'

'Are you threatening me, Vasu?' I asked.

'No, no . . . just speak to Mercedes. She knows. Speak to Mercedes.'

I knew right then my instincts were right. I thought, *Yep, you're an arsehole, a total bastard.* He hung up abruptly. I knew they were empty threats, they had to be – I didn't do it. I rang Merc and her reaction was the same. 'Don't worry. He's just a complete bloody idiot!' Unsurprisingly, Vasu told the press a different story.

> 'We said if that's what you decided, good luck with it. We wish you all the best,' Mr Rasiah said.
>
> *The Australian*, 25 June 2005

But our relief at being able to make a fresh start turned to panic. Over the weekend, all our instincts were screaming *Danger*. Merc, Wayan and I were having exactly the same reactions. We all had bad vibes and bad dreams. Our decision to hire Walter had been rash, in the heat of the moment, thinking anyone was better than Lily and Vasu. By Sunday, Merc came in to see me, sobbing. It was another wrong decision. We didn't know a thing about this man. The payment worried me, too. I might be in debt for ever; I'd never be free.

Merc calmed down a little and we changed strategies. We'd rehire Erwin and Hotman – if they'd take me back. Merc rang them that afternoon, explaining we were scared and asking if they'd please take the case back. They were delighted. Hotman instantly organised a press conference in Jakarta with Merc. We knew these two people; we had no suspicions about them, no anxiety. Merc and I felt we finally had the right team. We knew they'd try as hard as they could.

Merc then rang Walter and gave him the news, which he didn't want to accept. For months afterwards, he harassed my sister, phoning and texting, wanting the case back. Our instincts had been spot on.

We knew that firing Lily and Vasu would also get rid of Ron and Robin. The four of them were so close and got along so well from the very first day they met that I was suspicious they'd known each other well before my case. They denied it. But from day one, Ron and Robin had given Lily and Vasu rave reviews. Ron even did a bit of PR spinning before he'd supposedly met them. The day he flew to Bali to meet them and me for the first time he was quoted saying, 'We have been talking at length with Schapelle Corby's Indonesian lawyers, and they are certainly on the ball.' Ron and Robin seemed like the only people who thought Lily and Vasu were any good. We were ready to fire them.

Looking back, it all seemed to be a game to them. I was terrified and desperate, and as soon as they sprang from nowhere, I clung to them, put my faith and hopes in them. But I believe I was just a pawn. Apart from the media, music and movies that Ron talked about so obsessively, all four regularly talked about suing Qantas for millions of dollars. Merc was always hosing them down with a firm 'No! Not yet, we have to get her home first!' But that was their plan: that was how the big bucks would roll in.

Things had already started to unravel two days before the sackings, as earlier that week in an interview with *Bulletin* magazine Mum had called Ron my 'black knight' and told the truth about him asking me for half a million dollars. All of Team Corby jumped in to defend him – frantically, desperately doing interviews, telling blatant lies to undo the truth.

> Mr Bakir denied yesterday that he had asked Corby to repay him up to $500,000 for his part in the failed campaign to secure her freedom. 'It is an outright lie that never happened,' he said. 'I'm not the only one saying it never happened, Schapelle Corby is saying it never happened.'
>
> *Herald Sun*, 25 June 2005

Mr Rasiah said Corby's mother, Rosleigh Rose, was wrong to claim that Queensland businessman Ron Bakir had told Corby she owed him the $500,000 he had spent on the case.

Sydney Morning Herald, 23 June 2005

'Her lawyer Lily Lubis went into the prison and asked Schapelle if I had ever asked her to repay money and Schapelle said that I hadn't done that.'

Gold Coast Bulletin, 24 June 2005

Reporter: Is there any truth in the suggestion that you've asked Schapelle Corby for money?

Ron Bakir: Absolutely not. And not only do I deny it, Schapelle has simply stated to her Indonesian lawyer that I have not asked her for five hundred thousand dollars.

Sunday, 26 June 2005

Bakir laughs at the $500,000 figure and denies he told Schapelle he would like her to pay him back. 'No, that wasn't said. There was a discussion that took place between myself and the family. I said if I can recoup any money, then thanks. If I can't so be it . . . I never mentioned a figure. I'm planning to disclose publicly the figure soon.'

Bulletin, 28 June 2005

It was all total lies, but I was stuck behind the grimy walls of Hotel K. Despite the media continually stating that Ron was 'bankrolling' my defence and calling him my 'financial backer', he was not, he did not pay for my defence. The Australian Government paid all my Indonesian lawyers' fees, and my family had also given the legal team money for operational costs. The government paid for four witnesses to fly to Bali, and my mum paid for the other three – James, Ally and Katrina. Ron and Robin certainly knew the government would be paying, as Robin's law firm filled out the forms. Ron kept threatening to give a breakdown of the money he'd spent but never did. He did not bankroll my defence; he was not my financial backer.

They got malicious and vindictive, telling more lies. It was unbelievable. Two days after I'd fired them all, Robin went on Channel 9's *Sunday* programme and lied with almost everything he said. *Sunday* did not check the facts. One of his lies was claiming that members of my family were doing interviews to line their pockets and kept things from me. In fact, Merc told me about all interviews they did, always running it by me first. I was relieved whenever my family made any money from the media. Merc had already spent all her savings on me, Dad, all his superannuation. But his lies hit. People started sending me letters saying, 'I sent you this amount, did you ever get it?' The only thing Merc ever kept from me was hurtful rumours that I couldn't do anything about. She protected me from some media coverage and tried to deal with it herself, though I'd see the pain etched on her face and know something was very wrong. But sometimes I preferred not to know. I had enough to deal with in here. Merc was very hurt by all the lies. She's a totally selfless person, always helping people. Being selfish or self-serving is one of life's greatest sins to Merc, and to be accused of such behaviour hurt her deeply. I guess that was what they wanted.

> *Reporter:* When Indonesian prosecutors recommended a twenty-year sentence to Corby nearly two months ago, it was undoubtedly a terrible shock for Schapelle. A time when she needed support from her family. But Robin Tampoe also makes this serious accusation against Schapelle's sister Mercedes about a conversation he had with her that day.
>
> *Robin Tampoe:* This is one of the things which I think upset me greatly, was the day the prosecution recommended a twenty-year sentence and I had a conversation with Mercedes before I went into court and she said to me, 'If the prosecutor asks for a hard sentence, I won't be able to deal with this, I'm going to run out of here. Will you see Schapelle in the holding cell?'
>
> I said, 'Of course I will.'

The prosecutor asked for life. I went to the holding cell among all the chaos to see Schapelle. I was holding her hand while she was crying. I find out down the track that she [Mercedes] ran out of there to do a live interview for thirty thousand dollars with *New Idea*. So that is the situation I find myself in. I'm holding her sister's hand while she's making thirty thousand dollars with *New Idea* and that, from my point of view, sickens me.

What I would love is for Schapelle to have her say. It seems to me when I see her that so much of what is going on outside that jail cell is not disclosed to her.

Sunday, 26 June 2005

The truth was I'd explicitly and repeatedly told Robin, 'Do not come to the holding cell.' Merc certainly did not ask him to look after me there, she knew I hated being their show pony – especially so if I got bad news in court. Merc did do an interview for *New Idea* a bit later, but Robin knew about it days beforehand. Merc was sobbing when we hugged in court that day, anything but the cold heartless response that man claimed.

Two days after his vindictive, vicious lies on the *Sunday* programme, Robin released his 'insurance letter', the one I was pressured to write the day after my verdict. It was clearly calculated to look like I'd just written it and was siding with him and not my devoted sister and mum. How could anyone be so evil?

Convicted drug smuggler Schapelle Corby has pleaded for a Gold Coast lawyer to rejoin her fight for freedom. Corby, 27, has written a letter to Australian lawyer Robin Tampoe from her prison cell in Bali, begging him to continue working on her defence. The latest twist in the Corby saga followed days of conflict between Corby's mother, Rosleigh Rose, and Mr Tampoe and mobile phone entrepreneur Ron Bakir.

In the letter obtained by the Philip Clark *Drive* program on 2GB, Corby said she 'needs' Mr Tampoe but will 'understand' if he does not accept her offer.

AAP Bulletin, 28 June 2005

I felt an awful sense of total betrayal, mixed with loathing. When I'd trusted someone and then lost that trust in them, I found myself wanting so much to believe and to once again trust. I've now learnt that once lost – it's lost, finished, gone, no more, the end.

Life in jail didn't get any easier. I spent hours sitting on my bed looking out my cell window, just people-watching, assessing every individual female prisoner, getting information that would help me choose my friends carefully. I was slowly becoming introverted and more often in my own faraway world, lost in my thoughts, lost in nothingness with nothing to do, nowhere to go and no one to really talk to.

The deep pain of my situation infiltrated every single moment. During the night, I'd wake up crying, every hour on the hour. I'd realise, *Yeah, I'm still here*, and lie down, crying myself to sleep again. A little wooden box of my belongings was right at my head, and because we were all so squashed up with little room to sleep, I'd wake up with a start, then lie back down and hit my head almost every time. But I couldn't move it because there was nowhere else to put it.

I had to hold everything inside, which might be why when I woke each morning the horror of my situation hit me again. I had to say to myself, *OK, you can be strong today*. I had to change the way I was thinking, because I didn't know how long I'd be in this hellhole. I'd start the day by clearing out all the bad energy and thoughts, fighting to get rid of the negativity. *This is today; you never know what tomorrow is going to hold.* I was living from moment to moment, the only way I could survive.

18

The Bali Nine Check In

I HATED THE BALI NINE. I FELT SURE THEIR CRIME OF trafficking heroin a month before my verdict had contributed to me getting twenty years. I believed the judge hit me hard because their brazen drug-smuggling racket had mocked Indonesian drug laws. Three of nine Australians – most of them teenagers or in their early twenties – were caught with heroin strapped to their thighs at Denpasar airport. One guy was already seated on the plane, while another four were nabbed in a local hotel room surrounded by heroin and drug paraphernalia.

Renae Lawrence was the only female in the group. I was terrified of her before she arrived. I didn't want to share a cell with her. I had panicked thoughts that she'd cause problems for me, pick on me, start fights and ram my head into the cement walls. I even taught Dewi, one of the girls in my cell, a line to say if Renae attacked me: 'Who are you? You're a prisoner, you're a criminal . . . you're lower than a snake's belly. How dare you come in here and do this!'

My fears were fuelled by news stories, scary photographs and frenzied gossip. All the girls who'd shared a cell with her at Polda had been telling crazy stories about this *freak* for weeks. She refused to let anyone else sleep if she was awake. She'd kick them in the head, sexually hit on them, punch them. So, by the time she checked in at Kerobokan, I imagined Renae as an aggressive, psychopathic lesbian. I was scared to death of her.

A frantic whisper swept around the women's block as soon as she walked through the door. Her myth made her larger than life.

'Oh, Renae's here! It's Renae!'

Everyone was staring, pointing and whispering at the notorious psychopath. All eyes were on her, including mine. As I sat watching her through the bars on my cell window, my fears instantly vanished. This girl couldn't have contrasted more with the images in my head. She looked like a frightened mouse as she took that first terrifyingly lonely walk up the gravel path towards the guards' table. When she reached it, she stood timidly giving her details, saying nothing to the thirty or forty girls ferreting wildly through her bags in their usual scavenging fashion.

As she was walked to her new cell, her face was full of terror, like she was about to be put in a cage and fed to the lions. She almost was. She was to share with the Black Monster, until Sonia viciously objected, screaming, kicking and slamming the cage door shut. The guards didn't argue; they just walked Renae to another cell, her big blue eyes spilling tears as she trailed behind them like a lost lamb, clinging to her pilfered bags. I felt sorry for her as I sat listening to her cries, knowing exactly what she was going through. But I didn't go to her. I kept my distance for a few hours to let her breathe and take in the dump that was her home for now . . . and maybe for ever.

I finally went to meet Renae just before lock-up. She was a mess. She was sitting on the cell floor, sobbing and broken, with her head hopelessly hanging.

'Come on, this isn't going to help you,' I told her.

She slowly looked up at me, her eyes red and swollen. 'How do you do it? How do you do it, Schapelle?'

'You just have to, Renae. You *have* to.' It was impossible not to see the fresh scars on her sliced-up wrists. 'And you can't do *that* – you can't. Just forget about doing that again.'

But she had so much anger inside. She was living hour by hour and didn't know how to control her emotions. She'd already tried to kill herself at Polda and then lost it a couple of days after checking in, slamming her fist into the cell wall over and over until the bones in her hand were broken. The guards unlocked my cell so I could go and try to calm her down, settle her a bit. But I couldn't. I had no chance of holding her back, as she kept smashing her swollen fist into the concrete wall and screaming like a tortured animal. A few male prisoners ran in and began grabbing her arms. She went crazy until we finally got her to the ground. I pushed a little blue sleeping tablet into her mouth, and within a minute she calmed down.

One night about two weeks later, she again started smashing her already broken hand into the wall. The guards came in and unlocked my cell to help and when I got to her cell, she was shaking, crying hysterically and gasping for air. I tried to soothe her, giving her a hug and holding her good hand while we waited for the doctor to arrive. She had to let out her anger and said it was either the wall or one of the girls. Luckily, she chose the wall.

I soon told Dewi she had to forget the snake's-belly line I'd taught her. Renae and I were unlikely friends: we were worlds apart as people, and outside in the real world I doubt we'd have even met, let alone become friends. She spent her spare time blowing up cars, I spent mine having facials. But inside Hotel K, we bonded as easily as kids in kindergarten. We both needed someone to talk to and support us through our black days. The broad brushstrokes of being Australian, speaking English and being stuck in here were enough to draw us together, and we became friends . . . for a while.

But I tried to avoid talking about her crime. I didn't want to know, I didn't want to think about what she'd undeniably been involved in. I also blamed Renae and the other eight for hurting my case.

When they were arrested, there were headlines everywhere screaming: 'Corby death penalty!' Bali was making an example of me. They were showing the world that this little holiday isle really was tough on drug traffickers. The prosecutors regularly told my lawyers I would be a lesson to the world. But the lesson wasn't working, the headlines weren't hitting home, no one was listening if nine Australians were trafficking drugs a month before my verdict. They were arrested in April; I was sentenced in May. The judges felt they really had to make a point. They hit hard. My sentence was one of the highest-ever for trafficking marijuana.

Merc looked into it and easily found plenty of cases to highlight the wildly disparate sentences for drug cases.

Two Indonesian brothers were caught importing 8.5 kilograms of marijuana through Jakarta airport. Like me they were charged under Article 82, which carries the maximum punishment of death. But unlike me they didn't get anything close to twenty years – one brother got five years, the other six.

Another man, who was on exactly the same charges as me but had been caught with 160 kilograms of marijuana – forty times more than the amount found in my boogie-board bag – was sentenced to five years less than me.

Even people caught with harder drugs received lighter sentences than mine. A man who flew into Bali with 5.2 kilograms of cocaine hidden in the lining of his surfboard bag was sentenced to life but got fifteen years on appeal. A known drug dealer caught smuggling forty kilos of crystal meth from Hong Kong to Indonesia in gravestones got seven and a half years.

A man caught with 4,700 Ecstasy pills strapped to his legs as he flew into Indonesia from Taiwan was sentenced to four years and six months. Another man caught boarding a flight to Australia with 5,852 Ecstasy pills strapped to his thighs and stomach was sentenced to ten years in jail. A brother and sister who were caught with 2.62 kilograms of pure heroin in their shoes when they were spotted walking strangely as they came off a flight from Taiwan were each sentenced to twelve years.

It was impossible to understand and comprehend how the Indonesian justice system worked, how they decided on what sentences to hand down. They seemed to just pluck a number from thin air, rather than relying on legal precedents like courts in most countries did. There was no uniformity, no fairness.

What was even more incredible were the ridiculously low sentences given out for murder. There were several people in Kerobokan Prison doing just five or six years for gruesome slayings. Or, in the most extreme and obscene case, Bali bomber Abu Bakar Bashir, guilty of conspiring to bomb the Kuta nightclubs in October 2002, which killed 202 people, was sentenced to just thirty months. This terrorist, who'd given his 'blessings' for the bombings, was freed four and a half months early for good behaviour! He was out in two years, showing absolutely no remorse for all those killed and injured in the bombings.

The man who'd supplied the equipment for the bombs in the second Bali attack, in 2005, which killed twenty people and injured a hundred, was so happy with his eighteen-year sentence the day before his twenty-ninth birthday that he called it 'the sweetest birthday gift'. He warmly shook hands with the judges and gave the thumbs up, smiling, when his sentence was delivered. This terrorist obviously knew he'd got away lightly.

It was also ironic that the murderers were often given jail privileges, allowed out at weekends and sent on errands to get the guards cigarettes from the local shop. My visitors have often been shocked to learn that the friendly man at the front door who obligingly called them a cab on his mobile phone or hailed one for them was a murderer who'd punched a man to death. He got five years and would soon be released. He was fit and well toned, as he regularly worked out at a local gym.

I stepped back into the courtroom almost exactly six weeks after I'd left it on my blackest day. It was hard to sit in front of those same judges again, but I felt like I might finally get justice in this unfair system. My whole family was over the moon when Hotman miraculously got my case reopened. We thought it was a sign that the judges could see that I didn't get a fair trial. But it turned out to be yet another sharp plunge on the roller-coaster.

After the usual five-minute photo session in the hot seat, I walked over to sit next to Hotman. He was colourful, dramatic, feisty and constantly leapt up to fight for me. *Yes, this is more like it!* I finally had a professional lawyer.

My translator was also a pro. He was late on the first day of my original trial, so Eka, who spoke conversational English, had been sworn in. 'Where were you? Do you know what happened to me?' I asked him. 'Yes.' He apologised for being late, telling me that Lily had given him the wrong court start time. I wondered if it had been intentional – why else had Eka unusually been in court that first day? She was an employee of Lily and Vasu's. They billed big bucks for her translation work. When this guy started translating, I realised how much I must have missed with Eka. It wasn't her fault; she was untrained and it was a hard job. She should never have been put in that position by her masters.

We had two days in court, and it went nowhere. All Hotman was able to introduce were a legal expert and two Qantas employees from Brisbane airport – one who had checked me in and one who'd taken the boogie board at the oversized-luggage counter. They told the court they'd noticed nothing unusual, no smell of marijuana. I wanted to scream out: 'That's because it wasn't there!'

At the end of the second day, the judges shut down the retrial and crushed my hopes. I sobbed in court. How much longer did I have to live this nightmare?

They now had two months to consider my appeal. I couldn't stop crying as I was led out and driven back to Hotel K, where fate seemed to want to keep me caged. It was the last time I set foot outside Kerobokan for more than a year.

I was having a lot of black days and Renae would often come and sit with me in my cell. She had her share of dark days, too, although she'd started taking the tranquiliser Xanax, which often zonked her right out, almost turning her into a walking zombie. Her eyes would be half closed and I'd have to keep hitting her, saying, 'Come on, Renae. Think of what you look like. Cut it out!'

I tried to tell her to maybe just take half a tablet. But she wasn't coping, she needed to blur reality and numb the fear and pain. It wasn't easy living under the dark shadow of the death penalty. Renae felt sure she would get death, or life at best. I'd help wean her off the tablets after the verdict. Right now, she was living on a dangerous edge.

One night around 7 p.m. I heard yelling and screaming coming from her cell. It sounded like someone was being possessed. I was laughing to myself as I pictured Renae's reaction: she'd be sitting there, going 'Oh . . . what's going on?' with that wide-eyed, spaced-out look on her face. It was my twisted sense of humour, one that Renae shared, too.

But suddenly I heard angry shouting. 'Stop it . . . stop it!' Then, bang, bang – 'Stop it, *stop it!*' It was Renae's voice. Whatever was going on, she definitely wasn't finding it funny.

After about an hour of yelling and screaming, the guards turned up and opened her cell. She walked over to my cage window.

'Renae, what's going on?' I could see something in her eyes, so I leant in closer. She was giving me a scary, glassy-eyed stare. 'Renae, stop it. What are you thinking? Can you just stop it, Renae? Come on . . .'

She put her hand up to my cell window. I flinched.

'OK, Renae, don't move.' She held a razor blade between her thumb and first finger. 'I'm just moving my hand slowly, and I'm going to take this out of your hand.' She was edgy. I didn't want to spook her. 'Just let it go – don't squeeze it, just let it go. Give it to me, Renae, give it to me.' I touched her hand. 'Now, undo your fingers!' My eyes were locked on hers, willing her to give up the blade.

It had all been a cry for help. Her eyes were full of pain, pleading: *This place sucks, but I don't want to do this. Can you help me? Take it away from me! Help me!* She finally dropped it into my hand. The suicidal moment passed . . . for now.

I wrapped the blade in a tissue and put it away. We decided after that night that I'd look after all her razors and she'd come and take one when she needed to shave her legs. Emotions were volatile and changed dangerously fast in Hotel K. It was better to be safe than sorry.

Three weeks after meeting Renae Lawrence, I heard the unbelievable news that another Australian had been arrested with drugs, this time outside a dance party. Bali was cracking down. Our cells were full of girls who'd been picked up at a club with one or two Ecstasy pills. The police would randomly choose a club or restaurant, shut it down and search everyone at the door as they left. Unusually, it seemed they were handing out pretty standard sentences for Ecstasy: most people got four years and six months, whether they were caught at an airport with 4,700 pills wrapped in plastic and strapped to their legs or found at a club with one or two.

One of the girls in my cell was doing four years and six months for being spotted throwing an Ecstasy tablet in the bin during a police raid on a nightclub. She had a negative urine test. Another prisoner was serving the same amount of time just for a positive urine test.

A Brazilian girl who was on holiday in Bali with three friends was caught in the crackdown. She was out enjoying dinner with her girlfriends when the police randomly raided the restaurant and found a speck of hashish wrapped in a little tissue in her handbag. She received a four-month imposed extension on her paradise holiday, stuck in the confines of a shabby hotel. This girl was in Polda on the night that model Michelle Leslie was arrested with two pink Ecstasy tablets in her handbag.

My first reaction at hearing the news of yet another Aussie caught with drugs was pure shock. I immediately thought this girl must have done it for publicity. How could anyone from Australia have anything to do with drugs in Bali after the Bali Nine and I had been front-page news for months? It was unfathomable.

But Michelle became the eleventh Australian in Hotel K, arriving one afternoon after we'd all been locked up. Michelle was placed in Salma's 'elite' cell. In the morning, I went down to say hello, but from then on we had little to do with each other. She occasionally came to my cell and poked around, asking a bunch of questions like what I was reading, how many pairs of jeans I had and what I ate. She kept pushing me to do a story and a 'photo shoot' with her for one of the women's magazines. She'd already been given a little camera. She regularly told me that she had 'the ultimate story': 'The media is all over this, they're so onto me. I've got the ultimate story, babe! I've got fame, modelling, drugs and religion. It's the *ultimate* story! It can't get better than this, darl.'

I wanted my story to be over. But it was far from it. Poor Merc had broken the bad news to me the same day Michelle Leslie arrived at Kerobokan: on appeal, my sentence had been cut by only five years. I was shattered. It was nothing. I sobbed uncontrollably. My chances of undoing this injustice were evaporating fast. Maybe I really was going to be stuck for ever with someone else's miserable fate. Merc tried to calm me. 'We've still got another appeal, Schapelle.'

I had one last shot, in the Supreme Court in Jakarta. It had to work. It was Hotman's turf – he was the best, he'd weave his magic, and I'd get out then. This insane situation would unravel. I didn't hold out any hope for new evidence, just a new perspective: the judges had to see that the investigation had been non-existent, that I'd never had the chance to find a shred of evidence to defend myself, and that I didn't get a fair trial. In my heart and soul, I still believed that this would end soon. I was innocent, and I believed something would snap me out of the nightmare as fast as it had snapped me in.

The Bali Nine were just starting their trials. I'd see them lining up with handcuffs on, waiting for the sardine bus, when I sat out at visits. I knew the hell they were all going through. Watching Renae go to court was hard. In the early stages of her trial, I could never sleep on nights before she was due in court, and during the days I felt a sense of anger, just knowing what she'd be going through with the media. I'd try not to let it affect me so much, but it was useless. All of my own dark memories and emotions came flashing back strongly. I couldn't escape them.

I tried to help Renae look her best for court by doing her make-up. She'd never been the type to wear make-up and was reluctant at first, but I soon converted her; she even asked me to do it. Sometimes I put little clips in her hair, though she'd rip them out faster than a two year old. Renae really did care about how she looked, and often if I was sitting in a visit while she was handcuffed and waiting to go out to the bus, she'd dash over and ask me to fix her hair. I'd ruffle it a bit and then she'd run back to the line, singing out, 'Thanks, beauty therapist!' One morning, she ran over to me with tears in her eyes and whispered, 'I want my mum.' I knew exactly how she felt.

I didn't see much of the Bali Nine guys, apart from when they were standing handcuffed before court or when I'd walk past them in the visiting hall, where many of them often sat talking to their devoted and distraught parents. Andrew Chan and Matt Norman regularly went to church, so I'd see them there, too. Andrew was always really friendly and incredibly upbeat, shaking hands with people and giving them high-fives. Sometimes I'd talk to him, though Renae asked me not to. Unsurprisingly, there were definite tensions between the Nine.

Two weeks after the Bali Nine trials started, Michelle Leslie also began her trial and was distressed to be handcuffed to Renae on her first day. She didn't like Renae and tried to keep her distance, especially publicly. But within a few weeks her court case was finished and a success. Five weeks after checking into Hotel K and three months after her arrest, Michelle was going home.

As soon as I heard the news, I walked down to her cell to congratulate her. She was straightening her hair and busy packing, so I told her, 'I'll see you again before you go, to say goodbye.'

'Yeah, OK, babe,' she replied.

Then she was gone. She didn't come to say goodbye.

I always felt conflicting emotions when any girl was released: pleased for her but upset and agitated that it wasn't me, too. It was a kick in the guts, a reminder that I was stuck, trapped, caged in this soul-sucking dump. It super-sensitised me and brought on the strong emotions I usually tried to suppress: a deep, all-consuming, heartbreaking longing to go home. Watching someone walk free left me trembling and teary for days.

'Why can't it be me?' I'd cry to Merc. 'How much longer do you think it'll be?'

My beautiful sister would always be positive, but she felt the same frustrations. How much longer did we all have to live this life for? I was so tired.

I often got lost in a world of my own, withdrawing into myself, no longer interested in getting to know the new prisoners being endlessly crammed into my cell. I didn't know these girls, and often didn't like them, but I spent fifteen hours a day just inches from them, usually getting tangled up at night when we slept. There were now fifteen of us jammed in. I no longer knew half their names. Many times I didn't even realise a new prisoner had been put in our cage until I felt her staring at me. New girls would sit staring at me for days. I was Schapelle Corby!

I felt I was living under a permanent dark cloud of bad luck. After more than a year, I was still stuck in the primitive pre-sentencing cells. Renae had been moved after two days; Michelle Leslie didn't spend a single night in one.

> *I woke at 4 a.m., wondering how long it will be before I can go home. I fell asleep amongst the chaotic noises of the girls getting up, banging pots and pans, dropping things, yelling. My head is aching. They speak so loud. This is how it is every morning, but some mornings it affects me more. I feel so, so heavy and so sad. I've felt this so long now that I can't even cry about it any more. It just builds up inside and slowly releases the pressure of pain from my whole being during the day.*
>
> Diary entry, 5 December 2005

My cell was always so irritatingly noisy, with girls endlessly gossiping, chanting prayers and fighting over everything from cooking gas and money to bottled water. Whether it was 2 a.m. or 6 a.m., there was always someone awake making noise. Girls would often play cards until about five in the morning, squealing at the top of their lungs if they won, or screaming and fighting if someone cheated. Ironically, playing cards was why many of them were in here. Each night, I would try to go to sleep at about 8 p.m. I'd lie down and say a little prayer to myself: *Please, God, please give me strength to get through this. Give me the heart of forgiveness so I can forgive the*

*guards, because they know not what they do. Please protect my family,
ease my father's pain . . .*

Then I'd lie there hopelessly trying to sleep for the next few hours,
usually filling up with rage at the ceaseless yelling and screaming.
Sometimes I'd picture myself walking around strangling them,
smashing their heads against the walls, screaming 'Shuttttupp!!'
in their faces. But I didn't. *Stop, Schapelle – stop! stop! stop!* I kept
telling myself. *Breathe, breathe . . .*

My heart would feel like it was going to explode. I'd bite my
tongue, control myself, control my energy. But it was too easy to
do the wrong thing. I did explode occasionally, jumping up and
shouting: 'Shut the fuck up!' But it never did any good; it didn't
make them quiet. I always felt so ashamed at my outbursts that
I'd spend the next day going around saying sorry.

With so many women, there were always bitter domestic politics.
We had a cleaning roster, but most of the girls were lazy and no one
stuck to it. Girls stole each other's food, money, toothpaste, which
caused screaming rows. No one took their turn to buy cleaning
products but always expected someone else to do it – usually me.

And jealousy was rife. A girl having two visits a day, a new
shirt, a good laugh or a delicious lunch always provoked vicious
backstabbing. I didn't replace my worn-out mattress, because I knew
the knives would come out – also, I'd feel bad for all the girls
sleeping on the bare concrete. My cooking gas often evaporated in
a single day, and my shirts often walked past me on someone else's
back. But I tried to minimise the theft of my clothes by doing my
washing on Sundays when I had no visits and could keep a close
eye on the clothesline. If I put drinks in the ice cooler overnight,
by morning they'd often be empty.

Whenever I came back from a visit with my mail and bags of
shopping (which Dad often did and always went overboard with),
I'd usually give the girls whatever they wanted. I shared all my
things, but it wasn't enough – they still had to steal. I couldn't trust
anyone. I wanted to, but I always got burned.

I'd become good friends with Dewi, sharing all my food with
her, giving her whatever she wanted out of my packages and money

whenever she needed it. I confided in her, I trusted her. But one day she spoke to the local media, saying some vile things about me. I'm sure she didn't realise she was talking to a reporter, as they so often sidled up, pretending to be tourists. But it ended our friendship. We stopped talking. It hurt me deeply.

One of the older women in my cell saw how upset I was. 'Schapelle, don't ever forget where you are,' she told me. 'You are living among liars and cheats – you can't trust anybody.'

It was the best bit of advice anyone's given me. I instinctively wanted to trust people and make friends, but I couldn't, I wasn't living in normal society. After Dewi hurt me, I withdrew further and started fading more into black. Sometimes I'd go three weeks without speaking to anyone in my cell. It was as if I'd taken a vow of silence, or a vow of silence had taken me. Some new girls probably wondered what my voice sounded like. It was easier to live in fairyland. Sweet insanity.

But I did care about other people, and I'd often come back to reality with a thud. I'd see something horrible, like a poor girl boiling up filthy tap water and tipping it into a bottle. 'What are you doing?' She couldn't afford to buy bottled water and no one would let her drink theirs. I couldn't believe it had been going on for weeks. This was *water*: a necessity, not some luxury item like chocolate. I felt so ashamed. I'd become so self-centred that I hadn't noticed what was going on around me. I bought the girl some bottled water and told her to be sure to tell me when she needed more.

I felt sorry for the poorer girls, as they were usually treated badly by those with more money. There was a real class system in the cells. The poor girls, who had no visits, no money and often no self-esteem, were used as lackeys by the richer girls. They'd order them to wash and massage their feet. Sometimes they gave them money, but often they'd just order them about because they could.

One girl, Murna, was taken full advantage of during her six months in Hotel K. She'd stolen a mobile phone. She had no visits, no money and was quite shy, with no self-confidence; she would run around slaving for girls who gave her nothing in return, knowing she never stood up for herself. Murna wasn't a pretty girl; actually, to be truthful, she was awful to look at, and I had a feeling she thought 'pretty' people had the right of way. I spoke to her often, as she could speak English fluently. I helped her out by giving her toiletries, food, clothes, bottled water and hugs. I occasionally asked her to massage my feet, so she wouldn't feel like she was just taking from me.

Her profession on the outside was prostitution. She got her clients through the Internet, where she advertised herself. Foreign men would hire her online and pay her flight from Jakarta, where she lived with her parents, to wherever they were staying – usually the tourist island of Bali. Her last client had her arrested. He told her to fly to Bali and that he'd reimburse her for the ticket when she arrived. So she borrowed money from her mum and flew to meet this man at his hotel room. He was an animal. After hours of rough sex, she was so tired and sore that she pleaded with him to stop, even for a short rest to get some food. He refused and kept at it. A little later she was crying in pain. He told her he'd ease it with anal sex. But she refused. She stood up, feeling weak and crying, got dressed and asked for her pay. He just laughed. She grabbed his phone and left. The man then called down to reception and had her arrested on her way out. He gave a statement to the police before flying home to Australia to his wife and kids.

Murna was thirty-two years old and had been working as a prostitute for more than ten years. Being in Hotel K, where AIDS was rife, heightened her awareness of it and she began to confide in me her fears that she may have contracted the virus. She'd never had any tests done in all her working years, and she was scared. Eventually, I talked her into going to the prison clinic. I knew if she didn't have tests done here, she'd never have them. We arranged for an appointment, and I waited outside for her. Then we had to wait a couple of weeks for the results. She was very tense, living on the edge until finally she was called to the clinic and given two envelopes. One contained HIV results, the other STD results. The doctor told her to take them away and open them in her own time.

She left it another week. In that time, she became a walking time bomb, a complete wreck, falling down crying and screaming. The fact that she was sharing a cell with Sonia didn't help her stress. I'd sit with Murna, hold her tight with her head on my shoulder, rocking her like a baby until she calmed down, usually using one of my hands to shoo away all the onlookers. Murna finally opened the envelopes. HIV: negative. STD: syphilis positive.

The doctor immediately started her on a course of shots, telling her that if she'd left it any longer, her body would have broken out in sores. Because she was regularly off at the clinic, Murna became the hot topic of gossip. Rumours flew around that she had AIDS. People were so rude and ignorant, staying well away from her and humiliating her by blurting out in conversation, 'She's got AIDS.' It made me furious, but I'd calm myself and tell them: 'Stop gossiping – *educate* yourselves. She doesn't have what you say, anyway. I know, I went with her to the clinic.'

I asked the gossip girls if they'd ever have an AIDS test. They all answered no. My response to them was they should shut up then, because this girl was brave enough to get tested, to make sure that, if she had been HIV positive, she wouldn't pass the virus on.

Although time was stagnant, it also seemed to fly. I spent my time reading, writing letters, lying in my pool listening to my iPod, giving myself facials, cooking up curries and stir-fries on my little gas cooker, or just sitting on my mattress people-watching or daydreaming about going home. I'd often imagine my future dream home, picturing myself lazing back on a cosy couch in my large lounge room, watching a pub-size flat-screen TV or cooking in my big kitchen. Upstairs would be my big bedroom (which maybe would turn into a parents' retreat, with any luck!), while outside there'd be a quality vegetable garden, an in-ground swimming pool and a barbecue – not forgetting a puppy picked up and rescued from the pound and a granny flat for Dad.

I enjoyed playing with my fantasies of life outside, but I still couldn't look at photos of beaches, my friends or my home, or read contemporary books about girls my age shopping, going to parties or the movies, and having love affairs. It would only hurt too much and sharply remind me of what I was missing. I preferred books set in ancient history and to remain numb to the life stolen from me.

The guards weren't making life in hell any easier. I still couldn't play tennis. If I stood at the door of the women's block longingly watching the men play, the guards would enjoy slamming it shut in my face. I'd uselessly scream, 'I was just *watching* . . .', but they'd just smirk, relishing their pathetic power. Often I'd go to pick up the hose to fill my pool and a guard would snatch it away, claiming she needed it that very instant. They all found it amusing when my pool was slashed by a prisoner or nicked by a careless gardener.

They were always using and abusing their power, demanding cash, food, cigarettes or anything else that caught their eye. We had to give them cash to leave the block, in fact. And I was blatantly told to buy cartons of cigarettes for the guards so that I could get my mail, even though I paid a hefty fee to collect it anyway.

They'd come into my cell, pointing at my shopping or parcels, and screech: 'I want! Gimme! Gimme!' It was pathetic, but it wasn't worth fighting. I'd usually give them what they wanted, although sometimes I'd rebelliously make them wait a few days. I lived in hope that one day they'd give something back or somehow come around, maybe let me play a bit of tennis. But I soon learnt to expect nothing back.

I felt they were always trying to beat me down, break my spirit and turn me into a zombie. I wasn't going to let them; I might be physically caged, but my mind and spirit were free to fly. But they did something that really hurt me when they moved my friend Eddie to another jail. Eddie and I had become close – definitely nothing sexual, but he was a real support, helping to take the edge off my loneliness. They moved him before I was unlocked, so we didn't even get the chance to say goodbye. I felt so vulnerable, so frightened and alone. Eddie had been my rock. Now he was gone. I felt deeply depressed and didn't eat for a couple of days, until

Renae walked into my cell one afternoon with a bowl of vegetable soup she'd chopped up and cooked. It was such a nice gesture, as Renae didn't cook. I ate it and realised I had to stop feeling sorry for myself.

All I had control over at this point were my emotions and my mind, but I'd even lose control of those during my down times. Sometimes I'd start to believe I had early-onset Alzheimer's disease. I often felt so terribly vague, forgetful, my mind coddled and foggy as if I was losing my grip on reality. But I'd snap out of it and put it down to stress, trauma and my groundhog-day existence: nowhere to go, nothing to do, no mental stimulation, trapped in hell. I was trying desperately to stay positive, make the best of it, spend my time improving my character – learning to be patient, trying to help others as I watched the hurt and damage the bitchy gossip girls caused.

But as my second Christmas loomed, it was hard to keep my spirits up. I'd had a severe ear infection for weeks, with all my requests to go outside to a specialist refused. I had excruciating conjunctivitis in both eyes, and my longing to go home was agonising. On Christmas Eve, I lay on my mattress with tears pouring down my face as I visualised my mum running around her kitchen, preparing all the food, trifles and cheesecakes, as my little sister Mele frantically wrapped last-minute presents in the bedroom while outside someone cut the lawn in preparation for all the guests.

Mum would be wearing my white Haviana flip-flops, which she'd taken on her last visit to feel closer to her baby. I knew I would be on her mind almost every minute, even more than usual, and it hurt me that she'd be hurting. This was painful for us all. My family wasn't physically locked up, but mentally and emotionally they were caged in here with me. We all thought I'd be home by Christmas 2004; then we thought I'd be home for my twenty-eighth birthday in July; then we thought I'd be home for this Christmas. But I was still here.

When I turned twenty-eight, I kept it quiet from the other prisoners. I didn't want a fuss and a reminder of where I was. Only

Dewi knew, and I asked her not to tell anyone. I spent it sitting alone under the banana trees at the back of the cells near the clothesline. My pool was unusable, a bit of useless plastic strewn on the ground after a girl had slashed it with a knife the day before. It was jail – there was no point getting upset. I improvised by using a bucket of water and ladle to sporadically splash water over myself to cool down in the scorching heat. I tried not to think too much about spending a birthday in prison. It was painful and also embarrassing. I ate some Japanese food that Merc had dropped off, although as it was Sunday we didn't get to see each other.

But Christmas was a bit harder to ignore, as everyone tried to get into the Christmas spirit, even loudly singing Christmas carols in the cells. I couldn't believe it when I heard a musical voice singing carols in English, endlessly, one after the other – almost every carol I knew. This sweet voice echoed around all our cells. I discovered it was Renae. She seemed to know all the words to all the carols, and she could really sing. (Maybe I should call Ron!) In the morning, all the girls in the cell went around to each other giving hugs, but I excused myself, not wanting to start the day in tears.

Many of the Bali Nine parents were in Bali for the trials and came in bearing armfuls of Christmas presents and food. I was invited to join a few groups but ended up just popping out to Scott Rush's parents' little party wearing my fake pink Chanel sunglasses to hide my red, infected eyes. They had brought decorations and had done a good job of making things feel Christmassy. In the afternoon, Dad, Merc, Wayan and the kids came in laden with food and presents. Merc had gone to so much trouble organising a feast of hams, chickens, rolls, chocolates and beer. She'd even organised little presents for me to give to the kids. We all tried to be upbeat, but the undertone was unmistakably pain. Having to lay out Christmas dinner on a filthy concrete floor in jail, with male prisoners staring at us through a window, wasn't much of a celebration.

Back in the women's block, Renae came into my cell and handed me a present: a new pair of sneakers. She didn't like me skipping or exercising in my flip-flops. I gave her a big juicy steak and some mushrooms.

By New Year's Eve, my eyes were better, but I had no hearing in my infected ear and was extremely worried about permanent deafness. I was living on painkillers but still couldn't get out to see a specialist.

I wanted to end my most horrible year imaginable by fasting for forty-eight hours, thinking pure thoughts, and praying. My plan was to rid myself of the past year and start the new one with fresh body, mind and spirit. But I fell to temptation early, eating when I got really hungry and later having a couple of shots of arak, a potent Indonesian spirit.

The year before, I had a sleepover in Salma's cell on New Year's Eve for what I thought was going to be a bit of fun. It wasn't. She didn't speak much English and, to my embarrassment, refused to let the other two girls share a glass of beer with us. I was also stressed about girls in my cell rifling through all my things – which was exactly what they did.

This year we were told our monkey cages would be left open until midnight, a special treat that cost each cell 70,000 rupiah. But unsurprisingly they slammed us away at 5.30 p.m. Why did I expect anything else? I sat on my mattress, refusing to let my mind think about what my friends were doing. It hurt too much; it was better to block, suppress and stay numb.

A bit later, we heard a noise at the main door and were shocked to see that the guards had returned to unlock us. All the girls excitedly blew trumpets, set up a tape player in the sewing room and danced wildly. I did my usual, I watched. But it was good to be outside. I desperately missed standing underneath the night sky, looking up at the twinkling stars. This night the stars and moon were hidden behind clouds, but it was a beautiful feeling when raindrops started splashing on my skin and hair in the dark. By 9 p.m., we were back in our cages, and as I looked through the bars at the rain still falling, I realised how much I'd come to appreciate the preciousness of life . . . any life.

The next day, I decided to treat myself to a long shower and told all the girls to do what they needed to do in the shower room first. It was a self-indulgent half hour: washing my hair, putting a treatment in, shaving my legs and using a chocolate-ginger-coconut body scrub. As I was ladling water over myself to wash it off, I focused on the spit on the floor. It was disgusting. It was nothing new, but I'd never get used to it. I held my heart and told myself: *Not too much longer, Pelle, and you'll be having a real shower. This year will be better, it will be!*

'The darkest hour is just before the dawn. Schapelle, that hour is now.' I contemplated those words when someone wrote them to me. It was a good sentiment, but was this really the darkest time that I would experience on this awful journey? Or was there still more to come?

I didn't have to wait long to find out the answer.

19

No Dawn

CHAPELLED: TO BE SCREWED – BRUTALLY. Urban online
dictionary of slang

Police have seized photographs of Schapelle Corby with a
man who has just been charged with marijuana smuggling.
The alleged drug dealer is pictured alone with Corby in
some photographs and with Corby and another couple in
others. They were found during a recent police search of
the alleged dealer's home in South Australia. He was the
target of a joint SA–Queensland police operation into a
hydroponic marijuana smuggling ring allegedly operating
between two states.

The photographs were taken before Corby was charged
in October last year with importing 4.1 kg of marijuana
into Bali in her body board bag . . . The chance discovery
of the photos comes as Corby, 28, is preparing to appeal
against her drug smuggling conviction and sentence . . .
Balinese prosecutors are expected to seek access to the
photographs seized by police in SA. They will want them
to try to cast doubt on claims by Corby in her trial that she
had no connection with drugs or drug dealers.

Herald Sun, 10 December 2005

When Merc came in stressed and upset to tell me about this story, I was almost blasé. I shrugged it off; I was tired of the lies that I could do nothing about from in here. Being cut off from the outside world made me lose my reality compass. I didn't fully understand how bad it was. I had no idea who was in the shots or when or where they were taken, but I knew I'd never knowingly been involved with any drug dealers.

Merc was asking me if I could remember ever being photographed with a guy in his forties, as a couple.

'I'd never go out with a guy that old, Merc!' I was more pissed off with this implication than anything else.

But poor Mum and Merc had a true perspective of the damage it was causing me as people across Australia read the Saturday-morning headlines. They both knew that public opinion was now in the balance – 90 per cent of Australians were no longer so sure of my innocence, no longer swept up in the hysteria of my trial, but more calmly asking, did she or didn't she? Is Schapelle a drug dealer or a very unlucky traveller? People were seesawing, ready to be tipped either way. Then bang . . . a smoking gun, photographic proof of a drug past.

The Melbourne journalist who wrote the story had a red-hot scoop – even if the story was all wrong.

It made me look like a liar and a drug smuggler. But it was worse . . . much worse. It was an extremely crucial and sensitive time for me. I was in the middle of my last appeal when these headlines were splashed in newspapers right across Indonesia. The prosecutors were instantly clamouring for copies of the photos to use against me – as proof they'd been right all along. The Indonesian courts could still give me the death sentence.

My mum was beside herself, turning into a protective lioness, fighting to find the truth and protect her baby from this deadly journalistic beat-up. She and Merc started scrambling for answers, but as it was the weekend, they didn't have much luck. They didn't sleep; they spent every single hour of that stressful weekend twisting their brains, trying to work out where those photos could possibly have been taken. They were dreaming up theories: maybe

I'd been unwittingly snapped in the background of a restaurant or party, or maybe they were digitally mocked-up fakes.

Then, on Monday morning, Mum rang the journalist, quickly uncovering disturbing news.

First, he revealed that she was also in the photographs. Mum asked what she was wearing – hopeful it would be a clue to finding out when and where they were taken. But the reporter was hedging. 'You look like you're going out to dinner.' She was baffled: 'I don't go out for dinner! What am I wearing?' He couldn't say. He didn't know. He dropped his bombshell. He hadn't actually *seen* the photos. It took a split second for Mum to absorb what she'd heard. Then she lost it.

'How dare you! How dare you write this about my girl, when you haven't even seen the photos?'

He promised to 'fix' it if he was wrong. But his story had already hit its mark. People believe what they read, they remember the bad stuff. How can you fix it? How do you undo a front-page story? Surely he should have checked his facts *before* it went to print, before he hurt me and my family.

Mum was fuming. 'You're bloody wrong!' She hung up in disgust.

Her next call was to the South Australian Police. She spoke to a senior policeman on the investigation, who admitted that he'd been warned by his superiors to say nothing. Mum was desperate, hurting badly. She wouldn't let him hang up. He didn't. He had a heart. He also knew the truth . . . he knew that the story was all wrong. He didn't want to lose his job, but he did want to help, so he spoke cryptically. 'You'll know where the photos were taken the instant you see them.' Then it was like a game of verbal charades: he gave her clues, she put it together. It was her best chance yet of unravelling the truth.

'There are other people in the shots,' he hinted.

'Who are the other people?'

'Friends.'

'Schapelle doesn't have forty-year-old friends.'

'They were your friends. You took them into the jail to see Schapelle . . . That's all I'm saying.'

It was her first major break. The photos were taken in Kerobokan Prison *after* my arrest.

'My friends don't go to Bali!'

'But you used to drink at a bar . . .'

Mum nearly dropped the phone. She'd just solved it. She started shaking and called out to Greg downstairs, '*I* did it, I took them there!' She was devastated. 'It's my fault!' she cried. She'd hurt her baby.

The policeman was still on the line. She spoke to him again.

'I know who you mean . . . I met them at a bar . . .'

She couldn't think of its name. The policeman prompted her: 'The Secret Garden.'

'Yes!' Mum clearly recalled two men from Adelaide whom she'd met at a bar and brought in to see me. She so rarely brought anyone in, knowing I usually hated it. But she remembered one of them telling her his granddaughter had followed my case and that the other man was a postman.

Mum was distraught. She hung up. Game over.

Mum stood in her kitchen and broke down sobbing, bent over and gasping for breath. She doesn't usually cry, but she couldn't stop. My beautiful mum was hurting so much, shaking so fiercely that she couldn't even call Merc, who she knew was also deeply distressed. She couldn't believe how a journalist could get it so wrong.

When she'd calmed down a bit, she phoned the journalist, yelling, 'Look what you've done, look what you've done!' She told him the photos were taken in Kerobokan Prison. He sounded shocked. She hung up.

Anyone who'd seen the photographs knew where they were taken. Maybe the journalist had been played, used as a patsy to smear my name with lies he'd been given. Whoever had leaked him his scoop had to have known they were *not* taken before my arrest – it was impossible not to know that if you'd sighted the photos. In one of the pictures, Mum and Greg and the two Adelaide men were standing right outside the front doors of Kerobokan. In another they were holding 'Free Schapelle' stubby holders and most of the packet was of shots taken all around Bali.

But this reporter blindly wrote a story that made me look like I had a drug past, without even eyeballing the evidence he was using against me. His entire story hinged on photos he had not seen, but his bullshit would be read and accepted as fact by hundreds of thousands of people, millions once it hit radio and TV and the Indonesian media. The only reason this was a red-hot story was because it had supposedly shown I'd been involved with drugs before Bali. The true facts didn't add up to a story at all.

Making a front-page story using evidence he hadn't seen was a gamble for this journalist but obviously worth the risk to him. For me, it wasn't just a flutter, it was Russian roulette. This blatantly false story could be the bullet the prosecutors needed to finally get me life or even the death penalty.

The journalist clearly knew the potentially lethal repercussions of his 'scoop', writing this in the days following:

> The photographs have led to speculation doubting Corby's claims of innocence after she was arrested in Bali with 4.1 kg of cannabis, and Indonesian prosecutors now want to see them as they try to have her 15-year jail sentence lengthened.
>
> *News Ltd*, 13 December 2005

Even after we knew the photos were taken in jail, and we knew the police also knew it – as they'd interviewed the alleged drug dealer in the centre of this fiasco well before the story was printed – this reporter kept slinging more mud day after day after day, refusing to admit the photos were taken in jail. My family wanted to strangle him.

Then, after a week of headlines, the story died. We had the photos, indisputable proof the story was wrong. Mum didn't get the photos from the police – they'd refused to even show them to her, despite her flying to Adelaide to try to clear it all up. The Adelaide postman, who was in the photos but not on drugs charges, felt for us and gave Mum his set of copies. But the damage had been done. This Melbourne reporter did not write a retraction, he did not admit he'd been wrong and certainly didn't *fix* it. He wrote a short story with the correct facts . . . which sure didn't add up to a red-hot front-page scoop.

> The *Herald Sun* revealed a week ago that police in South Australia had seized photos of Corby with a man who was recently charged with marijuana smuggling. The alleged drug dealer is pictured alone with Corby in some photographs. Police initially thought they were taken before Corby was charged in October last year with importing 4.1 kg of marijuana in Bali.
>
> *Herald Sun*, 17 December 2005

He'd lost his little gamble but clearly didn't want to make too much noise about it.

He was also onto a new story, busy packing his bags to go on a trip to the Solomon Islands a few days later with my nemesis, police boss Mick Keelty. So who was his source? Who'd leaked these lies? It must have been a trusted informant for the newspaper's editors to run a story based on *hearsay*. We'd been told by the good-hearted SA cop that it was not leaked by the South Australian Police, which was believable, given it went to a Victorian reporter.

We were not the only ones speculating that Mick Keelty was his source. The police boss was under journalistic fire about it, his denials making headlines. But, as usual, he couldn't help slinging more mud, adding weight to the story, twisting the knife. Despite admitting he'd seen the photos, he told the media on 12 December: 'If any evidence existed about Schapelle Corby, there was always a risk that it would come to light eventually.'

Five weeks later I learnt my appeal had failed. My sentence was reinstated to twenty years. It was brutal.

It blew out the small flame of hope that had kept me sane. It was the first time that I really lost all hope of ever being freed. I spiralled into a deep black depression. I will never know what impact that story had on the judges' decision, but my lawyers believed it did hurt me. It also helped the mud to stick when two more stories broke in quick succession. I felt battered.

My brother James was arrested for breaking into the house of a drug dealer, stealing money and marijuana, which he'd taken home and stashed in Mum's coffee jar. I got this bad news the same day as the news of my reinstatement. It was devastating. I have no idea why James committed this crime. But I do know he had nothing to do with the marijuana in my bag, because I saw inside it before checking in, and James didn't go anywhere near it.

But James gave the police a perfect chance to attack us again. Without a shred of evidence linking him to the marijuana in my bag, a senior Queensland policeman stated in an affidavit given to the court that there was a link. This same policeman had marched James in front of all the cameras outside court, rather than taking him through a more discreet entrance with the other two defendants.

> He (Mr Kisina) is suspected of some involvement in the exportation of cannabis for which his sister has received a 20-year imprisonment sentence, the affidavit says.
>
> *The Australian*, 21 January 2006

A few days later the senior policeman was made to retract his words:

> Queensland police admitted yesterday they did not have evidence to support allegations that Schapelle Corby's half brother was involved in the Bali drug run that put her in jail.
>
> *The Australian*, 24 January 2006

But he'd already inflamed the story, increased the damage caused by James himself, undoubtedly confirming what many people were already thinking. But no more claims about a link between James's crime and my arrest have ever been made — because it simply doesn't exist.

About ten days later, my family was headline news again. It was more lies and more hack journalism, but this time the source was no secret – it was the Australian Federal Police. The ABC's *7.30 Report* ran a story about my dad's former neighbour being charged with 'running a sophisticated, commercial marijuana operation just one month before Schapelle Corby's fateful trip to Bali'.

None of us had seen Dad's old neighbour Tony for more than a year before I went to Bali. We all knew Tony and his girlfriend but had no idea he grew marijuana. Central to this story was that my lawyers had rejected an offer by the AFP to DNA-test the marijuana from my bag. Therefore, no comparison between it and Tony's marijuana could be made. Friends told me that even morning chat-show hosts were talking about how I'd refused to allow testing of the marijuana, which could have proved it was from Tony's place.

> The Australian Federal Police have told the ABC's investigative unit that when the AFP offered to forensically test Schapelle Corby's boogie-board bag and its contents, her lawyers rejected the offer.
>
> *7.30 Report*, 30 January 2006

We'd seen a lot of untruth reported, but this was the trusted ABC. It had it blatantly wrong. The request for assistance to test the marijuana had been my request, as legally it was my decision to make. I'd given my consent to the Australian consul back on 3 December 2004. Vasu had also been pushing hard for the tests. It wasn't shades of grey, it was black and white. The ABC was wrong: wrong to trust the AFP and wrong not to independently check its facts.

There were press reports stating that we were pushing for DNA testing, and even the AFP had issued a press release of its own stating that the Bali police had refused its help to test the marijuana: 'The head of the Bali Police wrote back in January 2005, stating the AFP assistance was not required.' Also, if we'd refused an offer to test the marijuana, it would have made major headline news – no doubt about that whatsoever.

But in an interview the day after the ABC story, Mr Keelty unbelievably repeated the lies, sticking the knife in yet again.

> 'I think the reality was if it was tested, and the tests didn't come out with what the defence counsel expected, then it may assist the prosecution and not the defence,' AFP Commissioner Mick Keelty said today.
>
> *The Australian*, 31 January 2006

My family and I believed Mr Keelty was running a media campaign against me. My case had caused him major headache, turning airport crime into news that people were suddenly hungry to read. It had opened a can of worms, and the AFP was trying to screw the lid back on. In the process, they had to discredit me to try to calm public fears about our airports. I felt they wanted to turn people against me, make them believe I was just a lowlife drug smuggler who got lucky getting my big bag of dope through their airports.

Right throughout my trial, Mr Keelty undermined my defence at every turn. I was fighting for my life, in a foreign country with the death penalty lurking. I just wanted him to shut up. It would have been contempt of court anywhere else, surely. It seemed unfathomable to me and my family that the boss of the Australian Federal Police could make such damaging and prejudicial comments while I was before the courts. But that is what he did.

He started his attacks on me as soon as John Ford went public with a plausible explanation of how the dope got into my bag – baggage handlers. It put the fear of God into people who used airlines, and Mr Keelty knew he was sitting on the explosive cocaine news and a world of airport crime. The day Merc and Lily told me the news of Mr Ford, Commissioner Keelty was already publicly ridiculing him and his evidence, before the police had even interviewed this man.

'At best it's hearsay on hearsay . . . To actually transfer drugs from one part of the country to another, from state to state, and end up overseas, is a big leap. Then to connect to a person coming off a plane, it's very wild. There are a lot of things to have gone wrong for that to have happened like that.

'It is a bit of a long shot here that it's connected to the Corby case in any event . . . At best, a person is giving hearsay evidence about what other parties supposedly said. It is very light on,' Mr Keelty said of Ford's evidence, effectively scuttling the Corby team's best hope of an acquittal.

Sydney Morning Herald, 18 March 2005

Before news of the cocaine syndicate broke, Mr Keelty had been denying the airports had a problem with airport workers – baggage handlers – involved in drug crime.

Keelty is under fire for strenuously denying – in relation to the Corby case – the existence of baggage handler drug smuggling operations when his officers were investigating one.

Daily Telegraph (Australia), 14 May 2005

Then, after the news broke, he instantly hit out with negative comments, undermining my lawyers, who were trying to use it to help in my defence. He did it knowing his comments made news in Indonesia and regardless of the fact it was just two weeks from my verdict – with death or life still highly possible. But he didn't shut up.

Despite the new allegations about baggage handlers, Mr Keelty said the Sydney cocaine syndicate case had no bearing on the defence of accused Bali drug smuggler Schapelle Corby. 'This is very different to the sort of scenario that has been drawn around the Corby case,' Mr Keelty said.

The Australian, 11 May 2005

'These are baggage handlers who are part of the international syndicate, who are operating to help import drugs into Australia,' Mr Keelty said. 'These people were part of the syndicate. This is quite different to the suggestion about domestic transfer of drugs on the domestic side.'

Daily Telegraph (Australia), 11 May 2005

'I have never said publicly one way or the other about Schapelle Corby's innocence or guilt,' he told Macquarie Radio ... 'There are tens of thousands of people who travel to Bali each and every year. The evidence and intelligence of interference with those bags or drugs suddenly arriving in Bali just doesn't exist.'

AAP Bulletin, 16 May 2005

'It's rare that the person carrying drugs doesn't realise that they're carrying the drugs on behalf of a syndicate.'

Herald Sun, 17 May 2005

The truth was our airports were riddled with crime, and our bags were tampered with. Qantas chief executive Geoff Dixon admitted the airline had a complaint a day about things stolen from people's checked-in luggage. While Mr Keelty was trying to put the lid back on the can of worms, they were squirming out everywhere. Reports, new and old, kept leaking out, showing that drug crimes by airport staff had been rife for years, well before my boogie board and I flew to Bali in 2004. My case simply put a public focus on it all.

It was revealed that since 2003 police had been running Operation Flora, a specialist police drug squad to target 'drug activity' at Sydney's domestic airport terminals.

'The purpose of this operation was to target the transportation of prohibited drugs between cities via the domestic airline system,' a police statement of facts tendered to the court said.

AAP, 14 July 2005

A customs report done a month before I travelled to Bali, but not made public until it was leaked to the *Australian* newspaper after my verdict, revealed that there were two customs operations – called Berlap and Tempest – that had been targeting two groups of baggage handlers, each working in a gang of six.

> It [the report] says baggage handlers had diverted bags containing large amounts of narcotics from incoming international flights to domestic baggage carousels, sometimes changing baggage tags, to avoid Customs examination. Baggage handlers are suspected of large-scale pillage and may use the roof area to gain illegal entry to passenger baggage, the report says. The roster system makes it easy for baggage handlers to get their 'mates' working in the same gang, it says.
>
> *The Australian*, 31 May 2005

Then there was an investigation into airport security by British aviation expert Sir John Wheeler, done four months after my verdict, which found that 'cannabis is moved through [Australian] airports' and that criminals involved in drugs were responsible for 'subverting or suborning airline or airport employees'.

The authorities no doubt want the public interest in airport crime to get back in its box. Perhaps that's why it all went quiet about the baggage handlers involved in the cocaine syndicate. There has been no news of any baggage handler ever convicted, despite Qantas boss Geoff Dixon stating, at the time the story broke: 'We have for many months and have continued to have full knowledge, I mean full knowledge, of the activities of those baggage handlers alleged to have been involved.'

There was without question a major crime issue at Sydney airport, otherwise why did the government spend an extra $200 million of taxpayers' money on upgraded airport security? And why did Sydney Airport Corporation spend $2.8 million on extra surveillance? None of it makes me innocent, but it shows it was not only possible for someone to put drugs in my bag, it was easy.

I felt, and still do, that the authorities saw me as just a little person, a little sacrifice, only a nuisance for making too much noise. They needed to squash me, shut me up.

I was a victim of airport crime. But I was stuck in jail for twenty years. My appeals were over, my life was over, my dreams shattered. My belief that life was fair was lost. The only thing keeping me going was my family and their untiring love and devotion to me, their undying optimism and strength.

Erwin was being optimistic and told me we could apply for an extraordinary appeal. I asked bleakly, 'Who's ever had any success with that?'

'The former president's son!' Great!

Now after my hopes of appeal to finally go home have been squashed, so have I.

My heart feels black, full of holes that leak sadness and sorrow, hope and despair trickling through my veins, weighing me down ever so heavily. I can't decide if time goes by fast or slowly, it doesn't matter really, as long as the days keep ending and time doesn't stop.

I'm finding it hard to sleep at night and am finding it harder and harder to wake up in the mornings. When I do wake up, I'm drained, don't want to get dressed, don't want to move. I push myself to do everything, even clean my teeth, it's like 'why bother'. For the past three months, due to ear infections, eye sickness, sinus, I haven't done any form of exercise.

I keep it together for my visitors' sakes, my family's sakes. I have to keep them, the ones I love so dearly, in the understanding that I'm doing fine, I'm strong, I can wait on a while longer.

If I'm weak and let depression take a strong hold of my thoughts and body, that would be it. There would be no surviving for me. I realise it in this place, realise it because I feel it, I'm aware of the darkness of depression creeping in to be a part of me. If I'm weak it could quite easily consume me and take over my life.

I will not allow this to happen. I'm aware it's trying to dig into me now. I have to protect myself and my family from this.

If I allow myself to be consumed, then my family will also be consumed, my dad in particular. He suffers from small bouts of depression due to his cancer. And if I can prevent my dad's depression by taking hold of my own, then that's what I must do – a new task for myself.

Diary entry, 2 February 2006

20

Pass the Salt

WHEN LIFE HANDS YOU A LEMON, ASK FOR THE TEQUILA
AND SALT!

Today is Valentine's Day. Dad came in early and, how sweet he is, brought me a big bunch of flowers – first time in my life. Merc and Nyeleigh came in a bit later with a cute cuddly companion for me – well, for me and Renae to share – a little puppy, one of the puffball dogs that old people usually have. I named him Stanley. Merc had put a yellow ribbon in his hair and he's so, so gorgeous. He's quite content to sit on my lap for hours while I brush his hair.

Renae and I both showered Stanley, dried him and combed his hair to get him ready for her afternoon visit with Renae's dad and stepmum. The guards were OK with Stanley in our block, apart from one who kept sneering. They could see how much this little cuddly companion had changed both our depressed, angry demeanours. It's truly amazing how much an animal can have a positive effect on people's lives. I tell you, this puppy is brightening my world. And Renae was in total shock, her world had just caved in massively, but today this puppy here has lit up her face all day.

Diary entry, 14 February 2006

The day before Valentine's, Renae was sentenced to life imprisonment. Her lawyer Anggia, Lily's sister, had been promising her ten years. She was shattered. When she'd returned to Kerobokan, she was lost, in a state of shock. I went into her cell and gave her a hug. Tears rolled down my cheeks as she told me she didn't understand, she'd been mentally prepared for twenty years – as the prosecutors had demanded – or anything less.

Andrew Chan and Myuran Sukumaran, the so-called Bali Nine ringleaders, were both sentenced to death on Valentine's Day, with local newspaper headlines screaming: 'Valentine is Dead'. I couldn't imagine how they were feeling. They were so young. Andrew had only turned twenty-two in January, receiving the prosecutors' request for death on his birthday. Myuran was twenty-five years old.

All the rest of the Bali Nine were sentenced to life.

While they were considering the risk of appeal, I was praying that Erwin could successfully win me the chance to have an extraordinary appeal, as it wasn't automatic. Hotman had walked away. He'd failed and didn't like the taste of it, telling the press it was time to make money so he could buy the latest-model Ferrari. There were no hard feelings. He'd tried his best, and I was grateful to him. But ever-faithful Erwin promised to keep on fighting on.

Meanwhile, I had to keep living in this dump. I'd allowed myself to slip into a black hole for two weeks after my failed appeal, but then it was time to use all my energy to pull myself out. I didn't want to fall too far and crumble with self-pity. So despite the heaviness around my heart, I grabbed my new purple hand weights from Mum, put on the new sneakers Renae had given me for Christmas and did some lifting, some sit-ups and some skipping. After an hour, I felt a great sense of achievement at dragging my sorry arse off my mattress and putting my visions of exercise into action. I felt pretty good.

Exercise always helped to lift my spirits. I'd never succumb to the temptation of drugs to blur and numb my pain, like prisoners all around me did. I wouldn't do that to myself or my family. But I was always shocked to see how quickly prisoners start doing drugs in here, often when they hadn't ever touched them before. Drugs were so common that when twenty-four females were randomly plucked from their cells one day for drug testing, nineteen came back with positive results. People were quick to lose their way. Some women also turned to other women for sex, sometimes within days of checking in, and often with husbands and children at home.

The women's block was full of lesbians who could often be heard having very noisy sex in their cells. If I was out the back, hanging up clothes or lying in my pool, I could usually hear them. When the guards did the cell checks, they regularly found carrots with condoms in the bathrooms. I very rarely had lesbians living in my cell, as usually we'd pay a guard to discreetly move them. All the straight girls would feel timid and uncomfortable if two girls were fooling around or staring while we were getting undressed. I liked to take my top off and sit in my bra because it was so hot and sticky, but the lesbians would overtly sit and stare. Or if we were showering, they'd often put their head over the top of the door to watch. I'd yell, 'Excuse me!' But they still did it.

The sexual activity got so bad in one cell, so loud and fierce, that the guards actually yelled at roll call, 'Stop eating each other.' It was unbelievable. My dad half-jokingly asked me one day if I'd ever be tempted. I can speak for now and until the end of time . . . that will never happen. I will not have any kind of sex in this dirty and disgusting place.

But Kerobokan is a seedy, sex-crazed little world. Merc and I were completely shocked when we first saw all the sex going on around us during a visit. It was not subtle; it was as blatant as a porn channel. I often saw girls giving oral sex, then coming up, wiping their mouths and checking their faces in a little mirror. Women were often sitting awkwardly on a guy's lap, thrusting away, sometimes with small children nearby – who may well have been conceived in this romantic way.

In the beginning, Merc and I didn't believe they were actually having sex. We saw couples sitting close in weird and ridiculous positions but thought maybe they'd just really missed each other. We'd be sitting there asking each other, 'Do you think they're doing it?' 'No, they couldn't.' 'I think they are . . .' It wasn't just naivety, as the girls seemed to always have their jeans done up. But I soon discovered that it didn't matter.

I was sitting in my cell one day, people-watching, when the sex mystery was obscenely solved. It was gross. A girl was squatting at the entrance to the women's block, with her knees apart, waiting to be called to a visit. It was full exposure. I copped an eyeful. She wasn't wearing underpants, and in the crotch of her jeans was a trap door hanging wide open. She was unbuttoned and well prepared for her visit. It turned out the sewing lady did big business cutting trap doors. Disgusting!

Merc now refuses to sit on the stain-covered straw mats in the visiting hall.

It didn't take long for the sight of public sex to become familiar, but I will never get used to it — it makes me feel awkward and uncomfortable, especially when my dad or mum comes to visit. We've all had to learn to put blinkers on and focus on each other.

But it doesn't always work. Sometimes it is impossible to shut out what is going on. One afternoon, a husband and wife, sitting just a metre across from me, used their little baby to try to hide what they were doing. They held the baby strategically while she was masturbating him. But it didn't hide her hand thrusting up and down or the look on his face. It was sick. It was surely child abuse.

Some male prisoners used prostitutes for quick sex during a visit, despite having girlfriends or wives. Sometimes they'd have sex with the prostitute in the morning, then with their wife in the afternoon. Male and female prisoners also often got together.

I've seen and heard so many twists of sexual betrayal in here that it makes the soap operas I watched at home seem dull. There was one prisoner who was doing a long sentence for drugs, whose wife came in daily; she did everything for him, including fight for his freedom. His thanks to her was to regularly have sex with female prisoners behind the visiting hall. The devoted wife had no idea.

One female prisoner stole another one's husband. We were all completely shocked, as we thought this girl was a lesbian. She was the girl who used to stroke my arms as we queued for water, before she scratched them. The married woman, who used to invite this girl to visits with her husband, had no clue of the fires she was lighting. It was a bitter betrayal. The husband stopped calling his wife to visits, so he and this girl could enjoy sex. The wife heard all the gory details from the gossip girls. This girl was freed first and ran off with the husband. The wife never saw him again.

If there is a betrayal, it's impossible to do anything about it from in here. I've seen the pain of several women who've found out their husbands were cheating or had simply vanished, no doubt with another woman. One morning, such a betrayal almost ended in a suicide. A female prisoner called home, only to hear another woman answer the phone. She went crazy but could do nothing, so she lashed out at herself, overdosing on her medication. She had AIDS. She was in very bad shape, but she survived.

The most sickly, grotesque sexual scene I've witnessed was when I walked in on a female guard sitting on the cement floor of my cell, kissing – full tongue kissing – and fondling a new attractive female prisoner. The look on my face stopped them quickly. I was so disgusted and had to ask the girl why . . . why would she do such a thing? She wasn't poor, she had food to eat, visitors coming to see her – including her boyfriend. Why would she possibly need to sell herself short like that? The answer was: 'She lets me use her hand phone.' And the guard herself is married with three daughters.

They kissed in our cell a few more times but, knowing I didn't approve, soon moved their kissing and canoodling out the back. This guard was one of the more friendly ones, often helping me on occasions. When I didn't have a hose to fill my pool, she took me for a walk to the kitchen to get one. Another day, I was standing at the door watching some of the Western guys play tennis. She could see the sadness and desperation on my face, so she took my hand, walked me to the tennis court and let me watch for five minutes. One of the guys gave me his racquet and I had a couple of shots. I'm not good at tennis, but it didn't matter . . . I had fun. When the precious five minutes were up, she took me back to the block. I really hoped this guard would help me to play more tennis. She didn't.

But despite being helpful, she always made me feel very uncomfortable – always way too touchy-feely. One day she actually pulled me down onto her knee while she sat at the guards' table, and cupped my breasts. I leapt up quickly, but as it was early days I was pretty timid and didn't get angry. She soon learnt I wasn't bisexual, though it didn't stop her trying to get close, sitting on my mattress and often asking me to sit beside her. I found it very unsettling.

Unsurprisingly, women regularly fall pregnant in here, often using the stomach-massage technique to abort. But when they choose to have the baby, women are allowed to live with it in Kerobokan for the first two years – at least that's what the prison rulebook states. Only twice since I've been here have women brought their newborns back to Hotel K, both very briefly. One girl brought hers in for a single day before releasing it to her family to nurture. She did it for the baby's sake, as this place isn't exactly baby-friendly. But she's had a haunted look in her eyes ever since. The other woman had her baby live here for just two weeks before she was freed. I was shocked to see her washing it under the putrid brown tap water.

One of the guards also had a baby girl she used to bring in with her each day, leaving her with us prisoners to babysit. She was often left lying on a mattress in any old cell, usually full of girls playing cards and smoking. She'd be put on the bed, with a towel under her bum because the guard didn't give her a nappy. The poor little thing was always being passed around. Unbelievably, most of the girls would let the baby suckle their breasts. She didn't have a dummy, so they'd just get their breasts out to pacify her. The guard didn't mind. I saw her pacified on almost every female's breast. Some of the more educated people would cringe at how disgusting it was. But most didn't think there was anything wrong with it.

Often those men and women prisoners who started sexual relationships in here would get engaged and married in the jail church or the mosque. I guess it lifted their spirits, but for me I think having a relationship in here would be more lonely and upsetting than being alone. Just knowing your husband or boyfriend was in a nearby cell but never being able to spend a night together and fall asleep on his chest would exacerbate the agonising loneliness. Male prisoners are sometimes allowed to have their girlfriends from outside come in for the night, if they pay the guards. There is no such luxury for the women. We are never allowed out for a night, or to have anyone in, no matter how much money we've got.

One woman, the informer prisoner Wiwin, who was serving four and a half years for possession of ten Ecstasy tablets, found herself a prisoner boyfriend after seven months. When she quickly fell pregnant, they were married in the prison mosque. The day after, she started wearing the traditional Muslim clothing and stopped kissing her husband in full view of people. I thought to myself, *Poor guy, his girl's really changed on him.* When he was released about a month later, Wiwin started hiding away in her cell, only coming out for roll call and rice, and always wearing her Muslim clothes. People started forgetting what she looked like. Being pregnant, she got permission one day to go to the hospital outside. Her husband met her at the hospital. Then they were gone. Wiwin was the first woman in all of Kerobokan history to escape. The female guard who'd accompanied Wiwin copped a fair bit of flack and laughs from jail authorities and prisoners for about a week. Then all was forgotten. Wiwin was a smart woman after all.

Escape is something I often fantasise about, imagining a helicopter dropping a rope made into a swing with a seat. Or I see myself sailing off in a homemade boat, using my bedcover as a sail, dangling my legs over the side and fishing as the winds sweep me home to the closest Australian shores. They are silly daydreams. Escape would mean spending the rest of my life as a fugitive and not seeing my family. I would never do it. (Though, never say never.)

Men don't just dream about it, they seem to do it quite often. One old man simply walked straight out Hotel K's front door. It was ingenious. He'd only been here a couple of days and no one recognised him as he slipped out with all the visitors. He was well into the hills before the guards even realised he was gone.

Another guy went out to the dentist and on the way back got the guard to stop at the ATM. He sprinted straight past the machine and into freedom. The guard tried to run after him but didn't have the speed, or maybe the heart, to catch him. But it wasn't at all unusual to see men beaten within an inch of their lives after failed escape attempts.

One of the most frightful sights I've seen was a guy who didn't make it. He was caught, beaten, brought back into prison and beaten again. He'd cut down a tall thin tree, carved footholds into it, then climbed like a circus performer to the top of the wall before leaping to freedom. (What an amazing feeling *that* would be.) But other, jealous prisoners had seen him and alerted the guards. They were ready and waiting for him. Merc and I were sitting in the visiting hall when he staggered past in his blood-splattered underpants. He had huge welts across his back where he'd already been whipped. I couldn't recognise his face: it was too distorted.

After they took him out to the isolation tower, the guards started pulling out axes from the little gardening room beside us. I was sure they were going to hit him with them. I started hyperventilating and getting really upset. Merc tried to settle me down but was shaking, too. It turned out they were just hacking down a tree to stop other prisoners getting ideas about climbing over the walls. We saw them dragging branches and bits of the tree past us.

As the months passed, I tried to keep my spirits up. Stanley was a big help. We put him on the list for roll call and would hold him up and say 'woof' when the guards called his name. He was as pampered as any Paris Hilton pooch. He slept next to me most nights, ate peanut butter and honey sandwiches and walked with me to visits, usually with pretty coloured ribbons in his hair. He was shampooed, brushed and cuddled regularly, and even got his own parcels in the post. He was far better company than most humans.

One day, I caught a girl unwittingly stealing a tin of Stanley's gourmet dog food. She was just finishing it off when I walked into the cell. It was the first time someone thieving from me had actually brightened my day.

Reluctantly, I had to give Stanley back to Merc after a few months, as there were too many Muslims in my cell who couldn't go near him for religious reasons. Jail life hadn't always been the best for my little puppy anyway. I once found him playing with a syringe left lying on the floor by one of the two heroin addicts in my cell.

Continuing to create a bit of fun and soak up any moment of life that is uplifting is vital for my survival, to fight the pain and depression. It might be as subtle as a beautiful sentiment in a letter or a laugh in a visit, or as crude as watching a fight. One afternoon, I had ringside seats to a session of rock 'n' roll wrestling between Renae and a Chinese lesbian who we nicknamed 'Andrew Chan' – because she looked like him.

The wrestling was in knee-high water, as the whole block was completely flooded from a heavy tropical downpour. I sat on my bed eating a hamburger to watch the fight through my window. It was showtime. A crowd of girls quickly gathered around to watch. Renae and Andrew were really going for it, both looking like blokes, with their tough demeanour, body language, stance and shouted words. They both had their fists up, slightly hunched like boxers, circling each other. Then they'd go in for the kill. Renae was winning. She'd dunked Andrew's head under the water four times.

But then it turned ugly. On the fifth dunk, Renae's right arm hooked Andrew's head and took her down under the water again. This time, Renae reared up aggressively. She'd been bitten on her inner arm where she'd hooked Andrew. She was raging. She started yelling and showing the screaming crowd a huge bite mark, then angrily holding Andrew's head under the water, gripping her around the neck. I sat watching, waiting with my heart in my throat to see what would happen next and thinking about my mum's old mantra: 'Don't play-fight, you kids, it will always end up in a fight.'

Renae was still holding Andrew under the water, so a couple of girls broke it up, pulling Renae away. By then it was 4.30 p.m., and the guards were locking us down for the night. Renae quickly ran over to my cell window, excitedly asking, 'Did you see that, Schapelle?', holding up her arm to show me the deep bite mark. 'Yeah, I saw it, and it looked like an accident!' It was the big topic of conversation that night in my cell. Everyone thought Andrew had accidentally bitten Renae's arm when it came forcefully swinging into her face. The fight had at least been a bit of jailhouse entertainment, something to do, something different to look at.

These days, I spend a bit of time with the real Andrew Chan and Matthew Norman, as they're both pretty funny guys, though we never talk about their crimes or their life and death sentences. Matthew's sentence was increased to death on appeal but has just been returned to life imprisonment after a further appeal. Andrew is incredibly positive by anyone's standards, let alone a prisoner on death row. One morning, he had almost the whole visitors' area laughing with his antics. I was opening some of my parcels on the floor of the mail room and pulled out a pair of size 14 pastel-blue lace underpants. He grabbed them from me and pulled them on over his little short shorts, which showed off his skinny white legs perfectly. Then, with the lace underpants ballooning out from the puckering of his shorts, he pranced around the visitors' area like a catwalk model.

My brother Michael also often gives me a good laugh whenever he comes over to visit me. He came in one day, after a gap of about three months since his last visit, and gave me a big hug and a smile. I was shocked when I saw that his perfectly straight white teeth were all brown and grossly decaying. My smile quickly faded and my heart broke as I looked at him. With all the stress I'd been under, my teeth were looking a bit worse for wear – but his stress was far more evident. I felt sorry for him, as he'd always taken good care of his teeth. I didn't want to say anything or look too closely and hurt him. But he quickly realised my discomfort and started laughing at me. 'What?' I asked. He kept laughing and trying to talk normally, and I tried to also, though it was hard. Then he looked away for a second, before quickly turning back with perfectly normal pearly-white teeth. He laughed hysterically and held the fake plastic teeth in his hand. I burst out laughing, too. I thought they were so gross and funny that I washed them before putting them in and walking around to speak to a few people I knew. Everyone had a good laugh.

Michael was also the one to finally convince me to chop off my long hair. I told him I'd been contemplating it for a few months, maybe even shaving it off. It was so hot and washing it was such a hassle, with the dirty water constantly giving me ear infections. I was going as long as humanly – or womanly – possible between washes, sometimes three or four weeks. But I kept putting off the cut, thinking I'd be going home soon, and meanwhile living like a stinky matted piggy.

'Just do it! It'll be so much easier and you'll wonder why you hadn't done it sooner,' Michael said.

'Do you think I'll look ugly, though?'

'Yes!' was his blunt reply, and we both laughed.

After his visit, I walked back to the block, borrowed a pair of pink-handled kindergarten-type scissors from another cell and marched into my own cell, complete with thirteen-plus girls lying around in it. I then got a small mirror and placed it on top of a turned-over bucket. I put the rubbish bin beside me, and I was ready.

Sitting on the ground, I took a long look at myself in the mirror, then pulled up small clumps of hair, just enough so the blunt scissors could cut through without having to hack at it too much. I started at the front. I knew if I started chopping from the back, I'd get scared and stop. I couldn't stop when starting at the front, otherwise I'd be left with an awful '80s-style mullet and fit perfectly into this place . . . no, thanks.

I didn't speak, as I didn't want anyone talking me out of it. There was no turning back, this hair had to go. I was focused. To the other girls, I must have looked like a depressed, stressed, out-of-control wreck as I just kept hacking and hacking. I heard all the girls whispering among themselves, 'What's she doing?' Women from other cells came in to sneak a peek. This was an event, anything to kill time – glad I could help them.

When Yohanna, the knitting lady, saw me, she pushed everyone out of the cell, knelt down beside me and asked what I was doing. I didn't speak. She started crying, hugging me and saying, 'Tell me what's happened, Schapelle.' I just kept looking in the mirror, chopping an inch away from my scalp. She tried taking the scissors off me. I stopped for a second, started crying and turned to her.

'It's OK, Yohanna. I'm OK, it's just too hot!' Cutting my hair was emotionally hard as I loved that hair and it also represented more of the life I'd lost.

I took a photograph of my beloved chopped-off hair and then threw the hair in the bin. A few days later, I found out that one of the girls had buried it in front of our cell. I thought that was a bit weird, but it was an Indonesian custom. I didn't realise what a nightmare cutting my hair would cause. Suddenly, prisoners all over Hotel K, and visitors, were trying to take the first lucrative shots of my new short hairdo. It was worth a lot of cash. It was the beginning of my hat-and-scarf phase.

Each time I begin to feel something slightly resembling a comfort zone in here, something, a person, a problem, a change, whatever, will come along and throw me off course, out of whack, placing a hole in the road. Always something to disrupt, making it impossible for me to gain any illusion of a half-hearted sense of security.

My cell was the worst it had ever been. We were up to fifteen girls, including the two drug addicts who regularly shot up next to me. And though we now had running water, we were often worse off. Sonia regularly stuck her hand out of her cell to turn off the water pump. She liked doing it at 5 p.m. so we had no water until the guards came in at 7 a.m. It usually meant the bathroom floor would be covered with more floating shit, without any water to flush it away. Sometimes I found it hard to believe I was still actually a woman.

The septic tank also blocked up a few times, and our cell was the first to overflow. I went with Renae and a girl from my cell, Sumila, behind the block to try to fix it. Sumila didn't mind getting her hands dirty. She lifted the cement lid of the septic tank and, as she did, all its gross contents came alive, spurting thirty centimetres into the air. I felt Renae grab my shoulders and shove me out of the way and then run for it. She couldn't get away fast enough. I heard her screams over the top of my own. All the slop was gushing out all over Sumila's bare feet. Then, with her bare hands, she replaced the lid. That would without doubt be the most grotesque image I have ever been witness to – an overflowing septic tank.

Back in the block, Sumila rinsed her feet and hands using water from the fish pond. She then gave Renae and me one of her biggest smiles. We stood in shock as we watched the simplicity of her hygiene.

Finally, after a year and a half in the pre-sentencing cell, I was allowed to move into Salma's elite cell. It was a relief, but I had to be careful of a prisoner called Michelle. She was an expatriate Dutch woman living in Bali and in jail for drugs. She was nasty, always making snide remarks and always walking around with a camera, taking shots of everything . . . especially me.

She was odd and no one really liked her except Renae, and as they started becoming buddies, it caused a rift in our friendship. I spent one night in the same cell as this woman before she moved into Renae's cell, lying at night with a sheet over my head so she didn't take photos of me asleep. I'd already caught her taking sneaky shots of me a few times. I had done nothing to this girl but try to be nice.

My concerns about this woman were confirmed after she was released and sold a story about me to *New Idea*. Incredibly, the magazine just took her lies, publishing a story full of errors without bothering to check its facts. They even stated that Stanley was dead. It was unbelievable. Not only do I not have any privacy but complete lies are made up.

Journalists keep coming in trying to get stories about me by paying other prisoners to talk. I don't understand why people won't just leave me alone. It's never-ending, and I know it will continue until the day someone comes to say, 'Pack your bags, you're checking out.'

21

Stealing My Soul

THIS IS LIKE THE DEATH OF MY LIFE BEFORE. IT'S BEEN A mourning process, a grieving, all the emotions of shock, disbelief, denial, then anger, then trying to deal with it, then numbness and acceptance.

I have to accept that I'm here: accept that this is my life, at least for now.

But I will not accept my sentence – I don't know why I call it 'my sentence'. It's not mine. I will never accept twenty years. I'm just waiting. I'm not putting a number on my years in this shit hole. No way can I think about twenty years. I live in hope that something will happen, something has to. I will fight, my family will fight. Even if we fight for twenty years, we will keep fighting.

I am strong enough, capable enough of surviving in prison for twenty years. If I have no choice; if I have to, if there is no alternative. I am not capable of hurting myself, not capable of suicide or hurting my family in that way. I will come through without damaging myself; I will not allow anger or bitterness to eat away at me.

I feel paralysed inside these walls, my heart is still beating full of love – well, half full of love. I am still alive, but I'm stuck, I can't move, no one can hear me. People care for me, people work for me, but as yet, with all their efforts, no one can save me. The people who have died within these walls have died of loneliness, helplessness, of a broken heart, broken spirit.

Like a small child, I've had to learn to walk again. I can't do anything for myself, everything is relied on from the outside world – my friends, family – everything I need has to be brought in, from my food, toilet paper and medicines to emotional support. Without constant contact through my visits, it is very possible that I might go insane, a depressed, angry, crazy, psychopathic Aussie chick.

I think I am back to my normal mental state . . . not so religious. I keep all my relationships personal, as with my relationship with God. It's personal, between Him and me. No one else. I still pray, in my cell.

As part of accepting that this is for now my fate, I've also realised there's nothing to be gained in this place by letting anger overcome you, rebelling against discipline, screaming at the guards. It's not going to help me walk out those doors; it just causes more problems. I work every day at staying calm, on an even keel, replacing negative thoughts with positive ones.

I've become numbed to things. I have changed in some ways: I can sit calmly reading my book on my bed with a cell full of girls screaming at each other and barely notice; I can switch off, I'm like the calm in the eye of a storm.

Most days and nights we can hear the cries of prisoners in other cells humming through the concrete walls, like a dull constant aching all night long. I've grown accustomed to this sound, so now it doesn't affect me. It used to sadden me greatly that I couldn't reach through the walls to comfort the girl whose heart was breaking. My own heart would be burdened by that sound, and I'd usually lie on my bed listening and end up crying myself to sleep with them.

Now I still hear this sound, but I've grown to not let it affect me as it did. I can't allow myself to drown with every sound of pain that penetrates these walls, as it eats away my strength and energy; I need to be in control of my mind and feelings, it's my mind and feelings that I need to concentrate on, not others, for me to get through this.

But I am slowly losing myself. When I go back to the women's block, I change, I disappear. I can go three weeks without talking to anyone. I keep to myself. I've become introverted. Only on the rare occasion when the Schapelle I once knew comes out to give me a visit do I realise how alone and terribly lonely and lost I am.

It's so lonely in here. I see my family, I'm surrounded by lots of people, but I long for male company: that of a cute guy, nothing naughty and rude, just small stuff like a caring hand to move the hair out of my teary eyes and kiss my forehead, give me a warm hug, hold my hand. Little things like that. I'm usually a very touchy person. When will I have that again?

I do not want a relationship in this place, but I have thought that if I'm here years from now, maybe I would have a child – somehow. It is life's most precious gift, and I don't want to miss my chance. The prison rules would allow me to keep my baby here for two years. Maybe it seems cruel, but he or she would be just as loved as any other child. Maybe I could build a cell, so that it's clean. It's just all silly daydreams at the moment.

Maybe I will serve this sentence in an Australian prison. It is a question everyone seems to try to answer for me but one I have not seriously contemplated. I will wait and decide in time.

I long to be free and live again outside these walls. So many simple things from the outside world now seem so precious. When my brother Michael comes in to visit me straight after a surf, his feet are always covered in wet sand. I forget what it feels like to get sand between my toes. I rub the sand off his feet and onto mine. In a weird way it gives me a little comfort, makes me feel a little closer to where I long to be.

But I do realise that this is where I must stay until that day in the future when someone in authority grows some balls to help fight for my innocence, my freedom, for what is right, to get that cage door unlocked. The culprits who did this have watched this play out like a sick TV soap opera. I'd like to think they'd put their cowardly hands up, but I gave up any hope of that a long time ago.

I will never understand *WHY*, why this happened to me. Why my bag? I still sometimes go over it in my head but never get an answer. I live day by day but don't look into the future, as the future means only these four walls, heat, dirt and too many stinky people. The future means sixteen more years locked in a cage. I feel sad and broken – my hopes have faded to nothing. They're dead. I waited for justice for four years, since that very first Monday in Polda when I was sure I'd be free to finally go and enjoy my holiday. I always seemed to be waiting, waiting for the next answer, for the court's decisions, waiting on my appeals. But my wait is over. I've lost. My judicial review was rejected on 28 March 2008, exhausting the last legal avenue.

Right now, I'm empty, lost and numb. I used to have a clear fresh sparkle radiating within, showing through my laugh and my eyes, I never had a problem looking in the mirror, I knew who I was, I didn't question myself. Lately now, four years on from that fatal date, and after repeated blows, I'm finding a confusing, distant reflection in the mirror; it's dull, my eyes don't seem to speak any more, they're lifeless, as though my soul is drying up. Where have I gone, where am I going? I can feel I'm gradually losing the essence that makes me me.

It's strange and it hurts, indescribably, to become aware of your own fading soul reflected through your eyes each time you look in the mirror.

I was once so vain and preoccupied with trying to keep my face youthful and line-free. I'd buy all the latest creams and products, fighting the signs of ageing. Now, how I've changed; I would love to be the owner of deep ingrained laughter lines. It's been so long since I've felt peaceful and happy. So long since I've smiled and laughed on the inside and out.

I want touch, affection, to feel as a woman being loved, I want daily life responsibility, normal life problems. I want to feel angry at the price of petrol or bananas in Australia.

I'm breathing in a dull anger with each breath from this injustice, from who put me here. I breathe it in daily in this monotonous existence.

I sound like a broken record, but I will keep saying it: *I'm innocent, I'm innocent, I'm innocent.*

Epilogue

As I left a visit with Schapelle recently, I told her, 'Don't lose hope.' She looked at me with her piercing blue eyes and stated matter of factly: 'It's gone. It's already gone!'

This has been a shattering year for Schapelle, perhaps the most deeply shattering of all so far. After five years of battling prostate and bone cancer, her beloved father, Michael Corby, finally passed away in January.

Schapelle didn't get a chance to say goodbye.

It has broken her heart. Tears spring to her eyes at the mention of her dad. She is in such unbearable pain that she is unable to write about his passing herself.

Michael Corby lived for his three children, Schapelle, Mercedes and Michael – they were his whole world. He shared a special bond with his youngest daughter that was clear to see. She put a sparkle in his eyes. She lit him up. She was always his baby girl, and he adored her.

His last words before slipping into unconsciousness were to ask if Schapelle was OK.

Seeing her unjustly caged in a cell, losing her precious life day by day in a dark nightmare that he was powerless to do anything about, devastated him. He moved to Bali in 2005 to do whatever he could to help, devoting his last good months to being with his daughters. Despite being in pain and terribly sick, he regularly did Schapelle's grocery shopping and visited her almost daily in Kerobokan prison – sitting on the dirty concrete floor of the jail, ignoring the intense pain that caused him. But in 2006 he was forced to return to Australia for further medical treatment. Schapelle never saw him again.

He failed to recover his health sufficiently to make a return trip. Father and daughter were each trapped, oceans apart, by their own tragic circumstances. The shocking injustice that keeps her locked behind the white walls of Kerobokan Prison stole her chance to say goodbye to her dad. His death has crushed her to a point where her family is seriously worried about her mental state for the first time.

She's acutely aware that life on the outside has now changed irreversibly. A few months after her dad's death, her stepfather, Greg Martin, who was a big part of her life for the past fifteen years, also lost his fight with cancer. It is a devastatingly sad time for Schapelle and her family.

But there was another cruel blow to compound her agony. After living with a flame of hope for the past two years while three judges in Jakarta reviewed her case, they finally delivered their deadly decision in March – her sentence will stand at 20 years.

She has now exhausted all appeals. The flame is out. Her hopes are dead. She truly believes there are no more tomorrows.

Kathyrn Bonella
April 2008

Acknowledgements

THANKS . . . FOR MY SUPPORTERS, A BIG HEARTFELT THANKS goes out to all – you keep my name alive: your thoughts, prayers, letters all contribute to finding the light. The 'Schapelle' support action groups throughout Australia and New Zealand and the website administrators for all the hard work and dedication – you are all very much appreciated.

Mum, Dad, Greg, Michael, Clinton, James, Meleane, Mercedes and Wayan – your lives have been shaken, but never once have you stopped the fight. Little Wayan and Nyeleigh – for being brats and making me laugh.

Nyoman – though we are yet to meet, you've brought us all a renewed energy and excitement of new life, a welcome addition in our lives.

Cus Melissa and friends – for organising such a successful fundraiser, and Morrison for support and keeping my fashion senses alive with your great clothes. Thanks to the founders of Natural Glow for putting colour back in my cheeks.

Aunty Julianne, all my family, my friends, extended family, including you, Jet, and my Indonesian family – you are always there for me. Always. On verdict day, you were all there; it meant so much to me. Thank you. You are all a part of me, of who I am. This is so hard to understand but know I love you all so preciously; I couldn't ask for a better family and friends. You do so much. I think of you all more than I see you.

Pak Erwin – you're a good man. I have faith in your ability as a lawyer and a trusted friend. If anyone is capable of bringing me home a free woman, it's you. I know you always do your absolute best for me.

Kathryn – it's taken frustration, tears, patience, sleepless nights and a lot of time, but we've done it. Thank you for being so understanding, so caring, especially on the odd awkwardness of my down days. You're a true and wonderful woman with such qualities – one being a major asset in the world of journalism.

Thank you, K, may this help to open the eyes to open the heart to open the door.

Schapelle Corby,
Kerobokan Prison, October 2006

My heartfelt thanks to Christine Marie and James Foster for always being available to bounce things off, to Caroline Frith for her endless encouragement, to my mum Sue and sisters Louise and Simone for their love and support, and to my late dad Rod for showing me a passion for human stories. Thanks to publisher Tom Gilliatt for his patience and dedication, as well as to editor Jon Gibbs for his hard work.

A very special thanks to the Corby family. They are an amazingly supportive and loving family. Thanks to Wayan for his untiring help. Thanks to Schapelle and Mercedes for letting me share their lives for almost a year to work with them on this book. They are beautiful women with huge hearts and very wicked senses of humour. I feel privileged to know them.

Schapelle is one of the most inspiring people I've ever met. She is innocent, stuck in a hellhole for something she didn't do, yet handles her situation with so much grace and dignity. Despite living in so much pain, her first concern is always her family. She tries to be upbeat and always – even through tears – finds something funny or interesting to talk about. She's incredible and is loved by so many friends and family and even strangers who write and visit constantly.

There is no question that Schapelle is innocent. None at all.

It is a travesty that she has already spent four horrendous years locked up in hell for someone else's crime. Every day, she hopes for justice, and if she doesn't get it soon, her story will be one of Australia's greatest travesties.

To anyone who has ever flown overseas: her story could be yours.

Kathryn Bonella

Author Information

KATHRYN BONELLA FIRST GOT INVOLVED IN SCHAPELLE Corby's story while working as a TV producer for Australian current-affairs programme *60 Minutes*. She produced the first exclusive TV interview with Schapelle a month after her arrest and then covered the verdict day in May 2005.

To write this book, Kathryn spent ten months living in Bali to work closely with Schapelle. Together, they spent hours in the visiting area of Kerobokan Prison, doing interviews and working on chapters. Schapelle also spent time in her cell writing diary notes and stories too painful to relive in conversation.

Since completing a Bachelor of Arts in Journalism in Melbourne, Kathryn has worked in television and print. She moved to London eighteen months after graduating and spent several years freelancing for *60 Minutes* as well as numerous English and American television programmes, magazines and newspapers.

She returned to Australia in 2000 to work as a full-time producer for *60 Minutes*, travelling the world to cover stories ranging from the Bali bombings to Princess Mary's wedding in Denmark. At the end of 2005, she resigned to write this book with Schapelle.

Since the book's release in Australia in November 2006, Kathyrn has returned to freelancing for various magazines, newspapers and television programmes.